THE OMNIBUS
P. D. JAMES

The Omnibus
P. D. James

A TASTE FOR DEATH

DEVICES AND DESIRES

ORIGINAL SIN

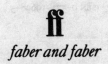

faber and faber

This P. D. James Omnibus
first published in 1998
by Faber and Faber Limited
3 Queen Square London WC1N 3AU

Export paperback edition not for sale in
the United Kingdom, the United States or Canada

Printed in England by Clays Ltd, St Ives plc

A Taste for Death © 1986 P. D. James
For permission to quote the lines by A. E. Housman on page 9
the publishers acknowledge the Society of Authors
as the literary representative of the Estate of A. E. Housman,
and Jonathan Cape Ltd., publishers of A. E. Housman's
Collected Poems.

Devices and Desires © 1989 P. D. James

Original Sin © 1994 P. D. James
The quotation from Wilfred Owen on page 54 is taken from
The Complete Poems and Fragments edited by Jon Stallworthy,
by permission of the Owen Estate and Chatto and Windus.

P. D. James is hereby identified as author of this
work in accordance with Section 77 of the
Copyright, Designs and Patents Act 1988.

A CIP record for this book
is available from the British Library

ISBN 0-571-19698-5

A Taste for Death

To my daughters,
Clare and Jane
and in memory of their father,
Connor Bantry White

Author's Note

My apologies are due to the inhabitants of Campden Hill Square for my temerity in erecting a Sir John Soane house to disrupt the symmetry of their terraces and to the Diocese of London for providing, surplus to pastoral requirements, a Sir Arthur Blomfield basilica and its campanile on the banks of the Grand Union Canal. Other places described are recognizably part of London. It is the more important to state, therefore, that all the events described in the novel are fictional and all the characters, living and dead, wholly imaginary.

I am grateful to the Director and staff of the Metropolitan Police Forensic Science Laboratory for their generous help with the scientific details.

Contents

Some can gaze and not be sick,
But I could never learn the trick.
There's this to say for blood and breath,
They give a man a taste for death.
                                    A.E. Housman

BOOK ONE

Death of a Baronet

1

The bodies were discovered at eight forty-five on the morning of Wednesday 18 September by Miss Emily Wharton, a 65-year-old spinster of the parish of St Matthew's in Paddington, London, and Darren Wilkes, aged 10, of no particular parish as far as he knew or cared. This unlikely pair of companions had left Miss Wharton's flat in Crowhurst Gardens just before half past eight to walk the half-mile stretch of the Grand Union Canal to St Matthew's church. Here Miss Wharton, as was her custom each Wednesday and Friday, would weed out the dead flowers from the vase in front of the statue of the Virgin, scrape the wax and candle stubs from the brass holders, dust the two rows of chairs in the Lady Chapel, which would be adequate for the small congregation expected at that morning's early Mass, and make everything ready for the arrival at nine twenty of Father Barnes.

It was on a similar mission seven months earlier that she had first met Darren. He had been playing alone on the towpath, if anything as purposeless as hurling old beer cans into the canal could be described as playing, and she had paused to say good morning to him. Perhaps he had been surprised to be greeted by an adult who didn't either admonish or cross-examine him. For whatever reason, after his initial expressionless stare, he had attached himself to her, at first dawdling behind, then circling round her, as might a stray dog, and finally trotting at her side. When they had reached St Matthew's church he had followed her inside as naturally as if they had set out together that morning.

It was apparent to Miss Wharton, on that first day, that he had never been inside a church before, but neither then nor on any subsequent visit did he evince the least curiosity about its purpose. He had prowled contentedly in and out of the vestry and bellroom while she got on with her chores, had watched critically while she had arranged her six daffodils eked out with foliage in the vase at the foot of the Virgin, and had viewed with the bland indifference of childhood Miss Wharton's frequent genuflections, obviously taking these sudden bobbings to be one more manifestation of the peculiar antics of adults.

But she had met him on the towpath the next week and the one following. After the third visit he had, without invitation, walked

13

home with her and had shared her tin of tomato soup and her fish fingers. The meal, like a ritual communion, had confirmed the curious, unspoken, mutual dependence which bound them. But by then she had known, with a mixture of gratitude and anxiety, that he had become necessary to her. On their visits to St Matthew's he always left the church, mysteriously present one moment and the next gone, when the first members of the congregation began to trickle in. After the service, she would find him loitering on the towpath, and he would join her as if they hadn't parted. Miss Wharton had never mentioned his name to Father Barnes or to anyone else at St Matthew's and, as far as she knew, he had never, in his secretive world of childhood, mentioned hers. She knew as little about him now, his parents, his life, as she had at their first meeting.

But that had been seven months ago, a chill morning in mid-February, when the bushes which screened the canal walk from the neighbouring council estate had been tangled thickets of lifeless thorn; when the branches of the ash trees had been black with buds so tight that it seemed impossible they could ever crack into greenness; and the thin denuded wands of willow, drooping over the canal, had cut delicate feathers on the quickening stream. Now high summer was browning and mellowing into autumn. Miss Wharton, briefly closing her eyes as she trudged through the mush of fallen leaves, thought that she could still scent, above the smell of sluggish water and damp earth, a trace of the heady elderberry flowers of June. It was that smell that on summer mornings most clearly brought back to her the lanes of her Shropshire childhood. She dreaded the onset of winter, and on waking this morning she had thought that she could smell its breath in the air. Although it hadn't rained for a week, the path was slippery with mud, deadening sound. They walked under the leaves in an ominous quietness. Even the tinny clatter of the sparrows was stilled. But to their right the ditch which bordered the canal was still lush with its summer greenness, its grasses thick over the split tyres, discarded mattresses and scraps of clothing rotting in its depths, and the torn and laden boughs of the willows dropped their thin leaves on to a surface which seemed too oily and stagnant to suck them in.

It was eight forty-five and they were nearing the church, passing now into one of the low tunnels that spanned the canal. Darren, who liked best this part of the walk, gave a whoop and rushed into the tunnel, hollering for an echo and running his hands, like pale starfish, along the brick walls. She followed his leaping figure, half-dreading the moment when she would pass through the arch into that claustrophobic, dank, river-smelling darkness and would hear, unnaturally loud, the suck of the canal against the paving stones and the slow drip of water from the low roof. She quickened her pace and within minutes the half moon of brightness at the end of the tunnel had widened to receive them again into the daylight and he was back, shivering at her side.

She said:

'It's very cold, Darren. Oughtn't you to be wearing your parka?' He hunched his thin shoulders and shook his head. She was amazed at how little he wore and how impervious he was to the cold. Sometimes it seemed to her that he preferred to live in a perpetual shiver. Surely wrapping up well on an autumn chill morning wasn't considered unmanly? And he looked so nice in his parka. She had been relieved when he first appeared in it; it was bright blue striped with red, expensive, obviously new, a reassuring sign that the mother she had never met and of whom he never spoke, tried to take good care of him.

Wednesday was her day for replacing the flowers, and this morning she was carrying a small tissue-wrapped bunch of pink roses and one of small white chrysanthemums. The stems were wet and she felt the dampness seeping through her woollen gloves. The flowers were tight budded but one was beginning to open and a transitory evocation of summer came to her, bringing with it an old anxiety. Darren often arrived on their church morning with a gift of flowers. These, he had told her, were from Uncle Frank's stall at Brixton. But could that really be true? And then, there was the smoked salmon, last Friday's gift, brought to her flat just before suppertime. He told her he had been given it by Uncle Joe who kept a café up Kilburn way. But the slivers, so moist, so delicious, had been interleaved with greaseproof paper, and the white tray in which they lay had looked so very like the ones she had looked at with hopeless longing in Marks and Spencer, except that someone had torn off the label. He had sat opposite her, watching her while she ate, making an extravagant moue of distaste when she suggested that he share it, but staring at her with a concentrated, almost angry, satisfaction; rather, she thought, as a mother might watch a convalescent child taking her first mouthful. But she had eaten it, and with the delicious taste still lingering on her palate it had seemed ungrateful to cross-question him. But the presents were getting more frequent. If he brought her any more, then they would have to have a little talk.

15

Suddenly, he gave a yell, raced furiously ahead and leapt up at an overhanging bough. There he swung, thin legs jerking, the white, thick-soled running shoes looking incongruously heavy for the bony legs. He was given to these sudden spurts of activity, running ahead to hide among the bushes and jump out at her, leaping across puddles, rummaging for broken bottles and cans in the ditch and hurling them with a desperate intensity into the water. She would pretend to be frightened when he jumped out, would call out to him to be careful when he crept along an overhanging branch and hung, skimming the water. But on the whole, she rejoiced in his liveliness. It was less worry than the lethargy which so often seemed to overcome him. Now, watching his grinning monkey face as he swung, arm over arm, the frantic twisting of his body, the silver of the delicate ribcage under the pale flesh where the jacket had parted from his jeans, she felt a surge of love so painful that it was like a thrust to the heart. And with the pain came again the old anxiety. As he dropped beside her she said:

'Darren, are you sure your mother doesn't mind your helping me with St Matthew's?'

'Naw, that's OK, I told ya.'

'You come to the flat so often. It's lovely for me but are you quite sure she doesn't mind?'

'Look, I told ya. It's OK.'

'But wouldn't it be better if I came to see her, just to meet her, so that she knows who you're with?'

'She knows. Anyway, she ain't at home. She's off visiting me Uncle Ron at Romford.'

Another uncle. How could she possibly keep track of them? But a fresh anxiety surfaced.

'Then who is looking after you, Darren? Who is at home?'

'No one. I'm sleepin' with a neighbour till she comes back. I'm OK.'

'And what about school today?'

'I told ya. I don't have to go. It's a holiday, see, it's a holiday! I told ya!'

His voice had become high, almost hysterical. Then, as she didn't speak, he fell in beside her and said more calmly:

'They got Andrex at forty-eight pee a double roll up at Notting Hill. That new supermarket. I could get ya a couple of rolls if you're interested.'

He must, she thought, spend a lot of time in supermarkets, shopping for his mother, perhaps, on his way home from school.

16

He was clever at finding bargains, reporting back to her about the special offers, the cheaper lines. She said:

'I'll try to get up there myself, Darren. That's a very good price.'

'Yeah, that's what I thought. It's a good price. First time I seen 'em under fifty pee.'

For almost the whole of their walk their objective had been in sight: the green copper cupola of the soaring campanile of Arthur Blomfield's extraordinary Romanesque basilica, built in 1870 on the bank of this sluggish urban waterway with as much confidence as if he had erected it on the Venetian Grand Canal. Miss Wharton, on her first visit to St Matthew's, nine years previously, had decided that it was expedient to admire it since it was her parish church and offered what she described as Catholic privileges. She had then put its architecture firmly out of her mind, together with her yearnings for Norman arches, carved reredos and familiar Early English spires. She supposed that she had now got used to it. But she was still slightly surprised when she found Father Barnes showing round groups of visitors, experts interested in Victorian architecture, who enthused over the baldachin, admired the Pre-Raphaelite paintings on the eight panels of the pulpit, or set up their tripods to photograph the apse, and who compared it, in confident, unecclesiastical tones (surely even experts ought to lower their voices in church) with the Cathedral of Torcello near Venice or with Blomfield's similar basilica at Jericho in Oxford.

And now, as always, with dramatic suddenness, it loomed before them. They passed through the turnstile in the canal railings and took the gravel path to the porch of the south door, the one to which Miss Wharton had a key. This led to the Little Vestry where she would hang up her coat and to the kitchen where she would wash out the vases and arrange the fresh flowers. As they reached the door she glanced down at the small flower bed which gardeners in the congregation were trying to cultivate with more optimism than success in the unrewarding soil at the side of the path.

'Oh look, Darren, how pretty. The first dahlias. I never thought they'd flower. No, don't pick them. They look so nice there.' He had bent down, his hand among the grasses but as she spoke he straightened up and thrust a grubby fist into his pocket.

'Don't you want 'em for the BVM?'

'We've got your uncle's roses for Our Lady.' If only they were his uncle's! I shall have to ask him, she thought. I can't go on like this, offering Our Lady stolen flowers, if they were stolen. But suppose they weren't and I accuse him? I shall destroy everything there is

17

between us. I can't lose him now. And it might put the idea of theft into his head. The half-remembered phrases fell into her mind; corrupting innocence, an occasion of sin. She thought, I shall have to think about it. But not now, not yet.

She rummaged in her handbag for the key on its wooden key ring and tried to fit it into the lock. But she couldn't get it in. Puzzled, but not yet worried, she tried the doorknob and the heavy iron bound door swung open. It was already unlocked, a key in place on the other side. The passage was quiet, unlit, the oak door to the Little Vestry on the left tightly closed. So Father Barnes must already be here. But how strange that he should arrive before her. And why hadn't he left on the passage light? As her gloved hand found the switch, Darren scampered past her, up to the wrought iron grille which separated the passage from the nave of the church. He liked to light a candle when they arrived, thrusting thin arms through the grille to reach the candleholder and the coin box. Early in their walk she had handed him the usual tenpenny piece, and now she heard a faint tinkle and watched while he stuck his candle in the socket, and reached for the matches in their brass holder.

And it was then, in that moment, that she felt the first twitch of anxiety. Some premonition alerted her subconscious; earlier disquiets and a vague sense of unease came together and focused into fear. A faint smell, alien yet horribly familiar; the sense of a recent presence; the possible significance of that unlocked outer door; the dark passageway. Suddenly she knew that something was dreadfully wrong. Instinctively she called out:

'Darren!'

He turned and looked at her face. And then, immediately, he was back at her side.

Gently at first, and then with one sharp movement, she opened the door. Her eyes dazzled with light. The long fluorescent tube which disfigured the ceiling was on, its brightness eclipsing the gentle glow from the passageway. And she saw horror itself.

There were two of them and she knew instantly, and with absolute certainty, that they were dead. The room was a shambles. Their throats had been cut and they lay like butchered animals in a waste of blood. Instinctively she thrust Darren behind her. But she was too late. He, too, had seen. He didn't scream but she felt him tremble and he made a small, pathetic groan, like an angry puppy. She pushed him back into the passage, closed the door, and leaned against it. She was aware of a desperate coldness, of the tumultuous

18

thudding of her heart. It seemed to have swollen in her chest, huge and hot, and its painful drumming shook her frail body as if to burst it apart. And the smell, which at first had been tentative, elusive, no more than an alien tincture on the air, now seemed to seep into the passage with the strong effluvium of death.

She pressed her back against the door, grateful for the support of its solid carved oak. But neither its strength nor her tightly closed eyes could shut out horror. Brightly lit as on a stage, she saw the bodies still, more garish, more brightly lit than when they had first met her horrified eyes. One corpse had slipped from the low single bed to the right of the door and lay staring up at her, the mouth open, the head almost cleft from the body. She saw again the severed vessels, sticking like corrugated pipes through the clotted blood. The second was propped, ungainly as a rag doll, against the far wall. His head had dropped forward and over his chest a great mat of blood had spread like a bib. A brown and blue woollen cap was still on his head but askew. His right eye was hidden but the left leered at her with a dreadful knowingness. Thus mutilated, it seemed to her everything human had drained away from them with their blood; life, identity, dignity. They no longer looked like men. And the blood was everywhere. It seemed to her that she herself was drowning in blood. Blood drummed in her ears, blood gurgled like vomit in her throat, blood splashed in bright globules against the retinas of her closed eyes. The images of death she was powerless to shut out swam before her in a swirl of blood, dissolved, reformed, and then dissolved again, but always in blood. And then she heard Darren's voice, felt the tug of his hand on her sleeve.

'We gotta get outer here before the filth arrive. Come on. We ain't seen nothin', nothin'. We ain't been 'ere.'

His voice squeaked with fear. He clutched at her arm. Through the thin tweed, his grubby fingers bit, sharp as teeth. Gently she prised them loose. When she spoke, she was surprised at the calmness of her voice.

'That's nonsense, Darren. Of course they won't suspect us. Running away . . . now that would look suspicious.'

She hustled him along the passage.

'I'll stay here. You go for help. We must lock the door. No one must come in. I'll wait here and you fetch Father Barnes. You know the Vicarage? It's the corner flat in that block on Harrow Road. He'll know what to do. He'll call the police.'

'But you can't stay 'ere on your own. Suppose 'e's still here? In the church, waitin' and watchin'? We gotta keep together. OK?'

The authority in his childish voice disconcerted her.

'But it doesn't seem right, Darren, to leave them. Not both of us. It seems, well, callous, wrong. I ought to stay.'

'That's daft. You can't do nothin'. They're dead, stiff. You saw 'em.'

He made a swift gesture of drawing a knife across his throat, rolled up his eyes and gagged. The sound was horribly realistic, a gush of blood in the throat. She cried out:

'Oh don't, Darren, please don't!'

Immediately he was conciliatory, his voice calmer. He put his hand in hers. 'Better come along with me to Father Barnes.' She looked down at him, piteously, as if she were the child.

'If you think so, Darren.'

He had regained his mastery now. The small body almost swaggered. 'Yeah, that's what I think. Come along with me.' He was excited. She heard it in the raised treble, saw it in the bright eyes. He was no longer shocked and he wasn't really upset. It had been silly to think that she needed to protect him from the horror. That spurt of fear at the thought of the police had passed. Brought up on those bright flickering images of violence, could he distinguish between them and reality, she wondered. Perhaps it was more merciful that, protected by his innocence, he shouldn't be able to. He put a thin arm around her shoulders, helping her to the door and she leaned against him, feeling the sharp bones under her arm.

'How kind he is,' she thought, 'how sweet, this dear, dear child.' She would have to talk to him about the flowers and the salmon. But she needn't think about that now, not now.

They were outside. The air, fresh and cold, smelled to her as sweet as a sea breeze. But when, together, they had pulled shut the heavy door with its iron decorated bands, she found she couldn't fit the key into the lock. Her fingers were jumping rhythmically, as if in spasm. He took the key from her and, stretching high, thrust it into the lock. And then her legs gently folded and she subsided slowly on the step, ungainly as a marionette. He looked at her.

'You all right?'

'I'm afraid I can't walk, Darren. I'll be better soon. But I have to stay here. You fetch Father Barnes. But hurry!'

As he still hesitated, she said:

'The murderer, he can't still be inside. The door was unlocked when we arrived. He must have left after he'd – he wouldn't hang about inside waiting to be caught, would he?'

How odd, she thought, that my mind can reason that out while my body seems to have given up.

But it was true. He couldn't still be there, hiding in the church, knife in hand. Not unless they had died very recently. But the blood hadn't looked fresh . . . Or had it? Her bowels suddenly churned. Oh God, she prayed, don't let that happen, not now. I'll never get to the lavatory. I can't make it past that door. She thought of the humiliation, of Father Barnes coming, the police. It was bad enough to be slumped here like a heap of old clothes.

'Hurry,' she said. 'I'll be all right. But hurry!'

He made off, running very fast. When he had gone, she still lay there, fighting the terrible loosening of her bowels, the need to vomit. She tried to pray but, strangely, the words seemed to have got muddled up. 'May the souls of the righteous, in the mercy of Christ, rest in peace.' But perhaps they hadn't been the righteous. There ought to be a prayer that would do for all men, all the murdered bodies all over the world. Perhaps there was. She would have to ask Father Barnes. He would be sure to know.

And then came a new and different terror. What had she done with her key? She looked down at the one clutched in her hand. This was weighted with a large wooden tag charred at the end where Father Barnes had put it down too close to a gas flame. So this was his spare key, the one he kept at the Vicarage. It must be the one they had found in the lock and she had handed it to Darren to relock the door. So what had she done with hers? She rummaged frantically in her handbag as if the key were a vital clue, its loss disastrous, seeing in imagination a phalanx of accusing eyes, the police demanding she account for it, Father Barnes's tired and dispirited face. But her scrabbling fingers found it safe between her purse and the bag lining, and she drew it out with a moan of relief. She must have automatically put it away when she found the door already open. But how odd that she couldn't remember! Everything was a blank between their arrival and the moment in which she had thrust open the Little Vestry door.

She was aware of a dark shadow looming beside her. She looked up and saw Father Barnes. Relief flooded her heart. She said:

'You've rung the police, Father?'

'Not yet. I thought it was better to see for myself, in case the boy was playing tricks.'

So they must have stepped past her, into the church, into that dreadful room. How odd that, huddled in the corner, she hadn't even noticed. Impatience rose like vomit in her throat. She wanted to cry out, 'Well now you've seen!' She had thought that when he

21

arrived everything would be all right. No, not all right but better, made sense of. Somewhere there were the right words and he would speak them. But looking at him, she knew that he brought no comfort. She looked up at his face, unattractively blotched by the morning chill, at the grubby stubble, at the two brittle hairs at the corners of his mouth, at the trace of blackened blood in the left nostril, as if he had had a nose bleed, at the eyes, still gummy with sleep. How silly to think that he would bring his strength, would somehow make the horror bearable. He didn't even know what to do. It had been the same over the Christmas decorations. Mrs Noakes had always done the pulpit, ever since Father Collins's time. And then Lilly Moore had suggested that it wasn't fair, that they ought to take turns at the pulpit and the font. He should have made up his mind and stood firm. It was always the same. But what a time to be thinking of Christmas decorations, her mind a tangle of hollyberries and gaudy poinsettias, red as blood. But it hadn't been so very red, more a reddish brown.

Poor Father Barnes, she thought, irritation dissolving into sentimentality. He's a failure like me, both failures. She was aware of Darren shivering beside her. Someone ought to take him home. Oh God, she thought, what will this do to him, to both of us? Father Barnes was still standing beside her, twisting the doorkey in his ungloved hands. She said, gently:

'Father, we have to get the police.'

'The police, Of course. Yes, we must call the police. I'll phone from the Vicarage.'

But still he hesitated. On an impulse she asked:

'Do you know them, Father?'

'Oh yes, yes. The tramp. That's Harry Mack. Poor Harry. He sleeps in the porch sometimes.'

He didn't need to tell her that. She knew that Harry liked to doss down in the porch. She had taken her turn at clearing up after him, the crumbs, the paper bags, the discarded bottles, sometimes even worse things. She ought to have recognized Harry, that woollen hat, the jacket. She tried not to dwell on why it was that she hadn't. She asked, with the same gentleness:

'And the other, Father. Did you recognize him?'

He looked down at her. She saw his fear, his bewilderment, and above all, a kind of astonishment at the enormity of the complications that lay ahead. He said slowly, not looking at her:

'The other is Paul Berowne, Sir Paul Berowne. He is – he was – a Minister of the Crown.'

2

As soon as he had left the Commissioner's office and was back in
his own room Commander Adam Dalgliesh rang Chief Inspector
John Massingham. The receiver was snatched at the first ring and
Massingham's disciplined impatience came across as strongly as
his voice. Dalgliesh said:

'The Commissioner has had a word with the Home Office. We're
to take this one, John. The new squad will officially be in existence
on Monday anyway, so we're only jumping the gun by six days.
And Paul Berowne may still technically be the Member for Hertfordshire North East. He wrote to the Chancellor of the Exchequer
to apply for the Chiltern Hundreds on Saturday, apparently, and
no one seems quite sure whether the resignation dates from the
day the letter was received or the date the warrant is signed by the
Chancellor. Anyway all that is academic. We take the case.'

But Massingham was uninterested in the procedural details for
the resignation of a parliamentary seat. He said:

'Division are sure, sir, that the body is Sir Paul Berowne?'

'One of the bodies. Don't forget the tramp. Yes, it's Berowne.
There's evidence of identity at the scene, and the parish priest
knew him, apparently. It wasn't the first time Berowne had spent
the night in St Matthew's church vestry.'

'An odd place to choose to sleep.'

'Or to die. Have you spoken to Inspector Miskin?'

Once they had begun working together they would both be calling
her Kate, but now Dalgliesh gave her her rank. Massingham said:

'She's off today, sir, but I managed to get her at her flat. I've
asked Robins to collect her gear and she'll meet us at the scene. I've
alerted the rest of the team.'

'Right, John. Get the Rover, will you. I'll meet you outside. Four
minutes.'

It crossed his mind that Massingham might not have been too
displeased had Kate Miskin already left her flat and been impossible
to contact. The new squad had been set up in C1 to investigate
serious crimes that, for political or other reasons, needed particularly sensitive handling. It had been so self-evident to Dalgliesh
that the squad would need a senior woman detective that he had
devoted his energy to choosing the right one, rather than to specu-

23

lating how well she would fit into the team. He had selected the 27-year-old Kate Miskin on her record and her performance at interview, satisfied that she had the qualities for which he was looking. They were also the ones he most admired in a detective: intelligence, courage, discretion and common sense. What else she might have to contribute remained to be seen. He knew that she and Massingham had worked together before when he had been a newly promoted divisional detective inspector and she a sergeant. It was rumoured that the relationship had at times been stormy. But Massingham had learned to discipline some of his prejudices since then, as he had the notorious Massingham temper. And a fresh, even an iconoclastic, influence, even a little healthy rivalry, could be more effective operationally than the collusive and macho freemasonry which frequently bound together a team of all male officers.

Dalgliesh began rapidly but methodically to clear his desk, then checked his murder bag. He had told Massingham four minutes, and he would be there. Already he had moved, as if by a conscious act of will, into a world in which time was precisely measured, details obsessively noticed, the senses preternaturally alert to sounds, smell, sight, the flick of an eyelid, the timbre of a voice. He had been called from this office to so many bodies, in such different settings, such different states of dissolution, old, young, pathetic, horrifying, having in common only the one fact, that they were violently dead and by another's hand. But this body was different. For the first time in his career, he had known and liked the victim. He told himself that it was pointless to speculate what difference, if any, this would make to the investigation. Already he knew that the difference was there.

The Commissioner had said:

'His throat is cut, possibly by his own hand. But there's a second body, a tramp. This case is likely to be messy in more ways than one.'

His reaction to the news had been partly predictable and partly complex and more disturbing. There had been the natural initial shock of disbelief at hearing of the unexpected death of any person even casually known. He would have felt no less if he'd been told that Berowne was dead of a coronary or killed in a car smash. But this had been followed by a sense of personal outrage, an emptiness and then a surge of melancholy, not strong enough to be called grief but keener than mere regret, which had surprised him by its intensity. But it hadn't been strong enough to make him say:

24

'I can't take this case. I'm too involved, too committed.'

Waiting briefly for the lift he told himself that he was no more involved than he would be in any other case. Berowne was dead. It was his business to find out how and why. Commitment was to the job, to the living, not to the dead.

He had hardly passed through the swing doors when Massingham drove up the ramp with the Rover. Getting in beside him Dalgliesh asked:

'Fingerprints and photography, they're on their way?'

'Yes, sir.'

'And the lab?'

'They're sending a senior biologist. She'll meet us there.'

'Did you manage to get Doctor Kynaston?'

'No, sir, only the housekeeper. He's been in New England visiting his daughter. He always goes there in the autumn. He was due back at Heathrow on BA flight 214 arriving at seven twenty-five. It's landed, but he's probably stuck on the Westway.'

'Keep on trying his home until he arrives.'

'Doc Greeley is available, sir. Kynaston will be jet-lagged.'

'I want Kynaston, jet-lagged or not.'

Massingham said:

'Only the best for this cadaver.'

Something in his voice, a tinge of amusement, even contempt, irritated Dalgliesh. He thought, my God, am I getting over-sensitive about this death even before I've seen the body? He fastened his seat belt without speaking and the Rover slid gently into Broadway, the road he had crossed less than a fortnight earlier on his way to see Sir Paul Berowne.

Gazing straight ahead, only half-aware of a world outside the claustrophobic comfort of the car, of Massingham's hands stroking the wheel, the almost soundless changing of the gears, the pattern of traffic lights, he deliberately let his mind slip free of the present and of all conjecture about what lay ahead, and remembered, by an exercise of mental recall, as if something important depended on his getting it right, every moment of that last meeting with the dead man.

3

It was Thursday 5 September and he was about to leave his office to drive to Bramshill Police College to begin a series of lectures to the Senior Command Course when the call came through from the private office. Berowne's private secretary spoke after the manner of his kind. Sir Paul would be grateful if Commander Dalgliesh could spare a few minutes to see him. It would be convenient if he could come at once. Sir Paul would be leaving his office to join a party of his constituents at the House in about an hour.

Dalgliesh liked Berowne, but the summons was inconvenient. He was not expected at Bramshill until after luncheon and had planned to take his time over the journey to north Hampshire, visiting churches at Sherborne St John and Winchfield and lunching at a pub near Stratfield Saye before arriving at Bramshill in time for the usual courtesies with the Commandant before his two-thirty lecture. It occurred to him that he had reached the age when a man looks forward to his pleasures less keenly than in youth but is disproportionately aggrieved when his plans are upset. There had been the usual time-consuming, wearying and slightly acrimonious preliminaries to the setting up of the new squad in C1 and already his mind was reaching out with relief to the solitary contemplation of alabaster effigies, sixteenth-century glass and the awesome decorations of Winchfield. But it looked as if Paul Berowne wasn't proposing to take much time over their meeting. His plans might still be possible. He left his grip in the office, put on his tweed coat against a blustery autumnal morning and cut through St James's Station to the Department.

As he pushed his way through the swing doors he thought again how much he had preferred the Gothic splendour of the old building in Whitehall. It must, he recognized, have been infuriating and inconvenient to work in. It had, after all, been built at a time when the rooms were heated by coal fires tended by an army of minions and when a score of carefully composed handwritten minutes by the Department's legendary eccentrics were adequate to control events which now required three divisions and a couple of under secretaries. This new building was no doubt excellent of its kind, but if the intention had been to express confident authority tempered by humanity he wasn't sure that the architect had suc-

26

ceeded. It looked more suitable for a multinational corporation than for a great Department of State. He particularly missed the huge oil portraits which had dignified that impressive Whitehall staircase, intrigued always by the techniques by which artists of varying talents had coped with the challenge of dignifying the ordinary and occasionally unprepossessing features of their sitters by the visual exploitation of magnificent robes and by imposing on their pudgy faces the stern consciousness of imperial power. But at least they had removed the studio photograph of a royal princess which until recently had graced the entrance hall. It had looked more suitable for a West End hairdressing salon.

He was smilingly recognized at the reception desk, but his credentials were still carefully scrutinized and he was required to await the escorting messenger, even though he had attended enough meetings in the building to be reasonably familiar with these particular corridors of power. Few of the elderly male messengers now remained, and for some years the Department had recruited women. They shepherded their charges with a cheerful, maternal competence as if to reassure them that the place might look like a prison but was as gently beneficent as a nursing home and that they were only there for their own good.

He was finally shown into the outer office. The House was still in recess for the summer and the room was unnaturally quiet. One of the typewriters was shrouded and a single clerk was collating papers with none of the urgency which normally powered a minister's private office. It would have been a very different scene a few weeks earlier. He thought, not for the first time, that a system which required ministers to run their departments, fulfil their parliamentary responsibilities, and spend the weekend listening to the grievances of their constituents, might have been designed to ensure that major decisions were made by men and women tired to the point of exhaustion. It certainly ensured that they were heavily dependent on their permanent officials. Strong ministers were still their own men; the weaker degenerated into marionettes. Not that this would necessarily worry them. Departmental heads were adept at concealing from their puppets even the gentlest jerk of strings and wire. But Dalgliesh hadn't needed his private source of department gossip to know that there was nothing of this limp subservience about Paul Berowne.

He came forward from behind his desk and held out his hand as if this were a first meeting. His was a face, stern, even a little melancholy in repose, which was transfigured when he smiled. He smiled now. He said:

27

'I'm sorry to bring you here at short notice. I'm glad we managed to catch you. It isn't particularly important but I think it may become so.'

Dalgliesh could never see him without being reminded of the portrait of his ancestor, Sir Hugo Berowne, in the National Portrait Gallery. Sir Hugo had been undistinguished except for a passionate, if ineffective, allegiance to his king. His only notable recorded act had been to commission Van Dyke to paint his portrait. But it had been enough to ensure him, at least pictorially, a vicarious immortality. The manor house in Hampshire had long since passed from the family, the fortune was diminished; but Sir Hugo's long and melancholy face framed by a collar of exquisite lace still stared with arrogant condescension at the passing crowd, the definitive seventeenth-century Royalist gentleman. The present baronet's likeness to him was almost uncanny. Here was the same long-boned face, the high cheekbones tapering to a pointed chin, the same widely spaced eyes with the droop of the left eyelid, the same long-fingered pale hands, the same steady but slightly ironic gaze.

Dalgliesh saw that his desk top was almost clear. It was a necessary ploy for an overworked man who wanted to stay sane. You dealt with one thing at a time, gave it your whole attention, decided it, then put it aside. At this moment he managed to convey that the one thing requiring attention was comparatively unimportant, a short communication on a sheet of quarto-sized white writing paper. He handed it over. Dalgliesh read:

'The member for Hertfordshire North East, despite his fascist tendencies, is a notable liberal when it comes to women's rights. But perhaps women should beware; proximity to this elegant baronet can be lethal. His first wife was killed in a car accident; he was driving. Theresa Nolan, who nursed his mother and slept in his house, killed herself after an abortion. It was he who knew where to find the body. The naked body of Diana Travers, his domestic servant, was found drowned at his wife's Thames-side birthday party, a party at which he was expected to be present. Once is a private tragedy, twice is bad luck, three times looks like carelessness.'

Dalgliesh said:

'Typed with an electric golfball machine. They're not the easiest to identify. And the paper is from a pad of ordinary commercial bond sold in thousands. Not much help there. Have you any idea who could have sent it?'

28

'None. One gets used to the usual abusive or pornographic letters. They're part of the job.'

Dalgliesh said:

'But this is close to an accusation of murder. If the sender is traced I imagine your lawyer would advise that it's actionable.'

'Actionable, yes, I imagine so.'

Dalgliesh thought that whoever had composed the message hadn't been uneducated. The punctuation was careful, the prose had a certain rhythm. He or she had taken trouble over the arrangement of the facts and in getting in as much relevant information as possible. It was certainly a cut above the usual filth and drivel which dropped unsigned into a minister's postbag, and it was the more dangerous for that.

He handed it back and said:

'This isn't the original, of course. It's been photocopied. Are you the only person to receive it, Minister, or don't you know?'

'It was sent to the press, at least to one paper, the *Paternoster Review*. This is in today's edition. I've only just seen it.'

He opened his desk drawer, took out the journal and handed it to Dalgliesh. There was a folded marker at page eight. Dalgliesh let his eyes slide down the page. The paper had been running a series of articles on junior members of the Government and it was Berowne's turn. The first part of the article was innocuous, factual, hardly original. It briefly reviewed Berowne's previous career as a barrister, his first unsuccessful attempt to enter Parliament, his success at the 1979 election, his phenomenal rise to junior ministerial rank, his probable standing with the Prime Minister. It mentioned that he lived with his mother, Lady Ursula Berowne, and his second wife in one of the few extant houses built by Sir John Soane and that he had one child by his first marriage, 24-year-old Sarah Berowne, who was active in left-wing politics and who was thought to be estranged from her father. It was unpleasantly snide about the circumstances of his second marriage. His elder brother, Major Sir Hugo Berowne, had been killed in Northern Ireland and Paul Berowne had married his brother's fiancée within five months of the car accident which had killed his wife. 'It was, perhaps, appropriate that the bereaved fiancée and husband should find mutual consolation although no one who has seen the beautiful Barbara Berowne could suppose that the marriage was merely a matter of fraternal duty.' It went on to prognosticate with some insight but little charity about his political future. But much of that was little more than Lobby gossip.

29

The sting lay in the final paragraph and its origin was unmistakable. 'He is a man who is known to like women; certainly most find him attractive. But those women closest to him have been singularly unlucky. His first wife died in a car smash while he was driving. A young nurse, Theresa Nolan, who nursed his mother, Lady Ursula Berowne, killed herself after an abortion, and it was Berowne who found the body. Four weeks ago a girl who worked for him, Diana Travers, was found drowned following a party given for his wife on her birthday, a party at which he was expected to be present. Bad luck is as lethal for a politician as halitosis. It could yet follow him into his political career. It could be the sour smell of misfortune rather than the suspicion that he doesn't know what he really wants which could mock the prediction that here is the next Conservative Prime Minister but one.'

Berowne said:

'The *Paternoster Review* isn't circulated in the Department. Perhaps it should be. Judging from this we might be missing entertainment if not instruction. I read it occasionally at the club, mainly for the literary reviews. Do you know anything about the paper?'

He could, thought Dalgliesh, have asked the Department's own public relations people. It was interesting that apparently he hadn't chosen to. He said:

'I've known Conrad Ackroyd for some years. He owns and edits the *Paternoster*. His father and grandfather had it before him. In those days it was printed in Paternoster Place in the City. Ackroyd doesn't make money out of it. Papa left him reasonably well provided for through more orthodox investments, but I imagine it just about breaks even. He likes to print gossip occasionally, but the paper isn't a second *Private Eye*. Ackroyd hasn't the guts for one thing. I don't think he has ever risked being sued in the history of the paper. It makes it less audacious and less entertaining than the *Eye*, of course, except for the literary and dramatic reviews. They have an enjoyable perversity.' Only the *Paternoster*, he recalled, would have described a revival of Priestley's *An Inspector Calls* as a play about a very tiresome girl who caused a great deal of trouble to a respectable family. He added: 'The facts will be accurate as far as they go. This will have been checked. But it's surprisingly vicious for the *Paternoster*.'

Berowne said:

'Oh yes, the facts are accurate.' He made the statement calmly, almost sadly, without explanation and apparently without the intention of offering any.

Dalgliesh wanted to say 'Which facts? The facts in this journal or the facts in the original communication?' But he decided against the question. This wasn't yet a case for the police, least of all for him. For the present, anyway, the initiative must lie with Berowne. He said:

'I remember the Theresa Nolan inquest. This Diana Travers drowning is new to me.'

Berowne said:

'It didn't make the national press. There was a line or two in the local paper reporting the inquest. It made no mention of my wife. Diana Travers wasn't a member of her birthday party but they did dine at the same restaurant, the Black Swan on the river at Cookham. The authorities seem to have adopted that slogan of the insurance company. Why make a drama out of a crisis?'

So there had been a cover up, of sorts anyway, and Berowne had known it. The death by drowning of a girl who worked for a Minister of the Crown and who died after dining at the restaurant where that Minister's wife was also dining, whether or not he himself was present, would normally have justified at least a brief paragraph in one of the national papers. Dalgliesh asked:

'What do you want me to do, Minister?'

Berowne smiled.

'Do you know, I'm not exactly sure. Keep a watching brief, I suppose. I'm not expecting you to take this on personally. That would obviously be ridiculous. But if it does develop into open scandal I suppose someone eventually will have to deal with it. At this stage I wanted to put you in the picture.'

But that was precisely what he hadn't done. With any other man Dalgliesh would have pointed this out and with some asperity. The fact that he felt no temptation to do so with Berowne interested him. He thought, there'll be reports on both the inquests. I can get most of the facts from official sources. For the rest, if it does blow up into an open accusation, he'll have to come clean. And if that happened, whether it became a matter for him personally and for the proposed new squad would depend on how great the scandal, how real the suspicion and of what precisely. He wondered what Berowne was expecting him to do, find a potential blackmailer or investigate him for double murder? But it seemed likely that a scandal of some sort would eventually break. If the communication had been sent to the *Paternoster Review*, it had almost certainly been sent to other papers or journals, possibly to some of the nationals. They might at present be choosing to hold their fire, but that didn't mean they'd have thrown the communication into their wastepaper baskets. They had probably spiked it while they checked with their lawyers. In the meantime, to wait and watch was probably the wisest option. But there would be no harm in having a word with Conrad Ackroyd. Ackroyd was one of the greatest gossips in London. Half an hour spent in his wife's elegant and comfortable drawing room was usually more productive and a great deal more entertaining than hours spent beavering through official files.

Berowne said:

'I'm meeting a party of constitutents at the House. They want to be shown round. Perhaps if you've time you could walk over with me.' Again the request was a command.

But when they left the building he turned without explanation to the left and down the steps to Birdcage Walk. So they were to walk to the House the longest way, along the fringe of St James's Park. Dalgliesh wondered if there were things his companion wished to confide which could more easily be said out of the office. The ninety acres of entrancing if formalized beauty of the park, crossed by paths so convenient that they might have been purposefully designed to lead from one centre of power to another, must, he thought, have heard more secrets than any other part of London.

But if that were Berowne's intention, it was destined to be thwarted. They had hardly crossed Birdcage Walk when they were hailed by a cheerful shout and Jerome Mapleton trotted up beside them, rubicund, sweaty-faced, a little out of breath. He was the member for a South London constituency, a safe seat which he nevertheless hardly ever left, as if fearing that even a week's absence might put it in jeopardy. Twenty years in the House still hadn't dampened his extraordinary enthusiasm for the job and his not unappealing surprise that he should actually be there. Talkative, gregarious and insensitive, he attached himself as if by magnetic force to any group larger or more important than the one he was actually in. Law and order was his chief interest, a concern popular with his prosperous middle-class constituents cowering behind their security locks and decorative window bars. Adapting his subject to his captive audience, he plunged at once into parliamentary small talk about the newly appointed committee, bobbing up and down between Berowne and Dalgliesh like a small craft on bumpy water.

'This committee, "Policing a Free Society: The Next Decade", isn't that what it's called? Or is it "Policing in a Free Society: The Next Decade"? Didn't you spend the first session deciding whether to include that little preposition? So typical. You're looking at policy as well as technical resources aren't you? Isn't that a tall order? It's made the committee larger than is usually thought effective hasn't it? Wasn't the original idea to look again at the application of science and technology to policing? The committee seems to have enlarged its terms of reference.'

Dalgliesh said:

'The difficulty is that technical resources and policy aren't easily separated, not when you get to practical policing.'

'Oh I know, I know. I quite appreciate that, my dear Commander. This proposal to monitor vehicle movements on the motorways, for example. You can do it, of course. The question is, should you do it? Similarly with surveillance. Can you examine advanced scientific methods divorced from the policy and ethics of their actual use? That's the question, my dear Commander. You know it, we all know it. And, come to that, can we any longer rely on the received doctrine that it's for the Chief Constable to decide on the allocation of resources?'

Berowne said:

'You aren't, of course, about to utter heresy – that we ought to have a national force?' He spoke without apparent interest, his eyes fixed ahead. It was as if he were thinking: Since we're lumbered with this bore, let's throw him a predictable subject and hear his predictable views.

'No. But it might be better to have one by will and intention than by default. De jure, Minister, not de facto. Well, you'll have plenty to keep you busy, Commander, and given the membership of the working party it won't be dull.' He spoke wistfully. Dalgliesh suspected that he had hoped to be a member. He heard him add: 'I suppose that's the attraction of the job for the sort of man you are.'

What sort of man, thought Dalgliesh. The poet who no longer writes poetry. The lover who substitutes technique for commitment. The policeman disillusioned with policing. He doubted whether Mapleton intended his words to be offensive. The man was as insensitive to language as he was to people.

He said:

'I've never been quite sure what the attraction is except that the job isn't boring and it gives me a private life.'

Berowne spoke with sudden bitterness:

33

'It's a job with less hypocrisy than most. A politician is required to listen to humbug, talk humbug, condone humbug. The most we can hope for is that we don't actually believe it.' The voice rather than the words disconcerted Mapleton. Then he decided to treat it as a joke and giggled. He turned to Dalgliesh.

'So what now for you personally, Commander? Apart from the working party, of course?'

'A week of lectures to the Senior Command Course at Bramshill. Then back here to set up the new squad.'

'Well, that should keep you busy. What happens if I murder the member for Chesterfield West when the working party is actually sitting?' He giggled again at his own audacity.

'I hope you'll resist the temptation, sir.'

'Yes, I must try. The committee is too important to have the senior police detective interest represented on a part-time basis. And by the way, talking of murder, there's a very odd paragraph about you, Berowne, in today's *Paternoster Review*. Not altogether friendly, I thought.'

'Yes,' said Berowne shortly. 'I've seen it.' He increased his pace so that Mapleton, already out of breath, had to choose between talking or using his energy to keep up. When they reached the Treasury, he obviously decided that the reward was no longer worth the effort and with a valedictory wave disappeared up Parliament Street. But if Berowne had been seeking a moment for further confidences it had disappeared. The pedestrian signal had turned to green. No pedestrian, seeing the lights in his favour at Parliament Square, hesitates. Berowne gave him a rueful glance as if to say: 'See how even the lights conspire against me,' and walked briskly across. Dalgliesh watched as he crossed Bridge Street, acknowledged the salute of the policeman on duty and disappeared into New Palace Yard. It had been a brief and unsatisfactory encounter. He had the feeling that Berowne was in some trouble deeper and more subtly disturbing than poison pen messages. He turned back to the Yard telling himself that if Berowne wanted to confide he would do it in his own good time.

But that time had never come. And it had been on his drive back from Bramshill a week later that he had turned on his radio and heard the news of Berowne's resignation of his ministerial post. The details had been sparse. Berowne's only explanation had been that he felt it was time for his life to take a new direction. The Prime Minister's letter, printed in the next day's *Times* had been conventionally appreciative but brief. The great British public, most of whom would have been hard pressed to name three members of the Cabinet of this or any administration, were preoccupied with chasing the sun in one of the rainiest summers in recent years and took the loss of a junior minister with equanimity. Those parliamentary gossips still in London enduring the boredom of the silly season waited in happy expectation for the scandal to break. Dalgliesh waited with them. But there was, apparently, to be no scandal. Berowne's resignation remained mysterious.

Dalgliesh had already sent while at Bramshill for the reports of the inquests on Theresa Nolan and Diana Travers. On the face of it there was no cause for concern. Theresa Nolan, after having a medical termination on psychiatric grounds, had left a suicide note for her grandparents which they had confirmed was in her handwriting and which made her intention to kill herself plain beyond any doubt. And Diana Travers, after drinking and eating unwisely, had apparently herself dived into the Thames to swim out to her companions who were messing about in a punt. Dalgliesh had been left with an uneasy feeling that neither case was as straightforward as the reports made it appear, but certainly there was no prima facie evidence of foul play in connection with either of the two deaths. He was uncertain how much further he was expected to probe or whether, in the light of Berowne's resignation, there was any point in his probing. He had decided to do nothing further for the present and to leave it to Berowne to make the first move.

And now Berowne, the harbinger of death, was himself dead, by his hand or another's. Whatever secret he had been hoping to confide on that short walk to the House would remain for ever unspoken. But if he had, indeed, been murdered then the secrets would be told; through his dead body, through the intimate detritus of his life, through the mouths, truthful, treacherous, faltering, reluctant of his family, his enemies, his friends. Murder was the first destroyer of privacy as it was of so much else. And it seemed to Dalgliesh an ironic twist of fate that it should be he, whom Berowne had shown a disposition to trust, who should now be travelling to begin that inexorable process of violation.

35

4

They were almost at the church before he wrenched his mind back to the present. Massingham had driven in, for him, an unusual silence as if sensing that his chief was grateful for this small hiatus between knowledge and discovery. And he had no need to inquire the way. As always, he had mapped his route before setting out. They were driving up the Harrow Road and had just passed the complex of St Mary's Hospital when the campanile of St Matthew's came suddenly into view on their left. With its crossed bands of stone, its high arched windows and copper cupola it reminded Dalgliesh of the brick towers he had laboriously erected as a child, brick on precarious brick, until they toppled in noisy disorder on the nursery floor. It held for him some of the same hubristic impermanence and, even as he gazed, he half expected it to bend and sway.

Without speaking, Massingham took the next turning to the left and drove towards it down a narrow road bordered on each side by a terrace of small houses. They were identical with their small upper windows, narrow porches and square bays, but it was obvious that the road was coming up in the world. Some few still showed the tell-tale signs of multiple occupation, dishevelled lawns, peeling paint and drawn secretive curtains. But these were succeeded by bright little bandboxes of social aspiration; newly painted doors, carriage lamps, an occasional hanging basket, the front garden paved to provide standing for the car. At the end of the road the huge bulk of the church with its soaring walls of smoke-blackened brick looked as much out of keeping as it was out of scale with this small domestic self-sufficiency.

The huge north door, large enough for a cathedral, was closed. Beside it a grime encrusted board gave the name and address of the parish priest and the time of services, but there was nothing else to suggest that the door was ever opened. They drove slowly down a narrow asphalt drive between the southern wall of the church and the railing bordering the canal, but still there was no sign of life. It was obvious that the news of a murder hadn't yet spread. There were only two cars parked outside the south porch. One, he guessed, belonged to Detective Sergeant Robins and the red Metro to Kate Miskin. He wasn't surprised that she was there before them. She opened the door before Massingham had time to ring, her handsome shield-shaped face composed under the light brown fringe, and looking in her shirt, slacks and leather jerkin as elegantly informal as if she had just come in from a country walk. She said:

'The DI's compliments, sir, but he had to get back to the station. They've got a homicide at Royal Oak. He left as soon as Sergeant Robins and I arrived. He'll be available from midday if you need him. The bodies are here, sir. They call it the Little Vestry.'

It was typical of Glyn Morgan not to have disturbed the scene. Dalgliesh had a respect for Morgan as a man and a detective but was grateful that either duty, tact or a mixture of both had taken him away. It was a relief not to have to soothe and propitiate an experienced detective who could hardly be expected to welcome a commander from the new C1 squad intruding on his patch.

Kate Miskin pushed open the first door on the left and stood aside for Dalgliesh and Massingham to enter. The Little Vestry was garishly lit like a film set. Under the glare of the fluorescent light the whole bizarre scene, Berowne's sprawled body and severed throat, the clotted blood, the tramp propped like a stringless marionette against the wall, looked for a moment unreal, a Grand Guignol tableau too overdone and too contrived to be convincing. Hardly glancing at Berowne's body Dalgliesh picked his way across the carpet to Harry Mack and squatted beside him. Without turning his head he asked:

'Were the lights on when Miss Wharton found the bodies?'

'Not in the passage, sir. But she says this light was on. The boy confirms it.'

'Where are they now?'

'In the church, sir. Father Barnes is with them.'

'Have a word with them will you, John? Tell them I'll speak to them as soon as I'm free. And try to contact the boy's mother. We ought to get him away from here as soon as possible. Then I want you here.'

Harry looked as derelict in death as he must have done in life. If it hadn't been for the breastplate of blood, he could have been asleep, legs stuck out, head slumped forward, his woollen cap slipped over his right eye. Dalgliesh put his hand under the chin and gently lifted the head. He had the sensation that it would come apart from the body and roll over into his hands. He saw what he had expected to find, the single slash across the throat, apparently from left to right, cutting through the trachea to the vertebrae. Rigor mortis was already well established and the skin was ice cold

37

and goosefleshed as the erector muscles of the hairs contracted with the onset of rigor. Whatever concatenation of chance or desire had brought Harry Mack to this place, there was no mystery about the cause of death.

He was wearing old plaid trousers, over-large and loose as pantaloons, and tied at the ankles with string. Above them, as far as it was possible to see for the blood, he wore a striped knitted pullover over a navy jumper. A malodorous checked jacket, stiff with grime, was unbuttoned, the left flap lying open. Dalgliesh raised it with careful fingers touching only the extreme edge of the cloth and saw underneath a smudge of blood on the carpet about two centimetres long and thicker at the right end than at the left. Peering closer he thought he could see a smear roughly the same length on the jacket pocket, but the cloth was too dirty for him to be sure. But the implication of the smear on the carpet was plain enough. One or more drops of blood must have fallen or been spilt from the weapon before Harry fell and had then been smeared along the carpet as the body was dragged against the wall. But whose blood? If it proved to be Harry's, the discovery was of small significance. But suppose it were Berowne's? Dalgliesh felt impatient for the arrival of the forensic biologist, although he knew he couldn't hope for the answer, not yet. Samples of both victims' blood would be taken from the bodies at the post-mortem, but it would be three days at least before he could expect to get the result of the analysis.

He wasn't sure what impulse had made him go first to Harry Mack's body. But now he trod carefully across the carpet to the bed and stood silently looking down at the body of Berowne. Even as a 15-year-old boy, standing at the side of the bed of his dead mother, he hadn't felt the need to think, far less to utter, the word goodbye. You couldn't speak to someone who was no longer there. He thought: we can vulgarize everything but not this. The body in its stiff ungainliness, beginning already, or so it seemed to his over-sensitive nose, to emit the first sour-sweet stink of decay, yet had an inalienable dignity because it once had been a man. But he knew, none better, how quickly this spurious humanity would drain away. Even before the pathologist had finished at the scene and the head was wrapped, the hands mittened in their plastic bags, even before Doc Kynaston got to work with his scalpels, the corpse would be an exhibit, more important, more cumbersome and more difficult to preserve than other exhibits in the case, but still an exhibit, tagged, documented, dehumanized, invoking only

38

interest, curiosity or disgust. But not yet. He thought: I knew this man, not well but I knew him. I liked him. Surely he deserves better of me than to gaze at him with my policeman's eyes.

He lay head towards the door and at an angle of forty-five degrees from the bed, his shoes touching the end. The left hand was flung out, the right lay closer to the body. The bed had been covered with a blanket of hand-knitted squares of bright wool. It looked as if Berowne had clutched it as he fell, half-pulling it from the bed, so that it lay partly bunched at his right side. An open razor, the blade thick with clotted blood lay on top of it, a few inches from his right hand. It was extraordinary how many details simultaneously impressed themselves on Dalgliesh's mind. A thin wedge of what looked like mud caked between the heel and the sole of the left shoe; the pattern of blood stiffening the fine fawn cashmere of the sweater; the half-open mouth fixed in a rictus between a smile and a sneer; the dead eyes seeming as he watched to shrink into their sockets; the left hand with its long pale fingers, curved and delicate as a girl's; the palm of the right hand thick with blood. But the whole picture struck him as wrong, and he knew why. Berowne couldn't both have held the razor in his right hand and clutched at the blanket as he fell. But if he had first dropped the razor, why should it be lying on top of the blanket and so conveniently close to his hand as if it had slipped from the opening fingers? And why should the palm be so thickly clotted, almost as if another's hand had lifted it and smeared it into the blood at the throat? If Berowne himself had wielded the razor, surely the palm which had clutched it would have been less bloodied.

He was aware of a small noise at his side and looked round to see Detective Inspector Kate Miskin looking, not at the corpse, but at him. She quickly turned her eyes away but not before he had detected, to his discomfort, a look of grave, almost maternal solicitude. He said roughly:

'Well, Inspector?'

'It looks obvious, sir, murder followed by suicide. The classical pattern of self-inflicted wounds – three cuts, two tentative, the third cutting through the trachea.' She added:

'It could be used as an illustration in a textbook of forensic medicine.'

He said:

'There's no difficulty in recognizing the obvious. One should be slower to believe it. I want you to break the news to his family. The address is 62 Campden Hill Square. There is a wife and an elderly mother, Lady Ursula Berowne, and a housekeeper of sorts. Use your discretion about which is best able to take it. And take a DC. When the news breaks they may be pestered and need protection.'

'Yes, sir.'

She showed no resentment at being ordered from the scene. She knew that the job of breaking the news wasn't a routine chore, that she hadn't been chosen merely because she was the only woman in his team and he saw this as a woman's job. She would break the news with tact, discretion, even with compassion. God knew she had had enough practice in ten years of policing. But she would still be a traitor to grief, watching and listening, even as she spoke the formal words of condolence, for the flicker of an eyelid, the tensing of hands and face muscles, for the unwise word, for any sign that for someone in that waiting house in Campden Hill Square this might not be news at all.

5

Before he concentrated on the actual scene of the crime, Dalgliesh always liked to make a cursory survey of the surroundings to orientate himself, and, as it were, to set the scene of murder. The exercise had its practical value, but he recognized that, in some obscure way, it fulfilled a psychological need, just as in boyhood he would explore a country church by first walking slowly round it before, with a frisson of awe and excitement, pushing open the door and beginning his planned progress of discovery to the central mystery. And now, in these few remaining minutes, before the photographer, the fingerprint officers, the forensic biologists arrived at the scene, he had the place almost to himself. Moving into the passage he wondered whether this quiet air tinctured with the scent of incense, candles, and the more solidly Anglican smell of musty prayer books, metal polish and flowers, had held for Berowne also the promise of discovery, of a scene already set, a task inevitable and inescapable.

The brightly lit passage with its floor of encaustic tiles and its white painted walls ran the whole west end of the church. The Little Vestry was the first room on the left. Next to it and with a connecting door, was a small kitchen about ten feet by eight. Then came a narrow lavatory with an old-fashioned bowl of decorated porcelain and a mahogany seat with, above it, a hanging chain set under a single high window. Lastly an open door showed him a high square room, almost certainly set under the campanile, which was obviously both the vestry proper and the bell room. Opposite it the passage was separated from the body of the church by a ten foot long grille in delicate wrought iron which gave a view up the nave to the cavernous glitter of the apse and the Lady Chapel on the right. A central door in the grille topped with figures of two trumpeting angels gave entry to the church for the processing priest and choir. To the right a padlocked wooden box was fixed to the grille. Behind it, but within reach of stretching hands, stood a branching candlestand, also in wrought iron, with a box of matches in a brass holder attached to it with a chain, and a tray containing a few small candles. Presumably this was to enable people who had business in the vestry to light a candle when the grille door to the church was locked. Judging from the cleanness of the candle-

41

holders it was a facility of which they seldom, if ever, took advantage. There was only one candle in place, stuck upright like a pale wax finger, and this had never been lit. Two of the brass chandeliers suspended above the nave gave a gentle diffused light but the church looked dimly mysterious compared with the glare of the passage and the figures of Massingham and the detective sergeant quietly conferring, of Miss Wharton and the boy patiently sitting like hump-backed dwarfs on low chairs in what must be the children's corner, seemed as distanced and insubstantial as if they moved in a different dimension of time. As he stood watching Massingham looked up, caught his eye, and moved down the nave towards him.

He returned to the Little Vestry and, standing in the doorway, drew on his latex gloves. It always surprised him a little that it was possible to fix the attention on the room itself, its furniture and objects, even before the bodies had been packaged and taken away, as if in their fixed and silent decrepitude they had for a moment become part of the room's artefacts, as significant as any other physical clue, no more and no less. As he moved into the room he was aware of Massingham behind him, alert, already drawing on his gloves but, for him, unnaturally subservient, pacing quietly behind his chief like a recently qualified houseman deferentially attendant on the consultant. Dalgliesh thought: Why is he behaving as if I need tactful handling, as if I'm suffering from a private grief? This is a job like any other. It promises to be difficult enough without John and Kate treating me as if I'm a sensitive convalescent.

Henry James, he remembered, had said of his approaching death, 'So here it is at last, the distinguished thing!'. If Berowne had thought in these terms, then this was an incongruous place in which to receive so honoured a visitation. The room was about twelve foot square and lit by a fluorescent tube running almost the full length of the ceiling. The only natural light came from two high curved windows. They were covered outside by a protective mesh which looked like chicken wire on which the dirt of decades had accumulated, so that the panes were honeycombs of greenish grime. The furniture, too, looked as if it had been gradually acquired over the years; gifts, rejects, the unregarded remnants of long-forgotten jumble sales. Opposite the door and set under the windows was an ancient oak desk with three right hand drawers, one without handles. On its top was a simple oak cross, a much used blotter in a leather pad, and an old fashioned black telephone, the receiver off the rest and lying on its side.

Massingham said:

'Looks as if he took it off. Who wants the telephone to ring just when he's concentrating on slitting his jugular?'

'Or his killer was taking no chances on the bodies being discovered too soon. If Father Barnes took it into his head to ring and got no reply he'd probably come round to see if Berowne was all right. If he continued to get the engaged sound he'd probably assume that Berowne was having an evening of telephoning and let it go.'

'We might get a palm print, sir.'

'Unlikely, John. If this is murder, we're not dealing with a fool.'

He continued his exploration. With his gloved hands, he pulled open the top drawer and found a stack of white writing paper, of cheap quality, headed with the name of the church, and a box of envelopes. Apart from these, the desk held nothing of interest. Against the left-hand wall was an assortment of canvas and metal chairs neatly stacked, presumably for the occasional use of the parochial church council. Beside them was a five-drawer metal filing cabinet, and next to it a small glass-fronted bookcase. He slipped the catch and saw that it contained an assortment of old prayer books, missals, devotional pamphlets, and a pile of booklets about the history of the church. There were only two easy chairs, one set on each side of the fireplace; a compact brown chair in torn leather with a patchwork cushion, and a grubby, more modern chair with fitted pads. One of the stacked chairs had been up-righted. A white towel hung over its back and on the seat rested a brown canvas bag, its zip open. Massingham rummaged gently inside and said:

'A pair of pyjamas, a spare pair of socks, and a table napkin wrapped round half a sliced loaf, wholemeal, and a piece of cheese. Roquefort by the look of it. And there's an apple. A Cox if that's relevant.'

'Hardly. Is that all, John?'

'Yes, sir. No wine. Whatever he thought he was doing here, it doesn't look like an assignation, not with a woman anyway. And why choose this place with the whole of London open to him? Bed too narrow. No comfort.'

'Whatever he was looking for, I don't think it was comfort.'

Dalgliesh had moved over to the fireplace, a plain wooden overmantel with an iron surround patterned with grapes and convolvulus set in the middle of the right-hand wall. It must, he thought, have been decades since a fire was lit in it for warmth.

43

In front of the grate was a tall electric fire with artificial coals, a high curved back and a triple set of burners. He moved it gently forward and saw that the grate had, in fact, been recently used; someone had tried to burn a diary. It lay open in the firebasket, its leaves curled and blackened. Some pages had apparently been torn out and separately burnt; the brittle fragments of black ash had floated down to lie on top of the debris under the grate, old twisted matchends, coal dust, carpet fluff, the accumulated grit of years. The blue cover of the diary with the year clearly printed had been more resistant to the flames; one corner only was slightly scorched. Whoever had burnt it had evidently been in a hurry, unless, of course, he had been concerned only to destroy certain pages. Dalgliesh made no attempt to touch it. This was a job for Ferris, the scene of crime officer, already hovering impatiently in the passage. The Ferret was never happy when anyone other than himself was examining a scene of crime and it seemed to Dalgliesh that his impatience to get on with the job came through the wall as a palpable force. He crouched low and peered into the debris under the grate. Among the fragments of blackened paper he saw a used safety match, the unburnt half of the stem clean and white as if it had only recently been struck. He said:

'He could have used this to burn the diary. But, if so, where is the box? Have a look in the jacket pockets will you, John.'

Massingham walked over to Berowne's jacket hanging on a hook at the back of the door and felt in the two outer and one inner pockets. He said:

'A wallet, sir, a Parker fountain pen and a set of keys. No lighter and no matches.'

And there were none, either, visible in the room.

With mounting excitement which neither betrayed they moved over to the desk and peered intently at the blotter. It, too, must have been there for years. The pink blotting paper tattered at the edges was marked with a criss-cross of different inks blodged with faded blots. It wasn't, thought Dalgliesh, surprising; most people now used ballpoints rather than ink. But peering more closely he could see that someone had recently been writing with a fountain pen. Superimposed on the older markings were more recent blottings, a pattern of broken lines and half curves in black ink extending over some six inches of the blotter. Their newness was obvious. He went over to Berowne's jacket, and brought out the fountain pen. It was elegantly slim, one of the newest models, and filled, he saw, with black ink. It should be possible for the lab to match the ink even if the letters couldn't be deciphered. But if Berowne had been writing and had blotted the paper at the desk, where was it now? Had he himself disposed of it, torn it up, flushed it down the lavatory, burnt it among the debris of the diary pages? Or had someone else found it, perhaps even come specifically to find it, and either destroyed it or taken it away?

Lastly, he and Massingham passed through the open door to the right of the fireplace, careful not to brush against Harry's body, and explored the kitchen. There was a gas boiler, comparatively modern, mounted above a deep square porcelain sink much stained and with a clean but crumpled tea towel hanging on a hook beside it. Dalgliesh peeled off his gloves and felt the towel. It was slightly damp not in patches but all over as if it had been soaked in water then wrung out and left to dry through the night. He handed it to Massingham who took off his own gloves and ran it through his hand. He said:

'Even if the murderer were naked, or half-naked he would have needed to wash his hands and arms. He could have used this. Berowne's towel is presumably the one hanging on the chair and that looked dry enough.'

He went out to check while Dalgliesh continued his exploration. On the right was a cupboard with a Formica top, brown with tea stains, on which stood one large kettle, one smaller more modern kettle and two teapots. There was also a chipped enamel mug stained almost black inside and smelling of spirits. Opening the cupboard he saw that it contained a collection of unmatched crockery and two folded clean tea towels, both dry, and on the bottom shelf an assortment of flower vases and a battered cane basket containing folded dusters, and tins of metal and furniture polish. Here presumably Miss Wharton and her fellow helpers would arrange the flowers, wash out their dusters, refresh themselves with tea.

Attached to the pipe of the gas boiler by a brass chain was a box of safety matches in a brass holder, similar to the one chained to the candlestand; hinged at the top to allow the insertion of a fresh box. There had been a similar holder and brass chain in the parish room of his father's Norfolk church but he couldn't remember seeing one since. They were clumsy to use, the striking surface barely adequate. It was difficult to believe that the boxes had been removed, then replaced and even more difficult to credit that a match from either of the chained boxes had been struck, then carried lit and precariously flickering into the Little Vestry and used to burn the diary.

Massingham was back beside him. He said:

'The towel next door is perfectly dry and only slightly dirtied. It looks as if Berowne could have washed his hands when he arrived and that's all. It's odd that he didn't leave it in here, except that there's nowhere convenient to hang it. Odder, though, that the killer, assuming there is a killer, didn't use it to dry himself rather than the smaller tea towel.'

Dalgliesh said:

'If he remembered to take it out with him to the kitchen. If he didn't, he'd hardly want to go back for it. Too much blood, too much risk of leaving a clue. Better to use what he found to hand.'

It was apparent that the kitchen was the only room with water and a sink; hand washing as well as washing up must be done here, if at all. Above the sink was a mirror composed of glass tiles stuck to the wall, and under it a simple glass shelf. Upon this was a sponge bag, its zip open, containing a toothbrush and a tube of paste, a dry face flannel and a used bar of soap. Beside this was a more interesting find, a narrow leather case with the initials PSB stamped on it in faded gold. With his gloved hands Dalgliesh lifted the lid and found what he had expected to see, the twin to the cut throat razor lying so incriminatingly close to Berowne's right hand. On the satin lining of the lid was a sticker with the maker's name in old-fashioned twirls, P.J. Bellingham, and the Jermyn Street address. Bellingham, the most expensive and prestigious barber in London and supplier still of razors to those clients who had never adjusted to the shaving habits of the twentieth century.

There was nothing of apparent interest in the lavatory and they made their way into the robing vestry. It was obvious that this was where Harry Mack had settled himself for the night. What looked like an old army blanket, frayed at the edges and stiff with dirt, had been loosely spread in a corner, its fumy stink mingling with the smell of incense to produce an incongruous amalgam of piety and squalor. Beside it was an overturned bottle, a length of grubby cord and a sheet of newspaper on which lay a crust of brown loaf, the core of an apple and some crumbs of cheese. Massingham picked them up and rubbed them between his palms and thumbs and sniffed. He said:

'Roquefort, sir. Hardly a cheese which Harry would have provided for himself.'

There was no evidence that Berowne had started his own meal

– that in itself might be of some help in deciding on the approximate time of death – but he had apparently either cajoled Harry into the church with the promise of a meal or, more likely, had supplied an obvious and immediate need before he was ready for his own share of the supper.

The vestry itself was so familiar from childhood memories that Dalgliesh could have taken one quick glance, shut his eyes and spoken aloud an inventory of high church piety: the packets of incense on top of the cupboard; the incense holder and censer; the crucifix and, behind the faded red serge curtain, the lace-trimmed vestments and the short starched surplices of the choir. But now his mind was on Harry Mack. What had roused him from his half-drunken sleep; a scream, the sound of a quarrel, a falling body? But could he have heard it from this room? As if echoing his thoughts, Massingham said:

'He could have been roused by thirst, gone to the kitchen for a drink of water and stumbled into the crime. That enamel mug looked as if it might be his. Father Barnes will know whether it belongs to the church and with luck there may be prints. Or he could have gone to the lavatory, but I doubt whether he would have heard anything from there.'

And, thought Dalgliesh, he was unlikely to have gone afterwards into the kitchen to wash. Massingham was probably right. Harry had settled himself for the night and then felt the need for a drink of water. But for that fatal thirst, he might still be quietly sleeping.

Outside in the passage Ferris was prancing gently on his toes like a runner limbering for a race.

Massingham said:

'The blotter, the enamel mug, the tea towel and the diary are all important and there's what looks like a recently struck match in the grate; we need that. But we shall want all the debris in the fireplace and the S-bends in the pipes. The probability is that the murderer washed himself in the kitchen.'

None of it really needed saying, least of all to Charlie Ferris. He was the most expert of the Met's scene of crime officers and the one Dalgliesh always hoped would be available when he began a new case. It was inevitable that he should be nicknamed 'the Ferret', although seldom in his hearing. He was very small, sandy-haired, sharp-featured and with his sense of smell so well developed that it was rumoured that he had sniffed out a suicide in Epping Forest even before the animal predators got to it. In his spare time he sang in one of the most famous of London's amateur choirs. Dalgliesh, who had heard him at a police concert, never ceased to be surprised that so narrow a chest and so slight a frame could produce such a powerful organ-toned bass. He was fanatical about his job and had even designed the most appropriate clothes for searching: white shorts and a sweat shirt, a plastic swimming cap, tight fitting to prevent the spilling of hairs, latex gloves as fine as a surgeon's and rubber bathing shoes over his bare feet. His creed was that no murderer ever left the scene of a crime without leaving some physical evidence of his crime behind him. If it were there, Ferris would find it.

There were voices in the passage. The photographer and fingerprint officers had arrived. Dalgliesh could hear George Matthews's booming voice cursing the traffic in Harrow Road and Sergeant Robins's quieter answer. Someone laughed. They were neither callous nor particularly insensitive, but neither were they undertakers, required to assume a professional reverence in the face of death. The forensic biologist hadn't yet arrived. Some of the most distinguished scientists at the Metropolitan Laboratory were women and Dalgliesh, recognizing in himself an old-fashioned sensitivity which he certainly wouldn't have confessed to them, was always glad when it was possible to remove the more horrific bodies before they arrived to track and photograph the bloodstains and supervise the collection of samples. He left Massingham to greet and brief the new arrivals. It was time to talk to Father Barnes. But first he wanted a word with Darren before the boy was driven home.

6

Sergeant Robins said:

'He'd have been gone by now, sir, but the little devil's been playing us up. We couldn't get an address out of him, and when he did come up with one it was wrong, a non-existent road. Could have been a bloody waste of time. I think he's telling the truth now but I had to threaten him with the Juvenile Bureau, the Welfare and God knows what before he did. And then he tried to give us the slip and run off. I was lucky to grab him.'

Miss Wharton had already been driven back to Crowhurst Gardens by a WPC, there to be solaced no doubt with tea and sympathy. She had made gallant efforts to pull herself together but had still been confused about the precise sequence of events between arriving at the church and the moment when she had pushed open the door of the Little Vestry. The important fact for the police to ascertain was whether she or Darren had actually entered the room with the risk that the scene had been contaminated. Both were adamant that they had not. Beyond this there was little of importance which she could tell and Dalgliesh had briefly heard her story and let her go.

But it was irritating that Darren was still with them. If he needed to be questioned again it was right that it should be at home and with his parents present. Dalgliesh knew that his present insouciance in the face of death was no guarantee that the horror hadn't touched him. It wasn't always an obvious trauma which disturbed a child the most. And it was odd that the boy was so resistant to being driven home. Normally, a ride in a car, even a police car, would be something of a treat for a child particularly now that a gratifying crowd was beginning to collect to witness his notoriety, drawn by the yards of white tape which sealed off the whole of the south part of the church and by the police cars and the unmistakable black and sinister mortuary van parked between the church wall and the canal. Dalgliesh went up to the car and opened the door. He said:

'I'm Commander Dalgliesh. It's time we got you home, Darren. Your mother will be worried.' And surely the boy should be at school. The term must have started. But that, thank God, was hardly his concern.

49

Darren, looking small and extremely disgruntled, was slumped in the front left-hand seat. He was an odd-looking child with an engaging monkey-like face, pale under the rash of freckles, snub-nosed and bright-eyed beneath the spiked almost colourless lashes. He and Sergeant Robins had obviously tried each other's patience to the limits, but he cheered up at the sight of Dalgliesh and enquired with childish belligerence:

'You the boss man round here?'

A little disconcerted, Dalgliesh replied cautiously:

'You could say that.'

Darren looked round with bright suspicious eyes, then said:

'She never did it, Miss Wharton. She's innercent.'

Dalgliesh said, seriously:

'No, we didn't think she did. You see, it needed more strength than an elderly lady or a boy could have. You're both in the clear.'

'Yeah, that's all right then.'

Dalgliesh said:

'You're fond of her?'

'She's all right. She wants lookin' after, mind you. She's daft. She hasn't got the sense she was born with. I keep an eye on her, like.'

'I think she relies on you. It was lucky you were together when you found the bodies. It must have been horrible for her.'

'Turned her up proper. She don't like blood, you see. That's why she won't have a coloured TV. She makes out she can't afford it. That's daft. She's always buying flowers for that BVM.'

'BVM?' said Dalgliesh, his mind scurrying after some unrecog-nized make of car.

'That statue in the church. The lady in blue with the candles in front of her. They're called BVMs. She's always puttin' flowers there and lightin' candles. Ten pee, they are. Five pee for the small ones.'

His eyes shifted as if he had been lured on to dangerous ground. He added quickly:

'I reckon she won't have a coloured TV 'cause she don't like the colour of blood.'

Dalgliesh said:

'I think you're probably right. You've been very helpful to us, Darren. And you're quite sure that you didn't go into that room, either of you?'

'Naw, I told yer. I was behind 'er all the time.' But the question had been unwelcome and for the first time some of his cockiness seemed to have drained from him. He slumped back in his seat and stared resentfully through the windscreen.

Dalgliesh went back into the church and found Massingham.

'I want you to go home with Darren. I've a feeling there's something he's keeping back. It might not be important but it would be helpful to have you there when he talks to his parents. You've got brothers, you know about small boys.'

Massingham said, 'You want me to go now, sir?'

'Obviously.'

Dalgliesh knew that the order was unwelcome. Massingham hated to leave a scene of crime even temporarily while the body was still there, and he would go the more unwillingly because Kate Miskin, back now from Campden Hill Square, was to stay. But if he had to go he would go alone. He ordered the police driver out of the car with unusual curtness and drove off at a speed which suggested that Darren was about to enjoy a gratifyingly exciting ride.

Dalgliesh passed through the grille door into the body of the church, turning to close it gently behind him. But even so the soft clang rang sharply in the silence and echoed around him as he made his way down the nave. Behind him out of sight, but always present to the mind, was the apparatus of his trade; lights, cameras, equipment, a busy silence broken only by voices unhushed and confident in the presence of death. But here, guarded by the elegant whorls and bars of wrought iron, was another world as yet uncontaminated. The smell of incense strengthened and he saw ahead a haze of gold where the gleaming mosaics of the apse stained the air and the great figure of Christ in glory, his wounded hands stretched out, glared down the nave with cavernous eyes. Two more of the nave lights had been switched on but the church was still dim compared with the harsh glare of the arc lights trained on the scene and it took him a minute to locate Father Barnes, a dark shape at the end of the first row of chairs under the pulpit. He walked up to him, aware of the ring of his feet on the tiled floor, wondering whether they sounded as portentous to the priest as they did to him.

Father Barnes was sitting bolt upright on his chair, his eyes staring ahead at the gleaming curve of the apse, his body taut and contracted, like that of a patient expecting pain, willing himself to endure. He didn't turn his head as Dalgliesh approached. He had obviously been summoned in a hurry. His face was unshaved and the hands, rigidly clamped together in his lap, were grubby, as if he had gone to bed unwashed. The cassock, whose long black lines etiolated still further his lean body, was old and stained with what

51

looked like gravy. One spot he had tried ineffectively to rub away. His black shoes were unpolished, the leather cracked at the sides, the toes scuffed into greyness. There came from him a smell, half-musty, half disagreeably sweet, of old clothes and incense, overlaid with stale sweat, a smell which was a pitiable amalgam of failure and fear. As Dalgliesh eased his long limbs in the adjoining chair and rested his arm along its back, it seemed to him that his body encompassed and, by its own calm presence, gently eased a core of fear and tension in his companion, so strong that it was almost palpable. He felt a sudden compunction. The man would, of course, have come fasting to the first Mass of the day. He would be craving hot coffee and food. Normally someone at or near the scene would be brewing tea but Dalgliesh had no intention of using the washroom even to boil a kettle until the scene of crime officer had done his work.

He said:

'I won't keep you long, Father. There are just a few questions and we'll let you go back to the Vicarage. This must have been a horrible shock to you.' Father Barnes still didn't look at him. He said in a low voice:

'A shock. Yes, it was a shock. I shouldn't have let him have the key. I don't know really why I did. It isn't easy to explain.' The voice was unexpected. It was low with an agreeable trace of huskiness and with a hint of more power than the frail body would suggest; not an educated voice but one on which education had imposed a discipline which hadn't quite obliterated the provincial, probably East Anglian, accent of childhood. He turned now to Dalgliesh and said again:

'They'll say I'm responsible. I shouldn't have let him have the key. I'm to blame.'

Dalgliesh said:

'You aren't responsible. You know that perfectly well and so will they.' The ubiquitous, frightening, judgemental 'they'. He thought, but did not say, that murder provided its own dreadful excitement for those who neither mourned nor were directly concerned and that people were commonly indulgent to those who helped provide the entertainment. Father Barnes would be surprised – agreeably or otherwise – by the size of next Sunday's congregation. He said:

'Could we start at the beginning? When did you first meet Sir Paul Berowne?'

'Last Monday, just over a week ago. He called at the Vicarage at about half past two and asked if he could see the church. He'd come here first and found he couldn't get in. We'd like to keep the church open all the time but you know how it is today. Vandals, people trying to break open the offertory box, stealing the candles. There's a note in the north porch saying that the key is at the Vicarage.'

'I suppose he didn't say what he was doing in Paddington?'

'Yes, he did, actually. He said that an old friend was in St Mary's Hospital and he'd been to see him. But the patient was having treatment and couldn't see visitors so he had an hour to spare. He said he'd always wanted to see St Matthew's.'

So that was how it had started. Berowne's life, like that of all busy men, was dominated by the clock. He had set aside an hour to visit an old friend. The hour had become unexpectedly available for a private indulgence. He was known to be interested in Victorian architecture. However fantastic the labyrinth into which that impulse had led him, his first visit to St Matthew's at least had had the comforting stamp of normality and reason.

Dalgliesh said:

'Did you offer to accompany him?'

'Yes, I offered but he said not to trouble. I didn't press it. I thought he might want to be alone.' So, Father Barnes was not without sensitivity. Dalgliesh said:

'So you gave him the key. Which key?'

'The spare one. There are only three to the south porch. Miss Wharton has one and I keep the other two at the Vicarage. There are two keys on each ring, one to the south door and a smaller key which opens the door in the grille. If Mr Capstick or Mr Pool want a key – they're our two churchwardens – they come to the Vicarage. It's quite close, you see. There's only one key to the main north door. I always keep that in my study. I never lend it out in case it gets lost. It's too heavy, anyway, for general use. I told Sir Paul that he would find a booklet describing the church in the bookstand. It was written by Father Collins and we've always meant to revise it. It's over there on the table by the north porch. We only charge three pence.' He turned his head painfully, like an arthritic patient, as if inviting Dalgliesh to buy a copy. The gesture was pathetic and rather appealing. He went on:

'I think he must have taken one because two days later I found a five pound note in the box. Most people just put in three pence.'

'Did he tell you who he was?'

'He said his name was Paul Berowne. I'm afraid it didn't mean anything to me at the time. He didn't say he was an MP or a baronet, nothing like that. Of course, after he'd resigned I knew who he was. It was in the papers and on the television.'

Again there was a pause. Dalgliesh waited. After a few seconds the voice began again, stronger now and more resolute.

'I suppose he was away about an hour, perhaps less. Then he returned the key. He said he would like to sleep that night in the Little Vestry. Of course he didn't know it was called that. He said in the small room with the bed. The bed has been there since Father Collins's time, in the war. He used to sleep in the church during air raids so that he could put out the fire bombs. We've never taken it away. It's useful if people feel ill during services or if I want to rest before midnight Mass. It doesn't take up much room. It's only a narrow collapsible bed. Well, you've seen it.'

'Yes. Did he give any reason?'

'No. He made it sound quite an ordinary request and I didn't like to ask why. He wasn't a man you could cross-question. I did say what about sheets, a pillowcase. He said he'd bring anything he needed.'

He had brought one double sheet and had slept between it, doubled over. Otherwise he had used the existing old army blanket folded beneath him and on top the blanket of multicoloured woollen squares. The pillowcase on what was obviously a chair cushion was also presumably his.

Dalgliesh asked:

'Did he take the key away with him then or call back for it that night?'

'He called back for it. That must have been about eight o'clock or a little earlier. He was standing at the door of the Vicarage carrying a grip. I don't think he came by car. I didn't see one. I gave him the key. I didn't see him again until next morning.'

'Tell me about the next morning.'

'I used the south door as usual. It was locked. The door to the Little Vestry was open and I could see that he wasn't there. The bed was made up very tidily. Everything was tidy. There was a sheet and a pillowcase folded on top. I looked through the grille into the church. The lights weren't on but I could just see him. He was sitting in this row, a little further along. I went into the vestry and robed for the Mass, then through the grille door into the church. When he saw that Mass was to be in the Lady Chapel he moved across and sat in the back row. He didn't speak. No one else was there. It wasn't Miss Wharton's morning and Mr Capstick, who likes to come to the nine thirty Mass, had influenza. There were just the two of us. When I'd finished the first prayer and turned to face him, I saw that he was kneeling. He took Communion. Afterwards, we walked together to the Little Vestry. He handed me back the key, thanked me, picked up his grip and left.'

'And that was all on that first occasion?'

Father Barnes turned and looked at him. In the dimness of the church his face looked lifeless. Dalgliesh saw in his eyes a mixture of entreaty, resolution, and pain. There was something he feared to say yet needed to confide. Dalgliesh waited. He was used to waiting. At last Father Barnes spoke.

'No, there is something. When he lifted his hands and I placed the wafer in his palms – I thought I saw –' he paused then went on, 'there were marks, wounds. I thought I saw stigmata.'

Dalgliesh fixed his eyes on the pulpit. The painted figure of a Pre-Raphaelite angel carrying a single lily, its yellow hair crimped under the wide halo, looked back at him with its bland, uncurious gaze. He asked:

'On his palms?'

'No. On his wrists. He was wearing a shirt and a pullover. The cuffs were a little loose. They slipped back. That's when I saw.'

'Have you told anyone else about this?'

'No, only you.'

For a full minute neither of them spoke. In all his career as a detective Dalgliesh couldn't remember a piece of information from a witness more unwelcome and – there was no other word – more shocking. His mind busied itself with images of what this news could do to his investigation if it ever became public; the newspaper headlines; the half-amused speculation of the cynics; the crowds of sightseers, the superstitious, the credulous, the genuine believers, thronging the church in search of . . . what? A thrill, a new cult, hope, certainty? But his distaste went deeper than irritation at an unwelcome complication to his inquiry, at the bizarre intrusion of irrationality into a job so firmly rooted in the search for evidence which would stand up in court, documented, demonstrable, real. He was shaken, almost physically, by an emotion far stronger than distaste and one of which he was half-ashamed; it seemed to him both ignoble and in itself hardly more rational than the event itself. What he was feeling was a revulsion amounting almost to outrage. He said:

'I think you should continue to say nothing. It isn't relevant to Sir Paul's death. It isn't even necessary to include it in your

55

statement. If you do feel the need to confide in anyone, tell your bishop.'

Father Barnes said simply:

'I shan't tell anyone else. I think I did have a need to speak about it, to share it. I've told you.'

Dalgliesh said:

'The church was dimly lit. You said the lights weren't on. You were fasting. You could have imagined it. Or it could have been a trick of the light. And you saw the marks only for a couple of seconds when he lifted his palms to receive the Host. You could have been mistaken.'

He thought: Who am I trying to reassure, him or me?

And then came the question which against reason he had to ask:

'How did he look? Different? Changed?'

The priest shook his head then said, with great sadness:

'You don't understand. I wouldn't have recognized it, the difference, even if it had been there.' Then he seemed to recover himself. He went on resolutely:

'Whatever it was I saw, if it was there, it didn't last long. And it's not so very unusual. It has been known before. The mind works on the body in strange ways; an intense experience, a powerful dream. And as you say the light was very dim.'

So Father Barnes didn't want to believe it either. He was arguing it away. Well that, thought Dalgliesh wryly, was better than a note in the parish magazine, a telephone call to the daily papers or a sermon next Sunday on the phenomenon of stigmata and the inscrutable wisdom of providence. He was interested to find that they shared the same distrust, perhaps the same revulsion. Later there would be a time and a place to consider why this was so. But now there were more immediate concerns. Whatever had brought Berowne again to that vestry it had been a human hand, his or another's, which had wielded that razor. He said:

'What about yesterday night? When did he ask you if he could come back?'

'In the morning. He rang shortly after nine. I said I'd be in any time after six that evening and he came for the key precisely on the hour.'

'Are you sure of the time, Father?'

'Oh yes, I was watching the six o'clock news. It had only just started when he rang the bell.'

'And again, no explanation?'

'No. He was carrying the same grip. I think he came by bus or underground or walked. I didn't see a car. I handed him the key at the door, the same key. He thanked me and left. I didn't come to the church that night, I had no reason to. The next I knew was when the boy came for me and told me that there were two dead bodies in the Little Vestry. You know the rest.'

Dalgliesh said:

'Tell me about Harry Mack.'

The change of subject was obviously welcome and Father Barnes was voluble on the subject of Harry. Poor Harry was a problem for St Matthew's. For some reason, no one knew why, he had for the last four months taken to sleeping in the south porch. He usually bedded down on newspapers and covered himself with an old blanket which he sometimes left in the porch, ready for the next night, and sometimes took away, rolled into a long wad and tied around his stomach with string. Father Barnes, when he found the blanket, hadn't liked to remove it. After all, it was Harry's only covering. But it wasn't really convenient to have the porch used as a shelter or as a storage for Harry's odd and rather smelly belongings. The Parochial Church Council had actually discussed whether they ought to install railings and a gate, but that had seemed uncharitable and there were more important things to spend their money on. They had difficulty in meeting their diocesan quota as it was. They had all tried to help Harry, but he wasn't easy. He was known at the Wayfarers' Refuge in Cosway Street in St Marylebone, an excellent place, where he usually got a midday meal and medical attention for minor ailments when he needed it. He was a little too fond of drink and would occasionally get into fights. St Matthew's had liaised with the Refuge about Harry but they hadn't known what to suggest. They had tried to persuade Harry to have a bed in their dormitory but he wouldn't agree. He couldn't bear the intimate contact with other people. He wouldn't even eat his dinner at the refuge. He'd put it between slabs of bread then take it away to eat in the streets. The porch was his place, snug, south-facing, out of public view.

Dalgliesh said:

'So he's not likely to have knocked on the door yesterday evening and asked Sir Paul to let him in.'

'Oh no, Harry wouldn't have done that.'

But somehow he had got in. Perhaps he'd already settled down under his blanket when Berowne arrived. Berowne had asked him in out of the cold to share his meal. But how had he persuaded Harry? He asked Father Barnes what he thought.

'It must have happened that way, I suppose. Harry could already have been here in the porch. He usually dosses down fairly early. And it was unexpectedly cold last night for September. But it's very odd. There must have been something about Sir Paul that gave him confidence. He wouldn't have done it for most people. Even the warden at the Refuge, so experienced with the city's derelicts, couldn't persuade Harry to spend the night there. But they only have the dormitory, of course. It was sleeping or eating with other people Harry couldn't stand.'

And here, thought Dalgliesh, he had had the larger vestry to himself. It could have been the assurance of that privacy and, perhaps, the promise of food which had persuaded him in from the cold. He asked:

'When were you last here in the church, Father? I'm talking about yesterday.'

'From four thirty till about quarter past five, when I read Evensong in the Lady Chapel.'

'And when you locked up after you, how certain could you be that there was no one here, perhaps hidden? Obviously you didn't search the church. Why should you? But if someone were hiding here, would you have been likely to have seen him?'

'I think so. You see how it is. We've no high pews, only the chairs. There's nowhere he could have hidden.'

Dalgliesh said:

'Perhaps under the altar, the high altar or in the Lady Chapel? Or in the pulpit?'

'Under the altar? It's a horrible thought, sacrilege. But how could he have got in? I found the church locked when I arrived at four thirty.'

'And no one had collected the keys during the day, not even the churchwardens?'

'No one.'

And Miss Wharton had assured the police that her key hadn't left her handbag. He said:

'Could anyone have got in during Evensong? Perhaps while you were praying? Were you alone in the Lady Chapel?'

'Yes. I came in by the south door as usual and locked both it and the door in the grille after me. Then I unlocked the main door. That would be the natural way in for any stranger wanting to attend a service. My people know that I always unlock the main door for Evensong and it's very heavy. It squeaks dreadfully. We're always meaning to oil it. I don't think anyone could have entered without my hearing.'

58

'Did you tell any other person that Sir Paul was spending the night here yesterday?'

'Oh no. There wasn't anyone to tell. And I wouldn't have said anything. He didn't ask for secrecy; he didn't ask for anything. But I don't think he would have liked another person to know. No one else knew anything about him, not until this morning.'

Dalgliesh went on to question him about the blotter and the spent match. Father Barnes said that the Little Vestry had last been used two days ago on Monday the sixteenth when the Parochial Church Council had met as usual at five thirty, immediately after Evensong. He had presided, sitting at the desk, but hadn't used the blotter. He always wrote with a biro. He hadn't been aware of any recent marks but, then, he wasn't very clever at noticing that kind of detail. He was sure that the match couldn't have been left there by anyone in the PCC. Only George Capstick smoked and he used a pipe which he lit with a lighter. But he hadn't been at the PCC because of recovering, still, from the flu. People had remarked how pleasant it was not to be enveloped in smoke.

Dalgliesh said:

'These are small details and probably of no importance. But I would be grateful if you would keep them to yourself. And I'd like you to have a look at the blotter and see whether you can remember what it looked like on Monday. And we've found a rather dirty enamel mug. It would be helpful to know if that belonged to Harry.'

Seeing Father Barnes's face, he added:

'You won't need to go back into the Little Vestry. When the photographer has finished we'll bring out the items to you. And then I expect you'll be glad to get back to the Vicarage. We shall need a statement later, but that can wait.'

They sat for a minute in silence as if what had passed between them needed to be assimilated in peace. So here, thought Dalgliesh, lay the secret of Berowne's quixotic decision to give up his job. It had been something more profound, less explicable, than disillusionment, mid-life restlessness, the fear of a threatened scandal. Whatever had happened to him on that first night in St Matthew's vestry had led him, the next day, to change the whole direction of his life. Had it also led him to his death?

As they both got up they heard the clang of the grille door. Inspector Miskin was walking down the aisle. When she came up to them she said:

'The pathologist has arrived, sir.'

59

7

Lady Ursula Berowne sat immobile in her sitting room on the fourth floor of 62 Campden Hill Square and gazed out over the top boughs of the plane trees as if at some far distant unseeable vista. It seemed to her that her mind was like an overfilled glass which only she could hold steady. One jerk, one shudder, one small loss of control and it would spill over into a chaos so terrible that it could only end in death. It was strange, she thought, that her physical response to shock should be the same now as it had been after Hugo was killed, so that to her present grief was added a grief for him as keen, as new as when she had first heard that he was dead. And the physical symptoms had been the same; a raging thirst, her body parched and shrivelled, her mouth dry and sour as if infected with her own breath. Mattie had brewed her pot after pot of strong coffee which she had gulped down scalding hot, black, unaware of its oversweetness. Afterwards she had said:

'I would like something to eat, something salty. Anchovy toast.' She had thought: I'm like a woman pregnant with grief, subject to odd fancies.

But that was over now. Mattie had wanted to put a shawl over her shoulders, but she had shrugged it off and demanded to be left alone. She thought: There is a world outside this body, this pain. I shall take hold of it again. I shall survive. I must survive. Seven years, ten at the most, that's all I need. Now she waited, husbanding strength for the first of many visitors. But this was someone she herself had summoned. There were things which had to be said to him and there might not be much time.

Shortly after eleven she heard the doorbell ring, then the groaning of the lift and a soft clatter as the grille door closed. The door of her sitting room opened and Stephen Lampart came quietly in.

It seemed to her important that she should meet him standing. But she couldn't restrain the grimace of pain as her arthritic hip took the weight and she knew that the hand grasping the knob of her cane was trembling. Immediately he was at her side. He said:

'Oh no. Please, you mustn't.'

With one firm hand on her arm he solicitously helped her back into the chair. She disliked casual touching, the assumption of acquaintances or strangers that her disablement entitled them to handle her, as if her body were a despised encumbrance which it was proper gently to push and pull into place. She wanted to shrug off his firm, proprietorial grasp but managed to resist. But she couldn't prevent the tightening of her muscles at his touch and she knew that he hadn't missed this instinctive revulsion. When he had settled her, gently and with professional competence, he seated himself in the chair opposite. They were separated by a low table. A circle of polished rosewood established his dominance; strength against weakness, youth against age, doctor and sub-servient patient. Except that she wasn't his patient. He said:

'I believe you're waiting for a hip replacement.' It was Barbara, of course, who had told him, but he wouldn't be the first one to mention her name.

'Yes, I'm on the list of the orthopaedic hospital.'

'Forgive me, but why not go private? Aren't you suffering unnecessarily?'

It was, she thought, an almost indecently incongruous remark with which to begin a visit of condolence; or was this his way of confronting her grief and stoicism by taking refuge on professional ground, the only one on which he felt confident and could speak with authority?

She said:

'I prefer to be treated as a National Health patient. I enjoy my privileges but that is one I don't happen to want.'

He smiled gently, humouring a child.

'It seems a little masochistic.'

'Possibly. But I haven't called you here for a professional opinion.'

'Which as an obstetrician I wouldn't, in any case, be competent to give. Lady Ursula, this news about Paul is horrifying, unbeliev-able. Shouldn't you have sent for your own doctor? Or a friend? You should have someone with you. It's wrong for you to be alone at a time like this.'

She said:

'I have Mattie if I need the usual palliatives, coffee, alcohol, warmth. At 82, the few people one might wish to see are all dead. I have outlived both my sons. That is the worst thing that can happen to a human being. I have to endure it. But I don't have to talk about it.' She could have added: 'least of all with you' and it seemed to her that the words, unspoken, hung on the air between them. He was for a moment silent as if considering them, accepting their justice. Then he said:

61

'I would, of course, have called on you later even if you hadn't telephoned. But I wasn't sure that you'd want to see anyone so soon. You got my letter?'

He must have written it as soon as Barbara had telephoned the news and had sent it round by one of his nurses who, in a hurry to get home after night duty, hadn't even stopped to hand it in but had slipped it through the letter box. He had used all the obvious adjectives. He hadn't needed a thesaurus to decide on the appropriate response. Murder, after all, was appalling, terrible, horrific, unbelievable, an outrage. But the letter, a social obligation too promptly performed, had lacked conviction. And he should have known better than to have his secretary type it. But that, she thought, was typical. Scrape away the carefully acquired patina of professional success, prestige, orthodox good manners, and the real man was there; ambitious, a little vulgar, sensitive only when sensitivity paid. But much of this, she knew, was prejudice and prejudice was dangerous. She must be careful to betray it as little as possible if the interview were to go the way she wanted. And it was hardly fair to criticize the letter. Dictating condolences to the mother of a murdered husband whom you've been cuckolding for the last three years would take more than his limited social vocabulary.

She hadn't seen him for nearly three months and she was struck anew by his good looks. He had been an attractive youth, tall, rather ungainly, with a thatch of black hair. But now the gangling figure had been smoothed and tailored by success, he carried his height with easy assurance and the grey eyes – which he knew so well how to use – held a basic wariness. His hair, frosted now with grey, was still thick with an unruliness that expensive cutting still hadn't completely disciplined. It added to his attractiveness, hinting at an untamed individuality which was far removed from the tedium of conventional male good looks.

He leaned forward and looked across at her intently, his grey eyes softened with sympathy. She found herself resenting his easy assumption of professional concern. But he did it very well. She almost expected him to say, 'We did all we could, all that was humanly possible.' Then she told herself that the concern could be genuine. She had to resist the temptation to underrate him, to stereotype him as the handsome, experienced seducer of cheap fiction. Whatever he was, he wasn't as uncomplicated as that. No human being could be. And he was, after all, acknowledged as a fine gynaecologist. He worked hard, he knew his job.

When Hugo was at Balliol, Stephen Lampart had been his closest friend. She had liked him in those days and some of that liking still remained, resented, only half-acknowledged, but bound up with memories of sunlit walks in Port Meadow, luncheon and laughter in Hugo's rooms, with the years of hope and promise. He had been the clever, handsome, ambitious boy from a lower-middle-class home, likeable, amusing, buying himself into the company he wanted by looks and wit, clever at concealing the itch of ambition. Hugo had been the privileged one, his mother an earl's daughter, his father a baronet and a distinguished soldier, possessor of the Berowne name, inheritor of what remained of the Berowne money. For the first time she found herself wondering whether he had resented not only Hugo but all the family, and whether that subsequent betrayal could have had long roots in the soil of an old envy. She said:

'There are two things we have to discuss and there may not be much time or another opportunity. Perhaps I ought to say first that I didn't ask you here to criticize my daughter-in-law for infidelity. I'm not in a position to criticize anyone's sexual life.'

The grey eyes grew cautious. He said:

'How wise of you. Few of us are.'

'But my son was murdered. The police will know that soon if they don't already. And I know it now.'

He said:

'Forgive me, but can you be sure? All Barbara could tell me when she rang this morning was that the police had found Paul's body and that of a tramp,' he paused, 'with injuries to their throats.'

'Their throats were cut. Both their throats. And from the careful tact with which the news was broken, I imagine that the weapon was one of Paul's razors. I suppose Paul could have been capable of killing himself. Most of us are, given sufficient pain. But what he wasn't capable of was killing that tramp. My son was murdered, and that means that there are certain facts the police will make it their business to discover.'

He asked, calmly:

'What facts, Lady Ursula?'

'That you and Barbara are lovers.'

The hands clasped loosely in his lap tightened then relaxed. But he was still able to meet her eyes.

'I see. Was it Paul or Barbara who told you that?'

'Neither. But I've lived in the same house with my daughter-in-law for four years. I'm a woman. I may be crippled but I have the use of my eyes and my intelligence.'

'How is she, Lady Ursula?'

'I don't know. But before you leave I suggest that you make it your business to find out. I've only seen my daughter-in-law for three minutes since I got the news. She is, apparently, too distressed to talk to visitors. It seems that I count as a visitor.'

'Is that quite fair? Sometimes other people's grief is harder to bear, to face, than one's own.'

'Particularly if one's own isn't acute?'

He leaned forward and said quietly:

'I don't think we have any right to assume that. Barbara's feelings may not be intense but Paul was her husband. She cared for him, probably more than either of us understand. This is a horrible business for her, for all of us. Look, do we have to talk now? We're both in shock.'

'We have to talk, and there isn't much time. Commander Adam Dalgliesh is coming to see me as soon as they've finished with whatever it is they're doing at the church. Presumably he'll want to interview Barbara, too. In time, probably sooner than later, they'll get round to you. I have to know what you propose to tell them.'

'This Adam Dalgliesh, isn't he some kind of poet? An odd hobby for a policeman.'

'If he's as good a detective as he is a poet, he's a dangerous man. Don't underestimate the police because of what you read in the upmarket papers.'

He said:

'I don't underestimate the police, but I've no reason to fear them. I know that they combine a macho enthusiasm for selective violence with a rigid adherence to middle-class morality, but you aren't seriously suggesting that they'll suspect me of cutting Paul's throat because I go to bed with his wife? They may be out of touch with social reality but, surely, not that much out of touch.'

She thought: This is more like it, this is the real man.

She said calmly:

'I'm not saying they'll suspect you. I've no doubt you'll be able to provide a satisfactory alibi for last evening. But it will cause less trouble if neither of you lies about your relationship. I'd prefer not to have to lie about it myself. Naturally, I shan't volunteer the information. But it is possible that they will ask.'

'And why should they, Lady Ursula?'

'Because Commander Dalgliesh will liaise with Special Branch. My son was a Minister of the Crown, however briefly. Do you suppose there's anything about a minister's private life, particularly a minister in that Department, which isn't known to those people whose business it is to discover and document this kind of potential scandal? What sort of world do you think we're living in?'

He got up and began slowly pacing in front of her. He said:

'I suppose I ought to have thought of that. I would have thought of it given time. Paul's death has been such an appalling shock. I don't think my mind is working properly yet.'

'Then I suggest that it begins working. You and Barbara have to agree on your story. Better still, agree to tell the truth. I take it that Barbara was your mistress when you first introduced her to Hugo and that she remained your mistress after Hugo was killed and she married Paul.'

He stopped and turned to her.

'Believe me, Lady Ursula, it wasn't intended, it wasn't like that.'

'You mean that she and you graciously decided to abstain from your sexual liaison, at least until the honeymoon was over?'

He came and stood in front of her and looked down.

'I think there's something I ought to say but I'm afraid it isn't, well, gentlemanly.' She thought but did not speak: That word is meaningless now. With you it probably always was. Before 1914, one could talk like that without sounding false or ridiculous, but not now. That word and the world it represented have gone for ever, trodden into the mud of Flanders. She said:

'My son's throat was cut. In the light of that brutality, I don't think we need concern ourselves about gentility, spurious or otherwise. It's about Barbara, of course.'

'Yes. There's something you ought to understand if you don't already. I may be her lover but she doesn't love me. She certainly doesn't want to marry me. She's as satisfied with me as she can be with any man. That's because I understand her needs and I don't make demands. Not many demands. We all make some. And, of course, I'm in love with her as far as I'm capable of loving anyone. That's necessary to her. And she feels safe with me. But she wouldn't get rid of a perfectly good husband and a title to marry me. Not by divorce. Certainly not by conniving at murder. You have to believe that if you and she are going to go on living together.'

She said:

'That at least was frank. You seem well suited to each other.'

He accepted the subtle insult behind the irony.

'Oh yes,' he said sadly, 'we suit each other.' He added, 'I suspect she doesn't even feel particularly guilty. Less so than I do, oddly enough. It's difficult to take adultery seriously if you're not getting much pleasure out of it.'

'Your role must be exhausting and hardly satisfying. I admire your self-sacrifice.'

His smile was reminiscent, secretive.

'She's so beautiful. It's absolute, isn't it? It doesn't even depend on whether she's well or happy or not tired or on what she wears. It's always there. You can't blame me for trying.'

'Oh yes,' she said, 'I can, and I do.'

But she knew that she was being less than honest. All her life she had been beguiled by physical beauty in men and in women. It was what she had lived by. When, in 1918, with her brother and fiancé both killed, she, an earl's daughter, had gone on the stage in defiance of tradition, what else had she to offer? Not, she thought with wry honesty, any great dramatic talent. She had, almost casually and instinctively, demanded physical beauty in her lovers and had been unjealous and over-indulgent of it in her women friends. They had been the more surprised when, at the age of 32, she had married Sir Henry Berowne, apparently for less obvious qualities, and had given him two sons. She thought now of her daughter-in-law as she had watched her many times, standing motionless in front of the glass in the hall. Barbara was incapable of passing a mirror without that moment of narcissistic stillness, that calm reflective gaze. What had she been watching for? That first droop from the corner of the eyes, the fading blue, the dry fold of skin, the first crêping of the neck which would show how transitory it was, this overprized perfection.

He was still restlessly pacing, still talking.

'Barbara likes to feel that attention is being paid to her. You have to admit that about the sexual act. Attention, specific and intense, is certainly being paid. She needs men to desire her. She doesn't much want them actually to touch her. If she thought I had a hand in killing Paul she wouldn't thank me. I don't think she'd forgive me. And she certainly wouldn't protect me. I'm sorry. I've been too frank. But I think it had to be said.'

'Yes, it had to be said. Who would she protect?'

'Her brother, possibly, but not, I should have thought for long and certainly not at any risk to herself. They've never been particularly close.'

She said dryly:

'No sibling loyalty will be demanded of her. Dominic Swayne

was here in this house with Mattie for the whole of yesterday evening.'

'Is that his story or hers?'

'Are you accusing him of having a hand in my son's death?'

'Of course not. The idea is ridiculous. And if Mattie says he was with her, I've no doubt he was. We all know that Mattie is a model of rectitude. You asked me if there was anyone Barbara would protect, I can think of no one else.'

He had stopped his pacing now and sat down again opposite to her.

He said:

'Your reasons for telephoning me. You said there were two things we needed to discuss.'

'Yes. I should like to be sure that the child Barbara is carrying is my grandchild, not your bastard.'

His shoulders stiffened. For a moment, it could have been a second only, he sat rigidly gazing down at his clasped hands. In the silence she heard the ticking of the carriage clock. Then he looked up. He was still calm but she thought that his face was paler.

'Oh, there's no doubt about that. No possible doubt. I had a vasectomy three years ago. I'm not suited to fatherhood and I hadn't any wish to be made ridiculous by paternity suits. I can give you the name of my surgeon if you want proof. That's probably simpler than relying on blood tests once he's born.'

'He?'

'Oh yes, it's a boy. Barbara had an amniocentesis. Your son wanted an heir and he's going to get an heir. Didn't you know?'

She sat for a moment in silence. Then she said:

'Isn't that a risky procedure for the foetus, particularly so early in the pregnancy?'

'Not with the new techniques and in expert hands. And I saw that she was in expert hands. No, not mine. I'm not that kind of fool.'

She asked:

'Did Paul know about the child before he died?'

'Barbara hasn't said. I imagine not. After all, she's only just heard of it herself.'

'The pregnancy? Surely not.'

'No, the sex of the child. I rang and told her first thing yesterday morning. But Paul may have suspected that there was a child on the way. After all, he did go back to that church, presumably to ask his God for further and better instructions.'

She was seized by an anger so intense that, for a moment, she couldn't speak. And when her voice did come it quavered like the voice of an old, impotent woman. But at least her words could sting. She said:

'You never could resist it, even as a boy, the temptation to combine vulgarity with what you imagined was wit. Whatever happened to my son in that church, and I don't pretend to understand it, in the end he died because of it. When next you're tempted to indulge in a cheap witticism you might remember that.'

His own voice was low and as cold as steel.

'I'm sorry. I thought from the beginning that this conversation was a mistake. We're both too shocked to be rational. And now, if you'll excuse me, I'll go down to see Barbara before the police descend on her. She's alone I take it?'

'As far as I know she is. Anthony Farrell should be arriving soon. I sent for him to his private address as soon as I got the news but he has to get up from Winchester.'

'The family lawyer? Having him here when the police arrive – won't that look suspicious? Too like a necessary precaution?'

'He's a family friend as well as a lawyer. It's natural for both of us to want him here. But I'm glad you're seeing her before he arrives. Tell her to answer Dalgliesh's questions but not to volunteer information, any information. I've no reason to suppose the police will take an unnecessarily dramatic view of what, after all, was common adultery. But it isn't something they'll expect her to confide even if they know about it. Too much candour looks as suspicious as too little.'

He asked:

'Were you with her when the police broke the news?'

'The police didn't break the news. I did. It seemed to me advisable in all the circumstances. A competent woman officer told me first, then I went down alone to see Barbara. She behaved very prettily. Barbara has always known what emotion it is appropriate for her to feel. And she's a good actress. She should be. She's had plenty of practice. Oh, and another thing. Tell her to say nothing about the child. That's important.'

'If it's what you want, what you think is wise. But it could be helpful to mention the pregnancy. They'd be particularly gentle with her.'

'They'll be gentle. They won't be sending a fool.'

They were speaking like confederates, precariously allied in a conspiracy which neither would acknowledge. She felt a cold disgust as physical as nausea and with it there swept over her a weakness which shrivelled her in her chair. Immediately, she was aware of him at her side, of his fingers, gentle, firm, pressing her wrist. She knew that she should have resented his touch, but now it comforted her. She lay back, her eyes closed, and her pulse strengthened under his fingers. He said:

'Lady Ursula, you really should see your doctor. Malcolm Hancock, isn't it? Let me ring him.' She shook her head.

'I'm all right. I can't cope with another person yet. Until the police arrive I need to be alone.' It was a confession of weakness which she hadn't expected to make, not to him and not at such a moment. He walked to the door. When his hand was on the knob she said:

'There's one more thing. What do you know about Theresa Nolan?'

'No more than you, I imagine, probably less. She only worked at Pembroke Lodge for four weeks and I hardly set eyes on her. She nursed you, lived in this house, for over six. And when she came to me she was already pregnant.'

'And Diana Travers?'

'Nothing, except that she was unwise enough to overeat, drink too much and then dive into the Thames. As you must know, Barbara and I had left the Black Swan before she drowned.' He was silent for a moment and then said, gravely:

'I know what you're thinking about, that ludicrous article in the *Paternoster Review*. Lady Ursula, may I give you some advice? Paul's murder, if it is murder, is perfectly simple. He let someone into that church, a thief, another derelict, a psychopath, and that person killed him. Don't complicate his death which, God knows, is horrible enough, with old, irrelevant tragedies. The police will have enough to get their teeth into without that.'

'Are they both irrelevant?'

He didn't answer. Instead he said:

'Has Sarah been told?'

'Not yet. I tried to telephone her this morning at the flat but there was no reply. She was probably out getting a paper. I'll try again as soon as you leave.'

'Would you like me to go round? She is Paul's daughter, after all. This will be a terrible shock to her. She oughtn't to learn it from the police or the television news.'

'She won't. If necessary, I'll go round myself.'

'But who will drive you? Isn't Wednesday Halliwell's day off?'

69

'There are taxis.'

She resented the way in which he seemed to be taking over, insinuating himself into the family as cunningly as he once had in Oxford. And then, again, she reproached herself for unfairness. He had never lacked his measure of kindness. He said:

'She ought to have time for preparation before the police burst in on her.'

Time for what? she wondered. To make a decent pretence that she cared? She didn't reply. Suddenly she wanted him gone so urgently that it was all she could do not to order him to get out. Instead she held out her hand. Bending, he took it in his and then raised it to his lips. The gesture, theatrical and ludicrously inappropriate disconcerted but did not disgust her. After he had left, she found herself looking down at her thin, ring encrusted fingers, at the age-mottled knuckles against which, briefly, his lips had rested. Was the gesture a tribute to an old woman facing with dignity and courage a last tragedy? Or had it been something more subtle, a pledge that, despite everything, they were allies, that he understood her priorities and would make them his?

8

Dalgliesh remembered a surgeon once telling him that Miles Kynaston had shown promise of becoming a brilliant diagnostician, but had given up general medicine for pathology at registrar level because he could no longer bear to watch human suffering. The surgeon had sounded a note of amused condescension as though he were betraying a colleague's unfortunate weakness, wryly observed, which a more prudent man would have detected before beginning his medical training, or at least would have come to terms with before his second year. It could, Dalgliesh thought, have been true. Kynaston had fulfilled his promise, but now he applied his diagnostic skills to the unrepining dead, whose eyes couldn't implore him to offer hope, whose mouths could no longer cry out. Certainly he had a taste for death. Nothing about it disconcerted him; its messiness, its smell, the most bizarre of its trappings. Unlike most doctors, he saw it, not as the final enemy, but as a fascinating enigma, each cadaver, which he would gaze at with the same intent look as he must once have fixed on his living patients, a new piece of evidence which might, if rightly interpreted, bring him closer to its central mystery.

Dalgliesh respected him more than any other pathologist with whom he had worked. He came promptly when called, and was equally prompt reporting on a post-mortem. He didn't indulge in the crude autopsy humour which some of his colleagues found necessary to bolster their social self-esteem; dinner guests could know themselves safe from distasteful anecdotes about carving knives or missing kidneys. Above all he was good in the witness box, too good for some people. Dalgliesh remembered the sour comment of a defending counsel after a verdict of guilty: 'Kynaston's getting dangerously infallible with juries. We don't want another Spilsbury.'

He never wasted time. Even as he greeted Dalgliesh he was taking off his jacket and was drawing his fine latex gloves over stubby-fingered hands which looked unnaturally white, almost bloodless. He was tall and stolidly built, giving an impression of shambling clumsiness until one saw him working in a confined space when he would seem physically to contract and become compact, even graceful, moving about the body with the lightness

71

and precision of a cat. His face was fleshy, the dark hair receding from a high speckled forehead, the long upper lip as precisely curved as an arrow, and the full, heavily lidded eyes dark and very bright, giving his face a look of sardonic, humorous intelligence. Now he squatted, toad-like, by Berowne's body, his hands hanging loosely in front of him, palely disembodied. He gazed at the throat wounds with extraordinary concentration, but made no move to touch the body except to run his hand lightly over the back of the head, like a caress. Then he said:

'Who are they?'

'Sir Paul Berowne, late MP and junior minister, and a tramp, Harry Mack.'

'On the face of it, murder followed by suicide. The cuts are textbook; two fairly superficial from left to right, then one above, swift, deep, severing the artery. And the razor neatly to hand. As I say, on the face of it obvious. A little too obvious?'

Dalgliesh said:

'I thought so.'

Kynaston stepped gingerly over the carpet to Harry, prancing on tiptoe like an inexpert dancer.

'One cut. Enough. Again from left to right. Which means that Berowne, if it were Berowne, stood behind him.'

'So why isn't Berowne's right shirt-sleeve soaked with blood? All right, it's heavily bloodstained, his own or Harry's blood or both. But if he killed Harry, wouldn't you expect a greater amount of soaking?'

'Not if he turned up his shirt-sleeve first and took him from behind.'

'And turned it down again before slitting his own throat? Unlikely, surely.'

Kynaston said:

'Forensic should be able to identify Harry's blood, or what could be Harry's blood, on the shirt-sleeve as well as Berowne's own. There seem to be no visible stains between the bodies.'

Dalgliesh said:

'Forensic have been over the carpet with the fibre-optic lamp. They may get something. And there is one discernible smudge under Harry's jacket and a trace of what looks like blood on the jacket lining immediately above it.'

He lifted the corner. Both of them looked at the stain on the carpet in silence. Dalgliesh said:

'It was under the jacket when we found it. That means it was there before Harry fell. And if it proves to be Berowne's blood, then he died first, unless, of course, he staggered across to Harry after making one or more of the superficial cuts in his own throat. As a theory, it strikes me as ludicrous. If he were in the very act of cutting his own throat, how could Harry have stopped him? So why bother to kill him? But is it possible, medically possible?'

Kynaston looked at him. Both knew the importance of the question. He said:

'After the first superficial cut, I'd say that it was.'

'But would he still have had the strength to kill Harry?'

'With his own throat partly cut? Again, after that first superficial cut, I don't think one can rule it out. He'd be in a state of high excitement, remember. It's amazing what strength people do find. After all, we're supposing that he was interrupted in the act of suicide. Hardly the moment when a man is at his most rational. But I can't be certain. No one can. You're asking the impossible, Adam.'

'I was afraid so. But it's too neat.'

'Or you want to believe it's too neat. How do you see it?'

'From the position of the body I think he could have been sitting on the edge of the bed. Assuming he was murdered, assuming that the murderer went first into the kitchen, then he could have crept back silently and attacked Berowne from behind. A blow, a cord round the throat. Or he grabs him by the hair, drags back the head, makes the first deep cut. The others, the ones designed to look tentative, could have come afterwards. So we look for any mark under the cuts, or for a bump on the back of the head.'

Kynaston said:

'There is a bump but it's small. It could have been caused by the body falling. But we'll know more at the PM.'

'An alternative theory is that the killer knocked him out first, then went into the washroom to strip and came back for the final throat-cutting before Berowne had a chance to come round. But that raises obvious objections. He'd have to judge the force of the blow very carefully and you'd expect it to leave more than a slight bump.'

Kynaston said:

'But it raises fewer objections than the first theory, that he came in half-naked and armed with a razor and yet there are no obvious signs that Berowne put up any resistance.'

'He could have been taken by surprise. He would expect his visitor to come back through the door to the kitchen. It's possible

that he tiptoed down the passage and came in by the main door. That's the most likely theory, given the position of the body.'
Kynaston said:
'You're assuming premeditation then? That the killer knew he'd find a razor to hand?'
'Oh yes. If Berowne were murdered then the killing was premeditated. But I'm theorizing in advance of the facts, the unforgivable sin. All the same, there's something contrived about it, Miles. It's too obvious, too neat.'
Kynaston said:
'I'll finish the preliminary examination and then you can take them away. I would normally do the PM first thing tomorrow but they aren't expecting me back at the hospital until Monday and the PM room is tied up until the afternoon. Three thirty is the earliest. Is that all right for your people?'
'I don't know about the lab. The sooner the better for us.'
Something in his voice alerted Kynaston. He said:
'Did you know him?'
Dalgliesh thought: this is going to come up again and again. You knew him. You're emotionally involved. You don't want to see him as mad, a suicide, a killer. He said:
'Yes, I knew him slightly, mostly across a committee table.'
The words seemed to him grudging, almost a small treachery. He said again:
'Yes, I knew him.'
'What was he doing here?'
'He had some kind of religious quasi-mystical experience here in this room. He may have been hoping to recapture it. He'd arranged with the parish priest to stay the night here. He gave no explanation.'
'And Harry?'
'It looks as if Berowne let him in. He may have found him sleeping in the porch. Apparently Harry couldn't tolerate being with other people. There's evidence that he was proposing to sleep further along the passage in the larger vestry.'
Kynaston nodded and got down to his familiar routine. Dalgliesh left him to it and went out into the passage. Watching this violation of the body's orifices, preliminaries to the scientific brutality to follow, had always made him feel uncomfortably like a voyeur. He had often wondered why he found it more offensive and ghoulish than the autopsy itself. Was it, perhaps, because the body was so recently dead, sometimes hardly cold. A superstitious man might fear that the spirit, so recently released, hovered around

74

to be outraged at this insult to the discarded, still vulnerable, flesh. There was nothing for him to do now until Kynaston had finished. He was surprised to find himself tired. He expected to be exhausted later in an investigation when he would be working a sixteen-hour day, but this early heaviness, the feeling that he was already spent in mind and body was new to him. He wondered whether it was the beginning of age, or one more sign that this case was going to be different.

He went back into the church, sat down in a chair in front of a statue of the Virgin. The huge nave was empty now. Father Barnes had gone, escorted home by a police constable. He had been readily helpful about the mug, identifying it as one Harry had often had with him when he was found sleeping in the porch. And he had tried to be helpful about the blotter, staring at it with almost painful intensity before saying that he thought that the black markings hadn't been there when he had last seen the blotter on Monday evening. But he couldn't be sure. He had taken a sheet of writing paper from the desk and used it to make notes during the meeting. This had covered the blotter so that he had really only seen it for a short time. But, as far as his memory went, the black markings were new.

Dalgliesh was grateful for these minutes of quiet contemplation. The scent of incense seemed to have intensified, but it smelled to him overlaid with a sickly, more sinister smell, and the silence wasn't absolute. At his back he could hear the ring of footsteps, an occasional raised voice, calm, confident and unhurried, as the unseen professionals went about their work behind the grille. The sounds seemed very far off and yet distinct and he had the sensation of a secret, sinister busy-ness, like the scrabbling of mice behind the wainscot. Soon, he knew, the two bodies would be neatly parcelled in plastic sheeting. The rug would be carefully folded to preserve bloodstains, and in particular, that one significant stain of dried blood. The scene of crime exhibits, packed and tagged, would be carried to the police car; the razor, the crumbs of bread and cheese from the larger room, the fibres from Harry's clothing, that single burnt matchhead. For the moment he would keep possession of the diary. He needed to have it with him when he went to Campden Hill Square.

At the foot of the statue of the Virgin and Child stood a wrought-iron candleholder bearing its triple row of clotted sockets, the tips of burnt wick deep in their rims of wax. On impulse he felt in his pocket for a tenpenny piece and dropped it in the box. The clatter was unnaturally loud. He half-expected to hear Kate or Massingham moving up beside him to watch, unspeaking but with interested eyes, this untypical act of sentimental folly. There was a box of matches in a brass holder chained to the candlerack, similar to the one at the back of the church. He took one of the smaller candles and, striking a match, held it to the wick. It seemed to take an unduly long time before it took hold. Then the flame burnt steadily, a limpid, unflickering glow. He stuck the candle upright in a socket then sat and gazed at the flame, letting it mesmerize him into memory.

9

It was over a year ago but it seemed even longer. They had both
been attending a seminar on judicial sentencing at a northern
university, Berowne to open it formally with a brief speech,
Dalgliesh to represent the police interest; and they had travelled by
rail in the same first class compartment. For the first hour Berowne,
with his private secretary, had dealt with official papers while
Dalgliesh, after a final perusal of the agenda, had settled down to
re-read Trollope's *The Way We Live Now*. When the last file had
been placed in the briefcase, Berowne had looked across at him and
had seemed to want to talk. The young Principal, with a tact that
would help ensure he remained a 'high flyer' had suggested that
he should take first luncheon if that were agreeable to the Minister,
and had disappeared. And for a couple of hours they had talked.

Looking back on it, Dalgliesh was still amazed that Berowne
should have been so frank. It was as if the train journey itself, the
old-fashioned intimate compartment in which they had found
themselves, the freedom from interruptions and the tyranny of the
telephone, the sense of time visibly flying, annihilated under the
pounding wheels, not to be accounted for, had released both of
them from a carefulness which had become so much a part of living
that they were no longer aware of its weight until they let it slip
from their shoulders. Both were very private men. Neither needed
the masculine camaraderie of club or golf course, pub or grouse
moor which so many of their colleagues found necessary to solace
or sustain their over-busy lives.

Berowne had spoken at first spasmodically, then easily, and
finally intimately. From the ordinary subjects of casual conversation
– books, recent plays, acquaintances they had in common – he had
gone on to talk about himself. Both had leaned forward, hands
loosely clasped. To a casual passenger, glancing in as he lurched
down the corridor, they must, thought Dalgliesh, have looked like
two penitents in a private confessional absolving each other.
Berowne had seemed not to expect a reciprocal confidence, indiscretion traded for indiscretion. He spoke; Dalgliesh listened.
Dalgliesh knew that no politician would have talked with such
freedom unless he had had absolute confidence in his listener's
discretion. It was impossible not to feel flattered. He had always

respected Berowne; now he warmed to him and was honest enough about his own reactions to know why Berowne had spoken of his family:

'We're not a distinguished family, merely an old one. My great grandfather lost a fortune because he was fascinated by a subject for which he had absolutely no talent – finance. Someone told him that the way to make money was to buy when the shares were low and sell when they were high. A simple enough rule which struck his rather undeveloped mind with the force of divine inspiration. He had absolutely no difficulty in following the first precept. The problem was that he never had the opportunity to follow the second. He had a positive genius for picking losers. So had his father. In his case the losers were on four legs. But I feel grateful to great grandfather nevertheless. Before he lost his money he had the good sense to commission John Soane to design the Campden Hill Square house. You're interested in architecture, aren't you? I'd like you to see it when you can spare a couple of hours. It needs at least that. In my view it's even more interesting than the Soane museum in Lincoln's Inn Fields; a perverse neo-classicism I suppose you'd call it. I find it satisfying, architecturally anyway. But I'm not sure that it isn't a house to admire rather than to live in.'

Dalgliesh had wondered how Berowne knew about his fondness for architecture. It could only have been because he read his poetry. A poet may heartily dislike having to talk about his verse but the knowledge that someone has actually read it is never unwelcome.

And now, sitting legs stretched, on a chair too low comfortably to accommodate his six feet two inches, eyes fixed on that single taper, unflickering in the incense-heavy stillness, he could hear again the tone, taut with self-disgust, in which Berowne had explained why he had given up the law:

'Such odd things determine why and when one makes that kind of decision. I suppose I had persuaded myself that sending men to prison wasn't something I cared to do for the rest of my life. And appearing only for the defence has always seemed too easy an option. I was never really good at pretending that I could assume my client to be innocent because I or my instructing solicitor had been careful to ensure that he didn't actually confess. By the time you've seen your third rapist walk free because you've been cleverer than the prosecuting counsel, you lose the taste for that particular victory. But that's just the easy explanation. I suspect it wouldn't have happened if I hadn't lost an important case, important to me anyway. You won't remember it – Percy Matlock. He killed his wife's lover. It wasn't a particularly difficult case and we were confident we'd get it reduced to manslaughter. Even with that lesser verdict there was plenty of mitigation. But I didn't prepare carefully enough. I suppose I thought I didn't need to. I was pretty arrogant in those days. But it wasn't only that. At the time I was very much in love, one of those adventures which seem of overwhelming import-ance at the time but, afterwards, leave one wondering if it wasn't a kind of sickness. But I just wasn't giving the case what it needed. Matlock was convicted of murder and died in prison. He had one child, a daughter. Her father's conviction unhinged what precarious stability she'd managed to maintain and after she came out of the psychiatric hospital she got in touch with me and I gave her a job. She still keeps house for my mother. I don't think she's otherwise employable, poor girl. So I live with a constant and uncomely reminder of folly and failure, and no doubt it does me good. The fact that she's actually grateful to me, devoted is the word people use, doesn't make it easier.'

He had gone on to talk of his brother, killed five years earlier in Northern Ireland:

'The title came to me through his death. Most of the things I expected to value in life have come to me through death.'

Not, Dalgliesh remembered, the 'things I value'. The 'things I expected to value'.

He could smell above the all-pervading redolence of incense, the faint acrid smoke of the candle. Getting up from his chair, he left it burning, the pale flame staining the air, and moved down the nave through the grille and into the back of the church.

In the bell room Ferris had set up his metal exhibits table and had neatly laid out his spoils, each tagged and shrouded in its plastic envelope. Now he was standing back regarding them with the faintly anxious proprietorial air of a stallholder at a church bazaar wondering whether he has set out his wares to best advantage. And indeed, thus dignified and labelled, these diverse and ordinary objects had assumed an almost ritualistic significance; the shoes, one with its wedge of mud behind the heel, the stained beaker, the blotter with its criss-cross of dead marks made by dead hands, the diary, the remains of Harry Mack's last meal, the closed razor case and, occupy-ing the centre of the table, the prize exhibit, the open cut-throat razor, its blade and bone handle gummy with blood. Dalgliesh asked:

'Anything interesting?'

'The diary, sir.' He made a move as if to take it out of its packet. Dalgliesh said:

'Leave it. Just tell me.'

'It's the last page. It looks as if he tore out the entries for the last two months and burned those pages separately, then chucked the book open on the flames. The cover is only singed. The last page is the one which sets out the summary of the calendars for last year and next. There's no sign even of singeing, but the top half is missing. Someone has torn the page in two.' He added:

'I suppose he could have folded it and used it as a spill to get a light from the pilot on the gas water heater.'

Dalgliesh picked up the bag containing the shoes. He said:

'It's possible.'

But it struck him as unlikely. For a murderer in a hurry, and this murderer had been in a hurry, it would have been a tedious and uncertain way to get a light. If he'd come without a lighter or matches, surely the obvious thing would have been to remove the box from the chained brass holder attached to the heater. He turned the shoes over in his hands and said:

'Handmade. There are some extravagances it's difficult to forgo. The toes are still polished, the sides and heels dull and slightly smeared. It looks as if they've been washed. And there are still traces of mud at the sides as well as under the left heel. The lab will probably find scrape marks.'

They were hardly, he thought, the shoes you'd expect to find on a man who had spent the day in London unless he had walked in the parks or along the towpath of the canal. But he could hardly have walked to St Matthew's that way; there were no signs that he had cleaned his shoes anywhere in the church. But this, again, was theorizing in advance of the facts. They could hope to learn later where Berowne had spent his last day on earth.

Kate Miskin appeared in the doorway. She said:

'Doc Kynaston has finished, sir. They're ready to remove the bodies.'

10

Massingham had expected that Darren would live in one of the high rise local authority housing estates in Paddington. Instead the address which he had at last been persuaded to give was in a short and narrow street off the Edgware Road, an enclave of cheap, unsmart cafés chiefly Goan and Greek. As they turned into it Massingham realized that it wasn't strange to him, he had been here before. It was surely in this street that he and old George Percival had picked up two excellent vegetarian take-aways when they were both detective-sergeants on Division. Even the names, exotic, until now almost forgotten, came back to him: Alu Ghobi, Sag Bhajee. It had changed little since then, a street where people minded their own business, principally that of supplying their own kind with meals remarkable for value and cheapness. Although it was morning and the quietest time of the day the air was already pungent with the smell of curry and spices, reminding Massingham that it was some hours since breakfast and that there was no certainty when he would get his lunch.

There was only one pub, a high narrow Victorian building squeezed between a Chinese take-away and a Tandoori café, darkly uninviting, with a painted scrawl on the window advertising with defiant Englishness: 'Bangers and mash', 'Bangers and bubble-and-squeak' and 'Toad-in-the-hole'. Between the pub and the café was a small door with a single bell and a card with the one name 'Arlene'. Darren stooped, took a key from the side of his canvas trainer shoes, then tiptoeing, inserted it in the lock. Massingham followed him up the narrow uncarpeted stairs. At the top he said:

'Where's your ma?'

Still without speaking, the boy pointed to the door on the left. Massingham knocked gently, then, getting no reply, pushed it open.

The curtains were drawn but they were thin and unlined and even in the subdued light he could see that the room was spectacularly untidy. There was a woman lying on the bed. He moved over and putting out his hand found the switch of the bedside light. As it clicked on she gave a small grunt but didn't move. She was lying on her back, naked except for a short wrapover dressing gown from which one blue-veined breast had escaped and lay like a quivering jellyfish against the pink satin. A thin line of lipstick outlined the moistly open mouth from which a bleb of mucus ballooned and fell. She was snorting gently, small guttural sounds as if there were phlegm in her throat. Her eyebrows had been plucked in the manner of the thirties, thin arches high above the natural line of the brow. They gave the face, even in sleep, a look of clownish surprise, enhanced by the circles of rouge on both cheeks. On a chair beside the bed was a large jar of Vaseline, the lid open, a single fly gummed to the rim. The back of the chair and the floor were strewn with clothes and the top of a chest of drawers which served as a dressing table under an oval mirror was crowded with bottles, dirty glasses, jars of make-up and packets of tissues. Set incongruously among the mess was a jam jar with a bunch of freesias still bound with a rubber band, whose delicate sweetness was lost in the stink of sex, scent and whisky. He said:

'Is this your ma?'

He wanted to ask 'Is she often like this?', but instead, he drew the boy out and closed the door. He had never liked questioning a child about its parents and he didn't propose to do it now. It was a common enough tragedy, but it was a job for the Juvenile Bureau not for him and the sooner one of their officers arrived the better. He was fretted by the thought of Kate, back at the scene of crime by now, and he felt a spurt of resentment against Dalgliesh who had involved him in this irrelevant mess. He asked:

'Where do you sleep, Darren?'

The boy pointed to a back bedroom and Massingham pushed him gently before him.

It was very small, hardly more than a box room, with a single high window. Under it was a narrow bed covered with a brown army blanket and beside it a chair with a collection of objects neatly arranged. There was a model of a fire engine; a glass dome which shaken would produce a miniature snow storm; two models of racing cars; three large veined marbles; and another jam jar, this one holding a bunch of roses, whose heads were already bending on their high thornless stems. An old chest of drawers, the only other furniture, was piled with an incongruous collection of objects, shirts still in their transparent packets, women's underwear, silk scarves, tins of salmon, baked beans, soup, a packet of ham and one of tongue, three model kits for making boats, a couple of lipsticks, a box of model soldiers, three packets of cheap scent.

Massingham had been a policeman too long to be easily moved. Some offences, cruelty to children or animals, violent crime against the vulnerable old, could still produce a flare of the spectacular Massingham temper which had resulted in more than one of his forebears facing a duel or a court martial. But even this he had learned to discipline. But now, viewing with angry eyes this childish room with its pathetic neatness, its evidence of small self-sufficiency, the single jar of flowers which he guessed the boy himself had arranged, he was seized with an impotent anger against the drunken slut next door. He said:

'Did you steal these things, Darren?'

Darren didn't reply, then he nodded.

'Matey, you're in trouble.'

The boy sat on the edge of the bed. Two tears rolled down his cheeks, followed by sniffs and heaves of the narrow chest. Suddenly he shouted:

'I ain't going to one of them council homes, I ain't! I ain't!'

'Stop crying,' said Massingham urgently, hating the tears, wanting to get away. Christ, why had AD let him in for this? What was he supposed to be, a childminder? Torn between pity, anger and his impatience to be back on his proper job, he said more roughly:

'Stop crying!'

There must have been something urgent in his voice. Darren's gulps were immediately checked although the tears flowed on. Massingham said more gently:

'Who said anything about a home? Look, I'm going to ring the Juvenile Bureau. Someone will come to look after you. It will probably be a WPC, you'll like her.' Darren's face expressed an immediate and lively scepticism which in other circumstances, Massingham would have found amusing. The boy looked up and asked:

'Why can't I go 'ome with Miss Wharton?'

Why not, indeed, thought Massingham. The poor little bugger seemed to be attached to her. Two waifs supporting each other. He said:

'I don't really think that's on. Wait here, I'll be back.'

He looked at his watch. He would have to stay, of course, until the WPC arrived but she shouldn't be too long and at least AD would have an answer to his question. He knew now what had been worrying Darren, what he had been concealing. One small mystery, at least, was solved. AD could relax and get on with the inquiry. And so, with luck, could he.

11

Even Father Barnes's predecessor, Father Kendrick, hadn't been able to do much with St Matthew's Vicarage. It occupied the corner of St Matthew's Court, an undistinguished three-storey, red brick block of flats bordering the Harrow Road. After the war, the Church Commissioners had finally decided that the existing huge Victorian house was unmanageable and uneconomic, and had sold the site to a developer on the understanding that a maisonette on the ground and first floor should be made over, in perpetuity, to house the parish priest. It was the only maisonette in the block but was otherwise indistinguishable from the others, with their mean windows and small, badly proportioned rooms. At first the flats had been let to carefully chosen tenants and an attempt made to preserve the modest amenities; the square of lawn bordering the road, the two rose beds, the hanging windowboxes on each of the balconies. But the block, like most of its kind, had had a chequered history. The first property company had gone into liquidation and it had been sold to a second and then a third. The rents were raised, to general dissatisfaction, but were still inadequate to cover the maintenance costs of a poorly constructed building and there were the usual acrimonious disputes between the tenants and the land-lords. Only the church maisonette was well maintained, its two storeys of white windows an incongruous badge of respectability among the peeling paint and disintegrating windowboxes.

The original tenants had been replaced by the transients of the city, the peripatetic young, sharing three to a room, unmarried mothers on social security, foreign students; a racial mix which, like some human kaleidoscope, was continually being shaken into new and brighter colours. Those few who did attend church found a congenial home with Father Donovan at St Anthony's with its steel bands, carnival processions, and general interracial bonhomie. None of them ever knocked on Father Barnes's door. They saw, with watchful and expressionless eyes, his almost furtive comings and goings. But he was as much an anachronism at St Matthew's Court as was the church he represented.

He had been escorted back to the Vicarage by a plainclothes officer, not the one who had been working most closely with Commander Dalgliesh, but an older man, broad-shouldered, stolid, reassuringly calm, who had spoken to him in a soft country accent which he couldn't recognize but was most certainly not local. He said he was from the Harrow Road Station but had only recently been transferred there from West Central. He waited while Father Barnes unlocked the front door, then followed him in and offered to make a cup of tea, the British specific against disaster, grief and shock. If he was surprised by the grubbiness of the ill-equipped Vicarage kitchen he concealed it. He had made tea in worse places. When Father Barnes reiterated that he was perfectly all right and that Mrs McBride who did for him was due at ten thirty, he didn't persist. Before he left he handed Father Barnes a card with a number on it.

'That's the number Commander Dalgliesh said you were to ring if you need anything. If you're worried like. Or if anything new occurs to you. Just give a ring. It'll be no trouble. And when the press come bothering, just tell them as little as you need. No speculating. No use in speculating, is there? Just tell it how it was. A lady from your congregation and a boy found the bodies and the boy fetched you. Better not give any names unless you have to. You saw that they were dead and rang for the police. No need to say more. That's all there is to it.'

The statement, stupendous in its over-simplification, opened a new abyss before Father Barnes's horrified eyes. He had forgotten about the press. How soon would they arrive? Would they want to take photographs? Ought he to call an emergency meeting of the PCC? What would the Bishop say? Ought he to ring the Archdeacon at once and leave it to him? Yes, that would be the best plan. The Archdeacon would know what ought to be done. The Archdeacon was capable of coping with the press, the Bishop, the police and the Parochial Church Council. Even so, he feared that St Matthew's was fated to be the centre of a dreadful attention.

He always went to Mass fasting and, for the first time that morning, he was aware of feeling weak, even paradoxically a little sick. He sank down on to one of the two wooden chairs at the kitchen table and looked rather helplessly at the card with its seven clearly written digits, then glanced round as if seeking inspiration where to put it for safe keeping. Finally, he dug in his cassock pocket for his wallet and slipped it in with his bank card and single credit card. He let his eyes roam round the kitchen, seeing it as that pleasant policeman must have seen it, in all its sad decrepitude. The plate from which he had eaten his hamburgers and frozen green beans, which had been last night's supper, still unrinsed in the sink; the splatter of grease marks above the ancient gas stove; the viscous mess of grime gumming the narrow gap between stove and cupboard; the soiled and smelly teacloth hanging from its hook at the side of the sink; last year's calendar askew on its nail; the two open shelves jammed with a conglomeration of half-used cereal packets, jars of stale jam, cracked mugs, packets of detergent; the cheap, unstable table with its two chairs, their backs grubby from numerous clutching hands; the linoleum curving at the wall where it had become unstuck; the general air of discomfort, uncaring, negligence, dirt. And the rest of the flat wasn't much better. Mrs McBride took no pride in it because there was nothing to take a pride in. She didn't care because he didn't. Like him, she had probably ceased to notice the slow accretion of dirt over their lives.

After thirty years of marriage to Tom McBride, Beryl McBride sounded more Irish than did her husband. Sometimes, indeed, Father Barnes suspected that the brogue was less acquired than assumed, a music hall stereotype of Irishness adopted either out of marital togetherness or from some less recognizable need. He had noticed that in rare moments of stress she was apt to revert to her original Cockney. She was employed by the parish for twelve hours a week and her nominal duties were to come in on Mondays, Wednesdays and Fridays, clean the flat, wash and spin dry any linen or articles in the soiled linen basket, and prepare and leave for him a simple lunch on a tray. On the other weekdays and at weekends, Father Barnes was expected to look after himself. There had never been a job description. Mrs McBride and the current incumbent were expected to work out a mutually agreed arrangement of hours and duties.

Twelve hours a week had been an adequate, even generous allocation of time when young Father Kendrick had been priest-in-charge. He was married to the prototype of an ideal parson's wife, a capable and buxom physiotherapist, well able to run her part-time hospital job and the parish simultaneously and to pound Mrs McBride into shape as vigorously as, no doubt, she did her patients. No one, of course, had expected Father Kendrick to stay. He had only been a stop-gap, to fill in after Father Collins's long, twenty-five-year ministry and the appointment of a permanent successor, if there were to be a successor. St Matthew's, as the Archdeacon was never tired of pointing out, was surplus to the Church's pastoral ministry in inner London. With two other Anglican churches within a three-mile radius, both with vigorous young clergy and enough parochial organizations to provide serious competition for the social services department, St Matthew's, with its small and ageing population, was an uncomfortable reminder of the declining authority of the established church in the inner cities. But as the Archdeacon said, 'Your people are remarkably loyal. It's a pity they aren't also rich. The parish is a drain on resources, no doubt about it. But we can hardly sell it. The building is supposed to be of some importance, architecturally. I can never see it myself. That extraordinary campanile. Hardly English, is it? One isn't, after all, on the Venetian Lido, whatever the architect thought.' For the Archdeacon, who had, in fact, never seen the Venetian Lido, had been reared in the Close at Salisbury and, making some allowance for scale, had known from childhood exactly what a church should look like.

Before Father Kendrick had set off for his new city parish – racial mix, boys' club, mothers' union, young people's fellowship; the proper challenge for a mildly high-church, ambitious young priest with one eye on a mitre – he had had a brief word about Beryl McBride.

'Frankly, she terrifies me. I keep well out of her way. But Susan seems able to manage her. Better have a word with her about the domestic arrangements. I wish Mrs McBride had taken her husband's religion instead of his accent. That way St Anthony's would have had the benefit of her cooking. I did hint to Father Donovan that here was a brand ready for plucking, but Michael knows when to leave well alone. Now, if you can seduce his housekeeper Mrs Kelly into Anglicanism, you'll be in clover.'

Susan Kendrick, expertly wrapping china in newspaper and ankle-deep in shavings from her packing cases, had been briskly informative but hardly more reassuring.

'She needs watching. Her plain cooking is quite good although the repertoire is a bit limited. But she isn't so dependable when it comes to housework. You need to begin as you mean to go on. If you set the right standards and she knows that she can't fool you, you'll be all right. She's been here a long time, of course, from Father Collins's days. She wouldn't be easy to dislodge. And she's a very loyal member of the congregation. St Matthew's seems to suit her for some reason. As I said, just begin as you mean to go on. Oh, and watch the sherry. There's no real dishonesty. You can leave anything out, money, your watch, food. It's just that she likes the odd nip. Better offer her one occasionally. That way there's less temptation. You can hardly lock the stuff up.'

'No, of course not,' he had said. 'No, I quite see that.'

But it had been Mrs McBride who had started as she meant to go on. It had been hopeless from the start. He still recalled, with a flush of shame, that first, all-important interview. He had sat in front of her, in the square little room which was used as a study, as if he were the suppliant, and had seen her sharp little eyes, black as currants, move round the room, noting the gaps in the shelves where Father Kendrick's leatherbound volumes had been stacked, the meagre rug in front of the gas fire, his few prints stacked against the wall. And that wasn't all she had taken in. She had had him summed up, all right. She had seen his timidity, his ignorance of housekeeping, his lack of authority as a man or a priest. And he suspected that she had known more intimate secrets. His virginity, his half-shameful fear of her close, warm-smelling, overwhelming femaleness, his social insecurity, born in that small, terraced house near the river at Ely, where he had lived with his widowed mother, nurtured by the desperate contrivings, the small deceptions of respectable poverty, the deprivation that was so much more humiliating than the real poverty of the inner cities. He could imagine the words in which she would later report to her husband.

'He's not really a gentleman, not like Father Kendrick. You can see that. Father Kendrick's father was a bishop, after all, and Mrs Kendrick is the niece of Lady Nichols, when all's said and done. There's no knowing where this one comes from.' Sometimes he suspected that she had even known how diminished was his remaining store of faith, that it was this essential lack and not his general inadequacy which was at the core of her disdain.

His most recent library book had been a Barbara Pym. He had read with envious disbelief the gentle and ironic story of a village parish where the curates were entertained, fed, and generally spoilt by the female members of the congregation. Mrs McBride, he thought, would soon put a stop to anything like that at St Matthew's. Indeed, she had put a stop to it. During his first week, Mrs Jordan had visited him with a homemade fruitcake. She had seen it on the table on her Wednesday visit and had said:

'One of Ethel Jordan's, is it? You want to watch her, Father, an unmarried priest like you.' The words had hung on the air, heavy with innuendo, and an act of simple kindness had been spoiled. Eating the cake, he had felt it like tasteless dough in his mouth, every mouthful an act of shared indecency.

She arrived on time. Whatever her other negligences, Mrs McBride was a stickler for punctuality. He heard her key in the door and a minute later she was in the kitchen. She didn't seem surprised to see him sitting there still in his cloak and obviously only just returned from Mass, and he knew at once that she had been told about the murders. He watched while she carefully removed her headscarf to reveal the upswept waves of unnaturally dark hair, hung up her coat in the hall cupboard, donned her overall from its hook behind the kitchen door, took off her outdoor shoes and eased her feet into her house slippers. It wasn't until she had put on the kettle for their morning coffee that she spoke.

'Well, here's a nice thing for the parish, Father. Two of 'em dead, so Billy Crawford was saying in the newsagent's. And one of 'em old Harry Mack.'

'I'm afraid so, Mrs McBride. One of them was Harry.'

'And who would the other be? Or aren't the police knowing yet?'

'I think we'll have to wait until they notify the next of kin before they release that information.'

'But you saw him, Father. Wasn't it with your own eyes now? And were you not recognizing him?'

'You really musn't ask me that, Mrs McBride. We must wait for the police.'

'And who'd be wantin' to kill Harry? Sure, he wouldn't be killed for anything he had on him, the poor soul. It wasn't suicide, was it, Father? One of those suicide pacts? Or do the police think Harry did it?'

'They don't know what happened yet. We really ought not to speculate.'

'Well, I don't believe it. Harry Mack's no murderer. As well believe that the other chap, the one you're keeping so quiet about, the one you're not telling about, did in Harry. Harry was a nasty, thieving, foul-mouthed old devil, God rest him, but he was harmless enough. The police have no call to be pinning it on Harry.'

'I'm sure they won't try to. It could have been anyone, someone who broke in to steal. Or someone Sir Paul Berowne himself let in. Anyone. The door of the vestry was open when Miss Wharton arrived this morning.'

He turned towards the stove so that she shouldn't see the flush of shame and dismay that he had let slip Berowne's name. And she hadn't missed it, not she. And why had he told her about that unlocked door? Was he trying to reassure her, or himself? But what did it matter? The details would be out soon enough and it would look odd if he were too reticent, odd and suspicious. But why suspicious? Surely no one, not even Mrs McBride, was going to suspect him. He recognized, with a familiar confusion of self-disgust and hopelessness, that he was telling more than he ought in his usual attempt to propitiate her, to get her on his side. It had never worked and it wouldn't now. She didn't pick up the name Berowne although he knew that it was safely stowed in her mind. Sitting across from her, he saw the triumph in her cunning little eyes, heard in her voice the note of ghoulish relish.

'Bloody murder, is it then? That's a nice thing for the parish. You'll be needing to get the church fumigated, Father.'

'Fumigated?'

'Well, sprinkled with holy water, that sort of thing. Maybe my Tom had better speak to Father Donovan. He could let us have some from St Anthony's.'

'We have our own holy water, Mrs McBride.'

'In a case like this, you can't take chances. Better get some from Father Donovan. Be on the safe side. My Tom can bring it along after Mass on Sunday. Here's your coffee, Father. I've made it extra strong. You've had a nasty shock and that's the truth of it.'

The coffee, as always, was the cheapest kind of bottled grains. It was even less palatable now that its strength made the taste discernible. On the brown surface a few globules of half-sour milk swam and coalesced. There was a smear of what looked like lipstick on the brim of the cup and he turned it away from him slowly, so that she shouldn't notice. He knew that he could have carried the coffee into the comparative serenity of his study but he hadn't the courage to get to his feet. And to leave before both cups had been drained would only offend her. She had said, on her first morning with him, 'Mrs Kendrick and me always had a cup of coffee together before I got started, nice and friendly like.' He had had no way of knowing whether this was the truth, but the pattern of spurious intimacy had been established.

'That Paul Berowne, he was an MP wasn't he? Resigned or something. I remember reading about him in the *Standard*.'

'Yes, he was an MP.'

'And a Sir, too, didn't you say?'

'A baronet, Mrs McBride.'

'What was he doing in the Little Vestry, then? I never knew we had any baronets attending St Matthew's.'

It was too late now to take refuge in discretion.

'He didn't. He was just someone I knew. I gave him the key. He wanted to spend some time quietly in the church,' he added in a vain hope that a confidence so dangerously close to intimacy, to his job as priest, might flatter her, might even silence curiosity. 'He wanted somewhere quiet to think, to pray.'

'In the Little Vestry? A funny place to choose. Why wasn't he on his knees in a pew? Why wasn't he in the Lady Chapel in front of the Blessed Sacrament? That's the proper place to be praying for them who can't wait till Sunday.' Her voice with its note of aggrieved disapproval suggested that both the place and the praying were equally reprehensible.

'He could hardly sleep in the church, Mrs McBride.'

'And why should he want to be sleeping? Hadn't he his own bed to be going home to?'

Father Barnes's hands had begun to shake again. The coffee cup lurched in his fingers and he felt two scalding drops on his hand. Carefully, he replaced the cup in its saucer, willing the dreadful shaking to stop. He almost lost her next words.

'Well, if he did kill himself, he died clean, I'll say that for him.'

'Died clean, Mrs McBride?'

'Wasn't he washing himself when Tom and I passed by last night just after eight o'clock? Him or Harry Mack? And you can't be telling me that Harry went near running water if he could help it. Fairly gushing out of the drainpipe it was. 'Course we thought you were there. "Father Barnes is having a stripwash in the vestry washroom." That's what I said to Tom. "Perhaps he's saving on the gas bill back at the Vicarage." We had a laugh about it.'

'When exactly was this, Mrs McBride?'

'I told you, Father, just after eight. We were on our way to the Three Feathers. We wouldn't have been passing the church except that we called in to collect Maggie Sullivan and it's a shortcut from her place to the Feathers.'

'But the police ought to know. This could be important information. They'll be interested in anyone who was near St Matthew's last night.'

'Interested? Is that what they'll be? And what are you getting at then, Father? You're saying that Tom and old Maggie Sullivan and I cut his throat for him?'

'Of course not, Mrs McBride. That's ridiculous. But you could be important witnesses. That gushing water. It means that Sir Paul was alive at eight o'clock.'

'Someone was alive in there at eight and that's for sure. And a fine rush of water he was using.'

Father Barnes was struck with a terrible possibility and, without thinking, gave it voice:

'Did you notice what colour it was?'

'And what would I be doing peering down drains? Of course I didn't notice what colour it was. What colour would it be? But it was running away, fast and furious, that's for sure.'

Suddenly, she pushed her face over the table towards him. Her huge breasts, so much at odds with the thin face and the bony arms, were pushed into great half moons by the table edge. Her coffee cup clattered in the saucer. The sharp little eyes widened. She whispered with alliterative relish:

'Father, are you saying that it would be running red?'

He said, weakly:

'I suppose it's possible.'

'You think he was in there do you, Father, washing his bloody hands? Oh my God! Suppose he had come out and seen us. We could have been murdered on the spot, Tom and Maggie and me. He could have slit our throats for us then and there and thrown us in the canal, likely as not. Holy Mother of God!'

The conversation had become bizarre, unreal, totally uncontrollable. He had been told by the police to say as little as possible to anyone. He had meant to say nothing. But now she knew the names of the victims, she knew who had found them, she knew that the door had been unlocked, she knew how they had died, although surely he hadn't mentioned the slitting of throats. But that could have been guesswork. A knife was, after all, a more likely weapon in London than a gun. She knew all that and, more, she had actually been passing at the time. He gazed back at her across the stained table with appalled eyes, linked to her by that bloodstained gurgle of water which was gushing through both their minds, sharing the same dreadful imagining of that silently emerging figure, the raised and bloody knife. And he was aware of something else. Horrible as was the deed that bound them in a fascinated confederacy of blood they were, for the first time, having a conversation. The eyes which met his across the table top were bright with horror and with an excitement which was too close to relish to be comfortable. But the familiar glance of insolence and contempt had gone. He could almost deceive himself that she was confiding in him. The relief was so great that he found that his hand was creeping across the table towards hers in some gesture of mutual comfort. Ashamed, he quickly drew it back.

She said:

'Father, what shall we do?' It was the first time she had ever asked him that question. He was surprised at the confidence in his voice.

'The police have given me a special telephone number. I think we ought to ring now, at once. They'll send someone round, either here or to your house. After all, you and Tom and Maggie are very important witnesses. And then when we've done that, I shall need to be undisturbed in the study. I wasn't able to say Mass. I shall read Morning Prayer.'

'Yes, Father,' she said, her voice almost meek. And there was something else he ought to do. Strange that thought hadn't occurred to him before. Surely it must be his duty to call in the next day or so on Paul Berowne's wife and his family. Now that he knew what had to be done, it was remarkable how different he felt. A biblical phrase dropped into his mind, 'Doing evil that good may come'. But he quickly put it away from him. It was too close to blasphemy to be comfortable.

BOOK TWO

Next of Kin

1

After leaving the church Dalgliesh went briefly back to the Yard to pick up his files on Theresa Nolan and Diana Travers and it was after midday before he arrived at 62 Campden Hill Square. He had brought Kate with him, leaving Massingham to supervise what remained to be done at the church. Kate had told him that at present there were only women in the house and it seemed sensible that he should have a woman with him, particularly as it was Kate who had first broken the news. It was not a decision he had expected Massingham to welcome, and nor had he. These first interviews with the next of kin were crucial and Massingham wanted to be there. He would work with Kate Miskin loyally and conscientiously because he respected her as a detective and that was what he was required to do. But Dalgliesh knew that Massingham still half-regretted the days when women police officers were content to find lost children, search female prisoners, reform prostitutes, comfort the bereaved and, if they hankered for the excitement of criminal investigation, were suitably occupied coping with the peccadilloes of juvenile delinquents. And, as Dalgliesh had heard him argue, for all their demands for equality of status and opportunity, putting them in the front line behind the riot shields, taking the petrol bombs, the hurled stones and now the bullets, only made the job of their male colleagues even more onerous. In Massingham's view the instinct to protect a woman in moments of high danger was deep-seated and ineradicable, and the world would be a worse place if it wasn't. He had, as Dalgliesh knew, grudgingly respected Kate's ability to look down at the butchered bodies in St Matthew's vestry and not be sick, but he hadn't liked her the better for it.

He knew that he would find no police officer at the house. Lady Ursula had gently but firmly rejected the suggestion that someone should stay. Kate had reported her words:

'You are not, presumably, expecting this murderer, if he exists, to turn his attention to the rest of the family. That being so, I hardly see the need for police protection. You, I am sure, have a better use for your manpower and I would prefer not to have an officer sitting in the hall like a bailiff.'

She had, too, insisted on herself breaking the news to her

daughter-in-law and the housekeeper. Kate was given no opportunity to observe the reaction of anyone other than Lady Ursula to Paul Berowne's death.

Campden Hill Square lay in its midday calm, an urban oasis of greenery and Georgian elegance rising from the ceaseless grind and roar of Holland Park Avenue. An early morning mist had cleared and a fugitive sun glinted on leaves which were only now beginning to yellow and which hung in heavy swathes, almost motionless in the still air. Dalgliesh couldn't remember when he had last seen the Berowne house. Living as he did high above the Thames on the fringe of the city, this wasn't his part of London. But the house, one of the rare examples of Sir John Soane's domestic architecture, was pictured in so many books on the capital's buildings that its elegant eccentricity was as familiar to him as if he commonly walked these streets and squares. The conventional Georgian houses each side of it were as high, but its neo-classical façade in Portland stone and brick dominated the terrace and the whole square, inalienably a part of them, yet looking almost arrogantly unique.

He stood for a minute looking up at it, Kate unspeaking at his side. On the second floor rose three very high, curved windows, originally, he suspected, an open loggia but now glazed and fronted with a low stone balustrade. Between the windows, mounted on incongruous corbels which looked more Gothic than neo-classical, were stone caryatids, whose flowing lines, reinforced by the typically Soanian pilasters at the corners of the house, drew the eye upwards, past the square windows of the third storey to a fourth storey faced in brick and, finally, to the stone balustrade with its row of curved shells echoing the curve of the lower windows. As he stood contemplating it, as if hesitating to violate its calm, there was a moment of extraordinary silence in which even the muted roar of the traffic in the avenue was stilled and in which it seemed to him that two images, the shining façade of the house and that dusty blood-boltered room in Paddington, were held suspended out of time, then fused so that the stones were blood splattered, the caryatids dripped red. And then the traffic lights released the stream of cars, time moved on, the house lay uncontaminated in its pale pristine silence. But he had no sense that they were being watched, that somewhere between these walls and the windows glinting in the transitory sun there were people waiting for him in anxiety, grief, perhaps in fear. Even when he rang the doorbell it was a full two minutes before the door was opened and he faced a woman who he knew must be Evelyn Matlock.

She was, he guessed, in her late thirties, and was uncompro-
misingly plain in a way it struck him few women nowadays were.
A small sharp nose was imbedded between pudgy cheeks on
which the threads of broken veins were emphasized rather than
disguised by a thin crust of make-up. She had a primly censorious
mouth above a slightly receding chin already showing the first
slackness of a dewlap. Her hair, which looked as if it had been
inexpertly permed, was pulled back at the sides but frizzed over
the high forehead rather in the poodle-like fashion of an Edwardian.
But as she stood aside to let them enter he saw that her wrists and
ankles were slim and delicate, curiously at odds with the sturdy
body, heavy-busted, almost voluptuous under the high-necked
blouse. He remembered what Paul Berowne had said of her. Here
was the woman whose father he had unsuccessfully defended, to
whom he had given a home and a job, who was supposed to be
devoted to him. If that were true, she was concealing her grief at
his death with remarkable stoicism. A police officer, he thought, is
like a visiting doctor. One is greeted with no ordinary emotions.
He was used to seeing relief, apprehension, dislike, even hatred;
but now, for a moment, he saw in her eyes naked fear. It passed
almost at once and gave place to what seemed to him an assumed
and slightly truculent indifference, but it had been there. She
turned her back on them, saying:
    'Lady Ursula is expecting you, Commander. Will you please
follow me.'
    The words, spoken in a high, rather forced voice, had the
repressive authority of a nurse-receptionist greeting a patient
from whom she expects nothing but trouble. They passed through
the outer vestibule then under the fluted dome of the inner hall.
To their left, the finely wrought balustrade of a stone cantilevered
staircase rose like a border of black lace. Miss Matlock opened
the double door to the right and stood back to let them enter.
She said:
    'If you will wait in here I will let Lady Ursula know that you have
arrived.'
    The room in which they found themselves ran the whole length
of the house and was obviously both the formal dining-room and
library. It was full of light. At the front, two high curved windows
gave a view of the square garden while at the rear one huge
expanse of glass looked out over a stone wall with three niches,
each containing a marble statue; Venus, naked, one hand delicately
shielding the mons Veneris, one pointing at her left nipple, a

second female figure, half robed and wearing a wreath of flowers and, between them, Apollo with his lyre, laurel-crowned. The two sections of the room were divided by projecting piers formed of mahogany glass-fronted bookcases from which sprang a canopy of three semi-circular arches decorated and painted in green and gold. High bookcases lined the library walls and stood between the windows, each topped with a marble bust. The volumes, bound in green leather and tooled in gold, were identical in size and fitted the bookshelves so precisely that the effect was more of an artist's *trompe-l'œil* than of a working library. Between the shelves and in the recesses over them were mirrors so that the rich splendour of the room seemed to be endlessly reflected, a vista of painted ceilings, leather books, of marble, gleaming mahogany and glass. It was difficult to imagine the room being used for dining, or indeed, for any purpose other than the admiring contemplation of the architect's romantic obsession with spatial surprise. The oval dining table stood before the rear window, but it held in the middle a model of the house on a low plinth as if it were a museum exhibit, and the eight high-backed dining chairs had been set back against the walls. Over the marble fireplace was a portrait, presumably of the baronet who had commissioned the house. Here the delicate fastidiousness of the painting in the National Portrait Gallery was metamorphosed into a sturdier nineteenth-century elegance, but with the unmistakable Berowne features still arrogantly confident above the faultlessly tied cravat. Looking up at it, Dalgliesh said:

'Lady Ursula Berowne, remind me of what she said, Kate.'

'She said: "After the first death there is no other." It sounded like a quotation.'

'It is a quotation.' He added without explanation, 'Her elder son was killed in Northern Ireland. Do you like this room?'

'If I wanted to settle down for a quiet read I'd prefer the Kensington public library. It's for show rather than use, isn't it? Odd idea, having a library and dining room in one.' She added: 'But I suppose it's splendid in its way. Not exactly cosy, though. I wonder if anyone has ever been murdered for a house.'

It was a long speech for Kate.

Dalgliesh said:

'I can't say that I remember a case. It might be a more rational motive than murdering for a person; less risk of subsequent disenchantment.'

'Less chance of betrayal, too, sir.'

100

Miss Matlock appeared in the doorway; she said with cold formality:

'Lady Ursula is ready to see you now. Her sitting room is on the fourth floor, but there is a lift. Would you please follow me.'

They could have been a couple of unpromising applicants for a minor domestic job. The lift was an elegant gilded birdcage in which they were borne slowly upwards in a repressive silence. When it jerked to a stop they were led out into a narrow carpeted passage. Miss Matlock opened a door immediately opposite and announced:

'Commander Dalgliesh and Miss Miskin are here, Lady Ursula.' Then without waiting for them to step into the room, she turned and left.

And now, as he entered Lady Ursula Berowne's sitting room, Dalgliesh felt for the first time that he was in a private house, that this was a room which the owner had made peculiarly her own. The two high beautifully proportioned windows with their twelve panes gave a view of sky delicately laced with the top boughs of the trees and the long narrow room was full of light. Lady Ursula was sitting very upright to the right of the fireplace, her back to the window.

There was an ebony cane with a gold knob leaning against her chair. She did not rise when they came in but held out her hand as Kate introduced Dalgliesh. Her clasp, quickly released, was surprisingly strong but it was still like holding briefly a disconnected set of bones loosely enclosed in dry suede. She gave Kate a quick appraising glance and a nod which could have been acknowledgement or approval and said:

'Please sit down. If Inspector Miskin is required to make notes, then she may find that chair by the window convenient. Perhaps you will sit opposite me, Commander.'

The voice, with its timbre of upper-class arrogance, an arrogance of which its owner so often seems unaware, was exactly as he would have expected. It seemed artificially produced, as if in an attempt to control any quavering she had had to gather both breath and energy to produce the measured cadences. But it was still a beautiful voice. As she sat facing him, rigidly upright, he saw that her chair was one designed for the disabled with a button in the armrest to raise the seat when she wanted help in rising. Its functional modernity struck a discordant note in a room which was otherwise cluttered with eighteenth-century furniture; two chairs with embroidered seats, a Pembroke table, a bureau, each a fine

101

example of its period, were strategically placed to provide an island of support if she needed to make her painful progress to the door, so that the room looked rather like an antique shop with its treasures ineptly displayed. It was an old woman's room, and above the smell of beeswax and the faint summer scent from a bowl of pot-pourri on the Pembroke table, his sensitive nose could detect a whiff of the sour smell of old age. Their eyes met and held. Hers were still remarkable, immense, well-spaced and heavily lidded. They must once have been the focus of her beauty, and although they were sunken now, he could still see the glint of intelligence behind them. Her skin was cleft with deep lines running from the jaw to the high jutting cheekbones. It was as if two palms had been placed against the frail skin and forced it upwards so that he saw with a shock of premonitory recognition the shine of the skull beneath the skin. The scrolls of the ears flat against the side of the skull were so large that they looked like abnormal excrescences. In youth she would have dressed her hair to cover them. Her face was devoid of make-up and with the hair drawn back tightly and twisted into a high roll it looked naked, a face stripped for action. She was wearing black trousers topped with a belted tunic in thin grey wool, high-buttoned almost to the chin, and deep-cuffed. Her feet were lodged in wide black-barred shoes and in their immobility gave the impression of being clamped to the carpet. There was a paperback on the round table to the right of her chair. Dalgliesh saw that it was Philip Larkin's *Required Writing*. She put out her hand and laid it on the book, then said:

'Mr Larkin writes here that it is always true that the idea for a poem and a snatch or line of it come simultaneously. Do you agree, Commander?'

'Yes, Lady Ursula, I think I do. A poem begins with poetry, not with an idea for poetry.'

He betrayed no surprise at the question. He knew that shock, grief, trauma took people in different ways, and if this bizarre opening was helping her, he could conceal his impatience. She said:

'To be a poet and a librarian, even if unusual, had a certain appropriateness, but to be a poet and a policeman seems to me eccentric, even perverse.'

Dalgliesh said:

'Do you see the poetry as inimical to the detection, or the detection to the poetry?'

'Oh, the latter, surely. What happens if the muse strikes – no, that is hardly the appropriate word – if the muse visits you in the middle of a case? Although if I remember, Commander, your muse in recent years has been somewhat fugitive.' She added with a note of delicate irony: 'to our great loss.'

Dalgliesh said:

'It hasn't so far happened. Perhaps the human mind can deal with only one intense experience at a time.'

'And poetry is, of course, an intense experience.'

'One of the most intense there is.'

Suddenly she smiled at him. It lit up her face with the intimacy of a shared confidence, as if they were old sparring partners.

'You must excuse me. Being interrogated by a detective is a new experience for me. If there is an appropriate dialogue for this occasion, I haven't yet found it. Thank you, anyway, for not burdening me with your condolences. I have received too many official condolences in my time. They have always seemed to me either embarrassing or insincere.'

Dalgliesh wondered what she would reply if he had said: 'I knew your son. Not well, but I did know him. I accept that you don't want my condolences, but if I had been able to speak the right words, they would not have been insincere.'

She said:

'Inspector Miskin broke the news to me with tact and consideration. I am grateful. But she was, of course, unable or unwilling to tell me much more than that my son was dead, and that there were certain wounds. How did he die, Commander?'

'His throat was cut, Lady Ursula.'

There was no way of softening that brutal reality. He added:

'The tramp with him, Harry Mack, died the same way.'

He wondered why he had felt it important to speak Harry's name. Poor Harry, so incongruously yoked in the forced democracy of death, whose stiffening body would receive far more attention in its dissolution than it had ever received in life. She said:

'And the weapon?'

'A bloodstained razor, his apparently, was close to your son's right hand. There are a number of forensic tests to be carried out but I expect to find that the razor was the weapon.'

'And the door to the church – the vestry, or wherever he was – that was open?'

'Miss Wharton, who with a young boy discovered the bodies, says that she found it unlocked.'

'Are you treating this as suicide?'

'The tramp, Harry Mack, didn't kill himself. My preliminary view is that neither did your son. It's too early to say more until we get the results of the post-mortem examination and the forensic tests. Meantime I am treating it as a double murder.'

'I see. Thank you for being so frank.'

Dagliesh said:

'There are questions I need to ask. If you would rather wait I could come back later, but it is, of course, important to lose as little time as possible.'

'I would prefer to lose none, Commander. And two of your questions I can anticipate. I have no reason to believe that my son was contemplating ending his life and he had to my knowledge no enemies.'

'As a politician that makes him unusual, surely.'

'He had political enemies, obviously. Some few from his own party, no doubt. But none as far as I know is a homicidal maniac. And terrorists, surely, use bombs and guns not their victim's razor. Forgive me, Commander, if I'm stating the obvious, but isn't it most likely that someone unknown to him, a tramp, a psychopath, a casual thief, killed both him and this Harry Mack?'

'It is one of the theories we have to consider, Lady Ursula.' He asked: 'When did you last see your son?'

'At eight o'clock yesterday morning when he carried up my breakfast tray. That was his usual practice. He wished to reassure himself, no doubt, that I had survived the night.'

'Did he tell you then or at any time that he intended returning to St Matthew's?'

'No. We didn't discuss his plans for the day, only mine, and those I presume are hardly of interest to you.'

Dalgliesh said:

'It could be important to know who was here in the house during the day and at what time. Your own timetable could help us to that.'

He gave no further explanation and she asked for none.

'My chiropodist, Mrs Beamish, arrived at ten thirty. She always comes to the house. I was with her for about an hour. Then I was driven to a luncheon engagement with Mrs Charles Blaney at her club, the University Women's. After luncheon we went to look at some watercolours in which she is interested at Agnew's, in Bond Street. We had tea at the Savoy together and I dropped Mrs Blaney at her Chelsea house before returning here at about half past five. I asked Miss Matlock to bring me up a thermos of soup and a plate of

104

smoked salmon sandwiches at six o'clock. She did so and I told her I preferred not to be disturbed again that evening. The luncheon and exhibition had been more tiring than I had expected. I spent the evening reading, and rang for Miss Matlock to help me to bed shortly before eleven.'

'Did you see any other member of the household during the day apart from your son, Miss Matlock and the chauffeur?'

'I saw my daughter-in-law briefly when I had occasion to go into the library. That was some time during the early part of the morning. I presume that this is relevant, Commander?'

'Until we know how your son died it is difficult to be sure what is or is not relevant. Did any other member of the household know that Sir Paul intended revisiting St Matthew's yesterday evening?'

'I have had no opportunity to ask them. I can't believe it likely that they did. No doubt you will inquire. We have only a small staff. Evelyn Matlock, whom you have met, is the housekeeper. Then there is Gordon Halliwell. He is an ex-sergeant in the Guards, who served with my elder son. He, I suppose, would describe himself as a chauffeur-handyman. He came here just over five years ago, before Hugo was killed, and has stayed on.'

'He drove your son?'

'Rarely. Paul, of course, had the use of his ministerial car before he resigned; otherwise he drove himself. Halliwell drives me almost daily, and occasionally my daughter-in-law. He has a flat over the garage. You will have to wait, Commander, to hear anything he may disclose. Today is his day off.'

'When did he leave, Lady Ursula?'

'Either very late last night or early this morning. That is his usual practice. I have no idea where he is. I don't question my servants about their private lives. If the news of my son's death is broadcast this evening, as I expect it will be, no doubt he will return early. In any case he is normally back before eleven. Incidentally, I spoke to him by house telephone yesterday evening shortly after eight o'clock and, again, at about nine fifteen. Apart from Halliwell, there is now only one other member of the staff, Mrs Iris Minns, who comes here four days a week to do general housework. Miss Matlock can give you her address.'

Dalgliesh asked:

'This experience of your son's in the vestry of St Matthew's, did he talk to you about it?'

'No. It was not a subject with which he would expect me to sympathize. I have not since 1918 been a religious woman. I doubt if I ever was in any real sense. Mysticism, in particular, is as meaningless to me as music must be to the tone deaf. I accept, of course, that people do have these experiences. I would expect the causes to be physical and psychological; overwork, the *ennui* of middle age, or a need to find some meaning to existence. That to me has always been a fruitless quest.'

'Did your son find it fruitless?'

'Until this happened, I would have described him as a conventional Anglican. I suspect that he used the offices of his religion as a reminder of fundamental decencies, an affirmation of identity, a brief breathing space when he could think without fear of interruption. Like most upper-class Anglicans he would have found the incarnation more understandable if God had chosen to visit His creation as an eighteenth-century English gentleman. But like most of his class, he got over that little difficulty by more or less refashioning Him in the guise of an eighteenth-century English gentleman. His experience – his alleged experience – in that church is inexplicable, and to do him justice, he didn't attempt to explain it, at least not to me. I hope you won't expect me to discuss it. The subject is unwelcome, and it can surely have had nothing to do with his death.'

It was a long speech and he could see that it had tired her. And she could not, thought Dalgliesh, be as naive as that; he was surprised that she could expect him to believe that she was. He said:

'When a man changes the whole direction of his life and is dead – possibly murdered – within a week of that decision, it must be relevant, at least to our investigation.'

'Oh yes, it's relevant to that I've no doubt. There will be very few privacies in this family which won't be relevant to your investigation, Commander.'

He saw that in the last few seconds, she had been overcome with exhaustion. Her body looked diminished, almost shrivelled, in the huge chair, and the gnarled hands on the arms began very gently to shake. But he controlled his compassion as she was controlling her grief. There were questions he still needed to ask and it wouldn't be the first time that he had taken advantage of tiredness or grief. He bent and took from his case the half-burnt diary still in its protective transparent wrapping. He said:

'It's been examined for fingerprints. We shall need in time to check which belong to people who had a right to handle the diary; Sir Paul, yourself, members of the household. I wanted you to confirm that it is in fact his. It would be helpful if you could do that without unwrapping it.'

She took the package and it lay for a moment in her lap while she stared down at it. He had a sense that she was unwilling to meet his eyes. She sat with extraordinary stillness, then she said:

'Yes, this is his. But it's unimportant surely. A mere record of engagements. He wasn't a diarist.'

'It's odd, in that case, that he should wish to burn it – if he did burn it. And there's another oddity; the top half of the last page has been torn away. It's the page setting out last year's calendar and the calendar for 1986. Can you recall what else, if anything, was on that page, Lady Ursula?'

'I can't remember that I ever saw that page.'

'Can you recall when and where you last saw the diary?'

'I'm afraid that's the kind of detail it's impossible for me to remember. Is there anything else, Commander? If there is, and it isn't urgent, perhaps it could wait until you are sure that you are, in fact, investigating murder.'

Dalgliesh said:

'We know that already, Lady Ursula. Harry Mack was murdered.'

She didn't reply, and for about a minute they sat in silence, facing each other. Then she lifted her great eyes to his and he thought he detected a mixture of fleeting emotions: resolution, appeal, defiance. He said:

'I am afraid I've kept you too long and tired you. There is really only one more matter. Is there anything you can tell me about the two young women who died after they had been working in this house, Theresa Nolan and Diana Travers?'

The production of the half-burnt diary had shocked her deeply, but this question she took in her stride. She said calmly:

'Very little, I'm afraid. I've no doubt you know most of it already. Theresa Nolan was a gentle, considerate nurse and a competent, but not, I think, very intelligent, young woman. She came as night-nurse on the second of May when I had a bad attack of sciatica and left on the fourteenth of June. She had a room in this house but was on duty only at night. She went, as I expect you know, to a maternity nursing home in Hampstead. I accept that she probably became pregnant while she was working here, but I can assure you that no one in this house was responsible. Pregnancy is not an occupational hazard of nursing an 82-year-old arthritic woman. I know even less of Diana Travers. She was, apparently, an un-employed actress who was doing domestic work while she was

107

"resting" – I think that's the euphemism they use. She came to the house in response to a card Miss Matlock had placed in a local newsagent's window and Miss Matlock took her on to replace a cleaning woman who had recently left.'

'After consulting you, Lady Ursula?'

'It was hardly a matter on which she needed to consult me and, in fact, she did not. I know, of course, why you are inquiring about both women. One or two of my friends made it their business to send me the cutting from the *Paternoster Review*. I'm surprised that the police should trouble themselves with what is surely no more than cheap journalistic spite. It can hardly be relevant to my son's murder. If that is all, Commander, perhaps you would like to see my daughter-in-law now. No, don't bother to ring. I prefer to take you down myself. And I can manage perfectly well without your help.'

She pressed the knob in the arm of her chair and the seat slowly rose. It took her a moment to establish her balance. Then she said:

'Before you meet my daughter-in-law there is something I should, perhaps, say. You may find her less apparently distressed than you expect. That is because she has no imagination. Had she found my son's body she would have been disconsolate, certainly too shocked and distressed to talk to you now. But what her eyes don't actually see she finds it difficult to imagine. I say this only in justice to both of you.'

Dalgliesh nodded but didn't reply. It was, he thought, the first mistake she had made. The implication of her words was obvious, but it would have been wiser of her to have left them unspoken.

2

He watched while she braced herself for the first step, steeling herself for the expected gripe of pain. He made no move to help her; he knew that the gesture would be as presumptuous as it was unwelcome and Kate, sensitive as always to unspoken commands, closed her notebook then waited in watchful silence. Slowly Lady Ursula made her way to the door, steadying herself with her cane. Her hand shook on the gold knob, the veins starting out like blue cords. They followed her slowly down the carpeted corridor and into the lift. There was barely room in its elegantly curved interior for three and Dalgliesh's arm was against hers. Even through the tweed of his sleeve he could sense its brittleness and could feel its gentle, perpetual shaking. He was aware that she was under intense strain and he wondered how much it would take to break her and whether it would be his job to see that she did break. As the lift ground slowly down the two floors he knew that she was as aware of him as he was of her, and that she saw him as the enemy.

They followed her into the drawing room. This room, too, Paul Berowne would have shown him, and for a moment he had the illusion that it was the dead man, not his mother, who stood at his side. Three tall curved windows, ornately curtained, gave a view of the garden trees. They looked unreal, a one-dimensional woven tapestry in an infinite variety of green and gold. Under the elaborately enriched ceiling with its curious mixture of the Classic and Gothic, the room was sparsely furnished and the air had the melancholy, unbreathed atmosphere of a seldom-visited country house drawing room, an amalgam of pot-pourri and wax polish. Almost he expected to see a white looped cord marking off the area where tourists' feet were forbidden to tread.

The bereaved mother had received him alone, presumably by choice. The widow had thought it prudent to be solaced and protected by her doctor and her lawyer. Lady Ursula briefly introduced them then immediately went out and Dalgliesh and Kate were left to walk alone across the carpet to a scene which looked as contrived as a tableau. Barbara Berowne was sitting in a high-backed armchair to the right of the fire. Opposite her, and leaning forward in his chair was her lawyer, Anthony Farrell. Standing beside her with his hand on her wrist was her doctor. It was he who spoke first:

'I'll leave you now, Lady Berowne, but I'll look in again this evening, about six o'clock if that is convenient, and we'll try to do something to help you sleep tonight. If you need me earlier, get Miss Matlock to ring. Try to eat a little supper if you can. Get her to make you something light. You won't feel like food, I know, but I want you to try. Will you?'

She nodded and held out her hand. He held it for a moment, then turned his gaze on Dalgliesh, shifted his eyes and muttered:

'Appalling, appalling.'

As Dalgliesh made no response, he said:

'I think Lady Berowne is strong enough to talk to you now, Commander, but I hope it won't take long.'

He spoke like an amateur actor in a murder play, predictable dialogue predictably delivered. It surprised Dalgliesh that a doctor, presumably not unused to tragedy, should be more ill at ease than his patient. When he reached the door, Dalgliesh asked quietly:

'Were you also Sir Paul's physician?'

'Yes, but only recently. He was a private patient of Dr Gillespie who died last year. Sir Paul and Lady Berowne then registered with me under the National Health Service. I now have his medical records but he has never consulted me professionally. He was a very healthy man.'

So part of the unease was explained. Here was no old and valued family physician but an overworked local general practitioner, understandably anxious to get back to a crowded surgery, or his round of visits, perhaps unhappily aware that the situation required a social skill and concentrated attention which he hadn't the time to give, but trying, not very convincingly, to play the part of a family friend in a drawing room which he probably had not entered until that moment. Dalgliesh wondered whether Paul Berowne's decision to register as a National Health patient had been a matter of political expediency, conviction or economy, or of all three. There was a rectangle of faded wallpaper above the carved marble fireplace. It was half-obscured by a not particularly distinguished family portrait, but Dalgliesh suspected that a more valuable oil had once hung there. Barbara Berowne said:

'Please sit down, Commander.'

She waved vaguely towards a sofa set against the wall. It was inconveniently placed and looked too insubstantial for use, but Kate went over to it, sat down and unobtrusively took out her notebook. Dalgliesh walked over to one of the upright chairs, carried it across to the fireplace and set it down to the right of Anthony Farrell. He said:

'We are sorry to have to bother you at a time like this, Lady Berowne, but I'm sure you'll understand that it is necessary.'

But Barbara Berowne was gazing after Dr Piggott. She said resentfully:

'What a funny little man! Paul and I only registered with him last June. His hands are sweaty.'

She gave a little moue of distaste and rubbed her fingers stiffly together. Dalgliesh said:

'Do you feel able to answer some questions?'

She looked across at Farrell rather like a child expecting guidance. He said in his smooth professional voice:

'I'm afraid, my dear Barbara, that in a murder investigation the usual civilized conventions have to go. Delay is a luxury the police can't afford. I know that the Commander will make it as short as possible, and you'll be brave and make it as easy for him as you can.'

Before she had a chance to reply, he said to Dalgliesh:

'I'm here as Lady Berowne's friend as well as her lawyer. The firm has looked after the family for three generations. I had a great personal regard for Sir Paul. I've lost a friend as well as a client. That's partly why I'm here. Lady Berowne is very much alone. Her mother and stepfather are both in California.'

Dalgliesh wondered what Farrell would say if he replied: 'But her mother-in-law is only a couple of floors away.' He wondered if the implication of their separateness at a time when the family would naturally seek support, if not comfort, from each other, was lost on them, or on Farrell, or whether they were so used to living their lives under one roof but apart that even in a moment of high tragedy neither could cross the psychological barrier represented by that caged lift, those two floors.

Barbara Berowne turned her remarkable violet-blue eyes on Dalgliesh and he was for a second disconcerted. After the first fleeting glimmer of curiosity the glance was deadened, almost lifeless, as if he were looking into coloured contact lenses. Perhaps after a lifetime of seeing the effect of her gaze she no longer needed to animate it with any expression other than a casual interest. He had known that she was beautiful, how he couldn't remember, probably it was an accumulation of casually dropped comments when her husband was talked of, of press photographs. But it wasn't a beauty to stir his heart. It would have given him pleasure to

111

sit unnoticed and look at her as he might at a picture, to note with dispassionate admiration the delicate, perfectly curved arch above the slanting eyes, at the curve of the upper lip, the shadowed hollow between the cheekbone and the jaw, the rise of the slim throat. He could look and admire and leave without regret. For him this blonde loveliness was too exquisite, too orthodox, too perfect. What he loved was a more individual and eccentric beauty, vulnerability allied to intelligence. He doubted whether Barbara Berowne was intelligent, but he didn't underrate her. Nothing in police work was more dangerous than to make superficial judgements about human beings. But he wondered briefly whether here now was a woman for whom a man would kill. He had known three such women in his career; none would have been described as beautiful.

She was sitting in her chair with a still, relaxed elegance. Above her skirt of light grey, finely-pleated wool, she wore a silk shirt of pale blue with a grey cashmere cardigan slung loosely over her shoulders. Her only jewellery was a couple of gold chains and small gold stud earrings. Her hair, with its strands of pale and darker corn yellow, was drawn back and hung over her shoulder in a single thick pleat fastened at the end with a tortoiseshell clamp. Nothing, he thought, could have been more discreetly fitting. Black, particularly in so recent a widow, would have been ostentatious, theatrical, even vulgar. This gentle arrangement of grey and blue was entirely appropriate. Kate had, he knew, arrived with her news before Lady Berowne had dressed. She had been told that her husband was dead with his throat cut, and she had still been able to take trouble with her dressing. And why not? He was too old a hand to assume grief wasn't genuine because it was appropriately clad. There were women whose self-respect demanded perpetual attention to detail no matter how violent events, others for whom it was a matter of confidence, of routine, or of defiance. In a man such punctiliousness was normally regarded as commendable. Why not, then, in a woman? Or was it merely that her appearance had for over twenty years been the major preoccupation of her life and she couldn't change that habit merely because someone had slit her husband's throat? But he couldn't help noticing the details, the intricate buckle at the side of the shoes, the lipstick meticulously applied and precisely matching the pink of her nail varnish, the trace of eye-shadow. Her hands at least had been steady. When she spoke her voice was high and, to him, unpleasing. It would, he thought, easily degenerate into a childish whine. She said:

'Of course I want to help, but I don't know I can. I mean it's all so incredible. Who could have wanted to kill Paul? He hadn't any enemies. Everyone liked him. He was very popular.'

The banal, inadequate tribute in that high, slightly jarring tone must have struck even her as gauche. There was a short silence which Farrell thought it prudent to break; he said:

'Lady Berowne is, of course, deeply shocked. We were hoping, Commander, that you would be able to give us more information than we have at present. We gather that the weapon was some kind of knife and that there were injuries to the throat.'

And that, thought Dalgliesh, was as tactful a way of saying that Sir Paul's throat had been slit as even the most skilled lawyer could devise. He said:

'Both Sir Paul and the tramp were apparently killed in the same way.'

'Was the weapon at the scene?'

'A possible weapon was at the scene. They may both have been killed with Sir Paul's razor.'

'And that was left by the murderer in the room?'

'We found it there, yes.'

The implication of his careful words wasn't lost on Farrell. For his part he wouldn't use the word 'suicide', but it lay between them with all its implications. He went on:

'And the church door. Had that been forced?'

'It was unlocked when Miss Wharton, the church worker, found the bodies this morning.'

'So anyone could have got in and someone, presumably, did?'

'Certainly. You will understand that the investigation is still in its early stages. We can be sure of nothing until we have the result of the autopsy and the forensic reports.'

'Of course. I ask because Lady Berowne prefers to know the facts, or as many of them as are available. And she has a right, of course, to be kept fully informed.'

Dalgliesh made no reply, nor did he need to; they understood each other perfectly. Farrell would be polite, studiously so, but not affable. His carefully controlled demeanour, so much a part of his professional life that it no longer seemed assumed, was saying: 'We're both professionals with something of a reputation in our jobs. We both know what we're about. You will excuse a certain lack of amiability but we may be required to be on different sides.'

The truth was that they were already on different sides and both knew it. It was as if Farrell emanated an ambiguous ectoplasm which folded Barbara Berowne in its comforting aura saying: 'Here I am, I'm on your side, leave this to me. There's nothing to worry about.' It came to Dalgliesh as a subtle, masculine understanding, close to conspiracy, from which she was excluded. He did it very well.

His city firm of Torrington, Farrell and Penge, with its many ramifications, had enjoyed an unsullied legal reputation for over two hundred years. Its criminal department had represented some of the most ingenious villains in London. Some were holidaying in their Riviera villas, some on their yachts. Very few were behind bars. Dalgliesh had a sudden picture of a prison van which two days previously he had driven past on his way to the Yard, of the row of anonymous, hostile eyes gazing out through the slots as if they were expecting to see nothing more. The ability to pay for a couple of hours of Farrell's time at a crucial stage of their misfortunes would have made all the difference. Barbara Berowne said peevishly:

'I don't see why I have to be bothered. Paul didn't even tell me he was going to spend the night in that church. Dossing down with a tramp. I mean, it was all so silly.'

Dalgliesh said:

'When did you last see him?'

'At about nine fifteen yesterday morning. He came up to see me just before Mattie brought up my breakfast tray. He didn't stay long. About fifteen minutes.'

'How did he seem, Lady Berowne?'

'He seemed himself. He didn't say very much. He never did. I think I told him how I was going to spend the day.'

'And how was that?'

'I had a hair appointment at Michael and John in Bond Street at eleven. Then I lunched in Knightsbridge with an old school friend and we did some shopping in Harvey Nichols. I got home here at teatime and by then he'd left. I never saw him after nine fifteen.'

'And, as far as you know, he didn't return to the house?'

'I don't think so, but I wouldn't have seen him anyway. After I got back I changed and then took a taxi to Pembroke Lodge. That's my cousin's nursing home in Hampstead. He's an obstetrician, Mr Stephen Lampart. I was with him until midnight when he brought me home. We drove to Cookham to have dinner at the Black Swan. We left Pembroke Lodge at seven forty and drove straight to the Black Swan. I mean, we didn't stop on the way.'

It was, he thought, remarkably pat. He had expected her to come out with an alibi sooner or later, but hardly so soon and in such detail. He asked:

'And when you last saw Sir Paul at breakfast time, he didn't tell you how he proposed to spend the day?'

'No. But couldn't you look in his diary? He keeps it in his desk drawer in the study.'

'We found part of his diary in the vestry. It had been burnt.'

He was watching her face closely as he spoke. The blue eyes flickered, grew wary, but he could have sworn that this was news to her. She turned again to Farrell:

'But this is extraordinary! Why should Paul burn his diary?'

Dalgliesh said:

'We don't know that he did. But the diary was there in the grate. A number of the pages were burnt and the final page torn in half.'

Farrell's eyes met Dalgliesh's. Neither spoke. Then Dalgliesh said:

'So we need to try to establish his movements some other way. I had hoped you might be able to help.'

'But does it matter? I mean, if someone broke in and killed him, how does it help to know that he went to the estate agent a few hours earlier?'

'And did he?'

'He said he had an appointment.'

'Did he say with which one?'

'No, and I didn't ask. I suppose God told him to sell the house. I don't think He told him which estate agent to use.'

The words were as shocking as an indecency. Dalgliesh felt Farrell's dismayed surprise as clearly as if the man had gasped. He could detect neither bitterness nor irony in that high, slightly petulant voice. She could have been a mischievous child, daring in the presence of adults to say the unpardonable thing and half-surprised by her own temerity. Anthony Farrell decided that the time had come to intervene. He said smoothly:

'I myself was expecting to see Sir Paul yesterday afternoon. He had made an appointment at two thirty with me and two of my colleagues on the financial side of the firm to discuss certain arrangements made necessary, I understand, by his decision to give up his parliamentary career. But he rang yesterday shortly before ten to cancel the appointment and to make a new appointment for the same time today. I hadn't myself arrived at the office when he telephoned, but he left a message with my clerk. If you are able to prove that his death was murder, then I naturally accept that every detail of his affairs will properly come under scrutiny. Both Lady Ursula and Lady Berowne would wish that they should.'

He might be a pompous ass, thought Dalgliesh, but he was no fool. He knew or guessed, that most of these questions were premature. He was prepared to allow them, but he could stop them when he chose. Barbara Berowne turned on him her remarkable eyes.

'But there isn't anything to discuss. Paul left everything to me. He told me he had after we were married. The house too. It's quite straightforward. I'm his widow. It's all mine, well nearly all.'

Farrell said smoothly:

'Perfectly straightforward, my dear. But it's hardly necessary to discuss it now.'

Dalgliesh took from his wallet a copy of the poison pen letter and handed it to her.

He said:

'I expect you saw this.'

She shook her head and gave it to Farrell, who read it, taking his time, his face expressionless. If he had seen it before, he certainly wasn't admitting to the knowledge.

He said:

'That on the face of it is a malicious and possibly actionable attack on Sir Paul's character.'

'It may have nothing to do with his death but, obviously, we should like to clear it out of the way.'

He turned again to Barbara Berowne.

'Are you sure that your husband didn't show it to you?'

'No, why should he? Paul didn't believe in worrying me with things I couldn't do anything about. Isn't it the usual kind of poison pen letter? I mean, politicians get them all the time.'

'You mean, this wasn't unusual, that your husband had received similar communications?'

'No, I don't know, I don't think he did. He never said so. I meant that anyone in public . . .'

Farrell broke in, smoothly professional:

'Lady Berowne means, of course, that anyone in public life and particularly in politics has to expect a certain amount of this kind of malice and unpleasantness.'

Dalgliesh said:

'But not quite as specific as this, surely. There was a subsequent article, obviously based on this, in the *Paternoster Review*. Did you see that, Lady Berowne?'

She shook her head.

Farrell said:

'I suppose this has to be relevant, but do we need to talk about it now?'

Dalgliesh said:

'Not if Lady Berowne finds it too distressing.'

The implication was plain and Farrell didn't like it. His client helped him. She turned to him with a look in which appeal, surprise and distress were beautifully mingled.

'But I don't understand. I've told the Commander all I know. I've tried to help, but how can I? I don't know anything about Diana Travers. Miss Matlock, Mattie, looks after the house. I think this girl answered an advertisement and Mattie took her on.'

Dalgliesh said:

'Wasn't that rather unusual for these days? Young people don't often want to do housework.'

'Mattie said that she was an actress who only wanted to work a few hours each week. It suited her.'

'Did Miss Matlock consult you before taking on the girl?'

'No. I expect she asked my mother-in-law. They look after the house between them. They don't bother me with it.'

'And the other dead girl, Theresa Nolan. Did you have anything to do with her?'

'She was my mother-in-law's nurse, nothing to do with me. I hardly saw her.'

She turned to Anthony Farrell:

'Do I have to answer all these questions? I want to help but how can I? If Paul did have enemies, I don't know about them. We didn't really talk about politics, things like that.'

The sudden blaze of blue conveyed that no man would wish to burden her with matters so irrelevant to the essential fact about her.

She added:

'It's too dreadful. Paul dead, murdered – I can't believe it. I haven't really taken it in. I don't want to go on talking about it. I just want to be left alone and to go to my room. I want Mattie.'

The words were a piteous appeal for sympathy, for understanding, but the voice was that of a querulous child.

Farrell went over to the fireplace and pulled on the bell cord. He said:

'I'm afraid that one of the dreadful facts about murder is that the

117

police are obliged to intrude on grief. It's their job. They have to be sure that there is nothing your husband said to you which could give them a clue to suggest that he had an enemy. Someone who might know that he would be in St Matthew's Church that night, someone who had a grudge against him, might want him out of the way. It seems most likely that Paul was killed by a casual intruder, but the police have to exclude other possibilities.'

If Anthony Farrell thought that he was going to conduct the interview on his terms, he was mistaken. But before Dalgliesh could speak, the door burst open and a young man flung himself across the room to Barbara Berowne. He cried:

'Barbie darling! Mattie rang me with the news. It's awful, unbelievable. I'd have come earlier only she couldn't reach me until eleven. Darling, how are you? Are you all right?'

She said rather faintly:

'This is my brother, Dominic Swayne.'

He nodded at them as if their presence were an intrusion and turned again to his sister.

'But what happened, Barbie? Who did it? D'you know?'

Dalgliesh thought, this isn't genuine, he's acting. And then he told himself that the judgement was certainly premature and possibly unjust. One thing policing taught you was that in moments of shock and grief, even the most articulate could sound platitudinous. If Swayne were over-acting the part of a devoted consoling brother, that didn't necessarily mean that he wasn't both genuinely devoted and anxious to console. But Dalgliesh hadn't missed Barbara Berowne's small shudder as his arms went round her shoulders. It could, of course, have been a small manifestation of shock, but Dalgliesh wondered if it hadn't also been one of mild revulsion.

He wouldn't have known at first that they were brother and sister. True Swayne had the same corn-yellow hair, but his, either by nature or art, was tightly curled above a round pale forehead. The eyes, too, were alike, the same remarkable violet blue under the curved brows. But there the resemblance ended. He had none of his sister's classical heart-catching beauty. But his face, delicately featured, wasn't without a certain puckish charm with its well-formed rather petulant mouth, ears as tiny as a child's, milk-white and slightly jutting like incipient wings. He was short, little more than five foot three, but broad shouldered and with long arms. This simian strength grafted on to the delicate head and face were so discordant that the first impression was of a minor physical deformity.

But Miss Matlock had answered the bell and was standing in the doorway. Without saying goodbye and with a little moan Barbara Berowne half-stumbled over to her. The woman gazed first at her, then at the men in the room impassively, then, placing an arm across her shoulder, guided her out. There was a moment of silence, then Dalgliesh turned to Dominic Swayne:

'As you are here, perhaps you would answer one or two questions. It's possible you may be able to help us. When did you last see Sir Paul?'

'My revered brother-in-law? Do you know, I can't remember. Not for some weeks anyway. Actually I was in this house all yesterday evening, but we didn't meet. Evelyn, Miss Matlock, wasn't expecting him back for dinner. She said that he had left after breakfast and no one knew where he had gone.'

Kate asked from her seat by the wall:

'When did you arrive, sir?'

He turned to look at her, the blue eyes amused, frankly appraising, as if signalling a sexual invitation.

'Just before seven. The neighbour was coming out of his door and saw me arrive so he'll be able to confirm the time if it's important. I can't see why it should be. Miss Matlock too, of course. I stayed until just before ten thirty then went over to the local pub, the Raj, for a last drink. They'll remember me there. I was one of the last to leave.'

Kate asked:

'And you were here the whole time?'

'Yes. But what's it got to do with Paul's death? I mean is it important?

He couldn't, thought Dalgliesh, be as naive as that. He said:

'It could be helpful in tracing Sir Paul's movements yesterday. Could he have returned to the house while you were here?'

'I suppose so, but it doesn't seem likely. I was having a bath for about an hour, that's principally why I came, and he might have come back then, but I think that Miss Matlock would have mentioned it. I'm an actor, out of work at present. Just auditioning. They call it resting, God knows why. It seems more like feverish activity to me. I lodged here for a week or two in May, but Paul wasn't all that welcoming, so I moved in with Bruno Packard. He's a theatre designer. He has a small flat, a conversion, at Shepherd's Bush. But what with his model sets and gear there's not a lot of room. On top of that there isn't a bath, only a shower, and that's in the loo, so it isn't exactly convenient for anyone reasonably fastidious. I've taken to turning up here for an occasional bath and meal.'

119

It was, thought Dalgliesh, almost suspiciously pat as if the whole speech had been rehearsed. And he was certainly being unusually confiding for a man who hadn't even been asked to explain his movements, who could have no reason to suppose that this was a case of murder. But if the times were confirmed, it looked as if Swayne could be in the clear. Swayne said:

'Look, if there's nothing else you want I'll go up to Barbie. This is an appalling shock for her. Mattie will give you Bruno's address if you want it.'

After he had left, no one spoke for a moment, then Dalgliesh said:

'I am interested that Lady Berowne inherits the house. I would have expected it to be entailed.'

Farrell took the question with professional calm:

'Yes, the situation is unusual. I have, of course, authority from both Lady Ursula and Lady Berowne to give you any information you need. The old Berowne property, the one in Hampshire, was entailed, but that has long since gone, together with most of the fortune. This house has always been willed from one baronet to the next. Sir Paul inherited it from his brother, but he had absolute discretion about its disposal. After his marriage he made a new will and left it to his wife absolutely. The will is quite straightforward. Lady Ursula has her own money but there is a small bequest to her and a larger one to his only child, Miss Sarah Berowne. Halliwell and Miss Matlock get £10,000 each and he has left an oil painting, an Arthur Devis if I remember rightly, to the Chairman of his local Party. There are other minor bequests. But the house, its contents, and an adequate provision goes to his wife.'

And the house alone, thought Dalgliesh, must be worth at least three-quarters of a million, probably considerably more given its position and unique architectural interest. He recalled as he so often did the words of an old detective sergeant when he, Dalgliesh, had been a newly appointed DC. 'Love, Lust, Loathing, Lucre, the four Ls of murder, laddie. And the greatest of these is lucre.'

3

Their last interview that afternoon at Campden Hill Square was
with Miss Matlock. Dalgliesh had asked to be shown where
Berowne had kept his diary and she had led them into the ground
floor study. It was, he knew, architecturally one of the most eccentric rooms in the house, and the one, perhaps, most typical of
Soane's style. It was octagonal, each wall fitted from floor to ceiling
with glass fronted bookcases between which fluted pilasters rose to
a dome topped by an octagonal lantern decorated with richly
coloured glass. It was, he thought, an exercise in the clever organization of limited space, an eminently successful example of the
architect's peculiar genius. But it was still a room to wonder at
rather than to live in, to work in, or to enjoy.

Solidly placed in the centre of the room was Berowne's mahogany
desk. Dalgliesh and Kate moved over to it while Miss Matlock
stood in the doorway and watched them, her eyes fixed on
Dalgliesh's face, as if a momentary lapse of concentration might
cause him to spring at her. Dalgliesh said:

'Could you show me, please, exactly where the diary was kept?'

She moved forward and, without speaking, pulled open the top
right hand drawer. It was empty now except for a box of writing
paper and one of envelopes. He asked:

'Did Sir Paul work here?'

'He wrote letters. He kept his parliamentary papers in his office
at the House and everything to do with his constituency at his
office at Wrentham Green.' She added:

'He liked things separate.'

Dalgliesh thought: Separate, impersonal, under control. Again
he had the sense that he was in a museum, that Berowne had sat in
this richly ornamented cell like a stranger. He said:

'What about his private papers? Do you know where those are
kept?'

'I suppose in the safe. It's concealed behind the books in the case
to the right of the door.'

If Berowne had, indeed, been murdered the safe and its contents
would have to be examined. But that, like much else, could wait.

He moved over to the bookcases. It was, of course, popular
wisdom that personality could be diagnosed from the shelves of a

private library. These revealed that Berowne had read more biography, history and poetry than he had fiction, and yet, scanning the shelves, it struck Dalgliesh that he could have been browsing in the library of a private club, or a luxury cruise ship, although admittedly one where the object of the voyage was cultural enrichment rather than popular entertainment, and the fares high. Here, tidily shelved, was essentially the predictable, unexceptional choice of a well-educated, cultured Englishman who knew what it was proper to read. But he couldn't believe that Berowne was a man whose idea of choosing fiction was to order routinely the Booker shortlist. Again he had the sense of a personality escaping him, of even the room and its objects conspiring to hide from him the essential man. He asked:

'How many people had access to this room yesterday?'

The formal impersonality of the library must have affected him. The question sounded oddly phrased even to his own ears, and she made no attempt to hide the tone of contempt.

'Access? The study is part of a private house. We don't keep it locked. All the family and their friends have what you call access.'

'And who did, in fact, come in here yesterday?'

'I can't be sure. I suppose Sir Paul must have done if you found his diary with him in the church. Mrs Minns would have come in to dust. Mr Frank Musgrave, who is chairman of the Constituency party was shown in here at lunchtime, but he didn't wait. Miss Sarah Berowne called in during the afternoon to see her grandmother, but I think she waited in the drawing room. She left before Lady Ursula returned.'

Dalgliesh asked:

'Mr Musgrave and Miss Berowne were let in by you?'

'I opened the door to them. There's no one else to do it.' She paused, then added:

'Miss Berowne used to have her own keys to the front door, but she didn't take them with her when she left home.'

'And when did you last see the diary?'

'I can't remember. I think it was about two weeks ago when Sir Paul rang from his office in the Department and asked me to check on a dinner engagement.'

'And when did you last see Sir Paul?'

'Just before ten o'clock yesterday. He came into the kitchen to collect some food for a picnic lunch.'

'Then perhaps we could go to the kitchen now.'

She led him along the tiled passage, down a couple of steps, then through a baize-covered door to the back of the house. Then she stood aside to let him in, and again stood at the door, hands clasped, the parody of a cook awaiting judgement on the cleanliness of the kitchen. And indeed there would be nothing to fault. Like the study it was curiously impersonal, lacking cosiness without being actually uncomfortable or poorly equipped. There was a central table in well-scrubbed pine with four chairs and a large and very old gas-cooker in addition to a more modern solid-fuel stove. It was obvious that little money had been spent on the kitchen in recent years. From the low window he could see the back of the wall dividing the house from the mews garages, and the feet only of the marble statues in their niches. Thus truncated, a row of delicately carved toes, they seemed to emphasize the room's colourless deprivation. The only individual note was a pink geranium in a pot on the shelf over the sink, and beside it a second pot with a couple of cuttings. He said:

'You told me that Sir Paul collected his lunch. Did he do that himself or did you get it for him?'

'He did. He knew where things were kept. He was often in the kitchen when I prepared Lady Ursula's breakfast tray. He used to take it up to her.'

'And what did he take away with him yesterday?'

'Half a loaf of bread which he sliced ready to eat, a piece of Roquefort cheese, two apples.' She added:

'He seemed preoccupied. I don't think he much minded what he was taking.'

It was the first time she had volunteered any information, but when he went on to question her gently about Berowne's mood, what, if anything he had said, she seemed to regret the moment of confidence and became almost surly. Sir Paul had told her that he wouldn't be in to luncheon, but nothing else. She hadn't known that he was going to St Matthew's church, nor whether he would be back for dinner. Dalgliesh said:

'So you prepared dinner in the usual way and at the usual time?'

The question disconcerted her. She flushed and the clasped hands tightened. Then she said:

'No. No, not in the usual way. Lady Ursula asked me when she got back after her tea engagement to bring up a tray with a flask of soup and a plate of smoked salmon sandwiches on brown bread. She didn't want to be disturbed again that evening. I took it up shortly after six. And I knew that Lady Berowne was dining out. I decided to wait and see if Sir Paul actually came back. There were things I could cook quickly if he did. I had soup I could warm up. I could make him an omelette. There's always something.' She sounded as defensive as if he had accused her of dereliction of duty.

He said:

'But it was, perhaps, a little inconsiderate of him not to let you know whether he would be in to dinner.'

'Sir Paul was never inconsiderate.'

'And to stay out all night without a word was surely unusual? It must have been worrying for all the household.'

'Not for me. It isn't my busines what the family choose to do. He could have been staying in the constituency. At eleven o'clock I asked Lady Ursula if it was all right to go to bed and leave the front door unbolted. She said that I should. Lady Berowne knew that it was necessary to bolt it after her when she came in.'

Dalgliesh changed the tack of his questions.

'Did Sir Paul take matches with him yesterday morning?'

Her surprise was obvious and, he thought, unfeigned.

'Matches? He didn't need matches. Sir Paul doesn't – he didn't – smoke. I didn't see him with any matches.'

'If he had taken them, where would he have got them?'

'From here at the side of the stove. It isn't self-lighting. Or there is a packet of four boxes in the cupboard above.'

She opened and showed him. The paper wrapping round the four boxes had been torn and one box taken, presumably that now lying at the side of the stove. She was gazing at him now with a fixed attention, her eyes very bright, her face a little flushed, as if she had a slight fever. His questions about the matches, which had first surprised her, now seemed to disconcert her. She was more on her guard, warier, much more tense. He was too experienced and she too poor an actress for him to be deceived. Up to now she had answered his questions in the tone of a woman performing a necessary if disagreeable duty. But now the interview had become an ordeal. She wanted him gone. He said:

'We would like to see your sitting room, if you have no objection?'

'If you think it necessary. Lady Ursula said that you were to be given every facility.'

Dalgliesh thought it unlikely that Lady Ursula had said any such thing, and certainly not in those words. He and Kate followed her across the passage and into the opposite room. It must, Dalgliesh thought, once have been the butler's or housekeeper's sanctum. As with the kitchen there was no view except of the courtyard and the door leading through to the mews garages. But the furniture was comfortable enough; a chintz-covered sofa for two, a matching armchair, a gate-legged table and two dining chairs set against the wall, a bookcase filled with volumes of an identical size, obviously from a book club. The fireplace was of marble with a wide over-mantel on which was crowded, with no attempt at arrangement, a collection of modern and prettily sentimental figurines, women in crinolines, a child hugging a puppy, shepherds and shepherdesses, a ballet dancer. These presumably belonged to Miss Matlock. The pictures were prints in modern frames, one of Constable's *Hay Wain* and, more surprising, Monet's *Women in a Field*. They and the furniture were innocuous, predictable, as if someone had said, 'We need to employ a housekeeper, furnish a room for her.' Even rejects from the rest of the house would have had more character than these impersonal objects. What again was missing was the sense that someone had impressed on this place her own personality. He thought: They live here their separate cabined lives. But only Lady Ursula is at home in this house. The rest are no more than squatters.

He asked her where she had spent the previous evening. She said:

'I was here or in the kitchen. Mr Dominic Swayne came for a meal and a bath, and afterwards we played Scrabble. He arrived shortly before seven and left before eleven. Our neighbour, Mr Swinglehurst, was garaging his car and saw Mr Swayne arrive.'

'Did anyone else in the house see him while he was here?'

'No, but he did take a telephone call at about twenty to nine. It was from Mrs Hurrell, the wife of the last agent at the constituency. She wanted to try and contact Sir Paul. I told her that no one knew where he was.'

'And Mr Swayne, where did he bath?'

'Upstairs, in the main bathroom. Lady Ursula has her own bathroom, and there is a shower room down here, but Mr Swayne wanted a proper bath.'

'So you were either in this room or the kitchen and Mr Swayne was upstairs for at least part of the evening. The back door, was it locked?'

'Locked and bolted. It always is after tea. The key is here on the keyboard in that cupboard.'

She opened it and showed him the wall-mounted board with its rows of hooks and tagged keys. He asked:

'Could anyone have gone out without your noticing, perhaps while you were in the kitchen?'

'No. I usually keep the door to the passage open. I should have seen or heard. No one left the house last night by that door.' She seemed to rouse herself then said with sudden vigour:

'All these questions. What was I doing? Who was here? Who could have left without being seen? Anyone would think he was murdered.'

Dalgliesh said:

'It is possible that Sir Paul was murdered.'

She gazed at him, appalled, then sank down on to the chair. He saw that she was shaking. She said in a low voice:

'Murdered. No one said anything about murder. I thought . . .' Kate moved over to her, glanced at Dalgliesh, then placed her hand on Miss Matlock's shoulder. Dalgliesh asked:

'What did you think, Miss Matlock?'

She looked up at him and whispered so quietly that he had to bend his head to hear.

'I thought he might have done it himself.'

'Had you any reason to suppose that?'

'No. No reason. Of course not. How could I? And Lady Berowne said . . . There was something about his razor. But murder . . . I don't want to answer any more questions, not tonight. I don't feel well. I don't want to be badgered. He's dead. That's terrible enough. But murder! I can't believe it's murder. I want to be left alone.'

Looking down at her, Dalgliesh thought: The shock is real enough, but part of this is acting, and not very convincing acting at that. He said coolly:

'We're not allowed to badger a witness, Miss Matlock, and I don't think you really believe that we have been badgering you. You've been very helpful. I'm afraid we shall have to talk again, to ask you more questions, but it needn't be now. We can see ourselves out.'

She got out of the chair as clumsily as an old woman and said:

'No one sees themselves out of this house. That's my job.'

In the Rover Dalgliesh rang the Yard. He said to Massingham:

'We'll see Mr Lampart as early as we can tomorrow. It would be helpful if we could fit that in before the PM at three thirty. Is there any news of Sarah Berowne?'

'Yes sir. She's a professional photographer, apparently, and has had sessions all today. She's got another booked for tomorrow afternoon, a writer who's due to leave for the States in the evening. It's rather important so she hopes it won't be necessary to cancel. I told her we'd come along in the evening at six thirty. And Press

Office want an urgent word. The news will break at six o'clock and they want to set up a press conference first thing tomorrow.'

'That's premature. What on earth do they expect us to be able to say at this stage? Try to get it postponed, John.'

If he could prove that Berowne had been murdered the whole investigation would take place against a background of feverish media interest. He knew that, although he didn't welcome it, but there was no reason why it should start yet. As Kate manoeuvred the Rover out of its restricted parking place and began to move slowly down Campden Hill he looked back at the elegant façade of the house, at the windows like dead eyes. And then, on the top floor, he saw the twitch of a curtain and knew that Lady Ursula was watching them leave.

4

It was six twenty before Sarah Berowne managed to reach Ivor Garrod by telephone.She had been in her flat for most of the early part of the afternoon but hadn't dared ring from there. It was an absolute rule of his, born, she had sometimes felt, from his obsession with secrecy, that nothing important should ever be told over her own telephone. So the whole afternoon from the time her grandmother had left her had been dominated by the need to find a convenient public kiosk, to have sufficient coins ready. But he had always been unavailable and she hadn't liked to risk leaving a message, not even her name.

Her only appointment of the day had been to photograph a visiting writer staying with friends in Hertfordshire. She always worked with the minimum of equipment and had travelled by train. She couldn't remember very much of the short session. She had worked like an automaton choosing the best setting, testing the light, fitting the lenses. She supposed it had gone reasonably well, the woman had seemed satisfied, but even as she worked she had been impatient to get away to find a public telephone, to try once again to reach Ivor.

She had jumped down from the train almost before it drew to a stop at King's Cross and had looked round with desperate eyes for the arrows pointing to the telephones. They were open instruments banked each side of a malodorous passageway leading from the main concourse, its walls scribbled with numbers and graffiti. The rush hour was in progress and it was a couple of minutes before an instrument was free. She almost snatched it, still warm, from the relinquishing hand. And this time she was lucky; he was in his office, it was his voice that answered. She gave a small sob of relief:

'It's Sarah. I've been trying to reach you all day. Can you talk?'

'Briefly. Where are you?'

'At King's Cross. You've heard?'

'Only now, on the six o'clock news. It hasn't made the evening papers.'

'Ivor, I have to see you.'

He said calmly:

'Naturally. There are things we need to talk about, but not tonight. That isn't possible. Have the police been in touch with you?'

'They've been trying to get me, but I told them that I was tied up all today and wouldn't be free until six thirty tomorrow.'

'And are you?'

What does that matter, she thought. She said:

'I've got two appointments in the afternoon.'

'Hardly being tied up all day. Never lie to the police unless you can be sure that they have no way of finding out. They only have to check with your diary.'

'But I couldn't let them come until we'd spoken. There are things they might ask. About Theresa Nolan, about Diana. Ivor, we have to meet.'

'We shall. And they won't ask about Theresa. Your father killed himself, his final and most embarrassing folly. His life was a mess. The family will want it decently buried, not dragged out stinking into the daylight. How did you learn the news, by the way?'

'Grandmama. She rang me, then came round by taxi after the police had left her. She didn't tell me very much. I don't think she knew all the details. She doesn't believe that Daddy killed himself.'

'Naturally. The Berownes are expected to put on uniform and kill other people, not themselves. But that, come to it, was apparently what he did, kill another person. I wonder how much sympathy Ursula Berowne will waste on that dead tramp.'

A small burr of doubt caught at her mind. Could they possibly have said on the news that the second victim was a tramp? She said:

'But it isn't only Grandmama. The police, a Commander Dalgliesh, he doesn't seem to think that Daddy killed himself either.'

The level of noise had risen. The narrow hallway was crowded with people needing to telephone before catching their trains. She felt their bodies thrusting against her. The air was a jabber of voices against the background tramp of feet, the raucous, unintelligible litany of the station announcer. She bent her head more closely over the mouthpiece. She said:

'The police don't seem to think it was suicide.'

There was a silence. She dared to speak more loudly against the noise.

'Ivor, the police don't think . . .'

He cut in:

'I heard you. Look, stay where you are. I'll come now. We can only have half an hour but you're right, we ought to talk. And don't worry, I'll be with you in the flat when they arrive tomorrow. It's important you don't see them alone. And, Sarah . . .'

'Yes, I'm here.'

'We were together the whole of yesterday evening. We were together from six o'clock when I arrived from work. We stayed together all night. We ate in the flat. Get that into your mind. Start concentrating on it now. And stay where you are. I'll be there in about forty minutes.'

She replaced the receiver and stood for a moment motionless, her head against the cold metal of the instrument. A furious female voice said: 'Do you mind. Some of us have trains to catch', and she felt herself pushed aside. She fought her way out of the hall and leaned against the wall. Small waves of faintness and nausea flowed over her, each leaving her more desolate, but there was nowhere to sit, no privacy, no peace. She could go to the coffee bar but he might get there early. Suppose she became disorientated, lost track of time. He had said 'stay where you are', and obeying him had become a habit. She leaned back and closed her eyes. She had to obey him now, rely on his strength, rely on him to tell her what to do. She had no one else.

He hadn't once said he was sorry that her father was dead, but he wasn't sorry and he didn't expect her to be. He had always been brutally unsentimental; that was what he meant by honesty. She wondered what he would do if she said: 'He was my father and he's dead. I loved him once. I need to mourn for him, for myself. I need to be comforted. I'm lost, I'm frightened. I need to feel your arms around me. I need to be told that it wasn't my fault.'

The marching horde flowed past her, a phalanx of grey intent faces, eyes staring ahead. They were like a flood of refugees from a stricken city, or a retreating army, still disciplined, but dangerously on the edge of panic. She closed her eyes and let the tramp of their feet engulf her. And, suddenly, she was in another station, another crowd. But then she had been six years old and the station had been Victoria. What were they doing there, she and her father? Probably meeting her grandmother, returning by overland and by boat from her house rising out of the Seine at Les Andelys. For one moment she and her father had been parted. He had paused to greet an acquaintance and she had momentarily slipped his hand and run to look at the brightly coloured poster of a seaside town. Looking round she saw with panic that he was no longer there. She was alone, menaced by a moving forest of endless, tramping, terrifying legs. They could have been parted only for seconds, but the terror had been so dreadful that, recalling it now, eighteen years later, she felt the same loss, the same engulfing terror, the same absolute despair. But suddenly he had been there, striding towards her, his long tweed coat flapping open, smiling, her father, her safety, her god. Not crying, but shuddering with terror and relief, she had run into his outstretched arms and felt herself lifted high, had heard his voice: 'It's all right, my darling, it's all right, it's all right.' And she had felt the dreadful shaking dissolving in his strong clasp.

She opened her eyes and blinking away the smarting tears she saw the drab blacks and greys of the marching army fudge, dissolve, then whirl into a kaleidoscope shot through with flashes of bright colour. It seemed to her that the moving feet were pounding over and through her, that she had become invisible, a brittle, empty shell. But suddenly the mass parted and he was there, still in that long tweed coat, moving towards her, smiling, so that she had to restrain herself from crying 'Daddy, Daddy', and running into his arms. But the hallucination passed. This wasn't he, this was a hurrying stranger with a briefcase who glanced with momentary curiosity at her eager face and outstretched arms, then looked through her and passed on. She shrank back, wedging herself more firmly against the wall, and began her long, patient wait for Ivor.

5

It was just before ten o'clock and they were thinking of locking up their papers for the night when Lady Ursula rang. Gordon Halliwell had returned and she would be grateful if the police could see him now. He himself would prefer it. Tomorrow was going to be a busy day for both of them, and she couldn't say when they would be available. Dalgliesh knew that Massingham, if in charge, would have said firmly that they would arrive next morning, if only to demonstrate that they worked at their own convenience, not that of Lady Ursula. Dalgliesh, who was anxious to question Gordon Halliwell and who had never felt the need to bolster either his own authority or his self-esteem, said that they would arrive as soon as possible.

The door of number sixty-two was opened by Miss Matlock who gazed at them for a couple of seconds with tired, resentful eyes before standing to one side to let them in. Dalgliesh could see that her skin was grey with weariness, the set of her shoulders a little too rigid to be natural. She was wearing a long dressing gown in flowered nylon, strained across the breast, the belt double-knotted as if she were afraid they would tear it off. She made a clumsy flutter of her hands towards it and said peevishly:

'I'm not dressed for visitors. We were hoping to get to bed early. I wasn't expecting you to come back tonight.'

Dalgliesh said:

'I'm sorry to have to disturb you again. If you want to go to bed, perhaps Mr Halliwell could let us out.'

'It isn't his job. He's only the chauffeur. Locking up the house is my responsibility. Lady Ursula has asked him to take the telephone calls tomorrow, but it isn't suitable, it isn't right. We've had no peace since the six o'clock news. This will kill her if it goes on.'

It was, thought Dalgliesh, likely to go on for a very long time but he doubted whether it would kill Lady Ursula.

Their footsteps rang on the marble floor as Miss Matlock led them down the passage past the octagonal study then through the baize door to the back of the house and finally down three stairs to the outside door. The house was very quiet but portentously expectant like an empty theatre. He had the sense, as he often did in the houses of the recently murdered, of a thin denuded air, a voiceless presence. She drew the locks and they found themselves in the rear courtyard. The three statues in their niches were subtly lit with concealed lighting and seemed to float, gently gleaming, in the still air. The night was surprisingly balmy for autumn, and there came from some nearby garden the transitory smell of cypress so that he felt for a moment displaced, disorientated as if transported to Italy. It seemed to him inappropriate that the statues should be lit, the beauty of the house still celebrated when Berowne lay frozen like a carcass of meat in his plastic shroud, and he found himself instinctively putting out his hand for a switch before following Miss Matlock through a second door which led to the old mews and the garages.

The rear of the wall with the statues was unadorned; the spoils of the eighteenth-century grand tour were not for the eyes of the footmen or coachmen who once must have inhabited the mews. The yard was cobbled and led to two large garages. The double doors of the left were open and in the glare of two long tubes of fluorescent light they saw that the entrance to the flat was by way of a wrought-iron staircase leading up the side of the garage wall. Miss Matlock merely pointed to the door at the top and said:

'You'll find Mr Halliwell there.' And then, as if to justify the formal use of his name, she said: 'He used to be a sergeant in the late Sir Hugo's regiment. He's been decorated for bravery, the Distinguished Service Medal. I expect Lady Ursula told you. He isn't the usual kind of chauffeur-handyman.'

And what in these egalitarian, servantless days, thought Dalgliesh, did she suppose the usual kind of chauffeur-handyman to be?

The garage was large enough comfortably to hold the black Rover with its A registration and a white Golf, both of which were neatly parked with room for a third car. Making their way down the side of the Rover through a strong smell of petrol they saw that the garage was obviously also used as a workshop. Under a high, long window at the rear was a wooden bench with fitted drawers, and on the wall above, a pegboard on which tools were neatly displayed. Propped against the right-hand wall was a man's bicycle.

They had hardly set foot on the bottom step of the staircase when the door above opened and the figure of a man stood stockily silhouetted against the light. As they came up to him Dalgliesh saw that he was both older and shorter than he had expected, surely only just the statutory height for a soldier, but broad shouldered and giving an immediate impression of disciplined strength. He was very dark, almost swarthy, and the straight hair, longer than it would have been in his Army days, fell across his forehead almost touching eyebrows straight as black gashes above the deep-set eyes. His nose was short with slightly flared nostrils, the mouth uncompromising above a square chin. He was wearing well-cut fawn slacks and a woollen checked shirt, open-necked, and gave no sign of tirednesss, seeming as fresh as if this were a morning visit. He looked at them with keen but untroubled eyes; eyes that had seen worse things than a couple of CID officers arriving at night. Standing aside to let them in, he said in a voice which held only a trace of roughness:

'I'm just making coffee, or there's whisky if you'd prefer it.'

They accepted the coffee and he went through a door at the back of the room from which presently they heard the noise of running water, the clatter of a kettle lid. The sitting room was long but narrow, its low windows looking out on the blank rear of the wall. Soane, as a good architect, would have ensured that the privacy of the family was protected; the mews would be unseen from all but the top windows of the house. At the far end of the room a door stood open and Dalgliesh could glimpse the end of a single bed. At the back was a small, delicately wrought Victorian fireplace with a carved wooden surround and an elegant fire-basket reminding him of the grate in St Matthew's Church. A modern three-bar electric fire was plugged in to a socket at its side.

A pine table with four chairs occupied the middle of the room and two rather battered armchairs stood each side of the fireplace. Between the windows was a worktop with, above it, a pegboard of tools, smaller and more delicate than those in the garage. They saw that Halliwell's hobby was wood carving and that he was working on a Noah's Ark with a set of animals. The ark was beautifully constructed with dove-tail joints and an elegant clapboard roof; the completed animals, a pair of lions, tigers and giraffes were more crudely carved but instantly recognizable and with a certain vigorous life.

The far wall was fitted with a bookshelf from floor to ceiling. Dalgliesh moved across to it and saw with interest that Halliwell owned what looked like a complete set of the *Notable British Trials*. And there was one other volume even more interesting: he drew out and leafed through the eighth edition of Keith Simpson's *Textbook on Forensic Medicine*. Replacing it, and glancing round the room he was struck with its tidiness, with its self-containment. It was the room of a man who had organized his living space and

134

probably his life to fulfil his needs, who knew his own nature and was at peace with it. Unlike Paul Berowne's study, this was the room of a man who felt he had a right to be there.

Halliwell came in carrying a tray with three stoneware mugs, a bottle of milk and one of Bell's whisky. He motioned towards the whisky and when Dalgliesh and Massingham shook their heads added a generous measure to his own black coffee. They sat round the table.

Dalgliesh said:

'I see you've got what looks like a complete set of the *Notable British Trials*. That must be comparatively rare.'

Halliwell said:

'It's an interest of mine. I could have fancied being a criminal lawyer if things had been different.'

He spoke without resentment. It was a statement of fact; but there was no need to ask which things. The law was still a privileged profession. It was rare for a working-class boy to end up eating his dinners in the Inns of Court.

He added:

'It's the trials I find interesting, not the defendants. Most murderers seem pretty stupid and commonplace when you see them in the dock. Same will be true of this chap, no doubt, when you get your hands on him. But maybe a caged animal is always less interesting than one running wild, especially when you've glimpsed his spoor.'

Massingham said:

'So you're assuming it's murder.'

'I'm assuming that a Commander and a Chief Inspector of the CID wouldn't come here after ten at night to discuss why Sir Paul Berowne should want to slit his throat.'

Massingham leaned across to reach the milk bottle. Stirring his coffee he asked:

'When did you hear of Sir Paul's death?'

'On the six o'clock news. I rang Lady Ursula and said I'd drive back at once. She said I wasn't to hurry. There was nothing I could do here and she wouldn't be wanting the car. She said the police had asked to see me, but that you'd have plenty to occupy yourselves until I got back.'

Massingham asked:

'How much has Lady Ursula told you?'

'As much as she knows, which isn't a great deal. She said that their throats were cut and that Sir Paul's razor had been the weapon.'

135

Dalgliesh had asked Massingham to do most of the questioning. This apparent reversal of role and status was often disconcerting to a suspect, but not to this one. Halliwell was either too confident or too unworried to be troubled by such niceties. Dalgliesh had the impression that, of the two, it was Massingham who was, unaccountably, the less at ease. Halliwell, who answered his questions with what seemed deliberate slowness, had an odd and disconcerting trick of fixing his dark eyes intently on the questioner as if it were he who was the interrogator, he who was seeking to fathom an unknown, elusive personality.

He admitted that he had known that Sir Paul used a cut-throat razor; anyone in the house would know that. He knew that the diary was kept in the top right-hand drawer. It wasn't private. Sir Paul might ring and ask whoever answered the telephone to check on the time of an engagement. There was a key to the drawer, kept usually in the lock or in the drawer itself. Occasionally Sir Paul had been known to lock the drawer and take the key with him, but that wasn't usual. These were the sort of details you got to know if you lived or worked in a house. But he couldn't remember when he had last seen the razors or the diary, and he hadn't been told that Sir Paul would be visiting the church that previous evening. He couldn't say whether anyone else in the house had known; no one had mentioned the matter to him.

Asked for his movements during the day, he said that he had got up at about half-past six and had gone for a half-hour jog in Holland Park before boiling an egg for his breakfast. At eight thirty he had gone over to the house to see if there were any odd jobs which Miss Matlock had needed doing. She had given him a table lamp to mend and an electric kettle. He had then driven to collect Mrs Beamish, Lady Ursula's chiropodist who lived in Parsons Green and who no longer ran a car. That was a regular arrangement on the third Tuesday in the month. Mrs Beamish was over seventy and Lady Ursula was the only patient she now saw. The session was over by eleven thirty and he had then driven Mrs Beamish home and returned to take Lady Ursula to a luncheon engagement with a friend, Mrs Charles Blaney, at the University Women's Club. He had parked the car near the club, gone for a solitary pub lunch and returned at two forty-five to drive both ladies to an exhibition of watercolours at Agnew's. Afterwards he had driven them to the Savoy for afternoon tea, then returned to Campden Hill Square by way of Chelsea where he had dropped Mrs Blaney at her house. He and Lady Ursula were back at number sixty-two by five thirty-three. He could remember the time exactly because he had looked at the car clock. He was used to organizing his life by time. He had helped Lady Ursula into the house, had then garaged the Rover and had spent the rest of the evening in his flat until leaving for the country just after ten o'clock. Massingham said:

'I believe Lady Ursula telephoned you twice during the evening. Can you remember when that was?'

'Yes. Once at about eight, and again at nine fifteen. She wanted to discuss next week's arrangements and to remind me that she had said I could take the Rover. I drive one of the early Cortinas but it's having its MOT test.'

Massingham asked:

'When the cars are garaged, the Rover, your own and the Golf, is the garage kept locked?'

'It's kept locked whether or not the cars are garaged. The outer gate is, of course, always secure so there isn't much risk of theft, but it's possible that kids from the comprehensive school could climb over the wall, perhaps as a dare. There are dangerous tools in the larger garage and Lady Ursula thinks it wiser always to keep it locked. I didn't bother to lock it tonight because I knew you were coming.'

'And yesterday evening?'

'It was locked after five forty.'

'Who has the keys except yourself?'

'Sir Paul and Lady Berowne both have a set and there's a spare bunch on the keyboard in Miss Matlock's sitting room. Lady Ursula wouldn't need them. She relies on me to drive her.'

'And were you here in this flat all yesterday evening?'

'From five forty. That's right.'

'Is there any chance that someone from the house or from outside could have taken out a car or the bicycle without your knowing?'

Halliwell paused, then he said:

'I don't see how that would be possible.'

Dalgliesh interposed quietly:

'I'd like you to be more definite than that, Mr Halliwell, if you can be. Could they or couldn't they?'

Halliwell looked at him.

'No, sir, they couldn't. I must have heard the garage being unlocked. I've got sharp ears.'

Dalgliesh went on:

'So last night from about five forty until you left for the country

137

shortly after ten you were here alone in this flat and the garage door was bolted?'

'Yes, sir.'

'Is it usual for you to keep the doors bolted when you're in the flat?'

'If I know I'm not going out, it is. I rely on the garage door for my security. The flat lock is only a Yale. It's become a habit to bolt the doors.'

Massingham asked:

'And where did you go when you left here?'

'Into the country. To Suffolk, to see a friend. It's a two-hour drive. I arrived about midnight. It's the widow of one of my mates killed in the Falklands. There's a boy. He doesn't miss his dad, he was killed before he was born, but his mother reckons that it's good for him to have a man about the place occasionally.'

Massingham asked:

'So you went to see the boy?'

The smouldering eyes were fixed on him. Halliwell answered simply:

'No. I went to see his mother.'

Massingham said:

'Your private life is your affair, but we need confirmation about when you arrived at your friend's house. That means we need to know her address.'

'Maybe, sir, but I don't see why I need to give it. She's had enough to put up with in the last three years without the police bothering her. I left here just after ten. If Sir Paul was dead before then, what I did later that night isn't relevant. Maybe you know when he died, maybe not. But when you get the autopsy report you'll get a clearer idea. If I need to give you her name and address then, OK, I'll give it. But I'll wait until you convince me that it's necessary.'

Massingham said:

'We shan't bother her. She merely has to answer one simple question.'

'A question about murder. She's had enough of death and dying. Look, I left here shortly after ten and I arrived almost exactly at midnight. If you do ask her, she'll say the same, and if it's relevant, if I had anything to do with Sir Paul's death, then I'll have fixed a time with her anyway, won't I?'

Massingham asked:

'Why did you start out so late? Today was your day off. Why hang about until ten before starting on a two-hour journey?'

138

'I prefer driving when the worst of the traffic is over, and I had some jobs I wanted to get finished first, a plug to fix on the table lamp, the electric kettle to mend. They're on the side if you want to check on the work. Then I bathed, changed, cooked myself a meal.'

The words, if not the voice, were on the edge of insolence, but Massingham held his temper. Dalgliesh, his own well under control, thought he knew why. Halliwell was a soldier, decorated, a hero. Massingham would have dealt less gently with any man for whom he felt less instinctive respect. If Halliwell had murdered Paul Berowne then the Victoria Cross wouldn't save him, but Dalgliesh knew that Massingham would prefer almost any other suspect to be guilty. Massingham asked:

'Are you married?'

'I had a wife and a daughter. They're both dead.'

He turned and looked directly at Dalgliesh. He said:

'What about you, sir? Are you married?'

Dalgliesh had reached out behind him and taken up one of the carved lions. Now he turned it gently in his hands. He said:

'I had a wife and a son. They, too, are dead.'

Halliwell turned again to Massingham and bent on him his dark unsmiling eyes.

'And if that question was none of my business, neither are my wife and daughter any of yours.'

Massingham said:

'Nothing is irrelevant when it comes to murder. This lady you visited yesterday night, are you engaged to her?

'No. She's not ready for that. After what happened to her husband I don't know that she ever will be. That's why I don't want to give you her address. She's not ready for that kind of question from the police, or for any other question.'

Massingham rarely made that kind of mistake and he didn't compound it by explanation or excuse. Dalgliesh didn't press the matter. The important hour was eight o'clock. If Halliwell had an alibi for the hours until ten he was in the clear and was entitled to his privacy for the following day. If he were trying with difficulty to build up a relationship with a bereaved and vulnerable woman it was understandable that he didn't want the police arriving with unnecessary questions however tactful. He said:

'How long have you been working here?'

'Five years three months, sir. I took the job when Major Hugo was alive. After he was killed Lady Ursula asked me to stay on. I stayed. The money suits, the place suits, you could say Lady Ursula suits. Apparently I suit her. I like living in London and I haven't decided yet what to do with my gratuity.'

'Who pays your wages? Who actually employs you?'

'Lady Ursula. It's my job to drive her mostly. Sir Paul used to drive himself or use the ministerial car. Occasionally I'd drive him and her young ladyship if they were out in the evening. There wasn't much of that. They weren't a social couple.'

'What sort of couple were they?' Massingham's voice was carefully uninterested.

'They didn't hold hands in the back of the car, if that's what you mean.' He paused, then added: 'I think that she was a bit afraid of him.'

'With reason?'

'Not that I could see, but I wouldn't describe him as an easy man. Nor a happy one, come to that. If you can't cope with guilt, best avoid doing things that make you feel guilty.'

'Guilt?'

'He killed his first wife didn't he? All right it was an accident; wet road, bad visibility, a notorious bend. That all came out at the inquest. But he was the one driving. I've seen it before. They never quite forgive themselves. Something here' – he gave his chest a gentle thump – 'keeps asking them whether it really was an accident.'

'There's no evidence that it wasn't, and he was as likely to kill himself as his wife.'

'Maybe that wouldn't have worried him that much. Still he didn't die, did he? She did. And then, five months later, he married again. He got his brother's fiancée, his brother's house, his brother's money, his brother's title.'

'But not his brother's chauffeur?'

'No. He didn't take over me.'

Dalgliesh asked:

'Did the title matter to him? I shouldn't have thought so.'

'Oh it mattered all right, sir. It wasn't much, I suppose, a baronetcy, but it was old. 1642. He liked it all right, the sense of continuity, his little bit of vicarious immortality.'

Massingham said:

'Well, we can all hope for that. You don't sound as if you much liked him.'

'Liking didn't come into it between him and me. I drove his mother, she paid me. And if he disliked me he didn't show it. But I reckon I reminded him of things he'd rather forget.'

Massingham said:

'And now it's all gone, ended with him, even the title.'

'Maybe. Time will show. I think I'd wait nine months before I was sure of that.'

It was a hint of a possibility Dalgliesh had already suspected, but he didn't pursue it. Instead he asked:

'When Sir Paul gave up his ministerial job and then his parliamentary seat, what was the feeling in the house among the staff?'

'Miss Matlock didn't discuss it. This isn't the sort of house where the staff sit in the kitchen drinking tea and gossiping about the family. We leave upstairs, downstairs to the telly. Mrs Minns and I thought we might be in for a scandal.'

'What sort of a scandal?'

'Sexual, I suppose. That's the kind it usually is.'

'Had you any reason to suspect that?'

'None, except that bit of dirt in the *Paternoster Review*. I've no evidence. You asked me what I thought, sir. That was what I thought most likely. Turns out I was wrong. It was more complicated apparently. But then he was a complicated man.'

Massingham went on to ask him about the two dead women. Halliwell said:

'I hardly saw Theresa Nolan. She had a room here but she either stayed in it most of the time, or went out. Kept herself to herself. She was employed as a night-nurse and wasn't supposed to be on duty until seven. Miss Matlock nursed Lady Ursula during the day. She seemed a quiet, rather shy girl. A bit timid for a nurse, I thought. Lady Ursula had no complaints as far as I know. You'd better ask her.'

'You know that she got pregnant while she was working here?'

'Maybe, but she didn't get pregnant in this flat, nor in the house for all I know. There's no law which says you can only have sex between seven at night and seven next morning.'

'And Diana Travers?'

Halliwell smiled:

'A different girl altogether. Lively. Very bright, I'd say. I saw more of her although she only worked the two days, Monday and Friday. Odd sort of job for a girl like that to take, I thought. And a bit of a coincidence seeing Miss Matlock's advert just when she was looking for a part-time job. Those cards usually stick in the windows until they get too brown and faded to be read.'

Massingham said:

'Apparently Lady Berowne's brother, Mr Swayne, was here last
evening. Did you see him?'

'No.'

'Is he often here?'

'More often than Sir Paul liked. Or other people for that matter.'

'Including you?'

'Me and his sister, I reckon. He has a habit of turning up for a
bath or a meal when it suits him, but he's harmless. Spiteful, but
about as dangerous as a wasp.'

It was, Dalgliesh thought, too facile a judgement.

Suddenly all three men, keen-eared, raised their heads and
listened. Someone was coming through the garage. There was a
rush of footfalls, soft soled, on the iron staircase, the door was
almost flung open and Dominic Swayne stood in the entrance.
Halliwell must have left the latch of the Yale up. It was, thought
Dalgliesh, a curious oversight unless, of course, he had been half-
expecting this sudden intrusion. But he made no sign, merely
fixing on Swayne his dark unwelcoming gaze before turning again
to his mug of coffee. Swayne must have known that they were
there since, presumably, Miss Matlock had let him into the house,
but his start of surprise and the tentative embarrassed smile were
nicely judged.

'Oh my God! Sorry, sorry! I seem to have an unlucky habit of
bursting in when the police are doing their stuff. Well, I'll leave you
to the third degree.'

Halliwell said coldly:

'Why not try knocking first?'

But it was to Dalgliesh that Swayne turned:

'I only wanted to tell Halliwell that my sister says I can borrow
the Golf tomorrow.'

Halliwell said without moving from his seat:

'You can borrow the Golf without prior notice. You usually do.'

Swayne kept his eyes on Dalgliesh.

'That's OK then. Look, I'm here. Is there anything you want to
ask me? If so, go ahead.'

Massingham had got up from the table and had picked up one of
the carved elephants. His voice was carefully devoid of emphasis.

'Just to confirm again that you were here in the house the whole
of last evening from the time you arrived, just before seven, till
you left for the Raj at half past ten?'

'That's right, Inspector. Clever of you to remember.'

'And during that time you didn't leave number sixty-two?'

'Right again. Look, I'm hardly everyone's favourite brother-in-law, I admit, but I had nothing to do with Paul's death. And I don't see why Paul should have resented me so much unless I reminded him of someone he'd rather not be reminded of. I mean I don't drug unless someone else is paying, which they so rarely do. I'm comparatively sober. I work when there's work to be had. I admit I bath and eat at his expense occasionally, but I don't see why he should resent that – he's hardly on the bread line – or my having a game of Scrabble with poor Evelyn. No one else bothers to. And I didn't slit his throat for him. I'm not in the least bloodthirsty. I don't think I've got the nerve. I'm not like Halliwell, trained to creep about among the rocks with my face blacked and a knife between my teeth. That's not my idea of amusement.'

Massingham put the elephant down. It was like a rejection.

He said:

'You prefer an evening's Scrabble with your lady friend? Who won?'

'Oh, Evelyn won, she usually does. Yesterday she got "zephyr" on a treble, clever girl. Three hundred and eighty-two points to my two hundred. It's extraordinary how often she picks the high numbers. If she weren't so depressingly honest, I'd suspect her of cheating.'

Massingham said:

'"Zig-zag" would have scored even higher.'

'Ah, but there aren't two Zs in Scrabble. I can see that you aren't an addict. You should try it sometime, Inspector. It's excellent for sharpening the wits. Well, if that's all I'll be off.'

Dalgliesh said:

'Not quite all. Tell us about Diana Travers.'

Swayne stood for a couple of seconds very still, the bright eyes rapidly blinking. But the shock, if it were shock, was quickly mastered. Dalgliesh could see the muscles of his hands and shoulders relaxing. He said:

'What about her? She's dead.'

'We know that. She drowned after a dinner party given by you at the Black Swan. You were there when she died. Tell us about it.'

'There's nothing to tell. I mean, you must have read the report of the inquest. And I don't see what it's got to do with Paul. She wasn't his girl or anything like that.'

'We didn't suppose that she was.'

He shrugged and held out his palms in a parody of resigned reasonableness.

'Well, what do you want to know?'

'Why not begin by telling us why you invited her to the Black Swan.'

'No particular reason. Call it a generous impulse. I knew my dear sister was having what she would describe as an intimate dinner party for her birthday, too intimate to invite me apparently. So I thought I'd organize a little celebration of my own. I was here bringing Barbara my birthday present, and I saw Diana dusting the hall as I left. So I asked her to come along. I picked her up outside Holland Park tube at six thirty and drove her to meet the gang at the Black Swan.'

'Where you had dinner.'

'Where we had dinner. Do you want the details of the menu?'

'Not unless it's relevant. Suppose you go on from there.'

'After dinner we went out to the riverbank and found this punt moored upstream. The rest of the party thought it would be amusing to mess about on the river. Diana and I decided that it would be even more amusing to mess about on the bank. She was pretty high. Drink not drugs. Then we thought it would be fun to swim out to the punt and bob up beside them.'

'Having first taken off your clothes.'

'They were already off. Sorry if I shock you.'

'And you dived in first.'

'Not dived, waded. I never dive into unknown water. Anyway, I struck out with my usual elegant crawl and reached the punt. Then I looked back for Diana. I couldn't see her on the bank, but then, there are quite a few bushes at that spot, Jean Paul trying to make some sort of a garden I suppose, and I thought she might have changed her mind and be dressing. I was a bit worried, but not frantically worried, if you see what I mean. But I thought I'd better go back and check. And the whole idea of the swim was losing its charm. The water was icy cold and very dark and the chums hadn't greeted me with quite the enthusiasm I expected. So I let go of the punt and struck back towards the bank. She wasn't there, but her clothes were. So then I really was scared. I called out to the party in the punt but they were rocking about, giggling, and I don't think they heard me. And then they found her. They struck the body with the punt pole just as she surfaced. Pretty ghastly for the girls. They managed to hold her head above water and paddled to the bank, nearly upsetting the punt in the process. I helped drag her out and we tried the usual mouth to mouth. It was a god awful mess. The girls crying and trying to get some clothes on her. Me dripping wet and shivering. Tony forcing his breath into her mouth as if he were pumping up a balloon. Diana lying there, eyes staring, with the water running off her hair and the weeds wrapped round her neck like a green scarf. . . They made her look decapitated. Erotic in a horrible way. And then one of the girls ran to the restaurant for help and that chef chap came out and took over. He seemed to know what he was doing. But no good. End of Diana. End of jolly evening. End of story.'

There was a scrape of wood as Halliwell violently pushed himself up from the table and disappeared swiftly into the kitchen. Swayne looked after him.

'What's he upset about? I was the one who had to look at her. You'd think he'd heard worse things than that.'

Neither Dalgliesh nor Massingham spoke and almost immediately Halliwell was back. He was carrying another half bottle of Scotch and set it down. It seemed to Dalgliesh that his face was paler but he poured himself another tot of whisky with a perfectly steady hand. Swayne glanced at the bottle as if wondering why he wasn't invited to drink then turned again to Dalgliesh.

'I'll tell you one thing about Diana Travers. She wasn't an actress. I found that out on our drive to the Black Swan. No Equity card. No drama school. No theatrical jargon. No agent. No parts.'

'Did she say what her job really was?'

'She said she wanted to be a writer and was collecting material. It was easier to tell people you were on the stage. That way, they never asked why you wanted a temporary job. I can't say I cared one way or the other. I mean, I was taking the girl out to dinner, I wasn't proposing to shack up with her.'

'And during the time you were with her on the river bank, before the swim and when you went back to find her, did you see or hear any other person?'

The blue eyes widened and became so like his sister's that the resemblance was uncanny. He said:

'I don't think so. We were a bit preoccupied, if you get me. You mean, a peeping Tom, someone spying on us? The thought didn't occur to me.'

'Let it occur to you now. Were you absolutely alone?'

'We must have been, mustn't we? I mean, who else would be there?'

'Think back. Did you see or hear anything suspicious?'

'I can't say that I did, but then there was all the jolly girlish screaming from the punt. And I don't think I would have seen or heard anything very clearly once I'd waded in and begun swimming. I do seem to remember that I heard Diana diving in after me, but that's what I expected her to do so maybe I imagined it. And there could have been someone watching us I suppose. In the bushes, maybe. But I didn't see him. Sorry, if that's the wrong answer. And sorry for barging in. Oh, by the way, I'll be staying here in the house if you want me. Brotherly consolation for the widow.'

He gave a shrug and a smile which seemed bestowed on the room generally rather than anyone in it. Then he was gone. They heard the soft thud of his descending footsteps on the iron staircase. No one made any comment. As they rose to go, Massingham asked his last question. He said:

'We can't be certain yet how Sir Paul and Harry Mack died, but we think the probability is that both were murdered. Have you seen or heard anything in this house or outside it which would give you a suspicion of who might be responsible?'

It was the question they always asked, expected, formal, almost crudely direct. Because of this, it was often the one least likely to elicit the truth.

Halliwell poured himself another whisky. It looked as if he were settling in for a night's hard drinking. Without looking up he said:

'I didn't slit his throat for him. If I knew who had, I'd probably tell you.'

Massingham persevered:

'Sir Paul had no enemies as far as you are aware?'

'Enemies?'

Halliwell's smile was nearer a grin. It transformed his swarthy good looks into a mask at once sinister and sardonic, giving force to Swayne's description of him creeping black-faced among the rocks.

'He must have had, mustn't he, sir, being a politician? But that's all over now. Done with. Finished. Like the Major, he's moved out of their gunshot now.'

And with that echo of Bunyan, which Dalgliesh suspected might have been a deliberate half-quotation, the interview was at an end.

Halliwell went down with them through the garage and dragged the heavy doors shut behind them. They heard the rasp of the two bolts. The lights in the niches had been switched off and the cobbled yard was in darkness except for twin wall mounted lights at each end of the garage wall. In the half-darkness the smell of cypress had strengthened, but was overlaid with a scent sicklier and funereal as if somewhere close was a dustbin of dead and rotting flowers. As they approached the back door to the house the figure of Miss Matlock stepped noiselessly out of the shadows. In the folds of the long dressing gown she seemed taller, hierarchic, almost graceful in her watching stillness. Dalgliesh wondered how long she had stood silently waiting for them.

He and Massingham followed her in silence through the quiet house. As she turned the key and drew back the bolts of the front door Massingham said:

'That game of Scrabble you played last night with Mr Swayne. Who won?'

The ploy was deliberately naive, the trap obvious. But her reaction was surprising. In the subdued light of the hall they watched the flush mottle her throat then flare up to crimson her face.

'I did. I got three hundred and eighty-two points in case you should be interested. That game was played, Inspector. You may be used to talking to liars. I'm not one of them.'

Her body was rigid with fury but the clasped hands shook as if they were palsied. Dalgliesh said gently:

'No one is suggesting that you are, Miss Matlock. Thank you for waiting up for us. Goodnight.'

Outside as he unlocked the Rover, Massingham said:

'Now why should that simple question shake her? Literally.'

Dalgliesh had met with it before, the clumsy aggression of women who were both shy and insecure. He wished that he could feel more sorry for her. He said:

'It wasn't particularly subtle, John.'

'No sir, it wasn't meant to be. She played that game of Scrabble all right. The question is, when?'

Dalgliesh took the wheel. He drove away from the house then drew into a vacant space half-way down Campden Hill Square and rang the Yard. Kate Miskin's answering voice sounded as strong and lively as it had in the early hours of the inquiry.

'I've traced and seen Mrs Hurrell, sir. She confirms that she did ring the Campden Hill Square house just before eight forty-five to ask for Sir Paul. A man answered. He said: "Swayne speaking". Then when she told him what she wanted he handed her over to Miss Matlock. Miss Matlock said that she didn't know where Sir Paul was, and nor did anyone else in the house.'

It was, thought Dalgliesh, an odd way for Swayne to answer the telephone when in someone else's house. One might almost believe that he wanted to establish that he was there. He asked:

'Anything from the door-to-door inquiries?'

'Nothing yet, sir, but I've spoken again to the McBrides and Maggie Sullivan. All three are definite about the gush of water from the church drain. Someone was using the sink in the washroom just after eight o'clock. They all agree about the time.'

'And the lab?'

'I've had a word with the senior biologist. If they can get the blood samples immediately after the PM, say by late afternoon, they'll set up the electrophoresis overnight. The director has agreed that they can work over the weekend. We should know about the bloodstains by Monday morning.'

'No news from the document examiner yet, I suppose. And what about the match end?'

'The document examiner hasn't been able to start on the blotter yet, but he'll give it priority. The usual problems with the match, sir. They'll do an analysis with the S.E.M. and look for print marks, but they're unlikely to be able to say more than that the wood is the usual poplar. They couldn't possibly say that it was from a particular box, and it's too short for a length comparison.'

'Right, Kate. We'll call it a day. Better get home. Goodnight.'

'Goodnight, sir.'

As the car slid down Campden Hill Square and turned into Holland Park Avenue Dalgliesh said:

'Halliwell has expensive tastes. That set of the *Notable British Trials* must have cost close on a thousand pounds, unless he collected them volume by volume over the years.'

'Not as expensive as Swayne's though, sir. That's a Fellucini jacket he was wearing, silk and linen, silver-crested buttons. They sell for four fifty.'

'I'll take your word for it. I wonder why he burst in like that. It was an unconvincing performance. Probably hoping to find out how much Halliwell was telling. It's significant, though, that he did burst in and as if he made a habit of it. And when Halliwell isn't there, he'd have no problem in getting hold of a key or even manipulating the Yale if necessary.'

'Is it important, sir, whether he could get into the mews flat?'

'I think so. This murderer was aiming at verisimilitude. There's a copy of Simpson's *Textbook on Forensic Medicine* in Halliwell's bookcase. It's all set out there in Chapter Five with the writer's usual clarity, a table showing the distinction between suicidal and

148

homicidal cuts of the throat. Swayne could have seen it at any time, browsed through it, remembered it. So, too, could anyone else at Camden Hill Square with access to the garage flat, and most easily, of course, Halliwell himself. Whoever slit Berowne's throat knew exactly what effect he was aiming to produce.'

Massingham asked:

'But would Halliwell have left the Simpson there for us to find?'

'If other people knew of its existence, to destroy it would be more incriminating than to leave it on the shelf. But Halliwell has to be in the clear if Lady Ursula is telling the truth about those two telephone calls, and I can't see her giving Halliwell an alibi for the murder of her son. Or any other suspect for that matter.'

Massingham said:

'Or Halliwell giving Swayne an alibi unless he had to. There's no love lost there. He despises the man. Incidentally, I knew I'd seen Swayne somewhere before. I've remembered now. He was in that play at the Coningsby Theatre in Camden Town a year ago. *The Garage*. The cast actually constructed a garage on the stage. In the first act they put it up, in the second they knocked it down.'

'I thought it was a wedding tent.'

'Wrong play, sir. Swayne played the local psychopath, one of the gang who pulled it down. So he must have an Equity card.'

'How did he strike you as an actor?'

'Energetic but unsubtle. Not that I'm much of a judge. I prefer films. I only went because Emma was going through her cultural stage. The play was highly symbolic. The garage was supposed to represent Britain, or capitalism, or imperialism, or, maybe, the class struggle. I'm not sure the author knew. You could tell that it was going to be a great critical success. No one spoke a literate line and a week later I couldn't remember a word of the dialogue. There was some fairly energetic fighting in the second act. Swayne knows how to handle himself. Still, kicking in a garage wall isn't the most suitable training for slitting a throat. I can't see Swayne as a killer, not this killer, anyway.'

They were both experienced detectives, they knew the importance at this stage of keeping the detection rational, of concentrating on the physical, ascertainable facts. Which of the suspects has the means, the opportunity, the knowledge, the physical strength, the motive? It was unproductive so early in the investigation to begin asking: has this man the ruthlessness, the nerve, the desperation, the psychological make-up to commit this particular crime? And yet, seduced by the fascination of human personality, they nearly always did.

6

In the small back bedroom on the second floor of 49 Crowhurst Gardens, Miss Wharton lay rigidly awake and stared into the darkness. Her body, pressed into the hard mattress, felt unnaturally hot and heavy as if weighted with lead. Even to turn in search of greater comfort was too great an effort. She hadn't expected to sleep soundly, but she had gone through her nightly routine with a dogged hope that adhering to these small and comforting rituals would deceive her body into slumber, or at least into quietude; the chapter of scripture prescribed in her book of devotions, the hot milk, the one digestive biscuit, final indulgence of the day. None had worked. The passage from St Luke's Gospel had been the parable of the good shepherd. It was one of her favourites, but tonight she had read it with a sharpened, perversely questioning mind. What, after all, was a shepherd's job? Only to care for the sheep, to make sure they didn't escape so that they could be branded, sheared and then slaughtered. Without the need for their wool, their flesh, there would be no job for the shepherd.

Long after she had closed her Bible she lay rigid for what seemed an endless night, her mind burrowing and scurrying like a tormented animal. Where was Darren? How was he? Who was making sure that he wasn't lying uncomforted or distressed? He hadn't seemed too affected by the horror of that awful scene, but with a child one never knew. And it was her fault that they were cut off from each other. She should have insisted on knowing where he lived, meeting his mother. He had never spoken of his mother and when she had asked him he had shrugged and not replied. She hadn't liked to press it. Perhaps she could reach him through the police. But ought she to worry Commander Dalgliesh when he had two murders to solve?

And the word 'murder' brought on a new anxiety. There was something she ought to remember but couldn't; something she ought to have told Commander Dalgliesh. He had questioned her briefly, gently, sitting beside her on one of the small chairs in the children's corner of the church, as if uncaring, even unaware, how oddly it suited his tall figure. She had tried to be calm, accurate, matter-of-fact, but she knew there were gaps in her memory, that there was something the horror of the scene had blotted out. Yet what could it be? It was something small, possibly insignificant, but he had said she must tell him every detail, however trivial.

But now another and more immediate worry surfaced. She needed to go to the lavatory. She switched on her bedside light, fumbled for her spectacles and peered at the carriage clock ticking gently on her bedside table. It was only ten past two. There was no hope of waiting until morning. Although she had her own sitting room, bedroom and kitchen, Miss Wharton shared the bathroom with the McGraths in the flat below. The plumbing was old-fashioned and if she had to use the lavatory in the night, Mrs McGrath would complain next morning. The alternative was to use her chamberpot but that had to be emptied and the whole morning would be dominated by her anxious listenings to know when it would be safe to carry it down to the lavatory without meeting Mrs McGrath's bold, contemptuous eyes. Once she had bumped into Billy McGrath on the stairs with the covered pot in her hand. The memory of it still burned her cheeks. But she would have to use it. The night was still so quiet she couldn't face creeping down to shatter its peace with cascades of swirling water, those long drawn-out shakes and grumbles of the pipe.

Miss Wharton didn't know why the McGraths disliked her so much, why her inoffensive gentility should be so provocative to them. She tried to keep out of their way, although this wasn't easy when they shared the same front door, the same narrow entrance passage. She had explained Darren to them on his first visit to her room by telling them that his mother worked at St Matthew's. The lie, blurted out in panic, had seemed to satisfy them and she had subsequently put it resolutely out of her mind since she could hardly include it in her weekly confession and Darren was so swift in his comings and goings that there was little risk they would question him. It was as if he sensed that the McGraths were enemies, better avoided than encountered. She attempted to propitiate Mrs McGrath with a desperate overpoliteness and even by small acts of kindness; taking her milk bottles in out of the sun in summer, leaving a jar of homemade jam or chutney on her doorstep when she came home from St Matthew's Christmas Fair. But these signs of weakness seemed only to increase their enmity, and she knew in her heart that there was nothing to be done about it. People, like countries, needed someone weaker and more vulnerable than themselves to bully and despise. This was what the world was like. As she gently dragged the chamberpot from under the bed and crouched over it, muscles tense, trying to regulate and

151

quieten the flow, she thought again how much she would have liked to have a cat. But the garden, twenty yards of unmown grass, hummocky as a field, surrounded by an almost obliterated border of overgrown rose bushes, and torn, unflowering shrubs, belonged to the bottom flat. The McGraths would never let her have use of it and it wouldn't be fair to keep a cat cooped up all night and day in her own two small rooms.

Miss Wharton had been taught to fear in her childhood and it isn't a lesson children can ever unlearn. Her father, a schoolmaster in an elementary school, had managed to maintain a precarious tolerance in the classroom by a compensating tyranny in his own home. His wife and three children were all afraid of him. But shared fear hadn't brought the children closer. When, with his usual irrationality, he would single out one child for his displeasure, the siblings would see in each other's shamed eyes their relief at this reprieve. They learned to lie to protect themselves, and were beaten for lying. They learned to be afraid, and were punished for cowardice. And yet, Miss Wharton kept on her side table a silver framed photograph of both her parents. She never blamed her father for past or present unhappiness. She had learned her lesson well. She blamed herself.

She was now virtually alone in the world. Her younger brother, John, to whom she had been closest, more psychologically robust than his siblings, had fared best. But John had been burnt alive in the rear gun turret of his Lancaster bomber the day before his nineteenth birthday. Miss Wharton, mercifully ignorant of the steel-bound inferno in which John had screamed away his life, had been able to prettify his death into the peaceful picture of the single German bullet finding the heart, the young, pale-faced warrior being gently wafted earthwards, his hand still resting on his gun. Her older brother, Edmund, had emigrated to Canada after the war and now, divorced and childless, worked as a clerk in some small northern town whose name she could never remember since he so seldom wrote.

She slid the chamberpot back under the bed, then put on her dressing gown and padded on naked feet across the narrow hall and into her front sitting room to the single window. The house was very quiet. Under the lights the street ran like a slimy river between the banks of parked cars. Even with her window closed she could hear the muted roar of night traffic along the Harrow Road. It was a night of low cloud, stained red with the glare of the restless city. Sometimes it seemed to Miss Wharton, looking out into that eerie half-darkness, that London was built on coal and was perpetually smouldering, that Hell, unrecognized, was all around her. To the right, silhouetted against the hectic glow, was the campanile of St Matthew's. Usually it gave her comfort. Here was a place where she was known, valued for the small services she could give, kept busily occupied, solaced, shriven and at home. But now the thin, alien tower, stark against the ruddy sky was a symbol of horror and death. And her twice-weekly walk to St Matthew's along the towpath; how could she face that now? The path had seemed to her mysteriously exempt from the terrors of the city streets, except for those brief stretches under the bridges. Even on the darkest morning she had walked there in blessed freedom from fear. And in recent months she had had Darren. But now Darren was gone, safety was gone, the towpath would always be slippery with imagined blood. Creeping back to bed her mind journeyed across the roofs to the Little Vestry. It would be empty now, of course. The police would have taken the bodies away. The black windowless van had been parked there ready even before she had left. There would be nothing now but the bloodstains browning on the carpet – or would that, too, have been taken away? Nothing but emptiness and darkness and the smell of death, except in the Lady Chapel where the sanctuary light would still be gleaming. Was she to lose even this, she wondered? Was this what murder did to the innocent? Took away the people they loved, loaded their minds with terror, left them bereft and unfriended under a smouldering sky.

7

It was after eleven thirty when Kate Miskin clanged the lift door behind her and unlocked the security lock of her flat. She had wanted to wait at the Yard until Dalgliesh and Massingham had returned from seeing Halliwell. But AD had suggested that it was time she called it a day and there was little more that she or anyone could do until the morning. If AD was right, and Berowne and Harry Mack had both been murdered, she and Massingham could be regularly working a sixteen-hour day, sometimes longer. It wasn't a possibility she feared; she had done it before. As she switched on the light and double-locked the door behind her it struck her as odd, perhaps even reprehensible, that she should be hoping that AD was right. Then almost immediately she absolved herself with the universal and comforting platitude. Both Berowne and Harry were dead; nothing could bring them back. And if Sir Paul Berowne hadn't slit his own throat, then the case promised to be fascinating as well as important, and not only to her personally, to her chance of promotion. There had been a certain amount of opposition to the setting-up in C1 of a special squad to investigate serious crimes which were thought to be politically or socially sensitive and she could name a number of senior officers who wouldn't be sorry if this, their first case, collapsed into a commonplace tragedy of murder followed by suicide.

She entered her flat, as always, with a sense of satisfaction, of coming home. She had lived in Charles Shannon House for just over two years. Buying the flat on a carefully calculated mortgage had been the first step in a planned upward progress; even eventually to one of the converted warehouses on the Thames, wide windows overlooking the river, huge rooms with their bare rafters, a distant view of Tower Bridge. But this was a beginning. She rejoiced in it, and sometimes had to prevent herself from prowling round, touching the walls, the furniture, to reassure herself of its reality.

The flat, a long sitting room with a narrow iron balcony running its whole width, two small bedrooms, a kitchen and a bathroom and separate lavatory, was on the top floor of a Victorian block just off Holland Park Avenue. It had been built in the early 1860s to provide studios for artists and designers in the growing arts and

154

crafts movement, and a couple of blue commemorative plaques over the door testified to its historic interest. But architecturally it was without merit, an aberration of yellowish London brick set amidst the surrounding Regency elegance, immensely tall, castel-lated and incongruous as a Victorian castle. The soaring walls, broken by numerous carved and oddly proportioned windows and criss-crossed with iron fire escapes, rose to a roof topped with rows of chimney pots between which sprouted a variety of television aerials, some long defunct.

It was the only place she had ever thought of as home. She was illegitimate and had been brought up by her maternal grand-mother who had been nearly sixty when she was born. Her mother had died within days of her birth and was known to her only as a thin serious face in the front row of a school photograph, a face in which she could recognize none of her own strong features. Her grandmother had never spoken of her father and she had assumed that her mother had never divulged his identity. She was fatherless even in name, but it had long ceased to worry her, if it ever had. Apart from the inevitable fantasies of early childhood when she had pictured her father seeking her out, she hadn't known any urgent need to discover her roots. Two half-remembered lines of Shakespeare which had met her eyes when she had casually opened the book in the school library had become for her the philosophy by which she intended to live.

'What matters it what went before or after
Now with myself I will begin and end.'

She hadn't chosen to furnish her flat in a period style. She had little feeling for the past; all her life had been a striving to struggle free of it, to make a future fashioned to her own need for order, security, success. So she had lived for a couple of months with nothing but a folding table, one chair and a mattress on the floor, until she had saved the money to buy the austere, well-designed modern furniture she liked; the sofa and two easy chairs in real leather, the dining table and four chairs in polished elm, the fitted bookcase completely covering one wall, the sleek, professionally designed kitchen which held the minimum of necessary utensils and crockery but nothing superfluous. The flat was her private world kept inviolate from colleagues in the police. Only her lover was admitted, and when Alan had first stepped through the door, uncurious, unthreatening, carrying as always his plastic bag of books, even his gentle presence had seemed for a moment a dangerous intrusion.

She poured herself an inch of whisky, mixed it with water, then unlocked the security lock of the narrow door which led from the sitting room to the iron balcony. The air rushed in, fresh and clean. She closed the door then stood, glass in hand, leaning back against the brickwork and staring out eastward over London. A low bank of heavy cloud had absorbed the glare of the city's lights and lay, palely crimson, like a colour-wash carefully laid against the richer blue-black of night. There was a light breeze just strong enough to stir the branches of the great limes lining Holland Park Avenue, and to twitch the television aerials which sprouted like frail exotic fetishes from the patterned roofs fifty feet below. To the south the trees of Holland Park were a black curdle against the sky, and ahead the spire of St John's church gleamed like some distant mirage. It was one of the pleasures of these moments, seeing how the spire appeared to move, sometimes so close that she felt that she would only have to stretch out a hand to feel its harshly textured stones, sometimes, like tonight, as distant and insubstantial as a vision. Far below to her right under the high arc lights the avenue ran due west, greasy as a molten river, bearing its unending cargo of cars, trucks and red buses. This, she knew, had once been the old Roman road leading westward straight out of Londinium; its constant grinding roar came to her only faintly like the surge of a distant sea.

Whatever the time of year, except in the worst of winter weather, this was her nightly routine. She would pour herself a whisky, Bell's, and take out the glass for these minutes of contemplation, rather, she thought, like a caged prisoner reassuring herself that the city was still there. But her small flat was no prison, rather the physical affirmation of a freedom hard won and jealously maintained. She had escaped from the estate, from her grandmother, from that meanly proportioned, dirty, noisy flat on the seventh floor of a post-war tower block, Ellison Fairweather Buildings, monument to a local councillor passionately dedicated, like most of his kind, to the destruction of small neighbourhood streets and the erection of twelve-storey monuments to civic pride and sociological theory. She had escaped from the shouting, the graffiti, the broken lifts, the stink of urine. She remembered the first evening of her escape, the eighth of June over two years ago. She had stood where she stood now and poured her whisky like a libation, seeing the momentary arc of liquid light as it fell between the grating, saying aloud 'Sod you, Councillor Bloody Fairweather. Welcome freedom.'

156

And now she was really on her way. If she made a success of this new job anything, well almost anything, was possible. It was perhaps not surprising that AD would choose at least one woman for his squad. But he wasn't the man to make routine gestures to feminism, or to any other fashionable cause come to that. He had selected her because he needed a woman in the squad and because he knew her record, knew that he could rely on her to do a good job. Looking out over London she felt confidence surge through her veins strong and sweet as the first conscious breath of morning. The world stretched out below her was one she was at home in, part of that dense, exciting conglomerate of urban villages which made up the Metropolitan Police district. She pictured it stretching away over Notting Hill Gate, over Hyde Park and the curve of the river, past the towers of Westminster and Big Ben, briefly over that anomaly, the patch of the City of London Police, then on to the eastern suburbs to the boundary with the Essex Constabulary. She knew almost to a yard where that boundary lay. This was how she saw the capital, patterned in police areas, districts, divisions and sub-divisions. And immediately below her lay Notting Hill, that tough, diverse, richly cosmopolitan village where she had been posted after leaving the preliminary training school. She could remember every sound, colour, smell as strongly as on that torrid August night eight years ago when it had happened, the moment when she knew that her choice had been right and that this was her job.

She had been on foot patrol in Notting Hill with Terry Read on the hottest August night in living memory. A boy, almost squealing with excitement, had rushed at them and, gibbering, had pointed to a nearby tenement. She saw it again; the huddle of frightened neighbours at the foot of the stairs, faces gleaming with sweat, stained shirts stuck to steaming bodies, a smell of hot, unwashed humanity. And above the whispers a raucous voice from upstairs shouting its unintelligible protest. The boy said:

'He got a knife, miss. George tried to get in but he threatened him. That's right, ain't it, George?'

George, white, small, weasel-like in the corner:

'Yeah, that's right.'

'And he's got Mabelle in with him, Mabelle and the kid.'

A woman whispered:

'Blessed Jesus, he's got the kid in there.'

They had fallen back to let her through, her and Terry. She asked:

'What's his name?'

'Leroy.'

'His other name?'

'Price. Leroy Price.'

The hallway was dark, the room itself, unlocked since the lock was smashed, was even darker. The harsh glare filtered through a torn piece of carpet nailed over the window. She could see dimly the stained double mattress on the floor, a folding table, two chairs, one on its side. There was a smell of vomit, of sweat, of beer overlaid with the strong oily smell of fish and chips. Against the wall cowered a woman, a child in her arms.

She said gently:

'It's all right, Mr Price. I'll have that knife. You don't mean to hurt them. She's your kid. You wouldn't want to hurt either of them. I know what it is, it's too hot, and you've had enough. We all have.'

She had seen it before, on the estate as well as on the beat, that moment when the burden of frustration, hopelessness and misery suddenly became too heavy and the mind exploded into an anarchy of protest. He had indeed had too much. Too many unpaid, unpayable bills, too much worry, too many demands, too much frustration and, of course, too much drink. She had walked up to him not speaking, calmly meeting his eyes, holding out her hand for the knife. She wasn't aware of fear, only the fear that Terry might come crashing in. There was no sound; the group at the foot of the stairs was frozen into silence, the street outside stilled in one of those strange moments of quietness which sometimes fall on even the rowdiest quarters of London. She could hear only her own quiet breathing and his harsh grating breaths. Then with a wild sob he had dropped the knife and flung himself towards her. She had held him, murmuring as she might to a child, and it was over.

She had overplayed Terry's part in the affair, and he had let her. But old Moll Green, never absent when there was a chance of excitement and the hope of bloodshed, had been one of those waiting, bright-eyed, at the foot of the stairs. The following Tuesday Terry had busted her for carrying hash, admittedly with small provocation, but he was behind with his self-imposed weekly quota of arrests. Moll, motivated either by an unexpected surge of female solidarity, or a revulsion against men in general and Terry in particular, had given her own version of the incident to the station sergeant. Little was subsequently said to Kate, but enough to make it plain that the truth was known, and that her reticence had done her no harm. Now she wondered briefly what had

158

happened to that man, to Mabelle, to the child. For the first time it struck her as odd that, the incident over, her report made, she had never given any of them another thought.

She came in, closed the door and drew the heavy linen curtains, then went to telephone Alan. They had planned to see a film the following night but this would no longer be possible. It was pointless to make any plans until the case was finished. He took the news calmly as he always did when she had to break a date. One of the many things she liked about him was that he never fussed.

He said:

'It looks then as if dinner next Thursday may not be possible either.'

'We may be through by then, but it's unlikely. Still, keep it free and if I have to I'll ring and cancel.'

'Well, good luck with the case. I hope it won't be love's labour's lost.'

'What?'

'Sorry. Berowne is the name of an attendant lord in Shakespeare. It's an unusual and interesting name.'

'It was an unusual and interesting death. See you next Thursday at about eight.'

'Unless you find it necessary to cancel. Goodbye, Kate.'

She thought that she detected a trace of irony in his voice, then decided that tiredness had made her imaginative. It was the first time he had wished her good luck with a case, but he had still asked no questions. He was, she thought, as punctiliously discreet about her job as she was herself. Or was it merely that he didn't care? Before he put the receiver down she said quickly:

'That attendant lord, what happened to him?'

'He loved a woman called Rosaline, but she told him to go and nurse the sick. So he went off to jest a twelvemonth in a hospital.'

There was hardly, she thought, much inspiration to be gained from that. She smiled as she put down the receiver. It was a pity about next Thursday's dinner. But there would be other dinners, other evenings. He would come when she rang and asked him. He always did.

She suspected that she had met Alan Scully just in time. Her early sexual education in the concrete underpasses of the high-rise flats and behind the bicycle sheds of her north London comprehensive, the mixture of excitement, danger and disgust, had been a good preparation for life but a poor preparation for loving. Most of the boys had been less intelligent than herself. This might not have

159

mattered to her if they had had looks or some wit. She was amused, but also a little dismayed, to realize by the time she was eighteen that she was thinking of men as they were alleged so often to regard women, an occasional sexual or social diversion, but too unimportant to be allowed to interfere with the serious business of life; passing her A-levels, planning her career, getting away from Ellison Fairweather Buildings. She found that she could enjoy sex while despising the source of her pleasure. It wasn't, she knew, an honest basis for any relationship. And then, two years ago, she had met Alan. His flat in a narrow street behind the British Museum had been burgled and it was she who had arrived with the fingerprint and scene of crime officers. He told her that he worked in a theological library in Bloomsbury and that he was an amateur collector of books of early Victorian sermons – it seemed to her an extraordinary choice – and that two of the most valuable volumes had been taken. They had never been recovered and she sensed from the calm resignation with which he answered her questions that he had hardly expected that they would be. His flat, small, cluttered, a repository for books rather than a space for living, was unlike any place she had ever seen, as he was unlike any man. She had had to make a return visit and they had spent about an hour chatting over coffee. He had then asked her, simply, to go with him to see a Shakespearian production at the National Theatre.

It was less than a month after that evening that they first went to bed together and he had demolished one of her firmly held assumptions, that intellectuals weren't interested in sex. He was both interested in and very good at it. They had settled into a comfortable, apparently mutually satisfactory, loving friendship in which each saw the other's job, without resentment or envy, as foreign territory, its speech and mores so far removed from any possibility of comprehension that they rarely spoke of it. Kate knew that he was intrigued, not so much by her lack of religious faith as by the fact that she apparently had no intellectual curiosity about its diverse and fascinating manifestations. She sensed, too, although he never said so, that he thought that her literary education had been neglected. She could, if challenged, quote angry modern verse about unemployed youth in the inner cities and the subjection of the Blacks in South Africa, but this he saw as a poor substitute for Donne, Shakespeare, Keats or Eliot. She, for her part, saw him as an innocent, so deficient in the skills necessary for survival in the urban jungle that it amazed her that he should walk

160

with such apparent indifference through its perils. Apart from the burglary, which remained mysterious, nothing untoward ever seemed to happen to him or, if it did, he failed to notice. It amused her to ask him to recommend books and she persevered with those which, diffidently, he produced for her. At present her bedtime reading was Elizabeth Bowen. The life of her heroines, their private incomes, their charming houses in St John's Wood, their uniformed parlourmaids and formidable aunts, above all the delicate sensitivity of their emotions amazed her. 'Not enough washing-up, that's their trouble,' she told Alan, having in mind the author as well as her characters. But it interested her that she needed to go on reading.

And now it was close to midnight. She was both too excited and too tired to feel much hunger, but she supposed that she ought to cook something light, perhaps an omelette, before she went to bed. But first she switched on the answerphone. And with the first sound of the familiar voice euphoria died to be replaced by a confusion of guilt, resentment and depression. It was her grandmother's social worker. There were three messages, each at two hourly intervals, controlled professional patience gradually giving way to frustration and, finally, an irritation that was close to hostility. Her grandmother, weary of incarceration in her seventh-floor flat, had gone out to the post office to collect her pension and had come back to find that the window had been smashed and an attempt made to force the door. It was the third such incident in less than a month. Mrs Miskin was now too apprehensive to go out. Would Kate please ring the local authority social services department as soon as she got in, or, if it were after five thirty, ring her grandmother direct. It was urgent.

It always was, she thought wearily. And this was a ridiculously late hour at which to ring. But it couldn't wait until morning. Her grandmother wouldn't sleep until she had rung. Her call was answered after the first burr and she guessed that the old lady had been sitting waiting by the telephone.

'Oh, there you are. Fine time to ring. Nearly bloody midnight. Mrs Mason's been trying to get you.'

'I know. Are you all right, Gran?'

'Course I'm not all right. Bloody hell, I'm not. When are you coming round?'

'I'll try to look in sometime tomorrow but it won't be easy. I'm in the middle of a case.'

'Better come at three o'clock. Mrs Mason said she'll look in at three. She wants to see you 'specially. Three o'clock, mind.'

'Gran, that's just not possible.'

'How'm I goin' to get my shopping, then? I'm not leaving this flat alone, I tell you that.'

'There should be enough in the freezer for at least another four days.'

'I don't fancy that made-up muck. I told you before.'

'Can't you ask Mrs Khan? She's always so helpful.'

'No I can't. She don't go out now, not unless her husband's with her, not since that lot from the National Front were up this way. Besides, it's not fair. More than enough trouble luggin' up her own stuff. The kids have broken the bloody lift again in case you didn't know.'

'Gran, is the window mended?'

'Oh, they've been and mended the window.' Her grandmother's voice suggested that this was no more than an unimportant detail.

She added:

'You gotta get me out of this place.'

'I'm trying, Gran. You're on the waiting list for a one-person flat in one of those blocks with a warden, sheltered housing. You know that.'

'I don't need any bloody warden. I ought to be with my own kith and kin. See you tomorrow then at three o'clock. Mind you come. Mrs Mason wants to see you.'

She put down the receiver.

Kate thought: Oh God, I can't cope with this again, not now, not just at the beginning of a new case.

She told herself with angry self-justification, that she wasn't irresponsible, that she did what she could. She had bought her grandmother a new refrigerator topped with a small freezer and visited every Sunday to stock it with meals for the week ahead only, more often than not, to be met with the familiar complaint:

'I can't eat that fancy stuff. I want to do my own shopping. I want to get out of here.'

She had paid for a telephone to be installed and had taught her grandmother not to be afraid of it. She had liaised with the local authority and arranged for a weekly visit from a home help to clean the flat. She would willingly have cleaned it herself if her grandmother would have tolerated the interference. She would take any trouble, spend any money, to avoid taking her grandmother to live with her in Charles Shannon House. But that, she knew, was what the old lady, in alliance with her social worker,

162

was inexorably pressing her to accept. And she couldn't do it. She couldn't give up her freedom, Alan's visits, the spare room where she did her painting, her privacy and peace at the end of the day for an old woman's impedimenta, the ceaseless noise of her television, the mess, the smell of old age, of failure, the smell of Ellison Fairweather Buildings, of childhood, of the past. And now, more than ever, it was impossible. Now, with her first case with the new squad, she needed to be free.

She was seized with a spurt of envy and resentment against Massingham. Even if he had a dozen difficult and demanding relatives no one would expect him to have to cope. And if she did have to take time off from the job he would be the first to point out that, when the going got really tough, you couldn't rely on a woman.

8

In her bedroom on the second floor Barbara Berowne lay back on her bank of pillows and stared ahead at the television screen mounted on the wall opposite her uncurtained four-poster. She was waiting for the late-night movie, but had switched on the set as soon as she had got into bed, and was now tuned to the last ten minutes of a political discussion. She had turned down the sound so low that she could hear nothing, but she still gazed intently at the restless mouths as if she were lip-reading. She remembered how Paul's mouth had tightened with disapproval when he had first seen the television set, mounted on its swivel, obtrusively over-large, spoiling the wall and dwarfing into insignificance the two Cotman watercolours of Norwich Cathedral each side of it. But he had said nothing, and she had told herself defiantly that she didn't care. But now she could watch the late film without being uneasily aware that he was there in the next room, perhaps lying sleepless in rigid disapproval, hearing the muted screams and gunfire like the noisy manifestations of their own subtler, undeclared warfare.

He had disliked, too, her untidiness, an unconscious protest against the impersonality, the obsessive neatness of the rest of the house. In the light of her bedside lamp she gazed untroubled over the muddle in the room; the clothes strewn where she had dropped them; the sheen of her satin dressing-gown thrown across the foot of the bed, the grey skirt splayed fan-like over a chair, her pants lying like a pale shadow on the carpet, her brassière hanging by one strap from the dressing table. What an indecent, silly garment it looked, thus casually discarded; so precisely shaped and moulded and looking surgical for all its lace and delicacy. But Mattie would tidy up her things in the morning, gather up her underclothes for washing, hang jackets and skirts in the wardrobe. And she would lie with the breakfast tray on her knees, and watch; then get up, bath, dress and face the world, as always immaculate.

It had been Anne Berowne's room and she had moved into it after their marriage. Paul had suggested that they might change bedrooms but she hadn't seen why she should sleep in a smaller, inferior room, deprived of the view of the square garden, simply because this had been Anne's bed. First it had been Anne's room, then it was Paul's and hers, then it was hers alone, but always with the knowledge that he was sleeping next door. And now it was hers absolutely. She remembered the afternoon when they had first stood in the bedroom together after their marriage, his voice so formal that she had hardly recognized it. He could have been showing round a prospective purchaser.

'You may care to choose different pictures; there are some in the small salon. Anne liked watercolours and the light here is good for them, but you don't have to keep them.'

She hadn't cared about the pictures which had seemed to her rather dull, insignificant English landscapes by painters Paul seemed to think she ought to recognize. She still didn't care, not even enough to change them. But the bedroom had, from her first possession, taken on a different personality; softer, more luxurious, scented and feminine. And gradually it had become as cluttered as an indiscriminately stocked antique shop. She had gone round the house and moved up to her room the items of furniture, the oddly assorted objects which had taken her fancy, as if obsessively raping the house, leaving no space for those rejected but insidious ghosts. A Regency two-handed vase under a glass dome filled with multi-coloured flowers intricately devised from shells, a gilt-bronze Tudor wood cabinet decorated with porcelain ovals of shepherds and shepherdesses, a bust of John Soane on a marble pedestal, a collection of eighteenth-century snuff boxes, taken from their showcase and now casually littering her dressing table. But there were still ghosts, living ghosts, voices on the air which no object, however desired, had power to exorcise. Propped against the scented pillows she was back in her childhood bed, a 12-year-old lying rigid and sleepless, hands clutching the bedclothes. Snatches of endless argument half-heard over weeks and months, then only partly understood, had come together into a coherent whole, refined by her imagination and now unforgettable. First her mother's voice:

'I thought you'd want custody of the children. You're their father.'

'And leave you free of responsibility to enjoy yourself in California? Oh no, my dear, you were the one who wanted children, you take them. I suppose Frank didn't bargain for two step-children? Well, he's got them. I hope he likes them.'

'They're English. Their place is here.'

'What did you tell him? That you were coming without encumbrances? A little shop-soiled, darling, but unencumbered? Their

165

place is with their mother. Even a bitch has some maternal instincts. You take them or I fight the divorce.'

'My God, they're your children. Don't you care? Don't you love them?'

'I might have done if you'd let me and if they'd been less like you. As it is, I'm frankly indifferent. You want freedom, so do I.'

'All right, we'll share. I'll take Barbie, you have Dicco. A boy's place is with his father.'

'Then we're in a difficulty. You'd better consult the father, that is if you know which one it was. By all means let him have Dicco. I won't stand in his way. If there was anything of me in that boy I'd have recognized it. He's grotesque.'

'My God, Donald, you bastard!'

'Oh no, my dear, I'm not the bastard in this family.'

She thought: I won't listen, I won't remember, I won't think about it, and pressed the volume button, letting the rancorous voices batter at her ears. She didn't hear the door open, but suddenly there was an oblong of pale light and Dicco stood there, wrapped in his knee-length dressing gown, his springing hair a tangled halo. He stood watching her in silence, then moved bare-footed across the room and the bedsprings bounced as he settled himself close against her. He said:

'Can't you sleep?'

She turned off the set, feeling the familiar guilt.

'I was thinking about Sylvia and father.'

'Which one? We've had so many.'

'The first. Our proper father.'

'Our proper father? Our improper father. I wonder if he's dead yet. Cancer was too good for him. Don't think about them, think about the money. That's always a comfort. Think about being free, your own person. Think how well you always look in black. You aren't frightened, are you?'

'No, of course not. There's nothing to be frightened about. Dicco, go back to bed.'

'His bed. You knew that, didn't you? You know where I'm sleeping. In his bed.'

'Mattie won't like that, nor will Lady Ursula. Why couldn't you sleep in the spare room? Or go back to Bruno?'

'Bruno doesn't want me in the flat. He never did. There isn't room. And I wasn't comfortable. You want me to be comfortable, surely? And I'm getting a little tired of Bruno. My place is here. I'm your brother. This is your house now. You're not being very

166

welcoming, Barbie. I thought you'd want me near you, in case you wanted to talk in the night, confide, confess. Come on, Barbie, confess. Who do you think killed him?'

'How do I know? Someone broke in, I suppose, a thief, another tramp, someone who wanted to steal the church collection. I don't want to talk about it.'

'Is that what the police think?'

'I suppose so. I don't know what they think.'

'Then I can tell you. They think it was an odd church for a thief to choose. I mean, what was there worth stealing?'

'There are things on the altar, aren't there? Candlesticks, a cross. There were in the church where I was married.'

'I wasn't there when you were married, Barbie. You didn't invite me, remember?'

'Paul wanted a quiet wedding, Dicco. What does it matter?'

And that, she thought, was another thing Paul had cheated her out of. She had imagined a grand wedding, herself floating up the aisle of St Margaret's Westminster, the sheen of white satin, a veil like a cloud, the flowers, the crowds, the photographers. Instead he had suggested a registrar's office and when she had protested had insisted on their local parish church and the quietest of ceremonies, almost as if the wedding were something to be ashamed of, something furtive and indecent.

Dicco's voice came to her in a low insinuating whisper:

'But they don't keep them on the altar any more, not at night. Crosses and candlesticks, they lock them away. Churches are dark, empty. No silver, no gold, no lights. Nothing. Do you suppose that's when their God comes down from his cross and walks about, goes up to the altar and finds that it's only a wooden table with a piece of fancy cloth pinned round it?'

She wriggled under the bedclothes.

'Don't be silly, Dicco. Go to bed.'

He leaned forward, and the face so like hers and yet so different gleamed within inches of her eyes, so that she could actually see the sheen of sweat on his brow, and smell the wine on his breath.

'That nurse, Theresa Nolan, the one who killed herself. Was Paul the father of her baby?'

'Of course not. Why does everyone go on about Theresa Nolan?'

'Who goes on about her? Did the police ask about her?'

'I can't remember. I think they asked why she left. Something like that. I don't want to think about it.'

His soft, indulgent laugh was like a conspiracy.

'Barbie, you've got to think. You can't go through life not thinking about things just because they're inconvenient or unpleasant. It was his child, wasn't it? That's what your husband was up to while you were cavorting with your lover, fucking his mother's nurse. And that other girl, Diana Travers, the one who drowned. What was she doing in this house?'

'You know what she was doing. Helping Mattie.'

'A dangerous occupation, though, isn't it, working for your husband? Look, if someone did murder Paul it was someone very clever and cunning; someone who knew he was there in that church; someone who knew he would find a cut-throat razor ready to hand; someone with the nerve to take one enormous risk; someone used to cutting human flesh. Do you know someone like that, Barbie? Do you? It's lucky, isn't it, that you and Stephen have an alibi.'

'You have an alibi, too?'

'And Mattie, of course. And Lady Ursula. And Halliwell. It's a bit suspicious, all these iron-clad alibis. What about Sarah?'

'I haven't spoken to her.'

'Well let's hope she hasn't an alibi too, otherwise the police will begin to scent conspiracy. When you rang to tell me that he was going to chuck you, I said that it would be all right. Well, it is all right. I said not to worry about the money. Well, you don't have to worry. It's all yours.'

'Not so very much.'

'Come off it, Barbie, enough. The house to begin with, that must be worth a cool million. And he was insured, wasn't he? Was there a suicide clause? That would be awkward.'

'Mr Farrell said that there wasn't. I asked.'

Again that soft inward laugh, something between a grunt and a giggle:

'So you actually got round to asking about the insurance! You don't waste time do you? And that's what the lawyers think, is it? That Paul killed himself?'

'Lawyers never say. Mr Farrell told me not to talk to the police unless he was there.'

'The family won't want it to be suicide; they'd rather he was murdered. And perhaps he was. If he'd wanted to kill himself, why didn't he use the gun? His brother's gun. A man doesn't cut his throat if he's got a gun. And he had ammo, too, didn't he?'

'Ammo?'

'Bullets. Where is the gun? Still in his safe?'

'No. I don't know where it is.'

'What do you mean you don't know? Have you looked?'

'Yesterday after he'd left. Not for the gun, I wanted to look for some papers, his will. I opened the safe and it wasn't there.'

'Are you sure?'

'Of course I'm sure. It's a very small safe.'

'And you didn't tell the police, naturally. It wouldn't be easy to explain why you wanted to take a look at your husband's will just a few hours before he so conveniently died.'

'I haven't told anyone. How did you know about the gun, anyway?'

'My God, Barbie, you are extraordinary! Your husband has his throat slit, his gun is missing and you tell no one.'

'I expect he got rid of it. Anyway, what does it matter? He didn't shoot himself. Dicco, go to bed. I'm tired.'

'But you aren't frightened about the gun, are you? Barbie, why aren't you frightened? It's because you know who's taken it, don't you? You know, or you suspect. Who was it, Lady Ursula, Halliwell, Sarah, your lover?'

'Of course I don't know! Dicco, leave me alone. I'm tired. I don't want to talk any more. I want to sleep.'

Her eyes brimmed with tears. It was unfair of him to upset her like this. She felt an immense sorrow for herself, widowed, alone, vulnerable. And pregnant. Lady Ursula didn't want her to tell anyone about the baby yet, not the police, not Dicco. But he would have to know some time. Everyone would. And they ought to know so that they could look after her, see that she wasn't worried. Paul would have looked after her, but Paul wasn't here. And she had only told him about the baby yesterday morning. Yesterday. But she wouldn't think about yesterday, not now, not ever again. And the film was due to begin, a Hitchcock repeat, and she had always liked Hitchcock. It wasn't fair of Dicco to come in, badgering her, making her remember.

He smiled and patted her on the head as he would a dog, and then he was gone. She waited until the door was closed and she could be certain he wouldn't reappear, then she pressed on the TV button. The screen glowed into light and the credits for the previous programme began to roll. She was in time. She settled more comfortably against her pillows, keeping the sound low so that he shouldn't hear.

9

Massingham had hung about at the Yard longer than was strictly necessary and it was a minute to midnight by the time he drove up to the villa in St Petersburgh Place. But the downstairs light was still on; his father hadn't yet gone up to bed. He turned the key in the lock as quietly as possible and pushed open the door as stealthily as if he were making an illegal entrance. But it was no good. His father must have been waiting for the noise of the car. Almost at once the door of the small front sitting room opened and Lord Dungannon shuffled out. The words 'slippered pantaloon' fell into Massingham's mind bringing with them the familiar dragging weight of pity, irritation and guilt.

His father said:

'Oh, here you are then, my dear boy. Purves has just brought in the grog tray. Would you care to join me?'

His father never used to call him my dear boy. The words sounded false, over-rehearsed, ridiculous. And his answering voice struck the same note of embarrassed insincerity.

'No thank you, Father. I'd better get up. It's been a tiring day. We're working on the Berowne case.'

'Of course. Berowne. She was Lady Ursula Stollard before she married. Your Aunt Margaret was presented in the same year. But she must be over eighty. It can't have been unexpected.'

'It's not Lady Ursula who's dead, Father. It's her son.'

'But I thought Hugo Berowne was killed in Northern Ireland.'

'Not Hugo, Father. Paul.'

'Paul.' His father seemed to contemplate the word then said:

'Then I must, of course, write to Lady Ursula. Poor woman. If you're sure you won't come in . . .' His voice, which since April had become the quaver of an old man, broke off. But Massingham was already bounding up the stairs. Half-way along the landing he paused and glanced down over the banisters expecting to see his father shuffling back into the sitting room to his solitude and his whisky. But the old man was still there, gazing up at him with what seemed almost indecent longing. In the strong light from the hall lamp he saw clearly what the last five months had done to the craggy Massingham features. The flesh seemed to have slipped from the bones so that the beaked nose cleft the skin sharp as a knife edge while the jowls hung in slack mottled pouches like the flesh of a plucked fowl. The flaming Massingham hair was bleached and faded now to the colour and texture of straw. He thought: He looks as archaic as a Rowlandson drawing. Old age makes caricatures of us all. No wonder we dread it.

Mounting the short flight of stairs to his flat he was caught in the same old muddle. It really was becoming intolerable. He had to get away and soon. But how? Apart from a brief spell in the Section House he had lived in his separate rooms in his parents' house ever since he had joined the police. While his mother had been alive, the arrangement had suited him admirably. His parents, absorbed in each other as they had been ever since his father's late marriage in his mid-forties, had left him alone, hardly noticing whether he was in or out. The shared front door had been an inconvenience but nothing more. He had lived comfortably, paid a nominal rent, saved money, told himself that he would buy his own flat when he was ready. He had even found it possible to conduct his love affairs in privacy, while at the same time being able to call on his mother's depleted staff if he wanted a meal cooked, his clothes washed, his rooms cleaned, his parcels taken in.

But with his mother's death in April, all that had changed. While the House of Lords was sitting his father managed to get through his days, padding out with his bus pass to catch the number 12 or the 88 to Westminster, lunching at the House, occasionally sleeping through the evening debates. But at the weekends, even more in the Parliamentary recess, he had become as clinging as a possessive woman, watching his son's comings and goings with almost obsessive interest, listening for his key in the lock, making his quiet but desperate pleas for companionship. Massingham's two youngest brothers were still at school and escaped from their father's grief during the holidays by staying with friends. His only sister was married to a diplomat and lived in Rome. His younger brother was at Sandhurst. The burden fell almost entirely on him. And now he knew that even the rent he paid had become a necessary contribution, almost as important to his father's dwindling resources as the daily attendance payment at the Lords.

Suddenly repentant he thought: I could have spared him ten minutes. Ten minutes of embarrassing non-communication, of small talk about his job which, until now, his father had never thought worthy of interest. Ten minutes of boredom only partly alleviated by alcohol, and setting a precedent for nights of boredom to come.

171

Closing the door of his flat behind him he thought of Kate Miskin, less than a couple of miles to the west, relaxing in her flat, pouring herself a drink, free of responsibility, free of guilt, and felt a surge of envy and irrational resentment so strong that he could almost persuade himself that it was all her fault.

BOOK THREE

Helping with Inquiries

1

The message from Pembroke Lodge was polite but unambiguous. Mr Lampart would be operating all morning but would be happy to see Commander Dalgliesh when he was free. That would be at about one o'clock or a little later, depending on the length of his list. Translated, this meant that Mr Lampart was a busy man concerned with saving life and alleviating pain, who could legitimately claim that these benign activities took precedence over the sordid preoccupations of a policeman, however distinguished. And the time of the appointment was nicely judged, too. Dalgliesh could hardly complain about going without his lunch since Mr Lampart, more importantly occupied, was obviously unconcerned about his.

He took Kate with him and asked her to drive. She slid into the right-hand seat without fuss and drove as she always did, competently and strictly according to the book, with none of Massingham's occasional impatience or sudden spurts of speed. When they had climbed Haverstock Hill and were passing the Round Pond he said:

'Pembroke Lodge is about a half mile after the Spaniards. The entrance could be easy to miss.' She slowed down, but even so, they saw it only just in time, a wide, white painted gate, set well back from the road and screened with horse chestnuts. A wide gravel drive curved to the left, then divided to circle an immaculate lawn fronting the house. They saw a low elegant Edwardian villa set on the edge of the heath, obviously built when a rich man could indulge his fancy for fresh air, an open view, and convenient proximity to London without being thwarted by planning authorities or conservationists concerned about encroachment on public land. As the Rover crunched slowly over the gravel Dalgliesh saw that the former stables to the right of the house had been converted to garages, but little other architectural change was apparent, at least outwardly. He wondered how many beds the nursing home could accommodate. Probably not more than thirty at most. But Stephen Lampart's activities wouldn't be restricted to his private facilities here. He was, as Dalgliesh had already checked, on the staff of two major London teaching hospitals, and no doubt operated at private clinics other than Pembroke Lodge. But this was his personal domain and Dalgliesh had no doubt that it was a highly profitable one.

The outer door was open. It led into an oval and elegant vestibule with a pair of ornate doors and a notice inviting visitors to enter. They found themselves in an entrance hall, square and very light. The staircase, with its delicate carved balustrade, was lit by a huge stained glass window. To the left was a carved fireplace in veined marble. Above it hung an oil painting in the manner of a late Gainsborough, a young mother, serious faced, her white arms encircling her two daughters in folds of blue satin and lace. To the right was a desk in polished mahogany, decorative rather than utilitarian, complete with its bowl of roses and presided over by a white-coated receptionist.

The smell of disinfectant was discernible, but overlaid with a heavier scent of flowers. It was apparent that a consignment had recently been delivered. Great sheaves of roses and gladioli, formal arrangements in beribboned baskets and more outré examples of the florist's ingenuity were piled by the door awaiting distribution. The aura of pampered femininity was almost overwhelming. It was not a place in which a man could feel at home, yet Dalgliesh sensed that it was Kate who felt the more ill at ease. He saw her give a glance of fascinated disgust at one of the more bizarre offerings of conjugal congratulations: a baby's cot, over two feet long, tightly covered with the wired heads of rosebuds, dyed blue, and with a pillow and coverlet of white carnations similarly decapitated, the whole monstrosity embellished with a huge blue bow. As they moved to the reception desk across a carpet thick enough to drag at their feet, a trolley of coloured bottles, nail varnishes and assorted jars, was pushed across the hall by an elegant older woman in a pale pink trousersuit, obviously the beautician. Dalgliesh was reminded of a conversation overheard at a dinner party some months earlier. 'But darling, the place is divine. One is pampered from the moment one arrives. Hairdresser, facials, cordon bleu menu, champagne instead of Valium for the blues. The lot. The thing is, though, that I'm not sure they don't overdo it. One feels absolutely outraged when labour starts and one realizes that there are some humiliations and discomforts that even dear Stephen can't do much about.' Dalgliesh wondered suddenly and irrelevantly whether Lampart's patients ever died on him. Probably not, not here anyway. Those at risk would be admitted elsewhere. The place had its own subtle aura of bad taste, but the ultimate bad taste of death and failure would be rigorously excluded.

The receptionist, like the decor, had been carefully chosen to reassure, not to threaten. She was middle-aged, pleasant looking rather than beautiful, well-groomed, immaculately coiffured. They were, of course, expected. Mr Lampart wouldn't keep the Commander more than a few minutes. Would they care for some coffee? No? Then perhaps they wouldn't mind waiting in the drawing room.

Dalgliesh looked at his watch. He estimated that Lampart would arrive in about five minutes, a nicely calculated delay long enough to demonstrate lack of anxiety, but short enough not to antagonize a man who was, after all, a senior officer of the Yard.

The drawing room into which they were shown was large and high-ceilinged with a central bay window and two flanking smaller ones overlooking the lawn and giving a distant view of the heath. Something of its Edwardian formality and plush comfort remained in the Axminster carpet, the heavy sofas set at right angles to the fire, and the open fire itself in which synthetic nuggets were roasting under the carved overmantel. Stephen Lampart had resisted any temptation to combine the room's domesticity with a consulting room. There was no couch tactfully secreted behind screens, no washbasin. This was a room where clinical realities could be, for a moment, forgotten. Only the mahogany desk reminded the visitor that it was also a room for business.

Dalgliesh glanced at the pictures. There was a Frith over the fireplace and he walked over to study more closely its meticulous romanticizing of Victorian life. It showed a London railway terminus; uniformed heroes returning from some colonial adventure. The first class carriages were in the foreground. Richly mantled and beribboned ladies, with their decorously pantalooned daughters, decorously greeted their returning menfolk while the more unrestrained welcomes of the common soldiery occupied the periphery of the canvas. On the opposite wall was a bank of stage designs, drawings and costumes for what looked like Shakespearian productions. Dalgliesh supposed that the stage provided some of Lampart's most notable patients and that these were a thank-offering for services rendered. A side table was covered with signed photographs in silver frames. Two, flamboyantly signed, were from minor European ex-royalty. The rest were of impeccably groomed mothers, wishful, sentimental, triumphant, or reluctant, who displayed their babies in unpractised arms. There was the unmistakable aura of nanny in the background. This phalanx of maternity in a room which otherwise was essentially male, struck an incongruous note. But at least, thought Dalgliesh, the man hadn't displayed his medical diplomas over the sideboard.

Dalgliesh left Kate studying the Frith and walked over to the windows. The huge horse chestnut in the middle of the lawn was still heavy with its summer foliage, but the screen of beech trees which partly hid the heath were already showing the first bronze of autumn. The morning light was diffused through a sky which had at first been as opaque as thin milk but which had now lightened into silver. There was no sun but he was aware that it shone above the gauze of clouds and the air was light. Along the path two figures were slowly walking, a nurse wearing a white cap and cloak and a woman with a helmet of yellow hair and a ponderous fur coat which looked far too heavy for a day in early autumn.

It was six minutes precisely before Stephen Lampart arrived. He came in without hurry, apologized for the delay, and greeted them with calm courtesy as if this were a social call. If he was surprised to find Dalgliesh accompanied by a woman detective, he concealed it admirably. But, as Dalgliesh introduced them and they shook hands, he caught Lampart's sharp appraising glance. He could have been greeting a prospective patient, assessing from long experience, in this their first meeting, whether he was likely to have trouble with her.

He was expensively but not formally dressed. The dark grey tweed with its almost invisible stripe and the immaculate blue shirt were, no doubt, designed to distance him from the more intimidating orthodoxy of the successful consultant. He could, thought Dalgliesh, have been a merchant banker, an academic, a politician. But whatever the job, he would have been good at it. His face, his clothes, the confident gaze, all bore the unmistakable imprint of success.

Dalgliesh had expected him to seat himself at the desk with the advantage of dominance which this would give. Instead, he motioned them to the low sofa and sat opposite them in a higher and straight-backed armchair. It gave him a more subtle advantage while reducing the interview to the level of an intimate, even cosy, discussion of a mutual problem. He said:

'I know, of course, why you're here. This is an appalling business. I still find it difficult to believe. I suppose relations and friends all tell you that. Brutal murder is the sort of thing that happens to strangers, not to the people one knows.'

Dalgliesh said:

'How did you learn about it?'

'Lady Berowne telephoned me soon after your people brought the news, and as soon as I was free I called in at the house. I wanted to offer any help I could to her and Lady Ursula. I still don't have any details. Are you any clearer yet what exactly happened?'

'Both their throats were cut. We don't yet know why or by whom.'

'I understood that much from the press and television, but the reports seemed almost wilfully uncommunicative. I take it you're treating it as murder.'

Dalgliesh said, drily:

'There's no evidence to suggest that it was a suicide pact.'

'And the church door, the one leading to this vestry or wherever it was where the bodies were found, may I ask whether you found it open or is that the sort of question that you're not supposed to answer?'

'It was unlocked.'

He said:

'Well, that at least will reassure Lady Ursula.' He didn't elucidate. But then, he didn't need to. After a pause he asked:

'What do you want of me, Commander?'

'I'd like you to talk to us about him. This murder could be what at first sight it appears. He let someone in and that person, a stranger, killed them both. But if it isn't as simple as that, then we need to know as much about him as we can get.'

Lampart said:

'Including who could have known where he was yesterday night and who hated him enough to cut his throat.'

'Including anything you can tell us which could be even remotely relevant.'

Lampart paused as if to collect and marshal his thoughts. It was unnecessary. Both of them knew that his thoughts had been marshalled long before. Then he said:

'I don't think I can give much help. Nothing I know or could guess about Paul Berowne is remotely relevant to his death. If you ask about his enemies, I suppose he must have had them, political enemies. But I should suppose that Paul had fewer than most people in government and, anyway, they're not the sort to go in for murder. The idea that this could be a political crime is absurd. Unless, of course' – again he paused and Dalgliesh waited – 'unless someone on the extreme Left had a personal animosity. But it seems unlikely. More than unlikely, ridiculous. Sarah, his daughter,

179

strongly disliked his politics. But I've no reason to suppose that the set she's mixed up with or even her Marxist boyfriend go in for razor slashing.'

'What set is that?'

'Oh, some minor revolutionary outfit on the extreme Left. I don't suppose Labour would have them. I'd have thought you would already have known. Don't Special Branch make it their business to keep track of these people?' His gaze was open and mildly inquiring but Dalgliesh caught the bite of contempt and dislike in the careful voice and wondered if Kate had heard it too. He asked:

'Who is the boyfriend?'

'Oh really, Commander, I'm not accusing him. I'm not accusing anyone.' Dalgliesh didn't speak. He wondered what length of silence Lampart would think convincing before he came across with the information. After a pause he said: 'He's Ivor Garrod. Banner carrier for all the fashionable shibboleths. I've only met him once. Sarah brought him to dinner at Campden Hill Square about five months ago, principally, I imagine, to annoy Papa. It was a meal I prefer to forget. From the talk then, the violence he advocates is on a somewhat grander scale than merely cutting the throat of a single Tory ex-minister.'

Dalgliesh asked quietly:

'When did you last see Sir Paul Berowne?' The change of questioning almost disconcerted Lampart but he answered calmly enough:

'About six weeks ago. We're not as friendly as we used to be. Actually I was proposing to telephone him today and ask if he could have dinner with me tonight or tomorrow, unless, of course, religious conversion had destroyed his taste for good food and wine.'

'Why did you want to see him?'

'I wanted to ask him what he intended to do about his wife. You know, of course, that he'd recently resigned his seat as well as his job as junior minister and you probably know as much as I do why. He was proposing apparently to drop out of public life. I wanted to know if that included dropping out of his marriage. There was the question of financial provision for Lady Berowne, for Barbara. She is my cousin, I've known her since childhood. I have an interest.'

'How strong an interest?'

Lampart looked sideways over his shoulder at the fair-haired woman and her nurse, still patiently circling the lawn. He seemed momentarily to transfer his interest to them then recollected himself, a little too obviously, and turned again to Dalgliesh.

'I'm sorry. How strong an interest? I don't want to marry her if that's what you're implying, but I am concerned about her. For the past three years I've been her lover as well as her cousin. You could call that a strong interest, I suppose.'

'Did her husband know that you and she were lovers?'

'I've no idea. Husbands usually do get to know these things. Paul and I didn't see each other often enough to make it an embarrassment. We're both busy men with little in common now. Except Barbara, of course. Anyway, he was hardly in a position to object, morally speaking. He had a mistress as I've no doubt you've discovered. Or haven't you grubbed out that piece of dirt yet?'

Dalgliesh said:

'I'm interested in knowing how you managed to grub it out.'

'Barbara told me. She guessed, or rather she knew. She employed a private detective about eighteen months ago and had him followed. To be accurate, she told me of her suspicions and I got hold of a suitably discreet man on her behalf. I don't think it bothered her particularly, the infidelity. It was just that she liked to know. I don't think she saw the woman as a serious rival. Actually, I suspect she was quite pleased. It amused her and it gave her something to hold over Paul if the need arose. And, of course, freed her from the disagreeable necessity of sleeping with him, at least on an inconveniently regular basis. But she didn't lock her door. Barbara liked an occasional assurance that he was still suitably enthralled.'

He was, thought Dalgliesh, being remarkably candid, unnecessarily so. He wondered whether this apparently naive willingness to confide his own and other people's more intimate emotions arose from over-confidence, arrogance and vanity, or whether there was a more sinister motive. Lampart wouldn't be the first murderer to argue that if you told the police details they had no particular right to demand they would be less likely to suspect other more dangerous secrets.

He asked:

'And was he still suitably enthralled?'

'I imagine so. What a pity he isn't here to be asked.' With a quick and surprisingly clumsy gesture he got up from the desk and walked to the window as if seized by restlessness. Dalgliesh turned in his chair and watched him. Suddenly he strode over to the desk, picked up the telephone and dialled. He said:

'Sister, I think Mrs Steiner has had enough outdoor exercise. It's too cold this morning for slow walking. Tell her I'll be along to see her again in,' he glanced at his watch, 'in about fifteen minutes. Thank you.' He put down the receiver, came back to his chair and said almost roughly: 'Let's get down to it, shall we? What you want from me, I suppose, is some sort of statement. Where was I, what was I doing, who was I with when Paul got himself killed? If it was murder, I'm not naive enough to deceive myself that I'm not a suspect.'

'It isn't a question of suspicion. We have to ask those questions of anyone who was closely connected with Sir Paul.'

He laughed, a sudden explosion of sound, harsh and mirthless.

'Closely connected! You could say that I suppose. And it's all just a matter of routine. Isn't that what you usually tell your victims?' Dalgliesh didn't reply. The silence seemed to irritate Lampart. He said: 'Where do I make it, this statement? Here, or at the local police station? Or are you operating from the Yard?'

'You could make it there, in my office, if that's convenient for you. Perhaps you could come in this evening. Or it could be taken at the local station if that would save time. But it would be helpful to have the gist of it now.'

Lampart said:

'You've noticed, I suppose, that I haven't asked to have my solicitor present. That shows rather a touching confidence in the police, wouldn't you say?'

'If you want him to be present that, of course, is your right.'

'I don't want him. I don't need him. I hope you won't be disappointed, Commander, but I think I have an alibi. That is if Berowne died between seven and midnight.' Still Dalgliesh didn't speak. Lampart went on: 'I was with Barbara for the whole of that time as, no doubt, you already know. You must have seen her. Earlier, from two o'clock until five I was here operating. The list is available and theatre sister and the anaesthetist can corroborate. I know I was gloved, gowned and masked, but I can assure you that my staff recognize my work even if they don't actually see my face. But, of course, they did see it, before I gowned up. I mention that in case you had some fanciful idea that I might have persuaded a colleague to stand in for me.'

Dalgliesh said:

'That might work in fiction but hardly in real life.'

'And afterwards, Barbara and I had tea in this room then spent some time in my private flat, upstairs. Then I changed and we left here together at about seven forty. The night porter saw us go and can probably confirm the time. We drove to the Black Swan at

182

Cookham where we had dinner together. I wasn't particularly noticing the time but I suppose we got there at about eight thirty. I drive a red Porsche, in case that's significant. The table was booked for eight forty-five. Jean Paul Higgins is the manager. He'll be able to confirm it. No doubt he'll also confirm that it was after eleven when we left. But I'd be grateful for a little tact. I'm not oversensitive about reputation, but I can't afford to have half of fashionable London gossiping about my private life. And while some of my patients have their little foibles like giving birth under water or squatting on the drawing room carpet, being delivered by a murder suspect isn't everyone's fancy.'

'We'll be discreet. When did Lady Berowne arrive here? Or did you call for her earlier at Campden Hill Square?'

'No. I haven't been inside number sixty-two for weeks. Barbara came by cab. She dislikes driving in London. She arrived about four, I suppose. She was in the theatre watching me operate from about four fifteen until I finished. Did I mention that?'

'She was with you the whole time?'

'Most of the time. I think she slipped out for a few minutes after I'd completed the third Caesarean.'

'And she was masked and gowned too?'

'Of course. But what possible relevance is that? He couldn't have died, surely, before seven.'

'Is that something she often does? Watch you operate?'

'It isn't uncommon. It's a fancy she has,' he paused and added, 'from time to time.'

They were both silent. There were some things, thought Dalgliesh, that even Stephen Lampart, with his pose of ironic detachment and contempt for reticence, couldn't bring himself actually to say. So that was how she got her kicks. That was what turned her on; watching, masked and gowned, while his hands cut into another woman's body. The erotic charge of the medical priesthood. The attendant nurses moving in patterned ceremony about him. The grey eyes meeting the blue above the mask. And afterwards, watching, while he peeled off his gloves, held out his arms in a parody of benediction while an acolyte lifted the gown from his shoulders. The heady mixture of power, mystery, ruthlessness. The rituals of knife and blood. Where, he wondered, had they made love. His bedroom, a private sitting room? It was surprising that they didn't couple on the operating table. Perhaps they did.

The telephone on the desk rang. With a muttered apology, Lampart picked up the receiver. The conversation, apparently with a colleague, was highly clinical and one-sided with Lampart doing most of the listening. But he made no attempt to cut it short. Dalgliesh gazed out over the garden while his mind busied itself with its preliminary assessment. If they had left Pembroke Lodge at seven forty it would need fast driving to get to the Black Swan by eight thirty. Time to take in a murder on the way? It was feasible provided he could make an excuse to leave her in the car. No man in his senses would take her with him into the church on such a bloody mission even if she knew or guessed what he had in mind. So there would have to be an excuse. Someone he had briefly to see. Some business to be transacted. The car would have to be parked close to the church. That in itself would be risky. A red Porsche was conspicuous. And then what? The knock on the church door. Berowne letting him in. The rehearsed excuse for calling. How long for these preliminaries? Less than a minute perhaps. The sudden blow to knock Berowne out. Then to the washroom for the razor which he could be sure he would find, the quick stripping off of jacket and shirt and back to the vestry, razor in hand. The careful tentative cuts followed by the final slash to the bone. He must have done some forensic medicine when a student, if not since. He would know better than any other suspect how to simulate a suicide.

And then the disaster. Harry appears, stumbling, probably half-drunk, half-asleep, but not so asleep that he couldn't see, couldn't remember. And now, there would be no time for finesse and none needed. And afterwards: the quick wash; the razor placed near Berowne's hand; the rapid glance to left and right; the covering darkness; the door left unlocked since he couldn't take away the key; the unhurried return to the car. He would have to depend on her silence, of course. He would need to be certain that she would stick to their story and say that they had driven straight to the Black Swan. But it was an easy lie, no complicated fabrication, no difficult details or timing to remember. She would say what in fact she had in effect already said. 'We drove straight there. No, I can't remember the route. I wasn't noticing. But we didn't stop.' He would have to fabricate a good reason for asking her to lie. 'I needed to see one of my patients, a woman.' But why not tell the police that? There's nothing wrong about a quick professional visit. The need to stop would have to be faintly disreputable. Either that or something he had suddenly remembered. A telephone call which had been unanswered. Too quick. He would need longer than that. And why not wait and make it from the Black Swan? But, of course, there was

184

the obvious ploy. He would say he had called at the church, spoken to Berowne, left him alive and well. That way, she would back up his alibi in her own interest as well as his. And if, in the end, she didn't, he would still have his story. 'I called to talk to Berowne about his wife. I only stayed for ten minutes at the most. The discussion was perfectly amicable. I saw no one but Berowne and I left him alive and well.'

Lampart replaced the receiver. He said:

'Sorry about that. Where were we, Commander? At the Black Swan?'

But Dalgliesh changed the tack of the questioning. He said:

'You knew Sir Paul Berowne intimately once, even if you weren't particularly close at the end. No two men share a woman without being interested in each other.' He could have added, 'sometimes obsessed with each other'. He went on: 'You're a doctor. I'm wondering what you make of it, this experience he had in the vestry at St Matthew's.' The flattery was hardly subtle and Lampart was too clever a man to miss it. But he wouldn't be able to resist it. He was used to being asked his opinion, to being listened to with deference. It was partly what he lived by. He said:

'I'm an obstetrician, not a psychiatrist. But I shouldn't have thought the psychology of it was particularly complicated. The usual story. It's only the manifestations that are a little bizarre. Call it the mid-life crisis. I don't like the expression "male menopause". It's inaccurate anyway. The two things are fundamentally different. I think he looked at his life, what he'd achieved, what he could hope for, and didn't much care for it. He'd tried law and politics and neither satisfied him. He had a wife he lusted after but didn't love. A daughter who didn't love him. A job which constrained any hope he might have of breaking out into spectacular or exuberant protest. All right; he'd got himself a mistress. That's the easy expedient. I haven't seen the lady but from what Barbara told me it's more a question of comfort and cocoa, a bit of mild office gossip on the side rather than any breaking of the straitjacket he got himself strapped into. So he needed an excuse for chucking it all. What better one than proclaiming that God himself has told you you're on the wrong tack? I don't think it would be my way out. But you can argue that it's preferable to a nervous breakdown, alcoholism or cancer.'

When Dalgliesh didn't speak he went on quickly, with a kind of nervous sincerity which was almost convincing.

'I see it all the time. The husbands. They sit where you're sitting

185

now. Ostensibly, they come to talk to me about their wives. But they're the ones with the problem. They can't win. It's the tyranny of success. They spend most of their youth working to qualify, most of their young manhood building up success – the right wife, the right house, the right schools for the children, the right clubs. For what? For more money, more comfort, a bigger house, a faster car, more taxation. And they don't even get much of a kick out of it. And there's another twenty years to be got through. And it isn't much better for those who aren't disillusioned, who find their niche, who actually enjoy what they do. Their fear is the prospect of retirement. Overnight you're nobody. The walking dead. Haven't you seen those dreadful old men, trawling for a committee, angling for a royal commission, a job, any kind of a job, as long as it gives them the illusion that they're still important.'

Dalgliesh said:

'Yes, I've seen them.'

'Christ, they practically go down on their knees and slaver for it.'

'I think that's true enough, but it didn't apply to him. He was still only a junior minister. His success was ahead. He was still at the striving stage.'

'Oh yes, I know. The next Tory Prime Minister but one. Do you think that was a serious possibility? I don't. He hadn't the fire in the belly, not for politics anyway. Not even one little smouldering coal.'

He spoke with a kind of triumphant bitterness. He said:

'I'm all right, Jack. I'm one of the lucky ones. No hostages to fortune. The job gives me what I need. And when I'm ready for the scrapheap, I've got the *Mayflower*, a sloop, fifty feet. She's berthed at Chichester. I don't get much time for her now. But once retired, I'll provision her and be off. And you, Commander? No *Mayflower*?'

'No *Mayflower*.'

'But you've your poetry, of course. I was forgetting.' He spoke the word as if it were an insult. As if he were saying, 'you've got your woodwork, your stamp collection, your embroidery'. Worse, he spoke it as if he knew there hadn't been a poem for four years, that there might never be one again. Dalgliesh said:

'For someone who wasn't intimate, you know a lot about him.'

'He interested me. And at Oxford his elder brother and I were friends. I dined at Campden Hill Square fairly often when he was alive and the three of us used to sail together. To Cherbourg specifically, in 1978. You get to know a man when you've survived a force ten gale together. Actually, Paul saved my life. I went overboard and he got me back.'

186

'But isn't yours a rather superficial assessment, the obvious explanation?'

'It's surprising how often the obvious explanation is the correct one. If you were a diagnostician, you'd know that.'

Dalgliesh turned to Kate:

'Is there anything you wanted to ask, Inspector?' Lampart wasn't quite quick enough to restrain his momentary frown of surprise and discomfiture that a woman he had taken to be no more than Dalgliesh's helot, whose role was to take unobtrusive notes and sit as a meek and silent witness, was apparently licensed to question him. He turned on her a half-smiling over-attentive gaze but his eyes were wary.

Kate said:

'This dinner at the Black Swan, is that a favourite place of yours? Do you and Lady Berowne go there often?'

'Fairly often in summer. Less so in winter. The ambience is agreeable. It's a convenient distance from London and now that Higgins has changed his chef the food is good. If you're asking for a recommendation for a quiet dinner, yes, I can recommend it.' The sarcasm was unsubtle and he had made his resentment too obvious. The question, innocuous enough, if apparently irrelevant, had rattled him. Kate said:

'And you were there, both of you, on the evening of the seventh of August, when Diana Travers was drowned?'

He said dryly:

'You obviously already know that we were there so there seems little point in asking. It was Lady Berowne's twenty-seventh birthday party. She was born on the seventh of August.'

'And you escorted her, not her husband?'

'Sir Paul Berowne was otherwise engaged. I gave the party for Lady Berowne. He was expected to join us later but rang to say that he couldn't make it. Since you know that we were there, you obviously know, too, that we left before the tragedy.'

'And the other tragedy, sir, Theresa Nolan? You were not, of course, present when that happened either?' Careful, Kate, thought Dalgliesh. But he didn't interfere, and he wasn't anxious.

'If you mean did I sit by her side in Holland Park when she swallowed a bottle of Distalgesic tablets and washed them down with cooking sherry, no I wasn't. If I had been, obviously I should have stopped her.'

'She left a note making it plain that she'd killed herself because of guilt over her abortion. A perfectly legal abortion. She was one

187

of your nurses here. I wonder why she didn't have the operation at Pembroke Lodge?'

'She didn't ask. And if she had, I wouldn't have done it. I prefer not to.operate on my own staff. If there appear to be medical reasons for termination, I refer them to a fellow gynaecologist. I did so with her. Actually, I can't see how her death or that of Diana Travers has anything to do with the business that brings you here this morning. Ought we to be wasting time with irrelevant questions?'

Dalgliesh said:

'Not irrelevant. Sir Paul received letters suggesting, obliquely but fairly unmistakably, that he was somehow connected with those two deaths. Anything that happened to him during the last weeks of his life has to be relevant. The letters were probably the usual malicious nonsense that politicians expose themselves to but it's as well to clear them out of the way.'

Lampart turned his gaze from Kate to Dalgliesh.

'I see. I'm sorry if I sounded uncooperative but I know absolutely nothing of the Travers girl except that she worked at Campden Hill Square as a part-time domestic and that she was at the Black Swan on the night of the birthday party. Theresa Nolan came here from Campden Hill Square where she'd been nursing Lady Ursula who was laid low with sciatica. I understand they got her from a nursing agency. When Lady Ursula no longer needed a night nurse, she suggested to the girl that she apply here. She had a midwifery qualification. She was perfectly satisfactory. She must have got pregnant when she was working at Campden Hill Square. But I didn't ask by whom and I don't think she ever said.'

Dalgliesh said:

'Did it occur to you that the child could have been Sir Paul Berowne's?'

'Yes. It occurred to me. I imagine it occurred to quite a number of people.' He said no more and Dalgliesh didn't press him. He asked:

'What happened when she discovered she was pregnant?'

'She came to me and said that she couldn't face having a baby and wanted a termination. I referred her to a psychiatrist and left him to make the necessary arrangements.'

'Did you think that the girl's condition at the time, I mean her mental condition, was such that she was likely to qualify legally for an abortion?'

188

'I didn't examine her. I didn't discuss it with her. And it wasn't a medical decision I was qualified to make. As I said, I referred her to a psychiatric colleague. I told her that she could have leave with pay until a decision was made. She only came back here for a week after the operation. And the rest you know.'

Suddenly he got to his feet and began restlessly pacing. Then he turned to Dalgliesh.

'I've given some thought to this business of Paul Berowne. Man is an animal and he lives most at ease with himself and the world when he remembers that. Admittedly he's the cleverest and most dangerous of animals, but he's still an animal. The philosophers, and poets too, for all I know, make it all too complicated. It isn't. Our basic needs are pretty straightforward – food, shelter, warmth, sex, prestige, in that order. The happiest people go after them and are satisfied with them. Berowne wasn't. God knows what unattainable intangibles he thought he'd a right to. Eternal life, probably.'

Dalgliesh said: `

'So you believe the probability is that he killed himself?'

'I haven't enough evidence. But let's say that if you finally decide it was suicide, then I for one won't be surprised.'

'And the tramp? There were two deaths.'

'That's more difficult. Did he kill Paul or did Paul kill him? Obviously the family won't want to believe the latter. Lady Ursula will never accept that explanation, whatever the final verdict.'

'But you . . .' .

'Oh, I feel that if a man has sufficient violence in him to slit his own throat, he's certainly capable of slitting another's. And now, perhaps you'll excuse me,' he glanced at Kate, 'both of you. I have a patient waiting. I'll call in at the Yard between eight and nine thirty and sign my statement.' He added, rising: 'Perhaps by then I shall manage to think of something else to help you. But don't be too sanguine.' He made it sound like a threat.

2

There was an almost unbroken stream of traffic past the front gate and Kate had to wait for over a minute before it was safe to filter in. She thought: I wonder just how he does it. The interview was all there in her notebook in her neat, unorthodox shorthand but she had the gift of almost perfect verbal recall and she could have typed most of it out without reference to the hieroglyphics. She let her mind slide over each question and response and she still couldn't see where AD had been so clever.

He had said very little, his questions short and sometimes apparently unrelated to the line of inquiry. But Lampart, and that after all was the intention, had been seduced into saying a great deal too much. And all that guff about the male mid-life crisis, popular psychology which you could have sent to you in a plain envelope if you wrote to the agony aunties inquiring what was wrong with your old man. He could be right, of course. But, after all, medically speaking, varieties of the male menopause weren't Stephen Lampart's field. He'd been asked for his opinion and he'd given it, but you'd expect a man as fond of his own voice as he was to be even more forthcoming about the psychological problems of pregnancy and abortion. But when it came to Theresa Nolan, what had they got? A brush off, the keep off signs clearly posted. He hadn't even wanted to think about her, let alone talk about her. And it wasn't just because she, Kate, had been the one to do the questioning and had done it with that undeferential over-politeness which she had known would be more offensive to his vanity than rudeness or open antagonism. She had hoped that, with luck, it might goad him into an indiscretion, but it wouldn't have worked if there had been nothing to conceal. She heard AD's voice:

'That touching detail, about Sir Paul saving his life. Did you believe it?'

'No, sir. Not as he told it. I think something of the sort probably happened. He went overboard and his friend yanked him back. He wouldn't have mentioned it if there weren't some corroboration. But I think he was really saying, "Look, I might have pinched his wife but I wouldn't have killed him, would I? He saved my life."' She added: 'It wasn't very subtle the way he fingered Garrod.' She glanced at him quickly. He smiled with wry distaste as he sometimes did when a colleague used an Americanism. But he let it pass, merely saying:

'Nothing about him was subtle.'

Suddenly she felt a surge of optimism, heady, intoxicating and dangerously close to the euphoria which always came when a case was going well but which she had learned to distrust and subdue. If this goes all right, if we get him, whoever he is, and we will, then I'm on my way. I'm really on my way. But the elation went deeper than mere ambition or the satisfaction of a test passed, a job well done. She had enjoyed herself. Every minute of her brief confrontation with that self-satisfied poseur had been deeply pleasurable. She thought of her first months with the CID, the plugging, conscientious, door-to-door inquiries which had made up her day, the pathetic victims, the even more pathetic villains. How much more satisfying was this sophisticated manhunt; the knowledge that they were up against a killer with the intelligence to think and plan, who wasn't an ignorant, feckless victim of circumstance or passion. She had learned facial control long before she had joined the police. She drove carefully, her face calmly set on the road ahead. But something of what she was feeling must have communicated itself to her companion. He said:

'Did you enjoy yourself, Inspector?' The question and the rare use of her rank jolted her but she decided to answer it honestly, knowing that she had no option. She had done her homework. She knew his reputation, and when colleagues had spoken about him she had made it her business to listen. They had said: 'He's a bastard, but a just bastard.' She knew that there were some inadequacies he could forgive and some foibles he could tolerate. But dishonesty wasn't among them. She said:

'Yes, sir. I liked the sense of being in control, that we were getting somewhere.' Then she added, knowing as she spoke that this was dangerous territory, but hell, she thought, why should he get away with it:

'Was the question meant as a criticism, sir?'

'No. No one joins the police without getting some enjoyment out of exercising power. No one joins the murder squad who hasn't a taste for death. The danger begins when the pleasure becomes an end in itself. That's when it's time to think about another job.'

She wanted to ask: 'Have you ever thought of another job, sir?' But she knew the temptation was illusory. There were some senior officers of whom one could ask that question after a couple of whiskies in the senior officers' mess, but he wasn't among them.

191

She remembered the moment when she had told Alan that Dalgliesh had chosen her for the new squad. He had said, smiling: 'So isn't it about time you tried reading his verse?' and she had replied: 'I'd better come to terms with the man before I try coming to terms with his poetry.' She wasn't sure that she had succeeded. Now she said:

'Mr Lampart spoke about razor slashing. We deliberately didn't tell him how Sir Paul died. So why should he have mentioned a razor?'

Dalgliesh said:

'Reasonably enough. He was an old friend, one of the people who would know how Berowne shaved. He must have guessed what weapon was used. It's interesting that he couldn't bring himself to ask us outright if it was. Incidentally, we'll have to check that timing fairly quickly. It's a job for Saunders, I think. He'd better make three runs, the same time, the same make of car, the same night of the week, and, with luck, the same weather conditions. And we'll need to know everything possible about Pembroke Lodge. Who owns the freehold, who holds shares, how the business operates, what its reputation is.' She couldn't make a written note of his instructions. But then, she didn't need to.

She said:

'Yes, sir.'

Dalgliesh went on:

'He had the means, he had the knowledge, he had the motive. I don't think he wanted marriage with the lady but he certainly didn't want an impoverished mistress who might begin thinking in terms of divorce. But if he wanted Berowne dead, and dead before he threw away his money on some half-baked scheme for housing derelicts, he didn't need to slit his throat. He's a doctor. There are more subtle methods. This murderer didn't kill merely from expediency. There had been hatred in that room. Hate isn't an easy emotion to hide. I didn't see it in Stephen Lampart. Arrogance, aggression, sexual jealousy of the man in possession. But not hate.'

Kate had never lacked courage and she didn't now. After all, he'd selected her for the team. Presumably he thought her opinion worth having. He wasn't looking for a female subordinate to massage his ego. She said:

'But couldn't it have been expediency rather than hate, sir? Killing without arousing suspicion isn't easy even for a doctor. He wasn't Sir Paul's general practitioner. And this, if he could pull it off, would be the perfect murder, one that isn't even suspected as

192

murder. It was Harry Mack who did for him. Without that second killing, wouldn't we have taken it at its face value . . . suicide?'

Dalgliesh said:

'Followed by the usual euphemistic verdict 'while the balance of his mind was disturbed'. Perhaps. If he hadn't made the mistake of taking away the matches and of half-burning the diary. That was an unnecessary refinement. In some ways, the clue of that half-burned match is the most interesting in the case.'

Suddenly she felt at ease with him, almost companionable. She was no longer thinking of the impression she might be making but of the case. She did what she would have done with Massingham. With her eyes fixed on the road ahead, she thought it through aloud:

'Once the killer decided to burn the diary, he'd know he needed to take the matches with him to the church. Berowne didn't smoke so there wouldn't be a lighter on the body. Obviously, he'd be unwise to risk using his own lighter if he had one, and he couldn't be sure he'd find matches in the vestry. And when he did, they were chained and it was easier and quicker to use the box he'd brought with him. Time was vital. So we get back to someone who knew Sir Paul, knew his habits, knew where he was on Tuesday night but who wasn't familiar with the church. But he'd hardly be carrying the diary in his hand when he arrived. So he was wearing a jacket or coat with largish pockets. Or he had a bag of some kind, a carrier, a tote bag, a briefcase, a medical bag.'

Dalgliesh said:

'Or he could have carried it folded inside an evening paper.'

Kate went on:

'He rings. Sir Paul lets him in. He asks to go to the washroom. He leaves his bag there together with the matches and the diary. He strips. Perhaps he strips naked. Then it's back to the Little Vestry. But this is getting bizarre, sir. His victim isn't going to sit there quietly waiting for it. Not confronted by a man, stark naked with an open razor in his hand. Paul Berowne wasn't old or sick or weak. He would have defended himself. It couldn't have happened that way.'

'Concentrate on the matches.'

'But he must have been naked when he killed. Naked to the waist anyway. He must have known that it would be a bloody business. He couldn't have risked getting his clothes splashed. But of course! He knocks out his victim first. Then he goes for the razor, strips, does the fancy bit. Then back to the washroom. He has a

193

quick but thorough sluice down and gets back into his clothes. Then, last of all, he burns the diary. That way he can be sure there's no blood on the cover or in the grate. It must have happened in that order. Finally, perhaps a matter of habit, he slips the matchbox in his jacket pocket. That suggests he was used to carrying matches. A smoker, perhaps. It must have given him a shock when he put his hands in his pocket later and found them and realized that he should have left them at the scene. Why didn't he go back? Too late, perhaps. Or perhaps he couldn't face the shambles.'

Dalgliesh said:

'Or he knew that a second visit would add to the risk of being seen, of leaving some trace of himself in the vestry. But let's assume that the killer took his own box away on purpose. What does that suggest?'

'That the box he used could be traced to him. But that's unlikely, surely. He'd use an ordinary brand, one of a million similar boxes. And he couldn't have known that we'd find that half-burnt match. Perhaps he took it away because it was a box someone might miss. Perhaps he always planned to return it. And that means he didn't go to the church from his own home. Logically, he came from Campden Hill Square, where he'd helped himself both to the diary and to the box of matches. But if so, if the matchbox came from Berowne's own home, why not leave it at the scene? Even if the box were traced, it would only lead us back to Berowne himself. So we get back to a simple mistake. A matter of habit. He slipped the box into his pocket.'

Dalgliesh said:

'If he did it might not have worried him too much after the first shock of discovery. He'd tell himself that we'd assume Berowne used the matches from the chained box, or that we'd think that the matches had been burned with the diary. Or perhaps we'd argue that he could have used a match from one of those packets you can pick up in hotels and restaurants, small enough to burn away without a trace. Admittedly, Berowne wasn't a man likely to collect restaurant matches but defense counsel could argue that it happened that way. This isn't exactly a propitious time to ask for a conviction on forensic evidence alone, certainly not on one inch of a half-burned match.'

Kate asked:

'How do you think it happened, sir?'

'Possibly much as you've described. If Sir Paul had been faced with a naked and armed assailant, I doubt if we'd have found what we did find at the scene. There was no sign of a struggle. That suggests that he must have been knocked out first. That done, the killer got to work swiftly, expertly, knowing just what he was about. And he didn't need much time. A couple of minutes to strip and lay his hands on the razor. Less than ten seconds to do the killing. So the knockout blow need not have been heavy. In fact, it would have had to be nicely judged if it weren't to leave a suspiciously large bruise. But there's another possibility. He could have slipped something over Berowne's head and dragged him down. Something soft, a scarf, a towel, his own shirt. Or a noose, a cord, a handkerchief.'

Kate said:

'But he'd have to be careful not to pull it too tight, not to throttle his victim. The cause of death had to be the slit throat. And wouldn't a scarf or handkerchief leave a mark?'

Dalgliesh said:

'Not necessarily. Not when he'd finished his butchery. But we may get something from this afternoon's PM.'

And suddenly, she was back in the Little Vestry, looking down again at that half-severed head, seeing the whole picture, vivid, clear-edged, bright as a coloured print. And this time there was no blessed moment of preparation, no chance to compose her mind and muscles for what she knew she would have to face. Her hands, white knuckled, tightened on the wheel. For a moment she imagined the car had stalled, that she had stepped on the brake. But they were still riding smoothly, down the Finchley Road. How strange, she thought, that the horror, briefly recalled, should be more terrible than reality. But her companion was speaking. She must have lost a few seconds of what he was saying. But now she heard him talking about the time of the post-mortem, saying that she might like to watch. Normally the suggestion, which she translated as an order, would have pleased her. She would have welcomed it as one more affirmation that she was really part of his team. But now for the first time she felt a spasm of distaste, almost a revulsion. She would be there, of course. This wouldn't be her first autopsy. She had no fear of disgracing herself. She could gaze and not be sick. In detective training school, she had seen her male colleagues topple in the PM room while she had stood firm. It was important to be present at the PM if the pathologist would allow it. You could learn a lot, and she was eager to learn. Her grandmother and the social worker would be waiting for her at three o'clock but they would have to wait. She had tried, but not too hard, to find a

195

moment in the day to ring and say that she couldn't be there. But she told herself that it wasn't necessary; her grandmother knew that already. She would try to drop in at the end of the day if it wasn't too late. But for her, now at this moment, the dead had to take priority over the living. But for the first time since she had joined the CID, a small treacherous voice, whispering in self-distrust, asked her what exactly it was that her job was doing to her.

She had chosen to be a police officer deliberately, knowing that the job was right for her. But she had never, even from the first, had any illusions about it. It was a job where people when they needed you demanded that you should be there at once, unquestionably, effectively, and when they didn't preferred to forget you existed. It was a job where you were sometimes required to work with people you'd rather not work with and show respect for senior officers for whom you felt little or none; where you could find yourself allied to men you despised and against some for whom, more often than you'd bargained for, more often than was comfortable, you felt sympathy, even pity. She knew the comfortable orthodoxies, that law and order were the norms, crime the aberration, that policing in a free society could only be done with the consent of the policed, even presumably in those areas where the police had always been seen as the enemy and had now been elevated into convenient stereotypes of oppression. But she had her own credo. You kept sane by knowing that hypocrisy might be politically necessary but that you didn't have to believe it. You kept honest; there was no point in the job otherwise. You did the job so that your male colleagues had to respect you even if it was too much to expect that they would like you. You kept your private life private, unmessy. There were men enough in the world without being trapped by propinquity into sexual entanglement with your colleagues. You didn't fall into the easy habit of obscenity; you had heard enough of that in Ellison Fairweather Buildings. You knew how far you could reasonably hope to rise and how you proposed to get there. You made no unnecessary enemies; it was hard enough for a woman to climb without getting kicked in the ankles on the way up. Every job, after all, had its disadvantages. Nurses got used to the smell of dressings and bedpans, unwashed bodies, other people's pain, the smell of death. She had made her choice. And now, more than ever, she had no regrets.

3

The hospital where Miles Kynaston held his appointment as consultant pathologist had needed a new PM room for years but facilities for the living patients had taken priority over accommodation for the dead. Kynaston grumbled but Dalgliesh suspected that he didn't really care. He had the equipment he needed and the pm room in which he worked was sparse familiar territory in which he felt as comfortably at home as he might in an old dressing gown. He had no real wish to be banished to some larger, more remote and more impersonal quarters, and his occasional complaints were no more than ritual noises made to remind the medical committee that the Forensic Pathology Department existed.

But there was, inevitably, always something of a squash. Dalgliesh and his officers were there primarily from interest rather than necessity, but the exhibits sergeant, the fingerprint officer, the scene of crime and exhibit officers with their envelopes, bottles and tubes, took up necessary room. Kynaston's secretary, a plump, middle-aged woman, cheerfully efficient as a president of the Women's Institute, sat in her twin-set and tweeds, squashed in the corner with a bulging bag at her feet. Dalgliesh always expected her to take out her knitting. Kynaston had always disliked using a tape-recorder and from time to time he turned towards her and dictated his findings in low, staccato sentences which she seemed to understand. He always worked to music, usually baroque and often a string quartet, Mozart, Vivaldi, Haydn. This afternoon's recording was one Dalgliesh immediately recognized since he, too, owned it, Neville Marriner conducting Telemann's Viola Concerto in G. Dalgliesh wondered if its enigmatic, richly melancholic tone provided Kynaston with a necessary catharsis; whether it was his way of attempting to dramatize the routine indignities of death; or whether, like house painters or others less singularly employed, he simply liked music while he worked.

Dalgliesh noted with a mixture of interest and irritation that Massingham and Kate kept their eyes fixed on Kynaston's hands with an attention which suggested that they were afraid to shift their gaze in case inadvertently they should happen to meet his eyes. He wondered how they could possibly suppose that he saw this ritual disembowelment as having anything to do with Berowne.

The detachment, which had become second nature to him, was helped by the matter-of-fact efficiency with which the organs were drawn out, examined, bottled and labelled. He felt exactly as he had when, as a young probationer, he had watched his first autopsy; a surprise at the bright colours of the coils and pouches dangling in the pathologist's gloved and bloody hands, and an almost childish wonder that so small a cavity should be capable of accommodating such a large and diverse collection of organs.

Afterwards, as they scrubbed their hands in the washroom, Kynaston from necessity, Dalgliesh from a fastidiousness which he would have found difficult to explain, he asked:

'What about the time of death?'

'No reason to alter the estimate I made at the scene. Seven o'clock would be the earliest. Say between seven and nine. I may be able to be a little more precise when the stomach contents have been analysed. There were no signs of a struggle. And if Berowne were attacked he made no attempt to protect himself. There are no cuts across the gripping aspect of his palm. Well, you saw that for yourself. The blood on his right palm came from the razor not from defensive cuts.'

Dalgliesh said:

'From the razor or from the blood on his throat?'

'That's possible. The palm was certainly more thickly coated than one might expect. Nothing complicated about the cause of death in either case. In both, it's a classical fine cut, through the thyro-hyoid ligament, severing everything from the skin to the spine. Berowne was healthy, no reason why he shouldn't have lived to a good old age if someone hadn't cut his throat for him. And Harry Mack was in better shape, medically speaking, than I expected. Liver not too good but it could have stood a few more years' abuse before it actually gave out on him. The lab will get the throat tissue under the microscope, but I don't think you'll get any joy. There is no obvious sign of a ligature at the edge of the wound. The bump on the back of Berowne's head is superficial, probably made when he fell.'

Dalgliesh said:

'Or was pulled down.'

'Or was pulled down. You'll have to wait for the lab report on the blood smear before you can go much further, Adam.'

Dalgliesh said:

'And even if that smear isn't Harry Mack's blood you still aren't prepared to say that Berowne wasn't capable of stumbling across to Harry even with those two superficial cuts in his throat.'

Kynaston said:

'I could say it was improbable. I couldn't say that it was impossible. And we're not just talking about the superficial cuts. Remember that case quoted by Simpson? The suicide practically severed his head yet remained conscious long enough to kick the ambulance man downstairs.'

'But if Berowne killed Harry why move back to the bed to finish himself off?'

'A natural association, bed, sleep, death. If he had decided to die on his bed, why should he change his mind because it was necessary to kill Harry first?'

'It wasn't necessary. I doubt whether Harry could have reached him in time to stop that final cut. It offends against common sense.'

'Or it offends against your idea of Paul Berowne.'

'Both. This was double murder, Miles.'

'I believe you, but it's going to be the devil to prove and I don't think my report will be much help. Suicide is the most private and mysterious of acts, inexplicable because the chief actor is never there to explain it.'

Dalgliesh said:

'Unless, of course, he leaves his testimony behind. If Berowne did decide to kill himself I'd have expected to find some kind of note, an attempt at explanation.'

Kynaston said enigmatically:

'The fact that you didn't find it doesn't necessarily mean that he didn't write it.'

He drew on a fresh pair of gloves and pulled his face mask over his mouth and nose. Already a new cadaver was being wheeled in. Dalgliesh looked at his watch. Massingham and Kate could drive back to the Yard and get on with the paperwork. He had another appointment. After the frustrations of the day he needed a little light relief, even a little cosseting. He proposed to extract information by more agreeable ways than a police interrogation. He had earlier that morning telephoned Conrad Ackroyd and had been invited to take a civilized afternoon tea with the owner and editor of the *Paternoster Review*.

4

Conrad and Nellie Ackroyd lived in a gleamingly neat stucco Edwardian villa in St John's Wood with a garden running down to the canal, a house reputedly built by Edward the Seventh for one of his mistresses and inherited by Nellie Ackroyd from a bachelor uncle. Ackroyd had moved into it from his city flat above the *Paternoster* office three years previously following his marriage and had happily accommodated his books, his belongings and his life to Nellie's taste for comfort and domesticity. Now, although they had a servant, he himself welcomed Dalgliesh at the door, his black eyes as brightly expectant as a child's.

'Come in, come in. We know what you're here for, dear boy. It's about my little piece in the *Review*. I'm glad you haven't felt it necessary to come in pairs. We're quite prepared to help the police with their inquiries, as you so tactfully put it, when you've caught your man and he's having his arms twisted in a little backroom, but I draw the line at giving afternoon tea to some oversized minion who wears out the springs in my sofa and eats my cucumber sandwiches with one hand while taking down everything I say with the other.'

Dalgliesh said:

'Be serious, Conrad. We're talking about murder.'

'Are we? There was a rumour – just a rumour, of course – that Paul Berowne could have made his own quietus. I'm glad it isn't true. Murder is more interesting and far less depressing. It's inconsiderate of one's friends to commit suicide; too like setting a good example. But all that can wait. Tea first.'

He called up the stairs:

'Nellie, darling, Adam is here.' Looking at him as he led the way into the drawing room, Dalgliesh thought that he never seemed a day older than when they had first met. He gave the impression of plumpness, perhaps because of his almost round face and the chubbiness of his marsupial cheeks. But he was firm fleshed, active, moving with the nimble grace of a dancer. His eyes were small and upward-slanting. When he was amused he would narrow them into twin creases of flesh. The most remarkable thing about his face was the restless mobility of his small, delicately formed mouth which he used as a moist focus of emotion. He

200

would press it in disapproval, turn it down like a child's in disappointment or disgust, lengthen and curve it when he smiled. It seemed never still, never the same shape. Even in repose he would munch with it as if relishing the taste of his tongue.

Nellie Ackroyd, in contrast, was slim where he was plumpish, fair where he was dark, and out-topped him by three inches. She wore her long blonde hair twined in a plait round her head in the fashion of the twenties. Her tweed skirts were well cut but longer than had been fashionable for half a century and topped invariably by a loose cardigan. Her shoes were pointed and laced. Dalgliesh remembered one of his father's Sunday-school teachers who could have been her double. As she came into the room, he was for a moment back in that village church hall, sitting in a circle with the other children on the low wooden chairs and waiting for Miss Mainwaring to hand out that Sunday's stamp, a coloured biblical picture which he would lick and stick with infinite care on that week's space on his card. He had liked Miss Mainwaring – dead now for over twenty years, of cancer, and buried in that distant Norfolk churchyard – and he liked Nellie Ackroyd.

The Ackroyds' marriage had astounded their friends and been a source of prurient speculation to their few enemies. But whenever he was with them Dalgliesh never doubted that they were genuinely happy together and he marvelled anew at the infinite variety of marriage, that relationship at once so private and public, so hedged with convention and yet so anarchical. In his private life Ackroyd was reputed to be one of the kindest men in London. His victims pointed out that he could afford to be: one issue of the *Paternoster Review* commonly contained sufficient spleen to satisfy a normal lifespan. The reviews of new books and plays were always clever and entertaining, sometimes perceptive and occasionally cruel and were a form of fortnightly entertainment cherished by all except the victims. Even when the *Times Literary Supplement* changed its practice, the *Paternoster* continued to preserve the anonymity of its reviewers. Ackroyd took the view that no reviewer, not even the most scrupulous or disinterested, could be completely honest if his copy were signed and he preserved the confidence of his contributors with all the high-minded zeal of an editor who knows that he is hardly likely to be presented with a court injunction. Dalgliesh suspected that the most vicious reviews were written by Ackroyd himself, abetted by his wife, and indulged a private picture of Conrad and Nellie sitting up in their separate beds and calling their happier inspirations through the open communicating door.

201

Whenever he was with them he was struck anew by the self-sufficiency amounting to conspiracy of their connubial felicity. If ever there were a marriage of convenience, this was it. She was a superb cook. He loved food. She liked nursing, and he suffered each winter from a mild recurrent bronchitis and from attacks of sinus headache which exacerbated his mild hypochondria and which kept her happily busy with chest rubs and inhalations. Dalgliesh, although the least prurient of men about the sex lives of his friends, couldn't resist wondering occasionally whether the marriage had ever been consummated. On the whole he thought that it had. Ackroyd was a stickler for legality and on one honeymoon night at least he must have closed his eyes and thought of England. After which necessary sacrifice to legal and theological requirements they had both settled down to the more important aspects of matrimony, the decoration of their house and the state of Conrad's bronchial tubes.

He hadn't come empty-handed. His hostess was a passionate collector of 1920s and 1930s girls' school stories, her series of early Angela Brazil being particularly notable. The shelves of her sitting room were witness to her addiction for this potent nostalgia; stories in which a succession of sloping-bosomed heroines, bloused and booted, called Dorothy or Madge, Marjorie or Elspeth, whacked hockey sticks with vigour, exposed the cheat in the upper fourth or were instrumental in unmasking German spies. Dalgliesh had found his first edition some months earlier in a second-hand bookshop in Marylebone. The fact that he couldn't recall precisely when or where reminded him how long it had been since he had last seen the Ackroyds. He suspected that they were most often visited by people who, like himself, wanted something, usually information. Dalgliesh reflected again on the oddness of human relationships in which people could describe themselves as friends who were content not to see each other for years, yet when they did meet could resume their intimacy as if there had been no interval of neglect. But their mutual liking was genuine enough. Dalgliesh might only call when there was something he needed, but he was never less than glad to sit in Nellie Ackroyd's elegant sitting room and gaze out through the Edwardian conservatory to the shimmer of the canal. Resting his eyes on it now, it was difficult to believe that this light-dappled water seen through hanging baskets of variegated ivy and pink geraniums was the same which, a couple of miles upstream, slid like a liquid menace through the dark tunnels and flowed sluggishly past the south door of St Matthew's Church.

202

He handed over his offering with the customary chaste kiss which seemed to have become a social convention even among comparatively recent acquaintances.

'For you,' he said. 'I think it's called *Dulcy on the Game*.'

Nellie Ackroyd unwrapped it with a little squeak of pleasure.

'Don't be naughty, Adam. *Dulcy Plays the Game*. How lovely! And it's in perfect condition. Where did you find it?'

'In Church Street, I think. I'm glad you haven't got it already.'

'I've been looking for it for years. This completes my pre-1930 Brazils. Conrad, darling, look what Adam has brought.'

'Very civil of you, dear boy. Ah, here comes tea.'

It was brought in by an elderly maid and set down in front of Nellie Ackroyd with almost ritual care. The tea was substantial. Thin crustless bread and butter, a plate of cucumber sandwiches, homemade scones with cream and jam, a fruitcake. It reminded him of childhood rectory teas, of visiting clergy and parish workers balancing their wide-brimmed cups in his mother's shabby but comfortable drawing room, of himself, carefully schooled, handing round plates. It was odd, he thought, that the sight of a coloured plate of thinly cut bread and butter could still evoke a momentary but sharp pain of grief and nostalgia. Watching Nellie as she carefully aligned the handles, he guessed that all their life was governed by small diurnal rituals; early morning tea, the cocoa or milk last thing at night, beds carefully turned down, nightdress and pyjamas laid out. And now it was five fifteen, the autumn day would soon be darkening into evening and this small, very English tea ceremony was designed to propitiate the afternoon furies. Order, routine, habit, imposed on a disorderly world. He wasn't sure that he would like to live with it, but as a visitor he found it soothing and he didn't despise it. He had, after all, his own contrivances for keeping reality at bay. He said:

'This piece in the *Review*. I hope you're not thinking of turning the paper into a new gossip magazine.'

'Not at all, dear boy. But people like an occasional titbit. I'm thinking of including you in our new column, "What They Find to Talk About".' Incongruous people seen dining together. Adam Dalgliesh, poet-detective, with Cordelia Gray at Mon Plaisir, for example.'

'Your readers must lead very dull lives if they can find vicarious excitement in a young woman and myself virtuously eating duck à l'orange.'

'A beautiful young woman dining with a man over twenty years her senior is always interesting to our readers. It gives them hope. And you're looking very well, Adam. The new adventure obviously suits you. All right, I meant the new job, of course. Aren't you in charge of the sensitive crime squad?'

'It doesn't exist.'

'No, that's my name for it. The Met probably call it C3A or something equally boring. But we know about it. If the Prime Minister and the leader of the Social Democrats imbibe arsenic while secretly dining together to plan a coalition and the Cardinal Archbishop of Westminster and His Grace of Canterbury are seen tiptoeing mysteriously from the scene we don't want the local CID charging in to dirty the carpets with their size twelves. Isn't that rather the idea?'

'A fascinating if unlikely scenario. What about the editor of a literary review found battered to death and a senior detective observed tiptoeing from the scene? Your piece about Paul Berowne, Conrad, what started it off?'

'An anonymous communication. And you needn't assume a look of pained disgust. We all know that your people sit in pubs paying out taxpayers' money to the most sordid ex-cons for information received, most of it no doubt of highly dubious accuracy. I know all about snouts. And I didn't even have to pay for this. It came through the post, free and gratis.'

'Who else had it, do you know?'

'It went to three of the dailies, to the gossip writers. They decided to wait and see before using it.'

'Very prudent. You checked it.'

'Naturally I checked it. At least Winifred did.'

Winifred Forsythe was nominally Ackroyd's editorial assistant but there were few jobs connected with the *Review* that she couldn't turn her hand to and there were those who claimed that it was Winifred's financial nous that kept the journal afloat. She had the appearance, dress and voice of a Victorian governess, an intimidating woman who was accustomed to getting her own way. Perhaps because of some atavistic fear of female authority, few people stood up to her and when Winifred asked a question she expected to get an answer. There were times when Dalgliesh wished that he had her on his staff.

Ackroyd said:

'She began by telephoning the Campden Hill Square house and asking for Diana Travers. A woman answered, not Lady Berowne

204

or Lady Ursula. Either a servant or housekeeper, Winifred said she didn't sound like a secretary, not authoritative enough, not that competent kind of voice. Anyway, Berowne never had a living-in secretary. It was probably the housekeeper. When she heard the question there was a silence and she gave a kind of gasp. Then she said: "Miss Travers isn't here, she's left." Winifred asked if they had an address and she said: "No" and put down the receiver rather sharply. It wasn't well handled. If they wanted to conceal the fact that Travers had worked there they should have schooled the woman more efficiently. There was no mention at the inquest that the girl had worked for Berowne and no one else seems to have caught on to it. But it looked as if our poison pen was right in at least one of his facts. Travers was certainly known at Campden Hill Square.'

Dalgliesh asked:

'And after that?'

'Winifred went down to the Black Swan. I have to admit her cover story wasn't particularly convincing. She told them that we were thinking of doing an article on drowning accidents in the Thames. We could confidently expect that no one would have heard of the *Paternoster Review* so that the essential incongruity of it wouldn't be apparent. Even so, everyone was remarkably cagey. The proprietor – what's his name, some Frenchman? – wasn't there when Winifred called but the people she did talk to had been well rehearsed. After all, no restaurant owner wants a death on the premises. In the midst of life we are in death, but not, one hopes, in the midst of dinner. Dropping unfortunate live lobsters into boiling water is one thing – really, how can people believe that they don't feel it? – but a drowned customer on the premises is quite another. Not that the Thames exactly counts as his premises, but the general theory holds. Much too close to be comfortable. From the moment one of the party she was with came dripping in to say the girl was dead, he and his staff took up their defensive positions and I must say they seemed to have carried it off very neatly.'

Dalgliesh didn't say that he had already studied the local police reports. He asked:

'What happened exactly? Did Winifred find out?'

'The girl, Diana Travers, came with a party of five friends. I gather they were mostly theatrical people, on the fringe anyway. No one well known. They got a little noisy after dinner and went out to the riverbank where there was a certain amount of larking about. That isn't encouraged at the Black Swan, tolerated if you're a

205

young viscount with the right connections no doubt, but this particular lot weren't rich enough, aristocratic enough, or famous enough for that kind of licence. The owner was wondering whether to send someone out to remonstrate when the party moved further downstream and more or less out of earshot.'

Dalgliesh said:

'Presumably they'd paid their bill by then.'

'Oh yes, everything settled.'

'Who paid?'

'Now this may surprise you. Dominic Swayne, Barbara Berowne's brother. It was his party. He booked the table, he paid.'

Dalgliesh said:

'The young man must have plenty of money if he could settle a bill for six at the Black Swan. Why wasn't he a member of his sister's birthday party?'

'Now that wasn't a question Winifred thought it would be productive to ask. But it did occur to her that he might have held his own party on the same night to embarrass his sister or, of course, her escort.'

It had also occurred to Dalgliesh. He recalled the police report. There had been six in the party; Diana Travers, Dominic Swayne, two female drama students whose names he couldn't recall, Anthony Baldwin, a stage designer, and Liza Galloway, who was taking a course in stage management at the City College. None had a criminal record, and it would have been a matter of mild surprise if they had. None had been investigated by the Thames Valley police and that wasn't surprising either. There had been nothing suspicious, at least on the surface, about the Travers death. She had dived naked into the Thames and drowned with unspectacular efficiency, in twelve feet of reed-infested water on a warm summer night.

Ackroyd went on with his story:

'Apparently the party had the good sense, from the restaurant's point of view, not to carry a dead and weed-wrapped body straight through the french windows into the dining room. Luckily the side door which leads to the kitchen quarters was the one closest. The girls rushed in bleating that one of their party had drowned, while Baldwin, who seems to have behaved with more good sense than the rest of them, was trying to give the girl the "kiss of life", not very efficiently. The chef ran out and took over with rather more expertise and worked on her until the ambulance arrived. By then she was dead by any criteria. She probably had been from the moment they brought her out. But you know all this. Don't tell me that you haven't studied the inquest report.'

Dalgliesh said:

'Did Winifred ask whether Paul Berowne had been there that evening?'

'Yes, she did, with as much tact as she's capable of. Apparently he was expected. He had some business that prevented him joining the party for dinner but he said that he would try to get there in time for coffee. Just before ten there was a telephone call to say that he had been delayed and couldn't make it. The interesting thing is that he was there . . . at least his car was.'

'How did Winifred discover that?'

'Well, I must say, by a great deal of cleverness and even more good luck. You know the car park at the Black Swan presumably?'

Dalgliesh said:

'No, I've never been there. It's a pleasure to come. Tell me.'

'Well, the proprietor dislikes the sound of cars arriving and leaving and I don't blame him, so the park is about fifty yards from the restaurant and surrounded by a high beech hedge. They haven't got valet parking, presumably that would be too expensive. People just have to walk the fifty yards and if it's raining they drop their guests at the door first. So the car park is secluded and reasonably private. Even so, the doorman does keep an eye on it from time to time and it occurred to Winifred that Berowne would hardly leave his car there if he were actually telephoning to say that he couldn't arrive. After all, any of the party might have taken it into their heads to leave soon afterwards and would have recognized it. So she made some further inquiries further down the lane. There's a kind of lay-by just before you reach the A3 opposite a farm cottage lying a little back from the road. She inquired there.'

Dalgliesh asked:

'On what pretext?'

'Oh she just said that she was a private inquiry agent trying to trace a stolen car. People will answer almost anything as long as you ask with sufficient assurance. You should know that, my dear Adam.'

Dalgliesh said:

'And she struck lucky.'

'Indeed she did. A boy, he's fourteen, was doing his homework upstairs in his front bedroom in the cottage and saw a black Rover parked. Being a boy he was naturally interested. He was quite definite about the make. It was there from about ten o'clock and was still there when he went to bed.'

'Did he get the number?'

'No, that would have meant going out of the house, of course, and he wasn't sufficiently intrigued to take that kind of trouble. What interested him was that there was only one man in the car. He parked it, locked it, and walked off towards the Black Swan. It's not unusual to have cars parked there, but they're usually courting couples and they stay in the car.'

'Was he able to give a description?'

'Only a very general one, but as far as it went it corresponded more or less with Berowne. I'm satisfied myself that it was his car and that he was there. But I admit there's no proof. It was ten at night when the boy glimpsed him and there are no lights in the lane. I couldn't be certain that he was at the Black Swan when Diana Travers drowned and as you'll have noticed from my piece, I very carefully didn't say that he was.'

'Did you check it with your lawyers before you printed it?'

'Indeed I did. They weren't exactly happy but they had to admit that it wasn't libellous. After all, it was purely factual. Our gossip always is.'

And gossip, thought Dalgliesh, was like any other commodity in the marketplace. You only received it if you had something of value to give. And Ackroyd, one of London's most notorious gossips, had a reputation for accuracy and value. He collected small titbits of information as other men hoarded screws and nails. They might not be wanted for the job on hand but sooner or later they would come in useful. And he liked the sense of power which gossip gave him. Perhaps it reduced for him the vast amorphous city to manageable proportions, a few hundred people who counted in his world and who gave him the illusion of living in a private village, intimate but diverse and not unexciting. And he wasn't vicious. He liked people and he enjoyed pleasing his friends. Ackroyd crouched spider-like in his study and spun his web of mild intrigue. It was important to him that at least one thread connected him to a senior police officer as others, rather stronger, did to the parliamentary lobby, the theatre, Harley Street, the Bar. Almost certainly he would have tapped his sources, ready to offer Dalgliesh a small bonus of information. Dalgliesh thought it was time he fished for it. He said:

'What do you know of Stephen Lampart?'

'Not a great deal, since nature has mercifully spared me the experience of childbirth. Two dear friends had their babies at his place in Hampstead, Pembroke Lodge. Everything went very well; an heir to a dukedom and a future merchant banker, both safely delivered and both boys, which, after a succession of girls, was what was wanted. He's reputedly a good gynaecologist.'

'What about women?'

'Dear Adam, how prurient you are. Being a gynaecologist must present particular temptations. Women after all are so ready to show their gratitude in the only way some of the poor dears know. But he protects himself, and not only where his sex life is concerned. There was a libel case eight years ago. You may remember it. A journalist, Mickey Case, was so ill-advised as to suggest that Lampart had carried out an illegal abortion at Pembroke Lodge. Things were a little less liberal in those days. Lampart sued and got exemplary damages. It ruined Mickey. There's not been a hint of scandal since. There's nothing like a reputation for being litigious to save you from slander. It is occasionally rumoured that he and Barbara Berowne are rather more than cousins but I don't think anyone has actual proof. They've been remarkably discreet, and Barbara Berowne, of course, played the part of the MP's adoring and beautiful wife to perfection when called upon to do so, which wasn't very often. Berowne was never a social chap. A small dinner party occasionally, the usual mild constituency beanfeasts, fund raising and so on. But otherwise, she wasn't required to exhibit herself in that particular role inconveniently often. The odd thing about Lampart is that he spends his life delivering babies but he dislikes children intensely. But then I rather agree with him. Up to four weeks they're quite enchanting. After that all one can say in favour of children is that they eventually grow up. He took his own precautions against procreation. He's had a vasectomy.'

'How on earth did you get to know that, Conrad?'

'My dear boy, it isn't a secret. People used to boast about it. When he first had it done he used to wear one of those revolting ties advertising the fact. A little vulgar, I admit, but then there is a streak of vulgarity in Lampart. He keeps it under better control now, the vulgarity I mean. The tie is folded away in a drawer along, no doubt, with other mementos from his past.'

And this indeed was a bonus, thought Dalgliesh. If Barbara Berowne were pregnant and Lampart wasn't the father, then who was? If it were Berowne himself and he had known of the fact, would he have been more or less likely to have killed himself? A jury would probably think less likely. To Dalgliesh, who had never believed the suicide theory, this wasn't particularly relevant. But it would be highly relevant to the prosecution if he caught his man and the case came to trial.

Ackroyd said:

'How did you get on with the formidable Lady Ursula? Had you met her before?'

'No. In my life, I don't often meet the daughter of an earl. Until now I haven't met one in my job either. What should I think of her? You tell me.'

'What everyone wants to know about her – everyone of her generation, anyway – is why she married Sir Henry. Now I happen to know the answer. I've thought it out all on my own. You may think my theory is obvious but it's none the worse for that. It explains why so many beautiful women choose such ordinary men. It's because a beautiful woman – and I'm talking about beauty, not just prettiness – is so ambivalent about her beauty. With part of her mind she knows it's the most important thing about her. Well, of course, it is. But with another part she distrusts it. After all, she knows how transitory it is. She has to watch it fading. She wants to be loved for some other quality, usually one she doesn't possess. So when Lady Ursula got tired of all the importunate young men badgering and praising her she chose dear old Henry who had loved her devotedly for years, would obviously continue to love her until he died, and seemed not to notice that he'd got himself the most admired beauty in England. Apparently it worked out very well. She gave him two sons and was faithful to him, well, more or less. And now, poor dear, she's left with nothing. Her father's title became extinct when her only brother was killed in 1917. And now this. Unless, of course, Barbara Berowne is pregnant with an heir which, on the face of it, seems unlikely.'

Dalgliesh asked:

'Isn't that the least important part of the tragedy, the extinction of the baronetcy?'

'Not necessarily. A title, particularly an old one, confers a comforting sense of family continuity, almost a kind of personal immortality. Lose it and you really begin to understand that all flesh is grass. I'll give you a word of advice, my dear Adam. Never underestimate Lady Ursula Berowne.'

Dalgliesh said:

'I'm in no danger of that. Did you ever meet Paul Berowne?'

'Never. I knew his brother, but not well. We met when he was first engaged to Barbara Swayne. Hugo was an anachronism, more like a First World War hero than a modern soldier. You half-expected to see him slapping his cane against khaki breeches, carrying a sword. You expect his kind to get killed. They're born for it. If they didn't, what on earth would they do with themselves in old age? He was very much the favourite son, of course. He was the kind of man his mother understood, was brought up with, that mixture of physical beauty, recklessness and charm. I began to get interested in Paul Berowne when we decided to do that short feature, but I admit that most of my information about him is second hand. Part of Paul Berowne's private tragedy, admittedly a small one viewed sub specie aeternitatis, was neatly summed up by Jane Austen. "His temper might, perhaps, be a little soured by finding, like many others of his sex, that through some unaccountable bias in favour of beauty he was the husband of a very silly woman." *Pride and Prejudice*, Mr Bennet.'

'*Sense and Sensibility*, Mr Palmer. And when one meets Barbara Berowne the bias doesn't seem so very unaccountable.'

'*Sense and Sensibility*? Are you sure? Anyway, I'm glad that I'm immune to that particular enthralment and the urge for possession that seems inseparable from it. Beauty suborns the critical faculty. God knows what Berowne thought he was getting, apart from a load of guilt. Probably the Holy Grail.'

All in all, thought Dalgliesh, the visit to St John's Wood had been even more fruitful than he had hoped. He took his time over finishing his tea. He owed his hostess at least the appearance of a decent civility and he had no particular wish to hurry away. Soothed by Nellie Ackroyd's solicitous attention, comfortably ensconced in a gently rocking button-backed armchair whose arms and headrest seemed precisely designed to suit his body, and with his eyes soothed by the distant sheen of the canal seen through the light-filled conservatory, he had to make an effort to rouse himself to make his farewells and set off to drive back to the Yard, pick up Kate Miskin and take her with him to interview Berowne's only child.

5

Melvin Johns hadn't intended to make love. He had met Tracy at
their usual place, the gate leading to the towpath, and they had
walked together, her arm tucked under his, her thin body tugging
against him until they came to their secret place, the patch of
flattened grass behind the thick elderberries, the straight, dead
stump of tree. And it had happened, as he knew it would. The
brief, unsatisfactory spasm and what went before were no different
than they had always been. The potent smell of loam and dead
leaves, the soft earth under his feet, her eager body straining under
his, the smell of her armpits, her fingers scratching at his scalp, the
scrape of the bark of the tree against his cheek, the gleam of the
canal seen through a thicket of leaves. All over. But afterwards the
depression that always followed was worse than he had ever
known. He wanted to sink into the earth and groan aloud. She
whispered:

'Darling, we have to go to the police. We must tell them what we
saw.'

'It wasn't anything. Just a car parked outside the church.'

'Outside the vestry door. Outside where it happened. The same
night. And we know the time, about seven o'clock. It could be the
murderer's car.'

'It isn't likely he'd be driving a black Rover, and it isn't as if we
noticed the number, even.'

'But we have to tell. If they never find who did it, if he kills again,
we'd never forgive ourselves.'

The note of unctuous self-righteousness nauseated him. How
was it, he wondered, that he'd never noticed before that perpetual
whine in her voice. He said hopelessly:

'You said your dad would kill us if he knew we'd been meeting.
The lies, telling him you were at evening classes. You said he'd kill
us.'

'But, darling, it's different now. He'll understand that. And we
can get engaged. We'll tell them all that we were engaged.'

Of course, he thought, suddenly enlightened. Dad, that respectable lay preacher, wouldn't mind as long as there was no scandal.
Dad would enjoy the publicity, the sense of importance. They
would have to marry. Dad, Mum, Tracy herself, would ensure that.

It was as if his life was suddenly revealed to him in a slow unwinding reel of hopelessness, picture succeeding picture down the inescapable years. Moving into her parents' small house; where else could they afford to live? Waiting for a council flat. The first baby crying in the night. Her whining, accusing voice. The slow death, even of desire. A man was dead, an ex-minister, a man he had never known, never seen, whose life and his had never until this moment touched. Someone, his murderer or an innocent motorist, had parked his Rover outside the church. The police would catch the killer, if there was a killer, and he would go to prison for life and in ten years he would be let out, free again. But he was only 21 and his life sentence would end only with his death. And what had he done to deserve his punishment? Such a little sin compared with murder. He almost groaned aloud with the injustice of it.

'All right,' he said with dull resignation. 'We'll go to the Harrow Road police station. We'll tell them about the car.'

6

Sarah Berowne's flat was in a gaunt Victorian terrace of five-storey houses whose over-ornate and grimy façade was set back some thirty feet from the Cromwell Road behind a hedge of dusty laurel and spiky, almost leafless privet. Next to the entry-phone was a bank of nine bells, the top one bearing only the single word 'Berowne'. The door opened to their push as soon as they rang and Dalgliesh and Kate passed through a vestibule into a narrow hall, the floor linoleum-covered, the walls painted the ubiquitous glossy cream, the only furniture a table for letters. The caged box of a lift was only large enough for two passengers. Its back wall was almost completely mirrored, but as it groaned slowly upwards, the image of their two figures standing so close that he could smell the clean sweet scent of her hair, could almost imagine that he could hear her heart beat, did nothing to dispel his incipient claustrophobia. They stopped with a jerk. As they stepped out into the corridor and Kate turned to close the lift grille he saw that Sarah Berowne was standing waiting for them at her open door.

The family resemblance was almost uncanny. She stood framed against the light from her flat like a frail feminine shadow of her father. Here were the same wide spaced grey eyes, the same droop of the eyelid, the same finely boned distinction but devoid of the patina of masculine confidence and success. The fair hair, not layered in gold like Barbara Berowne's but darker, almost ginger, already showed its first grey and hung in dry lifeless strands framing the tapering Berowne face. She was, he knew, only in her early twenties but she looked much older, the honey-coloured skin drained with weariness. She didn't even bother to glance at his warrant card and he wondered whether she didn't care or was making a small gesture of contempt. She gave only a nod of acknowledgement as he introduced Kate, then stood aside and motioned them across the hall into the sitting room. A familiar figure rose to meet them and they found themselves facing Ivor Garrod.

Sarah Berowne introduced them but didn't explain his presence. But then there was no reason why she should; this was her flat, she could invite in whom she wished. It was Kate and he who were the interlopers, there at best by invitation or on sufferance, tolerated, seldom welcome.

After the dimness of the hall and the claustrophobic lift they had walked into emptiness and light. The flat was a conversion from the mansard roof, the low sitting room running almost the whole length of the house, its northern wall composed entirely of glass with sliding doors opening on to a narrow balustraded balcony. There was a door at the far end, presumably leading to the kitchen. The bedroom and bathroom would, he assumed, open from the entrance-hall at the front of the house. Dalgliesh had developed a knack of taking in the salient features of a room without that preliminary frank appraisal which he himself would have found offensive from any stranger, let alone a policeman. It was odd, he sometimes thought, that a man morbidly sensitive about his own privacy should have chosen a job that required him to invade almost daily the privacy of others. But people's living-space, and the personal possessions with which they surrounded themselves, were inevitably fascinating to a detective, an affirmation of identity, intriguing both in themselves and as a betrayal of character, interests, obsessions.

This room was obviously both her living room and her studio. It was sparsely but comfortably furnished. Two large and battered sofas sat against opposite walls with shelves over them for books, stereo and a drinks cupboard. Before the window there was a small round table with four dining chairs. The wall facing the window was covered with a cork board on which was pinned a collection of photographs. To the right were pictures of London and Londoners obviously designed to make a political point; couples over-dressed for a Palace garden party drifting across the grass of St James's Park against the background of the bandstand; a group of Blacks in Brixton staring resentfully into the lens; the Queen's Scholars of Westminster School filing decorously into the Abbey; an over-crowded Victorian playground with a thin wistful-eyed child grasping the railings like an imprisoned waif; a woman with a face like a fox choosing a fur in Harrods; a couple of pensioners, gnarled hands curled in their laps sitting stiff as Staffordshire figures one each side of their single-bar electric fire. The political message was, he thought, too facile to carry much weight but, as far as he was capable of judging, the pictures were technically clever; they were certainly well composed. The left of the board displayed what had probably been a more lucrative commission: a line of portraits of well-known writers. Some of the photographer's concern with social deprivation seemed to have infected even her work here. The men, unshaven, fashionably under-dressed in their tieless open-necked shirts, looked as if they had either just taken part in a literary discussion on Channel Four, or were on their way to a 1930s labour exchange, while the women looked either haunted or defensive, except for a buxom grandmother noted for her detective stories, who gazed mournfully at the camera as if deploring either the bloodiness of her craft or the size of her advance.

Sarah Berowne motioned them to the sofa at the right of the door and seated herself on the one opposite. It was hardly, thought Dalgliesh, a convenient arrangement for other than shouted conversation. Garrod perched himself on the arm of the sofa further from her as if deliberately distancing himself from all three of them. In the last year he had, it seemed deliberately, moved out of the political limelight and was now less often heard propounding the views of the Workers' Revolutionary Campaign, concentrating, apparently, on his job as a community social worker, whatever that might mean. But he was immediately recognizable, a man who even in repose held himself as if well aware of the power of his physical presence but with that power under conscious control. He was wearing denim jeans with a white open-necked shirt and contrived to look both casual and elegant. He could, thought Dalgliesh, have stepped down from a portrait in the Uffizi with his long arrogant Florentine face, the generously curved mouth under the short upper lip, the high arched nose and tumble of dark hair, the eyes which gave nothing away. He said:

'Would you like something to drink? Wine, whisky or coffee?'

His tone was almost studiously polite, but neither sardonic nor provocatively obsequious. Dalgliesh knew his opinion of the Metropolitan Police; he had proclaimed it often enough. But he was playing this very carefully. They were all to be on the same side, at least for the present. Dalgliesh and Kate refused his offer of a drink and there was a small silence broken by Sarah Berowne. She said:

'You're here about my father's death, of course. I don't think there's very much I can say to help. I haven't seen or spoken to him for over three months.'

Dalgliesh said:

'But you were at 62 Campden Hill Square on Tuesday afternoon.'

'Yes, to see my grandmother. I had an hour to spare between appointments and I wanted to try to find out what was happening, my father's resignation, the rumour about his experience in that church. There was no one else to ask, to talk to. But she was out to tea. I didn't wait. I left at about four thirty.'

216

'Did you go into the study?'

'The study?'

She looked surprised, then asked:

'I suppose you're thinking of his diary. Grandmama told me that you'd found it half-burned in the church. I was in the study but I didn't see it.'

Dalgliesh said:

'But you knew where he kept it?'

'Of course. In the desk drawer. We all knew that. Why do you ask?'

Dalgliesh said:

'Just in the hope that you might have seen it. It would have been useful to know if the diary was there at four thirty. We can't trace your father's movements after he left the office of an estate agent in Kensington High Street at half past eleven. If you had happened to look in the drawer and seen the diary then there is the possibility that he came back to the house unnoticed sometime during the afternoon.'

That was only one possibility and Dalgliesh didn't deceive himself that Garrod, for one, was ignorant of the others. Now he said:

'We don't even know what happened except what Sarah has learned from her grandmother, that Sir Paul and the tramp had their throats cut and that it looks as if his razor was the weapon. We were hoping you would be able to tell us more. Are you suggesting that it was murder?'

Dalgliesh said:

'Oh, I don't think there can be any doubt that this was murder.'

He watched as the two bodies opposite seemed visibly to stiffen, then added calmly:

'The tramp, Harry Mack, certainly didn't slit his own throat. His death may not be of shattering social significance but no doubt his life had some importance, at least to him.'

He thought: If that doesn't provoke Garrod then I wonder what would. But Garrod merely said:

'If you're asking us to provide an alibi for Harry Mack's murder, then we were here together from six o'clock on Tuesday until nine o'clock Wednesday morning. We had supper here. I bought a mushroom flan from Marks and Spencer's in Kensington High Street and we ate that. I could tell you what wine we drank with it but I don't suppose that's relevant.'

217

It was the first sign of irritation but his voice was still mild, the gaze clear and unflustered. Sarah Berowne said:

'But Daddy! What happened to Daddy?'

Suddenly she sounded as frightened and helpless as a lost child. Dalgliesh said:

'We're treating it as a suspicious death. We can't say much more until we get the result of the post-mortem and the forensic tests.'

Suddenly she got up and moved over to the window staring out over the thirty yards of dishevelled autumnal garden. Garrod slid down from the arm of the sofa and went to the drinks cupboard, then poured a couple of glasses of red wine. He took one over to her and offered it silently, but she shook her head. He moved back to the sofa and sat holding his own glass, not drinking. He said:

'Look, Commander, this isn't exactly a visit of condolence, is it? And although it's reassuring to hear of your concern for Harry Mack, you're not here because of a dead tramp. If Harry's body had been the only one in that church vestry it would have ranked a detective sergeant at best. I would have thought Miss Berowne had a right to know whether she's being questioned in a murder investigation or whether you're just curious to know why Paul Berowne should have slit his own throat. I mean, either he did or he didn't. Criminal investigation is your job, not mine, but I should have thought that, by now, it ought to be pretty clear cut one way or the other.'

Dalgliesh wondered whether the dreadful pun had been intentional. Either way, Garrod saw no reason to apologize for it. Watching that still figure by the window Dalgliesh saw Sarah Berowne give a little shudder. Then, as if by an act of will, she turned from the window and faced him. He ignored Garrod and spoke directly to her.

'I should like to be more positive but, at the moment, that just isn't possible. Suicide is obviously one possibility. I was hoping that you might have seen your father recently and been able to say how he seemed to you, whether he said anything that could be relevant to his death. I know this is painful for you. I'm sorry that we have to ask these questions, that we have to be here.'

She said:

'He did speak to me once about suicide, but not in the way you mean.'

'Recently, Miss Berowne?'

'Oh no, we haven't spoken for years. Not really spoken, really talked to each other as opposed to making sounds with our mouths.

218

No, this was when I was home from Cambridge after my first term. One of my friends had killed himself and my father and I talked about his death, about suicide generally. I've always remembered it. He said that some people thought of suicide as one of the options open to them. It wasn't. It was the end of all options. He quoted Schopenhauer: "Suicide may be regarded as an experiment, a question which man puts to nature trying to force her to an answer. It is a clumsy experiment to make; for it involves the destruction of the very consciousness which puts the question and awaits the answer." Daddy said that while we live there is always the possibility, the certainty of change. The only rational time for a man to kill himself is not when life is intolerable but when he would prefer not to live it even if it became tolerable, even pleasant.'

Dalgliesh said:

'That sounds like the ultimate despair.'

'Yes. I suppose that's what he could have felt, ultimate despair.'

Suddenly Garrod spoke. He said:

'He could more reasonably have quoted Nietzsche. "The thought of suicide is a great consolation: by means of it one gets successfully through many a bad night."'

Ignoring him, Dalgliesh still spoke directly to Sarah Berowne. He said:

'So your father didn't see you or write to you? He didn't explain what had happened in that church, why he was giving up his job, his parliamentary seat?'

He almost expected her to say: 'What has that to do with this inquiry and what has it to do with you?' Instead she said:

'Oh no! I don't suppose he thought that I cared one way or the other. I only learned about it when his wife telephoned me. That was when he gave up his ministerial job. She seemed to think I might have some influence over him. It showed how little she understood either of us. If she hadn't telephoned, I should have had to learn about his resignation from the newspapers.' Then she suddenly broke out:

'My God! He couldn't even get converted like an ordinary man. He had to be granted his own personal beatific vision. He couldn't even resign his job with decent reticence.'

Dalgliesh said mildly:

'He seems to have acted with considerable reticence. He obviously felt that it was a private experience to be acted upon rather than discussed.'

'Well, he could hardly splash it on the front pages of the Sunday heavies. Perhaps he realized that he'd only make himself ridiculous. Himself and the family.'

Dalgliesh asked:

'Would that have mattered?'

'Not to me, but Grandmama would have minded – will mind now, I suppose. And his wife, of course. She thought she was marrying the next prime minister but one. She wouldn't relish being tied to a religious crank. Well, she's free of him now. And he's free of us, all of us.'

She was silent for a moment, then said with sudden vehemence:

'I'm not going to pretend. Anyway you know perfectly well that my father and I were, well, estranged. There's no secret about it. I didn't like his politics, I didn't like the way he treated my mother, I didn't like the way he treated me. I'm a Marxist, there's no secret about that either. Your people will have me on one of their little lists somewhere. And I care about my political beliefs. I don't believe he really did. He expected me to discuss politics as if we were chatting about a recent play we'd both seen, or a book we'd read, as if it were an intellectual diversion, something you could have what he would call a civilized argument about. He said that was one of the things he deplored about the loss of religion, it meant that people elevated politics into a religious faith and that was dangerous. Well that's what politics are for me, a faith.'

Dalgliesh said:

'Feeling as you do about him, his bequest to you must present you with a dilemma of conscience.'

'Is that your tactful way of asking me if I killed my father for his money?'

'No, Miss Berowne. It's a not particularly tactful way of finding out what you feel about a not uncommon moral dilemma.'

'I feel fine, just fine. There's no dilemma as far as I'm concerned. Anything I get will be put to good use for a change. It won't be much. Twenty thousand, isn't it? It's going to need more than twenty thousand pounds to change this world.'

Suddenly she went back to the sofa, sat down, and they saw that she was crying. She said:

'I'm sorry, I'm sorry. This is ridiculous. It's only shock. And tiredness. I didn't sleep much last night. And I've had a busy day, things I couldn't cancel. Why should I cancel them, anyway? There's nothing I can do for him.'

The phenomenon wasn't new to him. Other people's tears, other people's grief were inseparable from a murder inquiry. He had

220

learned not to show surprise or embarrassment. The response varied, of course. A cup of hot, sweet tea if there was someone around to make it, a glass of sherry if the bottle was to hand, a slug of whisky. He had never been good at the comforting hand on the shoulder, and here, he knew, it wouldn't be welcome. He felt Kate stiffen at his side as if to make an instinctive move towards the girl. Then she looked at Garrod, but Garrod didn't move. They waited silently. The sobbing was quickly checked and Sarah Berowne again raised her face to them. She said:

'I'm sorry, I'm sorry. Please don't mind me. I'll be all right in a minute.'

Garrod said:

'I don't think there's anything else we can usefully tell you but if there is, perhaps it could wait until another time. Miss Berowne is upset.'

Dalgliesh said:

'I can see that. If she wants us to go, of course we shall.'

She looked up and said to Garrod:

'You go. I'm all right. You've said what you came to say. You were here with me on Tuesday night, all night. We were together. And there's nothing you can say about my father. You never knew him. So why don't you go?'

Dalgliesh was surprised by the sudden venom in her voice. Garrod could have hardly welcomed this curt dismissal, but he was too controlled and too astute to protest. He looked at her with what seemed detached interest rather than resentment and said:

'If you need me, just ring.'

Dalgliesh waited until he was at the door then said quietly:

'One moment. Diana Travers and Theresa Nolan. What do you know about them?'

Garrod was motionless for a second then swung slowly round. He said:

'Only that they're both dead. I do occasionally see the *Paternoster Review*.'

Dalgliesh said:

'The recent article about Sir Paul in the *Review* was partly based on a scurrilous communication sent to him and to a number of papers. This communication.'

He took it from his briefcase and handed it to Garrod. There was a silence while he read it. Then, his face devoid of expression, he handed it to Sarah Berowne. He said:

'You aren't, surely, suggesting that Berowne cut his throat

221

because someone sent him an unkind letter? Wouldn't that be a little over-sensitive for a politician? And he was a barrister. If he thought it was actionable, he had his remedy.'

Dalgliesh said:

'I'm not suggesting that it provides a motive for suicide. I was wondering whether you or Miss Berowne had any idea who could have sent it?'

The girl handed it back, merely shaking her head. But Dalgliesh saw that its production had been unwelcome. She was neither a good actress nor a good liar. Garrod said:

'I admit that I took it for granted that the child Theresa Nolan aborted was Berowne's, but I didn't feel called upon to do anything about it. If I had, I'd have done something more effective than this farrago of unsubstantiated spite. I only met the girl once, at an unfortunate dinner party at Campden Hill Square. Lady Ursula was convalescent; it was her first night down. The poor girl certainly didn't look happy. But then, Lady Ursula was brought up to know what room people are entitled to dine in and, of course, their proper placement at table. Nurse Nolan, poor child, was eating out of her station and was made to feel it.'

Sarah Berowne said softly:

'Not intentionally.'

'Oh, I didn't say it was intentional. Women like your grand-mother are offensive merely by existing. Intention doesn't come into it.'

Then without touching Sarah Berowne, without even a glance at her, he said his goodbyes to Kate and Dalgliesh as formally as if they had been fellow guests at a dinner party, and the door closed behind him. The girl tried to control herself, then broke into open sobbing. Kate got up, went through the opposite door and after what seemed to Dalgliesh an unnecessarily long time, came back with a glass of water, then sat down beside Sarah Berowne and silently offered it. The girl drank it thirstily, then said:

'Thank you. This is silly. It's just that I can't believe he's dead, that I'll never see him again. I suppose I always thought that sometime, somehow, things would be right between us. I suppose I thought that there was plenty of time. All the time in the world. They've all gone now, Mummy, Daddy, Uncle Hugo. Oh God, I feel so hopeless.'

There were things that he would liked to have asked but now wasn't the time. They waited until she was calm again and then asked if she was sure she was all right before they left. The

222

question struck him as insincere, a formal hypocrisy. She was as right as she would ever be when they were there.

As they drove away Kate was for a time silent, then she said:

'It's an all-electric kitchen, sir. There's one wrapped packet of four boxes of Bryant and May matches in the cupboard, that's all. But that doesn't prove anything. They could have bought a single box and chucked it away afterwards.'

Dalgliesh thought: She was fetching the glass of water showing genuine sympathy, genuine concern. But her mind was still on the evidence. And some of my officers think women are more sentimental than men. He said:

'We shan't get much joy trying to trace a single box of matches. A safety match is the easiest thing to lay hands on, the most difficult to identify.'

'There's another thing, though, sir. I looked in the waste bin. I found the cardboard packet from the Marks and Spencer mushroom flan. They ate it all right, but it was two days past its last marked date of sale on Tuesday. He couldn't have bought it then. Since when have Marks and Spencer sold stale food? I wasn't sure whether you'd want the package or not.'

Dalgliesh said:

'We haven't yet a right to take anything out of that flat. It's too early. You could argue that it's a clue in their favour. If they'd planned this crime I suspect Garrod would have bought the food on Tuesday morning and have made sure that the girl at the desk remembered him. And there's another thing, they've produced an alibi for the whole night. That suggests that they may not know the relevant time.'

'But isn't Garrod too clever to fall into that trap?'

'Oh, he wouldn't produce an alibi neatly timed for eight o'clock, but the somewhat over-generous one he has produced to cover every hour from six to nine the next morning does suggest that he's playing safe.'

And like the other alibis it wouldn't be an easy one to break. They had briefed themselves before this visit as they did before every interview. They knew that Garrod lived alone in a single-bedroom mansion flat in Bloomsbury, a large, anonymous block, without a porter. If he claimed to have spent the night elsewhere it was difficult to see who could prove otherwise. Like everyone else concerned with the case whom they had interviewed to date, Sarah Berowne and her lover had produced an alibi. The police might not consider it a particularly convincing one, but Dalgliesh had too high an opinion of Garrod's intelligence to suppose that it could be easily broken and certainly not by a date stamp on the carton of a mushroom flan.

Back at the Yard, Dalgliesh had hardly entered his office before Massingham came in. He prided himself on his ability to control his excitement and his voice was carefully nonchalant.

'Harrow Road have just been on the phone, sir. There's an interesting development. A couple walked into the station ten minutes ago, a 21-year-old and his girl. They say they were on the towpath on Tuesday evening, courting apparently. They passed through the turnstile of St Matthew's just before seven. There was a large black Rover parked outside the south door.'

'Did they get the number?'

'No such luck. They can't even be sure of the make. But they are definite about the time. The girl was expected home by seven thirty and they looked at their watches just before leaving the towpath. And the boy, Melvin Johns, thinks that it could have been an A registration. Harrow Road think he's telling the truth. The poor kid seems petrified. He's certainly not a nutcase looking for publicity. They've asked the couple to wait until I get over.' He added:

'That parking lot by the church could be useful for anyone who knew it. But the local people obviously prefer to park their cars where they can keep an eye on them. And it isn't as if the area has a theatre, fashionable restaurants. For my money, there's only one black Rover one might expect to see parked outside that church.'

Dalgliesh said:

'That's premature, John. It was dusk, they were in a hurry. They can't even be sure of the make.'

'You're depressing me, sir. I'd better get over there. It'll be just my luck to discover it was the local undertaker's hearse!'

7

She knew that Ivor would come back that night. He wouldn't telephone first, partly out of excessive caution, partly because he always expected her to be there waiting when she knew he was likely to arrive. For the first time since they had become lovers she found herself dreading his signal, the one long ring of the entry-phone followed by the three short. Why couldn't he telephone, she thought resentfully, let her know when to expect him? She tried to settle to work on her newest project, the montage of two black-and-white photographs taken last winter in Richmond Park of the naked boughs of huge oak trees under a sky of tumbling clouds, and which she now planned to mount, one reversed under the other, so that the tangled boughs looked like roots reflected in water. But it seemed to her as she shifted the prints with increasing dissatisfaction that the device was meaningless, a cheap derivative effect; that this, like all her work, was symbolic of her life, thin, insubstantial, second-hand, pilfered from other people's experience, other people's ideas. Even the London pictures, cleverly composed, were without conviction, stereotypes seen through Ivor's eyes not her own. She thought: I must learn to be my own person, however late, however much it hurts, I have to do it. And it seemed to her strange that it should have taken her father's death to show her what she was.

At eight o'clock she was aware of hunger and cooked herself scrambled eggs, stirring them carefully over the slow flame, taking as much trouble as if Ivor had been there to share them. If he did arrive while she was eating he could cook his own. She washed up and he still hadn't arrived. Walking out to the balcony she gazed over the garden to the darkening bulk of the opposite terrace whose windows were beginning to light up like signals from space. Those unknown people would be able to see her window too, the huge expanse of lighted glass. Would the police call on them, ask them whether they had seen a light here on Tuesday night? Had Ivor, for all his cleverness, thought of that?

Gazing out over the darkness she made herself think of her father. She could recall the precise moment at which things had changed between them. They had been living then in the Chelsea house, just her parents, herself and Mattie. It had been seven

225

o'clock on a misty August morning and she had been alone in the dining room, pouring her first cup of coffee, when the call came. She had answered the telephone from the hall and had been given the news just as her father came down the stairs. He had seen her face, stopped, his hand on the banister and she had looked up at him.

'It's Uncle Hugo's Colonel. He wanted to ring himself. Daddy, Hugo's dead.' And then their eyes had met, had for a moment held, and she had seen it clearly; the mixture of exultation and wild hope, the knowledge that now he could have Barbara. It had lasted only a second. Time had moved on. And then he had taken the receiver from her and, without speaking, she had walked back into the dining room, through the french windows and into the enclosing greenness of the garden shaking with the horror of it.

Nothing afterwards could ever be right between them. Everything that followed, the car accident, her mother's death, his marriage to Barbara less than five months later, had seemed only the inevitable consequence of that moment of realization, not willed by him, not even connived at, but accepted as inescapable. And even before the marriage the enormity of that mutual knowledge made it impossible for them to meet each other's eyes. He was ashamed that she knew. She was ashamed of knowing. And it seemed to her that when they moved into Hugo's house, the house which from their first moment of possession had seemed to resent and reject them, she carried her knowledge like a secret infection, that if Halliwell, Mattie, her grandmother knew, they had caught the knowledge from her.

At Campden Hill Square she and her father had been like fellow guests at a hotel who had met by chance, aware of a shared and shameful history, creeping down the passages in case the other should suddenly appear, planning to take meals at different times, harassed by the knowledge of the other's presence, the footstep in the hall, the key in the door. Ivor had been her escape and her revenge. She had been desperate for a cause, for an excuse to distance herself from her family, for love; but most of all for revenge. Ivor, whom she had met when he had commissioned a series of photographs, had provided them all. Before her father's marriage to Barbara she had moved out, borrowing against her modest legacy from her mother's will to put down a deposit on the Cromwell Road flat. She had tried, by embracing with passion everything he most disliked or despised, to free herself of her father. But now he was gone and she would never be free of him, never again.

One of the dining chairs was still pulled out from the table. Here, only yesterday, her grandmother had painfully seated herself and told her the news in brutal monosyllables, the taxi-meter ticking away outside. She had said:

'No one expects you to show much grief but try, when the police arrive, as they will, to behave with reasonable discretion. If you have any influence over him, persuade your lover to do the same. And now perhaps you could help me with the lift door.'

She had always been a little afraid of her grandmother, knowing from childhood that she was a disappointment, that she should have been a son. And she had none of the qualities her grandmother admired; beauty, intelligence, wit, not even courage. There was no comfort for her in that cluttered top-floor sitting room at Campden Hill Square where the old lady had sat since Hugo's death like some archaic prophetess awaiting the inevitable doom. It was her father who had always come first with her, in her childhood and afterwards. It was her father who had been the more supportive when she had left Cambridge at the end of her first year and had gone to a London polytechnic to study photography. How much had she really cared about her mother's anguish when the infatuation with Barbara became obvious? Wasn't it just that she had hated the threat to her comfortable, ordered, conventional life, resented the fact that, entranced, her father no longer seemed even to notice her? Perhaps, she thought, the belated acknowledgement of that old jealousy was one small step towards becoming her own person.

It was after eleven before he arrived, and she was very tired. He made no excuses and wasted no time on preliminaries. Throwing himself down on the sofa, he said:

'It wasn't very clever, was it? The idea of my being here was to have a witness. You let yourself be left alone with probably the most dangerous detective of the Yard and a female sidekick brought along to reassure you that he wasn't going to stop behaving like a gentleman.'

She said:

'Don't worry. I didn't reveal the Boy Scout password. And they're human, I suppose. Inspector Miskin was rather kind.'

'Don't be ridiculous. The girl's a fascist.'

'Ivor, how can you say that? How can you know?'

'I make it my business to know. I suppose she held your hand, made you a nice cup of tea.'

'She fetched me a drink of water.'

'Which gave her an excuse to ferret around in the kitchen without the trouble of getting a search warrant.'

She cried:

'It wasn't like that! She wasn't like that!'

'You haven't an idea what any of the police are like. The trouble with you middle-class liberals is that you're conditioned to see them as allies. You never accept the truth about them. You can't. To you they're always the avuncular Sergeant Dixon tugging his forelock and telling the kids the time. It's what you're brought up on. "If you're ever in difficulty, darling, if a nasty man approaches you and wiggles his johnny at you, always find a policeman." Look, Dalgliesh knows your politics, he knows about the legacy, he knows you've got a lover who's a committed Marxist and who might like to get his hands on the cash for the best or worst of reasons. So he's got a motive and a suspect, a very satisfactory suspect from his point of view, just what the Establishment are hoping for. Then he can get down to the business of fabricating the evidence.'

'You don't really believe that.'

'For Christ's sake, Sarah, there are precedents. You can't have lived for over twenty years with your eyes shut. Your grand-mother prefers to believe that her son wasn't a murderer or a suicide. Fair enough. She may even persuade the police to play along with her fantasy. She's nearly in her dotage but these old women still have extraordinary influence. But she's not making me the sacrificial victim to Berowne family pride. There's only one way to treat the police. Tell them nothing, nothing. Let the bastards find out the hard way. Make them do some work for their index-linked pensions.'

She said:

'I suppose if it really comes to it you'll let me tell them where I was Tuesday night?'

'If it comes to what? What are you talking about?'

'If they actually arrest me.'

'For cutting your father's throat? Is it likely? Come to think of it, a woman could have done it. Given a razor it wouldn't need much strength, only immense nerve. But it would have to be a woman he trusted, one who could get close to him. That could explain why there wasn't a struggle.'

She said:

'How do you know that there wasn't a struggle, Ivor?'

'If there had been, the press and the police would have said so. It

228

would have been one of the strongest indications that it wasn't suicide. You must have read the sort of thing they print: "Sir Paul put up a desperate struggle for life. There were considerable signs of disorder in the room." Your father killed himself, but that doesn't mean that the police won't use his death to make nuisances of themselves.'

She said:

'Suppose I decide to tell?'

'Tell what? Give them the code names of eleven people whose addresses, whose real names you don't even know? Give them the address of a suburban terraced house where they'll find nothing incriminating? The moment a police officer sets foot in the safe house the cell is disbanded, reformed, rehoused. We're not fools. There is a procedure for treachery.'

'What procedure? Throwing me in the Thames? Slitting my throat?'

She saw the surprise in his eyes. Was it her imagination that it was tinged with respect? But he only said:

'Don't be ridiculous.'

He unwound himself from the sofa and made for the door. But there was something she needed to ask. Once she would have been afraid, she was still a little afraid, but perhaps it was time to take a small step towards courage. She said:

'Ivor, where were you on Tuesday night? You've never been late for a cell meeting before, you've always been there before the rest of us. But it was after ten past nine before you arrived.'

'I was with Cora at the bookshop and there was a hold-up on the tube. I explained at the time. I wasn't at St Matthew's Church cutting your father's throat, if that's what you're implying. And until the police are forced to accept that he killed himself we'd better not meet. If it's necessary I'll be in touch in the usual way.'

'And the police? Suppose they come back?'

'They'll come back. Stick to the alibi and don't try to be clever. Don't embroider. We were here together from six o'clock all night. We ate a mushroom flan, we drank a bottle of Riesling. All you have to do is to remember what we did on Sunday night and transpose it to Tuesday. Don't think you're doing me any great favour, it's yourself you need to protect.'

And without touching her he was gone. So that, she thought wearily, was how love ended, with the slam of a grille door, the grind of the lift bearing him slowly downwards out of her life.

BOOK FOUR

Devices and Desires

1

The Black Swan, despite its name, didn't derive from a riverside pub but from an elegant two-storey villa built at the turn of the century by a prosperous Kensington painter seeking a weekend retreat with country quiet and a river view. After his death it had suffered the usual vicissitudes of a private residence too damp and inconveniently situated to be suitable as a permanent home and too large for a weekend cottage. It had been a restaurant of sorts for twenty years under its original name, but hadn't flourished until Jean Paul Higgins took it over in 1980, renamed it, built on a new dining room with wide windows overlooking the river and the far water meadows, employed a French chef, Italian waiters, and an English doorman, and set out to win his first modest mention in *The Good Food Guide*. Higgins's mother had been a Frenchwoman and he had obviously decided that, as a restaurateur, it was that half of his parentage he had better emphasize. His staff and customers called him Monsieur Jean Paul and it was only his bank manager who, to his chagrin, insisted on greeting him with cheerful exuberance as Mr Higgins. He and his bank manager were on excellent terms and for the best of reasons: Mr Higgins was doing very well. In the summer it was necessary to book a table for luncheon or dinner at least three days in advance. In autumn and winter the place was less busy and the luncheon menu offered only three main dishes but the standard of cooking and service never varied. The Black Swan was close enough to London to attract a number of city regulars willing to drive twenty odd miles for the Black Swan's peculiar advantages; an attractive ambience, tables spaced at a reasonable distance, a low noise level, no piped music, unostentatious service, discretion and excellent food.

Monsieur Jean Paul was small and dark with melancholy eyes and a thin moustache which made him look like a stage Frenchman, an impression strengthened when he spoke. He himself greeted Dalgliesh and Kate at the door with unflurried courtesy as if there were nothing he had been looking forward to more than a visit from the police. But Dalgliesh noticed that despite the early hour and the quietness of the house, they were shown into his private office at the rear of the building with the minimum of delay. Higgins was of the school which believes, not without

233

reason, that even when the police come visiting in plainclothes and don't actually kick down the door, they are always unmistakably the police. Dalgliesh didn't miss his quick glance of appraisal at Kate Miskin, the quickly suppressed look of surprise changing to modified approval. She was wearing slacks in fawn gaberdine with a well-cut, unobtrusive checked jacket over a rollneck cashmere jumper and with her hair bound back in a short, thick plait. Dalgliesh wondered what Higgins expected a plainclothes policewoman to look like, an over-made-up harpy in black satin and a trenchcoat?

He offered refreshment, at first carefully ambiguous about the kind, and then more specific. Dalgliesh and Kate accepted coffee. It came quickly, served by a young waiter in a short white jacket, and it was excellent. When Dalgliesh had swallowed his first sip, Higgins gave a small sigh of relief as if his guest, now irrevocably compromised, had lost some of his power.

Dalgliesh said:

'As I expect you know, we are investigating the death of Sir Paul Berowne. You may have information which can help fill in some of the background.'

Jean Paul spread his palms and launched into his voluble Frenchman act. But the melancholy eyes were wary.

'The death of Sir Paul, so terrible, so tragic. I ask myself what the world is coming to when such violence is possible. But how can I help the Commander? He was murdered in London, not here, thank God. If it was murder. There's a rumour that, maybe, Sir Paul himself . . . But that, too, would be terrible, more terrible for his wife than murder, perhaps.'

'He came here regularly?'

'From time to time, not regularly. He was a busy man, of course.'

'But Lady Berowne was here more often, usually with her cousin, I understand?'

'A delightful lady. She adorned my dining room. But, of course, one does not always notice who is dining with whom. We concentrate on the food and the service. We are not gossip writers, you understand.'

'But presumably you can remember whether she was dining with her cousin, Mr Stephen Lampart, on the Tuesday of this week, just three days ago?'

'On the seventeenth. That was so. They were seated at twenty minutes to nine. It is a little foible of mine, to note the time the customer is actually seated. The booking was for eight forty-five but they were a little early. Monsieur may wish to inspect the book.'

He opened his desk drawer and produced it. Obviously, thought Dalgliesh, he had been expecting a visit from the police and had placed the evidence to hand. The time against the name Lampart was written clearly and there was no sign that the figures had been altered.

He asked:

'When was the table booked?'

'That morning. At ten thirty, I believe. I cannot, I regret, be more precise.'

'Then he was fortunate to get it.'

'We can always find a table for an old and valued customer, but it is, of course, easier if a booking is made. The notice was sufficient.'

'How did Mr Lampart and Lady Berowne seem when they arrived?'

The dark eyes lifted reproachfully to his as if in silent protest at so tactless a question.

'How should they seem, Commander? Hungry.' Then he added as if fearing the answer had been imprudent:

'They were as usual. The lady is always gracious, most friendly. They were content that I was able to give them their usual table, in the corner by the window.'

'What time did they leave?'

'At eleven or a little after. One does not hurry a good dinner.'

'And during dinner? They talked presumably.'

'They talked, monsieur. It is a pleasure of dining, to share good food, good wine and good talk with a friend. But as for what they said, we are not eavesdroppers, Commander. We are not the police. These are good customers you understand.'

'Unlike some of the customers you had here on the night Diana Travers drowned. You had time to notice them, I suppose?'

Higgins showed no surprise at the sudden change in questioning. He spread his hands in a Gallic gesture of resignation.

'Alas, who could overlook them? They were not the kind of client we usually attract. At dinner they were quiet enough but afterwards, well, it was not agreeable. I was relieved when they left the dining room.'

'Sir Paul Berowne wasn't with his wife's party, I understand.'

'That is so. When they arrived, Mr Lampart said that Sir Paul hoped to join them later, in time for coffee. But as you may know, he telephoned at ten o'clock or a little later maybe and said that it would not, after all, be possible.'

'Who took the call?'

235

'My doorman, Henry. Sir Paul asked to speak to me and I was called to the telephone.'

'Did you recognize his voice?'

'As I have said, he was not here so very often, but I knew his voice. It was a voice, how you say, a distinctive voice, surprisingly like your own, Commander, if I may be permitted to say so. I cannot swear to these things, but I had no doubt at the time who was speaking.'

'Have you any doubt now?'

'No, Commander, I cannot say that I have.'

'The two parties for dinner, Mr Lampart's and the young people, did they mix, greet each other?'

'They may have done, on arrival, but the tables were not close.' He would have seen to that, thought Dalgliesh. If there had been the slightest sign of embarrassment on Barbara Berowne's part, or of insolence on her brother's, Higgins would have noticed it.

'And the members of Diana Travers's party, had you ever seen them here before?'

'Not that I remember, except for Mr Dominic Swayne. He has dined here once or twice with his sister, but the last time was some months ago. But for the others, I cannot be sure.'

'It was strange, surely, that Mr Swayne wasn't included in Lady Berowne's birthday party?'

'Monsieur, it is not for me to dictate which guests my customers should invite. No doubt there were reasons. There were four only in the birthday group, an intimate party. The table was balanced.'

'But would have become unbalanced if Sir Paul had arrived?'

'That is so, but then he was expected only for coffee and he was, after all, the lady's husband.'

Dalgliesh went on to ask Higgins about the events leading up to the drowning.

'As I have said, I was glad when the young people left the dining room and went out through the conservatory to the garden. They took two bottles of wine with them. It was not the best claret but for them it was good enough. I do not like to see my wine swung about as if it were beer. There was much laughter and I was wondering whether to send Henry or Barry to deal with them, but they moved along the bank out of earshot. It was there that they found the punt. It was tied up, wedged you might say, in a small inlet about eighty yards upstream. Now, of course, it has been

236

removed. Perhaps it should not have been there, but how can I blame myself? They were not children although they behaved like children. I cannot control what my patrons do when they are off the premises, nor indeed when they are here.'

He used the word blame but the regret was perfunctory. No voice could have held less concern. Dalgliesh suspected that the only thing Higgins ever blamed himself for was a spoilt dinner or poor service. He went on:

'The next thing I know is the chef beckoning me from the door of the dining room. That was unusual, you understand. Immediately I could see something is wrong. I go quickly out. In the kitchen is one of the girls crying and saying that this other girl, Diana, is dead, drowned. We go out to the riverbank. The night is dark, you understand, the stars high and the moon not full. But there is some light from the car park which is always brightly lit, and some from the kitchen wing of the house. But I take with me a torch. Monsieur may imagine the distress. The girls crying, one of the young men working on the body, Mr Swayne standing there with his clothes dripping. Marcel takes over the respiration – he has many talents, that one – but it is of no use. I could see she was dead. The dead are not like the living, monsieur, never, never, never.'

'And the girl was naked?'

'As you no doubt have been told. She had taken off all her clothes and dived in for a swim. It was a great folly.'

There was a silence while he contemplated the folly. Then Dalgliesh put down his coffee cup. He said:

'It was convenient that Mr Lampart should have been dining that night. It was natural, of course, to call on him for help.'

The dark eyes, carefully expressionless, looked straight into his.

'That was my first thought, Commander. But it was too late. When I reached the dining room, I was told that Mr Lampart's party had only that moment left. I myself saw the Porsche as it turned out of the drive.'

'So Mr Lampart could have been fetching his car from the park shortly before you learned of the tragedy?'

'That is possible, certainly. I understand that the rest of his party waited at the door.'

'Surely an early, and somewhat hurried, end to the evening?'

'As to hurried, that I cannot say. But the party had been seated early, shortly after seven. If Sir Paul had been able to join them, no doubt they would have stayed later.'

Dalgliesh said:

'There has been a suggestion that Sir Paul may have arrived here that night after all.'

'I have heard that, Commander. There was a woman who came to question my staff. It was not agreeable. I was not here at the time but I would have dealt with her. No one saw Sir Paul on that night I assure you. And his car was not seen in the parking lot. It may have been there but it was not seen. And how can this concern his death I ask myself.' Dalgliesh could usually tell when he wasn't getting the truth or was getting only part of it. It was less a matter of instinct than of experience. And Higgins was lying. Now he decided to take a chance. He said:

'But someone did see Sir Paul Berowne that night. Who was it?'

'Monsieur, I assure you . . .'

'I need to know and I'm quite prepared to hang around until I do. If you want to get rid of us, a perfectly reasonable wish on your part, you'll succeed most quickly by answering my questions. The verdict at the inquest was accidental death. No one, to my knowledge, has suggested that it was anything else. She had eaten too much, drunk too much, she got caught in the reeds and panicked. It is of academic interest whether she died of shock or was drowned. So what are you hiding and why?'

'We are hiding nothing, Commander, nothing. But as you have just said, the death was an accident. Why then make trouble? Why add to distress? And one cannot be sure. A figure quickly walking, glimpsed in the darkness, in the shadow of the hedge, who can tell who it was?'

'So who was it saw him? Henry?'

It was less a lucky guess than a reasonable assumption. Berowne almost certainly hadn't shown himself on the premises and the doorman was the member of staff most likely to have been outside.

'It was Henry, yes.' Higgins admitted the fact with a sad defeatism. The mournful eyes gazed reproachfully at Dalgliesh as if to say: 'I have been helpful, I have given you information and coffee, and look where it has led me.'

'Then perhaps you'll send for him. And I'd like to speak to him alone.'

Higgins lifted the telephone receiver and dialled a single digit. It connected him to the front entrance. Henry answered it and was summoned. When he appeared, Higgins said:

'This is Commander Dalgliesh. Please tell him what you thought you saw the night that girl was drowned.' Then he gave him a half-rueful glance, shrugged his shoulders and left. Henry, unruffled, stood at attention. Dalgliesh saw that he was older than his confident, upright figure would suggest. Certainly nearer seventy than sixty.

He said:

'You're ex-Army, aren't you?'

'That's right, sir, the Gloucesters.'

'How long have you been working here for Mr Higgins, for Monsieur Jean Paul?'

'Five years, sir.'

'You live in?'

'No, sir. The wife and I, we live at Cookham. This place is handy as places go.' He added, as if hoping that a personal touch would demonstrate his willingness to cooperate frankly: 'I've got my Army pension but a little extra never hurts.'

And it wouldn't be so little, thought Dalgliesh. The tips would be good and most of them, given human frailty about the depredations of the Inland Revenue, would be tax free. Henry would want to keep his job.

He said:

'We're investigating the death of Sir Paul Berowne. We're interested in anything that happened to him during the last weeks of his life, however unimportant and irrelevant it might seem. Apparently he was here on the night of the seventh of August and you saw him.'

'Yes, sir, crossing the car park. One of our guests that night was leaving and I was fetching his Rolls. We haven't valet parking, sir, it would take me off the door too often. But occasionally guests like to have their cars parked and they hand me their keys on arrival. Antonio, he's one of the waiters, gave me the word that my party was ready to leave and I went for the car. I was standing there putting the key in the lock when I saw Sir Paul cross the car park walking along the line of the hedge and out through the gate leading to the river.'

'How certain are you it was Sir Paul Berowne?'

'Pretty certain, sir. He isn't here often but I've a good eye for faces.'

'Do you know what car he drives?'

'A black Rover, I think. An A registration. I can't remember the number.' Couldn't or wouldn't, thought Dalgliesh. A black Rover would be difficult to identify; a registration number was irrefutable evidence. He asked:

'And there was no black Rover parked that night?'

'Not that I noticed, sir, and I think I would have noticed.'

'And you said he was walking briskly?'

'Very briskly, sir, purposefully you might say.'

'When did you tell Monsieur Jean Paul about this?'

'The next morning, sir. He said that there was no need to tell the police. Sir Paul had a right to walk by the river if he chose. He said we had better wait until the inquest. If there had been marks on the body, any suggestion of foul play, that would be different. The police would want to know the names of anyone who had been here that night. But it was accidental death. The coroner was satisfied that the young lady had herself dived into the river. After that, Monsieur Jean Paul decided we should say nothing.'

'Even after Sir Paul's death?'

'I don't think Monsieur thought the information would be helpful, sir. Sir Paul Berowne was dead. How could it matter if he'd taken a walk by the river six weeks earlier.'

'Have you told this story to anyone else? Anyone at all? Your wife, a member of the staff here?'

'To no one, sir. There was a lady came inquiring. I was off sick that day. But even if I'd been here, I would have said nothing, not unless Monsieur had told me it was all right.'

'And about ten minutes after you saw him walking across the car park, Sir Paul rang to say he wouldn't be arriving after all?'

'Yes, sir.'

'Did he say where he was ringing from?'

'No, sir. It couldn't have been from here. The only public telephone we have is in the hall. There's a telephone kiosk in Mapleton, that's the nearest village, but I happen to know that it was out of order that night. My sister lives there and wanted to ring me. There's no box nearer, not that I know of. That call was a proper mystery, sir.'

'When you mentioned the matter next day, what did you and Monsieur think Sir Paul might have been doing here? I take it you discussed it.'

Henry paused, then he said:

'Monsieur thought Sir Paul might have been keeping an eye on his wife.'

'Spying on her?'

'I suppose it was possible, sir.'

'By walking along the riverbank?'

'It doesn't seem very likely, not put like that.'

'And why should he have wished to spy on his wife?'

240

'I can't say, I'm sure, sir. I don't think Monsieur was serious. He just said: "It is none of our business, Henry. Maybe he is keeping an eye on her Ladyship."'

'And that's all you can tell me?'

Henry hesitated. Dalgliesh waited. Then he said:

'Well, there is something else, sir. But it seems daft when I come to think about it. The car park is well lit, sir, but he was walking quickly and in the shadow of the hedge at the far side. But there was something about the way his jacket was clinging, his trousers, too. I think, sir, he'd been in the river, and that's why I say it was daft. He wasn't walking away from the river, sir, he was walking towards it.'

He looked from Dalgliesh to Kate, his eyes puzzled as if the full peculiarity of it had only now struck him.

'I'll swear he was wet, sir, soaking wet. But like I said, he was walking towards the river, not away from it.'

Dalgliesh and Kate had driven separately to the Black Swan. She was returning directly to the Yard and he driving north-east to Wrentham Green to lunch with the Chairman and Vice-Chairman of Berowne's constituency party. They would meet at the Yard in the mid-afternoon to attend the brief formalities of the preliminary inquest before going on to what promised to be a more interesting appointment, to interview Paul Berowne's mistress. As Kate unlocked the door of her Metro he said:

'We'd better have a word with the couple who were dining here with Mr Lampart and Lady Berowne on August the seventh. They might be able to say when exactly Lampart left the table to fetch the car, how long he was away. Get their names and addresses, will you, Kate? I suggest from the lady, rather than Lampart. And it would be useful to know more about the mysterious Diana Travers. According to the police report on the drowning she emigrated with her parents to Australia in 1963. They stayed, she came back. Neither of them came over for the inquest or the funeral. Thames Valley had some difficulty in finding someone to identify her. They dug up an aunt and she made the funeral arrangements. She hadn't seen her niece for over a year but she had absolutely no doubt about the identification. And while you're at number sixty-two, see if you can get anything more out of Miss Matlock about the girl.'

Kate said:

'Mrs Minns might be able to tell us something, sir. We're seeing her first thing tomorrow.' She added:

'There was one thing Higgins said about the Travers drowning which struck me as odd. It doesn't tie up.'

241

So she had noticed the anomaly. Dalgliesh said:

'It seems to have been an evening for river sports. It was almost as odd as Henry's story. Paul Berowne with his wet clothes clinging to him, but walking towards the river, not away from it.'

Kate still lingered, her hand on the car door. Dalgliesh gazed out over the high beech hedge which separated the car park from the river. The day was changing. The early morning air had held a brittle and transitory brightness, but now the storm clouds, forecast for the afternoon, were rolling in from the west. But it was still warm for early autumn and there came to him as he stood in the almost deserted car park, cleansed of the smell of hot metal and petrol, the scent of river water and sun-warmed grasses. He stood for a moment savouring it like a truant, feeling the pull of the water, wishing that there were time to follow the wraith of that dripping figure through the gateway to the peace of the riverbank. Kate, coming out of her momentary trance, opened the car door and slid in. But she seemed to have shared his mood. She said:

'It all seems so far away from that dingy Paddington vestry.' He wondered if she was implying, not daring to say:

'It's Berowne's murder we're supposed to be investigating, not the coincidental drowning of a girl he may hardly have seen.'

But now, more than ever, he was convinced that the three deaths were linked, Travers, Nolan, Berowne. And the main purpose of their visit to the Black Swan had been achieved. Lampart's alibi held. Even driving a Porsche it was hard to see how he could have killed Berowne and still been seated by eight forty.

2

With the electrification of the north-east suburban line, Wrentham Green had increasingly become a commuter town despite the protestations of its older inhabitants that it was a county town of character not a dormitory suburb of London. The town had woken up sooner than some of its less vigilant neighbours to the post-war despoliation of England's heritage by developers and local authorities, and had checked the worst excesses of that unholy alliance just in time. The broad eighteenth-century high street, although desecrated by two modern multiple stores, was essentially intact, and the small close of Georgian houses facing the river was still regularly photographed for Christmas calendars even if it required some contortions on the part of the photographer to exclude the end of the car park and the municipal lavatories. It was in one of the smaller houses of the close that the Constituency Conservative Party had its headquarters. Passing through the porticoed door with its gleaming brass plate, Dalgliesh was met by the Chairman, Frank Musgrave, and the Vice-Chairman, General Mark Nollinge.

As always he had prepared himself for the visit. He knew more about both of them than he suspected either would have thought necessary. Together in amicable harness they had for the last twenty years run the local Party. Frank Musgrave was an estate agent who ran a family business, still independent of the large conglomerates, which he had originally inherited from his grandfather. From the number of house boards Dalgliesh had noticed on his drive through the town and the neighbouring villages, the business was flourishing. The single word, 'Musgrave', bold black lettering on white, had met him at every turn. Its reiteration had become an irritating, almost premonitory, reminder of his destination.

He and the General were an incongruous pair. It was Musgrave who at first sight looked like a soldier, indeed his resemblance to the late Field-Marshal Montgomery was so marked that Dalgliesh wasn't surprised to hear him speak in a parody of that formidable warrior's staccato bark. The General barely came up to his shoulder. He held his slight body so rigidly that it seemed as if his vertebrae were fused, and his bald head, tonsured with fine white hair, was speckled as a thrush's egg. As Musgrave made the introductions he

243

looked up at Dalgliesh with eyes as innocently candid as a child's, but strained and puzzled as if he had looked too long on unattainable horizons. In contrast to Musgrave's formal business suit and black tie, the General was wearing an ancient tweed jacket cut according to some personal whim with two oblong patches of suede on each elbow. His shirt and regimental tie were immaculate. With his shining face he had the polished vulnerability of a well-tended child. Even in the first minutes of casual conversation the mutual respect of the two men was immediately apparent. Whenever the General spoke, Musgrave would gaze from him to Dalgliesh with the slightly anxious frown of a parent, worried lest his offspring's brilliance should be underrated.

Musgrave led the way through the wide hall, down a short passage to the room at the back of the house which Berowne had used as his office. He said:

'Kept it locked since Berowne's death. Your people rang, but we'd have locked it anyway. The General and I thought it the right thing to do. Not that there's anything here to shed light. Shouldn't think so, anyway. Welcome to look, of course.'

The air smelt stale and dusty, almost sour, as if the room had been locked for months rather than days. Musgrave switched on the light, then strode over to the window and vigorously tugged back the curtains with a rattle of rings. A thin northern light filtered through the plain nylon curtains beyond which Dalgliesh could see a small walled car park. He had seldom, he thought, been in a more depressing room, and yet it was difficult to explain why he should feel this sudden weight of dejection. The room was no worse than any of its kind, functional, uncluttered, impersonal, and yet he felt that the very air he breathed was infected by melancholy.

He said:

'Did he stay in this house when he was in the constituency?'

'No. Just used this room here as an office. He always stayed at the Courtney Arms. Mrs Powell kept a bed for him. It was cheaper and less trouble than having a flat in the constituency. Talked occasionally about asking me to find one, but it never came to anything. I don't think his wife was keen.'

Dalgliesh asked casually:

'Did you see very much of Lady Berowne?'

'Not a lot. Did her bit, of course. Annual fête, appearances at the local elections, that sort of thing. Decorative and gracious all round. Not much interested in politics, would you say, General?'

'Lady Berowne? No, not greatly. The first Lady Berowne was different, of course. But then, the Manstons have been a political family for four generations. I used to wonder sometimes whether Berowne entered politics to please his wife. I don't think he felt the same commitment after she was killed.'

Musgrave gave him a sharp glance as if this were a heresy, previously unacknowledged, which even now was better left unspoken. He said quickly:

'Yes, well, water under the bridge. A sad business. He was driving at the time. I expect you've heard.'

Dalgliesh said:

'Yes. I had heard.'

There was a short, uncomfortable pause during which it seemed to him that the golden image of Barbara Berowne glimmered, unacknowledged and disturbing, in the still air.

He began his examination of the room, aware of the General's anxious, hopeful gaze, of Musgrave's sharp eyes on him as if watching a trainee clerk taking his first inventory. Set in the middle of the floor and facing the window was a solid Victorian desk and a button-backed swivel chair. In front of it were two smaller leather armchairs. There was a modern desk with a heavy old-fashioned typewriter to one side and two more chairs and a low coffee table in front of the fireplace. The only memorable piece of furniture was a bureau-bookcase with brass bound panes which occupied the recess to the right of the fireplace. Dalgliesh wondered if his companions knew its value. Then he guessed that respect for tradition would forbid its sale. Like the desk, it was part of the room, inviolate, not to be disposed of for a quick profit. Strolling over to it, he saw that it held an oddly assorted collection of reference books, local guides, biographies of notable Tory politicians, *Who's Who*, parliamentary reports, Stationery Office publications, even a few classical novels, apparently gummed together by immutable time.

On the wall behind the desk was a copy of a well-known oil portrait of Winston Churchill with a large colour photograph of Mrs Thatcher hung to its right. But it was the picture above the fireplace which immediately caught the eye. Moving to it from the bookcase, Dalgliesh saw that it was an eighteenth-century oil painting by Arthur Devis of the Harrison family. The young Harrison, legs elegantly crossed in their satin breeches, stood with proprietorial arrogance beside a garden seat on which sat his thin-faced wife, her arm round a young child. A small girl sat demurely beside her holding a basket of flowers, while to the left her brother's arm was raised to the string of a kite, luminous in the summer sky. Behind the group stretched a gentle English land-scape in high summer, smooth lawns, a lake, a distant manor house. Dalgliesh recalled from his interview with Anthony Farrell that Musgrave had been left a Devis. This, presumably, was it. The General said:

'Berowne brought it here from Campden Hill Square. He moved the Churchill portrait and hung it here instead. There was some feeling about it at the time. The Churchill had always hung over the mantelpiece.'

Musgrave had moved up beside Dalgliesh. He said:

'I'll miss that picture. Never tired of looking at it. It was painted in Hertfordshire, only six miles from here. You can still see that landscape. The same oak tree, same lake. And the house. It's a school now. My grandfather was agent when it was sold. It couldn't be anywhere else but England. I never knew that painter's work till Berowne brought it here. Rather like a Gainsborough, isn't it? But I'm not sure I don't like it better than that one in the National Gallery – Mr and Mrs Robert Andrews. The women are a bit alike, though, aren't they? Thin-faced, arrogant, wouldn't care to be married to either of them. But it's lovely, lovely.'

The General said quietly:

'I'll be relieved when the family send for it. It's a responsibility.'

So neither of them knew about the legacy, unless they were better actors than he thought likely. Dalgliesh kept a prudent silence, but he would have given much to have seen Musgrave's face when he learned of his good luck. He wondered what spurt of quixotic generosity had prompted the gift. It was surely an exceptionally generous way of rewarding political loyalty. And it was an irritating complication. Common sense and imagination protested at the thought of Musgrave slitting a friend's throat to possess a picture, however obsessively desired, which there was no evidence he even knew had been willed to him. But in the normal course of human life he would have been lucky to have outlived Berowne. He had been at the Campden Hill Square house on the afternoon of Berowne's death. He could have taken the diary. He almost certainly knew that Berowne used a cut-throat razor. Like everyone else who benefited from the death, he would have to be tactfully investigated. It was almost certainly a waste of effort; it would take time; it complicated the main thrust of the inquiry; but it still had to be done.

They were, he knew, waiting for him to talk about the murder. Instead he walked over to the desk and seated himself in Berowne's chair. That, at least, was comfortable, fitting his long limbs as if made for him. There was a thin film of dust on the desk surface. He pulled open the right-hand drawer and found nothing but a box of writing paper and envelopes, and a diary similar to the one found by the body. Opening it, he saw that it contained only engagements and an *aide-mémoire* for the days he spent in his constituency. Here, too, his life had been ordered, compartmentalized.

Outside, a thin drizzle was beginning to fall, misting the window, so that he saw the brick wall of the car park and the bright curved roofs of the cars as if in a pointillist oil painting. What burden, he wondered, had Berowne brought with him into this sunless and depressing office? Disenchantment with the second job to which he had committed himself? Guilt over his dead wife, his failed marriage? Guilt over the mistress whose bed he had so recently left? Guilt over his neglect of his only child, over the baronetcy which had been rightly his brother's? Guilt because that better loved elder son was dead and he was still alive? 'Most of the things I expected to value in life have come to me through death.' And had there been, perhaps, a more recent guilt, Theresa Nolan, who had killed herself because she had aborted a child? His child? And what was there for him here amid these files and papers, mocking in their meticulous order his disordered life, but the Catch 22 of the well-intentioned? The miserable batten on their victims. If you provide them what they crave, open your heart and mind to them, listen with sympathy, they come in ever increasing numbers, draining you emotionally and physically until you have nothing left to give. If you repel them they don't come back and you're left despising yourself for your inhumanity. He said:

'I suppose this room is the place of last resort.'

It was Musgrave who understood him the quicker.

'Nine times out of ten that's what it is. They've exhausted the patience of their families, DHSS staff, local authorities, friends. Then it's here. "I voted for you. Do something." Some Members like it, of course. Find it the most fascinating part of the job. They're the social workers *manqué*. I suspect he didn't. What he tried to do, seemed almost obsessed with at times, was explaining to people the limits of government power, any government. Remember the last debate on the inner cities? I was in the public gallery. There was a lot of suppressed anger in his irony. "If I understand the Honourable Member's somewhat confused argument the Government are asked to ensure equality of intelligence, talent, health, energy and wealth while, at the same time, abolishing original sin as from the beginning of the next financial year. What divine providence has singularly failed to do, Her Majesty's Government are to achieve by Statutory Order." The House didn't much like it. Not their kind of humour.'

He added:

'It was a lost battle anyway, educating the electorate in the limits of executive power. No one wants to believe it. And anyway, in a democracy there's always an opposition to tell them that anything is possible.'

The General said:

'He was a conscientious constituency MP, but it took a lot out of him, more than we realized. I think he was sometimes torn between compassion and irritation.'

Musgrave jerked open the drawer of a filing cabinet, and pulled out a file at random:

'Take this one, spinster, aged 52. In the middle of the change and feeling like hell. Dad dead. Mum at home and virtually bedridden, demanding, incontinent, getting senile. No hospital bed, and Mum wouldn't go voluntarily even if there were. Or this one. Two kids, both of them 19. She gets pregnant, they marry. Neither set of parents like it. Now they're living with the in-laws in a small terraced house. No privacy. Can't make love. Mum will hear through the walls. Baby squalling. Family saying "I told you so". No hope of a council house for another three years, maybe longer. And that's typical of what he got every Saturday. Find me a hospital bed, a house, work. Give me money, give me hope, give me love. It's partly what the job is all about, but I think he found it frustrating. I'm not saying he wasn't sympathetic to the genuine cases.'

The General said quietly:

'All the cases are genuine. Misery always is.'

He gazed out of the window to where the drizzle had now strengthened to steady rain, and then said:

'Perhaps we should have found him a more cheerful room.'

Musgrave expostulated:

'But the Member has always used this room for his surgery, General, and it's only once a week.'

The General said quietly:

'Nevertheless, when we get the new Member he should have something better.'

248

Musgrave capitulated without rancour.

'We could oust George. Or use that front room on the top floor for the surgery. But then the elderly would have to manage the stairs. I don't see how we could rehouse the bar.'

Dalgliesh half-expected him to call at once for plans and begin the reallocation, his own concerns half-forgotten. He said:

'Did his resignation come as a surprise?'

It was Musgrave who answered:

'Absolutely. A complete shock. A shock and a betrayal. It's no good beating about the bush, General. It's a bad time for a by-election, and he must have known.'

The General said:

'Hardly a betrayal. We've never seen ourselves as a marginal seat.'

'Anything under fifteen thousand is marginal these days. He should have soldiered on until the Election.'

Dalgliesh asked:

'Did he explain his reasons? I take it that he did see you both, he didn't merely write.'

Again it was Musgrave who answered:

'Oh he saw us all right. Actually deferred writing to the Chancellor until he'd told us. I was on holiday – my usual short autumn break – and he had the decency to wait until I was back. Came up here late last Friday, Friday the thirteenth appropriately enough. He said that it wouldn't be right for him to continue as our Member. It was time that his life took a different turn. Naturally I asked what he meant by a different turn. "You're a Member of Parliament," I said. "You're not driving a bloody bus." He said that he didn't know yet. He hadn't been shown. "Hadn't been shown by whom?" I asked. He said "God". Well, there's not much a man can say to that. Nothing like an answer like that for putting a stopper on rational discussion.'

'How did he seem?'

'Oh, perfectly calm, perfectly normal. Too calm. That's what was so odd about it. A bit eerie really, wouldn't you say, General?'

The General said very quietly:

'He looked to me like a man released from pain, physical pain. Pale, drawn, but very peaceful. You can't mistake the look.'

'Oh, he was peaceful enough. Obstinate too. You couldn't argue. His decision had nothing to do with politics, though. We did at least establish that. I asked him outright. "Are you disillusioned with policy, with the Party, with the PM, with us?" He said it was nothing like that. He said: "It's nothing to do with the Party. It's myself I have to change." He seemed surprised by the question, almost amused as if it were irrelevant. Well, it wasn't irrelevant to me. The General and I have given a lifetime of service to the Party. It matters to us. It's not some kind of game, a trivial pursuit that you can pick up and put down when you're bored. We deserved a better explanation and a bloody sight more consideration than we got. He seemed almost to resent having to talk about it. We could have been discussing arrangements for the summer fête.'

He began pacing the narrow room, his outrage a palpable force. The General said mildly:

'I'm afraid we were no help to him. None at all.'

'He wasn't asking for help, was he? Or for advice. He'd gone to a higher power for that. It's a pity he ever set foot in that church. Why did he, anyway? D'you know?' He shot the question at Dalgliesh like an accusation. Dalgliesh said mildly:

'Out of an interest in Victorian church architecture apparently.'

'Pity he didn't take up fishing or stamp collecting. Oh well, he's dead, poor devil. No point in feeling bitter now.'

Dalgliesh said: 'You saw that article in the *Paternoster Review*, of course?'

Musgrave had got himself under control. He said:

'I don't read that kind of journal. If I want book reviews I get them from the Sunday papers.' His tone suggested that he was occasionally given to such odd indulgencies.

'But someone read it and cut it out; it was round the constituency pretty sharply. The General's view was that it was actionable.'

General Nollinge said:

'I thought that it might be. I advised him to consult his lawyer. He said he'd think about it.'

Dalgliesh said:

'He did more than that. He showed it to me.'

'Asked you to investigate, did he?' Musgrave's tone was sharp.

'Not really. He wasn't specific.'

'Exactly. He wasn't specific about anything in those last few weeks.'

He added:

'Of course, when he first told us that he'd written to the PM and was applying for the Chiltern Hundreds, we remembered that *Review* article and braced ourselves for the scandal. Quite wrong, of course. Nothing as human or understandable. There's one odd thing, though, which we thought we'd better mention. Now that he's dead it can't do any harm. It happened on the night that girl was drowned. Diana Something-or-other.'

Dalgliesh said:

'Diana Travers.'

'That's right. He turned up here that night, well, early morning really. He didn't arrive until well after midnight but I was still here working on some papers. Something or someone had scratched his face. It was superficial, but deep enough to have bled. The scab had just formed. It could have been a cat, I suppose, or he may have fallen into a rosebush. Equally the claws could have been a woman's.'

'Did he give you any explanation?'

'No. He didn't mention it and neither did I, either then or later. Berowne had a way of making it impossible for you to ask unwelcome questions. It couldn't have had anything to do with the girl, of course. Apparently, he wasn't dining at the Black Swan that night. But afterwards when we read that article, it struck me as an odd coincidence.'

It was indeed, thought Dalgliesh. He asked, because the question was necessary, not because he expected any useful information, whether anyone in the constituency could have known that Berowne would be in St Matthew's Church on the night of his death. Catching Musgrave's sharp, suspicious glance and the General's pained frown, he added:

'We have to consider the possibility that this was a planned murder, that the killer knew he would be there. If Sir Paul told someone in the constituency – telephoned perhaps – there has to be the chance that the conversation was overheard or passed on unwittingly.'

Musgrave said:

'You're not suggesting that he was killed by an aggrieved constituent? A bit far-fetched, surely.'

'But not impossible.'

'Aggrieved constituents write to the local press, cancel their subs and threaten to vote SDP next time. Can't see this as political in any sense. Damn it, man, he'd resigned his seat. He was out, finished, spent, no danger to anyone. After that nonsense in the church no one was going to take him seriously any more.'

The General's soft voice broke in:

'Not even the family knew where he was that night. It would be strange if he told someone here when he hadn't told them.'

'How do you know, General?'

'Mrs Hurrell rang Campden Hill Square shortly after eight thirty and spoke to the housekeeper, Miss Matlock. At least, I understand that it was a young man who answered the telephone but he handed her over to Miss Matlock. Wilfred Hurrell was the agent here. He died at three o'clock the next morning in St Mary's Hospital, Paddington. Cancer, poor devil. He was devoted to Berowne and Mrs Hurrell rang Campden Hill Square because he was asking for him. Berowne had told her to ring at any time. He'd see that he could always be reached. That's what I find so odd. He knew that Wilfred hadn't long to go, yet he didn't leave a number or an address. That wasn't like him.'

Musgrave said:

'Betty Hurrell rang me afterwards to see if he were in the constituency. I wasn't at home. I hadn't got back from London by then, but she spoke to my wife. She couldn't help her, of course. A bad business.'

Dalgliesh gave no sign that the call wasn't news to him. He asked:

'Did Miss Matlock say that she'd ask any of the family whether they knew how to contact Sir Paul?'

'She just told Mrs Hurrell that he wasn't at home and that no one in the house knew where he was. Mrs Hurrell could hardly press the matter. Apparently he left home shortly after ten thirty and never returned. I called at the house just before lunch hoping to catch him, but he never came back. I expect they told you I was there.'

The General said:

'I tried to reach him later, just before six o'clock, to make an appointment for the next day. I thought it might be helpful if we could have a quiet talk. He wasn't at home then. Lady Ursula answered the telephone. She said she'd look at his diary and ring back.'

'Are you sure, General?'

'That I spoke to Lady Ursula? Oh yes. Usually Miss Matlock answers, but sometimes one gets Lady Ursula.'

'Are you sure that she said she'd consult the diary?'

'She may have said that she'd see if he were free and ring back. Something like that. Naturally I assumed that meant she would consult his diary. I said not to worry if it was any trouble. She's crippled with arthritis, you know.'

'Did she ring back?'

'Yes, about ten minutes later. She said that Wednesday morning seemed all right, but she'd ask Berowne to ring me and confirm next morning.'

Next morning. That suggested that she knew that her son wouldn't be back that night. More importantly, if she had, indeed, gone down to the study and had consulted the diary, then it had been there in the study drawer shortly after six on the day of Berowne's death. And at six o'clock, according to Father Barnes, he had arrived at the Vicarage. Here at last could be the vital clue linking the murder with Campden Hill Square. This had been a carefully planned killing. The murderer had known where to find the diary, had taken it with him to the church, had partly burned it in an attempt to add verisimilitude to the suicide theory. And that placed the heart of the murder firmly in Berowne's household. But wasn't that where he had always known that it lay?

He recalled that moment in Lady Ursula's sitting room when he had revealed the diary. The clawed hands shrivelled with age tightening on the plastic. The frail body frozen into immobility. So she had known. Shocked as she was, her mind had still been working. But would any mother shield her son's murderer? Under one circumstance he thought it possible that this mother might. But the truth was probably less complicated and less sinister. She couldn't believe that anyone she personally knew had been capable of this particular crime. She could accept only two possibilities. Either her son had killed himself or, more likely and more acceptably, his murder had been the work of casual unpremeditated violence. If Lady Ursula could bring herself to believe this, then she would see any connection with Campden Hill Square as irrelevant, a potential source of scandal and, worse, a damaging diversion of police energies from their job of finding the real killer. But he would have to question her about that telephone call. He had never in his professional life been afraid of a witness or a suspect. But this was one interview to which he wasn't looking forward. But if the diary had been in the desk at six o'clock, then at least Frank Musgrave was in the clear. He had left Campden Hill Square before two. But his suspicion of Musgrave had immediately struck him as an irrelevance. And then another thought, possibly equally irrelevant, fell into his mind. What was it that Wilfred Hurrell, lying on his deathbed, had been so anxious to say to Paul Berowne? And was it possible that someone had been determined that he shouldn't have the opportunity to say it?

Afterwards the three of them lunched together in the elegant first-floor dining room overlooking the river, now running thick and turbulent under the driving rain. As they were seated, Musgrave said:

'My great-grandfather once dined with Disraeli at this table. They looked out over much the same view.'

The words confirmed what Dalgliesh had suspected, that it was Musgrave whose family had always voted Tory and who would find any other allegiance unthinkable, the General who had come to his political philosophy by a process of thought and intellectual commitment.

It was an agreeable meal, stuffed shoulder of lamb, fresh vegetables beautifully cooked, a gooseberry tart with cream. He guessed that both his companions had tacitly agreed not to pester him with inquiries about the progress of the police investigation. They had earlier asked the obvious questions and had met his reticence with tactful silence. He was inclined to put this restraint down to a wish that he should enjoy a meal over which they had obviously taken trouble, rather than to any reluctance to discuss a painful subject, or any fear that they might let slip things best left unspoken. They were served by an elderly black-coated waiter with the face of an anxiously amiable toad, who poured an excellent Niersteiner with shaky hands, but without spilling a drop. The dining room was almost empty – there were only two couples and they were at distant tables. Dalgliesh suspected that his hosts had tactfully ensured that he should enjoy his luncheon in peace. But both men found an opportunity to give him their opinion. When, after coffee, the General remembered the need to make a telephone call, Musgrave leaned confidingly across the table:

'The General can't believe it was suicide. It isn't something he'd do himself so he can't imagine it in his friends. I'd have said the same myself once, about Berowne, I mean. Not so sure now. There's a madness in the air. Nothing's certain any more, least of all people. You think you know them, know how they'd behave. But you don't, you can't. We're all strangers. That girl now, the nurse, the one who killed herself. If it was Berowne's child she aborted, that couldn't have been easy for him to live with. Not trying to interfere, you understand. Your job, of course, not mine. But the case seems pretty straightforward to me.'

And it was in the car park when Musgrave had left them to go to his car that the General said:

'I know that Frank thinks that Berowne killed himself, but he's wrong. Not malicious, or disloyal or unkind; just wrong. Berowne wasn't the kind of man to kill himself.'

Dalgliesh said:

'I don't know whether he was or wasn't. What I am reasonably sure of is that he didn't.'

They watched in silence while Musgrave, with a final wave, negotiated the gate and accelerated out of sight. It seemed to Dalgliesh an additional perversity of fate that he should be driving a black Rover with an A registration.

* * *

Half an hour later Frank Musgrave turned into the drive of his house. It was a small but elegant red-bricked country house designed by Lutyens and bought by his father forty years earlier. Musgrave had inherited it with with the family business and regarded it with as much obsessional pride as if it had been a two-hundred-year-old family seat. He maintained it with jealous care as he looked after everything that was his, his wife, his son, his business, his car. Usually he drove up to it with no more than customary satisfaction at the old man's good eye for a house, but every six months, as if in obedience to some unstated law, he would halt the car and make a deliberate revaluation of its market price. He did that now.

He had hardly entered the hall when his wife, anxious faced, came out to meet him. Taking the coat from his shoulders, she said:

'How did it go, dear?'

'All right. He's an odd man. Not altogether friendly but perfectly civil. Seemed to enjoy his lunch.' He paused and added:

'He knows that it was murder.'

'Oh Frank, no! Not that! What are you going to do?'

'What everyone else concerned with Berowne will do, try to limit the damage. Has Betty Hurrell rung?'

'About twenty minutes ago. I told her that you'd be coming to see her.'

'Yes,' he said heavily, 'I must do that.'

He laid his hand momentarily on his wife's shoulder. Her family hadn't wanted her to marry him, hadn't thought him good enough for the only child of a previous Lord Lieutenant of the County. But he had married her and they had been happy, were still happy. He thought with sudden anger: He's done enough damage, but this is where it stops. I'm not going to risk everything I've worked for, everything I've achieved and my father before me, just because Paul Berowne goes off his head in a church vestry.

255

3

Scarsdale Lodge was a large, L-shaped, modern block of flats, brick-built, its front disfigured rather than enhanced by a series of irregular, jutting balconies. A path of stone blocks led between twin lawns to the canopied entrance porch. In the middle of each lawn, a small circular flower bed closely packed with dwarf dahlias ranging in circles through white to yellow and, finally, red glared upwards like a bloodshot eye. To the left a driveway brought them to the rear garage block and to a marked parking lot with a notice warning that it was strictly for the use of visitors to Scarsdale Lodge. It was overlooked by the smaller windows at the back of the building and Dalgliesh, knowing how paranoid flat residents became over unlicensed parking, guessed that a watch would be kept on it for alien cars. Almost certainly Berowne would have judged it safer to leave his car in the public park at Stanmore Station and would have walked the last quarter of a mile uphill, an anonymous commuter with the ubiquitous briefcase, the carrier bag of wine, the offering of flowers probably bought from a stall near Baker Street or Westminster Underground. And Stanmore wasn't so very far out of his way. It was, in fact, conveniently on the route to his Hertfordshire constituency. He would be able to snatch the odd hour on a Friday night, that hiatus between his London life and his Saturday morning constituency surgery.

He and Kate walked in silence to the front door. It was fitted with an intercom; hardly the most effective security but better than none, and with the advantage that there was no porter to watch comings and goings. Kate's ring and her careful announcement of their names through the grille was answered only by the burr of the released door and they passed through a hall that was typical of a thousand in similar apartment blocks in suburban London. The floor was of checkered vinyl, polished to mirror brightness. On the left wall was a cork board with notices from the managing agents about the date of lift maintenance and the cleaning contract. To the right an immense cheese plant in a green plastic pot, inadequately supported, drooped its bifurcated leaves. Ahead of them were the twin lifts. The silence was absolute. Somewhere up there, people must be living their cabined lives, but the air, sharp with the tang of floor polish, was as silent as if this were an apartment house of the dead. The tenants would be Londoners, transients most of them, young professionals on their way up, secretaries sharing with each other, retired couples living their self-contained lives. And a visitor could be coming to any one of the forty-odd flats. If Berowne were sensible he would have taken the lift to a different floor each time and walked up. But the risk would be small. Stanmore, for all its high leafiness, was no longer a village. There would be no peeping eyes behind the curtains to watch when he came or went. If Berowne had bought it for his mistress, as a convenient, anonymous meeting place he had chosen well.

Number forty-six was the corner flat on the top floor. They trod silently along a carpeted corridor to the white unnamed door. When Kate rang he wondered whether an eye was regarding them through the peephole, but the door was opened at once as if she had been standing there waiting for them. She stood aside and motioned them in. Then she turned to Dalgliesh and said:

'I've been expecting you. I knew you'd come sooner or later. And at least I'll know now what happened. I can hear someone speak his name, even if it's only a policeman.'

She was ready for them. She had done her crying; not all the crying she would do for her lover, but that dreadful howling anguish that tears the body apart was over now, at least for a time. He had had to witness its effects too often to miss the signs; the puffy eyelids, the skin dulled by grief's despoiling power, the lips swollen and unnaturally red, as if the lightest blow would burst them open. It was difficult to know how she normally looked. He thought that she had a pleasant, intelligent face, long-nosed but with high cheekbones and a firm jaw and a good skin. Her hair, mid-brown, strong and straight, was drawn back from her face and tied with a tag of crumpled ribbon. A few hairs lay damply across her forehead. Her voice was cracked and strained with recent crying but she had it well under control. He felt a respect for her. If grief was the criterion, she was the widow. As they followed her into the sitting room, he said:

'I'm very sorry to have to trouble you, and so soon. You know why we're here, of course. Do you feel able to talk about him? I need to know him better than I do if I'm to get anywhere.' She seemed to understand what he meant, that the victim was central to his death. He died because of what he was, what he knew, what he did, what he planned to do. He died because he was uniquely himself. Murder destroyed privacy, laid bare with brutal thoroughness all the petty contrivances of the dead life. Dalgliesh would rummage through Berowne's past as thoroughly as he rummaged through a victim's cupboards and files. The victim's privacy was the first to go, but no one intimately concerned with murder was left unscathed. The victim had at least escaped beyond earthbound considerations of dignity, embarrassment, reputation. But for the living, to be part of a murder investigation was to be contaminated by a process which would leave few of their lives unchanged. But at least, he thought, it had the merit of democracy. Murder remained the unique crime. Peer and pauper stood equal before it. The rich were, of course, advantaged in this as in everything. They could afford the best lawyer. But in a free society there was little else they could buy. She asked:

'Would you like some coffee?'

'Very much please, if it's not too much trouble.' Kate asked:

'Can I help?'

'It won't take long.'

Kate apparently took the words as an acceptance and followed the girl into the kitchen leaving the door ajar. It was typical of her, thought Dalgliesh, this unsentimental, practical response to people and their immediate concerns. Without hectoring or presumption, she could reduce the most embarrassing situation to something approaching normality. It was one of her strengths. Now, above the tinkle of kettle lid and crockery, he could hear their voices, conversational, almost ordinary. From the few phrases he could catch, they seemed to be discussing the merits of a make of electric kettle which both possessed. Suddenly he felt that he shouldn't be there, that he was redundant as a detective and a man. They would both get on better without his male, destructive presence. Even the room seemed inimical to him, and he could almost persuade himself that the low broken sibilants of female voices were in conspiracy.

There was the grinding roar of a coffee mill. So, she used fresh ground beans. But of course. She would take trouble over the coffee. It was the drink she and her lover must most often have shared. He looked around the sitting room with its long window giving a distant view of the London skyline. The furniture represented a rather orthodox good taste. The sofa, covered with fawn linen, uncrumpled, still pristine, looked expensive and was probably Scandinavian in the austerity of the design. On each side of the fireplace were matching armchairs, the covers more worn than that on the sofa. The fireplace itself was modern, a simple shelf of white wood above a plain surround. And the fire, he saw, was one of the newest gas models which gave an illusion of burning coals and a living flame. She would have been able to turn it on as soon as she heard his ring; instant comfort, instant warmth. And if he didn't come, if there was business at the House or at home or in the constituency which kept him from her, there would be no cold ash the next morning to mock her with its easy symbolism.

Above the sofa was a line of watercolours; gentle English landscapes, their quality unmistakable. He thought he recognized a Lear and a Cotman. He wondered if these had been Berowne's gifts, a way perhaps of transferring to her something of value which both could enjoy and which her pride could accept. The wall opposite the fireplace was covered with wooden adjustable units reaching from floor to ceiling. These held a simple stereo system, racks for records, a television set, and her books. Walking over to inspect them and flicking them open, he saw she had read history at Reading University. Take away the books and substitute popular prints for the watercolours and the room could have been a showroom in a newly built block of flats, seducing the prospective buyer with a depressingly orthodox good taste. He thought; there are rooms designed to be got away from, bleak anterooms where the armour is buckled on to confront the real world outside. There are rooms to come back to, claustrophobic refuges from the arduous business of work and striving. This room was a world in itself, a still centre provisioned with economy and care but containing everything necessary to its owner's life; the flat itself an investment in more than property. All her capital had been tied up here, monetary and emotional. He looked at the row of plants, varied, well-tended, glossily healthy, which were ranged on the window sill. But then, why shouldn't they be healthy? She was always there to tend them.

The two women came back into the room, Miss Washburn carrying a tray with a percolator, three large white cups, a jug of hot milk, and sugar crystals. She set it down on the coffee table. Dalgliesh and Kate seated themselves on the sofa. Miss Washburn poured the coffee, including a cup for herself, then carried it over to her seat by the fire. As Dalgliesh had expected, the coffee was excellent, but she didn't drink. She gazed across at them and said:

'The television newsreader said knife wounds. What wounds?'

'Is that how you heard, on the television news?'

She said with great bitterness:

'Of course. How else would I hear?'

Dalgliesh was shaken by a pity so unexpected and so acute that for a moment he dared not speak. And with the pity came a resentment against Berowne which frightened him with its intensity. Surely the man had faced the possibility of sudden death. He was a public figure; he must have known there was always a risk. Hadn't there been someone that he could trust with his secret? Someone who could have broken the news to her, visited her, brought her at least the comfort that he had thought about saving her pain. Couldn't he have found time in his over-busy life to write a letter which could have been privately taken to her if he died unexpectedly? Or had he been arrogant enough to think himself immune from the risks of lesser mortals; a coronary, a car accident, an IRA bomb? The tide of anger ebbed, leaving a slough of self-disgust. It had been directed against himself. He thought: Isn't that how I might have behaved? We're alike even in this. If he had a splinter of ice in the heart, then so have I.

She repeated stubbornly:

'What knife wounds?'

There was no way of telling it gently.

'His throat was cut. His and the tramp's who was with him, Harry Mack.' He didn't know why telling her Harry's name should be important as it had been important to speak it to Lady Ursula. It was as if he were determined that none of them should forget Harry.

She asked:

'With Paul's razor?'

'It's probable.'

'And the razor was still there, by the body?'

She had said body, not bodies. There was only one which concerned her. He said:

'Yes, by his outstretched hand.'

'And the outside door, was it unlocked?'

'Yes.'

She said:

'So he let in his murderer just as he let in the tramp. Or did the tramp kill him?'

'No, the tramp didn't kill him. Harry was a victim, not a killer.'

'Then it was an outsider. Paul couldn't have killed anyone, and I don't believe he killed himself.'

Dalgliesh said:

'We don't believe it either. We're treating it as murder. That's why we need your help. We need you to talk about him. You probably knew him better than any other person.'

She said, so low that he could only just catch the whisper:

'I thought I did. I thought I did.'

She took up her cup and tried to lift it to her lips, but couldn't control it. Dalgliesh felt Kate stiffen at his side and wondered whether she was controlling an impulse to put her arms round the girl's shoulder and raise the cup to her lips. But she didn't move and, at the second attempt, Miss Washburn managed to get her mouth to the brim. She gulped in the coffee, noisily, like a thirsty child.

Watching her, Dalgliesh knew what he was doing and the more fastidious part of his mind was repelled by it. She was alone, unacknowledged, denied the simple human need to share her grief, to talk about her lover. And it was that need which he was about to exploit. He sometimes thought bitterly that exploitation was at the heart of successful detection, particularly with murder. You exploited the suspect's fear, his vanity, his need to confide, the insecurity that tempted him to say that one vital sentence too many. Exploiting grief and loneliness was only another version of the same technique.

She looked at him and said:

'Can I see where it happened? I mean without making a fuss about it or being noticed. I should like to sit there alone when they have the funeral. It would be better than sitting at the back of the congregation trying not to make a fool of myself.'

He said:

'At the moment the back of the church is being kept locked. But I'm sure it could be arranged once we've finally finished with the place. Father Barnes, he's the parish priest, would let you in. It's a very ordinary room. Just a vestry, dusty, rather cluttered, smelling of hymn books and incense, but a very peaceful place.' He added, 'I think it happened very quickly. I don't think he felt any pain.'

'But he must have felt fear.'

'Perhaps not even that.'

She said:

'It's such an unlikely thing to have happened, that conversion, divine revelation, whatever it was. That sounds foolish. Of course it's unlikely. I meant that it's an unlikely thing to have happened to Paul. He was, well, worldly. Oh I don't mean in the sense that he only cared about success, money, prestige. But he was so in the world, of the world. He wasn't a mystic. He wasn't even particularly religious. He usually went to church on Sundays and on the major feast days because he enjoyed the liturgy – he wouldn't attend if they used the new Bible or Prayer Book. And he said he

261

liked an hour when he could think without interruptions, without the telephone ringing. He once said that formal religious observance confirmed identity, reminded one of the limits of behaviour, something like that. Belief wasn't meant to be a burden. Nor was disbelief. Does any of this make sense?'

'Yes.'

'He liked food, wine, architecture, women. I don't mean that he was promiscuous. But he loved the beauty of women. I couldn't give him that. But I could give him something no one else could, peace, honesty, total trust.'

It was odd, he thought. It was the religious experience not the murder that she needed most to talk about. Her lover was dead and even the enormity of that final, irrevocable loss couldn't blot out the pain of that earlier betrayal. But they would get round to the murder in time. There was no hurry. He wouldn't get what he wanted by rushing her now. He asked:

'Did he explain it to you, that experience in the vestry?'

'He came round the following night. He'd had a meeting in the House and it was late. He couldn't stay long. He told me that he had had an experience of God. That's all. An experience of God. He made it sound perfectly matter-of-fact. But it wasn't, of course. Then he left. I knew then I'd lost him. Not as a friend, perhaps, but then I didn't want him as a friend. I'd lost him as a lover. I'd lost him for ever. He didn't need to tell me that.'

There were, he knew, women to whom secrecy, risk, treachery, conspiracy, gave a love affair that extra erotic charge. They were women as uncommitted as their men, as fond of personal privacy, who wanted an intense relationship but not at the price of their careers, women to whom sexual passion and domesticity were irreconcilable. But she, he thought, had not been one of them. He recalled word for word his conversation with Higginson of Special Branch. Higginson, in his carefully tailored tweeds, straight-backed, clear-eyed, firm-jawed under the cropped moustache, so like the conventional image of an army officer that, for Dalgliesh, he walked in an aura of bogus respectability; a conman deferential on suburban doorways, a second-hand car salesman loitering at Warren Street Underground. Even his cynicism seemed as carefully calculated as his accent. Yet the accent was perfectly genuine and so was the cynicism. The worst you could say of Higginson was that he liked his job too well.

'It's the usual thing, my dear Adam. A decorative wife for show, the devoted little woman on the side for use. Only in this case I'm

262

not sure what use precisely. The choice is a little surprising. You'll see. But there's no security problem, never has been. They've both been remarkably discreet. Berowne has always made it plain that he accepted any necessary security precautions but that he was entitled to take some risks where his private life was concerned. She has never made trouble. I'd be surprised if she makes it now. There'll be no embarrassing little bundle in eight months' time.'

Could she, he wondered, have really shut her eyes to the reality, that the affair was documented, every step of its progress noted with almost clinical detachment by those cynical watchers who had decided, no doubt after the normal bureaucratic processes, that she could be classified as a harmless diversion, that Berowne could enjoy his weekly entertainment without official harassment. Surely she couldn't have deceived herself, and neither could he. She was, after all, herself a bureaucrat, a Principal. She must know how the system worked. She was still comparatively junior, but it was her world. One sign that she was a security risk and he would have been warned off. And he would have taken the warning. You didn't become a Minister of State if you hadn't enough ambition, egotism, and ruthlessness to know where your priorities had to lie.

He asked:

'How did you meet?'

'How do you expect? At work. I was a Principal in his private office.'

So it had been as he had expected.

'And then when you became lovers, you asked for a transfer?'

'No, I was due for a transfer. You don't stay long in private office.'

'Did you ever meet his family?'

'He didn't take me home, if that's what you mean. He didn't introduce me to his wife or Lady Ursula and say, "Meet Carole Washburn. Meet my mistress."'

'How often did you see him?'

'As often as he could get away. Sometimes we had a half-day. Sometimes a couple of hours. He tried to drop in on his way to his constituency if he were alone. Sometimes we couldn't meet for weeks.'

'And he never suggested marriage? Forgive me, this question could be important.'

'If you mean that someone could have slit his throat to prevent him asking for a divorce to marry me, you're wasting your time. The answer to your question, Commander, is no, he never suggested marriage. And neither did I.'

263

'Would you describe him as happy?'

She didn't seem surprised by the apparent irrelevance of the question nor did she need to give it much thought. She had known the answer for a long time. 'No, not really. What happened to him – I don't mean the murder – what happened to him in that church, whatever it was, I don't think it would have happened if he'd been satisfied with his life, if our love had been enough for him. It was enough for me; all I wanted, all I needed. It wasn't enough for him. I've always known that. Nothing was enough for Paul, nothing.'

'Did he tell you that he'd had a poison pen letter about Theresa Nolan and Diana Travers?'

'Yes, he told me. He didn't take it seriously.'

'He took it seriously enough to show it to me.'

She said:

'Theresa Nolan's child, the one she aborted, it wasn't his if that's what you're thinking. It couldn't have been. He would have told me. Look, it was just a poison pen letter. Politicians get them all the time. They're used to them. Why worry about it now?'

'Because anything that happened during the last weeks of his life could be important. You must see that.'

'What does it matter, the scandal or the lies. They can't touch him now. They can't hurt him. Nothing can. Not any more.'

He asked, gently:

'Were there things that hurt him?'

'He was human, wasn't he? Of course there were things that hurt him.'

'What things? His wife's infidelity?'

She didn't reply.

He said:

'Miss Washburn, my priority is catching his murderer, not preserving his reputation. They needn't be incompatible. I'll try to see that they aren't. But I'm clear which has to come first. Shouldn't you be?'

She spoke with sudden fierceness:

'No. I've preserved his privacy – not reputation, privacy – for three years. It's cost me a lot. I haven't complained to him. I'm not complaining now. I knew the rules. But I'm going to go on preserving his privacy. It was important to him. If I don't, all those years of discretion, never being seen together, never being able to say "This is my man, we're lovers", always taking second place to his job, his wife, his constituents, his mother, what has been the point of it? You can't bring him back.'

That was always the cry when the going got rough, 'You can't bring them back.' He remembered his second child murderer; the hidden cache of pornographic photographs the police had uncovered in the killer's flat, indecent poses of his victims, pathetic childish bodies violated and exposed. It had been his job as a newly promoted detective inspector to ask a mother to identify her daughter. The woman's eyes had glanced at the photograph once only and then stared ahead, denying knowledge, denying truth. There were some realities which the mind refused to accept even in the cause of retribution, of justice. You can't bring them back. It was the cry of the whole defeated, anguished, grieving world.

But she was speaking.

'There were a lot of things I couldn't give him. But I could give him secrecy, discretion. I've heard about you. There was that business down in the Fens, the forensic scientist who was murdered. Paul told me about it. It was quite a triumph for you, wasn't it? You say, "What about the victim?" But what about your victims? I expect you'll catch Paul's murderer. You usually do, don't you? Does it ever occur to you to count the cost?'

Dalgliesh felt Kate stiffen at the clear note of dislike and contempt. The girl went on:

'But you'll have to do it without me. You don't really need my help. I'm not going to break Paul's confidences just so that you can notch up another success.'

He said:

'There's the matter of the dead tramp, Harry Mack.'

'I'm sorry, but I've nothing left over to spare for Harry Mack, not even sympathy. I'm leaving Harry Mack out of my calculations.'

'I can't leave him out of mine.'

'Of course not, that's your job. Look, I know nothing that can help solve this murder for you. If Paul had enemies I don't know about them. I've told you about him and me. You knew anyway. But I'm not getting involved any deeper. I'm not ending up in the witness box, photographed on my way into court, pictured on the front page "Paul Berowne's Little Bit On The Side".'

She got to her feet. It was the sign for them to go. When they reached the door, she said:

'I want to get away, just for a couple of weeks. I've plenty of leave in hand. If the papers find out about me then I don't want to be here when it happens. I couldn't bear that. I want to get out of London, out of England. You can't stop me.'

Dalgliesh said:

'No. But we'll still be here when you come back.'

'And if I don't come back?' She spoke with the weary acceptance of defeat. How could she live abroad, dependent as she was on her job, her salary? This flat might have lost its meaning for her but London was still her home and the job would be important to her for more reasons than money. A young woman didn't become a Principal without intelligence, hard work, ambition. But he answered her question as if it had reality.

'Then I should have to come to you.'

Outside in the car, buckling on his seatbelt, he said:

'I wonder if we would have got more out of her if you'd seen her alone. She might have spoken more freely if I hadn't been there.'

Kate said:

'Possibly, sir, but only if I'd promised to keep it confidential, and I don't see how I could have done that.'

Massingham, he suspected, would have promised secrecy and then had no compunction in telling. That was one of the differences between them.

'No,' he said, 'you couldn't have done that.'

4

Back in New Scotland Yard, Kate burst into Massingham's office. She found him alone, surrounded by paper, and had pleasure in interrupting his conscientious but unenthusiastic perusal of the door-to-door inquiry reports with a vehement account of the interview. She had controlled her sense of outrage with difficulty on the drive back to the Yard and was in the mood for a confrontation, preferably with a male.

'The man was a shit!'

'Oh, I don't know. Aren't you being a bit hard?'

'It's the same old story. He basks in his success; she's tucked away in the equivalent of a Victorian love-nest to serve his purpose when he has an odd moment to spare for her. We could be back in the nineteenth century.'

'But we aren't. It's her choice. Come off it, Kate! She has a good job, her own flat, a good salary, a career with a pension. She could have chucked him any day she chose. He wasn't coercing her.'

'Not physically, perhaps.'

'Don't start singing a variation of the old song "It's the Man What Gets the Pleasure, It's the Girl What Gets the Blame". Recent history is against you anyway. There was nothing to stop her having it out with him. She could have given him an ultimatum. "You've got to choose, it's her or me".'

'Knowing what his choice would be?'

'Well that's the risk isn't it? She might have struck lucky. This isn't the nineteenth century. And he's not Parnell. Divorce wouldn't have harmed his career, not for long, not much.'

'It wouldn't have helped it.'

'OK. Take your chap, whoever he is. Or any chap you might fancy. If you had to choose between him and your job, would that be so easy? When you're feeling censorious, better ask yourself which you'd choose.'

The question disconcerted her. He probably either knew or had guessed about Alan. You didn't keep many secrets in the CID and her very reticence about her private life would have stimulated curiosity. But she hadn't expected such perception from him or such frankness and she wasn't sure she liked it. She said:

'Well, it hasn't made me respect him.'

'We don't have to respect him. We're not asked to respect him or like him or admire his politics, his ties or his taste in women. Our job is to catch his murderer.'

She sat down opposite him, suddenly weary, and let her shoulder bag slip to the floor, then watched him as he began putting his papers together. She liked his office, intrigued by the difference between its sparse masculinity and the murder squad room down the corridor. There the atmosphere was heavily masculine, reminiscent, she thought, of an officers' mess, but as she had once overheard Massingham say to Dalgliesh with the sly malice which his subordinates found offensive and which reminded them of his old nickname of the Honjohn . . . 'Not altogether a first class regiment would you say, sir?' The squad were called in to investigate crime at sea and were usually rewarded with a framed photograph of the ship concerned. These were mounted in regular lines along the walls together with signed portraits of chiefs of police from Commonwealth countries, emblems and badges, signed testimonials, even the occasional photograph of a celebratory dinner. Massingham's walls were decorated only with colour prints of early cricket matches borrowed, she guessed, from his home. These gentle evocations of long dead summers, the oddly shaped bats, the top hats of the players, the familiar cathedral spires piercing an English sky, the shadowed grass, and the crinolined ladies with their parasols, had at first been a source of mild interest to his colleagues but were now hardly noticed. Kate thought his choice showed a nice compromise between masculine conformity and personal taste. And he could hardly have mounted his school photographs. Eton wasn't exactly unacceptable to the Met but it wasn't a school to boast about. She asked:

'How is the house-to-house going?'

'As you'd expect. No one saw or heard anything. They were all sitting glued to the box, down at the Dog and Duck, or at bingo. No big fish, but we've netted the usual minnows. Pity we can't throw them back. Still, it'll keep Division busy.'

'And the cab drivers?'

'No luck. One chap remembered driving a middle-aged gent to within forty yards of the church at the relevant time. We traced the fare. He was visiting his lady friend.'

'What? In a love-nest off the Harrow Road?'

'He had somewhat specific requirements. Remember Fatima?'

'Good God, is she still on the job?'

'Very much so. She's also taken to doing a little snouting for

Chalkey White. The lady's none too pleased with us at present. And neither is Chalkey.'

'And the fare?'

'Well, he's putting in an official complaint. Harassment, interference with personal liberty, the usual. And we've had six confessions to the murder.'

'Six. So soon?'

'Four of them we've met before. All certifiable. One did it to protest against Tory policy on immigration, one because Berowne had seduced his granddaughter, and one because the Archangel Gabriel told him to. They've all got the time wrong. They all used a knife not a razor and you won't be surprised to hear that none of them can produce it. With a singular lack of originality, they all claim to have chucked it in the canal.'

She said:

'Do you ever wonder how much of our job is really cost effective?'

'From time to time. What do you expect us to do about it?'

'Waste less time on the minnows to begin with.'

'Come off it, Kate. We can't pick and choose. Only within strict limits anyway. And it's no different with a doctor. He can't make the whole society healthy, he can't heal the world. He'd go crazy if he tried. He just treats what comes his way. Sometimes he wins, sometimes he loses.'

She said:

'But he doesn't spend all his time cauterizing warts while the cancers go untreated.'

He said:

'Hell, if bloody murder isn't a cancer, what is? Actually, it's probably a murder investigation, not common crime, which isn't cost effective. Think what it cost to put the Yorkshire Ripper behind bars. Think what this killer will cost the taxpayer before we get him.'

'If we get him.' And for the first time she was tempted to add: 'And if he exists.'

Massingham got up from the desk.

'You need a drink. I'll buy you one.'

Suddenly she almost liked him.

'OK,' she said, 'thanks.' She picked up her shoulder bag and they went out together to the senior officers' mess.

Mrs Iris Minns lived in a council flat on the second floor of a block off the Portobello Road. To park anywhere close on a Saturday, the day of the street market, was impossible, so Massingham and Kate left the car at the Notting Hill Gate police station and walked. The Saturday market was, as always, a carnival; a cosmopolitan, peaceable if noisy celebration of human gregariousness, curiosity, gullibility and greed. It brought back to Kate memories of her early days in the division. She always walked through the cluttered street with pleasure, although she seldom bought; she had never shared the popular obsession with the trivia of the past. And for all its air of cheerful camaraderie, the market was, she knew, less innocent than it looked. Not all the bundles of notes in various currencies changing hands would find their way into tax returns. Not all the trading was in the harmless artefacts of the past. The usual number of unwary visitors would be relieved of their wallets or purses before they reached the bottom of the road. But few London markets were as gentle, as entertaining or as good-humoured. This morning, as always, she entered the narrow, raucous thoroughfare with a lifting of the spirits.

Iris Minns lived in flat twenty-six of Block Two, a building separated from the main block and from the road by a wide courtway. As they crossed it, watched by several pairs of carefully incurious but wary eyes, Massingham said:

'I'll do the talking.' She felt the familiar spurt of resentment but said nothing.

The appointment had been made by telephone for nine thirty, and from the speed with which the front door was opened to their ring, Mrs Minns must have been among those watching their arrival from behind their curtains. They found themselves facing a small compact figure with a square face, a round determined chin, a long mouth which twitched into a brief smile which seemed less one of welcome than of satisfaction that they were on time, and a pair of dark, almost black, eyes which gave them a quick, appraising glance as if inspecting them for dust. She took the trouble to examine Massingham's warrant card with some care, then stood aside and motioned them in, saying:

'Well, you're on time, I'll say that for you. There's tea or coffee if you fancy it.'

Massingham quickly refused it for both of them. Kate's first instinct was to say quickly that she would like coffee, but she resisted the temptation. This could be an important interview; there was no point in jeopardizing its success out of personal pique. And Mrs Minns wouldn't miss any overt antagonism between them. She couldn't have been mistaken in the flash of intelligence in those dark eyes.

The sitting room into which they were shown was so remarkable that she hoped that her surprise didn't show too clearly on her face. Provided by local bureaucracy with an oblong box fifteen feet by ten, a single window and a door opening to a balcony too small for any purpose but giving air to a few pot plants, Mrs Minns had created a small Victorian sitting room, dark, cluttered, claustrophobic. The wallpaper was a dark olive-green patterned with ivy and lilies, the carpet a faded but serviceable Wilton, while occupying almost the whole of the middle of the room was an oblong table of polished mahogany with curved legs, its surface mirror-bright, and four high-backed carved chairs. A smaller octagonal table was set against one wall holding an aspidistra in a brass pot while the walls were hung with sentimental prints in maple frames; the *Sailor's Farewell* and *Sailor's Return*, a child reaching for a flower above a brook, its heedless steps protected by a winged angel wearing an expression of pious imbecility. In front of the window stood a long plant-holder of wrought iron painted white, filled with pots of geraniums, and outside on the balcony they could glimpse terracotta pots holding ivy and climbing plants whose variegated leaves were entwined with the railings.

The focus of the room was a seventeen-inch television set, but this was less of an anachronism than might first appear since it was placed against a background of green ferns whose fronds curled against the screen like an ornate but living frame. The window-ledge was covered with small tubs of African violets, deep purple and a freckled paler mauve. Kate thought that they were planted in yoghurt tubs, but it was difficult to be sure since each was decorated with a plaited paper doily. A sideboard with an elaborately carved back was covered with china animals, dogs discordant in size and breed, a spotted fawn, and half a dozen china cats in unconvincing feline attitudes, each one on a starched linen mat, presumably to protect the polished mahogany.

The whole room was spotlessly clean, the pungent smell of polish overwhelming. When in winter the heavy red velvet curtains

271

were drawn it would be possible to believe oneself in another setting, another age. And Mrs Minns could have been part of it. She was wearing a black skirt and a white blouse buttoned to the neck and fastened with a cameo brooch and with her greying hair dressed high at the front and coiled in a small bun at the nape of the neck, she looked, thought Kate, like an ageing actress dressed for the part of a Victorian housekeeper. The only criticism one could make was that the rouge and eyeshadow had been over-lavishly applied. She seated herself in the right-hand armchair and motioned Kate to the other, leaving Massingham to seat himself by turning round one of the dining chairs. In it he looked uncomfortably high and, thought Kate, somewhat at a disadvantage, a male intruder into comfortable female domesticity. In the autumn light, filtered through lace curtains and the green of the balcony plants, his face under the thatch of red hair looked almost sickly, the freckles over the forehead standing out like a splutter of pale blood. He said:

'Can't we have the door closed? I can't hear myself speak.'

The door on to the balcony was ajar. Kate got up and went over to close it. To the right she could glimpse the huge blue and white teapot hanging outside the Portobello Pottery and the painted wall panel of the porcelain market. The noise of the street came up to her like the clatter of shingle on a seashore. Then she closed the door and the sound was deadened. Mrs Minns said:

'It's only on a Saturday. Mr Smith and I don't much mind it. You get used to it. I always say it's a bit of life.' She turned to Kate:

'You live in these parts, don't you? I'm sure I've seen you shopping up at the Gate.'

'Very possibly, Mrs Minns. I'm not far away.'

'Oh well, it's a village, isn't it? You see everyone up at the Gate sooner or later.'

Massingham said impatiently:

'You mentioned a Mr Smith.'

'He lives here, but you can't see him. Not that he'd be able to tell you anything. But he's off roamin'.'

'Roaming? Where?'

'How do I know. On his bicycle. His folk used to live in Hillgate Village in the old days. Proper little slum it was when his grandad was alive. A hundred and sixty thousand they're asking for the houses now. I reckon he's got gypsy blood, has Mr Smith. There was a lot of gypsies settled round here after they pulled down the Hippodrome racecourse. He's always roamin'. It's easier for him now that British Rail let his bike go free. Lucky for you he isn't here. He's not too keen on the police. Too many of your chaps pick him up for nothing only sleeping under a hedge. That's what's wrong with this country, too much pickin' on decent people. And other things I could mention what we're not allowed to say.'

Kate could sense Massingham's anxiety to get on with the matter in hand. As if she too had sensed it, Mrs Minns said:

'It was a proper shock for me, I don't mind telling you. Lady Ursula rang me up just before nine o'clock that night. She told me you'd be sure to be along sooner or later.'

'So that was the first you'd heard of Sir Paul's death, when his mother rang to warn you?'

'Warn me? No call to warn me. I didn't slit his throat for him, poor gentleman, nor I don't know who did. You'd have thought Miss Matlock might have taken the trouble to phone earlier. That would have been better for me than hearing it on the six o'clock news. I wondered whether to ring the house, find out if there was anything I could do, but I reckoned they'd be bothered with enough calls without me on the line. Better wait, I thought, until someone rings.'

Massingham said:

'And that was Lady Ursula, just before nine?'

'That's right. Nice of her to trouble. But then we've always got on well, me and Lady Ursula. You call her Lady Ursula Berowne because she's the daughter of an earl. Lady Berowne is only the wife of a baronet.'

Massingham said impatiently.

'Yes, we know that.'

'Oh you do, do you. Millions don't, nor don't care neither. Still, it's as well to get it right if you're thinking of hanging about Campden Hill Square.'

Massingham asked:

'How did she sound when she rang you?'

'Lady Ursula? How do you expect? She wasn't laughing, was she? Wasn't crying neither. That's not her way. She was calm like she always is. Couldn't tell me much, though. What happened? Suicide was it?'

'We can't be sure, Mrs Minns, until we know more, get the results of some tests. We have to treat this as a suspicious death. When did you last see Sir Paul?'

'Just before he went out on Tuesday, about half past ten that would be. We was in the library. I'd gone in to polish the desk and there he was, sitting there. So I said I'd come back later, and he said "No, come in, Mrs Minns, I won't be long."'

273

'What was he doing?'

'Like I said, he was sitting at the desk. He had his diary open.'

Massingham said, sharply:

'Are you sure?'

'Of course I'm sure. He had it open in front of him and he was looking through it.'

'How can you be certain that it was his diary?'

'Look, it was open in front of him and I could see it was a diary. It had different days on the page, it had dates in it and he'd written in it. Think I don't know a diary when I see one? Afterwards he closed it up and put it in the top right-hand drawer where it's usually kept.'

Massingham asked:

'How do you know where it's usually kept?'

'Look, I've worked in that house nine years. I was taken on by her Ladyship when Sir Hugo was baronet. You get to know things.'

'What else happened between you?'

'Nothing much. I asked him if I could borrow one of his books.'

'Borrow one of his books?' Massingham frowned his surprise.

'That's right. I'd seen it on the bottom shelf when I'd been dusting and I fancied reading it. It's there, under the television set, if you're interested. *A Rose by Twilight* by Millicent Gentle. I haven't seen a book by her for years.'

She reached for it and handed it to Massingham. It was a slim book still in its dust cover, a picture of an egregiously handsome dark-haired hero holding a blonde girl half-swooning in his arms against a background riot of roses. Massingham flicked through it and said with a note of amused contempt:

'Hardly his kind of reading, I should have thought. Sent to him, I imagine, by one of his constituents. It's signed by the author. I wonder why he bothered to keep it.'

Mrs Minns said sharply:

'Why shouldn't he keep it? She's a good writer is Millicent Gentle. Not that she's been doing much lately. I'm very partial to a good romantic novel. Better than all those horrible murders. I can't be doing with them. So I asked if I could borrow it and he said I could.'

Kate took the book and opened it. On the flyleaf was written: 'To Paul Berowne, with every good wish from the author'. Underneath was the signature, Millicent Gentle and the date, the seventh of August. It was the date of Diana Travers' drowning, but apparently Massingham hadn't noticed. She closed the book and said:

'We'll take this book back to Campden Hill Square if you've finished with it, Mrs Minns.'

'Please yourself. I wasn't thinking of pinchin' it if that's what you're thinking.'

Massingham asked:

'What else happened after he'd said you could borrow the book?'

'He asked me how long I'd been working at Campden Hill Square. I said nine years. Then he said "Have they been good years for you?" I said, as good for me as they have for most.'

Massingham smiled. He said:

'I don't think that's what he meant.'

'I know what he meant all right. But what did he expect me to say? I do the work, they pay me; four pounds an hour which is above the going rate, and a taxi home if I'm there after dark. I wouldn't stay if the job didn't suit. But what do they expect for their money? Love? If he'd wanted me to say that I'd spent the best years of my life at Campden Hill Square then he was disappointed. Mind you, it was different when the first Lady Berowne was alive.'

'How do you mean, different?'

'Just different. The house seemed more alive then. I liked the first Lady Berowne. She was a very pleasant lady. Not that she lasted long, poor soul.'

Kate asked:

'Why did you continue to work at number sixty-two, Mrs Minns?'

Mrs Minns turned her bright little eyes on Kate and said simply:

'I like polishing furniture.'

Kate guessed that Massingham was tempted to ask what she thought of the second Lady Berowne, but he decided to keep to his main line of questioning.

'And what then?' he asked.

'He went out, didn't he?'

'Out of the house?'

'That's right.'

'Can you be sure?'

'Look, he had his jacket on, he picked up that hold-all he had, he went through the hall and I heard the front door open and shut. If it wasn't him going out then who was it?'

'But you didn't actually see him go?'

'I never followed him to the door to kiss him goodbye, if that's what you mean. I have my work to do. But that's the last time I saw him in this world, and I've no expectations of seeing him in the next, that's for sure.'

275

Perhaps prudently Massingham did not pursue this thought. He said:

'And you're certain that he put the diary back in the drawer?'

'He didn't take it with him. Look, what is it about the diary? Are you saying I stole it or something?'

Kate broke in:

'It isn't in the drawer now, Mrs Minns. Of course, we don't suspect anyone of taking it. It hasn't any value. But it does seem to be missing, and it could be important. You see, if he did make an appointment for the next day, then it wouldn't be very likely that he set out from home meaning to kill himself.'

Mrs Minns, mollified, said:

'Well, he didn't take it with him. I saw him put it back with my own eyes. And if he did come back for it later, it wasn't while I was in the house.'

Massingham asked:

'That's possible, of course. When did you leave?'

'Five o'clock. My usual time. I wash up the lunch things and I have my special afternoon job. Some days it might be the silver, some days the linen cupboard. On Tuesday it was dusting the books in the library. I was there from half past two until four, when I went to help Miss Matlock with the tea. He certainly didn't come back then. I'd have heard anyone if they'd come through the hall.'

Suddenly Kate asked:

'Would you say it was a happy marriage, Mrs Minns?'

'Hardly ever saw them together to tell. When I did they seemed all right. They never shared a bedroom, though.'

Massingham said:

'That's not so very unusual.'

'Maybe. But there's not sharing and not sharing if you get my meaning. I make the beds, you see. That may be your idea of a marriage but it's not mine.'

Massingham said:

'Hardly the way to produce the next baronet.'

'Well, I did wonder about that a few weeks ago. Off her breakfast she was and that isn't like her. But not much chance I reckon. Too worried about her figure. Mind you, she's not bad when she's in a good mood. Too gushing though. "Oh Mrs Minns be a darling and fetch my dressing gown." "Mrs Minns, be an angel and run a bath for me." "Be a dear and make a cup of tea." Sweet as sugar as long as she gets her own way. Well, she more or less has to be. Same with Lady Ursula. She doesn't much care for Miss Matlock helping her to bath and dress. I can see that even if Matlock can't. But there it is. If you get used to having your bath run and your breakfast in bed and your clothes hung up, you have to put up with some inconvenience in return. Different when Lady Ursula was a girl, of course. Servants were seen and not heard then. Pressed back against the wall when the gentry go by in case they have to look at you. Hand the post with a glove so as not to contaminate it. Think yourself lucky to have a good place. My gran was in service; I know.'

Massingham said:

'There were no quarrels, then, as far as you know?'

'It would have been better, maybe, if there had been. He was too polite, formal you could say. Now that's not natural in a marriage. No, there were no quarrels, not till Tuesday morning anyway. And then you could hardly call it a quarrel. Takes two to quarrel. She was screeching fit to reach the whole house, but I didn't hear much from him.'

'When was this, Mrs Minns?'

'When I took up her breakfast tray at half past eight. I do that every morning. Sir Paul used to take up Lady Ursula's. She only has orange juice, two slices of wholemeal bread, toasted, marmalade and coffee, but Lady Berowne has the whole hog. Orange juice, cereal, scrambled egg, toast, the lot. Never puts on an ounce though.'

'Tell me about the quarrel, Mrs Minns. What did you hear?'

'I got to the bedroom door when I heard her screeching: "You're going to that whore. You can't, not now. We need you, we both need you. I won't let you go." Something like that. And then I could hear his voice, very low. I couldn't hear what he was saying. I stood outside the door and wondered what to do. I put the tray down on the table by the door. I usually do that while I knock. But it didn't seem right to go barging in. On the other hand I couldn't stand there like a daft thing. Then the door opened and he came out. White as paper he was. He saw me and said: "I'll take the tray, Mrs Minns." So I gave it to him. The way he looked it was a wonder he didn't drop it there and then.'

Massingham said:

'But he took it into the bedroom?'

'That's right, and shut the door. And I went back to the kitchen.'

Massingham changed the direction of his questions. He asked:

'Did anyone else enter the library that Tuesday as far as you know?'

'That Mr Musgrave from the constituency did. He waited from about half past twelve to nearly two o'clock hoping Sir Paul would be back for lunch. Then he gave up and went away. Miss Sarah was there about four o'clock. She'd come to see her grandmother. I told her Lady Ursula wasn't expected back to tea, but she said she'd wait. Then she got fed up too, seemingly. Must have let herself out. I didn't see the going of her.'

Massingham went on to ask her about Diana Travers. Kate sensed that he had less faith than had she in AD's belief that the deaths of both girls were somehow connected with Paul Berowne's murder, but he dutifully did what was expected of him. The result proved a great deal more interesting than either of them had thought possible. Mrs Minns said:

'I was there when Diana arrived. We'd just lost Maria. She was Spanish, her husband worked as a cook in Soho, then she got pregnant with her third and the doctor said to cut down on her outside jobs. She was a good worker, was Maria. Those Spanish girls know how to house-clean, I'll say that for them. Anyway, Miss Matlock put a card in the newsagent's window at the end of Ladbroke Grove and Diana turned up. The card couldn't have been there more than an hour. A bit of luck, really, I never thought she'd get any answers. Good cleaning ladies don't have to look in newsagents for jobs these days.'

'And was she a good cleaner?'

'Never done it in her life before, you could see that. But she was willing enough. Of course Miss Matlock never let her touch the best china or polish in the drawing room. She took over the bathrooms, bedrooms, prepared vegetables, did a bit of shopping. She was all right.'

'A strange job for her to choose, though, a girl like that.'

Mrs Minns understood what he meant.

'Oh, she was educated all right, you could see that. Well it wasn't badly paid, four pounds an hour, a good midday meal if you're there for it and no tax unless you're daft enough to pay it. She said she was an actress looking for work and wanted a job she could chuck at once if something turned up. What's so interesting about Diana Travers anyway?'

Massingham ignored the question. He said:

'Did you and she get on well together?'

'No reason why we shouldn't. I told you, she was all right. A bit nosey. Found her one day looking in the drawer of Sir Paul's desk. Didn't hear me till I was on top of her. Bold as brass about it. Just laughed. Asked a lot about the family, too. She didn't get much out of me, nor from Miss Matlock either. No harm in her though, just a bit too keen on chat. I liked her all right. If I hadn't I wouldn't have let her come here.'

'You mean she lived here? We weren't told that at Campden Hill Square.'

'Well, they didn't know, did they? No reason why they should. She was buying herself a flat in Ridgmount Gardens and there was a hold-up. The owners weren't ready to move into their new place. You know how it is. Anyway, she had to leave her old place and find somewhere for a month. Well, I've got the two bedrooms so I told her she could move in here. Twenty-five pounds a week including a good breakfast. Not bad. I don't know that Mr Smith was all that keen but he was due to be off roamin' anyway.'

And there were the two bedrooms, thought Kate. Mrs Minns' black eyes stared at Massingham, defying him to inquire about the usual sleeping arrangements. And then she said:

'My gran said every woman should marry once, she owes it to herself. But no point in making a habit of it.'

Kate said:

'A flat in Ridgmount Gardens? Isn't that a bit upmarket for an out-of-work actress?'

'That's what I thought, but she said Daddy was helping. Maybe he was, maybe he wasn't. Maybe it was Daddy, maybe someone else. Anyway, he was in Australia, or so she told me. No business of mine.'

Massingham said:

'So she moved in here. When did she leave?'

'Just ten days before she was drowned, poor kid. And you're not telling me there was anything suspicious about that death. I was at the inquest. Natural interest you might say. Never a mention of where she worked though, was there? You'd have thought they might have sent a wreath to the funeral. Didn't want to know, did they?'

Massingham asked:

'What did she do with herself while she was living here with you?'

'I hardly saw her. No business of mine, was it? Two mornings a week she worked at Campden Hill Square. The rest of the time she said she was off for auditions. She went out a good bit at night, but she never brought anyone here. She was no trouble, neat and tidy always. Well, I wouldn't have had her here if I hadn't known that.

279

Then, the evening after she drowned, before the inquest even, she hadn't been dead twenty-four hours, these two chaps turn up.'

'Here?'

'That's right. Just when I got back from Campden Hill Square. Sitting in their car watching out for me if you ask me. Said they were from her solicitors, come to collect any of her things she might have left here.'

'Did they show you any identity, any authority?'

'A letter from the firm. Posh writing paper. And they had a card, so I let them in. I stayed by the door and watched them, mind you. They didn't like it, but I wanted to see what they were up to. "There's nothing here," I told them. "Look for yourselves. She left nearly a fortnight ago." They properly turned the place over, even turned the mattress up. Found nothing, of course. Funny business, I thought, but nothing came of it so I let it go. No point in making trouble.'

'Who do you think they were?'

Mrs Minns gave a sudden shout of laughter.

'You tell me! Come off it! They were two of your lot. Fuzz. Think I don't know a policeman when I see one?'

Even in the room's dim arboreal light Kate saw the faint flush of excitement on Massingham's face. But he was too experienced to press further. Instead he asked a few harmless questions about the domestic arrangements at Campden Hill Square and prepared to bring the interview to a close. But Mrs Minns had her own ideas. Kate sensed that she had something private to communicate. Getting up she said:

'D'you mind if I use your lavatory, Mrs Minns?'

She doubted whether Massingham was deceived, but he could hardly follow them. Waiting for her outside the door of the bathroom Mrs Minns almost hissed:

'You saw the date in that book?'

'Yes, Mrs Minns. The day Diana Travers was drowned.'

The sharp little eyes gleamed with satisfaction.

'I thought as how you'd noticed. He didn't though, did he?'

'I expect so. He just didn't mention it.'

'He never noticed. I know his sort. Too sharp for their own good and then miss what's under their noses.'

'When did you first see the book, Mrs Minns?'

'The next day, August the eighth. In the afternoon it was, after he came home from the constituency. Must have brought it with him.'

280

'So she may have given it to him then.'

'Maybe. Maybe not. Interesting though, isn't it? I thought as how you'd noticed. Keep it to yourself, that's my advice. He thinks too much of himself, that Massingham fellow.'

They had turned out of Portobello Road and were walking down Ladbroke Grove before Massingham spoke, then he laughed.

'My God, that room! I pity the mysterious Mr Smith. If I had to live there and with her, I'd go roaming.'

Kate flared:

'What's wrong with it or with her? At least it's got character, not like the bloody building, designed by some bureaucrat with a brief to fit in as many living units with the least possible public expenditure. Just because you've never had to live in one doesn't mean that the people who do like it.' She added with fierce defensiveness: 'Sir.'

He laughed again. She was always punctilious about acknowledging his rank when she was angry.

'All right, all right, I admit the character. They've both got character, she and her room. And what's so wrong with the block? I thought it was rather decent. If the council offered me a flat there I'd take it quickly enough.'

And he would, she thought. He was probably less concerned about the details of his life, where he ate, where he lived, even what he wore, than she was herself. And it was irritating to discover, once more, how easily in his company she was trapped into insincerity. She had never believed that buildings were all that important. It was people, not architects, who made slums. Even Ellison Fairweather Buildings would have been all right if it had been put up in a different place and filled with different people. He went on:

'And she was useful, wasn't she? If she's right and he did put the diary back in the drawer, and if we can prove that he didn't return . . .'

She broke in:

'That won't be easy, though. It'll mean accounting for every minute of his time. And so far we haven't a clue where he went after he left the estate agent's. He had a key. He could have let himself in and been out again in a minute.'

'Yes, but the probability is that he didn't. After all he went out with his bag, he obviously intended to stay out all day and go straight to the church. And if Lady Ursula did consult the diary before six o'clock when General Nollinge rang, then we

281

know who has to be our chief suspect don't we? Dominic Swayne.'

None of it needed saying. She had seen the importance of the diary as soon as he had. She said:

'Who do you think those men were, the ones who did the search? Special Branch?'

'That's my guess. Either she worked for them and they planted her in Campden Hill Square or she worked for someone or something a great deal more sinister and they rumbled her. Of course they could have been who they said they were, men from a solicitor's firm looking perhaps for papers, a will.'

'Under the mattress? It was a pretty professional search.'

If it were Special Branch, she thought, there was going to be trouble. She said:

'They did tell us about Berowne's mistress.'

'Knowing that we'd have discovered that for ourselves quickly enough. That's typical of Special Branch. Their idea of cooperation is like a minister answering a PQ in the House; keep it short, keep it accurate, make sure you don't tell them anything they don't know already. God, if she was tied up with Special Branch there's going to be trouble.'

She said:

'Between Miles Gilmartin and AD?'

'Between everyone.'

They walked in silence for a moment, then he said:

'Why did you bring away that novel?'

She was for a moment tempted to prevaricate. She knew that when the significance of the date had first struck her she had planned to keep quiet about it, to do a little private detection, trace the writer, see if there was anything in it. Then prudence had prevailed. If it proved important, AD would have to know and she could imagine what his response would be to that particular kind of personal initiative. It was hypocritical to complain about the lack of interdepartmental cooperation while trying to run her own show within the squad. She said:

'The signature is dated the seventh of August, the day Diana Travers died.'

'So what? She signed and posted it on the seventh.'

'Mrs Minns saw it the following afternoon. Since when has the London post arrived that promptly?'

'It's perfectly possible if she sent it first class.'

She persisted:

'It's far more likely that he met Millicent Gentle that day and she gave it to him personally. I thought it would be interesting to know when and why.'

He looked at her and said:

'Could be. It's just as likely that she signed it on the seventh then left it for him at his constituency office.' Then he smiled.

'That's what you and Mrs Minns were having your girlish gossip about.'

He gave a slow, secret smile and she knew, with a spurt of irritation, that he had guessed about her temptation to conceal the evidence and was amused by it.

6

Once back in the Rover and on their way to the Yard she suddenly said:

'I don't understand it, religious experience.'

'You mean you don't know how to categorize it.'

'You were brought up in it, I suppose. They indoctrinated you from the cradle: nursery prayers, school chapel, that sort of thing.'

She had seen the school chapel once on an outing to Windsor. It had impressed her. That, after all, was its purpose. She had felt interest, admiration, even awe, walking under that soaring fan vaulting. But it had still remained a building in which she had felt herself an alien, speaking to her of history, privilege, tradition, an affirmation that the rich, having inherited the earth, could hope to ensure similar privileges in heaven. Someone had been playing the organ and she had sat listening with pleasure to what she thought must have been a Bach cantata, but for her there had been no secret harmonies.

He said, his eyes on the road:

'I'm reasonably familiar with the external forms. Not as much as my father. Compulsory chapel every day for him or so he claims.'

'I don't even feel the need of it, religion, praying.'

'That's perfectly natural. A lot of people don't. You're probably in the respectable majority. It's a matter of temperament. What's worrying you?'

'Nothing's worrying me. But it's odd about praying. Most people do pray apparently. Someone did a survey about it. They pray even if they're not sure who to. What about AD?'

'I don't know what he feels the need of except his poetry, his job and his privacy. And probably in that order.'

'But you've worked with him before, I haven't. Don't you think that there's something about this case that's got under his skin?'

He looked at her as if he were sharing the car with a stranger, wondering just how much he could prudently confide. Then he said:

'Yes, yes I do.'

Something, Kate felt, had been achieved, a confidence, a trust established. She pressed further.

'What's bugging him then?'

'What happened to Berowne in that church, I suppose. AD likes life to be rational. Odd for a poet, but there it is. This case isn't, not altogether.'

'Have you talked to him about it, what happened in that church I mean?'

'No. I did try once but all I could get out of him was: "The real world is difficult enough, John. Let's try to stay in it." So I shut my mouth, not being a fool.'

The light changed. She slipped out the clutch, the Rover moved quickly and smoothly away. They were meticulous in taking turns to drive. He yielded up the seat readily enough but like all good drivers he disliked being a passenger and it was a matter of pride for her to match his fast competence. She knew that she was tolerated by him, respected even, but they didn't really like each other. He accepted that the team needed a woman but without being overtly chauvinistic, he would have preferred a man as partner. Her feeling towards him was more positive, compounded of resentment and antipathy. Some of it she knew was class resentment. But at heart there was a dislike more instinctive and fundamental. She found red-haired men physically unattractive. Whatever there was between them it certainly wasn't the antagonism of an unacknowledged sexuality. Dalgliesh, of course, knew that perfectly well. He made use of it as he made use of so much. For a moment she felt a spurt of active dislike of all men. I'm an oddity, she thought. How much would I care, really care, if Alan chucked me? Suppose I had the choice, promotion or Alan, my flat or Alan? She was given to these awkward self-examinations, imaginary choices, ethical dilemmas, none the less intriguing because she knew she would never have to confront them in real life.

She said:

'Do you believe that something really did happen to Berowne in that vestry?'

'It must have, mustn't it? A man doesn't chuck his job and change the direction of his whole life for nothing.'

'But was it real? OK, don't ask me what I mean by real. Real in the sense this car is real, you're real, I'm real. Was he deluded, drunk, drugged? Or did he really have, well, some kind of supernatural experience, I suppose?'

'It seems unlikely for a practising member of the good old C of E, which is what he's supposed to have been. That's the sort of thing you expect of characters in a Graham Greene novel.'

She said:

285

'You make it sound as if it were in poor taste, eccentric, a bit presumptuous.' She was silent for a moment and then asked:

'If you have a kid will you have him christened?'

'Yes. Why do you ask?'

'So you believe in it, God, the Church, religion.'

'I didn't say so.'

'Then why?'

'My family have been christened for 400 years, longer I suppose. Yours, too, I imagine. It doesn't seem to have done us any harm. I don't see why I should be the first to break the tradition, not without some positive feelings against it which I don't happen to have.'

And wasn't that, she thought, one of the things which Sarah Berowne had resented in her father, the ironic detachment which is too arrogant even to care. She said:

'So it's a matter of class.'

He laughed:

'Everything with you is a matter of class. No, it's a matter of family, of family piety if you like.'

She said, carefully not looking at him:

'I'm hardly the person to talk to about family piety. I'm illegitimate, if you didn't know.'

'No, I didn't know.'

'Well, thank you for not telling me it isn't important.'

He said:

'It only concerns one person. You. If you think it's important then OK, it has to be important.'

Suddenly she almost liked him. She glanced at the freckled face under a shock of red hair and tried to see him against the background of that college chapel. Then she thought of her own school. Ancroft Comprehensive had certainly had a religion all right, fashionable and, in a school with twenty different nationalities, expedient. It was anti-racism. You soon learned that you could get away with any amount of insubordination, indolence or stupidity if you were sound on this essential doctrine. It struck her that it was like any other religion; it meant what you wanted it to mean: it was easy to learn, a few platitudes, myths and slogans; it was intolerant, it gave you the excuse for occasional selective aggression, and you could make a moral virtue out of despising the people you disliked. Best of all, it cost nothing. She liked to pretend that this early indoctrination had absolutely nothing to do with the cold fury which seized her when she met its opposite, the obscene

286

graffiti, the shouted insults, the terror of Asian families afraid to leave their barricaded homes. If you had to have a school ethos to give the illusion of togetherness then for her money anti-racism was as good as any. And whatever she might think about its more absurd manifestations, it wasn't likely to lead you to see visions in a dusty church.

7

Dalgliesh had decided to drive alone on the Saturday afternoon to see the Nolans in their Surrey cottage. It was the kind of chore he would normally have entrusted to Massingham and Kate, or even to a detective sergeant and DC, and he could see the surprise in Massingham's eyes when he told him that he had no need of a witness nor of anyone to take notes. The journey itself wasn't unnecessary. If Berowne's murder were linked to Theresa Nolan's suicide, anything he could discover about the girl, who was at present no more than a photograph in a police file, a pale, childish face under a nurse's cap, could be important. He needed to clothe that shadowy ghost with the living girl. But in intruding on her grandparents' grief he could at least make it as easy as possible for them. One police officer must surely be more tolerable than two.

But there was, he knew, another reason for going himself and alone. He needed an hour or two of solitude and quietness, an excuse to get away from London, from his office, from the insistent telephone, from Massingham and the squad. He needed to escape from the AC's carefully unspoken criticism that he was making a mystery out of a tragic but unremarkable suicide and murder, that they were all wasting time on a manhunt without a quarry. He needed to escape, however briefly, from the clutter of his desk and the pressure of personalities, to see the case with clearer, unprejudiced eyes.

It was a warm, blustery day. Torn shreds of clouds dragged across a sky of clear azure blue and cast their frail shadows over the shorn, autumnal fields. He was travelling via Cobham and Effingham, and once off the A3 he drove the Jaguar XJS into a layby and thrust open the car roof. After Cobham, with the wind tearing at his hair, he thought he could smell in its fitful gusts the rich, pine-scented woodsmoke of autumn. The narrow country roads, bleached white between the grass verges, wound through the Surrey woodlands which would suddenly clear to give him a wide view to the South Downs and Sussex. He found himself wishing that the road would straighten before his wheels and run empty, unsignposted, for ever, that he could press down the accelerator and lose all his frustrations in the surge of power, that this rush of autumn-scented air screaming in his ears could cleanse his mind as well as his eyes of the colour of blood for ever.

He half-dreaded his journey's end, and it came unexpectedly quickly. He passed through Shere and found himself climbing a short hill; and there on the left-hand side of the road, bounded by oaks and silver birch, and separated from the road by a short garden, was an unremarkable Victorian cottage with its name, 'Weaver's Cottage', painted on the white gate. About twenty yards beyond it the road straightened and he drove the Jaguar gently on to the sandy verge. When he had turned off the engine the silence was absolute, birdless, and he sat for a moment, motionless and exhausted, as if he had come through some self-imposed ordeal.

He had telephoned, so he knew that they must be expecting him. But all the windows were fastened, there was no woodsmoke from the stack and the cottage had the secretive, oppressive air of a place not deserted but deliberately closed against the world. The front garden was untended with none of the haphazard exuberance of the normal cottage garden. All the plants were in rows, chrysanthemums, Michaelmas daisies, dahlias, with between them half-denuded rows of vegetables. But the ground was unweeded and the small patch of lawn on each side of the door unmown and shaggy. There was an iron knocker in the form of a horse-shoe, but no bell. He let it fall gently, guessing that they must have heard the car, must surely be expecting the knock, but it was a full minute before the door opened.

He said:

'Mrs Nolan?' and took out his card, feeling as he always did, like an importunate door-to-door salesman. She barely looked at it, but stood aside to let him in. She must, he thought, be nearer seventy than sixty, a small-boned woman with a sharp, anxious face. The exophthalmic eyes, so like her granddaughter's, gazed into his with a look with which he was only too familiar: a mixture of apprehension, curiosity and then relief that at least he looked human. She was wearing a suit in blue and grey crimplene, ill-fitting at the shoulders and puckered where she had shortened it at the hem. In her lapel was a round brooch of coloured stones in silver. It dragged at the thin crimplene. He guessed that this wasn't her usual wear for a Saturday afternoon, that she had dressed up for his visit. Perhaps she was a woman who dressed up to meet all life's ordeals and tragedies; a small gesture of pride and defiance in the face of the unknown.

The square sitting room with its single window looked to him more typical of a London suburb rather than these deep country

289

woods. It was neat, very clean, but characterless and rather dark. The original fireplace had been replaced by one of mock marble with a wooden overmantel and was furnished with an electric fire, one bar of which was burning. Two walls had been papered in a lurid mixture of roses and violets, and two with a plain paper in blue stripes. The thin, unlined curtains were hung with the patterned side towards the road so that the afternoon sunshine was filtered through a pattern of bulbous pink roses and ivy clad latticework. There were two modern armchairs, one each side of the fireplace, and a square central table with four chairs. Against the far wall was a large television set, high on a trolley. Except for a copy of both the *Radio Times* and *TV Times*, there were no magazines and no books. The only picture was a garish print of the Sacred Heart over the fireplace.

Mrs Nolan introduced her husband. He was sitting in the right-hand armchair, facing the window, a huge, gaunt man, who responded to Dalgliesh's greeting with a stiff nod, but didn't get up. His face was rigid. In the shaft of sunlight between the curtains its planes and angles looked as if they had been carved in oak. His left hand, crossed in his lap, was beating a ceaseless, involuntary tattoo.

Mrs Nolan said:

'You'd like some tea, I dare say?'

He said:

'Very much, thank you, if it isn't too much trouble,' and thought: I seem to have heard that question and spoken those words all my life.

She smiled and nodded as if satisfied, and bustled out. Dalgliesh thought: I say the conventional insincerities and she responds as if I were the one doing the favour. What is it about this job that makes people grateful that I can act like a human being?

The two men waited in silence, but the tea came very quickly. So that, he thought, accounted for the delay in opening the door. She had hurried at his knock to put on the kettle. They sat at the table in stiff formality waiting while Albert Nolan raised himself stiffly from his chair and edged his way painfully into his seat. The effort set up a new spasm of shaking. Without speaking his wife poured his tea and set the cup before him. He didn't grasp it, but bent his head and slurped his tea noisily from the side. His wife didn't even look at him. There was a half-cut cake which she said was walnut and marmalade and she smiled again when Dalgliesh accepted a slice. It was dry and rather tasteless, rolling into a soft dough in his mouth. Small pellets of walnut lodged in his teeth and the occasional sliver of orange-peel was sour to the tongue. He washed it down with a mouthful of strong, over-milked tea. Somewhere in the room a fly was making a loud intermittent buzz.

He said:

'I'm sorry that I have to trouble you, and I'm afraid it may be painful for you. As I explained on the telephone, I'm investigating the death of Sir Paul Berowne. A short time before he died he had an anonymous letter. It suggested that he might have had something to do with your granddaughter's death. That's why I'm here.'

Mrs Nolan's cup rattled in her saucer. She put both hands under the table like a well-behaved child sat a party. Then she glanced at her husband. She said:

'Theresa took her own life. I thought you'd know that, sir.'

'We did know it. But anything which happened to Sir Paul in the last weeks of his life could be important, and one thing that happened was the arrival of that anonymous letter. We should like to know who sent it. You see, we think it probable that he was murdered.'

Mrs Nolan said:

'Murdered? That letter wasn't sent from this cottage, sir. God help us, we've no call to do such a thing.'

'I know that. We never for a moment thought that it was. But I wondered whether your granddaughter ever talked to you about anyone, a close friend perhaps, someone who might have blamed Sir Paul for her death.'

Mrs Nolan shook her head. She said:

'You mean, someone who might have killed him?'

'It's a possibility we have to consider.'

'Who could there be? It doesn't make sense. She hadn't anyone else, only us, and we never laid hands on him, though God knows we were bitter enough.'

'Bitter against him?'

Suddenly her husband spoke:

'She got pregnant while she was in his house. And he knew where to find her body. How did he know? You tell me that.'

His voice was harsh, almost expressionless, but the words came out with such force that his body shook. Dalgliesh said:

'Sir Paul said at the inquest that your granddaughter spoke to him one night about her love of the woods. He thought that if she had decided to end her life, she might choose the only piece of wild woodland in central London.'

Mrs Nolan said:

'We never sent that letter to him, sir. I did see him at the inquest. Dad didn't go but I thought one of us ought to be there. He just spoke to me, Sir Paul. He was kind really. Said he was sorry. Well, what else can people say?'

Mr Nolan said:

'Sorry. Ay, I dare say.'

She turned to him:

'Dad, there's no proof. And he was a married man. Theresa wouldn't . . . Not with a married man.'

'There's no knowing what she might have done. Or him. What does it matter? She killed herself, didn't she? First getting the baby, then the abortion, then suicide. What's one more sin when you've got that on your conscience?'

Dalgliesh said gently:

'Can you tell me something about her? You brought her up, didn't you?'

'That's right. She hadn't anyone else. We only had the one child, her dad. Her mum died ten days after Theresa was born. She had appendicitis and the operation went wrong. A chance in a million, the doctor said.'

Dalgliesh thought: I don't want to hear this. I don't want to listen to their pain. That was what the consultant obstetrician had said to him when he had gone to take a last look at his dead wife with her newborn son in the crook of her arm, both of them composed in the secret nothingness of death. A chance in a million. As if there could be comfort, almost pride, in the knowledge that chance had singled out your family to demonstrate the arbitrary statistics of human fallibility. Suddenly the buzzing of the fly was intolerable. He said:

'Excuse me,' and seized the copy of the *Radio Times*. He swiped at it violently, but missed. It took another two vehement slaps against the glass before the buzzing finally stopped and it dropped out of sight leaving only a faint smear. He said:

'And your son?'

'Well, he couldn't look after the baby. It wasn't to be expected. He was only 21. And I think he wanted to get away from the house, from us, even from the baby. In a funny way I think he blamed us. You see, we didn't really want the marriage. Shirley, his wife, she wasn't the girl we would have chosen. We told him no good would come of it.'

And when no good had come of it, it was them he had blamed, as if their disapproval, their resentment, had hovered over his wife like a curse. He asked:

292

'Where is he now?'

'We don't know. We think he went to Canada, but he never writes. He had a good trade, mechanic. He understood cars. And he was always clever with his hands. He said he'd have no trouble finding a job.'

'So he doesn't know that his daughter is dead?'

Albert Nolan said:

'He hardly knew she was alive. Why should he care now she's dead?'

His wife bent her head as if to let his bitterness wash over her. Then she said:

'I think she always felt guilty, poor Theresa. She thought she'd killed her mum. It was nonsense, of course. And then her dad leaving her, that didn't help. She grew up like an orphan and I think she resented it. When bad things happen to a child, she always thinks it's her fault.'

Dalgliesh said:

'But she must have been happy here with you. She loved the woodlands, didn't she?'

'Maybe. But I think she was lonely. She had to go to school by bus and couldn't stay for after-school activities. And there weren't other girls of her age anywhere near. She used to love walking in the woods, but we didn't encourage that, not on her own. These days you never know. Nobody's safe any more. We hoped that she'd make friends when she started nursing.'

'And did she?'

'She never brought them home. But then there wasn't much here for young people. Not really.'

'And you found nothing among her papers, among things she left, to give you any idea who the father of her child could have been?'

'She didn't leave anything, not even her nursing books. She was living in a hostel near Oxford Street after she left Campden Hill Square and she cleared the whole room, threw everything out. All we had from the police was the letter, her watch, the clothes she was wearing. We threw the letter away. No point in keeping it. You can see her room if you like, sir. It's the one she had since she was a little girl. There's nothing there, just an empty room. We gave everything here, her clothes and her books, to Oxfam. We thought that was what she would have wanted.'

It was, he thought, what they had wanted. She led him up the narrow staircase, showed him the room and then left. It was at the back of the cottage, small, narrow, north-facing, with one latticed window. Outside the pine trees and silver birch were so close that the leaves almost trembled against the panes. The room held a green luminosity as if it were under water. A branch of climbing rose with drooping leaves and one tight cankered bud, tapped at the window. It was, as she had said, only an empty room. The air was very still and held a faint smell of disinfectant as if the walls and floor had been scrubbed. It reminded him of a hospital room from which a dead body had been removed, impersonal, functional, a calculated space between four walls, waiting for the next patient to bring his apprehension, his pain, his hope to give it meaning. They had even stripped the bed. A white coverlet was spread over the bare mattress and the single pillow. The shelves of the wall-hung bookcase were empty; surely they were too fragile ever to have held many books. Nothing else remained except for a crucifix over the bed. Having nothing to remember but grief they had divested the room even of her personality and had closed the door.

Looking down at the stripped and narrow bed he recalled the words of the girl's suicide note. He had read it only twice when studying the report of the inquest but he had no difficulty in remembering it word for word.

'Please forgive me. I can't go on in so much pain. I killed my baby and I know that I shall never see her or you again. I suppose I'm damned but I can't believe in hell any more. I can't believe in anything. You were good to me but I was no use to you, ever. I thought when I became a nurse that everything would be different but the world was never friendly. Now I know that I don't have to live in it. I hope that it won't be children who find my body. Forgive me.'

It was not, he thought, a spontaneous letter. He had read so many suicide notes since he was a young DC. Sometimes they were written out of a pain and anger which produced its own unselfconscious poetry of despair. But this, despite its pathos and seeming simplicity, was more contrived, the tone of self-regard subdued but unmistakable. She may, he thought, have been one of those dangerously innocent young women, often more dangerous and less innocent than they seem, who are the catalysts of tragedy. She stood on the periphery of his investigation like a pale wraith in her nurse's uniform, unknown and now unknowable and yet, he was convinced, central to the mystery of Berowne's death.

He had no hope now of learning anything useful at Weaver's Cottage, but his instinct to search made him pull open the drawer of the bedside cabinet, and he saw that something of her remained: her missal. He picked it up and leafed casually through it. A small square of paper torn from a notebook fell out. He picked it up and found himself looking at three columns of figures and letters:

R	D3	S
B	D2	S
P	D1	S
S–N	S2	D

Downstairs the Nolans were still sitting at the table. He showed them the paper. Mrs Nolan thought that the figures and letters were in Theresa's handwriting, but said she couldn't be sure. Neither of them had any explanation to offer. Neither showed any interest. But they made no difficulty when he said that he would like to take the paper away.

Mrs Nolan went with him to the front door and, somewhat to his surprise, walked with him down the path to the gate. When they reached it she looked across at the dark shadows of the wood and said with barely suppressed passion:

'This cottage is tied to Albert's job. We ought to have been out three years ago when he got really bad, but they've been very kind to us. But we'll be leaving as soon as the local authority finds us a flat, and I won't be sorry. I hate these woods, hate them, hate them. Nothing but the wind forever whistling, sodden earth, darkness pressing in on you, small animals screaming in the night.'

And then as she closed the gate behind him she looked up into his face:

'Why didn't she tell me about the baby? I'd have understood. I'd have looked after her. I could have made Dad understand. That's what hurts. Why didn't she tell me?'

Dalgliesh said:

'I expect she wanted to save you pain. That's what we all try to do, save those we love from pain.'

'Dad's so bitter. He thinks she's damned. But I've forgiven her. God can't be less merciful than I am. I can't believe that.'

'No,' he said, 'I don't think we need believe that.'

She stood at the gate watching him. But when he had got into the car and fastened his seatbelt he looked back at her and found that, almost mysteriously, she had gone. The cottage had returned to its secret reticence. He thought: There's too much pain in this job. To think I used to congratulate myself, to think it useful, God help me, that people found it easy to confide in me. And what has today's brush with reality brought me? A scrap of paper torn from a notebook with a few jottings, letters and digits which she may not even have written. He felt himself contaminated by the Nolans' bitterness and pain. He thought: And if I tell myself that enough is enough, twenty years of using people's weakness against them, twenty years of careful non-involvement, if I resign, what then? Whatever Berowne found in that dingy vestry, it isn't open to me even to look for it. As the Jaguar bumped gently back on to the road he felt a spurt of irrational envy and anger against Berowne who had found so easy a way out.

8

It was six fifteen on Sunday evening and Carole Washburn stood gripping the rail of the balcony and looking down over the panorama of North London. She had never needed to draw the curtains when Paul had been with her, even late at night. They could gaze out together over the city and know themselves unwatched, inviolate. Then it had been good to step outside, feeling the warmth of his arm through his sleeve, and stand there together, secure, private, gazing down at the busy preoccupations of a world patterned in light. Then she had been a privileged spectator; but now she felt like an outcast, yearning for this distant unattainable paradise from which she was for ever excluded. Each night since his death she had stood watching as the lights had come on, block by block, house by house, squares of light, oblongs of light, light glimmering through curtains of rooms where people were living their shared, or secret, lives.

And now what seemed the longest Sunday she had ever endured was drawing to its close. In the afternoon, desperate to get out of the cage of the flat, she had driven to the nearest open supermarket. There was nothing she needed, but she had taken a trolley and pushed it aimlessly between the shelves, automatically reaching out for tins, packages, rolls of toilet paper, piling the trolley high, oblivious of the glances of her fellow shoppers. But then the tears had started to flow again, splashing over her hand, dropping in an unstoppable stream, splodging the packets of cereal, wrinkling the toilet rolls. She had abandoned her trolley laden with unwanted, unsuitable goods and had walked out to the car park and driven home again, slowly and carefully like a novice driver, seeing the world blurred and disorientated, the people jerking like puppets, as if reality were dissolving in perpetual rain.

By evening she had been seized by a desperate need for human companionship. It wasn't the need to begin some sort of life for herself, to plan some sort of future, to cast out her unpractised net into the void she had made around her secret life and begin to draw other people close. Perhaps that would come in time, impossible as it now seemed. It had been a simple uncontrollable longing to be with another human being, to hear a human voice making ordinary, unremarkable human sounds. She had telephoned

Emma, who had come into the Civil Service with her from Reading, and who was now a Principal in the Department of Health and Social Security. Before she became Paul's mistress she had spent a fair proportion of her spare time with Emma, quick lunches at a pub or café convenient for both their offices, films, the occasional theatre, even a weekend together in Amsterdam to visit the Rijksmuseum. It had been an undemanding, unconfiding friendship. She had known that Emma would never give up the chance of a date with a man to spend an evening with her; and Emma had been the first victim to her obsessional need for privacy, the reluctance to commit even an hour of time which could be given to Paul. She looked at her watch. It was six forty-two. Unless Emma was spending the weekend out of town she would probably be at home.

She had to look up the number. The familiar digits sprang from the page at her like the key to an earlier, half-forgotten existence. She hadn't spoken to a human being since the police had left, and she wondered if her voice sounded as gruff and false to Emma as it did to her own ears.

'Hello? Emma? You won't believe it. This is Carole, Carole Washburn.'

There was the sound of music, joyous, contrapuntal. It could have been Mozart or Vivaldi. Emma called:

'Turn it down, darling,' and then to Carole:

'Good God! How are you?'

'Fine. It's ages since we met. I wondered if you'd like to see a film or something. Tonight perhaps.'

There was a small silence, and then Emma's voice, carefully uncommitted, surprise and perhaps a small note of resentment carefully controlled.

'Sorry, we've got people coming in for dinner.'

Emma had always said dinner rather than supper even when they were proposing to eat a take-away Chinese meal at the kitchen table. It had been one of those minor snobberies which Carole had found irritating. She said:

'Next weekend perhaps?'

'Not possible, I'm afraid. Alistair and I are driving down to Wiltshire. Visiting his parents, actually. Another time perhaps. Lovely to hear from you. I must fly, the guests are due at seven thirty. I'll give you a ring sometime.'

It was all she could do not to cry out: 'Include me, include me! Please, I need to come.' The receiver was replaced, voice, music, communication cut off. Alistair. But of course, she had forgotten that Emma was engaged. A Principal at the Treasury. So he had moved into the flat. She could imagine what they were saying now.

'Three years without a word and she suddenly rings and wants to see a film. And on Sunday evening for God's sake.'

And Emma wouldn't ring back. She had Alistair; a shared life, shared friends. You couldn't cut people out of your life and expect to find them complaisant, readily available, just because you needed to feel human again.

There were two more days of her leave to get through before she was due back in the office. She could go home, of course, except that this flat was home. And it was hardly worth the drive to Clacton, to the square, high-roofed bungalow outside the town where her widowed mother had lived since her father's death twelve years earlier. She hadn't been home for fourteen months. Friday night was sacrosanct; she could hope for a couple of hours with Paul on his way to his constituency. Sunday she had always kept free for him. Her mother, used to her neglect, seemed no longer to be particularly worried by it. Her mother's sister had the bungalow next door and the two widows, early acrimonies forgotten, had settled into a cosy routine of mutual support, their brick-boxed lives measured out by small treats: shopping, morning coffee at their favourite café, returning their library books, the evening television programmes, supper on a trolley. Carole had almost given up wondering about their lives, why they had chosen to live by the sea when they never went near it, what they talked about. She could telephone now and her mother would be grudgingly acquiescent, resenting the chore of making up the spare bed, the interruption to the weekend programme, the problem of stretching the food. She told herself that she had trained her mother over the past three years to expect neglect, had been grateful that her time with Paul hadn't been threatened by demands from Clacton. It seemed to her ignoble to telephone now, to rush home in search of a comfort for which she couldn't ask and which her mother, even if she had known the truth, wouldn't be able to give.

Six forty-five. If this were a Friday he would have arrived by now, timing his entrance to ensure that there was no one in the hall to see him. There would be the one long ring, the two short peals on the bell which were his signal. And then the bell rang, one long insistent peal. She thought she heard a second and then a third, but that might have been her imagination. For one miraculous second, no more, she thought that he had come, that it had all been an idiotic mistake. She called: 'Paul, Paul my darling!' and almost flung herself against the door. And then her mind took hold of reality and she knew the truth. The receiver slid through her moist hands and almost fell and her lips were so dry that she could hear them cracking. She whispered:

'Who is it?' The answering voice was high, a female voice. It said:

'Could I come up? I'm Barbara Berowne.'

She pressed the button almost without thinking and heard the burr of the released lock, the click of the door as it closed. It was too late now to change her mind, but she knew that there had been no choice. In her present desperate loneliness she would have sent no one away. And this encounter had been inevitable. Ever since her affair with Paul had started she had wanted to see his wife, and now she was going to see her. She opened the door and stood waiting, listening for the whine of the lift, the muted footfalls on the carpet, as she had once waited for his.

She came down the corridor, light-footed, casually elegant, golden, her scent, subtle and elusive, seeming to precede her and then waste itself on the air. She was wearing a coat of cream broadcloth, its wide arms and shoulders pleated, the sleeves fashioned in some finer and differently textured cloth. Her black leather boots looked as soft as her black gloves and she carried a shoulder bag on a slim strap. She was hatless, the corn coloured hair with its streaks of paler gold twisted at the back into a long roll. It surprised Carole that she could notice the details, could actually wonder about the material of the coat sleeves, speculate where it had been bought, how much it had cost.

As she came in it seemed to Carole that the blue eyes looked round the room with a frank, faintly contemptuous appraisal. She said in a voice which even to her own ears sounded harsh, ungracious:

'Please sit down. Would you like something to drink? Coffee, sherry, some wine?'

She, herself, moved over to Paul's chair. It seemed to her impossible that his wife should sit where she had been used to seeing him. They faced each other a few yards apart. Barbara Berowne looked down at the carpet as if satisfying herself that it was clean before placing her bag at her feet. She said:

'No thank you. I can't stay long. I have to get back. We've got some people coming, some of Paul's colleagues. They want to talk

300

about the memorial service. We shan't have it until the police discover who killed him, but these things have to be settled weeks in advance if one wants St Margaret's. Apparently they don't think he really qualifies for the Abbey, poor darling. You'll come, of course; to the memorial service I mean. There will be so many people there that you won't be noticed. I mean you needn't feel embarrassed about me.'

'No, I've never felt embarrassed about you.'

'I think it's all rather gruesome actually. I don't think Paul would have wanted all that fuss. But the constituency seemed to feel that we ought to have a memorial service. After all, he was a Minister. The cremation will be private. I don't think you ought to go to that anyway, do you? It will be just the family and really intimate friends.'

Intimate friends. Suddenly she wanted to laugh aloud. She said:

'Is that why you're here? To tell me about the funeral arrangements?'

'I thought Paul would want you to know. After all, we both loved him in our different ways. We're both concerned to safeguard his reputation.'

She said:

'There's nothing you can teach me about safeguarding his reputation. How did you know where to find me?'

'Oh I've known where to find you for months. A cousin of mine employed a private detective. It wasn't very difficult, just a matter of following Paul's car on a Friday evening. And then he eliminated all the couples in this block, all the old women and all the single men. That left you.'

She had drawn off her black gloves and had lain them on her knee. Now she was smoothing them out, finger by finger, with pink tipped hands. She said without looking up:

'I'm not here to make trouble for you. After all we're in this together. I'm here to help.'

'We aren't in anything together. We never have been. And what do you mean by help? Are you offering me money?'

The eyes looked up, and Carole thought she detected a flicker of anxiety, as if the question needed to be taken seriously.

'Not really. I mean, I didn't think you were actually in need. Did Paul buy this flat for you? It's rather cramped, isn't it? Still, it's quite pleasant if you don't mind living in a suburb. I'm afraid he hasn't mentioned you in his will. That's another thing I thought you ought to know, in case you were wondering.'

301

Carole said, her voice over-loud and harsh even to her own ears:
'This flat is mine. The deposit was paid by me, the mortgage is paid with my money. Not that it's any of your business. But if you have a conscience about me, forget it. There's nothing I want from you or from anyone else connected with Paul. Women who prefer to be kept by men all their lives can never get it into their heads that some of us like to pay our own way.'
'Did you have any choice?'
Speechless, she heard the high, childish voice continuing:
'After all, you've always been discreet. I admire you for that. It can't have been easy only seeing him when he hadn't anything better to do.'
The amazing thing was that the insult wasn't deliberate. She was capable of being intentionally offensive, of course, but this had been a casual remark born of an egotism so insensitive that she spoke what she thought, not wanting particularly to wound, but incapable of caring whether she wounded or not. Carole thought: Paul, how could you have married her? How could you have been taken in? She's stupid, third-rate, spiteful, insensitive, mean minded. Is beauty really so important?
She said:
'If that's all you've come to say, perhaps you'll go. You've seen me. You know what I look like. You've seen the flat. This is the chair he used to sit in. That's the table he used for his drink. If you want I can show you the bed we made love on.'
'I know what he came for.'
She wanted to cry out 'Oh no you don't. You know nothing about him. I was as happy lying with him on that bed as I've ever been or ever shall be. But that wasn't what he came for.' She had believed, still believed, that only with her had he been wholly at peace. He had lived his over-busy life neatly compartmentalized; the Campden Hill Square house, the House of Commons, his ministerial suite at the department, his constituency headquarters. Only in this high, ordinary, suburban flat did the disparate elements fuse together and he could be a whole person, uniquely himself. When he had come in and sat opposite her, had dropped his briefcase at his feet and smiled at her she had watched with joy, time and time again, the taut face soften and relax, become already smooth as if they had just made love. There were things about his private life which she knew he had held back from her, not consciously or out of lack of trust, but because, when they were together, they had no longer seemed important. But he had never held back himself.

Barbara Berowne was admiring her engagement ring, holding out her hand and moving it slowly in front of her face; the huge diamond in its setting of sapphires twinkled and flashed. She gave a secretive reminiscent smile then looked across at Carole and said:

'There's one other thing which you might as well know. I'm having a baby.'

Carole cried:

'It isn't true! You're lying! You can't be!'

The blue eyes widened.

'Of course it's true. It isn't something you can lie about, not for long anyway. I mean the truth will be obvious to the whole world in a couple of months.'

'It isn't his child!'

She thought: I'm shouting, screaming at her. I must keep calm. O God, help me not to believe.

And now Barbara Berowne actually laughed.

'Of course it's his child. He always wanted an heir, didn't you know that? Look, you may as well accept it. The only other man I've slept with since my marriage is sterile. He's had a vasectomy. I'm going to have Paul's son.'

'He wouldn't have done it. You couldn't have made him do it.'

'But he did. There is one thing you can always make a man do. That is if he likes women at all. Haven't you found that out? You're not pregnant, too, are you?'

Carole buried her face in her hands. She whispered:

'No.'

'I thought I ought to be sure.' She giggled. 'That would have been a complication, wouldn't it?'

Suddenly all control was gone. There was nothing left but naked anger, naked shame. She heard herself bawling like a shrew.

'Get out! Get out of my flat!'

Even in the middle of her anguish and fury she didn't miss the sudden flicker of fear in the blue eyes. She saw it with a spurt of pleasure and triumph. So she wasn't inviolate after all, she could be frightened. But the knowledge was vaguely unwelcome; it made Barbara Berowne vulnerable, more human. Now she got up almost gracelessly, bent to pick up her shoulder bag by the strap, then scampered to the door ungainly as a child. Only when Carole had opened it and stood aside to let her out did she turn and speak.

'I'm sorry you've taken it like this. I think you're being rather silly. After all, I was his wife, I'm the injured party.'

303

And then she was hurrying down the corridor. Carole called after her:

'The injured party! My God that's good. The injured party!'

She closed the door and leaned against it. Sickness heaved at her stomach. She rushed to the bathroom, spewed into the basin grasping the taps for support. And then came anger, cleansing, almost exhilarating. Between fury and grief she wanted to fling her head back and howl like an animal. She groped her way back into the sitting room and felt for her own chair like a blind woman, then sat gazing at his empty seat, willing herself to calm. When she had herself under control, she fetched her handbag and took out the card with the Scotland Yard extension she had been asked to telephone.

It was Sunday, but someone would be on duty. Even if she couldn't speak to Inspector Miskin now, she could leave a message, ask that she be rung back. It couldn't wait until tomorrow. She had to commit herself irrevocably, and now.

A male voice answered, one she didn't recognize. She gave her name and asked for Inspector Miskin.

She said:

'It's urgent. It's about the Berowne murder.'

There was a delay of only seconds before the Inspector answered. Although she had only heard the voice once before, it came to her with a shock of recognition. She said:

'This is Carole Washburn. I want to see you. There's something I've decided to tell you.'

'We'll come round now.'

'Not here. I don't want you to come here, not ever again. I'll meet you tomorrow morning. Nine o'clock. The formal garden in Holland Park, the one near the Orangery. Do you know it?'

'Yes, I know it. We'll be there.'

'I don't want Commander Dalgliesh. I don't want any male officer. Just you. I won't talk to anyone else.'

There was a pause, then the voice spoke again, unsurprised, accepting:

'Nine o'clock tomorrow. The garden, Holland Park. I'll be on my own. Can you give me any idea what it's about?'

'It's about the death of Theresa Nolan. Goodbye.'

Then she replaced the receiver and leaned her forehead against the cold stickiness of the metal. She felt empty, light-headed, shaken by her heartbeats. She wondered what she would feel, how she could go on living when she was capable of knowing what she had done. She wanted to cry aloud: 'My darling, I'm sorry, I'm sorry. I'm sorry.' But she had made her decision. There was no going back now. And it seemed to her that there still hung in the room the fugitive scent of Barbara Berowne's perfume, like the taint of betrayal, and that the air of her flat would never be free of it.

BOOK FIVE
Rhesus Positive

1

Miles Gilmartin of Special Branch was protected from the impor-
tunities of casual visitors and the attention of the ill-intentioned by
a series of checks and counterchecks which to Dalgliesh, waiting in
thwarted anger and impatience while each was negotiated, seemed
more childishly ingenious than necessary or effective. It wasn't a
game he was in the mood to play. By the time he was finally
ushered into Gilmartin's office by a PA who irritatingly combined
exceptional beauty with an obvious consciousness of her unique
privilege in serving the great man, Dalgliesh was beyond considerations of prudence or discretion. Bill Duxbury was with Gilmartin
and they hardly got beyond the few preliminary courtesies before
anger found its relief in words.

'We're supposed to be on the same side, if you people acknowledge any side but your own. Paul Berowne was murdered. If I can't
get cooperation from you, where can I expect to get it?'

Gilmartin said:

'I can understand a certain resentment that we didn't tell you
earlier that Travers was one of our operatives . . .'

'Operatives. You make it sound as if she were on a production
line. And you didn't tell me. I had to discover it for myself. Oh, I
can see the fascination of your world. It reminds me of my prep
school. We had our little secrets, our code words, initiation ceremonies. But when the hell are you people going to grow up? All
right, I know it's necessary, some of it anyway, and for some of the
time. But you make it into an obsession. Secrecy for its own sake,
the whole vast paper-ridden bureaucracy of spying. No wonder
your kind of organization breeds your own traitors. In the meantime I'm investigating an actual murder and it would help if you
stopped playing games and joined the real world.'

Gilmartin said mildly:

'I'm not sure that speech wouldn't have been more appropriately
made to MI5. There's something in what you say. One ought to
guard more against over-enthusiasm, and we're certainly over-
bureaucratized. But then what organization isn't? We deal in
information after all and information is valueless if it isn't properly
documented and easily available. Still, pound for pound, I think we
give the taxpayers value for money.'

Dalgliesh looked at him.

'You really haven't understood a word I've been saying.'

'Oh yes I have, Adam. But it's all so unlike you. Such vehemence! You've been reading too many of those espionage novels.'

Three years ago, thought Dalgliesh bitterly, Gilmartin might have thought even if he hadn't dared to speak it: It's all that poetry you write. But he couldn't say that now. Gilmartin went on:

'Are you sure this Berowne murder isn't getting under your skin? You knew him, didn't you?'

'For God's sake, if another person suggests I can't handle the case because I knew the victim, I'll resign.' For the first time, a look of concern like a brief spasm of pain passed over Gilmartin's bland, almost colourless face.

'Oh, I shouldn't do that. Not over a small sin of omission on our part. I suppose that Berowne was murdered, by the way. There's a rumour that it could have been suicide. After all, he was hardly normal at the time. This habit he'd developed of sleeping in church vestries. And isn't he supposed to have had some kind of divine revelation? Listening to his voices when he should have been listening to the Prime Minister. And such a very curious church to choose. I can understand an enthusiasm for English Perpendicular but a Romanesque basilica in Paddington is surely an improbable choice for a good night's sleep let alone one's personal road to Damascus.'

Dalgliesh was tempted to ask him whether he would have found St Margaret's Westminster a more acceptable choice. Gilmartin, having neatly demonstrated at least a superficial knowledge of church architecture and scripture to his own evident satisfaction, got up from his desk and began to pace between the windows as if suddenly aware that he was the only one sitting down at a desk and that this lower status might put him at a disadvantage. He could afford a good tailor and dressed with a careful formality which, in a less confident man, might suggest that he was aware of the slightly ambiguous reputation of the security service and was anxious not to reinforce it by any slovenliness in manner or appearance. But Gilmartin dressed to please himself as he did everything. Today he was elegant in grey. Above the formal suit with its almost invisible darker stripe, the square almost bloodless face and the sleek hair, prematurely white and brushed straight back from the high forehead, reinforced both image and colour scheme; a carefully composed arrangement in grey and silver against which his old school tie, despite its comparative sobriety, hung like a garish flag of defiance.

310

In contrast Bill Duxbury, stocky, ruddy-faced and loud-voiced, looked like a gentleman farmer whose farming is more successful than his gentility. He stood half looking out of the window as if he had been ordered to distance himself from the adults and their concerns. Dalgliesh saw that he had recently got rid of his moustache. Without it his face looked incomplete and naked, as if he had been forcibly shaved. He was wearing a tweed checked suit, rather too heavy for the comparatively mild autumn, the jacket cut with a back flap which strained over his large, rather feminine buttocks. When Gilmartin looked at him, which was infrequently, it was with a pained, slightly surprised expression as if deploring both his subordinate's figure and his tailor.

It had early been apparent that Gilmartin was to do the talking. Duxbury would have briefed him but Duxbury would remain silent unless invited to speak. Dalgliesh was suddenly reminded of a dinner party conversation some years previously. He had found himself sitting with a woman on one of those three-person sofas which can only comfortably hold two. It had been a Georgian drawing room in a north Islington square but he couldn't now remember the name of his hostess and God knew what he thought he had been doing there. His companion had been slightly drunk, not offensively so but enough to make her flirtatious, merry, and then confiding. Memory refused to come up with her name and it didn't matter. They had sat together for half an hour before their hostess, with practised tact, had separated them. He could remember only part of their conversation. She and her husband had a penthouse overlooking a street which was commonly used for student demonstrations and the police – she was sure they were Special Branch – had asked if they could use their front sitting room to take photographs from the window.

'We said they could, of course, and they were really very sweet about it. But part of me wasn't really happy. I wanted to say: "They're British subjects. They've got the right to march if they want to. If you want to photograph them, can't you do it openly, in the street?" But I didn't. After all, it was rather fun in a way. The sense of conspiracy, being in the know. And it wasn't up to us to make a stand. They know what they're doing. And it never does to antagonize these people.'

It had seemed to him then, and it did now, to sum up the attitude of decent liberals all over the world: 'They know what they're doing. It isn't up to us to make a stand. It never does to antagonize these people.'

311

He said bitterly:

'I'm surprised that you and MI5 don't encourage regular second-ments to the KGB. You've more in common with them than you have with any outsider. It might be instructive to see how they deal with their paperwork.'

Gilmartin lifted an eyelid at Duxbury as if inviting solidarity in the face of unreason. He said mildly:

'As far as paperwork is concerned, Adam, it would help us if your people were a little more conscientious. Massingham, when requesting information about Ivor Garrod, should have put in an IR49.'

'In quadruplicate, of course.'

'Well, registry need a copy and so, presumably, do you. We're supposed to keep MI5 in the picture. We could look at the procedure again, of course, but I would say that four copies were the minimum.'

Dalgliesh said:

'This girl, Diana Travers. Was she the most suitable person you could find to spy on a Minister of State? Even for Special Branch, it seems an odd choice.'

'But we weren't spying on a Minister of State, she wasn't assigned to Berowne. As we told you when you inquired about his mistress, Berowne never was a risk. No IR49 submitted there either, inciden-tally.'

'I see. You infiltrated Travers into Garrod's group or cell, what-ever he calls it, and conveniently forgot to mention the fact when we inquired about him. You must have known that he was a suspect. He still is.'

'It hardly seemed relevant. We all operate, after all, on the "need to know" principle. And we didn't infiltrate her into Campden Hill Square. Garrod did. Travers's little job for us had nothing to do with Berowne's death.'

'But Travers's death might have.'

'There was nothing suspicious about her death. You must have studied the autopsy report.'

'Which wasn't, I noticed, carried out by the usual Home Office pathologist for Thames Valley.'

'We like to use our own people. He's perfectly competent, I assure you. She died from natural causes, more or less. It could have happened to anyone. She had eaten too much, drunk too much, and she plunged into cold water, got tangled in the reeds, gasped and drowned. There were no suspicious marks on the

312

body. She had had, as you no doubt remember from the PM report, a sexual connection just before death.' He hesitated a little before the phrase. It was the only time Dalgliesh had seen him even slightly discomposed. It was as if he felt the words 'making love' were inappropriate and couldn't bring himself to use a coarser soubriquet.

Dalgliesh was silent. Anger had led him into a protest that now seemed to him humiliatingly childish as well as ineffectual. He had achieved nothing except possibly to exacerbate the simmering professional rivalry between C Division, the Special Branch and MI5 whose uneasy relationship could so easily spill over into high politics. Next time Gilmartin might say: 'And for God's sake, put AD in the picture. He's apt to get his knickers in a twist if he doesn't get his share of the lollipops.' But what depressed him most and left him with a sour taste of self-disgust, was how close he had come to losing his control. He realized how important it had become to him, his reputation for coolness, detachment, uninvolvement. Well, he was involved now. Perhaps they were right. You shouldn't take on a case if you knew the victim. But how could he claim to have known Berowne? What time had they spent together, except for a three-hour train journey, a brief ten-minute spell in his office, an interrupted walk in St James's Park? And yet he knew that he had never felt so great an empathy with any other victim. That impulse to connect his fist with Gilmartin's jaw, to see blood spurting over that immaculate shirtfront, that old school tie; well, fifteen years ago he might have done it and it would have cost him his job. For a moment he almost yearned for the lost uncomplicated spontaneity of youth.

He said:

'I'm surprised that you thought Garrod worth the trouble. He was a left-wing activist at university. It hardly needs an undercover agent to discover that Garrod doesn't vote Tory. He's never made any secret of his beliefs.'

'Not of his beliefs, but he has of his activities. His group are rather more than the usual middle-class malcontents looking for an ethically acceptable outlet for aggression and some kind of cause, preferably one that gives them the illusion of commitment. Oh yes, he's worth it.'

Gilmartin signalled a glance at Duxbury who said:

'It's only a small group – cell he calls it. At present four are women. Thirteen of them altogether. He never recruits more nor less. A nice touch of counter-superstition, and, of course,

313

it adds to the mystique of conspiracy. The magic number, the closed circle.'

Dalgliesh thought that the number also had a certain operational logic. Garrod could organize three groups of four or two of six for field work and still free himself as coordinator, director, recognized leader. Duxbury went on:

'They're all from the privileged middle class which makes for cohesion and obviates class tensions. The comrades, after all, aren't notable for brotherly love. This lot speak the same language including, of course, the usual Marxist jargon, and they're all intelligent. Silly, maybe, but intelligent. A potentially dangerous bunch. None is a member of the Labour Party, incidentally. Not that the Party would have them. Six of them, including Garrod, are paid up members of the Workers' Revolutionary Campaign but they don't hold office. My guess is that the WRC is little more than a front. Garrod prefers to run his own show. A natural fascination with conspiracy, I suppose.'

Dalgliesh said:

'He should have joined Special Branch. And Sarah Berowne is a member?'

'For the last two years. A member and Garrod's mistress, which gives her a peculiar prestige in the group. In some ways the comrades are remarkably old-fashioned.'

'And what did you get from Travers? All right, let me guess. Garrod introduced her into the Campden Hill Square house. That wouldn't be difficult given the shortage of reliable domestic help. Sarah Berowne would have tipped them off about the advertisement, if she didn't actually suggest it. Anyone willing to do housework and turning up with good references – and you'd have seen to that – would be pretty sure of a job. That was his cell's function presumably, to discredit selected MPs.'

It was Gilmartin who answered:

'One of their functions. They mostly went for the moderate socialists. Dig up the muck, an illicit love affair, preferably homosexual, an ill-advised friendship, a half-forgotten sponsored trip to South Africa, a suggestion of sticky fingers in the party funds. Then when the poor devil goes up for re-selection, spread the manure around judiciously and draw delicate attention to the smell. Discrediting members of the present administration is probably more a matter of occasional duty than enjoyment. I imagine Garrod chose Paul Berowne for personal rather than political reasons. Sarah Berowne dislikes more than her Papa's party.'

314

So it had been Garrod who had sent the poison pen message to Ackroyd and the gossip writers of the nationals. Well, he had always been Dalgliesh's most likely suspect for that particular mischief. As if hearing his thoughts, Gilmartin said:

'I doubt whether you'll be able to prove he sent that message to the press. They do it very cleverly. A member of the group visits one of those shops where they sell new and second-hand typewriters and let you try out the machines. You know the scene, rows of chained typewriters for the customers to bang away on. The chance of a single prospective customer being recognized is almost nil. We can't keep perpetual watch on all the cell members. They don't warrant that intensity of effort and I'm not sure, anyway, what particular section or subsection of the criminal law they'd be infringing. The information they use is accurate. It's no use to them if it isn't. How did you get on to Travers by the way?'

'Through the woman she lodged with before she moved into her flat. Women have a profound contempt for masculine secret societies and a knack of seeing through them.'

Gilmartin said:

'The whole sex is one secret society. We wanted Travers to live alone. We should have insisted. But I'm surprised that she talked.'

'She didn't. Her landlady didn't altogether believe in an unemployed actress who could yet afford to buy a flat. But it was your men turning up to search her room that confirmed her suspicions. Incidentally, what was your real interest in Garrod, apart from getting some additional names in your activist files?'

Gilmartin pursed his lips.

'There could have been an IRA connection.'

'And was there?'

For a moment Dalgliesh thought that he would refuse to answer. Then he glanced at Duxbury and said:

'Not as far as we've been able to discover. Do you think Garrod is your man?'

'He could be.'

'Well, good hunting.' He seemed suddenly ill at ease as if uncertain how to bring the interview to an end. Then he said:

'It has been useful talking to you, Adam. We've taken notes of the points you've raised. And you'll watch the procedures, won't you? The IR49. A modest little form but it has its uses.'

As the lift bore him down to his own floor it seemed to Dalgliesh that he had been closeted with Special Branch for days rather than less than an hour. He felt contaminated by a kind of sick hopelessness. He knew that he would shake off its symptoms soon enough; he always did. But the infection would still be there in his bloodstream, part of that sickness of the spirit which he was beginning to think he must learn to endure.

But the interview, humiliatingly fractious as it had been, had served its purpose, clearing away a tangle of extraneous brushwood from the main path of his inquiry. He knew now the identity and motive of the poison pen writer. He knew what Diana Travers had been doing at Campden Hill Square, who had put her there, and why, after the drowning, her room had been searched. Two young women were dead, one by her own hand, one by accident. There was no mystery about why and how they had died and little now about how they had lived. Why then was he still obstinately convinced that these two deaths were not only linked but central to the mystery of Paul Berowne's murder?

2

When he got back from that secretive and self-sufficient world on
the eighteenth and nineteenth floors, Dalgliesh found that his own
corridor was unusually silent. He put his head in his secretary's
office but Susie's typewriter was shrouded, her desk cleared, and
he remembered that she had a dental appointment that morning.
Kate was meeting Carole Washburn in Holland Park. Irked by his
own bad temper he had hardly given a thought to the possibilities
of that encounter. Massingham was, he knew, visiting the Wayfarers' Refuge in Cosway Street to talk to the warden there about
Harry Mack before going on to interview two of the girls who had
been in the punt on the Thames when Diana Travers had drowned.
According to their evidence at the inquest neither of them had seen
the girl dive into the river. They and the rest of the party had left
her with Dominic Swayne on the bank when they pushed out the
punt and had seen and heard nothing of her until that awful
moment when the punt pole had struck her body. Both had
admitted at the inquest that they had been half-drunk at the time.
Dalgliesh doubted whether they would have anything more useful
to say now that they were sober but, if they had, Massingham was
the one best suited to get it out of them.

But Massingham had left a message. As he entered his room,
Dalgliesh saw a single sheet of white paper pinned to his blotter
with Massingham's paper knife, a long and remarkably sharp
dagger which he claimed to have won at a fairground when a child.
The dramatic gesture and the few lines of letters and figures in a
stark black upright hand said it all. The forensic science laboratory
had telephoned the result of the blood analyses. Without pulling
out the dagger, Dalgliesh stood silently and looked down at the
evidence which, more than any other, was vital to his theory that
Berowne had been murdered.

Berowne	Mack	Smears on carpet and jacket lining
Rhesus Pos	Pos	Pos
ABO A	A	A
AK 2–1 (7.6%) (enzymes)	1 (92.3%)	2–1

PGM   1+ (40%)   2 + 1 − (4.8%)   1+
(enzymes)
Razor blade:
AK   2–1
PGM   2+, 1−, 1+,

The PGM system was, he knew, a strong one. There would have been no need to set up a control reaction with the dirty carpet. But the lab must have worked over the weekend despite their heavy load and the fact that, as yet, there was no suspect in custody, and he was grateful. There was blood of two different types on the razor, but that was hardly surprising, the analysis a mere formality. But, more important, the smear on the carpet under Harry's coat wasn't his blood. Dalgliesh had another interview booked for late in the afternoon which promised, in its different way, to be as irritating as the session with Gilmartin. It was helpful that this important piece of scientific evidence had arrived in time.

3

Holland Park was only a few minutes' walk from Charles Shannon House. Kate had woken early shortly after six and by seven had breakfasted and was impatient to get away. After prowling restlessly round an already immaculate flat trying to find jobs to occupy the time she stuffed a paper bag of crumbs for the birds in her jacket pocket and left three-quarters of an hour early, telling herself that it would be less frustrating to walk in the park than to stay cooped up wondering whether Carole Washburn would actually turn up, whether she might already be regretting her promise.

Dalgliesh had accepted that the agreement with the girl must be kept; she would meet Carole Washburn alone. He had given her no instructions and offered no advice. Other senior officers would have been tempted to remind her of the importance of the meeting, but this wasn't his way. She respected him for it, but it increased her burden of responsibility. Everything might depend on how she handled their encounter.

Just before nine she made her way to the terrace above the formal gardens. When she had last visited the park the beds had been richly patterned with the summer display of geraniums, fuchsias, heliotropes and begonias. But now the time had come for the autumn stripping. Half the beds were already bare; expanses of soft loam littered with broken stems, petals like blobs of blood and a scatter of dying leaves. A council cart, like the dread tumbrel of winter, stood ready for the new strippings. And now, as the minute finger of her watch clicked to the hour the squeals and shouts from the grounds of Holland Park School were suddenly hushed and the park lay in its early morning calm. An old woman, bent as a witch, with a team of six small discouraged dogs on a lead shuffled along the side path, then paused to pull and sniff at the last flowers of the lavender. A solitary jogger loped down the steps and disappeared through the arches leading to the orangery.

And suddenly Carole Washburn was there. Almost precisely on the hour a solitary female figure appeared at the far end of the garden. She was wearing a short grey jacket over a matching skirt, her head covered by a voluminous blue and white scarf which almost obscured her face. But Kate knew immediately and with a lift of the heart, who it was. They stood for a moment regarding each other, then advanced between the denuded flower beds in measured, almost ceremonial, paces. Kate was reminded of spy thrillers, the exchange of defectors at some border crossing, a sense of unseen watchers, ears pricked for the crack of a rifle. When they met the girl nodded but did not speak. Kate said simply:

'Thank you for coming.' Then she turned and together they passed up the steps out of the garden, across the spongy turf of the wide lawn and into the path between the rose gardens. Here the freshness of the morning air was tinged with the remembered scent of summer. Roses, thought Kate, were never finished. There was something irritating about a flower which couldn't recognize that its season was over. Even in December there would be tight and browning buds destined to wither before they opened, a few anaemic heavy heads drooping towards the petal-strewn earth. Pacing slowly between the spiked bushes, aware of Carole's shoulder almost brushing hers, she thought: I must have patience. I must wait for her to speak first. She has to be the one to choose the time and place.

They came up to the statue of Lord Holland, seated on his pedestal, gazing benignly towards his house. Still without speaking, they walked on down the mushy path between the woodlands. Then her companion paused. She looked into the wilderness and said:

'That's where he found her, over there, under that slanting silver birch, the one by the holly bush. We came here together a week later. I think he needed to show me.'

Kate waited. It was extraordinary that this wilderness of trees could be close to the centre of a great city. Once over the low palisade it would be possible to believe oneself deep in the country-side. No wonder that Theresa Nolan, reared among the Surrey woodlands, should have chosen this quiet leafy place in which to die. It must have been like a return to early childhood; the smell of leaf loam, the rough bark of the tree against her back, the scurry of small birds and squirrels in the undergrowth, the softness of the earth making death as natural and friendly as falling asleep. For one extraordinary moment it seemed to her that she entered into that death, was mysteriously one with that lonely dying girl under the far tree. She shivered. The moment of empathy was quickly over but its power astonished and a little disturbed her. She had seen enough suicides in her first five years of policing to have learnt detachment, and, for her, it had never been a difficult lesson.

She had always been able to distance emotion, to think: This is a dead body. Not: This was a living woman. So why should an imagined death be more distressing than a body actually seen? Perhaps, she thought, I can afford a little involvement, a little pity. But it was strange that it should begin now. What was it, she wondered, about the Berowne case which seemed to be changing even her perception of her job? She turned her eyes again to the path and heard Carole Washburn's voice:

'When Paul learned that she was missing, when the nursing home rang to ask if anyone at Campden Hill Square had seen her or knew where she was, he guessed that she might be here. Before he became a minister and security became a nuisance he often walked through the park to work. He could cross Kensington Church Street, get into Hyde Park and then into Green Park at Hyde Park Corner, walking nearly all the way to the House on grass and under trees. So it was natural to come and look – I mean, he didn't have to go much out of his way. He wasn't putting himself to any great trouble.'

The sudden bitterness in her voice was shocking. Still Kate didn't speak. She dug in her jacket pocket for the small bag of crumbs and held them out on her palm. A sparrow, tame as only London sparrows are, hopped on her fingers with a delicate scrape of claws. His head jerked, and she felt the beak like a pin-prick, and then he was gone.

She said:

'He must have known Theresa Nolan very well.'

'Perhaps. She used to talk to him in the night hours when Lady Ursula was asleep; tell him about herself, her family. He was easy for women to talk to, some women.'

Both of them were for a moment silent. But there was one question which she had to ask. She said:

'The child Theresa Nolan was carrying, could it have been his?' To her relief the question was taken calmly, almost as if it were expected. The girl said:

'Once I would have said no and been absolutely certain. I'm not certain of anything any more. There were things he didn't tell me, I always knew that. I know it even better now. But I think he would have told me that. It wasn't his child. But he did blame himself for what happened to her. He felt responsible.'

'Why?'

'She tried to see him the day before she killed herself. She went to his office, to the Department. It was tactless – the kind of thing

321

only an innocent would do – and she couldn't have chosen a worse time. He was just due to go into an important meeting. He could have made five minutes to see her, but it wouldn't have been convenient and it wouldn't have been prudent. When the young HEO in his private office brought in the news that a Miss Theresa Nolan was in the front hall asking to see him urgently, he said that she was probably one of his constituents and sent down a message asking her to leave her address and he'd get in touch. She went away without saying a word. He never heard from her again. I think he would have got in touch, given time. But he wasn't given time. The next day she was dead.'

It was interesting, thought Kate, that this piece of news hadn't come out when Dalgliesh was interviewing Sir Paul's civil servants. Those careful men, by training and instinct, protected their Minister. Were they extending this protection beyond death? They had spoken of Paul Berowne's speed and skill in mastering a complicated submission, but there had been no mention of the inconvenient arrival of an importunate young woman. But perhaps it wasn't surprising. The officer who had taken the message had been comparatively junior. It was another example of the man who had the interesting information not even being questioned. But even if he had been, he might not have thought it important, unless he had read the inquest report and recognized the girl and, perhaps, not even then.

Carole Washburn still stood gazing into the woodlands, hands deep in her jacket pockets, her shoulders hunched as if there blew from the tangled wilderness the first chill wind of winter. She said:

'She was slumped against the trunk – that trunk. You can barely see it now and in high summer it's invisible. She could have been there for days.'

Not for long, thought Kate. The smell would soon have alerted the park-keepers. Holland Park might be a small paradise in the middle of the city, but it was no different from any other Eden. There were still predators on four legs prowling in the under-growth and predators on two walking the paths. Death was still death. Bodies still stank when they rotted. She glanced at her companion. Carole Washburn was still staring into the woodland with a painful intensity as if conjuring up that slumped figure at the foot of the silver birch. Then she said:

'Paul told the truth about what happened, but not the whole truth. There were two letters in her jacket pocket, one addressed to her grandparents asking forgiveness, the one read out at the

322

inquest. But there was another, marked confidential and addressed to Paul. That's what I've come to tell you.'

'Did you see it? Did he show it to you?' Kate tried to keep the eagerness out of her voice. Could this, she thought, be physical evidence at last?

'No. He brought it to the flat but he didn't give it to me to read. He told me what was in it. Apparently while Theresa was nursing at Pembroke Lodge she was transferred to night duty. One of the patients had been brought some bottles of champagne by her husband and they'd had a party. It's that kind of place. Anyway she was a little tipsy. She was gloating over the baby, a son after three girls, and said "thanks to darling Stephen". Then she let out that if patients wanted a child of a particular sex Lampart would do an early amniocentesis and abort an unwanted foetus. Women who hated childbirth and weren't prepared to go through with it just to get a child of the wrong sex knew where to go.'

Kate said:

'But he was – he is – taking a terrible risk.'

'Not really. Not if there's never anything on paper, never anything specifically said. Paul wondered if some of the pathological reports were falsified to show an abnormality in the foetus. Most of his lab work is done on the premises. Afterwards Theresa tried to get some evidence, but it wasn't easy. When she questioned the patient the next day she laughed and said that she was joking. But she was obviously terrified. That afternoon she discharged herself.'

So this was the explanation of those mysterious jottings which AD had found in Theresa's missal. She had been trying to collect evidence about the sex of the patients' previous children. Kate asked:

'Did Theresa speak to anyone at Pembroke Lodge?'

'She didn't dare. She knew that someone had libelled Lampart once, and been made bankrupt as a result. He was – he is – notoriously litigious. What could she hope to do, a young nurse, poor, without powerful friends, against a man like that? Who would believe her? And then she found that she was pregnant and had her own problems to think about. How could she speak against what she saw as his sin when she was about to commit mortal sin herself? But when she was preparing to die she felt that she had to do something to put a stop to it. She thought about Paul. He wasn't weak, he had nothing to fear. He was a Minister, a powerful man. He would see that it was stopped.'

'And did he?'

'How could he? She hadn't any idea what kind of burden she was putting on him. As I said, she was an innocent. They're always the ones who do the most harm. Lampart is his wife's lover. If he tackled him it would look like blackmail or, worse, revenge. And his own guilt over her death, the lie about her being a constituent, his failure to help her, that must have seemed morally worse than anything Lampart was doing.'

'What did he decide?'

'He tore up the letter while he was with me and flushed it down the lavatory.'

'But he was a lawyer. Wasn't his instinct to preserve evidence?'

'Not that evidence. He said: "If I haven't the courage to use it, then I must get rid of it. There's no compromise. Either I do what Theresa wanted or I destroy the evidence." I suppose he thought that hoarding it might be degrading, might smack of potential blackmail, carefully preserving evidence against your enemy in case you needed it in future.'

'Did he ask your advice?'

'No. Not advice. He needed to think it through and I was there to listen. That's what he usually needed me for, to listen. I realize that now. And he knew what I would say, what I wanted. I would say: "Divorce Barbara and use that letter to make sure that she and her lover make no trouble over it. Use it to get your freedom." I don't know whether I would have said it so brutally, but he knew that's what I wanted him to do. Before he destroyed it he made me promise to say nothing.'

Kate said:

'He took absolutely no action, you're sure of that?'

'I think he may have spoken to Lampart. He told me that he would, but we never discussed it again. He was going to tell Lampart what he knew and admit that he had no evidence. And he took his money out of Pembroke Lodge. There was quite a bit, I think, originally invested by his brother.'

They began walking slowly down the path. Kate thought: Suppose Paul Berowne had spoken to Lampart. With the evidence destroyed, and pathetically inadequate evidence at that, the doctor would have little to fear. A scandal could hurt Paul Berowne as much as it harmed Lampart. But after Sir Paul's experience in that vestry things might be very different. Perhaps the changed Berowne, his own career thrown away, would see it as his moral duty to expose and ruin Lampart, evidence or no evidence. And what of Barbara Berowne, faced on one hand with a husband who

324

had chucked away both job and prospects, and was even proposing to sell their home, and on the other with a lover who might be facing ruin. Kate decided on a blunt question which, in other circumstances, she might have felt unwise:

'Do you think Stephen Lampart killed him, with or without her connivance?'

'No. He'd be a fool to involve her in anything like that. And she hasn't the courage or the wit to plan it alone. She's the kind of woman who gets a man to do her dirty work for her and then persuades herself that she knows nothing about it. But I've given you a motive, a motive for both of them. It ought to be enough to make life uncomfortable for her.'

'Is that what you want?'

The girl turned round on her and said with sudden passion:

'No, that's not what I want. I want her to be harried and grilled and frightened. I want her disgraced. I want her arrested, imprisoned for life. I want her dead. It won't happen, none of it will happen. And the awful thing is that I've hurt myself more than I can ever hurt her. Once I'd made that call to you, once I'd said I'd be here, then I knew I had to come. But he told me in confidence, he trusted me, he always trusted me. Now there's nothing left, nothing I can remember about our loving that will ever be free of pain and guilt.'

Kate looked at her and saw that she was crying. She was making no sound, not even a sob, but from eyes fixed and staring as if in terror the tears ran in a steady stream over the drained face and the half-open quivering mouth. There was something frightening about this steady, silent grief. Kate thought: There isn't a man, any man in the world who is worth this agony. She felt a mixture of sympathy, helplessness and irritation which she recognized was tinged with slight contempt. But the pity won. There was nothing she could find to say which might comfort, but at least she could make some practical response, ask Carole back to the flat for coffee before they parted. She was opening her mouth to speak, then checked herself. The girl wasn't a suspect. Even if it were reasonable to think of her in those terms, she had an alibi, a late meeting out of London for the time of death. But suppose Carole were required to give evidence in court, then any suggestion of friendship, of an understanding between them could be prejudicial to the prosecution. And more than to the prosecution; it could be prejudicial to her own career. It was the kind of sentimental error of judgement which wouldn't exactly displease Massingham if he came to hear of it. And then she heard herself saying:

325

'My flat is very close, just across the avenue. Come and have coffee before you go.'

In the flat Carole Washburn moved over to the window like an automaton and gazed out without speaking. Then she moved over to the sofa and stood regarding the oil painting on the wall above, three triangles, partly superimposed, in a browny-red, clear green and white. She asked, but not as if she greatly cared:

'Do you like modern art?'

'I like experimenting with shapes and different colours laid against each other. I don't like reproductions and I can't afford originals so I paint my own. I don't suppose they're art, but I enjoy them.'

'Where did you learn to paint?'

'I just bought the canvas and oils and taught myself. The small bedroom is a kind of studio. I haven't had time to do much lately.'

'It's clever. I like the texture of the background.'

'Done by pressing a tissue over the paint just before it dried. Texture's the easy part, it's applying the oil smoothly that I find tricky.'

She went into the kitchen to grind coffee beans. Carole followed and stood listlessly watching from the doorway. She waited until the grinder had been switched off then suddenly asked:

'What made you choose the police?'

Kate was tempted to reply: For much the same reasons that you chose the Civil Service. I thought I could do the job. I was ambitious. I prefer order and hierarchy to muddle. Then she wondered whether Carole needed to ask, not answer, questions, to reach out, however tentatively, to another's life. She said:

'I didn't want an office job. I wanted a career where I could earn well from the start, hope for promotion. I suppose I like pitting myself against men. And they were rather against the idea at the school I went to. That was an added inducement.'

Carole Washburn made no response but watched her for a moment then drifted back into the sitting room. Kate, hands busy with percolator, mug and saucers, tray and biscuits found herself recalling that last interview with Miss Shepherd, the careers adviser:

'We had rather hoped that you would set your sights higher, university, for example. You're safe, I'd say, for two As and a B at A-level.'

'I want to start earning.'

'That's understandable, Kate, but you'll get a full grant, remember. You can manage.'

'I don't want to have to manage. I want a job, a place of my own. University would be three wasted years.'

'Education is never wasted, Kate.'

'I'm not giving up education. I can go on educating myself.'

'But a policewoman . . . We had rather hoped that you would choose something more, well, socially significant.'

'You mean more useful.'

'More concerned, perhaps, with basic human problems.'

'I can't think of anything more basic than helping to make sure that people can walk safely in their own city.'

'I'm afraid, Kate, that recent research shows that walking in safety has little to do with the level of policing. Why not read that pamphlet in the library, "Policing the Inner City: A Socialist Solution"? But if this is your choice, naturally we shall do what we can to help. How do you see yourself? In the Juvenile Bureau?'

'No. I see myself as a senior detective.' She had been tempted to add mischievously: 'and as the first woman Chief Constable.' But that, she had known, was as unrealistic as a recruit to the WRAC seeing herself as commanding the Household Cavalry. Ambition, if it were to be savoured, let alone achieved, had to be rooted in possibility. Even her childhood fantasies had been anchored to reality. The lost father would reappear, loving, prosperous, repentant, but she had never expected him to descend from a Rolls-Royce. And in the end he hadn't come, and she had known that she had never really expected him.

There were no sounds from the sitting room and when she carried in the tray of coffee she saw that Carole was sitting on a chair, stiffly upright, gazing down at her clasped hands. Kate set down the tray and at once Carole slopped milk into her mug, then clasped both hands round it and gulped avidly, hunched in her chair like an old starved woman.

It was strange, thought Kate, that the girl seemed more distraught, less under control, than at their first meeting when they had briefly chatted in her own kitchen. What, she wondered, had happened since then to prompt her betrayal of Berowne's confidence, to produce this bitterness and resentment? Had she somehow learned that there was no mention of her in his will? But that, surely, was what she must have expected. But perhaps it mattered more than she had ever thought possible, the public and final confirmation that she had always been on the periphery of his life,

327

officially non-existent after death as she had been in their years together. She thought that she had been indispensable to him, that he had found with her in that ordinary, seldom visited flat, a still centre of fulfilment and peace. Maybe he had, at least for a few snatched hours. But she hadn't been indispensable to him; no one had. He had compartmentalized people as he had the rest of his over-organized life, filing them away in the recesses of his mind until he needed what they had to offer. But then, she asked herself, is that so very different from what I do with Alan?

She knew that she wouldn't be able to bring herself to ask what had brought the girl to this meeting, and it wasn't really important to the inquiry. What was important was that Berowne's confidence had been broken and Lampart's motive immensely strengthened. But how far did that really get them? One piece of hard physical evidence was worth a dozen motives. They were back to the old question, could Lampart and Barbara Berowne really have had the time? Someone, Berowne or his killer, had been using the wash-room at St Matthew's at eight o'clock. Three people had seen the gush of water, none of them could be shaken. So either Berowne was alive at eight or the murderer was still on the premises. Either way it was difficult to see how Lampart could have driven to the Black Swan by eight thirty.

When she had finished her coffee Carole managed a weak smile and said:

'Thank you. I'd better go now. I suppose you want all this on paper.'

'We'd like a statement. You could call in at the Harrow Road station, there's an incident room there, or come to the Yard.'

'I'll call in at Harrow Road. There won't be any more questions will there?'

'There could be, but I don't think we'll want you for long.'

At the door they stood for a moment facing each other. Suddenly Kate thought that Carole was going to step forward and fall into her arms, and knew that her unpractised arms might even know how to hold and comfort, that she might even be able to find the right words. But the moment passed and she told herself that the thought had been embarrassing and ridiculous. As soon as she was alone she rang Dalgliesh, careful to keep any note of triumph out of her voice:

'She came, sir. There's no new physical evidence but she has strengthened one of the suspects' motives. I think you'll want to go to Hampstead.'

328

He said:

'Where are you ringing from? Your flat?'

'Yes sir.'

'I'll be there in about half an hour.'

But it was less than that when the bell of the entry-phone rang.
He said:

'I'm parked further up Lansdowne Road. Could you come down
now?'

He didn't suggest that he should come up, and she hadn't
expected it. No senior officer was more scrupulous in respecting
the privacy of his subordinates. She told herself that in him it
hardly counted for virtue. He was too scrupulously careful to
protect his own. Going down in the lift it occurred to her that the
more she learned of Berowne the more alike he seemed to Dalgliesh.
She felt a spurt of irritation against both of them. Here waiting for
her was a man who might also cause that extremity of grief for a
woman unwise enough to love him. She told herself that she was
glad that she had that temptation at least well under control.

4

Stephen Lampart said:

'It isn't true. Theresa Nolan was psychologically disturbed; or, if you prefer bluntness, mad enough to kill herself. Nothing she wrote before that act counts as reliable evidence, even if you have this alleged letter, which I assume you haven't. I mean, if it were actually in your possession you'd be flourishing it in my face, surely. What you're relying on is third-hand information. We both know what that's worth in a court of law, or anywhere else for that matter.'

Dalgliesh said:

'Are you telling me that the girl's story is untrue?'

'Let's be charitable and say mistaken. She was lonely, guilt-ridden, particularly about sex, depressed, losing touch with reality. There's a psychiatrist's report on her medical file which, stripped of its jargon, says precisely that. Or you can argue that she was deliberately lying, she or Berowne. Neither was a particularly reliable witness. Both, as it happens, are dead. If this is meant to give me a motive, it's absurd. It's also close to slander and I know how to deal with that.'

Dalgliesh said:

'As you knew how to deal with libel. A police officer, carrying out a murder investigation, isn't so easily ruined.'

'Not financially, perhaps. The courts are so ridiculously indulgent to the police.'

The nurse who had received them at Pembroke Lodge had said, 'Mr Lampart has just finished operating, if you would come this way,' and they had been shown into a room adjacent to the theatre. Lampart had joined them almost at once, pulling off his green operating cap, peeling off his gloves. The room was small, clinical, seeming full of rushing water and the sound of feet passing in the room next door, of confident voices above the unconscious body of the patient. It was a temporary place, a room for quick clinical exchanges not for confidences. Dalgliesh wondered if the ploy had been deliberate, a way of demonstrating the subtle power of his professional status, of reminding the police that there was more than one kind of authority. Dalgliesh didn't think that Lampart had dreaded the interview, even if he had thought it prudent to face it

330

on his own territory. He hadn't shown the least sign of apprehension. After all, he had enjoyed power, one kind of power, long enough to have acquired the self-assertive hubris of success. A man who had developed the confidence of a successful obstetrician certainly had the confidence to confront an investigating officer of the Metropolitan Police.

Now he said:

'I didn't kill Berowne. Even if I were capable of a particularly brutal and bloody murder, I certainly wouldn't take Berowne's wife with me and expect her to wait in the car while I slit her husband's throat. As for this other nonsense, even if it were true that I aborted healthy foetuses because they weren't the sex the mother wanted, how do you propose to prove it? The operations were done here. The pathological reports are on the medical records. There's nothing incriminating on any file in this building. And even if there were, you wouldn't have access to it, not without a great deal of trouble. I have strong feelings about the sanctity of medical records. So what can you do? Start interviewing a succession of patients in the hope of tricking or bullying one of them into an indiscretion? And how would you track them down without my cooperation? Your allegation is ridiculous, Commander.'

Dalgliesh said:

'But Paul Berowne believed it. He got rid of his shares in Pembroke Lodge after Theresa Nolan's death. I think he spoke to you. I don't know what he said to you but I can guess. You could trust him to keep silent at that time, but after his experience in that church, his conversion, whatever it was, could you trust his silence then?'

He wondered whether he had been wise to show his hand so soon and so clearly. But the doubt was momentary. Lampart had to be confronted by the new evidence, tenuous as it might be. He had to be given the right to reply. And if it were irrelevant, the sooner it was cleared out of the way, the better.

Lampart said:

'It wasn't like that. We never spoke. And, assuming that he did believe it, he would have been in a somewhat invidious position, rather more invidious than you realize. He wanted a son but he certainly didn't want another daughter. Nor incidentally, did Barbara. Barbara might be willing to bear him an heir, if only to consolidate her position. She saw that as part of the bargain. But nine months' discomfort to produce another daughter for him to resent, despise and ignore was asking rather too much of a woman,

331

particularly one who dislikes and fears the thought of childbirth. Assuming the story is true, you could say that Berowne found himself in a curious position, morally anyway. He couldn't stomach the means but I suspect he wasn't entirely displeased with the ends. That has never been a particularly dignified moral stance, not in my book. Barbara had one miscarriage – a female – eight months after their marriage. Do you suppose he grieved over that? No wonder the poor devil was in a mess psychologically. No wonder he took a razor to his throat. What you've discovered, Commander, if true, is an added reason for suicide, not a motive for murder.'

Lampart took down his jacket from a peg, then opened the door for Dalgliesh and Kate with a smiling courtesy that was almost insulting. Then he led the way to his private drawing room, shut the door and motioned them towards the easy chairs before the fire. Sitting opposite he leaned forward, legs apart, and almost thrust his face at Dalgliesh. Dalgliesh could see the handsome features magnified, the pores of the skin glistening with sweat as if he were still in the heat of the theatre, the taut muscles straining at the neck, the smudge of tiredness under the eyes and the threads of scarlet around the irises, the flecks of dandruff at the roots of the undisciplined forelock. It was still a comparatively young face, but the signs of ageing were there and he could suddenly see how Lampart would look in another thirty years; the skin speckled and bleached, the bones less firmly fleshed, the macho confidence soured into the cynicism of old age. But now his voice was strong and harsh and the aggression came over to Dalgliesh, powerful as a force.

'I'll be frank with you, Commander, more frank than I would probably think prudent if what you're saying were true. If I had aborted those unwanted foetuses, it wouldn't be giving me a single pang of what you would probably call conscience. Two hundred years ago, anaesthesia in childbirth was regarded as immoral. Less than a hundred years ago birth control was virtually illegal. A woman has a right to choose whether she bears a child. I happen to think she also has a right to choose which sex. An unwanted child is usually a nuisance to itself, to society, to its parents. And a two-month foetus isn't a human being, it's a complicated collection of tissue. You probably don't personally believe that the child has a soul before birth, at birth, or after birth. Poet or no poet, you're not the kind of man who sees visions and hears voices in church vestries. I'm not a religious man. I was born with my share of

332

neuroses, but not that one. But what surprises me about those who claim to have faith is that they seem to think that we can find out scientific facts behind God's back. That first myth, the Garden of Eden, is remarkably persistent. We always feel we haven't a right to knowledge or that, when we get it, we haven't the right to use it. In my book we've the right to do anything we can to make human life more agreeable, safer, less full of pain.'

His voice grated and there was a gleam in the grey eyes uncomfortably close to fanaticism. He could, thought Dalgliesh, have been a seventeenth-century religious mercenary reciting his credo with drawn sword.

Dalgliesh said, mildly:

'Provided, presumably, we don't hurt other people and the act isn't illegal.'

'Provided we don't hurt other people. Yes, I'd accept that. Getting rid of an unwanted foetus hurts no one. Either abortion is never justified or it's justified on grounds which the mother happens to think important. The wrong sex is as good a reason as any. I've more respect for those Christians who oppose abortion on any grounds than for those ingenious compromisers who want life on their own terms and a good conscience at the same time. At least the former are consistent.'

Dalgliesh said:

'The law is consistent. Indiscriminate abortion is unlawful.'

'Oh, but this would have been highly discriminatory. All right, I know what you mean. But the law has no place when it comes to private morality, sexual or otherwise.'

Dalgliesh said:

'Where else is it supposed to operate?'

He got up and Lampart saw them out, deferential, smiling, confident. Except for perfunctory courtesies, neither spoke another word.

In the car Kate said:

'It was practically a confession, sir. He didn't even bother to deny it.'

'No. But it isn't one he'd ever make on paper or which we could use in court. And it was a confession to medical malpractice, not murder. And he's right, of course. It would be the devil to prove.'

'But it gives him a double motive. His affair with Lady Berowne and the fact that Berowne might have felt he had a duty to expose him. Under all that bluff and arrogance, he must know that he's as vulnerable to scandal as any other doctor. Even a rumour wouldn't have done him any good. And coming from someone of Berowne's standing, it would have been taken seriously.'

Dalgliesh said:

'Oh, yes, Lampart has got it all – means, motive, opportunity, knowledge, and the arrogance to think he can get away with it. But I accept one thing he told us. He wouldn't have taken Barbara Berowne with him into that vestry and I can't see her agreeing to be left alone in a car parked in a not particularly salubrious area of Paddington whatever the excuse. And, always, we get back to the timing. The night porter saw them leaving Pembroke Lodge together. Higgins saw them arriving at the Black Swan. Unless one or both are lying Lampart has to be in the clear.'

And then he thought: Unless we've been misled by that gush of water from the waste pipe. Unless we've got the time of death totally wrong. If Berowne had died at the earliest time Dr Kynaston had thought possible, say seven o'clock, what happened to Lampart's alibi then? He had claimed to be at Pembroke Lodge with his mistress, but there had to be more ways than one of leaving the Lodge and returning unseen. But someone had been in the church kitchen at eight o'clock; unless, of course, the water had been left deliberately running. But by whom? Someone who had come earlier, at seven o'clock, someone who had arrived in a black Rover? If Berowne had died at seven o'clock, there were suspects other than Stephen Lampart. But what possible purpose would be served by leaving the tap running? There was, of course, always the possibility that it had been left on by accident. But if that were the case, then how and when had it been turned off?

5

Lady Ursula's friends had expressed their condolences with flowers and her sitting room was incongruously festive with long stemmed thornless roses, carnations and imported boughs of white lilac which looked like plastic artefacts sprayed with scent. The flowers had been less arranged than stuck into a variety of vases placed around the room for convenience rather than effect. By her side on the rosewood table was a small cut glass bowl of freesias. Their scent, sweet and unmistakable, came up to Dalgliesh as he neared her chair. She made no attempt to rise, but held out her hand and he took it. It felt cold and dry and there was no responsive pressure. She was sitting, as always, bolt upright, wearing an ankle-length black wrapover skirt with above it a high-necked blouse in fine grey wool. Her only jewellery was a double chain in old gold and her rings; the long fingers resting on the arms of her chair were laden with great flashing stones so that the blue-corded hands with their parchment skin seemed almost too frail to hold the weight of gold.

She motioned Dalgliesh to the opposite chair. When he had seated himself and Massingham had found a place on a small sofa set against the wall, she said:

'Father Barnes called here this morning. Perhaps he thought he had a duty to bring me spiritual comfort. Or was he apologizing for the use made of his vestry? He could hardly suppose I thought it was his fault. If he intended to offer spiritual consolation I'm afraid he found me a disappointing mourner. He's a curious man. I found him rather unintelligent, commonplace. Was that your opinion?'

Dalgliesh said:

'I wouldn't describe him as commonplace, but it's difficult to see him influencing your son.'

'He seemed to me a man who had long ago given up the expectation of influencing anyone. Perhaps he has lost his faith. Isn't that fashionable in the Church today? But why should that distress him? The world is full of people who have lost faith; politicians who have lost faith in politics, social workers who have lost faith in social work, schoolteachers who have lost faith in teaching and, for all I know, policemen who have lost faith in policing and poets who have lost faith in poetry. It's a condition of

335

faith that it gets lost from time to time, or at least mislaid. And why doesn't he get his cassock cleaned? It is a cassock, isn't it? There were what I assumed were egg stains on the right cuff and the front looked as if he's dribbled on it.'

Dalgliesh said:

'It's a garment he practically lives in, Lady Ursula.'

'He could buy a spare, surely.'

'If he could afford one. And he had made an attempt to sponge off the stain.'

'Had he? Not very effectively. Well, that's the sort of thing you're trained to notice, of course.'

It did not surprise him that they were discussing ecclesiastical garb while what remained of her son lay headless and disembowelled in a mortuary ice box. Unlike herself and Father Barnes, they had been able to communicate from their first meeting. She shifted a little in her chair, then she said:

'But you are not, of course, here to discuss Father Barnes's spiritual problems. What are you here to say, Commander?'

'I'm here to ask you again, Lady Ursula, whether or not you saw your son's diary in the desk drawer when General Nollinge rang this house at six o'clock last Tuesday.'

The remarkable eyes looked straight into his.

'You have asked that question twice before. I am, of course, always happy to talk to the poet who wrote "Rhesus Negative" but your visits are becoming rather frequent and your conversation predictable. I've nothing to add to what I told you before. I find this reiteration rather offensive.'

'You do understand the implication of what you're saying?'

'Naturally I understand it. Is there anything else you need to ask?'

'I should like you to confirm that you did, in fact, speak to Halliwell twice on the evening your son died and that, to your knowledge, the Rover was not taken out that night before ten o'clock.'

'I've already told you, Commander. I spoke to him at about eight o'clock and then at nine fifteen. That must have been about forty-five minutes before he left for Suffolk. And I think you can safely assume that, if anyone had taken the Rover, Halliwell would have known. Anything else?'

'Yes, I should like to see Miss Matlock again.'

'In that case I would prefer that you see her here and that I remain. Perhaps you will ring the bell.'

336

He tugged at the bell-cord. Miss Matlock didn't hurry. But three minutes later she stood in the doorway wearing again the long grey skirt with its gaping pleat, the same ill-fitting blouse.

Lady Ursula said:

'Sit down will you, Mattie. The Commander has some questions for you.'

The woman took one of the chairs against the wall and brought it over, placing it beside Lady Ursula's chair. She looked stolidly at Dalgliesh. This time she seemed almost without anxiety. He thought, she's beginning to get confidence. She knows how little we're able to do if she sticks to her story. She's beginning to think that it could be easy after all. He went through her account again. She answered his questions about the Tuesday evening in almost the same words she had previously used. At the end he said:

'It wasn't, of course, unusual for Mr Dominic Swayne to call here for a bath, perhaps a meal?'

'I've told you. He did it from time to time. He's Lady Berowne's brother.'

'But Sir Paul wasn't necessarily aware of these visits?'

'Sometimes he was, sometimes not. It wasn't my place to tell him.'

'What about the time before last, not the Tuesday but the time before? What did you do then?'

'He had a bath as usual, then I cooked him supper. He doesn't always have supper here when he comes for his bath but that night he did. I cooked him a pork chop with mustard sauce, sauté potatoes and green beans.'

A more substantial meal, thought Dalgliesh, than the omelette she had cooked on the night of Berowne's death. But on that night he had arrived at shorter notice. Why? Because his sister had telephoned him after her quarrel with her husband? Because she had told him where Berowne would be that night? Because his plan of murder was beginning to take shape?

He asked:

'And after that?'

'He had apple tart and cheese.'

'I mean, what did you do after the meal?'

'After that we played Scrabble.'

'You and he seem extraordinarily fond of Scrabble.'

'I like it. I think he plays to please me. There's no one here to give me a game.'

'And who won that time, Miss Matlock?'

'I think I did. I can't remember by how much, but I think I won.'

'You think you won? It was only ten days ago, can't you be sure?'

Two pairs of eyes looked into his, hers and Lady Ursula's. They were not, he thought, natural allies, but now they sat side by side rigidly upright, motionless as if held in a field of force which both sustained and linked them. Lady Ursula was, he sensed, almost at the end of her endurance, but he thought he saw in Evelyn Matlock's defiant gaze a glint of triumph. She said:

'I can remember perfectly. I won.'

It was, he knew, the most effective way of fabricating an alibi. You described events which had, in fact, happened, but on a different occasion. It was the most difficult of all alibis to break since, apart from the alteration in time, the parties concerned were speaking the truth. He thought she was lying, but he couldn't be sure. She was, he knew, a neurotic, and the fact that she was now beginning to enjoy pitting her wits against his might be no more than the self-dramatization of a woman whose life had afforded few such heady excitements. He heard Lady Ursula's voice:

'Miss Matlock has answered all your inquiries, Commander. Should you propose to continue badgering her, then I think we shall have to arrange for my solicitor to be present.'

He said coldly:

'That, of course, is her right, Lady Ursula. And we're not here to badger either you or her.'

'In that case, Mattie, perhaps you will show the Commander and Chief Inspector Massingham out.'

They were driving down Victoria Street when the telephone rang. Massingham answered it, listened, then handed the receiver to Dalgliesh.

'It's Kate, sir. I detect a note of girlish enthusiasm. Can't wait until we get back apparently. But I think she'd like to tell you herself.'

Kate's voice, like her enthusiasm, was under control but Dalgliesh, too, couldn't miss the note of heady optimism. She said:

'Something interesting has turned up, sir. Hearne and Collingwood rang ten minutes ago with Millicent Gentle's address. She's moved since they last published her and hadn't told them where so it took a little time to trace her. She's at Riverside Cottage, Coldham Lane, near Cookham. I've looked at the ordnance survey. Coldham Lane runs almost opposite the Black Swan. Sir, she must have handed Sir Paul her book on August the seventh.'

'It seems likely. Have you a telephone number?'

'Yes, sir. The firm wouldn't give me either the address or the number until they'd rung her and checked that she agreed.'

'Ring her then, Kate. Ask if she'll see us as early as possible tomorrow morning.'

He replaced the receiver. Massingham said:

'The clue of the romantic novelist. I can't wait to meet the author of *A Rose by Twilight*. Do you want me to go to Cookham, sir.'

'No, John, I'll go.'

At the Yard entrance he got out of the Rover, leaving Massingham to garage it, then hesitated and strode off vigorously to St James's Park. The office was too claustrophobic to contain this sudden surge of irrational optimism. He needed to walk free and alone. It had been a hellish day, beginning in Gilmartin's office with peevish ill-temper, ending in Campden Hill Square with unprovable lies. But now the vexations and frustrations fell from his shoulders. He thought:

Tomorrow I shall know exactly what happened at the Black Swan on the night of the seventh of August. And when I know that, I shall know why Paul Berowne had to die. I may not yet be able to prove it. But I shall know.

6

Brian Nichols, recently promoted Assistant Commissioner, resented Dalgliesh and found this dislike the more irritating because he wasn't sure that it was justified. After twenty-five years of policing he regarded even his antipathies with a judicial eye; he liked to be confident that the case against the accused would stand up in court. With Dalgliesh he wasn't sure. Nichols was the senior in rank but this gave him small satisfaction when he knew that Dalgliesh could have outstripped him had he chosen. This lack of concern about promotion, which Dalgliesh never condescended to justify, he saw as a subtle criticism of his own more ambitious preoccupations. He deplored the poetry, not on principle, but because it had conferred prestige and, therefore, couldn't be regarded as a harmless hobby like fishing, gardening or woodwork. A policeman, in his view, should be satisfied with policing. An added grievance was that Dalgliesh chose most of his friends from outside the force and those fellow officers he consorted with weren't always of an appropriate rank. In a junior officer that would have been regarded as a dangerous idiosyncrasy and in a senior it had a taint of disloyalty. And to compound these delinquencies, he dressed too well. He was standing now with easy assurance looking out of the window wearing a suit in a subtle brown tweed which Nichols had seen him wearing for the last four years. It bore the unmistakable stamp of an excellent tailor, probably, thought Nichols, the firm his grandfather had patronized. Nichols, who enjoyed buying clothes, sometimes with more enthusiasm than discrimination, felt that it was becoming in a man to own rather more suits and those not so well tailored. Finally, whenever he was with Dalgliesh, he felt inexplicably that he ought perhaps to shave off his moustache and would find his hand moving involuntarily to his upper lip as if to reassure himself that the moustache was still a respectable appendage. This impulse, irrational, almost neurotic, irritated him profoundly.

Both men knew that Dalgliesh needn't be here in Nichols's tenth-floor office, that the casual suggestion that the AC should be put in the picture was no more than an invitation, not a command. The new squad was now formally set up; but Berowne's murder had happened six days too soon. In future, Dalgliesh would report directly to the Commissioner. But for now Nichols could claim a legitimate interest. It was his department, after all, which had provided most of the men for Dalgliesh's supporting team. And with the Commissioner temporarily away at a conference, he could argue that he had a right at least to a brief progress report. But, irrationally, part of him wished that Dalgliesh had objected, had given him the excuse for one of those departmental wrangles which he provoked when the job offered less excitement than his restless spirit craved and which he was adept at winning.

While Nichols looked through the file on the case Dalgliesh looked out earthward over the city. He had seen many capitals from a similar height, all different. When he looked down on Manhattan from his hotel bedroom its spectacular soaring beauty always seemed to him precarious, even doomed. Images would rise from films seen in his boyhood, prehistoric monsters towering above the skyscrapers to claw them down, a vast tidal wave from the Atlantic obliterating the skyline, the light-spangled city darkening into the final holocaust. But London, laid out beneath him under a low ceiling of silver-grey cloud, looked eternal, rooted, domestic. He saw the panorama, of which he never tired, in terms of painting. Sometimes it had the softness and immediacy of watercolour; sometimes, in high summer, when the park burgeoned with greenness, it had the rich texture of oil. This morning it was a steel engraving, hard-edged, grey, one-dimensional.

He turned away from the window with reluctance. Nichols had closed the file but was swivelling his chair and moving his body restlessly as if to emphasize the comparative informality of the proceedings. Dalgliesh moved over and took a seat opposite him. He gave a concise summary of his investigation as far as it had gone and Nichols listened with a show of disciplined patience, still swivelling, his eyes on the ceiling. Then he said:

'All right, Adam, you've convinced me that Berowne was murdered. But then I'm not the one who has to be convinced. But what have you got by way of direct evidence? One small smudge of blood under a fold of Harry Mack's jacket.'

'And a matching stain on the lining. Berowne's blood. He died first. There's no room for doubt. We can prove that the smear is identical with his blood.'

'But not how it got there. You know what defending counsel will argue if it ever gets to court. One of your chaps carried it there on his shoes. Or the boy did, the one who found the body. Or that spinster – what's her name – Edith Wharton.'

'Emily Wharton. We examined their shoes and I'm confident neither went into the Little Vestry. And, even if they had, it's difficult to see how they could have left a smudge of Berowne's blood under Harry's jacket.'

'It's a very convenient smudge from your point of view. From the family's too, I suppose. But without it there's nothing to suggest that this isn't exactly what it first appeared – murder followed by suicide. A politician, prominent, successful, has some kind of religious conversion, quasi-mystical experience, call it what you will. He throws over his job, his career, possibly his family. Then, don't ask me how or why, he discovers that it's all a chimera.' Nichols repeated the word as if to reassure himself of the pronunci-ation. Dalgliesh wondered where he had come across it. Then he went on:

'Why did Berowne go back to that church, incidentally? Do you know?'

'Possibly because of a new complication to do with his marriage. I think his wife told him that morning that she was pregnant.'

'There you are then. He was already having doubts. He goes back, faces the reality of what he's given up. There's nothing ahead but failure, humiliation, ridicule. He decides to end it then and there. He has the means to hand. While he's making his prep-arations, burning his diary, Harry comes in and tries to stop him. Result? Two bodies instead of one.'

'That assumes he didn't know Harry Mack was there. I think he did, he let him in. That's hardly the action of a man contemplating suicide.'

'You've no proof that he let him in. None that would satisfy a jury.'

'Berowne gave Harry part of his supper, wholemeal bread, Roquefort cheese, an apple. It's on the file. You aren't suggesting that Harry Mack bought his own Roquefort? He couldn't have surprised Berowne. He'd been in the church for some time before Berowne died. He was bedded down in the larger vestry. There's physical evidence, hair, fibres from his coat, apart from the crumbs of food. And he wasn't in the vestry or in the church when Father Barnes locked up after Evensong.'

Nichols said:

'He thinks he locked up. Would he swear in the witness box that he turned the key in the south door, that he'd searched every pew? And why should he search? He wasn't expecting a murder. There are plenty of places where Harry, or a murderer for that matter, could have concealed himself. The church was dark presumably; a dim religious light.'

The AC had this habit of spattering his conversation with the odd half-quotation. Dalgliesh could never decide whether he knew that he was doing it or whether the words swam into his consciousness from some half-forgotten pool of schoolroom lore. Now he heard him say:

'How well did you know Berowne personally?'

'I saw him a couple of times across a committee room table. We travelled together to the conference on sentencing. He asked to see me once in his office. We walked through St James's Park to the House together. I liked him but I'm not obsessed with him. I don't identify with him more than anyone does with any victim. This isn't a personal crusade. But I admit to a perfectly reasonable objection to seeing him branded as the brutal murderer of a man who died after he did.'

Nichols said:

'On the evidence of one small smudge of blood?'

'What evidence do we need?'

'To the fact of murder, none. As I said you don't have to convince me. But I don't see how you're going to get any further unless you find one irrefutable piece of evidence linking one of your suspects to the scene of the crime.' Nicholas added, 'Sooner rather than later.'

'The Commissioner is getting complaints, I suppose.'

'The usual thing, two dead bodies, two throats severed, a murderer at large. Why aren't we arresting this dangerous lunatic instead of examining the cars, clothes and houses of respectable citizens? Did you find any traces on the suspects' clothes by the way?'

It was ironic, thought Dalgliesh, but not surprising; the new division set up to investigate serious crimes with sensitive undertones already accused of crass insensitivity. And he knew where the criticisms would have come from. He said:

'No, but I didn't expect any. This killer was naked or nearly naked. He had the means of washing himself to hand. Three passers-by heard the water gushing away shortly after eight.'

'Berowne washing his own hands before supper?'

'If so he was doing it very thoroughly.'

'But his hands were clean when you found him?'

'The left hand was. The right was heavily bloodied.'

'There you are then.'

343

Dalgliesh said:

'Berowne's towel was hanging over a chair in the vestry, I think his murderer dried himself with the tea towel in the kitchen. It was still slightly damp, not in places but all over, when I touched it. And he was killed with one of his own razors. Berowne had two, Bellinghams, in a case by the washbasin. A casual intruder, or Harry Mack for that matter, wouldn't have known they were there, probably wouldn't even have recognized the case for what it was.'

'And what's a Bellingham for God's sake? Why couldn't the man use a Gillette or an electric razor like the rest of us? OK, so it was someone who knew he shaved with a cut-throat, knew he'd be at the church that night, had access to the Campden Hill Square house to collect the matches and the diary. You know who best fits that list of requirements? Berowne himself. And all you've got against the suicide theory is one smudge of blood.'

Dalgliesh was beginning to think that those four monosyllables would haunt him to the end of the case. He said:

'You're not suggesting, I suppose, that Berowne half-cut his throat, staggered over to Harry to murder him, dripping blood in the act, then staggered back again to the other end of the room to make the third and final cut in his own throat?'

'No, but defence counsel might. And Doc Kynaston hasn't entirely ruled it out. You and I have known more ingenious defences succeed.'

Dalgliesh said:

'He wrote something while he was in that vestry. The lab can't identify the words although they think it possible that he signed his name. The ink on the blotter is the same as the ink in his pen.'

'So he wrote a suicide note?'

'Possibly, but where is it now?'

The AC said:

'He burnt it with the diary. All right, I know what you're going to say, Adam. Is it likely a suicide would burn a note once written? Well it's not impossible. He could have been dissatisfied with what he'd said. Inadequate words, too trite, let it go. After all, the action speaks for itself. Not every suicide goes documented into that good night.'

A flicker of pleased surprise passed over his face as if he were gratified at the aptness of the allusion but would rather like to be able to remember where it came from. Dalgliesh said:

'There's one thing he could have written which it's unlikely he would have blotted immediately, and that is something that another person might well wish to destroy.'

344

Nichols was sometimes a little slow in grasping the point, but he was never afraid to take his time. He took it now. Then he said:

'That would need three signatures, of course. It's an interesting theory and it would certainly strengthen the motive for at least two of your suspects. But, again, there's no proof. We get back to that all the time. It's an ingenious edifice you've built up, Adam, I'm half-convinced by it. But what we need is solid, physical evidence.' He added: 'You could say it's like the church, an ingenious edifice erected on an unproved supposition, logical within its terms, but only valid if one can accept the basic premise, the existence of God.'

He seemed pleased with the analogy. Dalgliesh doubted if it were his own. He watched while the AC skimmed over the remaining pages of the file almost dismissively. Closing the file, he said:

'Pity that you haven't been able to trace Berowne's movements after he left 62 Campden Hill Square. He seems to have walked into thin air.'

'Not altogther. We know that he went to Westertons, the estate agents, in Kensington High Street and saw one of their negotiators, Simon Follett-Briggs. He asked someone from the firm to visit the next day to inspect and value the house. Again, hardly the action of a man contemplating suicide. Follett-Briggs says that he was as unconcerned as if he were giving them instructions to sell a forty-thousand one-bedroom basement flat. He did tactfully express his regrets that the family should be selling a house they'd lived in since it was first built. Berowne replied that they'd had it for a hundred and fifty years; it was time someone else had a turn. He didn't want to discuss it, only to ensure that someone came next morning to carry out the valuation. It was a short interview. He was away by eleven thirty. After that, we haven't been able to trace him. But he could have walked in one of the parks or by the river. His shoes were muddied and subsequently washed and scraped clean.'

'Cleaned where?'

'Exactly. It suggests that he could have returned home, but no one admits to having seen him. He might escape notice if he slipped quickly in and out but hardly if he stopped long enough to clean his shoes. And Father Barnes is certain that he arrived at the church by six. We've seven hours to account for.'

'You saw this Follett-Briggs? Extraordinary names these fellows have. He must be feeling pretty sick. That would have been quite a commission. He might get it yet, I suppose, if the widow decides to sell.'

Dalgliesh didn't reply.

'Did Follett-Briggs say what he expected it to fetch?'

He could, thought Dalgliesh, have been speaking of a second-hand car.

'He wouldn't commit himself, of course. He hasn't inspected the house and he took the view that Berowne's instructions no longer held. But under a little tactful pressure he did murmur that he would expect to get in excess of a million. That's excluding the contents, of course.'

'And it all goes to the widow?'

'It goes to the widow.'

'But the widow has an alibi. So has the widow's lover. So, as far as I can see, has every other suspect in the case.'

As he picked up his file and moved to the door, the AC's voice pursued him like a plea.

'Just one piece of physical evidence, Adam. That's what we need. And for God's sake try to get it before we have to call the next press conference.'

7

Sarah Berowne found the postcard on the hall table on Monday morning. It was a card from the British Museum of a bronze cat wearing earrings with Ivor's message written in his cramped upright hand. 'Have tried to ring you but no luck. Hope you're feeling better. Any chance of dinner next Tuesday?'

So he was still using their code. He kept ready a small collection of postcards from the main London museums and galleries. Any mention of telephoning meant a proposal to meet, and this message deciphered, asked her to be near the postcard gallery of the British Museum on Tuesday next. The time varied with the day. On Tuesdays the assignation was always for three o'clock. Like similar messages, this assumed that she could make it. If not she was expected to ring back to say that dinner was impossible. But he had always taken it for granted that she would cancel all other engagements when the cards arrived. A message sent in this way was always urgent.

It was, she thought, hardly a code that would defeat the ingenuity of the police let alone the security forces if they became interested, but perhaps its very openness and simplicity was a safeguard. There was, after all, no law against friends spending an hour looking round museums together, and the rendezvous was a sensible one. They could pore over the same guidebook, talk in the almost obligatory whispers, move about at will to find the deserted galleries.

In those first heady months after he had recruited her to the Cell of Thirteen, when she was beginning to fall in love with him, she had looked for these cards as she might for a love letter, lurking in the hall for the post to fall through the letter box, seizing on the card and poring over its message as if these cramped letters could say everything that she needed so desperately to be told but which she knew he would never write still less speak. But now, for the first time, she read the summons with a mixture of depression and irritation. The notice was ridiculously short; it wouldn't be easy to get to Bloomsbury by three. And why on earth couldn't he telephone? Tearing up the card she felt as she never had before, that the code was a childish and unnecessary device born of his obsessional need to manipulate and conspire. It made them both ridiculous.

He was, as usual, there on time, selecting cards from the stand. She waited while he paid and, without speaking, they moved out of the gallery together. He was fascinated by the Egyptian antiquities and, almost instinctively, they made their way first to the ground-floor galleries and stood together while he contemplated the huge granite torso of Rameses the Second. It had seemed to her once that these dead eyes, this finely chiselled half-smiling mouth above the jutting beard, had been a powerfully erotic symbol of their love. So much had been whispered between them in sly elliptical phrases while they had stood regarding it as if seeing the Pharaoh for the first time, shoulders touching, and she had fought the need to stretch out her hand, to feel his fingers in hers. But now all its power had drained away. It was an interesting artefact, a huge slab of cracked granite, no more. He said:

'Shelley is supposed to have used these features as a model when he wrote "Ozymandias".'

'I know.'

A couple of Japanese tourists, their scrutiny completed, drifted away. With no change in the level or tone of his voice, he said:

'The police seem more certain now that your father was murdered. I imagine they've got the PM and forensic reports. They've been to see me.'

A sliver of fear slid down her spine liked iced water.

'Why?'

'In the hope of breaking our alibi. They didn't, and of course they can't. Not unless they break you. Have they been back?'

'Once. Not Commander Dalgliesh, the woman detective and a younger man, a Chief Inspector Massingham. They asked about Theresa Nolan and Diana Travers.'

'What did you tell them?'

'That I'd seen Theresa Nolan twice, once when I'd called to see Grandmama when she was ill, and once at that dinner party and that I'd never seen Diana. Wasn't that what you expected me to say?'

He answered:

'Let's go and visit Ginger.'

Ginger, named from the colour of the remnants of his hair, was the body of a pre-dynastic man, mummified by the hot desert sands three thousand years before Christ. Ivor had always been intrigued by him and they never left the museum without this almost ritual visit. Now she gazed down at the emaciated body curled on its left side, the pathetic collection of pots to hold the food and drink which would nourish his spirit on its long journey through the underworld, the spear with which he would defend himself against its ghostly terrors until he reached his Egyptian heaven. Perhaps, she thought, if that spirit could awake now and see the bright lights, the huge room, the moving forms of twentieth-century man, he would think that he had attained it. But she had never been able to share Ivor's pleasure in this *memento mori*; the body's emaciation, even its attitude, evoked too strongly a modern horror; the pictures and newsreels of the dead at Belsen. She thought: Even when we're here he never asks what I think, what I feel, what I'd like most to see. She said:

'Let's go to the Duveen Gallery. I want to look at the Parthenon screen.'

They moved slowly away. As they paced, their eyes on the open guidebook, she said:

'Diana Travers. You told me that she wasn't put into Campden Hill Square to spy on Daddy's private life. You said it was only his job you were interested in, finding out what was in the new Police Tactical Options Manual. I must have been naive. I can't think why I believed you. But that's what you told me.'

'I don't need to have a cell member polishing the Berowne family silver to discover what's in the Tactical Options Manual. And she wasn't put there to spy on his private life, not primarily. I put her there to make her think she had a job to do, that she was trusted. It kept her occupied while I decided what to do about her.'

'What do you mean, do about her? She was a member of the cell. She replaced Rose when Rose went back to Ireland.'

'She thought she was a member, but she wasn't. There's no reason why you shouldn't know. After all, she's dead. Diana Travers was a Special Branch spy.'

He had trained her not to look at him when they were talking but to keep her eyes on the exhibits, the guidebook or straight ahead. She gazed straight ahead now. She said:

'Why didn't you tell us?'

'Four of you were told, not the whole cell. I don't tell the cell everything.'

She had, of course, known that his membership of the Workers' Revolutionary Campaign was a cover for the Cell of Thirteen. But even the cell, apparently, had only been a cover for his private inner cabinet. Like a Russian doll, you unscrewed one deceit to find another nestling within it. There were only four people whom he trusted completely, confided in, consulted, and she hadn't been among them. Had he ever trusted her, she wondered, even from the beginning? She said:

'That first time, when you rang me nearly four years ago and asked me to take photographs of Brixton, was that all part of a plan to recruit me, to get the daughter of a Tory MP into the WRC?'

'Partly. I knew where your political sympathies lay. I guessed you wouldn't exactly welcome your father's second marriage. It seemed a propitious time to make an approach. Afterwards, my interest became, well, more personal.'

'But was there ever love?'

He frowned. She knew how much he hated any intrusion of the personal, the sentimental. He said:

'There was, there still is, great liking, respect, physical attraction. You can call that love if you want to use the word.'

'What do you call it, Ivor?'

'I call it liking, respect, physical attraction.'

They had moved into the Duveen Gallery. Above them pranced the horses on the Parthenon frieze, the naked riders with their flying cloaks, the chariots, the musicians, the elders and maidens approaching the seated gods and goddesses. But she looked up at this marvel with unseeing eyes. She thought: I need to know, I need to know everything. I have to face the truth. She said:

'And it was you who sent that poison pen note to Daddy and to the *Paternoster Review*? Doesn't it seem rather petty even to you, the people's revolutionary, the great campaigner against oppression, prophet of the new Jerusalem, reduced to gossip, slander, to childish spite? What did you think you were doing?'

He said:

'Making a little mild mischief.'

'Is that what you call it – helping to discredit decent men? And not only my father. Most of them on your own side, men who've given years to the Labour movement, a cause you're supposed to support.'

'Decency doesn't come into it. This is a war. Wars may be fought by decent men but they're not won by them.'

A small group of visitors had drifted up. They moved away and walked slowly down the side of the gallery. He said:

'If you're in the job of organizing a revolutionary group, even a small one, and they're going to have to wait for real action, real power, then you must keep them occupied, keen, give them the illusion that they're achieving something. Talk isn't enough. There has to be action. It's partly a matter of training for the future, partly of keeping up morale.'

350

She said:

'From now on you're going to have to do it without me.'

'I realize that. I knew that after Dalgliesh had seen you. But I expect you to stay on, at least nominally, until this murder inquiry is over. I don't want to say anything to the others while Dalgliesh is nosing around. Then you can join the Labour Party. You'll be happier there. Or the SDP, of course. Take your choice, there's no difference. By the time you're forty you'll be a Tory anyway.'

She said:

'And you still trust me? You've told me all this knowing that I want to get out?'

'Of course. I know you. You've inherited your father's pride. You wouldn't want people saying that your lover chucked you so you took your revenge by betraying him. You wouldn't want your friends, your grandmother even, to know that you've conspired against your father. You can say I rely on your bourgeois decencies. But there isn't much of a risk. The cell will be dissolved, re-formed, meet elsewhere. That's necessary now anyway.'

She thought: That's another aspect of the revolutionary struggle, getting to know people's decencies and using them against them. She said:

'Daddy, there's something I've learned about him, something I didn't realize until he died. He tried to be good. I suppose those words don't mean anything to you.'

'They mean something. I'm not sure what exactly you expect them to mean. I suppose he tried to behave so that he wasn't made uncomfortable by too much guilt. We all do. Given his politics and lifestyle that can't have been easy. Perhaps in the end he gave up trying.'

She said:

'I wasn't talking about politics. It had nothing to do with politics. I know you think everything has, but there is another view. There is a world elsewhere.'

'I hope you'll be happy in it.'

They were moving out of the gallery now and she knew that this was the last time they would be there together. It surprised her how little she cared. She said:

'But Diana Travers; you said you put her into Campden Hill Square until you decided what to do with her. What did you do? Drown her?'

And now for the first time she saw that he was angry.

'Don't be melodramatic.'

'But it was convenient for you, wasn't it?'

'Oh yes, and not only for me. There's someone else who had a much stronger motive for getting rid of her. Your father.'

Forgetting the need for secrecy, she almost cried:

'Daddy? But he wasn't there! He was expected, but he never arrived.'

'Oh, but he was there. I followed him that night. You could call it an exercise in surveillance. I drove behind him all the way to the Black Swan and watched him turn into the drive. And if you should decide to talk to Dalgliesh, who seems for some reason to induce in you the need for sentimental girlish confidences, then that is one piece of information that I shall feel it necessary to pass on.'

'But you can't, can you? Not without admitting that you were there, too. If it's a question of motive, Dalgliesh might think there's not a lot to choose between you. And you're alive; he's dead.'

'But unlike your father, I have an alibi. A genuine one this time. I drove straight back to London, to a meeting of senior social workers at the town hall. I'm in the clear. But is he? His memory is unsavoury enough as it is. D'you want another scandal linked to his name? Isn't poor Harry Mack enough for you? Think about that if you're tempted to make an anonymous call to Special Branch.'

8

Tuesday morning couldn't have heralded a better day for a drive out of London. The sunlight was fitful but surprisingly strong and the sky was a high ethereal blue above the scudding clouds. Dalgliesh drove fast, but almost in silence. Kate had expected that they would drive straight to Riverside Cottage but the road passed the Black Swan and when they reached it Dalgliesh stopped the car, appeared to think, then turned into the drive. He said:

'We'll have a beer. I'd like to walk along the river, view the cottage from this bank. It's Higgins's property, most of it anyway. We'd better let him know we're here.'

They left the Rover in the car park, which was empty except for a Jaguar, a BMW, and a couple of Fords, and made their way to the entrance hall. Henry greeted them with impassive courtesy as if unsure whether he was expected to recognize them and, in reply to Dalgliesh's question, told them that Monsieur was in London. The bar was empty except for a quartet of businessmen conspiratorially bent over their whiskies. The barman, baby-faced above his white starched jacket and bow tie, served them with a notable brew of real ale which the Black Swan took some pride in obtaining, then began industriously washing glasses and rearranging his bar as if hoping that a show of busy-ness might inhibit Dalgliesh from asking any questions. Dalgliesh wondered by what extraordinary alchemy Henry had managed to signal their identities. They carried their beer to the chairs each side of the log fire, drank in companionable silence, then returned to the car park and passed through the gate in the hedge to the riverbank.

It was one of those perfect English autumnal days which occur more frequently in memory than in life. The rich colours of grass and earth were intensified by the mellow light of a sun almost warm enough for spring and the air was a sweet evocation of all Dalgliesh's boyhood autumns; woodsmoke, ripe apples, the last sheaves of harvest, and the strong sea-smelling breeze of flowing water. The Thames was running strongly, under a quickening breeze. It flattened the grasses fringing the river edge and eddied the stream into the little gullies which fretted the bank. Under a surface iridescent in blues and greens, on which the light moved and changed as if on coloured glass, the blade-like weeds streamed

353

and undulated. Beyond the clumps of willows on the far bank, a herd of Friesians were peacefully grazing.

Opposite and about twenty yards upstream he could see a bungalow, little more than a large white shack on stilts, which he guessed must be their destination. And he knew too, as he had known walking under the trees of St James's Park, that here he would find the clue he sought. But he was in no hurry. Like a child postponing the moment of assured satisfaction he was glad that they were early, grateful for this small hiatus of calm. And suddenly he experienced a minute of tingling happiness so unexpected and so keen that he almost held his breath as if he could halt time. They came to him so rarely now, these moments of intense physical joy, and he had never before experienced one in the middle of a murder investigation. The moment passed and he heard his own sigh. Breaking the mood with a commonplace, he said:

'I suppose that must be Riverside Cottage.'

'I think so, sir. Shall I get the map?'

'No. We shall find out soon enough. We'd better get on.'

But he still lingered feeling the wind lift his hair and grateful for another minute of peace. He was grateful, too, that Kate Miskin could share it with him without the need to speak and without making him feel that her silence was a conscious discipline. He had chosen her because he needed a woman in his team and she was the best available. The choice had been partly rational, partly instinctive, and he was beginning to realize just how well his instinct had served him. It would have been dishonest to say that there was no hint of sexuality between them. In his experience there nearly always was, however repudiated or unacknowledged, between any reasonably attractive heterosexual couple who worked closely together. He wouldn't have chosen her if he had found her disturbingly attractive, but the attraction was there and he wasn't immune to it. But despite this pinprick of sexuality, perhaps because of it, he found her surprisingly restful to work with. She had an instinctive knowledge of what he wanted; she knew when to be silent; she wasn't over-deferential. He suspected that with part of her mind she saw his vulnerabilities more clearly, understood him better, and was more judgemental than were any of his male subordinates. She had none of Massingham's ruthlessness, but she wasn't in the least sentimental. But then in his experience, women police officers seldom were.

He took a final look at the bungalow. If he had walked along the riverbank on that first visit to the Black Swan, as he had been tempted to do, he would have viewed its pathetic pretensions with an incurious and disparaging eye. But now as its fragile walls seemed to shimmer in the slight haze from the river it held for him an infinite and disturbing promise. It was built about thirty yards from the water's edge with a wide veranda, a central stack and to the left, downstream, a small landing stage. He thought he could see a patch of broken earth with clumps of mauve and white, perhaps a patch of Michaelmas daisies. Some attempt had been made at a garden. From a distance the bungalow looked well-maintained, the white paintwork gleaming. But even so, it had a summer look; temporary, a little ramshackle. Higgins, he thought, would hardly relish having it in full view of his lawns.

As they looked, the dumpy figure of a woman came out of the side door and made her way to the landing stage, a large dog trotting at her heels. She lowered herself into a dinghy, leaned over to cast off and began rowing purposefully across the river towards the Black Swan, humpbacked over the oars, the dog sitting bolt-upright in the prow. As the dinghy crawled closer they could see that he was a cross between a poodle and some kind of terrier with a woolly body and an anxious, amiable face almost entirely obscured by hair. They watched as the woman bent and rose over the dipping oars, making slow progress against a current that was bearing her downstream towards them. When the dinghy finally bumped the bank, Dalgliesh and Kate walked up to her. Bending down, he caught the bow of the dinghy and held it steady. He saw that her landing place had not been fortuitous. There was a steel stake driven deep into the grass at the water's edge. He slipped the painter over it and held out his hand. She grasped it and almost hopped ashore, one-footed, and he saw that she wore a surgical boot on her left foot. The dog leapt out after her, sniffed at Dalgliesh's trousers, then flopped, discouraged, on the grass as if the physical effort of the journey had all been his. Dalgliesh said:

'I think you must be Miss Millicent Gentle. If so, we're on our way to see you. We telephoned from Scotland Yard this morning. This is Inspector Kate Miskin and my name is Adam Dalgliesh.'

He looked down at a face round and crumpled like an overstored apple. The striped russet cheeks were hard balls under small eyes which, when she smiled up at him, creased into narrow slits, then opened to reveal irises as brightly brown as polished pebbles. She was wearing a shapeless pair of brown Terylene slacks and a padded sleeveless jerkin in faded red over a jumper matted with age. Drawn well down over her head was a pixie cap in knitted green and red stripes and with earflaps each ending in a pigtail of plaited wool, decorated with a red bobble. She had an air of slightly battered puckishness like an elderly garden gnome which has weathered too many winters. But when she spoke her voice, deep and resonant, was one of the most beautiful female voices he had ever heard.

'I am expecting you, of course, Commander, but not for another half hour. How pleasant to meet you so unexpectedly. I would row you across but with Makepeace it would mean one at a time and that would be rather slow. I'm afraid it's five miles by road, but perhaps you have a car.'

'We have a car.'

'Of course, you would have, being police officers. How silly of me. Then I'll be waiting for you. I've just rowed across with my letters. Mr Higgins lets me put them on the hall table to be posted with his. My postbox is a two-mile walk. It's very kind of him considering that he doesn't really like my cottage. I'm afraid he considers it rather an eyesore. You can't miss the road. Take the first left marked Frolight, then over the hump-backed bridge, then left again at Mr Roland's farm – there's a sign with a Friesian cow on it – then you'll see a track leading to the river and my cottage. As you can see, you can't really miss it. Oh, and you'll have some coffee, I hope.'

'Thank you, we should like that.'

'I thought you might. That's partly why I rowed over. Mr Higgins is kind about selling me an extra pint of milk. It's about Sir Paul Berowne, isn't it?'

'Yes, Miss Gentle, it's about Sir Paul.'

'I thought it might be when you telephoned and said you were police. That dear good man. I shall see you both then in about ten minutes.'

They watched her for a moment as she limped briskly towards the Black Swan, the dog lurching at her heels, then turned and made their way slowly back to the car park. They followed her instructions without difficulty but Dalgliesh drove slowly knowing them to be still ahead of their appointment and wanting to give Miss Gentle time to row back and be waiting for them. Gentle was, apparently, her real name not a pseudonym; it had seemed almost too appropriate for a romantic novelist. Driving with irritating slowness, he was aware of Kate's controlled impatience at his side. But ten minutes later they left the side road and turned up the rough track to the cottage.

It ran across an unhedged field and would, thought Dalgliesh, be little more than an impassable quagmire in the worst of the winter. The bungalow looked more substantial than it had from a distance. A flowerbed, now in its shaggy autumnal decrepitude, bordered the cinder path to the side steps beneath which he could glimpse cans, presumably of paraffin, stacked under a tarpaulin. Behind the bungalow was a vegetable patch; stunted cabbages, and the scarred stems of Brussels sprouts, bulbous onions, broken-leaved, and the last of the runner beans whose dying swathes hung from their poles like rags. The river smell was stronger here and he could picture the scene in winter, the cold mist rising from the water, the soggy fields, the single mud track to a desolate country road.

But when Miss Gentle opened the door to them and smilingly stepped aside they walked into cheerfulness and light. From the wide sitting-room windows it was possible to imagine oneself on a ship with nothing in view but the white veranda rail and the sheen of the river. Despite an incongruous wrought iron stove, the room was indeed more typical of a cottage than a riverside shack. One wall, incongruously papered with rosebuds and robins, was almost covered with pictures; dated watercolours of country scenes, twin engravings of Winchester and Wells Cathedrals, four early-Victorian fashion plates mounted in one frame, an embroidered picture in wool and silk of the Angel greeting the Apostles at the empty tomb, a couple of rather good miniature portraits in oval frames. The far wall was covered with books, some of them, Dalgliesh noticed, were Miss Gentle's own, still pristine in their jackets. On each side of the stove was an easy chair and between them a gate-legged table on which a jug of milk and three flowered cups and saucers had already been placed. Miss Gentle, helped by Kate, drew up a small rocking chair for her second guest. Makepeace, having ambled with his mistress to greet them, slumped down in front of the empty stove and heaved a malodorous sigh.

Miss Gentle brought in the coffee almost immediately. The kettle had been on the boil, she had only to pour the water over the grains. Taking his first sip, Dalgliesh had a moment's compunction. He had forgotten how inconvenient it was for the solitary to be faced with unexpected visitors. That row across to the Black Swan had, he suspected, been more for the milk than to get the letters posted. He said, gently:

'You know, of course, that Sir Paul Berowne is dead.'

'Yes, I know. He was murdered, and that's why you're here. How did you find me?'

Dalgliesh explained about the finding of her book. He said:

'Anything that happened to him during the last weeks of his life is important to us. That's why we'd like you to tell us exactly what happened on the night of August the seventh. You did see him?'

'Oh, yes, I saw him.' She put down her cup and gave a little shiver as if she was suddenly cold. Then she settled down to tell her story as if they were children round the nursery fire.

'I really get on very well with Mr Higgins. Of course, he would like to buy the cottage and pull it down, but I've said that he can have first refusal from my executors when I'm dead. We have our little joke about it. And the Black Swan is really very respectably run. A nice type of customer, very quiet. But on that night they weren't. I was trying to work and it got very irritating. Young people shouting and screaming. So I went out to the bank and I could just see that there were four of them in a punt. They were rocking very dangerously and two of them were standing up and trying to change places. I thought I would row across and speak to Mr Higgins. Perhaps Henry could deal with them. Apart from the noise they were behaving very foolishly. So Makepeace and I rowed across. I made for my usual spot – it would have been most imprudent to row up to them and remonstrate, I'm not as strong as I used to be. As I turned the boat to draw up to the bank, I saw the other two men.'

'Did you know who they were?'

'Not at the time. It was, of course, dark by then. There was only the reflected light coming over the hedge from the car park. Afterwards I knew one of them, Sir Paul Berowne.'

'What were they doing?'

'Fighting.' Miss Gentle spoke the words without the least disapproval, almost, Dalgliesh thought, with a note of surprise that he should have needed to ask. Her tone implied that fighting on the riverbank and partly in the dark was an activity to be expected of two gentlemen who had nothing better to do. She said:

'They didn't notice me, of course. Only my head was above the level of the bank. I was afraid Makepeace would bark but I told him not to and he was really very controlled although I could see that he wanted to jump out and join in. I rather wondered if I ought to intervene myself but I decided it would be undignified and really quite ineffective. And it was obviously a private fight. I mean, it didn't look like an unprovoked attack which I feel one has a duty to try to put a stop to. The second man looked much shorter than Sir Paul, which made it rather unfair in a way. But then he was the younger so that redressed the balance. They were getting on very well without me or Makepeace.'

Dalgliesh couldn't resist a glance at Makepeace, steaming in somnolent calm. It seemed unlikely that he could have raised the energy for a bark let alone a bite. He asked:

'Who won?'

'Oh, Sir Paul. He landed what I think is called a hook to the jaw. It looked very satisfying. The younger man fell, then Sir Paul picked him up by the collar of his coat and his trousers, very like a puppy, and threw him into the river. He made quite a splash. "My goodness," I said to Makepeace, "what an extraordinary evening we're having!"'

Dalgliesh thought that the scene was beginning to resemble a chapter from one of Miss Gentle's own genre. He said:

'What happened next?'

'Sir Paul waded into the river and fished him out. I expect he didn't actually want him to drown. Perhaps he didn't know whether he could swim. Then he threw him down on the grass, said something which I couldn't hear and walked upstream towards me. As he drew alongside, I popped up my head. I said: "Good evening. I don't suppose you remember me but we met last June at the Hertfordshire Conservative fête. I was visiting a niece. I'm Millicent Gentle."'

'What did he do?'

'He came over, squatted down by the dinghy, and shook hands. He was quite unflustered, not in the least disconcerted. He was dripping wet, of course, and his cheek was bleeding. It looked like a scratch. But he was as self-possessed as he had been when we'd met at the Conservative fête. I said: "I saw the fight. You haven't killed him, have you?" He said: "No, I haven't killed him. I only wanted to." Then he apologized and I said there was really no need. He was beginning to shiver – it really wasn't warm enough to be standing around in wet clothes – so I suggested he should come back to the cottage and dry off. He said: "That's very kind of you but I think I ought first to move the car." I knew what he meant, of course. It would be better if he left the Black Swan before anyone saw him or knew that he was there. Politicians have to be so careful. I suggested that he park it somewhere at the side of the road and I'd wait for him a little further upstream until he came back. He could have driven round, of course, but it would have been five miles or more and he really was very cold. He disappeared and I waited. It wasn't long. He was back in less than five minutes.'

'And what happened to the other man?'

'I didn't wait to see. I knew he'd be all right. He wasn't alone, you see. He had a girl with him.'

'A girl? Are you sure?'

'Oh yes, quite sure. She came out of the bushes and watched when Sir Paul threw him into the river. I couldn't have missed her. She was quite naked.'

'Could you recognize her?' Without being asked, Kate opened her shoulder bag and handed over the photograph.

Miss Gentle said:

'Isn't that the girl who was drowned? It's possible it was the same one, but I didn't see her face clearly. The light was very poor, as I've said, and they must have been forty yards away.'

'What did she do?'

'She laughed. It was most extraordinary. Peal on peal of laughter. When Sir Paul waded in to help him out, she sat on the bank, quite naked and roared with laughter. One ought not to laugh at another's misfortune, but he really did look very funny. The scene was quite bizarre. Two men stumbling out of the river and a naked girl sitting on the bank and laughing. She had rather an infectious laugh, full-throated, joyous. Ringing across the water, it didn't sound malicious. But I suppose it must have been.'

'And what was happening to the party in the punt?'

'They were paddling downstream towards the Black Swan. Perhaps they were beginning to feel a little frightened. The river is so black at night and so strange, almost sinister. I'm used to it now, I feel at home with it. But I think they wanted to get back to the lights and the warmth.'

'So the last you saw of the man and the girl they were together on the bank and you began rowing quietly upstream without being noticed?'

'Yes. The river bends just slightly there and the rushes are taller at the water edge. They were quickly out of sight. I sat quietly and waited until Sir Paul appeared.'

'From what direction?'

'From further upstream, the same direction as I had been rowing. He'd come through the car park, you see.'

'Still out of earshot and sight of the boy and girl?'

'Well, out of sight, but I could still hear her laughing as we rowed across. I had to go carefully. With Makepeace and a passenger we were very low in the water.'

The picture of the two of them in that bucket of a dinghy with

Makepeace rigid at the prow was ridiculous but endearing. Dalgliesh wanted to laugh. It wasn't an impulse he had expected to feel in the middle of any murder investigation, least of all this one, and he was grateful. He asked:

'The girl, for how long was she laughing?'

'Until we were almost on the opposite bank. And then, suddenly, the laughing stopped.'

'Did you hear anything at that moment, a cry, a splash?'

'Nothing. But then, if she had dived cleanly in there wouldn't have been much of a splash. And I don't think I would have heard it above the noise of the oars.'

'What happened then, Miss Gentle?'

'First Sir Paul asked if he could use the telephone to make a local call. He didn't say to where and, naturally, I didn't ask. I left him here and went into the kitchen so that he could feel quite private. Then I suggested that he ought to have a hot bath. I switched on the electric wall heater in the bathroom and lit all my paraffin stoves. It didn't seem a time for economy. And I gave him some disinfectant for his face. I don't think I mentioned that the boy had scratched him quite badly on his cheek. Not a very masculine way to fight I thought. Then, while he was in the bathroom, I dried his clothes in the spin-dryer. I haven't got a washing machine. Well, I don't really need one, just being on my own. I can even manage the sheets now that we have drip-dry. But I don't think I could manage without my spin-dryer. Oh, and I handed him my father's old dressing gown to wear while the clothes were drying. It's all wool and beautifully warm. They don't make that quality now. When he came out of the bathroom I thought how handsome he looked in it. We settled down in front of the fire and I made some hot cocoa. Being a gentleman I thought he might prefer something stronger and I offered my elderberry wine. He said he'd rather have the cocoa. Well, he didn't actually say he preferred the cocoa. He would have liked to taste the wine, he was sure it was excellent, but he thought a hot drink might be better. I quite agreed. There's really nothing quite as comforting as good strong cocoa when one is famished with cold. I made it with all milk. I had ordered an extra pint because I planned to have cauliflower cheese for supper. Wasn't that lucky?'

Dalgliesh said:

'Very lucky. Have you spoken of this to any other person?'

'No one. I wouldn't have spoken to you if you hadn't telephoned and he hadn't been dead.'

'Did he ask for your silence?'

'Oh, no, he wouldn't have done that. He wasn't that kind of man, and he knew that I wouldn't tell. You know when you can trust a person about something like that, don't you find? If you can, why ask? If you can't, there's no point in asking.'

'Please continue to say nothing, Miss Gentle. It could be important.'

She nodded but didn't speak. He asked, wondering why it should matter so, why he needed so urgently to know:

'What did you talk about?'

'Not about the fight, at least not very much. I said: "I expect it was about a woman, wasn't it?" And he said it was.'

'The woman who laughed, the naked girl?'

'I don't think so. I'm not sure why, but I don't think so. I've a feeling it was rather more complicated than that. And I don't think he would have fought in front of her, not if he'd known she was there. But then, I don't suppose he did know. She must have concealed herself in the bushes when she saw him coming.'

He thought he knew why Berowne had been on the riverbank. He had arrived to join the dinner party, to greet his wife and his wife's lover, to take part in a civilized charade, the complaisant husband, stock figure of farce. And then he had heard the murmur of running water, had smelt, as had Dalgliesh, that strong nostalgic river smell with its promise of a few moments of solitude and peace. So he had hesitated, then walked through the gate in the hedge from the car park to the riverbank. Such a small thing, a simple impulse obeyed, and it had led him to that blood-boltered vestry.

And it must have been then that Swayne, perhaps pulling his shirt over his head, had stepped out of the bushes to confront him like the personification of everything he despised in his own life, in himself. Had he challenged Swayne about Theresa Nolan, or did he already know? Was that one other secret that the girl had confided to him in that final letter, the name of her lover?

Dalgliesh asked again, gently insistent:

'What *did* you talk about, Miss Gentle?'

'Mainly about my work, my books. He was really very interested in how I started writing, where I got my ideas. Of course, I haven't published anything for six years now. My kind of fiction isn't very fashionable. Dear Mr Hearne, always so kind, so helpful, explained it to me. Romantic fiction is more realistic now. I'm afraid I'm too old-fashioned. But I can't change. People are sometimes a little unkind about romantic novelists, I know, but we're just like other

362

writers. You can only write what you need to write. And I'm very lucky. I have my health, my old-age pension, my home, and Makepeace for company. And I still keep writing. The next book may be the lucky one.'

Dalgliesh asked:

'How long did Sir Paul stay?'

'Oh, for hours, until nearly midnight. But I don't think that he was being polite. I think he was happy here. We sat and talked and I made scrambled eggs when we got hungry. There was enough milk for that but not, of course, for the cauliflower cheese. At one point he said: "No one in the world knows where I am at this moment, not a single soul. No one can get at me." He said it as if I had given him something precious. He sat in that chair, the one you're in now and he looked so comfortable in father's old dressing gown and so at home. You're very like him, Commander. I don't mean your features. He was fair and you're so dark. But you are like him; the way you sit, your hands, the way you walk, even your voice a little.'

Dalgliesh put down his cup and got up. Kate looked at him, surprised, then rose too and picked up her shoulder bag. Dalgliesh heard himself thanking Miss Gentle for the coffee, emphasizing the need for silence, explaining that they would like a written statement and that a police car would call and take her to New Scotland Yard, if that were convenient. They had reached the door when Kate asked, on impulse:

'And when he left you that night, that was the last time you saw him?'

'Oh no. I saw him on the afternoon of his death. I thought you knew.'

Dalgliesh said gently:

'But Miss Gentle, how could we have known?'

'I thought he would have told someone where he was going. Is it important?'

'Very important, Miss Gentle. We've been trying to trace his movements that afternoon. Tell us what happened.'

'There isn't much to tell. He arrived, quite unexpectedly, just before three o'clock. I remember that I was listening to Woman's Hour on Radio Four. He was on foot and he was carrying a bag. He must have walked the four miles from the station but he seemed surprised when I pointed out how far it was. He said he had felt like a walk along the river. I asked him if he'd had any lunch and he said he had some cheese in his bag and that would do. He must have been famished. Luckily I'd made myself a beef stew for lunch and there was some over so I made him come in and he ate that and then we had coffee together. He didn't talk very much. I don't think he'd come to talk. Then he left his bag with me and set off for his walk. He came back about four-thirty and I made tea. His shoes were very dirty – the river meadows have been so waterlogged this summer – so I gave him my shoe cleaning box and he sat outside on the steps and cleaned them. Then he took up his bag, said goodbye and was on his way. It was as simple as that.'

As simple as that, thought Dalgliesh. The lost hours accounted for, the wedge of mud on his shoe explained. He had gone, not to his mistress but to a woman whom he had seen only once before in his life, who asked no questions, made no demands, who had given him those remembered moments of peace. He had wanted to spend those few hours where no one in the world knew where to find him. And he must have gone straight from Paddington to St Matthew's Church. They would have to check the times of the trains, how long the whole journey was likely to have taken. But whether or not Lady Ursula was lying, it seemed highly unlikely that Berowne could have called in at his house, collected his diary, and still arrived at the church by six.

Looking back at the closing door, Kate said:

'I know an old lady who, in her place, would say: "No one wants my books, I'm poor, I'm lame, and I live in a damp cottage with only a dog for company." She says: "I've got my health, my pension, my home, Makepeace for company, and I go on writing."'

Dalgliesh wondered who it was she had in mind. There was a bitterness in her voice which was new to him. Then he remembered that there was an elderly grandmother somewhere in the picture, and wondered. It was the first time that she had ever hinted at a private life. Before he could answer she went on:

'So that explains why Higgins said that Swayne's clothes were dripping wet. It was a night in August, after all. If he'd been swimming naked and then pulled on his clothes after the drowning, why should they be dripping?' She added:

'It's a new motive, sir, a double motive. Swayne must have hated him. The thrashing, the humiliation, thrown into the river and dragged out like a dog, and in front of the girl.'

Dalgliesh said:

'Oh, yes, Swayne must have hated him.'

So he had it at last, the motive not only for murder but for this particular murder with its mixture of planning and impulse, its brutality, its over-ingenuity, the cleverness which hadn't quite been clever enough. It was there before him in its pettiness, its arrogance, its essential inadequacy, but in all its terrible strength. He recognized the mind behind it. He had met it before, the mind of a killer who isn't content merely to take a life, who avenges humiliation with humiliation, who cannot bear the searing knowledge that his enemy breathes the same air, who wants his victim not only dead but disgraced, the mind of a man who has felt despised and inferior all his life but who will never feel inferior again. And if his instinct were right and Dominic Swayne were his man, then to get him he would have to break a vulnerable, lonely and obstinate woman. He shivered and turned up the collar of his coat. The sunlight was fading over the meadows but the wind was freshening and there came from the river a smell, dank and ominous, like the first breath of winter. He heard Kate's voice:

'Do you think we'll be able to break his alibi, sir, by any method we're allowed to use?'

Dalgliesh roused himself and strode to the car.

'We must try, Inspector, we must try.'

BOOK SIX

Mortal Consequences

1

When Father Barnes had first told Miss Wharton of Susan Kendrick's suggestion that she might like to spend a day or so with them in the Nottingham vicarage until the fuss had died down, she had accepted with gratitude and relief. It was agreed that she would travel to Nottingham immediately after the inquest and that Father Barnes would himself go by tube with her to King's Cross to carry her one case and see her off. The whole plan had seemed like an answer to a prayer. The half-lubricous respect with which she was now treated by the McGraths who seemed to regard her as a prize exhibit, bolstering their esteem in the road, she found more terrifying than their previous antagonism. It would be a relief to get away from their avid eyes and endless questions.

The inquest had been less of an ordeal than she had feared. Only evidence of identity and of the finding of the bodies had been briefly taken, before, at the request of the police, the proceedings were adjourned. The coroner had treated Miss Wharton with grave consideration and her time in the witness box had been so brief that she was hardly aware of standing there before she was released. Her anxiously searching eyes had failed to see Darren. She had a confused recollection of being introduced to a number of strangers including a fair-haired young man who said that he was Sir Paul's brother-in-law. No one else from the family was present, although there were a number of sombre-suited men who Father Barnes told her were lawyers. He himself, resplendent in a new cassock and biretta, had been extraordinarily at ease. He had shepherded her with a proprietorial arm, past the photographers, had greeted members of the congregation with an assurance she had never before seen in him, and had seemed quite at ease with the police. Miss Wharton, for one appalled moment, found herself thinking that the murders seemed to have done him good.

She had known after the first day at St Crispin's that the visit wasn't going to be a success. Susan Kendrick was heavily pregnant with her first child but her energy was undiminished and every minute of her day seemed occupied either with parish or domestic concerns or with her part-time physiotherapy clinic at the local hospital. The rambling inner-city vicarage was never empty and, except for Father Kendrick's study, never peaceful. Miss Wharton was constantly introduced to people whose names she couldn't quite catch, and whose functions in the parish she never divined. Where the murders were concerned, her hostess was dutifully sympathetic but obviously took the view that it was unreasonable for anyone to be lastingly distressed by dead bodies, however unpleasant their ends, and that dwelling on the experience was at best self-indulgent and at worst morbid. But Miss Wharton had reached the stage when it would have been helpful to talk, and she was missing Darren with a need which was becoming desperate, wondering where he was, what was happening to him, whether he was happy.

She had expressed her pleasure at the coming baby but nervousness had made her sound coy and her words had sounded gushingly sentimental even to her own ears. Confronted with Susan's robust common sense about her pregnancy she had been made to feel an absurd old maid. She had offered to help in the parish, but her hostess's inability to find a job suitable to her abilities had drained her confidence further. She had begun to creep about the vicarage like the church mouse they probably thought she resembled. After a couple of days she had nervously suggested that she ought to be thinking of home, and no one had made any attempt to dissuade her.

But on the morning of departure she had brought herself to confide in Susan her worries about Darren, and here her hostess had been helpful. Local bureaucracy held no terrors for her. She had known whom to ring, how to discover the number, and had spoken to the unknown voice at the end of the line in the accents of conspiratorial, mutually acknowledged authority. She had made the call from her husband's study with Miss Wharton seated in the chair conveniently placed for those seeking the vicar's counsel. During the telephone conversation, she had felt like the unworthy recipient of patient professional concern, vaguely conscious that she would have done better had she been an unmarried mother or a delinquent, preferably both, and had been black.

Afterwards Susan Kendrick had given her the verdict. She couldn't see Darren at present; his social worker felt that it wasn't at all desirable. He had been taken before the Juvenile Court and a supervision order made. They were hoping to arrange a programme of intermediate treatment for him, but until this was satisfactorily under way they didn't think it wise for him to see Miss Wharton. It might only provoke unfortunate memories. He had been very reluctant to talk about the murders, and his social worker felt that

370

when he was ready to do so it should be with someone suitably qualified in social work skills who could work through the trauma with him. He'll hate it all, thought Miss Wharton. He never did like interference.

Lying in bed on her first night at home, wakeful, as she so often was now, she came to a decision. She would go to Scotland Yard and ask the police to help. Surely they would have some authority, or at least some influence, over Darren's social worker. They had always been kind and helpful to her. They would be able to reassure the local authority that she could be trusted with Darren. The decision brought a measure of peace to her troubled mind and she fell asleep.

The next morning found her less confident, but with her resolution unshaken. She would set out after ten o'clock; there was no point in getting caught up in the rush hour. She dressed carefully for the excursion; first impressions were always important. Before setting out she knelt to pray briefly that the visit might be a success, that she would be met with understanding, that Scotland Yard wouldn't be the terrifying place of her imagination, that Commander Dalgliesh or Inspector Miskin would be willing to talk to the local authority, to explain that she wouldn't even mention the murders to Darren if his social worker thought it unwise. She walked to Paddington underground station and took the Circle Line. At St James's Park station she came out of the wrong exit, was for a few minutes lost and had to inquire the way to the Yard. And suddenly across the road, she saw the revolving sign, and the great glass oblong building so familiar from television news pictures.

The entrance hall surprised her. She wasn't sure what she had imagined; a uniformed officer on duty, perhaps a steel grille, even a succession of manacled prisoners being escorted to the cells. Instead she found herself facing an ordinary reception desk with a couple of young women on duty. The hall was very busy with an air of purposeful but relaxed activity. Men and women showed their passes, and passed happily gossiping through to the lifts. Except for the flame of remembrance burning on its plinth it could, she thought, be almost any office. She asked for Inspector Miskin, having decided that this was a matter on which a woman might be more sympathetic than a man and that she could hardly worry Commander Dalgliesh with something so unimportant, except to her. No, she admitted, she hadn't an appointment. She was asked to sit down on one of the chairs set against the left-hand wall, and watched while the girl telephoned. Her confidence grew, and the

371

hands clutching her handbag gradually relaxed. She was able to take an interest in the busy comings and goings, to feel that she had a right to be there.

And suddenly Inspector Miskin was standing beside her. She hadn't expected her to appear. Somehow she had thought that she would be taken by messenger to the Inspector's office. She thought: she's saving time. If she thinks it's important then she'll take me up. And Inspector Miskin obviously didn't think it important. When Miss Wharton had explained her purpose she sat down beside her and was for a moment silent. Miss Wharton thought: she's disappointed. She hoped I was bringing her some news about the murders, that I'd remembered something new and important. Then the Inspector said:

'I'm sorry, but I don't see how we can help. The Juvenile Court has made a supervision order to the local authority. It's their concern now.'

'I know. That's what Mrs Kendrick told me, but I thought you might be able to use your influence. After all, the police . . .'

'We have no influence, not in this.'

The words sounded dreadfully final. Miss Wharton found herself pleading:

'I wouldn't talk to him about the murder, although I sometimes think that boys are tougher than we are in some ways. But I'd be very careful. I'd feel so much better if only I could see him again, even if briefly, just to know that he's all right.'

'Why can't you? Did they say?'

'They think he ought not to talk about the murders until he can work through the trauma with someone experienced in social work skills.'

'Yes, that sounds like the jargon.'

Miss Wharton was surprised by the sudden bitterness in the Inspector's voice. She sensed that she had an ally. She opened her mouth to make an appeal and decided against it. If anything could be done, Inspector Miskin would do it. The Inspector seemed to be thinking, then she said:

'I can't give you his address; anyway I can't remember it. I'd have to consult the file. I'm not even sure if they've left him at home with his mother, although I suppose they'd have gone for a care order if they'd wanted to remove him. But I can remember the name of his school, Bollington Road Junior. Do you know it?'

Miss Wharton said eagerly:

'Oh yes, I know where Bollington Road is. I can get there.'

'They still come out at about three thirty, don't they? You could try passing at the right time. If you met him accidentally I don't see how they could object to that.'

'Thank you, thank you.'

Miss Wharton, her perceptions sharpened by anxiety and now relief, guessed that Inspector Miskin was wondering whether to ask her again about the murders; but she said nothing. As they got up and the Inspector walked with her to the door, she looked up at her and said:

'You've been very kind. If I remember anything new about the murders, anything I haven't told you, I'll get in touch at once.'

Sitting in the tube on her way to St James's Park station she had planned that, if all went well, she would treat herself afterwards to coffee in the Army and Navy Stores. But her visit to the Yard seemed to have taken more out of her than she had expected, and even the thought of negotiating the traffic of Victoria Street depressed and discouraged her. Perhaps it would be less exhausting to go without the coffee and make for home. While she was hesitating at the edge of the pavement she felt a shoulder brush against hers. A male voice, young, pleasant, said:

'Excuse me, but aren't you Miss Wharton? I met you at the Berowne inquest. I'm Dominic Swayne, Sir Paul's brother-in-law.'

She blinked, confused for a second, and then recognized him. He said:

'We're blocking the pavement,' and she felt his hand on her arm, firmly guiding her across the street. Then, without releasing her, he said:

'You must have been to the Yard. So have I. I feel in need of a drink. Please have one with me. I was thinking of the St Ermin's Hotel.'

Miss Wharton said:

'You're very kind, but I'm not sure . . .'

'Please. I need someone to talk to. You'd be doing me a kindness.'

It really was impossible to refuse. His voice, smile, the press of his arm were persuasive. He was steering her gently but firmly forward through the station and into Caxton Street. And, suddenly here was the hotel, looking so solidly welcoming, its wide court-yard flanked by heraldic beasts. It would be good to have a quiet sit before she started the journey home. He guided her through the left-hand door and into the foyer.

It was, she thought, all very grand; the branching staircase leading to a curved balcony, the glittering chandeliers, the mirrored walls and elegantly carved pillars. Yet she felt strangely at home. There was something reassuring about this Edwardian elegance, this atmosphere of assured, respectable comfort. She followed her companion over the blue and fawn carpet to a couple of high-backed chairs before the fireplace. After they had seated themselves he asked:

'What would you like? There's coffee, but I think you should have something stronger. Sherry?'

'Yes, that would be very nice, thank you.'

'Dry?'

'Well, not too dry, perhaps.'

Mrs Kendrick had brought out the sherry decanter before dinner every evening at St Crispin's vicarage. It had invariably been dry, a pale sour sharpness not really to her taste. But she had missed the evening ritual on her return home. There was no doubt one did get quickly used to these little luxuries. He lifted his finger and the waiter came, swiftly deferential. The sherry arrived, a rich amber, half-sweet, immediately reviving. There was a little bowl of nuts and one of small dry biscuits. How elegant, how soothing it all was. The raucous life of Victoria Street could have been miles away. She sat back, glass at her lips, and looked with tremulous wonder at the ornately carved ceiling, the twin wall-lights with their fringed shades, the huge urns of flowers at the foot of the stair. And suddenly she knew why she felt so at home. Sight, sound, sensation, even the young man's face bent smiling towards her, all fused into a long-forgotten picture. She was in a hotel lounge, surely this same hotel, this very place, sitting with her brother on his first leave after he had gained his sergeant's stripes. And then she remembered. He had been stationed at Bassingbourn in East Anglia. They must have met at a hotel near Liverpool Street, not Victoria. But it had been so very similar. She remembered her pride in the smartness of his uniform, the one winged badge of an air-gunner on his breast, the pristine brightness of his three stripes, her sense of importance at being escorted by him, how she had revelled in the unaccustomed luxury, in the assured way in which he had summoned the waiter; ordered sherry for her, beer for himself. And her present companion reminded her a little of John. Like John, he was barely her own height. 'They like us small, we tail-end Charlies,' John had said. But he had John's fairness, something of John in the blue eyes and the high curve of the eyebrows, and all of John in his kindness and courtesy. Almost she could imagine that she saw the single-winged emblem of the air-gunner on his chest. He said:

'They've been questioning you again about the murders, I suppose. Did they give you a bad time?'

'Oh no, it wasn't at all like that.'

She explained the purpose of her visit, finding it easy to talk to him about Darren, their walks along the towpath, their visits to the church, her need to see him. She said:

'Inspector Miskin couldn't do anything about the local authority, but she has told me where Darren goes to school. She was really very kind.'

'The police are never kind, only when it suits them. They weren't kind to me. You see, they think I know something. They've got a theory. They think my sister might have done it, she and her lover together.' Miss Wharton cried:

'Oh no! But that's a terrible idea. Surely not a woman – and his own wife! A woman couldn't have done it, not this murder. Surely they can't think that.'

'Perhaps not. Perhaps they're only pretending to think it. But they're trying to make me say that she confided in me, confessed even. We're very close, you see; we always have been. We only have each other. They know she'd tell me if she were in any trouble.'

'But that's awful for you. I can't believe that Commander Dalgliesh really believes that.'

'He needs to make an arrest, and the wife or husband is always the obvious suspect. I've had a couple of bad hours.'

Miss Wharton had finished her sherry, and, miraculously it seemed, another was in its place. She took a sip and thought: You poor dear. You poor young man. He, too, was drinking, a paler liquid in a tumbler, mixed with water. Perhaps it was whisky. Now he put down the glass and leaned across the table towards her. She could smell the spirit on his breath, masculine, sour, a little disquieting. He said:

'Talk to me about the murders. Tell me what you saw, what it was like.'

She could feel his need, strong as a force; and her own need rose to meet it. She, too, needed to talk. She had spent too many sleepless nights fighting off horror, willing herself not to think about it, not to remember. It was better to open that vestry door again and confront reality. So she told him, whispering it across the table. She was back again in that slaughterhouse. She described it all; the wounds like flaccid mouths, Harry Mack with his rigid breastplate of dried blood, the stench, more insistent in imagination than it had been in reality, the pale lifeless hands, drooping like flowers. He leaned over the table towards her, mouth to mouth. Then she said:

'And that's all I can remember. Nothing that happened before, nothing afterwards, only the dead bodies. And afterwards, when I dream about them, they're always naked, quite naked. Isn't that extraordinary?'

She gave a little giggle, and lifted her glass carefully to her lips.

She heard him sigh as if the dreadful recital had released something in him. He leaned back in his chair, breathing heavily as if he had been running. Then he said:

'And you didn't go into the room, the vestry where they were found?'

'That's what the Commander kept asking us. He even looked at the soles of our shoes. That wasn't at first, he did that just before we left. And then next day a policeman came and took the shoes away. Wasn't that strange?'

'They were looking for blood.'

'Oh yes,' she said sadly, 'there was so much blood.'

Again, he leaned across the table towards her his face pale and intent. She could see a small blob of mucus at the corner of the left eye, a dewing of moisture along the upper lip. She took another gulp of the sherry. How warming, how comforting it was. He said:

'Whoever did that, whoever it was, he can't be an ordinary, common intruder. This murder was carefully planned, brilliantly planned too. You're looking for someone with intelligence and nerve. To come back into that room, naked, razor in hand. To confront him, and then to kill. My God, it must have taken courage!' He leaned towards her even closer. 'You must see that. You do see it, don't you?'

Courage, she thought. But courage was a virtue. Could a man be as evil as this and yet show courage? She would have to ask Father Barnes, except that it wasn't so easy to talk to Father Barnes nowadays. But it was easy to talk to this young man looking at her with John's eyes.

She said:

'I had a feeling while Darren and I were sitting there in the church waiting to be interviewed, that there was something he knew, something he was keeping back, something he was feeling, well, perhaps a little guilty about.'

'You've told the police about this?'

'Oh, no, I haven't told them. It would sound so stupid. There

376

isn't anything he could be keeping back, not really. We were together the whole time.'

'But he might have noticed something, something you didn't see.'

'But then the police would have seen it too. It's just a feeling I had. You see, I really know Darren quite well. I know when he's feeling . . . well, a little ashamed. But this time I must be wrong. Perhaps I shall know more when I'm able to see him.'

'What are you planning to do? Meet him outside the school?'

'I thought so. The Inspector said they come out at three thirty.'

'But he'll be with other boys. You know what they are, shouting and rushing home. He might not want to leave the gang. He might be embarrassed to see you waiting there.'

Miss Wharton thought: Perhaps he'll be ashamed of me. Boys are so odd. It will be terrible if I see him and he won't stop, won't acknowledge me.

Her companion said:

'Why not write him a note and ask him to meet you at the usual place. He'll know that means the towpath. I could take it to him if you like.'

'Oh could you? But you won't know him.'

'I'll give it to one of the other kids to deliver. Give him a tip and tell him it's secret. Or I'll ask one of them to point him out. Darren will get it, I promise. Look, let me write it for you. He can read, can't he?'

'Oh yes, I'm sure he can read. He can read the notices in church. He's really an intelligent little boy. His social worker told Mrs Kendrick that Darren hasn't been going to school. Apparently his mother moved with him to Newcastle but she didn't find the same opportunities there for her job so they moved back. But she never told the school and I'm afraid it was all too easy for Darren to truant. It was naughty of him. But I'm sure he can read.'

He crooked his finger. The waiter came on silent feet. A few minutes later he was back with a sheet of headed paper and an envelope. Miss Wharton's glass was taken away and a filled one put in place of it.

He said:

'I'll print the message and your name. That'll make it easier for him. And we'd better say to meet you after school. That will be simpler for him than slipping out in the early morning. I may not be able to contact him today but I shall by tomorrow. Suppose we

377

make it Friday at four o'clock on the towpath. Will that be all right for you?'

'Oh yes, yes, perfectly. And I won't let him be too late home.'

He wrote quickly, folded the paper then, without showing it to her, put it in the envelope. 'What is his name?' he asked. 'His surname.'

'Wilkes. He's Darren Wilkes. And the school is Bollington Road Junior, near Lisson Grove.'

She watched while he printed it on the envelope and slipped it into his jacket pocket. He smiled across at her.

'Drink up your sherry,' he said, 'and don't worry. It's going to be all right. He'll be there. You'll see him, I promise.'

As they left the hotel and stepped into the wan sunlight it seemed to Miss Wharton that she was floating in an ecstasy of gratitude and relief. She was hardly aware of giving him her address, of being handed into a taxi, of the five-pound note being slipped into the cabbie's hand. His face, unnaturally large, blocked the cab window.

'Don't worry,' he said again. 'I've paid the cabbie. There'll be a little change. And don't forget. It's Friday at four o'clock.'

Tears of gratitude sprang to her eyes. She held out her hand, seeking for words, but none came. And then the cab moved forward jerking her back in her seat and he was gone. For the whole of the journey home she sat bolt upright, hugging her handbag to her chest as if it symbolized this new found intoxicating happiness. Friday she said aloud. Friday at four.

After the taxi was out of sight, Swayne took out and read the message again, his face expressionless. Then he licked the flap and sealed the envelope. The time and place were exactly as he had said. But the date was the following afternoon, Thursday not Friday. And it was he, not Miss Wharton, who would be waiting on the towpath.

378

2

Ten minutes after Kate got back to her office, Massingham came in. He and Dalgliesh had been interviewing Swayne. She had concealed her disappointment at being excluded from this first important encounter after the finding of the new evidence, telling herself that her time would come. Unless they broke Swayne quickly, the interrogations, carefully structured, conducted within judges' rules and Force regulations, but planned, varied, persistent, would continue inexorably day after day until that moment when they would either have to charge him or, for the time being at least, leave him in peace. From the look on Massingham's face she would get her chance. He almost threw the file on the desk, then walked over to the window as if the spectacular view of Westminster's towers and the curve of the river could help soothe his frustration.

She said:

'How did it go?'

'It didn't. He sits there with his brief at his side smiling, saying less and less. Or rather, saying the same thing over and over. "Yes, Berowne and I did meet on the riverbank. Yes, we did have a scuffle. He accused me of seducing Theresa Nolan and I resented him trying to father his bastard on me. He went for me as if he were crazy. He was crazy. But he didn't throw me in the river. Berowne had left before I swam out to the punt. And I didn't kill him. I was with Miss Matlock all that evening. I was seen arriving at Campden Hill Square. I took Mrs Hurrell's telephone call at eight forty. I was there until I left for the pub. I was seen there from ten forty-five to closing time. If you think otherwise, prove it."'

'And his brief, who has he got? Someone from Torrington, Farrell and Penge?'

'No. No one from the Berowne connection. I have a feeling Barbara Berowne is distancing herself from her slightly disreputable brother. He's dredged up a bright young pin-stripe from Maurice and Sheldon, perfectly competent and already calculating his fees. There's nothing like a notorious case for getting your name before the public. His strength is that he really believes his client; that must be a rare pleasure for a brief from that firm. You could see how his mind was working. He doesn't think that Swayne has the guts for this particular murder; he can't believe that the motive is strong enough; he can't see how Swayne could have left Campden Hill Square for long enough to commit the murder and returned without Matlock knowing; and he certainly can't see why she should lie. But mainly, of course, he makes it plain that he doesn't believe that Berowne was murdered, and in that he's getting to be one of the majority. He and the AC should get together.'

And so, thought Kate, we try again to break Evelyn Matlock. And she will sit there, chaperoned by Lady Ursula and advised by the family lawyers, half-obstinate, half-triumphant, with that look of dedicated virtue, enjoying her self-imposed martyrdom. In what cause, she wondered. Hatred, revenge, self-glorification, love? For the first time she faced the realization that the case, the first undertaken by the new squad, could end without an arrest in ignominious failure. Massingham turned from the window:

'There still isn't a single piece of physical evidence linking him to the scene. OK, so he had a motive. So did half a dozen others.'

'But if he killed out of hate, surely he couldn't conceal it even now?'

'Oh yes he could, well enough, anyway. He's purged it, hasn't he, the worst of his hatred? He's rid himself of its power. He can sit there smiling, the arrogant bastard, because he's free of his enemy for ever. He had himself well under control, but he was exulting like a man in love.'

She said:

'He killed him and we know he killed him. But we've got to break that alibi. And more than that, we've got to find some physical evidence.'

'Oh, Swayne knows that, none better. He's confident that the evidence doesn't exist. It's all circumstantial. If we'd got anything stronger, we'd have produced it by now. And he's actually saying what other people are thinking, that Berowne got Theresa Nolan pregnant, rejected her, and killed himself, partly out of remorse and partly because the dirt in the *Paternoster Review* warned him that the scandal was going to break. My God, Kate, if the old man's got this wrong it'll be one hell of a fuck-up.'

She glanced at him in surprise. It was rare to hear him use an obscenity. And she guessed that he wasn't only thinking of the success of the new squad, or of those colleagues in C1, and not the most junior, who wouldn't be unhappy to see the maverick Dalgliesh taken down a peg. He had planned his career as carefully as she had hers and the last thing he wanted was a spectacular failure chalked up against him. But he should worry, she thought bitterly. He was hardly likely to find himself back in Division.

She said:

'They'll hardly hold it against you. You'll be off to the Senior Command Course in January anyway, the next step towards the chairmanship of ACPO.'

He spoke almost as if he had forgotten she was there:

'It's not going to be so easy when my father dies.'

'He's not ill, is he?'

'Not ill, but he's over seventy, and a lot of life seems to have gone out of him since my mother died last April. I'd like to move out, buy a flat, but it's difficult just now.'

It was the first time he had ever spoken of his family. The confidence surprised her. The fact that he had made it must, she supposed, say something about their changing relationship, but she sensed that it would be imprudent to probe.

She said:

'I shouldn't lose any sleep over the title. You can always disclaim it. Anyway, the police'll find it easier to accommodate Chief Constable the Lord Dungannon than they would Chief Constable Kate Miskin.'

He grinned.

'Oh well,' he said easily, 'You could have chosen to join the Wrens but you'd hardly expect to end up First Sea Lord. It will come in time; the first woman Chief Constable: about a decade after the first female Archbishop of Canterbury, I'd say. Not in my time, thank God.'

She didn't respond to the provocation. She was aware of his sudden glance, then he said:

'What's the matter? Something worrying you?'

Is it so obvious, she thought, not altogether pleased at his unusual perception. There was little point in never inviting him to the flat if her mind had become so accessible. She said:

'Miss Wharton turned up while you were with Swayne. She wants to see Darren.'

'Well, what's to stop her?'

'His social worker, apparently, in the interests of good social work practice. Miss Wharton's fond of the boy. She obviously understands him. They get on well together. He likes her. D'you wonder his social worker is determined to keep them apart?'

He smiled, amused, a little indulgent, a man in whose privileged life the word welfare had meant its dictionary definition, nothing more.

'You really hate them, don't you?'

'Anyway, I told her the name of his school. I suggested she could loiter outside and meet him coming out.'

'And you're wondering whether the social services will like it?'

'I know damn well they won't like it. I'm wondering if it was wise.' She added, as if to reassure herself: 'All right, so she'll hang around the school, and with luck get the chance to walk home with him. I can't see what possible harm it can do.'

'None I should think,' he said easily. 'No possible harm in the world. Come and have a drink.'

But before they could reach the door his telephone rang. He went to answer it then held out the receiver to Kate.

'It's for you.'

Kate took it from him, listened in silence for a minute then said briefly:

'All right, I'll come now.'

Watching her face as she put down the receiver Massingham asked:

'What's the matter?'

'It's my grandmother. She's been mugged. That was the hospital. They want me to collect her.'

He said with easy sympathy.

'That's tough. Is it serious? Is she all right?'

'Of course she's not all right! She's over eighty and the bastards have mugged her. She's not seriously hurt if that's what you're asking. But she's not fit to be alone. I'll have to take the rest of today off. Probably tomorrow, too, by the sound of it.'

'Can't they get someone else to cope?'

'If there was anyone else they wouldn't be ringing me.' Then she added more calmly:

'She brought me up. There is no one else.'

'Then you'd better go. I'll tell AD. Sorry about the drink.' He added, his eyes still on her face: 'It's not going to be convenient.'

She said fiercely:

'Of course, it's not bloody convenient. You don't have to tell me. When would it ever be?'

Walking beside him down the corridor to her room she suddenly asked:

'What would happen if your father fell ill?'

'I hadn't thought. I suppose my sister would fly home from Rome.'

382

Of course, she thought. Who else? The resentment against him which she had begun to think was fading spurted into angry life. The case was at last beginning to break and she wouldn't be there. She might be away only for a day and a half but it couldn't be at a worse time. And it could be longer, much longer. Looking up at Massingham's carefully controlled face as they parted at her door she thought: He and AD are on their own now. It'll be like the old days. He might be sorry about our missed drink. But that's all he's sorry about.

3

Thursday was one of the most frustrating days that Dalgliesh could remember. They had decided to give Swayne a rest and there was no further interrogation, but a press conference called for the early afternoon had been particularly difficult. The media were getting impatient, not so much with the lack of progress as with the lack of information. Either Sir Paul Berowne had been murdered or he had killed himself. If the latter, then the family and the police should admit the fact; if the former it was time for the new squad to be more forthcoming about their progress in bringing the murderer to book. Both within and outside the Yard there were snide comments about the squad being more noted for its sensitivity than for its effectiveness. As a super in C1 muttered to Massingham in the bar:

'It'll be a nasty one to leave unsolved, the sort that breeds its own mythology. Lucky that Berowne was on the Right, not the Left, or someone would be writing a book by now to prove that MI5 slit his throat for him.'

Even the tidying of loose ends, although satisfying, hadn't lifted his depression. Massingham had reported on a visit to Mrs Hurrell. He must have been persuasive; Mrs Hurrell had admitted that her husband, in the hours before his death, had confided in her. There had been a small bill for posters overlooked when the final accounts were prepared after the last General Election. It would have put the Party's expenses over the statutory limit and invalidated Berowne's victory. Hurrell had himself covered the discrepancy and had decided to say nothing, but it had been on his conscience and he had wanted to confess to Berowne before he died. What purpose he thought would be served by the confession was difficult to envisage. Mrs Hurrell wasn't a good liar and Massingham reported that she had been rather unconvincingly insistent that her husband hadn't at any time confided in Frank Musgrave. But it wasn't a path they needed to explore. They were investigating murder not malpractice and Dalgliesh was convinced that he knew his man.

And Stephen Lampart had been cleared of any possible part in Diana Travers's death. His two guests on the night of the drowning, a fashionable plastic surgeon and his young wife, had been seen by Massingham. They apparently knew him slightly, and between pressing drink on him and the gratifying discovery of shared acquaintances, had confirmed that Stephen Lampart hadn't left the table during the meal and had spent less than a couple of minutes fetching the Porsche while they waited chatting with Barbara Berowne at the door of the Black Swan.

But it was useful to clear this detail out of the way as it was useful to know from Sergeant Robins's inquiries that Gordon Halliwell's wife and daughter had been drowned while on holiday in Cornwall. Dalgliesh had briefly wondered whether Halliwell could have been Theresa Nolan's father. It had never seemed very likely but the possibility had had to be explored. These were all loose ends neatly tied up but the main line of the inquiry was still blocked. The words of the AC rang in his brain as insistent and irritating as a television jingle: 'Find me the physical evidence'.

Strangely, it was a relief rather than an additional irritation to hear that Father Barnes had telephoned while he was in the press conference and would like to see him. The message was somewhat confused but hardly more so than Father Barnes himself. Apparently the priest wanted to know whether the Little Vestry could now be unsealed and brought into use and when, if at all, the church was likely to get back the carpet. Would the police arrange for it to be cleaned, or was that a matter for him? Would they have to wait until it had been produced at the trial? Was there a chance that the Criminal Injuries Compensation Board might pay for a new carpet? It seemed odd that even someone as unworldly as Father Barnes should seriously expect the statutory powers of the CICB to include supplying carpets, but, for a man beginning seriously to fear that a murder case might never be brought to trial, this innocent preoccupation with trivia was reassuring, almost touching. He decided on impulse that he might as well call on Father Barnes.

There was no answer at the vicarage and all the windows were dark. And then he remembered from his first visit to the church that the noticeboard had shown Evensong at four on Thursdays. Father Barnes would presumably be in church. And so it proved. The great north door was unbolted and when he turned the heavy iron handle and pushed it open he was met by the expected waft of incense and saw that the lights were on in the Lady Chapel and that Father Barnes, robed only in his surplice and stole, was leading the responses. The congregation was larger than Dalgliesh had expected and the mutter of voices came to him clearly in a gentle, disjointed murmur. He seated himself in the front row just inside the door and sat to listen in patience to Evensong, that most neglected and aesthetically satisfying portion of the Anglican

385

liturgy. For the first time since he had known it the church was being used for the purpose for which it had been built. But it seemed to him subtly changed. In the branched candleholder where, only last Wednesday, his single light had burned, there was now a double row of candles, some newly lit, others flickering with their last tremulous flame. He felt no impulse to add to the glitter. In their light the Pre-Raphaelite face of the Madonna with her flare of crimped and yellow hair under the high crown shone glossily as if newly painted and the distant voices came to him like the ominous premonitory mutterings of success.

The service was short; there was no address and no singing and within minutes Father Barnes's voice, as if from a far distance but very clear, perhaps because the words were so familiar, was speaking the Third Collect for aid against all perils: 'Lighten our darkness we beseech Thee, O Lord; And by Thy great mercy defend us from all perils and dangers of this night for the love of Thine only Son, our saviour Jesus Christ.'

The congregation murmured their amens, got to their feet and began to disperse. Dalgliesh stood up and moved forward. Father Barnes came briskly up to him in a flutter of white linen. He had certainly gained in confidence, almost, Dalgliesh could believe, in physical stature since their first meeting. Now he looked cleaner, more tidily dressed, even plumper as if a little and a not unwelcome notoriety had put flesh on his bones.

He said:

'How kind of you to come, Commander. I'll be with you in a moment. I just have to clear the offertory boxes. My churchwardens like me to keep to schedule. Not that we expect to find much.'

He took a key from his trouser pocket and unlocked the box attached to the votive candlestand in front of the statue of the Virgin, and began counting the coins into a small leather drawstring bag. He said:

'Over three pounds in small change and six one-pound coins. We've never done as well as that before. And the ordinary collections are well up too since the murders.' His face might make an attempt at solemnity but his voice was as happy as a child's.

Dalgliesh moved with him down the nave to the second candlestand in front of the grille. Miss Wharton, who had finished hanging up the kneelers and straightening the chairs in the Lady Chapel, bustled up beside him. As Father Barnes unlocked the box, she said:

'I don't expect there will be more than eighty pence. I used to

386

give Darren a tenpenny piece to light a candle, but really no one else uses this box. He loved stretching his hands out through the grille and striking the match. He could just reach. It's funny, but I'd forgotten about that until now. I suppose it was because he didn't have time to light the candle that dreadful morning. There it is, you see, still unlit.'

Father Barnes's hands were busy in the box.

'Only seven coins this time, and a button – rather an unusual one. It looks like silver. I thought at first it was a foreign coin.'

Miss Wharton peered closer. She said:

'That must have been Darren. How naughty of him. I remember now, he bent down by the path and I thought he was picking a flower. It really was very wrong of him to steal from the church. Poor child, it must have weighed on his conscience. No wonder I thought he was feeling guilty about something. I'm hoping to see him tomorrow. I'll have a little word about it. But perhaps we should light the candle now, Commander, and say a prayer for the success of your investigation. I think I have tenpence.'

She began rummaging in her bag.

Dalgliesh said quietly to Father Barnes:

'May I see the button, Father.'

And there at last it was, resting on his palm, the piece of physical evidence they had been seeking. He had seen such a button before, on Dominic Swayne's Italian jacket. A single button. So small a thing, so commonplace, but so vital. And he had two witnesses to its finding. He stood looking at it and there came over him a feeling not of excitement or of triumph, but of immense weariness, of completion.

He said:

'When was this box last cleared, Father?'

'Last Tuesday, it must have been the seventeenth, after morning Mass. As I said, I should have cleared it this Tuesday but I'm afraid in all the excitement I forgot.'

So it had been cleared the morning Berowne was murdered. Dalgliesh said:

'And it wasn't in the box then? Could you have missed it?'

'Oh no, that really wouldn't have been possible. It certainly wasn't there then. '

And the whole west end of the church had been closed after the finding of the bodies until today. In theory, of course, someone in the church itself, a member of the congregation or a visitor, could have put the button in the box. But why should they? The obvious box to use, even for a practical joke, was the one in front of the statue of the Virgin. Why walk the length of the nave to the back of the church? And it couldn't have been put in the box by mistake for a coin. No candle had been lit in this stand. But all this was academic. He was countering arguments like a defence counsel. There was surely only one jacket from which this button could have come. It was too great a coincidence to suppose that someone connected with St Matthew's Church other than Swayne should have dropped it outside the south door.

He said:

'I'm going to place this in one of the envelopes from the Little Vestry and I shall then seal it and ask both of you to sign across the flap. We can unseal the room now, Father.'

'You mean this button is important? It's a clue?'

'Oh yes,' he said, 'It's a clue.'

Miss Wharton said nervously:

'But the owner, do you suppose he'll come looking for it?'

'I don't think for one moment that he's missed it yet. But, even if he has, no one will be in any danger once he knows that the police have it. But I'll send a man round to stay in the church, Father, until we pick him up.'

Neither of them asked whose button it was and he saw no reason to tell them. He went outside to the car and rang Massingham. Massingham said:

'We'd better pick up the boy now.'

'Yes, at once. That's the first priority. Then Swayne. And we shall need the jacket. Check the lab report on it will you, John? There were no buttons missing when we saw Swayne at Campden Hill Square. This is probably the spare. The lab will have noticed if there was a tag on the hem. And see if you can get proof of sale to Swayne. We need the name of the importers and the retailers. But that will probably have to wait now until tomorrow.'

'I'll put it in hand, sir.'

'But we need a duplicate button now. I'm going to get this one sealed and certified and I haven't a transparent envelope. You recognized the jacket. I suppose it's too much to hope you've got one.'

'Much too much. Three hundred-odd quid too much. My cousin has one. I can get hold of a button.' He added:

'Do you think there's any danger to Miss Wharton or Father Barnes?'

'Obviously Swayne either hasn't missed the button or has no

idea when he lost it. But I'd like someone here in the church until we lay hands on him. But first get hold of Darren and quickly. I'm coming straight back and then I'd like you to come with me to 62 Campden Hill Square.'

'Yes, sir. There's a lot to do. It's a pity we haven't Kate. This tends to happen with women officers, the inconvenient domestic emergency.'

Dalgliesh said coldly:

'Not noticeably, John, particularly not with that officer. In twenty minutes then.'

4

It was only the second time since her father's murder that Sarah had called at 62 Campden Hill Square. The first had been on the morning after the news broke. Then there had been a small group of photographers outside the railings and she had turned instinctively as they had called her name. Next morning she had seen a newspaper picture of herself scurrying furtively up the steps like a delinquent housemaid sneaking in at the wrong door under the caption 'Miss Sarah Berowne was among the callers today at Campden Hill Square'. But now the square was empty of people. The great elms waited in sodden acquiescence for winter, their boughs moving sluggishly in the rain-drenched air. Although the storm was over the evening was so dark that lights shone palely from first-floor drawing rooms as if it were already night. She supposed that, behind those windows, people lived their secretive, separate even desperate lives, yet the lights seemed to shine out with the promise of unattainable security.

She had no key. Her father had offered her one when she had walked out with, or so it had seemed to her at the time, the stiff formality of a Victorian father reluctant to have her under his roof but recognizing that, as an unmarried daughter, she was entitled to his protection and to a room in his house should she need it. Looking up at the famous façade, at the high elegantly curved windows, she knew that it never had been and that it never could be her home. How much, she wondered, had it really mattered to her father? It had always seemed to her that he lodged in it but had never made it his own any more than it was hers. But had he in boyhood envied his elder brother these dead prestigious stones? Had he lusted after the house as he had lusted after his brother's fiancée? What had he been thinking of when, her mother at his side, he had jammed down his foot at that dangerous corner? What was it out of his past which had finally confronted him in that dingy vestry at St Matthew's Church?

Waiting for Mattie to answer the door she wondered how to greet her. It seemed natural to ask 'How are you, Mattie?' but the question was meaningless. When had she ever cared how Mattie felt? What possible answer other than an equally meaningless courtesy could she expect? The door opened. Gazing at her with a

390

stranger's eyes, Mattie said her quiet 'Good evening'. There was something different about her; but then, hadn't they all changed since that awful morning? She had the drained look which Sarah had seen on a friend's face who had recently given birth, bright eyed, flushed, but bloated and somehow diminished, as if virtue had gone out of her.

She said:

'How are you, Mattie?'

'I am well thank you, Miss Sarah. Lady Ursula and Lady Berowne are in the dining room.'

The oval dining table was spread with correspondence. Her grandmother sat stiffly upright, her back to the window. In front of her was a large blotter and to her left boxes of writing paper and envelopes. She was folding a handwritten letter as Sarah came up to her. The girl was intrigued, as always, that her grandmother should be so meticulous over the niceties of social behaviour, having all her life flouted its sexual and religious conventions. Her stepmother apparently either had no letters of condolence to answer or was leaving the chore to someone else. Now she sat at the end of the table preparing to varnish her nails, her hands hesitating over the ranked bottles. Sarah thought: Surely not blood red? But no, it was to be a soft pink, entirely innocuous, entirely suitable. She ignored Barbara Berowne and said to her grandmother:

'I've come in answer to your letter. The memorial service, it isn't possible. I am sorry but I shan't be there.'

Lady Ursula gave her a long speculative gaze, rather, thought Sarah, as if she were a new lady's maid arriving with somewhat suspect references. She said:

'It is not my wish particularly that there should be a memorial service, but his colleagues expect it and his friends seem to want it. I shall be there and I expect his widow and his daughter to be there with me.'

Sarah Berowne said:

'I told you, it's not possible. I'll come to the cremation, of course, but that will be private and for the family only. But I'm not going to display myself suitably clad in black in St Margaret's, Westminster.'

Lady Ursula drew a stamp across the dampened pad and stuck it precisely in the right-hand corner of the envelope.

'You remind me of a girl I knew in childhood, the daughter of a bishop. She caused something of a scandal in the diocese when she resolutely refused to be confirmed. What struck me as strange even

391

at thirteen was that she hadn't the wit to see that her scruples had nothing to do with religion. She merely wanted to embarrass her father. That, of course, is perfectly understandable, particularly given the bishop in question. But why not be honest about it?'

Sarah Berowne thought: I shouldn't have come. It was stupid to believe that she would understand or even want to try. She said:

'I suppose, Grandmama, you would have wanted her to conform even if the scruples had been genuine.'

'Oh yes, I think so. I would put kindness above what you would call conviction. After all, if the whole ceremony were a charade, which as you know is my opinion, then it could do her no possible harm to let the episcopal hands rest momentarily upon her head.'

Sarah said quietly:

'I'm not sure I'd want to live in a world that put kindness before conviction.'

'No? But it might be more agreeable than the one we have and considerably safer.'

'Well this is one charade which I prefer not to have any part in. His politics weren't mine. They still aren't. I should be making a public statement. I shan't be there and I hope that people will know why.'

Her grandmother said drily:

'Those who notice will; but I shouldn't expect too much propaganda value from it. The old will be watching their contemporaries and wondering how long it will be before their turn comes, hoping their bladders will hold out, and the young will be watching the old. But I dare say enough of them will notice your absence to get the message that you hated your father and are pursuing your political vendetta beyond the grave.'

The girl almost cried:

'I didn't hate him! Most of my life I loved him, I could have gone on loving him if he had let me. And he wouldn't want me to be there, he wouldn't expect it. He would have hated it himself. Oh, it will all be very tasteful, carefully chosen words and music, the right clothes, the right people, but you won't be celebrating him, not the person, you will be celebrating a class, a political philosophy, a privileged club. You can't get it into your head, you and your kind, that the world you grew up in is dead, it's dead.'

Lady Ursula said:

'I know that, my child. I was there in 1914 when it died.'

She took the next letter from the top of a pile and without looking up, went on:

'I've never been a political woman and I can understand the poor and the stupid voting for Marxism or one of its fashionable variants. If you've no hope of being other than a slave, you may as well opt for the most efficient form of slavery. But I must say that I have an objection to your lover, a man who has enjoyed privilege all his life, working to promote a political system which will ensure that no one else gets a chance of what he has so singularly enjoyed. It would be excusable if he were physically ugly; that misfortune tends to breed envy and aggression in a man. But he isn't. I can understand the sexual attraction even if I am fifty years too old to feel it. But you could have gone to bed with him, surely, without taking on all the fashionable baggage.'

Sarah Berowne turned wearily away, walked over to the window and looked out over the square. She thought: My life with Ivor and the cell is over, but it was never honest, it never had any reality, I never belonged. But I don't belong here. I'm lonely and I'm afraid. But I have to find my own place. I can't run back to Grandmama, to an old creed, a spurious safety. And she still dislikes and despises me, almost as much as I despise myself. That makes it easier. I'm not going to stand beside her in St Margaret's like a prodigal daughter.

Then she was aware of her grandmother's voice. Lady Ursula had stopped writing and was leaning both hands on the table. She said:

'Now that you are both here, there is something that I need to ask. Hugo's gun and the bullets are missing from the safe. Does either of you know who has taken them?'

Barbara Berowne's head was buried over her tray of bottles. She glanced up but didn't reply. Sarah, startled, turned quickly round.

'Are you sure, Grandmama?'

Her surprise must have been obvious. Lady Ursula looked at her.

'So you haven't taken it, and presumably, you don't know who has?'

'Of course I haven't taken it. When did you find it was missing?'

'Last Wednesday morning, shortly before the police arrived. I thought then that it was possible that Paul had killed himself and that there might be a letter to me with his papers. So I opened the safe. There was nothing new. But the gun had gone.' Sarah asked:

'When was it taken, do you know?'

'I haven't had occasion to look in the safe for some months. That is one reason why I have said nothing to the police. It could have been missing for weeks. It could have had nothing to do with

Paul's death, and there was no point in concentrating their attention on this house. Later I had another reason for silence.'

Sarah asked:

'What possible other reason could you have had?'

'I thought his murderer might have taken it to use on himself if the police got too close to the truth. That would seem an eminently sensible thing for him to do. I saw no reason to prevent it. Now I think it is time for me to tell the police.'

'Obviously you must tell them.' Sarah frowned, then she said:

'I suppose Halliwell wouldn't have taken it as a sort of memento. You know how devoted he was to Uncle Hugo. He might not like the idea of it getting into someone else's hands.'

Lady Ursula said drily:

'Very probably. I share his concern. But whose hands?'

Barbara Berowne looked up and said in her little girl voice:

'Paul threw it away weeks ago. He told me that it wasn't safe to keep it.'

Sarah looked at her:

'Nor particularly safe, I should have thought, to throw it away. He could have handed it into the police, I suppose. But why? He has a licence and it was perfectly safe where it was.'

Barbara Berowne shrugged:

'Well, that is what he said. And it doesn't matter, does it? He wasn't shot.'

Before either of the other women could reply, they heard the ring of the front door bell. Lady Ursula said:

'That may well be the police. If so, they're back rather sooner than I expected. I have a feeling that they may be getting to the end of their inquiries.'

Sarah Berowne said roughly:

'You know, don't you? You have always known.'

'I don't know and I have no real evidence. But I am beginning to guess.'

They listened in silence for Mattie's footfalls on the marble hall, but she seemed not to have heard the bell. Sarah Berowne said impatiently:

'I'll go. And I hope to God that it is the police; it's time that we faced the truth, all of us.'

5

He went first to the Shepherd's Bush flat to collect the gun. He wasn't sure why he needed it, any more than he was sure why he had stolen it from the safe. But it couldn't be left at Shepherd's Bush; it was time he found a new hiding place for it. And to have the gun with him reinforced his sense of power, of being inviolate. The fact that it had once been Paul Berowne's and was now his made it a talisman as well as a weapon. When he held it, pointed it, stroked the barrel, something of that first triumph returned. He needed to feel it again. It was strange how quickly it faded, so that he was sometimes tempted to tell Barbie what he had done for her, tell her now, long before it was safe or wise to confide, seeing in imagination the blue eyes widening with terror, with admiration, with gratitude and, at last, with love.

Bruno was in his workroom, busy with his latest model. Swayne thought how disgusting he was with his huge half-naked chest on which a lucky charm, a silver goat's head on a chain, moved repulsively among the hairs, his pudgy fingers on which the delicate pieces of cardboard seemed to stick while he edged them with infinite care into place. Without looking up, he said:

'I thought you'd moved out for good.'

'I have. I'm just collecting the last of my gear.'

'I'd like the key, then.'

Without speaking, Swayne placed it on the table.

'What shall I say if the police turn up?'

'They won't. They know I've moved out. Anyway, I'm off to Edinburgh for a week. You can tell them that if they come snooping around.'

In the small back room, its walls covered with shelves, which was both Bruno's spare bedroom and a repository for his old models, nothing was ever moved, nothing ever tidied. He stood on the bed to reach the topmost high cluttered shelf, felt under the stage of a model of Dunsinane Castle and drew out the Smith and Wesson and the ammunition. He slipped them into a small canvas bag together with the last of his socks and a couple of shirts. Then, without a final word to Bruno, he left. It had been a mistake to come in the first place. Bruno had never really wanted him. And the place was a hovel, he wondered how he had stuck it for so long.

Paul's bedroom at Campden Hill Square was much more suitable. He ran lightly down the stairs to the front door, rejoicing that he need never enter it again.

He was on the canal path too early, just after three thirty, but it wasn't because he was anxious. He knew that the boy would come. Since the meeting with Miss Wharton, he had had the sensation of being carried along by events, not a mere passenger of fate, but triumphantly borne forward on a crest of luck and euphoria. He had never felt stronger, more confident, more in control. He knew that the boy would come, just as he knew that the meeting would be important in ways that he couldn't at present begin to guess.

Even getting the message to Darren had been easier than he had dared to hope. The school was a two storey building of grimy Victorian brick set behind railings. He had loitered close but not directly outside, anxious not to attract the attention of the little group of waiting mothers, and hadn't moved up to the gate until he heard the first squeals of the released children. He had chosen a boy as his messenger. A girl, he felt, might be more curious, more noticing, more likely to question Darren about the message. He picked on one of the younger boys and asked:

'Do you know Darren Wilkes?'

'Yeah. He's over there.'

'Give him this, will you? It's from his mum. It's important.'

He handed over the envelope with a fifty-pence piece. The boy had taken it with hardly a glance at him, snatching the coin as if afraid that he would change his mind. He had run across the playground to where a boy was kicking a football against the wall. Swayne had watched until he saw the envelope change hands and then had turned and walked quickly away.

He had chosen the meeting place with care; a tangled hawthorn growing close to the canal in whose shelter he could stand and watch the long stretch of path to his right and the forty yards which led to the mouth of the tunnel to his left. Behind him, a few yards to the right, was one of the iron gates to the canal path. His brief exploration had shown that it led to a narrow road bounded by lock-up garages, padlocked yards, the blank faces of anonymous industrial buildings. It wasn't a road to tempt the canal walker on a dark autumn afternoon, and it would give him an escape route from the towpath in case of need. But he wasn't seriously worried. He had been standing here for over twenty minutes and had seen no one.

And the boy, too, was early. Just before ten to four the small figure came into sight, loitering along the canal bank. He looked unnaturally tidy in his obviously new jeans topped with a brown and white zipped jacket. Swayne stepped a little back against the bark of a tree and watched his approach through a shield of leaves. Suddenly he wasn't there and Swayne felt a wild apprehension until he saw that the boy had climbed down into the ditch and was now reappearing, his hands stretched round the rim of an old cycle wheel. He began bowling it along the towpath. The wheel lurched and bounded. Swayne stepped out of his hiding place and caught it. The boy, no more than twelve yards away, stopped short, looked at him, wary as an animal, seemed about to turn and run. At once Swayne smiled and bowled the wheel back. The boy caught it, still fixing on him his steady, unsmiling gaze. Then he swung it round, clumsily twirling, staggered and let it go. It rose out over the water, then fell with a splash which seemed to Swayne so loud that he half-expected the canal path to be suddenly alive with people. But there was no one, no calling voices, no running feet.

The ripples widened, then died. He strolled up to the boy and said easily:

'It made a good splash. Do you find many of those in the ditch?'

The boy shifted his glance. Looking out over the canal, he said:

'One or two. Depends.'

'You're Darren Wilkes, aren't you? Miss Wharton told me I'd find you here. I was looking for you. I'm an inspector of Special Branch. Do you know what that means?'

He took out his wallet with its credit cards and his old university identity card. How lucky that he'd never given that in after his first and last disastrous semester. It bore his photograph and he flashed it at the boy, not giving him a chance to see more.

'Where is she then, Miss Wharton?'

The question was carefully casual. He didn't want to betray his need, if he had a need. But he had bothered to come. He was here. Swayne said:

'She can't come. She told me to say that she's sorry but she isn't feeling very well. Did you bring the note she sent you?'

'What's wrong with 'er then?'

'Only a cold. It's nothing to worry about. Did you bring the note, Darren?'

'Yeah. I've got it.'

He thrust a small fist into his jeans pocket and brought it out. Swayne took the crumpled page, glanced at it, then tore it deliberately into small pieces. The boy watched silently as he threw them into the water. They lay on the surface like frail spring petals, then moved sluggishly, darkened, and were lost.

He said:

'Better take no chances. You see, I had to be certain that you really are Darren Wilkes. That's why the note was so important. We ' have to have a talk.'

'What about?'

'The murder.'

'I don't know nothin' about the murder. I've talked to the cops.'

'The ordinary police, yes I know. But they're a bit out of their depth. There's more to this than they understand. Much more.'

They were moving together slowly upstream towards the entrance to the tunnel. The bushes were thicker here, in one place so thick that even with their summer greenness dropping away they still provided a safe screen from the path. He drew the boy with him into the semi-darkness and said:

'I'm going to trust you, Darren. That's because I need your help. You see, we in the Special Branch think that this wasn't an ordinary murder. Sir Paul was killed by a gang, a terrorist gang. You know what I mean by the Special Branch, don't you?'

'Yeah. Somethin' to do with spying.'

'That's right. It's our job to catch the enemies of the state. It's called special because that's what it is. Special and secret. Can you keep secrets?'

'Yeah. I keep plenty.'

The small body seemed to swagger. He looked up at Swayne, the face so like an intelligent monkey, suddenly sharp and knowing.

'Is that why you was there then? Watching 'im?'

The shock was like a physical punch on the chest, painful, disabling. When he could speak Swayne was surprised how calm his voice sounded.

'What makes you think I was there?'

'Them fancy buttons on yer jacket. I found one.'

His heart leaped, then for a second seemed to stop, a dead thing in his chest, dragging him down. But then he felt again its regular thudding, pulsing back warmth and life and confidence. He knew now why he was here, why both of them were here. He said:

'Where, Darren? Where did you find it?'

'On the path by the church. I picked it up. Miss Wharton thought I were picking a flower. She never seed me. She give me ten pee for a candle, see, same as always. I always have ten pee for the BVM.'

For a moment Swayne's mind seemed to whirl out of control. The boy's words no longer made sense. He saw the peaked face, a sickly green in the gloom of the bush, look up at him with something like contempt.

'The BVM. The statue of the lady in blue. Miss Wharton always give me ten pee for the box. Then I lit a candle, see? For the BVM. Only this time I kept the ten pee and I never 'ad time to light the candle 'cos she called me.'

'And what did you do with the button, Darren?'

He had to clench his fists to keep his hands from the boy's neck.

'Put it in the box, didn't I? Only she never knowed. I never tell 'er.'

'And you've told no one else?'

'No one arsed me.'

He looked up again, suddenly sly:

'I don't reckon Miss Wharton would like it.'

'No. Nor would the police – the ordinary police. They'd call it stealing, taking the money for your own use. You know what they do to boys who steal, don't you? They're trying to get you put away, Darren. They want an excuse to put you in a home. You know that too, don't you? You could be in real trouble. But you keep my secret and I'll keep yours. We'll both swear on my gun.'

'You got a gun then?'

For all the childish assumption of nonchalance he couldn't keep the excitement out of his voice.

'Of course. The Special Branch always go armed.'

He drew the Smith and Wesson out of his shoulder bag and held it out in his palm. The boy's eyes fastened on it fascinated. Swayne said:

'Put your hand on it and swear to tell no one about the button, about me, about this meeting.'

The small hand was stretched out eagerly. Swayne watched as it was laid on the barrel. The boy said:

'I swear.'

Swayne put his own hand over Darren's and pressed it down. It felt small and very soft and curiously detached from the boy's body as if it had a separate life like a young animal.

He said solemnly:

'And I swear not to reveal anything that passes between us.'

He was aware of the boy's longing. He said:

'Would you like to hold it?'

'Is it loaded?'

'No. I'm carrying the bullets but it isn't loaded.'

The boy took it and began to point it, first at the canal, then with a grin at Swayne, then again over the canal. He held it as he must have seen it held by cops on the television, straight out, grasping it with both hands. Swayne said:

'You've got the right idea. We could do with you in the Branch when you're older.'

Suddenly they were aware of the swish of bicycle wheels. Both drew back instinctively into the deeper shelter of the bushes. They had a brief glimpse of a middle-aged man in a cloth cap slowly pedalling against the squelch of the mud, his eyes fixed on the towpath. They stood motionless, hardly breathing, until he had disappeared. But he had reminded Swayne that there wasn't very much time. The canal path would become busier. There could be people taking a short cut home. He must do what he had to do quickly and silently. He said:

'You want to be careful, playing by the canal. Can you swim?'

The boy shrugged.

'Didn't they teach you how to swim at school?'

'Naw. I ain't been to school that much.'

It was almost too easy. He fought back a sudden impulse to laugh aloud. He wanted to lie back there on the mushy earth and gaze upwards through the knotted boughs and shout his triumph. He was invincible, out of their reach, protected by luck and cleverness, and something which had nothing to do with either, but which was now part of him for ever. The police couldn't have found the button; if they had they would have confronted him with it, would have taken back the jacket with its tell-tale tag of knotted cotton on the hemline. They must have seen that tag, must have known the spare button was missing when they examined the jacket. But a serious-faced young constable had returned it without comment, and he had worn it almost daily since, feeling superstitiously ill at ease without it. Getting the button wouldn't be difficult. He would first deal with the boy, then go at once to the church. No, not at once. He'd need a chisel to break open the offertory box. He could fetch one from Campden Hill Square, or better, buy one from the nearest Woolworth's. One purchaser among so many wouldn't be noticed. And he wouldn't buy the chisel only. It would be safer to collect a number of small items before queuing at the cash point, that way the cashier would be less likely to remember the chisel. And breaking open the offertory box would look like a simple burglary. It was always happening. He doubted whether anyone would bother to inform the police, and if they did why should anyone connect it with the murder? And then it struck him that the box might have been emptied. The thought sobered his triumph, but for a moment only. If it had, the button would either have been given to the police or thrown away as useless. And it couldn't have been given to the police, they would have produced it. And even if by ill-chance it was still in someone's possession, only the boy knew where it had been found. And the boy would be dead, accidentally drowned, one more child unwisely playing on the canal bank.

He moved out of the shelter of the bushes and the boy followed. On either side the path stretched in empty desolation, the canal sliding thick and brown as sludge between the fretted banks. He shivered. For a second he had been seized with the illusion that no one was coming because there was no one left to come, that he and Darren were the last survivors of a dead, deserted world. Even the silence was eerie, and it struck him that since arriving on the path he hadn't heard the rustle of a single animal, nor the note of a bird.

He was aware that Darren had moved from his side and was squatting beside the water. Pausing beside him, Swayne saw that there was a dead rat caught in the crook of a broken twig; the sleek body, elongated, rippled the surface, its snout pointing like a prow. He squatted beside the boy and they contemplated it in silence. The rat, he thought, looked curiously human in death with its glazed eye and the small paws raised as if in a last despairing supplication. He said: 'Lucky rat', and then it struck him how senseless was that casual statement. The rat, no longer rat, was neither lucky nor unlucky. It didn't exist. No statement about it had any meaning.

He watched while the boy grasped the end of the twig and began moving the body under the water. Then he lifted it. Small eddies broke over its head, and it rose glistening, hump-backed from the suck of the stinking water. He said sharply:

'Don't do that, Darren.'

The boy let go the twig and the rat plopped back and began drifting sluggishly downstream.

They walked on. And then suddenly his heart lurched. Darren darted from his side, and with a high shout ran leaping into the tunnel mouth. For one appalled second Swayne thought that his victim must have divined his purpose and was dashing to escape. He rushed after him in the semi-darkness; and then he breathed easily again. Darren, whooping and hollering, was running his hands along the tunnel wall, then leaping, arms outflung, in a vain

401

attempt to touch the roof. In his relief Swayne almost leaped with him.

And this, of course, was the place, none better. He would need only a minute, perhaps only seconds. It would have to be swift and sure. Nothing must be left to chance; he would have to do more than merely throw him in. He would need to kneel and hold the head under the water. The boy might struggle, but it would only be brief. He looked too frail to put up much of a struggle. He slipped his arms out of his jacket and folded it over his shoulder; there was no sense in getting an expensive jacket splashed. But the edge of the towpath was concrete here, not earth. He would be able to kneel if necessary without the risk of getting tell-tale mud on his trousers.

He called quietly:

'Darren.'

The boy, still leaping at the roof, took no notice. Swayne had drawn breath to call again when suddenly the small figure in front of him swayed, crumpled, fell, silently as a leaf, and lay still. His first thought was that Darren was playing games; but when he came up to him he saw that the boy had fainted. He lay sprawled, so close to the canal that one thin arm was flung out over it, the small half-clenched fist almost touching the water. He was so motionless that he could have been dead; but Swayne knew that he would have recognized death when he saw it. He squatted and gazed intently into the still face. The boy's mouth was moistly open and he thought he could hear the gentle sigh of the breath. In the half-light the freckles stood out against the whiteness of the skin like splashes of gold paint and he could just see the sparse lashes spiked against the cheek. He thought: There must be something wrong with him. He's sick. Boys don't faint for no reason. And then he was visited by a sensation which was half-pity, half-anger. Poor little bastard. They drag him before the Juvenile Court, put him under supervision and they can't even look after him. They can't even see he's sick. Sod them. Sod the whole fucking lot of them.

But now that what he had to do was made easier than ever, no more than a gentle nudge away, it had suddenly become difficult. He put his foot under the boy and lifted him gently. The body rose on his shoe, seemingly weightless so that he could hardly feel it. But Darren didn't stir. One tip, he thought, one small thrust. If he had believed in a god, he would have said to him: 'You shouldn't have made it this easy. Nothing should be this easy.' It was very

402

quiet in the tunnel. He could hear the slow drip of moisture from the roof, the faint slap of the canal against the pavement edge, the clicking of his digital watch, loud as a time-bomb. The smell of the water came up to him, strong and sour. The two half-moons gleaming at the tunnel ends seemed suddenly very far away. He could imagine them receding and shrinking into thin curves of light, and then fading completely, leaving him and the quietly breathing boy sealed up together in black, damp-smelling nothingness.

And then he thought: Do I need to do it? He hasn't done me any harm. Berowne deserved to die, but he doesn't. And he won't talk. The police have lost interest in him, anyway. And once I have the button it won't matter if he does talk. It will be his word against mine. And without the button, what can they prove? He plucked the jacket from his shoulder and knew as he felt the slip of the lining against his arms that this was the decisive action. The boy would be allowed to live. He savoured for one extraordinary moment a new sensation of power, and it seemed to him sweeter, more exhilarating than even the moment when he had finally turned to gaze down on Berowne's body. This was what it felt like to be a god. He had the power to take life or to bestow it. And this time he had chosen to be merciful. He was giving the boy the greatest gift in his power, and the boy wouldn't even know that it was he who had given it. But he would tell Barbie. Some day, when it was safe, he would tell Barbie, about the life he had taken, the life he had graciously spared. He pulled the body a little further from the water's edge and heard the boy moan. The eyelids flickered. As if afraid to meet the opening gaze, Swayne sprang to his feet then almost ran to the tunnel end suddenly desperate to gain that half-moon of light before the darkness closed in on him for ever.

6

It was Sarah Berowne who let them in. Without speaking, she led them across the hall to the library. Lady Ursula was seated at the dining-room table on which were stacked letters and documents in three neat piles. Some of the writing paper was edged with black as if the family had rummaged in their drawers for the mourning paper which must have been fashionable in her youth. As Dalgliesh entered she looked up and gave him a nod then inserted her silver paper knife in yet one more envelope and he heard the faint rasp as the paper slit open. Sarah Berowne walked over to the window and stood looking out, her shoulders hunched. Beyond the rain-washed panes the heavy swathes of the sycamores drooped dankly in the drenched air, the dead leaves torn by the storm hanging like brown dusters among the green. It was very quiet. Even the hiss of the traffic on the avenue was muted like a spent tide on a far distant shore. But inside the room some of the heaviness of the day seemed still to linger and the diffused frontal headache which had plagued him since the morning intensified and focused behind his right eye, a stabbing needle of pain.

He had never felt in this house an atmosphere of peace or ease but now the tension quivered on the air. Barbara Berowne alone seemed impervious to it. She, too, was sitting at the table. She was painting her nails; small gleaming bottles and tufts of cotton wool were set out before her on a tray. As he entered the brush was for a moment poised, its bright tip motionless in the air.

Without looking round, Sarah Berowne said:

'My grandmother is concerned, among other matters, with the arrangements for the memorial service. I suppose you have no views, Commander, on the relative appropriateness of "Fight the Good Fight" and "O Lord and Master of Mankind"?'

Dalgliesh walked across to Lady Ursula and held out the button on the palm of his hand. He said:

'Have you seen a button like this, Lady Ursula?'

She beckoned him nearer, then bent her head close to his fingers as if about to smell the button. Then she looked up at him expressionlessly and said:

'Not to my knowledge. It looks as if it came from a man's jacket, probably an expensive one. I can offer no other help.'

'And you, Miss Berowne?'

She came over from the window, looked at it briefly, and said: 'No, it isn't mine.'

'That wasn't my question. I asked if you'd seen it, or one like it.'

'If I have, I can't remember. But then, I'm not very interested in clothes or in trivia. Why not ask my stepmother?'

Barbara Berowne was holding up her left hand and blowing gently on her nails. Only the thumbnail remained unpainted. It looked like a dead deformity among the four pink tips. As Dalgliesh came up to her she took up the brush and began to draw careful sweeps of pink along the thumbnail. This done, she glanced at the button, then turned quickly away and said:

'It isn't off anything of mine. I don't think it belonged to Paul either. I haven't seen it before. Is it important?'

She was, he knew, lying, but not, he thought, through fear or any sense of danger. For her, to lie when in doubt was the easiest, even the most natural, response, a way of buying time, fending off unpleasantness, postponing trouble. He turned to Lady Ursula:

'I should like to speak to Miss Matlock, too, please.'

It was Sarah Berowne who went across to the fireplace and tugged at the bell.

When Evelyn Matlock came in, all three Berowne women turned as one and gazed at her. She stood for a moment her eyes fixed on Lady Ursula, then marched across to Dalgliesh stiff as a soldier on a charge. He said:

'Miss Matlock, I'm going to ask you a question. Don't answer it in a hurry. Think carefully before you speak and then tell me the truth.'

She glared at him. It was the look of a recalcitrant child, obstinate, malicious. He couldn't remember when he had seen so much hate in a face. Again he took his hand from his pocket and held out on his palm the silver-crested button. He said:

'Have you ever seen this button or one like it?'

He knew that Massingham's eyes as well as his own would be fixed on her face. It was easy to speak a lie, one short syllable. To act a lie was more difficult. She could just about control the tone of her voice, could make herself look up and gaze resolutely into his eyes, but the damage was already done. He hadn't missed that instantaneous flicker of recognition, the small start, the quick flush across the forehead; that, most of all, was beyond her control. As she paused, he said:

'Come closer, look at it carefully. It's a distinctive button, probably from a man's jacket. Not the kind you find on ordinary jackets. When did you last see one like it?'

But now her mind was working. He could almost hear the process of thought.

'I can't remember.'

'Are you saying that you can't remember seeing a button like this, or that you can't remember when you saw it last?'

'You're muddling me.'

She turned her face to Lady Ursula who said:

'If you want a lawyer before you answer, you're entitled to one. I can ring Mr Farrell.'

She said:

'I don't want a lawyer. Why should I want a lawyer? And if I did, I wouldn't choose Anthony Farrell. He looks at me as if I'm dirt.'

'Then I suggest you answer the Commander's question. It seems a plain enough one to me.'

'I've seen something like it. I can't remember where. There must be hundreds of similar buttons.'

Dalgliesh said:

'Try to remember. You think you've seen something like it. Where? In this house?'

Massingham, carefully avoiding Dalgliesh's eyes, must have been waiting his moment. His voice was a careful balance of brutality, contempt and amusement.

'Are you his mistress, Miss Matlock? Is that why you're shielding him? Because you are shielding him, aren't you? Is that how he paid you, a quick half hour on your bed between his bath and his supper? He was getting it cheap, wasn't he, his alibi for murder.'

No one did it better than Massingham. Every word was a calculated insult. Dalgliesh thought: My God, why do I always let him do my dirty work for me?

The woman's face flared. Lady Ursula laughed, a tiny cackle of derision. She spoke to Dalgliesh:

'Really, Commander, apart from being offensive, I find that suggestion ridiculous. It's grotesque.'

Evelyn Matlock turned on her, hands clenched, her body quivering with resentment:

'Why is it ridiculous, why is it grotesque? You can't bear to believe it, can you? You've had lovers enough in your time, everyone knows that. You're notorious. Well, you're old now, crippled and ugly and no one wants you, man or woman, and you can't bear to think that someone might want me. Well he did and he does. He loves me. We love each other. He cares. He knows what my life is like in this house. I'm tired, I'm overworked and I hate you all. You didn't know that, did you? You thought I was grateful. Grateful for the job of washing you like a baby, grateful for waiting on a woman too idle to pick up her own underclothes from the floor, grateful for the worst bedroom in the house, grateful for a home, a bed, a roof, the next meal. This place isn't a home. It's a museum. It's dead. It's been dead for years. And you think of no one but yourselves. Do this, Mattie, fetch that, Mattie, run my bath, Mattie. I do have a name. He calls me Evelyn. Evelyn, that's my name. I'm not a cat or a dog, I'm not a household pet.' She turned on Barbara Berowne: 'And what about you? There are things I could tell the police about that cousin of yours. You planned to get Sir Paul even before your fiancé was buried, before his own wife was dead. You didn't sleep with him. Oh no, you were too cunning for that. And what about you, his daughter? How much did you care about him? Or that lover of yours? You only used him to hurt your father. Not one of you knows what caring is, what love is.' She turned again on Lady Ursula: 'And then there's Daddy. I'm supposed to be grateful for what your son did. But what did he do? He couldn't even keep Daddy out of prison. And prison was torture for him. He was claustrophobic. He couldn't take it. He was tortured to death. And how much do you care, any of you? Sir Paul thought that giving me a job, a home, what you call a home, was enough. He thought he was paying for his mistake. He never did pay. I did all the paying.'

Lady Ursula said:

'I didn't know that you felt like this. I should have known. I blame myself.'

'Oh no you don't! Those are just words. You never have blamed yourself. Not ever. Not for anything. Not all your life. Yes, I did sleep with him. And I shall again. You can't stop me. It's no affair of yours. You don't own me body and soul, you only think you do. He loves me and I love him.'

Lady Ursula said:

'Don't be ridiculous. He was using you. He used you to get a free meal, a hot bath, his clothes washed and ironed. And in the end he used you to get an alibi for murder.'

Barbara Berowne had finished her manicure. Now she surveyed her finished nails with the pleased complacency of a child. Then she looked up.

'I know that Dicco made love to her, he told me. Of course he didn't murder Paul, that's silly. That's what he was doing when Paul died. He was making love to her on Paul's bed.'

Evelyn Matlock swung round on her. She cried:

'It's a lie! He couldn't have told you! He wouldn't have told you.'

'Well he did. He thought it would amuse me. He thought it was funny.'

She looked at Lady Ursula, a conspiratorial glance of mingled amusement and contempt, as if inviting her to share a private joke. Barbara Berowne's high, childish voice went on:

'I asked him how he could bear to touch her, but he said he could make love to any woman if he shut his eyes and imagined it was someone else. He said he kept his mind on the hot bathwater and a free meal. Actually, he didn't mind the love-making. He said she hasn't a bad figure and he could quite enjoy it as long as he kept the light off. It was all the sloppy talk, all that messing over him afterwards that he couldn't bear.'

Evelyn Matlock had sunk down on one of the chairs against the wall. She put her face in her hands, then looked up into Dalgliesh's face and said in a voice so low that he had to bend his head to hear:

'He did go out that night, but he told me he wanted to talk to Sir Paul. He wanted to find out what was going to happen to Lady Berowne. He told me they were dead when he arrived. The door was open and they were dead. They were both dead. He loved me. He trusted me. Oh God, I wish he'd killed me too.'

Suddenly she began crying, great retching sobs which seemed to tear her chest apart and rose to a whooping crescendo of agony. Sarah Berowne moved swiftly over to her and awkwardly cradled her head. Lady Ursula said:

'This noise is appalling. Take her to her room.'

As if the half-heard words were a threat, Evelyn Matlock made some attempt to control herself. Sarah Berowne looked across to Dalgliesh and said:

'But surely he couldn't have done it. There wouldn't have been time to commit the murders, clean up afterwards. Not unless he went by car or by bicycle. He'd never have risked a cab. And if he took the cycle, Halliwell must have seen or heard him.'

Lady Ursula said: 'Halliwell wasn't there to hear him.'

She lifted the receiver and dialled a number. They heard her say: 'Could you please come over, Halliwell.'

No one spoke. The only sound in the room was Miss Matlock's muted sobbing. Lady Ursula looked at her with a calmly speculative gaze, without pity, almost, it seemed to Dalgliesh, without interest.

And then they heard footsteps on the marble floor of the hall and Halliwell's stocky figure stood in the doorway. He was wearing jeans and a short-sleeved, open-necked shirt, and stood there completely at ease. The dark eyes flicked briefly from the police to the three Berownes, then to the sobbing, huddled figure in Sarah Berowne's arms. Then he closed the door and looked calmly at Lady Ursula, undeferential, relaxed, wary, shorter than the other two men, but seeming in his calm self-confidence momentarily to dominate the room.

Lady Ursula said:

'Halliwell drove me to St Matthew's Church on the night my son died. Describe to the Commander what happened, Halliwell.'

'Everything, my Lady?'

'Of course.'

He spoke directly to Dalgliesh:

'Lady Ursula rang me at ten to six and asked me to have the car ready. She said that she would come out to the garage and we were to leave as quietly as possible by the back door. When she was seated in the car she said that I was to drive to St Matthew's Church, Paddington. It was necessary for me to consult the road map and I did so.'

So they had left, thought Dalgliesh, nearly an hour before Dominic Swayne arrived. The flat over the garage would have been empty. Swayne would have assumed that Halliwell had already left for his next day's leave. The chauffeur went on:

'We arrived at the church and Lady Ursula asked me to park outside the south door at the back. Her Ladyship rang the bell and Sir Paul answered it. She went inside. About half an hour later she returned and asked me to join them. That must have been about seven o'clock. Sir Paul was there with another man, a tramp. There was a sheet of paper on the table covered with about eight lines of handwriting. Sir Paul said he was about to sign his name and wanted me to witness his signature. Then he signed and I wrote my name underneath. The tramp did the same.'

Lady Ursula said:

'It was fortunate that Harry could write. But then he was an old man. He was at a state school when the young were taught these skills.'

Dalgliesh asked:

'Was he sober?'

It was Halliwell who answered.

409

'His breath smelt, but he was steady enough on his feet, and he could write his name. He wasn't so drunk that he didn't know what he was doing.'

'Did you read what was written on the paper?'

'No sir. It wasn't my business to read it and I didn't.'

'How was it written?'

'Apparently with Sir Paul's fountain pen. He used the pen to sign his name and then handed it to me and to the tramp. When we had signed, he blotted the paper. Then the tramp went out through the door to the right of the fireplace and Lady Ursula and I left. Sir Paul stayed in the vestry. He didn't see us to the door. Lady Ursula then said that she would like to be taken for a drive before returning home. We drove to Parliament Hill Fields and then to Hampstead Heath. She sat in the car on the edge of the heath for about twenty minutes. Then I drove her home and we arrived back about half past nine. Lady Ursula asked me to drop her at the front door so that she could enter the house unobserved. She told me to park the car in Campden Hill Square and I did so.'

So they had been able to leave and return unobserved. And she had asked for her supper to be brought up on a tray, the thermos of soup, the smoked salmon. No one would disturb her until Miss Matlock came to put her to bed.

He said to Halliwell:

'After you had signed that paper, did Sir Paul say anything?'

Halliwell looked at Lady Ursula but, this time, he got no help. Dalgliesh asked again:

'Did he say anything, to you, to Harry Mack, to his mother?'

'Harry wasn't there. Like I said, he signed and stumbled off. Not much of a man, I'd say, for company or conversation. Sir Paul did speak, to her Ladyship. Only the three words. He said: "Look after him."'

Dalgliesh looked across at Lady Ursula. She was sitting very still, her hands in her lap, looking out across the room beyond the green tapestry of the trees to some imagined future, and he thought he saw the trace of a smile on her lips. He turned again to Halliwell:

'So you now admit that you lied when I asked if a car or the bicycle could have been taken out that night? You lied about being in your flat the whole of that evening?'

Halliwell said, calmly:

'Yes sir, I lied.'

Lady Ursula broke in:

'I asked him to lie. What had happened between me and my son

410

in that vestry wasn't relevant to his death, whether or not he killed himself. It seemed to me important that you should spend your time and effort finding his killer, not meddling in the private affairs of the family. My son was alive when I left him. I asked Halliwell to say nothing about our visit. He is a man accustomed to obeying orders.'

Halliwell said:

'Some orders, my Lady.'

He looked across at her and gave her a grim fleeting smile. She answered his glance with a small self-satisfied nod. It seemed to Dalgliesh that they were for a moment oblivious of anyone else in the room, united in their private conspiratorial world which had its own compulsions. They stood together now as they had from the first. And he had no doubt what it was that bound them. Hugo Berowne had been his commanding officer; she was Sir Hugo's mother. He would have done a great deal more than lie for her.

They had almost forgotten Barbara Berowne. But now she sprang up from the table and almost threw herself at Dalgliesh. The pink fingers scrabbled at his jacket. The spurious sophistication dropped away and he was being clutched by a frightened child. She cried:

'It isn't true, he didn't do it! Dicco didn't leave the house. Can't you see? Mattie is jealous because he never really cared for her. How could he? Look at her. And the family have always hated him, him and me.' She turned to Lady Ursula. 'You never wanted him to marry me. You never thought I was good enough for your precious sons, either of them. Well, this house is mine now, and I think it would be better if you left.'

Lady Ursula said quietly:

'I'm afraid it isn't.'

With difficulty she turned and lifted the strap of her handbag from the back of her chair. They watched as the distorted fingers fumbled at the clip. Then she took out a folded sheet of paper. She said:

'What my son signed was his will. You are adequately, but not extravagantly, provided for. This house and the rest of his property is left to me in trust for his unborn child. If that child does not survive, then it comes to me.'

Barbara Berowne had tears brimming her eyes, a frustrated child. She cried:

'Why did he do it? How did you make him?'

But it was to Dalgliesh that Lady Ursula turned as if it were he who was owed the answer. She said:

411

'I had gone there to remonstrate with him, to make sure that he knew about the child, knew whether it was his, to ask what he intended. It was the presence of the tramp that gave me the idea. You see, I had the necessary two witnesses. I told him: "If she's carrying your child, I want to ensure that he's born safely. I want to safeguard his future. If you should die tonight, she'll inherit everything and your child will have Lampart as a stepfather. Is that what you want?" He didn't reply. He sat down at the table. I took a sheet of paper from the top drawer of the desk and placed it in front of him. Without speaking he wrote out the will, just the eight lines. A reasonable annual income for his wife and everything else in trust for the child. He may have wanted to get rid of me; I think he did. He may have been beyond caring; that is possible. He may have taken it for granted that he would be alive to make more formal arrangements next day. Most of us make that assumption. Or he may, somehow, have known that he wouldn't survive the night. But that, of course, is ridiculous.'

Dalgliesh said:

'You lied about speaking to Halliwell later that evening. Once the bodies were discovered you knew that he could be at risk. He would lie at your request. You felt you owed him at least an alibi. And you lied about your son's diary. You knew that it was in this house at six o'clock that evening. You went down to the study and took it from the desk drawer when the General telephoned.'

She said:

'At my age the memory is bound to be a little defective.' She added, with what sounded like grim satisfaction: 'I don't think I've ever lied to the police before. My class seldom has the need to. But if we do, then I can assure you that we're quite as ready to and just as good at it, probably better, than other people. But then I don't think you've ever doubted that.'

Dalgliesh said:

'You were waiting, of course, to see how much we had discovered, to be sure that your grandchild's mother wasn't a murderess or the accomplice of a murderer. You knew that you were concealing vital information, information which could have helped your son's butcher go free. But that wouldn't have mattered, would it? Not if the family line continued, not if your daughter-in-law produced an heir.'

She corrected him gently:

'A legitimate heir. It may not seem very important to you, Commander, but I am over eighty and we have different priorities.

412

She isn't an intelligent woman, not even an admirable one, but she'll be an adequate mother, I'll see to that. He'll do all right. He'll survive. But to grow up knowing that your mother was her lover's accomplice in the brutal murder of your father, that's not a heritage any child could cope with. I didn't intend that my grandson should have to cope with it. Paul asked me to look after his son. That is what I have been doing. There is a peculiar authority about the last wishes of the recently dead. In this case they coincided with my own.'

'That is all you care about?'

She said:

'I am 82, Commander. The men I have loved are all dead. What on earth else is left for me to care about?'

Dalgliesh said:

'We shall want new statements, of course, from all of you.'

'Naturally, you people always want statements. Aren't you sometimes in danger of believing that everything important in life can be put down in words, signed and admitted in evidence? I suppose that's the attraction of the job. All the messy, incomprehensible muddle reduced to words on a sheet of paper, exhibits with tags and numbers. But you're a poet – or were once. You can't possibly believe that what you deal in is the truth.'

Dalgliesh said:

'Dominic Swayne is living here now, isn't he? Do any of you know where he is?' There was no reply. 'Then we shall leave a police officer here until he returns.'

It was then that the telephone began ringing. Barbara Berowne gave a gasp and glanced from the instrument to Dalgliesh with something very like fear. Lady Ursula and Sarah Berowne ignored it as if neither the room nor anything in it was any longer their concern. Massingham moved over to it and lifted the receiver. He gave his name, listened in silence for a couple of minutes during which no one moved, then spoke so quietly that the words were unintelligible and replaced the receiver. Dalgliesh moved over to him. Massingham said very quietly:

'Darren has arrived home, sir. He won't say where he's been and Robins says it's obvious he's hiding something. His mother isn't back yet and no one knows where she is. They're trying her usual pubs and clubs. Two officers are staying with Darren until we pick up Swayne and they've rung the social services to try to contact his supervisor. No luck there. It's after office hours.'

'And Swayne?'

413

'No trace yet. That designer he shared a flat with says that he looked in at Shepherd's Bush earlier to collect his gear. Said he was off to Edinburgh.'

'Edinburgh?'

'He has friends there, apparently, people he met when he was doing a fringe show at this year's festival. Robins is in touch with Edinburgh. They may be able to pull him off the train.'

'If he took it.'

He walked over to Evelyn Matlock. She lifted to him a face devastated by grief and he saw in her eyes something so like trust that it turned his heart over. He said:

'He used your affection for him to make you lie for him; that was a betrayal. But what he felt for you and what you felt for him is your business and his, no one else's, and no one but you can know the truth about it.'

She said, looking up at him, willing him to understand:

'He did need me. He never had anyone else. It was love. It was love.'

Dalgliesh didn't reply.

Then she said in a voice so low that he could hardly catch the words:

'He did take a box of matches with him when he left. I wouldn't have known only the electric kettle in the kitchen was broken. Halliwell was mending it for me. I had to light the gas with a match and I needed a new box. The one by the stove was missing.'

She began to cry again, but now almost soundlessly, a stream of silent tears washing down her face as if she wept out of a weariness and hopelessness that had gone beyond pain.

But there were still questions that he needed to ask and to ask now while she had passed beyond the extremity of misery and loss into an acceptance of defeat. He said:

'When Mr Swayne arrived, did he go alone into any part of the house other than your sitting room and the kitchen?'

'Only to take his toilet bag to the bathroom.'

So he would have had the chance to enter the study. He asked:

'And when he came back, was he carrying anything?'

'Only his evening paper. He had it with him when he arrived.'

But why not leave it in the back of the house? Why carry a newspaper with him to the bathroom unless he proposed to use it to conceal something, a book, a file, private letters. Suicides commonly destroyed their papers; he would find something in the house to take with him and burn. It had probably been fortuitous that he had opened the drawer and found the diary ready to hand.

He turned to Sarah Berowne and said:

'Miss Matlock is obviously distressed. I think she would like a cup of tea. Perhaps one of you could go to the trouble of making it for her.'

She said:

'You despise us, don't you? Every one of us.'

He said:

'Miss Berowne, I am in this house as an investigating officer. I have no other right here and no other function.'

He and Massingham had reached the door before Lady Ursula spoke, her voice high, unwavering.

'Before you leave, Commander, I think you should know that a gun is missing from the study safe. It belonged to my elder son, a Smith and Wesson .08. My daughter-in-law tells me that Paul got rid of it, but I think it would be safer to assume that she is – ' She paused and then added with delicate irony, 'that she is mistaken.'

Dalgliesh turned to Barbara Berowne.

'Could your brother have got hold of it? Did he know the combination of the safe?'

'Of course he didn't. Why should Dicco want it? Paul got rid of it. He told me. He thought it was dangerous. He threw it away. He threw it in the river.'

Lady Ursula spoke as if her daughter-in-law were not present.

'I think you can assume that Dominic Swayne knows the combination of the safe. My son changed it three days before he died. He had the habit of noting the new combination in pencil on the last page of his diary until he was sure that he and I had memorized it. His practice was to circle the digits on next year's calendar. That was the page which I think you showed me, Commander, had been torn out.'

7

It was nearly five o'clock by the time he had bought the chisel, the strongest the shop had on display. There hadn't in the end been time to get to a Woolworth's, but he had told himself that it didn't matter and had bought the chisel in a hardware shop off the Harrow Road. The assistant might remember him, but then, who was going to ask? The theft would be seen as an unimportant break-in. And afterwards he would throw the chisel in the canal. Without the chisel to match with the marks on the edge of the box, how could they possibly link him with the crime? It was too long for his jacket pocket, so he placed it with the gun in the canvas bag. It amused him to carry over his shoulder that innocuous commonplace bag, to feel the weight of the gun and the chisel bumping against his side. He had no fear of being stopped. Who would want to stop him, a respectably dressed young man walking quietly home at the end of the day? But the assurance was more deeply rooted. He walked the drab streets head high, invincible, and could have laughed aloud at the grey, stupid faces, staring ahead as they passed him, or bent to the ground as if instinctively searching the pavement in the hope of finding a dropped coin. They were corralled in their hopeless lives, endlessly trudging the same bare perimeters, slaves of routine and convention. He alone had had the courage to break free. He was a king among men, a free spirit. And in a few hours he would be on his way to Spain to the sun. No one could stop him. The police had nothing to justify holding him, and now the only physical evidence linking him with the scene of crime was within his reach. He had enough money to last for the next two months and then he would write to Barbie. The time wasn't ripe to tell her yet, but one day he would tell her and it had to be soon. The need to tell someone was becoming an obsession. He had nearly confided in that pathetic spinster over drinks at the St Ermin's Hotel. Afterwards he had been almost frightened by that urge to confess, to have someone marvel at his brilliance, his courage. Most of all he needed to tell Barbie. It was Barbie who had a right to know. He would tell her that she owed her money, her freedom, her future to him. She would know how to be grateful.

The afternoon was so dark now that it could have been night, the sky thick and furred as a blanket, the air heavy to breathe and with the sharp metallic taste of the coming storm. Just as he turned the corner of the road and saw the church, it broke. The air and sky glittered with the first flash of lightning, then almost at once there came the crack of thunder. Two large drops stained the pavement in front of him and the rain sheeted down. He ran into the shelter of the church porch, laughing aloud. Even the weather was on his side; the main approach road to the church had been empty, and now he looked out from the porch into a wash of rain. Already the terraced houses seemed to shiver behind a curtain of water. From the glistening road spurts rose like fountains and the gutters ran and gurgled in torrents.

Gently he turned the great iron handle of the door. It was unlocked, slightly ajar. But he had expected to find it open. With part of his mind he believed that churches, buildings of sanctuary and superstition, were always left open for their worshippers. But nothing could surprise him, nothing could go wrong. The door squeaked as he closed it behind him and stepped into the sweet-smelling quietness.

The church was larger that he had imagined, so cold that he shuddered and so still that he thought for a second that he heard an animal panting before he realized that it was his own breath. There was no artificial light except for a single chandelier and a lamp in a small side chapel where a crimson glow stained the air. Two rows of candles burning before the statue of the Madonna gusted in the draught from the closing door. There was a locked box attached to the branching candleholder but he knew that it wasn't this that he sought. He had questioned the boy carefully. The box containing the button was at the west end of the church in front of the iron ornamental grille. But he didn't hurry. He moved into the middle of the nave facing the altar and spread his arms wide as if to take possession of the vast emptiness, the holiness, the sweet-smelling air. In front of him the mosaics of the apse gleamed richly gold and turning to look up at the clerestory he could see in the half-light the ranks of painted figures, one-dimensional, harmlessly sentimental as cut-outs from a child's picture book. The rainwater ran down his hair to wash over his face, and he laughed as he tasted its sweetness on his tongue. A small pool gathered at his feet. Then slowly, almost ceremoniously, he paced down the nave to the candleholder in front of the grille.

There was a padlock on the box, but it was only small, and the box itself more fragile than he had expected. He inserted the chisel

417

under the lid and heaved. At first it resisted, and then he could hear the gentle splinter of the wood and the gap widened. He gave one more heave and suddenly the padlock sprang apart with a crack so loud that it echoed through the church like a pistol shot. Almost at once it was answered by a crack of thunder. The gods, he thought, are applauding me.

And then he was aware of a dark shadow moving up to him and heard a voice, quietly untroubled, gently authoritative.

'If you're looking for the button, my son, you've come too late. The police have found it.'

8

Last night Father Barnes had dreamed again the same dream which had visited him on the night of the murder. It had been terrible; terrible on first waking and no less terrible when he thought about it later, and like all nightmares it had left him feeling that it had been no aberration but was firmly lodged in his subconscious, powered with its own terrible reality, crouched ready to return. The dream had been a Technicolor horror. He had been watching a procession, not part of it but standing on the edge of the pavement, alone, disregarded. At its head was Father Donovan in his richest chasuble, prancing in front of the processional cross while the congregation streamed out of his church behind him; laughing faces, bodies leaping and steaming, the clash of the steel drums. David, he thought, leaping before the Ark of the Lord. And then came the sacrament borne high under a canopy. But when he drew close, he saw that it wasn't a proper canopy but the faded, grubby carpet from the Little Vestry of St Matthew's, its fringe swaying as the poles lurched, and what they were carrying wasn't the sacrament but Berowne's body, pink and naked like a stuck pig with its gaping throat.

He had woken up calling out, fumbling for the bedside lamp. Night after night the nightmare had returned and then, last Sunday, mysteriously, he had been free of it and for several nights his sleep had been deep and undisturbed. As he turned to lock the dark and empty church after Dalgliesh and Miss Wharton had left he found himself praying that it wouldn't revisit him tonight.

He glanced at his wristwatch. It was only quarter past five, but the evening was as dark as midnight. And when he reached the edge of the porch the rain began falling. First came a flash of thunder, so loud that it seemed to shake the church. He thought how unmistakable and how eerie it was, that unearthly sound, something between a growl and an explosion. No wonder, he thought, men have always feared it, like the anger of God. And then, immediately, came the rain spilling from the porch roof in a solid wall of water. It would be ridiculous to set out for the Vicarage through such a storm. He would be soaking wet in seconds. If he hadn't insisted on staying on for a few minutes after Dalgliesh had left to enter the candle money in his petty cash register he could probably have had a lift home. The Commander was dropping Miss Wharton at her flat on his way to the Yard. But now there was nothing for it but to wait.

And then he remembered Bert Poulson's umbrella. Bert, who sang tenor in the choir, had left it in the bellroom after Sunday's Mass. He could borrow it. He went back into the church leaving the north door ajar, unlocked the door in the grille and made his way into the bellroom. The umbrella was still there. Then it occurred to him that he ought, perhaps, to leave a note on the peg. Bert might turn up early on Sunday and begin agitating when he found it was missing; he was that sort of man. Father Barnes went into the Little Vestry and taking a sheet of paper from the desk drawer wrote: 'Mr Poulson's umbrella is at the Vicarage'.

He had hardly finished writing, and was putting his biro back in his pocket when he heard the sound. It was a loud crack and it was very close. Instinctively he moved out of the Little Vestry and into the passage. Behind the grille was a young man, fair-haired, chisel in hand, and the collection box gaped open.

And then Father Barnes knew. He knew both who it was and why he was here. He remembered Dalgliesh's words: 'No one will be at risk once he knows that we've found the button.' But for one second, no more, he felt fear, an overwhelming, incapacitating terror which rendered him speechless. And then it passed, leaving him cold and faint but perfectly clear-headed. What he felt now was an immense calm, a sense that there was nothing he could do and nothing he need fear. Everything was taken care of. He walked forward as firmly as if he were greeting a new member of his congregation and knew that his face showed the same conscious, sentimental concern. His voice was perfectly steady. He said:

'If you're looking for the button, my son, you've come too late. The police have found it.'

The blue eyes blazed into his. Water was flowing like tears over the young face. It looked suddenly like the face of a desolate and terrified child, the mouth, half-open, gaped at him, speechless. And then he heard a groan and saw with disbelieving eyes the two hands stretched towards him, shaking; and in the hands was a gun. He heard himself say: 'No, oh no, please!' and knew that he wasn't pleading for pity because there was none. It was a last impotent cry against the inescapable. And even as he made it he felt a thud and his body leaped. It was only seconds later as he hit the ground that he heard the gunshot.

Someone was bleeding over the tiles of the nave. He wondered where it was coming from, this steadily spreading stain. Extra cleaning, he thought. Difficult to get off. Miss Wharton and her ladies wouldn't be pleased. The red stream crept, viscous as oil, between the tiles. Like that TV advert, liquid engineering. Somewhere someone was groaning. It was a horrible noise, very loud. They really ought to stop. And then he thought: This is my blood, this is me bleeding. I'm going to die. There was no fear, but only a moment of dreadful weakness, followed by a nausea more terrible than any physical sensation he had ever experienced. But then that, too, passed. He thought: If this is dying, it is not so very difficult. He knew there were words he ought to say, but he wasn't sure he could remember them and it didn't matter. He thought: I must let go, just let go. After that thought there was no other.

He was unconscious when at last the blood stopped flowing. He was beyond hearing when almost an hour later the door was pushed slowly open and the heavy footsteps of a police officer moved down the nave towards him.

9

From the moment she walked into the casualty department and
saw her grandmother, Kate had known that there was no longer
any choice. The old lady had been sitting on a chair against the
wall, a red hospital blanket around her shoulders, and had a pad of
gauze taped to her forehead. She had looked very small and
frightened, her face greyer and more wizened than ever before, her
anxious eyes fixed on the entrance door. Kate was reminded of a
stray dog brought into the Notting Hill nick and awaiting transfer
to the Battersea Dogs' Home which, tied by a string to a bench,
had gazed quivering at the door with just such an intensity of
longing. Walking up to her, it seemed that she was seeing her
grandmother with shocked eyes as if they had been parted for
months. The tell-tale signs of deterioration, of the draining away of
strength and self-respect that she had either ignored or pretended
not to see, were suddenly all too plain. The hair, which her grandmother had always tried to dye back to its original red, now
hanging in vertical stripes of white, grey and a curious orange each
side of the sunken cheeks; the blotched hands thin as talons; the
ridged nails on which the remnants of polish, months old, clung
like dried blood; the eyes still sharp, but glittering now with the
first glint of paranoia; the sour smell of unwashed clothes, unwashed flesh.

Without touching her, Kate sat beside her on the vacant chair.
She thought: I mustn't make her ask, not now, not when it has
become so important. At least I can spare her that humiliation.
Where did I get my own pride if not from her? She said:

'It's all right, Gran. You're coming home with me.' There had
been no hesitation and no choice. She couldn't look into those eyes
and see for the first time real fear, real despair and still say no. She
had left her side only for a few minutes to speak to the staff nurse
and confirm that it was all right for her to leave. Then she had led
her, docile as a child, to the car, driven her to the flat, and put her to
bed. After all the scheming and agonizing, the self-justification, the
determination that she and her grandmother would never again
live under the same roof, it had been as simple and inevitable as
that.

The next day had been hectic for both of them. By the time Kate had seen the local CID, driven her grandmother back to her flat and packed a case with Mrs Miskin's clothes and the odd collection of possessions from which she couldn't bear to be parted, left notes for the neighbours to explain what had happened, and spoken to the social service department and the housing office it was mid-afternoon. Then on their arrival back at Charles Shannon House there had been tea to make, drawers and a cupboard to clear for her grandmother's things, her own painting gear to be stowed away in the corner. God knows, she thought, when I'll be able to use that again.

It was after six before she was free to set off to the Notting Hill Gate supermarket to shop for enough food to leave ready for the next few days. She only hoped that she would be able to get back to work the next morning, that her grandmother would be well enough to leave. She had insisted on accompanying Kate and had stood up well to the day's exertions. But now she was looking tired and Kate was filled with a desperate worry that she might refuse to be left next morning. She had struck her head and bruised her right arm when the youths had jumped on her. But they had been content to grab her purse without kicking in her teeth and the physical damage was superficial. Her head and arm had been X-rayed; the hospital were satisfied that she was fit to be at home if there was someone to keep an eye on her. Well, there was someone to keep an eye on her, the only person in the world she had left.

Pushing her trolley along the aisles at the supermarket, Kate marvelled at the amount of additional food which one other person made necessary. She needed no list. These were the familiar items demanded by her grandmother which she had shopped for every week. As she placed them in the basket she could still hear the echo of that old, confident, disgruntled voice in her ears. Ginger biscuits ('not those soft ones, I like them hard for dipping'), tinned salmon ('red, mind you, I can't be doing with that pink muck'), tinned pears ('at least you can get your teeth into them'), custard powder, packets of cut ham ('keeps fresher that way and you can see what you're getting'), the strongest tasting teabags ('I wouldn't bath a newt in that stuff you bought last week'). But this afternoon had been different. Since coming to the flat she had sat without com-plaint, a pitiable, tired, docile old woman. Even her expected criticism of Kate's latest painting – 'I don't know why you want to stick that thing on the wall, looks like a kid's drawing' – had sounded more like a ritual objection, an attempt to revive her old

423

bravado, than genuine outrage. She had let Kate set off for the shops with nothing but a sudden deepening of fear in the faded eyes and an anxious:

'You'll not be long then?'

'Not long, Gran. Just off to the supermarket at Notting Hill Gate.'

Then, as Kate reached the door, she called her back and raised her small gallant pennant of pride:

'I'm not asking to be kept. I've got me pension.'

'I know, Gran. There's no problem.'

Manoeuvring her trolley down the aisles stacked with tinned fruit, she thought: I don't seem to need a supernatural religion. Whatever happened to Paul Berowne in that church vestry, it's as closed to me as painting is to the blind. Nothing is more important to me than my job. But I can't make the law the basis of my personal morality. There has to be something more if I'm to live at ease with myself.

And it seemed to her that she had made a discovery about herself and about her job which was of immense importance, and she smiled that it should have happened while she was hesitating between two brands of tinned pears in a Notting Hill Gate supermarket. Odd, too, that it should have happened during this particular case. If she was still with the squad at the end of the inquiry she would like to say to AD: 'Thank you for having me on the case, for choosing me. I've learnt something about the job and myself.' But immediately she realized that it wouldn't be possible. The words would be too revealing, too confiding, the sort of girlish enthusiasm she wouldn't be able to recall afterwards without a flush of shame. And then she thought: For God's sake why not? He's not going to demote me, and it's the truth. I shouldn't be saying it to embarrass him, or impress him or for any other reason except that it's true and I need to say it. She knew that she was over-defensive, probably she always would be. Those early years couldn't be wiped out and they couldn't be forgotten. But surely she could let down one small drawbridge without yielding the whole fortress. And would it matter so much if it were yielded?

She was too clearsighted to expect this mood of exaltation to last long but it depressed her how quickly it drained away. A wind was blustering around Notting Hill Gate, shaking out the sodden litter from the raised flower-beds and swirling it damply against her ankles. On the parapet an old man, corded in rags and surrounded by bulging plastic bags, lifted his querulous voice and ranted feebly against the world. She hadn't brought the car. It was hopeless to try to park near Notting Hill. But the two bags were heavier than she had expected and their weight began to drag on her spirits as well as her shoulder muscles. It was all very well to indulge in self-congratulation, to muse on the imperatives of duty, but now the reality of the situation struck her like a physical blow, filling her with a misery close to despair. She and her grandmother would be locked together now until the old lady died. She was getting too old to cope with independence and soon she would compensate for its loss by persuading herself that she didn't really want it. And who now would give her priority for a single-person flat or a place in an old people's home, even if she would accept it, with so many more urgent cases on the waiting list? And when she was too old to be left during the day, what then? How could she, Kate, carry on her job and at the same time nurse a geriatric patient? She knew what officialdom would say. 'Can't you ask for three months' compassionate leave, or find a part-time job?' And the three months would become a year, the year might be two or three, her career would be finished. No hope now of a place on the Bramshill course, of planning for a senior command. What hope even of staying on in the special squad with its long unpredictable hours, its demand for total commitment.

The storm was over now but the great plane trees in Holland Park Avenue still shook down heavy drops of rain which seeped, disagreeably cold, under the collar of her coat. The evening rush hour was in full spate and her ears were battered by the grind and roar of traffic, a noise which normally she hardly noticed. As she waited to cross Ladbroke Grove, a van hissing too fast through the running gutters splashed her ankles with dirt. She shouted her protest, unheard above the thunder of the road. The storm had brought down the first autumn fall of leaves. They drifted sluggishly against the barks of the trees and lay, delicately veined skeletons, on the tacky pavement. As she trudged past Campden Hill Square she gazed up towards the Berowne house. It was hidden by the trees of the square garden but she could picture its secret life and had to resist the temptation to cross the road and walk up to it to see if the police Rover was parked outside. She seemed to have been away from the squad for weeks rather than a single day.

She was glad to turn from the roar of the avenue into the comparative quiet of her own road. Her grandmother didn't speak when she rang the bell and called her own name into the entry-phone. But there was a burr and the door was released with surprising speed. The old lady must have been near the door. She humped her carrier bags into the lift and was borne upwards past floor after floor of empty and silent corridors.

She let herself into the flat and, as she always did, turned her key in the security lock. Then she hauled the bags of groceries on to the kitchen table and turned to walk the three yards across the hall to the sitting room door. The flat was silent, unnaturally so. Surely her grandmother would have turned on the television? Small facts, unregarded in her self-obsessed mood of resentment and misery, suddenly came together; the sitting room door tight closed when she had left it open, the swift but voiceless response to her ring at the street door, the unnatural silence. Even as her hand touched the knob and she pushed open the sitting room door, she knew with absolute certainty that something was wrong. But by then it was too late.

He had gagged her grandmother and tied her to one of the dining chairs with strips of white cloth, probably, she thought, a ripped sheet. He himself stood behind her, eyes blazing above the smiling mouth like a bizarre tableau of triumphant youth and age. He was holding the gun with both hands, steadying the barrel, his arms stretched rigid. She wondered if he were used to firearms or whether this was how he had seen a gun held in TV crime series. Her mind was curiously detached. She had often wondered how she would feel if faced with this kind of emergency and it interested her that her reactions were so predictable. Disbelief, shock, fear. And then the surge of adrenalin, the gears of the mind taking hold.

As their eyes met he slowly lowered his arms, then placed the nozzle of the gun against her grandmother's head. Her eyes above the mouth gag were immense, great black pools of terror. It was extraordinary that those restless eyes could be filled with such an intensity of pleading. Kate was seized with such pity and such anger that, for a moment, she dared not speak. Then she said:

'Take off that gag. Her mouth's bleeding. She's had one shock already. D'you want to kill her with pain and fright?'

'Oh, she won't die. They don't, these old bitches. They live for ever.'

'She isn't strong and a dead hostage isn't much use to you.'

'Ah, but I'll still have you. A policewoman, rather more valuable.'

'Will you? D'you think I care a damn except for her. Look, if you want any cooperation from me take off that gag.'

'And have her hollering like a stuck pig? Not that I know what a stuck pig sounds like, but I know the kind of noise she'd make. I'm in a particularly sensitive mood and I never could stand noise.'

426

'If she does then you can gag her again, can't you? But she won't. I'll see to that.'

'All right. Come and take it off yourself. But be careful. Remember I've got this gun against her head.'

She moved across, knelt and put her hand against her grandmother's cheek.

'I'm going to take off the gag. Now you mustn't make a noise. Not a sound. If you do, he'll put it on again. Promise?' There was no response, nothing but terror in the glazed eyes. But then her head jerked twice.

Kate said:

'Don't worry, Gran. I'm here. It's going to be all right.'

The stiff hands with their parched swollen knuckles clasped the chair ends as if fastened to the wood. She put her own hands over them. They felt like dry crêpe, cold and lifeless. She pressed down her warm palms and felt the physical transfer of life, of hope. Gently she put her right hand against her grandmother's cheek and wondered how she could ever have found this crumpled flesh repulsive. She thought: We haven't touched each other for fifteen years. And now I am touching her, and with love.

When the gag dropped off, he waved her back and said:

'Stand over there against the wall. Now.' She did as she was ordered. His eyes followed her.

Bound in her chair, her grandmother was rhythmically opening and shutting her mouth like a fish gasping for air. A thin dribble of bloodstained mucus dripped over her chin. Kate waited until she could control her voice. Then she said coolly:

'Why this panic? We've got no real evidence. You must know that.'

'Ah, but now you have.'

Without moving the gun he turned up the corner of his jacket with his left hand.

'My spare button. Your people at the lab won't have missed this broken twist of thread. Pity the buttons are so distinctive. This comes of having expensive taste in clothes. Papa always said it would be my undoing.'

His voice was high, brittle, the eyes large and bright as if he were on drugs. She thought: he's not really as calm as he wants to sound. And he's been drinking. Probably got at my whisky while he was waiting. But that made him more dangerous not less. She said:

'That's not enough, a single button. Look, don't be a fool. Stop play-acting. Hand over the gun. Go home and call your lawyer.'

427

'Ah, but I don't think I can do that, not now. You see there's this damned officious priest. Or rather, there was this damned officious priest. He had a taste for martyrdom, poor sod. I hope he's enjoying it.'

'You've killed him? Father Barnes?'

'Shot him. So you see I haven't anything to lose. If I'm aiming for Broadmoor rather than a high-security jail, you could say the more the merrier.'

There was, she remembered, a mass murderer who had said just that. Who was it? Haigh?

She said:

'How did you find me?'

'The telephone directory, how else? Rather a coy and uncommunicative entry, but I guessed it was you. No difficulty in getting the old woman to open the door, incidentally. I just said I was Chief Inspector Massingham.'

'All right, so what's the plan?'

'I'm getting out. Spain. There's a boat at Chichester harbour which I can handle. The *Mayflower*. I've sailed on her. She belongs to my sister's lover in case you're interested. You're going to drive me there.'

'Not now I'm not. Not till the roads are clear. Look, I'm as anxious to live as you are. I'm not Father Barnes, I'm no martyr. The police pay me well, but not that well. I'll get you to Chichester but we have to wait until the A3 is clear if we're going to get through. For God's sake, it's the rush hour! You know what the traffic's like getting out of London. I don't fancy getting stuck in a traffic jam with a gun at my back and every other motorist peering into the car.'

'Why should they? The police will be looking for a single man, not a man, wife and his dear old grandma.'

She said:

'They won't be looking for anyone yet, button or no button. Not unless they've found the priest or know that you've got the gun. As far as the police know, there's no hurry. They don't even know that you've found out about the button. If we're to get well away fast and unnoticed we have to have a clear drive to Chichester. And there's no point in carting along my grandmother. She'll only be a hindrance.'

'Possibly, but she's coming. I need her.'

Of course he needed her. His plan was plain enough. She would be expected to drive, he would sit at the back the gun against the old lady's head. And when they reached the harbour she would be expected to help with the boat, at least until they got out to sea. And what then? Two gun shots, two bodies bundled over the side? He seemed to be considering, then he said:

'All right, we'll wait. Just for an hour. How much food is there?'

'Are you hungry?'

'I shall be, and we'll need provisions. Everything portable that you've got.'

This she knew could be important. Hunger, shared need, shared food, a natural human want satisfied. It was one way of establishing that empathy on which their survival might depend. She remembered what she had been taught about sieges. The prisoners identified with their captors. It was those sinister watching eyes outside, those unseen intelligences, their guns, their listening devices leeched to the walls, their false insinuating voices which became the enemy. She wouldn't identify with him or with his kind if they were together until they starved, but there were things she could do. Use 'we' not 'you'. Try not to provoke him. Try to ease the tension and, if necessary, cook for him. She said:

'I could go and see what we've got. I don't keep much fresh food but there'll be eggs, tins, pasta, and I could cook what I had planned for tonight: spaghetti bolognese.'

He said:

'No knives.'

'You can't do much cooking without a knife of some sort. I'll need to chop onions and the liver. My recipe uses chopped liver.'

'Then do without them.'

Spaghetti bolognese. Strong tasting. Was there anything that she could put into the sauce which would incapacitate him? Her thoughts ranged over the contents of her medicine chest. But she rejected the idea as nonsensical. There would be no opportunity. He wasn't a fool. He'd see to that. And he wouldn't eat anything which she didn't share. Her grandmother began muttering. Kate said:

'I've got to speak to her.'

'All right. But keep your hands behind your back and be careful.'

She had to get hold of the gun, but now wasn't the time. It was pressed hard against her grandmother's skull. One suspicious move on her part and he would press the trigger. She went up again to the chair and bent her head. Her grandmother whispered. Kate said:

'She wants to go to the lavatory.'

'That's too bad. She's staying where she is.'

Kate said angrily:

'Look, d'you want a stink in the room for the next hour? And in the car come to that. I'm fastidious if you're not. Let me take her. What possible danger can she be?'

Again there was a moment's silence while he thought:

'All right. Untie her. But leave the door open. And remember I'll be watching you.'

It took her a full minute to undo the clumsy knots, but at last the linen dropped away and her grandmother fell forward into her arms. She drew her up, marvelling at the lightness of her body, brittle as a bird's. Holding her gently and murmuring encouragement as she might to a child, Kate half-carried her into the lavatory. Supporting her with one arm, she pulled down her knickers and lowered her on to the seat, aware of him standing braced against the passage wall less than two yards away, the gun pointed at her head. Her grandmother whispered:

'He's going to kill us.'

'Nonsense, Gran. Of course he won't kill us.'

The old lady directed a look of venomous hatred across Kate's shoulder. She hissed:

'He's been at your whisky. Bloody cheek.'

'I know, Gran. It doesn't matter. Better not talk, not now.'

'He's going to shoot us. I know.' Then she said. 'Your dad was a copper.'

A policeman! Kate could have laughed aloud. It was extraordinary to learn that now, in this place, at this moment, astonishing to learn it at all. Still shielding her grandmother's body with her own she said:

'Why didn't you tell me?'

'You never asked. No point in telling anyway. He was killed before you were born, in a car smash, chasing a villain. And he had a wife and two kids. Little enough for them on a police pension without letting on about you.'

'So he never knew?'

'That's right. And no point in telling his wife. Nothing she could do about it. More grief, more trouble.'

'So you were landed with me. Poor Gran. I haven't been much use.'

'You've been all right. No worse than any other kid. I never felt right about you. I always felt guilty.'

'Guilty! You! Why on earth?'

'When she died, your ma, I wished it had been you.'

So that had been at the root of all the estrangement. She felt a spring of joy. Here crouching by a lavatory seat, a gun at her head with death perhaps seconds away she could have laughed. She put her arm round the old lady, helping her to her feet, then let her rest against her while she drew up her knickers. She said:

'But of course you did. It was natural. It was right. She was your daughter. You loved her. Of course you wish it had been me who died if one of us had to go.' But she couldn't make herself say: it would have been better if it had been me. Her grandmother muttered:

'I've felt bad about it all these years.'

'Well stop feeling bad about it. We've got a lot of years ahead.'

And then she heard his step as he moved into the doorway, felt his breath on the back of her neck. He said:

'Get her out of here and start cooking that meal.'

But there was something she needed to ask. For over twenty years she hadn't asked, hadn't even cared. But now amazingly, it had become important. Ignoring him she said to her grandmother:

'Was she glad about me? My mother?'

'Seemingly. Before she died she said "my sweet Kate". So that's what I called you.'

So it had been as simple as that, as wonderful as that.

His voice rasped with impatience:

'I said, get her out of here. Take her into the kitchen. Tie her to one of the chairs, against the wall, by the door. I want my gun against her head while you're cooking.'

She did as she was told, fetching the strips of sheeting from the sitting room, drawing her grandmother's wrists gently behind her back, tying them as loosely as she dared, careful not to hurt her. Keeping her eyes on the knots, she said:

'Look, there's something I must do. I've got to ring my boyfriend. He's coming to supper at eight.'

'It doesn't matter. Let him come. We'll be gone by then.'

'It does matter. If he finds the flat empty he'll know something is wrong. He'll check the car. Then he'll ring the Yard. We've got to put him off.'

'How do I know he's expected?'

'You'll find his initials on that wall diary behind you on the clipboard.' She was grateful now that, absorbed with the business of settling in her grandmother, she had telephoned Alan to cancel

431

their date but hadn't rubbed out those faint pencilled initials and the time. She said:

'Look, we've got to get to Chichester before anyone knows we've gone. He won't be altogether surprised to be chucked. We had one hell of a row last time he was here.'

He was silent considering. Then he said:

'All right. What's his name and the number?'

'Alan Scully and he works at the Hoskyns Theological Library. He won't have left yet. He stays late on Thursday.'

He said:

'I'll ring from the sitting room. You stand back against the wall. Don't come to the telephone till I tell you. What's the number?'

She followed him into the sitting room. He motioned her back against the wall to the left of the door then moved over to where the telephone stood on a shelf of the wall unit, the answering machine beside it, the directories neatly stacked beneath. She wondered if he would remember the risk of leaving his palm print. As if the thought had communicated itself to him, he took a handkerchief from his pocket and draped it over the receiver. He said:

'Who will answer, this man Scully or a secretary?'

'At this hour, he will. He'll be alone in his office.'

'Let's hope he is. And don't try anything. If you do I'll shoot you first and then the old witch. And maybe she won't die quickly. You will, but not her. I might have a little fun with her first, switch on the electric stove, clamp down her hand on the hot plate. Think about that if you're tempted to be clever.'

She couldn't believe that, even now, he'd bring himself to do it. He was a killer but not a torturer. But the words, the horror of the picture they evoked, made her shudder. And the threat of death was real enough. He had already killed three men. What had he got to lose? He would prefer a live hostage, prefer to let her do the driving, to have an extra pair of hands on the boat. But if he needed to kill he would, trusting that he could get well on his way before their bodies were found.

He said:

'Right, what's the number?'

She gave it and watched, heart pounding, while he dialled. The call must have been quickly answered. He didn't speak but after less than four seconds he held out the receiver and she moved across and took it from his hand. She began speaking loudly and very fast, desperate to drown any questions, any response.

'Alan? It's Kate. Tonight's off. Look I'm tired, I've had one hell of

432

a day and I'm fed up with cooking for you every bloody time we meet. And don't ring back. Just come tomorrow if you feel like it. Maybe you'll take me out for a change. And Alan, remember to bring me that book you promised. The Shakespeare *Love's Labour's Lost* for Christ's sake. See you tomorrow. And remember the Shakespeare.' She banged down the receiver. She found that she was holding her breath, and let it out gently and silently, afraid that he would notice the release of tension. Had her words sounded even remotely credible? The message seemed to her so obviously false. Could he possibly have been deceived? But after all, he didn't know Alan, he didn't know her. That might be typical of the way they spoke to each other. She said:

'That's OK. He'll keep away.'

'He'd better.'

He motioned her back to the kitchen and took up his stance beside her grandmother, the gun again to her head.

He said:

'You've got wine, I suppose?'

'You should know. You've been at the drinks cupboard.'

'So I have. We'll have the Beaujolais. And we'll take the whisky and a half-dozen bottles of the claret with us. I've a feeling I'm going to need alcohol before I get across the Channel.'

How experienced a sailor was he? she wondered. And what kind of boat was the *Mayflower*? Stephen Lampart had described it but she couldn't now remember. And how could he be sure that the craft would be fuelled and ready for sea, that the tides would be right? Or had he passed beyond the borders of reason, of precarious sanity, into a fantasy in which even the tides would run to his bidding?

He asked:

'Well, aren't you going to get on with it? We haven't much time.'

She knew that every action must be slow, deliberate, unfrightening, that any sudden movement might be fatal. She said:

'I'm going to reach up and take a frying pan from that top cupboard. Then I'll need the minced beef and the liver from the refrigerator and a tube of tomato paste and the herbs from this cupboard on my right. OK?'

'I don't need a cookery lesson. And remember, no knives.'

As she started her preparations she thought of Alan. What was he doing? What was he thinking? Would he stand still for a moment, consider, come to the conclusion that she was drunk, hysterical or mad, then go back to his books? But he couldn't! He

433

must know that she was none of these things, that if she did go mad, it wouldn't be in that way. But it was impossible to picture him actually taking action, ringing the Yard, asking for Commander Dalgliesh. It seemed to her that she was expecting him to act a part as out of character as it would be for her to take over his job, catalogue his library. But surely that reference to *Love's Labour's Lost* had been unmistakable. He must know that she was trying to convey an urgent message, that she was under duress. He couldn't have forgotten their talk about Berowne, the attendant lord. She thought: He reads the newspapers, he must know that these things happen. He can't not know what sort of world we live in. And she would never normally speak to him in those terms, in that tone of voice. He knew her well enough to be sure of that. Or did he? They had been happily making love for over two years. There wasn't anything about her body that wasn't familiar to him as his was to her. Since when did that mean that two people knew each other?

Standing back against the wall, the gun still pressed to her grandmother's head, Swayne kept his eyes fixed on her while she took the package of minced steak and the one of liver out of the refrigerator for the frying pan. He said:

'Ever been to California?'

'No.'

'It's the only place to live. Sun. Ocean. Brightness. People who aren't grey and frightened and half-dead. You wouldn't like it. Not your kind of place.'

She asked:

'Why don't you go back?'

'I can't afford to.'

'The air fare or the expense of living there?'

'Neither. My stepfather pays me to stay away. I'll lose my allowance if I go back.'

'Couldn't you get a job?'

'Ah, but then I might lose something else. There is a little matter of step-papa's Seurat.'

'That's a painting, isn't it? What did you do to it?'

'Clever. How did you know that? The history of art isn't in the police curriculum, is it?'

'What did you do to it?'

'Stuck a knife through it several times. I wanted to spoil something he cared about. Actually he didn't much care about it. But he cared about what it cost. Well, it wouldn't have been much good sticking a knife in Mama, would it?'

434

'What about your mother?'

'Oh, she keeps in with my stepfather. She more or less has to. He's the one with the money. Anyway, she's never much cared for children, not her own, anyway. Barbara's too beautiful for her. She doesn't really like her. That's because she's afraid my step-papa does, too much.'

'And you?'

'They don't want to know about me, either of them. They never have. Not this stepfather, nor the one before. But they will. They will.'

She tipped the mince from the paper into the frying pan and began moving it around with a spatula. Keeping her voice calm as if this were an ordinary dinner and he an ordinary guest, she said above the hiss of singeing meat:

'This really ought to have onions in it.'

'Forget about the onions. What about your mother?'

'My mother's dead and I never knew my father. I'm a bastard.' She thought, I might as well tell him. It could evoke some emotion, curiosity, pity, contempt. No, not pity. But even contempt would be something. Contempt was a human response. If they were to survive she had to get some relationship established that was other than fear, hatred, conflict. But when he spoke his voice held nothing but an amused tolerance.

'One of those, are you? They've all got chips on their shoulders, bastards. I should know. I'll tell you something about my father. When I was eleven he made me have a blood test. A doctor came and stuck a needle in my arm. I could see my own blood flowing out into the syringe. I was terrified. He did it to try and prove that I wasn't his son.'

She said, and meant it:

'That was a terrible thing to do to a child.'

'He was a terrible man. But I got my own back. Is that why you're a policewoman, getting your own back on the rest of us?'

'No, just earning a living.'

'There are other ways. You could have been a decent whore. There aren't enough of those around.'

'Are those the women you fancy, whores?'

'No, what I fancy isn't so easily come by. Innocence.'

'Like Theresa Nolan?'

'So you know about that? I didn't kill her. She killed herself.'

'Because you made her abort your child?'

'Well, she could hardly expect to have it, could she? And how are

435

you so sure that it was mine? You never can be sure, any of you. If Berowne didn't sleep with her he wanted to. By God he wanted to. Why else should he have thrown me into that river? I could have done a lot for him, helped him if he'd let me. He couldn't be bothered even to talk to me. Who did he think he was? He was going to leave my sister, my sister, for his dreary whore or for his God. Who the hell cares which? He was going to sell his house, make us poor and despised. He humiliated me in front of Diana. Well, he chose the wrong man.'

His voice was still low but it seemed to her that it rang out filling the room, charged with anger and triumph.

She thought:

I might as well ask him about it. He'll want to talk. They always do. She spoke almost casually, squeezing the tomato paste into the pan, reaching up for the jar of mixed herbs.

'You knew that he'd be in that vestry. He wouldn't have left home without saying where he could be found, not when there was a risk that a dying man would send for him. You told Miss Matlock to lie to us, but she knew where he was and she told you.'

'He gave her a telephone number. I guessed it was the number of the church but I rang directory enquiries. The number they gave me for St Matthew's was the one he'd given Evelyn.'

'How did you get from Campden Hill Square to the church? Cab? Car?'

'By bicycle, his bicycle. I took the key to the garage from Evelyn's cupboard. Halliwell had left by then, whatever he told the police. His lights were out and the Rover had gone. I didn't take Barbie's Golf. Too conspicuous. A bicycle was just as quick and I could wait in the shadows until the road was clear and pedal quickly away. And I didn't leave it outside the church where it might have been seen. I asked Paul if I could bring it in, leave it in the passage. It was a fine night so I didn't have to worry about muddy tyre marks on the floor. I thought of everything, you see.'

'Not everything. You took away the matches.'

'But I put them back. The matches prove nothing.'

She said:

'And he let you in, you and the bicycle. That's what I find odd. That he actually let you in.'

'It's odder than you think. Much odder. I didn't realize at the time, but I do now. He knew I was coming. He was expecting me.'

She felt a frisson of almost superstitious horror. She wanted to cry out: But he couldn't have known! It isn't possible!

She said:

'And Harry Mack. Did you really have to kill Harry?'

'Of course. It was his bad luck that he came blundering in. But he was better dead, poor sod. Don't worry about Harry. I did him a favour.'

Turning to face him Kate asked:

'And Diana Travers. Did you kill her too?'

He gave a sly smile and seemed to gaze straight through her as if reliving a secret pleasure.

'I didn't need to. The weeds did it for me. I trod water and watched as she dived in. There was a flash of whiteness cleaving the surface. And then it settled and there was nothing, only that liquid darkness. So I waited, counting the seconds. And then quite close to me, a hand rose out of the water. Just a hand, pale, disembodied. It was uncanny. Like this. See, like this.'

He shot up his left hand, the fingers tautly splayed. She could see the stretched sinews under the milk white flesh. She didn't speak. Gently he relaxed his fingers and let his arm fall. He said:

'And then that, too, disappeared. And I waited, still counting the seconds. But there was nothing, not even a ripple.'

'And you swam on, leaving her to drown?'

His eyes focused on her as if with an effort and she heard again in his voice the charge of hatred and triumph.

'She laughed at me. No one does that. No one will, ever again.'

'What did you feel like afterwards, knowing what you'd done in that vestry, the butchery, the blood?'

'You need a woman and I had one handy. Not the one I would have chosen but you have to take what you can get. It was clever too. I knew she'd never break after that.'

'Miss Matlock. You used her in more ways than one.'

'No more that the Berownes did. They think she's devoted to them. Do you know why? Because they never bother to ask themselves what she really thinks. So efficient, so devoted. Almost one of the family, except, of course, that she isn't is she? She never was. She hates them. She doesn't know it, not really, not yet, but she hates them and one day she'll wake up to it. Like me. That dreadful old bitch, Lady Ursula. I've seen her trying not to cringe when Evelyn touches her.'

'Evelyn?'

'Mattie. She does have a name of her own, you know. They found a pet name for her as they might for a cat or a dog.'

'If they've been overworking her for years why didn't she leave?'

'Too scared. She went off her head. Once you've had one spell in the funny farm and your dad's a murderer people get wary. They're not sure you're safe looking after their precious kids or let loose in the kitchen. Oh, the Berownes had her where they wanted her all right. Why should they think she got a kick out of it, fussing over that selfish old woman, washing under her droopy old tits. Christ, I hope I never get old.'

She said:

'You will. Where you're going, they take good care of you. Healthy diet, daily exercise, locked up safely at night. You'll grow old all right.'

He laughed:

'But they won't kill me, will they? They can't. And I'll be out again. Cured. You'll be surprised how quickly they'll cure me.'

'Not if you kill a police officer.'

'Let's hope I don't have to then. When is that stuff going to be ready? I want to get on.'

She said:

'Soon. It won't be long now.'

Already the kitchen was beginning to fill with the savoury smell of the sauce. She reached up for her pasta jar and tipped out a handful of spaghetti, breaking it. The thin cracks sounded unnaturally loud. She thought: If Alan has telephoned the police they could be outside already, boring through the wall, looking, watching, listening. How would they play it, she wondered. Telephone and begin the long process of negotiation? Crash in? Probably neither. As long as he was ignorant of their presence they would watch and listen, knowing that sooner or later he would leave the flat with his hostages. That would give them their best chance to disable him. If they were there. If Alan had acted.

Suddenly he said:

'My God, this place is bloody pathetic. You can't see it, can you? You think it's all right. No, you think it's better than all right. You think it's really something. You're proud of it, aren't you? Dull, orthodox, ghastly, conventional good taste. Six bloody awful mugs hanging on their little hooks. You don't need any more, do you? Six people are quite enough. No one else can drop in because there isn't a mug for him. And the same in the cupboard. I've had a look. I know. Six of everything. Nothing broken. Nothing chipped. Everything neatly arranged. Six dinner plates, side plates, soup bowls. Christ, I've only got to open this cupboard behind me to know what you're like. Don't you ever want to stop counting the crockery and start living?'

'If by living you mean mess and violence, no I don't. I had enough of that when I was a kid.'

Without moving the gun he reached up his left hand and slipped the catch on the cupboard. Then he took out the dinner plates one by one and placed them on the table. He said:

'They don't look real, do they? They don't look as if they'd break.' He took one of the plates and smashed it down against the side of the table. It cracked neatly into two. Then he took the next. She went quietly on with her cooking and heard as plate after plate was carefully smashed, the two pieces neatly arranged on the table. The pyramid grew. Each crack was like the small report of a gun. She thought: if the police are actually here, if they've got their listening devices on, they'll pick that up, try to identify it. The thought must have occurred to him. He said:

'Lucky for you the fuzz aren't outside. They'd wonder what I'm doing. It would be a shame for the old bitch if they broke in. Plates don't make a mess, but blood and brains, you can't stack those up neatly on the table.'

She said:

'How did you do it? How did you manage to surprise him? I mean you must have burst in on him half-naked, razor in hand.' She had asked the question to propitiate him, flatter him. What she hadn't expected was his reply. It almost burst out of him as if they were lovers and he had been longing to confide. He said:

'But you don't understand! He wanted to die, God rot him, he wanted it! He practically asked for it. He could have tried to stop me, pleaded, argued, put up a fight. He could have begged for mercy. "No, please don't do it. Please!" That's all I wanted from him. Please. Just that one word. The priest could say it, but not Paul Berowne. He looked at me with such contempt. And then he turned his back. I tell you he turned his back on me! When I came in half-naked, his razor in my hand, we stood and looked at each other. He knew then. Of course he knew. And I wouldn't have done it, not if he'd spoken to me as if I were even half-human. I spared the boy. I can be merciful. And that boy is sick. If you get out of here alive, do something about it for Christ's sake. Or don't you bloody care?'

The blue eyes were suddenly luminous. She thought: He's crying. He's actually crying. And he was crying soundlessly, without a twitch of the face. And now her blood ran cold because she knew that anything was possible. She felt no pity, only a detached curiosity. She hardly dared breathe, terrified that his hand would shake, that the gun pressed again against her grandmother's head would go off. She could see the old lady's eyes wide and glazed as if she were already dead, her figure rigid with terror, not daring even to wince at the hurt of the metal hard against the defenceless skull. He took control of himself. With a sound between a sob and a laugh he said:

'Christ, I must have looked daft. Naked, or practically. Just my pants. And the razor. He must have seen the razor. I mean I wasn't hiding it or anything. So why didn't he stop me? He didn't even look surprised. He was supposed to be terrified. He was supposed to prevent it happening. But he knew what I'd come for. He just looked at me as if he were saying "So it's you. How strange that it has to be you." As if I had no choice. Just an instrument. Mindless. But I did have a choice. And so did he. Christ, he could have stopped me. Why didn't he stop me?'

She said:

'I don't know. I don't know why he didn't stop you.' And then she asked: 'You said you spared the boy. What boy? Have you spoken to Darren?'

He didn't reply. He stood staring at her but as if he wasn't seeing her, suddenly remote as if he'd entered a private world. Then he said in a voice so cold, so full of menace, that she could hardly recognize it:

'That message about the Shakespeare: *Love's Labour's Lost*. That was a code, wasn't it?'

He smiled a grim self-satisfied smile and she thought: Oh God he knows and he's glad that he knows. Now he's got the excuse he wants, the excuse to kill us. Her heart began thumping, a leaping animal hurling itself against her chest. But she managed to keep her voice steady:

'Of course not. How could it be? What on earth gave you that idea?'

'Your bookcase. I had a look at it while I was exploring the flat before you came back. Quite a little self-improver, aren't you? All the usual boring stuff people think they ought to have when they are trying to make an impression. Or is the boyfriend trying to educate you? Some job. Anyway, you've got a Shakespeare.'

She said solidly through lips that seemed to have grown dry and huge:

'It wasn't a code. What possible code could it be?'

'I hope for your sake that it wasn't. I'm not going to get myself

440

banged up in this hole with the police outside waiting for an excuse to burst in and kill me. That would be tidy. No awkward questions. I know how they operate. No death penalty any more, so they set up their own execution squads. Well, it isn't going to work with me. So you'd better pray that we get away from here safely before they arrive. Look, you can leave that stuff. We're going now.'

Oh God, she thought, he means it. It would have been better to have done nothing, not to have telephoned Alan, to have got away from the flat as soon as possible, to trust to the hope of crashing the car. And then her heart seemed for a moment literally to stop and she was seized with a dreadful coldness. There was a difference in the room, in the flat. Something had changed. And then she knew what it was. The ceaseless background roar of the traffic along the avenue, faint but continuous, had stopped and nothing was moving down Ladbroke Road. The police were diverting the traffic. Both roads were closed. They weren't risking a shoot out. The siege had begun. And any minute he, too, would realize it.

She thought I can't bear it. He'll never be able to stand a siege. Neither of us will. He meant what he said. As soon as he realizes the police are outside, as soon as they ring, then he'll shoot us. I've got to get that gun. I've got to get it now.

She said:

'Look, this is ready now. I've cooked it. We may as well eat it. It'll only take a few minutes and it's not as if we can stop on the road.'

There was a silence and then he spoke again in a voice like ice.

'I want to see that Shakespeare. Go and fetch it.'

She forked a strand of spaghetti from the saucepan and tested it with trembling fingers. Without looking round, she said:

'It's about ready. Look, I'm busy. Can't you fetch it? You know where it is.'

'Go and fetch it, unless you want to rid yourself of this old bag.'

'All right.'

It had to be now.

She willed her hands into stillness. With her left fingers she slipped undone the two buttons at the top of her shirt as if the kitchen had suddenly become too hot. The slab of liver lay on the draining board in front of her, bleeding into its wrapping. She plunged her hands into it, tearing at it, squeezing it, smearing her hands until they were thick with blood. It was the work of seconds, no more. Then with an instantaneous gesture she drew her bloody hand fiercely across her throat and swung round, wide-eyed, head

441

thrown back and thrust out at him the bloodclotted hands. Without even waiting for the terror in his eyes, his gasp like a sob, she flung herself at him and they crashed down together. She heard the clatter of the gun as it spun out of his hand and then a thud as it ricocheted against the door.

He had been trained. He was as good at combat as she was and as desperate. And he was strong, far stronger than she had expected. With a sudden convulsive jerk, he was on top of her, mouth to mouth, fierce as a rapist, his harsh breath rasping down her throat. She ground her knee into his groin, heard his yelp of pain, prised his hands from her throat and slid her bloody hands over the floor, feeling for the gun. Then she almost screamed with agony as he jammed his thumbs into her eyes. With their bodies locked, both were reaching desperately for the gun. But she couldn't see. Her eyes were dancing stars of coloured pain, and it was his right hand which found the weapon.

The shot shattered the air like an explosion. Then there was a second explosion and the door of the flat burst open. She had a bizarre sensation of male bodies leaping through the air, then standing arms stretched, guns rigid, their bodies towering over her like dark colossi. Someone was pulling her up. There were shouts, commands, a cry of pain. And then she saw Dalgliesh in the doorway and he was moving towards her, deliberately, gently, like a film in slow motion, speaking her name and, as it seemed, willing her to fix her eyes only on him. But she turned and looked at her grandmother. The sunken eyes were still fixed in that glazed extremity of fear. The hair still hung in its multi-coloured strands. The pad of gauze was still taped to the forehead. But nothing else was there. Nothing. The bottom of her face had been shot away. And strapped to her execution chair by the linen bands which Kate herself had fixed she couldn't even fall. In that second in which she could bear to look it seemed to Kate that the rigid figure fixed on her a glance of sad, reproachful astonishment. Then she was sobbing wildly, burying her head against Dalgliesh's jacket, smearing it with her bloody hands. She could hear him whispering:

'It's all right, Kate. It's all right. It's all right.' But it wasn't. It never had been. It never would be.

He stood there, holding her in his strong clasp among the loud masculine voices, the commands, the sounds of scuffling. And then she pulled away from him, fighting for control and saw over his shoulder Swayne's blue eyes blazing, triumphant. He was handcuffed. An officer she didn't know was dragging him out. But he looked back at her as if she were the only person in the room. Then he jerked his head at her grandmother's body and said:

'Well, you're free of her now. Aren't you going to thank me?'

BOOK SEVEN
Aftermath

1

Massingham had never been able to understand why it was traditional for police officers to attend the funeral of a murder victim.
When the crime was still unsolved there might be some justification
for it although he had never himself believed in the theory that a
killer was likely to expose himself to the public gaze merely for the
satisfaction of watching his victim's corpse go underground or into
the fire. He had, too, an unreasonable aversion to cremation – his
family had for generations preferred to know where the bones of
their forebears lay – and disliked canned religious music, a liturgy
denuded of grace and meaning and the hypocrisy of attempting to
dignify a simple act of hygienic disposal with a spurious significance.

Mrs Miskin's funeral enabled him to indulge all these prejudices.
He was further disgusted when it came to the ritual of examining
the wreaths, a pathetically small line of floral contrivances set out
along the crematorium wall, to find that a particularly florid example
was from the squad. He wondered who had been given the job of
buying it and whether the somewhat fulsome message of sympathy was directed at Mrs Miskin who wouldn't see it or Kate who
wouldn't want it. But at least the affair had been brief and, by luck,
had coincided with the extravagant vulgarity of a pop star's funeral
in the neighbouring chapel, so that public and press interest in
their more subdued entertainment had been mercifully small.

They were to go back to the Lansdowne Road flat. Waiting for
Dalgliesh in the car he only hoped that Kate had provided an
adequate amount of refreshment; he badly needed a drink. The
experience, too, seemed to have soured his chief's temper. On the
drive south into London he was more than usually uncommunicative.
Massingham said:

'Did you read that article by Father Barnes in one of the Sunday
heavies, sir? Apparently he's claiming that some kind of miracle
happened at St Matthew's, that Paul Berowne had stigmata on his
wrists after his first night in that vestry.'

Dalgliesh's eyes were fixed on the road ahead.

'I read it.'

'Do you think it's true?'

'Enough people will want it to be to fill the church for the foreseeable future. They should be able to afford a new carpet for the Little Vestry.'

Massingham said:

'I wonder why he did it? Father Barnes, I mean. It won't exactly please Lady Ursula. And Berowne would have hated it, I imagine.'

Dalgliesh said:

'Yes, he'd have hated it. Or perhaps it would have amused him. How can I possibly know? As for why he did it, even a priest, apparently, isn't immune to the temptations of becoming a hero.'

They were driving down the Finchley Road before Massingham spoke again.

'About Darren, sir. Apparently his mum has finally taken off. The council are applying to the Juvenile Court to convert the supervision order into a care order. Poor little sod, he's fallen into the clutches of the Welfare State with a vengeance.'

Dalgliesh said, his eyes still on the road:

'Yes I heard, the Social Service Director found time to ring me. And it's just as well. They think he has leukaemia.'

'That's tough.'

'There's an excellent chance of a cure. They've got it early. They admitted him to Great Ormond Street yesterday.'

Massingham smiled, Dalgliesh glanced at him:

'What's amusing you, John?'

'Nothing, sir. I was thinking about Kate. She'll probably ask me if I seriously suppose that God would kill off Berowne and Harry to get young Darren cured of his leukaemia. It was Swayne, after all, who first pointed out that the kid was sick.'

It had been a mistake, his chief's voice was cold:

'It would argue a certain extravagant use of human resources, wouldn't you say? Watch your speed, John, you're over the limit.'

'Sorry, sir.'

He eased his foot from the accelerator, and drove on in silence.

An hour later, balancing a plate of cucumber sandwiches on his knee, Dalgliesh thought that all the funeral teas he had attended had been curiously alike in their mixture of relief, embarrassment and unreality. But this one evoked a stronger and more personal memory. He had been thirteen at the time and had returned with his parents to a Norfolk farmhouse after his father had conducted the funeral service of a local tenant farmer. Then, watching the young widow in new black clothes which she couldn't afford, passing round the home-made sausage rolls and sandwiches, pressing on him the fruit cake which she knew was his favourite, he had felt for the first time an adult and almost overwhelming sense of the sadness at the heart of life and had marvelled at the grace with which the poor and the humble could meet it. He had never thought of humility in connection with Kate Miskin and she had nothing in common with that country widow and her desolate and uncertain future. But when he saw the food brought in, the sandwiches made before she left for the crematorium, then covered with foil to keep them fresh, the fruit cake, he saw that it was almost exactly the same food and it evoked the same surge of pity. It had, he guessed, been difficult for her to decide what should suitably be offered, alcohol or tea. She had decided on tea and she was right; as far as he was concerned it was tea they needed.

It was a small and curiously assorted party; a Pakistani who had been her grandmother's neighbour and his very beautiful wife, both of them more at ease at this funeral than he guessed they might have been at a festivity, sat together in gentle dignity. Alan Scully helped hand round the teacups with a vague self-effacement. Dalgliesh wondered whether he were anxious not to give the impression that he had a right to treat the flat as his own, then decided that this interpretation was over-subtle. Here, surely, was a man supremely unworried about what other people might think. Watching Scully handing round plates with the air of a man unsure what exactly he was holding, or what he was expected to do with it, Dalgliesh recalled that surprising telephone conversation, the persistence with which he had ensured that he spoke only to himself, the clarity of the message, the extraordinary calmness of his voice, and not least, those perceptive last words.

'And there's another thing. There was a pause after I lifted the receiver before she spoke, and then she spoke very fast. I think someone else actually dialled the number and then handed over the receiver. I've given it some thought, and there's only one interpretation which fits all the facts. She's under some kind of duress.'

Watching Scully's gangling six-foot-two body, the mild eyes behind the horn-rimmed spectacles, the lean, rather handsome face, the long strands of fair untidy hair, he thought how unlikely a lover for Kate he seemed, if lover he were. And then he caught Scully's glance at Kate as she was talking to Massingham, speculative, intense, for a moment vulnerable in its open longing, and thought: 'He's in love with her.' And he wondered whether Kate knew, and if she did, how much she cared.

It was Alan Scully who was the first to leave, fading gently away rather than making a definite exit. When the two Khans had also said their goodbyes, Kate carried the tea things into her kitchen. There was a sense of anti-climax, the usual uncomfortable hiatus at the end of a vaguely social occasion. Both men wondered if they should offer to help wash up, or whether Kate wanted them out of the way. And then, suddenly, she said that she would like to go back to the Yard with them and, indeed, there seemed no good reason why she should stay at home.

But Dalgliesh was a little surprised when she followed him into his office and stood in front of the desk as rigid as if she had been summoned for a reprimand. He looked up and saw her face flushed and almost bloated with embarrassment, then she said gruffly:

'Thank you for choosing me for the squad. I've learnt a lot.' The words came out with a harsh ungraciousness which made him realize what it had cost her to say them. He said gently:

'One always does. That's what so often makes it painful.'

She nodded as if it were she dismissing him, then turned and walked stiffly to the door. Suddenly she swung round and cried:

'I shall never know whether I wanted it to happen like that. Her death. Whether I caused it. Whether I meant it. I shall never know. You heard what Swayne called out to me. "Aren't you going to thank me?" He knew. You heard him. How shall I ever be sure?'

He said what it was possible to say:

'Of course you didn't want it to happen. When you think about it calmly and sensibly you know that. You're bound to feel partly responsible. We all do when we lose someone we love. It's a natural guilt, but it isn't rational. You did what you thought was right at

450

the time. We can't any of us do more. You didn't kill your grandmother. Swayne did, his final victim.'

But with murder there never was a final victim. No one touched
by Berowne's death would remain unchanged, himself, Massingham,
Father Barnes, Darren, even that pathetic spinster, Miss Wharton.
Kate knew that perfectly well. Why should she suppose that she
was different? The well-worn reassuring phrases sounded false
and glib even as he spoke them. And some things were beyond his
reassurance. Berowne's foot, hard on the accelerator at that dangerous corner; her bloodstained hands thrust out to the killer. There
was action and there was consequence. But she was tough, she
would cope. Unlike Berowne, she would learn to accept and carry
her personal load of guilt, as he himself had learnt to carry his.

3

Miss Wharton's only experience of a children's hospital was fifty years ago when she had been admitted to her local cottage hospital to have her tonsils out. Great Ormond Street could hardly have been more different from her traumatic memories of that ordeal. It was like walking into a children's party, the ward so full of light, of toys, of mothers and happy activity that it was difficult to believe that this was a hospital until she saw the pale faces and the thin limbs of the children. Then she told herself: But they're ill, they're all ill, and some of them will die. Nothing can prevent it.

Darren was one of those in bed but sitting up, lively and occupied with a jigsaw on a tray. He said with happy self-importance:

'You can die with what I've got. One of the kids told me.'

Miss Wharton almost cried out her protest.

'Oh Darren, no, no! You aren't going to die!'

'I reckon I won't. But I could. I've gone to foster parents now. Did they tell you?'

'Yes, Darren; that's lovely. I'm so glad for you. Are you happy with them?'

'They're all right. Uncle's going to take me fishing when I get out of here. They're coming in later on. And I got a bicycle – a Chopper.'

Already his eyes were on the door. He had hardly looked at her since she had arrived and when she had walked up to the bed she had glimpsed in his face a curiously adult embarrassment and had suddenly seen herself as he saw her, as all the children must see her, a pathetic, rather silly old woman carrying her gift of an African violet in a small pot. She said:

'I miss you at St Matthew's, Darren.'

'Yeah. Well I reckon I won't have time for that now.'

'Of course not. You'll be with your foster family. I quite understand.'

She wanted to add: But we did have happy times together, didn't we? Then stopped herself. It was too like a humiliating plea for something she knew he couldn't give.

She had brought him the violet because it had seemed more manageable than a bunch of flowers. But he had seemed hardly to look at it and now gazing round the toy-filled ward, she wondered how she could possibly have imagined that it was a suitable gift. He didn't need it, and he didn't need her. She thought: He's ashamed of me. He wants to get rid of me before this new Uncle arrives. He hardly seemed to notice when she said goodbye and slipped away, handing the violet to one of the nurses on her way out.

She took the bus to the Harrow Road and walked to the church. There was plenty for her to do. Father Barnes, refusing a period of convalescence, had only been back two days but the number of services, and the size of the congregations, had increased since that article in the paper about a miracle and there would be a long line of penitents waiting for confession after this afternoon's Evensong. St Matthew's would never be the same again. She wondered how long there would be a place in it for her.

This was the first time she had gone alone to the church since the murder, but in her misery and loneliness she was hardly aware of apprehension until she tried to fit her key in the lock and found, as she had on that dreadful morning, that she couldn't get it in. The door, as then, was unlocked. She pushed it open, her heart pounding, and called:

'Father, are you there? Father?'

A young woman came out of the Little Vestry. She was an ordinary, respectable, unfrightening girl, wearing a jacket and a blue headscarf. Seeing Miss Wharton's white face, she said:

'I'm sorry. Did I startle you?'

Miss Wharton managed a faint smile:

'It's all right. It's just that I wasn't expecting anyone. Was there anything you wanted? Father Barnes won't be here for another half hour.'

The girl said:

'No, there's nothing. I was a friend of Paul Berowne. It's just that I wanted to visit the Little Vestry, to be alone here. I wanted to see where it happened, where he died. I'm going now. Father Barnes said to return the key to the vicarage but perhaps I could leave it with you as you're here.'

She held it out and Miss Wharton took it. Then she watched as the girl went to the door. When she reached it, she turned and said:

'He was right, Commander Dalgliesh. It's just a room, a perfectly ordinary room. There was nothing there, nothing to see.'

And then she was gone. Miss Wharton, still trembling, locked the outside door, went along the passage to the grille and gazed up through the church to the red glow of the sanctuary lamp. She thought: And that, too, is only an ordinary lamp made of polished brass with a red glass. You can take it apart, clean it, fill it with ordinary oil. And the consecrated wafers behind the drawn curtain, what are they? Only thin transparent discs of flour and water which come neatly packed in little boxes, ready for Father Barnes to take them in his hands and say the words over them which will change them into God. But they weren't really changed. God wasn't there in that small recess behind the brass lamp. He wasn't any longer in the church. Like Darren, he had gone away. Then she remembered what Father Collins had once said in a sermon when she first came to St Matthew's: 'If you find that you no longer believe, act as if you still do. If you feel that you can't pray, go on saying the words.' She knelt down on the hard floor, supporting herself with her hands grasping the iron grille and said the words with which she always began her private prayers: 'Lord I am not worthy that thou shouldest come under my roof, but speak but the word and my soul shall be healed.'

Devices and Desires

AUTHOR'S NOTE

This story is set on an imaginary headland on the north-east coast of Norfolk. Lovers of this remote and fascinating part of East Anglia will place it between Cromer and Great Yarmouth but they must not expect to recognize its topography nor to find Larksoken Nuclear Power Station, Lydsett village or Larksoken Mill. Other place names are genuine, but this is merely the novelist's cunning device to add authenticity to fictitious characters and events. In this novel only the past and the future are real; the present, like the people and the setting, exists only in the imagination of the writer and her readers.

CONTENTS

BOOK ONE

Friday 16 September to Tuesday 20 September

1

The Whistler's fourth victim was his youngest, Valerie Mitchell, aged fifteen years, eight months and four days, and she died because she missed the nine-forty bus from Easthaven to Cobb's Marsh. As always she had left it until the last minute to leave the disco and the floor was still a packed, gyrating mass of bodies under the makeshift strobe lights when she broke free of Wayne's clutching hands, shouted instructions to Shirl about their plans for next week above the raucous beat of the music and left the dance floor. Her last glimpse of Wayne was of his serious, bobbing face bizarrely striped with red, yellow and blue under the turning lights. Without waiting to change her shoes, she snatched up her jacket from the cloakroom peg and raced up the road past the darkened shops towards the bus station, her cumbersome shoulder bag flapping against her ribs. But when she turned the corner into the station she saw with horror that the lights on their high poles shone down on a bleached and silent emptiness and dashing to the corner was in time to see the bus already half-way up the hill. There was still a chance if the lights were against it and she began desperately chasing after it, hampered by her fragile, high-heeled shoes. But the lights were green and she watched helplessly, gasping and bent double with a sudden cramp, as it lumbered over the brow of a hill and like a brightly lit ship sank out of sight. 'Oh no!' she screamed after it, 'Oh God! Oh no!' and felt the tears of anger and dismay smarting her eyes.

This was the end. It was her father who laid down the rules in her family and there was never any appeal, any second chance. After protracted discussion and her repeated pleas she had been allowed this weekly visit on Friday evenings to the disco run by the church youth club, provided she caught the nine-forty bus without fail. It put her down at the Crown and Anchor at Cobb's Marsh, only fifty yards from her cottage. From ten fifteen her father would begin watching for the bus to pass the front room where he and her mother would sit half watching the television, the curtains drawn back. Whatever the programme or weather, he would then put on his coat and come out to walk the fifty yards to meet her, keeping her always in sight. Since the Norfolk Whistler had begun his killings her father had had an added justification for the mild domestic tyranny which, she half realized, he both thought right in dealing with his only child and rather enjoyed. The concordat had been early established: 'You do right by me, my girl, and I'll do right by you.' She both loved him and slightly feared him and she dreaded his anger. Now there would be one of those awful rows in which she knew she couldn't hope to look to her mother for support. It would be the end of her Friday evenings with Wayne and Shirl and the gang. Already they teased and pitied her because she was treated as a child. Now it would be total humiliation.

Her first desperate thought was to hire a taxi and to chase the bus, but she didn't know where the cab rank was and she hadn't enough money; she was sure of that. She could go back to the disco and see if Wayne and Shirl and the gang between them could lend her enough. But Wayne was always skint and Shirl too mean and by the time she had argued and cajoled it would be too late.

And then came salvation. The lights had changed again to red and a car at the end of a tail of four others was just drawing slowly to a stop. She found herself opposite the open left-hand window and looking directly at two elderly women. She clutched at the lowered glass and said breathlessly: 'Can you give me a lift? Anywhere Cobb's Marsh direction. I've missed the bus. Please.'

The final desperate plea left the driver unmoved. She stared ahead, frowned, then shook her head and let in the clutch. Her companion hesitated, looked at her, then leaned back and released the rear door.

'Get in. Quickly! We're going as far as Holt. We could drop you at the crossroads.'

Valerie scrambled in and the car moved forward. At least they were going in the right direction and it took her only a couple of seconds to think of her plan. From the crossroads outside Holt it would be less than half a mile to the junction with the bus route. She could walk it and pick it up at the stop before the Crown and Anchor. There would be plenty of time; the bus took at least twenty minutes meandering round the villages.

The woman who was driving spoke for the first time. She said: 'You shouldn't be cadging lifts like this. Does your mother know that you're out, what you're doing? Parents seem to have no control over children these days.'

Silly old cow, she thought, what business is it of hers what I do? She wouldn't have stood the cheek from any of the teachers at school. But she bit back the impulse to rudeness, which was her adolescent response to adult criticism. She had to ride with the two old wrinklies. Better keep them sweet. She said: 'I'm supposed to catch the nine-forty bus. My dad'ud kill me if he thought I'd cadged a lift. I wouldn't if you was a man.'

'I hope not. And your father's perfectly right to be strict about it. These are dangerous times for young women, quite apart from the Whistler. Where exactly do you live?'

'At Cobb's Marsh. But I've got an aunt and uncle at Holt. If you put me down at the crossroads he'll be able to give me a lift. They live right close. I'll be safe enough if you drop me there, honest.'

The lie came easily to her and was as easily accepted. Nothing more was said by any of them. She sat looking at the backs of the two grey, cropped heads, watching the driver's age-speckled hands on the wheel. Sisters, she thought, by the look of them. Her first glimpse had shown her the same square heads, the same strong chins, the same curved eyebrows above anxious, angry eyes. They've had a row, she thought. She could sense the tension quivering between them. She was glad when, still without a word, the driver drew up at the crossroads and she was able to scramble out with muttered thanks and watch while they drove out of sight. They were the last human beings, but one, to see her alive.

She crouched to change into the sensible shoes which her parents insisted she wear to school, grateful that the shoulder bag was now lighter, then began trudging away from the town towards the junction where she would wait for the bus. The road was narrow and unlit, bordered on the right by a row of trees, black cut-outs pasted against the star-studded sky and on the left, where she walked, by a narrow fringe of scrub and bushes at times dense and close enough to overshadow the path. Up till now she had felt only an overwhelming relief that all would be well. She would be on that bus. But now, as she walked in an eerie silence, her soft footfalls sounding unnaturally loud, a different, more insidious anxiety took over and she felt the first prickings of fear. Once recognized, its treacherous power acknowledged, the fear took over and grew inexorably into terror.

A car was approaching, at once a symbol of safety and normality and an added threat. Everyone knew that the Whistler must have a car. How else could he kill in such widely spaced parts of the

5

county, how else make his getaway when his dreadful work was done? She stood back into the shelter of the bushes, exchanging one fear for another. There was a surge of sound and the cat's-eyes momentarily gleamed before, in a rush of wind, the car passed. And now she was alone again in the darkness and the silence. But was she? The thought of the Whistler took hold of her mind, rumours, half-truths fusing into a terrible reality. He strangled women, three so far. And then he cut off their hair and stuffed it in their mouths, like straw spilling out of a Guy on 5 November. The boys at school laughed about him, whistling in the bicycle sheds as he was said to whistle over the bodies of his victims. 'The Whistler will get you,' they called after her. He could be anywhere. He always stalked by night. He could be here. She had an impulse to throw herself down and press her body into the soft, rich-smelling earth, to cover her ears and lie there rigid until the dawn. But she managed to control her panic. She had to get to the crossroads and catch the bus. She forced herself to step out of the shadows and begin again her almost silent walk.

She wanted to break into a run but managed to resist. The creature, man or beast, crouching in the undergrowth was already sniffing her fear, waiting until her panic broke. Then she would hear the crash of the breaking bushes, his pounding feet, feel his panting breath hot on her neck. She must keep walking, swiftly but silently, holding her bag tightly against her side, hardly breathing, eyes fixed ahead. And as she walked she prayed: 'Please God, let me get safely home and I'll never lie again. I'll always leave in time. Help me to get to the crossroads safely. Make the bus come quickly. Oh God, please help me.'

And then, miraculously, her prayer was answered. Suddenly, about thirty yards ahead of her, there was a woman. She didn't question how, so mysteriously, this slim, slow-walking figure had materialized. It was sufficient that she was there. As she drew nearer with quickening step she could see the swathe of long, blonde hair under a tight-fitting beret, and what looked like a belted trenchcoat. And at the girl's side, trotting obediently, most reassuring of all, was a small black and white dog, bandy-legged. They could walk together to the crossroads. Perhaps the girl might herself be catching the same bus. She almost cried aloud, 'I'm coming. I'm coming,' and, breaking into a run, rushed towards safety and protection as a child might to her mother's arms.

6

And now the woman bent down and released the dog. As if in obedience to some command, he slipped into the bushes. The woman took one swift backward glance and then stood quietly waiting, her back half turned to Valerie, the dog's lead held drooping in her right hand. Valerie almost flung herself at the waiting back. And then, slowly, the woman turned. It was a second of total, paralysing horror. She saw the pale, taut face which had never been a woman's face, the simple, inviting, almost apologetic smile, the blazing and merciless eyes. She opened her mouth to scream, but there was no chance and terror had made her dumb. With one movement the noose of the lead was swung over her head and jerked tight and she was pulled from the road into the shadow of the bushes. She felt herself falling through time, through space, through an eternity of horror. And now the face was hot over hers and she could smell drink and sweat and a terror matching her own. Her arms jerked upwards, impotently flailing. And now her brain was bursting and the pain in her chest, growing like a great red flower, exploded in a silent, wordless scream of 'Mummy! Mummy!' And then there was no more terror, no more pain, only the merciful, obliterating dark.

2

Four days later Commander Adam Dalgliesh of New Scotland Yard dictated a final note to his secretary, cleared his in-tray, locked his desk drawer, set the combination of his security cupboard and prepared to leave for a two-week holiday on the Norfolk coast. The break was overdue and he was ready for it. But the holiday wasn't entirely therapeutic; there were affairs in Norfolk that needed his attention. His aunt, his last surviving relative, had died two months earlier leaving him both her fortune and a converted windmill at Larksoken on the north-east coast of Norfolk. The fortune was unexpectedly large and had brought its own, as yet unresolved, dilemmas. The mill was a less onerous bequest but was not without its minor problems. He needed, he felt, to live in it alone for a week or two before finally making up his mind whether to keep it for occasional holidays, sell, or pass it over at a nominal price to the Norfolk Windmill Trust who were, he knew, always anxious to restore old windmills to working order. And then there were family papers and his aunt's books, particularly her comprehensive library of ornithology, to be looked at and sorted and their disposal decided upon. These were pleasurable tasks. Even in boyhood he had disliked taking a holiday totally without purpose. He didn't know from what roots of childhood guilt or imagined responsibility had grown this curious masochism which, in his middle years, had returned with added authority. But he was glad that there was a job to be done in Norfolk, not least because he knew that the journey had an element of flight. After four years of silence, his new book of poetry, *A Case to Answer and Other Poems*, had been published to considerable critical acclaim which was surprisingly gratifying, and to even wider public interest which, less surprisingly, he was finding more difficult to take. After his more notorious murder cases, the efforts of the Metropolitan Police press office had been directed to shielding him from egregious publicity. His publisher's rather different priorities took some getting used to and he was frankly glad of an excuse to escape from them, at least for a couple of weeks.

He had earlier said his goodbye to Inspector Kate Miskin and she was now out on a case. Chief Inspector Massingham had been seconded to the Intermediate Command Course at Bramshill Police College, one more step on his planned progress to a chief constable's braid, and Kate had temporarily taken over his place as Dalgliesh's second in command of the Special Squad. He went into her office to leave a note of his holiday address. It was, as always, impressively tidy, sparsely efficient and yet feminine, its wall enlivened by a single picture, one of her own abstract oils, a study in swirling browns heightened with a single streak of acid green, which Dalgliesh was growing to like more each time he studied it. On the uncluttered desktop was a small glass vase of freesias. Their scent, at first fugitive, suddenly wafted up to him, reinforcing the odd impression he always got that the office was more full of her physical presence empty than it was when she was seated there working. He laid his note exactly in the middle of the clean blotter, and smiled as he closed the door after him with what seemed unnecessary gentleness. It remained only to put his head round the AC's door for a final word and he was on his way to the lift.

The door was already closing when he heard running footsteps, a cheerful shout and Manny Cummings leapt in, just avoiding the bite of the closing steel. As always he seemed to whirl in a vortex of almost oppressive energy, too powerful to be contained by the lift's four walls. He was brandishing a large brown envelope. 'Glad I caught you, Adam. It is Norfolk you're escaping to, isn't it? If the Norfolk CID do lay their hands on the Whistler, take a look at him for me, will you, check he isn't our chap in Battersea.'

'The Battersea Strangler? Is that likely, given the timing and the MO? Surely it isn't a serious possibility?'

'Highly unlikely, but Uncle is never happy unless every stone is explored and every avenue thoroughly upturned. I've put together some details and the Identikit just in case. As you know, we've had a couple of sightings. And I've let Rickards know that you'll be on his patch. Remember Terry Rickards?'

'I remember.'

'Chief Inspector now, apparently. Done all right for himself in Norfolk. Better than he would have done if he'd stayed with us. And they tell me he's married, which might have softened him a bit. Awkward cuss.'

Dalgliesh said: 'I shall be on his patch but not, thank God, on his

9

team. And if they do lay hands on the Whistler, why should I do you out of a day in the country?'

'I hate the country and I particularly loathe flat country. Think of the public money you'll be saving. I'll come down – or is it up? – if he's worth looking at. Decent of you, Adam. Have a good leave.'

Only Cummings would have had the cheek. But the request was not unreasonable made, as it was, to a colleague his senior only by a matter of months and one who had always preached co-operation and the common-sense use of resources. And it was unlikely that his holiday would be interrupted by the need to take even a cursory glance at the Whistler, Norfolk's notorious serial killer, dead or alive. He had been at his work for fifteen months now and the latest victim – Valerie Mitchell wasn't it? – was his fourth. These cases were invariably difficult, time-consuming and frustrating, depending as they often did more on good luck than good detection. As he made his way down the ramp to the underground car park he glanced at his watch. In three-quarters of an hour he would be on his way. But first there was unfulfilled business at his publishers.

3

The lift at Messrs Herne & Illingworth in Bedford Square was almost as ancient as the house itself, a monument both to the firm's obstinate adherence to a bygone elegance and to a slightly eccentric inefficiency behind which a more thrustful policy was taking shape. As he was borne upwards in a series of disconcerting jerks Dalgliesh reflected that success, although admittedly more agreeable than failure, has its concomitant disadvantages. One of them, in the person of Bill Costello, Publicity Director, was waiting for him in the claustrophobic fourth-floor office above.

The change in his own poetic fortunes had coincided with changes in the firm. Herne & Illingworth still existed in so far as their names were printed or embossed on book covers under the firm's ancient and elegant colophon, but the house was now part of a multinational corporation which had recently added books to canned goods, sugar and textiles. Old Sebastian Herne had sold one of London's few remaining individual publishing houses for eight and a half million and had promptly married an extremely pretty publicity assistant who was only waiting for the deal to be concluded before, with some misgivings but a prudent regard for her future, relinquishing the status of newly acquired mistress for that of wife. Herne had died within three months, provoking much ribald comment but few regrets. Throughout his life Sebastian Herne had been a cautious, conventional man who reserved eccentricity, imagination and occasional risk-taking for his publishing. For thirty years he had lived as a faithful, if unimaginative husband and Dalgliesh reflected that if a man lives for nearly seventy years in comparatively blameless conventionality that is probably what his nature requires. Herne had died less of sexual exhaustion, assuming that to be as medically credible as puritans would like to believe, than from a fatal exposure to the contagion of fashionable sexual morality.

The new management promoted their poets vigorously, perhaps seeing the poetry list as a valuable balance to the vulgarity and soft pornography of their best-selling novelists whom they packaged with immense care and some distinction as if the elegance of the jacket and the quality of the print could elevate highly commercial banality into literature. Bill Costello, appointed the previous year as Publicity Director, didn't see why Faber & Faber should have a monopoly when it came to the imaginative publicizing of poetry, and was successful in promoting the poetry list despite the rumour that he never himself read a line of modern verse. His only known interest in verse was his presidency of the McGonagall Club whose members met on the first Tuesday of every month at a City pub to eat the landlady's famous steak and kidney pudding, put down an impressive amount of drink and recite to each other the more risible efforts of arguably Britain's worst poet ever. A fellow poet had once given Dalgliesh his own explanation: 'The poor devil has to read so much incomprehensible modern verse that you can't wonder that he needs an occasional dose of comprehensible nonsense. It's like a faithful husband occasionally taking therapeutic relief at the local cat-house.' Dalgliesh thought the theory ingenious but unlikely. There was no evidence that Costello read any of the verse he so assiduously promoted. He greeted his newest candidate for media fame with a mixture of dogged optimism and slight apprehension, as if knowing that he was faced with a hard nut to crack.

His small, rather wistful and childish face was curiously at odds with his Billy Bunter figure. His main problem was, apparently, whether to wear his belt above or below his paunch. Above was rumoured to indicate optimism, below a sign of depression. Today it was slung only just above the scrotum, proclaiming a pessimism which the subsequent conversation served only to justify.

Eventually Dalgliesh said firmly: 'No, Bill, I shall not parachute into Wembley Stadium holding the book in one hand and a microphone in the other. Nor shall I compete with the station announcer by bawling my verses at the Waterloo commuters. The poor devils are only trying to catch their trains.'

'That's been done. It's old hat. And it's nonsense about Wembley. Can't think how you got hold of that. No, listen, this is really exciting. I've spoken to Colin McKay and he's very enthusiastic. We're hiring a red double-decker bus, touring the country. Well, as much of the country as we can in ten days. I'll get Clare to show you the rough-out and the schedule.'

Dalgliesh said gravely: 'Like a political campaign bus; posters, slogans, loudspeakers, balloons.'

'No point in having it if we don't let people know it's coming.'

'They'll know that all right with Colin on board. How are you going to keep him sober?'

'A fine poet, Adam. He's a great admirer of yours.'

'Which doesn't mean he'd welcome me as a travelling companion. What are you thinking of calling it? Poets' Progress? The Chaucer Touch? Verse on Wheels – or is that too like the WI? The Poetry Bus? That has the merit of simplicity.'

'We'll think of something. I rather like Poets' Progress.'

'Stopping where?'

'Precincts, village halls, schools, pubs, motorway cafés, anywhere where there's an audience. It's an exciting prospect. We were thinking of hiring a train but the bus has more flexibility.'

'And it's cheaper.'

Costello ignored the innuendo. He said: 'Poets upstairs, drinks, refreshments downstairs. Readings from the platform. National publicity, radio and TV. We start from the Embankment. There's a chance of Channel Four and, of course, *Kaleidoscope*. We're counting on you, Adam.'

'No,' said Dalgliesh firmly. 'Not even for the balloons.'

'For God's sake, Adam, you write the stuff. Presumably you want people to read it – well, buy it anyway. There's tremendous public interest in you, particularly after that last case, the Berowne murder.'

'They're interested in a poet who catches murderers, or a policeman who writes poetry, not in the verse.'

'What does it matter as long as they're interested? And don't tell me that the Commissioner wouldn't like it. That's an old cop-out.'

'All right, I won't, but he wouldn't.'

And there was, after all, nothing new to be said. He had heard the questions innumerable times and he had done his best to answer them, with honesty if not with enthusiasm. 'Why does a sensitive poet like you spend his time catching murderers?' 'Which is the more important to you, the poetry or the policing?' 'Does it hinder or help being a detective?' 'Why does a successful detective write poetry?' 'What was your most interesting case, Commander? Do you ever feel like writing a poem about it?' 'The love poems, is the woman you've written them to alive or dead?' Dalgliesh wondered whether Philip Larkin had been badgered about what it felt like to be both poet and librarian, or Roy Fuller on how he managed to combine poetry with law.

He said: 'All the questions are predictable. It would save everyone a great deal of trouble if I answered them on tape, then you could broadcast them from the bus.'

'It wouldn't be at all the same thing. It's you personally they want to hear. Anyone would think you didn't want to be read.'

And did he want to be read? Certainly he wanted some people to read him, one person in particular, and having read the poems he wanted her to approve. Humiliating but true. As for the others; well, he supposed that the truth was that he wanted people to read the poems but not be coerced into buying them, an over-fastidiousness which he could hardly expect Herne & Illingworth to share. He was aware of Bill's anxious, supplicating eyes, like a small boy who sees the bowl of sweets rapidly disappearing from his reach. His reluctance to co-operate seemed to him typical of much in himself that he disliked. There was a certain illogicality, surely, in wanting to be published but not caring particularly whether he was bought. The fact that he found the more public manifestations of fame distasteful didn't mean that he was free of vanity, only that he was better at controlling it and that in him it took a more reticent form. After all, he had a job, an assured pension and now his aunt's considerable fortune. He didn't have to care. He saw himself as unreasonably privileged compared with Colin McKay who probably saw him – and who could blame Colin? – as a snobbish, oversensitive dilettante.

He was grateful when the door opened and Nora Gurney, the firm's cookery editor, came briskly in, reminding him as she always did of an intelligent insect, an impression reinforced by the bright exophthalmic eyes behind huge round spectacles, familiar fawn jumper in circular ribbing and flat pointed shoes. She had looked exactly the same since Dalgliesh had first known her.

Nora Gurney had become a power in British publishing by the expedience of longevity (no one could remember when she had first come to Herne & Illingworth) and a firm conviction that power was her due. It was likely that she would continue to exercise it under the new dispensation. Dalgliesh had last met her three months previously at one of the firm's periodic parties given for no particular reason so far as he could remember, unless to reassure the authors by the familiarity of the wine and canapés that they were still in business and basically same lovable old firm. The guest list had chiefly comprised their most prestigious writers in the main categories, a ploy which had added to the general atmosphere of inadvertence and fractionized unease; the poets had drunk too much and

14

had become lachrymose or amorous as their natures dictated, the novelists had herded together in a corner like recalcitrant dogs commanded not to bite, the academics, ignoring their hosts and fellow guests, had argued volubly among themselves and the cooks had ostentatiously rejected their half-bitten canapés on the nearest available hard surface with expressions of disgust, pained surprise or mild, speculative interest. Dalgliesh had been pinned in a corner by Nora Gurney who had wanted to discuss the practicality of the theory she had developed: since every set of fingerprints was unique, could not the whole country be printed, the data stored on a computer and research carried out to discover whether certain combinations of lines and whorls were indicative of criminal tendencies? That way crime could be prevented rather than cured. Dalgliesh had pointed out that, since criminal tendencies were universal, to judge from the places where his fellow guests had parked their cars, the data would be unmanageable, apart from the logistical and ethical problems of mass fingerprinting and the discouraging fact that crime, even supposing the comparison with disease to be valid, was, like disease, easier to diagnose than to cure. It had almost been a relief when a formidable female novelist, vigorously corseted in a florid cretonne two-piece which made her look like a walking sofa, had borne him off to pull out a crumple of parking-tickets from her voluminous handbag and angrily demand what he was proposing to do about them.

The Herne & Illingworth cookery list was small but strong, its best writers having a solid reputation for reliability, originality and good writing. Miss Gurney was passionately committed to her job and her writers, seeing the novels and verse as irritating if necessary adjuncts to the main business of the house which was to nourish and publish her darlings. It was rumoured that she herself was an indifferent cook, one more indication of the firm British conviction, not uncommon in more elevated if less useful spheres of human activity, that there is nothing so fatal to success as knowing your subject. It didn't surprise Dalgliesh that she had seen his arrival as fortuitous and the chore of delivering Alice Mair's proofs as a near-sacred privilege. She said: 'I suppose they've called you in to help catch the Whistler.'

'No, that, I'm thankful to say, is a job for the Norfolk CID. Calling in the Yard happens more often in fiction than real life.'

'It's convenient that you're driving to Norfolk, whatever the reason. I wouldn't really wish to trust these proofs to the post. But I thought your aunt lived in Suffolk? And surely someone said that Miss Dalgliesh had died.'

'She did live in Suffolk until five years ago when she moved to Norfolk. And yes, my aunt has died.'

'Oh well, Suffolk or Norfolk, there's not a lot of difference. But I'm sorry she's dead.' She seemed for a moment to contemplate human mortality and to compare the two counties to the disadvantage of both, then said: 'If Miss Mair isn't at home you won't leave this at the door, will you? I know that people are extraordinarily trusting in country districts but it would be quite disastrous if these proofs were lost. If Alice isn't at home her brother, Dr Alex Mair, may be. He's the Director of the nuclear power station at Larksoken. But perhaps, on second thoughts, you'd better not hand it to him either. Men can be extremely unreliable.'

Dalgliesh was tempted to point out that one of the country's foremost physicists who was responsible for an atomic power station and, if the papers were to be believed, was strongly tipped for the new post of nuclear power supremo, could presumably be trusted with a parcel of proofs. He said: 'If she's at home, I'll hand it to Miss Mair personally. If she isn't, I'll keep it until she is.'

'I've telephoned to say that it's on its way, so she'll be expecting you. I've printed the address very clearly. Martyr's Cottage. I expect you know how to get there.'

Costello said sourly: 'He can map-read. He's a policeman, remember.'

Dalgliesh said that he knew Martyr's Cottage and had briefly met Alexander Mair but not his sister. His aunt had lived very quietly but neighbours sharing the same remote district inevitably do get to know each other and, although Alice Mair had been away from home at the time, her brother had made a formal visit of condolence to the mill after Miss Dalgliesh's death.

He took possession of the parcel, which was surprisingly large and heavy and crisscrossed with an intimidating pattern of Sellotape, and was slowly borne downwards to the basement which gave access to the firm's small car park and his waiting Jaguar.

4

Once free of the knotted tentacles of the eastern suburbs, Dalgliesh made good time and by three he was driving through Lydsett village. Here a right turn took him off the coastal road on to what was little more than a smoothly macadamed track bordered by water-filled ditches and fringed by a golden haze of reeds, their lumbered heads straining in the wind. And now, for the first time, he thought that he could smell the North Sea, that potent but half-illusory tang evoking nostalgic memories of childhood holidays, of solitary adolescent walks as he struggled with his first poems, of his aunt's tall figure at his side, binoculars round her neck, striding towards the haunts of her beloved birds. And here, barring the road, was the familiar old farm gate still in place. Its continued presence always surprised him since it served no purpose that he could see except symbolically to cut off the headland and to give travellers pause to consider whether they really wanted to continue. It swung open at his touch but closing it, as always, was more difficult and he lugged and half lifted it into place and slipped the circle of wire over the gatepost with a familiar sensation of having turned his back on the workaday world and entered country which, no matter how frequent his visits, would always be alien territory.

He was driving now across the open headland towards the fringe of pine trees which bordered the North Sea. The only house to his left was the old Victorian rectory, a square, red-brick building, incongruous behind its struggling hedge of rhododendron and laurel. To his right the ground rose gently towards the southern cliffs and he could see the dark mouth of a concrete pillbox, undemolished since the war, and as seemingly indestructible as the great hulks of wave-battered concrete, remnants of the old fortifications which lay half-submerged in the sand along part of the beach. To the north the broken arches and stumps of the ruined Benedictine abbey gleamed golden in the afternoon sun against the crinkled blue of the sea and, breasting a small ridge, he glimpsed for the first time the topsail of Larksoken Mill and beyond it, against the skyline, the great grey bulk of Larksoken Nuclear Power Station. The road he was on, veering left, would lead eventually to the station but was, he knew, seldom used since normal traffic and all heavy vehicles used the new access road to the north. The headland was empty and almost bare, the few straggling trees, distorted by the wind, struggled to keep their precarious hold in the uncompromising soil. And now he was passing a second and more dilapidated pillbox and it struck him that the whole headland had the desolate look of an old battlefield, the corpses long since carted away but the air vibrating still with the gunfire of long-lost battles, while the power station loomed over it like a grandiose modern monument to the unknown dead.

On his previous visits to Larksoken he had seen Martyr's Cottage spread out beneath him when he and his aunt had stood surveying the headland from the small top room under the cone of the mill. But he had never been closer to it than the road and now, driving up to it, it struck him again that the description 'cottage' was hardly appropriate. It was a substantial, two-storey, L-shaped house standing to the east of the track with walls partly flint and partly rendered, enclosing at the rear a courtyard of York stone which gave an uninterrupted view over fifty yards of scrub to the grassy dunes and the sea. No one appeared as he drew up and, before lifting his hand to the bell, he paused to read the words of a stone plaque embedded in the flints to the right of the door.

In a cottage on this site lived Agnes Poley, Protestant martyr, burned at Ipswich, 15th August 1557, aged 32 years.
Ecclesiastes chapter 3, verse 15.

The plaque was unadorned, the letters deeply carved in an elegant script reminiscent of Eric Gill, and Dalgliesh remembered his aunt telling him that it had been placed there by previous owners in the late twenties, when the cottage was originally extended. One of the advantages of a religious education is the ability to identify at least the better-known texts of scripture and this was one which it needed no effort of memory to recall. As a delinquent nine-year-old at his prep school, he had once been required by the headmaster to write out in his best handwriting the whole of the third chapter of Ecclesiastes, old Gumboil, economical in this as in all matters, believing that writing lines should combine punishment with literary and religious education. The words, in that round childish script, had remained with him. It was, he thought, an interesting choice of text.

That which hath been is now; and that which is to be hath already been; and God requireth that which is past.

He rang and there was only a short delay before Alice Mair opened the door. He saw a tall, handsome woman dressed with careful and expensive informality in a black cashmere sweater with a silk scarf at the throat and fawn trousers. He would have recognized her from her strong resemblance to her brother, although she looked the elder by some years. She took it for granted that each knew who the other was, and standing aside to motion him in she said: 'It's good of you to be so accommodating, Mr Dalgliesh. I'm afraid Nora Gurney is implacable. Once she knew you were on your way to Norfolk you were a predestined victim. Perhaps you would bring the proofs through to the kitchen.'

It was a distinguished face with the deep-set, widely spaced eyes beneath straight brows, a well-shaped, rather secretive mouth and strong greying hair swept upwards and curled into a chignon. In her publicity photographs she could, he recalled, look beautiful in a somewhat intimidating, intellectual and very English mould. But seen face to face, even in the informality of her own house, the absence of a spark of sexuality and, he sensed, a deep-seated reserve, made her seem less feminine and more formidable than he had expected, and she held herself stiffly as if repelling invaders of her personal space. The handshake with which she had greeted him had been cool and firm and her brief smile was surprisingly attractive. He knew that he was oversensitive to the timbre of the human voice and hers, although not jarring or unpleasant, sounded a little forced as if she were deliberately speaking at an unnatural pitch.

He followed her down the hall to the kitchen at the back of the house. It was, he judged, almost twenty feet long and obviously served the triple purpose of sitting room, working place and office. The right-hand half of the room was a well-equipped kitchen with a large gas stove and an Aga, a butcher's chopping block, a dresser to the right of the door holding an assortment of gleaming pots, and a long working surface with a wooden triangle sheathing her assortment of knives. In the centre of the room was a large wooden table holding a stoneware jar of dried flowers. On the left-hand wall was a working fireplace, the two recesses fitted with wall-to-ceiling bookshelves. To each side of the hearth was a high-backed wicker armchair in an intricate closely woven design fitted with patchwork

19

cushions. There was an open roll-top desk facing one of the wide windows and, to its right, a stable door, the top half open, gave a view of the paved courtyard. Dalgliesh could glimpse what was obviously her herb garden planted in elegant terracotta pots carefully disposed to catch the sun. The room, which contained nothing superfluous, nothing pretentious, was both pleasing and extraordinarily comforting and, for a moment, he wondered why. Was it the faint smell of herbs and newly baked dough, the soft ticking of the wall-mounted clock which seemed both to mark the passing seconds and yet to hold time in thrall, the rhythmic moaning of the sea through the half-open door, the sense of well-fed ease conveyed by the two cushioned armchairs, the open hearth? Or was it that the kitchen reminded Dalgliesh of that rectory kitchen where the lonely only child had found warmth and undemanding, uncensorious companionship, been given hot dripping toast and small forbidden treats?

He placed the proofs on the desk, refused Alice Mair's offer of coffee and followed her back to the front door. She walked out with him to the car and said: 'I was sorry about your aunt – sorry for you, I mean. I expect that for an ornithologist death ceases to be terrible once sight and hearing begin to go. And to die in one's sleep without distress to oneself or inconvenience to others is an enviable end. But you had known her for so long that she must have seemed immortal.'

Formal condolences, he thought, were never easy to speak or accept and usually sounded either banal or insincere. Hers had been perceptive. Jane Dalgliesh had indeed seemed to him immortal. The very old, he thought, make our past. Once they go it seems for a moment that neither it nor we have any real existence. He said: 'I don't think death was ever terrible to her. I'm not sure that I really knew her and I'm left wishing I'd tried harder. But I shall miss her.'

Alice Mair said: 'I didn't know her either. Perhaps I should have tried harder too. She was a very private woman, I suspect one of those fortunate people who find no other company more agreeable than their own. It always seems presumptuous to encroach on that self-sufficiency. Perhaps you share it. But if you can tolerate company, I'm having a few people, mostly colleagues of Alex from the power station, tc dinner on Thursday night. Would you care to join us? Seven thirty for eight.'

It sounded, he thought, more like a challenge than an invitation.

Somewhat to his surprise, Dalgliesh found himself accepting. But then the whole encounter had been a little surprising. She stood regarding him with a serious intensity as he let in the clutch and turned the car and he had the impression that she was watching critically to see how he handled it. But at least, he thought as he gave a final wave, she hadn't asked him whether he had come to Norfolk to help catch the Whistler.

5

Three minutes later he raised his foot from the accelerator. Ahead of him, trudging along on the left of the path, was a little group of children, the eldest girl wheeling a pushchair with two smaller children, one each side of her, clutching the bars. Hearing the noise of the car she turned and he saw a peaked, delicate face framed with red-gold hair. He recognized the Blaney children, met once before with their mother walking along the beach. Obviously the eldest girl had been shopping: the folding pushchair had a shelf under the seat lumped high with plastic bags. Instinctively he slowed down. They were unlikely to be in real danger, the Whistler stalked at night, not in broad daylight, and no vehicle had passed him since he left the coastal road. But the child looked grossly overburdened and ought not to be so far from home. Though he had never seen their cottage he seemed to remember that his aunt had told him that it lay about two miles to the south. He recalled what he knew about them, that their father earned a precarious living as a painter whose innocuous, prettified watercolours were sold in cafés and tourist shops along the coast and that their mother had been desperately ill with cancer. He wondered whether Mrs Blaney was still alive. His instinct was to pile the children into the car and drive them home but that, he knew, was hardly sensible. Almost certainly the eldest child – Theresa, wasn't it? – had been taught not to accept lifts from strangers, particularly men, and he was virtually a stranger. On an impulse he reversed the Jaguar and drove quickly back to Martyr's Cottage. This time the front door was open and a swathe of sunlight lay across the red-tiled floor. Alice Mair had heard the car and came out to him from the kitchen, wiping her hands.

He said: 'The Blaney children are walking home. Theresa is wheeling a pushchair and trying to cope with the twins. I thought I could offer a lift if I had a woman with me, someone they know.'

She said briefly: 'They know me.'

Without another word she went back into the kitchen then came out to him, closed the front door after her without locking it and got into the car. Putting it into gear, his arm brushed her knee. He was aware of an almost imperceptible withdrawing, more emotional than physical, a small delicate gesture of self-containment. Dalgliesh doubted whether that half-imagined recoil had anything to do with him personally, nor did he find her silence disconcerting. Their conversation, when they did speak, was brief. He asked: 'Is Mrs Blaney still alive?'

'No. She died six weeks ago.'

'How are they managing?'

'Not particularly well, I imagine. But Ryan Blaney doesn't welcome interference. I sympathize. Once he lets down his defences half the social workers in Norfolk, amateur and professional, will move in on him.'

When they drew up beside the little band it was Alice Mair who opened the car door and spoke.

'Theresa, here is Mr Dalgliesh to give you all a lift. He's Miss Dalgliesh's nephew from Larksoken Mill. One of the twins had better sit on my lap. The rest of you and the pushchair can fit into the back.'

Theresa looked at Dalgliesh without smiling and said a grave thank you. She reminded him of pictures of the young Elizabeth Tudor, the same red-gold hair framing a curiously adult face both secretive and self-composed, the same sharp nose and wary eyes. The faces of the twins, softer editions of her own, turned towards her questioningly then broke into shy smiles. They looked as if they had been dressed in a hurry and not very suitably for a long walk on the headland, even in a warm autumn. One wore a tattered summer dress in pink spotted cotton with double flounces, the other a pinafore over a checked blouse. Their pathetically thin legs were unprotected. Theresa was wearing jeans and a grubby sweat shirt with a map of London's Underground across the front. Dalgliesh found himself wondering if it had been brought back from a school trip to the capital. It was too large for her and the wide sleeves of limp cotton hung from her freckled arms like rags thrown over a stick. In contrast to his sisters, Anthony was over-clad, a bundle of leggings, jumper and a padded jacket topped with a woollen helmet with a bobble pulled well down over his forehead, beneath which he surveyed their busyness, unsmiling, like a stout imperious Caesar.

Dalgliesh got out of the Jaguar and tried to extricate him from the pushchair, but the anatomy of the chair momentarily defeated him. There was a bar beneath which the child's rigid legs were obstinately

23

stuck. The solid uncooperative bundle was surprisingly heavy; it was like trying to manoeuvre a firm and rather smelly poultice. Theresa gave him a brief, pitying smile, dragged the plastic bags from beneath the seat then expertly freed her brother and settled him on her left hip while, with the other hand, she collapsed the pushchair, with a single vigorous shake. Dalgliesh took the baby from her while Theresa helped the children into the Jaguar and commanded with sudden fierceness, 'Sit still.' Anthony, recognizing incompetence, grasped Dalgliesh's hair firmly with a sticky hand and he felt the momentary touch of a cheek, so soft that it was like the fall of a petal. Throughout these manoeuvrings Alice Mair sat quietly watching from the car but made no move to help. It was impossible to know what she was thinking.

But once the Jaguar had moved away she turned to Theresa and said in a voice of surprising gentleness: 'Does your father know that you're out alone?'

'Daddy has taken the van to Mr Sparks. It's due for its MOT test. Mr Sparks doesn't think it's going to pass. And I found we'd run out of milk for Anthony. We have to have milk. And we wanted some more disposable nappies.'

Alice Mair said: 'I'm giving a dinner party on Thursday evening. If your father agrees, would you like to come and help with the table like you did last month?'

'What are you going to cook, Miss Mair?'

'Put your head close so that I can whisper. Mr Dalgliesh is going to be one of the guests. I want it to be a surprise.'

The pale golden head leaned forward towards the grey and Miss Mair whispered. Theresa smiled and then nodded with serious satisfaction in a moment of grave feminine conspiracy.

It was Alice Mair who directed him to the cottage. After about a mile they turned seaward and the Jaguar lurched and bounced down a narrow track between high, untended hedges of bramble and elderberry. The track led only to Scudder's Cottage, the name crudely painted on a board nailed to the gate. Beyond the cottage it widened to provide a rough, gravelled turning, backed by a forty-foot bank of shingle behind which Dalgliesh could hear the crash and suck of the tide. Scudder's Cottage, small-windowed, picturesque under its tiled, dipping roof, was fronted by a flowering wilderness which had once been a garden. Theresa led the way, between grass almost knee-high bordered by a riot of unpruned roses, to the porch, then reached for a key hung high on a nail, less, Dalgliesh supposed, for security reasons than to ensure that it wasn't lost. With Dalgliesh carrying Anthony they passed into the cottage.

It was much lighter than he had expected, largely because of a rear door, now open, which led to a glass extension giving a view of the headland. He was aware of the room's clutter, the central wooden table still covered with the remains of their midday meal, an assortment of plates smeared with tomato sauce, a half-eaten sausage, a large bottle of orangeade uncapped; the children's clothes thrown over the back of a low nursing chair before the fireplace, of the smell of milk and bodies and wood smoke. But what held his attention was a large oil painting propped on a chair and fronting the door. It was a three-quarter portrait in oils of a woman, painted with remarkable power. It dominated the room so that he and Alice Mair stood for a moment, silently regarding it. The painter had avoided caricature, if only just, but the portrait was, he felt, intended less as a physical likeness than an allegory. Behind the wide, full mouth, the arrogant stare of the eyes, the dark, crimped, Pre-Raphaelite hair streaming in the wind, was a careful delineation of the headland, its objects disposed and painted with the meticulous attention to detail of a sixteenth-century primitive; the Victorian rectory, the ruined abbey, the half-demolished pillbox, the crippled trees, the small white mill like a child's toy and, gaunt against a flaming evening sky, the stark outline of the power station. But it was the woman, painted more freely, who dominated the landscape, arms stretched, the palms facing outwards in a parody of blessing. Dalgliesh's private verdict was that it was technically brilliant, but overwrought and painted, he felt, in hatred. Blaney's intention to produce a study of evil was as clear as if the portrait had been labelled. It was so different from the artist's usual work that without the bold signature, the single surname, Dalgliesh might have wondered if it was, in fact, his work. He recalled Blaney's pallid and innocuous watercolours of the better-known beauty spots of Norfolk: Blakeney, St Peter Mancroft and the cathedral at Norwich, which he produced for the local shops. They could have been painted from picture postcards and probably were. And he could recall seeing one or two small oils hung in local restaurants and pubs, slap-dash in technique and economical of paint, but so different from the prettified watercolours that it was hard to believe that they too were by the same hand. But this portrait was different from either; the wonder was that the artist who could

25

produce this disciplined splurge of colour, this technical artistry and imagination, had been content to churn out meretricious souvenirs for the tourist trade.

'You didn't know I could do it, did you?'

Absorbed in the painting, their ears hadn't caught his almost silent approach through the open door. He moved round and joined them and stared intently at the portrait as if seeing it for the first time. His daughters, as though obedient to some unspoken command, grouped themselves around him in what in older children could have been a conscious gesture of family solidarity. Dalgliesh had last seen Blaney six months earlier splashing alone along the edge of the beach, painting gear slung over his shoulder, and was shocked by the change in the man. He stood a gaunt six foot three in his torn jeans, the checked, woollen shirt open almost to the waist, his long grubby feet in the open sandals looking like dry, brown bones. His face was a picture of red ferocity, the straggling red hair and beard, the bloodshot eyes, the gaunt-featured face burnt red by wind and sun, which yet showed on the cheekbones and under the eyes the bruising stain of tiredness. Dalgliesh saw Theresa slip her hand into his while one of the twins moved closer to him and clasped both arms firmly round one of his legs. Dalgliesh thought that however ferocious he might appear to the outside world his children had no fear of him.

Alice Mair said calmly: 'Good afternoon, Ryan,' but did not appear to expect an answer. She nodded towards the portrait and went on: 'It's remarkable, certainly. What are you proposing to do with it? I can hardly suppose that she sat for you or that it was commissioned.'

'She didn't need to sit. I know that face. I'm showing it at the Norwich Contemporary Arts Exhibition on October the third if I can get it there. The van is out of use.'

Alice Mair said: 'I'll be driving to London within the next week. I could collect it and deliver it if you let me have the address.'

He said: 'If you like.' The response was ungracious but Dalgliesh thought he detected relief. Then he added: 'I'll leave it packed and labelled to the left of the door in the painting shed. The light is just above it. You can collect it whenever it suits you. No need to knock.' The last words had the force of a command, almost of a warning.

Miss Mair said: 'I'll telephone you when I know when I'm going. By the way, I don't think you've met Mr Dalgliesh. He saw the children on the road and thought of giving them a lift.'

Blaney didn't say thank you, but after a moment's hesitation held out his hand which Dalgliesh grasped. Then he said gruffly, 'I liked your aunt. She telephoned offering to help when my wife was ill and when I said there was nothing she or anyone could do, she didn't keep fussing. Some people can't keep away from a deathbed. Like the Whistler, they get their kicks from watching people die.'

'No,' said Dalgliesh, 'she never fussed. I shall miss her. I'm sorry about your wife.'

Blaney didn't reply, but stared hard at Dalgliesh as if assessing the sincerity of that simple statement, and then said curtly, 'Thank you for helping the children,' and lifted his son from Dalgliesh's shoulder. It was a clear gesture of dismissal.

Neither of them spoke as Dalgliesh negotiated the track and finally turned on to the higher road. It was as if the cottage had exerted some spell which it was important to throw off before they talked. Then he asked: 'Who is that woman in the portrait?'

'I hadn't realized that you didn't know. Hilary Robarts. She's Acting Administrative Officer at the power station. Actually you'll meet her at dinner on Thursday night. She bought Scudder's Cottage when she first arrived here three years ago. She's been trying to get the Blaneys out for some time. There's been a certain amount of feeling about it locally.'

Dalgliesh asked: 'Why does she want to gain possession? Does she propose to live there?'

'I don't imagine so. I think she bought it as an investment and wants to sell. Even a remote cottage – particularly a remote cottage – has value on this coast. And she has some justice on her side. Blaney did say that his tenancy would be short-term. I think she feels a certain resentment that he used his wife's illness, her death, and now uses the children as an excuse for reneging on his undertaking to leave when she wanted the cottage back.'

Dalgliesh was interested that Alice Mair apparently knew so much about local affairs. He had thought of her as essentially a private woman who would be very little concerned with her neighbours or their problems. And what about himself? In his deliberations whether to sell or keep on the mill as a holiday home he had seen it as a refuge from London, eccentric and remote, providing a temporary escape from the demands of his job and the pressures of success. But how far, even as an occasional visitor, could he isolate himself from the community, from their private tragedies no less than their dinner parties? It would be simple enough to avoid their hospitality given sufficient ruthlessness and he had never lacked that when it came to safeguarding his privacy. But the less tangible demands of neighbourliness might be less easily shrugged away. It was in London that you could live anonymously, could create your own ambience, could deliberately fabricate the persona which you chose to present to the world. In the country you lived as a social being and at the valuation of others. So he had lived in childhood and adolescence in the same country rectory, taking part each Sunday in a familiar liturgy which reflected, interpreted, and sanctified the changing seasons of the farming year. It was a world he had relinquished with small regret and he had not expected to find it again on Larksoken headland. But some of its obligations were here, deep-rooted even in this arid and unfertile earth. His aunt had lived as privately as any woman he knew, but even she had visited and tried to help the Blaneys. He thought of the man, bereft and incarcerated in that cluttered cottage behind the great dyke of shingle, listening night after night to the never-ceasing moaning of the tide, and brooding on the wrongs, real or imaginary, which could inspire that hate-filled portrait. It could hardly be healthy for him or for his children. Come to that, he thought grimly, it could hardly be healthy for Hilary Robarts. He asked: 'Does he get much official help with the children? It can't be easy.'

'As much as he's prepared to tolerate. The local authority has arranged for the twins to attend some kind of daycare centre. They get collected most days. And Theresa, of course, is at school. She catches the bus at the end of the lane. She and Ryan between them cope with the baby. Meg Dennison – she housekeeps for the Reverend and Mrs Copley at the Old Rectory – thinks we ought to do more for them but it's difficult to see precisely what. As an ex-schoolmistress I should have thought she'd had her fill of children and I make no pretence at understanding them.' Dalgliesh remembered her whispered confidence to Theresa in the car, the child's intent face and brief transforming smile, and thought that she understood one child at least far better than she would probably claim.

But his thoughts returned to the portrait. He said: 'It must be uncomfortable, particularly in a small community, to be the object of so much malevolence.'

She understood at once what he meant. 'Hatred rather than

malevolence, wouldn't you say? Uncomfortable and rather frightening. Not that Hilary Robarts is easily frightened. But she's becoming something of an obsession with Ryan, particularly since his wife's death. He chooses to believe that Hilary practically badgered her into her grave. It's understandable, I suppose. Human beings need to find someone to blame both for their misery and for their guilt. Hilary Robarts makes a convenient scapegoat.'

It was a disagreeable story and coming as it did after the impact of the portrait it provoked in Dalgliesh a mixture of depression and foreboding which he tried to shake off as irrational. He was glad to let the subject drop and they drove in silence until he left her at the gate of Martyr's Cottage. To his surprise she held out her hand and gave him, once again, that extraordinary, attractive smile.

'I'm glad you stopped for the children. I'll see you, then, on Thursday night. You will be able to make your own assessment of Hilary Robarts and compare the portrait with the woman.'

6

As the Jaguar crested the headland Neil Pascoe was dumping rubbish into one of the two dustbins outside the caravan, two plastic bags of empty tins of soup and baby food, soiled disposable napkins, vegetable peelings and squashed cartons, already malodorous despite his careful sealing of the bags. Firmly replacing the lid he marvelled, as he always did, at the difference one girl and an eighteen-month-old baby could make to the volume of household waste. Climbing back into the caravan, he said: 'A Jag has just passed. It looks as if Miss Dalgliesh's nephew is back.'

Amy, fitting a recalcitrant new ribbon to the ancient typewriter, didn't bother to look up.

'The detective. Perhaps he's come to help catch the Whistler.'

'That isn't his job. The Whistler is nothing to do with the Met Police. It's probably just a holiday. Or perhaps he's here to decide what to do with the mill. He can hardly live here and work in London.'

'So why don't you ask him if we can have it? Rent-free, of course. We could caretake, see that no one squats. You're always saying it's antisocial for people to have second homes or leave property empty. Go on, have a word with him. I dare you. Or I will if you're too scared.'

It was, he knew, less a suggestion than a half-serious threat. But for a moment, gladdened by her easy assumption that they were a couple, that she wasn't thinking of leaving him, he actually entertained the idea as a feasible solution to all their problems. Well, almost all. But a glance round the caravan restored him to reality. It was becoming difficult to remember how it had looked fifteen months ago, before Amy and Timmy had entered his life; the home-made shelves of orange boxes ranged against the wall which had held his books, the two mugs, two plates and one soup bowl, which had been adequate for his needs, neatly stacked in the cupboard, the excessive cleanliness of the small kitchen and lavatory, his bed smooth under the coverlet of knitted woollen squares, the single hanging cupboard which had been sufficient for his meagre wardrobe, his other possessions boxed and tidily stowed in the chest under the seat. It wasn't that Amy was dirty; she was continually washing herself, her hair, her few clothes. He spent hours carrying water from the tap outside Cliff Cottage to which they had access. He was continually having to fetch new Calor-gas cylinders from the general store in Lydsett village and steam from the almost constantly boiling kettle made the caravan a damp mist. But she was chronically untidy; her clothes lying where she had dropped them, shoes kicked under the table, knickers and bras stuffed beneath cushions and Timmy's toys littering the floor and table top. The make-up, which seemed to be her sole extravagance, cluttered the single shelf in the cramped shower and he would find half-empty, opened jars and bottles in the food cupboard. He smiled as he pictured Commander Adam Dalgliesh, that no doubt fastidious widower, making his way through the accumulated mess to discuss their suitability as care-takers at Larksoken Mill.

And then there were the animals. She was incurably sentimental about wildlife and they were seldom without some maimed, deserted or starving creatures. Seagulls, their wings covered with oil, were cleansed, caged and then let free. There had been a stray mongrel whom they had named Herbert, with a large uncoordinated body and look of lugubrious disapproval who had attached himself to them for a few weeks and whose voracious appetite for dog-meat and biscuits had had a ruinous effect on the housekeeping. Happily Herbert had eventually trotted off and to Amy's distress had been seen no more, although his lead still hung on the caravan door, a limp reminder of her bereavement. And now there were the two black and white kittens found abandoned on the grass verge of the coast road as they came back in the van from Ipswich. Amy had screamed for him to stop and, scooping up the kittens, had thrown back her head and howled obscenities at the cruelty of human beings. They slept on Amy's bed, drank indiscriminately from any saucer of milk or tea put down for them, were remarkably docile under Timmy's boisterous caresses and, happily, seemed content with the cheapest kind of tinned cat food. But he was glad to have them because they too seemed to offer some assurance that Amy would stay.

He had found her – and he used the word much as he might of finding a particularly beautiful sea-washed stone – one late June afternoon the previous year. She had been sitting on the shingle

31

staring out to sea, her arms clasped round her knees, Timmy lying asleep on the small rug beside her. He was wearing a blue fleecy sleeping suit embroidered with ducks from which his round face seemed to have spilled over, still and pink as a porcelain, painted doll, the delicate lashes brush-tipped on the plump cheeks. And she, too, had something of the precision and contrived charm of a doll with an almost round head poised on a long delicate neck, a snub nose with a splatter of freckles, a small mouth with a full upper lip beautifully curved and a bristle of cropped hair, originally fair but with bright orange tips which caught the sun and trembled in the breeze so that the whole head seemed for a moment to have a vivid life separated from the rest of her body and, the image changing, he had seen her as a bright exotic flower. He could remember every detail of that first meeting. She had been wearing blue faded jeans, and a white sweat shirt flattened against the pointed nipples and the upturned breasts; the cotton seeming too thin a protection against the freshening onshore breeze. As he approached tentatively, wanting to seem friendly but not to alarm her, she had turned on him a long and curious glance from remarkable, slanted, violet-blue eyes.

Standing over her, he had said: 'My name's Neil Pascoe. I live in that caravan on the edge of the cliff. I'm just going to make some tea. I wondered if you'd like a mug.'

'I don't mind, if you're making it.' She had turned away at once and gazed again out to sea.

Five minutes later he had slithered down the sandy cliffs, a mug of tea slopping in each hand. He heard himself say: 'May I sit down?'

'Please yourself. The beach is free.'

So he had lowered himself to sit beside her and together they had stared wordlessly towards the horizon. Looking back on it he was amazed both at his boldness and at the seeming inevitability and naturalness of that first encounter. It was several minutes before he had found the courage to ask her how she had got to the beach. She had shrugged.

'By bus to the village and then I walked.'

'It was a long way carrying the baby.'

'I'm used to walking a long way carrying the baby.'

And then, under his hesitant questioning, the story had come out, told by her without self-pity, almost, it had seemed, without particular interest, as if the events had happened to someone else. It was not, he supposed, an unusual tale. She was living in one of the small private hotels in Cromer on Social Security. She had been in a squat in London but had thought it would be pleasant to have some sea air for the baby for the summer. Only it wasn't working out. The woman at the hotel didn't really want kids and with summer holidays approaching could get a better rate for her rooms. She didn't think she could be turned out, but she wasn't going to stay, not with that bitch.

He asked: 'Couldn't the baby's father help?'

'He hasn't got a father. He did have a father – I mean, he isn't Jesus Christ. But he hasn't got one now.'

'Do you mean that he's dead or that he's gone away?'

'Could be either, couldn't it? Look, if I knew who he was I might know where he was, OK?'

Then there had been another silence during which she took periodical gulps of her tea and the sleeping baby stirred and gave small pig-like grunts. After a few minutes he had spoken again.

'Look, if you can't find anywhere else in Cromer you can share the caravan for a time.' He had added hastily: 'I mean, there is a second bedroom. It's very small, only just room for the bunk, but it would do for a time. I know it's isolated here but it's close to the beach which would be nice for the baby.'

She had turned on him again that remarkable glance in which for the first time he had detected to his discomfiture a brief flash of intelligence and of calculation.

'All right,' she said. 'If I can't find anywhere else I'll come back tomorrow.'

And he had lain awake late that night half hoping, half dreading that she would return. And she had returned the following afternoon, carrying Timmy on her hip and the rest of her possessions in a backpack. She had taken over the caravan and his life. He didn't know whether what he felt for her was love, affection or pity, or a mixture of all three. He only knew that in his anxious and over-concerned life his second greatest fear was that she might leave.

He had lived in the caravan now for just over two years, supported by a research grant from his northern university to study the effect of the Industrial Revolution on the rural industries of East Anglia. His dissertation was nearly finished but for the last six months he had almost stopped work on it and had devoted himself entirely to his passion, a crusade against nuclear power. From the caravan on the very edge of the sea he could see Larksoken Power Station stark against the skyline, as uncompromising as his own will to oppose it,

33

a symbol and a threat. It was from the caravan that he ran People Against Nuclear Power, with its acronym PANUP, the small organization of which he was both founder and president. The caravan had been a stroke of luck. The owner of Cliff Cottage was a Canadian who, returning to his roots and seduced by nostalgia, had bought it on impulse as a possible holiday home. About fifty years earlier there had been a murder at Cliff Cottage. It had been a fairly commonplace murder, a henpecked husband at the end of his tether who had taken a hatchet to his virago of a wife. But if it had been neither particularly interesting nor mysterious, it had certainly been bloody. After the cottage had been bought the Canadian's wife had heard graphic accounts of spilt brains and blood-spattered walls and had declared that she had no intention of living there in summer or at any other time. Its very isolation, once attractive, now appeared both sinister and repellent. And to compound the problem, the local planning authority had shown themselves unsympathetic to the owner's over-ambitious plans for rebuilding. Disillusioned with the cottage and its problems, he had boarded up the windows and returned to Toronto, meaning eventually to come back and make a final decision about his ill-advised purchase. The previous owner had parked a large, old-fashioned caravan at the back and the Canadian had made no difficulty about letting this to Neil for two pounds a week, seeing it as a useful way of having someone to keep an eye on the property. And it was the caravan, at once his home and his office, from which Neil conducted his campaign. He tried not to think about the time, six months ahead, when his grant would finish and he would need to find work. He knew that he had somehow to stay here on the headland, to keep always in view that monstrous building which dominated his imagination as it did his view.

But now, to the uncertainty about his future funding, was added a new and more terrifying threat. About five months earlier he had attended an open day at the power station during which the Acting Administrative Officer, Hilary Robarts, had given a short preliminary talk. He had challenged almost everything she had said and what was meant as an informative introduction to a public relations exercise had developed into something close to a public brawl. In the next issue of his news-sheet he had reported on the incident in terms which he now realized had been unwise. She had sued him for libel. The action was due to be heard in four weeks' time and he knew that, successful or not, he was faced with ruin. Unless she died in the next few weeks – and why should she die? – it could be the end of his life on the headland, the end of his organization, the end of all he had planned and hoped to do.

Amy was typing envelopes, sending out the final copies of the newsletter. A pile was already to hand and he began folding the pamphlets and inserting them into the envelopes. The job wasn't easy. He had tried to economize with the size and quality and the envelopes were in danger of splitting. He now had a mailing list of 250, only a small minority of whom were active supporters of PANUP. Most never paid any dues towards the organization and the majority of the pamphlets went unsolicited to public authorities, local firms and industry in the vicinity of Larksoken and Sizewell. He wondered how many of the 250 were read and thought, with a sudden spasm of anxiety and depression, of the total cost of even this small enterprise. And this month's newsletter wasn't his best. Rereading one before he put it in the envelope, it seemed to him to be ill-organized, to have no coherent theme. The principal aim now was to refute the growing argument that nuclear power could avoid the damage to the environment through the greenhouse effect, but the mixture of suggestions ranging from solar power to replacing light bulbs with those which consumed seventy-five per cent less energy seemed naïve and hardly convincing. His article argued that nuclear-generated electricity couldn't realistically replace oil and fossil fuels unless all nations built sixteen new reactors a week in the five years from 1995, a programme impossible to achieve and one which, if practicable, would add intolerably to the nuclear threat. But the statistics, like all his figures, were culled from a variety of sources and lacked authority. Nothing he produced seemed to him to be genuinely his own work. And the rest of the newsletter was a jumble of the usual scare stories, most of which he had used before; allegations of safety breaches which had been covered up, doubts about the safety of the ageing Magnox stations, the unsolved problem of storing and transporting nuclear waste. And this issue he had been hard put to it to find a couple of intelligent letters for the correspondence page; sometimes it seemed that every crackbrain in north-east Norfolk read the PANUP newsletter but that no one else did.

Amy was picking at the letters of the typewriter which had a persistent tendency to stick. She said: 'Neil, this is a bloody awful machine. It would be quicker to write the addresses by hand.'

'It's better since you cleaned it and the new ribbon looks fine.'

'It's still diabolical. Why don't you buy a new one? It would save time in the end.'

'I can't afford it.'

'You can't afford a new typewriter and you think you're going to save the world.'

'You don't need possessions to save the world, Amy. Jesus Christ had nothing; no home, no money, no property.'

'I thought you said when I came here that you weren't religious.'

It always surprised him that, apparently taking no account of him, she could yet recall comments he had made months earlier. He said: 'I don't believe Christ was God. I don't believe there is a God. But I believe in what He taught.'

'If He wasn't a God, I don't see that it matters much what He taught. Anyway, all I can remember is something about turning the other cheek which I don't believe in. I mean, that's daft. If someone slaps your left cheek then you slap his right, only harder. Anyway, I do know they hung Him up on the cross so it didn't do Him a lot of good. That's what turning the other cheek does for you.'

He said: 'I've got a Bible here somewhere. You could read about Him if you wanted to. Make a start with St Mark's Gospel.'

'No thanks. I had enough of that in the home.'

'What home?'

'Just a home, before the baby was born.'

'How long were you there?'

'Two weeks. Two weeks too bloody many. Then I ran away and found a squat.'

'Where was that, the squat?'

'Islington, Camden, King's Cross, Stoke Newington. Does it matter? I'm here now, OK?'

'It's OK by me, Amy.'

Lost in his thoughts, he hardly realized that he had given up folding the pamphlets.

Amy said: 'Look, if you're not going to help with these envelopes you might as well go and put a new washer on that tap. It's been dripping for weeks and Timmy's always falling about in the mud.'

'All right,' he said, 'I'll do it now.'

He took down his tool kit from the high cupboard where it was kept well out of Timmy's reach. He was glad to be out of the caravan. It had become increasingly claustrophobic in the last few weeks. Outside he bent to talk to Timmy, caged in his playpen. He and Amy had collected large stones from the beach, looking for those with holes in them – and he had strung them on to strong cord and tied them along one side of the playpen. Timmy would spend hours happily banging them together or against the bars or, as now, slobbering against one of the stones in an attempt to get it into his mouth. Sometimes he would communicate with individual flints, a continuous admonitory prattle broken by sudden triumphant squeals. Kneeling down Neil clutched the bars, rubbed his nose against Timmy's, and was rewarded by his huge, heart-tugging smile. He looked very like his mother with the same round head on a delicate neck, the same beautifully shaped mouth. Only his eyes, widely spaced, were differently shaped, large blue spheres with, above them, straight bushy eyebrows which reminded Neil of pale and delicate caterpillars. The tenderness he felt for the child was equal to, if different from, the tenderness he felt for his mother. He could not now imagine life on the headland without either of them.

But the tap defeated him. Despite his tuggings with the wrench he couldn't get the screw to shift. Even this minor domestic task was apparently beyond his powers. He could hear Amy's derisive voice. 'You want to change the world and you can't change a washer.' After a couple of minutes he gave up the attempt, left the tool box by the cottage wall and walked to the edge of the cliff then slithered down to the beach. Crunching over the ridges of stones, he went down to the edge of the sea and almost violently wrenched off his shoes. It was thus, when the weight of anxiety about his failed ambitions, his uncertain future, became too heavy that he would find his peace, standing motionless to watch the veined curve of the poised wave, the tumult of crashing foam breaking over his feet, the wide inter-secting arches washing over the smooth sand as the wave retreated to leave its tenuous lip of foam. But today even this wonder, continually repeated, failed to comfort his spirit. He gazed out to the horizon with unseeing eyes and thought about his present life, the hopelessness of the future, about Amy, about his family. Thrusting his hands in his pocket, he felt the crumpled envelope of his mother's last letter.

He knew that his parents were disappointed in him, although they never said so openly since oblique hints were just as effective: 'Mrs Reilly keeps on asking me, what is Neil doing? I don't like to say that you're living in a caravan with no proper job.' She certainly didn't like to say that he was living there with a girl. He had written to tell them about Amy since his parents constantly threatened to visit and, unlikely as this was actually to happen, the prospect had added an intolerable anxiety to his already anxiety-ridden life.

'I'm giving a temporary home to an unmarried mother in return for typing help. Don't worry, I shan't suddenly present you with a bastard grandchild.'

After the letter had been posted he had felt ashamed. The cheap attempt at humour had been too like a treacherous repudiation of Timmy whom he loved. And his mother hadn't found it either funny or reassuring. His letter had produced an almost incoherent farrago of warnings, pained reproaches and veiled references to the possible reaction of Mrs Reilly if she ever got to know. Only his two brothers surreptitiously welcomed his way of life. They hadn't made university and the difference between their comfortable life style – houses on an executive estate, en suite bathrooms, artificial coal fires in what they called the lounge, working wives, a new car every two years and timeshares in Majorca – provided both with agreeable hours of self-satisfied comparisons which he knew would always end with the same conclusion, that he ought to pull himself together, that it wasn't right, not after all the sacrifices Mum and Dad had made to send him to college, and a fine waste of money that had proved.

He had told Amy none of this but would have happily confided had she shown the least interest. But she asked no questions about his past life and told him nothing about hers. Her voice, her body, her smell were as familiar to him as his own, but essentially he knew no more about her now than when she had arrived. She refused to collect any welfare benefits, saying that she wasn't going to have DHSS snoopers visiting the caravan to see if she and Neil were sleeping together. He sympathized. He didn't want them either, but he felt that for Timmy's sake she should take what was on offer. He had given her no money but he did feed both of them, and this was difficult enough on his grant. No one visited her and no one telephoned. Occasionally she would receive a postcard, coloured views usually of London with nondescript, meaningless messages, but as far as he knew she never replied.

They had so little in common. She helped spasmodically with PANUP but he was never sure how far she was actually committed. And he knew that she found his pacifism stupid. He could recall a conversation only this morning.

'Look, if I live next door to an enemy and he has a knife, a gun and a machine gun and I've got the same, I'm not going to chuck mine before he chucks his. I'll say, OK, let the knife go, then the gun maybe, then the machine gun. Him and me at the same time. Why should I throw mine away and leave him with his?'

'But one of you has to make a start, Amy. There has to be a beginning of trust. Whether it's people or nations, we have to find the faith to open our hearts and hands and say, "Look, I've nothing. I've only my humanity. We inhabit the same planet. The world is full of pain but we needn't add to it. There has to be an end of fear."'

She had said obstinately: 'I don't see why he should chuck his weapons once he knows I've got nothing.'

'Why should he keep them? He's got nothing to fear from you any more.'

'He'd keep them because he liked the feeling of having them and because he might like to use them some day. He'd like the power and he'd like knowing he had me where he wanted me. Honestly, Neil, you're so naïve sometimes. That's how people are.'

'But we can't argue like that any more, Amy. We aren't talking about knives and guns and machine guns. We're talking about weapons neither of us could use without destroying ourselves and probably our whole planet. But it's good of you to help with PANUP when you don't sympathize.'

She had said: 'PANUP's different. And I sympathize all right. I just think that you're wasting your time writing letters, making speeches, sending out all those pamphlets. It won't do any good. You've got to fight people their way.'

'But it's done good already. All over the world ordinary people are marching, demonstrating, making their voices heard, letting the people in power know that what they want is a peaceful world for themselves and their children. Ordinary people like you.'

And then she had almost shouted at him: 'I'm not ordinary! Don't you call me ordinary! If there are ordinary people, I'm not one of them.'

'I'm sorry, Amy. I didn't mean it like that.'

'Then don't say it.'

The only cause they had in common was a refusal to eat meat. Soon after she arrived at the caravan he had said: 'I'm vegetarian but I don't expect you to be, or Timmy.' He had wondered as he spoke whether Timmy was old enough to eat meat. He had added: 'You can buy a chop occasionally in Norwich if you feel like it.'

'What you have is all right by me. Animals don't eat me, and I don't eat them.'

'And Timmy?'

'Timmy has what I give him. He's not fussy.'

Nor was he. Neil couldn't imagine a more accommodating child nor, for most of the time, a more contented one. He had found the second-hand playpen advertised on a newsagent's board in Norwich and had brought it back on the top of the van. In it Timmy would crawl for hours or pull himself up and stand precariously balancing, his napkin invariably falling about his knees. When thwarted he would rage, shutting his eyes tight, opening his mouth and holding his breath before letting out a bellow of such terrifying power that Neil half expected the whole of Lydsett to come running to see which of them was tormenting the child. Amy never smacked him but would jerk him on to her hip and dump him on her bed saying: 'Bloody awful noise.'

'Shouldn't you stay with him? Holding his breath like that, he could kill himself.'

'You daft? He won't kill himself. They never do.'

And he knew now that he wanted her, wanted her when it was obvious that she didn't want him and would never again risk rejection. On the second night at the caravan she had slid back the partition between his bed and hers and had walked quietly up to his bed and had stood gravely looking down at him. She had been completely naked. He had said: 'Look, Amy, you don't have to pay me.'

'I never pay for anything, at least not like that. But have it your own way.' After a pause she had said: 'You gay or something?'

'No, it's just that I don't like casual affairs.'

'You mean you don't like them, or you don't think you ought to have them?'

'I suppose I mean that I don't think I ought to have them.'

'You religious, then?'

'No, I'm not religious, not in the ordinary way. It's just that I think sex is too important to be casual about. You see, if we slept together and I – if I disappointed you – we might quarrel and then you'd walk out. You'd feel that you had to. You'd leave, you and Timmy.'

'So what, I walk out.'

40

'I wouldn't want you to do that, not because of anything I'd done.'

'Or hadn't done. OK, I expect you're right.' Another pause, and then she had added: 'You'd mind then, if I walked out?'

'Yes,' he said, 'I'd mind.'

She had turned away. 'I always do walk out in the end. No one has ever minded before.'

It was the only sexual advance she had ever made to him and he knew it would be the last. Now they slept with Timmy's cot wedged between the partition and his bed. Sometimes in the night, wakeful because the child had stirred, he would put out his hands and clasp the bars and long to shake this frail barrier that symbolized the unbridgeable gulf between them. She lay there, sleek and curved as a fish or a gull, so close that he could hear the rise and fall of her breath faintly echoing the suspiration of the sea. His body ached for her and he would press his face into the lumpy pillow groaning with the hopelessness of his need. What could she possibly see in him to make her want him, except, as on that one night, out of gratitude, pity, curiosity or boredom? He hated his body, the scrawny legs on which the kneecaps protruded like deformities, the small blinking eyes too closely set, the sparse beard which couldn't disguise the weakness of the mouth and chin. Sometimes, too, he was tormented by jealousy. Without proof, he had convinced himself that there was someone else. She would say that she wanted to walk alone on the headland. And he would watch her go with the certainty that she was meeting a lover. And when she returned he would imagine that he could see the glow of the skin, the satisfied smile of remembered happiness, could almost smell that she had been making love.

He had already heard from the university that his research grant would not be extended. The decision wasn't surprising; he had been warned to expect it. He had been saving as much as possible from the grant in the hope of amassing a small sum which would tide him over until he could find a local job. It hardly mattered what. Anything that would pay enough to live and allow him to remain on the headland to carry on the campaign. In theory he supposed he could organize PANUP from anywhere in the UK, but he knew that it was irrevocably bound to Larksoken headland, to the caravan, to that concrete mass five miles to the north which had power, apparently, to dominate his will as it did his imagination. He had already put out feelers with local employers but they hadn't been too keen on employing a well-known agitator; even those who seemed sympathetic to the anti-nuclear

41

cause didn't actually have work on offer. Perhaps they feared that too many of his energies would be diverted to the campaign. And his small capital was draining away with the extra expense of Amy, Timmy and even the cats. And now there was the threat of this libel action, less of a threat than a certainty.

When, ten minutes later, he returned to the caravan Amy, too, had given up working. She was lying on her bed, looking up at the ceiling, Smudge and Whisky curled on her stomach.

Looking down at her, he said abruptly: 'If the Robarts legal action goes ahead I'll need money. We're not going to be able to go on as we are. We've got to make plans.'

She sat up smartly and stared at him. The kittens, affronted, squealed their protest and fled. 'You mean we might have to leave here?'

The 'we' would normally have lifted his heart, now he hardly noticed it. 'It's possible.'

'But why? I mean, you aren't going to find anything cheaper than the caravan. Try getting a single room for two pounds a week. We're bloody lucky to have this place.'

'But there's no work here, Amy. If I have huge damages to pay, I'll have to get a job. That means London.'

'What sort of a job?'

'Any sort. I've got my degree.'

'Well, I can't see the sense of leaving here, even if there isn't any work. You can go to the DHSS. Draw the dole.'

'That isn't going to pay damages.'

'Well, if you have to go, maybe I'll stay on. I can pay the rent here. After all, what's the difference to the owner? He'll get his two quid whoever pays it.'

'You couldn't live here alone.'

'Why not? I've lived in worse places.'

'On what? What would you do for money?'

'Well, with you gone I could go to the DHSS, couldn't I? They could send their snoopers round and it wouldn't matter. They wouldn't be able to say I was having sex with you then, not if you weren't here. Anyway, I've got a bit in my post office account.'

The casual cruelty of the suggestion struck at his heart. He heard with heavy disgust the note of self-pity which he was unable to suppress. He said: 'Is that what you really want, Amy, for me not to be here?'

'Don't be daft, I was only teasing. Honestly Neil, you should see yourself. Talk about misery. Anyway, it might not happen – the libel action, I mean.'

'It's bound to happen unless she withdraws it. They've set a date for the hearing.'

'She might withdraw it, or else she might die. She might drown on one of those night swims she takes after the headlines on the nine o'clock news, regular as clockwork, right up to December.'

'Who told you that? How do you know that she swims at night?'

'You did.'

'I can't remember telling you.'

'Then someone else did, one of the regulars in the Local Hero, maybe. I mean, it's no secret, is it?'

He said: 'She won't drown. She's a strong swimmer. She wouldn't take foolish risks. And I can't wish her dead. You can't preach love and practise hatred.'

'I can – wish her dead, I mean. Maybe the Whistler will get her. Or you might win the action and then she'll have to pay you. That'd be a laugh.'

'That's not very likely. I consulted a lawyer at the Citizens Advice Bureau when I was in Norwich last Friday. I could see he thought it was serious, that she did have a case. He said I ought to get myself a lawyer.'

'Well, get one.'

'How? Lawyers cost money.'

'Get legal aid. Put a note in the newsletter asking for contributions.'

'I can't do that. It's difficult enough keeping the newsletter going, what with the cost of paper and postage.'

Amy said, suddenly serious: 'I'll think of something. There's still four weeks to go. Anything can happen in four weeks. Stop worrying. It's going to be all right. Look, Neil, I promise you that libel action will never come to court.' And illogically, he was, for the moment, reassured and comforted.

7

It was six o'clock and at Larksoken Power Station, the weekly interdepartmental meeting was drawing to a close. It had lasted thirty minutes longer than usual; Dr Alex Mair took the view, which he could normally enforce by brisk chairmanship, that little original thought was contributed to a discussion after three hours of talking. But it had been a heavy agenda: the revised safety plan still in draft; the rationalization of the internal structure from the present seven departments to three under engineering, production and resources; the report of the district survey laboratory on their monitoring of the environment; the preliminary agenda for the local liaison committee. This annual jamboree was an unwieldy but useful public relations exercise which needed careful preparation, including as it did representatives from the interested government departments, local authorities, police, fire and water authorities, the National Farmers Union and the Country Landowners' Association. Mair sometimes grudged the work and time it involved but he knew its importance.

The weekly meeting was held in his office at the conference table set in front of the south window. Darkness was falling and the huge pane of glass was a black rectangle in which he could see their faces reflected, like the gaunt, disembodied heads of night travellers in a lighted railway carriage. He suspected that some of his departmental heads, particularly Bill Morgan, the Works Office Engineer, and Stephen Mansell, the Maintenance Superintendent, would have preferred a more relaxed setting in his private sitting room next door, the low, comfortable chairs, a few hours of chat with no set agenda, perhaps a drink together afterwards in a local pub. Well, that was one management style, but it wasn't his.

Now he closed the stiff cover of his folder in which his PA had meticulously tagged all the papers and cross-references, and said dismissively: 'Any other business.'

But he was not allowed to get away so easily. On his right, as usual, sat Miles Lessingham, the Operations Superintendent, whose reflection, staring back into the room, looked like a hydrocephalic death's head. Glancing from the image to the face, Mair could see

44

little difference. The stark overhead lights threw deep shadows under the deep-set eyes and the sweat glistened on the wide, rather knobbly forehead with its swathe of fair undisciplined hair. Now he stretched back in his chair and said: 'This proposed job – rumoured job, I should say – I suppose we're entitled to ask whether it has been formally offered to you yet? Or aren't we?'

Mair said calmly: 'The answer is that it hasn't; the publicity was premature. The press got hold of it somehow, as they usually do, but there's nothing official yet. One unfortunate result of our present habit of leaking any information of interest is that the people most concerned become the last to know. If and when it is official you seven will be the first to be told.'

Lessingham said: 'It will have serious implications here, Alex, if you do go. The contract already signed for the new PWR reactor, the internal reorganization which is bound to create disruption, electricity privatization. It's a bad time for a change at the top.'

Mair said: 'Is there ever a good time? But until it happens, if it does happen, there's little point in discussing it.'

John Standing, the station chemist, said: 'But the internal reorganization will go ahead presumably?'

'I hope so, considering the time and energy we've spent planning it. I should be surprised if a change at the top alters a necessary reorganization which is already under way.'

Lessingham asked: 'Who will they appoint, a director or a station manager?' The question was less innocent than it sounded.

'I imagine a station manager.'

'You mean that the research will go?'

Mair said: 'When I go, now or later, the research will go. You've always known that. I brought it with me and I wouldn't have taken the job if I couldn't have continued it here. I asked for certain research facilities and I got them. But research at Larksoken has always been somewhat of an anomaly. We've done good work, are still doing good work, but logically it should be done elsewhere, at Harwell or Winfrith. Is there any other business?'

But Lessingham was not to be discouraged. He said: 'Who will you be responsible to? The Secretary of State for Energy directly or the AEA?'

Mair knew the answer but had no intention of giving it. He said quietly: 'That is still under discussion.'

'Along, no doubt, with such minor matters as pay, rations, scope

45

of your responsibilities and what you are going to be called. Controller of Nuclear Power has a certain cachet. I like it. But what precisely will you control?'

There was a silence. Mair said: 'If the answer to that question were known, no doubt the appointment would have been made by now. I don't want to stifle discussion, but hadn't we better confine it to matters within the competence of this committee? Right, is there any other business?' and this time there was no reply.

Hilary Robarts, the Acting Administrative Officer, had already closed her file. She hadn't taken part in the questioning but the others, Mair knew, would assume that that was because he had already told her the answers.

Even before they had left, his PA, Caroline Amphlett, had come in to take away the tea cups and clear the table. Lessingham made it a habit to leave his agenda behind, a small personal protest against the amount of paper which the formal weekly meeting generated. Dr Martin Goss, head of the medical physics department, had, as always, doodled obsessively. His jotting pad was covered with hot-air balloons, intricately patterned and decorated; part of his mind had obviously been with his private passion. Caroline Amphlett moved, as always, with a quiet, efficient grace. Neither spoke. She had worked for Mair as his PA for the last three years and he knew her now no better than on that morning when she had sat in this same office being interviewed for the job. She was a tall, blonde girl, smooth-skinned with wide-spaced, rather small eyes of an extra-ordinary deep blue, who would have been thought beautiful if she had shown more animation. Mair suspected that she used her confidential job as his PA to preserve a deliberately intimidating reserve. She was the most efficient secretary he had ever had and it irked him that she had made it clear that, if and when he moved, she would wish to stay at Larksoken. She had told him that her reasons were personal. That, of course, meant Jonathan Reeves, a junior engineer in the workshop. He had been as surprised and chagrined at her choice as he had at the prospect of taking up a new job with an unknown PA, but there had been an additional and more disturbing reaction. Hers was not a type of female beauty which attracted him and he had always assumed that she was physically cold. It was disconcerting to think that an acned nonenity had discovered and perhaps explored depths which he, in their daily intimacy, hadn't even suspected. He had sometimes wondered, although with little real curiosity, whether she might not be less compliant, more complicated than he had supposed, had occasionally had a disconcerting sense that the façade she presented to the power station of dedicated, humourless efficiency had been carefully constructed to conceal a less accommodating, more complex personality. But if the real Caroline was accessible to Jonathan Reeves, if she really liked and wanted that unprepossessing wimp, then she hardly merited the tribute even of his curiosity.

8

He gave his departmental heads time to get back to their offices
before he rang for Hilary Robarts and asked her to come back. It
would have been more usual to have asked her with careful casual-
ness to wait behind after the meeting but what he had to say was
private and he had been trying for some weeks now to cut down the
number of times when they were known to be alone together. He
wasn't looking forward to the interview. She would see what he had
to say as personal criticism and that was something which in his
experience few women could take. He thought: She was my mistress
once. I was in love with her, as much in love as I thought I was
capable of being. And if it wasn't love, whatever that word means, at
least I wanted her. Will that make what I have to say easier or more
difficult? He told himself that all men were cowards when it came to a
showdown with a woman. That first post-natal subservience, bred of
physical dependence, was too ingrained ever to be totally eradi-
cated. He wasn't more cowardly than the rest of his sex. What was it
he had overheard that woman in the Lydsett stores saying? 'George
would do anything to avoid a scene.' Of course he would, poor sod.
Women with their womb-smelling warmth, their talcum powder
and milky breasts had seen to that in the first four weeks of life.

He stood up when she came in and waited until she had taken the
chair on the other side of the desk. Then he opened the right-hand
drawer and took out a duplicated news-sheet which he slid across
the desk towards her.

'Have you seen this? It's Neil Pascoe's latest news-sheet from
PANUP.'

She said: 'People Against Nuclear Power. That means Pascoe and
a few dozen other ill-informed hysterics. Of course I've seen it, I'm
on his mailing list. He takes good care that I see it.'

She gave it a brief glance, then pushed it back across the desk. He
took it up and read: 'Many readers will probably have learned by
now that I am being sued by Miss Hilary Robarts, the Acting
Administrative Officer at Larksoken Power Station, for alleged libel
arising from what I wrote in the May issue of the news-sheet. I shall,

of course, strenuously defend the action and, as I have no money to pay for a lawyer, will present my own defence. This is just the latest example of the threat to free information and even free speech presented by the nuclear energy lobby. Apparently now even the mildest criticism is to be followed by the threat of legal action. But there is a positive side. This action by Hilary Robarts shows that we, the ordinary people of this county, are making our impact. Would they bother with our small news-sheet if they weren't running scared? And the libel action, if it comes to trial, will give us valuable national publicity if properly handled. We are stronger than we know. Meanwhile I give below the dates of the next open days at Larksoken so that as many of us as possible can attend and strenuously put our case against nuclear power during the question time which normally precedes the actual tour of the station.'

She said: 'I told you, I've seen it. I don't know why you wasted your time reading it out. He seems determined to aggravate his offence. If he had any sense he'd get himself a good lawyer and keep his mouth shut.'

'He can't afford a lawyer. And he won't be able to pay damages.' He paused, and then said quietly: 'In the interests of the station I think you should drop it.'

'Is that an order?'

'I've no power to compel you and you know that. I'm asking you. You'll get nothing out of him, the man's practically penniless, and he isn't worth the trouble.'

'He is to me. What he describes as mild criticism was a serious libel and it was widely disseminated. There's no defence. Remember the actual words? "A woman whose response to Chernobyl is that only thirty-one people were killed, who can dismiss as unimportant one of the world's greatest nuclear disasters which put thousands in hospital, exposed a hundred thousand or more to dangerous radioactivity, devastated vast areas of land, and may result in deaths from cancer amounting to fifty thousand over the next fifty years, is totally unsuitable to be trusted to work in an atomic power station. While she remains there, in any capacity, we must have the gravest doubts whether safety will ever be taken seriously at Larksoken." That's a clear allegation of professional incompetence. If he's allowed to get away with that, we'll never get rid of him.'

'I wasn't aware that we were in the business of getting rid of inconvenient critics. What method had you in mind?' He paused, detecting in his voice the first trace of that reedy mixture of sarcasm and pomposity which he knew occasionally affected him and to which he was morbidly sensitive. He went on: 'He's a free citizen living where he chooses. He's entitled to his views. Hilary, he's not a worthy opponent. Bring him to court and he'll attract publicity for his cause and do your own no good at all. We're trying to win over the locals, not antagonize them. Let it go before someone starts a fund to pay for his defence. One martyr on Larksoken headland is enough.'

While he was speaking she got up and began pacing to and fro across the wide office. Then she paused and turned to him. 'This is what it's all about, isn't it? The reputation of the station, your reputation. What about my reputation? If I drop the action now it will be a clear admission that he was right, that I'm not fit to work here.'

'What he wrote hasn't hurt your reputation with anyone who matters. And suing him isn't going to help it. It's unwise to let policy be influenced, let alone jeopardized, by outraged personal pride. The reasonable course is quietly to drop the action. What do feelings matter?' He found that he couldn't remain seated while she was striding to and fro across the office. He got to his feet and walked over to the window hearing the angry voice but no longer having to face her, watching the reflection of her pacing figure, the swirling hair. He said again: 'What do feelings matter? It's the work that is important.'

'They matter to me. And that's something you've never under-stood, have you? Life is about feeling. Loving is about feeling. It was the same with the abortion. You forced me to have it. Did you ever ask yourself what I felt then, what I needed?'

Oh God, he thought, not this, not again, not now. He said, still with his back to her: 'It's ridiculous to say that I forced you. How could I? And I thought you felt as I did, that it was impossible for you to have a child.'

'Oh no, it wasn't. If you're so bloody keen on accuracy, let's be accurate about this. It would have been inconvenient, embarrassing, awkward, expensive. But it wasn't impossible. It still isn't imposs-ible. And, for God's sake, turn around. Look at me. I'm talking to you. What I'm saying is important.'

He turned and walked back to the desk. He said calmly: 'All right, my phrasing was inaccurate. Have a child by all means if that's what you want. I'll be happy for you as long as you don't expect me to father it. But what we're talking about now is Neil Pascoe and

PANUP. We've gone to a lot of trouble here to promote good relations with the local community and I'm not going to have all that good work vitiated by a totally unnecessary legal action, particularly not now when work will soon begin on the new reactor.'

'Then try to prevent it. And since we're talking about public relations, I'm surprised you haven't mentioned Ryan Blaney and Scudder's Cottage. My cottage, in case you've forgotten. What am I expected to do about that? Hand over my property to him and his kids rent-free in the interests of good public relations?'

'That's a different matter. It's not my concern as Director. But if you want my opinion, I think you're ill-advised to try and force him out simply because you've got a legal case. He's paying the rent regularly, isn't he? And it isn't as if you want the cottage.'

'I do want the cottage. It's mine. I bought it and now I want to sell it.'

She slumped back into the chair and he, too, sat. He made himself stare into the eyes in which, to his discomfort, he saw more pain than anger. He said: 'Presumably he knows that and he'll get out when he can, but it won't be easy. He's recently widowed and he's got four children. There's a certain amount of local feeling about it, I understand.'

'I've no doubt there is, particularly in the Local Hero where Ryan Blaney spends most of his time and money. I'm not prepared to wait. If we're moving to London in the next three months there's not much time to get the question of the cottage settled. I don't want to leave that kind of unfinished business. I want to get it on the market as soon as possible.'

He knew that this was the moment when he should have said firmly: 'I may be moving to London, but not with you.' But he found it impossible. He told himself that it was late, the end of a busy day, the worst possible time for rational argument. She was already overwrought. One thing at a time. He had tackled her about Pascoe and, although she had reacted much as he'd expected, perhaps she would think it over and do what he advised. And she was right about Ryan Blaney; it was none of his business. The interview had left him with two clear intentions more firmly fixed than ever in his mind. She wasn't coming to London with him and nor would he recommend her as Administrative Officer at Larksoken. For all her efficiency, her intelligence, her appropriate education, she wasn't the right person for the job. For a moment it crossed his mind that here was his bargaining card. 'I'm not offering you marriage but I am offering you the most senior job you could possibly aspire to.' But he knew there was no real temptation. He wouldn't leave the administration of Larksoken in her hands. Sooner or later she was going to have to realize that there would be no marriage and no promotion. But now was the wrong moment and he found himself wondering wryly when the right moment might be.

Instead he said: 'Look, we're here to run a power station efficiently and safely. We're doing a necessary and important job. Of course we're committed to it, we wouldn't be here otherwise. But we're scientists and technicians, not evangelists. We're not running a religious campaign.'

'They are, the other side. He is. You see him as an insignificant twit. He isn't. He's dishonest and he's dangerous. Look how he scrubs around in the records to turn up individual cases of leukaemia which he thinks he can ascribe to nuclear energy. And now he's got the latest Comare report to fuel his spurious concern. And what about last month's newsletter, that emotive nonsense about the midnight trains of death trundling silently through the northern suburbs of London? Anyone would think they were carrying open trucks of radioactive waste. Doesn't he care that nuclear energy has so far saved the world from burning five hundred million tons of coal? Hasn't he heard about the greenhouse effect? I mean, is the fool totally ignorant? Hasn't he any conception of the devastation caused to this planet by burning fossil fuels? Has no one told him about acid rain or the carcinogens in coal waste? And when it comes to danger, what about the fifty-seven miners buried alive in the Borken disaster only this year? Don't their lives matter? Think of the outcry if that had been a nuclear accident.'

He said: 'He's only one voice and a pathetically uneducated and ignorant one.'

'But he's having his effect and you know it. We've got to match passion with passion.'

His mind fastened on the word. We're not, he thought, talking about nuclear energy, we're talking about passion. Would we be having this conversation if we were still lovers? She's demanding from me a commitment to something more personal than atomic power. Turning to face her, he was visited suddenly, not by desire, but by a memory, inconveniently intense, of the desire he had once felt for her. And with memory came a sudden vivid picture of them together in her cottage, the heavy breasts bent over him, her hair falling across his face, her lips, her hands, her thighs.

He said roughly: 'If you want a religion, if you need a religion, then find one. There are plenty to choose from. All right the abbey is in ruins and I doubt whether that impotent old priest up at the Old Rectory has much on offer. But find something or someone; give up fish on Friday, don't eat meat, count beads, put ashes on your head, meditate four times a day, bow down towards your own personal Mecca. But don't, for God's sake, assuming He exists, ever make science into a religion.'

The telephone on his desk rang. Caroline Amphlett had left and it was switched through to an outside line. As he lifted the receiver he saw that Hilary was standing at the door. She gave him a last long look and went out, shutting it with unnecessary firmness behind her.

The caller was his sister. She said: 'I hoped I'd catch you. I forgot to remind you to call at Bollard's farm for the ducks for Thursday. He'll have them ready. We'll be six, incidentally. I've invited Adam Dalgliesh. He's back on the headland.'

He was able to answer her as calmly as she had spoken.

'Congratulations. He and his aunt have contrived with some skill to avoid their neighbours' cutlets for the last five years. How did you manage it?'

'By the expedient of asking. I imagine he may be thinking of keeping on the mill as a holiday home and feels it's time to acknowledge that he does have neighbours. Or he may be planning to sell, in which case he can risk a dinner party without being trapped into intimacy. But why not give him credit for a simple human weakness; the attraction of eating a good dinner which he hasn't had to cook?'

And it would balance her table, thought Mair, although that was hardly likely to have been a consideration. She despised the Noah's Ark convention which decreed that a superfluous man, however unattractive or stupid, was acceptable; a superfluous woman, however witty and well-informed, a social embarrassment.

He said: 'Am I expected to talk about his poetry?'

'I imagine he's come to Larksoken to get away from people who want to talk about his poetry. But it wouldn't hurt you to take a look at it. I've got the most recent volume. And it is poetry, not prose rearranged on the page.'

'With modern verse, can one tell the difference?'

'Oh yes,' she said. 'If it can be read as prose, then it is prose. It's an infallible test.'

'But not one, I imagine, that the English faculties would support. I'll be leaving in ten minutes. I won't forget the ducks.' He smiled as he replaced the receiver. His sister invariably had the power to restore him to good humour.

9

Before leaving he stood for a moment at the door and let his eyes range round the room as if he were seeing it for the first time. He was ambitious for the new job, had cleverly planned and schemed to get it. And now, when it was almost his, he realized how much he would miss Larksoken, its remoteness, its bleak uncompromising strength. Nothing had been done to prettify the site as at Sizewell, on the Suffolk coast, or to produce the pleasantly laid-out grounds of smooth lawn, flowering trees and shrubs which so agreeably impressed him on his periodic visits to Winfrith in Dorset. A low, curving wall faced with flint had been built on the seaward boundary behind whose shelter every spring a bright ribbon of daffodils strained and tossed in the March winds. Little else had been done to harmonize or soften the concrete's grey immensity. But this was what he liked, the wide expanse of turbulent sea, browny-grey, white-laced under a limitless sky, windows which he could open so that, at a touch of his hand, the faint continuous boom like distant thunder would instantaneously pour into his office in a roar of crashing billows. He liked best the stormy winter evenings when, working late, he could see the lights of shipping prinking the horizon as they made their way down the coast to the Yarmouth lanes, and see the flashing lightships and the beam from Happisburgh Light-house, which for generations had warned mariners of the treacher-ous offshore sands. Even on the darkest night, by the light which the sea seemed mysteriously to absorb and reflect, he could make out the splendid fifteenth-century west tower of Happisburgh Church, that embattled symbol of man's precarious defences against this most dangerous of seas. And it was a symbol of more than that. The tower must have been the last sight of land for hundreds of drowning mariners in peace and war. His mind, always tenacious of facts, could recall the details at will. The crew of HMS *Peggy*, driven ashore on 19 December 1770, the 119 members of HMS *Invincible* wrecked on the sands on 13 March 1801 when on her way to join Nelson's fleet at Copenhagen, the crew of HMS *Hunter*, the revenue cutter, lost in 1804, many of their crews buried under the grassy mounds in

Happisburgh Churchyard. Built in an age of faith, the tower had stood as a symbol, too, of that final unquenchable hope that even the sea would yield up her dead and that their God was God of the waters as he was of the land. But now mariners could see, dwarfing the tower, the huge rectangular bulk of Larksoken Power Station. For those who sought symbols in inanimate objects its message was both simple and expedient, that man, by his own intelligence and his own efforts, could understand and master his world, could make his transitory life more agreeable, more comfortable, more free of pain. For him this was challenging enough, and if he had needed a faith to live by it would have been starkly sufficient. But sometimes, on the darkest nights, when the waves pounded the shingle like bursts of distant gunfire, both the science and the symbol would seem to him as transitory as those drowned lives and he would find himself wondering if this great hulk would one day yield to the sea, like the wave-smashed concrete from the last war defences, and like them become a broken symbol of man's long history on this desolate coast. Or would it resist even time and the North Sea and still be standing when the final darkness fell over the planet? In his more pessimistic moments some rogue part of his mind knew this darkness to be inevitable, although he did not expect it to come in his time, maybe not even in his son's. He would sometimes smile wryly, telling himself that he and Neil Pascoe, on different sides, would under-stand each other well. The only difference was that one of them had hope.

10

Jane Dalgliesh had bought Larksoken Mill five years earlier when she had moved from her previous home on the Suffolk coast. The mill, which was built in 1825, was a picturesque brick tower, four storeys high with an octagonal dome cap and skeleton fantail. It had been converted some years before Miss Dalgliesh had bought it by the addition of a flint-faced, two-storey building with a large sitting room, smaller study and a kitchen on the ground floor and three bedrooms, two of them with their own bathrooms, on the floor above. Dalgliesh had never asked her why she had moved to Norfolk but he guessed that the mill's main attraction had been its remoteness, its closeness to notable bird sanctuaries and the impressive view of headland, sky and sea from the top storey. Perhaps she had intended to restore it to working order but with increasing age hadn't been able to summon the energy or enthusiasm to cope with the disturbance. He had inherited it as an agreeable but mildly onerous responsibility, together with her considerable fortune. The origin of that had only become plain after her death. It had originally been left to her by a noted amateur ornithologist and eccentric with whom she had been friendly for many years. Whether the relationship had gone beyond friendship Dalgliesh would now never know. She had, apparently, spent little of the money on herself, had been a dependable benefactress of the few eccentric charities of which she approved, had remembered them in her will, but without egregious generosity, and had left the residue of her estate to him without explanation, admonition or peculiar protestations of affection, although he had no doubt that the words 'my dearly beloved nephew' meant exactly what they said. He had liked her, respected her, had always been at ease in her company, but he had never thought that he really knew her, and now he never would. He was a little surprised how much he minded.

The only change she had made to the property was to build a garage, and after he had unloaded and put away the Jaguar he decided to climb to the top chamber of the mill while it was still light. The bottom room, with its two huge grinding-wheels of burr-granite propped against the wall and its lingering smell of flour, still held an air of mystery, of time held in abeyance, of a place bereft of its purpose and meaning, so that he never entered it without a slight sense of desolation. There were only ladders between the floors and, as he grasped the rungs, he saw again his aunt's long trousered legs ahead of him disappearing into the chamber above. She had used only the top room of the mill which she had furnished simply with a small writing table and chair facing the North Sea, a telephone and her binoculars. Entering it he could imagine her sitting there in the summer days and evenings, working on the papers which she occasionally contributed to ornithological journals and looking up from time to time to gaze out over the headland to the sea and the far horizon, could see again that carved, weather-browned Aztec face with its hooded eyes under the grey-black hair, drawn back into a bun, could hear again a voice which, for him, had been one of the most beautiful female voices he had ever heard.

Now it was late afternoon and the headland lay enriched by the mellow afternoon light, the sea a wide expanse of wrinkled blue with a painter's stroke of purple laid on the horizon. The colours and shapes were intensified by the sun's last strong rays so that the ruins of the abbey looked unreal, a golden fantasy against the blue of the sea, and the dry grass gleamed as richly as a lush water meadow. There was a window at each of the compass points, and, binoculars in hand, he made his slow perambulation. To the west his eyes could travel along the narrow road between the reed beds and the dykes to the flint-walled and Dutch-gabled cottages and the pantiled roofs of Lydsett village and the round tower of St Andrew's Church. To the north the view was dominated by the huge bulk of the power station, the low-roofed administration block with, behind it, the reactor building and the great steel, aluminium-clad building of the turbine house. Four hundred metres out to sea were the rigs and platforms of the intake structures through which the cooling sea water passed to the pump house and the circulating water pumps. He moved again to the eastern window and looked out over the cottages of the headland. Far to the south he could just glimpse the roof of Scudder's Cottage. Directly to his left the flint walls of Martyr's Cottage glistened like marbles in the afternoon sun and less than half a mile to the north, set back among the Californian pines which fringed that part of the coast, was the dull square cottage rented by Hilary Robarts, a neatly proportional suburban villa incongruously set down on this bleak headland and facing inland as if resolutely ignoring the sea. Further inland, and only just visible from the southern window was the Old Rectory, set like a Victorian dolls' house in its large, overgrown garden which, at this distance, looked as neatly green and formal as a municipal park.

The telephone rang. The strident peal was unwelcome. It was to get away from such intrusions that he had come to Larksoken. But the call was not unexpected. It was Terry Rickards saying that he would like to drop in for a chat with Mr Dalgliesh if it wouldn't be too much bother and would nine be convenient? Dalgliesh was unable to think of a single excuse why it shouldn't be. Ten minutes later he left the tower, locking the door after him. This precaution was a small act of piety. His aunt had always kept the door locked, fearing that children might venture into the mill and hurt themselves by tumbling down the ladders. Leaving the tower to its darkness and its solitude, he went into Mill Cottage to unpack and get his supper.

The huge sitting room with its York stone floor, rugs and open fireplace was a comfortable and nostalgic mixture of the old and the new. Most of the furniture was familiar to him from boyhood visits to his grandparents, inherited by his aunt as the last of her generation. Only the music centre and the television set were comparatively new. Music had been important to her and the shelves held a catholic collection of records with which he could refresh or console himself during the two weeks' holiday. And next door, the kitchen contained nothing superfluous but everything necessary to a woman who enjoyed food but preferred to cook it with a minimum of fuss. He put a couple of lamb chops under the grill, made a green salad and prepared to enjoy a few hours of solitude before the intrusion of Rickards and his preoccupations.

It still surprised him a little that his aunt had finally bought a television set. Had she been seduced into conformity by the excellence of the natural history programmes and then, like other late converts he had known, sat captive to virtually every offering as if making up for lost time? That at least seemed unlikely. He switched on to see if the set was still working. A jerking pop star was wielding his guitar as the credits rolled, his parodic sexual gyrations so grotesque that it was difficult to see that even the besotted young could find them erotic. Switching off, Dalgliesh looked up at the oil portrait of his maternal great-grandfather, the Victorian bishop, robed but unmitred, his arms in their billowing lawn sleeves confidently resting on the arms of the chair. He had an impulse to say, 'This is the music of 1988; these are our heroes; that building on the headland is our architecture and I dare not stop my car to help children home because they've been taught with good reason that a strange man might abduct and rape them.' He could have added, 'And out there somewhere is a mass murderer who enjoys strangling women and stuffing their mouths with their hair.' But that aberration, at least, was independent of changing fashions and his great-grandfather would have had his scrupulous but uncompromising answer to it. And with reason. After all, hadn't he been consecrated bishop in 1888, the year of Jack the Ripper? And probably he would have found the Whistler more understandable than the pop star whose gyrations would surely have convinced him that man was in the grip of his final, manic St Vitus's dance.

Rickards came promptly on time. It was precisely nine when Dalgliesh heard his car and, opening the door on the darkness of the night, saw his tall figure striding towards him. Dalgliesh hadn't seen him for more than ten years when he had been a newly appointed inspector in the Metropolitan CID and was surprised to see how little he had changed; time, marriage, removal from London, promotion, had left no apparent mark on him. His rangy, graceless figure, over six feet high, still looked as incongruous in a formal suit as it always had. The rugged, weatherbeaten face, with its look of dependable fortitude, would have looked more appropriate above a seaman's guernsey, preferably with RNLI woven across the chest. In profile his face, with the long, slightly hooked nose and jutting eyebrows, was impressive. In full face the nose was revealed as a little too wide and flattened at the base and the dark eyes, which when he was animated took on a fierce, almost manic gleam, in repose were pools of puzzled endurance. Dalgliesh thought of him as a type of police officer less common than formerly but still not rare; the conscientious and incorruptible detective of limited imagination and somewhat greater intelligence who had never supposed that the evil of the world should be condoned because it was frequently inexplicable and its perpetrators unfortunate.

He gazed round the sitting room at the long wall of books, the crackling wood fire, the oil of the Victorian prelate above the mantelshelf as if deliberately impressing each item on his mind, then sank into his chair and stretched out his long legs with a small grunt of satisfaction. Dalgliesh remembered that he had always drunk beer; now he accepted whisky but said he could do with coffee first. One habit at least had changed. He said: 'I'm sorry that you won't be meeting Susie, my wife, while you're here, Mr Dalgliesh. She's having our first baby in a couple of weeks and she's gone to stay with her mother in York. Ma-in-law didn't like the idea of her being in Norfolk with the Whistler on the prowl, not with me working the hours I do.'

It was said with a kind of embarrassed formality as if he, not Dalgliesh, were the host and he was apologizing for the unexpected absence of the hostess. He added: 'I suppose it's natural for an only daughter to want to be with her mother at a time like this, particularly with a first baby.'

Dalgliesh's wife hadn't wanted to be with her mother, she had wanted to be with him, had wanted it with such intensity that he had wondered afterwards whether she might have felt a premonition. He could remember that, although he could no longer recall her face. His memory of her, which for years, a traitor to grief and to their love, he had resolutely tried to suppress because the pain had seemed unbearable, had gradually been replaced by a boyish, romantic dream of gentleness and beauty now fixed for ever beyond the depredation of time. His newborn son's face he could still recall vividly and sometimes did in his dreams, that white unsullied look of sweet knowledgeable contentment, as if, in a brief moment of life, he had seen and known all there was to know, seen it and rejected it. He told himself that he was the last man who could reasonably be expected to advise or reassure on the problems of pregnancy and he sensed that Rickards's unhappiness at his wife's absence went deeper than missing her company. He made the usual inquiries about her health and escaped into the kitchen to make the coffee.

Whatever mysterious spirit had unlocked the verse, it had freed him for other human satisfactions, for love; or was it the other way around? Had love unlocked the verse? It seemed even to have affected his job. Grinding the coffee beans he pondered life's smaller ambiguities. When the poetry hadn't come, the job too had seemed not only irksome but occasionally repellent. Now he was happy enough to let Rickards impose on his solitude to use him as a sounding board. This new benignity and tolerance a little disconcerted him. Success in moderation was no doubt better for the character than failure but too much of it and he would lose his cutting edge. And five minutes later, carrying in the two mugs and settling

61

back in his chair, he could relish the contrast between Rickards's preoccupation with psychopathic violence and the peace of the mill. The wood fire, now past its crackling stage, had settled into a comfortable glow and the wind, seldom absent from the headland, moved like a benign, gently hissing spirit through the still and soaring clappers of the mill. He was glad that it wasn't his job to catch the Whistler. Of all murders serial killings were the most frustrating, the most difficult and the chanciest to solve, the investigation carried on under the strain of vociferous public demand that the terrifying unknown devil be caught and exorcized for ever. But this wasn't his case; he could discuss it with the detachment of a man who has a professional interest but no responsibility. And he could understand what Rickards needed; not advice – he knew his job – but someone he could trust, someone who understood the language, someone who would afterwards be gone, who wouldn't remain as a perpetual reminder of his uncertainties, a fellow professional to whom he could comfortably think aloud. He had his team and he was too punctilious not to share his thinking with them. But he was a man who needed to articulate his theories and here he could put them forward, embroider, reject, explore without the uncomfortable suspicion that his detective sergeant, deferentially listening, his face carefully expressionless, would be thinking, For God's sake, what's the old man dreaming up now? Or, The old man's getting fanciful.

Rickards said: 'We're not using Holmes. The Met say the system is fully committed at present, and anyway we've got our own computer. Not that there's much data to feed in. The press and public know about Holmes, of course. I get that at every press conference. "Are you using the Home Office special computer, the one named after Sherlock Holmes?" "No," I say, "but we're using our own." Unspoken question: "Then why the hell haven't you caught him?" They think that you've only got to feed in your data and out pops an Identikit of sonny complete with prints, collar-size and taste in pop music.'

'Yes,' said Dalgliesh, 'we're so sated now with scientific wonders that it's a bit disconcerting when we find that technology can do everything except what we want it to.'

'Four women so far and Valerie Mitchell won't be the last if we don't catch him soon. He started fifteen months ago. The first victim was found just after midnight in a shelter at the end of the Easthaven promenade, the local tart, incidentally, although he may not have known or cared. It was eight months before he struck again. Struck lucky, I suppose he'd say. This time a thirty-year-old schoolteacher cycling home to Hunstanton who had a puncture on a lonely stretch of road. Then another gap, just six months, before he got a barmaid from Ipswich who'd been visiting her granny and was daft enough to wait alone for the late bus. When it arrived there was no one at the stop. A couple of local youths got off. They'd had a skinful so weren't in a particularly noticing mood but they saw and heard nothing, nothing except what they described as a kind of mournful whistling coming from deep in the wood.'

He took a gulp of his coffee, then went on: 'We've got a personality assessment from the trick-cyclist. I don't know why we bother. I could have written it myself. He tells us to look for a loner, probably from a disturbed family background, may have a dominant mother, doesn't relate easily to people, particularly women, could be impotent, unmarried, separated or divorced, with a resentment and hatred of the opposite sex. Well, we hardly expect him to be a successful, happily married bank manager with four lovely kids just coming up to GCE or whatever they call it now. They're the devil, these serial murders. No motive – no motive that a sane man can understand anyway – and he could come from anywhere, Norwich, Ipswich, even London. It's dangerous to assume that he's necessarily working in his own territory. Looks like it, though. He obviously knows the locality well. And he seems to be sticking now to the same MO. He chooses a road intersection, drives the car or van into the side of one road, cuts across and waits at the other. Then he drags his victim into the bushes or the trees, kills and cuts back to the other road and the car and makes his getaway. With the last three murders it seems to have been pure chance that a suitable victim did, in fact, come along.'

Dalgliesh felt that it was time he contributed something to the speculation. He said: 'If he doesn't select and stalk his victim, and obviously he didn't in the last three cases, he'd normally have to expect a long wait. That suggests he's routinely out after dark, a night worker, mole-catcher, woodman, gamekeeper, that kind of job. And he goes prepared; on the watch for a quick kill, in more ways than one.'

Rickards said: 'That's how I see it. Four victims so far and three fortuitous, but he's probably been on the prowl for three years or more. That could be part of the thrill. 'Tonight I could make a strike, tonight I could be lucky. And, by God, he is getting lucky. Two victims in the last six weeks.'

'And what about his trademark, the whistle?'

'That was heard by the three people who came quickly on the scene after the Easthaven murder. One just heard a whistle, one said it sounded like a hymn and the third, who was a church woman, claimed she could identify it precisely, "Now the Day is Over". We kept quiet about that. It could be useful when we get the usual clutch of nutters claiming they're the Whistler. But there seems no doubt that he does whistle.'

Dalgliesh said: ' "Now the day is over / Night is drawing nigh / Shadows of the evening / Fall across the sky". It's a Sunday-school hymn, hardly the kind that gets requested on *Songs of Praise*, I should have thought.'

He remembered it from childhood, a lugubrious, undistinguished tune which, as a ten-year-old, he could pick out on the drawing-room piano. Did anyone sing that hymn now, he wondered? It had been a favourite choice of Miss Barnett on those long dark afternoons in winter before the Sunday school was released, when the outside light was fading and the small Adam Dalgliesh was already dreading those last twenty yards of his walk home where the rectory drive curved and the bushes grew thickest. Night was different from bright day, smelt different, sounded different; ordinary things assumed different shapes; an alien and more sinister power ruled the night. Those twenty yards of crunching gravel where the lights of the house were momentarily screened were a weekly horror. Once through the gate to the drive he would walk fast, but not too fast since the power that ruled the night could smell out fear as dogs smell out terror. His mother, he knew, would never have expected him to walk those yards alone had she known that he suffered such atavistic panic, but she hadn't known and he would have died before telling her. And his father? His father would have expected him to be brave, would have told him that God was God of the darkness as He was of the light. There were after all a dozen appropriate texts he could have quoted. 'Darkness and light are both alike to Thee.' But they were not alike to a sensitive ten-year-old boy. It was on those lonely walks that he had first had intimations of an essentially adult truth, that it is those who most love us who cause us the most pain. He said: 'So you're looking for a local man, a loner, someone who has a night job, the use of a car or van and a knowledge of *Hymns Ancient and Modern*. That should make it easier.'

Rickards said: 'You'd think so, wouldn't you.'

He sat in silence for a minute then said: 'I think I'd like just a small whisky now, Mr Dalgliesh, if it's all the same to you.'

It was after midnight when he finally left. Dalgliesh walked out with him to the car. Looking out across the headland Rickards said: 'He's out there somewhere, watching, waiting. There's hardly a waking moment when I don't think of him, imagine what he looks like, where he is, what he's thinking. Susie's ma is right. I haven't had much to give her recently. And when he's caught, that'll be the end. It's finished. You move on. He doesn't, but you do. And by the end you know everything, or think you do. Where, when, who, how? You might even know why if you're lucky. And yet, essentially, you know nothing. All that wickedness, and you don't have to explain it or understand it or do a bloody thing about it except put a stop to it. Involvement without responsibility. No responsibility for what he did or for what happens to him afterwards. That's for the judge and the jury. You're involved, and yet you're not involved. Is that what appeals to you about the job, Mr Dalgliesh?'

It was not a question Dalgliesh would have expected, even from a friend, and Rickards was not a friend. He said: 'Can any of us answer that question?'

'You remember why I left the Met, Mr Dalgliesh.'

'The two corruption cases? Yes, I remember why you left the Met.'

'And you stayed. You didn't like it any more than I did. You wouldn't have touched the pitch. But you stayed. You were detached about it all, weren't you? It interested you.'

Dalgliesh said: 'It's always interesting when men you thought you knew behave out of character.'

And Rickards had fled from London. In search of what? Dalgliesh wondered. Some romantic dream of country peace, an England which had vanished, a gentler method of policing, total honesty? He wondered whether he had found it.

BOOK TWO

Thursday 22 September to Friday 23 September

11

It was ten past seven and the saloon bar of the Duke of Clarence pub
was already smoke-filled, the noise level rising and the crowd at the
bar three feet deep. Christine Baldwin, the Whistler's fifth victim,
had exactly twenty minutes to live. She sat on the banquette against
the wall, sipping her second medium sherry of the evening, deliberately making it last, knowing that Colin was impatient to order the
next round. Catching Norman's eye, she raised her left wrist and
nodded significantly at her watch. Already, it was ten minutes past
their deadline and he knew it. Their agreement was that this was to
be a pre-supper drink with Colin and Yvonne, the limit both of time
and alcohol consumption clearly understood between her and
Norman before they left home. The arrangement was typical of their
nine-month-old marriage, sustained less by compatible interests
than by a carefully negotiated series of concessions. Tonight it had
been her turn to give way, but agreeing to spend an hour in the
Clarence with Colin and Yvonne didn't extend to any pretence that
she actually enjoyed their company.

She had disliked Colin since their first meeting; the relationship, at
a glance, had been fixed in the stereotyped antagonism between
newly acquired fiancée and slightly disreputable old schoolmate and
drinking partner. He had been best man at their wedding – a formidable pre-nuptial agreement had been necessary for that capitula-
tion – and had carried out his duties with a mixture of incompetence,
vulgarity and irreverence which, as she occasionally enjoyed telling
Norman, had spoilt for her the memory of her big day. It was typical
of him to choose this pub. God knew, it was vulgar enough. But at
least she could be certain of one thing: it wasn't a place where there
was a risk of meeting anyone from the power station, at least not
anyone who mattered. She disliked everything about the Clarence,
the rough scrape of the moquette against her legs, the synthetic
velvet which covered the walls, the baskets of ivy spiked with
artificial flowers above the bar, the gaudiness of the carpet. Twenty
years ago, it had been a cosy Victorian hostelry, seldom visited
except by its regulars, with an open fire in winter and horse brasses

polished to whiteness hung against the black beams. The lugubrious publican had seen it as his job to repel strangers and had employed to that end an impressive armoury of taciturnity, malevolent glances, warm beer and poor service. But the old pub had burnt down in the 1960s and been replaced by a more profitable and thrusting enterprise. Nothing of the old building remained and the long extension to the bar, dignified by the name Banqueting Hall, provided for the undiscriminating a venue for weddings and local functions and on other nights served a predictable menu of prawns or soup, steak or chicken, and fruit salad with ice-cream. Well, at least she had put her foot down over dinner. They had worked out their monthly budget to the last pound, and if Norman thought she was going to eat this overpriced muck with a perfectly good cold supper waiting in the refrigerator at home and a decent programme on the telly he could forget it. And they had better uses for their money than to sit here drinking with Colin and his latest tart who had opened her legs to half Norwich, if rumour were to be believed. There were the hire purchase repayments on the sitting-room furniture and the car, not to mention the mortgage. She tried again to meet Norman's eye but he was rather desperately keeping his attention on that slut Yvonne. And that wasn't proving difficult. Colin leaned over to her, his bold treacle-brown eyes half mocking, half inviting, Colin Lomas, who thought every woman would swoon when he beckoned.

'Relax, darling. Your old man's enjoying himself. It's your round, Norm.'

Ignoring Colin she spoke to Norman: 'Look, it's time we were going. We agreed we'd leave at seven.'

'Oh, come on, Chrissie, give the lad a break. One more round.'

Without meeting her eyes, Norman said: 'What'll you have, Yvonne? The same again? Medium sherry?'

Colin said: 'Let's get on to spirits. I'll have a Johnny Walker.'

He was doing it on purpose. She knew that he didn't even like whisky. She said: 'Look, I've had enough of this bloody place. The noise has given me a head.'

'A headache? Nine months married and she's started the headaches. No point in hurrying home tonight, Norm.'

Yvonne giggled.

Christine said, her face burning, 'You were always vulgar, Colin Lomas, but now you're not even funny with it. You three can do what you like. I'm going home. Give me the car keys.'

Colin leaned back and smiled. 'You heard what your lady wife said. She wants the car keys.'

Without a word, shamefaced, Norman took them out of his pocket and slid them over the table. She snatched them up, pushed back the table, struggled past Yvonne and rushed to the door. She was almost crying with rage. It took her a minute to unlock the car and then she sat shaking behind the wheel, waiting until her hands were steady enough to switch on the ignition. She heard her mother's voice on the day when she had announced her engagement: 'Well, you're thirty-two and if he's what you want I suppose you know your own mind. But you'll never make anything of him. Weak as water, if you ask me.' But she had thought that she could make something of him and that small semi-detached house outside Norwich represented nine months of hard work and achievement. Next year he was due for promotion at the insurance office. She would be able to give up her job as secretary in the medical physics department at Larksoken Power Station and start the first of the two children she had planned. She would be thirty-four by then. Everyone knew that you shouldn't wait too long.

She had only passed her driving test after her marriage and this was the first time that she had driven unaccompanied by night. She drove slowly and carefully, her anxious eyes peering ahead, glad that at least the route home was familiar. She wondered what Norman would do when he saw that the car had gone. Almost certainly he would expect to find her sitting there, fuming but ready to be driven home. Now he'd have to rely for a lift on Colin who wouldn't be so keen on coming out of his way. And if they thought that she was going to invite Colin and Yvonne in for a drink when they arrived they would get a shock. The thought of Norman's discomfiture at finding her gone cheered her a little and she pressed her foot down on the accelerator, anxious to distance herself from the three of them, to reach the safety of home. But suddenly the car gave a stutter and the engine died. She must have been driving more erratically than she thought for she found herself half skewed across the road. It was a bad place to be stranded, a lonely stretch of country lane with a thin band of trees on either side and it was deserted. And then she remembered. Norman had mentioned that they needed to fill up with petrol and must be sure to call at the all-night garage after they left the Clarence. It was ridiculous to have let the tank get so low but they had had an argument only three days earlier on whose turn

71

it was to call at the garage and pay for the petrol. All her anger and frustration returned. For a moment she sat there, beating her hands impotently on the wheel, desperately turning the key in the ignition, willing the engine to start. But there was no response. And then irritation began to give way to the first tricklings of fear. The road was deserted and even if a motorist came by and drew up, could she be certain that he wasn't a kidnapper, a rapist, even the Whistler? There had been that horrible murder on the A3 only this year. Nowadays you could trust no one. And she could hardly leave the car where it was, slewed across the road. She tried to recall when she had last passed a house, an AA box, a public telephone, but it seemed to her that she had been driving through deserted countryside for at least ten minutes. Even if she left the dubious sanctuary of the car she had no clue to the best direction in which to seek help. Suddenly a wave of total panic swept across her like nausea and she had to resist the urge to dash from the car and hide herself among the trees. But what good would that do? He might be lurking even there.

And then, miraculously, she heard footsteps and, looking round, saw a woman approaching. She was dressed in trousers and a trenchcoat and had a mane of fair hair beneath a tight-fitting beret. At her side on a leash trotted a small, smooth-haired dog. Immediately all her anxiety vanished. Here was someone who would help her push the car into the side of the road, who would know in which direction lay the nearest house, who would be a companion on her walk. Without even troubling to slam the door of the car she called out happily and ran smiling towards the horror of her death.

12

The dinner had been excellent and the wine, a Château Potensac '78, an interesting choice with the main course. Although Dalgliesh knew of Alice Mair's reputation as a cookery writer he had never read any of her books and had no idea to what culinary school, if any, she belonged. He had hardly feared being presented with the usual artistic creation swimming in a pool of sauce and accompanied by one or two undercooked carrots and mange-tout elegantly arranged on a side plate. But the wild ducks carved by Alex Mair had been recognizably ducks, the piquant sauce, new to him, enhanced rather than dominated the taste of the birds, and the small mounds of creamed turnip and parsnip were an agreeable addition to green peas. Afterwards they had eaten orange sorbet followed by cheese and fruit. It was a conventional menu but one intended, he felt, to please the guests rather than to demonstrate the ingenuity of the cook.

The expected fourth guest, Miles Lessingham, had unaccountably failed to arrive, but Alice Mair hadn't rearranged her table and the empty chair and unfilled wineglass were uncomfortably evocative of Banquo's ghost. Dalgliesh was seated opposite Hilary Robarts. The portrait, he thought, must have been even more powerful than he realized if it could so dominate his physical reaction to the living woman. It was the first time they had met although he had known of her existence as he had of all the handful of people who lived, as the Lydsett villagers said, 't'other side of the gate'. And it was a little strange that this was their first meeting; her red Golf was a frequent sight on the headland, her cottage had frequently met his eyes from the top storey of the mill. Now, physically close for the first time, he found it difficult to keep his eyes off her, living flesh and remembered image seeming to fuse into a presence both potent and disturbing. It was a handsome face, a model's face, he thought, with its high cheekbones, long, slightly concave nose, wide, full lips and dark, angry eyes deeply set under the strong brows. Her crimped, springing hair, held back with two combs, fell over her shoulders. He could imagine her posed, mouth moistly open, hips jutting and staring at the cameras with that apparently obligatory look of arrogant resentment. As she leaned forward to twitch another grape from the bunch and almost toss it into her mouth he could see the faint freckles which smudged the dark forehead, the glisten of hairs above a carved upper lip.

On the other side of their host sat Meg Dennison, delicately but unfussily peeling her grapes with pink-tipped fingers. Hilary Robarts's sultry handsomeness emphasized her own very different look, an old-fashioned, carefully tended but unselfconscious prettiness which reminded him of photographs of the late thirties. Their clothes emphasized the contrast. Hilary wore a shirtwaister dress in multicoloured Indian cotton, three buttons at the neck undone. Meg Dennison was in a long black skirt and a blue patterned silk blouse with a bow at the neck. But it was their hostess who was the most elegant. The long shift in fine dark brown wool worn with a heavy necklace of silver and amber hid her angularity and emphasized the strength and regularity of the strong features. Beside her Meg Dennison's prettiness was diminished almost to insipidity and Hilary Robarts's strong-coloured cotton looked tawdry.

The room in which they were dining must, he thought, have been part of the original cottage. From these smoke-blackened beams Agnes Poley had hung her sides of bacon, her bundles of dried herbs. In a pot slung over that huge hearth she had cooked her family's meals and, perhaps, at the end had heard in its roaring flames the crackling faggots of her dreadful martyrdom. Outside the long window had passed the helmets of marching men. But only in the name of the cottage was there a memory of the past. The oval dining table and the chairs were modern as were the Wedgwood dinner service and the elegant glasses. In the drawing room, where they had drunk their pre-dinner sherry, Dalgliesh had a sense of a room which deliberately rejected the past, containing nothing which could violate the owner's essential privacy; no family history in photograph or portrait, no shabby heirlooms given room out of nostalgia, sentimentality or family piety, no antiques collected over the years. Even the few pictures, three recognizably by John Piper, were modern. The furniture was expensive, comfortable, well designed, too elegantly simple to be offensively out of place. But the heart of the cottage wasn't there. It was in that large, warm-smelling and welcoming kitchen.

He had only been half listening to the conversation but now he forced himself to be a more accommodating guest. The talk was general, candlelit faces leaned across the table and the hands which peeled the fruit or fidgeted with the glasses were as individual as the faces. Alice Mair's strong but elegant hands with their short nails, Hilary Robarts's long, knobbled fingers, the delicacy of Meg Dennison's pink-tipped fingers, a little reddened with housework. Alex Mair was saying: 'All right, let's take a modern dilemma. We know that we can use human tissue from aborted foetuses to treat Parkinson's disease and probably Alzheimer's. Presumably you'd find that ethically acceptable if the abortion were natural or legal but not if it were induced for the purpose of providing the tissue. But you can argue that a woman has a right to the use that she makes of her own body. If she's particularly fond of someone who has Alzheimer's and wants to help him by producing a foetus, who has the right to say no? A foetus isn't a child.'

Hilary Robarts said: 'I notice that you assume the sufferer to be helped is a man. I suppose he'd feel entitled to use a woman's body for this purpose as he would any other. But why the hell should he? I can't imagine that a woman who's actually had an abortion wants to go through that again for any man's convenience.'

The words were spoken with extreme bitterness. There was a pause then Mair said quietly: 'Alzheimer's is rather more than an inconvenience. But I'm not advocating it. In any case, under present law, it would be illegal.'

'Would that worry you?'

He looked into her angry eyes. 'Naturally it would worry me. Happily it isn't a decision that I shall ever be required to make. But we're not talking about legality, we're talking about morality.'

His sister asked: 'Are they different?'

'That's the question, isn't it? Are they, Adam?'

It was the first time he had used Dalgliesh's Christian name. Dalgliesh said: 'You're assuming there's an absolute morality independent of time or circumstance.'

'Wouldn't you make that assumption?'

'Yes, I think I would, but I'm not a moral philosopher.'

Mrs Dennison looked up from her plate a little flushed and said: 'I'm always suspicious of the excuse that a sin is justified if it's done to benefit someone we love. We may think so, but it's usually to benefit ourselves. I might dread the thought of having to look after an Alzheimer patient. When we advocate euthanasia is it to stop pain

75

or to prevent our own distress at having to watch it? To conceive a child deliberately in order to kill it to make use of its tissue, the idea is absolutely repugnant.'

Alex Mair said: 'I could argue that what you are killing isn't a child and that repugnance at an act isn't evidence of its immorality.'

Dalgliesh said: 'But isn't it? Doesn't Mrs Dennison's natural repugnance tell us something about the morality of the act?'

She gave him a brief, grateful smile and went on: 'And isn't this use of a foetus particularly dangerous? It could lead to the poor of the world conceiving children and selling the foetuses to help the rich. Already I believe there's a black market in human organs. Do you think a multi-millionaire who needs a heart-lung transplant ever goes without?'

Alex Mair smiled. 'As long as you aren't arguing that we should deliberately suppress knowledge or reject scientific progress just because the discoveries can be abused. If there are abuses, legislate against them.'

Meg protested: 'But you make it sound so easy. If all we had to do was to legislate against social evils Mr Dalgliesh for one would be out of work.'

'It isn't easy but it has to be attempted. That's what being human means, surely, using our intelligence to make choices.'

Alice Mair got up from the table. She said: 'Well, it's time to make a choice now on a somewhat different level. Which of you would like coffee and what kind? There's a table and chairs in the courtyard. I thought we could switch on the yard lights and have it outside.'

They moved through to the drawing room and Alice Mair opened the french windows leading to the patio. Immediately the sonorous booming of the sea flowed into and took possession of the room like a vibrating and irresistible force. But once they had stepped out into the cool air, paradoxically, the noise seemed muted, the sea no more than a distant roar. The patio was bounded on the road side by a high flint wall which, to the south and east, curved to little more than four feet to give an unimpeded view across the headland to the sea.

The coffee tray was carried out by Alex Mair within minutes and, cups in hand, the little party wandered aimlessly among the terra-cotta pots like strangers reluctant to be introduced or like actors on a stage set, self-absorbed, pondering their lines, waiting for the rehearsal to begin.

They were without coats and the warmth of the night had proved illusory. They had turned as if by common consent to go back into the cottage when the lights of a car, driven fast, came over the southern rise of the road. As it approached its speed slackened.

Mair said: 'Lessingham's Porsche.'

No one spoke. They watched silently as the car was driven at speed off the road to brake violently on the turf of the headland. As if conforming to some prearranged ceremony they grouped themselves into a semicircle with Alex Mair a little to the front, like a formal welcoming party but one bracing itself for trouble rather than expecting pleasure from the approaching guest. Dalgliesh was aware of the heightening tension: small individual tremors of anxiety which shivered on the still, sea-scented air, unified and focused on the car door and on the tall figure which unwound from the driver's seat, leapt easily over the low stone wall and walked deliberately across the courtyard towards them. Lessingham ignored Mair and moved straight to Alice. He took her hand and gently kissed it, a theatrical gesture which Dalgliesh felt had taken her by surprise and which the others had watched with an unnaturally critical attention.

Lessingham said gently: 'My apologies, Alice. Too late for dinner, I know, but not, I hope, for a drink. And God, do I need one.'

'Where have you been? We waited dinner for forty minutes.' It was Hilary Robarts who asked the obvious question, sounding as accusatory as a peevish wife.

Lessingham kept his eye on Alice. He said: 'I've been considering how best to answer that question for the last twenty minutes. There are a number of interesting and dramatic possibilities. I could say that I've been helping the police with their inquiries. Or that I've been involved in a murder. Or that there was a little unpleasantness on the road. Actually it was all three. The Whistler has killed again. I found the body.'

Hilary Robarts said sharply: 'How do you mean, "found"? Where?'

Again Lessingham ignored her. He said to Alice Mair: 'Could I have that drink? Then I'll give you all the gory details. After unsettling your seating plan and delaying dinner for forty minutes that's the least I owe you.'

As they moved back into the drawing room Alex Mair introduced Dalgliesh. Lessingham gave him one sharp glance. They shook hands. The palm which momentarily touched his was moist and very cold.

77

Alex Mair said easily: 'Why didn't you ring? We would have kept some food for you.'

The question, conventionally domestic, sounded irrelevant, but Lessingham answered it. 'Do you know, I actually forgot. Not all the time, of course, but it honestly didn't cross my mind until the police had finished questioning me and then the moment didn't seem opportune. They were perfectly civil but I sensed that my private engagements had a pretty low priority. Incidentally, you get absolutely no credit from the police for finding a body for them. Their attitude is rather, "Thank you very much, sir, very nasty, I'm sure. Sorry you've been troubled. But we'll take over now. Just go home and try to forget all about it." I have a feeling that that isn't going to be so easy.'

Back in the drawing room, Alex Mair threw a couple of thin logs on to the glowing embers and went to get the drinks. Lessingham had refused whisky but had asked for wine. 'But don't waste your best claret on me, Alex. This is purely medicinal.' Almost imperceptibly they edged their chairs closer. Lessingham began his story deliberately, pausing at times to take gulps of the wine. It seemed to Dalgliesh that he was subtly altered since his arrival, had become charged with a power both mysterious and oddly familiar. He thought: He has acquired the mystique of the story-teller and, glancing at the ring of fire-lit and intent faces, he was suddenly reminded of his first village school, of the children clustered round Miss Douglas at three o'clock on a Friday afternoon for the half hour of story-time, and felt a pang of pain and regret for those lost days of innocence and love. He was surprised that the memory should have come back so keenly and at such a moment. But this was to be a very different story and one unsuited to the ears of children.

Lessingham said: 'I had an appointment with my dentist in Norwich at five o'clock and then briefly visited a friend in the Close. So I drove here from Norwich, not from my cottage. I'd just turned right off the B1150 at Fairstead when I nearly crashed into the back of this unlit car skewed across the road. I thought it was a damn silly place to park if someone wanted to take a leak in the bushes. Then it crossed my mind that there could have been an accident. And the right-hand door was open, that seemed a bit odd. So I drew into the side and went to take a look. There was no one about. I'm not sure why I walked into the trees. A kind of instinct I suppose. It was too dark to see anything and I wondered whether to call out. Then I felt a

78

fool and decided to leave it and mind my own business. And it was then that I almost tripped over her.'

He took another gulp of the wine. 'I still couldn't see anything, of course, but I knelt down and groped about with my hands. And it was then that I touched flesh. I think I touched her thigh, I can't be sure. But flesh, even dead flesh, is unmistakable. So I went back to the car and got my torch. I shone it on her feet and then slowly up her body to her face. And then, of course, I saw. I knew it was the Whistler.'

Meg Dennison asked gently: 'Was it very terrible?'

He must have heard in her voice what she obviously felt, not prurience but sympathy, an understanding that he needed to talk. He looked at her for a moment as if seeing her for the first time then paused, giving the question serious thought.

'More shocking than terrible. Looking back my emotions were complicated, a mixture of horror, disbelief and, well, shame. I felt like a voyeur. The dead, after all, are at such a disadvantage. She looked grotesque, a little ridiculous, with thin clumps of hair sticking out of her mouth as if she was munching. Horrible, of course, but silly at the same time. I had an almost irresistible impulse to giggle. I know it was only a reaction to shock but it was hardly admirable. And the whole scene was so, well, banal. If you had asked me to describe one of the Whistler's victims that's exactly how I should have seen her. You expect reality to be different from imaginings.'

Alice Mair said: 'Perhaps because the imaginings are usually worse.'

Meg Dennison said gently: 'You must have been terrified. I know I should have been. Alone and in darkness with such horror.'

He shifted his body towards her and spoke as if it were important that she, of all those present, should understand.

'No, not terrified, that was the surprising part. I was frightened, of course, but only for a second or two. After all, I didn't imagine he'd wait around. He'd had his kicks. He isn't interested in men anyway. I found myself thinking the ordinary, commonplace thoughts. I mustn't touch anything. I mustn't destroy the evidence. I've got to get the police. Then, walking back to the car, I started rehearsing what I'd say to them, almost as if I were concocting my story. I tried to explain why it was that I went into the bushes, tried to make it sound reasonable.'

Alex Mair said: 'What was there to justify? You did what you did. It sounds reasonable enough to me. The car was a danger slewed across the road. It would have been irresponsible just to drive on.'

'It seemed to need a lot of explaining, then and later. Perhaps because all the subsequent police sentences began with "why". You get morbidly sensitive to your own motives. It's almost as if you have to convince yourself that you didn't do it.'

Hilary Robarts said impatiently: 'But the body, when you first went back for the torch and saw her, you were certain she was dead?'

'Oh yes, I knew she was dead.'

'How could you have known? It could have been very recent. Why didn't you at least try to resuscitate her, give her the kiss of life? It would have been worth overcoming your natural repugnance.'

Dalgliesh heard Meg Dennison make a small sound between a gasp and a groan. Lessingham looked at Hilary and said coolly: 'It would have been if there had been the slightest point in it. I knew she was dead, let's leave it at that. But don't worry, if I ever find you *in extremis* I'll endeavour to overcome my natural repugnance.'

Hilary relaxed and gave a little self-satisfied smile, as if gratified to have stung him into a cheap retort. Her voice was more natural as she said: 'I'm surprised you weren't treated as a suspect. After all, you were the first on the scene, and this is the second time you've been, well almost, in at the death. It's becoming a habit.'

The last words were spoken almost under her breath but her eyes were fixed on Lessingham's face. He met her glance and said, with equal quietness: 'But there's a difference, isn't there? I had to watch Toby die, remember? And this time no one will even try to pretend that it isn't murder.'

The fire gave a sudden crackle and the top log rolled over and fell into the hearth. Mair, his face flushed, kicked it viciously back.

Hilary Robarts, perfectly calm, turned to Dalgliesh. 'But I'm right, aren't I? Don't the police usually suspect the person who finds the body?'

He said quietly: 'Not necessarily.'

Lessingham had placed the bottle of claret on the hearth. Now he leaned down and carefully refilled his glass. He said: 'They might have suspected me, I suppose, but for a number of lucky circumstances. I was obviously out on my lawful occasions. I have an alibi for at least two of the previous killings. From their point of view I was depressingly free of blood. I suppose they could see I was in a mild state of shock. And there was no sign of the ligature which strangled her, nor of the knife.'

Hilary said sharply: 'What knife? The Whistler's a strangler. Everyone knows that's how he kills.'

'Oh, I didn't mention that, did I? She was strangled all right, or I suppose she was. I didn't keep the torchlight on her face longer than was necessary. But he marks his victims, apart from stuffing their mouths with hair. Pubic hair, incidentally. I saw that all right. There was the letter L cut into her forehead. Quite unmistakable. A detective-constable who was talking to me later told me that it's one of the Whistler's trademarks. He thought that the L could stand for Larksoken and that the Whistler might be making some kind of statement about nuclear power, a protest perhaps.'

Alex Mair said sharply: 'That's nonsense.' Then added more calmly: 'There's been nothing on television or in the papers about any cut on the victims' foreheads.'

'The police are keeping it quiet, or trying to. It's the kind of detail they can use to sort out the false confessions. There have been half a dozen of those already apparently. There's been nothing in the media about the hair either, but that piece of unpleasantness seems to be generally known. After all, I'm not the only one to have found a body. People do talk.'

Hilary Robarts said: 'Nothing has been written or said, as far as I know, about it being pubic hair.'

'No, the police are keeping that quiet too, and it's hardly the sort of detail you print in a family newspaper. Not that it's so very surprising. He isn't a rapist but there was bound to be some sexual element.'

It was one of the details which Rickards had told Dalgliesh the previous evening but one, he felt, which Lessingham could well have kept to himself, particularly at a mixed dinner party. He was a little surprised at his sudden sensitivity. Perhaps it was his glance at Meg Dennison's ravaged face. And then his ears caught a faint sound. He looked across to the open door of the dining room and glimpsed the slim figure of Theresa Blaney standing in the shadows. He wondered how much of Lessingham's account she had heard. However little, it would have been too much. He said, hardly aware of the severity in his voice: 'Didn't Chief Inspector Rickards ask you to keep this information confidential?'

There was an embarrassed silence. He thought, They had forgotten for a moment that I'm a policeman.

Lessingham turned to him. 'I intend to keep it confidential. Rickards didn't want it to become public knowledge and it won't. No one here will pass it on.'

But that single question, reminding them of who he was and what he represented, chilled the room and changed their mood from fascinated and horrified interest to a slightly embarrassed unease. And when, a minute later, he got up to say his goodbyes and thank his hostess, there was an almost visible sense of relief. He knew that the embarrassment had nothing to do with the fear that he would question, criticize, move like a spy among them. It wasn't his case and they weren't suspects, and they must have known that he was no cheerful extrovert, flattered to be the centre of attraction while they bombarded him with questions about Chief Inspector Rickards's likely methods, the chance of catching the Whistler, his theories about psychopathic killers, his own experience of serial murder. But merely by being there he increased their awakening fear and repugnance at this latest horror. On each of their minds was imprinted the mental image of that violated face, the half-open mouth stuffed with hair, those staring, sightless eyes, and his presence intensified the picture, brought it into sharper focus. Horror and death were his trade and, like an undertaker, he carried with him the contagion of his craft.

He was at the front door when, on impulse, he turned back and said to Meg Dennison: 'I think you mentioned that you walked from the Old Rectory, Mrs Dennison. Could I walk home with you, that is if it's not too early for you?'

Alex Mair was beginning to say that he, of course, would drive her but Meg extricated herself clumsily from her chair and said, a little too eagerly: 'I'd be grateful if you would. I would like the walk and it would save Alex getting out the car.'

Alice Mair said: 'And it's time Theresa was on her way. We should have driven her home an hour ago. I'll give her father a ring. Where is she, by the way?'

Meg said: 'I think she was next door clearing the table a minute ago.'

'Well, I'll find her and Alex can drive her home.'

The party was breaking up. Hilary Robarts had been slumped back in her chair, her eyes fixed on Lessingham. Now she got to her feet and said: 'I'll get back to my cottage. There's no need for anyone to come with me. As Miles has said, the Whistler's had his kicks for tonight.'

Alex Mair said: 'I'd rather you waited. I'll walk with you once I've taken Theresa home.'

She shrugged and, without looking at him, said: 'All right, if you insist. I'll wait.'

She moved over to the window, staring out into the darkness. Only Lessingham stayed in his chair, reaching again to fill his glass. Dalgliesh saw that Alex Mair had silently placed another opened bottle in the hearth. He wondered whether Alice Mair would invite Lessingham to stay the night at Martyr's Cottage or whether he would be driven home later by her or her brother. He would certainly be in no state to drive himself.

Dalgliesh was helping Meg Dennison into her jacket when the telephone rang, sounding unnaturally strident in the quiet room. He felt her sudden shock of fear and for a moment, almost involuntarily, his hands strengthened on her shoulders. They heard Alex Mair's voice.

'Yes, we've heard. Miles Lessingham is here and gave us the details. Yes, I see. Yes. Thank you for letting me know.' Then there was a longer silence, then Mair's voice again. 'Completely fortui-tous, I should say, wouldn't you? After all, we have a staff of five hundred and thirty. But naturally everyone at Larksoken will find the news deeply shocking, the women particularly. Yes, I shall be in my office tomorrow if there's any help I can give. Her family have been told, I suppose? Yes, I see. Good night, Chief Inspector.'

He put down the receiver and said: 'That was Chief Inspector Rickards. They've identified the victim. Christine Baldwin. She is – she was – a typist at the station. You didn't recognize her then, Miles?'

Lessingham took his time refilling his glass. He said: 'The police didn't tell me who she was. Even if they had, I wouldn't have remembered the name. And no, Alex, I didn't recognize her. I suppose I must have seen Christine Baldwin at Larksoken, probably in the canteen. But what I saw earlier tonight wasn't Christine Baldwin. And I can assure you that I didn't shine the torch on her longer than I needed to satisfy myself that she was beyond any help that I could give.'

Without looking round from the window Hilary Robarts said: 'Christine Baldwin. Aged thirty-three. Actually, she's only been with us for eleven months. Married last year. Just transferred to the medical physics department. I can give you her typing and shorthand speeds if you're interested.' Then she turned round and looked Alex Mair in the face. 'It looks as if the Whistler's getting closer, doesn't it, in more ways than one.'

13

The final goodbyes were said and they stepped out from the smell of wood smoke, food and wine from a room which Dalgliesh was beginning to find uncomfortably warm into the fresh, sea-scented air. It took a few minutes before his eyes had adjusted to semi-darkness and the great sweep of the headland became visible, its shapes and forms mysteriously altered under the high stars. To the north the power station was a glittering galaxy of white lights, its stark geometric bulk subsumed in the blue-black of the sky.

They stood for a moment regarding it, then Meg Dennison said: 'When I first came here from London it almost frightened me, the sheer size of it, the way it dominates the headland. But I'm getting used to it. It's still disturbing but it does have a certain grandeur. Alex tries to demystify it, says its function is just to produce electricity for the National Grid efficiently and cleanly, that the main difference between this and any other power station is that you don't have beside it a huge pyramid of polluting coal dust. But atomic power to my generation always means that mushroom cloud. And now it means Chernobyl. But if it were an ancient castle standing there against the skyline, if what we looked out at tomorrow morning was a row of turrets, we'd probably be saying how magnificent it is.'

Dalgliesh said: 'If it had a row of turrets it would be a rather different shape. But I know what you mean. I should prefer the headland without it but it's beginning to look as if it had a right to be there.'

They turned simultaneously from contemplating the glittering lights and looked south to the decaying symbol of a very different power. Before them, at the edge of the cliff, crumbling against the skyline like a child's sandcastle rendered amorphous by the advancing tide, was the ruined Benedictine abbey. He could just make out the great empty arch of the east window and beyond it the shimmer of the North Sea while above, seeming to move through and over it like a censer, swung the smudged yellow disc of the moon. Almost without conscious will they took their first steps from the track on to the rough headland towards it. Dalgliesh said: 'Shall we? Can you spare the time? And what about your shoes?'

'Reasonably sensible. Yes, I'd like to, it looks so wonderful at night. And I don't really need to hurry. The Copleys won't have waited up for me. Tomorrow, when I have to tell them how close the Whistler is getting, I may not like to leave them alone after dark. This may be my last free night for some time.'

'I don't think they'd be in any real danger as long as you lock up securely. So far all his victims have been young women and he kills out of doors.'

'I tell myself that. And I don't think they'd be seriously frightened. Sometimes the very old seem to have moved beyond that kind of fear. The trivial upsets of daily living assume importance but the big tragedies they take in their stride. But their daughter is constantly ringing up to suggest they go to her in Wiltshire until he's caught. They don't want to but she's a strong-minded woman and very insistent, and if she telephones after dusk and I'm not there it will increase the pressure on them.' She paused and then said: 'It was a horrible end to an interesting but rather strange dinner party. I wish Mr Lessingham had kept the details to himself, but I suppose it helped him to talk about it, especially as he lives alone.'

Dalgliesh said: 'It would have needed superhuman control not to have talked about it. But I wish he'd omitted the more salacious details.'

'It will make a difference to Alex, too. Already some of the women staff demand to be escorted home after the evening shifts. Alice has told me that that isn't going to be easy for Alex to organize. They'll only accept a male escort if he has an unbreakable alibi for one of the Whistler murders. People cease to be rational even when they've known and worked with someone for the last ten years.'

Dalgliesh said: 'Murder does that, particularly this kind of murder. Miles Lessingham mentioned another death: Toby. Was that the young man who killed himself at the station? I seem to remember a paragraph in one of the papers.'

'It was an appalling tragedy. Toby Gledhill was one of Alex's most brilliant young scientists. He broke his neck by throwing himself down on top of the reactor.'

'So there was no mystery about it?'

'Oh no, absolutely none, except why he did it. Mr Lessingham saw it happen. I'm surprised you remember it. There was very little about it in the national press. Alex tried to minimize the publicity to protect his parents.'

And to protect the power station, thought Dalgliesh. He wondered why Lessingham had described Gledhill's death as murder but he didn't question his companion further. The allegation had been spoken so quietly that he doubted whether she had in fact heard it. Instead he asked: 'Are you happy living on the headland?'

The question did not appear to surprise her but it did surprise him, as did the very fact that they were walking so companionably together. She was curiously restful to be with. He liked her quiet gentleness with its suggestion of underlying strength. Her voice was pleasant and voices were important to him. But six months ago none of this would have been enough to make him invite her company for longer than was politely necessary. He would have escorted her back to the Old Rectory and then, a minor social obligation performed, turned with relief to walk alone to the abbey, drawing his solitude around him like a cloak. That solitude was still essential to him. He couldn't tolerate twenty-four hours in which the greater part wasn't spent entirely alone. But some change in himself, the inexorable years, success, the return of his poetry, perhaps the tentative beginning of love, seemed to be making him sociable. He wasn't sure whether this was something to be welcomed or resisted.

He was aware that she was giving his question careful thought.

'Yes, I think that I am. Sometimes very happy. I came here to escape from the problems of my life in London and, without really meaning to, I came as far east as I could get.'

'And found yourself confronting two different forms of menace, the power station and the Whistler.'

'Both frightening because both mysterious, both rooted in a horror of the unknown. But the menace isn't personal, isn't directed specifically against me. But I did run away and, I suppose, all refugees carry with them a small burden of guilt. And I miss the children. Perhaps I should have stayed and fought on. But it was becoming a very public war. I'm not suited to the role of popular heroine of the more reactionary press. All I wanted was to be left alone to get on with the job I'd been trained for and loved. But every book I used, every word I spoke was scrutinized. You can't teach in an atmosphere of rancorous suspicion. In the end I found I couldn't even live in it.'

She was taking it for granted that he knew who she was; but then anyone who had read the papers must know that.

He said: 'It's possible to fight intolerance, stupidity and fanaticism when they come separately. When you get all three together it's probably wiser to get out, if only to preserve one's sanity.'

They were approaching the abbey now and the grass of the headland was becoming more hillocky. She stumbled and he put out his hand to steady her. She said: 'In the end it came down to just two letters. They insisted that the blackboard should be called the chalkboard. Black or chalk. I didn't believe, I still don't believe that any sensible person, whatever his colour, objects to the word blackboard. It's black and it's a board. The word black in itself can't be offensive. I'd called it that all my life so why should they try to force me to change the way I speak my own language? And yet, at this moment, on this headland, under this sky, this immensity, it all seems so petty. Perhaps all I did was to elevate trivia into a principle.'

Dalgliesh said: 'Agnes Poley would have understood. My aunt looked up the records and told me about her. She went to the stake, apparently, for an obstinate adherence to her own uncompromising view of the universe. She couldn't accept that Christ's body could be present in the sacrament and at the same time physically in heaven at God's right hand. It was, she said, against common sense. Perhaps Alex Mair should take her as patron of his power station, a quasi-saint of rationality.'

'But that was different. She believed her immortal soul was in jeopardy.'

Dalgliesh said: 'Who knows what she believed? I think she was probably activated by a divine obstinacy. I find that rather admirable.'

Meg said: 'I think Mr Copley would argue that she was wrong, not the obstinacy, but her earthbound view of the sacrament. I'm not really competent to argue about that. But to die horribly for your own common-sense view of the universe is rather splendid. I never visit Alice without standing and reading that plaque. It's my small act of homage. And yet I don't feel her presence in Martyr's Cottage. Do you?'

'Not in the slightest. I suspect that central heating and modern furniture are inimical to ghosts. Did you know Alice Mair before you came here?'

'I knew no one. I answered an advertisement by the Copleys in *The*

Lady. They were offering free accommodation and food to someone who would do what they described as a little gentle housework. It's a euphemism for dusting, but of course it never works out like that. Alice has made a great difference. I hadn't realized how much I was missing female friendship. At school we only had alliances, offensive or defensive. Nothing ever cut across political divisions.'

Dalgliesh said: 'Agnes Poley would have understood that atmosphere too. It was the one she breathed.'

For a minute they walked in silence hearing the rustle of the long grasses over their shoes. Dalgliesh wondered why it was that, when walking towards the sea, there came a moment when its roar suddenly increased as if a menace, quiescent and benign, had suddenly realized and gathered up its power. Looking up at the sky, at the myriad pinpricks of light, it seemed to him that he could feel the turning earth beneath his feet and that time had mysteriously come to a stop, fusing into one moment the past, the present and the future; the ruined abbey, the obstinately enduring artefacts of the last war, the crumbling cliff defences, the windmill and the power station. And he wondered whether it was in such a disorientating limbo of time, listening to the ever-restless sea, that the previous owners of Martyr's Cottage had chosen their text. Suddenly his companion stopped and said: 'There's a light in the ruins. Two small flashes, like a torch.'

They stood still and watched in silence. Nothing appeared. She said, almost apologetically: 'I'm sure I saw it. And there was a shadow, something or somebody moving against the eastern window. You didn't see it?'

'I was looking at the sky.'

She said, almost with a note of regret: 'Well, it's gone now. I suppose I could have imagined it.'

And when, five minutes later, they made their way cautiously over the humpy grass into the heart of the ruins there was no one and nothing to be seen. Without speaking they walked through the gap of the east window and on to the edge of the cliff and saw only the moon-bleached beach stretching north and south, the thin fringe of white foam. If anyone had been there, thought Dalgliesh, there was plenty of opportunity for concealment behind the hunks of concrete or in the crevices of the sandy cliff. There was little point and no real justification in attempting to give chase, even if they had known the direction in which he had disappeared. People were entitled to walk

89

alone at night. Meg said again: 'I suppose I could have imagined it, but I don't think so. Anyway, she's gone now.'

'She?'

'Oh yes. Didn't I say? I had the distinct impression it was a woman.'

14

By four o'clock in the morning, when Alice Mair woke with a small despairing cry from her nightmare, the wind was rising. She stretched out her hand to click on the bedside light, checked her watch, then lay back, panic subsiding, her eyes staring at the ceiling while the terrible immediacy of the dream began to fade, recognized for what it was, an old spectre returning after all these years, conjured up by the events of the night and by the reiteration of the word 'murder' which, since the Whistler had begun his work, seemed to murmur sonorously on the very air. Gradually she re-entered the real world, manifested in the small noises of the night, the moan of the wind in the chimneys, the smoothness of the sheet in her clutching hands, the unnaturally loud ticking of her watch and, above all, in that oblong of pale light, the open casement and the drawn curtains which gave her a view of the faintly luminous star-studded sky.

The nightmare needed no interpretation. It was merely a new version of an old horror, less terrible than the dreams of childhood, a more rational, more adult terror. She and Alex were children again, the whole family living with the Copleys at the Old Rectory. That, in a dream, wasn't so surprising. The Old Rectory was only a larger, less pretentious version of Sunnybank – ridiculously named since it had stood on level ground and no sun ever seemed to penetrate its windows. Both were late Victorian, built in solid red brick, both had a strong, curved door under a high, peaked porch, both were isolated, each in its own garden. In the dream she and her father were walking together through the shrubbery. He was carrying his billhook and was dressed as he was on that last dreadful autumn afternoon, a singlet stained with his sweat, the shorts high cut, showing as he walked the bulge of the scrotum, the white legs, matted with black hair from the knees down. She was worried because she knew that the Copleys were waiting for her to cook lunch. Mr Copley, robed in cassock and billowing surplice, was impatiently pacing the back lawn seeming oblivious to their presence. Her father was explaining something to her in that over-loud, careful voice which he used to her mother, the voice which said: 'I know you are too stupid to understand this but I will talk slowly and loudly and hope that you won't try my patience too far.'

He said: 'Alex won't get the job now. I'll see that he doesn't. They won't appoint a man who's murdered his own father.'

And as he spoke he swung the billhook and she saw that its tip was red with blood. Then suddenly he turned towards her, eyes blazing, lifted it, and she felt its point pierce the skin of her forehead, and the sudden spurt of blood gushing into her eyes. Now wide awake, and breathing as if she had been running, she put her hand up to her brow and knew that the cold wetness she felt was sweat not blood.

There was little hope of falling asleep again; there never was when she woke in the early hours. She could get up, put on her dressing gown, go downstairs and make tea, correct her proofs, read, listen to the BBC World Service. Or she could take one of her sleeping tablets. God knew they were powerful enough to knock her into oblivion. But she was trying to wean herself off them and to give in now would be to acknowledge the potency of the nightmare. She would get up and make tea. She had no fear of waking Alex. He slept soundly, even through the winter gales. But first there was a small act of exorcism to be performed. If the dream were to lose its power, if she were somehow to prevent it recurring, she must face again the memory of that afternoon nearly thirty years ago.

It had been a warm autumnal day in early October and she, Alex and her father were working in the garden. He was clearing a thick hedge of brambles and overgrown shrubs at the bottom of the shrubbery and out of sight of the house, slashing at them with a billhook while Alex and she dragged the freed branches clear ready to build a bonfire. Her father was under clad for the time of year but was sweating heavily. She saw the arm lifting and falling, heard the crack of twigs, felt again the thorns cutting her fingers, heard his high commands. And then, suddenly, he gave a cry. Either the branch had been rotten or he had missed his aim. The billhook had sliced into his naked thigh and, turning, she saw the great curve of red blood begin to bubble in the air, saw him slowly sink like a wounded animal, his hands plucking the air. His right hand dropped the billhook and he held it out to her, shaking, palm upward, and looked at her beseechingly, like a child. He tried to speak but she couldn't make out the words. She was moving towards him, fascinated, when suddenly she felt a clutch on her arm

92

and Alex was dragging her with him down the path between the laurels towards the orchard.

She cried: 'Alex, stop! He's bleeding. He's dying. We've got to get help.'

She couldn't remember whether she actually said the words. All she later remembered was the strength of his hands on her shoulders as he forced her back against the bark of an apple tree and held her there, imprisoned. And he spoke a single word.

'No.'

Shaking with terror, her heart pounding, she couldn't have broken free even if she had wanted. And she knew now that this powerlessness was important to him. It had been his act and his alone. Compelled, absolved, she had been given no choice. Now, thirty years later, lying rigid, her eyes fixed on the sky, she remembered that single word, his eyes looking into hers, his hands on her shoulders, the bark of the tree scraping her back through her Aertex shirt. Time seemed to stop. She couldn't remember now how long he had held her imprisoned, only that it seemed an eternity of immeasurable time.

And then, at last, he gave a sigh and said: 'All right. We can go now.'

And that, too, amazed her, that he should have been thinking so clearly, calculating how long it would take. He dragged her after him until they stood over her father's body. And, looking down at the still-outstretched arm, the glazed and open eyes, the great scarlet pool soaking into the earth, she knew that it was a body, that he had gone for ever, that there was nothing she need fear from him ever again. Alex turned to her and spoke each word loudly and clearly as if she were a subnormal child.

'Whatever he's been doing to you, he won't do it again. Ever. Listen to me and I'll tell you what happened. We left him and went down to climb the apple trees. Then we decided that we'd better get back. Then we found him. That's all there is, it's as simple as that. You don't need to say anything else. Just leave the talking to me. Look at me, look at me, Alice. You understand?'

Her voice, when it came, sounded like an old woman's voice, cracked and tremulous, and the words strained her throat. 'Yes, I understand.'

And then he was dragging her by the hands, racing across the lawn, nearly pulling her arm from its socket, crashing through the kitchen door, crying aloud so that it sounded like a whoop of triumph. She saw her mother's face draining as if she too were bleeding to death, heard his panting voice.

'It's Father. He's had an accident. Get a doctor quick.'

And then she was alone in the kitchen. It was very cold. There were cold tiles under her feet. The surface of the wooden table on which she rested her head was cold to her cheeks. No one came. She was aware of a voice telephoning from the hall, and other voices, other steps. Someone was crying. Now there were more footsteps and the crunch of car wheels on gravel.

And Alex had been right. It had all been very simple. No one had questioned her, no one had been suspicious. Their story had been accepted. She didn't go to the inquest but Alex did, although he never told her what happened there. Afterwards some of the people concerned, their family doctor, the solicitor, a few of her mother's friends, came back and there was a curious tea party with sandwiches and home-made fruitcake. They were kind to her and Alex. Someone actually patted her head. A voice said, 'It was tragic that there was no one there. Common sense and a rudimentary knowledge of first aid would have saved him.'

But now the memory deliberately evoked had completed its exorcism. The nightmare had been robbed of its terror. With luck it might not return for months. She swung her legs out of bed and reached for her dressing gown.

She had just poured the boiling water on the tea and was standing waiting for it to brew when she heard Alex's footsteps on the stairs and, turning, she saw his tall figure blocking the kitchen door. He looked boyish, almost vulnerable, in the familiar corded dressing gown. He pushed both hands through his sleep-tousled hair. Surprised, because he was usually a sound sleeper, she said: 'Did I disturb you? Sorry.'

'No, I woke earlier and couldn't get off again. Holding dinner for Lessingham made it too late for comfortable digestion. Is this fresh?'

'About ready to pour.'

He took down a second mug from the dresser and poured tea for them both. She seated herself in a wicker chair and took her mug without speaking.

He said: 'The wind's rising.'

'Yes, it has been for the last hour.'

He went over to the door and unbolted the top wooden panel,

pushing it open. There was a sensation of rushing white coldness, scentless, but obliterating the faint tang of the tea and she heard the low growling roar of the sea. As she listened it seemed to rise in intensity so that she could imagine, with an agreeable *frisson* of simulated terror, that the low friable cliffs had finally crumbled and that the white foaming turbulence was rolling towards them across the headland, would crash against the door and throw its spume on Alex's face. Looking at him as he stared into the night, she felt a surge of affection as pure and as uncomplicated as the flow of cold air against her face. Its fleeting intensity surprised her. He was so much a part of her that she never needed nor wanted to examine too closely the nature of her feeling for him. She knew that she was always quietly satisfied to have him in the cottage, to hear his footfalls on the floor above, to share with him the meal she had cooked for herself at the end of the day. And yet neither made demands of the other. Even his marriage had made no difference. She had been unsurprised at the marriage since she had rather liked Elizabeth, but equally unsurprised when it ended. She thought it unlikely that he would marry again, but nothing between them would change, however many wives entered, or attempted to enter, his life. Sometimes as now she would smile wryly, knowing how outsiders saw their relationship. Those who assumed that the cottage was owned by him, not her, saw her as the unmarried sister, dependent on him for houseroom, companionship, a purpose in life. Others, more percep-tive but still nowhere near the truth, were intrigued by their appar-ent independence of each other, their casual comings and goings, their non-involvement. She remembered Elizabeth saying in the first weeks of her engagement to Alex, 'Do you know, you're a rather intimidating couple?' and she had been tempted to reply, 'Oh, we are, we are.'

She had bought Martyr's Cottage before his appointment as Director of the power station and he had moved in by an unspoken agreement that this was a temporary expedient while he decided what to do, keep on the Barbican flat as his main home or sell the flat and buy a house in Norwich and a smaller *pied à terre* in London. He was essentially an urban creature; she didn't see him settling perma-nently other than in a city. If, with the new job, he moved back to London she wouldn't follow him, and nor, she knew, would he expect her to. Here on this sea-scoured coast she had at last found a place which she was content to call home. That he could walk in and out of it unannounced never made it less than her own.

It must, she thought sipping her tea, have been after one o'clock when he returned from seeing Hilary Robarts home. She wondered what had kept him. Sleeping lightly as always in the early hours, she had heard his key in the lock, his foot on the stairs, before drifting again into sleep. Now it was getting on for five o'clock. He couldn't have had more than a few hours' sleep. Now, as if suddenly aware of the morning chill, he closed the top half of the door, drove home the bolt, then came and stretched himself out in the armchair opposite her. Leaning back, he cradled his mug in his hands.

He said: 'It's a nuisance that Caroline Amphlett doesn't want to leave Larksoken. I don't relish beginning a new job, particularly this job, with an unknown PA. Caroline knows the way I work. I'd rather taken it for granted that she'd come to London with me. It's inconvenient.'

And it was, she suspected, rather more than inconvenient. Pride, even personal prestige, were also at stake. Other senior men took their personal assistants with them when changing jobs. The reluctance of a secretary to be parted from her boss was a flattering affirmation of personal dedication. She could sympathize with his chagrin but it was hardly enough to keep him awake at night.

He added: 'Personal reasons, or so she says. That means Jonathan Reeves, presumably. God knows what she sees in him. The man isn't even a good technician.'

Alice Mair controlled her smile. She said: 'I doubt whether her interest in him is technical.'

'Well, if it's sexual she has less discrimination than I gave her credit for.'

He wasn't, she told herself, a poor judge of men or women. He rarely made fundamental mistakes and never, she suspected, about a man's scientific abililty. But he had no understanding of the extraordinary complexities and irrationalities of human motives, human behaviour. He knew that the universe was complex but that it obeyed certain rules, although, she supposed, he wouldn't have used the word 'obey' with its implication of conscious choice. This, he would say, is how the physical world behaves. It is open to human reason and, to a limited extent, to human control. People disconcerted him because they could surprise him. Most disconcerting of all was the fact that he occasionally surprised himself. He would have been at home as a sixteenth-century Elizabethan, categorizing people according to their essential natures; choleric, melancholic, mercurial, saturnine, qualities mirroring the planets that governed their birth. That basic fact established, then you knew where you were. And yet it could still surprise him that a man could be a sensible and reliable scientist in his work and a fool with women, could show judgement in one area of his life and act like an irrational child in another. Now he was peeved because his secretary, whom he had categorized as intelligent, sensible, dedicated, preferred to stay in Norfolk with her lover, a man he despised, rather than follow him to London.

She said: 'I thought you said once that you found Caroline sexually cold.'

'Did I? Surely not. That would suggest a degree of personal experience. I think I said I couldn't imagine ever finding her physically attractive. A PA who is personable and highly efficient but not sexually tempting is the ideal.'

She said drily: 'I imagine that a man's idea of the ideal secretary is a woman who manages to imply that she would like to go to bed with her boss but nobly restrains herself in the interests of office efficiency. What will happen to her?'

'Oh, her job's secure. If she wants to stay at Larksoken there will be plenty of competition to get her. She's intelligent as well as tactful and efficient.'

'But presumably not ambitious, else why should she be content to remain at Larksoken?' She added: 'Caroline may have another reason for wanting to stay in the area. I saw her in Norwich Cathedral about three weeks ago. She met a man in the Lady Chapel. They were very discreet but it looked to me like an assignation.'

He asked, but without real curiosity: 'What kind of man?'

'Middle-aged. Nondescript. Difficult to describe. But he was too old to be Jonathan Reeves.'

She said no more, knowing that he wasn't particularly interested, that his mind had moved elsewhere. And yet, looking back, it had been an odd encounter. Caroline's blonde hair had been bundled under a large beret and she was wearing spectacles. But the disguise, if it were meant as a disguise, had been ineffective. She herself had moved on swiftly, anxious not to be recognized or to seem a spy. A minute later she had seen the girl slowly walking along the aisle, guidebook in hand, the man strolling behind her carefully distanced.

They had moved together and had stood in front of a monument, seemingly absorbed. And when, ten minutes later, Alice was leaving the cathedral she had glimpsed him again. This time it was he who was carrying the guidebook.

He made no further comment about Caroline but after a minute's silence he said: 'Not a particularly successful dinner party.'

'An understatement. Beta-minus, except, of course, for the food. What's the matter with Hilary? Is she actually trying to be disagreeable or is she merely unhappy?'

'People usually are when they can't get what they want.'

'In her case, you.'

He smiled into the empty fire grate but didn't reply.

After a moment she said: 'Is she likely to be a nuisance?'

'Rather more than a nuisance. She's likely to be dangerous.'

'Dangerous? How dangerous? You mean dangerous to you personally?'

'To rather more than me.'

'But nothing you can't cope with?'

'Nothing I can't cope with. But not by making her Administrative Officer. She'd be a disaster. I should never have appointed her in an acting capacity.'

'When are you making the appointment?'

'In ten days' time. There's a good field.'

'So you've got ten days to decide what to do about her.'

'Rather less than that. She wants a decision by Sunday.'

A decision about what? she wondered. Her job, a possible promotion, her future life with Alex? But surely the woman could see that she had no future with Alex.

She asked, knowing the importance of the question, knowing, too, that only she would dare ask it, 'Will you be very disappointed if you don't get the job?'

'I'll be aggrieved, which is rather more destructive of one's peace of mind. I want it, I need it and I'm the right person for it. I suppose that's what every candidate thinks but in my case it happens to be true. It's an important job, Alice. One of the most important there is. The future lies with nuclear power, if we're going to save this planet, but we've got to manage it better, nationally and internationally.'

'I imagine you're the only serious candidate. Surely this is the kind of appointment which they only decide to make when they know they've got the right man available. It's a new job. They've managed perfectly well without a nuclear supremo up to now. I can see that, given the right man, the job has immense possibilities. But in the wrong hands it's just another public relations job, a waste of public money.'

He was too intelligent not to know that she was reassuring him. She was the only person from whom he ever needed reassurance or would ever take it.

He said: 'There's a suspicion that we could be getting into a mess. They want someone to get us out of it. Minor matters like his precise powers, who he'll be responsible to and how much he'll be paid have yet to be decided. That's why they're taking so long over the job specification.'

She said: 'You don't need a written job specification to know what they're looking for. A respected scientist, a proven administrator and a good public relations expert. They'll probably ask you to take a TV test. Looking good on the box seems to be the prerequisite for anything these days.'

'Only for future presidents or prime ministers. I don't think they'll go that far.'

He glanced at the clock. 'It's already dawn. I think I'll get a couple of hours' sleep.' But it was an hour later before they finally parted and went to their rooms.

15

Dalgliesh waited until Meg had unlocked the front door and stepped inside before saying his final goodnight, and she stood for a moment watching his tall figure striding down the gravel path and into the darkness. Then she passed into the square, tessellated hall with its stone fireplace, the hall which, on winter nights, seemed to echo faintly with the childish voices of Victorian rectors' children and which, for Meg, had always held a faintly ecclesiastical smell. Folding her coat over the ornate wooden newel post at the foot of the stairs, she went through to the kitchen and the last task of the day, setting out the Copleys' early-morning tray. It was a large, square room at the back of the house, archaic when the Copleys had bought the Old Rectory and unaltered since. Against the left-hand wall stood an old-fashioned gas stove so heavy that Meg was unable to move it to clean behind it and preferred not to think of the accumulated grease of decades gumming it to the wall. Under the window was a deep porcelain sink stained with the detritus of seventy years' washing-up and impossible to clean adequately. The floor was of ancient stone slabs, hard on the feet, from which in winter there seemed to rise a damp, foot-numbing miasma. The wall opposite the sink and the window was covered with an oak dresser, very old and probably valuable, if it had been possible to remove it from the wall without its collapse, and the original row of bells still hung over the door each with its Gothic script; drawing room, dining room, study, nursery. It was a kitchen to challenge rather than enhance the skills of any cook ambitious beyond the boiling of eggs. But now Meg hardly noticed its deficiencies. Like the rest of the Old Rectory it had become home.

After the stridency and aggression of the school, the hate-mail, she was happy to find her temporary asylum in this gentle household where voices were never raised, where no one obsessively analysed her every sentence in the hope of detecting racist, sexist or fascist undertones, where words meant what they had meant for generations, where obscenities were unknown or at least unspoken, where there was the grace of good order symbolized for her in Mr

Copley's reading of the Church's daily offices, Morning Prayer and Evensong. Sometimes she saw the three of them as expatriates, stranded in some remote colony, obstinately adhering to old customs, a lost way of life, as they did to old forms of worship. And she had grown to like both her employers. She would have respected Simon Copley more if he had been less prone to venial selfishness, less preoccupied with his physical comfort, but this she told herself was probably the result of fifty years of spoiling by a devoted wife. And he loved his wife. He relied on her. He respected her judgement. How lucky they were, she thought; secure in each other's affection and presumably fortified in increasing age by the certainty that if they weren't granted the grace of death on the same day there would be no lasting separation. But did they really believe this? She would like to have asked them, but knew that it would have been impossibly presumptuous. Surely they must have some doubts, made some mental reservations to the creed they so confidently recited morning and night. But perhaps what mattered at eighty was habit, the body no longer interested in sex, the mind no longer interested in speculation, the smaller things in life mattering more than the large and, in the end, the slow realization that nothing really mattered at all.

The job wasn't arduous, but she knew that gradually she was taking on much more than the advertisement had suggested and she sensed that the main anxiety of their life was whether she would stay. Their daughter had provided all the labour-saving devices: dishwasher, washing machine, spin-dryer, all housed in a disused still room near the back door, although until she came the Copleys had been reluctant to use them in case they couldn't turn them off, visualizing the machines whirling away all night, overheating, blowing up, the whole rectory pulsating with an uncontrollable power.

Their only child lived in a manor house in Wiltshire and rarely visited, although she telephoned frequently, usually at inconvenient times. It was she who had interviewed Meg for the Old Rectory and Meg now found it difficult to connect that confident, tweeded, slightly aggressive woman with the two gentle old people she knew. And she knew, although they would never have dreamt of telling her, perhaps didn't even admit it to themselves, that they were afraid of her. She bullied them, as she would have claimed, for their own good. Their second greatest fear was that they might be forced to comply with her frequently telephoned suggestion, made purely from a sense of duty, that they should go to stay with her until the Whistler was caught.

Unlike their daughter, Meg could understand why, after retirement, they had used all their savings to buy the rectory and had in old age burdened themselves with a mortgage. Mr Copley had in youth been a curate at Larksoken when the Victorian church was still standing. It was in that ugly repository of polished pine, acoustic tiles and garish, sentimental stained glass that he and his wife had been married, and in a flat in the rectory, living above the parish priest, that they had made their first home. The church had been partly demolished by a devastating gale in the 1930s, to the secret relief of the Church Commissioners who had been considering what to do with a building of absolutely no architectural merit serving a congregation at the major festivals of six at the most. So the church had been finally demolished and the Old Rectory, sheltering behind it and proving more durable, had been sold. Rosemary Duncan-Smith had made her views plain when driving Meg back to Norwich station after her interview.

'It's ridiculous for them to be living there at all, of course. They should have looked for a two-bedded, well-equipped flat in Norwich or in a convenient village close to the shops and post office, and to a church, of course. But Father can be remarkably obstinate when he thinks he knows what he wants and Mother is putty in his hands. I hope you aren't seeing this job as a temporary expedient.'

Meg had replied: 'Temporary, but not short-term. I can't promise that I'll stay permanently, but I need time and peace to decide on my future. And I may not suit your parents.'

'Time and peace. We'd all be glad of that. Well, I suppose it's better than nothing, but I'd be grateful for a month or two's notice when you do decide to go. And I shouldn't worry about suiting. With an inconvenient house and stuck out on that headland with nothing to look at but a ruined abbey and that atomic power station they'll have to put up with what they can get.'

But that had been sixteen months ago and she was still here.

But it was in that beautifully designed and equipped, but comfortable and homely kitchen at Martyr's Cottage that she had found her healing. Early in their friendship, when Alice had to spend a week in London and Alex was away, she had given Meg one of her spare keys to the cottage so that she could go in to collect and forward her post. On her return, when Meg offered it back, she had said: 'Better keep it. You may need it again.' Meg had never again used it. The door was usually open in summer and, when shut, she would always ring. But its possession, the sight and weight of it on her key ring, had come to symbolize for her the certainty and the trust of their friendship. She had been so long without a woman friend. She had forgotten, sometimes she told herself, that she had never before known the comfort of a close, undemanding, asexual companion-ship with another woman.

Before the accidental drowning of her husband four years earlier, she and Martin had needed only the occasional companionship of friendly acquaintances to affirm their self-sufficiency. Theirs had been one of those childless, self-absorbing marriages which uncon-sciously repel attempts at intimacy. The occasional dinner party was a social duty; they could hardly wait to get back to the seclusion of their own small house. And after his death it seemed to her that she had walked in darkness like an automaton through a deep and narrow canyon of grief in which all her energies, all her physical strength, had been husbanded to get through each day. She thought and worked and grieved only for a day at a time. To allow herself even to think of the days, the weeks, the months or years stretching ahead would have been to precipitate disaster. For two years she had hardly been sane. Even her Christianity was of little help. She didn't reject it, but it had become irrelevant, its comfort only a candle which served fitfully to illumine the dark. But when, after those two years, the valley had almost imperceptibly widened and there was for the first time, not those black enclosing cliffs, but the vista of a normal life, even of happiness, a landscape over which it was possible to believe the sun might shine, she had become unwittingly embroiled in the racial politics of her school. The older members of staff had moved or retired, and the new headmistress, specifically appointed to enforce the fashionable orthodoxies, had moved in with crusading zeal to smell out and eradicate heresy. Meg realized now that she had, from the first, been the obvious, the predestined victim.

She had fled to this new life on the headland and to a different solitude. And here she had found Alice Mair. They had met a fortnight after Meg's arrival when Alice had called at the Old Rectory with a suitcase of jumble for the annual sale in aid of St Andrew's Church in Lydsett. There was an unused scullery leading off a passage between the kitchen and the back door which was used as a collecting point for unwanted items from the headland; clothes, bric-à-brac, books and old magazines. Mr Copley took an occasional service at St Andrew's when Mr Smollett, the vicar, was on holiday, an involvement in church and village life which, Meg suspected, was as important to him as it was to the church. Normally, little jumble could be expected from the few cottages on the headland, but Alex Mair, anxious to associate the power station with the community, had put up a notice on the staff board and the two tea chests were usually fairly full by the time the October sale came round. The back door of the Old Rectory, giving access to the scullery, was normally left open during daylight hours and an inner door to the house locked, but Alice Mair had knocked at the front door and made herself known. The two women, close in age, both reserved, both independent, neither deliberately seeking a friend, had liked each other. The next week Meg had received an invitation to dinner at Martyr's Cottage. And now there was rarely a day when she didn't walk the half mile over the headland to sit in Alice's kitchen and talk and watch while she worked.

Her colleagues at school would, she knew, have found their friendship incomprehensible. Friendship there, or what passed for friendship, never crossed the great divide of political allegiance and in the acrimonious clamour of the staffroom could swiftly deteriorate into gossip, rumours, recriminations and betrayal. This peaceable friendship, asking nothing, was as devoid of intensity as it was of anxiety. It was not a demonstrative friendship; they had never kissed, had never indeed touched hands except at that first meeting. Meg wasn't sure what it was that Alice valued in her, but she knew what she valued in Alice. Intelligent, well-read, unsentimental, unshockable, she had become the focus of Meg's life on the headland.

She seldom saw Alex Mair. During the day he was at the power station and at weekends, reversing the normal peregrination, he was at his London flat, frequently staying there for part of the week if he had a meeting in town. She had never felt that Alice had deliberately kept them apart, fearing that her brother would be bored by her friend. In spite of all the traumas of the last four years Meg's inner self was too confidently rooted to be prone to that kind of sexual or social self-abasement. But she had never felt at home with him, perhaps because, with his confident good looks and the air of arrogance in his bearing, he seemed both to represent and to have absorbed something of the mystery and potency of the power he operated. He was perfectly amiable to her on the few occasions when they did meet; sometimes she even felt that he liked her. But their only common ground was in the kitchen of Martyr's Cottage and even there she was always more at home when he was away. Alice never spoke of him except casually but on the few occasions, like last night's dinner party, when she had seen them together they seemed to have the intuitive mutual awareness, an instinctive response to the other's needs, more typical of a long-standing successful marriage than of an apparently casual fraternal relationship.

And for the first time in nearly three years she had been able to talk about Martin. She remembered that July day, the kitchen door open to the patio, the scent of herbs and sea stronger even than the spicy, buttery smell of newly baked biscuits. She and Alice had sat opposite each other, across the kitchen table, the teapot between them. She could remember every word.

'He didn't get many thanks. Oh, they said how heroic he was and the headmaster said all the right things at the school memorial service. But they thought that the boys shouldn't have been swimming there anyway. The school disclaimed any responsibility for his death. They were more anxious to escape criticism than to honour Martin. And the boy he saved hasn't turned out very well. I suppose I'm silly to worry about that.'

'It would be perfectly natural to hope that your husband hadn't died for someone second-rate, but I suppose the boy has a point of view. It could be an awesome responsibility knowing that someone has died for you.'

Meg said: 'I tried to tell myself that. For a time I was – well, almost obsessed with that boy. I used to hang about the school waiting for him to come out. Sometimes I had the need almost to touch him. It was as if some part of Martin had passed into him. But he was only embarrassed, of course. He didn't want to see me or talk to me, he or his parents. He wasn't, in fact, a very nice boy, a bully and rather stupid. I don't think Martin even liked him although he never said so. He was spotty, too – oh dear, that wasn't his fault, I don't know why I even mentioned it.'

And she had wondered how it was she was speaking of him at all. For the first time after all these years. And that business about her obsession with him; she had never mentioned that to a living soul.

Alice had said: 'It's a pity your husband didn't leave him to drown and save himself, but I suppose that on the spur of the moment he didn't weigh up the relative value of a useful teaching career and pimpled stupidity.'

'Leave him to drown? Deliberately? Oh Alice, you know you couldn't do that yourself.'

'Perhaps not. I'm perfectly capable of irrational folly. I'd probably pull him out if I could do it without too much danger to myself.'

'Of course you would. It's human instinct, surely, to save others, particularly a child.'

'It's human instinct, and a thoroughly healthy one in my view, to save oneself. That's why, when people don't, we call them heroes and give them medals. We know they're acting against nature. I can't understand how you can have such an extraordinarily benign view of the universe.'

'Have I? I suppose I have. Except for the two years after Martin drowned I've always been able to believe that at the heart of the universe there is love.'

'At the heart of the universe there is cruelty. We are predators and are preyed upon, every living thing. Did you know that wasps lay their eggs in ladybirds, piercing the weak spot in their armour? Then the grub grows and feeds on the living ladybird and eats its way out, tying the ladybird's legs together. Whoever thought of that has, you have to admit, a peculiar sense of humour. And don't quote Tennyson at me.'

'Perhaps it doesn't feel anything, the ladybird.'

'Well, it's a comforting thought but I wouldn't bet on it. You must have had an extraordinarily happy childhood.'

'Oh, I did, I did! I was lucky. I would have liked brothers and sisters but I don't remember that I was ever lonely. There wasn't much money but there was a great deal of love.'

'Love. Is that so very important? You were a teacher, you ought to know. Is it?'

'It's vital. If a child has it for the first ten years hardly anything else matters. If he hasn't, then nothing does.'

There had been a moment's silence and then Alice had said: 'My father died, killed in an accident when I was fifteen.'

'How terrible. What kind of accident? Were you there? Did you see it?'

'He cut an artery with a billhook. He bled to death. No, we didn't see it, but we were on the scene soon afterwards. Too late, of course.'

'Alex too, and he was even younger. How awful for you both.'

'It had its effect on our lives undoubtedly, particularly mine. Why don't you try one of those biscuits? It's a new recipe but I'm not sure that it's entirely successful. A little too sweet, and I may have overdone the spice. Tell me what you think.'

Recalled to the present by the cold of the flagstones numbing her feet and automatically aligning the cup handles, she suddenly realized why she had remembered that summer teatime in Martyr's Cottage. The biscuits she would add to the tray next morning were a later batch of the same recipe provided by Alice. But she wouldn't take them from the tin until tomorrow. There was nothing more to do tonight except to fill her hot-water bottle. There was no central heating in the Old Rectory and she seldom switched on the two-bar electric fire in her bedroom, knowing how worried the Copleys were by their fuel bills. Finally, hugging the bottle's warmth to her chest, she checked on the bolts of the front and back doors and made her way up the uncarpeted stairs to bed. On the landing she met Mrs Copley, dressing-gowned, scurrying furtively to the bathroom. Although there was a cloakroom on the ground floor the Old Rectory had only one bathroom, a defect which necessitated embarrassed, low-voiced inquiries before anyone upset their carefully worked out rota by taking an unexpected bath. Meg waited until she heard the main bedroom door shut before going herself to the bathroom.

Fifteen minutes later she was in bed. She knew rather than felt that she was very tired and recognized the symptoms of an overstimu- lated brain in an exhausted body, the restless limbs and inability to get comfortable. The Old Rectory was too far inland for her to hear the crash of the waves but the smell and the throb of the sea were always present. In summer the headland would vibrate with a gentle rhythmic humming which, on stormy nights or at the spring tides would rise to an angry moan. She slept always with her window open and would drift into sleep soothed by that distant murmur. But tonight it had no power to lull her into unconsciousness. Her bedside book, often reread, was Anthony Trollope's *The Small House at Allington* but tonight it could no longer translate her to the reassur- ing, comfortable, nostalgic world of Barsetshire, to croquet on Mrs Dale's lawn and dinner at the squire's table. The memories of the evening were too traumatic, too exciting, too recent to be easily assuaged by sleep. She opened her eyes to the darkness, a darkness too often populated before sleep by those familiar, reproachful, childish faces, brown, black and white, bending over her, asking why she had deserted them when they loved her and thought that she had loved them. Usually it was a relief to be free of those gentle and accusing ghosts, which in the last few months had visited her less often. And sometimes they were replaced by a more traumatic memory. The headmistress had tried to insist that she go on a racial awareness course, she who had taught children of different races for over twenty years. There was one scene which for months she had tried resolutely to put out of her mind, that last meeting in the staffroom, the circle of implacable faces, brown, black and white, the accusing eyes, the insistent questions. And in the end, worn down by bullying, she had found herself helplessly weeping. No nervous breakdown, that useful euphemism, had been more humiliating.

But tonight even that shameful memory was replaced by more recent and more disquieting visions. She glimpsed again that girlish figure momentarily outlined against the walls of the abbey only to slip away like a wraith and be lost among the shadows of the beach. She sat again at the dinner table and saw in the candlelight Hilary Robarts's dark, discontented eyes staring intently at Alex Mair; watched the planes of Miles Lessingham's face fitfully lit by the leaping flames of the fire, saw his long-fingered hands reaching down for the bottle of claret, heard again that measured rather high voice speaking the unspeakable. And then, on the verge of sleep, she was crashing with him through the bushes of that dreadful wood, feeling the briars scratching her legs, the low twigs whipping against her cheeks, staring with him as the pool of light from the torch shone down on that grotesque and mutilated face. And in that twilight world between waking and sleeping she saw that it was a face she knew, her own. She jerked back to consciousness with a little cry of terror, switched on the bedside lamp, reached out for her book and began resolutely to read. Half an hour later, the book slipped out of her hand and she fell into the first of the night's uneasy periods of slumber.

16

It took only two minutes of lying stretched and rigid on his bed for Alex Mair to realize that sleep was unlikely to come. To lie in bed wakeful had always been intolerable to him. He could manage with little sleep but that was invariably sound. Now he swung his legs out of bed, reached for his dressing gown and walked over to the window. He would watch the sun rise over the North Sea. He thought back over the last few hours, the acknowledged relief of talking to Alice, the knowledge that nothing shocked her, nothing surprised her, that everything he did, if not right in her eyes, was judged by a different standard from the one she rigorously applied to the rest of her life.

The secret that lay between them, those minutes when he had held her shaking body against the tree trunk and stared into her eyes, compelling obedience, had bound them with a cord so strong that it couldn't be frayed, either by the enormity of their shared guilty secret, or by the small rubs of living together. And yet they had never spoken of their father's death. He didn't know whether Alice ever thought of it, or whether the trauma had erased it from her mind so that she now believed the version he had formulated, had taken the lie into her unconscious and made it her truth. When, quite soon after the funeral, seeing how calm she was, he had imagined that possibility he had been surprised at his reluctance to believe it. He didn't want her gratitude. It was degrading even to contemplate that she would feel an obligation towards him. Obligation and gratitude were words they had never needed to use. But he did want her to know and to remember. The deed was to him so monstrous, so surprising, that it would have been intolerable not to have shared it with a living soul. In those early months he had wanted her to know the magnitude of what he had done and that he had done it for her.

And then, six weeks after the funeral, he had suddenly found himself able to believe that it hadn't happened, not in that way, and that the whole horror was a childhood fantasy. He would lie awake at night and see his father's crumbling figure, the leap of blood like a scarlet fountain, would hear the harshly whispered words. In this revised and comforting version there had been a second of delay, no more, and then he had raced for the house shouting for help. And there was a second and even more admirable fantasy in which he had knelt at his father's side, had pressed his clenched fist hard into the groin, quenching the spurting blood, had whispered reassurance into those dying eyes. It had been too late, of course; but he had tried. He had done his best. The coroner had praised him, that precise little man with his half-moon spectacles, his face like a querulous parrot. 'I congratulate the deceased's son who acted with commendable promptness and courage and did everything possible to try to save his father's life.'

The relief of being able to believe in his innocence was at first so great that temporarily it overwhelmed him. He had lain in bed night after night drifting into sleep on a tide of euphoria. But he had known, even then, that this self-administered absolution was like a drug in the bloodstream. It was comforting and easy, but it wasn't for him. That way lay a danger more destructive even than guilt. He had told himself: 'I must never believe that a lie is the truth. I may tell lies all my life if it's expedient but I must know them for what they are and I must never tell them to myself. Facts are facts. I have to accept them and face them and then I can learn how to deal with them. I can look for reasons for what I did and call those reasons excuses; what he did to Alice, how he bullied Mother, how I hated him. I can attempt to justify his death at least to myself. But I did what I did and he died as he died.'

And with that acceptance came a kind of peace. After a few years he was able to believe that guilt itself was an indulgence, that he didn't need to suffer it unless he chose. And then there came a time when he felt a pride in the deed, in the courage, the audacity, the resolution which had made it possible. But that, too, he knew was dangerous. And for years afterwards he hardly thought of his father. Neither his mother nor Alice ever spoke of him except in the company of casual acquaintances who felt the need to utter embarrassed condolences from which there was no escape. But in the family only once was his name mentioned.

A year after the death his mother had married Edmund Morgan, a widowed church organist of mind-numbing dullness, and had retired with him to Bognor Regis where they lived on his father's insurance money in a spacious bungalow in sight of the sea, in an obsessive mutual devotion which mirrored the meticulous order and tidiness of their world. His mother always spoke of her new husband as Mr Morgan. 'If I don't talk to you about your father, Alex, it isn't that I've forgotten him, but Mr Morgan wouldn't like it.' The phrase had become a catchword between him and Alice. The conjunction of Morgan's job and his instrument offered endless possibilities of adolescent jokes, particularly when he and their mother were on honeymoon. 'I expect Mr Morgan is pulling out all his stops.' 'Do you suppose Mr Morgan is changing his combinations?' 'Poor Mr Morgan, labouring away. I hope he doesn't run out of wind.' They were wary, reticent children, yet this joke would reduce them to screams of helpless laughter. Mr Morgan and his organ releasing them into hysterical laughter had anaesthetized the horror of the past.

And then, when he was about eighteen, reality of another kind intruded itself and he said aloud, 'I didn't do it for Alice, I did it for myself', and thought how extraordinary it was that it had taken four years to discover that fact. And yet was it a fact, was it the truth, or was it merely a psychological speculation which in certain moods he found it interesting to contemplate?

Now, looking out over the headland to the eastern sky already flushed with the first faint gold of dawn, he said aloud: 'I let my father die deliberately. That is a fact. All the rest is pointless speculation.' In fiction, he thought, Alice and I should have been tormented by our joint knowledge, distrustful, guilt-ridden, unable to live apart yet miserable together. Yet since his father's death there had been nothing between him and his sister but companionship, affection, peace.

But now, nearly thirty years later, when he thought he had long come to terms with the deed and his own reaction to it, memory had begun to stir again. It had started with the first Whistler murder. The word 'murder' itself constantly on someone's lips, like a sonorous curse, seemed to have the power to evoke those half-suppressed images of his father's face which had become as unclear, as devoid of any life, as an old photograph. But in the last six months his father's image had begun to intrude on his consciousness at odd moments, in the middle of a meeting, across a boardroom table, in a gesture, the droop of an eyelid, the tone of a voice, the line of a speaker's mouth, the shape of fingers splayed to an open fire. His father's ghost had returned in the tangle of late-summer foliage, the first fall of the leaves, the tentative autumn smells. He wondered if the same thing was happening to Alice. For all their mutual sympathy, for all the sense he had of their being irrevocably bound together, this was the one question he knew he would never ask.

And there were other questions, one question in particular, which he had no need to fear from her. She wasn't in the least curious about his sexual life. He knew enough psychology to have at least some insight into what those early shaming and terrifying experiences had done to her. Sometimes he thought that she regarded his affairs with a casual, slightly amused indulgence as if, herself immune to a childish weakness, she was nevertheless indisposed to criticize it in others. Once, after his divorce, she had said: 'I find it extraordinary that a straightforward if inelegant device for ensuring the survival of the species should involve human beings in such emotional turmoil. Does sex have to be taken so seriously?' And now he found himself wondering whether she knew or guessed about Amy. And then, as the flaming ball rose from the sea, the gears of time slipped, went into reverse and he was back only five days ago lying with Amy in the deep hollow of the dunes, smelling again the scent of sand and grasses and the salt tang of the sea as the late afternoon warmth drained out of the autumn air. He could recall every sentence, every gesture, the timbre of her voice, could feel again the hairs rising on his arms at her touch.

17

She turned towards him, her head propped on her hand, and he saw the strong afternoon light shafting with gold the cropped brightly dyed hair. Already the warmth was draining from the air and he knew that it was time they were moving. But lying there beside her, listening to the susurration of the tide and looking up at the sky through a haze of grasses he was filled, not with post-coital sadness, but with an agreeable languor as if the long-committed Sunday afternoon still stretched ahead of them.

It was Amy who said: 'Look, I'd better be getting back. I told Neil I wouldn't be more than an hour and he gets fussy if I'm late because of the Whistler.'

'The Whistler kills at night not in daylight. And he'd hardly venture on the headland. Too little cover. But Pascoe's right to be concerned. There isn't much danger, but you shouldn't be out alone at night. No woman should until he's caught.'

She said: 'I wish they would catch him. It'd be one thing less for Neil to worry about.'

Making his voice carefully casual, he asked: 'Doesn't he ever ask where you're going when you sneak out on Sunday afternoons leaving him to look after the child?'

'No, he doesn't. And the child is called Timmy. And I don't sneak. I say I'm going and I go.'

'But he must wonder.'

'Oh, he wonders all right. But he thinks people are entitled to their privacy. He'd like to ask but he never will. Sometimes I say to him, "OK, I'm off now to fuck my lover in the sand dunes." But he never says a word, just looks miserable because he doesn't like me saying "fuck".'

'Then why do you? I mean, why torment him? He's probably fond of you.'

'No, he isn't, not very fond. It's Timmy he likes. And what other word is there? You can't call it going to bed. I've only been in your bed with you once and then you were as jumpy as a cat thinking that

113

sister of yours might come back unexpectedly. And you can't say we sleep together.'

He said: 'We make love. Or, if you prefer it, we copulate.'

'Honestly, Alex, that's disgusting. I think that word is really disgusting.'

'And do you do it with him? Sleep, go to bed, make love, copulate?'

'No, I don't. Not that it's any business of yours. He thinks it would be wrong. That means he doesn't really want to. If men want to they usually do.'

He said: 'That has been my experience, certainly.'

They lay side by side like effigies, both staring at the sky. She seemed content not to talk. So the question had at last been put and answered. It had been with shame and some irritation that he had recognized in himself for the first time the nagging of jealousy. More shaming had been his reluctance to put it to the test. And there were those other questions he wanted to ask but daren't. 'What do I mean to you?', 'Is this important?', 'What do you expect of me?' And most important of all, but unanswerable, 'Do you love me?' With his wife he had known precisely where he was. No marriage had begun with a more definite understanding of what each required of the other. Their unwritten, unspoken, only half-acknowledged pre-nuptial agreement had needed no formal ratification. He would earn most of the money, she would work if and when she chose. She had never been particularly enthusiastic about her job as interior designer. In return his home would be run with efficiency and reasonable economy. They would take separate holidays at least once every two years; they would have at most two children and at a time of her choosing; neither would publicly humiliate the other; the spectrum of marital offences under this heading ranging from spoiling the other's dinner-party stories to a too-public infidelity. It had been a success. They had liked each other, got on with remarkably little rancour and he had been genuinely upset, if principally in his pride, when she had left him. Fortunately marital failure had been mitigated by the public knowledge of her lover's wealth. He realized that to a materialistic society losing a wife to a millionaire hardly counted as failure. In their friends' eyes it would have been unreasonably proprietorial of him not to have released her with a minimum of fuss. But to do her justice, Liz had loved Gregory, would have followed him to California money or no money. He saw again in memory that transformed laughing face, heard her ruefully apologetic voice.

'It's the real thing this time, darling. I never expected it and I can still hardly believe it. Try not to feel too badly, it isn't your fault. There's nothing to be done.'

The real thing. So there was this mysterious real thing before which everything went down, obligations, habit, responsibility, duty. And now, lying in the dunes, seeing the sky through the rigid stalks of marram grasses, he thought about it almost with terror. Surely he hadn't found it at last and with a girl less than half his age, intelligent but uneducated, promiscuous and burdened with an illegitimate child. And he didn't deceive himself about the nature of her hold on him. No lovemaking had ever been as erotic or as liberating as their half-illicit couplings on unyielding sand within yards of the crashing tide.

Sometimes he would find himself indulging in fantasy, would picture them together in London in his new flat. The flat, as yet unsought, no more than a vague possibility among others, would assume dimensions, location, a horribly plausible reality in which he found himself arranging his pictures carefully on a non-existent wall, thinking over the disposal of his household goods, the exact location of his stereo system. The flat overlooked the Thames. He could see the wide windows giving a view over the river as far as Tower Bridge, the huge bed, Amy's curved body striped with bands of sunlight from the slatted wooden blinds. Then the sweet, deluding pictures would dissolve into bleak reality. There was the child. She would want the child with her. Of course she would. Anyway, who else could look after it? He could see the indulgent amusement on the faces of his friends, the pleasure of his enemies, the child lurching, sticky-fingered, about the flat. He could smell in imagination what Liz had never let him know in actuality – the smell of sour milk and dirty nappies, could picture the dreadful lack of peace and privacy. He needed these realities, deliberately emphasized, to bring him back to sanity. He was horrified that even for a few minutes he could seriously have contemplated such destructive stupidity. He thought: I'm obsessed by her. All right, just for these last few weeks I'll enjoy my obsession. This late summer would be brief enough, the warm unseasonable days of mellow sunshine couldn't last. Already the evenings were darkening. Soon he would smell the first sour tang of winter on the sea breezes. There would be no more lying in the warm sand dunes. She couldn't visit Martyr's Cottage again, that would be recklessly stupid. It was easy to convince himself that with care, when Alice was in London and no visitors expected, they could be together in his bedroom perhaps even for a whole night, but he knew that he would never risk it. Little on the headland was private for long. This was his St Martin's summer, an autumnal madness, nothing that the first cold of winter couldn't wither.

But now she said, as if there had been no period of silence between them, 'Neil's my friend, OK? Why do you want to talk about him anyway?'

'I don't. But I wish he'd civilize his living arrangements. That caravan is in direct line of my bedroom windows. It's an eyesore.'

'You'd need binoculars to see it from your windows. And so is your bloody great power station an eyesore. That's in everyone's direct line; we all have to look at that.'

He put out his hand to her shoulder, warm under the gritty film of sand and said with mock pomposity: 'It's generally agreed that, given the constraints imposed by its function and the site, the power station is rather successful architecturally.'

'Agreed by whom?'

'I think so for one.'

'Well, you would, wouldn't you? Anyway, you ought to be grateful to Neil. If he didn't look after Timmy I wouldn't be here.'

He said: 'That whole thing is primitive. He's got a wood stove in there, hasn't he? If that blows up you won't last a minute, all three of you, particularly if the door jams.'

'We don't lock it. Don't be daft. And we let the fire go out at night. And suppose your place blows up. It won't be just the three of us, will it? Bloody hell it won't. Not only humans either. What about Smudge and Whisky? They've got a point of view.'

'It won't blow up. You've been listening to his scaremongering nonsense. If you're worried about nuclear power ask me. I'll tell you what you want to know.'

'You mean while you're poking me you'll explain all about nuclear power? Oh boy, I'll certainly be able to take it in.'

And then she turned to him again. The pattern of sand on her shoulder glistened and he felt her mouth moving over his upper lip, his nipples, his belly. And then she knelt over him and the round childish face with its bush of bright hair shut out the sky.

Five minutes later she rolled apart from him and began shaking the

116

sand from her shirt and jeans. Tugging the jeans over her thighs, she said: 'Why don't you do something about that bitch at Larksoken, the one suing Neil? You could stop her. You're the boss.'

The question – or was it a demand – shocked him out of his fantasy as crudely as if, unprovoked, she had suddenly slapped his face. In their four meetings she had never questioned him about his job, had seldom mentioned the power station except, as on this afternoon, to complain half seriously that it spoilt the view. He hadn't made a deliberate decision to keep her out of his private and professional life. When they were together that life hardly entered into his own consciousness. The man who lay with Amy in the dunes had nothing to do with that burdened, ambitious, calculating scientist who ran Larksoken, nothing to do with Alice's brother, with Elizabeth's ex-husband, with Hilary's ex-lover. Now he wondered, with a mixture of irritation and dismay, whether she had deliberately chosen to ignore those invisible keep-out signs. And if he had been unconfiding, then so had she. He knew little more about her now than when they had first encountered each other in the abbey ruins on a blustery August evening less than six weeks earlier, had for a minute stood and gazed and had then moved silently towards each other in a wordless, amazed recognition. Later that evening she had told him that she came from Newcastle, that her widowed father had remarried and that she and her stepmother couldn't get on. She had moved down to London and lived in squats. It had sounded commonplace enough but he hadn't quite believed it and nor, he suspected, did she care whether or not he did. Her accent was more Cockney than Geordie. He had never asked about the child, partly from a kind of delicacy but mainly because he preferred not to think of her as a mother, and she had volunteered no information about Timmy or his father.

She said: 'Well, why don't you? Like I said, you're the boss.'

'Not over my staff's private lives. If Hilary Robarts thinks she has been libelled and seeks redress I can't prevent her from going to law.'

'You could if you wanted to. And Neil only wrote what was true.'

'That is a dangerous defence to a libel action. Pascoe would be ill advised to rely on it.'

'She won't get any money. He hasn't got any. And if he has to pay costs it will ruin him.'

'He should have thought of that earlier.'

She lay back with a little thud and for a few minutes they were both

117

silent. Then she said as casually as if the previous conversation had been trivial small talk which was already half forgotten: 'What about next Sunday? I could get away late afternoon. OK by you?'

So she bore no grudge. It wasn't important to her, or if it was, she had decided to drop it, at least for now. And he could put from him the treacherous suspicion that their first meeting had been contrived, part of a plan devised by her and Pascoe to exploit his influence with Hilary. But that, surely, was ridiculous. He had only to recall the inevitability of their first coming together, her passionate, uncomplicated, animal gusto in their lovemaking to know that the thought was paranoid. He would be here on Sunday afternoon. It might be their last time together. Already he had half decided that it had to be. He would free himself from this enslavement, sweet as it was, as he had freed himself from Hilary. And he knew, with a regret which was almost as strong as grief, that with this parting there would be no protests, no appeals, no desperate clinging to the past. Amy would accept his leaving as calmly as she had accepted his arrival.

He said: 'OK. About four thirty then. Sunday the twenty-fifth.'

And now time, which in the last ten minutes seemed mysteriously to have halted, flowed again and he was standing at his bedroom window five days later watching the great ball of the sun rise out of the sea to stain the horizon and spread over the eastern sky the veins and arteries of the new day. Sunday the twenty-fifth. He had made that appointment five days ago and it was one that he would keep. But lying there in the dunes he hadn't known what he knew now, that he had another and very different appointment to keep on Sunday, September the twenty-fifth.

18

Shortly after lunch Meg walked across the headland to Martyr's Cottage. The Copleys had gone upstairs to take their afternoon rest and for a moment she wondered whether to tell them to lock their bedroom door. But she told herself that the precaution was surely unnecessary and ridiculous. She would bolt the back door and lock the front door after her as she left and she wouldn't be gone for long. And they were perfectly happy to be left. Sometimes it seemed to her that old age reduced anxiety. They could look at the power station without the slightest premonition of disaster and the horror of the Whistler seemed as much beyond their interest as it was their comprehension. The greatest excitement in their lives, which had to be planned with meticulous care and some anxiety, was a drive into Norwich or Ipswich to shop.

It was a beautiful afternoon, warmer than most in the past disappointing summer. There was a gentle breeze and from time to time Meg paused and lifted her head to feel the warmth of the sun and the sweet-smelling air moving against her cheeks. The turf was springy beneath her feet and to the south the abbey stones, no longer mysterious or sinister, gleamed golden against the blue untroubled sea.

She did not need to ring. The door at Martyr's Cottage stood open as it often did in sunny weather, and she called out to Alice before, in response to her answering voice, moving down the corridor to the kitchen. The cottage was redolent with the zesty smell of lemon overlaying the more familiar tang of polish, wine and wood smoke. It was a smell so keen that it momentarily brought back the holiday she and Martin had spent in Amalfi, the trudge hand-in-hand up the winding road to the mountain-top, the pile of lemons and oranges by the roadside, putting their noses to those golden, pitted skins, the laughter and the happiness. The image experienced in a flash of gold, a flush of warmth to her face, was so vivid that for a second she hesitated at the kitchen door as if disorientated. Then her vision cleared and she saw the familiar objects, the Aga and the gas stove with the nearby working surfaces, the table of polished oak in the middle of the room with its four elegantly crafted chairs, and at the far end Alice's office with the walls covered with bookshelves and her desk piled with proofs. Alice was standing working at the table, wearing her long fawn smock.

She said: 'As you can see, I'm making lemon curd. Alex and I enjoy it occasionally and I enjoy making it, which I suppose is sufficient justification for the trouble.'

'We hardly ever had it – Martin and I, that is. I don't think I've eaten it since childhood. Mother bought it occasionally as a treat for Sunday tea.'

'If she bought it, then you don't know what it ought to taste like.'

Meg laughed and settled into the wicker chair to the left of the fireplace. She never asked if she could help in the kitchen since she knew Alice would be irritated by an offer which she knew to be impractical and insincere. Help was neither needed nor welcomed. But Meg loved to sit quietly and watch. Was it perhaps a memory of childhood, she wondered, that made watching a woman cooking in her own kitchen so extraordinarily reassuring and satisfying. If so, modern children were being deprived of yet one more source of comfort in their increasingly disordered and frightening world.

She said: 'Mother didn't make lemon curd but she did enjoy cooking. It was all very simple, though.'

'That's the difficult kind. And I suppose you helped her. I can picture you in your pinafore making gingerbread men.'

'She used to give me a piece of the dough when she was making pastry. By the time I'd finished pounding it, rolling it and shaping it, it was dun-coloured. And I used to cut out shaped biscuits. And yes, I did make gingerbread men with currants for their eyes, didn't you?'

'No. My mother didn't spend much time in the kitchen. She wasn't a good cook and my father's criticism destroyed what little confidence she had. He paid for a local woman to come in daily to cook the evening meal, virtually the only one he ate at home except on Sundays. She wouldn't come at weekends so that family meals then tended to be acrimonious. It was an odd arrangement and Mrs Watkins was an odd woman. She was a good cook but worked in a perpetual lather of bad temper and she certainly didn't welcome children in her kitchen. I only became interested in cookery when I was taking my degree in modern languages in London and spent a term in France. That's how it began. I found my necessary passion. I realized that I didn't have to teach or translate or become some man's over-qualified secretary.'

Meg didn't reply. Alice had only once before spoken of her family or her past life and she felt that to comment or question might cause her friend to regret the moment of rare confidence. She leaned comfortably back and watched as the deft, familiar, long-fingered hands moved confidently about their business. Before Alice on the table were eight large eggs in a blue shallow bowl and, beside it, a plate with a slab of butter and another with four lemons. She was rubbing the lemons with lumps of sugar until the lumps crumbled into a bowl, when she would pick up another and again begin patiently working away.

She said: 'This will make two pounds. I'll give you a jar to take to the Copleys if you think they'd like it.'

'I'm sure they would, but I'll be eating it alone. That's what I've come to tell you. I can't stay long. Their daughter is insisting that they go to her until the Whistler is caught. She rang again early this morning as soon as she heard the news of the latest murder.'

Alice said: 'The Whistler's getting uncomfortably close, certainly, but they're hardly at risk. He only stalks at night and all the victims have been young women. And the Copleys don't even go out, do they, unless you drive them?'

'They sometimes walk by the sea, but usually they take their exercise in the garden. I've tried to persuade Rosemary Duncan-Smith that they're not in danger and that none of us is frightened. But I think her friends are criticizing her for not getting them away.'

'I see. She doesn't want to have them, they don't want to go, but the friends, so-called, must be propitiated.'

'I think she's one of those masterful, efficient women who can't tolerate criticism. To be fair to her, I think she's genuinely worried.'

'So when are they going?'

'Sunday night. I'm driving them to Norwich to catch the eight thirty getting into Liverpool Street at ten fifty-eight. Their daughter will meet them.'

'That's not very convenient, is it? Sunday travel is always difficult. Why can't they wait till Monday morning?'

'Because Mrs Duncan-Smith is staying at her club in Audley Square for the weekend and has taken a room for them there. Then they can all drive down to Wiltshire first thing on Monday morning.'

'And what about you? Will you mind being left alone?'

'Not in the least. Oh, I expect I'll miss them when they've gone, but at present I keep thinking of all the work I'll be able to catch up on. And I'll be able to spend more time here, helping with the proofs. I don't think I'll be afraid. I can understand the fear and sometimes I find myself almost playing at being frightened, deliberately dwelling on the horror as if I'm testing my own nerve. It's all right in the daytime. But when night falls and we're sitting there by the fire, I can imagine him out there in the darkness, watching and waiting. It's that sense of the unseen, unknowable menace which is so disquieting. It's rather like the feeling I get from the power station, that there's a dangerous unpredictable power out on the headland which I can't control or even begin to understand.'

Alice said: 'The Whistler isn't in the least like the power station. Nuclear power can be understood and it can be controlled. But this latest murder is certainly a nuisance for Alex. Some of the secretaries live locally and bus or cycle home. He's arranging for the staff with cars to take them and pick them up in the morning, but with shift work that means more organizing than you'd expect. And some of the girls are beginning to panic and say they'll only be driven by another woman.'

'But they can't seriously think it's a colleague, someone from the power station?'

'They don't seriously think, that's the trouble. Instinct takes over and their instinct is to suspect every man, particularly if he hasn't an alibi for the last two murders. And then there's Hilary Robarts. She swims almost every evening until the end of October, and sometimes through the winter. She still intends to swim. The chances of her getting murdered may be a million to one but it's an act of bravado which sets a bad example. I'm sorry about yesterday evening, by the way. Not a very successful dinner party. I owed a meal to Miles and Hilary but I hadn't realized just how much they dislike each other. I don't know why. Alex probably does, but I'm not really interested enough to ask. How did you get on with our resident poet?'

Meg said: 'I liked him. I thought he'd be rather intimidating but he isn't, is he? We walked together to the abbey ruins. They look so wonderful by moonlight.'

Alice said: 'Appropriately romantic for a poet. I'm glad you didn't find his company disappointing. But I can never look at the moon without visualizing that litter of hardware. Man leaves his polluting mess behind him like metal turds. But it will be full moon on Sunday night. Why not come here for a quiet supper when you get back from the station and we'll walk to the ruins together. I'll expect you at nine thirty. It will probably just be the two of us. Alex usually goes into the station after a weekend in town.'

Meg said regretfully: 'I'd love to, Alice, but I'd better not. The final packing and getting them off will be a formidable business and by the time I get back from Norwich I'll be ready for bed. And I shan't be hungry. I need to make a high tea for them before we leave. I could only stay for an hour, anyway. Mrs Duncan-Smith says that she'll ring from Liverpool Street to say that they've arrived safely.'

Uncharacteristically Alice dried her hands and walked with her to the door. Meg wondered why in chatting about the dinner party and her walk with Adam Dalgliesh, she hadn't mentioned that mysterious female figure glimpsed among the ruins. It wasn't just that she feared to make too much of it; without Adam Dalgliesh's corroboration she could so easily have been mistaken. Something else, a reluctance she could neither explain nor understand, held her back. As they reached the door and Meg gazed out over the curve of the sunlit headland she experienced a moment of extraordinary perception in which it seemed to her that she was aware of another time, a different reality, existing simultaneously with the moment in which she stood. The external world was still the same. She saw every detail with a keener eye; the motes of dust dancing in the swathe of sunlight which fell across the stone floor, the hardness of each time-worn slab beneath her feet, every nail mark pitting the great oak door, each individual grass of the tussock at the fringe of the heath. But it was the other world which possessed her mind. And here there was no sunlight, only an everlasting darkness loud with the sound of horses' hoofs and tramping feet, of rough male voices, of an incoherent babble as if the tide were sucking back the shingle on all the beaches of the world. And then there was a hiss and crackling of faggots, an explosion of fire, and then a second of dreadful silence broken by the high, long-drawn-out scream of a woman.

She heard Alice's voice: 'Are you all right, Meg?'

'I felt strange for a moment. It's over now. I'm perfectly all right.'

'You've been overworking. There's too much for you to do in that house. And last night was hardly restful. It was probably delayed shock.'

Meg said: 'I told Mr Dalgliesh that I never felt Agnes Poley's presence in this house. But I was wrong. She is here. Something of her remains.'

There was a pause before her friend replied. 'I suppose it depends on your understanding of time. If, as some scientists tell us, it can go backwards, then perhaps she is still here, still alive, burning in an everlasting bonfire. But I'm never aware of her. She doesn't appear to me. Perhaps she finds me unsympathetic. For me, the dead remain dead. If I couldn't believe that I don't think I could go on living.'

Meg said her final goodbye and walked out resolutely over the headland. The Copleys, facing the formidable decisions of what to pack for an indeterminate visit, would be getting anxious. When she reached the crest of the headland she turned and saw Alice still standing at the open doorway. She raised her hand in a gesture more like a blessing than a wave and disappeared into the cottage.

BOOK THREE

Sunday 25 September

19

By a quarter past eight on Sunday night Theresa had finished the last of her long-deferred homework and thought she could safely put away her arithmetic book and tell her father that she was tired and ready for bed. He had earlier helped her wash up after supper, the last of the Irish stew to which she had added extra carrots from a tin, and had settled as he always did in front of the television, slumped back in the battered armchair by the empty fire grate with his bottle of whisky on the floor by his side. Here, she knew, he would sit until the last programme had ended, staring fixedly at the screen but not, she felt, really watching those black and white flickering images. Sometimes it was almost dawn when, awake, she would hear his heavy feet on the stairs.

Mr Jago had rung just after half-past seven and she had answered the telephone and taken a message saying that Daddy was in his painting shed and couldn't be disturbed. It wasn't true. He had been in the privy at the bottom of the garden. But she hadn't liked to tell that to Mr Jago and she wouldn't have dreamed of fetching her father, of knocking on the privy door. Sometimes she thought, with a curiously adult perception, that he took his torch and went there when he didn't really need to, that the ramshackle hut with its cracked door and wide comfortable seat was a refuge for him from the cottage, from the mess and muddle, Anthony's crying, her own ineffectual efforts to take her mother's place. But he must have been on his way back. His ears had caught the ring and, coming in, he had asked her who had telephoned.

'It was a wrong number, Daddy,' she had lied, and from habit made a quick act of contrition. She was glad that he hadn't spoken to Mr Jago. Daddy might have been tempted to meet him at the Local Hero knowing that it would be safe to leave her in charge for an hour or two, and tonight it was vitally important that he didn't leave the cottage. He had only half a bottle of whisky left, she had checked on that. She would be gone for only forty minutes or so and if there were a fire, the secret fear which she had inherited from her mother, he wouldn't be too drunk to save Anthony and the twins.

She kissed him briefly on a cheek which was prickly to her lips and smelt the familiar smell of whisky, turpentine and sweat. As always, he put up his hand and gently ruffled her hair. It was the only gesture of affection which he now made to her. His eyes were still on the old black and white screen where the familiar Sunday faces could be glimpsed through an intermittent snowstorm. He wouldn't, she knew, disturb her once the door to the back bedroom she shared with Anthony was closed. Since her mother's death he had never entered her bedroom when she was there, either by night or day. And she had noticed the difference in his attitude towards her, almost a formality, as if in a few short weeks she had grown into womanhood. He would consult her as if she were an adult about the shopping, the next meal, the twins' clothes, even the problem with the van. But there was one subject he never mentioned: her mother's death.

Her narrow bed was directly under the window. Kneeling on it, she gently drew back the curtains letting moonlight stream into the room, seeking out the corners, laying its swathes of cold, mysterious light on the bed and across the wooden floor. The door to the small box room at the front of the cottage where the twins slept was open and she passed through and stood for a moment looking down at the small humps closely curved together under the bedclothes then, bending low, listened for the regular hiss of their breath. They wouldn't wake now until the morning. She closed the door and went back into her own room. Anthony lay, as he always did, on his back, his legs splayed like a frog, his head to one side and both arms stretched high as if trying to seize the bars of the cot. He had wriggled free of his blanket and she drew it up gently over his sleeping suit. The impulse to snatch him into her arms was so strong that it was almost a pain. But, instead, she carefully let down the side of the cot and, for a moment, laid her head beside his. He lay as if drugged, his mouth pursed, his eyelids delicately veined films under which she could imagine the upturned, unseeing eyes.

Returning to her own bed, she pushed the two pillows down under the blankets and moulded them to the semblance of her body. Her father was very unlikely to look in, but if the unexpected should happen at least he wouldn't see in the moonlight an obviously empty bed. She felt beneath it for the small canvas shoulder bag in which she had placed ready what she knew she would need; the box of matches, the single white household candle, the sharp penknife, the pocket torch. Then she climbed on the bed and opened wide the casement window.

The whole headland was bathed in the silver light which she and her mother loved. Everything was transformed into magic; the outcrops of rock floated like islands of crumpled foil above the still grasses and the broken ill-kept hedge at the bottom of the garden was a mystic thicket woven from thin shafts of light. And beyond it, like a silken scarf, lay the wide untrammelled sea. She stood for a moment transfixed, breathing quickly, gathering up her strength, then climbed out on to the flat roof over the extension. It was covered with shingles and she crept forward with infinite care, feeling the grittiness of the stones through the soles of her plimsolls. It was a drop of only six feet and, with the help of the drainpipe, she made it easily, then scurried down the garden, stooping low, to the rotting wooden lean-to at the rear of her father's painting shed where she and her father kept their bicycles. In the moonlight streaming through the open door she disentangled hers, then wheeled it across the grass and lifted it through a gap in the hedge to avoid using the front gate. It was not until she reached the safety of the sunken lane where the old coastal railway had once run that she dared mount, and began bumping over the humpy grass northwards, towards the fringe of pine trees and the ruined abbey.

The old railway track ran behind the wood of pines which fringed the shore, but here it was less sunken, no more than a gentle depression in the headland. Soon, that too would flatten and there would be nothing, not even the rotting planks of old sleepers, to show where the coastal railway had once run, taking Victorian families with their spades and buckets, their nursemaids, their great portmanteaux, for their summer holiday by the sea. Less than ten minutes later she was in the open headland. She switched off the bicycle lamp, dismounted to check that there was no one in sight, and began bumping across the tough turf towards the sea.

And now the five broken arches of the abbey ruins came into sight, gleaming in the moonlight. She stood for a moment and stared in silence. It looked unreal, ethereal, an insubstantial edifice of light which would dissolve at a touch. Sometimes when, as now, she came to it by moon or starlight, the feeling was so strong that she would put out a hand and touch the stones and feel a physical shock at their rough hardness. Propping her bicycle against the low stone wall, she walked into the space where the great west door must once have been and into the body of the abbey.

It was on calm moonlit nights like this when she and her mother would make their little expeditions together. Her mother would say, 'Let's go and talk to the monks', and they would cycle here together and walk in companionable silence among the ruined arches or stand hand in hand where the altar must once have stood, hearing what those long-dead monks had once heard, but more remotely: the melancholy booming of the sea. It was here, she knew, where her mother liked best to pray, feeling more at home on this rough age-hallowed earth than in that ugly red-brick building outside the village where Father McKee visited every Sunday to say Mass.

She missed seeing Father McKee, missed his jokes, his praise, his funny Irish accent. But since her mother's death he visited only rarely and was never made welcome.

She remembered the last time, the briefness of the visit, her father seeing him out of the door, Father McKee's parting words: 'Her dear mother, God rest her, would want Theresa to be regular at Mass and confession. Mrs Stoddard-Clark would be glad to call for her in the car next Sunday and she could go back to the Grange afterwards for lunch. Now wouldn't that be nice for the child?'

And her father's voice: 'Her mother isn't here. Your God has chosen to deprive her of her mother. Tess is on her own now. When she feels like going to Mass, she'll go, and she'll go to confession when she has something to confess.'

The grass had grown high here, spiked with tall weeds and dried flowerheads, the ground so humpy that she had to walk with care. She moved up under the highest arch of all where the great eastern window had once shone in an imagined miracle of coloured glass. Now it was an empty eye through which she could see the gleam of the sea and above it the sailing moon. And now, by the light of her torch and very quietly, she began her task. She went over to the wall, knife in hand, and began searching for a large, flat-surfaced stone which would form the basis of her altar. Within minutes she had found one and had prised it loose with her penknife. But there was something hidden in the crevice behind it, a thin piece of cardboard pushed deep into the crevice. She took it out and unfolded it. It was half of a coloured postcard of the west front of Westminster Abbey. Even with the right-hand side cut away she recognized the familiar twin towers. She turned it over and saw that there were a few lines of message which she couldn't read by moonlight and felt no particular curiosity to decipher. It seemed quite new, but with the date stamp unreadable there was no way of knowing how long it had lain there. Perhaps it had been hidden during the summer season as part of a family game. It didn't worry her, indeed, preoccupied as she was, it hardly interested her. This was the kind of secret message her friends left for each other at school, hidden in the bicycle shed, slipped into a blazer pocket. She hesitated for a moment, started to tear it, then smoothed it out and put it carefully back.

Working her way along the wall, she found another suitable stone and the few smaller ones she needed to prop up the single candle. The altar was soon complete. She lit the candle, the hiss of the match sounding unnaturally loud and the sudden flare of the light almost too bright for her eyes. She let the first blobs of wax fall on the stone, then wedged the candle into it, propping it up with pebbles. Then she sat cross-legged before it and gazed into the candle's steady glow. She knew that her mother would come, unseen but known to be present, silent but speaking clearly. She had only to wait in patience and gaze steadily into the candle's unflickering light.

She tried to empty her mind of everything except the questions which she was here to ask. But her mother's death was too recent, the memory too painful to be shut out of her thoughts.

Mummy hadn't wanted to die in hospital and Daddy had promised that she wouldn't. She had heard his whispered assurances. She knew that Dr Entwhistle and the district nurse had opposed them both. There were snatches of conversation she wasn't supposed to overhear but which, standing silently in the darkness of the stairs behind the oak door which led to the sitting room, came to her clearly as if she was standing by her mother's bed.

'You really need twenty-four-hour nursing, Mrs Blaney, more care than I can give. And you'd be more comfortable in hospital.'

'I am comfortable. I have Ryan and Theresa. I have you. You're all so good to me. I don't need anyone else.'

'I do what I can, but twice a day isn't enough. It's a lot to expect of Mr Blaney and Theresa. It's all right saying you've got her, but she's only fifteen.'

'I want to be with them. We want to be together.'

'But if they're frightened . . . it's difficult for children.'

Then that gentle implacable voice, thin and unbreakable as a reed, carrying the obstinate selfishness of the dying. 'They won't be frightened. Do you think we'd let them be frightened? There isn't anything frightening about birth or death if they've been properly taught.'

'There are things you can't teach children, Mrs Blaney, things you can only experience.'

And she, Theresa, had done her best to convince everyone that they were all right, that they could manage. There had been small subterfuges. Before Nurse Pollard and the doctor arrived she would wash the twins, put on clean dresses, change Anthony's nappy. It was important that everything looked under control, so that Dr Entwhistle and the nurse couldn't say that Daddy couldn't cope. One Saturday she cooked buns and handed them gravely round on a plate, the best plate, her mother's favourite, with the delicately painted roses and the holes in the border where you could thread a ribbon. She remembered the doctor's embarrassed gaze as he said, 'No thank you, Theresa, not just now.'

'Please have one. Daddy made them.'

And as he left he had said to her father: 'You may be able to bear this, Blaney, I'm not sure that I can.'

Only Father McKee seemed to notice her efforts. Father McKee, who spoke so like an Irishman on the telly that Theresa thought he was doing it on purpose as a joke and tried always to reward him with a laugh.

'My and isn't it grand the way you have this cottage shining. Couldn't the blessed Virgin herself eat off that floor now? Made by your dad, are they? And very nice too. See, I'm putting one in my pocket for later. Now you be making a nice cup of tea, that's a good girl, while I chat to your ma.'

She tried not to think about the night when they had taken her mother away; waking to hear those awful groaning noises which had made her think that there was an animal in agony snuffling round the cottage; realizing that the noise wasn't outside at all; the sudden terror; her father's figure in the bedroom doorway commanding her to stay there, not to come out, to keep the children quiet. Watching at the window of the little front bedroom with the twins' frightened faces staring from the bed and seeing the ambulance arrive; the two men with the stretcher; that blanket-shrouded figure, quiet now, being carried down the garden path. It was then that she had rushed down the stairs and almost hurled herself at her father's restraining arms.

'Better not, better not. Get her inside.'

She wasn't sure who had spoken the words. Then she was breaking free and running after the ambulance as it turned at the bottom of the lane, beating her hands against the closed doors. She remembered her father lifting her in his arms, carrying her back into the cottage. She remembered the strength of him, the smell and roughness of his shirt, her impotently flailing arms. She had never seen her mother again. It was how God had answered her prayers, her mother's prayers, to be able to stay at home, her mother who asked for so little. And nothing Father McKee could say would make her forgive God.

The chill of the September night was seeping through her jeans and jumper and the small of her back was beginning to ache. For the first time she felt a prick of doubt. And then, in a tremble of the candle flame, her mother was with her. Everything was all right.

There were so many things she needed to ask. Anthony's nappies. The disposable ones were so expensive and so bulky to carry, and Daddy didn't seem to realize how much they cost. Her mother said she should use the terries and rinse them out. Then the twins didn't really like Mrs Hunter who came and collected them to take them to the playgroup. The twins must be polite to Mrs Hunter and not mind. She was doing her best. It was important that they kept going to the playgroup for Daddy's sake. Theresa must tell them that. And then there was Daddy. There was so much to say about him. He didn't go to the pub often because he didn't like to leave them, but there was always whisky in the house. Her mother said that she was not to worry about the whisky. He needed it now, but soon he would begin painting again and then he wouldn't need it so much. But if he really became drunk and there was another bottle in the house she had better pour it away. She needn't be frightened that it would make him angry. He would never be angry with her.

The silent communication went on. She sat as if in a trance, watching while the wax of the candle slowly burned down. And then there was nothing. Her mother had gone away. Before blowing out the candle she scraped away the traces of wax from the stone with her knife. It was important that no evidence remained. Then she replaced the stones in the wall. The ruins held nothing for her now but a cold emptiness. It was time to go home.

Suddenly she was overcome with tiredness. It seemed impossible that her legs would carry her as far as the bicycle and she couldn't face the thought of the bumpy ride across the headland. She didn't know what impulse led her through the great east window to stand on the edge of the cliff. Perhaps it was the need to gather her strength, to look out over the moonlit sea and recapture for a moment that lost communion with her mother. But instead her mind was seized with a very different memory, as recent as that afternoon, and one that was still so frightening that she hadn't spoken of it, even to her mother. She saw again the red car, moving at speed down the lane towards Scudder's Cottage, called the children from the garden, bundled them upstairs and shut the sitting-room door. But later she had stood behind it and listened. It seemed to her that no word of that conversation would ever be forgotten.

First Hilary Robarts's voice: 'This place was totally unsuitable for a sick woman who had to undergo long journeys for radiotherapy. You must have known she was ill when you took it. She couldn't manage.'

And then her father: 'And I suppose you thought that after she'd gone I wouldn't be able to manage either. How many months did you give her? You used to pretend that you were concerned but she knew what you were at. Watching how much weight she was losing each week, more bone showing through, wrists like sticks, the cancer skin. Not much longer now, you thought. You made a bloody good investment in this cottage. You invested in her death and you made her life a bloody misery for her last weeks.'

'That isn't true. Don't load your guilt on me. I had to come here, there were things I had to see. That patch of damp in the kitchen, the problem with rain coming in the roof. You wanted them seen to, presumably. You were the first to point out that I had obligations as a landlady. And if you won't get out I shall have to apply for a rise in the rent. What you pay is derisory. It doesn't even cover repairs.'

'Try. Go to the Rent Tribunal. Let them come and see for themselves. The freehold may be yours but I'm the man in possession. And I pay the rent regularly. You can't get me out, I'm not that daft.'

'You pay the rent, but for how long? You could get by when you had that part-time teaching job, but I can't see you managing now. I suppose you call yourself an artist, but what you are is a cheap hack painter turning out rubbish for undiscriminating tourists who think any fourth-rate original is better than a first-rate print. But they aren't selling as well now, are they? Those four watercolours Ackworth has in his window have been there for weeks. They're beginning to brown. Even tourists are getting a little particular these days. Junk doesn't sell just because it's cheap.'

But the twins, tired of incarceration, began quarrelling and she had to hurry upstairs to tell them it wouldn't be long now, that they mustn't come out until the witch had gone. Then she crept down again. But it wasn't necessary to descend further than the fourth step. The voices were shouting now.

'I want to know if you sent that woman here, that bloody social worker from the local authority who came to spy on me and question my children about me. Did you send her?'

The witch's voice was cool, but she could hear every word: 'I'm not required to answer that. If I did alert them, then it was about time someone did.'

'My God, you're evil, aren't you? You'd do anything to get me and my children out of this cottage. They used to burn people like you four hundred years ago. If it wasn't for the children I'd kill you. But I'm not having them taken into so-called care just for the satisfaction of putting my hands round your throat. But, by God, don't tempt me, don't tempt me. So get out. Get out of my cottage and off my ground. Take your rent and be thankful you're alive to take it. And don't ever interfere with my life again. Not ever, not ever.'

The witch said: 'Don't be hysterical. That's all you're good for, threats and violence. If the local authority took those children into care it would be the best thing for them. Oh, I dare say you'd like to kill me. Your sort always react to reason with threats and violence. Kill me and expect the state to support your children for the next fifteen years. You're ridiculous and pathetic.'

And then her father's voice, not shouting any more but so quiet that she could only just catch the words: 'If I do kill you, no one will lay their hands on me or my children. No one.'

With the reliving of that last awful encounter came anger and the anger flowing into her legs seemed to give them strength. She could cope now with the ride home. And it was time she was leaving. And then she saw that the beach was no longer empty. Suddenly she began shaking like a young puppy and then backed into the shelter of the arch. To the north, running down from the pine trees towards the sea, was a woman, her dark hair streaming, her white body almost naked. And she was shouting, shouting in triumph. It was the witch, Hilary Robarts.

20

Hilary ate an early supper. She wasn't hungry but she took a French roll from the freezer and heated it in the oven, then made herself a herb omelette. She washed up and left the kitchen tidy, then took papers from her briefcase and settled down at the sitting-room table to work. There was a paper to be written about the implications of the reorganization for her department, figures to be collated and presented, an argument for the redeployment of staff logically and elegantly presented. The task was important to her and normally she would have enjoyed it. She knew that she could be faulted when it came to personnel management but no one had been able to criticize her as organizer and administrator. Shuffling the papers she wondered how much, if at all, she would miss it when she and Alex were married and in London. She was surprised how little she cared. This part of her life was over and she would relinquish it without regret, this over-tidy cottage which had never been her own and never could be, the power station, even her job. And now there would be a different life, Alex's job, her status as his wife, entertaining the right people in the right way, some carefully chosen voluntary work, travel. And there would be a child, his child.

This overpowering need for a child had strengthened in the last year, growing in intensity as his physical need for her decreased. She tried to persuade herself that a love affair, like a marriage, couldn't always be maintained at the same pitch of sexual or emotional excitement, that essentially nothing had changed between them and nothing really could. How much commitment, physical or emotional, had there been at the start of the relationship? Well, that had suited her all right at the time; she hadn't wanted any more than he was prepared to give, a mutually satisfactory exchange of pleasure, the kudos of being his half-acknowledged mistress, the careful dissimulation when they were in company together which was hardly necessary or successful and wasn't seriously meant to be but which, for her part at least, had held a powerful erotic charge. It was a game they played; their almost formal greeting before meetings or in the presence of strangers, his twice weekly visits to her cottage.

When she had first come to Larksoken she had looked for a modern flat in Norwich and had, for a time, rented one close to the city centre. But once the affair began it was necessary to be near him and she had found a holiday cottage less than a quarter of a mile from Martyr's Cottage. He was, she knew, both too proud and too arrogant to visit her surreptitiously, sneaking out at night like a randy schoolboy. But no degrading pretence was necessary; the headland was invariably deserted. And he never stayed the night. The careful rationing of her company seemed almost a necessary part of the relationship. And in public they behaved as colleagues. He had always discouraged informality, too many first names, except to his immediate colleagues, too much easy camaraderie. The station was as disciplined as a tightly run ship in wartime.

But the affair, begun with such discipline, such emotional and social propriety, had deteriorated into messiness and longing and pain. She thought she knew the moment when the need for a child had begun to grow into an obsession. It was when the theatre sister at that expensive and discreet nursing home, only half concealing her disapproval and disgust, had taken away the kidney-shaped bowl with that quivering mass of tissue which had been the foetus. It was as if her womb, so clinically robbed, was taking its revenge. She hadn't been able to conceal her longing from Alex even though she knew that it repelled him. She could hear again her own voice, truculent, whining, an importunate child, and could see his look, half laughing, of simulated dismay which she knew concealed a genuine repugnance.

'I want a child.'

'Don't look at me, darling. That's one experiment I'm not prepared to repeat.'

'You have a child, healthy, living, successful. Your name, your genes will go on.'

'I've never set store on that. Charles exists in his own right.'

She had tried to argue herself out of the obsession, forcing the unwelcome images on her unreceptive mind, the broken nights, the smell, the constant demands, the lessening of freedom, the lack of privacy, the effect on her career. It was no good. She was making an intellectual response to a need where intellect was powerless. Sometimes she wondered if she was going mad. And she couldn't control her dreams, one in particular. The smiling nurse, gowned and masked, placing the newborn baby in her arms, herself looking down at the gentle, self-contained face bruised with the trauma of birth. And then the sister, grim-visaged, rushing in, snatching the bundle away. 'That isn't your baby, Miss Robarts. Don't you remember? We flushed yours down the lavatory.'

Alex didn't need another child. He had his son, his living hope, however precarious, of vicarious immortality. He might have been an inadequate and scarcely known parent, but he was a parent. He had held in his arms his own child. That wasn't unimportant to him, whatever he might pretend. Charles had visited his father last summer, a golden-bronzed, hefty-legged, sun-bleached giant who had seemed in retrospect to blaze through the station like a meteor, captivating the female staff with his American accent, his hedonistic charm. And Alex, she saw, had been surprised and slightly disconcerted by his pride in the boy, attempting unsuccessfully to conceal it with heavy-handed banter.

'Where is the young barbarian, swimming? He'll find the North Sea an unwelcome change from Laguna Beach.'

'He tells me he proposes to read law at Berkeley. There's a place waiting for him in step-papa's firm, apparently, once he qualifies. Next thing Liz will be writing to say that he's engaged to some socially acceptable sophomore, or do I mean preppy?'

'I'm managing to feed him, by the way. Alice has left me a recipe for hamburgers. Every shelf of the refrigerator is stuffed with ground beef. His vitamin C requirements seem abnormally high even for a boy of his height and weight. I press oranges constantly.'

She had squirmed in a mixture of embarrassment and resentment, the pride and the juvenile humour had both seemed so out of character, almost demeaning. It was as if he, as much as the typists, had been captivated by his son's physical presence. Alice Mair had left for London two days after Charles had arrived. Hilary wondered whether this had been perhaps a ploy to give father and son some time alone together or whether, and more likely from what she knew or guessed of Alice Mair, it had been a reluctance both to spend time cooking for the boy and to witness his father's embarrassing excess of paternalism.

She thought again of his last visit when he had walked home with her after the dinner party. She had deliberately sounded reluctant to be escorted, but he had come and she had meant that he should. After she had finished speaking he had said quietly: 'That sounds like an ultimatum.'

'I wouldn't call it that.'

'What would you call it then, blackmail?'

'After what's happened between us, I'd call it justice.'

'Let's stick to ultimatum. Justice is too grandiose a concept for the commerce between us two. And like every ultimatum it will have to be considered. It's usual to set a time limit. What's yours?'

She had said: 'I love you. In this new job you're going to need a wife. I'm the right wife for you. It could work. I'd make it work. I could make you happy.'

'I'm not sure how much happiness I'm capable of. Probably more than I've any right to. But it isn't in anyone's gift, not Alice's, not Charles's, not Elizabeth's, not yours. It never has been.'

Then he had come over to her and kissed her on the cheek. She had turned to cling to him but he had put her gently aside. 'I'll think about it.'

'I'd like to announce it soon, the engagement.'

'You're not thinking of a church wedding, I suppose. Orange blossom, bridesmaids, Mendelssohn's "Wedding March", "The voice that breathed o'er Eden".'

She had said: 'I'm not thinking of making either of us ridiculous, now or after marriage. You know me better than that.'

'I see, just a quick, painless turning-off at the local registrar's office. I'll give you my decision next Sunday night after I get back from London.'

She had said: 'You make it sound so formal.'

And he had replied: 'But it has to be formal, doesn't it, the response to an ultimatum?'

He would marry her and, within three months, he would know that she had been right. She would win because, in this, her will was stronger than his. She remembered the words of her father. 'There's only this one life, girlie, but you can live it on your own terms. Only the stupid and the weak need to live like slaves. You've got health, looks, brains. You can take what you want. All you need is the courage and the will.' The bastards had nearly got him in the end, but he had lived life on his own terms and so would she.

Now she tried to put thoughts of Alex, of their future, on one side and concentrate on the task in hand. But she couldn't settle. Restless, she went through the kitchen into the small back parlour which held her wine store and brought out a bottle of claret. She took down a glass from the dresser and poured. Taking her first mouthful, she felt on the corner of her lip the minute scrape of a chip. It was intolerable to her to drink from a chipped glass. Instinctively she took down another and emptied the first glass into it. She was about to throw the defective glass away when she hesitated, her foot on the pedal of the refuse bin. It was one of a set of six that Alex had given her. The defect, unnoticed before, was slight, little more than a roughness on the brim. The glass could be used to hold flowers. She had a picture of them, snowdrops, primroses, small sprigs of rosemary. When she had finished drinking she washed up both glasses and turned them over to drain. The bottle of claret she left uncorked on the table. It had really been too cold to drink, but in another hour it would be about right.

It was time for her swim, just after nine, and tonight she wouldn't bother with the news. Upstairs in her bedroom she stripped naked, put on the bottom half of a black bikini and over it her blue and white tracksuit. On her feet she wore old sandals, the leather stained and toughened by sea water. From the hall peg she took down a small steel locket on a leather thong just large enough to hold her Yale key, which she wore round her neck when swimming. It had been Alex's gift for her last birthday. Touching it, she smiled and felt, strong as the metal against her fingers, the certainty of hope. Then she took a torch from the drawer in the hall table and, closing the door carefully behind her, set off for the beach, her towel slung over her shoulder.

She smelt the resin of the pines before she passed between their slim, spiky trunks. There were only fifty yards of sandy path, thick with their fallen needles, between her and the shore. It was dimmer here, the moon glimpsed fitfully, sailing in majestic splendour above the high spires of the trees, now seen and now obscured, so that for a few seconds she had to switch on her torch. And now she passed out of the shadows and saw before her the white moon-bleached sand and the tremble of the North Sea. Dropping her towel in her usual place, a small hollow on the fringe of the wood, she slipped off her tracksuit and stretched her arms high above her head.

Then she kicked off her sandals and began running, over the narrow band of shingle, over the dusty sand above the watermark, over the smooth, sea-washed eddies of the foam, splashing through the small waves which seemed to be falling without a sound, to hurl herself at last into cleansing peace. She gasped at the coldness of it, fierce as a pain. But almost at once that passed, as it always did, and it seemed to her that the water gliding over her shoulders had taken on her own body warmth and that she swam cocooned in self-sufficiency. With her strong rhythmic crawl she struck out from the shore. She knew how long she could safely stay in; just five minutes before the cold struck again and it was time to return.

And now she stopped swimming and lay for a moment on her back, floating, looking up at the moon. The magic worked again as it always did. The frustrations, the fears, the anger of the day fell away and she was filled instead with a happiness which she would have called ecstasy, except that ecstasy was too ostentatious a word for this gentle peace. And with the happiness came optimism. Everything was going to be all right. She would let Pascoe sweat for another week then withdraw her action. He was too unimportant even to hate. And her solicitor was right, possession of Scudder's Cottage could wait. It was increasing in value every month. The rent was being paid, she was losing nothing. And the daily irritations of the job, the professional jealousies, the resentments, what did they matter now? That part of her life was coming to an end. She loved Alex, Alex loved her. He would see the sense of everything she had said. They would be married. She would have his child. Everything was possible. And then, for a moment, there came a deeper peace in which even none of this mattered. It was as if all the petty preoccupations of the flesh were washed away and she was a disembodied spirit floating free, looking down at her body spreadeagled under the moon, and could feel a gentle, undemanding sorrow for this earth-grounded creature who could find only in an alien element this sweet but transitory peace.

But it was time to get back. She gave a vigorous kick, twisted herself over and began her powerful crawl towards the shore, towards that silent watcher waiting for her in the shadow of the trees.

21

Dalgliesh had spent Sunday morning revisiting Norwich Cathedral and St Peter Mancroft before lunching at a restaurant on the outskirts of the city where he and his aunt two years previously had eaten an unpretentious but excellently cooked meal. But here, too, time had wrought its changes. The exterior and the décor were deceivingly the same but it was quickly apparent that both proprietor and chef had changed. The meal, arriving with suspicious promptness, had obviously been cooked elsewhere and heated up, the grilled liver a grainy slab of indistinguishable grey meat blanketed with a synthetic, glutinous sauce and accompanied by potatoes which were underdone and cauliflower which was a mush. It was not a luncheon to deserve a wine, but he fortified himself with Cheddar and biscuits before setting out on the afternoon's programme, a visit to the fifteenth-century church of St Peter and St Paul at Salle.

During the last four years it had been rare for him to visit his aunt without driving with her to Salle, and she had left with her will a request that her ashes should be strewn in the churchyard there without ceremony and by him on his own. He knew that the church had exerted a powerful influence on her but she had not, as far as he knew, been a religious woman and the request had a little surprised him. It had seemed so much more likely that she would have wanted her physical remains thrown to the winds on the headland, or that she would have left no instructions, regarding this as a simple matter of expedient disposal requiring neither thought on her part nor ceremony on his. But now he had a task to perform and one of surprising importance to him. In recent weeks he had been visited by the nagging guilt of a duty unfulfilled, almost a spirit unpropitiated. He found himself wondering, as he had before in his life, at man's insistent need for ritual, for the formal acknowledgement of each rite of passage. Perhaps this was something his aunt had understood and in her quiet way had made provision for.

He turned off the B1149 at Felthorpe to take the country roads across the flat country. It was unnecessary to consult the map. The magnificent fifteenth-century tower with its four pinnacles was an unmistakable landmark and he drove towards it along the almost deserted roads with the familiar sense of coming home. It seemed strange that his aunt's angular figure wasn't beside him, that all that remained of that secretive but powerful personality was a plastic package, curiously heavy, of white grit. When he reached Salle he parked the Jaguar a little down the lane and made his way into the churchyard. As always, he was struck that a church as magnificent as a cathedral could be so isolated yet seem utterly right among these quiet fields where its effect was less of grandeur and majesty than of an unpretentious and reassuring peace. For a few minutes he stood quietly listening and heard nothing, not even a bird song or the rustle of an insect in the tall grasses. In the frail sunlight the surrounding trees were flushed with the first gold of autumn. The ploughing was over and the brown crust of the crumbled fields stretched in their Sunday calm towards the far horizon. He walked slowly round the church feeling the weight of the package dragging at his jacket pocket, glad that he had chosen a time between services and wondering whether it might not have been courteous, perhaps even necessary, to obtain the consent of the parish priest before carrying out his aunt's wishes. But he told himself that it was too late to think of that now, glad to be spared explanations or complications. Making his way to the eastern fringe of the churchyard he opened the package and tipped out the ground bones like a libation. There was a flash of silver and all that remained of Jane Dalgliesh sparkled among the brittle autumn stalks and the tall grasses. He knew the customary words for such an occasion; he had heard them often enough on his father's lips. But the ones which came unbidden to his mind were the verses from Ecclesiastes carved on the stone outside Martyr's Cottage and in this timeless place beside the dignity of the great church it seemed to him that they were not inappropriate.

The west door was unlocked and before leaving Salle he spent fifteen minutes in the church revisiting old pleasures: the carvings on the oak stalls, peasants, a priest, animals and birds, a dragon, a pelican feeding its young; the medieval wineglass pulpit, which after five hundred years still showed traces of its original colouring; the chancel screen; the great east window which once had glowed in the glory of red, green and blue medieval glass but which now let in only the clear Norfolk light. As the west door clanged gently behind him he wondered when he would return, or if he would return at all.

It was early evening before he got home. What he had eaten of lunch had been stodgily filling so that he was less hungry than he had expected. He heated up the last of yesterday's home-made soup and followed it with biscuits and cheese and fruit and then kindled the fire and sat on the low chair before it, listening to Elgar's Cello Concerto and making a start on the job of sorting out his aunt's photographs. Tipping them out of their faded envelopes he sorted them with his long fingers on the low mahogany table. It was a task which induced a gentle melancholy from which an occasional scribbled identification on the back of a print, a remembered face or incident, would stab him into pain. And the Elgar was an appropriate accompaniment, the plaintive notes evoking those long, hot Edwardian summers known to him only from novels and poetry, the peace, the certainty, the optimism of the England into which his aunt had been born. And here was her fiancé, looking ridiculously young in his captain's uniform. The photograph was dated 4 May 1918, only a week before he was killed. He gazed for a moment intently at that handsome, debonair young face which, God knew, must by then have seen enough of horror, but it told him nothing. Turning it over Dalgliesh saw that it bore a pencilled message written in Greek. The young man was to have read Classics at Oxford and his aunt had studied Greek with her father. But he knew no Greek; their secret was safe enough with him and soon would be safe for ever. The hand which had formed these fading characters had been dead now for seventy years, the mind that had first created them for nearly two thousand. And here, in the same envelope, was one of his aunt herself at about the same age. It must have been one she had sent to her fiancé at the Front or given to him before he left for war. One corner was stained browny-red with what must be his blood; perhaps the photograph had been returned to her with the rest of his effects. She stood in her long skirt with the high-buttoned blouse, laughing, her hair in two wings on either side and bound above the temples. Over the years her face had always had distinction, but he saw, almost with a shock of surprise, that once she had been beautiful. And now her death had freed him for a voyeurism which in her life would have been repugnant to them both. And yet she hadn't destroyed the photographs. She must have known, realist that she was, that other eyes than hers would eventually see them. Or did extreme old age free one from all such petty considerations of vanity or self-esteem, as the mind gradually distanced itself from the devices and desires of the flesh? It was with a sense of irrational reluctance, almost of betrayal, that eventually he threw both photographs into the fire and watched them curl, blacken and finally flare into ash.

And what was he to do with all these undocumented strangers, the women, sloping-bosomed, under immense hats piled with ribbons and flowers, the cycling parties, the men knickerbockered, the women with their long, bell-shaped skirts and their straw boaters; the wedding parties, bride and bridesmaids almost hidden behind their immense bouquets, the chief participants grouped in recognized hierarchy and staring into the lens as if the click of the shutter could for a second halt time, hold it in thrall, proclaiming that this rite of passage at least had importance, binding the ineluctable past to the unseeable future? As an adolescent boy he had been obsessed with time. For weeks before the summer holidays he would feel a sense of triumph that now he had time by the forelock and could say, 'Go as quickly as you like and the holiday will be here. Or if you must, go slowly, and the summer days will last longer.' Now, in middle age, he knew of no contrivance and no promised pleasure which could halt the inexorable thudding of those chariot wheels. And here was a photograph of himself in his prep-school uniform, taken in the rectory garden by his father, a stranger ridiculously over-clad in cap and striped blazer standing almost to attention, facing the lens as if defying the terror of leaving home. That, too, he was glad to see the end of.

When the concerto was finished, the half-bottle of claret empty, he shuffled the remaining photographs together, placed them in the bureau drawer and decided to shake off melancholy with a brisk walk by the sea before bed. The night was too calm and beautiful to be wasted in nostalgia and futile regrets. The air was extraordinarily still and even the sound of the sea was muted as it stretched, pale and mysterious, under the full moon and the bright pattern of stars. He stood for a moment under the soaring wings of the mill then began walking vigorously over the headland towards the north, past the fringe of pines, until, three-quarters of an hour later, he decided to make for the beach. He half slid down the sandy decline and saw before him the great square hunks of concrete half buried in the sand, the curls of rotting iron springing from them like bizarre antennae. Moonlight, strong as the last light of the setting sun, had changed the texture of the beach so that each grain of sand seemed separately illuminated, every pebble mysteriously unique. Suddenly he had a childish impulse to feel the sea washing over his feet and, taking off his shoes and socks, he stuffed the socks in his jacket pocket and, tying the laces, slung the shoes round his neck. The water, after the first sting of cold, was almost blood-warm and he splashed vigorously along the fringe of the waves, pausing from time to time to look back at his footprints as he had as a child. Now he had reached the narrow strip of pine trees. There was, he knew, a narrow path which cut inland through them past Hilary Robarts's cottage to the road. It was the simplest way of regaining the headland without having to scramble up the friable cliffs to the south. Sitting on a ridge of shingle, he tackled the familiar problem of the paddler: how, with an inadequate handkerchief, to rid the spaces between his toes of the gritty dusting of tenacious sand. That achieved, socks and shoes replaced, he trudged through the pebbles to the shore line.

When he reached the powdery sand on the upper reaches of the beach he saw that someone had been here before him; to his left was a double line of naked footprints, the mark of running feet. These, of course, would be Hilary Robarts's. She must, as usual, have taken her nightly swim. Subconsciously he noticed how distinct they were. She must have left the beach nearly an hour and a half ago, yet on this windless night the indentations were as plain in the dry sand as if they had just been made. The path through the trees lay in front of him leading out of moonlight into the enclosing shadows of the pine wood. And the night was suddenly darker. A low blue-black cloud had momentarily covered the moon, its ragged edges silvered with light.

He switched on his torch and played it over the path. It caught the gleam of something white to his left, a sheet of newspaper, perhaps, a handkerchief, a discarded paper bag. Feeling no more than mild curiosity he stepped from the path to investigate. And then he saw her. Her distorted face seemed to leap up at him and hang suspended in the bright glare of the torchlight like a vision from a nightmare. Staring down, and for a moment transfixed, he felt a shock in which incredulity, recognition and horror fused into a second which made his heart leap. She was lying in a shallow depression of flattened marram grass, hardly a hollow but deep enough for the grasses on each verge to shield her body until he was almost on top of her. To her right, and partly beneath her, was a crumpled beach towel, striped in red and blue, and above it, placed precisely side by side, a pair of open sandals and a torch. Beside them, neatly folded, was what looked like a blue and white tracksuit. It must have been the edge of this which had first caught his eye. She lay on her back, the head towards him, the dead eyes upturned as if they had been fixed on him in a last mute appeal. The small bush of hair had been pushed under the upper lip, exposing the teeth, and giving the impression of a snarling rabbit. A single black hair lay across her cheek and he had an almost irresistible impulse to kneel and pluck it away. She was wearing only the bottom half of a black bikini and that had been pulled down over her thighs. He could clearly see where the hair had been sliced away. The letter L precisely in the centre of the forehead looked as if it had been cut with deliberation, the two thin lines precisely at right angles. Between the splayed and flattened breasts with their dark areolas and pointed nipples, milk-white against the brown skin of her arms, rested a key-shaped metal locket on a chain. And as he gazed down, slowly moving the torchlight over her body, the cloud moved from the face of the moon and she lay stretched out before him clearly, the naked limbs pale and bloodless as the bleached sands and as clearly visible as if it were day.

He was inured to horror; few manifestations of human cruelty, violence or desperation were unfamiliar to his practised eye. He was too sensitive ever to view a violated body with crude indifference but only in one recent case, his last, had this sensitivity caused him more than momentary inconvenience. And with Paul Berowne at least he had been warned. This was the first time he had almost stumbled over a murdered woman. Now, as he looked down on her, his mind analysed the difference between the reaction of an expert summoned to the scene of crime knowing what to expect and this sudden exposure to ultimate violence. He was interested both in the difference and in the detachment which could so coolly analyse it.

Kneeling, he touched her thigh. It felt icy cold and as synthetic as inflated rubber. If he prodded it the mark of his fingers would surely remain. Gently he ran them through her hair. It was still slightly damp at the roots but the ends were dry. The night was warm for September. He looked at his watch: ten thirty-three. He remembered being told, he couldn't recall when or by whom, that it was her practice to take her nightly swim shortly after nine o'clock. The physical signs confirmed what he thought most likely, that she had been dead for less than two hours.

He had seen no footprints on the sand but his and hers. But the tide was ebbing; it must have been high at about nine, although the dustiness of the upper reaches of the beach suggested that it didn't reach the hollow where she lay. But the most likely path for the murderer to have taken was the one through the wood which she herself must have used. He would have had the protection of the trees and a place in their shadow where he could watch and wait unseen. The ground with its mat of pine needles on the sand was unlikely to yield footprints but it was important that it shouldn't be disturbed. Moving carefully, he backed away from the body then walked about twenty yards to the south along a ridge of fine shingle. By the light of his torch, half crouching, he tracked his way through the densely planted pine trees, snapping off the brittle lower twigs as he passed. At least he could be certain that no one had recently passed this way. Within minutes he had gained the road; another ten of brisk walking and he would be at the mill. But the nearest telephone would be at Hilary Robarts's cottage. The probability was that the cottage was locked and he had no intention of breaking in. It was almost as important to leave the victim's house undisturbed as it was not to violate the scene of the crime. There had been no handbag beside her body, nothing but the shoes and torch neatly placed at the head of the hollow, the tracksuit and the brightly striped red and blue beach towel on which she partly lay. Perhaps she had left the key at home, the cottage unlocked. On the headland, after dark, few people would worry if they left a cottage unlocked for half an hour. It was worth taking five minutes to look.

Thyme Cottage, seen from the windows of the mill, had always struck him as the least interesting house on the headland. It faced inland, a square, uncompromising building with a cobbled yard instead of a front garden and picture windows in modern glass which destroyed any period charm it once might have had and made it look like a modern aberration more appropriate to a rural housing estate than to this sea-scarred and remote headland. On three sides the pines grew so closely that they almost touched the walls. He had wondered from time to time why Hilary Robarts should have chosen to live here despite its convenient distance from the power station. After Alice Mair's dinner party he thought he knew why. Now all the lights were blazing in the ground-floor rooms, the large rectangle of the picture window to the left reaching almost to the ground and the smaller square to the right which he thought was probably the kitchen. Normally they would have been a reassuring signal of life, normality and welcome, of a refuge from the atavistic fears of the enclosing wood, the empty moonlit headland. But now those bright, uncurtained windows added to his mounting unease and as he approached the cottage it seemed to him that there floated between him and those bright windows, like a half-developed print, the mental picture of that dead and violated face.

Someone had been here before him. He vaulted over the low stone wall and saw that the pane of the picture window had been almost completely smashed. Small slivers of glass gleamed like jewels on the cobbled yard. He stood and gazed between the jagged edges of the broken glass into the brightness of the sitting room. The carpet was littered with glass fragments like winking beads of silver light. It was obvious that the force of the blow had come from outside the cottage and he saw at once what had been used. Below him, face upwards on the carpet, was the portrait of Hilary Robarts. It had been slashed almost to the frame with two right-angled cuts forming the letter L.

He didn't try the door to see if it was unlocked. It was more important not to contaminate the scene than to save ten or fifteen minutes in ringing the police. She was dead. Speed was important, but it was not vital. Regaining the road he set off towards the mill, half running, half walking. And then he heard the noise of a car and, turning, saw the lights coming at him fast from the north. It was Alex Mair's BMW. Dalgliesh stood in the middle of the road and waved his torch. The car slowed and stopped. Looking up to the open right-side window he saw Mair, his face bleached by moonlight, regarding him for a moment with an unsmiling intensity as if this encounter were an assignation.

Dalgliesh said: 'I'm afraid I have shocking news for you. Hilary Robarts has been murdered. I've just found the body. I need to get to a telephone.'

The hand lying casually on the wheel tightened then relaxed. The eyes fixed on his grew wary. But when Mair spoke his voice was controlled. Only in that involuntary spasm of the hand had he betrayed emotion. He said: 'The Whistler?'

'It looks like it.'

'There's a telephone in the car.'

Without another word he opened the door, got out and stood silently aside while Dalgliesh spent an irritating two minutes getting through to Rickards's headquarters. Rickards wasn't there but the message given, he rang off. Mair had moved about thirty yards from the car and was staring back at the glitter of the power station as if dissociating himself from the whole procedure.

Now, walking back, he said: 'We all warned her not to swim alone but she wouldn't listen. But I didn't really believe there was any danger. I suppose all the victims thought that until it was too late. "It can't happen to me." But it can and it does. But it's still extra- ordinary, almost unbelievable. The second victim from Larksoken. Where is she?'

'On the fringe of the pines, where she usually swam, I imagine.' As Mair made a move towards the sea, Dalgliesh said: 'There's nothing you can do. I'll go back and wait for the police.'

'I know there's nothing I can do. I want to see her.'

'Better not. The fewer people who disturb the scene the better.'

Suddenly Mair turned on him. 'My God, Dalgliesh, don't you ever stop thinking like a policeman? I said I wanted to see her.'

Dalgliesh thought, this isn't my case and I can't stop him by force. But at least he could ensure that the direct path to the body lay undisturbed. Without another word he led the way and Mair followed. Why this insistence, he wondered, on seeing the body? To satisfy himself that she was, in fact, dead, the scientist's need to verify and confirm? Or was he trying to exorcize a horror which he knew could be more terrible in imagination than in reality? Or was there, perhaps, a deeper compulsion, the need to pay her the tribute of standing over her body in the quietness and loneliness of the night before the police arrived with all the official paraphernalia of a murder investigation to violate for ever the intimacies they had shared.

Mair made no comment when Dalgliesh led him to the south of the well-beaten path to the beach and still without speaking followed him as he plunged into the darkness and began tracking his way between the shafts of the pines. The pool of light from his torch shone on the brittle spars snapped by his previous breakthrough, on the carpet of pine needles dusted with sand, on dried pine cones and the glint of an old battered tin. In the darkness the strong resinous smell seemed to intensify and came up to them like a drug, making the air as heavy to breathe as if it were a sultry night in high summer.

Minutes later they stepped out of stultifying darkness into the white coolness of the beach and saw before them like a curved shield of beaten silver the moonlit splendour of the sea. They stood for a moment side by side, breathing hard as if they had come through some ordeal. Dalgliesh's footprints were still visible in the dry sand above the last ridge of pebbles and they followed them until they stood at the foot of the body.

Dalgliesh thought, I don't want to be here, not with him, not like this, both of us staring down unrebuked at her nakedness. It seemed to him that all his perceptions were preternaturally sharpened in this cold, debilitating light. The blanched limbs, the aureole of dark hair, the gaudy red and blue of the beach towel, the clumps of marram grass, all had the one-dimensional clarity of a colour print. This necessary guard on the body until the police could arrive would have been perfectly tolerable; he was used to the undemanding companionship of the recently dead. But with Mair at his side he felt like a voyeur. It was this revulsion, rather than delicacy, which made him move a little apart and stand looking into the darkness of the pines while remaining aware of every slight move and breath of the tall, rigid figure looking down at her with the concentrated attention of a surgeon.

Then Mair said: 'That locket round her neck, I gave it to her on August the twenty-ninth for her birthday. It's just the right size to hold her Yale key. One of the metal workers in the workshop at Larksoken made it for me. It's remarkable the delicacy of the work they do there.'

Dalgliesh was not inexperienced in the various manifestations of shock. He said nothing. Mair's voice was suddenly harsh.

'For God's sake, Dalgliesh, can't we cover her up?'

With what? thought Dalgliesh. Does he expect me to jerk the towel from under her? He said: 'No, I'm sorry. We mustn't disturb her.'

'But it's the Whistler's work. Dear God, man, it's obvious. You said so yourself.'

'The Whistler is a murderer like any other. He brings something to the scene and leaves something behind him. That something could be evidence. He's a man, not a force of nature.'

'When will the police arrive?'

'They shouldn't be long. I wasn't able to speak to Rickards but they'll be in touch with him. I'll wait if you want to leave. There's nothing you can do here.'

'I can stay until they take her away.'

'That might mean a long wait unless they're able to get the pathologist quickly.'

'Then I'll have a long wait.'

Without another word he turned and walked down to the edge of the sea, his footprints parallel with Dalgliesh's own. Dalgliesh moved down to the shingle and sat there, his arms round his knees, and watched while the tall figure paced endlessly, backwards and forwards, along the fringes of the tide. Whatever evidence he had on his shoes, it wouldn't be there now. But the thought was ridiculous. No murderer had ever left his imprint more clearly on a victim than had the Whistler. Why then did he feel this unease, the sense that it was less straightforward than it seemed?

He wriggled his heels and buttocks more comfortably into the shingle and prepared to wait. The cold moonlight, the constant falling of the waves and the sense of that stiffening body behind him induced a gentle melancholy, a contemplation of mortality including his own. *Timor mortis conturbat me.* He thought: in youth we take egregious risks because death has no reality for us. Youth goes caparisoned in immortality. It is only in middle age that we are shadowed by the awareness of the transitoriness of life. And the fear of death, however irrational, was surely natural whether one thought of it as annihilation or as a rite of passage. Every cell in the body was programmed for life; all healthy creatures clung to life until their last breath. How hard to accept, and yet how comforting, was the gradual realization that the universal enemy might come at last as a friend. Perhaps this was part of the attraction of his job, that the process of detection dignified the individual death, even the death of the least attractive, the most unworthy, mirroring in its excessive interest in clues and motives man's perennial fascination with the mystery of his mortality, providing, too, a comforting illusion of a moral universe in which innocence could be avenged, right vindicated, order restored. But nothing was restored, certainly not life, and the only justice vindicated was the uncertain justice of men. The job certainly had a fascination for him which went beyond its intellectual challenge, or the excuse it gave for his rigorously enforced privacy. But now he had inherited enough money to make it redundant. Was this what his aunt had intended by that uncompromising will? Was she in fact saying, here is enough money to make any job other than poetry unnecessary? Isn't it time that you made a choice?

It wasn't his case. It would never be his case. But by force of habit he timed the arrival of the police and it was thirty-five minutes before his ears caught the first rustle of movement in the pine wood. They were coming the way he had directed and they were making a great deal of noise about it. It was Rickards who appeared first with a younger but stolidly built man at his shoulder and four heavily laden officers in a straggle behind them. It seemed to Dalgliesh, rising to meet them, that they were immense, huge moon men, their features square and blanched in this alien light, bearing with them their bulky and polluting paraphernalia. Rickards nodded but didn't speak other than briefly to introduce his sergeant, Stuart Oliphant.

Together they approached the body and stood looking down at what had been Hilary Robarts. Rickards was breathing heavily, as if he had been running, and it seemed to Dalgliesh that there emanated from him a powerful surge of energy and excitement. Oliphant and the four other officers dumped their equipment and stood silently, a little apart. Dalgliesh had a sense that they were all actors in a film, waiting for the director to give the command to shoot, or that a voice would suddenly shout 'cut' and the little group would break up, the victim stretch herself and sit up and begin rubbing her arms and legs and complaining of stiffness and the cold.

Then, still gazing down at the body, Rickards asked: 'Do you know her, Mr Dalgliesh?'

'Hilary Robarts, Acting Administrative Officer at Larksoken Power Station. I met her first last Thursday, at a dinner party given by Miss Mair.'

Rickards turned and gazed towards the figure of Mair. He was standing motionless with his back to the sea but so close to the surf that it seemed to Dalgliesh that the waves must be washing over his shoes. He made no move towards them, almost as if he were waiting for an invitation or for Rickards to join him.

Dalgliesh said: 'Dr Alex Mair. He's the Director of Larksoken. I used the telephone in his car to call you. He says he'll stay here until the body is removed.'

'Then he's in for a long wait. So that's Dr Alex Mair. I've read about him. Who found her?'

'I did. I thought I made that plain when I telephoned.'

Either Rickards was deliberately extracting information he already knew or his men were singularly inefficient at passing on a simple message.

Rickards turned to Oliphant. 'Go and explain to him that we'll be taking our time. There's nothing he can do here except to get in the

153

way. Persuade him to go home to bed. If you can't persuade, try ordering. I'll talk to him tomorrow.' He waited until Oliphant had started scrunching over the ridge of shingle then called: 'Oliphant. If he won't move, tell him to keep his distance. I don't want him any closer. Then get the screens round her. That'll spoil his fun.'

It was the kind of casual cruelty which Dalgliesh didn't expect from him. Something was wrong with the man, something that went deeper than professional stress at having to view yet another of the Whistler's victims. It was as if some half-acknowledged and imperfectly suppressed personal anxiety had been violently released by the sight of the body, triumphing over caution and discipline.

But Dalgliesh, too, felt a sense of outrage. He said: 'The man isn't a voyeur. He's probably not altogether rational at present. After all, he knew the woman. Hilary Robarts was one of his senior officers.'

'He can't do her any good now, even if she was his mistress.' Then, as if acknowledging the implied rebuke, he said: 'All right, I'll have a word with him.'

He began running clumsily over the shingle. Hearing him, Oliphant turned and together they went up to that silent, waiting figure on the fringe of the sea. Dalgliesh watched as they conferred together, then they turned and began walking up the beach, Alex Mair between the two police officers as if he were a prisoner under escort. Rickards returned to the body but it was obvious that Oliphant was going to accompany Alex Mair back to his car. He switched on his torch and plunged into the wood. Mair hesitated. He had ignored the body as if it were no longer there but now he looked over at Dalgliesh as if there were unfinished business between them. Then he said a quick 'Goodnight' and followed Oliphant.

Rickards didn't comment on Mair's change of mind or on his methods of persuasion. He said: 'No handbag.'

'Her house key is in that locket round her neck.'

'Did you touch the body, Mr Dalgliesh?'

'Only her thigh and the hair to test its wetness. The locket was a gift from Mair. He told me.'

'Lives close, does she?'

'You'll have seen her cottage when you drove up. It's just the other side of the pine wood. I went there after I found the body, thinking it might be open and I could telephone. There's been an act of vandalism, her portrait thrown through the window. The Whistler and criminal damage on the same night; an odd coincidence.'

Rickards turned and looked full at him. 'Maybe. But this wasn't the Whistler. The Whistler's dead. Killed himself in a hotel at Easthaven, sometime around six o'clock. I've been trying to reach you to let you know.'

He squatted by the body and touched the girl's face, then lifted the head and let it drop. 'No rigor. Not even the beginning of it. Within the last few hours, by the look of her. The Whistler died with enough sins on his conscience but this . . . this,' he stabbed his finger violently at the dead body, 'this, Mr Dalgliesh, is something different.'

22

Rickards rolled on his search gloves. The latex sliding over his huge fingers made them look almost obscene, like the udders of a great animal. Kneeling, he fiddled with the locket. It sprang open and Dalgliesh could see the Yale key nestling inside it, a perfect fit. Rickards extracted it, then said: 'Right, Mr Dalgliesh. Let's go and take a look at that criminal damage.'

Two minutes later he followed Rickards up the path to the front door of the cottage. Rickards unlocked it and they passed into a passage running to the stairs and with doors on either side. Rickards opened the door to the left and stepped into the sitting room with Dalgliesh behind him. It was a large room running the whole length of the cottage with windows at each end and a fireplace facing the door. The portrait lay about three feet from the window surrounded by jagged slivers of glass. Both men stood just inside the door and surveyed the scene.

Dalgliesh said: 'It was painted by Ryan Blaney who lives at Scudder's Cottage further south on the headland. I saw it first on the afternoon I arrived.'

Rickards said: 'A funny way of delivering it. Sat for him, did she?'

'I don't think so. It was painted to please himself, not her.'

He was going to add that Ryan Blaney would, in his view, be the last person to destroy his work. But then he reflected that it hadn't, in fact, been destroyed. Two single cuts in the form of an L wouldn't be too difficult to repair. And the damage had been as precise and deliberate as those cuts on Hilary Robarts's forehead. The picture hadn't been slashed in fury.

Rickards seemed for a moment to lose interest in it. He said: 'So this is where she lived. She must have been fond of solitude. That is if she lived alone.'

Dalgliesh said: 'As far as I know she lived alone.'

It was, he thought, a depressing room. It was not that the place was uncomfortable; it held the necessary furniture but the pieces looked as though they were rejects from someone else's house, not the conscious choice of the occupant. Beside the fireplace with its fitted gas fire were two armchairs in synthetic brown leather. In the centre of the room was an oval dining table with four discordant chairs. On either side of the front window were fitted bookshelves, holding what looked like a collection of textbooks and assorted novels. Two of the lower and taller shelves were packed with box files. Only on the longest wall facing the door was there any sign that someone had made this room a home. She had obviously been fond of watercolours and the wall was as closely hung with them as if it had been part of a gallery. There were one or two which he thought he could recognize and he wished he could walk over to examine them more closely. But it was possible that someone other than Hilary Robarts herself had been in this room before them and it was important to leave the scene undisturbed.

Rickards closed the door and opened the opposite one on the right of the passage. This led to the kitchen, a purely functional, rather uninteresting room, well enough equipped but in stark contrast to the kitchen at Martyr's Cottage.

Set in the middle of the room was a small wooden table, vinyl-covered, with four matching chairs all pushed well in. On the table was an uncorked bottle of wine with the cork and the metal opener beside it. Two plain wineglasses, clean and upturned, were on the draining board.

Rickards said: 'Two glasses, both washed, by her or her killer. We'll get no prints there. And an open bottle. Someone was drinking with her here tonight.'

Dalgliesh said: 'If so he was abstemious. Or she was.'

Rickards with his gloved hand lifted the bottle by its neck and slowly turned it. 'About one glass poured. Maybe they planned to finish it after her swim.' He looked at Dalgliesh and said: 'You didn't come earlier into the cottage, Mr Dalgliesh? I have to ask everyone she knew.'

'Of course. No, I didn't come earlier into the cottage. I was drinking claret tonight, but not with her.'

'Pity you hadn't been. She'd be alive now.'

'Not necessarily. I might have left when she went to change for her swim. And if she did have someone with her here tonight that's probably what he did.' He paused, wondered whether to speak, then said: 'The left-hand glass is slightly cracked at the rim.'

Rickards lifted it to the central light and turned it slowly.

'I wish I had your eyesight. It's hardly significant, surely.'

'Some people strongly dislike drinking from a cracked glass. I do myself.'

'In which case why didn't she break it and chuck it away? There's no point in keeping a glass you aren't prepared to drink from. When I'm faced with two alternatives I start by taking the more likely. Two glasses, two drinkers. That's the common-sense explanation.'

It was, thought Dalgliesh, the basis of most police work. Only when the obvious proved untenable was it necessary to explore less likely explanations. But it could also be the first fatally easy step into a labyrinth of misconceptions. He wondered why his instinct insisted that she had been drinking alone. Perhaps because the bottle was in the kitchen not in the sitting room. The wine was a '79 Château Talbot, hardly an all-purpose tipple. Why not carry it into the sitting room and do it justice in comfort? On the other hand, if she were alone and had needed only a quick swig before her swim she might hardly have bothered. And if two people had been drinking in the kitchen she had been meticulous in pushing back the chairs. But it was the level of the wine that seemed to him almost conclusive. Why uncork a fresh bottle to pour only two half-glasses? Which didn't, of course, mean that she wasn't later expecting a visitor to help finish it.

Rickards seemed to be taking an unnatural interest in the bottle and its label. Suddenly he said gruffly:

'What time did you leave the mill, Mr Dalgliesh?'

'At nine fifteen. I looked at the carriage clock on the mantelpiece and checked my watch.'

'And you saw no one during your walk?'

'No one, and no footprints other than hers and mine.'

'What were you actually doing on the headland, Mr Dalgliesh?'

'Walking, thinking.' He was about to add: 'And paddling like a boy,' but checked himself.

Rickards said consideringly: 'Walking and thinking.'

To Dalgliesh's oversensitive ears he made the activities sound both eccentric and suspicious. Dalgliesh wondered what his companion would say if he had decided to confide. 'I was thinking about my aunt and the men who loved her, the fiancé who was killed in 1918 and the man whose mistress she might or might not have been. I was thinking of the thousands of people who have walked along that shore and who are now dead, my aunt among them, and how, as a boy, I hated the false romanticism of that stupid poem about great men leaving their footprints on the sands of time, since that was essentially all that most of us could hope to leave, transitory marks which the next tide would obliterate. I was thinking how little I had known my aunt and whether it was ever possible to know another human being except on the most superficial level, even the women I have loved. I was thinking about the clash of ignorant armies by night, since no poet walks by the sea at moonlight without silently reciting Matthew Arnold's marvellous poem. I was considering whether I would have been a better poet, or even a poet at all, if I hadn't also decided to be a policeman. More prosaically, I was, from time to time, wondering how my life would be changed for better or worse by the unmerited acquisition of three-quarters of a million.'

The fact that he had no intention of revealing even the most mundane of these private musings, the childish secrecy about the paddling, induced an irrational guilt, as if he were deliberately withholding information of importance. After all, he told himself, no man could have been more innocently employed. And it was not as if he were a serious suspect. The idea would probably have struck Rickards as too ridiculous even for consideration, although with logic he would have had to admit that no one who lived on the headland and had known Hilary Robarts could be excluded from the inquiry, least of all because he was a senior police officer. But Dalgliesh was a witness. He had information to give or withhold, and the knowledge that he would have no intention of withholding it didn't alter the fact that there was a difference now in their relationship. He was involved, whether he liked it or not, and he didn't need Rickards to point out that uncomfortable reality. Professionally it was none of his business, but it was his business as a man and a human being.

He was surprised and a little disconcerted to discover how much he had resented the interrogation, mild as it had been. A man was surely entitled to walk along the beach at night without having to explain his reasons to a police officer. It was salutary for him personally to experience this sense of privacy violated, of virtuous outrage which the most innocent of suspects must feel when faced with police interrogation. And he realized anew how much, even from childhood, he had disliked being questioned. 'What are you doing? Where have you been? What are you reading? Where are you going?' He had been the much-wanted only child of elderly parents, burdened by their almost possessive parental concern and overconscientiousness, living in a village where little the rector's son did was safe from scrutiny. And suddenly, standing here in this anonymous, over-tidy kitchen, he recalled vividly and with heart-stopping pain the moment when his most precious privacy had been violated. He remembered that secluded place, deep in the laurels and elderberries, at the bottom of the shrubbery, the green tunnel of leaves leading to his own three square yards of moist, mould-rich sanctuary, remembered that August afternoon, the crackle of bushes, the cook's great face thrust between the leaves. 'Your ma thought you'd be in here, Master Adam. Rector wants you. What do you do in there, hiding yourself away in all those mucky bushes? Better be playing out in the sunshine.' So the last refuge, the one he had thought totally secret, had been discovered. They had known about it all the time.

He said: 'Oh God from You that I could private be.'

Rickards looked at him. 'What was that, Mr Dalgliesh?'

'Just a quotation that came into my mind.'

Rickards didn't reply. He was probably thinking: 'Well, you're supposed to be a poet. You're entitled.' He gave a last searching look around the kitchen as if by the intensity of his gaze he could somehow compel that unremarkable table and four chairs, the opened bottle of wine, the two washed glasses to yield up their secret.

Then he said: 'I'll lock up here and set someone on guard until tomorrow. I'm due to meet the pathologist, Dr Maitland-Brown, over at Easthaven. He'll take a look at the Whistler and then come straight on here. The forensic biologist should have arrived from the lab by then. You wanted to see the Whistler yourself, didn't you, Mr Dalgliesh? This seems as good a time as any.'

It seemed to Dalgliesh a particularly bad time. One violent death was enough in one night and he was seized with a sudden longing for the peace and solitude of the mill. But there seemed no prospect of sleep for him until the early hours of the morning and there was little point in objecting. Rickards said: 'I could drive you over and bring you back.'

Dalgliesh felt an immediate revulsion at the thought of a car journey tête-à-tête with Rickards. He said: 'If you'll drop me at the mill I'll take my own car. There won't be any reason for me to linger at Easthaven and you may have to wait.'

It surprised him a little that Rickards was willing to leave the beach. Admittedly he had Oliphant and his minions; procedures at the scene of a murder were well established, they would be competent to do what was necessary, and until the forensic pathologist arrived the body couldn't be moved. But he sensed that it was important to Rickards that he and Dalgliesh should see the Whistler's body together and he wondered what forgotten incident in their joint pasts had led to that compulsion.

23

Balmoral Private Hotel was the last house of an undistinguished nineteenth-century terrace at the unfashionable end of the long promenade. The summer lights were still strung between the Victorian lampposts but they had been turned off and now swung in uneven loops like a tawdry necklace which might scatter its blackened beads at the first strong wind. The season was officially over. Dalgliesh drew up behind the police Rover on the left-hand side of the promenade. Between the road and glittering sea was a children's playground, wire-enclosed, the gate padlocked, the shuttered kiosk pasted with fading and half-torn posters of summer shows, bizarrely shaped ice-creams, a clown's head. The swings had been looped high and one of the metal seats, caught by the strengthening breeze, rapped out a regular tattoo against the iron frame. The hotel stood out from its drabber neighbours, sprucely painted in a bright blue which even the dull street lighting could hardly soften. The porch light shone down on a large card with the words 'Under new management. Bill and Joy Carter welcome you to Balmoral'. A separate card underneath said simply 'Vacancies'.

As they waited to cross the road while a couple of cars cruised slowly past, the drivers peering for a parking space, Rickards said: 'Their first season. Done quite well up to now, so they say, despite the bloody awful summer. This won't help. They'll get the ghouls, of course, but parents will think twice before booking in with the kiddies for happy family hols. Luckily the place is half-empty at present. Two cancellations this morning, so they've only got three couples and they were all out when Mr Carter found the body and, so far, we've managed to keep them in happy ignorance. They're in bed now, presumably asleep. Let's hope they stay that way.'

The earlier arrival of the police must have alerted some of the locals but the plainclothes officer unobtrusively on duty inside the porch had dispersed any curious bystanders and now the road was empty except for a little group of four or five people about fifty yards down on the seaward side. They seemed to be muttering together and as

Dalgliesh glanced at them they began moving aimlessly as if stirred by the breeze.

He asked: 'Why here, for God's sake?'

'We know why. There's a hell of a lot we don't know but at least we know that. They've got a part-time barman here, Albert Upcraft, seventy-five if he's a day. He remembers. He's a bit vague about what happened yesterday but there's nothing wrong with his long-term memory. The Whistler came here as a kid, apparently. His auntie – his dad's sister – was manager here twenty years ago. Used to take him off his mum's hands for a free holiday when the place was quiet. Mainly when mum had a new man and the new uncle didn't want the kid around. Sometimes he was here for weeks at a time. No trouble to anyone. Helped with the guests, picked up the odd tip, actually went to Sunday school.'

Dalgliesh said: 'Now the Day is Over.'

'Well, his day's over, all right. He booked in at two thirty this afternoon. Asked for the same room, apparently. Single at the back. Cheapest in the house. The Carters should be grateful for small mercies. He might have chosen to go out in style, best double bedroom, private bathroom, view of the sea, the lot.'

The constable at the door saluted and they passed through the lobby into the hall, and into a smell of paint and polish overlaid with the faint tang of lavender disinfectant. The cleanliness was almost oppressive. The lurid flowered carpet was covered with a narrow strip of perspex. The wallpaper was obviously new, a different pattern on each wall and a glimpse through the open door of the dining room showed tables set for four with shining white cloths and small vases of artificial flowers, daffodils, narcissi and bulbous roses. The couple who came from the back to meet them were as spruce as their hotel. Bill Carter was a dapper little man who looked as if he came fresh from the ironing board, the creases down his white shirt sleeves and the front of his trousers knife sharp, his tie neatly knotted. His wife was wearing a summer dress in a flowered crimplene under a knitted white sweater. She had obviously been crying. Her plump, rather childish face under the carefully set blonde hair was bloated and bruised red as if she had been struck. Her disappointment at seeing just the two of them was pathetically obvious.

She said: 'I thought you'd come to take him away. Why can't you take him away?'

163

Rickards didn't introduce Dalgliesh. He said soothingly: 'We will, Mrs Carter, as soon as the pathologist has seen him. He shouldn't be long now. He's on his way.'

'Pathologist? That's a doctor, isn't it? Why do you want a doctor? He's dead, isn't he? Bill found him. His throat's cut. How much deader can you get?'

'He won't be with you much longer, Mrs Carter.'

'The sheet's covered with blood, Bill says. He wouldn't let me in. Not that I want to see. And the carpet, ruined. Blood's terrible to get out, everyone knows that. Who's going to pay for the carpet and the bed? Oh God, I thought things were really coming right for us at last. Why did he come back here to do it? Not very nice, was it, not very considerate?'

'He wasn't a considerate man, Mrs Carter.'

Her husband put his arm round her shoulders and led her away. Less than half a minute later he reappeared and said: 'It's the shock, naturally. She's upset. Well, who wouldn't be? You know the way up, Mr Rickards. Your officer is still there. I won't come up with you if you don't mind.'

'That's all right, Mr Carter, I know the way.'

Suddenly he turned and said: 'Get him out soon, sir, for God's sake.'

For a moment Dalgliesh thought that he, too, was crying.

There was no lift. Dalgliesh followed Rickards up three flights of stairs, down a narrow passage towards the back and a short turn to the right. A young detective constable got up from his chair outside the door and with his left hand opened it then flattened himself against the wall. The smell seemed to gust out of the room at them, a strong effluvium of blood and death.

The light was on and the main bulb in its cheap pink shade hung low and shone full on the horror on the bed. It was a very small room, little more than a box room, with a single window too high to give a view of more than the sky and enough space only for the single bed, a chair, a bedside cabinet and a low chest of drawers with a mirror hung above it which served as a dressing table. But this room, too, was obsessively clean, making that unclean thing on the bed even more horrible. Both the gaping throat with its white corrugated vessels and the sagging mouth above it seemed to be stretched in protest or outrage at this violence to decency and order. There were no preliminary cuts visible and that single act of annihilating violence must surely, Dalgliesh thought, have taken more strength than was possible from the childish hand lying, fingers curved, on the sheet and fixed now in its blackening carapace of dried blood. The knife, six inches of bloodied steel, lay close beside it. For some reason he had undressed himself for death and lay now wearing only a vest and pants and a pair of short blue nylon socks which looked like the onset of putrefaction. On the chair beside the bed a dark grey striped suit was neatly folded. A blue-striped drip-dry shirt was hung from the back of the chair with the tie folded over it. Under the chair his shoes, well worn but polished to mirror brightness, were precisely placed side by side. They looked small enough for a girl.

Rickards said: 'Neville Potter, aged thirty-six. Scrawny little sod. You wouldn't believe he'd got the strength in those arms to throttle a chicken. And he came properly dressed in his Sunday best to meet his Maker, but then thought better of it. Probably remembered that his ma wouldn't like him getting blood on his best suit. You should meet Ma, Mr Dalgliesh. She's a real education, that one. She explains a lot. But he's left the evidence. It's all there, all laid out for us. Neat little devil, wasn't he?'

Dalgliesh edged himself round the end of the bed, being careful not to tread in the blood. On the top of the chest of drawers were the Whistler's weapons and his trophies; a leather dog lead, neatly curled, a blond wig and blue beret, a clasp knife, a lamp with a battery ingeniously fixed to the centre of a metal headband. Beside these was a pyramid of tangled bushy hair: blond, dark brown, red. In front of the careful arrangement was a page of paper torn from a notebook with the single written message in biro, printed like a child's. 'It was getting worse. This is the only way I know to stop myself. Please look after Pongo.' The 'Please' was underlined.

Rickards said: 'His dog. Pongo, for God's sake.'

'What did you expect him to be called, Cerberus?'

Rickards opened the door and stood with his back to the gap breathing deeply as if hungry for fresh air. He said: 'He and his ma lived on one of the caravan sites outside Cromer. Been there for twelve years. He was a general handyman, did any easy repairs, kept an eye on the place at night, dealt with complaints. The boss has another site outside Yarmouth and he would go there some nights to relieve the permanent chap. A bit of a loner. Had a small van and the dog. Married a girl he picked up on the site there years ago but it only lasted four months. She walked out on him. Driven out by Ma or by the smell of the caravan. God knows how she stuck it for four months.'

Dalgliesh said: 'He was an obvious suspect. You must have checked him.'

'His ma gave him an alibi for two of the murders. Either she was drunk and didn't know whether he was there or not, or she was covering up for him. Or, of course, she couldn't give a bloody damn one way or the other.' He said with sudden violence, 'I thought we'd learned by now not to take that kind of alibi at its face value. I'm having a word with the DC who interviewed them, but you know how it is. Thousands of interviews, checks, the stuff all put on the computer. I'd give a dozen computers for a DC who can sense when a witness is lying. My God, haven't we learned anything from the Yorkshire Ripper fiasco?'

'Didn't your man search the van?'

'Oh, they searched the van, all right. They showed a modicum of initiative. It was clean. He cached his stuff elsewhere. Probably picked it up every evening, watched, waited, chose his moment.' He gazed down at the head contraption and said: 'Ingenious, isn't it? As his ma says, he was always clever with his hands.'

The small rectangle of sky outside the single high window was blue-black pricked with a single star. It seemed to Dalgliesh that he had experienced half a lifetime of sensations since he had woken that morning to the cool sea-scented autumnal dawn, to the beginning of a day which had included that calm meditative walk under the soaring roof of St Peter Mancroft, the nostalgic self-indulgent pain induced by those faded photographs of the long dead; the rush and pull of the tide over his naked feet, the mingled shock and recognition as his torch shone on Hilary Robarts's body. It was a day which, stretching interminably, seemed to have embraced all seasons. So this was one way of stretching time, time which for the Whistler had stopped with that great gush of blood. And now at the end of the day he had come to this neat box of an execution shed, imposing on his mind as if it were a memory the picture of a skinny child lying supine on that same bed and watching through the high window the same single star while arranged on the chest of drawers with careful art were the trophies of his day: the tips in pennies and sixpences, the shells and coloured stones from the beach, the dried swathe of pustulated seaweed.

And he himself was here because Rickards had willed it, had

wanted him here in this room and at this time. He could have viewed the Whistler's body tomorrow in the mortuary, or, since he could hardly claim that he hadn't the stomach for it, on the autopsy table, to confirm what hardly needed confirmation, that this scrawny killer wasn't the once-glimpsed, six-foot, Battersea strangler. But Rickards had needed an audience, had needed him, Dalgliesh, against whose dreadfully experienced and unshockable calm he could hurl the bitterness and frustrations of failure. Five women dead, and the murderer a suspect they had interviewed and cleared early in the inquiry. The smell of that failure would linger at least in his own nostrils long after the media interest, the official inquiries had run their course. And now there was this sixth death, Hilary Robarts who might not have died and certainly wouldn't have died as she had if the Whistler had been stopped in his tracks earlier. But Dalgliesh sensed that something more keenly personal even than professional failure was fuelling Rickards's anger with its uncharacteristic spurts of verbal brutality and he wondered whether it had something to do with his wife and the coming child. He asked: 'What will happen to the dog?'

Rickards seemed not to notice the irrelevance of the question.

'What do you think? Who's going to take on an animal that has been where he's been, seen what he's seen?' He looked down at the stiffening corpse and, turning to Dalgliesh, said harshly: 'You pity him, I suppose.'

Dalgliesh didn't reply. He could have said: 'Yes, I pity him. And his victims. And you. And myself occasionally, come to that.' He thought: Yesterday I was reading *The Anatomy of Melancholy*. Odd. Robert Burton, that seventeenth-century Leicestershire rector, had said all that could be said at such a moment and the words came to him as clearly as if he had spoken them aloud. 'Of their goods and bodies we can dispose; but what shall become of their souls God alone can tell; His mercy may come *inter pontem et fontem, inter gladium et jugulum*, betwixt the bridge and the brook, the knife and the throat.'

Rickards shook himself violently as if suddenly seized with cold. It was an odd gesture. Then he said: 'At least he's saved the country his keep for the next twenty years. One argument for keeping his kind alive instead of putting them down is that we can learn from them, stop it happening again. But can we? We've got Straffen banged up, Brady, Nielson. How much have we learned from them?'

Dalgliesh said: 'You wouldn't hang a madman, presumably?'

'I wouldn't hang anyone, I'd find a less barbaric method. But they aren't mad, are they? Not until they're caught. Until then they cope with life like most other people. Then we discover that they're monsters and decide, surprise, surprise, to classify them as mad. Makes it seem more comprehensible. We don't have to think of them as human any more. We don't have to use the word evil. Everyone feels better. Do you want to see the mother, Mr Dalgliesh?'

'There's no point in it. He obviously isn't our man. I didn't for a moment suppose that he would be.'

'You should see the mother. She's a right bitch, that one. And do you know what her name is? Lillian. L for Lillian. That's something for the trick-cyclist to chew over. She made him what he was. But we can't check on people and decide who's fit to have kids, let alone fit to bring them up. And I suppose that when he was born she must have felt something for him, had some hopes for him. She could hardly know what she'd brought forth. You never had a child, did you, Mr Dalgliesh.'

'I had a son. Briefly.'

Rickards kicked the door gently, looking away. He said: 'Bloody hell, I'd forgotten. Sorry. Wrong time to ask, for both of us.'

There were confident footsteps mounting the stairs and now they had reached the passage. Dalgliesh said: 'It sounds as if the pathologist has arrived.'

Rickards made no reply. He had moved over to the chest of drawers and, with his forefinger, gently urged the tangle of hairs across the polished wood.

He said: 'There's one sample which we won't find here. Hilary Robarts. Forensic will look to make doubly sure, but it won't be here. And now I start looking for a very different murderer. And, by God, Mr Dalgliesh, this time I'm going to get him.'

24

Forty-five minutes later Rickards was back at the scene of the murder. He seemed to have passed beyond conscious tiredness and to be operating in a different dimension of time and space in which his mind worked with unnatural clarity while his body had become almost weightless, a creature of light and air, as insubstantial as the bizarre scene in which he moved and spoke and gave his orders. The pale transparent disc of the moon was eclipsed by the glare of the mounted lights which illumined and solidified the hard outlines of trees and men and equipment, yet paradoxically robbed them of form and essence so that they were, at one and the same time, revealed and clarified and transformed into something alien and strange. And always, beyond the masculine voices, the scrunch of feet on pebbles, the sudden flap of canvas in a tentative breeze, was the continual fall and suck of the tide.

Dr Anthony Maitland-Brown had driven from Easthaven to the scene in his Mercedes and had arrived first. He was already gowned and gloved and crouching by the body by the time Rickards caught up with him. Wisely he left him to it. M-B strongly disliked being watched while he made his preliminary examination at the scene and was apt to protest with a peevish 'Do we really need all these people standing around?' if anyone came within ten feet of him, as if the police photographer, scene-of-crime officer and forensic biologist were all so many snap-happy sightseers. He was an elegant and extraordinarily handsome man, over six feet tall, who had once in youth – so it was rumoured – been told that he looked like Leslie Howard and had spent subsequent years sedulously promoting the image. He was amicably divorced, comfortably well-off – his mother had bequeathed him a private income – and well able to indulge his twin passions of clothes and the opera. In his free time he escorted a succession of young and extremely pretty actresses to Covent Garden and Glyndebourne, where they were apparently content to endure three hours of boredom for the prestige of his company or, perhaps, the *frisson* of knowing that the elegant hands which poured their wine or helped them out of the Mercedes were commonly engaged with more bizarre activities. Rickards had never found him an easy colleague but recognized that he was a first-class forensic pathologist, and God knew they were rare enough. Reading M-B's lucid and comprehensive autopsy reports he could forgive him even his aftershave.

Now, moving away from the body, he stirred himself to greet the recent arrivals, photographer, cameraman, forensic biologist. The stretch of beach fifty yards each side of the murder scene had been efficiently roped off and plastic sheeting laid over the path now lit by a string of overhead lights. He was aware of his sergeant's discip-lined excitement at his side.

Stuart Oliphant said: 'We've found a print, sir. About forty yards into the copse.'

'On grass and pine needles?'

'No, sir, on sand. Someone, a kid perhaps, must have tipped it from a bucket. The print's a good one, sir.'

Rickards followed him into the wood. The whole of the path had been protected but at one place a marker had been driven into the soft ground at the right-hand side. Sergeant Oliphant drew back the plastic then lifted the box covering the print. In the glow of the overhead lights slung along the path it showed clearly, a dusting of moist sand over the pine needles and flattened grass, covering no more than six inches by four, and printed on it the intricate pattern of the sole of a right shoe.

Oliphant said: 'We found it soon after you left, sir. Only the one, but it's pretty clear. The photographs have been taken and the measurements will be at the lab this morning. Size ten by the look of it. They'll be able to give us confirmation pretty quickly, but it's hardly necessary. It's a trainer shoe, sir. A Bumble. You know the make, the one that has a picture of a bee on the heel. And it has the outline of a bee on the sole. You can see the curve of the wing here, sir. It's quite unmistakable.'

A Bumble trainer. If you wanted a print you could hardly hope for anything more distinctive. Oliphant voiced his thoughts: 'Common enough, of course, but not all that common. Bumbles are the most expensive on the market, the Porsche of trainers. Most of the kids with money like to have them. It's a bloody silly name. Part of the firm is actually owned by a man called Bumble and they've only been on the market for a couple of years, but he promotes them fairly vigorously. I suppose he hopes that the name will catch on, that people will start yelling for their Bumbles as they do for their wellie-boots.'

Rickards said: 'It looks fresh enough. When did we last get rain? Late on Saturday night, wasn't it?'

'About eleven. It was over by midnight but it was a heavy shower.'

'And there's no tree cover on this part of the path. The print's perfectly smooth. If it were made before midnight on Saturday I'd expect some spotting. Interesting that there's only the one and that it's pointing away from the sea. If someone wearing Bumble trainers came along this path any time on Sunday you'd expect to find at least one similar print on the upper reaches of the beach.'

'Not necessarily, sir. The shingle comes up almost as high as the path in places. We'd get no prints if he stayed on the pebbles. But if it was made on Sunday before she died would it still be here? She must have come along this path.'

'No reason why she would have trodden on it. It's well to the right of the path. It's odd, though. Too plain, too distinctive, too oppor-tune. You could almost believe it's been deliberately made to deceive us.'

'They sell Bumble trainers at the sports shop in Blakeney, sir. I could send a chap to buy a pair of size ten as soon as they open.'

'See that he's in plain clothes and buys them as an ordinary purchaser. I need confirmation of the pattern before we start asking people to turn out their shoe cupboards. We're going to be dealing with intelligent suspects. I don't want a balls-up at the beginning of the case.'

'Pity to waste time, sir. My brother owns a pair of Bumbles. The print's unmistakable.'

Rickards said obstinately: 'I need confirmation, and I want it fast.'

Oliphant replaced the box and the plastic cover then followed him back to the beach. Rickards was uncomfortably aware of the almost physical weight of resentment, antagonism and slight contempt which seemed to flow from the sergeant. But he was lumbered with the man. Oliphant had been part of the team bearing the brunt of the Whistler investigation and, although this admittedly was a different inquiry, it would be difficult to replace him without causing personal or logistical problems which Rickards was anxious to avoid. During the fifteen-month hunt for the Whistler his mild dislike of the sergeant had grown into an antipathy which he knew to be not wholly reasonable and which he had tried to discipline both in the interests of the investigation and of his own self-regard. A serial murder was difficult enough without personal complications.

He had no real evidence that Oliphant was a bully; he only looked like one. He was six feet of disciplined flesh and muscle, dark and conventionally handsome with rather pudgy features, full-lipped and hard-eyed, with a fleshy chin like a doughnut, dented in the middle with a deep dimple. Rickards found it difficult to keep his eyes off it. His repugnance to the man had elevated it to a deformity. Oliphant drank too much but that was an occupational hazard for a policeman. The fact that Rickards had never seen him actually drunk only increased the offence. A man shouldn't be able to put away that amount of alcohol and still stand firmly on his feet.

He was meticulous in his attitude to senior officers, respectful without being servile, but subtly managed to give Rickards the impression that he wasn't quite measuring up to the standards Oliphant had privately set for him. He was popular enough with the less sensitive probationers; the others wisely kept clear of him. Rickards told himself that if he were ever in trouble, Oliphant was the last police officer he would wish to see on his doorstep. Oliphant would probably regard that sentiment as a compliment. And there had never been from the public even the whisper of a complaint against him. That too, unreasonably, made Rickards suspicious. It suggested that where his interests were at stake the man was devious enough to act against his essential nature. He was unmarried but managed, without the crudity of actual boasting, to give the impression that women found him irresistible. Probably a number did, but at least he kept clear of his colleagues' wives. In all, he represented most of the qualities in a young detective which Rickards disliked: aggression, only controlled because control was prudent, a frank relish for power, too much sexual assurance and an inflated opinion of his own capabilities. But those capabilities weren't negligible. Oliphant would make Chief Inspector at least and might go higher. Rickards had never managed to bring himself to use his sergeant's nickname of Jumbo. Oliphant, so far from resenting a sobriquet both childish and basically unsuitable, seemed to tolerate, even to like it, at least in those colleagues he had privately authorized to use it. Less favoured mortals only used it once.

Maitland-Brown was ready to make his preliminary report. Drawing himself up to his full six feet three inches he peeled off his gloves and tossed them to a DC, rather like an actor casually divesting himself of part of his costume. It wasn't his custom to discuss his findings at the scene. He did, however, condescend to announce them.

'I'll do the autopsy tomorrow and let you have a report by Wednesday. I doubt whether there will be any surprises. On a preliminary examination it's clear enough. Death by strangulation. The implement was smooth and two centimetres in width, perhaps a belt, a strap or a dog lead. She was a tall, well-muscled woman. It would have taken strength but not inordinate strength given the advantage of surprise. He probably stood in the shelter of the pines then stepped out and slung the strap over her head as soon as she got back from the swim. She had just time to pick up her towel. She made one or two convulsive movements with the feet, you can see where the grass is marked. I estimate on the present evidence that she died between eight thirty and ten.'

Maitland-Brown had pronounced and clearly expected no questions. Nor was there need for any. He put out a hand for his coat which was obligingly handed to him by a DC, then took his leave. Rickards almost expected him to bow.

Rickards looked down at the corpse. Now with the head, hands and feet covered with plastic she looked for a second like a gift-wrapped toy, a plaything for someone with expensive and peculiar tastes, an artifice of latex and synthetic hair, glass eyes, a mere simulation of a living woman. Oliphant's voice seemed to come from a far distance.

'Commander Dalgliesh didn't come back with you then, sir?'

'Why should he? This isn't his pigeon. He's probably in bed.'

He thought, And I wish to God I were too. Already the day was crowding in on him as if physical weight were being piled on exhausted body; the press conference about the Whistler's suicide, the Chief Constable, the press officer, this new investigation, suspects to be interviewed, facts established, the whole cumbersome business of a murder investigation set in motion with the knowledge of his previous failure dragging like a stone on his heart. And somehow or other he had to find time to ring Susie.

He said: 'Mr Dalgliesh is a witness, not the investigating officer.'

'A witness, but hardly a suspect.'

'Why not? He lives on the headland, he knew the girl, he knew how the Whistler killed. He may not be a serious suspect in our eyes but he makes his statement like everyone else.'

Oliphant looked at him stolidly. He said: 'That'll be a new experience for him. Let's hope he enjoys it.'

BOOK FOUR

Monday 26 September

25

Anthony woke her, as he usually did, just after six thirty. Theresa wrenched her mind through clogging layers of sleep to the familiar morning sounds, the creak and rock of the cot and the sniffs and grunts as Anthony grasped the rails and pulled himself up. She smelt the familiar nursery smell compounded of baby talc, stale milk and a sodden nappy. She felt for the switch of the bedside light under the grubby shade with its fringe of dancing Bambis and, opening her eyes, stared into Anthony's and was rewarded by his wide, gummy smile and his ritual small bounces of pleasure which shook the cot. Gently opening the door of the twins' room she could see that they were still asleep, Elizabeth a curled lump on the far end of the bed, Marie on her back one arm flung out. If she could change and feed Anthony before he became fretful they would sleep for another half hour, thirty more minutes of peace for her father.

She would look after Elizabeth and Marie for her mother's sake as long as they needed her and with all her strength, but it was Anthony whom she loved. For a moment she lay still regarding him, enjoying this moment of their quiet, mutual pleasure in each other. Then he let go of the cot rail with one hand, raised one leg in a parody of a clumsy ballet dancer, collapsed on to his mattress, then rolled over on to his back, stuffed his fist into his mouth and began noisily sucking. Soon he would tire of this substitute comfort. She swung her legs out of bed, waited for a moment until she felt the physical flow of strength into arms and legs, then went over to the cot, let down the side and gathered him into her arms. She would change him downstairs on newspaper spread on the kitchen table, then strap him into his chair so that he could watch her while she heated his milk. By the time he was fed the twins would be awake and she would be free to help dress them ready for Mrs Hunter from the welfare to collect them and drive them to the playgroup. Then there would be breakfast for her father and herself before it was time to set out with her father and Anthony to walk to the crossroads where she would pick up the school bus.

She had just turned out the gas under the saucepan of milk when the telephone rang. Her heart lurched, then settled into a rhythmic pounding. She snatched at the receiver, hoping that she had been quick enough to stop it waking her father. George Jago's voice came over strongly, conspiratorial, husky with excitement.

'Theresa? Is your dad up yet?'

'No, not yet, Mr Jago. He's still asleep.'

There was a pause as if he were thinking, then he said: 'OK, don't disturb him. When he wakes tell him Hilary Robarts is dead. Last night. Murdered. Found on the beach.'

'You mean the Whistler got her?'

'Looked like that, meant to look like that if you ask me. But it couldn't have been. The Whistler was dead, been dead three hours or more. Like I told you last night. Remember?'

'Yes, I remember, Mr Jago.'

'Good thing I rang last night, isn't it? You told him, your dad? You told your dad about the Whistler?'

She heard under the excitement the insistent note of anxiety. 'Yes,' she said, 'I told him.'

'That's all right then. Now you tell him about Miss Robarts. Ask him to give me a ring. I've got a call to take a party to Ipswich but I'll be back about twelve. Or I could have a word with him now if he's quick.'

'He wouldn't be quick, Mr Jago. He's sound asleep. And I'm trying to feed Anthony.'

'All right. But you tell him, mind.'

'Yes, I'll tell him.'

He said: 'Good thing I rang last night. He'll know why.'

She put down the receiver. Her hands were wet. She wiped them on her nightdress and went over to the stove. But when she picked up the pan of milk her hands were shaking so violently that she knew she wouldn't be able to pour it into the narrow neck of the bottle. She took it over to the sink and, very carefully, managed to half fill it. Then she unstrapped Anthony and seated herself in the low nursing chair before the empty fireplace. His mouth opened and she plugged in the teat of the bottle and watched as he began his vigorous chomping, his eyes, suddenly vacant, fixed on hers, his two chubby hands raised, palms down like the paws of an animal.

It was then that she heard the creak of the stairs, and her father came in. He never appeared in front of her in the mornings without what he used as a dressing gown, an old raincoat buttoned to the neck. Above it his face under the sleep-tousled hair was grey and swollen, the lips unnaturally red.

He said: 'Was that the phone?'

'Yes, Daddy, Mr Jago.'

'What did he want, then, at this hour?'

'He rang to say that Hilary Robarts is dead. She's been murdered.'

Surely he would notice how different her voice sounded. It seemed to her that her lips were so dry that they would look bloated and deformed, and she bent her head low over the baby so that he shouldn't see. But her father didn't look at her and he didn't speak. With his back to her he said: 'The Whistler then, was it? Got her, did he? Well, she was asking for it.'

'No, Daddy, it couldn't have been the Whistler. Remember Mr Jago phoned us last night at half-past seven to say that the Whistler was dead. He said this morning he was glad he rang to tell us and that you would know why.'

Still he didn't speak. She heard the hiss of water from the tap into the kettle and watched him as he took it slowly back to the table and plugged it in, then took down a mug from the shelf. She was aware of the thudding of her heart, of Anthony's warm body against her arm, of her chin gently resting on his downy head. She said: 'What did Mr Jago mean by that, Daddy?'

'He meant that whoever killed Miss Robarts meant to blame it on the Whistler. That means the police will only suspect people who didn't know that the Whistler was dead.'

'But you knew, Daddy, because I told you.'

Then he turned and said without looking at her. 'Your mother wouldn't like you to tell lies.'

But he wasn't cross and he wasn't rebuking her. She heard nothing in his voice but a great weariness. She said quietly: 'But it isn't a lie, Daddy. Mr Jago telephoned when you were out in the privy. When you came back I told you.'

And then he turned and their eyes met. She had never seen him look more hopeless, more defeated. He said: 'That's right, you told me. And that's what you'll tell the police when they ask you.'

'Of course, Daddy. I'll tell them what happened. Mr Jago told me about the Whistler and I told you.'

'And do you remember what I said?'

The teat of the bottle had flattened. She took it from Anthony's

179

mouth and shook the bottle to let in the air. He gave an immediate wail of fury which she plugged with the teat.

She said: 'I think you said that you were glad. We would all be safe now.'

'Yes,' he said, 'we're all safe now.'

'Does that mean that we won't have to leave the cottage?'

'It depends. We shan't have to leave at once anyway.'

'Who will it belong to now, Daddy?'

'I don't know. Whoever she leaves it to in her will, I suppose. They might want to sell it.'

'Could we buy it, Daddy? It would be nice if we could buy it.'

'That would depend on how much they want. There's no point in thinking about that yet. We're all right for the moment anyway.'

She said: 'Will the police be coming here?'

'Sure to. Today, most likely.'

'Why will they be coming here, Daddy?'

'To find out whether I knew if the Whistler was dead. To ask you if I left the cottage last night. They'll be here, most likely, when you get back from school.'

But she wasn't going to school. Today, it was important that she didn't leave her father's side. And she had an excuse ready, a stomach cramp. And that, at least, was true, or partly true. Crouched over the lavatory she had seen that first pink evidence of her monthly period almost with joy.

She said: 'But you didn't leave the cottage, did you, Daddy? I was here until I went to bed at a quarter past eight. I could hear you moving down here. I could hear the television.'

He said: 'The television isn't an alibi.'

'But I came down, Daddy. You remember. I went to bed early at eight fifteen but I couldn't sleep and I was thirsty. I came down just before nine o'clock for a drink of water. I sat in Mummy's chair reading. You must remember, Daddy? It was half-past nine before I went back to bed.'

He gave a groan. He said: 'Yes, I remember.'

Suddenly Theresa was aware that the twins had entered the kitchen and were standing silently side by side by the doorway regarding their father expressionlessly. She said sharply: 'Go back and get dressed. You shouldn't be down here undressed like that, you'll catch cold.'

Obediently they turned and padded up the stairs.

180

The kettle was spouting steam. Her father turned it off but made no move to make the tea. Instead he sat at the table, his head bowed. She thought she heard him whisper: 'I'm no good for you, I'm no good for you.' She couldn't see his face but for one terrible moment she thought that he was crying. Still holding the bottle and feeding Anthony, she got up and moved across to him. She had no free hand but she stood very close. She said: 'It's all right, Daddy. There's nothing to worry about. It's going to be all right.'

26

On Monday 26 September Jonathan Reeves was working the 8.15 to 14.45 shift and, as usual, he was early at his bench. But it was 8.55 before the telephone rang and he heard the expected voice. Caroline sounded perfectly calm; only the words were urgent.

'I have to see you. Now. Can you get away?'

'I think so. Mr Hammond isn't in yet.'

'Then I'll meet you in the library. At once. It's important, Jonathan.'

She had no need to tell him that. She wouldn't be making an assignation during working hours if it weren't important.

The library was housed in the administration block next to the registry. It was part staff sitting room, part library, with three walls covered with shelves, two free-standing racks, and eight comfortable chairs ranged round low tables. Caroline was already waiting when he arrived, standing at the publications display stand and glancing through the latest copy of *Nature*. No one else was there. He moved up to her wondering if she expected him to kiss her, but then she turned and looked at him and he saw that it would be a mistake. And yet this was their first meeting since Friday night, the night that had changed everything for him. Surely, when they were alone like this, they needn't meet as strangers.

He said humbly: 'There's something you want to say.'

'In a minute. It's just on nine o'clock. Pray silence for the voice of God.'

His head jerked up at her. He was as surprised at her tone as if she had uttered an obscenity. They had never talked about Dr Mair except on the most superficial level, but he had always taken it for granted that she admired the Director and was happy to be his PA. He recalled overhearing the whispered words of Hilary Robarts when Caroline had walked into a public meeting at Mair's elbow: 'Behold, the handmaid of the Lord.' That was how they had all seen her, the intelligent, discreet, beautiful but subservient handmaid to a man she was content to serve because she found him worthy of service.

The intercom crackled. There was a background, indecipherable voice and then Mair's measured, serious tones.

'There cannot be anyone on the station who doesn't now know that Hilary Robarts was found dead on the beach last night. She had been murdered. It appeared at first that she was the second Larksoken victim of the Norfolk Whistler, but it now seems almost certain that the Whistler himself died before Hilary. We shall in time find a way of expressing our corporate grief at her loss as we shall at Christine Baldwin's. In the meantime her death is a matter for police investigation and Chief Inspector Rickards of the Norfolk CID, who has been responsible for the investigation into the Whistler murders, has taken charge of the case. He will be on the station later in the morning and may ask to interview those of you who knew Hilary best and may be able to help with details of her life. If any of you has any information, however slight, which may assist the police, please get in touch with Chief Inspector Rickards, either when he is here or at the incident room at Hoveton. The telephone number is 499 623.'

The intercom crackled and was silent. She said: 'I wonder how many drafts it took before he got that right. Innocuous, non-committal, nothing crudely stated but everything understood. And he didn't irritate us by saying that he could rely on us all to get on with the job, as if we were a bunch of excitable sixth-formers. He never wastes time and words on inessentials. He'll make a good senior civil servant all right.'

Jonathan said: 'This Chief Inspector Rickards, do you think he'll want to interview all of us?'

'Anyone who knew Hilary. And that will include us. And that's what I want to talk about. When he sees me I propose telling him that you and I spent the whole of last evening together from six o'clock until about half-past ten. Obviously I'll need you to back me up. And it depends, of course, on whether anyone can disprove it. That's what we have to discuss.'

He stood for a moment appalled. 'But we weren't! You're asking me to lie. This is a murder investigation. It's terribly dangerous to lie to the police, they always find out.'

He knew what he must sound like, a frightened child, petulant, reluctant to take part in a dangerous game. He looked straight ahead, not wanting to meet her eyes, fearful of what he might see there, entreaty, anger, contempt.

She said: 'You told me on Friday that your parents were going to spend Sunday night at Ipswich with your married sister. They went, didn't they?'

He said miserably: 'Yes, they went.'

It was because he knew that they wouldn't be at home that he had hoped, had half expected, that Caroline would suggest that they should be together again in the bungalow. He remembered her words: 'Look, there are times when a woman needs to be on her own. Can't you understand that? What happened yesterday doesn't mean that we have to spend every second of our time together. I've told you that I love you. God knows, I've shown it. Isn't that enough?'

She said: 'So you were alone in the flat yesterday evening. Or weren't you? If anyone called or telephoned, then obviously I've got to think of something else.'

'No one called. I was on my own until after lunch. Then I went for a drive.'

'What time did you get back? Did anyone see you garaging the car? It's not a large block of flats, is it? Did you meet anyone when you got home? And what about lights from the windows?'

'I left the lights on. We always do when the flat is empty. Mother thinks it's safer, makes it look occupied. And I didn't get back until after dark. I wanted to be alone, to think. I drove to Blakeney and walked on the marshes. I wasn't home until ten forty-five.'

She gave a small contented sigh. 'Then it looks all right. Did you meet anyone on the walk?'

'Only in the distance. A couple with a dog. I don't think they could recognize me even if they knew me.'

'Where did you eat?' Her voice was sharp, the interrogation relentless.

'I didn't. Not until I got home. I wasn't hungry.'

'Well, that's all right then. We're safe. And no one spied on me in the bungalow. And no one would ring or call. No one ever does.'

Spy. It was, he thought, a strange word to use. But she was right. The bungalow, as uninspired as its name, Field View, stood totally isolated on a dull country road outside Hoveton. He had never been inside it, never even been allowed to escort her home before they had arrived together on Friday evening, and it had surprised and a little shocked him. She had told him that it was rented furnished from the owners who had gone to Australia for a year to stay with a married daughter and had decided to stay on. But why had she stayed on, he

184

wondered? Surely there was a more attractive house or cottage somewhere she could have rented, a small flat in Norwich she could have afforded to buy. And following her inside the front door he had been struck by the contrast between its meanness, its vulgarity and her serene loveliness. He could picture it now, the dun-coloured carpet in the hall, the sitting room with two walls papered in pink stripes, the other two with huge clusters of roses, the hard sofa and two chairs with their grubby covers, the small reproduction of Constable's *Hay Wain*, hung too high to be comfortably seen and placed in incongruous proximity to the ubiquitous print of a yellow-faced Chinese girl, the old-fashioned, wall-mounted gas fire. And she had done nothing to change it, nothing to impress on it her own personality. It was as if she hardly noticed its deficiencies, its ugliness. It served its purpose. She asked no more of it. And it had served theirs. But even the hall had struck him chill. He had wanted to cry out, 'This is our first time together, my first time ever. Can't we go somewhere else? Does it have to be here?'

He said miserably: 'I don't think I can do it, not convincingly. Chief Inspector Rickards will know I'm lying. I'll look guilty, embarrassed.'

But she had decided to be gentle with him, reassuring. She said patiently: 'He'll expect you to be embarrassed. You'll be telling him we spent the evening alone making love. That's convincing enough. That's natural enough. He'd find it more suspicious if you didn't look guilty. Don't you see the guilt and embarrassment will make your story more convincing.'

So even his inexperience, his insecurity, yes, even his shame was to be used for her ends.

She said: 'Look, all we need to do is to transpose the two nights. Friday night becomes yesterday. Don't fabricate, don't invent. Tell them what we did, what we ate, the food, the wine, what we talked about. It will sound true because it will be true. And they can't catch us out by asking about the TV programmes we didn't watch.'

'But what happened was private. It was for us alone.'

'Not any more. Murder destroys privacy. We made love. No doubt the police will use a coarser word. If they don't speak it, then they'll think it. But we made love in my bedroom, on my bed. You do remember?'

Remember. Oh yes, he remembered. His face flamed. He felt as if his whole body was burning. The tears that welled up despite his desperate will to hold them back were scalding tears. He squeezed his eyes shut so that he need not have to wipe them away. Of course, he remembered. That dull, square little back room, anonymous as a room in some cheap hotel, the mixture of excitement and terror which half paralysed him, his incompetent fumblings, the whispered endearments which had become commands. She had been patient, experienced and in the end she had taken charge. Well, he had never been naïve enough to suppose that for her it was the first time. For him, but not for her. But what had happened was, he knew, irrevocable. It was she who had possessed him not he her, and that possession was more than physical. For a moment he couldn't speak. It was difficult to believe that those grotesque but controlled writhings had anything to do with the Caroline who stood now so close to him, yet so distanced. He noticed with sharpened perception the pristine cleanness of the grey and white striped shirt, cut like a man's, the sway of the long grey skirt, the black patent court shoes, the simple gold chain and the matching gold cufflinks, the corn-coloured hair sculpted back into the single thick plait. Was this what he had loved, still loved, a boy's romantic ideal, the cold remote perfection of her? And he knew with an almost audible groan that their first coupling had destroyed more than it had affirmed, that what he had yearned for, still yearned for, and had lost for ever, was an unattainable beauty. But he knew, too, that she would only have to stretch out a hand and he would follow her again to that bungalow, to that bed.

He said miserably: 'But why? Why? They won't suspect you, they can't. It's ridiculous even to think it. You got on well with Hilary. You get on well with everyone in the station. You're the last person the police will be interested in. You haven't even a motive.'

'But I have. I've always disliked her and I hated her father. He ruined Mummy, forced her to spend her last years in poverty. And I lost the chance of a decent education. I'm a secretary, essentially a shorthand-typist, and that's all I'll ever be.'

'I've always thought you could be anything you chose.'

'Not without education. All right, I know you can get a grant, but I had to leave school and earn as quickly as possible. And it's not only me, it's what Peter Robarts did to Mummy. She trusted him. She put every penny she'd got, every penny Daddy left, into his plastics company. I've hated him all my life and I hated her because of him. Once the police discover that I'll get no peace. But if I can produce an alibi, that will be the end. They'll leave us alone, both of us. We only need to say that we were together and there will be the end of it.'

'But they can't see what Hilary's father did to your mother as a motive for murder. It's unreasonable. And it was all so long ago.'

'No motive for killing another human being is ever reasonable. People kill for the strangest reasons. And I've got a thing about the police. It's irrational, I know, but I've always had it. That's why I'm so careful when I'm driving. I know I couldn't stand up to a real interrogation. I'm frightened of the police.'

And she was, he remembered, seizing on this demonstrable truth as if it made the whole request legitimate, reasonable. She was obsessive about the speed limit even when the road was clear, obsessive about wearing her seat belt, the state of her car. And he remembered that time three weeks ago, when she had had her handbag snatched while shopping in Norwich and, despite his protest, hadn't even reported it. He remembered her words. 'It's no use, they'll never get it back. We'll only waste their time at the police station. Let it go, there wasn't much in it.' And then he thought, I'm checking up on what she's telling me, verifying it. And he felt an overpowering shame mixed with pity. He heard her voice.

'All right, I'm asking too much. I know how you feel about truth, honesty, your boy scout Christianity. I'm asking you to sacrifice your good opinion of yourself. No one likes doing that. We all need our self-esteem. I suppose yours is knowing that you're morally better than the rest of us. But aren't you a bit of a hypocrite? You say you love me, but you won't lie for me. It's not an important lie. It won't hurt anyone. But you can't do it. It's against your religion. Your precious religion didn't stop you going to bed with me, did it? I thought Christians were supposed to be too pure for casual fornication.'

Casual fornication. Each word was like a blow, not a fierce stabbing pain but a continuous thud like regular deliberate blows on the same bruised flesh. He had never, even in those first marvellous days together, been able to talk to her about his faith. She had made it plain from the beginning that this was a part of his life with which she had neither sympathy nor understanding. And how could he begin to explain that he had followed her into the bedroom without guilt because his need of her was stronger than his love for God, stronger than guilt, stronger than faith, needing no rationalization, no justification other than itself. How, he had told himself, could anything be wrong which every nerve and sinew told him was natural and right, even holy.

She said: 'All right, let it go. I'm asking too much.'

Stung by the contempt in her voice, he said miserably: 'It's not that. I'm not better, I'm not. And you could never ask too much. If it's important to you, of course I'll do it.'

She looked at him sharply as if judging his sincerity, his will. He heard the relief in her voice. She said: 'Look, there's no danger. We're both innocent, we know that. And what we tell the police could so easily have been true.'

But that was a mistake, and he saw the realization of it in her eyes. He said: 'It could have been true, but it isn't.'

'And that's what's important to you, more important than my peace of mind, more important than what I thought we felt for each other.'

He wanted to ask why her peace of mind needed to be built on a lie. He wanted to ask what they did, in fact, feel for each other, what she felt for him.

She said, looking at her watch: 'And after all it will be an alibi for you too. That's even more important. After all, everyone knows how unkind she's been to you since that local radio programme. God's little nuclear crusader. You haven't forgotten that?'

The crudity of the implication, the note of impatience in her voice, all repelled him. He said: 'But suppose they don't believe us.'

'Don't let's go over all that again. Why shouldn't they believe us? And it hardly matters if they don't. They can't ever prove we're lying, that's what's important. And after all it's natural that we should have been together. It isn't as if we've just started seeing each other. Look, I've got to get back to the office now. I'll be in touch, but we'd better not see each other tonight.'

He hadn't expected to see her that night. The news of this latest murder would have been broadcast on local radio, passed from mouth to mouth. His mother would be waiting anxiously for his return from work, avid for news.

But there was something he had to tell her before she left and somehow he found the courage. He said: 'I rang you last night. While I was driving around thinking. I stopped at a phone box and telephoned. You weren't in.'

There was a small silence. He glanced nervously at her face but it was expressionless. She said: 'What time was that?'

188

'About twenty to ten, perhaps a bit later.'

'Why? Why did you telephone?'

'The need to talk to you. Loneliness. I suppose I half hoped that you might change your mind and ask me to come round.'

'All right. You might as well know. I was on the headland last night. I took Remus for a run. I left the car down a cart track just outside the village and walked as far as the ruined abbey. I suppose I was there just after ten.'

He said in horrified wonder: 'You were there! And all the time she must have been lying dead within a few yards of you.'

She said sharply: 'Not a few yards, more like a hundred. There was never any chance that I'd find her, and I didn't see her killer if that's what you're thinking. And I stayed on the cliffs. I didn't go down to the beach. If I had, the police would have found my footprints, mine and Remus's.'

'But someone might have seen you. It was bright moonlight.'

'The headland was empty. And if the murderer was lurking in the trees and saw me, he's hardly likely to come forward. But it's not the happiest position to be in. That's why I need an alibi. I wasn't going to tell you, but now you know. I didn't kill her. But I was there and I've got a motive. That's why I'm asking you to help.'

For the first time Jonathan detected in her voice a note of tenderness, almost of pleading. She moved as if to touch him and then drew back and the tentative gesture, the withdrawal, was as endearing as if she had laid her hand against his face. The hurt and misery of the last ten minutes were swept away in a rush of tenderness. His lips seemed to have thickened so that speech was difficult, but he found the words. He said: 'Of course, I'll help. I love you. I won't let you down. You can depend on me.'

27

Rickards had arranged with Alex Mair to be at the power station by nine that morning but had planned to call first at Scudder's Cottage to see Ryan Blaney. The visit was one of some delicacy. He knew that Blaney had children and it would be necessary to question at least the eldest. But this couldn't be done until he had with him a woman police constable and there had been some delay in arranging this. It was one of those comparatively minor irritations which he found difficult to accept, but he knew that it would be unwise to pay more than a brief visit to the Blaneys without a WPC. Whether or not the man proved to be a serious suspect, he couldn't risk a later allegation that information had been extracted from a juvenile without the observance of proper procedures. At the same time Blaney had a right to know what had happened to his picture, and if the police didn't tell him someone else speedily would. And it was important that he was there to see the man's face when he heard the news, both of the slashed portrait and of Hilary Robarts's murder.

He thought that he had seldom seen a more depressing place than Scudder's Cottage. A thin drizzle was falling and he saw the cottage and the neglected garden through a shimmering mist which seemed to absorb shapes and colours so that the whole scene was one damp amorphous grey. Leaving DC Gary Price in the car, Rickards and Oliphant made their way up the weed-infested path to the porch. There was no bell and when Oliphant thudded on the iron knocker the door almost immediately opened. Ryan Blaney stood before them, six foot tall, lank, bleary-eyed and gave them a long unwelcoming stare. The colour seemed to have drained even from his ruddy hair and Rickards thought he had never seen a man look so exhausted and yet still be on his feet. Blaney didn't invite them in and Rickards didn't suggest it. That intrusion had better wait until he was accompanied by a WPC. And Blaney could wait. He was anxious now to get to Larksoken Power Station. He gave the news that the portrait of Hilary Robarts had been slashed and found at Thyme Cottage, but offered no other details. There was no response. He said: 'Did you hear me, Mr Blaney?'

'Yes, I heard you. I knew that the portrait was missing.'

'When?'

'Last night, at about nine forty-five. Miss Mair called for it. She was going to take it to Norwich with her this morning. She'll tell you. Where is it now?'

'We have it, what remains of it. We shall need it for forensic examination. We'll give you a receipt, naturally.'

'What good will that do? You can keep it, the picture and your receipt. Slashed to pieces, did you say?'

'Not to pieces, in two clean slashes. Perhaps it can be repaired. We'll bring it with us when we come so that you can identify it.'

'I don't want to see it again. You can keep it.'

'We'll need the identification, Mr Blaney. But we'll talk about it when we see you later today. When, incidentally, did you last see the portrait?'

'Thursday evening when I wrapped it and left it in the painting shed. I haven't been in the shed since. And what's the good of talking? It was the best thing I've ever done and that bitch destroyed it. Get Alice Mair or Adam Dalgliesh to identify it. They've both seen it.'

'Are you saying you know who's responsible?' Again there was a silence. Rickards broke it by saying: 'We'll be with you late this afternoon, probably between four and five if that's convenient. And we shall have to talk to the children. We'll have a WPC with us. They're at school, I suppose, the children?'

'The twins are at playgroup, Theresa is here. She isn't well. Look, you're not going to all this trouble about a slashed portrait. Since when have the police cared about pictures?'

'We care about criminal damage. But there is something more. I have to tell you that Hilary Robarts was murdered last night.'

He stared intently at Blaney's face as he spoke. This was the moment of revelation, perhaps the moment of truth. It was surely impossible for Blaney to hear the news without betraying some emotion: shock, fear, surprise, real or simulated. Instead he said calmly: 'You don't have to tell me that either. I knew. George Jago phoned early this morning from the Local Hero.'

Did he indeed, thought Rickards, and mentally added George Jago to his list of people to be questioned as soon as possible. He asked: 'Will Theresa be in and well enough to speak to us this afternoon?'

'She'll be here and she'll be well enough.'

And then the door was closed firmly in their faces.

Oliphant said: 'God knows why Robarts wanted to buy that slum in the first place. And she's been trying to force him and the kids out for months. There's been a great deal of feeling about it in Lydsett as well as on the headland.'

'So you told me on the way here. But if Blaney killed her he'd hardly draw attention to himself by hurling that portrait through the window of Thyme Cottage. And two unrelated criminal acts, murder and malicious damage on the same night, is too great a coincidence to swallow.'

It had been a bad start to the day. The drizzle, seeping coldly under the collar of his coat, added to his mild dejection. He hadn't noticed that it was raining on the rest of the headland and could almost believe that Scudder's Lane and that picturesque but sour little hovel generated their own depressing climate. He had a lot to get through before he returned for a more rigorous confrontation with Ryan Blaney, and he wasn't looking forward to any of it. Forcing the gate shut over a clump of weeds on the path, he took a last look at the cottage. There was no smoke from the chimney and the windows, hazed with salt, were tightly closed. It was difficult to believe that a family lived here, that the cottage hadn't long been abandoned to damp and decay. And then, at the right-hand window, he glimpsed a pale face framed with red-gold hair. Theresa Blaney was looking down at them.

28

Twenty minutes later the three police officers were at Larksoken Power Station. A place had been reserved for them in the car park outside the perimeter fence close to the guard house. As soon as they approached the gate it was unlocked and one of the security police came out and removed the cones. The preliminaries took only a little time. They were received with almost impassive civility by the uniformed security guard on duty, signed the book and were issued with their lapel badges. The guard telephoned the news of their arrival, reported that the Director's PA, Miss Amphlett, would be with them very shortly and then appeared to lose interest in them. His companion, who had opened the gates and removed the cones, stood casually chatting to a stocky man dressed as a diver and carrying his helmet under his arm, who had apparently been working on one of the water towers. Neither of them seemed particularly interested in the arrival of the police. If Dr Mair had instructed that they were to be received with courtesy but the minimum of fuss, his staff couldn't have done it better.

Through the window of the guard house they saw a woman, obviously Miss Amphlett, walking unhurriedly down the concrete path. She was a cool, self-possessed blonde who, on arrival, ignored Oliphant's bold stare as if he weren't present and gravely greeted Rickards. But she didn't respond to his smile, either because she thought a smile inappropriate to the occasion or, more likely, because in her view few visitors to Larksoken merited such a personal welcome and a police officer wasn't among them.

She said: 'Dr Mair is ready for you, Chief Inspector,' and turned to lead the way. It made him feel like a patient being shown into the presence of a consultant. You could tell a lot about a man from his PA and what she told him about Dr Alex Mair reinforced his private imaginings. He thought of his own secretary, tousled-haired, nineteen-year-old Kim, who dressed in the more bizarre extreme of contemporary youth fashion, whose shorthand was as unreliable as her timekeeping, but who never greeted even the lowliest visitor without a wide smile and the offer, which they were ill advised to accept, of office coffee and biscuits.

They followed Miss Amphlett between the wide lawns to the administration building. She was a woman who induced unease and Oliphant, obviously feeling the need to assert himself, began to prattle.

'That's the turbine house to our right, sir, and the reactor building and the cooling plant behind it. The workshop is to the left. It's a Magnox thermal reactor, sir, a type first commissioned in 1956. We had it all explained to us when we went round. The fuel is uranium metal. To conserve the neutrons and to allow natural uranium to be used the fuel is clad in a magnesium alloy called Magnox with a low neutron absorption. That's where the reactor gets its name. They extract the heat by passing carbon dioxide gas over the fuel in the reactor core. That transfers its heat to water in a steam generator and the steam drives a turbine coupled to an electric generator.'

Rickards wished that Oliphant didn't feel the need to demonstrate his superficial knowledge of nuclear power in the presence of Miss Amphlett, and only hoped that it was accurate. Oliphant went on: 'Of course this type of reactor is out of date now. It's being replaced by a PWR, pressurized water reactor, like the one being built at Sizewell. I've been shown over Sizewell as well as Larksoken, sir. I thought I might as well learn what's going on in these places.'

Rickards thought, And if you've learned that, Elephant Boy, you're even cleverer than you think you are.

The room on the second floor of the administration block into which they were shown struck Rickards as immense. It was almost empty, an arrangement of space and light deliberately deployed to make a statement about the man who now rose to his feet behind the huge black modern desk and stood gravely waiting while they walked across what seemed endless yards of carpet. Even as their hands touched, and Alex Mair's grasp was firm and disconcertingly cold, Rickards's eyes and mind took in the salient features of the office. Two of the walls were painted a smooth light grey, but to the east and south sheets of plate glass reached from ceiling to floor giving a panorama of sky, sea and headland. It was a sunless morning but the air was suffused with a pale ambiguous light, the horizon blurred so that sea and sky were one shimmering grey. Rickards had for a moment the sensation of being weightlessly suspended in outer space in some bizarre and futuristic capsule. And then another image supervened. He could almost hear the throb of the engines and feel the ship shudder as the great surge of ocean divided under the prow.

There was very little furniture. Alex Mair's uncluttered desk, with a high but comfortable armchair for visitors, faced the southern window before which stood a conference table set with eight chairs. In front of the east window was a display table holding a model of what Rickards presumed was the new pressurized water reactor shortly to be constructed on the site. Even at a glance he could see that it was beautifully made, a marvel in glass and steel and perspex, as intricately crafted as if it were a decorative object in its own right. On the north wall hung the only picture; a large oil showing a man with a rifle on a skinny horse, posed in a bleak landscape of sand and scrubland with, in the background, a range of distant mountains. But the man had no head. Instead he was wearing a huge square helmet of black metal with a slit for the eyes. Rickards found the picture disturbingly intimidating. He had a faint memory that he had seen a copy of it, or of something very like it, before, and that the artist was Australian. He was irritated to find himself thinking that Adam Dalgliesh would have known what it was and who had painted it.

Mair went over to the conference table and lifting one of the chairs, swung it lightly and placed it by the desk. They were to sit facing him. After a moment's hesitation, Gary Price took a chair for himself, placed it behind Mair, and unobtrusively took out his notebook.

Looking into the grey sardonic eyes Rickards wondered how Alex Mair saw him, and a snatch of conversation, overheard some years ago in the mess at New Scotland Yard, came unbidden into his mind. 'Oh, Ricky's nobody's fool. He's a bloody sight more intelligent than he looks.' 'He'd better be. He reminds me of one of those characters you get in every war film. The poor honest son-of-a-bitch who always ends up with his face in the mud and a bullet in his chest.'

Well, he wasn't going to end with his face in the mud in this inquiry. The room might look as if it were specifically designed to intimidate him, but it was only a working office. Alex Mair, for all his assurance, his rumoured brilliance, was only a man and if he had killed Hilary Robarts he would end up, as better men than he had done, looking at the sky through iron bars and watching the changing face of the sea only in his dreams.

As they seated themselves, Mair said: 'I expect you'll need

195

somewhere to interview people. I've made arrangements for a small room in the medical physics department to be made available when you're finished here. Miss Amphlett will show you the way. I don't know how long you'll need it, but we've moved in a small refrigerator and there are facilities for making tea or coffee or, if you prefer, tea and coffee can be brought to you from the canteen. And the canteen staff can, of course, provide you with simple meals. Miss Amphlett will let you have today's menu.'

Rickards said: 'Thank you. We'll make our own coffee.'

He felt at a disadvantage and wondered if this was intended. They would need an interview room and he could hardly complain if this need had been anticipated. But it would have been a better start if he could have taken the initiative and he felt, perhaps illogically, that there was something demeaning to his job in this careful reassurance that he would get his food and drink. The look bent on him across the desktop was unworried, speculative, almost, he could imagine, slightly judgemental. He knew that he was in the company of power and the kind of power with which he was unfamiliar; confident, intellectual authority. A clutch of chief constables would have been less formidable.

Alex Mair said: 'Your Chief Constable has already liaised with the Atomic Energy Authority Constabulary. Inspector Johnston would like a word with you this morning, probably before you begin your general interview. He realizes that the Norfolk Constabulary have the principal responsibility here, but naturally he has an interest.'

Rickards said: 'We recognize that and we shall be glad of his co-operation.'

And it would be co-operation not interference. He had already made himself familiar with the duties of the AEAC and he was aware that there was a potential risk of dissension and overlapping of powers. But this was essentially a matter for the Norfolk CID and was seen as an extension of the Whistler inquiries. If Inspector Johnston was prepared to be reasonable, then so was he, but it was not a problem which he proposed to discuss with Dr Mair.

Mair opened the right-hand drawer of his desk and took out a manila folder. He said: 'This is Hilary Robarts's personnel file. There's no objection to your seeing it, but it merely gives the background information; age, places of education, degrees, career before she came to us in 1984 as deputy to the Administrative Officer.

A curriculum vitae from which the vitae is, unusually, conspicuously absent. The dry bones of a life.'

Mair slid it across the desk. The action had a curious finality. A life closed, finished with. Taking it Rickards said: 'Thank you, sir. It will be helpful to have it. Perhaps you could flesh out some of the dry bones for us. You knew her well?'

'Very well. Indeed, for a time we were lovers. That doesn't, I admit, necessarily imply more than physical intimacy but I probably did know her as well as anyone here on the station.'

He spoke calmly and totally without embarrassment, as if it were as unimportant as stating that he and Robarts had shared the same university. Rickards wondered if Mair expected him to seize on the admission. Instead he asked: 'Was she popular?'

'She was highly efficient. The two, I find, do not invariably go together. But she was respected and, I think, generally liked by those staff who had dealings with her. She will be greatly missed, probably more deeply than would be more egregiously popular colleagues.'

'And missed by you?'

'By all of us.'

'When did your affair end, Dr Mair?'

'About three or four months ago.'

'Without rancour?'

'With neither a bang nor a whimper. We had been seeing less of each other for some time before then. My personal future is at present rather unsettled but I am unlikely to continue as Director for very much longer. One comes to the end of a love affair as to the end of a job; a natural feeling that a stage of life has run its course.'

'And she felt the same?'

'I imagine so. We both had some regrets at the break but I don't think either of us ever imagined that we were indulging in a grand passion, or indeed expected our relationship to be lasting.'

'There was no other man?'

'None that I know of, but then there's no reason why I should know.'

Rickards said: 'So you would be surprised to learn that she wrote to her solicitor in Norwich on Sunday morning to make an appointment to discuss her will and that she told him she was expecting shortly to be married? We found the unposted letter among her papers.'

Mair blinked rapidly but otherwise showed no sign of discomposure. He said evenly: 'Yes, it would surprise me, but I'm not sure why. I suppose because she seemed to live rather a solitary life here and it's difficult to see how she could have found time or opportunity to enter into a new relationship. Of course, it's perfectly possible that some man from her past had re-emerged and they had come to an arrangement. I'm afraid I can't help you.'

Rickards changed the tack of his questioning. He said: 'There seems to be a feeling locally that she wasn't much help to you during the public inquiry into the second reactor here. She didn't give evidence to the official inquiry, did she? I can't quite see how she was involved.'

'Officially she wasn't. But at one or two public meetings, unwisely, she got embroiled with hecklers, and on one of our open days the scientist who normally escorts the public was off sick and she took his place. She was, perhaps, less tactful than she should have been with some of the questioners. After that I arranged that she wasn't directly involved with the public.'

Rickards said: 'So she was a woman who provoked antagonism?'

'Not enough, I should have thought, to provoke murder. She was dedicated to the work here and found it difficult to tolerate what she saw as wilful obscurantism. She hadn't a scientific training but she did acquire considerable knowledge of the science done here and perhaps undue respect for what she saw as expert scientific opinion. I pointed out that it was unreasonable to expect this to be shared by the general public. After all they've probably been told by experts in recent years that high-rise flats don't collapse, that the London Underground is safe from fire and that cross-channel ferries can't keel over.'

Oliphant, who had until now remained silent, suddenly said: 'I was one of the visitors on that open day. Someone asked her about Chernobyl. She made a remark, didn't she, about "only thirty dead, so what were people worrying about?" Isn't that what she said? It rather begged the question: how many dead would Miss Robarts agree was an acceptable figure?'

Alex Mair looked at him as if surprised that he could actually speak and, after a moment's contemplation, said: 'In comparing the Chernobyl death toll with fatalities in industry and in mining fossil fuels she was making a perfectly reasonable point, although she could have done it with more tact. Chernobyl is a sensitive subject. We get rather tired of explaining to the public that the Russian RBMK-type of reactor had a number of design weaknesses, notably that it had a fast-acting positive power coefficient when the reactor was at low power. The Magnox, AGR and PWR designs don't have this characteristic at any power level so that a similar accident here is physically impossible. I'm sorry if that sounds over-technical. What I'm saying is: it won't happen here, it can't happen here and, in fact, it didn't happen here.'

Oliphant said stolidly: 'It hardly matters whether it happens here or not, sir, if we get the results of it. Wasn't Hilary Robarts suing someone in the community for alleged libel arising out of the meeting I attended?'

Alex Mair ignored him and spoke to Rickards. 'I think that's generally known. It was a mistake, I think. She had a legitimate case but she wasn't likely to get satisfaction by going to law.'

Rickards asked: 'You tried to persuade her not to in the interests of the station?'

'And in her own. Yes, I tried.'

The telephone on the desk rang. Mair pressed the button. He said: 'This shouldn't take much longer. Tell him I'll ring back in twenty minutes.' Rickards wondered whether he had arranged for the call to be put through. As if in confirmation of the suspicion, Mair said: 'In view of my past relationship with Miss Robarts you'll need to know my movements on Sunday. Perhaps I could give them to you now. Both of us have a busy day ahead, I imagine.' It was a less than subtle reminder that it was time they got down to business.

Rickards kept his voice steady. 'That would be helpful, sir.' Gary Price bent his head over his notebook as assiduously as if he had just been reprimanded for inattention.

'They're hardly relevant until Sunday evening, but I may as well cover the whole of the weekend. I left here just after ten forty-five on Friday and drove to London, lunched with an old university friend at the Reform Club and went on at two thirty to a meeting with the Permanent Secretary at the Department of Energy. I then went to my flat in the Barbican and in the evening attended a performance of *The Taming of the Shrew* at the Barbican Theatre with a party of three friends. If you later need their corroboration, which seems unlikely, I can of course, give you their names. I drove back to Larksoken on Sunday morning, lunched at a pub *en route* and arrived home at about four. I had a cup of tea and then went for a walk on the headland and got back to Martyr's Cottage about an hour later. I had a quick supper with my sister at about seven and left for the station at seven thirty, or soon afterwards. I was working here in the computer room alone until ten thirty when I left for home. I was driving along the coast road when I was stopped by Commander Dalgliesh with the news that Hilary Robarts had been murdered. The rest you know.'

Rickards said: 'Not altogether, Dr Mair. There was some delay before we arrived. You didn't touch the body?'

'I stood and looked down at her but I didn't touch her. Dalgliesh was rather conscientiously doing his job, or should I say yours. He very rightly reminded me that nothing should be touched and that the scene should be left undisturbed. I went down and walked by the sea until you arrived.'

Rickards asked: 'Do you usually come in to work on Sunday evenings?'

'Invariably if I have had to spend the Friday in London. There is a very heavy pressure of work at present which it is impossible to fit into a five-day week. Actually I stayed for less than three hours, but they were valuable hours.'

'And you were alone in the computer room. Doing what, sir?'

If Mair found the inquiry irrelevant he didn't say so. 'I was engaged on my research which is concerned with the study of reactor behaviour in hypothesized loss-of-coolant accidents. I'm not, of course, the only person working in what is one of the most important areas of research in nuclear reactor design. There's a great deal of international co-operation in these studies. Essentially what I'm doing is evaluating the possible effects of loss of coolant by mathematical models which are then evaluated by numerical analysis and advanced computer programmes.'

Rickards said: 'And you're working here at Larksoken alone?'

'At this station I am. Similar studies are being carried out at Winfrith and in a number of other countries including the USA. As I have said, there's a considerable amount of international co-operation.'

Oliphant asked suddenly: 'Is that the worst thing that can happen, a loss of the coolant?'

Alex Mair looked at him for a moment as if deciding whether the question coming from such a source warranted an answer, then he said: 'The loss of coolant is potentially extremely dangerous. There

are, of course, emergency procedures if the normal cooling arrangements fail. The incident at Three Mile Island in the United States has
emphasized the need to know more about the extent and nature of
the threat posed by that kind of incident. The phenomenon to be
analysed is in three main groups: severe fuel damage and core
melting, migration of released fission products and aerosols through
the primary coolant circuit, and the behaviour of fission products in
released fuel and steam in the reactor container building. If you have
a genuine interest in the research and enough knowledge to understand it I can provide you with some references, but this hardly
seems the time and place for scientific education.'

Oliphant smiled as if gratified by the rebuke. He asked: 'Wasn't
the scientist who killed himself, Dr Toby Gledhill, working on the
research side here with you? I thought I read something about that in
one of the local papers.'

'Yes. He was my assistant here. Tobias Gledhill was a physicist
who was also an exceptionally talented computer expert. He is very
much missed as a colleague and a man.'

And that, thought Rickards, disposes of Toby Gledhill. From
another man the tribute could have been moving in its simplicity.
From Mair it sounded like a bleak dismissal. But then, suicide was
messy and embarrassing. He would find repugnant its intrusion into
his neatly organized world.

Mair turned to Rickards. 'I have a great deal to do this morning,
Chief Inspector, and no doubt you have too. Is this really relevant?'

Rickards said stolidly: 'It helps fill in the picture. I suppose you
booked in when you arrived here yesterday night and subsequently
booked out?'

'You saw something of the system when you arrived. Every
member of the staff has a signed identity badge with a photograph
and a personal number which is confidential. The number is elec-
tronically registered when the man or woman enters the site and
there is, in addition, a visual check of the badge by the gate staff. I
have a total staff of five hundred and thirty people working in three
shifts covering the twenty-four hours. At the weekend there are two
shifts, the day staff coming on from eight fifteen until twenty fifteen
and the night from twenty fifteen until eight fifteen.'

'And no one could enter or leave undetected, not even the
Director?'

'No one, least of all, I imagine, the Director. My check-in time will be recorded and I was seen arriving and leaving by the gate officer on duty.'

'There is no other way into the station except through the guard house?'

'Not unless you emulate the heroes of old war films and tunnel deep under the wire. No one was tunnelling here on Sunday night.'

Rickards said: 'We shall need to know the movements of every member of the staff on Sunday from early evening until ten thirty when Commander Dalgliesh discovered the body.'

'Isn't that an unnecessarily large spread of time? Surely she was killed shortly after nine?'

'That seems the most likely time of death and we expect to get a more accurate estimate from the post-mortem report. At present I prefer to make no assumptions. We have copies of the forms which were distributed in connection with the Whistler inquiry which we would like to issue to all the staff. I imagine that the great majority can be easily eliminated. Most people who have any family or social life can provide an alibi for Sunday evening. Perhaps you could suggest how the forms can be distributed with as little disturbance to the work here as possible.'

Mair said: 'The simplest and most effective way would be to leave them in the guard house. Each member of staff could be given one when he or she checks in. Those staff who are off sick or on leave today will have to receive them at home. I can supply their names and addresses.' He paused and then added: 'It seems to me highly unlikely that this murder has anything to do with Larksoken Power Station, but as Hilary Robarts worked here and you will be interviewing members of staff, it might be helpful if you have some idea of the layout and organization. My PA has put up a file for you with a diagram of the site, a booklet describing the operation of the reactor which will help to give you some idea of the different functions carried out, a list of staff by name and grade and a copy of the existing managerial structure and the operations staff shift rota. If you want to see any particular department I can arrange for you to be escorted. Certain areas cannot, of course be entered without protective clothing and a subsequent radiological check.'

The file was ready in his right-hand drawer and he handed it over. Rickards took it and studied the organization chart. After a moment he said: 'You have seven divisions, each with a head of department; Medical Physicist, Station Chemist, Operations Superintendent, Maintenance Superintendent, Reactor Physicist, Works Office Engineer and the station Administrative Officer, the post held by Hilary Robarts.'

'Temporarily held. The station Administrative Officer died of cancer three months ago and the post has not yet been filled. We are also about to reorganize the internal administration into three main divisions as at Sizewell where they have what I think is a more effective and rational system. But the future here is uncertain, as you've probably heard, and there may be a case for waiting until a new Director or Station Manager is in post.'

Rickards said: 'And at present the station Administrative Officer is responsible to you through the Deputy Director?'

'Through Dr James Macintosh, that is right. Dr Macintosh is at present in the States studying their nuclear installations and has been for the past month.'

'And the Operations Superintendent – Op. Super. as it says here – is Miles Lessingham, who was one of the guests at Miss Mair's dinner party on Thursday.'

Alex Mair didn't reply.

Rickards went on: 'You've been unfortunate, Dr Mair. Three violent deaths of members of your staff within the space of two months. First Dr Gledhill's suicide, then Christine Baldwin's murder by the Whistler, and now Hilary Robarts.'

Mair asked: 'Have you any doubts that Christine Baldwin was killed by the Whistler?'

'None at all. Her hair was found with that of other victims when he killed himself, and her husband, who would normally be the obvious first suspect, has an alibi. He was driven home by his friends.'

'And Toby Gledhill's death was the subject of an inquest, "death while the balance of his mind was disturbed", that convenient sop to convention and religious orthodoxy.'

Oliphant asked: 'And was the balance of his mind disturbed, sir?'

Mair turned on him his ironic and speculative gaze. 'I have no way of knowing the state of his mind, Sergeant. What I am sure of is that he killed himself and that he did it unaided. No doubt at the time he felt he had sufficient reason. Dr Gledhill was a manic depressive. He coped courageously with his disability and it rarely interfered with his work. But with that psychological make-up, suicide is always an above-average risk. And if you agree that the three deaths are unrelated, then we needn't waste time on the first two. Or was your statement, Chief Inspector, intended as a general commiseration?'

Rickards said: 'Just a comment, sir.' He went on: 'One of your staff, Miles Lessingham, found Christine Baldwin's body. He told us then that he was on his way to have dinner with you and Miss Mair. I suppose he gave you all a graphic description of his experience. Natural I'd say. Difficult thing to keep to yourself.'

Mair said calmly: 'Virtually impossible, wouldn't you say?' He added 'Among friends.'

'Which he was, of course. All friends together, including Miss Robarts. So you got all the gory details fresh from the scene. Including the ones he'd been specifically told to keep to himself.'

'Which were they, Chief Inspector?'

Rickards didn't reply. Instead he asked: 'Could I have the names of everyone who was present in Martyr's Cottage when Mr Lessingham arrived?'

'My sister and I, Hilary Robarts, Mrs Dennison, the housekeeper from the Old Rectory, and Commander Adam Dalgliesh of the Metropolitan Police. And the Blaney child – Theresa, I think she's called – was helping my sister with the meal.' He paused and then added: 'These inquiry forms which you're proposing to issue to all members of staff; I suppose it is necessary to take up their time in this way. Isn't it fairly plain what happened here? Surely this is what your people call a copycat murder.'

Rickards said: 'It was that all right, sir. All the details correct. Very clever, very convincing. Just the two differences. This murderer knew his victim and this murderer is sane.'

Five minutes later, following Miss Amphlett down the corridor to the interviewing room, Rickards thought, And you're a cool customer, mate. No embarrassing expressions of horror and grief which always sounded insincere. No protestations of innocence. The assumption that no one in his rational mind could suspect you of murder. He hadn't asked for his solicitor to be present, but then he didn't need one. But he was far too intelligent to have missed the significance of those questions about the dinner party. Whoever had killed Hilary Robarts had known that she would be swimming by moonlight sometime after nine o'clock yesterday, had known, too, precisely how the Whistler killed his victims. There were quite a number of people who knew one of these facts, but the number who knew both was limited. And six of them had been present at that dinner party at Martyr's Cottage last Thursday night.

29

The interview room which had been assigned to them was a feature-less little office with a view to the west dominated by the great bulk of the turbine house. It was adequately furnished for their purpose, but only just; entirely appropriate, thought Rickards sourly, to visitors whose presence was tolerated but hardly welcomed. There was a modern pedestal desk, obviously brought in from someone's office, three upright chairs and one rather more comfortable one with arms, a small side table with an electric kettle on a tray, four cups and saucers (did Mair expect them to make coffee for the suspects?), a bowl full of wrapped sugar lumps and three caddies.

Rickards said: 'What have they given us, Gary?'

Gary Price busied himself with the tins. 'Coffee bags and tea bags, sir. And there's a tin of biscuits.'

Oliphant asked: 'What kind of biscuits?'

'Digestive, Sarge.'

'Chocolate?'

'No, Sarge, just plain digestives.'

'Well, let's hope they're not radioactive. Better get the kettle on; we may as well start with the coffee. Where do they expect us to get water?'

'Miss Amphlett said there was a tap in the cloakroom at the end of the passage, Sarge. The kettle's filled, anyway.'

Oliphant tried one of the upright chairs, stretching in it as if to assess its comfort. The wood creaked. He said: 'Cold fish, wasn't he? And clever with it. Not much out of him, sir.'

'I wouldn't say that, Sergeant. We've learned more about the victim than he probably realizes. Efficient but not much liked, prone to interfere with matters outside her scope of responsibility, prob-ably because she secretly yearned to be a scientist rather than an administrator. Aggressive, uncompromising, intolerant of criticism. Antagonized the locals and from time to time did the station a bit of no good. And, of course, the Director's mistress, for what that was worth.'

Oliphant said: 'Until three or four months ago. A natural end with no hard feelings on either side. His version.'

'And we're never going to get hers, are we? But one thing was odd. When Mair met Mr Dalgliesh he was on his way home from here. His sister presumably was expecting him, yet apparently he didn't telephone her. It never seems to have occurred to him.'

'Shocked, sir, something else on his mind. He's just discovered that his ex-girlfriend is the victim of a particularly vicious psychopathic killer. Tends to eclipse brotherly feelings and thoughts of your bedtime cocoa.'

'Maybe. I wonder whether Miss Mair rang here to find out why he was delayed. We'll ask.'

Oliphant said: 'If she didn't ring, I can think of one reason why. She expected him to be late. She thought he was at Thyme Cottage with Hilary Robarts.'

'If she didn't ring because she thought that, then she can't have known that Robarts was dead. Right, Sergeant, let's get started. First of all we'll have a word with Miss Amphlett. The boss's PA usually knows more about the organization than anyone, including her boss.'

But any information of interest that Caroline Amphlett might have she was adept at concealing. She seated herself in the armchair with the calm assurance of an applicant for a job which she has every confidence of getting, and answered Rickards's questions calmly and without emotion except when he attempted to probe into Hilary Robarts's relationship with the Director. Then she permitted herself a moue of distaste that anyone could be so vulgarly inquisitive about matters which were not his concern and answered repressively that Dr Mair had never confided in her about his private life. She admitted that she knew Hilary Robarts made a habit of swimming at night and kept this up well into the autumn months and sometimes later. She thought the fact was generally known at Larksoken. Miss Robarts had been a strong and enthusiastic swimmer. She was not particularly interested in the Whistler except to take reasonable precautions and avoid walking alone at night, and she knew nothing about his methods except what she had read in the newspapers, that he strangled his victims. She had known about the dinner party at Martyr's Cottage on Thursday, she thought Miles Lessingham might have mentioned it, but no one had discussed with her the events of the evening and she saw no reason why they should.

As for her own movements on Sunday, she had spent the whole of the evening from six o'clock at her bungalow with her boyfriend, Jonathan Reeves. They had been together continually until he had left at about ten thirty. Her cool glance at Oliphant challenged him to ask her what they had been doing and he resisted the temptation except to ask what they had drunk and eaten. Asked about her relationship with Hilary Robarts, she said that she had greatly respected her but hadn't particularly liked or disliked her. Their professional relationship had been perfectly friendly but as far as she could remember they had never met outside the power station. As far as she knew, Miss Robarts had no enemies and she had no idea who could have wished her dead. When the door had closed after her Rickards said: 'We'll check her alibi, of course, but there's no hurry. Let young Reeves sweat for an hour or so. I want to check first on the staff who actually worked for Robarts.'

But the next hour was unproductive. The people who had worked directly for Hilary Robarts were more shocked than distressed and their evidence strengthened the image of a woman more respected than liked. But none had an obvious motive, none admitted to knowing precisely how the Whistler had killed and, more to the point, all could produce an alibi for Sunday night. Rickards had hardly expected otherwise.

At the end of the sixty minutes he sent for Jonathan Reeves. He came into the room white-faced and as stiffly controlled as if it were an execution shed and Rickards's first reaction was surprise that a woman as attractive as Caroline Amphlett should have chosen such an unlikely mate. It wasn't that Reeves had a particularly unprepossessing face. You couldn't even describe him as plain if you discounted the acne. And his features, taken individually, were good enough. It was the whole face which was somehow unremarkable, ordinary, the kind of face which defeated any attempt at an Identikit image. Rickards decided that it was best described in terms of movement rather than features; the almost continual blinking behind the horn-rimmed spectacles, the nervous sucking of the lips, his habit of suddenly stretching his neck like a TV comedian. He knew from the list Alex Mair had provided that the staff at Larksoken was predominantly male. Was this the best Amphlett could do for herself? But sexual attraction was irrational anyway. Look at him and Susie. Seeing them together, her friends probably felt an equal surprise.

He left most of the detailed questioning to Oliphant, which was a mistake. Oliphant was always at his worst with a frightened suspect and he took his time extracting, not without pleasure, a straightforward story which confirmed Caroline Amphlett's account.

Afterwards, when Reeves had been finally released, Oliphant said: 'He was as jumpy as a cat, sir. That's why I took my time over him. I think he's lying.'

It was, thought Rickards, typical of Oliphant both to assume and hope for the worst. He said curtly: 'Not lying necessarily, Sergeant; just frightened and embarrassed. Tough luck when your first night of passion ends in a not particularly subtle police interrogation. But the alibi seems firm enough and neither of them has an obvious motive. And there's no evidence that either knew the details of the Whistler's little habits. Let's get on to someone who did. Miles Lessingham.'

Rickards had last seen Lessingham at the scene of Christine Baldwin's murder, since he hadn't himself been at the incident room when Lessingham had called in next morning to sign his statement. He realized that the sardonic attempt at humour, the controlled detachment the man had shown at the scene were mainly due to shock and distaste, but he had sensed, too, that Lessingham had a wariness of the police amounting to dislike. It was not an uncommon phenomenon nowadays, even among the middle classes, and no doubt he had his reasons. But it hadn't made him easy to deal with then and it didn't now. After the usual preliminaries Rickards asked: 'Were you aware of the relationship between Dr Mair and Miss Robarts?'

'He's the Director, she was Acting Administrator.'

'I meant the sexual relationship.'

'No one told me. But not being entirely insensitive to my fellow mortals I thought it likely that they were lovers.'

'And you knew that it had ended?'

'I assumed so. They didn't confide in me when it began and they didn't confide in me when it ended. You'd better ask Dr Mair if you want details of his personal life. I have enough trouble managing my own.'

'But you weren't aware of any difficulties caused by the relationship: resentment, accusations of favouritism, jealousy perhaps?'

'Not from me, I assure you. My interests lie elsewhere.'

209

'And what about Miss Robarts? Did you get the impression that the affair ended without rancour? Did she seem upset, for example?'

'If she was she didn't weep on my shoulder. But then mine is hardly the shoulder she would have chosen.'

'And you have no idea who killed her?'

'None.'

There was a pause, then Rickards asked: 'Did you like her?'

'No.'

For a moment Rickards was nonplussed. It was a question which he frequently asked in murder investigations and usually to some effect. Few suspects would admit to disliking the victim without blundering into an attempt at explanation or justification. After a moment's silence, during which it was obvious that Lessingham had no intention of amplifying his statement, he asked: 'Why not, Mr Lessingham?'

'There aren't many people I actually like as opposed to tolerate and she didn't happen to be one of them. There was no particular reason. Does there have to be? You and your sergeant may not like each other for all I know. It doesn't mean that either of you is planning murder. And talking about murder, which is why I assume I'm here, I have an alibi for Sunday night. Perhaps I had better give it to you now. I have a thirty-foot sailing boat berthed at Blakeney. I went out with her on the morning tide and stayed out until nearly ten at night. I have a witness to my departure, Ed Wilkinson who berths his fishing smack next to my boat, but no witness to my return. There was enough wind in the morning to sail and then I anchored, caught a couple of cod and some whiting and cooked them for lunch. I had food, wine, books and my radio. There was nothing else I needed. It may not be the most satisfactory of alibis but it has the merit of simplicity and truth.'

Oliphant asked: 'You had a dinghy with you?'

'I had my inflatable dinghy on the cabin roof. And at the risk of exciting you, I have to say that I also carried my collapsible bicycle. But I didn't put ashore either at Larksoken headland or anywhere else, not even for the purpose of murdering Hilary Robarts.'

Rickards asked: 'Did you see Miss Robarts at any time during your trip? Were you in sight of the beach where she died?'

'I didn't go that far south. And I saw no one, dead or alive.'

Oliphant asked: 'Do you make a habit of sailing alone at the weekend?'

'I don't make a habit of anything. I used to sail with a friend. Now I sail alone.'

Rickards asked him next about Blaney's portrait of Miss Robarts. He admitted that he had seen it. George Jago, the publican of the Local Hero at Lydsett, had put it up for a week in the bar, apparently at Blaney's request. He had no idea where Blaney normally kept it and he had neither stolen it nor destroyed it. If anyone had, he thought it was probably Robarts herself.

Oliphant said: 'And thrown it through her own window?'

Lessingham said: 'You think she would have been more likely to slash it and chuck it through Blaney's? I agree. But whoever slashed it, it wasn't Blaney.'

Oliphant asked: 'How can you be so sure?'

'Because a creative artist, whether he's a painter or a scientist, doesn't destroy his best work.'

Oliphant said: 'Miss Mair's dinner party; you gave your fellow guests a description of the Whistler's methods including information we had specifically asked you not to divulge.'

Lessingham said coolly: 'One could hardly arrive two hours late for a dinner party without some explanation, and mine was, after all, unusual. I thought they were entitled to a vicarious thrill. Apart from that, to keep silent would have needed more self-control than I was capable of at the time. Murdered and mutilated bodies are your trade, of course. Those of us who have chosen less exciting jobs tend to find them distressing. I knew I could trust my fellow guests not to talk to the press and as far as I know none of them did. Anyway, why ask me what happened on the Thursday night? Adam Dalgliesh was a guest at the dinner party so you have a more experienced and no doubt, from your point of view, a more reliable witness. I won't say a police spy: that would be unfair.'

Rickards spoke for the first time in minutes. He said: 'It would also be inaccurate and offensive.'

Lessingham turned on him with a cool 'Exactly. That's why I haven't used the word. And now, if you've no more questions, I have a power station to run.'

30

It was after midday before the interviews at the power station were completed and Rickards and Oliphant were ready to leave for Martyr's Cottage. They left Gary Price to cope with the inquiry forms and arranged to pick him up after the interview with Alice Mair which Rickards felt might be more fruitful with two officers rather than one. Alice Mair received them calmly at the door with no apparent sign either of anxiety or of curiosity, glanced perfunctorily at their identity cards and invited them in. They might, Rickards thought, have been technicians arriving later than expected to repair the television set. And they were, he saw, expected to interview her in the kitchen. At first it struck him as an odd choice but then, looking round, he supposed you could hardly call it a kitchen; more like an office, sitting room and kitchen combined. Its size surprised him and he found himself wondering irrelevantly whether she had knocked down a wall to provide such over-generous working space. He wondered, too, what Susie would think of it and decided that she would find it unsettling. Susie liked her house to be clearly defined by functions; the kitchen was for working, the dining room for eating, the lounge for watching television and the bedroom for sleeping and, once a week, for making love. He and Oliphant sat in two cushioned, high-backed wicker chairs on each side of the fireplace. His was extremely comfortable, gently containing his long limbs. Miss Mair took the chair at her desk and swivelled it round to face him.

'My brother, of course, gave me the news of the murder as soon as he got home last night. I can't help you about Hilary Robarts's death, I'm afraid. I was at home the whole of yesterday evening and saw and heard nothing. But I can tell you a little about her portrait. Would you and Sergeant Oliphant care for coffee?'

Rickards would have cared; he found himself unexpectedly thirsty; but he declined for both of them. The invitation had sounded perfunctory and he hadn't missed her quick glance towards the desktop stacked with orderly piles of printed pages and a typewritten manuscript. It looked as if they had interrupted her in the business of proofreading. Well, if she was busy, so was he. And he found himself irritated, unreasonably, he felt, by her self-possession. He hadn't expected to find her in hysterics or under sedation for grief. The victim wasn't her next of kin. But the woman had worked closely with Alex Mair, had been a guest at Martyr's Cottage, had, according to Dalgliesh, dined there only four days ago. It was disconcerting to find that Alice Mair could sit quietly correcting proofs, a job which surely required concentrated attention. The killing of Robarts had taken considerable nerve. His suspicion of her was hardly serious; he didn't really see this as a woman's crime. But he let suspicion enter his mind like a barb and lodge there. A remarkable woman, he thought. Perhaps this interview was going to be more productive than he had expected.

He asked: 'You keep house for your brother, Miss Mair?'

'No, I keep house for myself. My brother happens to live here when he is in Norfolk, which naturally is for most of the week. He could hardly administer Larksoken Power Station from his flat in London. If I'm at home and cook dinner he usually shares it. I take the view that it would be unreasonable to demand that he make himself an omelette merely to affirm the principle of shared domestic responsibilities. But I don't see what relevance my housekeeping arrangements have to Hilary Robarts's murder. Could we, perhaps, get on to what happened last night?'

They were interrupted. There was a knock at the door and, without an apology, Alice Mair got up and went through to the hall. They heard a lighter, feminine voice and a woman followed her into the kitchen. Miss Mair introduced her as Mrs Dennison from the Old Rectory. She was a pretty, gentle-looking woman, conventionally dressed in a tweed skirt and twinset, and was obviously distressed. Rickards approved both of her appearance and of the distress. This was how he expected a woman to look and behave after a particularly brutal murder. The two men had got up at her entrance and she took Oliphant's chair while he moved one for himself from the kitchen table.

She turned to Rickards impulsively: 'I'm sorry, I'm interrupting, but I felt I had to get out of the house. This is appalling news, Inspector. Are you absolutely certain that it couldn't have been the Whistler?'

Rickards said: 'Not this time, madam.'

Alice Mair said: 'The timing's wrong. I told you that when I rang

213

early this morning, Meg. The police wouldn't be here now if it wasn't. It couldn't have been the Whistler.'

'I know that's what you said. But I couldn't help hoping that there'd been a mistake, that he'd killed her and then himself, that Hilary Robarts was his last victim.'

Rickards said: 'In a sense she was, Mrs Dennison.'

Alice Mair said calmly: 'I think it's called a copycat murder. There's more than one psychopath in the world and that kind of madness can be infectious, apparently.'

'Of course, but how horrible! Having started, will he too go on, like the Whistler did, death after death, no one feeling safe?'

Rickards said: 'I shouldn't let that worry you, Mrs Dennison.'

She turned to him almost fiercely. 'But of course it worries me! It must worry us all. We've lived so long with the horror of the Whistler. It's appalling to think that it's started all over again.'

Alice Mair got up. 'You need coffee, Meg. Chief Inspector Rickards and Sergeant Oliphant have declined but I think we need it.'

Rickards wasn't going to let her get away with that. He said firmly: 'If you're making it, Miss Mair, I think I'll change my mind. I'd be glad of a coffee. You too no doubt, Sergeant.'

And now, he thought, there'll be a further delay while she grinds beans and no one can talk above the noise. Why can't she just pour boiling water on coffee grains like everyone else?

But the coffee, when it did come, was excellent and he found it unexpectedly comforting. Mrs Dennison took her mug in her hands and cradled it like a child at bedtime. Then she put it down on the hearth and turned to Rickards.

'Look, perhaps you'd rather I went. I'll just have my coffee and then go back to the rectory. If you want to talk to me I'll be there for the rest of the day.'

Miss Mair said: 'You may as well stay and hear what happened last night. It has its points of interest.' She turned to Rickards. 'As I told you, I was here the whole of the evening from half-past five. My brother left for the power station shortly after seven thirty and I settled down to work on my proofs. I switched on the answerphone to avoid interruptions.'

Rickards asked: 'And you didn't leave the cottage for any purpose during the whole of the evening?'

'Not until after half-past nine when I left for the Blaneys'. But perhaps I could tell the story in sequence, Chief Inspector. At about ten past eight I switched off the machine thinking that there might be an important call for my brother. It was then I heard George Jago's message that the Whistler was dead.'

'You didn't ring anyone else to let them know?'

'I knew that wasn't necessary. Jago runs his own information service. He'd make sure that everyone knew. I came back into the kitchen and worked on my proofs until about half-past nine. Then I thought that I'd collect Hilary Robarts's portrait from Ryan Blaney. I'd promised to drop it in at the gallery in Norwich on my way to London and I wanted to make an early start next morning. I tend to be a little obsessive about time and didn't want to go even a short distance out of my way. I rang Scudder's Cottage to let him know that I was collecting the portrait but the number was engaged. I tried several times and then got out the car and drove over. I'd written a note to him to slip through the door telling him that I'd taken the picture as arranged.'

'Wasn't that a little unusual, Miss Mair? Why not knock at the cottage and collect it from him personally?'

'Because he had taken the trouble to tell me, when I first saw it, precisely where it was kept and where I could find the light switch to the left of the door. I took that as a reasonable indication that he didn't expect, or indeed want, to be disturbed by a call at the cottage. Mr Dalgliesh was with me at the time.'

'But that was odd, wasn't it? He must have thought it was a good portrait. He wouldn't wish to exhibit it otherwise. You'd think he'd want to hand it over personally.'

'Would you? It didn't strike me that way. He's an extremely private man, more so since the death of his wife. He doesn't welcome visitors, particularly not women who might cast a critical eye on the tidiness of the cottage and the state of the children. I could understand that. I wouldn't have welcomed it myself.'

'So you went straight to his painting shed? Where is that?'

'About thirty yards to the left of the cottage. It's a small wooden shack. I imagine that it was originally a washhouse or a smoking shed. I shone my torch on the path to the door, although that was hardly necessary. The moonlight was exceptionally bright. It was unlocked. And if you're now about to say that that, too, was odd, you don't understand life on the headland. We're very remote here and we get into the habit of leaving doors unlocked. I don't think it would ever occur to him to lock his painting shed. I switched on the light to the left of the door and saw that the picture wasn't where I expected.'

'Could you describe exactly what happened? The details, please, as far as you can recall them.'

'We're talking about last night, Chief Inspector. It would be difficult not to recall them. I left the light on in the shed and knocked on the front door of the cottage. There were lights on, downstairs only, but the curtains were drawn. I had to wait for about a minute before he came. He half opened the door but didn't invite me in. I said, "Good evening, Ryan." He just nodded, but didn't reply. There was a strong smell of whisky. Then I said, "I've come to collect the portrait but it isn't in the shed, or if it is I haven't found it." Then he said, his speech rather slurred, "It's to the left of the door, wrapped in cardboard and brown paper. A brown paper parcel, Sellotaped." I said, "Not now." He didn't reply but came out to me leaving the door open. We went to the shed together.'

'Was he walking steadily?'

'He was very far from steady, but he could certainly keep on his feet. When I said he smelt of drink and his voice was slurred I didn't mean that he was totally incapable. But I got the impression that he had spent the evening in fairly continuous drinking. He stood in the doorway of the shed with me at his shoulder. He didn't speak for about half a minute. Then all he said was, "Yes, it's gone."'

'How did he sound?' As she didn't reply he asked patiently, 'Was he shocked? Angry? Surprised? Or too drunk to care?'

'I heard the question, Chief Inspector. Hadn't you better ask him how he felt? I'm only competent to describe what he looked like, what he said, and what he did.'

'What did he do?'

'He turned and beat his clenched hands against the lintel of the door. Then he rested his head against the wood for a minute. It seemed at the time a histrionic gesture but I imagine that it was perfectly genuine.'

'And then?'

'I said to him, "Hadn't we better telephone the police? We could do it from here if your telephone is working. I've been trying to get through to you but it's always engaged." He didn't reply and I followed him back to the cottage. He didn't invite me in, but I stood in the doorway. He went over to the recess under the stairs and then said: "The receiver isn't properly on. That's why you couldn't get through." I said again, "Why not telephone the police now? The sooner the theft is reported the better." He turned to me and just said "Tomorrow. Tomorrow." Then he went back to his chair. I persisted. I said, "Shall I ring, Ryan, or will you? This really is important." He said, "I will. Tomorrow. Goodnight." That seemed a clear indication to me that he wanted to be alone, so I left.'

'And during this visit you saw no one other than Mr Blaney. The children weren't up, for example?'

'I took it the children were in bed. I neither saw nor heard them.'

'And you didn't discuss the Whistler's death?'

'I assumed George Jago had telephoned Mr Blaney, probably before he rang me. And what was there to discuss? Neither Ryan nor I were in a mood for doorstep chatting.'

But it was, thought Rickards, a curious reticence on both their parts. Had she been so anxious to get away and he to see her go? Or, for one of them, had an event more traumatic than a missing portrait driven even the Whistler temporarily out of mind?

There was a vital question Rickards needed to ask. The implications were obvious and she was far too intelligent a woman not to see them.

'Miss Mair, from what you saw of Mr Blaney that night, do you think he could have driven a car?'

'Impossible. And he hadn't a car to drive. He has a small van but it has just failed its MOT.'

'Or ridden a bicycle?'

'I suppose he could have tried but he'd have been in the ditch within minutes.'

Rickards's mind was already busy with calculations. He wouldn't get the results of the autopsy until Wednesday but if Hilary Robarts had taken her swim, as was her custom, immediately after the headlines to the main news which, on Sunday, was at nine ten, then she must have died at about half-past nine. At nine forty-five or a little later, according to Alice Mair, Ryan Blaney was in his cottage and drunk. By no stretch of the imagination could he have committed a singularly ingenious murder, requiring a steady hand, nerves and the capacity to plan, and been back in his cottage by nine forty-five. If Alice Mair were telling the truth she had given Blaney an alibi. He, on the other hand, would certainly be unable to give one to her.

Rickards had almost forgotten Meg Dennison, but now he looked across to where she sat like a distressed child, hands in her lap, her untasted coffee still standing in the hearth.

'Mrs Dennison, did you know last night that the Whistler was dead?'

'Oh yes. Mr Jago telephoned me too, about a quarter to ten.'

Alice Mair said: 'He probably tried to get you earlier but you were on the way to Norwich station with the Copleys?'

Meg Dennison spoke directly to Rickards: 'I should have been, but the car broke down. I had to get Sparks and his taxi in a hurry. Luckily he could just do it but he had to go straight on to a job in Ipswich, so he couldn't bring me back. He saw the Copleys safely on the train for me.'

'Did you leave the Old Rectory at any time during the evening?'

Mrs Dennison looked up and met his eyes. 'No,' she said, 'no, after I'd seen them off I didn't leave the house.' Then she paused and said, 'I'm sorry, I did go out into the garden very briefly. It would be more accurate to say that I didn't leave the grounds. And now, if you'll all excuse me, please, I'd like to go home.'

She got up, then turned again to Rickards: 'If you want to question me, Chief Inspector, I'll be at the Old Rectory.'

She was gone before the two men could get to their feet, almost stumbling from the room. Miss Mair made no move to follow her and, seconds later, they heard the front door close.

There was a moment's silence, broken by Oliphant. Nodding towards the hearth he said: 'Funny. She hasn't even touched her coffee.'

But Rickards had a final question for Alice Mair. He said: 'It must have been getting on for midnight when Dr Mair got home yesterday night. Did you ring the power station to find out if he'd left or why he was delayed?'

She said coolly: 'It didn't occur to me, Chief Inspector. Since Alex is neither my child nor my husband I am spared the compulsion of checking on his movements. I am not my brother's keeper.'

Oliphant had been staring at her with his sombre, suspicious eyes. Now he said: 'But he lives with you, doesn't he? You do talk, don't you? You must have known about his relationship with Hilary Robarts, for example. Did you approve?'

Alice Mair's colour didn't change, but her voice was like steel.

'Either to approve or disapprove would have been as presumptuously impertinent as was that question. If you wish to discuss my brother's private life, I suggest that you do so with him.'

Rickards said quietly: 'Miss Mair, a woman has been brutally done to death and her body mutilated. She was a woman you knew. In the light of that outrage, I hope you won't feel the need to be oversensitive to questions which are bound to seem at times both presumptuous and impertinent.'

Anger had made him articulate. Their eyes met and held. He knew that his were hard with fury, both with Oliphant's tactlessness and her response. But the grey eyes which met his were less easy to read. He thought he could detect surprise, followed by wariness, reluctant respect, an almost speculative interest.

And when, fifteen minutes later, she escorted her visitors to the door he was a little surprised when she held out her hand. As he shook it, she said: 'Please forgive me, Chief Inspector, if I was ungracious. Yours is a disagreeable but necessary job and you are entitled to co-operation. As far as I'm concerned, you will get it.'

31

Even without the garishly painted sign no one from Norfolk would have been in any doubt about the identity of the local hero after whom the Lydsett pub was named, nor could a stranger fail to recognize the admiral's hat with the star, the much-decorated chest, the black patch over one eye, the pinned-up, empty sleeve. Rickards reflected that he had seen worse paintings of Lord Nelson but not many. This made him look like the Princess Royal in drag.

George Jago had obviously decided that the interview should take place in the saloon bar wrapped now in the dim quietness of the late afternoon doldrums. He and his wife led Rickards and Oliphant to a small pub table, wooden-topped and with ornate cast-iron legs, set close to the huge and empty fireplace. They settled themselves round it rather, thought Rickards, like four ill-assorted people proposing to conduct a seance in appropriately ill-lit seclusion. Mrs Jago was an angular, bright-eyed, sharp-featured woman who looked at Oliphant as if she had seen his type before and was prepared to stand no nonsense. She was heavily made up. Two moons of bright rouge adorned each cheek, her long mouth was painted with a matching lipstick and her fingers, blood-tipped talons, were heavy with a variety of rings. Her hair was so glossily black that it looked unnatural and was piled high in the front in three rows of tight curls and swept upwards and secured with combs at the back and sides. She was wearing a pleated skirt topped with a blouse in some shiny material striped in red, white and blue, buttoned high at the neck and hung about with gold chains in which she looked like a bit-part actress auditioning for the part of a barmaid in an Ealing comedy. No woman could have been less suitably dressed for a country pub, yet both she and her husband, seated side by side with the brightly expectant look of children on their best behaviour, looked perfectly at home in the bar and with each other. Oliphant had made it his business to find out something of their past and had relayed the information to Rickards as they drove to the pub. George Jago had previously been the licensee of a pub in Catford but the couple had moved to Lydsett four years ago partly because Mrs

Jago's brother, Charlie Sparks, owned a garage and car-hire business on the edge of the village and was looking for part-time help. George Jago occasionally drove for him leaving Mrs Jago in charge of the bar. They had settled happily in the village, took a lively part in community activities and appeared not to miss the raucous life of the city. Rickards reflected that East Anglia had accepted and absorbed more eccentric couples. Come to that, it had absorbed him.

George Jago looked more the part of a country publican, a stocky, cheerful-faced man with bright, blinking eyes and an air of suppressed energy. He had certainly expended it on the interior of the pub. The low, oak-beamed saloon bar was a cluttered and ill-arranged museum devoted to Nelson's memory. Jago must have scoured East Anglia in his search for objects with even a tenuous relationship with the Admiral. Above the open fireplace was a huge lithograph of the scene in the cockpit of the *Victory* with Nelson romantically dying in Hardy's arms. The remaining walls were covered with paintings and prints, including the principal sea battles, the Nile, Copenhagen, Trafalgar; one or two of Lady Hamilton including a lurid reproduction of Romney's famous portrait, while commemorative plates were ranged each side of the doors and the blackened oak beams were festooned with rows of decorated memorial mugs, few of them original to judge from the brightness of the decoration. Along the top of one wall a row of pennants spelled out what was presumably the famous signal and a fishing net had been slung across the ceiling to enhance the general nautical atmosphere. And suddenly, looking up into the brown tar-tangled netting, Rickards remembered. He had been here before. He and Susie had stopped here for a drink when they had been exploring the coast one weekend in the first winter of their marriage. They hadn't stayed for long; Susie had complained that the bar was too crowded and smoke-filled. He could recall the bench at which they had sat, the one against the wall to the left of the door. He had drunk half a pint of bitter, Susie a medium sherry. Then, with the fire blazing, the flames leaping from the crackling logs and the bar loud with cheerful Norfolk voices the pub had seemed interestingly nostalgic and cosy. But now, in the dim light of an autumn afternoon, the clutter of artefacts, so few of them either genuine or of particular merit, seemed to Rickards to trivialize and diminish both the building's own long history and the Admiral's achievements. He felt a sudden onrush of claustrophobia and had to resist an impulse to throw open the door and let in fresh air and the twentieth century.

As Oliphant said afterwards, it was a pleasure to interview George Jago. He didn't greet you as if you were a necessary but unwelcome technician of doubtful competence who was taking up your valuable time. He didn't use words as if they were secret signals to conceal thoughts rather than express them, nor subtly intimidate you with his superior intelligence. He didn't see an interview with the police as a battle of wits in which he necessarily had the advantage, nor react to perfectly ordinary questions with a disconcerting mixture of fear and endurance as if you were secret police from a totalitarian dictatorship. All in all, he pointed out, it made a pleasant change.

Jago admitted cheerfully that he had telephoned the Blaneys and Miss Mair shortly after half-past seven on Sunday with news that the Whistler was dead. How did he know? Because one of the police on the inquiry had telephoned home to let his wife know it was all right for their daughter to go alone to a party that night and the wife had telephoned her brother Harry Upjohn who kept the Crown and Anchor outside Cromer and Harry, who was a friend of his, had rung him. He remembered exactly what he had said to Theresa Blaney.

'Tell your dad they've found the Whistler's body. He's dead. Suicide. Killed himself at Easthaven. No need to worry now.'

He had phoned the Blaneys because he knew that Ryan liked his pints at nights but hadn't dared to leave the children while the Whistler was at large. Blaney hadn't come in that evening but that didn't really signify. With Miss Mair he had left the message on her answering machine in much the same terms. He hadn't telephoned Mrs Dennison because he thought she would be on her way to Norwich with the Copleys.

Rickards said: 'But you did ring her later?'

It was Mrs Jago who explained. 'That was after I reminded him. I was at half-past six evensong and afterwards I went home with Sadie Sparks to settle arrangements for the autumn jumble sale. She found a note from Charlie to say that he'd been called out on two urgent jobs, taking the Copleys to Norwich and then fetching a couple from Ipswich. So when I got back I told George that Mrs Dennison hadn't driven the Copleys to the train and that he ought to phone her straight away to tell her about the Whistler. I mean, she'd be more likely to get a good night's rest knowing he was dead than wondering if he was lurking in the rectory bushes. So George rang.'

Jago said: 'It was close on nine fifteen by then, I reckon. I would have telephoned later anyway expecting she'd be back by half-past nine.'

Rickards said: 'And Mrs Dennison answered the phone?'

'Not then she didn't. But I tried again about thirty minutes later and got her then.'

Rickards asked: 'So you didn't tell any of them that the body had been found at the Balmoral Hotel?'

'Didn't know, did I? All I was told by Harry Upjohn was that the Whistler had been found and that he was dead. I dare say the police kept it quiet, where exactly he was found I mean. You wouldn't want a lot of morbid sightseers round the place. Nor would the hotel manager, come to that.'

'And early this morning you rang round again to say that Miss Robarts had been murdered. How did you discover that?'

'Saw the police cars passing, didn't I? So I got on my bike and went up to the gate. Your chaps had left it open so I shut it again and waited. When they came back I opened the gate for them and asked what was up.'

Rickards said: 'You seem to have an extraordinary talent for extracting information from the police.'

'Well, I know some of them, don't I? The local chaps, anyway. They drink in the Hero. The driver of the first car through wouldn't say anything. Nor would the driver of the mortuary van. But when the third car came through and stopped while I opened and shut the gate again I asked who was dead and they told me. I mean, I know a mortuary van when I see one.'

'Who exactly told you?' asked Oliphant belligerently. George Jago turned on him his bright and innocent comedian's gaze.

'Couldn't say, could I? One policeman is much like another. Someone told me.'

'So you rang round early this morning? Why then? Why wait?'

'Because it was after midnight by then. Folk like a bit of news but they like their sleep more. But I rang Ryan Blaney first thing today.'

'Why him?'

'Why not? When you've got news it's human nature to pass it on to an interested party.'

223

Oliphant said: 'And he was certainly an interested party. Must have come as something of a relief.'

'Might have done, might not. I didn't speak to him. I told Theresa.'

Oliphant said: 'So you didn't speak to Mr Blaney either when you rang on Sunday or this morning. Bit odd wasn't it?'

'Depends how you look at it. The first time he was in his painting shed. He doesn't like being called to the phone when he's working. No point, anyway. I told Theresa and she told him.'

Rickards said: 'How do you know she told him?'

'Because she said so when I rang this morning. Why shouldn't she tell him?'

'But you can't know for certain that she did?'

Mrs Jago said suddenly: 'And you can't know for certain that she didn't. What does it matter, anyway? He knows now. We all do. We know about the Whistler and we know about Miss Robarts. And maybe if you'd caught the Whistler a year ago Miss Robarts would still be alive.'

Oliphant asked quickly: 'What do you mean by that, Mrs Jago?'

'What they call a copycat murder, isn't it? That's the talk in the village, anyway, apart from those who still think the Whistler did it and you've got your times all wrong. And old Humphrey, of course, who thinks it was the Whistler's ghost still on the job.'

Rickards said: 'We're interested in a portrait of Miss Robarts which was painted recently by Mr Blaney. Have either of you seen it? Did he talk about it?'

Mrs Jago said: 'Of course we've seen it. Had it hanging in the bar, didn't we? And I knew that it would bring bad luck. It was an evil picture if ever I saw one.'

Jago turned to his wife and explained with patient emphasis: 'I don't see how you can say a picture is evil, Doris, not a picture. Things can't be evil. An inanimate object is neither good nor evil. Evil is what is done by people.'

'And what is thought by people, George, and that picture came out of evil thoughts, so I say that picture was evil.'

She spoke firmly but with no trace of obstinacy or resentment. Obviously this was the kind of marital argument, conducted without acrimony, and with scrupulous fairness, which they both relished. For a few minutes their attention was solely on each other.

Jago went on: 'Granted it wasn't the kind of picture you'd want to hang on your sitting-room wall.'

'Or in the bar, come to that. Pity you ever did, George.'

'Right enough. Still I reckon it didn't give anyone any ideas they didn't have already. And you can't say that it was evil, not a picture, Doris.'

'All right, suppose you get an instrument of torture, something used by the Gestapo.' Mrs Jago looked round the bar as if among its clutter she might reasonably expect to find an example. 'I'd say that thing was evil. I wouldn't give it house room.'

'You could say it was used for an evil purpose, Doris, that's different.'

Rickards asked: 'Why exactly did you hang the portrait in the bar?'

'Because he asked me, that's why. I usually find room for one or two of his small watercolours and sometimes he sells them and sometimes not. I always tell him they've got to be seascapes. I mean, it's all the Admiral here, isn't it, it's all nautical. But he was dead keen on having this up and I said I'd keep it for a week. He brought it down on his bike on Monday the twelfth.'

'In the hope of selling it?'

'Oh, it wasn't for sale, not that picture wasn't. He made that very plain.'

Oliphant said: 'So what was the point of putting it up?'

'That's what I said.' Jago turned triumphantly to the sergeant as if recognizing a fellow expert in logic. ' "What's the point in putting it up if you don't want to sell it?" I said. "Let them look at it," he said. "I want them to see it. I want the whole world to see it." A bit optimistic, I thought. After all, we're not the National Gallery.'

'More like the National Maritime Museum really,' said Doris surprisingly and beamed at them happily.

'Where did you find room for it?'

'On that wall opposite the door. Took down the two pictures of the Battle of the Nile, didn't I?'

'And how many people did see it in those seven days?'

'You're asking me how many customers I had. I mean, if they came in they saw it. Couldn't hardly miss it, could they? Doris wanted to take it down but I promised I'd keep it up until the Monday, so I did. Glad when he came and took it away, though. Like I said, it's all commemorative here. It's all the Admiral. It didn't seem to go with the décor. It wasn't here long. He said he'd call for it on the morning of the nineteenth and he did.'

'Did anyone from the headland or the power station see it?'

'Those who came in. The Local Hero isn't really their regular local. Most of them want to get away from the place at the end of the day and who's to blame them? I mean, living over the shop is all right, but not that shop.'

'Was there much talk about it? Did anyone ask where he kept it, for example?'

'Not to me. I reckon most of them knew where he kept it. I mean, he talked a bit about his painting shed. And if he had wanted to sell, he wouldn't have got any offers. I'll tell you someone who did see it, though. Hilary Robarts.'

'When was this?'

'The evening after he brought it in, about seven o'clock. She used to come in here from time to time. Never drank much, just a couple of dry sherries. Took them over to the seat by the fire.'

'Alone?'

'Usually she was. Once or twice she had Dr Mair with her. But she was alone that Tuesday.'

'What did she do when she saw the picture?'

'Stood and looked at it. The pub was pretty full at the time and everyone fell silent. You know how it is. They were all watching. I couldn't see her face because her back was to me. Then she walked over to the bar and said: "I've changed my mind about drinking here. Obviously you don't welcome customers from Larksoken." Then she went out. Well, I welcome customers from anywhere if they can hold their drink and don't ask for credit, but I didn't reckon she'd be much loss.'

'So she wasn't particularly popular on the headland?'

'I don't know about the headland. She wasn't particularly popular in this pub.'

Doris Jago said: 'Scheming she was to turn the Blaneys out of Scudder's Cottage. And him a widower trying to bring up four kids. Where did she think he was going to go? He gets family allowance and other bits of welfare help but that isn't going to find him another cottage. But I'm sorry she's dead, of course. I mean you have to be, don't you? It's not a nice thing to happen to anybody. We'll be sending a wreath from the Local Hero.'

'Was that the last time you saw her?'

Mrs Jago said: 'The last time George did. I saw her on the headland on Sunday. Must have been only a few hours before she died. I said to George, maybe I was the last person to see her alive, well, me and

Neil Pascoe and Amy. You don't think at the time, do you? We can't see into the future, nor wouldn't want to. Sometimes I look at that power station and wonder if we'll all end up dead on the beach.'

Oliphant asked how she came to be on the headland.

'Delivering the church magazine, wasn't I? I always do on the last Sunday afternoon in the month. Collect them after morning service then take them round after dinner. Lunch to you, maybe, we call it dinner.'

Rickards had called the main meal dinner all his life and still did despite his mother-in-law's unceasing campaign to raise his social status. Her midday meal was luncheon and her evening meal dinner even if it consisted, as it often did, of sardines on toast. He wondered what they had eaten today. He said: 'I didn't realize that people on the headland were churchgoers, other than the Copleys, of course.'

'And Mrs Dennison. Very regular she is. I can't say the others actually come to church, well, not to say actually attend, not to the services, but they do take the parish magazine.' Mrs Jago's tone suggested that there were depths of irreligion to which even the headlanders would hardly sink. She added: 'All except the Blaneys, of course. Well, they wouldn't, being RC. At least she was RC, poor dear, and the children are of course. I mean they have to be, don't they? I don't think Ryan's anything. He's an artist. I never delivered to Scudder's Cottage even when his wife was alive. Anyway RCs don't have parish magazines.'

George Jago said: 'I wouldn't say that, Doris. I wouldn't go that far. They might.'

'We've lived here for four years, George, and Father McKee is in the bar often enough and I've never seen one.'

'Well, you wouldn't, would you?'

'I might have, George, if there was one to see. They're different from us. No Harvest Festival and no parish magazines.'

Her husband explained patiently: 'They're different because they have different dogmas. It's all to do with dogma, Doris, it's nothing to do with Harvest Festival and parish magazines.'

'I know it's to do with dogma. The Pope tells them that the blessed Virgin Mary ascended into Heaven and they all have to believe it. I know all about dogma.'

Before Jago could open his mouth to dispute this claim to infallibility Rickards said quickly: 'So you delivered the magazines to the headlanders on Sunday afternoon. When precisely?'

227

'Well, I reckon I started off at about three, or maybe a bit after. We have a latish dinner on Sundays and we didn't get started on the spotted-dick pudding much before two thirty. And then George loaded the dishwasher and I got ready to go. Say three fifteen, if you want to be particular.'

Jago said: 'You were well gone by three fifteen, Doris. I'd say it was nearer three ten.'

Oliphant said impatiently: 'I don't think five minutes matters either way.'

George Jago turned on him a glance of nicely judged surprise and mild rebuke. 'They might. They could be crucial. I'd say five minutes in a murder investigation could be crucial.'

Mrs Jago added her reproof: 'One minute could be crucial if that was the actual minute she died. Crucial for her, anyway. I don't see how you can say they don't matter.'

Rickards thought it was time to intervene: 'I agree that five minutes could be important, Mr Jago, but hardly these five minutes. Perhaps your wife would tell us exactly what she did and saw.'

'Well, I got on my bicycle. George always offers to drive me but he has enough driving in the week and I don't like to bother him to get out the car. Not Sundays. Not after roast beef and spotted dick.'

'It'd be no trouble, Doris. I've told you that. No trouble.'

'I know, George. Haven't I just said you'd be willing enough? I like the exercise and I'm always back before dark.' She turned to Rickards and explained: 'George never liked me to be out after dark, not with the Whistler around.'

Oliphant said: 'So you left between three ten and three fifteen and cycled off over the headland.'

'With the church magazines in the basket, same as usual. First I went to the caravan. I always go to the caravan first. It's a bit tricky now with Neil Pascoe.'

'How is it tricky, Mrs Jago?'

'Well, he's asked us more than once to put out his magazine – *Nuclear Newsletter* he calls it – in the bar for people to buy or maybe read for free. But George and I have always set our faces against it. I mean, we get some of the staff from Larksoken in the pub and it's not nice, is it, to be faced with a paper saying that what you're doing is wicked and ought to be put a stop to. Not when all you want is a quiet drink. Not everybody in Lydsett agrees with what he's doing. You can't deny that Larksoken Power Station has brought more business

228

into the village, and jobs too. And you've got to trust people, haven't you? I mean, if Dr Mair says nuclear power is safe, then it probably is. Then again, you can't help wondering, can you?'

Rickards said patiently: 'But Mr Pascoe took the church magazine?'

'Well, it's only ten pence and I suppose he likes to know what's going on in the parish. When he first arrived on the headland – two years ago it was now – I called on him and asked if he'd like to take the magazine. He seemed a bit surprised but he said he would and paid his ten pence and he's had it ever since. If he doesn't want it he's only got to say so.'

Rickards asked: 'And what happened at the caravan?'

'I saw Hilary Robarts, same as I said. I gave Neil the magazine and collected the money and was having a bit of a chat with him inside the caravan when she drove up in that red Golf of hers. Amy was outside with the kid, bringing in some of his clothes from a washing line they'd rigged up there. When he saw the car Neil got out of the caravan and went over and stood by Amy. Miss Robarts got out of the car and they both stood looking at her, not speaking, just standing side by side watching her. It wasn't much of a welcoming committee, but then what would you expect? Then, when Miss Robarts got within six yards or so of them Timmy trotted over to her and grabbed at her slacks. He's a friendly little beggar and he didn't mean any harm. You know how kids are. But he'd been mucking about in that muddy patch under the tap and started smearing the stuff all over her trousers. She pushed him away none too gently. The kid fell flat on his bum and started bawling, and then all hell was let loose.'

Oliphant asked: 'What was said?'

'Now that I can't exactly remember. There were a lot of words used which you don't expect to hear on a Sunday. Some beginning with f and some beginning with c. Use your imagination.'

Rickards said: 'Were any threats made?'

'Depends what you mean by threats. There was a lot of shouting and screaming. Not Neil. He was just standing there looking so white I thought he was going to faint. It was Amy who was making the most noise. Anyone would think Miss Robarts had gone for the kid with a knife. I can't remember the half of it. Ask Neil Pascoe. Miss Robarts didn't seem to notice that I was there. Ask Amy and Neil. They'll tell you.'

Rickards said: 'You tell me too. It's helpful to get different people's views of an incident. You get a more accurate picture that way.'

Jago interposed: 'More accurate? Different maybe. It'd only be more accurate if they were all telling the truth.'

For a moment Rickards feared that Mrs Jago was prepared to challenge the assertion with another demonstration of semantics. He said: 'Well, I'm sure that you're telling the truth, Mrs Jago. That's why we're starting with you. Can you remember what was actually said?'

'I think Miss Robarts said that she had called to say that she was thinking of dropping her legal action but that now she would bloody well go ahead with it and she hoped it would ruin them both. "You and your whore." Charming wasn't it?'

'She used those precise words?'

'And a good few others which I can't exactly remember.'

'What I mean is, Mrs Jago, Miss Robarts was the one making the threats?'

For the first time Mrs Jago seemed uneasy, then she said: 'Well, she always was the one making threats, wasn't she? Neil Pascoe wasn't suing her.'

'What happened next?'

'Nothing. Miss Robarts got into the car and drove away. Amy lugged the kid into the caravan and slammed the door. Neil looked so miserable I thought he'd burst out crying, so I thought I'd say something to cheer him up.'

'What was that, Mrs Jago?'

'I said she was a vicious evil-minded bitch and one day someone would do her in.'

Jago said: 'Not very nice, Doris. Not on a Sunday.'

Doris Jago said complacently: 'Not very nice any day of the week, but I wasn't far wrong, was I?'

Rickards asked: 'What happened then, Mrs Jago?'

'I got on with delivering the magazines, didn't I? First of all I went to the Old Rectory. I don't usually call there because the Copleys and Mrs Dennison are usually at morning service and collect their own magazines, but they weren't there yesterday and I was a bit worried. Thought something might be wrong. But it was just that they were too busy packing to attend. The Copleys were off to stay with their daughter in Wiltshire. Nice for them, I thought, and it'll give Mrs Dennison a bit of a rest. She offered me a cup of tea but I said I wouldn't wait because I could see she was busy getting on with their high tea. But I did sit in the kitchen with her for five minutes and had a bit of a chat. She said that some of the staff at Larksoken had given some very nice children's clothes for the jumble which might fit the Blaney twins and she wondered whether Ryan Blaney would be interested. She'd price them up and then he could have his choice before they were taken off for the sale. We've done that once before but we have to manage it very tactfully. If Ryan thought we were offering charity he wouldn't take the clothes. But it isn't a charity, is it? It's in aid of church funds. I see him when he comes into the pub and Mrs Dennison thought that the suggestion might come better from me.'

'And after calling at the Old Rectory?'

'Then I went on to Martyr's Cottage. Miss Mair has a bill enclosed with the magazine every six months so I never bother to collect the ten pence. Sometimes she's busy and sometimes she just isn't there so I usually just put the magazine through the letter box.'

'Did you see whether she was at home on Sunday?'

'I never saw skin nor hide of her. Then I went on to the last cottage where Hilary Robarts lived. She'd got home by then, of course. I could see the red Golf outside the garage door. But I don't usually knock with her either. She isn't the kind of woman who'd welcome you in for five minutes' chat and a cuppa.'

Oliphant said: 'So you didn't see her?'

'I'd already seen her, hadn't I? If you're asking whether I saw her again the answer is no, I didn't. But I heard her.'

Mrs Jago paused for effect. Rickards asked: 'How do you mean you heard her, Mrs Jago?'

'I heard her through the letter box, didn't I, when I was pushing the magazine through? And a fine old argument she was having with somebody. I'd say it was a real row. The second of the day for her. Or, maybe, the third.'

Oliphant asked: 'What do you mean by that, Mrs Jago?'

'Just wondered, that's all. It struck me when she arrived at the caravan she was pretty wrought up. High colour. Edgy. You know.'

'You could tell that just by looking at her from the caravan door?'

'That's right. Call it a gift.'

Rickards asked: 'Could you tell whether she was speaking to a man or a woman?'

'Could be either. I only heard the one voice and that was hers. But

231

she had someone in with her for certain, unless she was shouting at herself.'

'What time would this be, Mrs Jago?'

'About four, I reckon, or a little after. Say I got to the caravan at twenty-five past three and away by twenty-five to four. Then there was the quarter of an hour at the Old Rectory which would bring me up to five to four, and then the ride across the headland. It must have been soon after four.'

'And after that you went home?'

'That's right. And I was back here soon after half-past four, wasn't I, George?'

Her husband said: 'You might have been, dear. And then again you might not. I was asleep.'

Ten minutes later Rickards and Oliphant left.

George and Doris watched the police car until it turned the corner of the road and went out of sight.

Doris said: 'I can't say I took to that sergeant.'

'I can't say I took to either of them.'

'You don't think I was wrong, George, telling them about the quarrel?'

'Had no option, did you? This is murder, Doris, and you were one of the last people to see her alive. Anyway, they'll probably get it, or some of it from Neil Pascoe. No point in keeping back what the police will find out in the end. And you only spoke the truth.'

'I wouldn't say that, George, not the whole truth. I may have toned it down a bit. But I didn't tell them any lies.'

For a moment they contemplated this nice distinction in silence. Then Doris said: 'That mud which Timmy smeared on Miss Robarts's trousers, it came from the patch under the outside tap. Been like that for weeks. Be funny, wouldn't it, if Hilary Robarts was murdered because Neil Pascoe couldn't fix a new washer?'

George said: 'Not funny, Doris. I wouldn't exactly say that it was funny.'

32

Jonathan Reeves's parents had moved from their small terraced house in south London to a flat in a modern block overlooking the sea just outside Cromer. His appointment at the power station had coincided with his father's retirement and the idea had been that they would return to a place that they had known and liked on past holidays and, as his mother had said, 'to provide a home for you until the right girl comes along'. His father had worked for fifty years in the carpet department of a large store in Clapham, starting at fifteen straight from school and rising eventually to be head of the department. The firm let him have carpets at less than cost price; the off-cuts, sometimes large enough for a small room, he got for nothing, so that from childhood Jonathan had never known a room at home which wasn't carpeted from wall to wall.

Sometimes it seemed that their thick-pile wool and nylon had absorbed and deadened not only their footsteps. His mother's calm response to any event was either 'very nice', equally appropriate to an enjoyable dinner, a royal engagement or birth, or a spectacular sunrise, or 'Terrible, terrible, isn't it? You wonder sometimes what the world's coming to', which covered events as diverse as Kennedy's assassination, a particularly gruesome murder, children abused or violated, or an IRA bomb. But she didn't wonder what the world was coming to. Wonder was an emotion long since stifled by Axminster, mohair, underfelt. It seemed to him that they lived together in amity because their emotions, debilitated by under-use or undernourishment, couldn't cope with anything as robust as a row. At the first sign of it his mother would say 'Don't raise your voice, dear, I don't like rows.' Disagreement, never intense, was expressed in peevish resentment which died through lack of energy to keep it going.

He got on well enough with his sister Jennifer, eight years his senior but now married to a local authority officer in Ipswich. Once, watching her bending over the ironing board, her features set in their familiar mask of slightly resentful concentration, he had been tempted to say, 'Speak to me. Tell me what you think, about death, about evil, about what we're doing here.' But her reply was predictable. 'I know what I'm doing here. Ironing Dad's shirts.'

To her acquaintances and to those she might have called friends, his mother would always speak of her husband as Mr Reeves. 'Mr Reeves is very highly thought of by Mr Wainwright.' 'Of course, you could say that Mr Reeves *is* the carpet department of Hobbs and Wainwright.' The store represented those aspirations, traditions and orthodoxies that others found in their profession, in their school, regiment or religion. Mr Wainwright senior was headmaster, colonel, their high priest; their occasional Sunday attendances at the local United Reform Chapel merely a gesture to a lesser God. And they were never regular worshippers. Jonathan suspected that this was deliberate. People might want to get to know them, involve them in mothers' meetings, whist drives, Sunday-school outings, might even want to visit. On the Friday of his first week at secondary school the form bully had said, 'Reeves's dad is shopwalker at Hobbs and Wainwright. He sold my mum a rug last week,' and had minced across the room, hands obsequiously clasped. 'I know madam will find that mixture extremely hardwearing. It's a very popular line.' The laughter had been sycophantic but uneasy and the teasing, for lack of popular support, had quickly died. Most of their fathers had even less prestigious jobs.

Sometimes he thought: We can't be as ordinary, as dull as we seem, and wondered if it were some defect in himself which diminished them all so that he invested them with his own inadequacy, his own pessimism. Sometimes, too, he would take from the bureau drawer the family photograph album which seemed to document their ordinariness: his parents stiffly posed against the rail of Cromer promenade and at Whipsnade Zoo, himself ridiculous in cap and gown at his degree ceremony. Only one held any real interest for him, the sepia studio photograph of his great-grandfather in the First World War, perched sideways on an artificial wall with, beside him, a huge aspidistra in a Benares jar. He would gaze intensely across seventy-four years at that gentle-faced vulnerable boy who looked, in the ill-fitting, high-buttoned serge and the grotesquely over-large cap more like an orphaned poor-law child than a soldier. He must have been under twenty when it was taken. And he had survived Passchendaele, the Ypres Salient, and had been discharged wounded and gassed early in 1918 with strength enough at least to father a son, but for little else. That life, he told himself, could not

234

have been ordinary. His great-grandfather had survived four years of horror with courage, endurance and a stoical acceptance of what his God or luck had dealt him.

But if not ordinary, the life seemed now of absolutely no importance to anyone. It had preserved a family, that was all. And how much did that matter? But now it struck him that his father's life had held a not-dissimilar stoicism. You couldn't, perhaps, equate fifty years with Hobbs and Wainwright with four years in France, but both had required that same dignified and stoical acceptance. He wished that he could talk to his father about his great-grandfather, about his father's early life. But it never seemed possible and he knew that what held him back was less an inhibiting shyness than the fear that, even if he broke through this strange barrier of reticence and inarticulateness, there would be nothing there. And yet surely it hadn't always been like that. He remembered the Christmas of 1968 when his father had bought him his first science book, *The Wonder Book of Science for Children*. On Christmas morning they had sat for hours together, slowly turning the pages while his father first read and then explained. He still had the book. He still occasionally looked at the diagrams. 'How television works', 'What happens when we are X-rayed', 'Newton and the apple', 'The marvel of modern ships'. And his father had said, 'I would have liked to have been a scientist if things had been different.' It was the only time in his life that his father had given any indication that there could have been for him, for them, a fuller, a different life. But things had not been different and now he knew that they never would be. He thought, 'We need, all of us, to be in control of our lives, and we shrink them until they're small and mean enough so that we can feel in control.'

Only once had the routine of their predictable days been interrupted by an event which was unexpected, dramatic. Shortly after his sixteenth birthday his father had taken the family Morris and had disappeared. Three days later he was found, sitting in the car on the top of Beachy Head, looking out to sea. It had been called a nervous breakdown due to overwork and Mr Wainwright had given him two weeks' holiday. His father had never explained what had happened, colluding in the official view that it had been a temporary amnesia. Neither of his parents had ever referred to it again.

The flat was on the fourth and top floor of a rectangular modern block. The sitting room at the front had a glass door giving on to a narrow balcony sufficient to hold two chairs. The kitchen was small but had a flap which could be lifted to provide a table just large enough for the three of them to eat. There were only two bedrooms, his parents' at the front and his own, much smaller, giving a view of the car park, the row of breeze-block garages and the town. The sitting room had a wall-mounted gas fire to augment the background central heating, and after they had moved in his parents had surrounded this with a false mantelshelf on which his mother could display the small treasures brought from the Clapham home. He remembered the morning when they had viewed the flat, his mother stepping out on to the balcony and saying, 'Look, Father, it's just like being on the deck of a liner', and she had turned almost with animation as if remembering that store of old movie magazines she kept, the pictures of befurred film stars on the gangplanks, the ship festooned with streamers and flags, hearing in imagination the hoots of the pilot boat, the band playing on the quay. And indeed his parents had, from the start, seen the flat as a glamorous change from their small terraced house. In summer they would move the two easy chairs so that they faced the window and the sea. In winter they reversed them and huddled round the gas fire. But neither the winter gales, nor the uncomfortable heat when summer beat on the glass, ever drew from either of them a word of regret for the old life.

They had sold their car when his father retired and the single-car garage was used to house Jonathan's second-hand Ford Fiesta. He garaged it and swung back the door. Locking it he thought how very private the flats were. Nearly all of them were occupied by retired couples whose routine seemed to be to walk during the morning, meet their friends for afternoon tea and to be home before seven. By the time he returned from work the block was quiet and the rear curtains drawn. He wondered if Caroline had guessed or had known just how private his comings and goings could be. Outside the flat he hesitated for a moment, key in hand, wishing he could postpone the moment of meeting. But any longer wait would seem unnatural; they must have been listening for the lift.

His mother almost ran towards him.

'It's terrible, isn't it? That poor girl. Dad and I heard it on the local radio. But at least they found the Whistler. That's one worry over. He'll not go on killing again after her.'

He said: 'They think that he died before Miss Robarts did, so that it may not have been the Whistler.'

236

'But of course it was the Whistler. She died in the same way, didn't she? Who else would it be?'

'That's what the police are trying to find out. They've been at the station all morning. They didn't get round to seeing me until nearly twelve.'

'What did they want to see you for? They can't think you had anything to do with it?'

'Of course not, Mother. They're interviewing everyone, everyone who knew her, that is. Anyway, I have an alibi.'

'An alibi? What alibi? Why would you want an alibi?'

'I don't want one, but as it happens I have one. I went to supper last night with a girl from the station.'

Immediately her face brightened, pleasure at the news momentarily eclipsing the horror of the murder. She said: 'Who invited you then, Jonathan?'

'A girl at the station. I told you.'

'Well, I know it's a girl. What kind of girl? Why don't you bring her home? You know that this is your home just as much as it is Dad's and mine. You can always bring your friends here. Why not ask her to tea next Saturday or Sunday? I'd have everything very nice, your granny's best tea service, I wouldn't let you down.'

Torn with a dreadful pity he said: 'Perhaps I will one day, Mum. It's a bit early yet.'

'I don't see how it can be too early to meet your friends. It's as well you were with her if they're looking for alibis. What time did you get home, then?'

'About quarter to eleven.'

'Well, that's not so very late. You look tired. It must have been a shock for everyone at Larksoken, a girl you knew, Administrative Officer, too, so it said on the radio.'

Jonathan said: 'Yes, it has been a shock. I suppose that's why I don't feel very hungry. I'd like to wait a little bit before supper.'

'It's all ready, Jonathan. Lamb chops. They're half cooked already. I've only got to slip them under the grill. And the vegetables are cooked. It's only going to spoil.'

'All right. I won't be more than five minutes.'

He hung his jacket in the hall, then went into his own room and lay on the bed, staring at the ceiling. The thought of food nauseated him but he had said five minutes and if he lay there much longer she would be knocking at the door. She always knocked, but very gently, two distinct, discreet taps, like an assignation. What, he wondered, did she fear she might find him doing if she came in unannounced? He made himself sit up and swung his legs over the side of the bed but was immediately seized by nausea and a weakness which made him fear for a moment that he was actually going to faint. But he recognized it for what it was; a mixture of tiredness, fear and sheer misery.

And yet so far it hadn't been too bad. There had been three of them, Chief Inspector Rickards, a thickset serious-faced young man who had been introduced as Detective-Sergeant Oliphant and a younger man in the corner apparently taking notes whom no one had bothered to introduce. The small interviewing room attached to the medical physics department had been set aside for them, and they had been sitting side by side at a small table, both in plain clothes. The room, as always, smelt faintly of disinfectant. He had never understood why since no clinical procedures were carried out there. Two white coats still hung behind the door and someone had left a tray of test tubes on top of the filing cabinet, adding to the air of inadvertence and amateurism. It had all been very low-key, very matter-of-fact. He felt that he was being processed, one of the dozens who had known her or claimed to have known her and who had passed through this or a similar door to answer the same questions. Almost he expected them to ask him to roll up his sleeve and to feel the prick of a needle. He knew that the probing, if there were to be probing, would come later. But he had been surprised at his own initial lack of fear. He had somehow assumed that the police were endowed with an almost supernatural power to sniff out lying, that he would walk into that room bearing an all too visible load of guilt, prevarication and conspiracy to defeat the ends of justice.

At their request he gave his name and address. The sergeant wrote it down. Then he said almost wearily: 'If you could tell us, please, where you were yesterday between six and ten thirty.'

He remembered thinking, Why six and ten thirty? She had been found on the beach. She liked to swim most nights just after the nine o'clock news; everyone knew that, at least, everyone who knew her. And the news on Sunday was at nine ten. And then he remembered that they would know exactly when she had been found. There wouldn't have been time yet for the autopsy report. Perhaps they were still uncertain about the time of death or were playing it safe.

Six to ten thirty. But nine, or shortly after, was surely the relevant time. He was surprised that he could work it out so clearly.

He said: 'I was at home with my parents until after dinner, after the one o'clock meal I mean. Then I drove over to spend the evening with my girlfriend Miss Caroline Amphlett. I was with her until just after ten thirty. She lives in a bungalow outside Holt. She's PA to the Director, Dr Mair.'

'We know where she lives, sir. And we know who she is. Did anyone see you arrive or leave?'

'I don't think so. The bungalow is very isolated and there weren't many cars on the road. I think someone in the flats may have seen me leave.'

'And you spent the evening doing what?'

The officer in the corner wasn't writing now, only looking, but he didn't seem curious, not even interested, just slightly bored.

'Caroline cooked supper and I helped. She had some home-made soup already made and heated that. We had mushroom omelettes, fruit, cheese, wine. After dinner we chatted. Then we went to bed and made love.'

'I don't think we need go into the more intimate parts of the evening, sir. How long have you and Miss Amphlett been friends?'

'About three months.'

'And when was this evening together planned?'

'A few days before. I can't remember exactly when.'

'And when did you get home, sir?'

'Just after ten forty-five.' He added, 'I've no witnesses to that, I'm afraid. My parents were away for the night visiting my married sister at Ipswich.'

'Did you know they would be away when you and Miss Amphlett planned your evening together?'

'Yes. They always visit my sister on the last Sunday of the month. But it wouldn't have made any difference. I mean, I'm twenty-eight. I live with them but I don't have to give them an account of my movements.'

The sergeant looked at him and said: 'Free, white and twenty-eight', as if he were noting it down. He had blushed and thought, That was a mistake. Don't try to be clever, don't explain, just answer their questions.

The Chief Inspector said: 'Thank you, sir, that will be all for now.'

As he reached the door he heard Rickards's voice.

'She wasn't very nice to you, was she, Miss Robarts, about that local radio programme you took part in, *My religion and my job*? Did you hear it, Sergeant?'

The sergeant said stolidly: 'No, sir, I didn't hear it. Can't think how I came to miss it. Very fascinating, I'm sure.'

He turned and faced them. He said: 'She wasn't very kind about it. I'm a Christian. You don't expect it always to be easy.'

Rickards said: ' "Blessed are ye when men revile and persecute you for the gospel's sake." A bit of persecution, was there? Oh well, things could be worse. At least you don't get thrown to the lions any more.'

The sergeant seemed to think that it was very funny.

He wondered, for the first time, how they could have known about Hilary's mild persecution of him over the programme. For some reason his brief, rather pathetic notoriety, his affirmation of faith, had outraged her. Someone at the station must have mentioned it to the police. After all, they had interviewed plenty of people before they got round to him.

But surely it was over now. He had given the police his alibi, his and hers, and there was no reason why they should be questioned again. He must put the whole thing out of his mind. But he knew that this wouldn't be possible. And now, remembering Caroline's story, he was struck with its inconsistencies. Why had she chosen to park the car on an isolated part of the road, down a cart track under the trees? Why had she chosen to drive with Remus to the headland when there were plenty of walks nearer home? He could have understood it if she had wanted to let the dog run on the beach and splash into the sea, but according to her they hadn't gone down to the beach. And what proof was there that she hadn't reached the cliffs until ten o'clock, half an hour after Hilary Robarts was thought to have died?

Then there was that story about her mother. He found that he just didn't believe it, hadn't believed it when she had first told him, and he believed it even less now. But that, surely, was something he might be able to check. There were private detectives, firms in London who could carry out this kind of inquiry. The thought both appalled and excited him. The idea that he might actually get in touch with those kind of people, might pay them money to spy on her, astounded him by its audacity. It wasn't something she would expect him to do, that anyone would expect him to do; but why shouldn't he? He had enough money to pay. There was nothing shameful in the inquiry. But first he must find out her date of birth. That shouldn't be difficult. He knew Shirley Coles, the junior clerk in the establishment division. Sometimes he even thought that she liked him. She wouldn't let him see Caroline's personal file but she might be willing to look up a harmless piece of information. He could say that he wanted to give Caroline a birthday present and had a feeling that the date was getting close. Then, with her name and date of birth, surely her parents could be traced. It should be possible to know whether her mother was alive, where she was living, her financial circumstances. There would be a copy of the London yellow pages in the library where private detective firms would be listed. He didn't want to do it by letter, but he could telephone with a preliminary inquiry. If necessary he could take a day's leave and go up to London. He thought: I've got to know. If this is a lie, then everything is a lie; the walk on the cliffs, everything she said to me, even her love.

He heard the two knocks on the door. To his horror he found that he was crying, not noisily but with a silent welling forth of tears which no effort could control. He called out, 'I'm coming. I'm coming.' Then he went over to the washbasin and began bathing his face. Looking up, he saw himself in the mirror. It seemed to him that fear and tiredness and a sickness of spirit which lay too deep for healing had stripped away all his pathetic pretences, that the face which had at least been ordinary, familiar, had become as disgusting to him as it must be to her. He stared at his image and saw it through her eyes; the dull brown hair with the clinging specks of scurf which daily shampooing seemed only to exacerbate, the eyes red-rimmed, a little too close together, the damp pale forehead on which the acne pustules stood out like the stigma of sexual shame.

He thought: She doesn't love me and she has never loved me. She chose me for two reasons; because she knew I loved her and because she thought I was too stupid to discover the truth. But I'm not stupid and I shall discover it. And he would begin with the smallest lie, the one about her mother. And what of his own lies, the lie to his parents, the false alibi to the police? And that greatest lie of all. 'I'm a Christian. You don't expect it always to be easy.' He wasn't a Christian any more and perhaps he never had been. His conversion had been no more than the need to be accepted, taken seriously, befriended by that little coterie of earnest proselytizers who had at least valued him for himself. But it wasn't true. None of it was true. In one day he had learned that the two most important things in his life, his religion and his love, were delusions.

The two knocks on the door were more insistent this time. His mother called: 'Jonathan, are you all right? The chops are getting overcooked.'

'It's all right, Mother. I'm coming.'

But it took another minute of vigorous splashing before his face looked normal and it was safe to open the door and join them for supper.

BOOK FIVE

Tuesday 27 September to Thursday 29 September

33

Jonathan Reeves waited until he saw Mrs Simpson leave her office for coffee before going into the establishment office where the personnel files were kept. All the personnel records had, he knew, been computerized but the original files were still in existence guarded by Mrs Simpson as if they were repositories of dangerous and actionable information. She was nearing the end of her service and had never come to terms with computer records. For her the only reality was set down in black and white between the manila folders of an official file. Her assistant, Shirley Coles, was a newly appointed junior, a pretty eighteen-year-old who lived in the village. She had early been instructed in the importance of the Director and the heads of departments but hadn't yet assimilated the more subtle law which permeates any organization and which defines those whose wishes are to be taken seriously whatever their grade and those who can be safely ignored. She was a pleasant child, anxious to please and responsive to friendliness.

Jonathan said: 'I'm almost sure that her birthday is early next month. I know that the personnel records are confidential, but it's only her date of birth. If you could have a look and let me know.'

He knew that he sounded gauche and nervous but that helped; she knew what it was to feel gauche and nervous. He added: 'Only the date of birth. Honestly. And I won't tell anyone how I found out. She did tell me but I've forgotten.'

'I'm not supposed to, Mr Reeves.'

'I know, but there isn't any other way that I can find out. She doesn't live at home so I can't ask her mother. I really would hate her to think I'd forgotten.'

'Couldn't you come back when Mrs Simpson is here? I expect she'd tell you. I'm not supposed to open files when she's away.'

'I could ask her, I know, but I'd rather not. You know how she is. I'm afraid she'd laugh at me. About Caroline. I thought you'd understand. Where is she, Mrs Simpson?'

'Having her coffee break. She always takes twenty minutes. But you'd better stand by the door and let me know if anyone's coming.'

But he stood instead at the side of the cabinet and watched while she went over to the security cupboard with its combination lock and began twirling the dial. He said: 'Can the police see these personnel records if they ask?'

'Oh no, Mr Reeves, that wouldn't be right. No one sees them except Dr Mair and Mrs Simpson. They're confidential. The police did see Miss Robarts's file, though. Dr Mair asked for it first thing on Monday morning, even before the police arrived. It was the first thing he rang for as soon as he got into his office. Mrs Simpson took it in to him personally. But that's different. She's dead. There isn't anything private when you're dead.'

'No,' he said. 'Nothing is private once you're dead.' And he had a sudden picture of himself in that small rented house in Romford, helping his mother clear out his grandfather's things after the old man's heart attack; the greasy clothes, the smell, the larder with its store of baked beans on which he chiefly lived, the uncovered saucers of stale and mouldy food, those shameful magazines which he had discovered at the bottom of a drawer and which, scarlet-faced, his mother had snatched from him. No, there wasn't anything left private once you were dead.

She said, her back to him, 'Awful, isn't it, the murder? You can't sort of realize it. Not someone you actually knew. It's made a lot of extra work for us in Estabs. The police wanted a list of all the staff with their addresses. And everyone's had a form asking where they were on Sunday evening and who they were with. Well, you know. You've had one. We all have.'

The combination lock needed precision. Her first effort had been unsuccessful and now she was carefully turning the dial again. Oh God, he thought, why can't she get on with it? But now, at last, the door swung open. He could glimpse the edge of a small metal box. She took from it a bunch of keys and, returning to the filing cabinet, quickly selected one and inserted it in the lock. The tray slid out at a touch of her fingers. Now she seemed infected with his anxiety. She gave one anxious look at the door and quickly rifled through the suspended files.

'Here it is.'

He had to stop himself from snatching it. She opened it and he saw the familiar buff-coloured form which he had himself completed when he first came to the station, her application for her present job. What he wanted was laid out before him in her careful capitals.

Caroline Sophia St John Amphlett, date of birth 14 October 1957, place Aldershot, England, nationality British.

Shirley closed the file and quickly replaced it and slid back the drawer. As she locked it she said: 'There you are then. Fourteenth of October. Quite soon really. It's a good thing you checked. What will you do to celebrate? If the weather stays good you could have a picnic on the boat.'

He said, puzzled: 'What boat? We don't have a boat.'

'Caroline does. She bought Mr Hoskins's old cabin cruiser berthed at Wells-next-the-Sea. I know because he put a card in Mrs Bryson's window at Lydsett and my Uncle Ted thought he might have a look at it as it was going cheap. But when he rang, Mr Hoskins told him it had been sold to Miss Amphlett from Larksoken.'

'When was that?'

'Three weeks ago. Didn't she tell you?'

He thought: One more secret, innocent perhaps, but still strange. She had never shown the slightest interest in boats or the sea. An old cabin cruiser, going cheap. And it was autumn, hardly the best time to buy a boat.

He heard Shirley's voice: 'Sophia's rather a pretty name. Old-fashioned, but I like it. She doesn't look like a Sophia, though, does she?'

But Jonathan had seen more than her full name and the date of birth. Underneath were the names of her parents. Father, Charles Roderick St John Amphlett, deceased, army officer. Mother, Patricia Caroline Amphlett. He had brought with him a sheet of paper torn from a notebook and quickly wrote down both the date and the names. They were a bonus. He had forgotten that the application form was so detailed. Surely, with this information, a detective agency would be able to trace her mother without too great difficulty.

It was only when the keys had been replaced in the security cupboard that he could breathe freely. Now that he had gained what he wanted it seemed ungracious to hurry away. It was important to be gone before Mrs Simpson returned and Shirley was left to face the inevitable question about what he was doing there and might be forced into a lie. But he lingered a moment while she settled herself at her desk. She began threading paper clips together to make a chain.

She said: 'I feel really awful about this murder, I really do. Do you know, I was actually there on Sunday afternoon, I mean the actual place where she died. We went for a picnic so that Christopher could play on the beach. I mean Mum, Dad, Christopher and me. He's my baby brother, he's only four. We parked the car on the headland only about fifty yards from Miss Robarts's cottage, but of course we didn't see her. We didn't see anybody the whole afternoon, except Mrs Jago in the distance on her bicycle delivering the church magazines.'

Jonathan said: 'Have you told this to the police? I suppose they might be interested. I mean, they'd be interested in hearing that you hadn't actually seen anyone near her cottage.'

'Oh yes, I told them. And they were very interested. Do you know, they asked me whether Christopher had spilled any sand on the path. And he had. Wasn't that funny? I mean, it was funny they should think of it.'

Jonathan said: 'When were you there, then?'

'They asked me that as well. Not very long. Only from about half-past one to about half-past three. We actually ate our picnic in the car. Mum said it wasn't the time of year to sit around on the beach getting cold. Then we went down the path to that little cove and Christopher made a sandcastle near to the sea. He was happy enough but it wasn't warm enough for the rest of us to sit about. Mum more or less had to drag him away yelling. Dad went on to the car and we were lagging a bit behind. Mum said, "I'm not having you carrying that sand into the car, Christopher. You know your dad won't like it." So she made him tip it out. More yells from Christopher, of course. Honestly, that kid can be diabolical sometimes. Funny, isn't it? I mean, us being there on that very same afternoon.'

Jonathan said: 'Why do you think they were so interested in the sand?'

'That's what Dad wanted to know. That detective, the one who was here and interviewed me, said that they might find a footprint and want to eliminate it if it belonged to one of us. Dad reckons they must have found a footprint. A couple of young detectives, very nice they were, came to see Dad and Mum yesterday evening. They asked Dad and Mum what shoes they had been wearing and they actually asked if they could take them away. Well, they wouldn't do that, would they, if they hadn't found something?'

Jonathan said: 'It must have been a terrible worry to your dad and mum.'

'Oh no, it didn't bother them. After all, we weren't there when she died, were we? After we left the headland we drove to have tea with Gran at Hunstanton. We didn't leave until half-past nine. Far too late for Christopher, Mum said. He slept in the car all the way home, mind you. But it was funny though, wasn't it? Being there on the very day. If she'd been killed a few hours earlier we'd actually have seen the body. I don't think we'll go back to that part of the beach again. I wouldn't go there after dark for a thousand pounds. I'd be frightened I might see her ghost. Funny about the sand, though, isn't it? I mean, if they do find a footprint and it helps them to catch the murderer it will all be because of Christopher wanting to play on the beach and Mum making him spill out the sand. I mean, it was such a little thing. Mum said it reminded her of Vicar's sermon last Sunday when he preached about how even our smallest actions can have immense consequences. I didn't remember it. I mean, I like singing in the choir, but Mr Smollett's sermons are dead boring.'

So small a thing, a footprint in soft sand. And if that footprint was made in the sand spilled by Christopher from his bucket, then it was made by someone who had used that path after half-past three on Sunday afternoon.

He said: 'How many people here know·about this? Have you told anyone except the police?'

'No one but you. They said that we weren't to talk and I haven't, not until now. I know Mrs Simpson was curious why I asked to see Chief Inspector Rickards. She kept saying that she couldn't see what I could tell them and that I wasn't to waste police time trying to make myself important. I suppose she was worried thinking I'd tell them about the row she and Miss Robarts had when Dr Gledhill's personal file was missing and Dr Mair had it all the time. But you won't tell, will you? Not even Miss Amphlett?'

'No,' he promised. 'I won't tell. Not even her.'

34

There was a surprising number of detective agencies in the yellow pages and apparently very little to choose between them. He chose one of the largest and wrote down the London telephone number. It wouldn't do to telephone from the power station and he didn't want to wait until he got home where there would be even less privacy. He was anxious, too, to ring as soon as possible. His plan was to lunch at a local pub and find a public call box.

The morning seemed interminable but at twelve o'clock he said that he was taking an early lunch hour and left, checking first that he had sufficient small coins. The nearest kiosk was, he knew, in the village close to the general store. It was a public position but he told himself that there was no need for particular secrecy.

His call was quickly answered by a woman. He had prepared what he would say and she seemed to find nothing strange in the request. But it became apparent that it wouldn't be as easy as he had hoped. Yes, she said, the agency could certainly hope to trace an individual from the information provided but there was no fixed charge. Everything depended on the difficulty and how long it took. Until his request had been formally received it was impossible even to give an estimate. The cost might be as little as £200 or as much as £400. She suggested that he should write in immediately, setting out all the information in his possession and stating clearly what he required. The letter should be accompanied by a down payment of £100. They would certainly deal with it as a matter of urgency, but until the request was received they could give no assurance of how long it would take. He thanked her, said that he would write, and put down the receiver, glad that he hadn't given her his name. Somehow he had imagined that they would take the information down over the telephone, tell him what the cost would be, promise him a quick result. It was all too formal, too expensive, too slow. He wondered whether to try another agency, then told himself that in this highly competitive field they were unlikely to give him any more encouraging news.

By the time he had got back to the power station and parked his car he had almost persuaded himself not to proceed. And then it occurred to him that he might make his own inquiries. The name was unusual enough; there might be an Amphlett in the London telephone directory and if not in London it might be worth trying some of the larger cities. And her father had been a soldier. Perhaps there was an army directory – wasn't it called the Army List? – which he could consult. It would be worth doing a little research before committing himself to expenditure he might not be able to meet, and the thought of writing to a detective agency, of actually putting his request down on paper, discouraged him. He began to feel like a conspirator, an unfamiliar role which both excited and ministered to some part of his nature which he hadn't previously known existed. He would work alone and if he were unsuccessful it would be time to think again.

And the first step was remarkably straightforward, so simple that he blushed at his folly at not having thought of it earlier. Back in the library he consulted the London telephone directory. There was a P. C. Amphlett with an address in Pont Street, SW1. He stared at it for a moment then with trembling fingers took out his notebook and jotted down the telephone number. The initials were those of Caroline's mother, but the entry bore no prefix. The subscriber could easily be a man. It could be a coincidence. And the name Pont Street meant nothing to him although he didn't think that SW1 could be a poor area of London. But would she have told him a lie which could be detected merely by consulting the telephone directory? Only if she were so confident of her dominance, of his enslavement to her, so certain of his inadequacy and stupidity that she hadn't needed to care. She had wanted that alibi and he had given it. And if this were a lie, if he visited Pont Street and discovered that her mother wasn't living in poverty, what else that she had told him had been true? When exactly had she been on the headland and for what purpose? But these were suspicions which he knew he could not seriously entertain. The idea that Caroline had killed Hilary Robarts was ridiculous. But why hadn't she been willing to tell the police the truth?

But he knew now what his next move would be. On the way home he would telephone the Pont Street number and ask for Caroline. That at least should prove whether or not it was her mother's address. And if it was then he would take a day's leave or wait until

Saturday, make an excuse to have a day in London and check for himself.

The afternoon dragged on endlessly and it was difficult to keep his mind on his work. He was worried, too, in case Caroline should appear, should suggest that he go home with her. But she seemed to be avoiding him and he was grateful. He left ten minutes early, making the excuse of a headache, and within twenty minutes was back at the telephone kiosk in Lydsett. The number rang for almost half a minute and he had nearly given up hope when it was answered. A woman's voice slowly and distinctly spoke the number. He had decided to assume a Scottish accent. He knew himself to be quite a good mimic and his maternal grandmother had been a Scot. There would be no difficulty in making it convincing. He said: 'Is Miss Caroline Amphlett at home, please?'

There was a long silence, then the woman said repressively: 'Who is that speaking?'

'My name is John McLean. We're old friends.'

'Indeed, Mr McLean. Then how strange that I don't know you and that you, apparently, don't know that Miss Amphlett no longer lives here.'

'Then could you give me her address, please?'

Again there was a silence. Then the voice said: 'I hardly think I would care to do that, Mr McLean. But if you wish to leave a message I will see that it reaches her.'

He asked: 'Is that her mother speaking?'

The voice laughed. It was not an agreeable laugh. Then she said: 'No, I'm not her mother. This is Miss Beasley, the housekeeper, speaking. But did you really need to ask?'

And then it occurred to him that there could be two Caroline Amphletts, two mothers with the same initials. The chance was surely remote, but it would be as well to make sure. He said: 'Does Caroline still work at Larksoken Power Station?'

And this time there could be no mistake. Her voice was harsh with dislike as she answered. 'If you know that, Mr McLean, why bother to ring me.'

And the telephone receiver was firmly replaced.

35

It was after ten thirty on the Tuesday night when Rickards came for the second time to Larksoken Mill. He had telephoned his intention shortly after six o'clock and had made it clear that the visit, although late, was official; there were facts he wanted to check and a question he needed to ask. Earlier in the day Dalgliesh had called in at the incident room at Hoveton and made a statement describing the finding of the body. Rickards hadn't been there, but Oliphant, obviously on his way out, had stayed to receive him and had briefly filled him in on the state of the investigation, not unwillingly but with a certain formality which suggested that he was under instructions. And Rickards himself, as he dragged off his jacket and seated himself in the same high-backed chair to the right of the fire, seemed a little chastened. He was wearing a dark blue, pin-striped suit which, for all its over-careful tailoring, had the slightly seedy and rejected air of a suit relegated to second-best. But it still looked odd and inappropriately citified on his gangling limbs, particularly here on the headland, giving him the air of a man dressed for an informal wedding or a job interview from which he had little hope of success. The thinly veiled antagonism, the bitterness of failure after the death of the Whistler, and even the restless energy of Sunday night had left him. Dalgliesh wondered whether he had spoken to the Chief Constable and received advice. If so, he could guess what it had been. It was much the same as he himself would have given.

'It's irritating that he's on your patch, but he's one of the Met's senior detectives, the Commissioner's blue-eyed boy. And he knows these people. He was at the Mair dinner party. He found the body. He's got useful information. All right, he's a professional, he's not going to withhold it, but you'll get it more easily and make life more agreeable for both of you if you stop treating him like a rival, or worse, a suspect.'

Handing Rickards his whisky, Dalgliesh inquired after his wife.

'She's fine, fine.' But there was something forced in his tone.

Dalgliesh said: 'I suppose now the Whistler's dead, she'll be coming home.'

'You'd think so, wouldn't you? I'd like it, she'd like it, but there's the little problem of Sue's ma. She doesn't want her ewe-lamb mixed up with any unpleasantness, particularly murder, and particularly just now.'

Dalgliesh said: 'It's difficult to isolate yourself from unpleasantness, even murder, if you marry a police officer.'

'She never intended Sue to marry a police officer.'

Dalgliesh was surprised at the bitterness in his voice. Again, he was uncomfortably aware that he was being asked for some kind of assurance which he, of all men, was least competent to give. While he was searching for the anodyne phrase he glanced again at Rickards's face, at the look of weariness, almost of defeat, at the lines which the fitful light of the wood fire made even more cavernous, and took refuge in practicality.

He asked: 'Have you eaten?'

'Oh, I'll get myself something from the fridge when I get back.'

'There's the remains of a cassoulet, if you'd like it. It won't take a moment to heat up.'

'Wouldn't say no, Mr Dalgliesh.'

He ate the cassoulet from a tray on his lap, voraciously as if it was his first meal for days, and afterwards mopped up the sauce with a crust of bread. Only once did he look up from his plate to ask: 'Did you cook this, Mr Dalgliesh?'

'If you live alone you have to learn at least simple cooking if you're not prepared to be always dependent on someone else for one of the essentials of life.'

'And that wouldn't suit you, would it? Dependent on someone else for an essential of life?'

But he spoke without bitterness and carried the tray and the empty plate back into the kitchen with a smile. A second later Dalgliesh heard the splash of running water. Rickards was washing up his plate.

He must have been hungrier than he had realized. Dalgliesh knew how mistakenly easy it was, when working a sixteen-hour day, to suppose that one could function effectively on a diet of coffee and snatched sandwiches. Returning from the kitchen, Rickards leaned back in his chair with a small grunt of contentment. The colour had returned to his face and when he spoke his voice was strong again.

'Her dad was Peter Robarts. Remember him?'

'No, should I?'

'No reason. Nor did I, but I've had time to look him up. He made a packet after the war in which, incidentally, he served with some distinction. One of those chaps with an eye for the main chance, which in his case was plastics. It must have been quite a time for the wide boys, the 1950s and 60s. She was his only child. He made his fortune quickly and he lost it as fast. The usual reasons; extravagance, ostentatious generosity, women, throwing his money around as if he were printing it, thinking his luck would hold, whatever the odds. He was lucky not to end up inside. The fraud squad had put together a nice little case against him and were within days of making an arrest when he had his coronary. Slumped forward into his lunch plate at Simpson's as dead as the duck he was eating. It must have been difficult for her; daddy's little girl one day, nothing too good, and then near-disgrace, death, poverty.'

Dalgliesh said: 'Relative poverty, but that, of course, is what poverty is. You've been busy.'

'Some, but not much, we got from Mair, some we had to grub around for. The City of London police have been helpful. I've been speaking to Wood Street. I used to tell myself that nothing about the victim was irrelevant but I'm beginning to wonder if much of this grubbing about isn't a waste of time.'

Dalgliesh said: 'It's the only safe way to work. The victim dies because she is uniquely herself.'

'"And once you comprehend the life, you comprehend the death." Old Blanco White – remember him? – used to drum that into us when I was a young DC. And what do you get in the end? A jumble of facts like an upturned waste-paper basket. They don't really add up to a person. And with this victim the pickings are small. She travelled light. There was little worth finding in that cottage, no diary, no letters except one to her solicitor making an appointment for next weekend telling him she expected to be married. We've seen him, of course. He doesn't know the name of the man and nor, apparently, does anyone else, including Mair. We found no other papers of importance except a copy of her will. And there's nothing exciting about that. She left everything she had to Alex Mair in two lines of bald lawyer's prose. But I can't see Mair killing her for twelve thousand pounds on NatWest's special reserve account and a practically derelict cottage with a sitting tenant. Apart from the will and that one letter, only the usual bank statements, receipted bills, the place obsessively tidy. You could imagine she knew she was going to die and had tidied away her life. No sign of a recent search, incidentally. If there was something in the cottage the murderer wanted, and he smashed that window to get it, he covered his tracks pretty effectively.'

Dalgliesh said: 'If he did have to smash the window to get in then he probably wasn't Dr Mair. Mair knew that the key was in the locket. He could have taken it, used it and put it back. There would be an additional risk of leaving evidence at the scene, and some murderers dislike returning to the body. Others, of course, feel a compulsion to do so. But if Mair did take the key, he'd have had to put it back whatever the risk. An empty locket would have pointed directly to him.'

Rickards said: 'Cyril Alexander Mair, but he's dropped the Cyril. Probably thinks Sir Alexander Mair will sound better than Sir Cyril. What's wrong with Cyril? My grandfather was called Cyril. I've got a prejudice against people who don't use their proper names. She was his mistress, incidentally.'

'Did he tell you?'

'More or less had to, didn't he? They were very discreet but one or two of the senior staff at the station must have known, known or suspected it, anyway. He's too intelligent to keep back information he knows we're bound to discover sooner or later. His story is that the affair was over, a natural end by common consent. He expects to move to London; she wanted to stay here. Well, she more or less had to unless she gave up her job, and she was a career woman, the job was important. His story is that what they felt for each other wasn't robust enough to be sustained by occasional weekend meetings – his words not mine. You'd think that the whole affair was a matter of convenience. While he was here he needed a woman, she needed a man. The goods have to be handy. No point if you're a hundred miles apart. Rather like buying meat. He's moving to London, she decided to stay. Find another butcher.'

Dalgliesh remembered that Rickards had always been slightly censorious about sex. He could hardly have been a detective for twenty years without encountering adultery and fornication in their various guises, apart from the more bizarre and horrifying manifestations of human sexuality beside which adultery and fornication were comfortingly normal. But this didn't mean that he liked them. He had taken his oath as a police constable and kept it. He had made his marriage vows in church and no doubt intended to keep them.

And in a job where irregular hours, drink, macho camaraderie and the propinquity of women police officers made marriages vulnerable his was known to be solid. He was too experienced and basically too fair to allow himself to be prejudiced, but in one respect at least Mair was unlucky in the detective assigned to the case.

Rickards said: 'Her secretary, Katie Flack, has just given notice. Found her too demanding, apparently. There was a recent row over the girl's taking more than her allotted lunch hour. And one of her staff, Brian Taylor, admits that he found her impossible to work for and had asked for a transfer. Admirably frank about it all. He can afford to be. He was at a friend's stag party at the Maid's Head in Norwich with at least ten witnesses from eight o'clock onwards. And the girl hasn't anything to worry about, either. She spent the evening watching TV with her family.'

Dalgliesh asked: 'Just the family?'

'No. Luckily for her the neighbours called in just before nine to discuss the dresses for their daughter's wedding. She's to be a bridesmaid. Lemon dresses with bouquets of small white and yellow chrysanthemums. Very tasteful. We got a full description. I suppose she thought it added to the verisimilitude of the alibi. Anyway, they were neither of them serious suspects. These days if you don't like your boss you pack in the job. Both of them were shocked, of course, and slightly defensive. They probably felt she'd got herself killed on purpose to put them in the wrong. Neither of them pretended that they had liked her. But there was something stronger than dislike about this killing. And this may surprise you, Mr Dalgliesh. Robarts wasn't particularly unpopular with the senior staff. They respect efficiency and she was efficient. Besides, her responsibilities didn't directly impinge on theirs. It was her job to see that the station was efficiently administered so that the scientific and technical staff could do their job most effectively. Apparently that's what she did. They answered my questions without fuss but they weren't particularly forthcoming. There's a kind of camaraderie about the place. I suppose if you feel yourself constantly under criticism or attack it makes for a certain wariness in dealing with outsiders. Only one of them said he actually disliked her, Miles Lessingham. But he has produced an alibi of a kind. He claims to have been on his boat at the time of death. And he made no secret of his feelings. He didn't want to eat with her or drink with her or spend his spare time with her or go to bed with her. But, as he pointed out, he feels that about a

number of people and hasn't found any impulse to murder them.'
He paused for a moment, then said, 'Dr Mair showed you round the
power station on Friday morning, didn't he?'

Dalgliesh asked: 'Did he tell you that?'

'Dr Mair didn't tell me anything he didn't actually have to tell me.
No, it came out when were talking to one of the junior staff, a local
girl who works in the establishment department. Chatty little thing. I
got a lot of useful stuff out of her one way or another. I was
wondering if anything happened on your visit which could be
relevant.'

Dalgliesh resisted the temptation to reply that if there had been he
would have said so before now. He replied: 'It was an interesting
visit and the place rather impressive. Dr Mair attempted to explain to
me the difference between the thermal reactor and the new pressurized water reactor. Most of the talk was technical except when he
spoke briefly about poetry. Miles Lessingham showed me the high
fuelling machine from which Toby Gledhill plunged to his death. It
did strike me that Gledhill's suicide could be relevant but I don't see
how. It was obviously distressing to Lessingham, and not only
because he witnessed it. There was a rather cryptic exchange at the
Mairs' dinner party between him and Hilary Robarts.'

Rickards crouched forward, his huge hand cradling the whisky
glass. Without looking up, he said: 'The Mair dinner party. I reckon
that cosy little gathering – if it was cosy – is at the nub of this case.
And there's something I wanted to ask you. That's really why I'm
here. That child, Theresa Blaney, exactly how much of the conversation about the latest Whistler victim did she overhear?'

It was the question Dalgliesh had been expecting. What surprised
him was how long it had taken Rickards to ask it.

He said carefully: 'Some of it, undoubtedly. You know that, I've
told you already. I couldn't say how long she'd been standing behind
the dining-room door before I noticed her or how much of the
conversation she actually heard.'

'Can you remember what stage in his account Lessingham had
reached at the time you saw Theresa?'

'I can't be certain. I think he was describing the body, exactly what
he saw when he returned with his torch.'

'So she could have heard about the cut on the forehead and the
pubic hair.'

'But would she have told her father about the hair? She had a

258

devotedly religious mother, an RC. I don't really know the child but I imagine that she's unusually modest. Would a gently nurtured, modest girl tell that to any man, even to her father?'

'Gently nurtured? Modest? You're sixty years out of date. Spend half an hour in any secondary-school playground and you'll hear things that'll curl your hair. Today's kids will say anything to anyone.'

'Not that child.'

'All right, but she could have told her dad about the L-shaped cut and he could have guessed about the hair. Damn it, everyone knew that the Whistler's murders must have had a sexual connotation. He didn't rape them, but that wasn't how he got his kicks. You don't need to be Krafft – what's his name?'

'Krafft-Ebing.'

'Sounds like a cheese. You don't need to be Krafft-Ebing, you don't even need to be sexually sophisticated, to guess what kind of hair the Whistler helped himself to.'

Dalgliesh said: 'But this is important, isn't it, if you're casting Blaney as chief suspect? Would he, or anyone else, kill that way if he wasn't certain about the Whistler's method? He could only hope to pin it on the Whistler by getting all the details right. If you can't prove that Theresa told her father both about the hair and the L-shaped cut your case is considerably weakened. I would doubt whether you had one. Besides, I thought that Oliphant said that Blaney had an alibi both from Miss Mair, who said he was drunk and at home by nine forty-five, and from his daughter. Wasn't her story that she went to bed at eight fifteen and came down just before nine o'clock to get herself a drink of water?'

'That's what she said, Mr Dalgliesh. But I'll tell you this: that child would confirm any story that her dad chose to tell. And the timing is suspiciously accurate. Robarts dies at nine twenty or as near as damn it. Theresa Blaney goes to bed at eight fifteen and conveniently needs a drink of water forty-five minutes later. I wish you could have seen her, and seen that cottage. But of course you have. Two WPCs from the juvenile bureau were with me and they treated her as tenderly as a babe in arms. Not that she needed it. We all sat round the fire in a cosy little circle and she held the kid in her lap. Ever tried questioning a child to discover if her dad's a murderer while she's sitting there gazing at you with those huge reproachful eyes and nursing a baby? I suggested that she hand the kid over to one of the WPCs but as soon as she tried to take him he immediately started up a howling. Wouldn't let his dad take him either. You'd think that Theresa and he had arranged it between them. And Ryan Blaney was there too, of course, throughout the interview. You can't question a child without the parent being present if the parent wants to be. My God, when I arrest someone for this murder, and I shall, Mr Dalgliesh, this time I shall, I hope it doesn't have to be Ryan Blaney. Those kids have lost enough already. But he's got the strongest motive of all, and he hated Robarts. I don't think he could conceal that hatred if he tried, and he didn't even attempt to try. And it's not only that she was trying to force him out of Scudder's Cottage. It goes deeper than that. I don't know what's at the root of it. Something to do with his wife, maybe. But I'll find out. He left the kids in the cottage and walked out with us to the cars. The last thing he said was: "She was an evil bitch and I'm glad she's dead. But I didn't kill her, and you can't prove I did."

'And I know the objections. Jago says he telephoned at seven thirty to let him know the Whistler was dead. He spoke to Theresa and the kid says she told her dad. No reason why she shouldn't tell him. I think we take it that she did. He wouldn't have left the kids alone in that cottage with the Whistler alive and on the prowl. No responsible father would, and it's generally admitted he's a responsible father. We've got the local authority's word for that, by the way. A fortnight ago they sent a social worker just to check that everything was all right. And I'll tell you who instigated that, Mr Dalgliesh. Now, this is interesting. It was Robarts.'

'Did she make any specific allegations?'

'None. Her story was that she had to visit from time to time to discuss repairs and so on, and that she was concerned at the weight of responsibility he was carrying and thought he could do with some help. Talked about seeing Theresa lugging heavy shopping home with the twins tagging along, sometimes when Theresa should have been at school. Phoned the local authority to send a social worker along. The social worker satisfied herself, apparently, that things were going as well as could be expected. The twins are already attending a playgroup and she offered additional services including a home help, but she didn't find Blaney either welcoming or co-operative. Don't know that I blame him. I wouldn't want the welfare on my back.'

'Does Blaney know that Hilary Robarts instigated the visit?'

'The local authority didn't tell him; it isn't their policy. And I don't see how he could have found out. But if he did find out, it considerably strengthens his motive, doesn't it? That visit could have been the last straw.'

Dalgliesh said: 'But would he have killed in that way? Logically, the knowledge that the Whistler was dead negatives the method.'

'Not necessarily, Mr Dalgliesh. Suppose it's a double-bluff. Suppose he's saying in effect, "Look, I can prove I knew the Whistler was dead. Whoever killed Hilary Robarts didn't know. So why aren't you looking for someone who hadn't been told that the Whistler's body had been found?" And by God, Mr Dalgliesh, there's another possibility. Suppose he knew that the Whistler was dead but thought that it was very recent. I asked Theresa precisely what George Jago had said to her. She remembered accurately, anyway Jago confirmed it. Apparently he said, "Tell your dad the Whistler is dead. Killed himself. Just now, over at Easthaven." But no mention of the hotel, nor of when the Whistler booked in. Jago didn't know any of that. The message he'd got from his mate at the Crown and Anchor was pretty garbled. So Blaney could have assumed that the body was found in open country just five miles down the coast. He can kill with impunity. Everyone, including the police, will assume that the Whistler has claimed his last victim then done away with himself. My God, Mr Dalgliesh, that's neat.'

Dalgliesh privately thought that it was more neat than convincing. He said: 'So you're assuming that the smashed portrait isn't directly connected with the murder. I can't see Blaney destroying his own work.'

'Why not? From what I saw of it, it wasn't anything special.'

'I think it was to him.'

'The portrait is a puzzle, I'll grant you that. And that's not the only difficulty. Someone had a drink with Robarts before she took that last swim, someone she let into the cottage, someone she knew. There were those two glasses on the draining board and, in my book, that means two people were drinking. She wouldn't have invited Blaney to Thyme Cottage and if he turned up I doubt if she would have let him in, drunk or sober.'

Dalgliesh said: 'But if you believe Miss Mair, your case against Blaney collapses anyway. She claims to have seen him at Scudder's Cottage at nine forty-five, or shortly afterwards, and he was then half drunk. All right, he could have feigned his drunkenness; that wouldn't present much difficulty. What he couldn't do was to kill Hilary Robarts at about nine twenty and get home by nine forty-five, not without the use of a car or van which he didn't have.'

Rickards said: 'Or a bicycle.'

'It would need fast pedalling. We know that she died after her swim, not before. Her hair was still damp at the roots when I found her. So you're probably safe enough in putting the time of death at between nine fifteen and nine thirty. And he couldn't have taken the bicycle with him and ridden back along the shore. The tide was high; he'd have been riding over the shingle which would be more difficult than the road. There's only one part of the shore where you get a stretch of sand at high tide and that's the small cove where Hilary Robarts swam. And if he had been on the road Miss Mair must have seen him. She's given him an alibi which I don't think you'll be able to break.'

Rickards said: 'But he hasn't given her one, has he? Her story is that she was alone in Martyr's Cottage until she left just after nine thirty to collect the portrait. She and that housekeeper at the Old Rectory, Mrs Dennison, are the only ones who were at the Mairs' dinner party who made no attempt to produce an alibi. And she has a motive. Hilary Robarts was her brother's mistress. I know he tells us it was over, but we've only his word for that. Suppose they'd planned to marry when he goes to London. She's devoted her life to her brother. Unmarried. No other outlet for her emotions. Why give way to another woman just when Mair is about to achieve his ambition?'

Dalgliesh thought that this was an altogether too facile explanation of a relationship which, even on his brief acquaintance had seemed more complicated. He said: 'She's a successful professional writer. I imagine that success provides its own form of emotional fulfilment, assuming she needs it. She seemed to me very much her own woman.'

'I thought she wrote cookery books. Is that what you call being a successful professional writer?'

'Alice Mair's books are highly regarded and extremely lucrative. We share the same publisher. If he had to make a choice between us, he'd probably prefer to lose me.'

'So you think the marriage might almost be a relief, release her from responsibilities? Let another woman cook and care for him for a change?'

'Why should he need any woman to care for him? It's dangerous to theorize about people and their emotions, but I doubt whether she feels that kind of domestic, quasi-maternal responsibility or whether he either needs or wants it.'

'How do you see it then, the relationship? They live together, after all, most of the time anyway. She's fond of him, that seems to be generally accepted.'

'They'd hardly live together if they weren't, if you can call it living together. She's away a great deal, I understand, researching her books, and he has a London flat. How can someone who's only met them together across the table at a dinner party get to the heart of their relationship? I should have thought that there was loyalty, trust, mutual respect. Ask them.'

'But not jealousy, of him or his mistress?'

'If there is, she's clever at concealing it.'

'All right, Mr Dalgliesh, take another scenario. Suppose he was tired of Robarts, suppose she's pressing him to marry her, wants to quit the job, move to London with him. Suppose she's making herself a nuisance. Wouldn't Alice Mair feel like doing something about that?'

'Like devising and carrying out a singularly ingenious murder to relieve her brother of a temporary embarrassment? Isn't that carrying sisterly devotion to unreasonable lengths?'

'Ah, but they aren't temporary embarrassments, are they, these determined women? Think. How many men do you know who've been forced into marriages they didn't really want because the woman's will was stronger than theirs? Or because they couldn't stand all the fuss, the tears, recriminations, the emotional blackmail?'

Dalgliesh said: 'She could hardly blackmail him with the relationship itself. Neither was married; they weren't deceiving anyone; they weren't causing public scandal. And I can't see anyone, man or woman, coercing Alex Mair into something he didn't want to do. I know it's dangerous to make facile judgements, although that's what we've been doing for the last five minutes, but he seems to me a man who lives his life on his own terms and probably always has.'

'Which might make him vicious if someone tried to stop him.'

'So now you're casting him as murderer?'

'I'm casting him as a strong suspect.'

Dalgliesh asked: 'What about that couple at the caravan? Is there any evidence that they knew about the Whistler's methods?'

'None that we could discover, but how certain can you be? The man, Neil Pascoe, gets about in that van of his, drinks in local pubs. He could have heard some talk. Not every policeman on the case has necessarily been discreet. We've kept the details out of the papers but that doesn't mean that there hasn't been talk. He's got an alibi of sorts. He took the van just south of Norwich to talk to a chap there who'd written to him expressing interest in PANUP, that anti-nuclear organization of his. Had some hopes, apparently, of getting a group started there. I sent a couple of DCs to see the chap. He says they were together until just after eight twenty when Pascoe started for home – said he was starting for home, anyway. The girl he lives with, Amy Camm, says he got back to the caravan by nine and they were together for the rest of the evening. My guess is that he got back a bit later. In that van he must have been pushing it a bit to get from beyond Norwich to Larksoken in forty minutes. And he's got a motive, one of the strongest. If Hilary Robarts had gone ahead with her libel action it could have ruined him. And it's in Camm's interests to support the alibi. She's got herself very cosily fixed up with the kid in that caravan. I'll tell you something else, Mr Dalgliesh, they had a dog once. The lead is still hanging inside the caravan.'

'But if one or both of them used it to strangle Robarts, would it be?'

'People might have seen it. They might have thought it would have been more suspicious to destroy or hide it than to leave it there. We took it away, of course, but it was little more than a formality. Robarts's skin was unbroken. There'll be no physical traces. And if we do manage to get prints, they'll be hers and his. We shall go on checking the alibis, obviously. Every blasted employee at that station, and there are over five hundred of them. You'd never believe that, would you? You go in the place and hardly set sight on a soul. They seem to move through the countryside as invisibly as the energy they're generating. Most of them live at Cromer or Norwich. They want to be near schools and shops, presumably. Only a handful choose to live near the station. Most of the Sunday day shift were home well before ten and virtuously watching the telly or out with their friends. We shall check on them whether or not they had anything to do with Robarts at work. But it's only a formality. I know where to look for my suspects, the guests at that dinner party. Due to Lessingham's inability to keep his mouth shut they were told two crucial facts; that the hair stuffed into her mouth was pubic hair and the mark on the forehead was an L. So that narrows the field very conveniently. Alex Mair, Alice Mair, Margaret Dennison, Lessingham himself, and, assuming that Theresa Blaney reported the conversation to her father, you can add Blaney. All right, I may not be able to break his alibi, his or Mair's, but I shall have a damn good try.'

Ten minutes later Rickards got to his feet and said it was time to get home. Dalgliesh walked with him to his car. The cloud level was low, the earth and sky subsumed in the same obliterating darkness in which the cold glitter of the power station seemed to have moved closer, and there lay over the sea a pale blue luminosity, like the faint semblance of a newly discovered Milky Way. Even to feel the ground strike hard beneath their feet was disorientating in this blackness and for a few seconds both men hesitated as if the ten yards to the car, gleaming like some floating spacecraft in the light spilling from the open door, was an odyssey over dangerous and insubstantial ground. Above them the sails of the mill gleamed white and silent, potent with latent power. For a moment Dalgliesh had the illusion that they were about to begin slowly turning.

Rickards said: 'Everything on this headland is contrast. After I left Pascoe's caravan this morning I stood on those low sandy cliffs and looked south. There was nothing but an old fishing smack, a coiled rope, an upturned box, that awful sea. It must have looked like that for near on a thousand years. And then I faced north and saw that bloody great power station. There it is, glittering away. And I'm seeing it under the shadow of the windmill. Does it work, by the way? The mill, I mean.'

Dalgliesh said: 'I'm told so. The sails turn but it doesn't grind. The original millstones are in the lower chamber. Occasionally I have a wish to see the sails slowly turning, but I resist. I'm not sure, once started, whether I could stop them. It would be irritating to hear them creaking away all night.'

They had reached the car but Rickards, pausing with his hand on the door, seemed reluctant to get in. He said: 'We've moved a long way, haven't we, between this mill and the power station? What is it? Four miles of headland and three hundred years of progress. And then I think of those two bodies in the morgue and wonder if we've progressed at all. Dad would have talked about original sin. He was a lay preacher, was Dad. He had it all worked out.'

So had mine, come to that, thought Dalgliesh. He said: 'Lucky Dad.' There was a moment's silence broken by the sound of the telephone, its insistent peal clearly heard through the open door. Dalgliesh said: 'You'd better wait a moment. It could be for you.'

It was. Oliphant's voice asked if Chief Inspector Rickards was there. He wasn't at his home and Dalgliesh's number was one of those which he'd left.

The call was brief. Less than a minute later Rickards joined him at the open door. The slight melancholy of the last few minutes had fallen away and his step was buoyant.

'It could have waited until tomorrow but Oliphant wanted me to know. This could be the breakthrough we've needed. There's been a call from the lab. They must have been working on it non-stop. Oliphant told you, I imagine, that we found a footprint.'

'He did mention it. On the right-hand side of the path in soft sand. He didn't give any details.'

And Dalgliesh, punctilious in not discussing a case with a junior officer in the absence of Rickards, hadn't asked.

'We've just got confirmation. It's the sole of a Bumble trainer, the right foot. Size ten. The pattern on the sole is unique, apparently, and they have a yellow bee on each heel. You must have seen them.' Then, when Dalgliesh didn't reply, he said: 'For God's sake, Mr Dalgliesh, don't tell me that you own a pair. That's a complication I can do without.'

'No, I don't own them. Bumbles are too fashionable for me. But I've seen a pair recently and here on the headland.'

'On whose feet?'

'They weren't on any feet.' He thought for a moment, then said: 'I remember now. Last Wednesday morning, the day after I arrived, I took some of my aunt's clothes, including two pairs of her shoes, to the Old Rectory for the church jumble. They keep a couple of tea chests in an old scullery there where people can leave things they don't want. The back door was open as it usually is in daylight so I didn't bother to knock. There was a pair of Bumbles among the other shoes. Or, more accurately, I saw the heel of one shoe. I imagine the other was there but I didn't see it.'

'On top of the chest?'

'No, about a third down. I think they were in a transparent plastic bag. As I say, I didn't see the whole pair but I did glimpse one heel with the unmistakable yellow bee. It's possible that they were Toby

Gledhill's. Lessingham mentioned that he was wearing Bumbles when he killed himself.'

'And you left the trainers there. You see the importance of what you're saying, Mr Dalgliesh?'

'Yes, I see the importance of what I'm saying and yes, I left the shoe there. I was donating jumble, not stealing it.'

Rickards said: 'If there was a pair, and common sense suggests that there was, anyone could have taken them. And if they're no longer in the chest, it looks as though somebody did.' He glanced at the luminous dial of his watch and said: 'Eleven forty-five. What time do you suppose Mrs Dennison goes to bed?'

Dalgliesh said firmly: 'Earlier than this, I imagine. And she'd hardly go to bed without bolting the back door. So if someone did take them and they're still missing, they can't be returned tonight.'

They had reached the car. Rickards, with his hand on the door, didn't reply but gazed out over the headland as if in thought. His excitement, carefully controlled and unspoken, was as palpable as if he had banged his fists against the car bonnet. Then he unlocked the door and slipped inside. The headlights cut into the darkness like searchlights.

As he wound down the window to say a final goodnight, Dalgliesh said: 'There's something I ought perhaps to mention about Meg Dennison. I don't know whether you remember, but she was the teacher at the centre of that race row in inner London. I imagine that she's had about as much interrogation as she can take. That means the interview might not be easy for you.'

He had thought carefully before he spoke, knowing that it might be a mistake. It was a mistake. The question, however carefully phrased, had sparked off that latent antagonism of which he was uneasily aware in all his dealings with Rickards.

Rickards said: 'What you mean, Mr Dalgliesh, is that it might not be easy for her. I've already spoken to the lady and I know something about her past. It took a lot of courage to stand up for her principles as she did. Some might say a lot of obstinacy. A woman who is capable of that has guts enough for anything, wouldn't you say?'

36

Dalgliesh watched the car lights until Rickards reached the coastal road and turned right, then locked the door and began a desultory tidying-up before bed. Looking back over the evening he recognized that he had been reluctant to talk to Rickards at length about his Friday morning visit to Larksoken Power Station and less than open about his reactions, perhaps because they had been more complex and the place itself more impressive than he had expected. He had been asked to arrive by eight forty-five since Mair wanted to escort him personally and had to leave for a luncheon appointment in London. At the beginning of the visit he had asked: 'How much do you know about nuclear power?'

'Very little. Perhaps it might be wiser to assume that I know nothing.'

'In that case we'd better begin with the usual preamble about sources of radiation, and what is meant by nuclear power, nuclear energy and atomic energy, before we begin our tour of the plant. I've asked Miles Lessingham as Operations Superintendent to join us.'

It was the beginning of an extraordinary two hours. Dalgliesh, escorted by his two mentors, was garbed in protective clothing, divested of it, checked for radioactivity, subjected to an almost constant stream of facts and figures. He was aware, even coming as an outsider, that the station was run with exceptional efficiency, that a quietly competent and respected authority was in control. Alex Mair, ostensibly there to escort a man afforded the status of a distinguished visitor, was never uninvolved, always quietly watchful, obviously in charge. And the staff Dalgliesh met impressed him with their dedication as they patiently explained their jobs in terms which an intelligent layman could understand. He sensed beneath their professionalism a commitment to nuclear power amounting in some cases to a controlled enthusiasm combined with a defensiveness which was probably natural given the public's ambivalence about nuclear energy. When one of the engineers said: 'It's a dangerous technology but we need it and we can manage it', he heard, not the arrogance of scientific certainty but a reverence for the element which they controlled, almost the love–hate relationship of a sailor for the sea which was both a respected enemy and his natural habitat. If the tour had been designed to reassure, then it had to some extent succeeded. If nuclear power was safe in any hands then it would be safe in these. But how safe, and for how long?

He had stood in the great turbine hall, ears pulsating, while Mair produced his facts and figures about pressures, voltages and breaking capacity; had stood, garbed in protective clothing, and looked down where the spent elements lay like sinister fishes underwater in the fuel cooling pond for a hundred days before being dispatched to Sellafield for reprocessing; had walked to the edge of the sea to look at the cooling water plant and condensers. But the most interesting part of the visit had been in the reactor house. Mair, summoned by a bleep from his intercom, had temporarily left them and Dalgliesh was alone with Lessingham. They had stood on a high walkway looking down at the black charge floors of the two reactors. To one side of the reactor was one of the two immense fuelling machines. Remembering Toby Gledhill, Dalgliesh glanced at his companion. Lessingham's face was taut and so white that Dalgliesh feared that he was about to faint. Then he spoke almost like an automaton, reciting a lesson learned by rote.

'There are 26,488 fuel elements in each reactor and they're charged by the fuelling machinery over a period of five to ten years. Each of the fuelling machines is approximately 23 feet high and weighs 115 tons. It can hold 14 fuel elements as well as the other components which are necessary for the refuelling cycle. The pressure vessel is heavily shielded, with cast-iron and densified wood. What you see mounted on top of the machine is the hoist unit for lifting the fuel elements. There is also a connecting unit which couples the machine to the reactor and a television camera which allows viewing of the operations above the magazine.'

He broke off and, looking at him, Dalgliesh saw that the hands gripping the rail in front of him were shaking. Neither spoke. The spasm lasted less than ten seconds. Then Lessingham said: 'Shock is an odd phenomenon. I dreamed of watching Toby fall for weeks afterwards. Then the dream suddenly stopped. I thought I'd be able to look down at the reactor charge floor and put the image out of my mind. Most of the time I can. After all, I work here, this is my place. But the dream still recurs and sometimes, like now, I can see him lying there so clearly that it could be a hallucination.'

Dalgliesh felt that nothing he could say would be other than banal. Lessingham went on: 'I got to him first. He was lying prone but I couldn't turn him over. I couldn't make myself touch him. But I didn't need to. I knew that he was dead. He looked very small, disjointed, a rag doll. All I was aware of were those ridiculous symbols of a yellow bee on the heels of his trainers. Christ, was I glad to get rid of those bloody shoes.'

So Gledhill hadn't been wearing protective clothing. The impulse to suicide hadn't been completely spontaneous.

Dalgliesh said: 'He must have been a good climber.'

'Oh yes, Toby could climb. That was the least of his talents.'

And then, without a perceptible change in his voice, he continued with the description of the reactor and the procedure for loading new fuel into the reactor core. Five minutes later, Mair rejoined them. On their way back to his office at the end of the tour he had suddenly asked: 'Have you heard of Richard Feynman?'

'The American physicist? I saw a television programme about him a few months ago, otherwise the name wouldn't have meant anything to me.'

'Feynman said: "Far more marvellous is the truth than any artist of the past imagined. Why do poets of the present not speak of it?" You're a poet, but this place, the power it generates, the beauty of the engineering, the sheer magnificence of it, it doesn't particularly interest you, does it? You or any other poet?'

'It interests me. That doesn't mean that I can make poetry out of it.'

'No, your subjects are more predictable, aren't they? How does it go?

> Twenty per cent to God and to His saints,
> Twenty per cent to nature and her proxies.
> And all the rest devoted to the plaints
> Of guys pursued by or pursuing doxies.'

Dalgliesh said: 'The percentage for God and His saints is down but I'd agree that the doxies are more than holding their own.'

'And that poor devil out there, the Norfolk Whistler, he's not poetic either presumably.'

'He's human. That makes him a fit subject for poetry.'

'But not one you'd choose?'

Dalgliesh could have replied that a poet doesn't choose his subject, it chooses him. But one reason for escaping to Norfolk had been to avoid discussions about poetry and even if he had enjoyed talking about his writing, it wouldn't have been with Alex Mair. But he had been surprised how little he had resented the questions. It was difficult to like the man, impossible not to respect him. And if he had murdered Hilary Robarts then Rickards was faced with a formidable opponent.

As he raked out the last ashes of the fire he remembered again with extraordinary clárity that moment when he had stood with Lessingham and looked down at the dark charge floor of the reactor beneath which that potent and mysterious power was silently working away. He wondered how long it would be before Rickards asked himself why precisely the murderer had chosen that particular pair of shoes.

37

Rickards knew that Dalgliesh was right; it would have been an unwarranted intrusion to call on Mrs Dennison so late at night. But he couldn't drive past the Old Rectory without slowing down and glancing to see if there was any sign of life. There was none; the house stood dark and silent behind the wind-torn bushes. Entering his own darkened house he felt a sudden overwhelming tiredness. But there was paperwork to be got through before he could go to bed, including his final report on the Whistler inquiry; awkward questions to be answered, a defence to be argued which would stand a chance of rebutting the charges, private and public, of police incompetence, poor supervision, too much reliance on technology and not enough good old-fashioned detection. And that was before he could begin scrutinizing the latest reports on the Robarts murder.

It was nearly four o'clock before he tore off his clothes and slumped face downwards on to the bed. Sometime during the night he must have been aware that he was cold for he awoke to find himself under the bedclothes and, stretching out his hand to the bedside lamp, saw with dismay that he had slept through the alarm and that it was almost eight o'clock. Instantly awake, he threw back the bedclothes and stumbled over to peer at himself in the glass of his wife's dressing table. The dressing table, kidney-shaped, was trimmed with pink and white flowered voile, the pretty matching set of ring stand and tray still neatly in place, a stuffed doll which Susie had won at a fair as a child hanging from the side of the glass. Only her jars of make-up were missing and their absence suddenly struck him as poignantly as if she were dead and they had been disposed of with the unimportant detritus of a life. What, he wondered, bending low to look more closely into the glass, had anything in this pink and white, utterly feminine bedroom, to do with that gaunt face, that rough, masculine torso? He experienced again what he had felt initially when they first moved in a month after the honeymoon, that nothing in the house was truly his. When he was a young DC he would have been amazed had anyone told him that he would achieve such a house, a gravel sweep of drive, its own half acre of garden, a drawing room and separate dining room, each with its carefully chosen suite of furniture which still smelt pristine new, reminding him every time he entered of the Oxford Street department store in which it had been chosen. But with Susie away he was again as ill at ease in it as if he were a barely tolerated and despised guest.

Dragging on his dressing gown, he opened the door of the small room at the south of the house which was to be the nursery. The cot was in pale lemon and white, matching the curtains. The changing table with its lower shelf for baby paraphernalia, its hanging bag for clean nappies, stood against the wall. The wallpaper was a riot of rabbits and leaping lambs. It was impossible to believe that any child of his would one day be sleeping here.

And it wasn't only the house which rejected him. With Susie absent it was sometimes difficult even to believe in the reality of his marriage. He had met her on a cultural cruise to Greece on which he had booked as an alternative to the usual solitary walking holiday. She had been one of the few younger women on the ship, travelling with her mother, the widow of a dentist. He realized now that it was Susie who had made the running, who had determined on the marriage, who had chosen him long before he had thought of choosing her. But the realization when it came was flattering rather than disturbing and, after all, he hadn't been unwilling. He had reached that time of life when he would occasionally indulge in an idealized picture of a wife waiting at home, domestic comfort, someone to return to at the end of the day, a child who would be his stake in the future, someone to work for.

And she had married him despite the opposition from her mother who at first had seemed to collude in the enterprise, perhaps reminding herself that Susie was twenty-eight and time was not on her side, but who, once the engagement had been secured, had made it plain that her only child could have done better, and had embarked on a policy of ostentatiously making the best of it while undertaking a vigorous campaign of his social re-education. But even she hadn't been able to find fault with the house. It had cost him all his savings and the mortgage was the largest his income could support but it stood as a solid symbol of the two things which mattered most to him, his marriage and his job.

Susie had been trained as a secretary but had seemed glad to give it up. If she had wanted to carry on working he would have supported

273

her as he would in any interest she cared to take up. But he preferred her to be happily satisfied with the house and the garden, to find her waiting for him when he returned at the end of the day. It was not the kind of marriage that was currently fashionable, nor the kind that most couples could afford; but it was his kind of marriage and he was grateful that it was hers.

He hadn't been in love with her at the time of the marriage, he knew that now. He would, indeed, have said that he hardly knew the meaning of the word since it had certainly nothing to do with the half-shameful affairs, the humiliations of his earlier experiences with women. And yet not only poets and writers, the whole world used the word, seeming to know by instinct if not by direct experience exactly what it meant. Sometimes he felt uniquely disadvantaged, excluded from a universal birthright as a man might be who had been born without a sense of taste or smell. And when, three months after the honeymoon, he had fallen in love with Susie it had seemed like the revelation of something known but never experienced, as blinded eyes might suddenly open to the reality of light and colour and form. It was one night when, for the first time, she had found joy in his lovemaking and, half crying, half laughing, had clung to him whispering incoherent endearments. Tightening his arms about her he had known in what seemed a moment of amazed recognition that this was love. That moment of affirmation had been both a fulfilment and a promise, not the end of searching but the beginning of discovery. It left no room for doubts; his love, once acknowledged, seemed to him indestructible. Their marriage might have its moments of shared unhappiness and anxiety but it could never be less than it was at this moment. Was it really possible, he thought now, that it could be seriously threatened if not destroyed by its first serious test, her decision to give in to her mother's calculated mixture of bullying and entreaty and leave him when their first child was about to be born? When the baby was first placed in her arms he wanted to be there. Now he might not even be told when she went into labour. The picture which persistently haunted his imagination, before he fell asleep and at waking, of his mother-in-law standing triumphantly in the labour ward with his child in her arms deepened his dislike of her almost to paranoia.

To the right of the dressing table was one of their wedding photographs in a silver-plated frame, taken after a marriage cere-mony which could have been specifically designed to emphasize the

274

social differences between the two families. Susie was leaning a little towards him, her peaked, vulnerable face looking younger than her twenty-eight years, the fair head with its chaplet of flowers barely reaching his shoulder. The flowers had been artificial, rosebuds and lilies of the valley but, in memory as on the day, there rose from them a transitory sweetness. Her face, gravely smiling, revealed nothing, not even what the whole white mystique surely symbolized; this is what I worked for, what I want, what I've achieved. He was looking straight at the camera stolidly enduring what had after all been the last of the seemingly endless photographs taken outside the church. The family group had at last been released. Here were Susie and himself, legally yoked, an accepted pair. The photographic session had, it seemed in retrospect, been the most important part of the ceremony, the service merely a preliminary to this complicated arranging and rearranging of incongruously garbed strangers according to some hierarchy not wholly understood by nim but of which the hectoring photographer was obviously master. He heard again his mother-in-law's voice: 'Yes, a bit of a rough diamond, I'm afraid, but he's really very able. Chief constable material, I'm told.'

Well, he wasn't chief constable material and she had known it, but at least she hadn't been able to criticize the house which he had provided for her only child.

It was an early hour to telephone and he knew that his mother-in-law, who was a late riser, would make the most of the first grievance of the day. But if he didn't speak to Susie now it might well be late at night before he had another opportunity. For a moment he stood looking down at the bedside telephone, unwilling to stretch out his hand. If things had been different, if it hadn't been for this new murder, he could have got in the Rover, driven north to York and brought her home. Face to face with him she might have found the strength to resist her mother. Now she would have to travel alone, or with Mrs Cartwright if her mother insisted on accompanying her. Well, he would put up with her if she insisted on coming and it might be better for Susie than facing the long train journey alone. But he wanted her home; he wanted her here in this house.

The ringing tone seemed to last for an inordinate time and it was his mother-in-law who answered, enunciating the number with weary resignation as if this had been the twentieth call of the morning.

He said: 'This is Terry, Mrs Cartwright. Is Susie awake?'

275

He had never called her mother. That was a nonsense which he had not been able to get his tongue round and, to do her justice, she had never suggested it.

'Well, she will be now, won't she? Not very considerate, Terry, to ring before nine. Susie isn't sleeping very well just now and she needs her lie-in. And she was trying to get you all last evening. Hold on.'

And then, at least a minute later, came the small, tentative: 'Terry?'

'Are you all right, darling?'

'Yes, everything's fine. Mummy took me to Dr Maine yesterday. He used to look after me when I was a child. He's keeping an eye on me and he says that everything's going on very well. He's booked me a bed in the local hospital just in case.'

So she's even got that fixed up, he thought bitterly, and for a moment the treacherous thought lodged in his mind that the two of them might have planned it together, that this was what Susie wanted. He said: 'I'm sorry I couldn't spend longer on the phone yesterday. Things got pretty hectic. But I wanted you to know that the Whistler was dead.'

'It's been in all the papers, Terry. It's wonderful news. Are you all right? Are you feeding yourself properly?'

'Fine. I'm fine. Tired, but I'm OK. Look, darling, this new murder, it's different. We haven't got another serial murderer on the loose. The danger's over now. I'm afraid there's no chance I can get away to fetch you, but I could meet you at Norwich. Do you think you could make it today? There's a fast train at two minutes past three. If your mother would like to come, stay until after the baby is born, well that's all right, of course.'

It wasn't all right, but it was a small price to pay.

'Hold on, Terry. Mummy wants to talk to you.'

Then, after another long delay, he heard her mother's voice.

'Susie is staying here, Terry.'

'The Whistler is dead, Mrs Cartwright. The danger's over.'

'I know that the Whistler's dead. But you've had another murder down there, haven't you? There's still a killer at large and you're the man who's hunting him. This baby is due in less than two weeks and what Susie needs now is to get away from murder and death. Her health has to be my first consideration. What she needs is a little cosseting and kindness.'

'She's had that here, Mrs Cartwright.'

'I dare say you did your best, but you're never there, are you? Susie rang you four times last night. She really needed to talk to you, Terry, and you weren't there. It isn't good enough, not now it isn't. Out half the night catching murderers or not catching them. I know that's your job but it's hardly fair on Susie. I want my grandchild born safely. A girl's place is with her mother at a time like this.'

'I thought that a wife's place was with her husband.'

Oh, God, he thought, that I should ever hear myself speaking those words. A wave of utter misery swept over him compounded of self-disgust, anger and despair. He thought, If she doesn't come today she'll never come. The baby will be born in York and her mother will hold him in her arms before I do. She'll get her clutches into both of them, now and for ever. He knew how strong was that bond between widow and only child. There wasn't a day when Susie didn't telephone her mother, sometimes more than once. He knew with what difficulty and patience he had begun to wean her away from that obsessive maternal embrace. Now he had given Mrs Cartwright another weapon. He heard the triumph in her voice.

'Don't you talk to me about a wife's place, Terry. You'll be talking about Susie's duty next. And what about your duty to her? You've told her you can't get away to fetch her and I'm certainly not having my grandchild born on a British Rail train. Susie is staying here until this latest murder is solved and you can find time to fetch her.'

And then he was cut off. Slowly he replaced the receiver and stood waiting. Perhaps Susie would ring back. He could, of course, ring again but he knew with a sick hopelessness that there would be no use. She wasn't going to come. And then the telephone rang. He snatched up the receiver and said eagerly: 'Hello? Hello?'

But it was only Sergeant Oliphant ringing from the incident room at Hoveton, an early call letting him know that Oliphant had either been up all night or had snatched even less sleep than he. His own four hours now seemed an indulgence.

'The Chief Constable's trying to get you, sir. I told his PA there'd be no point in ringing home. You'd be on your way here by now.'

'I shall be on my way in five minutes. Not to Hoveton but to the Old Rectory at Larksoken. Mr Dalgliesh has given us a strong lead on the Bumble trainers. Meet me outside the rectory in three quarters of an hour. And you'd better ring Mrs Dennison now. Tell her to keep the back door locked and not to admit anyone to the house until we

277

come. Don't alarm her; just say that there are one or two questions we have to put to her and we'd rather she spoke to us this morning before she talked to anyone else.'

If Oliphant was excited at the news he managed to conceal it. He said: 'You haven't forgotten that PR have fixed a press conference for ten, sir? Bill Starling from the local radio has been on to me but I told him he'll have to wait until then. And I think the CC wants to know if we're going to release the approximate time of death.'

And the Chief Constable wasn't the only one. It had been useful to fudge the approximate time of the murder, to avoid stating categorically that this couldn't have been the work of the Whistler. But sooner or later they would have to come clean and once the post-mortem report was to hand, it would be difficult to parry the media's insistent questions. He said: 'We shan't release any forensic information until we get the written report of the autopsy.'

'We've got that now, sir. Doc Maitland-Brown dropped it in about twenty minutes ago on his way to the hospital. He was sorry he couldn't wait to see you.'

I'll bet he was, thought Rickards. Nothing, of course, would have been said; Dr Maitland-Brown didn't gossip with junior police officers. But there must have been a cosy atmosphere of mutual self-congratulation in the incident room on their joint early start to the day. He said: 'There's no reason why he should have waited. All the stuff we need from him will be in the report. Better open it now, give me the gist.'

He heard the receiver being placed down on the desk. There was a silence of less than a minute, then Oliphant spoke: 'No sign of recent sexual activity. She wasn't raped. Seems she was an exceptionally healthy woman until someone slung a ligature round her neck and strangled her. He can be a bit more precise about the time of death now he's seen the stomach contents, but he hasn't changed his first estimate. Between eight thirty and nine forty-five, but if we want to make it nine twenty he won't object. And she wasn't pregnant, sir.'

'All right, Sergeant. I'll be with you outside the Old Rectory in about forty-five minutes.'

But he was damned if he was going to face a heavy day without breakfast. Quickly he peeled a couple of rashers from the packet in the refrigerator and placed them under the grill, turning it to full power, then switched on the kettle and reached for a mug. Time for one mug of strong coffee, then he'd put the rashers between two hunks of bread and eat them in the car.

Forty minutes later, driving through Lydsett, he thought about the previous evening. He hadn't suggested to Adam Dalgliesh that he should come with the police to the Old Rectory. It wasn't necessary; his information had been precise and specific, and it hardly needed a Commander of the Metropolitan Police to point out a tea chest of discarded shoes. But there was another reason. He had been happy enough to drink Dalgliesh's whisky, eat his stew, or whatever it was he had called it, to discuss the salient points of the investigation. What else, after all, had they in common except their jobs? But that certainly didn't mean that he wanted Dalgliesh present while he was actually doing it. He had been glad the previous evening to call at the mill, grateful that he hadn't to return to an empty house, had sat companionably by the wood fire and had felt, by the end of the evening, at least comfortably at ease. But once away from Dalgliesh's physical presence, the old uncertainties returned as they had with such disconcerting force at the deathbed of the Whistler. He knew he would never be totally at one with the man and he knew why. He had only to think of the incident now and the old resentment would come flooding back. And yet it had happened nearly twelve years ago and he doubted whether Dalgliesh even remembered it. That, of course, was the greater part of the injury, that words which had remained in his memory for years, which at the time had humiliated him and almost destroyed his confidence as a detective, could be so easily spoken and apparently so quickly forgotten.

The place was a small top room in a narrow warren of a house behind the Edgware Road, the victim a fifty-year-old prostitute. She had been dead for over a week when they found her and the stink in the cluttered, airless hovel had been so disgusting that he had had to press his handkerchief against his mouth to hold back the vomit. One of the DCs had been less successful. He had rushed to throw open the window and might have made it if the pane hadn't been grimed fast. He himself had been unable to swallow, as if his own spittle had become contaminated. The handkerchief held against his mouth was soaked with saliva. She had been lying naked among the bottles, the pills, the half-eaten food, an obscene putrefying lump of flesh only a foot from the brimming chamber pot which she hadn't in the end been able to reach. But that had been the least of the stench in the room. After the pathologist had left he had turned to the nearest PC and said: 'For God's sake, can't we get this thing out of here?'

And then he had heard Dalgliesh's voice from the doorway like a whiplash. 'Sergeant, the word is "body". Of, if you prefer, there's "cadaver", "corpse", "victim", even "deceased" if you must. What you are looking at was a woman. She was not a thing when she was alive and she is not a thing now.'

He could still react physically to the memory of it, feel the tightening of the stomach muscles, the hot surge of anger. He shouldn't have let it pass, of course, not a public rebuke like that, not in front of the DCs. He should have looked the arrogant bastard in the face and spoken the truth, even if it had cost him his stripes.

'But she isn't a woman now is she, sir? She's not a human being any more, is she? So if she isn't human, what is she?'

It had been the unfairness that had rankled. There were a dozen of his colleagues who would have merited that cold rebuke, but not he. He had never at any time since his promotion to the CID seen the victim as an unimportant lump of flesh, never taken a prurient, half-shameful pleasure in the sight of a naked body, had rarely seen even the most degraded, most disgusting of victims without some pity and often with pain. His words had been totally out of character, torn from him out of hopelessness, tiredness after a nineteen-hour day, out of uncontrollable physical disgust. It was bad luck that they should have been overheard by Dalgliesh, a DCI whose cold sarcasm could be more devastating than another officer's bawled obscenities. They had continued working together for another six months. Nothing further had been said. Apparently Dalgliesh had found his work satisfactory; at least there hadn't been any further criticism. There hadn't been any praise, either. He had been scrupulously correct to his superior officer; Dalgliesh had acted as if the incident had never taken place. If he later regretted his words he had never said so. Perhaps he would have been amazed to know how bitterly, almost obsessively, they had been resented. But now, for the first time, Rickards wondered whether Dalgliesh too might not have been under strain, driven by his own compulsions, finding relief in the bitterness of words. After all, hadn't he at the time recently lost his wife and newborn child? But what had that to do with a dead prostitute in a London whorehouse? And he should have known better. That was the nub of it. He should have known his man. It seemed to Rickards that to remember the incident for so long and with such anger was almost paranoid. But the thought of Dalgliesh on his patch had brought it all back. Worse things had happened to him, more serious criticisms accepted and forgotten. But this he couldn't forget. Sitting by the wood fire in Larksoken Mill, drinking Dalgliesh's whisky, nearly equal in rank, secure on his own patch, it had seemed to him that the past might be put aside. But he knew now that it couldn't. Without that memory he and Adam Dalgliesh might have become friends. Now he respected him, admired him, valued his opinion, could even feel at ease with him. But he told himself that he could never like him.

38

Oliphant was waiting outside the Old Rectory, not sitting in the car but lolling cross-legged against the bonnet and reading a tabloid newspaper. The impression given and no doubt intended was that he had been wasting time there for the past ten minutes. As the car approached he straightened up and handed over the paper. He said: 'They've gone to town a bit, sir. Only to be expected, I suppose.'

The story hadn't made the front page but was spread over the two centre pages with black headlines and a screamer: 'Not again!' The byline was the paper's crime correspondent. Rickards read:

> I have today learned that Neville Potter, the man now identified as The Whistler, who killed himself in the Balmoral Hotel at Easthaven on Sunday, had been interviewed by the police early in their inquiry and eliminated. The question is, why? The police knew the type of man they were looking for. A loner. Probably unmarried or divorced. Unsociable. A man with a car and a job that took him out at night. Neville Potter was just such a man. If he had been caught when he was first interviewed the lives of four innocent women could have been saved. Have we learned nothing from the Yorkshire Ripper fiasco?

Rickards said: 'The usual predictable nonsense. Female murder victims are either prostitutes who presumably deserve what they get or innocent women.'

Walking up the drive to the Old Rectory he quickly scanned the rest of the article. Its argument was that the police relied too much on computers, on mechanical aids, fast cars, technology. It was time to get back to the bobby on the beat. What use was feeding interminable data into a computer when an ordinary DC wasn't competent to spot an obvious suspect? The article was no more acceptable to Rickards because it expressed some of his own views.

He threw it back at Oliphant and said: 'What are they suggesting, that we could have trapped the Whistler by stationing a uniformed bobby on the beat at every country road intersection? You told Mrs Dennison that we were coming and asked her to keep out visitors?'

'She sounded none too pleased, sir. Said the only visitors who were likely to call were the headlanders and what reason could she give for turning away her friends. No one has called so far, at least not at the front door.'

'And you checked on the back door?'

'You said to wait outside for you, sir. I haven't been round the back.'

It was hardly a promising beginning. But if Oliphant, with his usual tactlessness, had managed to antagonize Mrs Dennison she showed no sign of displeasure on opening the door but welcomed them in with grave courtesy. Rickards thought again how attractive she was with a gentle old-fashioned prettiness which he supposed people used to call the English rose type when English rose prettiness was in fashion. Even her clothes had an air of anachronistic gentility, not the ubiquitous trousers but a grey pleated skirt and a matching cardigan over a blue blouse with a single row of pearls. But despite her apparent composure she was very pale, the carefully applied pink lipstick almost garish against the bloodless skin, and he saw that her shoulders were rigid under the thin wool.

She said: 'Won't you come into the drawing room, Chief Inspector, and explain what this is all about? And I expect you and your sergeant would like some coffee.'

'It's good of you, Mrs Dennison, but I'm afraid we haven't the time. I hope we won't have to keep you for long. We're looking for a pair of shoes, Bumble trainers, which we have reason to believe may be in your jumble box. Could we see it please?'

She gave them one quick glance then, without speaking, led them through a door at the rear of the hall and down a short passage leading to another door which was bolted. She reached up to the bolt which slid easily and they found themselves in a second and shorter passage, stone-flagged, facing a formidably stout back door which was also bolted at the top and bottom. There was a room on either side. The door on the right stood open.

Mrs Dennison led them in. She said: 'We keep the jumble here. As I told Sergeant Oliphant when he telephoned, the back door was double-locked at five last evening and has remained bolted. During the daytime I usually open it so that anyone who has jumble can come in and leave it without bothering to knock.'

Oliphant said: 'Which means they could help themselves to the stuff as well as leave it. Aren't you afraid of theft?'

'This is Larksoken, Sergeant, not London.'

The room, stone-flagged, brick-walled and with a single high window, must originally have been either a pantry or perhaps a store room. Its present use was immediately apparent. Against the wall were two tea chests, the left one about three-quarters full of shoes and the right containing a jumble of belts, bags and men's ties knotted together. Next to the door were two long shelves. On one stood an assortment of bric-à-brac; cups and saucers, fairings, small statuettes, saucers and plates, a portable radio, a bedside lamp with a cracked and grubby shade. The second shelf held a row of old and rather tattered books, most of them paperbacks. A row of hooks had been screwed into the lower shelf on which hung hangers holding a variety of better-quality clothes; men's suits, jackets, women's dresses and children's clothes, some of them already priced on small scraps of paper pinned to the hem. Oliphant stood for no more than a couple of seconds surveying the room, and then turned his attention to the box of shoes. It took less than a minute of rummaging to confirm that the Bumbles weren't there, but he began a systematic search, watched by Rickards and Mrs Dennison. Each pair, most tied together by the laces, was taken out and placed on one side until the box was empty and then as methodically replaced. Rickards took a right-foot Bumble trainer from his brief case and handed it to Mrs Dennison.

'The shoes we are looking for are like this. Can you remember if a pair were ever in the jumble box and, if so, who brought them in?'

She said at once: 'I didn't realize they were called Bumbles but, yes, there was a pair like this in the box. Mr Miles Lessingham from the power station brought them in. He was asked to dispose of the clothes of the young man who killed himself at Larksoken. Two of the suits hanging up here also belonged to Toby Gledhill.'

'When did Mr Lessingham bring in the shoes, Mrs Dennison?'

'I can't remember exactly. I think it was late afternoon a week or so after Mr Gledhill died, sometime towards the end of last month. But you'd have to ask him, Chief Inspector. He may remember more precisely.'

'And he brought them to the front door?'

'Oh yes. He said he wouldn't stay to tea but he did have a word in the drawing room with Mrs Copley. Then he brought the suitcase of clothes out here with me and we unpacked them together. I put the shoes in a plastic bag.'

'And when did you last see them?'

'I can't possibly remember that, Chief Inspector. I don't come out here very often except occasionally to price up some of the clothes. And when I do I don't necessarily look in the shoe box.'

'Not even to see what's been brought in?'

'Yes, I do that from time to time, but I don't make any kind of regular inspection.'

'They're very distinctive shoes, Mrs Dennison.'

'I know that, and if I'd rummaged about in the box recently I must have seen them or even noticed that they were missing. But I didn't. I'm afraid I can't possibly say when they were taken.'

'How many people know about the system here?'

'Most of the headlanders know, and any staff at Larksoken Power Station who regularly donate jumble. They usually come by car, of course, on their way home and sometimes, like Mr Lessingham, ring at the front door. Occasionally I take the bags from them at the door or they may say that they'll drop them in at the back. We don't actually hold the jumble sale here, that takes place in the village hall in Lydsett in October. But this is a convenient collecting place for the headland and for the power station, and then Mr Sparks or Mr Jago from the Local Hero comes in a van and loads it up a day or two before the sale.'

'But I see you price up some of the stuff here.'

'Not all of it, Chief Inspector. It's just that occasionally we know of people who might like some of the items and who buy them before the sale.'

The admission seemed to embarrass her. Rickards wondered whether the Copleys might not benefit in this way. He knew about jumble sales. His ma had helped with the annual one at the Chapel. The helpers expected to get the pick of the goods; that was their perk. And why not? He said: 'You mean that anyone local wanting clothes, maybe for his kids, would know that he could buy them here?'

She flushed. He could see that the suggestion and perhaps his choice of pronoun had embarrassed her. She said: 'Lydsett people usually wait until the main sale. After all, it wouldn't be worthwhile, people coming in from the village just to see what we're collecting. But sometimes I sell to people on the headland. After all, the jumble is given in aid of the church. There's no reason why it shouldn't be sold in advance if someone local happens to want it. Naturally they pay the proper price.'

'And who has from time to time wanted it, Mrs Dennison?'

'Mr Blaney has occasionally bought clothes for the children. One

285

of Mr Gledhill's tweed jackets fitted Mr Copley so Mrs Copley paid for that. And Neil Pascoe called in about a fortnight ago to see if we had anything suitable for Timmy.'

Oliphant asked: 'Was that before or after Mr Lessingham brought in the trainers?'

'I can't remember, Sergeant. You'd better ask him. We neither of us looked in the shoe box. Mr Pascoe was interested in warm jumpers for Timmy. He paid for two. There's a tin with the money on a shelf in the kitchen.'

'So people don't just help themselves and leave the cash?'

'Oh no, Chief Inspector. No one would dream of doing that.'

'And what about the belts? Would you be able to say whether one of the belts or straps is missing?'

She said with a sudden spurt of impatience: 'How could I possibly do that? Look for yourself. This box is literally a jumble; straps, belts, old handbags, scarves. How could I possibly say if anything is missing or when it was taken?'

Oliphant said: 'Would it surprise you to be told that we have a witness who saw the trainers in this box last Wednesday morning?'

Oliphant could make the simplest and most innocuous question sound like an accusation. But his crudeness, sometimes bordering on insolence, was usually carefully judged and Rickards seldom attempted to discipline it knowing that it had its uses. It had, after all, been Oliphant who had got close to shaking Alex Mair's composure. But now he should perhaps have remembered that he was talking to an ex-schoolmistress. Mrs Dennison turned on him the mildly reproving look more appropriate to a delinquent child.

'I don't think you can have been listening carefully to what I've been saying, Sergeant. I have no idea when the shoes were taken. That being so, how could it surprise me to learn when they were last seen?' She turned to Rickards: 'If we're going to discuss this further, wouldn't it be more comfortable for all of us in the drawing room than standing about here?'

Rickards hoped that it might at least be warmer.

She led them across the hall into a room at the front of the house which faced south over the lumpy lawn and the tangle of laurels, rhododendrons and wind-stunted bushes which effectively screened the road. The room was large and barely warmer than the one they had left, as if even the strongest autumn sun had been unable to penetrate the mullioned windows and the heavy drapes of the velvet curtains.

And the air was a little stuffy, smelling of polish, pot-pourri and faintly of rich food as if still redolent with long-eaten Victorian afternoon teas. Rickards almost expected to hear the rustle of a crinoline.

Mrs Dennison didn't switch on the light and Rickards felt that he could hardly ask her. In the gloom he had an impression of solid mahogany furniture, side tables laden with photographs, of comfortably upholstered armchairs in shabby covers and of so many pictures in ornate frames that the room had the air of an oppressive and rarely visited provincial gallery. Mrs Dennison seemed aware of the cold if not of the gloom. She stooped to plug in a two-bar electric fire to the right of the huge carved grate then seated herself with her back towards the window, and gestured Rickards and Oliphant to the sofa on which they sat side by side solidly upright on stiff, unyielding cushions. She sat quietly waiting, her hands folded in her lap. The room with its weight of dark mahogany, its air of ponderous respectability diminished her and it seemed to Rickards that she gleamed like a pale and insubstantial wraith dwarfed by the huge arms of the chair. He wondered about her life on the headland and in this remote and surely unmanageable house, wondered what she had been seeking when she fled to this wind-scoured coast and whether she had found it.

He asked: 'When was it decided that the Reverend and Mrs Copley should go to stay with their daughter?'

'Last Friday, after Christine Baldwin was murdered. She'd been very anxious about them for some time and pressing them to leave, but it was the fact that the last murder was so very close that persuaded them. I was to drive them to Norwich to catch the eight thirty on Sunday evening.'

'Was that generally known?'

'It was talked about, I expect. You could say it was generally known in as far as there are people here to know it. Mr Copley had to make arrangements for the services he normally takes. I told Mrs Bryson at the stores that I would only be needing half a pint of milk a day instead of the normal two and a half pints. Yes, you could say it was generally known.'

'And why didn't you drive them to Norwich as arranged?'

'Because the car broke down while they were finishing the packing. I thought I'd explained that already. At about half-past six I went to get it out of the garage and drove it to the front door. It was all right then but when I finally got them into it at seven fifteen and we were ready to go it wouldn't start. So I rang Mr Sparks at Lydsett Garage and arranged for him to take them in his taxi.'

'Without you?'

Before she could answer Oliphant got to his feet, walked over to a standard lamp close to his chair and, without a word, switched it on. The strong light flowed down on her. For a moment Rickards thought that she was about to protest. She half rose from the chair, then sat down again and went on as if nothing had happened.

'I felt bad about that. I would have been much happier to have seen them on the train, but Mr Sparks could only take the job if he could go straight on to Ipswich where he had to pick up a fare. But he promised he wouldn't leave them until he'd seen them into the carriage. And, of course, they're not children, they're perfectly capable of getting out at Liverpool Street. It's the terminus, after all; and their daughter was meeting them.'

Why, Rickards wondered, was she so defensive? She could hardly suppose herself a serious suspect. And yet, why not? He had known less likely murderers. He could see fear in the dozen small signs which no experienced policeman could miss; the tremble of the hands which she tried to control when his glance fell on them, the nervous tic at the corner of the eye, the inability to sit still one moment followed by an unnatural, controlled stillness the next, the note of strain in the voice, the way in which she was resolutely meeting his eyes with a look compounded of defiance and endurance. Taken singly each was a sign of natural stress; together they added up to something close to terror. He had resented Adam Dalgliesh's warning the previous night. It had been uncomfortably close to teaching him his job. But perhaps he had been right. Perhaps he was facing a woman who had suffered more aggressive interrogations than she could take. But he had his job to do.

He said: 'You phoned for the taxi straight away? You didn't try to find out what was wrong with the car?'

'There was no time to fuss about under the bonnet. I'm not a mechanic anyway. I've never been particularly good with a car. It was lucky that I found out in time that it wouldn't go, and even luckier that Mr Sparks could oblige. He came at once. Mr and Mrs Copley were getting very agitated. Their daughter was expecting them; all the arrangements had been made. It was important to catch the train.'

'Where was the car normally kept, Mrs Dennison?'

'I thought I told you that, Chief Inspector. In the garage.'

'Locked?'

'There's a padlock. Quite a small one. I don't suppose it's very secure if someone really wanted to break it, but no one has ever tried. It was locked when I went for the car.'

'Three-quarters of an hour before you needed to leave.'

'Yes. I don't understand what you're getting at. Is that significant?'

'I'm just curious, Mrs Dennison. Why so much time?'

'Have you ever had to load a car with the luggage required by two elderly people leaving for an indefinite stay? I had been helping Mrs Copley with the final part of her packing. I wasn't needed for a minute or so and it seemed a good opportunity to get the car out.'

'And while it stood there in front of the house, was it continually under your eye?'

'Of course not. I was busy checking that the Copleys had everything that they needed, going over the things I needed to do while they were away, parish business, a few telephone calls.'

'Where was this happening?'

'In Mr Copley's study. Mrs Copley was in her bedroom.'

'And the car was unattended in the drive?'

'Are you suggesting that someone sabotaged it?'

'Well, that would be a little fanciful, wouldn't it? What gave you that idea?'

'You did, Chief Inspector. It wouldn't otherwise have occurred to me. And I agree, it's fanciful.'

'And when, at nine forty-five, Mr Jago rang from the Local Hero to tell you that the Whistler's body had been found, what did you do then?'

'There was nothing I could do. There was no way of stopping the Copleys; they were over an hour into their journey. I rang their daughter at her London club and managed to catch her before she set out for Liverpool Street. She said that she'd made all her arrangements so that they might as well stay for a week since they were on their way. Actually, they're coming home tomorrow afternoon. Mrs Duncan-Smith has been called to help nurse a sick friend.'

Rickards said: 'One of my officers has seen Mr Sparks. He was anxious to reassure you that the Copleys were safely on their way. He rang you as soon as convenient for him but could get no reply. That was at about nine fifteen, about the same time as Mr Jago first tried to get through to you.'

'I must have been in the garden. It was a beautiful moonlit night and I was restless. I needed to get out of the house.'

'Even with the Whistler, as you thought, still at large?'

'Strangely enough, Chief Inspector, I've never been very frightened of the Whistler. The threat always seemed remote, a little unreal.'

'You went no further than the garden?'

She looked at him straight in the eyes. 'I went no further than the garden.'

'Yet you didn't hear the telephone?'

'It is a large garden.'

'But it was a quiet night, Mrs Dennison.'

She didn't reply.

He asked: 'And when did you come in from wandering alone in the dark?'

'I wouldn't describe a stroll around the garden as wandering alone after dark. I suppose I was out for about half an hour. I had been back about five minutes when Mr Jago rang.'

'And when did you hear about the Robarts murder, Mrs Dennison? Obviously it wasn't news to you when we met at Martyr's Cottage.'

'I thought you already knew that, Chief Inspector. Miss Mair telephoned me shortly after seven on Monday morning. She herself knew when her brother returned late on Sunday night after seeing the body but she didn't want to disturb me at midnight, particularly with such distressing news.'

Oliphant asked: 'And was it distressing news, madam? You hardly knew Miss Robarts. Why should it be so distressing?'

Mrs Dennison gave him a long look, then turned away. She said: 'If you really have to ask that question, Sergeant, are you sure you're in the right job?'

Rickards rose to go. She came with him to the front door. As they were leaving she turned to him and said with sudden urgency: 'Chief Inspector, I'm not stupid. All these questions about the shoes. Obviously you've found a print at the scene and you think it could have been made by the murderer. But surely Bumbles aren't uncommon. Anyone could have been wearing them. The fact that Toby Gledhill's pair are missing could be simply coincidence. They weren't necessarily taken with evil purpose. Anyone needing a pair of trainers could have stolen them.'

Oliphant looked at her. 'Oh, I don't think so, madam, do you? As you said yourself only half an hour ago, this is Larksoken, not London.' And he smiled his thick-lipped, self-satisfied smile.

39

Rickards wanted to see Lessingham at once but the press conference
called for ten meant that the interview had to be postponed and, to
complicate matters further, a telephone call to Larksoken Power
Station revealed that Lessingham had taken a day's leave but had left
a message saying he could be reached at his cottage outside Blakeney. Luckily he was at home and, without explanation, Oliphant
made an appointment for midday.

They were less than five minutes late and it was the more
frustrating, therefore, to find when they arrived at the low-built
wood and brick cottage set back on the coastal road a mile to the
north of the village that he wasn't at home. A note in pencil was
tacked to the front door.

'Anyone wanting me, try the *Heron*, berthed at Blakeney quay.
That includes the police.'

'Bloody cheek!' complained Oliphant. As if unwilling to believe
that any suspect could be as wilfully uncooperative, he tried the
door, peered in at the window, then disappeared round the back.
Returning he said: 'Ramshackle. Could do with a lick of paint. Funny
place to choose to live. These marshes are pretty dreary in winter.
You'd think he'd want a bit of life around him.'

Rickards privately agreed that it was an odd place for Lessingham
to choose. His cottage looked as if it had once been a pair, now
converted into a single dwelling, and, although agreeably proportioned with a certain melancholy charm, it looked at first sight
unoccupied and neglected. Lessingham was a senior engineer after
all, or technician, he couldn't for the moment remember which.
Anyway, he hardly lived here because he was poor.

He said: 'He probably wants to be close to his boat. There's not
much choice of harbour on this coast. It was either there or Wells-
next-the-Sea.'

As they got back into the car, Oliphant gazed back at the cottage
resentfully as if it were concealing behind the peeling paint some
secret which a few vigorous kicks on the door might persuade it to

divulge. Fastening his seat belt, he grumbled: 'And when we get to the quay I suppose there'll be a notice telling us to try the pub.'

But Lessingham was where he said he'd be. Ten minutes later they came up to him, sitting on an upturned crate on the deserted quay, an outboard motor in front of him. Berthed beside him was a thirty-foot sailing boat with a central cabin. It was obvious that he hadn't yet started to work. A relatively clean rag drooped from fingers which seemed too listless to hold it and he was regarding the engine as if it posed an intractable problem. He looked up as they stood over him and Rickards was shocked at the change in him. In only two days he seemed to have aged ten years. He was barefoot and wore a faded dark blue guernsey over knee-length denim shorts fashionably tattered at the edges. But this informal garb seemed only to emphasize his urban pallor, the skin taut over the wide cheekbones, the smudges like bruises under the deep-set eyes. He was a part-time sailor after all, thought Rickards. Extraordinary that even this bad summer hadn't produced more than a biscuit-coloured tan.

Lessingham didn't get up, but said without preamble: 'You were lucky to catch me when you rang. A day's leave is too good to waste indoors, particularly now. I thought we could talk here as well as anywhere.'

Rickards said: 'Not altogether. Somewhere more private would be better.'

'This is private enough. The locals can recognize the police when they see them. Of course if you want me to make a formal statement or were thinking of arresting me, I'd prefer the police station. I like to keep my house and my boat uncontaminated.' He added: 'I mean uncontaminated by disagreeable sensations.'

Oliphant said stolidly: 'Why do you suppose we would want to arrest you? Arrest you for what exactly?' He added: 'sir', and made the word sound like a threat.

Rickards felt a spurt of irritation. It was like the man not to miss an easy opening but this childish preliminary sparring would hardly smooth the interrogation. Lessingham looked at Oliphant, seriously considering whether the question needed a reply.

'God knows. I suppose you could think of something if you put your minds to it.' Then, seeming to realize for the first time that they were having to stand, he got up. 'All right, better come on board.'

Rickards wasn't a sailor, but it seemed to him that the boat, all wood, was old. The cabin, which they had to crouch low to enter, had a narrow mahogany table down the whole length and a bench on either side. Lessingham seated himself opposite them and they regarded each other across two feet of polished wood, their faces so close that Rickards felt he could smell his companions, a masculine amalgam of sweat, warm wool, beer and Oliphant's aftershave, as if all three were claustrophobically caged animals. It could hardly have been a more unsuitable place in which to conduct an interview, and he wondered whether Adam Dalgliesh would have engineered things better and despised himself for the thought. He was aware of Oliphant's great bulk beside him, their thighs touching, Oliphant's unnaturally warm, and had to resist an impulse to edge further away.

He said: 'Is this your boat, sir? The one you were sailing last Sunday night?'

'Not sailing, Chief Inspector, for much of the time; there wasn't enough wind. But yes, this is my boat and this is the one I was on last Sunday.'

'You seem to have damaged the hull. There's a long fresh-looking scratch on the starboard side.'

'Clever of you to notice. I scraped the water tower offshore from the power station. Careless of me. I've sailed these waters often enough. If you'd come a couple of hours later it would have been repainted.'

'And do you still say that you were never at any time within sight of the beach where Miss Robarts took her last swim?'

'You asked me that question when you saw me on Monday. It depends what you mean by "in sight of". I could have seen the beach through my binoculars if I'd happened to look, but I can confirm that I never got to within half a mile of it and that I didn't land. Since I could hardly murder her without landing, that seems to me conclusive. But I don't suppose you've come all this way just to hear me repeat my alibi.'

Reaching down with difficulty, Oliphant dragged his grip on to the seat beside him, took out a pair of Bumble trainers and placed them on the table neatly, side by side. Rickards watched Lessingham's face. He controlled himself immediately but he hadn't been able to disguise the shock of recognition in the eyes, the tensing of the muscles around the mouth. The pair of trainers, pristine, new, grey and white, with the small bumblebee on each heel, seemed to dominate the cabin. Having placed them there, Oliphant ignored them.

He said: 'But you were south of the water towers at the power station. The scratch is on the starboard side. You must have been travelling north, sir, when you got that scrape.'

'I turned for home when I was about fifty yards beyond the towers. I'd planned to make the power station the limit of the journey.'

Rickards said: 'These trainers, sir, have you seen a pair like these?'

'Of course. They're Bumbles. Not everyone can afford them but most people have seen them.'

'Have you seen them worn by anyone who worked at Larksoken?'

'Yes, Toby Gledhill had a pair. After he killed himself his parents asked me if I'd clear out his clothes. There weren't very many. Toby travelled light, but I suppose there were a couple of suits, the usual trousers and jackets and half a dozen pairs of shoes. The trainers were among them. Actually, they were almost new. He bought them about ten days before he died. He only wore them once.'

'And what did you do with them, sir?'

'I bundled up all the clothes and took them to the Old Rectory for the next church jumble sale. The Copleys have a small room at the back of the house where people can leave their junk. From time to time Dr Mair puts a notice on the notice board asking people to donate anything they don't want. It's part of the policy of being part of the community, all one happy family on the headland. We may not always go to church but we show goodwill by bestowing on the righteous our cast-off clothes.'

'When did you take Mr Gledhill's clothes to the Old Rectory?'

'I can't remember exactly, but I think it was a fortnight after he died. Just before the weekend I think. Probably on Friday the twenty-sixth of August. Mrs Dennison may remember. I doubt whether it's worth asking Mrs Copley, although I did see her.'

'So you handed them over to Mrs Dennison?'

'That's right. Actually, the back door of the rectory is usually kept open during daylight hours and people can walk in and drop anything they want to leave. But I thought on this occasion that it would be better to hand the things over formally. I wasn't entirely sure they'd be welcome. Some people are superstitious about buying the clothes of the recently dead. And it seemed, well, inappropriate just to drop them.'

'What happened at the Old Rectory?'

'Nothing very much. Mrs Dennison opened the door and showed me into the drawing room. Mrs Copley was there and I explained why I had called. She produced the usual meaningless platitudes about Toby's death and Mrs Dennison asked me if I would like tea. I declined and followed her through the hall to the room at the back where they store the jumble. There's a large tea chest there which holds the shoes. The pairs are just tied by the laces and thrown in. I had Toby's clothes in a suitcase and Mrs Dennison and I unpacked it together. She said that the suits were really too good for the jumble sale and asked if I'd mind if she sold them separately, provided, of course, the money went to church funds. She thought she might get a better price. I had a feeling that she was wondering whether Mr Copley might not use one of the jackets. I said she could do what she liked with them.'

'And what happened to the trainers? Were they put into the tea chest with the rest of the shoes?'

'Yes, but in a plastic bag. Mrs Dennison said they were in too good a condition to be thrown in with the others and get dirty. She went off and returned with the bag. She seemed to be uncertain what to do with the suits so I said I'd leave the suitcase. It was Toby's after all. It could be sold at the jumble sale with the rest of the things. Ashes to ashes, dust to dust, jumble to jumble. I was glad to see the end of it.'

Rickards said: 'I read about Dr Gledhill's suicide, of course. It must have been particularly distressing for you who actually saw it happen. He was described as a young man of brilliant promise.'

'He was a creative scientist. Mair will confirm that if you're interested one way or the other. Of course, all good science is creative whatever the humanities try to tell you, but there are scientists who have this special vision, genius as opposed to talent, inspiration as well as the necessary patient conscientiousness. Someone, I forget who, described it rather well. Most of us edge forward, painfully advancing, yard by yard; they parachute behind enemy lines. He was young, only twenty-four. He could have become anything.'

Rickards thought, anything or nothing, like most of these young geniuses. Early death usually conferred a brief vicarious immortality. He'd never known a young DCI, accidentally killed, who wasn't at once proclaimed a potential Chief Constable. He asked: 'What exactly was he doing at the power station, what was his job?'

'Working with Mair on his PWR safety studies. Briefly, it's to do with the behaviour of the core in abnormal conditions. Toby never discussed it with me, probably because he knew I couldn't understand the complicated computer codes. I'm just a poor bloody engineer. Mair is due to publish the study before he leaves for his rumoured new job, no doubt under both their names and with a suitable acknowledgement to his collaborator. All that will last of Toby is his name under Mair's on a scientific paper.'

He sounded utterly weary and, looking towards the open door, made a half movement as if to get up, out of the claustrophobic little cabin and into the air. Then he said, his eyes still on the door: 'It's no use trying to explain Toby to you, you wouldn't understand. It would be a waste of your time and mine.'

'You seem very sure of that, Mr Lessingham.'

'I am sure, very sure. I can't explain why without being offensive. So why don't we keep it simple, stick to the facts. Look, he was an exceptional person. He was clever, he was kind, he was beautiful. If you find one of these qualities in a human being, you're lucky, if you find all three then you get someone rather special. I was in love with him. He knew because I told him. He wasn't in love with me and he wasn't gay. Not that it's any business of yours. I'm telling you because it was a fact and you're supposed to deal in facts, and because if you're determined to be interested in Toby you may as well get him right. And there's another reason. You're obviously grubbing about for all the dirt you can find. I'd rather you had facts from me than rumours from other people.'

Rickards said: 'So you didn't have a sexual relationship.'

Suddenly the air was rent with a wild screeching and there was a beating of white wings against the porthole. Outside someone must be feeding the seagulls.

Lessingham started up as if the sound was alien to him. Then he collapsed back in his seat and said with more weariness than anger: 'What the hell has that to do with Hilary Robarts's murder?'

'Possibly nothing at all, in which case the information will be kept private. But at this stage it's for me to decide what may or may not be relevant.'

'We spent one night together two weeks before he died. As I said, he was kind. It was the first and the last time.'

'Is that generally known?'

'We didn't broadcast it over local radio or write to the local paper or put up a notice in the staff canteen. Of course it wasn't generally known, why the hell should it be?'

'Would it have mattered if it had been? Would either of you have cared?'

'Yes, I would, we both would. I would care in the way you would care if your sex life was sniggered about in public. Of course we would have cared. After he died, it ceased to matter as far as I was concerned. There's this to be said for the death of a friend, it frees you from so much you thought was important.'

Frees you for what? thought Rickards. For murder, that iconoclastic act of protest and defiance, that single step across an unmarked, undefended frontier which, once taken, sets a man apart for ever from the rest of his kind? But he decided to defer the obvious question.

Instead he asked: 'What sort of family had he?' The question sounded innocuous and banal, as if they were casually discussing a common acquaintance.

'He had a father and a mother. That sort of family. What other sort is there?'

But Rickards had resolved on patience. It was not a ploy that came easily to him, but he could recognize pain when its taut and naked sinews were thrust so close to his face. He said mildly: 'I mean what sort of background did he come from? Had he brothers or sisters?'

'His father is a country parson. His mother is a country parson's wife. He was an only child. His death nearly destroyed them. If we could have made it look like an accident we would have. If lying could have helped, I would have lied. Why the hell didn't he drown himself? That way there would at least have been room for doubt. Is that what you meant by background?'

'It's helping to fill in the picture.' He paused and then, almost casually, asked the seminal question. 'Did Hilary Robarts know that you and Tobias Gledhill had spent a night together?'

'Whatever possible relevance . . . ? All right, it's your job to do the scavenging. I know the system. You trawl up everything you can get your nets to and then throw away what you don't want. In the process you learn a lot of secrets you've no particular right to know and cause a lot of pain. Do you enjoy that? Is that what gives you your kicks?'

'Just answer the question, sir.'

'Yes, Hilary knew. She found out by one of those coincidences

297

which seem a one in a million chance when they happen but which aren't really so remarkable or unusual in real life. She drove past my house when Toby and I were leaving just after seven thirty in the morning. She had taken a day's leave, apparently, and must have left home early to drive off somewhere. It's no use asking me where because I don't know. I suppose, like most other people, she has friends she visits from time to time. I mean, someone somewhere must have liked her.'

'Did she ever speak about the encounter, to you or to anyone else you know?'

'She didn't make it public property. I think she regarded it as too valuable a piece of information to cast before the swine. She liked power, and this was certainly power of a kind. As she drove past, she slowed down almost to walking pace and stared straight into my eyes. I can remember that look: amusement, changing to contempt, then triumph. We understood each other all right. But she never subsequently spoke a word to me.'

'Did she talk about it to Mr Gledhill?'

'Oh yes, she spoke to Toby all right. That's the reason he killed himself.'

'How do you know that she spoke to him? Did he tell you?'

'No.'

'You're suggesting that she blackmailed him?'

'I'm suggesting that he was unhappy, muddled, uncertain about every aspect of his life, his research, his future, his sexuality. I know that she attracted him sexually. He wanted her. She was one of those dominant, physically powerful women who do attract sensitive men like Toby. I think she knew that and she used it. I don't know when she got hold of him or what she said to him, but I'm bloody sure that he'd be alive now if it weren't for Hilary Robarts. And if that gives me a motive for her murder, you're damned right. But I didn't kill her and, that being so, you won't find any evidence that I did. Part of me, a very small part, is actually sorry that she's dead. I didn't like her and I don't think she was a happy woman, or even a particularly useful one. But she was healthy and intelligent and she was young. Death ought to be for the old, the sick and the tired. What I feel is a touch of *lachrymae rerum*. Even the death of an enemy diminishes us apparently, or so, in certain moods, it seems. But that doesn't mean I'd want her alive again. But it's possible I'm prejudiced, perhaps even unjust. When Toby was happy, no one was more joyous. When he was miserable he went down into his private hell. Perhaps she could reach him there, could help him. I know I couldn't. It's difficult to comfort a friend when you suspect that he sees it as a ploy to get him into your bed.'

Rickards said: 'You've been remarkably frank in suggesting a motive for yourself. But you haven't given us a single piece of concrete evidence to support your allegation that Hilary Robarts was in any way responsible for Toby Gledhill's death.'

Lessingham looked straight into his eyes and seemed to be considering, then he said: 'I've gone so far, I may as well tell you the rest. He spoke to me when he passed me on his way to death. He said, "Tell Hilary she doesn't have to worry any more. I've made my choice." The next time I saw him he was climbing the fuelling machine. He balanced on it for a second, then dived down on top of the reactor. He meant me to see him die, and I saw him die.'

Oliphant said: 'A symbolic sacrifice.'

'To the terrifying god of nuclear fission? I thought one of you might say that, Sergeant. That was the vulgar reaction. It's altogether too crude and histrionic. All he wanted, for God's sake, was the quickest way to break his neck.' He paused, seemed to consider, then went on: 'Suicide is an extraordinary phenomenon. The result is irrevocable. Extinction. The end of all choice. But the precipitating action often seems so commonplace. A minor setback, momentary depression, the state of the weather, even a poor dinner. Would Toby have died if he'd spent the previous night with me instead of alone? If he was alone.'

'Are you saying that he wasn't?'

'There was no evidence either way and now there will never be. But then the inquest was remarkable for the lack of evidence about anything. There were three witnesses, myself and two others, to the way he died. No one was near him, no one could have pushed him, it couldn't have been an accident. There was no evidence from me or anyone else about his state of mind. You could say that it was a scientifically conducted inquest. It stuck to the facts.'

Oliphant said quietly: 'And where do you think he spent the night before he died?'

'With her.'

'On what evidence?'

'None that would stand up in a court. Only that I rang him three times between nine and midnight and he didn't reply.'

'And you didn't tell that to the police or the coroner?'

'On the contrary. I was asked when I'd last seen him. That was in the canteen on the day before he died. I mentioned my telephone call, but no one regarded it as important. Why should they? What did it prove? He could have been out walking. He could have decided not to answer the phone. There was no mystery about how he died. And now, if you don't mind, I'd like to get out of here and on with cleaning that bloody engine.'

They walked in silence back to the car. Rickards said: 'Arrogant bastard, isn't he? He made his view brutally plain. No point in trying to explain anything to the police. He can't say why without being offensive. You bet he can't. We're too thick, ignorant and insensitive to understand that a research scientist isn't necessarily an unimaginative technocrat, that you can be sorry a woman is dead without necessarily wishing her alive again, and that a sexually attractive boy might actually be prepared to go to bed with either sex.'

Oliphant said: 'He could have done it if he used the engine at full power. He'd have had to come ashore north of where she bathed and kept to the tide line, or we'd have seen his footprints. It was a thorough search, sir, at least a mile north and south. We identified Mr Dalgliesh's prints but, otherwise, the upper beach was clean.'

'Oh yes, he'd have kept pretty clear of the killing ground. But he could have beached the inflatable dinghy on shingle without much problem. There are stretches which are practically all pebbled, or with narrow strips of sand which he could leap over.'

'What about the old beach defences, the hunks of concrete? It would be difficult to come close to shore anywhere north within easy walking distance without risking the boat.'

'He has risked the boat recently, hasn't he? There's this scrape along the bow. He can't prove that he made it on the water towers. Cool about it, too, wasn't he? Calmly admitted that if we'd been an hour later he'd have repaired it. Not that repainting would have done him much good, the evidence would still be there. All right, so he manages to manoeuvre the boat as close in shore as he can, say, a hundred yards north of where she was found, makes his way along the shingle and into the trees and waits quietly in their shadow. Or he could have loaded the folding bicycle into the dinghy and landed at a safer distance. He couldn't cycle along the beach at high tide, but he'd have been safe enough on the coast road if he cycled without a light. He gets back to the boat and berths her again at Blakeney, just catching the high tide. No trouble about the knife or the shoes, he drops them overboard. We'll get the boat examined, with his consent, of course, and I want a single-handed chap to make that journey. If we've got an experienced sailor among our chaps, use him. If not, get someone local and accompany him. We've got to time it to the minute. And we'd better make inquiries of the crab fishermen down Cromer way. Someone may have been out that night and seen his boat.'

Oliphant said: 'Obliging of him, sir, to hand us his motive on a plate.'

'So obliging that I can't help wondering whether it isn't a smoke-screen for something he didn't tell us.'

But as Rickards fastened his seat belt another possibility occurred to him. Lessingham had said nothing about his relationship with Toby Gledhill until he had been questioned about the Bumble trainers. He must know – how could he fail to? – that these linked the murder even more strongly to the headlanders and, in particular, to the Old Rectory. Was his new openness with the police less a compulsion to confide than a deliberate ploy to divert suspicion from another suspect? And if so, which of the suspects, Rickards wondered, was most likely to evoke this eccentric act of chivalry?

40

On Thursday morning Dalgliesh drove to Lydsett to shop at the village store. His aunt had shopped locally for most of her main provisions and he continued the practice, partly he knew to assuage a nagging guilt about having a second home, however temporary. The villagers did not on the whole resent weekenders despite the fact that their cottages remained empty for most of the year and their contribution to village life was minimal, but preferred them not to arrive with their car boots loaded with provisions from Harrods or Fortnum and Mason.

And patronizing the Brysons in their corner shop entailed no particular sacrifice. It was an unpretentious village store with a clanging bell on the door which, as the sepia photographs of the Victorian village showed, had hardly altered externally in the last 120 years. Inside, however, the last four years had seen more changes than in the whole of its history. Whether because of the growth of holiday homes or the more sophisticated tastes of the villagers, it now offered fresh pasta, a variety of French as well as English cheeses, the more expensive brands of jams, marmalade and mustard, and a well-stocked delicatessen, while a notice proclaimed that fresh croissants were delivered daily.

As he drew up in the side street, Dalgliesh had to manoeuvre past an old and heavily built bicycle with a large wicker basket which was propped against the kerb, and as he entered he saw that Ryan Blaney was just completing his purchases. Mrs Bryson was ringing up and bagging three brown loaves, packets of sugar, cartons of milk and an assortment of tins. Blaney gave Dalgliesh a glance from his blood-shot eyes, a curt nod, and was gone. He was still without his van, thought Dalgliesh, watching him load his basket with the contents of one carrier and hang the other two on the handlebars. Mrs Bryson turned on Dalgliesh her welcoming smile but did not comment. She was too prudent a shopkeeper to get a reputation as a gossip or to become too openly involved in local controversies, but it seemed to Dalgliesh that the air was heavy with her unspoken sympathy for Blaney and he felt obscurely that, as a policeman, she held him partly responsible although he was unsure precisely why and for what. Rickards or his men must have questioned the villagers about the headlanders, Ryan Blaney in particular. Perhaps they had been less than tactful.

Five minutes later he stopped to open the gate barring entry to the headland. On the other side a tramp was sitting on the bank which separated the narrow road from the reed-enclosed dyke. He was bearded and wearing a checked tweed cap beneath which two neat plaits of strong grey hair bound with a rubber band fell almost to his shoulders. He was eating an apple, slicing it with a short-handled knife and throwing the sections into his mouth. His long legs, clad in thick corduroy trousers, were stretched out widely in front of him almost as if he were deliberately displaying a pair of black, white and grey trainers, their obvious newness in stark contrast to the rest of his clothes. Dalgliesh closed the gate then walked over to him and looked down into a pair of bright and intelligent eyes set in a drawn and weatherbeaten face. If this was a tramp, the keenness of that first glance, his air of confident self-sufficiency and the cleanliness of his white rather delicate hands made him an unusual one. But he was surely too encumbered to be a casual hiker. His khaki coat looked like army surplus and was bound with a wide leather belt from which was suspended by string an enamel mug, a small saucepan and a frying pan. A small, but tightly packed backpack lay on the verge beside him.

Dalgliesh said: 'Good morning. I'm sorry if I seem impertinent, but where did you get those shoes?'

The voice that answered him was educated, a little pedantic, a voice, he thought, that might have once belonged to a schoolmaster.

'You are not, I hope, about to claim ownership. I shall regret it if our acquaintanceship, although no doubt destined to be brief, should begin with a dispute about property.'

'No, they're not mine. I was wondering how long they've been yours.'

The man finished his apple. He threw the core over his shoulder into the ditch, cleaned the blade of his clasp knife on the grass, and pushed it with care deep into his pocket. He said: 'May I ask if this inquiry arrives from – forgive me – an inordinate and reprehensible curiosity, an unnatural suspicion of a fellow mortal, or a desire to purchase a similar pair for yourself. If the last, I am afraid I am unable to help you.'

'None of these things. But the inquiry is important. I'm not being either presumptuous or suspicious.'

'Nor, sir, are you being particularly candid or explicit. My name, incidentally, is Jonah.'

'Mine is Adam Dalgliesh.'

'Then, Adam Dalgliesh, give me one good reason why I should answer your question and you shall have an answer.'

Dalgliesh paused for a moment. There was, he supposed, a theoretical possibility that here before him was the murderer of Hilary Robarts, but he did not for a moment believe it. Rickards had telephoned him the previous evening to inform him that the Bumbles were no longer in the jumble chest, obviously feeling that he owed Dalgliesh this brief report. But that did not mean that the tramp had taken them, nor did it prove that the two pairs were the same. He said: 'On Sunday night a girl was strangled here on the beach. If you recently found, or were given, those shoes or were wearing them on the headland last Sunday the police will need to know. They have found a distinct footprint. It is important to identify it if only to eliminate the wearer from their inquiries.'

'Well, that at least is explicit. You talk like a policeman. I should be sorry to hear that you are one.'

'This isn't my case. But I am a policeman and I know that the local CID are looking for a pair of Bumble trainers.'

'And these, I take it, are Bumble trainers. I had thought of them as shoes.'

'They don't have a label except under the tongue. That's the firm's sales gimmick. Bumbles are supposed to be recognizable without a blatant display of the name. But if these are Bumbles there will be a yellow bee on each heel.'

Jonah didn't reply, but with a sudden vigorous movement swung both feet into the air, held them for a couple of seconds, then dropped them again.

Neither spoke for a few moments, then Jonah said: 'You are telling me that I now have on my feet the shoes of a murderer?'

'Possibly, but only possibly, these are the shoes he was wearing when the girl was killed. You see their importance?'

'I shall no doubt be made to see it, by you or another of your kind.'

'Have you heard of the Norfolk Whistler?'

'Is it a bird?'

'A mass murderer.'

'And these shoes are his?'

'He's dead. This latest killing was made to look as if he were responsible. Are you telling me you haven't even heard of him?'

'I sometimes see a newspaper when I need paper for other more earthy purposes. There are plenty to pick up from the waste bins. I seldom read them. They reinforce my conviction that the world is not for me. I seem to have missed your murdering Whistler.' He paused then added: 'What now am I expected to do? I take it that I am in your hands.'

Dalgliesh said: 'As I said, it isn't my case. I'm from the Metropolitan Police. But if you wouldn't mind coming home with me I could telephone the officer in charge. It isn't far. I live in Larksoken Mill on the headland. And if you care to exchange these trainers for a pair of my shoes, it seems the least I can offer. We're about the same height. There should be a pair to fit you.'

Jonah got to his feet with surprising agility. As they walked to the car Dalgliesh said: 'I've really no right to question you, but satisfy my curiosity. How did you come by them?'

'They were bestowed on me, inadvertently I might say, some time on Sunday night. I had arrived on the headland after dark and made my way to my usual night shelter in these parts. It's the half-buried concrete bunker near the cliff. A pillbox I think it's called. I expect you know it.'

'I know it. Not a particularly salubrious place to spend the night I should have thought.'

'I have known better certainly. But it has the advantage of privacy. The headland is off the usual route for fellow wayfarers. I usually visit once a year and stay for a day or two. The pillbox is completely weatherproof and as the slit window faces the sea I can light a small fire without fear of discovery. I push the rubbish to one side and ignore it. It is a policy I would recommend to you.'

'Did you go straight there?'

'No. As is my custom I called at the Old Rectory. The elderly couple who live there are usually very obliging in allowing me to use their tap. I wanted to fill up my water bottle. As it happens, there was no one at home. There were lights on in the lower windows but no one responded to the bell.'

'What time would this be, do you remember?'

'I have no watch and I take little account of time between sunset and sunrise. But I did notice that St Andrew's Church clock in the village showed eight thirty as I passed. I was probably at the Old Rectory by nine fifteen, or shortly afterwards.'

'What did you do then?'

'I knew that there was an outside tap close to the garage. I took the liberty of filling my bottle without permission. They would hardly, I think, begrudge me clean water.'

'Did you see a car?'

'There was one standing in the drive. The garage was open but, as I have said, I saw no human beings. I then went straight to the shelter. I was by then exceedingly tired. I drank some of the water, ate a crust of bread and some cheese and fell asleep. The shoes were thrown in through the door of the bunker some time during the night.'

Dalgliesh said: 'Thrown in rather than placed?'

'I imagine so. Anyone who actually entered the bunker must have seen me. It is surely more likely that they were thrown in. There is a wayside pulpit at a church in Ipswich. Last week it said: "God gives every bird his worm, but He does not throw it into the nest." On this occasion apparently He did.'

'And they hit you without waking you? They're heavy shoes.'

'As I have said, you talk like a policeman. I had walked twenty miles on the Sunday. I have an easy conscience and I sleep sound. If they had fallen on my face I have no doubt they would have wakened me. As it was, I found them next morning when I woke up.'

'Neatly placed?'

'Not at all. What happened was that I woke and turned over from my left side on to my back. I felt something hard beneath me and lit a match. The lump was one of the shoes. The other I found near my foot.'

'They weren't tied together?'

'Had they been tied, my dear sir, it would hardly have been possible for me to find one near the small of my back and the other at my feet.'

'And you weren't curious? After all, the trainers were practically new, hardly the kind of shoe anyone would chuck away.'

'Naturally I was curious. But unlike members of your profession I am not obsessed by the need to find explanations. It did not occur to me that I had a responsibility to find the owner or take the shoes in to the nearest police station. I doubt whether they would have thanked me for my trouble. I took gratefully what fate or God had provided.

My old shoes were nearing the end of their usefulness. You will find them in the pillbox.'

'And you put on these.'

'Not immediately. They were too damp. I waited until they were dry.'

'Damp in parts or all over?'

'Damp all over. Someone had washed them very thoroughly, probably by holding them under a tap.'

'Or by walking into the sea.'

'I smelt them. It was not sea water.'

'Could you tell?'

'My dear sir, I have the use of my senses. My nose is particularly keen. I can tell the difference between sea and tap water. I can tell you what county I'm in by the smell of the earth.'

They had turned left at the crossroads, and the soaring white sails of the windmill were in sight. They sat in companionable silence for a few moments.

Then Jonah said: 'You have, perhaps, a right to know what manner of man you are inviting under your roof. I am, sir, a modern remittance man. I know that, originally, my kind were banished to the colonies but they are a little more discriminating now and, in any case, banishment from the smells and colours of the English country-side would not have suited me. My brother, a model of civil rectitude and a prominent member of his local community, transfers one thousand pounds per annum from his bank account into mine, providing I never embarrass him by intruding on his presence. The interdict, I may say, extends to the town of which he is mayor but, since he and his fellow planners have long destroyed whatever character it once possessed, I have deleted it from my itinerary without regret. He is indefatigable in good works and you could say that I am among the recipients of his charity. He has been honoured by Her Majesty. An OBE, merely, but he has, I am sure, hope of higher things.'

Dalgliesh said: 'Your brother seems to be getting off rather lightly.'

'You yourself would willingly pay more to ensure my perpetual absence?'

'Not at all. It's just that I assume that the one thousand pounds is to enable you to keep yourself and I was wondering how you managed to do it. One thousand pounds as an annual bribe could be considered generous; as a living allowance it's surely inadequate.'

'To do him justice, my brother would willingly make an annual increase in line with the Retail Price Index. He has an almost obsessive sense of bureaucratic propriety. But I have told him that twenty pounds a week is more than adequate. I have no house, no rent, no rates, no heating, no lighting, no telephone, no car. I pollute neither my own body nor the environment. A man who cannot feed himself on nearly three pounds a day must either be lacking in initiative or be the slave of inordinate desires. An Indian peasant would regard it as luxury.'

'An Indian peasant would have less problem in keeping warm. The winters must be trying.'

'A hard winter is, indeed, a discipline in endurance. Not that I complain. I am always healthiest in winter. And matches are cheap. I have never learned those boy scout tricks with a magnifying glass and rubbed sticks. Happily I know half a dozen farmers who are willing to let me sleep in their barns. They know that I don't smoke, that I am tidy, that I shall be gone by the morning. But one should never trespass on kindness. Human kindness is like a defective tap, the first gush may be impressive but the stream soon dries up. I have my annual routine and that, too, reassures them. In a farmhouse twenty miles north of here they will be saying soon, "Isn't this the time of year that Jonah drops in?" They greet me with relief rather than tolerance. If I am still alive then so are they. And I never beg. An offer to pay is far more efficacious. "Could you sell me a couple of eggs and half a pint of milk", spoken at the farm door – provided the cash is proffered – will usually produce six eggs and a full pint. Not necessarily of the freshest, but one must not expect too much of human generosity.'

Dalgliesh said: 'What about books?'

'Ah there, sir, you have hit on a difficulty. Classics I can read in public libraries, although it is sometimes a little irritating to have to break off when it is time to move on. Otherwise I rely on second-hand paperbacks from market stalls. One or two stall-holders allow you to exchange the book or get your money back at the second visit. It is a remarkably cheap form of public lending library. As for clothes, there are jumble sales, Oxfam and those useful shops that deal in army surplus. I save from my allowance for a new ex-army winter coat every three years.'

Dalgliesh said: 'How long have you been living this life?'

'Nearly twenty years now, sir. Most tramps are pitiful because they are the slaves of their own passions, usually drink. A man who is free of all human desires except to eat, sleep and walk is truly free.'

Dalgliesh said: 'Not entirely. You have a bank account apparently, and you rely on that thousand pounds.'

'True. You think I would be freer if I didn't take it?'

'More independent, perhaps. You might have to work.'

'I cannot work, to beg I am ashamed. Luckily the Lord has tempered the wind to his shorn lamb. I should be sorry to do my brother out of the satisfaction of his benevolence. True, I have a bank account to receive my annual subsidy and to that extent I conform. But since my income depends on my separation from my brother it would hardly be possible to receive the money personally and my cheque book and accompanying plastic card have a most gratifying effect on the police when, as occasionally happens, they take a presumptuous interest in my doings. I had no idea that a plastic card was such a guarantee of respectability.'

Dalgliesh asked: 'No luxuries? No other needs? Drink? Women?'

'If by women you mean sex then the answer is no. I am escaping, sir, from drink and sex.'

'Then you are on the run from something. I could argue that a man on the run is never entirely free.'

'And I could ask you, sir, from what you are escaping on this isolated headland. If from the violence of your job you have been singularly unlucky.'

'And now that same violence has touched your life. I'm sorry.'

'You needn't be. A man who lives with nature is used to violence and is companionable with death. There is more violence in an English hedgerow than in the meanest streets of a great city.'

When they reached the mill Dalgliesh telephoned Rickards. He wasn't at the incident room but Oliphant was and said that he would immediately drive over. Then Dalgliesh took Jonah upstairs to look over the half-dozen pairs of shoes he had with him at the mill. There was no problem over fit but Jonah tried them all on and examined each shoe minutely before making his choice. Dalgliesh was tempted to say that a life of simplicity and self-abnegation hadn't spoilt his guest's eye for good leather. He saw, with some regret, his favourite and most expensive pair chosen.

Jonah walked up and down the bedroom looking down at his feet with complacency. He said: 'I seem to have the best of the bargain. The Bumbles came at an opportune time but they were hardly suitable for serious walking and I intended to replace them as opportunity offered. The rules of the road are few and simple but they are imperative. I commend them to you. Keep your bowels open; bath once a week; wear wool or cotton next to the skin and leather on the feet.'

Fifteen minutes later his guest was ensconced in an armchair, a mug of coffee in hand, still regarding his feet with satisfaction. Oliphant was prompt in arriving. Apart from his driver he was alone. He came into the sitting room bringing with him an aura of masculine menace and authority. Even before Dalgliesh had made the introduction he said to Jonah: 'You must have known you'd no right to those trainers. They're new. Ever heard of stealing by finding?'

Dalgliesh said: 'A moment, Sergeant.' Drawing Oliphant aside he said in a low voice: 'You'll treat Mr Jonah with courtesy.' And before Oliphant could protest, he added, 'All right, I'll save you the trouble of saying it. This isn't my case. But he is a guest in my house. If your men had searched the headland more thoroughly on Monday all three of us might have been saved some embarrassment.'

'He has to be a serious suspect, sir. He's got the shoes.'

Dalgliesh said: 'He also has a knife and he admits to having been on the headland on Sunday night. Treat him as a serious suspect by all means if you can find a motive or proof that he knew how the Whistler killed or even knew that he existed. But why not listen to his story before you jump to conclusions about his guilt?'

Oliphant said: 'Guilty or not, Mr Dalgliesh, he's an important witness. I don't see how we can allow him to go wandering off.'

'And I don't see how, legally, you can prevent him. But that's your problem, Sergeant.'

A few minutes later Oliphant was leading Jonah towards the car. Dalgliesh went out to see him off. Before climbing in at the back, Jonah turned to him.

'It was an ill day for me when I met you, Adam Dalgliesh.'

'But a good day, perhaps, for justice.'

'Oh, justice. Is that the business you're in? I think you may have left it rather late. This planet earth is hurtling now to its destruction. That concrete bastion on the edge of a polluted sea may bring about the final darkness. If not it will be by some other folly of man. There comes a time when every scientist, even God, has to write off an experiment. Ah, I see a certain relief on your face. You are thinking,

So he is mad after all, this peculiar tramp. I need no longer take him seriously.'

Dalgliesh said: 'My mind agrees with you. My genes are more optimistic.'

'You know it. We all know it. How else can one explain the modern sickness of man. And when the final darkness falls I shall die as I have lived, in the nearest dry ditch.' And then he gave a singularly sweet smile and added: 'Wearing your shoes, Adam Dalgliesh.'

41

The encounter with Jonah had left Dalgliesh curiously restless. There were plenty of jobs to be done in the mill but he felt disinclined to tackle any of them. His instinct was to get into the Jaguar and drive very fast and very far. But he had tried that expedient too often to have any faith in its efficacy. The mill would still be standing when he returned, the problems still unsolved. He had no difficulty in recognizing the basis of his discontent; the frustrating involvement with a case which would never be his yet from which it was impossible to distance himself. He remembered some words of Rickards spoken before they had finally parted on the night of the murder.

'You may not want to be involved, Mr Dalgliesh, but you are involved. You may wish that you had never been near the body, but you were there.'

He seemed to remember using much the same words to a suspect in one of his own cases. He was beginning to understand why they had been so ill received. On an impulse he unlocked the mill and climbed up the ladders to the top storey. Here, he suspected, his aunt had found her peace. Perhaps some of that lost contentment might seep into him. But any hope of being left undisturbed was due to be frustrated.

As he looked over the headland from the southern window a bicycle came into sight. At first it was too distant to see who was riding but then he recognized Neil Pascoe. They had never spoken but, like all the headlanders, they knew each other by sight. Pascoe seemed to be cycling with a ponderous determination, his head low over the handlebars, his shoulders working. But as he came close to the mill he suddenly stopped, put both feet on the ground, stared towards the mill as if seeing it for the first time, then dismounted and began wheeling the bicycle over the rough scrubland.

For one second Dalgliesh was tempted to pretend that he wasn't home. Then he realized that the Jaguar was parked at the side of the mill and that it was possible that Pascoe in that long stare had glimpsed his face at the window. Whatever the purpose of this visit it looked as if it were one he couldn't avoid. He moved over to the window above the door, opened it and called down: 'Are you looking for me?'

The question was rhetorical. Who else would Pascoe expect to find at Larksoken Mill? Looking down at the upturned face, the thin jutting beard, Dalgliesh saw him curiously diminished and foreshortened, a vulnerable rather pathetic figure clutching his bicycle as if for protection.

Pascoe shouted up against the wind: 'Could I talk to you?'

An honest reply would have been 'If you must', but it was not one that Dalgliesh felt he could shout down against the noise of the wind without sounding ungracious. He mouthed 'I'll be down.'

Pascoe propped the machine against the wall of the mill and followed him into the sitting room.

He said: 'We haven't actually met but I expect you've heard of me. I'm Neil Pascoe from the caravan. I'm sorry if I'm butting in when you want some peace.' He sounded as embarrassed as a door-to-door salesman trying to reassure a prospective customer that he wasn't a con man.

Dalgliesh was tempted to say, 'I might want some peace but it doesn't look as if I'm likely to get it.' He asked: 'Coffee?'

Pascoe gave the predictable reply: 'If it isn't too much trouble.'

'No trouble. I was thinking of making it.'

Pascoe followed him into the kitchen and stood leaning against the door post in an unconvincing assumption of ease as Dalgliesh ground the coffee beans and put on the kettle. It struck him that he had spent a considerable time since his arrival at the mill providing food and drink for uninvited visitors. When the grinding had ceased, Pascoe said almost truculently: 'I need to talk to you.'

'If it's about the murder then you ought to be speaking to Chief Inspector Rickards not me. This isn't my case.'

'But you found the body.'

'That might in certain circumstances make me a suspect. But it doesn't give me the right to interfere professionally in another officer's case outside my own force area. I'm not the investigating officer. But you know that, you're not stupid.'

Pascoe kept his eyes on the bubbling liquid. He said: 'I didn't expect you to be particularly pleased to see me. I wouldn't have come if there were anyone else I could talk to. There are things I can't discuss with Amy.'

'As long as you remember whom you are talking to.'

'A policeman. It's like the priesthood, is it? Never off duty. Once a priest always a priest.'

'It isn't in the least like the priesthood. No guarantee of confidentiality in the confessional and no absolution. That's what I'm trying to tell you.'

They said nothing else until the coffee had been poured into the two mugs and carried by Dalgliesh into the sitting room. They sat, one each side of the fireplace. Pascoe took his mug but seemed uncertain what to do with it. He sat twisting it in his hands, looking down at the coffee, making no attempt to drink. After a moment he said: 'It's about Toby Gledhill, the boy – well, he was a boy really – who killed himself at the power station.'

Dalgliesh said: 'I've heard about Toby Gledhill.'

'Then I expect you know how he died. He hurled himself down on top of the reactor and broke his neck. That was on Friday the twelfth of August. Two days before, on the Wednesday, he came to see me at about eight o'clock in the evening. I was on my own in the caravan, Amy had taken the van into Norwich to shop and said she wanted to see a film and would be back late. I was looking after Timmy. Then there was this knock and there he stood. I knew him, of course. At least, I knew who he was. I'd seen him on one or two of those open days at the power station. I usually make time to go to those. They can't stop me, and it gives me an opportunity of putting one or two awkward questions, countering their propaganda. And I think he was present at some of the meetings of the new pressurized water reactor inquiry. But, of course, I'd never really met him. I couldn't think what he wanted of me, but I invited him in and offered him a beer. I'd lit the stove because there were a lot of Timmy's clothes which needed drying so the caravan was very hot and rather damp. When I remember that night I seem to see him through a haze of steam. After the beer he asked if we couldn't go out. He seemed restless as if he found the caravan claustrophobic and he asked more than once when Amy was expected back. So I lifted Timmy out of his cot and put him into the backpack and we set off to walk north along the shore. It was when we had got as far as the abbey ruins that he told me what he'd come to say. He came out with it quite baldly, without any preamble. He'd come to the conclusion that nuclear power was too dangerous to use and that, until we've solved the problem of radioactive waste, we ought not to build any more nuclear power stations. There was one rather odd expression he used. He said: "It's not only dangerous, it's corrupting." '

Dalgliesh asked: 'Did he say why he'd come to this conclusion?'

'I think it had been building up for quite a few months, and Chernobyl had probably brought it to a head. He said that something else had recently happened that had helped to make up his mind. He didn't say what but he promised he would tell me when he'd had more time to think. I asked him if he was merely going to give up his job and opt out or whether he was prepared to help us. He said he thought that he had to help. It wouldn't be enough just to resign his job. It was diff·cult for him and I could see just how difficult. He admired and liked his colleagues. He said they were dedicated scientists and very intelligent men who believed in what they were doing. It was just that he couldn't believe any more. He hadn't thought about the way ahead, not very clearly anyway. He was like I am now; he just needed to talk it through. I suppose I seemed to be the natural person. He knew about PANUP of course.' He looked up at Dalgliesh and said rather naïvely: 'That stands for People Against Nuclear Power. When the proposal was put forward for the new reactor here I formed a little local group to oppose it. I mean a group of ordinary concerned local residents, not the more powerful national protest bodies. It hasn't been easy. Most people try to pretend that the power station isn't really there. And of course quite a number welcome it because it does bring in some employment, new customers for the shops and pubs. Most of the opposition to the new reactor wasn't local, anyway, it was people from CND, Friends of the Earth and Greenpeace. Of course we welcomed them. They're the ones with the heavy guns. But I thought it important to get something going locally and I suppose I'm not really a joiner. I like to do my own thing.'

Dalgliesh said: 'And Gledhill would have been quite a catch for you.' The words were almost brutal in their implication.

Pascoe flushed then looked him in the eyes. 'There was that too. I suppose I realized it at the time. I wasn't entirely disinterested. I mean, I did know how important it would be if he came over. But I was, well, flattered I suppose that he'd come first to me. PANUP hasn't made much impact, really. Even the initials were a mistake. I wanted something that people would easily remember, but PANUP – a bit of a laugh. I can guess what you're thinking, that I might have done more good for the cause by joining an existing pressure group instead of ministering to my own ego. You'd be right.'

Dalgliesh asked: 'Did Gledhill say whether he'd spoken to anyone at the station?'

'He said that he hadn't, not yet. I think that was what he most dreaded. He particularly hated the thought of telling Miles Lessingham. While we walked along the beach with Timmy half asleep bumping on my back he felt free to talk and I think he found it a release. He told me that Lessingham was in love with him. He wasn't gay himself but he was ambivalent. But he did tremendously admire Lessingham and felt that in some way he was letting him down. He gave the impression that everything was a muddle, his feelings about atomic power, his personal life, his career, everything.'

Suddenly Pascoe seemed to realize that he was holding his coffee mug and, lowering his head, began to drink from it with great slurps, like a man desperate with thirst. When the cup was drained he put it down on the floor and wiped his mouth with his hand.

He said: 'It was a warm night after a rainy day, the night of the new moon. Funny how I remember that. We were walking just above the tide mark on the shingle. And then, suddenly, there she was, Hilary Robarts, splashing out of the foam. She was only wearing the bottom half of her bikini and she stood there for a moment with the water running off her hair, glistening in that eerie light which seems to come off the sea on a starry night. Then she came slowly up the beach towards us. I suppose we stood there almost as if mesmerized. She had lit a small fire of brushwood on the shingle and the three of us moved towards it. She picked up her towel but didn't wrap it round her. She looked – well, she looked marvellous, the drops of water glistening on her skin and that locket thing she wears resting between her breasts. I know it sounds ridiculous and, well, corny, but she looked like some goddess risen from the sea. She took absolutely no notice of me but she looked at Toby. She said: "Nice to see you, Toby. Why not come down to the cottage for a drink and a meal?" Such ordinary words. Harmless sounding words. But they weren't.

'I don't think he could resist her. I don't suppose I would have been able to either. Not at that moment. And I knew exactly what she was doing, and so did she. She was asking him to make a choice. On my side nothing but trouble, a lost job, personal anguish, possibly even disgrace. And on hers security, professional success, the respect of peers, colleagues. And love. I think she was offering him love. I knew what would happen in the cottage if he went with her and he knew too. But he went. He didn't even say goodnight to me. She slung her towel over her shoulder and turned her back on us as if absolutely confident that he would follow her. And he did follow her. And two days later, on Friday the twelfth of August, he killed himself. I don't know what she said to him. No one will know now. But after that meeting I think he just couldn't take any more. It was not what she threatened him with, or even if she threatened him at all. But if it hadn't been for that meeting on the beach I think he'd be alive now. She killed him.'

Dalgliesh said: 'None of this came out at the inquest?'

'No, none. There was no reason why it should. I wasn't called as a witness. It was all handled very discreetly. Alex Mair was anxious that there shouldn't be any publicity. As you've probably noticed, there hardly ever is when something goes wrong at an atomic power station. They all become experts at the cover-up.'

'And why are you telling me this?'

'I want to be sure that this is something Rickards needs to be told. But I suppose I'm really telling you because I need to share it with someone. I'm not sure why I picked on you. Sorry.'

A true, if hardly kind, reply would have been: 'You picked on me in the hope that I'd undertake to pass it on to Rickards and save you the responsibility.' Instead Dalgliesh said: 'You realize, of course, that this is information Chief Inspector Rickards should have.'

'But is it? That's what I want to be sure of. I suppose it's the usual fear when dealing with the police. What use are they going to make of it? Are they going to get the wrong idea? Could it point to someone who could be innocent? I suppose you have to have confidence in the integrity of the police, you wouldn't go on being a detective if you hadn't. But the rest of us know that things can go wrong, that the innocent can be harried, the guilty get off, that the police aren't always as scrupulous as they pretend to be. I'm not asking you to tell him for me, I'm not that childish. But I don't really see how it's relevant. Both of them are dead. I can't see how telling Rickards about that meeting can help to catch Miss Robarts's killer. And it can't bring either of them back to life.'

Dalgliesh refilled Pascoe's mug. Then he said: 'Of course it's relevant. You're suggesting that Hilary Robarts might have black-mailed Gledhill into staying in his job. If she could do it to one person she could do it to another. Anything about Miss Robarts could be relevant to her death. And don't worry too much about innocent suspects. I'm not going to pretend that the innocent don't suffer in a murder investigation. Of course they do. No one even remotely touched by murder goes unscathed. But Chief Inspector Rickards isn't a fool and he's an honest man. He's only going to use what is relevant to his inquiry and it's for him to decide what is relevant and what isn't.'

'I suppose that's the reassurance I wanted to hear. All right, I'll tell him.'

He finished his coffee very quickly as if anxious to be gone and, with only a final word of goodbye, mounted his bicycle and pedalled furiously down the path, bending himself against the wind. Dalgliesh took the two mugs back into the kitchen thoughtfully. That verbal picture of Hilary Robarts rising like a glistening goddess from the waves had been remarkably vivid. But one detail had been wrong. Pascoe had spoken of the key locket resting between her breasts. He remembered Mair's words as he stood looking down at the body. 'That locket round her neck. I gave it to her on August the twenty-ninth for her birthday.' On Wednesday 10 August Hilary Robarts couldn't have been wearing it. Pascoe had undoubtedly seen Hilary Robarts walking out of the sea with the locket resting between her naked breasts; but it couldn't have been on 10 August.

BOOK SIX

Saturday 1 October to Thursday 6 October

42

Jonathan had decided to wait until Saturday to visit London and continue his inquiries. His mother was less likely to question him about a trip on Saturday to visit the Science Museum, while taking a day's leave always provoked inquiries about where he was going and why. But he thought it prudent to spend half an hour in the museum before setting off to Pont Street and it was after three o'clock before he was outside the block of flats. One fact was immediately apparent: no one who lived in this building and employed a house-keeper could possibly be poor. The house was part of an imposing Victorian terrace, half stone, half brick, with pillars each side of the gleaming black door and ornate glass, like green bottle tops, in the two ground-floor windows. The door was open and he could see a square hall tiled with black and white marble, the lower balustrade of an ornate wrought-iron staircase, and the door of a golden cage lift. To the right was a porter's desk with a uniformed man on duty. Anxious not to be seen loitering he walked quickly on considering his next move.

In one sense none was necessary except to find his way to the nearest tube station, return to Liverpool Street and take the first train to Norwich. He had done what he had set out to do; he knew now that Caroline had lied to him. He told himself that he should be feeling shocked and distressed, both at her lie and at his own duplicity in discovering it. He had thought himself in love with her. He was in love with her. For the past year there had been hardly an hour in which she had been absent from his thoughts. That blonde, remote, self-contained beauty had obsessed him. Like a schoolboy he had waited at the corners of corridors where she might pass, had welcomed his bed because he could lie undisturbed and indulge his secret erotic fantasies, would wake wondering where and how they might next meet. Surely neither the physical act of possession nor the discovery of deceit could destroy love. So why was this confirmation of her deception almost agreeable, even pleasant? He should be devastated; instead he was filled with a satisfaction close to triumph. She had lied, almost carelessly, confident that he was too much in love, too enthralled, too stupid even to question her story. But now, with the discovery of the truth, the balance of power in their relationship had subtly shifted. He wasn't sure yet what use he would make of the information. He had found the energy and courage to act but whether he would have the courage to confront her with his knowledge was another matter.

He walked quickly to the end of Pont Street, his eyes on the paving stones, then turned and retraced his steps trying to make sense of his turbulent emotions, so tangled that they seemed to jostle each other for dominance: relief, regret, disgust, triumph. And it had been so easy. Every dreaded obstacle from contacting the detective agency to finding an excuse for this day in London had been surmounted with greater ease than he could believe possible. So why not chance one further step? Why not make absolutely sure? He knew the name of the housekeeper, Miss Beasley. He could ask to see her, say that he had met Caroline a year or two ago, in Paris perhaps, had lost her address, wanted to get in touch. If he kept his story simple, resisted the temptation to embroider, there was no possible danger. He knew that Caroline had taken her summer holiday in France in 1986, the year, he too, had been there. It was one of the facts that had come up in conversation on their early dates together, innocuous chat about travel and paintings, the attempt to find some common ground, a shared interest. Well, at least he had been in Paris. He had seen the Louvre. He could say that that was where they had met.

He would need a false name, of course. His father's Christian name would do. Percival. Charles Percival. It was better to choose something slightly unusual; a too common name would sound obviously false. He would say that he lived in Nottingham. He had been at the university there and knew the town. Somehow being able to picture those familiar streets made the fantasy believable. He needed to root his lies in a semblance of truth. He could say that he worked at the hospital there, a laboratory technician. If there were any other questions he could parry them. But why should there be any other questions?

He made himself walk with confidence into the hall. Only a day ago he would have found difficulty in meeting the porter's eyes. Now, filled with the self-assurance of success, he said: 'I want to visit Miss Beasley in flat three. Would you say that I'm a friend of Miss Caroline Amphlett.'

The porter left the reception desk and went into his office to

322

telephone. Jonathan thought, What's to prevent me just going up the stairs and knocking at the door? Then he realized that the porter would immediately telephone Miss Beasley and warn her not to let him in. There was security of a kind, but it wasn't particularly tight.

Within half a minute the man was back. He said: 'That's all right, sir. You can go up. It's on the first floor.'

He didn't bother to take the lift. The double mahogany door with its numeral of polished brass, its two security locks and central spyhole was at the front of the house. He smoothed back his hair then rang the bell and made himself stare at the peephole with an assumption of ease. He could hear nothing from inside the flat and the heavy door seemed as he waited to grow into an intimidating barricade which only a presumptuous fool would attempt to breach. For a second, picturing that single eyeball scrutinizing him through the peephole, he had to fight an impulse to flee. But then there was the faint clink of a chain, the sound of a lock turning, and the door was opened.

Since his decision to call at the flat he had been too preoccupied with fabricating his story to give much conscious thought to Miss Beasley. The word housekeeper had conjured up a soberly dressed, middle-aged woman, at worst a little condescending and intimidating, at best deferential, chatty, eager to help. The reality was so bizarre that he gave a perceptible start of surprise, then blushed at his own betrayal. She was short and very thin with straight red-gold hair, white at the roots and obviously dyed, falling in a gleaming helmet to her shoulders. Her pale green eyes were immense and shallowly set, the lower lids inverted and bloodshot so that the eyeballs seemed to be swimming in an open wound. Her skin was very white and creped with innumerable small lines except over the jutting cheekbones where it was stretched as fine as paper. In contrast to the skin's unpainted fragility her mouth was a thin gash of garish crimson. She was wearing high-heeled slippers and a kimono and was carrying a small, almost hairless dog with bulging eyes, its thin neck encircled with a jewelled collar. For a few seconds she stood silently regarding him, the dog pressed against her cheek.

Jonathan, his carefully husbanded confidence rapidly draining, said: 'I'm sorry to trouble you. It's just that I'm a friend of Miss Caroline Amphlett and I'm trying to trace her.'

'Well, you won't find her here.' The voice, which he recognized, was unexpected from so frail a woman, deep and husky, and not unattractive.

He said, 'I'm sorry if I've got the wrong Amphlett. You see, Caroline did give me her address two years ago but I've lost it, so I tried the telephone directory.'

'I didn't say that you'd got the wrong Amphlett, only that you won't find her here. But as you look harmless enough and are obviously unarmed you had better come in. One cannot be too careful in these violent times, but Baggott is very reliable. Very few impostors get past Baggott. Are you an impostor, Mr . . . ?'

'Percival. Charles Percival.'

'You must excuse my déshabillé, Mr Percival, but I do not normally expect afternoon visitors.'

He followed her across a square hall and through double doors into what was obviously the drawing room. She pointed imperiously to a sofa set in front of the fireplace. It was uncomfortably low and as soft-cushioned as a bed, each drop end festooned with thick tas-selled cords. Moving slowly as if deliberately taking her time, she placed herself opposite to him in an elegant high-winged chair, settled the dog on her lap and gazed down on him with the fixed unsmiling intensity of an inquisitor. He knew that he must look as gauche and ungainly as he felt, his thighs enclosed in the softness of the cushion, his sharp knees almost touching his chin. The dog, as naked as if it had been skinned and shivering perpetually like a creature demented with cold, turned first on him and then up at her its pleading exophthalmic eyes. The leather collar, with its great dollops of red and blue stones, lay heavily on the animal's frail neck.

Jonathan resisted the temptation to look round at the room but it seemed that every feature had entered his consciousness; the marble fireplace with above it a full-length oil painting of a Victorian army officer, a pale arrogant face with one lock of blond hair falling almost to the cheek, which bore an uncanny resemblance to Caroline; the four carved chairs with embroidered seats set against the wall; the pale, polished floor with its wrinkled carpets; the drum-shaped table in the centre of the room and the side tables with their photographs in silver frames. There was a strong smell of paint and turpentine. Somewhere in the flat a room was being decorated.

After a moment's silent scrutiny the woman spoke. 'So you're a friend of Caroline's. You surprise me, Mr . . . Mr . . . I'm afraid I have already forgotten your name.'

He said firmly: 'Percival. Charles Percival.'

'Mine is Miss Oriole Beasley. I am the housekeeper here. As I said, you surprise me, Mr Percival. But if you say you are Caroline's friend, naturally I accept your word.'

'Perhaps I shouldn't say friend. I only met her once, in Paris in 1986. We went round the Louvre together. But I would like to see her again. She did give me her address, but I lost it.'

'How careless. So you waited two years and then decided to trace her. Why now, Mr Percival? You have managed, apparently, to control your impatience for two years.'

He knew how he must look and sound to her; unconfident, shy, ill at ease. But that, surely, was what she would expect from a man gauche enough to believe that he could revive a dead and fleeting passion. He said: 'It's just that I'm in London for a few days. I work in Nottingham. I'm a technician at the hospital there. I don't often get the chance to come south. It was an impulse really, trying to trace Caroline.'

'As you see, she's not here. She has not, in fact, lived in this house since she was seventeen, and as I am only the housekeeper it is hardly my place to hand out information about the family's where-abouts to casual inquirers. Would you describe yourself as a casual inquirer, Mr Percival?'

Jonathan said: 'Perhaps it seems like that. It's just that I found the name in the telephone directory and thought it was worth a try. Of course she might not want to see me again.'

'I should imagine that is more than likely. And, of course, you have some identification, something to confirm that you are Mr Charles Percival of Nottingham.'

Jonathan said: 'Not really, I'm afraid. I didn't think . . .'

'Not even a credit card or a driving licence? You seem to have come singularly unprepared, Mr Percival.'

Something in the deep, arrogantly upper-class voice, the mixture of insolence and contempt, stung him into defiance. He said: 'I'm not from the gas board. I don't see why I need to identify myself. It was just a simple inquiry. I was hoping to see her, or perhaps Mrs Amphlett. I'm sorry if I've offended you.'

'You haven't offended me. If I were easily offended I wouldn't work for Mrs Amphlett. But I'm afraid you can't see her. Mrs Amphlett goes to Italy in late September and then flies to Spain for the winter. I'm surprised Caroline didn't tell you. In her absence I look after the flat. Mrs Amphlett dislikes the melancholy of autumn and the cold of winter. A wealthy woman need suffer neither. I'm sure you are perfectly well aware of that, Mr Percival.'

And here, at last, was the opening he needed. He made himself look into those terrible bleeding eyes and said: 'I thought Caroline told me that her mother was poor, that she'd lost all her money investing in Peter Robarts's plastics company.'

The effect of his words was extraordinary. She flushed scarlet, the mottled stain travelling like a rash from her neck to her forehead. It seemed a long time before she could bring herself to speak, but when she did her voice was perfectly under control.

'Either you wilfully misunderstood, Mr Percival, or your memory is as unreliable for financial facts as it is for addresses. Caroline could have told you nothing of the sort. Her mother inherited a fortune from her grandfather when she was twenty-one and has never lost a penny of it. It was my small capital – ten thousand pounds, in case you are interested – which was unwisely invested in the schemes of that plausible rogue. But Caroline would hardly confide that small personal tragedy to a stranger.'

He could think of nothing to say, could find no credible explanation, no excuse. He had the proof he wanted; Caroline had lied. He should have been filled with triumph that his suspicions had been justified, his small enterprise crowned with success. Instead, he was swept with a momentary but overwhelming depression and a conviction which seemed to him as frightening as it was irrational, that the proof of Caroline's perfidy had been bought at a terrible price.

There was a silence in which she continued to regard him, but did not speak. Then she suddenly asked: 'What did you think of Caroline? Obviously she made an impression on you or you wouldn't be wishing to renew the acquaintance. And no doubt she has been in your mind during the last two years.'

'I think – I thought she was very lovely.'

'Yes, isn't she? I'm glad you feel that. I was her nurse, her nanny, if one must use that ridiculous expression. You could say that I brought her up. Does that surprise you? I'm hardly the popular idea of a nanny. Warm lap, aproned bosom, *Winnie the Pooh*, *The Wind in the Willows*, prayers at bedtime, eat up your crusts or your hair won't curl. But I had my methods. Mrs Amphlett accompanied the Brigadier on his overseas postings and we stayed here together, just the two of us. Mrs Amphlett believed that a child should have stability provided she was not required to provide it. Of course, if Caroline had been a son it would have been different. The Amphletts have never valued daughters. Caroline did have a brother but he was killed in a friend's car when he was fifteen. Caroline was with them but survived almost without a scratch. I don't think her parents ever forgave her. They could never look at her without making it plain that the wrong child had been killed.'

Jonathan thought: I don't want to hear this, I don't want to listen. He said: 'She never told me that she had a brother. But she did mention you.'

'Did she indeed? She talked about me to you. Now you do surprise me, Mr Percival. Forgive me, but you are the last person I should have expected her to talk to about me.'

He thought: She knows; not the truth, but she knows that I'm not Charles Percival from Nottingham. And it seemed to him, meeting those extraordinary eyes in which the mixture of suspicion and contempt was unmistakable that she was allied to Caroline in a female conspiracy in which he had from the first been a hapless and despised victim. The knowledge fuelled his anger and gave him strength. But he said nothing.

After a moment, she went on: 'Mrs Amphlett kept me on after Caroline left home, even after the Brigadier passed on. But passed on is hardly an appropriate euphemism for a soldier. Perhaps I should say was called to higher service, recalled to the Colours, promoted to glory. Or is that the Salvation Army? I have a feeling that it's only the Salvation Army who get promoted to glory.'

He said: 'Caroline did tell me that her father was a professional soldier.'

'She has never been a very confiding girl but you seem to have gained her confidence, Mr Percival. So now I call myself a house-keeper rather than a nanny. My employer finds plenty to keep me occupied even when she isn't here. It would never do for Maxie and me to live here on board wages and enjoy ourselves in London, would it, Maxie? No indeed. A little skilled sewing. Private letters to be posted on. Bills to be paid. Her jewels to be taken to be cleaned. The flat to be redecorated. Mrs Amphlett particularly dislikes the smell of paint. And, of course, Maxie has to be exercised daily. He never thrives in kennels, do you, my treasure? I wonder what will happen to me when Maxie is promoted to glory?'

There was nothing he could say to that, nor, apparently, did she expect him to. After a moment's silence, during which she lifted the dog's paw and rubbed it gently against her face, she said: 'Caroline's old friends seem very anxious to get in touch with her all of a sudden. Someone telephoned to ask for her only on Tuesday. Or was it Wednesday? But perhaps that was you, Mr Percival?'

'No,' he said, and was amazed at the ease with which he could lie. 'No, I didn't telephone. I thought it better just to take my chance and call.'

'But you knew who to ask for. You knew my name. You gave it to Baggott.'

But she wasn't going to catch him like that. He said: 'I remembered it. As I said, Caroline did talk about you.'

'It might have been sensible to telephone first. I could have explained that she wasn't here, saved you time. How odd that it didn't occur to you. But that other friend didn't sound like you. Quite a different voice. Scottish, I think. If you will excuse my saying so, Mr Percival, your voice is without either character or distinction.'

Jonathan said: 'If you don't feel you can give me Caroline's address, perhaps I'd better go. I'm sorry if I came at an inconvenient time.'

'Why not write a letter to her, Mr Percival? I can let you have the writing paper. I don't think it would be right to give you her address but you can be confident that I will post on any communication that you care to trust to me.'

'She isn't in London, then?'

'No, she hasn't lived in London for over three years and she hasn't lived here since she was seventeen. But I do know where she is. We keep in touch. Your letter will be safe with me.'

He thought: This is an obvious trap. But she can't make me write. There must be nothing in my handwriting. Caroline would recognize it even if I tried to disguise it. He said: 'I think I'd rather write later when I've more time to think what to say. If I post it to this address then you can send it on.'

'I will do that with pleasure, Mr Percival. And now, I expect, you will want to be on your way. Your visit may have been less productive than you hoped, but I expect you have learned what you came to learn.'

But she didn't move and for a moment he felt himself trapped, immobilized as if the disagreeably soft and yielding cushions held him in a vice. He half expected her to leap up and bar his way to the door, to denounce him as an impostor, to keep him locked in the flat while she telephoned the police or the porter. What then would he do: attempt to seize the keys by force and make his escape, wait for the police and try to bluff his way to freedom? But the momentary panic subsided. She got to her feet and led the way to the door and, without speaking, held it open. She did not close it and he was aware that she was standing there, the dog shivering in her arms, both of them watching him leave. At the head of the stairs he turned to smile a final goodbye. What he then saw made him stand for a second immobile before he almost ran down the stairs and through the hall to the open door. He had never in all his life seen such concentrated hatred on a human face.

43

The whole enterprise had been more of a strain than Jonathan could have believed possible, and by the time he reached Liverpool Street he was very tired. The station was in the process of being rebuilt – improved, as the large displays designed to reassure and encourage proclaimed – and had become a clanging and confusing maze of temporary walkways and direction signs in which it was difficult actually to find the trains. Taking a false turn he found himself in a glossily floored piazza and felt momentarily as disorientated as if he were in a foreign capital. His arrival that morning had been less confusing, but now even the station reinforced his sense of having ventured both physically and emotionally on to alien ground.

Once the journey had started he leaned back, his eyes closed, and tried to make sense of the day and of his conflicting emotions. But instead, and almost immediately, he fell asleep and didn't stir into consciousness until the train was drawing into Norwich station. But the sleep had done him good. He strode towards the castle car park filled with renewed energy and optimism. He knew what he would do; drive at once to the bungalow, and confront Caroline with the evidence and ask her why she had lied. He couldn't go on seeing her and pretend not to know. They were lovers; they should be able to trust each other. If she was worried or frightened he was there to reassure and comfort her. He knew that she couldn't have murdered Hilary. The very thought was profanation. But she wouldn't have lied unless she was frightened. Something was dreadfully wrong. He would persuade her to go to the police, explain why she had lied and persuaded him to lie. They would go together, confess together. He didn't ask himself whether she would want to see him or even whether, late on a Saturday, she would be at home. All he knew was that the matter between them had to be settled now. There was a rightness and inevitability about his decision and he felt, too, a small surge of power. She had thought him a gullible and ineffectual fool. Well, he would show her that she was wrong. From now on there would be a subtle change in their relationship; she would have a more confident, less malleable lover.

330

Forty minutes later he was driving through the darkness across flat, undistinguished country towards the bungalow. Slowing down as it came into sight on his left, he was struck afresh by how remote and unattractive it was and wondered again why, with so many villages closer to Larksoken, with the attractions of Norwich and the coast, she should have rented this forbidding, almost sinister little box of crude red brick. And the very word bungalow seemed to him ridiculous, evoking a picture of suburban ribbon development, of cosy respectability, of old people who could no longer manage stairs. Caroline should live in a tower with a wide view of the sea.

And then he saw her. The silver Golf came out from the drive very fast and accelerated eastward. She was wearing what looked like a woollen cap pulled down over her yellow hair but he knew her immediately. He didn't know whether she had recognized him or the Fiesta, but instinctively he braked and let her get almost out of sight before he followed. And, waiting in the quietness of that flat landscape, he could hear Remus barking hysterically.

He was surprised how easy it was to keep her in sight. Sometimes another car passing him would obscure his view of the silver Golf and occasionally, when she slowed for traffic lights or because they had reached a village, he had quickly to reduce speed in case she realized that he was on her tail. They passed through Lydsett village and she took the right turn across the headland. By now he feared that she must have recognized him, must know that she was being followed, but she went on apparently uncaring. When she had negotiated the gate he waited until she was out of sight over the ridge before following, then stopped, put out the car lights and went a little way on foot. He saw that she was picking someone up; a slim girl with spiked yellow hair, orange at the tips, was briefly illuminated in the headlights. The car turned north along the coast road, inland at the power station, then north again. Forty minutes later their destination was known, the quay at Wells-next-the-Sea.

He parked the Fiesta beside the Golf and followed them, keeping Caroline's blue and white cap in sight. They walked quickly, apparently unspeaking and neither of them looked back. At the quay he momentarily lost them and then he saw that they were getting on a boat. And now was his chance; he had to speak to Caroline. He almost ran towards them. They were already on board. It was a small craft, no more than fifteen feet long with a low central cabin and an outboard motor. Both girls were standing in the cockpit. As he came up Caroline turned to him. 'What the hell do you think you're doing?'

'I want to talk to you. I've been following you since you left the bungalow.'

'I know that, you fool. You've been in my mirror practically the whole way. If I'd wanted to throw you off it wouldn't have been difficult. You should give up this cloak-and-dagger business. It doesn't suit you and you're no good at it.'

But there was no anger in her voice, only a kind of irritated weariness. He said: 'Caroline, I have to talk to you.'

'Then wait until tomorrow. Or stay where you are if you must. We'll be back in an hour.'

'But where are you going? What are you doing?'

'For Christ's sake, what do you think I'm doing? This is a boat, my boat. Out there is the sea. Amy and I are planning a short trip.'

Amy, he thought, Amy who? But Caroline didn't introduce her. He said weakly: 'But it's so late. It's dark and it's getting misty.'

'So it's dark and misty. This is October. Look, Jonathan, why don't you mind your own business and get off home to mother.'

She was busying herself in the cockpit. He leaned over and clutched the side of the boat, feeling the gentle rock of the tide. He said: 'Caroline, please talk to me! Don't go. I love you.'

'I doubt it.'

Both of them seemed to have forgotten Amy. He said desperately: 'I know that you lied about your mother being ruined by Hilary's father. That wasn't true, any of it. Look, if you're in trouble I want to help. We've got to talk. I can't go on like this.'

'I'm not in trouble, and if I were you'd be the last person I'd turn to. And take your hands off my boat.'

He said, as if it were the most important thing between them: 'Your boat? You never told me you had a boat.'

'There are a great many things that I didn't tell you.'

And then, suddenly, he knew. There was no longer room for doubt. 'So it wasn't real was it, any of it? You don't love me, you never did love me.'

'Love, love, love. Stop bleating the word, Jonathan. Look, go home. Stand in front of your glass and take a good long look at yourself. How could you ever have supposed that it was real? This is real, Amy and me. She is why I stay at Larksoken and I am why she stays. Now you know.'

'You used me.'

He knew that he sounded like a querulous child.

'Yes, I used you. We used each other. When we went to bed I was using you and you were using me. That's what sex is. And, if you want to know, it was bloody hard work and it made me sick.'

Even in the throes of his misery and humiliation he could sense an urgency in her that had nothing to do with him. The cruelty was deliberate but it had no passion in it. It would have been more bearable if it had. His presence was merely an irritating but minor intrusion into more important preoccupations. Now the end of the rope had whipped clear of the bollard. She had started the engine and the boat was edging away from the quay. And for the first time he really noticed the other girl. She hadn't spoken since he arrived. She stood silently beside Caroline in the cockpit, unsmiling, shivering slightly, and somehow vulnerable, and he thought he saw on her childish face a look of puzzled compassion before his tears began to sting and the boat and its occupants became an amorphous blur. He waited until they were almost out of sight moving on the dark water, and then he made another decision. He would find a pub, have a beer and some food and be there when they returned. They couldn't be away long or they would miss the tide. And he had to know the truth. He couldn't spend another night in this uncertainty. He stood on the quay staring out to sea as if the little boat with its two occupants was still in sight, then turned away and dragged his feet towards the nearest pub.

44

The throb of the engine, unnaturally loud, shook the quiet air. Amy half expected doors to open, people to come running down to the quay, to hear protesting voices calling after them. Caroline made a movement and the noise died in a gentle murmur. The boat gently moved away from the quay. Amy said angrily: 'Who is he? Who is that creep?'

'Just a man from Larksoken. His name's Jonathan Reeves. He's unimportant.'

'Why did you tell him lies? Why did you tell him lies about us? We're not lovers.'

'Because it was necessary. What does it matter anyway? It isn't important.'

'It's important to me. Look at me, Caroline. I'm talking to you.'

But still Caroline didn't meet her eyes. She said calmly: 'Wait until we get clear of the harbour. There's something I have to tell you, but I want to get into deep water and I need to concentrate. Get up to the prow and keep a lookout.'

Amy stood for a moment irresolute, and then she obeyed, working her way carefully along the narrow deck, clutching the rim of the low cabin roof. She wasn't sure she liked the hold that Caroline apparently had over her. It was nothing to do with the money, which was paid irregularly and anonymously into her post office account or left hidden in the abbey ruins. It wasn't even the excitement and the secret sense of power which she gained from being part of a conspiracy. Perhaps after that first meeting in the pub at Islington which had led to her recruitment to Operation Birdcall she had subconsciously made a decision to give her loyalty and obedience and, now that the test had come, she was unable to shake off that unspoken allegiance.

Looking back she could see that the lights in the harbour were growing fainter, the windows becoming little squares of light and then pinpricks. The engine stuttered into greater life and, standing on the prow, she could feel the great power of the North Sea beneath her, the hiss of the parting water, see the unbroken waves smooth and black as oil emerging out of the mist, could feel the boat lifting, shuddering, and then settling. After ten minutes of watching she left her post and made her way back to the cockpit. She said: 'Look, we're well away from land now. What's going on? Did you have to tell him that? I know I'm supposed to keep away from people at Larksoken, but I'll find him, and I'll tell him the truth.'

Caroline was still standing motionless at the tiller, looking straight ahead. In her left hand she held a compass. She said: 'We won't be going back. That's what I have to tell you.'

Before Amy could even open her mouth she said: 'Look, don't start getting hysterical and don't argue. You're entitled to an explanation and if you keep quiet you'll get it. I've no option now; you have to know the truth, or some of the truth.'

'What truth? What are you talking about? And why aren't we going back? You said we'd only be gone about an hour. You said we were going out to meet some comrades offshore and get some new instructions. I left a note for Neil saying I wouldn't be long. I've got to get back to Timmy.'

But still Caroline didn't look at her. She said: 'We're not going back because we can't. When I recruited you from that London squat I didn't tell you the truth. It wasn't in your interest and I didn't know how far I could trust you. And I didn't know the whole truth myself, only as much as I needed to know. That's the way the operation works. Operation Birdcall is nothing to do with taking over Larksoken in the cause of animal rights. It's nothing to do with animals. It's nothing to do with threatened whales and sick seals and tormented laboratory animals and abandoned dogs and all the other spurious miseries you agonize about. It's to do with something far more important. It's to do with human beings and their future. It's to do with the way we organize our world.'

She was speaking very low and with an extraordinary intensity. Amy said above the noise of the engine: 'I can't hear you! I can't hear you properly. Turn off that engine!'

'Not yet. We've still a long way to go. We're meeting them at a precise spot. We have to sail south-east then take a bearing on the power station offshore structures and the Happisburgh light: I hope this mist doesn't thicken.'

'Who? Who are we meeting?'

'I don't know their names and I don't know their place in the organization. As I said, we are all of us told only as much as we actually need to know. My instructions were that if Operation Birdcall was blown I was to ring a number and activate the emergency procedure for getting me out. That's why I bought this boat and made sure it was always ready. I was told precisely where they'll pick us up. Then they'll get us into Germany, provide false papers, a new identity, incorporate us into the organization, find us a job.'

'Not for me they bloody well won't!' Amy looked at Caroline with horror. 'They're terrorists, aren't they? And you're one too. You're a bloody terrorist!'

Caroline said calmly: 'And what else are the agents of capitalism? What are the armies, the police, the courts? What are the industrialists, the multinational corporations who hold down three-quarters of the world's population and keep them poor and hungry? Don't use words you don't understand.'

'I understand that word. And don't you patronize me. You crazy or something? What were you planning, for Christ's sakes, to sabotage the reactor, release all that radioactivity, worse than Chernobyl, kill everyone on the headland, Timmy and Neil, Smudge and Whisky?'

'We wouldn't need to sabotage the reactors or release any radioactivity. The threat would be sufficient once we'd taken over the power stations.'

'The stations? How many? Where?'

'One here, one in France, one in Germany. The action would be co-ordinated and it would be sufficient. It's not what we could do when we had taken them over, it's what people would think we could do. War is out of date and unnecessary. We don't need armies. All we need are a few trained, intelligent and dedicated comrades with the necessary skills. What you call terrorism can change the world, and it's more cost-effective in human life than the militaristic industry of death which my father made his career. They've only one thing in common. A soldier, in the end, has to be prepared to die for this cause. Well, so are we.'

Amy cried: 'It can't happen! Governments won't let it happen!'

'It is happening and they can't stop it. They aren't united enough and they haven't the will. This is just the beginning.'

Amy looked at her. She said: 'Stop this boat. I'm getting off.'

'And swim ashore? You'd either drown or freeze to death. And in this mist.'

Amy hadn't noticed the thickening mist. One moment it seemed to her that she could see the distant lights of the shore, like stars, almost she could see the blackness of the slopping waves, could peer ahead. But now, slowly and inexorably, there was a clammy wetness. She cried: 'Oh God, take me back. You've got to get me off. Get me off. I want Timmy. I want Neil.'

'I can't do that, Amy. Look, if you don't want to be part of all this just say so when the boat arrives. They'll put you ashore somewhere. It won't be on this coast necessarily, but somewhere. We don't want reluctant recruits. There would be enough trouble as it is fitting you up with a new identity. But if you didn't want to be part of it, didn't want to be committed, why did you kill Hilary Robarts? D'you think we wanted a murder investigation centred on Larksoken, police attention, Rickards actually on the site, every suspect's past scrutinized, nothing left private? And if Rickards had arrested you, how sure could I be that you wouldn't crack, tell him about Operation Birdcall, turn Queen's evidence?'

Amy cried: 'Are you crazy? I'm on this boat with a bloody crazy woman. I didn't kill her.'

'Then who did? Pascoe? That's almost as dangerous.'

'How could he? He was on his way back from Norwich. We lied to Rickards about the time but he was back at the caravan by nine fifteen and we were there together all the evening with Timmy. And all that business about the Whistler cutting her forehead, the hair, we never knew any of that. I thought you killed her.'

'Why should I?'

'Because she discovered Operation Birdcall. Isn't that why you're running, because you've got no option?'

'You're right that I've got no option. But it's not because of Robarts. She didn't find out. How could she? But someone did. It isn't only the Hilary Robarts murder. They've started checking up on me, the security services. Somehow they've got a lead, probably from one of the German cells or from a mole in the IRA.'

'How do you know? You could be running away for nothing.'

'There are too many coincidences. That last postcard you hid in the abbey ruins. I told you it was put back the wrong way. Someone had read it.'

'Anyone could have found it. And the message wouldn't have meant anything. It never meant anything to me.'

'Found it in late September when the picnic season's well over? Found it and carefully put it back? And that wasn't all. They've checked on my mother's flat. She has a housekeeper who used to be my nanny. She rang to let me know earlier today. I didn't wait after that. I sent the signal to say I was getting out.'

On their starboard side the occasional lights of the shore were blurred by the mist but still visible. And the throb of the engine sounded less intrusive now, almost a gentle companionable hum. Or perhaps, thought Amy, she had got used to it. But it seemed extraordinary to be moving so quietly and steadily through the darkness, hearing Caroline's voice saying unbelievable things, talking about terrorism and flight and betrayal as calmly as if she were discussing the details of a picnic. And Amy needed to hear, needed to know. She found herself saying: 'Where did you meet them, these people you're working for?'

'In Germany when I was seventeen. My nanny was ill and I had to spend the summer holiday with my parents. My father was stationed there. He didn't take much notice of me, but someone else did.'

'But that was years ago.'

'They know how to wait and so do I.'

'And this nanny-housekeeper, is she a member of Birdcall too?'

'She knows nothing, absolutely nothing. She's the last person I'd choose. She's a silly old fool who's hardly worth her bed and board, but my mother finds a use for her, and so do I. She hates my mother, and I've told her that Mummy is checking on my life and to let me know at once if there are any telephone calls for me or any visitors. It helps make her life with Mummy tolerable. It makes her feel important, helps her to believe that I care about her, that I love her.'

'Do you? Do you love her?'

'I did once. A child has to love someone. I grew out of it and I grew out of her. Well, there was a call and there was a visitor. On Tuesday a Scot, or someone pretending to be a Scot rang. And today a visitor came.'

'What sort of visitor?'

'A young man who said he'd met me in France. It was a lie. He was an impostor. He was from MI5. Who else could have sent him?'

'But you can't be sure. Not sure enough to send that signal, leave everything, put yourself in their mercy.'

'I can. Look, who else could it have been? There were three separate incidents, the postcard, the telephone call, the visitor. What else should I wait for? The security services kicking down my door?'

'What was he like, this man?'

'Young. Nervous. Not very attractive. Not particularly convincing either. Even Nanny didn't believe him.'

'Funny kind of MI5 officer. Couldn't they do better than that?'

'He was supposed to be someone I'd met in France who fancied me and wanted to see me again and had steeled himself actually to call at the flat. Of course he appeared young and nervous. That's the kind of man they'd send. They'd hardly choose a seasoned forty-year-old veteran from Curzon Street. They know how to select the right man for the job. That's their business. He was the right man, all right. Perhaps he wasn't even meant to be convincing. Perhaps they were trying to scare me, get me to react, flush me out.'

'Well, you have reacted, haven't you? But if you're wrong, wrong about it all, what will they do, the people you work for? You've blown Operation Birdcall by running away.'

'This operation has been aborted but the future won't be jeopardized. My instructions were to telephone if there was firm evidence that we'd been discovered. And there was. And that's not all. My telephone is being bugged.'

'You can't possibly tell that.'

'I can't tell it for certain, but I know.'

Suddenly Amy cried: 'What did you do about Remus? Did you feed him, leave him water?'

'Of course not. This has to look like an accident. They've got to believe that we're lesbian lovers who went for an evening boat trip and were drowned. They've got to believe that we only intended to be away for a couple of hours. He gets fed at seven. They've got to find him hungry and thirsty.'

'But they might not start looking for you until Monday! He'll be frantic, barking and whining. There's no one close to hear. You bloody bitch!'

Suddenly she flew at Caroline, screaming obscenities, clawing at her face. But the girl was too strong for her. Hands gripped her wrists like steel bands and she found herself hurled back against the boards. Through the tears of rage and self-pity she whispered: 'But why? Why?'

'For a cause worth dying for. There aren't many of those.'

'Nothing's worth dying for, except maybe another person, someone you love. I'd die for Timmy.'

'That's not a cause, that's sentimentality.'

'And if I want to die for a cause I'll bloody well choose it myself. And it won't be for terrorism. It won't be for bastards who put bombs in pubs and blow up my friends and don't give a damn about ordinary people, because we're not important, are we?'

Caroline said: 'You must have suspected something. You're not educated but you're not stupid, either. I wouldn't have chosen you if I couldn't be sure of that. You never questioned me and you wouldn't have got an answer if you had, but you couldn't have thought that we were going to all that trouble for frightened kittens or butchered seal pups.'

Had she thought that? Amy wondered. Perhaps the truth was that she had believed in the intention but never that it would actually be carried out. She hadn't doubted their will, only their ability. And in the meantime it had been fun to be part of the conspiracy. She had enjoyed the excitement, the knowledge that she had a secret from Neil, the half-simulated *frisson* of fear as she left the caravan after dark to plant the postcards in the ruins of the abbey. She had hidden behind a broken breakwater almost laughing aloud that night when she had nearly been caught by Mrs Dennison and Mr Dalgliesh. And the money had been useful, too; generous payment for so small a task. And there had been the dream, the picture of a flag whose design was as yet unknown, but which they would raise over the power station and which would command respect, obedience, instant response. They would be saying to the whole world, 'Stop it. Stop it now.' They would be speaking for the captive zoo animals, the threatened whales, the polluted, sick seals, the tormented laboratory animals, the terrified beasts driven into the abattoirs to the smell of blood and their own death, the hens crowded together, unable even to peck, for the whole of the abused and exploited animal world. But it had been only a dream. This was reality; the insubstantial boards under her feet, the dark suffocating mist, the oily waves slapping against their frail craft. The reality was death, there was no other. Everything in her life, from the moment she had met Caroline in that Islington pub and they had walked back to the squat together, had led to this moment of truth, this terror.

She moaned: 'I want Timmy. What about my baby? I want my baby.'

'You won't have to leave him, not permanently. They'll find a way of reuniting you.'

'Don't be daft. What sort of life would he have with a terrorist gang? They'll write him off like they write off everyone else.'

Caroline said: 'What about your parents? Won't they take him? Can't they look after him?'

'Are you crazy? I ran away from home because my stepfather knocked Ma about. When he started on me I walked out. Do you think I'd let him have Timmy, him or her?'

Her mother had seemed to like the violence, or at least had liked what came after it. Those two years before she ran away had taught Amy one lesson; have sex only with men who want you more than you want them.

Caroline asked: 'What about Pascoe? Are you sure he knows nothing?'

'Of course he doesn't. We weren't even lovers. He didn't want me and I didn't want him.'

But there was someone she had wanted, and she had a sudden vivid memory of lying with Alex in the dunes, the smell of sea and sand and sweat, his grave ironic face. Well, she wasn't going to tell Caroline about Alex. She had one secret of her own. She would keep it.

She thought of the curious paths by which she had come to this moment in time, to this place. Perhaps if she drowned her whole life would flash before her as it was said to do, everything experienced, understood, made sense of in that final annihilating moment. But now she saw the past as a series of coloured slides, clicking in quick succession, an image briefly received, an emotion barely experienced before it disappeared. Suddenly she was shivering violently. She said: 'I'm cold.'

'I said to come with warm clothes and nothing else. That jumper isn't enough.'

'These are the only warm clothes I've got.'

'On the headland? What do you wear in winter?'

'Sometimes Neil lends me his greatcoat. We share. Whichever one of us goes out gets the coat. We were thinking we might get one for me from the Old Rectory jumble.'

Caroline took off her jacket. She said: 'Here, put this round you.'

'No, that's yours. I don't want it.'

'Put it on.'

'I said I don't want it.'

But like a child she let Caroline push her arms into the sleeves, stood obediently while the jacket was fastened. Then she crouched down, almost wedging herself under the narrow seat which ran round the boat, shutting out the horror of those silently advancing waves. It seemed to Amy that she felt for the first time and with every nerve the inexorable power of the sea. She saw in imagination her pale and lifeless body plummeting through the miles of wet darkness to the sea bed, to the skeletons of long-drowned sailors where the uncaring creatures swam between the ribs of ancient ships. And the mist, less thick now but mysteriously more frightening, had become a living thing, gently swirling and soundlessly breathing, stealing her own breath so that she found herself panting, insinuating its damp horror into every pore. It seemed impossible to believe that somewhere there was land, lighted windows behind the drawn curtains, light spilling from the doors of pubs, laughing voices, people sitting in warmth and safety. She saw the caravan as she had seen it so often, returning from Norwich after dark, a sturdy rectangle of wood which seemed rooted to the headland defying the gales and the sea, the warm glow from its windows, the twist of smoke rising from the stack. She thought of Timmy and Neil. How long would Neil wait until he called the police? He wasn't one to act in a hurry. After all, she wasn't a child, she had a right to leave. He might do nothing until morning, and perhaps even then he would wait. But it wouldn't matter. There was nothing the police could do. No one except that desolate figure on the quay knew where they were and if he raised the alarm it would be too late. It was useless to believe even in the reality of the terrorists. They were marooned here in black dampness. They would circle and circle until the fuel ran out and then drift out to sea until a coaster ran them down.

She no longer had any sense of passing time. The rhythmic throbbing of the engine had lulled her, not into peace but into a dulled acquiescence in which she was aware only of the wood hard against her back, of Caroline standing intent and motionless in the cockpit.

The engine died. For a few seconds the silence was absolute. Then, as the boat gently lurched, Amy heard the creak of wood, the slap of water. She breathed a suffocating wetness, felt its cold seeping through the jacket, into her bones. It seemed impossible that anyone could find them in this bleak expanse of water and emptiness and she had ceased to care whether they did.

Caroline said: 'This is the place. This is where they're going to meet us. We'll just have to circle here until they come.'

Amy heard the engine again, but this time it was an almost imperceptible throb. And suddenly she knew. There was no conscious process of reasoning, only a blinding and terrifying certainty which burst upon her with the clarity of a vision. There was a second in which her heart froze, leapt and its strong drumming powered her body into life. She almost sprang to her feet. 'They're not going to put me ashore, are they? They're going to kill me. You know it. You've known it all along. You've brought me here to be killed.'

Caroline's eyes were fixed on the two lights, the intermittent flash from the lighthouse, the glitter from the offshore structures. She said coldly: 'Don't be hysterical.'

'They can't risk letting me go. I know too much. And you said yourself that I wouldn't be much use to them. Look, you've got to help me. Tell them how useful I was, make believe I'm worth keeping. If I can only get ashore, somehow I'll make a break for it. But I have to have a chance. Caroline, you've got me into this. You must help me. I have to get ashore. Listen to me! Listen to me, Caroline! We've got to talk.'

'You are talking. And what you're saying is ludicrous.'

'Is it? Is it, Caroline?'

She knew now that she mustn't plead. She wanted to throw herself at Caroline's feet and scream: 'Look at me. I'm human. I'm a woman. I want to live. My child needs me. I'm not much of a mother but I'm the only one he has. Help me.' But she knew with an instinctive wisdom born of desperation that abject pleading, clutching hands, sobs, whining entreaties, would only repel. She was speaking for her life. She had to stay calm, to rely on reason. She had somehow to find the right words. She said: 'It isn't only me, it's you too. This could be a choice of life or death for both of us. They won't want you either. You were only useful to them while you worked at Larksoken, while you could pass on to them details of how the place was run, who was on duty and when. Now you're a liability, the same as me. There's no difference. What kind of work can you do for them that will make it worthwhile supporting you, setting you up with a new identity? They can't find you a job in another power station. And if MI5 are really on to you they'll still be looking. They might not believe so easily in the accident, not if our bodies aren't washed up. And our bodies won't be washed up, will they? Not unless they kill us and that's what they're planning to do. What are two more bodies to them? Why meet us here? Why so far? They could have picked us up much closer to land. They could have got us out by air if they'd really needed us. Caroline, go back. It isn't too late. You could tell the people you work for that it wasn't safe to come, the mist was too thick. They'll find another way to get you out if you want to go. I won't talk, I wouldn't dare. I promise you with my life. We can go back now and it will just have been two friends who took a boat trip and came back safely. It's my life, Caroline, and it could be yours. You gave me your jacket. I'm asking for my life.'

She didn't touch Caroline. She knew that the wrong gesture, perhaps any gesture, could be fatal. But she knew, too, that the silent figure staring rigidly ahead was at the moment of decision. And, gazing at that carved intent face, Amy realized for the first time in her life that she was utterly alone. Even her lovers, seen now as a passing procession of strained beseeching faces and grasping exploring hands, had been only casual strangers giving her the fleeting illusion that a life could be shared. And she had never known Caroline, could never know her, never begin to understand what in her past, perhaps in her childhood, had led to this dangerous conspiracy, this moment of decision. They were physically so close that each could hear, could almost smell, the other's breath. But each was alone, as much alone as if this wide sea held no other craft, no other living soul. They might be fated to die together, but each could suffer only her own death as each had lived only her own life. And there was nothing left to say. She had pleaded her cause and the words were all spent. Now she waited in the darkness and the silence to know whether she would live or die.

It seemed to her that even time had stopped. Caroline put out her hand and switched off the engine. In the eerie silence Amy could hear, like a low insistent pounding, the beating of her heart. And then Caroline spoke. Her voice was calm, reflective, as if Amy had posed her a difficult problem which needed thought to solve.

'We have to get away from the meeting place. We haven't enough power to outrun them if they find us and give chase. Our only hope is to put out all the lights, get away from this place and lie silent hoping they won't find us in the mist.'

'Can't we get back to the harbour?'

'There isn't time. It's over ten miles and they'll have a powerful engine. If they find us they'll be on to us in seconds. The mist is our only chance.'

And then they heard, blunted by the fog but clearly, the sound of an approaching boat. Instinctively they moved closer together in the cockpit and waited, not daring even to whisper. Each knew that their only chance now lay in silence, the mist, the hope that their small craft would be undetected. But the engine noise increased and became a regular, directionless, vibrating throb. And then, when they had thought that the boat would loom out of the darkness and be on them, the noise grew no louder and Amy guessed that they were being slowly circled. Then suddenly she screamed. The searchlight cut through the mist and shone full on their faces. The light dazzled so that she could see nothing but its own giant cone in which the particles of mist swam like motes of silver light. A rough, foreign voice called: 'Is that the *Lark* out of Wells harbour?'

There was a moment's silence and then Amy heard Caroline's voice. It was clear and loud but to Amy's ears it signalled a high note of fear. 'No. We're a party of four friends from Yarmouth, but we'll probably put in at Wells. We're all right. No help needed, thank you.'

But the searchlight didn't move. The boat was held as if suspended between sea and sky in a blaze of light. The seconds passed. Nothing more was said. Then the light was switched off and they heard again the sound of the retreating engines. For a minute, still waiting, still frightened to speak, they shared a common desperate hope that the ruse had worked. And then they knew. The light held them again. And now the engines were roaring and the boat came straight at them out of the mist with only time for Caroline to place an icy cheek against Amy's. She said: 'I'm sorry. I'm sorry.'

And then the great hull towered above them. Amy heard the crack as the wood splintered and the boat leapt out of the water. She felt herself hurled through an eternity of wet darkness and then falling endlessly falling, spreadeagled in space and time. Then there was the smack of the sea and a coldness so icy that for a few seconds she felt nothing. She came back to consciousness as she surfaced, gasping and fighting for breath, no more aware of the cold, feeling only the agony of a metal band crushing her chest, terror, and the desperate fight to keep her head above water, to survive. Something hard scraped against her face, then floated free. She thrashed out with flailing arms and fastened on a plank of wood from the boat. It offered at least a chance. She rested her arms on it and felt the blessed release of strain. And now she was capable of rational thought. The plank might support her until morning light and the fog lifted. But she would be dead of cold and exhaustion long before then. Somehow to swim ashore was her only hope, but which way lay the shore? If the mist lifted she would be able to see the lights, perhaps even the light of the caravan. Neil would be there waving to her. But that was silly. The caravan was miles away. Neil would be desperately worried by now. And she had never finished those envelopes. Timmy might be crying for her. She had to get back to Timmy.

But in the end the sea was merciful. The cold that numbed her arms so that she could no longer hold on to the plank numbed also her mind. She was slipping into unconsciousness when the searchlight again found her. She was beyond thought, beyond fear when the boat turned and came driving at full power into her body. And then there was silence and darkness and a single plank of wood gently bobbing where the sea was stained red.

45

It was after eight before Rickards got home on Saturday night but this was still earlier than usual and, for the first time in weeks, he was able to feel that an evening stretched ahead with its choices; a leisurely meal, television, radio, a gentle undemanding catching-up with household chores, telephoning Susie, an early bed. But he was restless. Faced with a few hours of leisure he was uncertain what to do with them. For a moment he wondered whether to go out for a solitary restaurant meal, but the effort of choosing, the expense, even the bother of booking seemed disproportionate to any possible pleasure. He showered and changed as if the steaming water were a ritual cleansing away of his job, of murder and failure, which might give the evening before him some meaning, some pleasure. Then he opened a tin of baked beans, grilled four sausages and a couple of tomatoes and carried his tray into the sitting room to eat while watching television.

At nine twenty he switched off the set and, for a few minutes, sat immobile with the tray still on his lap. He thought that he must look like one of those modern paintings, *Man with a Tray*, a stiff figure immobilized in an ordinary setting made unordinary, even sinister. As he sat, trying to summon the energy even to wash up, the familiar depression settled on him, the sense that he was a stranger in his own house. He had felt more at home in that fire-lit, stone-walled room at Larksoken Mill, drinking Dalgliesh's whisky, than he did here in his own sitting room in his familiar, tightly upholstered chair, eating his own food. And it wasn't only the absence of Susie, the heavily pregnant ghost in the opposite chair. He found himself comparing the two rooms, seeking a clue to his different responses to a deepening dejection of which the sitting room seemed partly a symbol, partly a cause. It wasn't only that the mill had a real wood fire, hissing and spitting real sparks and smelling of autumn, while his was synthetic, nor that Dalgliesh's furniture was old, polished by centuries of use, arranged purely for convenience not for show, not even that the paintings were real oils, genuine watercolours, or that the whole room had been put together with no apparent sense that anything in it was particularly highly regarded for its own sake. Above all, he decided, the difference surely lay in the books, the two walls covered with shelves holding books of every age and description, books for use, for pleasure in the reading and the handling. His own small collection, and Susie's, was in the bedroom. Susie had decreed that the books were too diverse, too tattered to be worthy of a place in what she called the lounge, and there weren't many of them. In recent years he had had so little time for reading; a collection of modern adventure novels in paperback, four volumes of a book club to which, for a couple of years, he had belonged, a few hardback travel books, police manuals, Susie's school prizes for neatness and needlework. But a child should be brought up with books. He had read somewhere that it was the best possible beginning to life, to be surrounded with books, to have parents who encouraged reading. Perhaps they could fit shelves each side of the fireplace and make a start. Dickens: he had enjoyed Dickens at school; Shakespeare, of course, and the major English poets. His daughter – neither he nor Susie doubted that the baby would be a girl – would learn to love poetry.

But all that would have to wait. He could at least make a start with the housework. The room's air of dull pretentiousness was partly due, he realized, to dirt. It looked like an uncleaned hotel room in which no one took pride because no guest was expected and those few who came wouldn't care. He realized now that he should have kept on Mrs Adcock who came in to clean for three hours every Wednesday. But she had only worked for them in the last two months of Susie's pregnancy. He had hardly met her and he disliked the thought of handing over house keys to a comparative stranger, more from his love of privacy than from any lack of trust. So, despite Susie's misgivings, he had paid Mrs Adcock a retainer and had said that he could cope. Now he added his supper things to a load of crockery in the dishwasher and took a duster from those neatly folded in the drawer. Dust lay heavy on every surface. In the sitting room he drew the duster along the window sill and saw with wonder the black line of grimed dirt.

He moved next to the hall. The cyclamen on the table beside the telephone had unaccountably wilted despite his hurried daily watering, perhaps because of it. He was standing, duster in hand, wondering whether to throw it out or whether rescue was possible, when his ears caught the crunch of wheels on the gravel. He opened the door, then flung it wide with such force that it swung back and the latch clicked. Then he was at the taxi door, gently receiving the swollen figure into his arms.

'My darling, oh my darling, why didn't you ring?'

She leaned against him. He saw with compassion the white transparent skin, the smudges under her eyes. He seemed to feel even beneath the thick tweed of her coat the stirring of his child.

'I didn't wait. Mummy had only gone up the road to see Mrs Blenkinsop. I just had time to ring for a taxi and leave her a note. I had to come. You're not cross?'

'Oh, my love, my darling. Are you all right?'

'Only tired.' She laughed. 'Darling, you've let the door close. You'll have to use my key.'

He took her handbag from her, rummaged for the key and her purse, paid the driver who had placed her one case by the door. His hands were shaking so that he could hardly fit the key in the lock. He half lifted her over the threshold and lowered her on to the hall chair.

'Sit there a moment, darling, while I see to the case.'

'Terry, the cyclamen is dead. You've overwatered it.'

'No, I haven't. It died missing you.'

She laughed. The sound was strong, a happy, contented peal. He wanted to lift her up into his arms and shout aloud. Suddenly serious, she said: 'Has Mummy phoned?'

'Not yet, but she will.'

And then, as if on cue, the telephone rang. He snatched it up. This time, awaiting the sound of his mother-in-law's voice he was totally without fear, without anxiety. By that one magnificent, affirming action Susie had placed them both forever beyond her mother's destructive reach. He felt that he had been lifted out of misery as if by a huge wave and set for ever with his feet firmly on a rock. There was a second in which he saw Susie's look of anxiety, so acute that it was a spasm of pain, and then she got clumsily to her feet and leaned against him, slipping her hand into his. But the caller wasn't Mrs Cartwright.

Oliphant said: 'Jonathan Reeves has rung headquarters, sir, and they've put him on to me. He says that Caroline Amphlett and Amy Camm have gone boating together. They've been gone three hours now and the mist is getting thicker.'

'Then why did he ring the police? He should have got on to the coast guard.'

'I've already done that, sir. That wasn't really why he phoned. He and Amphlett didn't spend last Sunday evening together. She was on the headland. He wanted to tell us that Amphlett lied. So did he.'

'I don't suppose they're the only ones. We'll pull them in first thing tomorrow morning and hear their explanations. I've no doubt she'll come up with one.'

Oliphant said stolidly: 'But why should she lie if she's got nothing to hide? And it isn't just the false alibi. Reeves says that their love affair was only pretence, that she only pretended to care for him to cover up her lesbian affair with Camm. I reckon the two women were in it together, sir. Amphlett must have known that Robarts swam at night. All the staff at Larksoken knew that. And she worked closely with Mair, none closer. She's his PA. He could have told her all the details of that dinner party, how the Whistler operated. There'd be no problem in getting hold of the Bumbles. Camm knew about the jumble box even if Amphlett didn't. Her kid had clothes from it.'

Rickards said: 'There'd be no trouble in getting hold of the shoes. There might be trouble in wearing them. Neither woman is tall.'

Oliphant dismissed what he probably felt was a puerile objection. He said: 'But they would have had no time to try them on. Better to grab a pair too large than too small, a soft shoe rather than unyielding leather. And Camm's got a motive, sir. A double motive. She threatened Robarts after her kid was pushed over. We've got Mrs Jago's evidence of their quarrel. And if Camm wanted to stay on in the caravan, close to her lover, it was important to put a stop to Robarts's libel action against Pascoe. And Camm almost certainly knew exactly where Robarts took her nightly swim. If Amphlett didn't tell her, Pascoe probably did. He admitted to us that he used to sneak out occasionally to spy on her. Dirty-minded little devil. And there's another thing. Camm has a dog lead, remember. So has Amphlett, come to that. Reeves said that she was exercising her dog on the headland Sunday night.'

'There were no paw marks at the scene, Sergeant. Don't let's get too excited. She might have been at the scene, but the dog wasn't.'

'Kept in the car, sir. Maybe she didn't have him with her but I reckon she used the lead. There's another thing. Those two wine-glasses in Thyme Cottage. I reckon Caroline Amphlett was with Robarts before she went for that last swim. She's Mair's PA. Robarts would have let her in without question. It all adds up, sir. It's a watertight case, sir.'

Rickards thought that it was as watertight as a sieve. But Oliphant was right. There was a case, even if there wasn't as yet a scintilla of proof. He mustn't let his feelings about the man cloud his judgement. And one fact was depressingly obvious. If he arrested another suspect this theory, for all the lack of firm evidence, would be a gift to any defence counsel.

He said: 'Ingenious, but it's totally circumstantial. Anyway, it can wait until tomorrow. There's nothing we can do tonight.'

'We ought to see Reeves, sir. He may change his story before morning.'

'You see him. And let me know when Camm and Amphlett get back. I'll see you at Hoveton at eight. We'll pull them in then. And I don't want them questioned, either of them, until I see them tomorrow. Is that understood?'

'Yes, sir. Goodnight, sir.'

When he had replaced the receiver, Susie said: 'If you think you ought to go, darling, don't worry about me. I'll be all right now I'm home.'

'It's not urgent. Oliphant can cope. He likes being in charge. Let's make him a happy Jumbo.'

'But I don't want to be a trouble to you, darling. Mummy thought that life would be better for you with me away.'

He turned and took her in his arms. He felt his own tears warm on her face. He said: 'Life is never better for me when you're away.'

46

The bodies were washed up two days later two miles south of Hunstanton, or enough of them to make identification certain. On the Monday morning a retired tax officer, exercising his Dalmatian dog on the beach, saw the animal sniffing round what looked like a white slab of lard entwined with seaweed, rolling and gliding at the edge of the tide. As he drew close the object was sucked back by the receding wave then taken up by the next surge and flung at his feet and he found himself gazing in incredulous horror at the torso of a woman neatly severed at the waist. For a second he stood petrified, staring down as the tide boiled in the empty sockets of the left eye and swayed the flattened breasts. Then he turned away and was violently sick before shambling like a drunkard up the shingle of the beach, dragging the dog by its collar.

The body of Caroline Amphlett, unmutilated, was washed up on the same tide together with planks from the boat and part of the roof of the cabin. They were found by Daft Billy, a harmless and amiable beachcomber, on one of his regular sorties. It was the wood which first caught his eye and he dragged the planks ashore with squeals of glee. Then, his prize secure, he turned his puzzled attention to the drowned girl. It was not the first body he had found in forty years of beachcombing and he knew what he must do, who he must tell. First he placed his hands under the arms and pulled the body out of the reach of the tide. Then, moaning softly, as if mourning his clumsiness, her lack of response, he knelt beside her and, pulling off his jacket, spread it over the torn rags of her shirt and slacks.

'Comfy?' he asked. 'Comfy?'

Then, putting out his hand he carefully moved the strands of hair out of her eyes and, rocking himself gently, began crooning to her as he might to a child.

47

Dalgliesh made three visits on foot to the caravan after lunch on Thursday but on no occasion was Neil Pascoe at home. He was unwilling to telephone to check whether the man had returned. He could think of no valid excuse for wanting to see him and it seemed best to make the visit part of a walk, as if the decision to call at the caravan were merely an impulse. In one sense he supposed it could be a visit of condolence but he had only known Amy Camm by sight and that excuse seemed to him dishonest as well as unconvincing. Shortly after five o'clock, when the light was beginning to fade, he tried again. This time the door of the caravan was wide open but there was no sign of Pascoe. While he stood hesitating a billow of smoke rose from above the edge of the cliff, followed by a brief flash of flame, and the air was suddenly filled with the acrid smell of bonfire.

From the edge of the cliff he looked down on an extraordinary scene. Pascoe had built a fireplace of large stones and chunks of concrete and had lit a fire of brushwood on to which he was emptying papers, box files, cartons, bottles and what looked like an assortment of clothes. The pile awaiting burning was caged down against the strengthening wind by the bars of Timmy's cot; that too, no doubt, destined for the flames. A soiled mattress lay curled to one side like a makeshift and ineffectual windbreak. Pascoe, wearing only a pair of grubby shorts, was working like a demented demon, his eyes white saucers in his blackened face, his arms and naked chest glistening with sweat. As Dalgliesh slithered down the sandy slope of the cliff and moved up to the fire he nodded a brief acknowledgement of his presence, then began dragging a small, scuffed suitcase from under the cot bars with desperate haste. Then he sprang up and balanced himself on the wide rim of the fireplace, his legs wide apart. In the ruddy glow of the flames his whole body gleamed, seeming for a moment transparent as if it were lit from within, and the great dollops of sweat ran from his shoulders like blood. With a shout he swung the case high over the fire and wrenched it open. The baby clothes fell in a brightly coloured shower

353

and the flames leapt like living tongues to snatch at the woollen garments in mid-air, spinning them into briefly burning torches before they fell blackened into the heart of the fire. Pascoe stood for a moment breathing heavily, then sprang down with a cry half exultant, half despairing. Dalgliesh could understand and partly shared his exultation in this tumultuous juxtaposition of wind, fire and water. With each gust the tongues of flame roared and hissed so that he saw through a shimmering haze of heat the veins of the tumbling waves stained as if with blood. As Pascoe emptied into the fire yet another box file of papers the charred fragments rose and danced like frantic birds, blew gently against Dalgliesh's face and settled over the dry stones of the upper shingle like a black contagion. He could feel his eyes prickling with the smoke.

He called out: 'Aren't you polluting the beach?'

Pascoe turned to him and spoke for the first time, shouting above the roar of the fire. 'What does it matter? We're polluting the whole bloody planet.'

Dalgliesh shouted back: 'Shove some shingle on it and leave it until tomorrow. It's too windy for a bonfire this evening.'

He had expected Pascoe to ignore him, but to his surprise the words seemed to recall his companion to reality. The exultation and vigour seemed to drain out of him. He looked at the fire and said dully: 'I suppose you're right.'

There was a spade and a rusty shovel thrown down by the pile of rubbish. Together the two men scooped up a mixture of shingle and sand and flung it on to the flames. When the last red tongue had died with an angry hiss Pascoe turned and began scrunching his way up the beach towards the cliff. Dalgliesh followed. The question he had half feared – Are you here on purpose? Why do you want to see me? – was unspoken and apparently unthought.

In the caravan Pascoe kicked the door shut and slumped down at the table. He said: 'Want a beer? Or there's tea. I'm out of coffee.'

'Nothing, thanks.'

Dalgliesh sat and watched as Pascoe groped his way over to the refrigerator. Returning to the table, he wrenched open the seal, threw back his head and poured the beer down his throat in an almost continuous stream. Then he slumped forward silent, still clutching the tin. Neither spoke and it seemed to Dalgliesh that his companion hardly knew that he was still there. It was dark in the caravan and Pascoe's face across the two feet of wood was an indistinguishable oval in which the whites of the eyes gleamed unnaturally bright. Then he stumbled to his feet, murmuring something about matches, and a few seconds later there was a scrape and hiss and his hands stretched towards the oil lamp on the table. In its strengthening glow his face, beneath the dirt and smudges of smoke, looked drained and haggard, the eyes dulled with pain. The wind was shaking the caravan, not roughly but with a regular gentle sway as if it were being rocked by an unseen hand. The sliding door of the end compartment was open and Dalgliesh could see, on the narrow bed, a pile of female clothes topped with a jumble of tubes, jars and bottles. Apart from this, the caravan looked tidy but denuded, less a home than a temporary, ill-equipped refuge, but holding still the unmistakable milky and faecal smell of a child. The absence of Timmy and his dead mother filled the caravan as it did both their minds.

After minutes of silence Pascoe looked up at him: 'I was burning all my PANUP records out there with the rest of the rubbish. You probably guessed. It was never any use. I was only using PANUP to pander to my own need to feel important. You more or less said so that time I called at the mill.'

'Did I? I hadn't any right to. What will you do now?'

'Go to London and look for a job. The university won't extend my grant for a further year. I don't blame them. I'd prefer to go back to the north-east but I suppose London offers me more hope.'

'What sort of job?'

'Any job. I don't give a damn what I do as long as it makes money for me and is no possible use to anyone else.'

Dalgliesh asked: 'What happened to Timmy?'

'The local authority took him. They got a Place of Safety Order or something of the sort. A couple of social workers came for him yesterday. Decent enough women, but he didn't want to go with them. They had to tear him screaming from my arms. What sort of a society does that to its children?'

Dalgliesh said: 'I don't suppose they had any choice. They have to make long-term plans for his future. After all, he couldn't have stayed here indefinitely with you.'

'Why not? I cared for him for over a year. And at least I would have had something out of all this mess.'

Dalgliesh asked: 'Have they traced Amy's family?'

'They haven't had much time, have they? And when they do I

don't expect they'll tell me. Timmy lived here for over a year but I'm of less account than the grandparents he never saw and who probably don't give a damn about him.'

He was still holding the empty beer can. Twisting it slowly in his hands he said: 'What really gets to me is the deception. I thought she cared. Oh, not about me, but about what I was trying to do. It was all pretence. She was using me, using this place to be near Caroline.'

Dalgliesh said: 'But they can't have seen very much of each other.'

'How do I know? When I wasn't here she probably sneaked out to meet her lover. Timmy must have spent hours alone. She didn't even care for him. The cats were more important than Timmy. Mrs Jago has taken them now. They'll be all right. Sometimes on Sunday afternoons she used to go out blatantly telling me that she was off to meet her lover in the sand dunes. I thought it was a joke, I needed to believe that. And all the time she and Caroline were out there together making love, laughing at me.'

Dalgliesh said: 'You've only got Reeves's evidence to suggest they were lovers. Caroline could have been lying to him.'

'No. No, she wasn't lying. I know that. They used us both, Reeves and me. Amy wasn't – well, she wasn't undersexed. We lived here together for over a year. On the second night she – well, she did offer to come to my bed. But it was just her way of paying for board and lodging. It wouldn't have been right then for either of us. But after a time I suppose I began to hope. I mean, living here together, I suppose I grew fond of her. But she never really wanted me to be near her. And when she came in from those Sunday walks I knew. I pretended to myself that I didn't but I knew. She looked exultant. She was shining with happiness.'

Dalgliesh said: 'Look, is it really so important to you, the affair with Caroline, even if it is true? What you had here together, the affection, friendship, comradeship, caring for Timmy, does all that go for nothing because she found her sexual life outside the walls of this caravan?'

Pascoe said bitterly: 'Forget and forgive? You make it sound so easy.'

'I don't suppose you can forget, or perhaps even want to. But I can't see why you have to use the word forgive. She never promised more than she gave.'

'You despise me, don't you?'

Dalgliesh thought how unattractive it was, the self-absorption of the deeply unhappy. But there were questions he still had to ask. He said: 'And she left nothing, no papers, no records, no diary, nothing to say what she was doing on the headland?'

'Nothing. And I know what she was doing here, why she came. She came to be near Caroline.'

'Did she have any money? Even if you fed her she must have had something of her own.'

'She always had some cash but I don't know how she got it. She never said and I didn't like to ask. I know she didn't draw any welfare payments. She said she didn't want the DHSS snooping round here to check whether we were sleeping together. I didn't blame her. Nor did I.'

'And she got no post.'

'She got postcards from time to time. Pretty regularly really. So she must have had friends in London. I don't know what she did with them. Threw them away I suppose. There's nothing in the caravan but her clothes and make-up and I'm going to burn those next. After that there'll be nothing left to show that she was ever here.'

Dalgliesh asked: 'And the murder. Do you think that Caroline Amphlett killed Robarts?'

'Perhaps. I don't care. It doesn't matter any more. If she didn't, Rickards will make her a scapegoat, her and Amy together.'

'But you can't really believe that Amy connived at murder?'

Pascoe looked at Dalgliesh with the frustration and anger of an uncomprehending child. 'I don't know! Look, I really never knew her. That's what I'm telling you. I don't know! And now that Timmy's gone I don't really care. And I'm in such a muddle, anger at what she did to me, at what she was, and grief that she's dead. I didn't think you could be angry and grieving at the same time. I ought to be mourning her but all I can feel is this terrible anger.'

'Oh yes,' said Dalgliesh. 'You can feel anger and grief together. That's the commonest reaction to bereavement.'

Suddenly Pascoe began crying. The empty beer can rattled against the table and he bent his head low over it, his shoulders shaking. Women, thought Dalgliesh, are better at coping with grief than we are. He had seen them so many times, the women police officers moving unconsciously to take the grieving mother, the lost child, in their arms. Some men were good at it too, of course. Rickards had been in the old days. He himself was good with the words, but then words were his trade. What he found difficult was what came so

357

spontaneously to the truly generous at heart, the willingness to touch and be touched. He thought: I'm here on false pretences. If I were not, perhaps I, too, could feel adequate.

He said: 'I think the wind is less strong than it was. Why don't we finish the burning and clear up that mess on the beach?'

It was over an hour before Dalgliesh was ready to set off for the mill. As he said goodbye to Pascoe at the door of the caravan a blue Fiesta with a young man at its wheel came bumping over the grass.

Pascoe said: 'Jonathan Reeves. He was engaged to Caroline Amphlett, or thought he was. She fooled him like Amy fooled me. He's been round once or twice to chat. We thought we might walk to the Local Hero for a game of bar billiards.'

It was not, thought Dalgliesh, an agreeable picture, the two men, bound by a common grievance, consoling each other for the perfidy of their women with beer and bar billiards. But Pascoe seemed to want to introduce Reeves and he found himself grasping a surprisingly firm hand and making his formal condolences.

Jonathan Reeves said: 'I still can't believe it, but I suppose people always say that after a sudden death. And I can't help feeling that it was my fault. I should have stopped them.'

Dalgliesh said: 'They were adult women. Presumably they knew what they were doing. Short of physically dragging them off the boat, which would hardly have been practicable, I don't see how you could have stopped them.'

Reeves reiterated obstinately: 'I should have stopped them.' Then he added: 'I keep having this dream, well, nightmare really. She's standing at the side of my bed with the child in her arms and saying to me, "It's all your fault. All your fault." '

Pascoe said: 'Caroline comes with Timmy?'

Reeves looked at him as if surprised that he could be so obtuse. He said: 'Not Caroline. It's Amy who comes. Amy, whom I never met, standing there with water streaming from her hair, holding the child in her arms and telling me that it's all my fault.'

48

Just over an hour later Dalgliesh had left the headland and was driving west along the A1151. After twenty minutes he turned south along a narrow country road. Darkness had fallen and the low scudding clouds, torn by wind, moved like a tattered blanket over the moon and the high stars. He drove fast and unhesitatingly, hardly aware of the tug and howl of the wind. He had taken this route only once before, early that same morning, but he had no need to consult the map; he knew where he was going. On either side of the low hedges stretched the black, unbroken fields. The lights of the car silvered an occasional distorted tree flailing in the wind, briefly illuminated as if with a searchlight the blank face of an isolated farm cottage, picked out the pin-bright eyes of a night animal before it scuttled to safety. The drive was not long, less than fifty minutes, but, staring straight ahead and shifting the gear lever as if he were an automaton, he felt for a moment disorientated as if he had driven through the bleak darkness of this flat, secretive landscape for interminable hours.

The brick-built, early-Victorian villa stood on the outskirts of a village. The gate to the gravel drive lay open and he drove slowly between the tossing laurels and the high, creaking boughs of the beech trees and manoeuvred the Jaguar between the three cars already discreetly parked at the side of the house. The two rows of windows in the front were dark and the single bulb which illuminated the fanlight seemed to Dalgliesh less a welcoming sign of occupation than a private signal, a sinister indication of secret life. He did not need to ring. Ears had been alert for the approaching car and the door was opened just as he reached it by the same stocky, cheerful-faced janitor who had greeted him on his first summons earlier that morning. Now, as then, he was wearing blue overalls so sprucely well cut that they looked like a uniform. Dalgliesh wondered what was his precise role; driver, guard, general factotum? Or had he, perhaps, a more specialized and sinister function?

He said: 'They're in the library, sir. I'll bring in the coffee. Will you be wanting sandwiches, sir? There's some beef left or I could put up a bit of cheese.'

Dalgliesh said: 'Just the coffee, thank you.'

They were waiting for him in the same small room at the back of the house. The walls were panelled in pale wood and there was only one window, a square bay heavily curtained with faded blue velvet. Despite its name the function of the room was unclear. Admittedly the wall opposite the window was lined with bookshelves, but they held only half a dozen leather-bound volumes and piles of old periodicals which looked as if they were Sunday colour supplements. The room had an oddly disturbing air of being both makeshift yet not devoid of comfort, a staging post in which the temporary occupants were attempting to make themselves at home. Ranged round the ornate marble fireplace were six assorted armchairs, most of them leather and each with a small wine table. The opposite end of the room was occupied by a modern dining table in plain wood with six chairs. This morning it had held the remains of breakfast and the air had been oppressively heavy with the smell of bacon and eggs. But the debris had been cleared and replaced by a tray of bottles and glasses. Looking at the variety provided, Dalgliesh thought that they had been doing themselves rather well. The loaded tray gave the place the air of a temporary hospitality room in which little else was hospitable. The air struck him as rather chill. In the grate an ornamental fan of paper rustled with each moan of the wind in the chimney and the two-bar electric fire which stood in the fender was barely adequate, even for so meanly proportioned and cluttered a room.

Three pairs of eyes turned on him as he entered. Clifford Sowerby was standing against the fireplace in exactly the same pose as when Dalgliesh had last seen him. He looked, in his formal suit and immaculate linen, as fresh as he had at nine o'clock that morning. Now, as then, he dominated the room. He was a solid-fleshed, conventionally handsome man with the assurance and controlled benevolence of a headmaster or a successful banker. No customer need fear to enter his office, provided his account was well in credit. Meeting him for only the second time Dalgliesh felt again an instinctive and seemingly irrational unease. The man was both ruthless and dangerous and yet, in their hours apart, he had been unable accurately to recall either his face or his voice.

The same could not be said for Bill Harding. He stood over six foot tall and, with his pale freckled face and thatch of red hair, had

360

obviously decided that anonymity was impossible and that he might as well opt for eccentricity. He was wearing a checked suit in heavy tweed with a spotted tie. Raising himself with some difficulty out of the low chair he ambled over to the drinks and, when Dalgliesh said he'd wait for coffee, stood holding the whisky bottle as if unsure what to do with it. But there was one addition since the morning. Alex Mair, whisky glass in hand, stood against the bookcase as if interested in the assortment of leather-bound volumes and piled periodicals. He turned as Dalgliesh entered and gave him a long, considering look, then nodded briefly. He was easily the most personable and the most intelligent of the three waiting men but something, confidence or energy, seemed to have drained out of him and he had the diminished, precariously contained look of a man in physical pain.

Sowerby said, his heavily lidded eyes amused: 'You've singed your hair, Adam. You smell as if you've been raking a bonfire.'

'I have.'

Mair didn't move but Sowerby and Harding seated themselves each side of the fire. Dalgliesh took a chair between them. They waited until coffee had arrived and he had a cup in hand. Sowerby was leaning back in his chair and looking up at the ceiling and seemed to be prepared to wait all night.

It was Bill Harding who said: 'Well, Adam?'

Putting down his cup, Dalgliesh described what exactly had happened since his arrival at the caravan. He had total verbal recall. He had made no notes, nor was it necessary. At the end of his account he said: 'So you can relax. Pascoe believes what will, I imagine, become the official line, that the two girls were lovers, went for an unwise boat trip together and were accidentally run down in the fog. I don't think he'll make any trouble for you or for anyone else. His capacity for troublemaking seems to be over.'

Sowerby said: 'And Camm left nothing incriminating in the caravan?'

'I doubt very much whether there was anything to leave. Pascoe said that he read one or two of the postcards when they arrived but they were mostly the usual meaningless phrases, tourist's chat. Camm apparently destroyed them. And he, with my help, has destroyed the detritus of her life on the headland. I helped him carry the last of her clothes and make-up down to the fire. While he was busy burning it I had a chance to return and make a fairly thorough search. There was nothing there.'

Sowerby said formally: 'It was good of you to do this for us, Adam. Obviously as Rickards isn't in the picture as far as our interest is concerned we could hardly rely on him. And you, of course, had an advantage he lacked. Pascoe would see you more as a friend than a policeman. That's obvious from his previous visit to Larksoken Mill. For some reason he trusts you.'

Dalgliesh said: 'You explained all that this morning. The request you made then seemed to me to be reasonable in the circumstances. I'm neither naïve nor ambivalent about terrorism. You asked me to do something and I've done it. I still think you should put Rickards in the picture, but that's your business. And you've got your answer. If Camm were involved with Amphlett she didn't confide in Pascoe and he has no suspicions of either woman. He believes that Camm only stayed with him to be near her lover. Pascoe, for all his liberal ideas, is as ready as the next man to believe that a woman who doesn't persist in wanting to go to bed with him must be either frigid or a lesbian.'

Sowerby permitted himself a wry smile. He said: 'While you were playing Ariel to his Prospero on the beach I suppose he didn't confess to killing Robarts. It's of small importance, but one has a natural curiosity.'

'My brief was to talk to him about Amy Camm, but he did mention the murder. I don't think he really believes that Amy helped to kill Robarts, but he doesn't really care whether the two girls did or did not. Are you satisfied yourselves that they did?'

Sowerby said: 'We don't have to be. It's Rickards who has to be satisfied and I imagine that he is. Incidentally, have you seen or spoken to him today?'

'He telephoned briefly about midday, principally, I think, to tell me that his wife has come home. For some reason he thought I'd be interested. As far as the murder is concerned, he seems to be coming round to the view that Camm and Amphlett were in it together.'

Harding said: 'And he's probably right.'

Dalgliesh asked: 'On what evidence? And since he's not allowed to know that one of them at least is a suspected terrorist, where's the motive?'

Harding said impatiently: 'Come off it, Adam, what real evidence does he expect to get? And since when was motive the first consideration? Anyway, they had a motive, at least Camm did. She hated Roberts. There's one witness at least to a physical fight between them on the Sunday afternoon of the murder. And Camm was fiercely protective of Pascoe and connected to that pressure group he started. That libel action would have ruined him and put PANUP out of business for ever. It's precarious enough as it is. Camm wanted Roberts dead and Amphlett killed her. That will be the general belief locally and Rickards will go along with it. To do him justice, he probably believes it.'

Dalgliesh said: 'Camm fiercely protective of Pascoe? Who says so? That's supposition not evidence.'

'But he's got some evidence, hasn't he? Circumstantial evidence, admittedly, but that's all he's likely to get now. Amphlett knew that Roberts went swimming at night; practically everyone at the power station knew that. She concocted a false alibi. Camm had access, like anyone else, to the jumble room at the Old Rectory. And Pascoe now admits that it could have been nine fifteen when he got back from Norwich. All right, the timing is tight but it's not impossible if Roberts swam earlier than usual. It adds up to a reasonable case. Not one which would have justified arresting them if they were still living, but enough to make it difficult to get a conviction against anyone else.'

Dalgliesh said: 'Would Amy Camm have left the child?'

'Why not? He was probably asleep, and if he wasn't and started yelling, who would hear? You're not suggesting, Adam, that she was a good mother, for God's sake? She left him at the end, didn't she? Permanently, as it happens, although that may not have been intentional. If you ask me, that kid had a pretty low priority with his mother.'

Dalgliesh said: 'So you're postulating a mother who is so outraged by a minor assault on her child that she avenges it with murder, and that same mother leaves him alone in a caravan while she goes sailing with her girlfriend. Wouldn't Rickards find that difficult to reconcile?'

Sowerby said, with a touch of impatience: 'God knows how Rickards reconciles anything. Luckily we're not required to ask him. Anyway, Adam, we know of a positive motive. Roberts could have suspected Amphlett. After all she was Acting Administrative Officer. She was intelligent, conscientious – over-conscientious, didn't you say, Mair?'

They all looked towards the silent figure standing against the bookcase. Mair turned to face them. He said quietly: 'Yes, she was conscientious. But I doubt whether she was conscientious enough to detect a conspiracy which had eluded me.' He turned back to his contemplation of the books.

There was a moment's embarrassed silence which was broken by Bill Harding. He said briskly, as if Mair hadn't spoken: 'So who was better placed to smell out a spot of treason? Rickards may have no firm evidence and an inadequate motive, but essentially he'll probably get it right.'

Dalgliesh got to his feet and walked over to the table. He said: 'It would suit you to get the case closed, I see that. But if I were the investigating officer the file would stay open.'

Sowerby said wryly: 'Obviously. Then let us be grateful that you aren't. But you'll keep your doubts to yourself, Adam? That doesn't need saying.'

'Then why say it?'

He placed his coffee cup back on the table. He was aware of Sowerby and Harding watching his every move as if he were a suspect who might suddenly make a break for it. Returning to his chair he said: 'And how will Rickards or anyone else explain the boat trip?'

It was still Harding who answered: 'He doesn't have to. They were lovers, for God's sake. They fancied a sea trip. It was Amphlett's boat after all. She left her car on the quay perfectly openly. She took nothing with her and neither did Amy. She left a note to Pascoe saying she'd be back in about an hour. In Rickards's eyes and everyone else's that adds up to an unfortunate accident. And who is to say that it wasn't? We were nowhere near close enough to have scared Amphlett into making a run for it; not yet.'

'And your people have found nothing at the house?'

Harding looked at Sowerby. It was a question they preferred not to answer and one which should not have been asked. After a pause, Sowerby answered: 'Clean. No radio, no documents, no evidence of trade craft. If Amphlett did intend to do a bunk, she cleaned up efficiently before she left.'

Bill Harding said: 'OK, if she did panic and was getting out, the only mystery is why so precipitous? If she killed Robarts and thought that the police were getting close, that might have tipped the balance. But they weren't getting close. It could, of course, have been a genuine boat trip, and a genuine accident. Or, their own side could have killed them both. Once the Larksoken plan was obsolete they were expendable. What were the comrades going to do with them, for God's sake? Fit them out with new personalities, new papers, infiltrate them into a power station in Germany? They were hardly worth the trouble, I should have thought.'

Dalgliesh said: 'Is there any evidence that it was an accident? Has any ship reported bow damage in the fog, a possible collision?'

Sowerby said: 'None so far. I doubt whether there will be. But if Amphlett really was part of the organization we suspect recruited her, they'd have no compunction in providing a couple of involuntary martyrs for the cause. What sort of people did she think she was dealing with? The fog would have helped them, but they could have run down the boat without the fog. Or, for that matter, taken them off and killed them elsewhere. But to fake an accident was the sensible course particularly given the bonus of the fog. I'd have done it that way myself.' And he would, thought Dalgliesh. He would have done it without compunction.

Harding turned to Mair. He said: 'You never had the least suspicion of her?'

'You asked me that before. None. I was surprised – a little irritated even – that she preferred not to stay as my PA when I got the new job, and even more surprised at the reason. Jonathan Reeves was hardly the man I thought she'd have chosen.'

Sowerby said: 'But it was clever. An ineffectual man, one she could dominate. Not too intelligent. Already in love with her. She could have chucked him whenever she chose and he wouldn't have the wit to know why. And why should you suspect? Sexual attraction is irrational anyway.'

There was a pause, then he added: 'Did you ever see her, the other girl, Amy? I'm told that she did visit the power station on one of those open days but I don't suppose you'd remember her.'

Mair's face was like a white mask. He said: 'I did see her once, I think. Blonde dyed hair, a chubby, rather pretty face. She was carrying the child. What will happen to him, incidentally? Or is it a she?'

Sowerby said: 'Taken into care, I suppose, unless they can trace the father or the grandparents. He'll probably end up fostered or adopted. I wonder what the hell his mother thought she was doing.'

Harding spoke with sudden vehemence: 'Do they think? Ever? No faith, no stability, no family affection, no loyalty. They're blown like paper with every wind. Then when they do find something to believe in, something to give them the illusion that they're important, what do they choose? Violence, anarchy, hatred, murder.'

Sowerby looked at him, surprised and a little amused. Then he said: 'Ideas some of them think worth dying for. In that, of course, lies the problem.'

'Only because they want to die. If you can't cope with living look for an excuse, a cause you can kid yourself is worth dying for and indulge your death wish. With luck you can take a dozen or so poor sods with you, people who can cope with living, who don't want to die. And there's always the ultimate self-deception, the final arrogance. Martyrdom. Lonely and inadequate fools all over the world will clench their fists and shout your name and carry placards with your picture and start looking round themselves for someone to bomb and shoot and maim. And that girl, Amphlett. She hadn't even the excuse of poverty. Dad a senior army officer, security, a good education, privilege, money. She'd had it all.'

It was Sowerby who replied. He said: 'We know what she had. What we can't know is what she didn't have.'

Harding ignored him. 'And what did they expect to do with Larksoken if they did take it over? They wouldn't have lasted for more than half an hour. They'd have needed experts, programmers.'

Mair said: 'I think you can take it they knew what and who they'd need and had planned how they could get them.'

'Into the country? How?'

'By boat, perhaps.'

Sowerby looked at him and then said a little impatiently: 'They didn't do it. They couldn't have done it. And it's our job to see that they never can do it.'

There was a moment's silence, then Mair said: 'I suppose Amphlett was the dominant partner. I wonder what arguments or what inducements she used. The girl – Amy – struck me as an instinctive creature, not likely to die for a political theory. But that is obviously a superficial judgement. I only saw her once.'

Sowerby said: 'Without knowing them we can't be sure who was the dominant partner. But I'd say it was almost certainly Amphlett. Nothing is known or suspected about Camm. She was probably recruited as a runner. Amphlett must have had a contact in the organization, must have met him occasionally if only to receive instructions. But they'd be careful never to get in touch directly. Camm probably received the coded messages setting out time and place for the next meeting and passed them on. As for her reasons, she found life unsatisfactory no doubt.'

Bill Harding lunged over to the table and poured himself a large whisky. His voice was thick as if he were drunk. 'Life has always been unsatisfactory for most people for most of the time. The world isn't designed for our satisfaction. That's no reason for trying to pull it down about our ears.'

Sowerby smiled his sly superior smile. He said easily: 'Perhaps they thought that's what we're doing.'

Fifteen minutes later, Dalgliesh left with Mair. As they stood unlocking their cars he looked back and saw that the janitor was still waiting at the open door.

Mair said: 'Making sure that we actually leave the premises. What extraordinary people they are! I wonder how they got on to Caroline. There seemed no point in asking as they made it obvious that they had no intention of saying.'

'No, they wouldn't say. Almost certainly they got a tip-off from the security services in Germany.'

'And this house. How on earth do they find these places? D'you suppose that they own it, borrow it, rent it or just break into it?'

Dalgliesh said: 'It probably belongs to one of their own officers, retired, I imagine. He, or she, lets them have a spare key for such an occasional use.'

'And now they'll be packing up, I suppose. Dusting down the furniture, checking for fingerprints, finishing up the food, turning off the power. And in an hour no one will know that they were ever there. The perfect temporary tenants. They've got one thing wrong, though. There wasn't a physical relationship between Amy and Caroline. That's nonsense.'

He spoke with such extraordinary strength and conviction, almost with outrage, that Dalgliesh wondered for a moment whether Caroline Amphlett had been more than his PA. Mair must surely have sensed what his companion was thinking but he neither explained nor denied. Dalgliesh said: 'I haven't congratulated you yet on your new job.'

Mair had slipped into his seat and turned on the engine. But the car door was still open and the silent warder at the door still waited patiently.

He said: 'Thank you. These tragedies at Larksoken have taken away some of the immediate satisfaction, but it's still the most important job I'm ever likely to hold.' Then, as Dalgliesh turned away, he said: 'So you think we still have a killer alive on the headland.'

'Don't you?'

But Mair didn't reply. Instead he asked: 'If you were Rickards, what would you do now?'

'I'd concentrate on trying to find out whether Blaney or Theresa left Scudder's Cottage that Sunday night. If either of them did, then I think my case would be complete. It isn't one that I'd be able to prove, but it would stand up in logic and I think that it would be the truth.'

49

Dalgliesh drove first out of the drive but Mair, accelerating sharply, overtook him on the first stretch of straight road and remained ahead. The thought of following the Jaguar all the way back to Larksoken was, for some reason, intolerable. But there was no danger of it; Dalgliesh even drove like a policeman, inside, if only just inside, the speed limit. And by the time they reached the main road Mair could no longer see the lights of the Jaguar in his mirror. He drove almost automatically, eyes fixed ahead, hardly aware of the black shapes of the tossing trees as they rushed past like an accelerated film, of the cat's-eyes unfolding in an unbroken stream of light. He was expecting a clear road on the headland and, cresting a low ridge, saw almost too late the lights of an ambulance. Violently twisting the wheel, he bumped off the road and braked on the grass verge, then sat there listening to the silence. It seemed to him that emotions which for the last three hours he had rigorously suppressed were buffeting him as the wind buffeted the car. He had to discipline his thoughts, to arrange and make sense of these astonishing feelings which horrified him by their violence and irrationality. Was it possible that he could feel relief at her death, at a danger averted, a possible embarrassment prevented, and yet, at the same time, be torn as if his sinews were being wrenched apart by a pain and regret so overwhelming that it could only be grief? He had to control himself from beating his head against the wheel of the car. She had been so uninhibited, so gallant, so entertaining. And she had kept faith with him. He hadn't been in touch with her since their last meeting on the Sunday afternoon of the murder and she had made no attempt to contact him by letter or telephone. They had agreed that the affair must end and that each would keep silent. She had kept her part of the bargain, as he had known she would. And now she was dead. He spoke her name aloud, 'Amy, Amy, Amy.' Suddenly he gave a gasp which tore at the muscles of his chest as if he were in the first throes of a heart attack and felt the blessed releasing tears flow down his face. He hadn't cried since he was a boy and even now, as the tears ran like rain and he tasted their surprising saltiness on his lips, he told himself that these minutes of emotion were good and therapeutic. He owed them to her and, once over, the tribute of grief paid, he would be able to put her out of his mind as he had planned to put her out of his heart. It was only thirty minutes later, when switching on the engine, that he gave thought to the ambulance and wondered which of the few inhabitants of the headland was being rushed to hospital.

50

As the two ambulance men wheeled the stretcher down the garden path the wind tore at the corner of the red blanket and billowed it into an arc. The straps held it down but Blaney almost flung himself across Theresa's body as if desperately shielding her from something more threatening than the wind. He shuffled crab-like down the path beside her, half bent, his hand holding hers under the blanket. It felt hot and moist and very small and it seemed to him that he was aware of every delicate bone. He wanted to whisper reassurance but terror had dried his throat and when he tried to speak his jaw jabbered as if palsied. And he had no comfort to give. There was a too-recent memory of another ambulance, another stretcher, another journey. He hardly dared look at Theresa in case he saw on her face what he had seen on her mother's; that look of pale, remote acceptance which meant that she was already moving away from him, from all the mundane affairs of life, even from his love, into a shadow land where he could neither follow nor was welcome. He tried to find reassurance in the memory of Dr Entwhistle's robust voice.

'She'll be all right. It's appendicitis. We'll get her to hospital straight away. They'll operate tonight and with luck she'll be back with you in a few days. Not to do the housework mind; we'll discuss all that later. Now, let's get to the telephone. And stop panicking, man. People don't die of appendicitis.'

But they did die. They died under the anaesthetic, they died because peritonitis intervened, they died because the surgeon made a mistake. He had read of these cases. He was without hope.

As the stretcher was gently lifted and slid with easy expertise into the ambulance he turned and looked back at Scudder's Cottage. He hated it now, hated what it had done to him, what it had made him do. Like him, it was accursed. Mrs Jago was standing at the door holding Anthony in her unpractised arms with a twin standing silently on each side. He had telephoned the Local Hero for help and George Jago had driven her over immediately to stay with the children until he returned. There had been no one else to ask. He had telephoned Alice Mair at Martyr's Cottage but all he had got was the answerphone. Mrs Jago lifted Anthony's hand and waved it in a gesture of goodbye, then bent to speak to the twins. Obediently they too waved. He climbed into the ambulance and the doors were firmly shut.

The ambulance bumped and gently swayed up the lane, then accelerated as it reached the narrow headland road to Lydsett. Suddenly it swerved and he was almost thrown from his seat. The paramedic sitting opposite him cursed.

'Some bloody fool going too fast.'

But he didn't reply. He sat very close to Theresa, his hand still in hers, and found himself praying as if he could batten on the ears of the God he hadn't believed in since he was seventeen. 'Don't let her die. Don't punish her because of me. I'll believe. I'll do anything. I can change, be different. Punish me but not her. Oh God, let her live.'

And suddenly he was standing again in that dreadful little churchyard, hearing the drone of Father McKee's voice, with Theresa at his side, her hand still cold in his. The earth was covered with synthetic grass but there was one mound left bare and he saw again the newly sliced gold of the soil. He hadn't known that Norfolk earth could be so rich a colour. A white flower had fallen from one of the wreaths, a small, tortured, unrecognized bud with a pin through the wrapped stalk and he was seized with an almost uncontrollable compulsion to pick it up before it was shovelled with the earth into the grave, to take it home, put it in water and let it die in peace. He had to hold himself tautly upright to prevent himself bending to retrieve it. But he hadn't dared, and it had been left there to be smothered and obliterated under the first clods.

He heard Theresa whisper and bent so low to listen that he could smell her breath. 'Daddy, am I going to die?'

'No. No.'

He almost shouted the word, a howled defiance of death, and was aware of the paramedic half rising to his feet. He said quietly: 'You heard what Dr Entwhistle said. It's just appendicitis.'

'I want to see Father McKee.'

'Tomorrow. After the operation. I'll tell him. He'll visit you. I won't forget. I promise. Now lie still.'

'Daddy, I want him now, before the operation. There's something I have to tell him.'

'Tell him tomorrow.'

'Can I tell you? I have to tell someone now.'

He said almost fiercely: 'Tomorrow, Theresa. Leave it till tomorrow.' And then, appalled by his selfishness, he whispered: 'Tell me, darling, if you must,' and closed his eyes so that she should not see the horror, the hopelessness.

She whispered: 'That night Miss Robarts died. I crept out to the abbey ruins. I saw her running into the sea. Daddy, I was there.'

He said hoarsely: 'It doesn't matter. You don't have to tell me any more.'

'But I want to tell. I ought to have told you before. Please, Daddy.'

He put his other hand over hers. He said: 'Tell me.'

'There was someone else there, too. I saw her walking over the headland towards the sea. It was Mrs Dennison.'

Relief flowed through him, wave after wave, like a warm cleansing summer sea. After a moment's silence he heard her voice again: 'Daddy, are you going to tell anyone, the police?'

'No,' he said. 'I'm glad you've told me but it isn't important. It doesn't mean anything. She was just taking a walk in the moonlight. I'm not going to tell.'

'Not even about me being on the headland that night?'

'No,' he said firmly, 'not even that. Not yet, anyway. But we'll talk about it, what we ought to do, after the operation.'

And for the first time he could believe that there would be a time for them after the operation.

51

Mr Copley's study was at the back of the Old Rectory, looking out over the unkempt lawn and the three rows of wind-crippled bushes which the Copleys called the shrubbery. It was the only room in the rectory which Meg would not dream of entering without first knocking and it was accepted as his private place as if he were still in charge of a parish and needing a quiet sanctum to prepare his weekly sermon or counsel those parishioners who sought his advice. It was here that each day he read Morning Prayer and Evensong, his only congregation his wife and Meg, whose low feminine voices would make the responses and read alternate verses of the psalms. On her first day with them he had said gently but without embarrassment: 'I say the two main offices every day in my study, but please don't feel that you need to attend unless you wish to.'

She had chosen to attend, at first from politeness but later because this daily ritual, the beautiful, half-forgotten cadences, seducing her into belief, gave a welcome shape to the day. And the study itself, of all the rooms in the solidly ugly but comfortable house, seemed to represent an inviolable security, a great rock in a weary land against which all the rancorous, intrusive memories of school, the petty irritations of daily living, even the horror of the Whistler and the menace of the power station beat in vain. She doubted whether it had greatly changed since the first Victorian rector had taken possession. One wall was lined with books, a theological library which she thought Mr Copley now rarely consulted. The old mahogany desk was usually bare and Meg suspected that he spent most of his time in the easy chair which looked out over the garden. Three walls were covered with pictures; the rowing eight of his university days with ridiculously small caps above the grave moustached young faces; the ordinands of his theological college; insipid watercolours in golden mounts, the record by some Victorian ancestor of his grand tour; etchings of Norwich Cathedral, the nave at Winchester, the great octagon of Ely. To one side of the ornate Victorian fireplace was a single crucifix. It seemed to Meg to be very old and probably valuable but she had never liked to ask. The body of Christ was a young man's body, stretched taut in its last agony, the open mouth seeming to shout in triumph or defiance at the God who had deserted him. Nothing else in the study was powerful or disturbing; furniture, objects, pictures all spoke of order, of certainty, of hope. Now, as she knocked and listened for Mr Copley's gentle 'Come in', it occurred to her that she was seeking comfort as much from the room itself as from its occupant.

He was sitting in the armchair, a book in his lap, and made to get up with awkward stiffness as she entered. She said: 'Please don't get up. I wonder if I could talk to you privately for a few minutes.'

She saw at once the flare of anxiety in the faded blue eyes and thought, He's afraid I'm going to give notice. She added quickly but with gentle firmness: 'As a priest. I wish to consult you as a priest.'

He laid down his book. She saw that it was one he and his wife had chosen the previous Friday from the travelling library, the newest H. R. F. Keating. Both he and Dorothy Copley enjoyed detective stories and she was always slightly irritated that husband and wife took it for granted that he should always have first read. This inopportune reminder of his mild domestic selfishness assumed for a moment a disproportionate importance and she wondered why she had ever thought he could be of help. Yet was it right to criticize him for the marital priorities which Dorothy Copley had herself laid down and gently enforced over fifty-three years? She told herself, I am consulting the priest not the man. I wouldn't ask a plumber how he treated his wife and children before letting him loose on the leaking tank.

He gestured towards a second easy chair and she drew it up opposite him. He marked his page with his leather bookmark with careful deliberation and laid down the novel as reverently as if it were a book of devotions, folding both hands over it. It seemed to her that he had drawn himself together and was leaning slightly forward, head to one side, as if he were in the confessional. She had nothing to confess to him, only a question which in its stark simplicity seemed to her to go to the very heart of her orthodox, self-affirming but not unquestioning Christian faith. She said: 'If we are faced with a decision, a dilemma, how do we know what is right?'

She thought she detected in his gentle face an easing of tension as if grateful that the question was less onerous than he had feared. But he took his time before he replied.

'Our conscience will tell us if we will listen.'

375

'The still, small voice, like the voice of God?'

'Not *like*, Meg. Conscience *is* the voice of God, of the indwelling Holy Spirit. In the collect for Whit Sunday we do indeed pray that we may have a right judgement in all things.'

She said with gentle persistence: 'But how can we be sure that what we're hearing isn't our own voice, our own subconscious desires? The message we listen for so carefully must be mediated through our own experience, our personality, our heredity, our inner needs. Can we ever break free of the devices and desires of our own hearts? Might not our conscience be telling us what we most want to hear?'

'I haven't found it so. Conscience has usually directed me against my own desires.'

'Or what at the time you thought were your own desires.'

But this was pressing him too hard. He sat quietly, blinking rapidly as if seeking inspiration in old sermons, old homilies, familiar texts. There was a moment's pause and then he said: 'I have found it helpful to think of conscience as an instrument, a stringed instrument perhaps. The message is in the music, but if we don't keep it in repair and use it constantly in regular and disciplined practice we get only an imperfect response.'

She remembered that he had been an amateur violinist. His hands were too rheumatic now to hold the instrument, but it still lay in its case on top of the bureau in the corner. The metaphor might mean something to him but for her it was meaningless.

She said: 'But even if my conscience tells me what is right, I mean right according to the moral law or even the law of the country, that doesn't necessarily mean the end of responsibility. Suppose if I obey it, do what conscience tells me, I cause harm, even danger to someone else.'

'We must do what we know is right and leave the consequences to God.'

'But any human decision has to take account of the probable consequences; that is surely what decision means. How can we separate cause from effect?'

He said: 'Would it be helpful if you told me what is troubling you, that is if you feel you can?'

'It isn't my secret to tell, but I can give an example. Suppose I know that someone is regularly stealing, from his employer. If I expose him he'll be sacked, his marriage will be at risk, his wife and children injured. I might feel that the shop or firm could afford to lose a few pounds each week rather than cause all that hurt to innocent people.'

He was silent for a moment, then said: 'Conscience might tell you to speak to the thief rather than to his employer. Explain that you know, persuade him to stop. Of course the money would have to be returned. I can see that that might present a practical difficulty.'

She watched as he wrestled with the difficulty for a moment, brow creased, conjuring up the mythical thieving husband and father, clothing the moral problem in living flesh. She said: 'But what if he won't or can't stop his stealing?'

'Can't? If stealing is an irresistible compulsion then, of course, he needs medical help. Yes, certainly, that would have to be tried, although I'm never very sanguine about the success of psychotherapy.'

'Won't, then, or promises to stop and then goes on stealing.'

'You must still do what your conscience tells you is right. We cannot always judge the consequences. In the case you have postulated, to let the stealing go on unchecked is to connive at dishonesty. Once you have discovered what is happening you can't pretend not to know, you can't abdicate responsibility. Knowledge always brings responsibility; that is as true for Alex Mair at Larksoken Power Station as it is in this study. You said that the children would be injured if you told; they are being injured already by their father's dishonesty and so is the wife who benefits from it. Then there are the other staff to consider: perhaps they might be wrongly suspected. The dishonesty, if undetected, could well get worse so that at the end the wife and children would be in deeper trouble than if it were stopped now. That is why it is safer if we concentrate on doing what is right and leave the consequences to God.'

She wanted to say, 'Even if we're not sure any longer if He exists? Even if that seems only another way of evading the personal responsibility which you have just told me we can't and shouldn't evade?' But she saw with compunction that he was suddenly looking tired and she didn't miss the quick glance down at his book.

He wanted to get back to Inspector Ghote, Keating's gentle Indian detective who, despite his uncertainties, would get there in the end because this was fiction; problems could be solved, evil overcome, justice vindicated, and death itself only a mystery which would be solved in the final chapter. He was a very old man. It was unfair to bother him. She wanted to put her hand on his sleeve and tell him that it was all right, he mustn't worry. Instead she got up and, using for the first time the name that came naturally to her, spoke the comforting lie.

'Thank you, Father, you have been very helpful. It's plainer to me now. I shall know what to do.'

52

Every turn and hazard of the overgrown garden path leading to the gate which gave access to the headland was so familiar to Meg that she hardly needed to follow the jerking moon of her torch's beam and the wind, always capricious at Larksoken, seemed to have abated the worst of its fury. But when she reached a slight ridge and the light at the door of Martyr's Cottage came in sight, it renewed its strength and came swooping down on her as if it would pluck her from the earth and send her whirling back to the shelter and peace of the rectory. She didn't give battle but leaned against it, her head bent, her shoulder bag bumping at her side, clutching her scarf to her head with both hands until the fury passed and she could again stand upright. The sky, too, was turbulent, the stars bright but very high, the moon reeling frantically between the shredded clouds like a blown lantern of frail paper. Fighting her way towards Martyr's Cottage, Meg felt as if the whole headland was whirling in chaos about her so that she could no longer tell whether the roaring in her ears was the wind, her blood or the crashing sea. When at last, breathless, she reached the oak door she thought for the first time about Alex Mair and wondered what she would do if he were at home. It struck her as strange that the possibility hadn't previously occurred to her. And she knew that she couldn't face him, not now, not yet. But it was Alice who answered her ring. Meg asked: 'Are you alone?'

'Yes, I'm alone. Alex is at Larksoken. Come in, Meg.'

Meg took off and hung up her coat and headscarf in the hall and followed Alice to the kitchen. She had obviously been occupied in correcting her proofs. Now she reseated herself at her desk, swivelled round and looked gravely at Meg as she took her usual fireside chair. For a few moments neither spoke. Alice was wearing a long brown skirt of fine wool with a blouse high-buttoned to the chin and over it a sleeveless, pleated shift in narrow stripes of brown and fawn which reached almost to the floor. It gave her a hieratic dignity, an almost sacerdotal look of composed authority which was yet one of total comfort and ease. A small fire of logs was burning in the hearth, filling the room with a pungent autumnal smell, and the wind, muted by thick sixteenth-century walls, sighed and moaned companionably in the chimney. From time to time it gushed down and the logs flared into hissing life. The clothes, the firelight, the smell of burning wood overlaying the subtler smell of herbs and warm bread were familiar to Meg from their many quiet evenings together and they were dear to her. But tonight was dreadfully different. After tonight the kitchen might never be home to her again.

She asked: 'Am I interrupting?'

'Obviously, but that doesn't mean that I don't welcome interruption.'

Meg bent to extract a large brown envelope from her shoulder bag.

'I've brought back the first fifty pages of proofs. I've done what you asked, read the text and checked for printing errors only.'

Alice took the envelope and, without glancing at it, placed it on the desk. She said: 'That's what I wanted. I'm so obsessed with the accuracy of the recipes that errors in the text sometimes slip through. I hope it wasn't too much of a chore.'

'No, I enjoyed it, Alice. It reminded me of Elizabeth David.'

'Not too much, I hope. She's so marvellous that I'm always afraid of being overinfluenced by her.'

There was a silence. Meg thought: We're talking as if the dialogue has been scripted for us, not as strangers exactly, but as people who are careful of their words because the space between them is loaded with dangerous thoughts. How well do I really know her? What has she ever told me about herself? Just a few details of her life with her father, snatches of information, a few phrases dropped into our conversations like a falling match, briefly illuminating the contours of a vast unexplored terrain. I've confided almost everything about myself, my childhood, the racial trouble at the school, Martin's death. But has it ever been an equal friendship? She knows more about me than any other living creature. All I really know about Alice is that she's a good cook.

She was aware of her friend's steady, almost quizzical look. Alice said: 'But you didn't fight your way in this wind just to bring back fifty pages of proofs.'

'I have to talk to you.'

'You are talking to me.'

Meg held Alice's own unflinching gaze. She said: 'Those two girls,

Caroline and Amy, people are saying that they killed Hilary Robarts. Is that what you believe?'

'No. Why do you ask?'

'Nor do I believe it. Do you suppose the police will try to pin it on them?'

Alice's voice was cool. 'I shouldn't think so. Isn't that rather a dramatic idea? And why should they? Chief Inspector Rickards strikes me as an honest and conscientious officer, if not particularly intelligent.'

'Well, it's convenient for them, isn't it? Two suspects dead. The case closed. No more deaths.'

'Were they suspects? You seem to be more in Rickards's confidence than I am.'

'They didn't have alibis. The man at Larksoken Caroline was supposed to be engaged to – Jonathan Reeves, isn't it? – apparently he's confessed that they weren't together that night. Caroline forced him to lie. Most of the staff at Larksoken know that now. And it's all over the village, of course. George Jago rang to tell me.'

'So they didn't have alibis. Nor did other people – you, for example. Not having an alibi isn't proof of guilt. Nor did I, incidentally. I was at home all that evening but I doubt whether I could prove it.'

And this at last was the moment which had filled Meg's thoughts since the murder, the moment of truth which she had dreaded. She said through dry unyielding lips: 'But you weren't at home, were you? You told Chief Inspector Rickards that you were when I was here sitting in this kitchen on the Monday morning, but it wasn't true.'

There was a moment's silence. Then Alice said calmly: 'Is that what you've come to say?'

'I know that it can be explained. It's ridiculous even to ask. It's just that I've had it on my mind for so long. And you are my friend. A friend should be able to ask. There should be honesty, confidence, trust.'

'Ask what? Do you have to talk like a marriage guidance counsellor?'

'Ask why you told the police you were here at nine. You weren't. I was. After the Copleys left I had a sudden need to see you. I tried the telephone but got only the answerphone. I didn't leave a message; there was no point. I walked down. The cottage was empty. The light was on in the sitting room and the kitchen and the door was locked. I called out for you. The record player was on, very loud. The cottage was filled with triumphant music. But there was no one here.'

Alice sat in silence for a moment. Then she said calmly: 'I went for a walk to enjoy the moonlight. I didn't expect a casual caller. There are never casual callers except you, and I thought that you were in Norwich. But I took the obvious precaution against an intruder, I locked the door. How did you get in?'

'With your key. You can't have forgotten, Alice. You gave me a key a year ago. I've had it ever since.'

Alice looked at her and Meg saw in her face the dawning of memory, chagrin, even, before she turned briefly away, the beginning of a rueful smile. She said: 'But I had forgotten; completely. How extraordinary! It might not have worried me, even if I had remembered. After all, I thought you were in Norwich. But I didn't remember. We've got so many keys to the cottage, some here, some in London. But you never reminded me that you had one.'

'I did once, early on, and you told me to keep it. Like a fool I thought that the key meant something: trust, friendship, a sign that Martyr's Cottage was always open to me. You told me that I might one day need to use it.'

And now Alice did laugh aloud. She said: 'And you did need to use it. How ironic. But it isn't like you to come in uninvited, not while I wasn't here. You never have before.'

'But I didn't know you weren't here. The lights were on and I rang and I could hear the music. When I rang the third time and you still didn't come I was afraid that you might be ill, unable to summon help. So I unlocked the door. I walked into a surge of wonderful sound. I recognized it, Mozart's Symphony in G minor. It was Martin's favourite. What an extraordinary tape to choose.'

'I didn't choose it. I just turned on the player. What do you think I should have chosen? A requiem mass to mark the passing of a soul I don't believe in?'

Meg went on as if she hadn't heard: 'I walked through to the kitchen. The light was on here too. It was the first time I'd been in this room on my own. And suddenly I felt like a stranger. I felt that nothing in it had anything to do with me. I felt that I had no right here. That's why I went away without leaving you any message.'

Alice said sadly: 'You were quite right. You had no right here. And you needed to see me so badly that you walked alone over the headland before you knew that the Whistler was dead?'

'I didn't walk in fear. The headland is so deserted. There's nowhere anyone can lurk, and I knew when I reached Martyr's Cottage I'd be with you.'

'No, you're not easily frightened are you? Are you frightened now?'

'Not of you but of myself. I'm frightened of what I'm thinking.'

'So the cottage was empty. What else is there? Obviously there is something else.'

Meg said: 'That message on your answerphone; if you'd really received it at ten past eight you would have telephoned Norwich station and left a message for me to ring back. You knew how much the Copleys disliked the thought of going to their daughter. No one else on the headland knew that. The Copleys never spoke of it and nor did I, not to anyone except you. You would have rung, Alice. There could have been an announcement over the station loud-speaker and I could have driven them home. You would have thought of that.'

Alice said: 'One lie to Rickards which could have been a matter of convenience, a wish to avoid trouble, and one instance of insensitive neglect. Is that all?'

'The knife. The middle knife in your block. It wasn't here. It meant nothing at the time, of course, but the block looked odd. I was so used to seeing the five carefully graded knives, each in its sheath. It's back now. It was back when I called in on the Monday after the murder. But it wasn't here on the Sunday night.'

She wanted to cry out: 'You can't be going to use it! Alice, don't use it!' Instead she made herself go on, trying to keep her voice calm, trying not to plead for reassurance, understanding.

'And next morning, when you telephoned to say that Hilary was dead, I didn't say anything about my visit. I didn't know what to believe. It wasn't that I suspected you; that would have been impossible for me, it still is. But I needed time to think. It was late morning before I could bring myself to come to you.'

'And then you found me here with Chief Inspector Rickards and heard me lying. And you saw that the knife was back in the block. But you didn't speak then and you haven't spoken since, not even, I presume, to Adam Dalgliesh.'

It was a shrewd thrust. Meg said: 'I've told no one, how could I? Not until we'd spoken. I knew that you must have had what seemed to you a good reason for lying.'

'And then, I suppose, slowly, perhaps unwillingly, you began to realize what that reason might be?'

'I didn't think you'd murdered Hilary. It sounds fantastic, ludicrous even to speak those words, to think of suspecting you. But the knife was missing and you weren't there. You did lie and I couldn't understand why. I still can't. I wonder who it is you're shielding. And sometimes – forgive me, Alice – sometimes I wonder whether you were there when he killed her, kept guard, stood there watching, might even have helped him by cutting off her hair.'

Alice sat so still that the long-fingered hands resting in her lap, the folds of her shift, might have been carved in stone. She said: 'I didn't help anyone – and no one helped me. There were only two people on that beach, Hilary Robarts and I. I planned it alone and I did it alone.'

For a moment they sat in silence. Meg felt a great coldness. She heard the words and she knew that they were true. Had she, perhaps, always known? She thought: I shall never be with her in this kitchen again, never again find the peace and security which I found in this room. And there fell into her mind an incongruous memory; herself sitting quietly in the same chair and watching while Alice made short pastry; sieving the flour on to a marble slab, adding the squares of soft butter, breaking in the egg, her long fingers delicately dabbling the mixture, drawing in the flour, lightly forming the glistening ball of dough. She said: 'They were your hands. Your hands tightening the belt round her throat, your hands cutting off her hair, your hands slicing that L into her forehead. You planned it alone and you did it alone.'

Alice said: 'It took courage, but perhaps less than you would imagine. And she died very quickly, very easily. We shall be lucky to go with so little pain. She hadn't even time to feel terror. She had an easier death than most of us can look forward to. And as for what followed, that didn't matter. Not to her. Not even much to me. She was dead. It's what you do to the living that takes the strong emotions, courage, hatred and love.'

She was silent for a moment, then she said: 'In your eagerness to prove me a murderess, don't confuse suspicion with proof. You can't prove any of this. All right, you say the knife was missing, but that's only your word against mine. And if it was missing, I could say that I went for a short walk on the headland and the murderer saw his chance.'

'And put it back afterwards? He wouldn't even know that it was there.'

'Of course he would. Everyone knows that I'm a cook, and a cook has sharp knives. And why shouldn't he put it back?'

'But how would he get in? The door was locked.'

'There's only your word for that. I shall say that I left it open. People on the headland usually do.'

Meg wanted to cry out: 'Don't, Alice. Don't begin planning more lies. Let there at least be truth between us.' She said: 'And the portrait, the smashed window, was that you too?'

'Of course.'

'But why? Why all that complication?'

'Because it was necessary. While I was waiting for Hilary to come out of the sea I glimpsed Theresa Blaney. She suddenly appeared on the very edge of the cliff by the abbey ruins. She was only there for a moment and then she disappeared. But I saw her. She was unmistakable in the moonlight.'

'But if she didn't see you, if she wasn't there when you . . . when Hilary died . . .'

'Don't you see? It meant that her father wouldn't have an alibi. She has always struck me as a truthful child and she has had a strict religious upbringing. Once she told the police that she was out on the headland that night Ryan would be in terrible danger. And even if she had sense enough to lie, for how long could she keep it up? The police would be gentle questioning her. Rickards isn't a brute. But a truthful child would find it difficult to lie convincingly. When I got back here after the murder I played back the messages on the answerphone. It occurred to me that Alex might change his plans and telephone. And it was then, too late, that I got George Jago's message. I knew that the murder could no longer be pinned on the Whistler. I had to give Ryan Blaney an alibi. So I tried to ring him to say that I'd collect the picture. When I couldn't get through I knew I had to call at Scudder's Cottage and as quickly as possible.'

'You could just have collected the portrait, knocked at the door to say what you'd done, seen him then. That would be proof enough that he was at home.'

'But it would have looked too deliberate, too contrived. Ryan had made it plain that he didn't want to be disturbed, that I was merely to collect the portrait. He made that very clear. And Adam Dalgliesh was with me when he said it. Not any casual caller, but Scotland

Yard's most intelligent detective. No, I had to have a valid excuse to knock and speak to Ryan.'

'So you put the portrait in the boot of your car and told him that it wasn't in the shed?' It seemed to Meg extraordinary that horror could briefly be subsumed by curiosity, by the need to know. They might have been discussing complicated arrangements for a picnic.

Alice said: 'Exactly. He was hardly likely to think that it was I who had taken it only a minute earlier. It was convenient, of course, that he was half drunk. Not as drunk as I described to Rickards, but obviously incapable of killing Robarts and getting back to Scudder's Cottage by a quarter to ten.'

'Not even in the van or on his bicycle?'

'The van was out of commission and he couldn't have stayed on the bicycle. Besides, I would have passed him cycling home. My evidence meant that Ryan would be safe even if Theresa confessed that she'd left the cottage. After I left him I drove back over a deserted headland. I stopped briefly below the pillbox and threw the shoes inside. I had no way of burning them except on an open fire where I had burned the paper and string from the wrapped portrait, but I had an idea that burning rubber could leave some trace and a persistent smell. I didn't expect the police to search for them because I didn't believe they would find a print. But even if they did there would be nothing to link those particular shoes with the murder. I washed them thoroughly under the outside tap before I disposed of them. Ideally I could have returned them to the jumble box but I daren't wait and that night I knew that, with you gone to Norwich, the back door would be locked.'

'And then you threw the picture through Hilary's window?'

'I had to get rid of it somehow. That way it looked like a deliberate act of vandalism and hatred and there were plenty of possible suspects for that, not all of them on the headland. It complicated matters even further and it was one more piece of evidence to help Ryan. No one would believe that he would deliberately destroy his own work. But it had a double purpose: I wanted to get into Thyme Cottage. I smashed enough of the window to get through.'

'But that was terribly dangerous. You might have cut yourself, got a sliver of glass on your shoes. And they were your own shoes then; you had disposed of the Bumbles.'

'I examined the soles very thoroughly. And I was particularly

386

careful where I trod. She had left the downstairs lights on so I didn't have to use my torch.'

'But why? What were you looking for? What did you hope to find?'

'Nothing. I wanted to get rid of the belt. I curled it very carefully and put it in the drawer in her bedroom among her other belts, stockings, handkerchiefs, socks.'

'But if the police examined it, it wouldn't have her prints on it.'

'Nor would it have mine. I was still wearing my gloves. Anyway why should they examine it? One would assume that the murderer had used his own belt and had taken it away again. The least likely hiding place for the killer to choose would be the victim's own cottage. That's why I chose it. And even if they did decide to examine every belt and dog lead on the headland I doubt whether they'd get any useful prints from half an inch of leather which dozens of hands must have touched.'

Meg said bitterly: 'You took a lot of trouble to give Ryan an alibi. What about the other innocent suspects? They were all at risk, they still are. Didn't you think of them?'

'I only cared about one other, Alex, and he had the best alibi of all. He would go through security to get into the station and again when he left.'

Meg said: 'I was thinking of Neil Pascoe, Amy, Miles Lessingham, even myself.'

'None of you is a parent responsible for four motherless children. I thought it very unlikely that Lessingham wouldn't be able to provide an alibi and if he couldn't there was no real evidence against him. How could there be? He didn't do it. But I have a feeling that he guesses who did. Lessingham isn't a fool. But even if he knows, he'll never tell. Neil Pascoe and Amy could give each other an alibi and you, my dear Meg, do you really see yourself as a serious suspect?'

'I felt like one. When Rickards was questioning me it was like being back in that staffroom at school, facing those cold accusing faces, knowing I'd already been judged and found guilty, wondering if perhaps I wasn't guilty.'

'The possible distress of innocent suspects, even you, was very low on my list of priorities.'

'And now you'll let them blame the murder on Caroline and Amy, both dead and both innocent?'

'Innocent? Of that, of course. Perhaps you're right and the police will find it convenient to assume they did it, one of them or together in collusion. From Rickards's point of view it's better to have two dead suspects than no arrest. And it can't hurt them now. The dead are beyond harm, the harm they do and the harm that is done to them.'

'But it's wrong and it's unjust.'

'Meg, they are dead. Dead. It can't matter. Injustice is a word and they have passed beyond the power of words. They don't exist. And life is unjust. If you feel called upon to do something about injustice concentrate on injustice to the living. Alex had a right to that job.'

'And Hilary Robarts, hadn't she a right to life? I know that she wasn't likeable, nor even very happy. There's no immediate family to mourn, apparently. She doesn't leave young children. But you've taken from her what no one can ever give back. She didn't deserve to die. Perhaps none of us do, not like that. We don't even hang the Whistler now. We've learned something since Tyburn, since Agnes Poley's burning. Nothing Hilary Robarts did deserved death.'

'I'm not arguing that she deserved to die. It doesn't matter whether she was happy, or childless, or even much use to anyone but herself. What I'm saying is that I wanted her dead.'

'That seems to me so evil that it's beyond my understanding. Alice, what you did was a dreadful sin.'

Alice laughed. The sound was so full-throated, almost happy, as if the amusement were genuine. 'Meg, you continue to astonish me. You use words which are no longer in the general vocabulary, not even in the Church's, so I'm told. The implications of that simple little word are outside my comprehension. But if you want to see this in theological terms, then think of Dietrich Bonhoeffer. He wrote: "We have at times to be willing to be guilty." Well, I'm willing to be guilty.'

'To be guilty, yes. But not to feel guilt. That must make it easier.'

'Oh, but I do feel it. I've been made to feel guilty from childhood. And if at the heart of your being you feel that you've no right even to exist, then one more cause of guilt hardly matters.'

Meg thought, I shall never be able to unlearn, never forget what's happening here this evening. But I have to know the whole of it. Even the most painful knowledge is better than half-knowledge. She said: 'That night I came here to tell you the Copleys were going to their daughter . . .'

Alice said: 'On the Friday after the dinner party. Thirteen days ago.'

'Is that all? It seems in a different dimension of time. You asked me

388

to come and have supper with you when I got back from Norwich. Was that planned as part of your alibi? Did you use even me?'

Alice looked at her. She said: 'Yes. I'm sorry. You would have been here about half-past nine, just time for me to get back and be ready with a hot meal in the oven.'

'Which you would have cooked earlier in the evening. Safe enough with Alex at the power station, out of the way.'

'That's what I planned. When you declined I didn't press it. That would have looked suspicious later, too like trying to establish an alibi. Besides, you wouldn't have been persuaded to change your mind, would you? You never do. But the very fact of the invitation would have helped. A woman wouldn't normally invite a friend to even an informal supper if she's simultaneously planning a murder.'

'And if I had accepted, if I had turned up here at half-past nine, that would have been awkward, wouldn't it, given your later change of plan? You wouldn't have been able to drive over to Scudder's Cottage to give Ryan Blaney his alibi. And you would have been left in possession of the shoes and the belt.'

'The shoes would have been the greatest problem. I didn't think they'd ever be connected with the crime but I needed to get rid of them before next morning. I couldn't possibly explain my possession of them. I would probably have washed them and hidden them away, hoping for a chance to get them back to the jumble box the next day. Though I would have to have found a way of giving Ryan his alibi. Probably I would have told you that I couldn't get through by telephone and that we ought to drive over at once to tell him that the Whistler was dead. But it's all academic. I didn't worry. You said you wouldn't come and I knew you wouldn't.'

'But I did. Not to supper. But I came.'

'Yes. Why did you, Meg?'

'A feeling of depression after a heavy day, hating seeing the Copleys go, the need to see you. I wasn't looking for a meal. I had an early supper and then walked over the headland.'

But there was something else she needed to ask. She said: 'You knew that Hilary swam after watching the beginning of the main news. I suppose most people knew that who knew that she liked swimming at night. And you were taking trouble to see that Ryan had his alibi for nine fifteen or shortly after. But suppose the body hadn't been discovered until the next day? Surely she wouldn't normally be missed until she didn't turn up at the power station on

Monday morning, and then they would telephone to see if she were ill. It might even have been Monday evening before anybody made any inquiries. She could have swum in the morning and not at night.'

'The pathologist can usually estimate the time of death with reasonable accuracy. And I knew she'd be found that night. I knew that Alex had promised to visit her when he got back from the power station. He was on his way to the cottage when he met Adam Dalgliesh. And now, I think, you know it all, except for the Bumble trainers. I came through the back gardens at the Old Rectory late on Sunday afternoon. I knew that the back door would be open and it was the time when you would be having high tea. I had a bag with me with a few items of jumble in case I was seen. But I wasn't seen. I took soft shoes, easy to wear, a pair that looked roughly my size. And I took one of the belts.'

But there was one more question to ask, the most important of all. Meg said: 'But why? Alice, I have to know. Why?'

'That's a dangerous question, Meg. Are you sure you really want the answer?'

'I need the answer, need to try to understand.'

'Isn't it enough that she was determined to marry Alex and I was determined that she shouldn't?'

'That isn't why you killed her. It can't be. There was something more than that, there had to be.'

'Yes, there was. I suppose you have a right to know. She was blackmailing Alex. She could have stopped him getting that job, or, if he had got it, could have made it impossible for him to function successfully. She had the power to destroy his whole career. Toby Gledhill had told her that Alex had deliberately held up publishing the result of their research because it might have prejudiced the success of the inquiry into Larksoken's second reactor. They discovered that some of the assumptions made in generating the mathematical models were more critical than had been thought. People opposing the building of the new PWR at Larksoken could have exploited it to cause delay, whip up fresh hysteria.'

'You mean that he deliberately falsified the results?'

'That's something he's incapable of doing. All he did was to delay publishing the experiment. He'll publish it within the next month or two. But that's the kind of information which, once it got into the press, would have done irreparable harm. Toby was almost prepared to hand it over to Neil Pascoe but Hilary dissuaded him. It was far too valuable for that. She meant to use it to persuade Alex to marry her. She faced him with the knowledge when he walked home with her after the dinner party and late that night, he told me. I knew then what I had to do. The only way he might have been able to buy her off was by promoting her from Acting Administrator to Administrative Officer of Larksoken, and that was almost as impossible for him as deliberately falsifying a scientific result.'

'You mean he might actually have married her?'

'He might have been forced to. But how safe would he have been even then? She could have held that knowledge over his head until the end of his life. And what would that life have been, tied to a woman who had blackmailed him into marriage, a woman he didn't want, whom he could neither respect nor love?'

And then she said in a voice so low that Meg only just heard it, 'I owed Alex a death.'

Meg said: 'But how could you be sure, sure enough to kill her? Couldn't you have talked to her, persuaded her, reasoned with her?'

'I did talk to her. I went to see her on that Sunday afternoon. It was I who was with her when Mrs Jago arrived with the church magazine. You could say that I went to give her a chance of life. I couldn't murder her without making sure that it was necessary. That meant doing what I'd never done before, talking to her about Alex, trying to persuade her that the marriage wouldn't be in either of their interests, to let him go. I could have saved myself the humiliation. There was no argument, she was beyond that. She was no longer even rational. Part of the time she railed at me like a woman possessed.'

Meg said: 'And your brother, did he know about the visit?'

'He knows nothing. I didn't tell him at the time and I haven't told him since. But he told me what he planned; to promise her marriage and then, when the job was secure, to renege. It would have been disastrous. He never understood the woman he was dealing with, the passion, the desperation. She was a rich man's only child, alternately overindulged or neglected, trying all her life to compete with her father, taught that what you want is yours by right if you've only got the courage to fight for it and take it. And she had courage. She was obsessed by him, by her need for him, above all by her need for a child. She said that he owed her a child. Did he think she was like one of his reactors, tameable, that he could let down into that turbulence the equivalent of his rods of boron-steel and control the force which he'd let loose? When I left her that afternoon I knew I had no choice. Sunday was the deadline. He had arranged to call at Thyme Cottage on his way home from the power station. It was fortunate for him that I got to her first.

'Perhaps the worst part of all was waiting for him to come home that night. I daren't ring the power station. I couldn't be sure that he would be alone in his office or in the computer room, and I had never before telephoned him to ask when he would be home. I sat there and waited for nearly three hours. I expected that it would be Alex who would find the body. When he discovered that she wasn't in the cottage the natural move would be to check at the beach. He would find the body, telephone the police from the car and ring home to tell me. When he didn't I began to fantasize that she wasn't really dead, that somehow I'd bungled it. I pictured him desperately working on her, giving her the kiss of life, saw her eyes slowly open. I turned off the lights and moved to the sitting room to watch the road. But it wasn't an ambulance that arrived, it was the police cars, the paraphernalia of murder. And still Alex didn't come.'

Meg asked: 'And when he did?'

'We hardly spoke. I'd gone to bed; I knew I must do what I would normally have done, not waited up for him. He came to my room to tell me that Hilary was dead and how she had died. I asked "The Whistler?" and he answered, "The police think not. The Whistler was dead before she was killed." Then he left me. I don't think either of us could have borne to be together, the air heavy with our unspoken thoughts. But I did what I had to do, and it was worth it. The job is his. And they won't take it away from him, not after it's been confirmed. They can't sack him because his sister is a murderess.'

'But if they found out why you did it?'

'They won't. Only two people know that and I wouldn't have told you if I couldn't trust you. On a less elevated level, I doubt if they'd believe you in the absence of confirmation from another witness; and Toby Gledhill and Hilary Robarts, the only two who could give it, are dead.' After a minute's silence, she said: 'You would have done the same for Martin.'

'Oh no, no.'

'Not as I did. I can't see you managing to use physical force. But when he drowned, if you could have stood on that river bank and

392

had the power to choose which one should die and which live, would you have hesitated?'

'No, of course not. But that would have been different. I wouldn't have planned a drowning, wouldn't have wanted it.'

'Or if you were told that millions of people would live more safely if Alex got a job which he is uniquely capable of filling but at the cost of one woman's life, would you hesitate then? That was the choice which faced me. Don't evade it, Meg. I didn't.'

'But murder, how could it solve anything? It never has.'

Alice said with sudden passion: 'Oh, but it can, and it does. You read history, don't you? Surely you know that.'

Meg felt exhausted with weariness and pain. She wanted the talking to stop. But it couldn't. There was still too much to be said. She asked: 'What are you going to do?'

'That depends on you.'

But out of horror and disbelief Meg had found courage. And she had found more than courage: authority. She said: 'Oh no, it doesn't. This isn't a responsibility I asked for and I don't want it.'

'But you can't evade it. You know what you know. Call Chief Inspector Rickards now. You can use this telephone.' When Meg made no move to use it she said: 'Surely you aren't going to do an E. M. Forster on me. If I had a choice between betraying my country and my friend I hope I would have the guts to betray my country.'

Meg said: 'That is one of those clever remarks that, when you analyse them, either mean nothing or mean something rather silly.'

Alice said: 'Remember, whatever you choose to do, you can't bring her back. You've got a number of options, but that isn't one. It's very satisfying to the human ego to discover the truth; ask Adam Dalgliesh. It's even more satisfying to human vanity to imagine you can avenge the innocent, restore the past, vindicate the right. But you can't. The dead stay dead. All you can do is to hurt the living in the name of justice or retribution or revenge. If that gives you any pleasure, then do it, but don't imagine that there's virtue in it. Whatever you decide, I know that you won't go back on it. I can believe you and I can trust you.'

Looking at Alice's face Meg saw that the look bent on her was serious, ironic, challenging; but it was not pleading. Alice said: 'Do you want some time to consider?'

'No. There's no point in having time. I know now what I have to do. I have to tell. But I'd rather you did.'

'Then give me until tomorrow. Once I've spoken there'll be no more privacy. There are things I need to do here. The proofs, affairs to arrange. And I should like twelve hours of freedom. If you can give me that I'll be grateful. I haven't the right to ask for more, but I am asking for that.'

Meg said: 'But when you confess you'll have to give them a motive, a reason, something they can believe in.'

'Oh, they'll believe it all right. Jealousy, hatred, the resentment of an ageing virgin for a woman who looked as she did, lived as she did. I'll say that she wanted to marry him, take him from me after all I've done for him. They'll see me as a neurotic, menopausal woman gone temporarily off her head. Unnatural affection. Suppressed sexuality. That's how men talk about women like me. That's the kind of motive that makes sense to a man like Rickards. I'll give it to him.'

'Even if it means you end up in Broadmoor? Alice, could you bear it?'

'Well, that's a possibility, isn't it? It's either that or prison. This was a carefully planned murder. Even the cleverest counsel won't be able to make it look like a sudden, unpremeditated act. And I doubt whether there's much to choose between Broadmoor and prison when it comes to the food.'

It seemed to Meg that nothing ever again would be certain. Not only had her inner world been shattered but the familiar objects of the external world no longer had reality. Alice's roll-top desk, the kitchen table, the high-backed cane chairs, the rows of gleaming pans, the stoves all seemed insubstantial, as if they would disappear at her touch. She was aware that the kitchen round which her eyes ranged was now empty. Alice had left. She leaned back, faint, and closed her eyes and then, opening them, she was aware of Alice's face bending low over hers, immense, almost moon-like. She was handing Meg a tumbler. She said: 'It's whisky. Drink this, you need it.'

'No, Alice, I can't. I can't really. You know I hate whisky, it makes me sick.'

'This won't make you sick. There are times when whisky is the only possible remedy. This is one of them. Drink it, Meg.'

She felt her knees tremble, and simultaneously the tears started like burning spurts of pain and began flowing unchecked, a salt stream over her cheeks, her mouth. She thought, This can't be happening. This can't be true. But that was how she had felt when

Miss Mortimer, calling her from her class, had gently seated her in the chair opposite to her in the Head's private sitting room and had broken the news of Martin's death. The unthinkable had to be thought, the unbelievable believed. Words still meant what they had always meant; murder, death, grief, pain. She could see Miss Mortimer's mouth moving, the odd, disconnected phrases floating out, like balloons in a cartoon, noticing again how she must have wiped off her lipstick before the interview. Perhaps she had thought that only naked lips could give such appalling news. She saw again those restless blobs of flesh, noticed again that the top button on Miss Mortimer's cardigan was hanging loose on a single thread and heard herself say, actually say, 'Miss Mortimer, you're going to lose a button.'

She clasped her fingers round the glass. It seemed to her to have grown immensely large and heavy as a rock and the smell of the whisky almost turned her stomach. But she had no power to resist. She lifted it slowly to her mouth. She was aware of Alice's face still very close, of Alice's eyes watching her. She took the first small sip, and was about to throw back her head and gulp it down, when, firmly but gently, the glass was taken out of her hands, and she heard Alice's voice: 'You're quite right, Meg, it was never your drink. I'll make coffee for both of us then walk with you back to the Old Rectory.'

Fifteen minutes later Meg helped wash up the coffee cups as if this was the end of an ordinary evening. Then they set out together to walk over the headland. The wind was at their back and it seemed to Meg that they almost flew through the air, their feet hardly touching the turf, as if they were witches. At the door of the rectory Alice asked: 'What will you do tonight, Meg. Pray for me?'

'I shall pray for both of us.'

'As long as you don't expect me to repent. I'm not religious, as you know, and I don't understand that word unless, as I suppose, it means regret that something we've done has turned out less well for us than we hoped. On that definition I have little to repent of except ill luck that you, my dear Meg, are an incompetent car mechanic.'

And then, as if on impulse, she grasped Meg's arms. The grip was so fierce that it hurt. Meg thought for a moment that Alice was going to kiss her but her hold loosened and her hands fell. She said a curt goodbye and turned away.

Putting her key in the lock and pushing the door open, Meg looked back, but Alice had disappeared into the darkness and the wild sobbing, which for an incredible moment she thought was a woman weeping, was only the wind.

53

Dalgliesh had just finished sorting the last of his aunt's papers when the telephone rang. It was Rickards. His voice, strong, high with euphoria, came over the line as clearly as if his presence filled the room. His wife had given birth to a daughter an hour earlier. He was ringing from the hospital. His wife was fine. The baby was wonderful. He only had a few minutes. They were carrying out some nursing procedure or other and then he'd be able to get back to Susie.

'She's got home just in time, Mr Dalgliesh. Lucky, wasn't it? And the midwife says she's hardly known such a quick labour for a first pregnancy. Only six hours. Seven and a half pounds, just a nice weight. And we wanted a girl. We're calling her Stella Louise. Louise is after Susie's mother. We may as well make the old trout happy.'

Replacing the receiver after warm congratulations which he suspected Rickards felt were hardly adequate, Dalgliesh wondered why he had been honoured with such early news and concluded that Rickards, possessed by joy, was ringing everyone who might have an interest, filling in the minutes before he was allowed back to his wife's bedside. His last words were: 'I can't tell you what it feels like, Mr Dalgliesh.'

But Dalgliesh could remember what it had felt like. He paused for a moment, the receiver still warm under his hand, and faced reactions which seemed to him over-complicated for such ordinary and expected news, recognizing with distaste that part of what he was feeling was envy. Was it, he wondered, his coming to the headland, the sense there of man's transitory but continuing life, the everlasting cycle of birth and death, or was it the death of Jane Dalgliesh, his last living relative, that made him for a moment wish so keenly that he too had a living child?

Neither he nor Rickards had spoken about the murder. Rickards would no doubt have felt it an almost indecent intrusion into his private, almost sacrosanct, rapture. And there was, after all, little more to be said. Rickards had made it plain that he considered the case closed. Amy Camm and her lover were both dead and it was unlikely now that their guilt would ever be proved. And the case against them was admittedly imperfect. Rickards still had no evidence that either woman had known details of the Whistler killings. But that, apparently, now assumed less importance in the police mind. Someone could have talked. Scraps of information picked up by Camm in the Local Hero could have been pieced together. Robarts herself could have told Amphlett and what they hadn't learned they could have guessed. The case might officially be classified as unsolved but Rickards had now persuaded himself that Amphlett, helped by her lover Camm, had killed Hilary Robarts. Dalgliesh, when they had briefly met on the previous evening, had felt it right to put another view and had argued it calmly and logically, and Rickards had turned his own arguments against him.

'She's her own woman. You said so yourself. She's got her own life, a profession. Why the hell should she care who he marries? She didn't try to stop him when he married before. And it's not as if he needs protection. Can you imagine Alex Mair doing anything he doesn't want to do? He's the sort of man who'll die at his own convenience, not God's.'

Dalgliesh had said: 'The absence of motive is the weakest part of the case. And I admit there isn't a single piece of forensic or other physical evidence. But Alice Mair fulfils all the criteria. She knew how the Whistler killed; she knew where Robarts would be shortly after nine o'clock; she has no alibi; she knew where she could find those trainers and she is tall enough to wear them; she had an opportunity of throwing them into the bunker on her way back from Scudder's Cottage. But there's something else, isn't there? I think this crime was committed by someone who didn't know that the Whistler was dead when she did the murder and did know shortly afterwards.'

'It's ingenious, Mr Dalgliesh.'

Dalgliesh was tempted to say that it wasn't ingenious, merely logical. Rickards would feel obliged to question Alice Mair again, but he would get nowhere. And it wasn't his case. Within two days he would be back in London. Any more dirty work which MI5 wanted done they would have to do themselves. He had already interfered more than was strictly justified and certainly more than he had found agreeable. He told himself that it would be dishonest to blame either Rickards or the murderer for the fact that most of the decisions he had come to the headland to make were still undecided.

That unexpected spurt of envy had induced a mild self-disgust which wasn't helped by the discovery that he had left the book he was currently reading, A. N. Wilson's biography of Tolstoy, in the room at the top of the tower. It was providing satisfaction and consolation of which at the present he felt particularly in need. Shutting the front door of the mill firmly against the wind, he fought his way round the curve of the tower, switched on the lights and climbed up to the top storey. Outside, the wind whooped and screamed like a pack of demented demons but here, in this small domed cell it was extraordinarily quiet. The tower had stood for over 150 years. It had resisted far worse gales. On an impulse he opened the eastward window and let the wind rush in like a wild cleansing force. It was then that he saw, over the flint wall which bounded the patio at Martyr's Cottage, a light in the kitchen window. It was no ordinary light. As he watched, it flickered, then died, flickered again, and then strengthened into a ruddy glow. He had seen that kind of light before and knew what it meant. Martyr's Cottage was on fire.

He almost slid down the two ladders linking the mill floors and, dashing into the sitting room, paused only to telephone for the fire brigade and ambulance, grateful that he hadn't yet garaged the car. Seconds later he was hurtling at top speed across the rough grass of the headland. The Jaguar rocked to a stop and he rushed to the front door. It was locked. For a second he considered battering it open with the Jaguar. But the frame was solid sixteenth-century oak and valuable seconds could be lost in futile manoeuvring and accelerating. Racing to the side he sprang at the wall, grasped the top, swung his body over and dropped on to the rear patio. It took only a second to check that the back door, too, was bolted top and bottom. He had no doubt who was inside; he would have to get her out through the window. He tore off his jacket and wrapped it round his right arm while, at the same time, turning on full the outside tap and drenching his head and upper body. The icy water dripped from him as he flexed his elbow and crashed it against the glass. But the pane was thick, designed to keep out the winter gales. He had to stand on the sill, supporting himself by the window frame, and kick violently and repeatedly before the glass crashed inwards and the flames leapt at him.

Inside the window was a double sink. He rolled over it and, gasping in the smoke, dropped to his knees and began to crawl towards her. She was lying between the stove and the table, the long body rigid as an effigy. Her hair and clothes were alight and she lay there staring upwards, bathed in tongues of fire. But her face was as yet untouched and the open eyes seemed to gaze at him with such an intensity of half-crazed endurance that there flashed into his mind unbidden the image of Agnes Poley so that the blazing tables and chairs were the crackling faggots of her agonizing martyrdom, and he smelled above the acrid smoke the dreadful stink of burning flesh.

He tugged at Alice Mair's body but it was awkwardly wedged and the edge of the burning table had fallen across her legs. Somehow he had to buy a few seconds of time. He staggered coughing through the smoke to the sink, turned both taps full on and, seizing a pan, he filled it and threw water over the flames again and again. A small area of fire hissed and began to die. Kicking away the burning debris, he managed to lift her over his shoulder then stumbled to the door. But the bolts, almost too hot to touch, were jammed fast. He would have to get her out through the broken window. Gasping with the effort, he pushed the dead weight forward over the sink. But the rigid body caught on the taps and it took an eternity of agonizing time before he was able to free her, shove her forward to the window and at last see her tip forward out of sight. He gasped in the fresh air and, grasping the edge of the sink, tried to raise himself. But suddenly his legs had no strength. He felt them buckle and had to rest his arms on the sink edge to prevent himself from falling back into the strengthening fire. Until this minute he had been unaware of pain, but now it clawed and bit at his legs and back as if he were being savaged by a pack of dogs. He couldn't stretch his head to reach the running taps but he cupped his hands and threw the water against his face as if this cool benison could assuage the agony in his legs. And suddenly he was visited with an almost overwhelming temptation to let go, to fall back into the fire rather than make the impossible effort to escape. It was only a second's folly but it spurred him to a last desperate attempt. He seized the taps, one with each hand, and slowly and painfully lifted himself across the sink. And now his knees had a purchase on the hard edge and he could thrust himself forward to the windows. Smoke billowed around him and the great tongues of flame roared at his back. His ears hurt with the roaring. It filled the headland and he no longer knew whether he was hearing fire, wind or the sea. Then he made the last effort and felt himself falling on to the softness of her body. He rolled away from her. She was no longer burning. Her clothes had been burnt away and now clung like blackened rags to what was left of the flesh. He managed to get to his feet and half crawled, half stumbled towards the outside tap. He reached it just before he lost consciousness and the last thing he heard was the hiss as the stream of water quenched his burning clothes.

A minute later he opened his eyes. The stones were hard against his burnt back and when he tried to move the spasm of agony made him cry aloud. He had never known such pain. But a face, pale as the moon, was bending over him and he recognized Meg Dennison. He thought of that blackened thing by the window and managed to say: 'Don't look. Don't look.'

But she answered gently: 'She's dead. And it's all right, I had to look.'

And then he ceased to know her. His mind, disorientated, was in another place, another time. And suddenly, among the crowd of gaping spectators, the soldiers with their pikes guarding the scaffold, there was Rickards saying: 'But she isn't a thing, Mr Dalgliesh. She's a woman.' He closed his eyes. Meg's arms enclosed him. He turned his face and pressed it into her jacket, biting the wool so that he would not disgrace himself by groaning aloud. And then he felt her cool hands on his face.

She said: 'The ambulance is coming. I can hear it. Lie still, my dear. It's going to be all right.'

The last sound he heard was the clanging of the fire engine's bell as he let himself slide again into unconsciousness.

EPILOGUE

Wednesday 18 January

It was mid-January before Adam Dalgliesh came again to Larksoken Mill, a sunny day of such warmth that the headland lay bathed in the bright translucence of a premature spring. Meg had arranged to meet him at the mill in the afternoon to say goodbye and, passing through the rear garden gate to walk across the headland, she saw that the first snowdrops were already in bloom and squatted to gaze with pure pleasure at their delicate green and white heads trembling in the breeze. The turf of the headland was springy to her feet and, in the far distance, a flock of seagulls wheeled and swooped like a shower of white petals.

The Jaguar stood outside the mill and through the open door a swathe of sunlight lay over the denuded room. Dalgliesh was on his knees packing the last of his aunt's books into tea chests. The pictures, already wrapped, were propped against the wall. Meg knelt beside him and began to help by passing him the corded volumes. She said: 'How are your legs and back?'

'A little stiff and the scars still itch occasionally. But they seem fine.'

'No more pain?'

'No more pain.'

They worked for a few minutes in companionable silence. Then Meg said: 'I know you don't want to be told this, but we're all grateful for what you are doing for the Blaneys. The rent you're charging for the mill is derisory and Ryan knows it.'

Dalgliesh said: 'I'm doing him no favours. I wanted a local family to live here and he was the obvious choice. It isn't everyone's house, after all. If he's worried about the size of the rent he can regard himself as a caretaker. You could argue that I should be paying him.'

'Not many men looking for a caretaker would choose an eccentric artist with four children. But this place will be just right for them; two bathrooms, a proper kitchen and the tower for Ryan to paint in. Theresa is transformed. She's been so much stronger since her operation and now she looks radiant with happiness. She called in at the Old Rectory yesterday to tell us all about it and how she's been measuring up the rooms and planning where they'll put the furniture. It's much more suitable for them than Scudder's Cottage even if Alex hadn't wanted to sell and get rid of it for good. I can't blame him. Did you know that he's selling Martyr's Cottage, too? Now that he's so busy with the new job I think he wants to cut himself off from the headland and its memories. I suppose that's natural. And I don't think you know about Jonathan Reeves. He's engaged to a young girl from the power station, Shirley Coles. And Mrs Jago has had a letter from Neil Pascoe. After a couple of false starts he's got a temporary job as a social worker in Camden. She says he seems happy enough. And there's good news about Timmy, at least I suppose it's good news. The police have traced Amy's mother. She and her common-law husband don't want Timmy so he's being placed for adoption. He'll go to a couple who'll give him love and security.'

And then she stopped, afraid that she was prattling on, that he might not be interested in all this local gossip. But there was one question that had been in her mind for the last three months which she needed to ask, and which only he could answer. She watched for a moment in silence as the long sensitive hands fitted the corded books expertly into the case, then said: 'Does Alex accept that his sister killed Hilary? I've never liked to ask Inspector Rickards and he wouldn't tell me if I did. And I can't possibly ask Alex. We've never discussed Alice or the murder since her death. At the funeral we hardly spoke.'

But she knew that Rickards would have confided in Adam Dalgliesh. He said: 'I don't think Alex Mair is a man to deceive himself about uncomfortable facts. He must know the truth. But that doesn't mean that he'll admit it to the police. Officially he accepts their view that the murderess is dead but that it's now impossible to prove whether that murderess was Amy Camm, Caroline Amphlett or Alice Mair. The difficulty is that there still isn't a single piece of concrete evidence to connect Miss Mair with Hilary Robarts's death and certainly not enough circumstantial evidence posthumously to brand her as the killer. If she had lived and withdrawn her confession to you I doubt whether Rickards would have been justified even in making an arrest. The open verdict at the inquest means that even the suicide theory is unproved. The fire investigator's report confirms that the fire was caused by the overturn of a pan of boiling fat, probably while she was cooking, perhaps trying out a new recipe.'

Meg said bitterly: 'And it all rests on my story, doesn't it? The not-very-likely tale told by a woman who has made trouble before and who has a history of mental breakdown. That came out clearly when I was being questioned. Inspector Rickards seemed obsessed with the relationship, whether I had a grudge against Alice, whether we had quarrelled. By the time he had finished I didn't know whether he saw me as a malicious liar or her accomplice.'

Even three and a half months after the death it was difficult to think of those long interrogations without the familiar destructive mixture of pain, fear and anger. She had been made to tell her story over and over again under those sharp and sceptical eyes. And she could understand why he had been so reluctant to believe her. She had never found it easy to lie convincingly and he had known that she was lying. But why? he had asked. What reason did Alice Mair give for the murder? What was her motive? Her brother couldn't be forced to marry Hilary Robarts. And it's not as if he hadn't been married before. His ex-wife is alive and well, so what made this marriage so impossible for her? And she hadn't told him, except to reiterate obstinately that Alice had wanted to prevent it. She had promised not to tell, and she never would, not even to Adam Dalgliesh, who was the only man who might possibly have been able to make her. She guessed that he knew that too, but that he would never ask. Once when she was visiting him in hospital she had suddenly said: 'You know, don't you?'

And he had replied: 'No, I don't know, but I can guess. Blackmail isn't an uncommon motive for murder.'

But he had asked no questions, and for that she was grateful. She knew now that Alice had told her the truth only because she had planned that Meg wouldn't be alive the next day to reveal it. She had meant them to die together. But in the end she had drawn back. The whisky, almost certainly drugged with her sleeping tablets, had been gently but firmly taken from her hand. In the end Alice had kept faith with their friendship and she would keep faith with her friend. Alice had said that she owed her brother a death. Meg had pondered on those words but could still find no real meaning in them. But if Alice had owed Alex a death she, for her part, owed Alice her loyalty and her silence. She said: 'I'm hoping to buy Martyr's Cottage when the repairs are finished. I have some capital from the sale of the London house and the promise of a small mortgage which is all I'll need. I thought I could let it in summer to

407

help with the expenses. And then, when the Copleys no longer need me, I could move in and live there. I'd like the thought that it would be waiting for me.'

If he was surprised that she should want to return to a place with such traumatic memories, he didn't say so. As if she had a need to explain Meg went on: 'Terrible things have happened in the past to people living on this headland, not only to Agnes Poley, to Hilary, to Alice, to Amy and Caroline. But I still feel at home here. I still feel that this is my place. I still feel that I want to be part of it. And if there are ghosts at Martyr's Cottage, they will be friendly spirits.'

He said: 'It's a stony soil in which to put down roots.'

'Perhaps that's the kind of soil my roots need.'

An hour later she had said her last goodbye. The truth lay between them, unspoken, and now he was leaving and she might never see him again. She realized with a smile of happy surprise that she was a little in love with him. But it didn't matter. It was as devoid of pain as it was of hope. When she reached a low ridge on the headland she turned and looked north at the power station, the generator and symbol of the potent and mysterious power which she could never separate from the image of that curiously beautiful mushroom cloud, symbol too of the intellectual and spiritual arrogance which had led Alice to murder, and it seemed to her for a second that she heard the echo of the last warning siren screaming its terrible message over the headland. And evil didn't end with the death of one evildoer. Somewhere at this moment a new Whistler could be planning his dreadful revenge against a world in which he had never been at home. But that was in the unforeseeable future and the fear had no reality. Reality was here, in a single moment of sunlit time, in the shivering grasses of the headland, the sparkling sea layered in blue and purple to the horizon and winged with a single sail, the broken arches of the abbey in which the flints struck gold from the mellowing sun, the great sails of the mill, motionless and silent, the taste of the sea-salted air. Here the past and the present fused and her own life, with its trivial devices and desires, seemed only an insignificant moment in the long history of the headland. And then she smiled at these portentous imaginings and, turning to wave a final goodbye to the tall figure still standing at the mill door, she strode out resolutely for home. The Copleys would be waiting for their afternoon tea.

Original Sin

CONTENTS

BOOK ONE

Foreword to Murder

For a temporary shorthand-typist to be present at the discovery of a corpse on the first day of a new assignment, if not unique, is sufficiently rare to prevent its being regarded as an occupational hazard. Certainly Mandy Price, aged nineteen years two months, and the acknowledged star of Mrs Crealey's Nonesuch Secretarial Agency, set out on the morning of Tuesday, 14 September for her interview at the Peverell Press with no more apprehension than she usually felt at the start of a new job, an apprehension which was never acute and was rooted less in any anxiety whether she would satisfy the expectations of the prospective employer than in whether the employer would satisfy hers. She had learned of the job the previous Friday when she called in at the agency at six o'clock to collect her pay after a boring two-week stint with a director who regarded a secretary as a status symbol but had no idea how to use her skills, and she was ready for something new and preferably exciting although perhaps not as exciting as it was subsequently to prove.

Mrs Crealey, for whom Mandy had worked for the past three years, conducted her agency from a couple of rooms above a newsagent and tobacconist's shop off the Whitechapel Road, a situation which, she was fond of pointing out to her girls and clients, was convenient both for the City and for the towering offices of Docklands. Neither had so far produced much in the way of business, but while other agencies foundered in the waves of recession Mrs Crealey's small and underprovisioned ship was still, if precariously, afloat. Except for the help of one of her girls when no outside work was available, she ran the agency single-handed. The outer room was her office in which she propitiated clients, interviewed new girls and assigned the next week's work. The inner was her personal sanctum, furnished with a divan bed on which she occasionally spent the night in defiance of the terms of the lease, a drinks cabinet and refrigerator, a cupboard which opened to reveal a minute kitchen, a large television set and two easy chairs set in front of a gas fire in which a lurid red light rotated behind artificial logs. She referred to her room as the 'cosy', and Mandy was one of the few girls who was admitted to its privacies.

It was probably the cosy which kept Mandy faithful to the agency, although she would never have openly admitted to a need which would have seemed to her both childish and embarrassing. Her mother had left home when she was six and she herself had been hardly able to wait for her sixteenth birthday when she could get away from a father whose idea of parenthood had gone little further than the provision of two meals a day which she was expected to cook, and her clothes. For the last year she had rented one room in a terraced house in Stratford East where she lived in acrimonious camaraderie with three young friends, the main cause of dispute being Mandy's insistence that her Yamaha motor bike should be parked in the narrow hall. But it was the cosy in Whitechapel Road, the mingled smells of wine and take-away Chinese food, the hiss of the gas fire, the two deep and battered armchairs in which she could curl up and sleep which represented all Mandy had ever known of the comfort and security of a home.

Mrs Crealey, sherry bottle in one hand and a scrap of jotting pad in the other, munched at her cigarette holder until she had manoeuvred it to the corner of her mouth where, as usual, it hung in defiance of gravity, and squinted at her almost indecipherable handwriting through immense horn-rimmed spectacles.

'It's a new client, Mandy, the Peverell Press. I've looked them up in the publishers' directory. They're one of the oldest – perhaps the oldest – publishing firm in the country, founded in 1792. Their place is on the river. The Peverell Press, Innocent House, Innocent Walk, Wapping. You must have seen Innocent House if you've taken a boat trip to Greenwich. Looks like a bloody great Venetian palace. They do have a launch, apparently, to collect staff from Charing Cross pier, but that'll be no help to you, living in Stratford. It's your side of the Thames, though, which will help with the journey, I suppose you'd better take a taxi. Mind you get them to pay before you leave.'

'That's OK, I'll use the bike.'

'Just as you like. They want you there on Tuesday at ten o'clock.'

Mrs Crealey was about to suggest that, with this prestigious new client, a certain formality of dress might be appropriate, but desisted. Mandy was amenable to some suggestions about work or behaviour but never about the eccentric and occasionally bizarre creations with which she expressed her essentially confident and ebullient personality.

She asked: 'Why Tuesday? Don't they work Mondays?'

'Don't ask me. All I know is that the girl who rang said Tuesday. Perhaps Miss Etienne can't see you until then. She's one of the directors and she wants to interview you personally. Miss Claudia Etienne. I've written it all down.'

Mandy said: 'What's the big deal then? Why have I got to be interviewed by the boss?'

'One of the bosses. They're particular who they get, I suppose. They asked for the best and I'm sending the best. Of course they may be looking for someone permanent, and want to try her out first. Don't let them persuade you to stay on, Mandy, will you?'

'Have I ever?'

Accepting a glass of sweet sherry and curling into one of the easy chairs, Mandy studied the paper. It was certainly odd to be interviewed by a prospective employer before beginning a new job even when, as now, the client was new to the agency. The usual procedure was well understood by all parties. The harassed employer telephoned Mrs Crealey for a temporary shorthand typist, imploring her this time to send a girl who was literate and whose typing speed at least approximated to the standard claimed. Mrs Crealey, promising miracles of punctuality, efficiency and conscientiousness, dispatched whichever of her girls was free and could be cajoled into giving the job a try, hoping that this time the expectations of client and worker might actually coincide. Subsequent complaints were countered by Mrs Crealey's invariably plaintive response: 'I can't understand it. She's got the highest reports from other employers. I'm always being asked for Sharon.'

The client, made to feel that the disaster was somehow his or her fault, replaced the receiver with a sigh, urged, encouraged, endured until the mutual agony was over and the permanent member of staff returned to a flattering welcome. Mrs Crealey took her commission, more modest than was charged by most agencies, which probably accounted for her continued existence in business, and the transaction was over until the next epidemic of 'flu or the summer holidays provoked another triumph of hope over experience.

Mrs Crealey said: 'You can take Monday off, Mandy, on full pay of course. And better type out your qualifications and experience. Put

"Curriculum Vitae" at the top, that always looks impressive.'

Mandy's curriculum vitae, and Mandy herself – despite her eccentric appearance – never failed to impress. For this she had to thank her English teacher, Mrs Chilcroft. Mrs Chilcroft, facing her class of recalcitrant eleven-year-olds, had said: 'You are going to learn to write your own language simply, accurately and with some elegance, and to speak it so that you aren't disadvantaged the moment you open your mouths. If any of you has ambitions above marrying at sixteen and rearing children in a council flat you'll need language. If you've no ambitions beyond being supported by a man or the State you'll need it even more, if only to get the better of the local authority Social Services department and the DSS. But learn it you will.'

Mandy could never decide whether she hated or admired Mrs Chilcroft, but under her inspired if unconventional teaching she had learned to speak English, to write, to spell and to use it confidently and with some grace. Most of the time this was an accomplishment she preferred to pretend she hadn't achieved. She thought, although she never articulated the heresy, that there was little point in being at home in Mrs Chilcroft's world if she ceased to be accepted in her own. Her literacy was there to be used when necessary, a commercial and occasionally a social asset, to which Mandy added high shorthand-typing speeds and a facility with various types of word processor. Mandy knew herself to be highly employable, but remained faithful to Mrs Crealey. Apart from the cosy there were obvious advantages in being regarded as indispensable; one could be sure of getting the pick of the jobs. Her male employers occasionally tried to persuade her to take a permanent post, some of them offering inducements which had little to do with annual increments, luncheon vouchers or generous pension contributions. Mandy remained with the Nonesuch Agency, her fidelity rooted in more than material considerations. She occasionally felt for her employer an almost adult compassion. Mrs Crealey's troubles principally arose from her conviction of the perfidy of men combined with an inability to do without them. Apart from this uncomfortable dichotomy, her life was dominated by a fight to retain the few girls in her stable who were employable, and her war of attrition against her ex-husband, the tax inspector, her bank manager and her office landlord. In all these traumas Mandy was ally, confidante and sympathizer. Where Mrs Crealey's love-life was concerned this was more from an easy goodwill than from any understanding, since to Mandy's nineteen-year-old mind the possibility that her employer could actually wish to have sex with the elderly – some of them must be at least fifty – and unprepossessing males who occasionally haunted the office, was too bizarre to warrant serious contemplation.

After a week of almost continuous rain Tuesday promised to be a fine day with gleams of fitful sunshine shafting through the low clusters of cloud. The ride from Stratford East wasn't long, but Mandy left plenty of time and it was only a quarter to ten when she turned off The Highway, down Garnet Street and along Wapping Wall, then right into Innocent Walk. Reducing speed to a walking pace, she bumped along a wide cobbled cul-de-sac bounded on the north by a ten-foot wall of grey brick and on the south by the three houses which comprised the Peverell Press.

At first sight she thought Innocent House disappointing. It was an imposing but unremarkable Georgian house with proportions which she knew rather than felt to be graceful, and it looked little different from the many others she had seen in London's squares or terraces. The front door was closed and she saw no sign of activity behind the four storeys of eight-paned windows, the two lowest ones each with an elegant wrought-iron balcony. On either side was a smaller, less ostentatious house, standing a little distanced and detached like a pair of deferential poor relations. She was now opposite the first of these, number 10, although she could see no sign of numbers 1 to 9, and saw that it was separated from the main building by Innocent Passage, barred from the road by a wrought-iron gate, and obviously used as a parking space for staff cars. But now the gate was open and Mandy saw three men bringing down large cardboard cartons by a hoist from an upper floor and loading them into a small van. One of the three, a swarthy under-sized man wearing a battered bush-ranger's hat, took it off and swept Mandy a low ironic bow. The other two glanced up from their work to regard her with obvious curiosity. Mandy, pushing up her visor, bestowed on all three of them a long discouraging stare.

The second of these smaller houses was separated from Innocent House by Innocent Lane. It was here, according to Mrs Crealey's instructions, that she would find the entrance. She switched off the engine, dismounted, and wheeled the bike over the cobbles, looking

7

for the most unobtrusive place in which to park. It was then that she had her first glimpse of the river, a narrow glitter of shivering water under the lightening sky. Parking the Yamaha, she took off her crash helmet, rummaged for her hat in the side pannier and put it on, and then, with the helmet under her arm, and carrying her tote bag, she walked towards the water as if physically drawn by the strong tug of the tide, the faint evocative sea smell.

She found herself on a wide forecourt of gleaming marble bounded by a low railing in delicate wrought iron with at each corner a glass globe supported by entwined dolphins in bronze. From a gap in the middle of the railing a flight of steps led down to the river. She could hear its rhythmic slap against the stone. She walked slowly towards it in a trance of wonder as if she had never seen it before. It shimmered before her, a wide expanse of heaving sun-speckled water which, as she watched, was flicked by the strengthening breeze into a million small waves like a restless inland sea, and then, as the breeze dropped, mysteriously subsided into shining smoothness. And, turning, she saw for the first time, the towering wonder of Innocent House, four storeys of coloured marble and golden stone which, as the light changed, seemed subtly to change colour, brightening, then shading to a deeper gold. The great curved arch of the main entrance was flanked by narrow arched windows and above it were two storeys with wide balconies of carved stone fronting a row of slender marble pillars rising to trefoiled arches. The high arched windows and marble columns extended to a final storey under the parapet of a low roof. She knew none of the architectural details but she had seen houses like this before, on a boisterous ill-conducted school trip to Venice when she was thirteen. The city had left little impression on her beyond the high summer reek of the canal, which had caused the children to hold their noses and scream in simulated disgust, the over-crowded picture galleries and palaces which she was told were remarkable but which looked as if they were about to crumble into the canals. She had seen Venice when she was too young and inadequately prepared. Now for the first time in her life, looking up at the marvel of Innocent House, she felt a belated response to that earlier experience, a mixture of awe and joy which surprised and a little frightened her.

The trance was broken by a male voice: 'Looking for someone?'

Turning, she saw a man looking at her through the railings, as if he

8

had risen miraculously from the river. Walking over, she saw that he was standing in the bow of a launch moored to the left of the steps. He was wearing a yachting cap set well back on a mop of black curls and his eyes were bright slits in the weatherbeaten face.

She said: 'I've come about a job. I was just looking at the river.'

'Oh, she's always here is the river. The entrance is down there.' He cocked a thumb towards Innocent Lane.

'Yes, I know.'

To demonstrate independence of action, Mandy glanced at her watch, then turned and spent another two minutes regarding Innocent House. With a final glance at the river she made her way down Innocent Lane.

The outer door bore a notice: PEVERELL PRESS – PLEASE ENTER. She pushed it open and passed through a glass vestibule and into the reception office. To the left was a curved desk and a switchboard manned by a grey-haired, gentle-faced man who greeted her with a smile before checking her name on a list. Mandy handed him her crash-helmet and he received it into his small age-speckled hands as carefully as if it were a bomb, and for a few moments seemed uncertain what to do with it, finally leaving it on the counter.

He announced her arrival by telephone, then said: 'Miss Blackett will come to take you up to Miss Etienne. Perhaps you would like to take a seat.'

Mandy sat and, ignoring the three daily newspapers, the literary magazines and the carefully arranged catalogues fanned out on a low table, looked about her. It must once have been an elegant room; the marble fireplace with an oil painting of the Grand Canal set in the panel above it, the delicate stuccoed ceiling and the carved cornice contrasted incongruously with the modern reception desk, the comfortable but utilitarian chairs, the large baize-covered noticeboard and the caged lift to the right of the fireplace. The walls painted a dark rich green bore a row of sepia portraits. Mandy supposed they were of previous Peverells and had just got to her feet to have a closer look when her escort appeared, a sturdy, rather plain woman who was presumably Miss Blackett. She greeted Mandy unsmilingly, cast a surprised and rather startled look at her hat and, without introducing herself, invited Mandy to follow her. Mandy was unworried by her lack of warmth. This was obviously the managing director's PA, anxious to demonstrate her status. Mandy had met her kind before.

9

The hall made her gasp with wonder. She saw a floor of patterned marble in coloured segments from which six slim pillars rose with intricately carved capitals to an amazing painted ceiling. Ignoring Miss Blackett's obvious impatience as she lingered on the bottom step of the staircase, Mandy unselfconsciously paused and slowly turned, eyes upwards, while above her the great coloured dome spun slowly with her; palaces, towers with their floating banners, churches, houses, bridges, the curving river plumed with the sails of high-masted ships and small cherubs with pouted lips blowing prosperous breezes in small bursts like steam from a kettle. Mandy had worked in a variety of offices from glass towers furnished with chrome and leather and the latest electronic wonders to rooms as small as cupboards with one wooden table and an ancient typewriter, and had early learned that the office ambience was an unreliable guide to the firm's financial standing. But never before had she seen an office building like Innocent House.

They mounted the wide double staircase without speaking. Miss Etienne's office was on the first floor. It had obviously once been a library but the end had been partitioned to provide a small office. A serious-faced young woman, so thin she looked anorexic, was typing on a word processor and gave Mandy only a brief glance. Miss Blackett opened the interconnecting door and announced: 'It's Mandy Price from the agency, Miss Claudia', then left.

The room seemed to Mandy very large after the ill-proportioned outer office and she walked across an expanse of parquet flooring towards a desk set to the right of the far window. A tall dark woman got up to receive her, shook hands and motioned her to the opposite chair.

She said: 'You have your curriculum vitae?'

'Yes, Miss Etienne.'

Never before had she been asked for a CV, but Mrs Crealey had been right; obviously one was expected. Mandy reached down to her tasselled and garishly embroidered tote bag, a trophy from last summer's holiday in Crete, and handed over three carefully typed pages. Miss Etienne studied them and Mandy studied Miss Etienne.

She decided that she wasn't young, certainly over thirty. Her face was sharp-boned with a pale delicate skin, the eyes shallowly set with dark, almost black, irises under heavy lids. Above them the brows had been plucked to a high arch. The short hair, brushed to a sheen, was parted on the left side, the falling strands tucked behind her right ear. The hands which rested on the CV were ringless, the fingers very long and slender, the nails unpainted.

Without looking up, she asked: 'Is your name Mandy or Amanda Price?'

'Mandy, Miss Etienne.' In other circumstances Mandy would have pointed out that if her name were Amanda the CV would have said so.

'Have you had any previous experience of working in a publishing house?'

'Only about three times during the last two years. I've listed the names of the firms I've worked for on page three of my CV.'

Miss Etienne read on, then looked up, the bright luminous eyes under the curved brows studying Mandy with more interest than she had previously shown.

She said: 'You seem to have done very well at school, but you've had an extraordinary variety of jobs since. You haven't stuck to any of them for more than a few weeks.'

In three years of temping Mandy had learned to recognize and circumvent most of the machinations of the male sex, but was less assured when it came to dealing with her own. Her instinct, sharp as a ferret's tooth, told her that Miss Etienne might need careful handling. She thought, that's what being a temp is, you silly old cow. Here today and gone tomorrow. What she said was: 'That's why I like temporary work. I want to get as wide a variety of experience as possible before I settle down to a permanent job. Once I do, I'd like to stay on and try to make a success of it.'

Mandy was being less than candid. She had no intention of taking a permanent job. Temporary work, with its freedom from contracts and conditions of service, its variety, the knowledge that she wasn't tied down, that even the worst job experience could end by the following Friday, suited her perfectly; her plans, however, lay elsewhere. Mandy was saving for the day when, with her friend Naomi, she could afford a small lock-up shop in the Portobello Road. There Naomi would fashion her jewellery and Mandy would design and make her hats, both of them rising rapidly to fame and fortune.

Miss Etienne looked again at the curriculum vitae. She said drily: 'If your ambition is to find a permanent job then make a success of it, you are certainly unique in your generation.'

11

She handed back the curriculum vitae with a quick impatient gesture, rose to her feet, and said: 'All right, we'll give you a typing test. Let's see if you're as good as you claim. There's a second word processor in Miss Blackett's office on the ground floor. That's where you'll be working so you may as well do the test there. Mr Dauntsey, our poetry editor, has a tape he wants transcribed. It's in the little archives office.' She got up and added, 'We'll fetch it together. You may as well get some idea of the layout of the house.'

Mandy said: 'Poetry?' This could be tricky, typing from tape. From her experience it was difficult with modern verse to know where the lines began and ended.

'Not poetry. Mr Dauntsey is examining and reporting on the archives, recommending which files should be retained, which destroyed. The Peverell Press has been publishing since 1792. There's some interesting material in the old files and it ought to be properly catalogued.'

Mandy followed Miss Etienne down the wide curved stairs, across the hall and into the reception room. Apparently they were to use the lift and it ran only from the ground floor. It was hardly, she thought, the best way to get an idea of the layout of the house, but the comment had been promising; it looked as if the job was hers if she wanted it. And from that first view of the Thames, Mandy knew that she did want it.

The lift was small, little more than five feet square, and as they groaned upwards she was sharply aware of the tall silent figure whose arm almost brushed her own. She kept her eyes fixed on the grid of the lift but she could smell Miss Etienne's scent, subtle and a little exotic but so faint that perhaps it wasn't scent at all but only an expensive soap. Everything about Miss Etienne seemed to Mandy expensive, the dull sheen of the shirt which could only be silk, the double gold chain and gold stud earrings, the cardigan casually slung around her shoulders which had the fine softness of cashmere. But the physical closeness of her companion and her own heightened senses, stimulated by the novelty and excitement of Innocent House, told her something more; that Miss Etienne wasn't at ease. It was she, Mandy, who should have been nervous. Instead she was aware that the air of the claustrophobic lift, jerking upwards with such maddening slowness, was quivering with tension.

They shuddered to a stop and Miss Etienne hauled back the

double-grille gates. Mandy found herself in a narrow hall with a facing door and one on the left. The door ahead was open and she saw a large cluttered room filled from floor to ceiling with metal shelves tightly packed with files and bundles of papers. The racks ran from the windows to the door with just enough room to walk between them. The air smelt of old paper, musty and stale. She followed Miss Etienne between the ends of the shelves and the wall and to another smaller door, this time closed.

Pausing, Miss Etienne said: 'Mr Dauntsey works on the files in here. We call it the little archives office. He said that he'd leave the tape on the table.'

It seemed to Mandy that the explanation was unnecessary and rather odd, and that Miss Etienne hesitated for a second, hand on the knob, before turning it. Then with a sharp gesture, almost as if she expected some obstruction, she pushed the door wide open.

The stink rolled out to meet them like an evil wraith, the familiar human smell of vomit, not strong but so unexpected that Mandy instinctively recoiled. Over Miss Etienne's shoulder her eyes took in at once a small room with an uncarpeted wooden floor, a square table to the right of the door and a single high window. Under the window was a narrow divan bed and on the bed sprawled a woman.

It had needed no smell to tell Mandy that she was looking at death. She didn't scream; she had never screamed from fear or shock; but a giant fist mailed in ice clutched and squeezed her heart and stomach and she began shivering as violently as a child lifted from an icy sea. Neither of them spoke but, with Mandy close behind Miss Etienne, they moved with quiet almost imperceptible steps closer to the bed.

She was lying on top of a tartan rug but had taken the single pillow from beneath it to rest her head as if needing this final comfort even in the last moments of consciousness. By the bed stood a chair holding an empty wine bottle, a stained tumbler and a large screw-top jar. Beneath it a pair of brown laced shoes had been neatly laid side by side. Perhaps, thought Mandy, she had taken them off because she hadn't wanted to soil the rug. But the rug was soiled and so was the pillow. There was a slime of vomit like the track of a giant snail gummed to the left cheek and stiffening the pillow. The woman's eyes were half open, the irises turned upward, her grey hair, worn in a fringe, was hardly disarranged. She was wearing a brown high-necked jumper and a tweed skirt from which two skinny legs, oddly

13

twisted, stuck out like sticks. Her left arm was flung outwards, almost touching the chair, the right lay across her breast. The right hand had scrabbled at the thin wool of the jumper before death, drawing it up to reveal a few inches of white vest. Beside the empty pill bottle there was a square envelope addressed in strong black handwriting.

Mandy whispered as reverently as if she were in church: 'Who is she?'

Miss Etienne's voice was calm. 'Sonia Clements. One of our senior editors.'

'Was I going to work for her?'

Mandy knew the question was irrelevant as soon as she asked it, but Miss Etienne replied: 'For part of the time, yes, but not for long. She was leaving at the end of the month.'

She picked up the envelope, seeming to weigh it in her hands. Mandy thought, she wants to open it but not in front of me. After a few seconds Miss Etienne said: 'Addressed to the coroner. It's obvious enough what's happened here even without this. I'm sorry you've had this shock, Miss Price. It was inconsiderate of her. If people wish to kill themselves they should do so in their own homes.'

Mandy thought of the small terrace in Stratford East, the shared kitchen and one bathroom, her own small back room in a house in which you'd be lucky to find enough privacy to swallow the pills, let alone die of them. She made herself gaze again at the woman's face. She felt a sudden urge to close the eyes and shut the slightly gaping mouth. So this was death, or rather this was death before the undertakers got their hands on you. Mandy had seen only one other dead person, her gran; neatly shrouded with a frill at her neck, packaged into her coffin like a doll in a gift box, curiously diminished and looking more peaceful than Gran ever had in life, the bright restless eyes closed, the over-busy hands folded in quietude at last. Suddenly grief came upon her in a torrent of pity, perhaps released by delayed shock or the sudden acute memory of the gran whom she had loved. At the first hot prick of tears she wasn't sure whether they were for Gran or for this stranger sprawled in such defenceless ungainliness. She seldom cried but when she did her tears were unstoppable. Terrified she would disgrace herself she fought for control and, gazing round, her eyes lit on something familiar, unfrightening, something she could cope with, an assurance that there was an ordinary world continuing outside this death-cell. On the table was a small tape recorder.

Mandy went over to it and closed her hand round it as if it were an icon. She said, 'Is this the tape? Is it a list? Do you want it tabulated?'

Miss Etienne regarded her for a moment in silence, then she said, 'Yes, tabulate it. And two copies. You can use the word processor in Miss Blackett's office.'

And in that moment Mandy knew that she had the job.

2

Fifteen minutes earlier Gerard Etienne, chairman and managing director of Peverell Press, was leaving the boardroom to return to his office on the ground floor. Suddenly he stopped, stepped back into the shadows, delicate-footed as a cat, and stood watching from behind the balustrade. Below him in the hall a girl was slowly pirouetting, her eyes upward to the ceiling. She was wearing thigh-length black boots flared at the top, a short tight fawn skirt and a velvet jacket in a dull red. One thin and delicate arm was raised to hold on her head a remarkable hat. It seemed to be made of red felt and was wide-brimmed, turned up at the front and decorated with an extraordinary array of objects: flowers, feathers, strips of satin and lace, even small fragments of glass. As she turned it flashed and gleamed and glittered. She should, he thought, have looked ridiculous, the peaked childish face half-hidden by untidy swathes of dark hair, topped by such a grotesque confection. Instead she looked enchanting. He found himself smiling, almost laughing, and was suddenly seized with a madness he hadn't felt since he was twenty-one, the urge to rush down the wide staircase, sweep her into his arms and dance with her across the marble floor, out through the front door and to the rim of the glittering river. She had finished her slow turn and followed Miss Blackett across the hall. He stood for a moment savouring this upsurge of folly which, it seemed to him, had nothing to do with sex but the need to hold distilled a memory of youth, of early loves, of laughter, of freedom from responsibility, of sheer animal delight in the world of the senses. None of it had any part in his life now. He was still smiling as he waited until the hall was clear and then slowly descended to his office.

Ten minutes later the door opened and he recognized his sister's footsteps. Without looking up he said: 'Who is the child in the hat?'

'The hat?' For a moment she seemed not to understand, then she said: 'Oh, the hat. Mandy Price from the secretarial agency.'

There was an odd note in her voice and he turned, giving her his full attention. He said, 'Claudia, what's happened?'

'Sonia Clements is dead. Suicide.'

'Where?'

'Here. In the little archives office. The girl and I found her. We were fetching one of Gabriel's tapes.'

'That girl found her?' He paused and added, 'Where is she now?'

'I've told you, in the little archives office. We didn't touch the body. Why should we?'

'I mean where is the child?'

'Next door with Blackie working on the tape. Don't waste your pity. She wasn't alone and there isn't any blood. That generation is tough. She didn't blink an eye. All she worried about was getting the job.'

'You're sure it was suicide?'

'Of course. She left this note. It's open but I haven't read it.'

She handed over the envelope then walked to the window and stood looking out. After a couple of seconds he slid out the flap and drew the paper carefully from the envelope, then read aloud. ' "I am sorry to cause a nuisance but this seemed the best room to use. Gabriel will probably be the one to find me and he's too familiar with death to be shocked. Now that I live alone I might not have been discovered at home until I began to stink and I find that one has the need to preserve some dignity, even in death. My affairs are in order, and I have written to my sister. I am under no obligation to give a reason for my act, but in case anyone is interested it is simply that I prefer annihilation to continued existence. It is a reasonable choice and one which we are all entitled to make." '

He said: 'Well that's clear enough, and in her own hand. How did she do it?'

'With drugs and drink. There isn't much mess, as I said.'

'Have you phoned the police?'

'The police? I haven't had time yet. I came straight to you. And is it really necessary Gerard? Suicide isn't a crime. Can't we just ring Dr Frobisher?'

He said curtly, 'I don't know whether it's necessary but it's certainly expedient. We don't want any doubts about this death.'

'Doubts?' she said. 'Doubts? Why should there be doubts?'

She had lowered her voice and now they were almost whispering. Almost imperceptibly they moved further from the partition towards the window.

17

He said: 'Gossip then, rumours, scandal. We can phone the police from here. There's no point in going through the switchboard. If they bring her down in the lift we can probably get her out of the building before the staff know what's happened. There's George of course. I suppose that the police had better come in by that door. George will have to be told to keep his mouth shut. Where is the agency girl now?'

'I've told you. Next door in Blackie's room, doing her typing test.'

'Or, more likely, describing to Blackie and anyone else who comes by how she was taken upstairs to get a tape and found a dead body.'

'I've instructed them both to say nothing until we've told all the staff. Gerard, if you think you can keep this quiet even for a couple of hours, forget it. There'll be an inquest, publicity. And they'll have to bring her down by the stairs. You can't possibly fit a body bag on a stretcher in the lift. My God, though, this is all we needed! Coming on top of the other business it's going to be great for staff morale.'

There was a moment's silence in which neither moved towards the telephone. Then she looked at him and asked: 'When you sacked her last Wednesday, how did she take it?'

'She didn't kill herself because I gave her the push. She was a rational woman, she knew she had to go. She must have known that from the day I took over here. I always made it clear that I thought we had one editor too many, that we could farm out the work to a freelance.'

'But she's fifty-three. It wouldn't have been easy for her to get another job. And she's been here for twenty-four years.'

'Part-time.'

'Part-time but working almost full-time. This place was her life.'

'Claudia, that's sentimental nonsense. She had an existence outside these walls. What the hell has that to do with it anyway? Either she was needed here or she wasn't.'

'And is that how you broke it to her? No longer needed.'

'I wasn't brutal, if that's what you're implying. I told her that I proposed to employ a freelance for some of the non-fiction editing and that her post was therefore superfluous. I said that although she didn't legally qualify for maximum redundancy pay we would come to some financial arrangement.'

'Arrangement? What did she say?'

'She said that it wouldn't be necessary. She would make her own arrangements.'

'And she has. Apparently with distalgesic and a bottle of Bulgarian cabernet. Well at least she's saved us money but, by God, I'd rather have paid out than be faced with this. I know I ought to feel pity for her. I suppose I shall when I've got over the shock. Just now it isn't easy.'

'Claudia, it's pointless to reopen all those old arguments. It was necessary to sack her and I sacked her. That had nothing to do with her death. I did what had to be done in the interests of the firm and at the time you agreed. Neither you nor I can be blamed for her suicide and her death has nothing to do with the other mischief here either.' He paused then said: 'Unless of course she was the one responsible.'

She didn't miss the sudden note of hope in his voice. So he was more worried than he would admit. She said bitterly: 'That would be a neat way out of our troubles, wouldn't it? But how could she have been, Gerard? She was off sick, remember, when the Stilgoe proofs were tampered with and visiting an author in Brighton when we lost the illustrations for the Guy Fawkes book. No, she's in the clear.'

'Of course. Yes, I'd forgotten. Look, I'll ring the police now while you go round the office and explain what's happened. That's less dramatic than getting everyone together for a general announcement. Tell them to stay in their rooms until the body has been removed.'

She said slowly: 'There is one thing. I think I was the last person to see her alive.'

'Someone had to be.'

'It was last night, just after seven. I was working late. I came out of the cloakroom on the first floor and saw her going up the stairs. She was carrying a bottle of wine and a glass.'

'You didn't ask her what she was doing?'

'Of course I didn't. She wasn't a junior typist. For all I knew she was taking the wine to the archives room to do a spot of secret drinking. If so it was hardly my concern. I thought it odd that she was working so late, but that's all.'

'Did she see you?'

'I don't think so. She didn't look round.'

'And no one else was about?'

'Not at that hour. I was the last.'

'Then say nothing about it. It isn't relevant. It doesn't help.'

'I did have a feeling, though, that there was something strange about her. She did look – well – furtive. She was almost scurrying.'

'That's hindsight. You didn't check on the building before you locked up?'

'I looked in her room. The light wasn't on. There was nothing there, no coat, no bag. I suppose she'd locked them in her cupboard. Obviously I thought she'd left and gone home.'

'You can say that at the inquest, but no more. Don't mention seeing her earlier. It might only lead the coroner to ask why you didn't check the top of the building.'

'Why should I?'

'Exactly.'

'But Gerard, if I'm asked when I saw her last . . .'

'Then lie. But for God's sake, Claudia, lie convincingly and stick with the lie.' He moved over to the desk and lifted the receiver. 'I suppose I'd better dial 999. It's odd, but this is the first time in my memory that we've ever had the police at Innocent House.'

She turned from the window and looked full at him. 'Let's hope that it's the last.'

3

In the outer office Mandy and Miss Blackett sat each at her word processor, each typing, eyes fixed on the screen. Neither spoke. At first Mandy's fingers had refused to work, trembling uncertainly over the keys as if the letters had been inexplicably transposed and the whole keyboard had become a meaningless jumble of symbols. But she clasped her hands tightly in her lap for half a minute and by an effort of will brought the shaking under control, and when she actually began typing the familiar skill took over and all was well. From time to time she glanced quickly at Miss Blackett. The woman was obviously deeply shocked. The large face with its marsupial cheeks and small, rather obstinate mouth, was so white that Mandy feared that at any moment she would slump forward over the keyboard in a faint.

It was over half an hour since Miss Etienne and her brother had left. Within ten minutes of closing the door Miss Etienne had put her head round it and had said: 'I've asked Mrs Demery to bring you some tea. It's been a shock for both of you.'

The tea had come within minutes, carried in by a red-haired woman in a flowered apron who had put down the tray on top of a filing cabinet with the words: 'I'm not supposed to talk so I won't. No harm in telling you, though, that the police have just arrived. That's quick work. No doubt they'll be wanting tea now.' She had then disappeared, as if aware that there was more excitement to be had outside the room than in.

Miss Blackett's office was an ill-proportioned room, too narrow for its height, the discordancy emphasized by the splendid marble fireplace with its formal patterned frieze, the heavy mantelshelf supported by the heads of two sphinxes. The partition, wooden for the bottom three feet with paned glass above, cut across one of the narrow arched windows as well as bisecting a lozenge-shaped decoration on the ceiling. Mandy thought that if the large room had had to be divided, it could have been done with more sensitivity to the architecture, not to mention Miss Blackett's convenience. This way it gave the impression that she was grudged even enough space in which to work.

Another but different oddity was the long snake in striped green velvet curled between the handles of the two top drawers of the steel filing cabinets. Its bright button eyes were crowned with a minute top hat and its forked tongue in red flannel hung from a soft open mouth lined with what looked like pink silk. Mandy had seen similar snakes before; her gran had had one. They were intended to be laid along the bottom of doors to exclude draughts, or wound round the handles to keep the door ajar. But it was a ridiculous object, a kind of kid's toy, and hardly one she had expected to see in Innocent House. She would have liked to have asked Miss Blackett about it but Miss Etienne had told them not to talk and Miss Blackett was obviously interpreting this as prohibiting all speech except about work.

The minutes passed silently. Mandy would shortly be at the end of her tape. Then Miss Blackett, looking up, said: 'You can stop that now. I'll give you some dictation. Miss Etienne wanted me to test your shorthand.'

She took one of the firm's catalogues from her desk drawer, handed Mandy a notebook, moved her chair beside her and began reading in a low voice, hardly moving her almost bloodless lips. Mandy's fingers automatically formed the familiar hieroglyphics but her mind took in few of the details of the forthcoming non-fiction list. From time to time Miss Blackett's voice faltered and Mandy knew that she too was listening to the sounds outside. After the initial sinister silence, they could now hear footsteps, half-imagined whispering, and then louder footfalls echoing on the marble and confident masculine voices.

Miss Blackett, her eyes on the door, said tonelessly: 'Perhaps you'd read it back now?'

Mandy read back her shorthand faultlessly. Again there was a silence. Then the door opened and Miss Etienne came in. She said: 'The police have arrived. They are just waiting for the police surgeon and then they'll be taking Miss Clements away. You'd better stay here until it's all clear.' She looked at Miss Blackett. 'Have you finished the test?'

'Yes, Miss Claudia.'

Mandy handed up her typed lists. Miss Etienne glanced at them dismissively and said: 'Right, the job is yours if you want it. Start tomorrow at nine-thirty.'

4

Ten days after Sonia Clements' suicide and exactly three weeks before the first of the Innocent House murders, Adam Dalgliesh lunched with Conrad Ackroyd at the Cadaver Club. It was at Ackroyd's invitation, given by telephone with that conspiratorial and slightly portentous air with which all Conrad's invitations were invested. Even a duty dinner party given to pay off outstanding social obligations promised mystery, cabals, secrets to be imparted to the privileged few. The date suggested was not really convenient and Dalgliesh rearranged his diary with some reluctance while reflecting that one of the disadvantages of advancing age was an increasing disinclination for social engagements combined with an inability to summon the wit or energy to circumvent them. The friendship between them – he supposed the word was appropriate enough; they were certainly not mere acquaintances – was based on the use each occasionally made of the other. Since both acknowledged the fact, neither could see that it needed justification or excuse. Conrad, one of the most notorious and reliable gossips in London, had often been useful to him, notably in the Berowne case. On this occasion Dalgliesh would obviously be expected to confer the benefit, but the demand in whatever form it came would probably be more irritating than onerous, the food at the Cadaver was excellent and Ackroyd, although he could be facetious, was seldom dull.

Later he was to see all the horrors that followed as emanating from that perfectly ordinary luncheon, and would find himself thinking: if this were fiction and I were a novelist, that's where it would all begin.

The Cadaver Club is not among the most prestigious of London's private clubs but its coterie of members find it among the most convenient. Built in the 1800s, it was originally the house of a wealthy if not particularly successful barrister who, in 1892, bequeathed it, suitably endowed, to a private club formed some five years earlier which had regularly met in his drawing-room. The club was and remains exclusively masculine, the main qualification for membership being a professional interest in murder. Now, as then, it lists among the members a few retired senior police officers, practising and retired barristers, nearly all of the most distinguished professional and amateur criminologists, crime reporters, and a few eminent crime-novelists, all male and there on sufferance since the club takes the view that, where murder is concerned, fiction cannot compete with real life. The club had recently been in danger of moving from the category of eccentric to the dangerous one of fashionable, a risk which the committee had promptly countered by blackballing the next six applicants for admission. The message was received. As one disgruntled applicant complained, to be blackballed by the Garrick is embarrassing, but to be blackballed by the Cadaver is ridiculous. The club kept itself small and, by its eccentric standards, select.

Crossing Tavistock Square, in the mellow September sunshine, Dalgliesh wondered how Ackroyd qualified as a member until he recalled the book his host had written five years earlier on three notorious murderers: Hawley Harvey Crippen, Norman Thorne and Patrick Mahon. Ackroyd had sent him a signed copy and Dalgliesh, dutifully reading it, had been surprised at the careful research and the even more careful writing. Ackroyd's thesis, not entirely original, had been that all three were innocent in the sense that none had intended to kill his victim, and Ackroyd had made a plausible, if not entirely convincing case, based on a detailed examination of the medical and forensic evidence. For Dalgliesh the main message of the book had been that men wishing to be acquitted of murder should avoid dismembering their victims, a practice for which British juries have long demonstrated their distaste.

They were to meet in the library for a sherry before luncheon and Ackroyd was already there ensconced in one of the leather high-backed chairs. He got to his feet with surprising agility for one of his size and came towards Dalgliesh with small, rather prancing steps, looking not a day older than when they had first met.

He said: 'It's good of you to make time, Adam. I realize how busy you are now. Special adviser to the Commissioner, member of the working party on regional crime squads and an occasional murder investigation to keep your hand in. You mustn't let them overwork you, dear boy. I'll ring for sherry. I thought of inviting you to my other club but you know how it is. Lunching there is a useful way of reminding people that you're still alive, but the members will come up and congratulate you on the fact. We'll be downstairs in the Snug.'

Ackroyd had married in late middle age, to the astonishment and consternation of his friends, and lived in connubial self-sufficiency in an agreeable Edwardian villa in St John's Wood where he and Nelly Ackroyd devoted themselves to their house and garden, their two Siamese cats and Ackroyd's largely imaginary ailments. He owned, edited and financed from a substantial private income *The Paternoster Review*, that iconoclastic mixture of literary articles, reviews and gossip, the last carefully researched, occasionally discreet, more often as malicious as it was accurate. Nelly, when not ministering to her husband's hypochondria, was an enthusiastic collector of 1920s and 1930s girls' school stories. The marriage was a success although Conrad's friends still had to remind themselves to ask after Nelly's health before enquiring about the cats.

The last time Dalgliesh had been in the library the visit had been professional and he had been in search of information. But then the case had been murder and he had been greeted by a different host. Little seemed to have changed. The room faced south over the square and this morning was warm with sunlight which, filtering through the fine white curtains, made the thin fire almost unnecessary. Originally the drawing-room, it now served both as sitting-room and library. The walls were lined with mahogany cases which held what was probably the most comprehensive private library of books on crime in London, including all the volumes of the Notable British Trials and Famous Trials series, books on medical jurisprudence, forensic pathology and policing and the club's few first editions of Conan Doyle, Poe, Le Fanu and Wilkie Collins, in a smaller case as if to demonstrate fiction's innate inferiority to reality. The large mahogany showcase was still in place, filled with articles collected or donated over the years; the prayer book with the signature, Constance Kent, on the flyleaf, the flintlock duelling pistol, supposedly used by the Reverend James Hackman for the murder of Margaret Wray, mistress of the Earl of Sandwich, a phial of white powder, allegedly arsenic, found in the possession of Major Herbert Armstrong. There was an addition since Dalgliesh's last visit. It lay curled, sinister as a lethal snake, in pride of place beneath a label stating that this was the rope with which Crippen had been hanged. Dalgliesh, turning to follow Ackroyd out of the library, mildly suggested that the public display of this distasteful object was barbaric, a protest which Ackroyd as mildly repudiated.

'A trifle morbid, perhaps, but barbaric is going a little far. After all, this isn't the Athenaeum. It probably does some of the older members good to be reminded of the natural end of their previous professional activities. Would you still be a detective if we hadn't abolished hanging?'

'I don't know. Abolition doesn't help with that particular moral dilemma as far as I'm concerned, since personally I would prefer death to twenty years in prison.'

'Not death by hanging?'

'No, not that.'

Hanging, for him, as he suspected for most people, had always held a particular horror. Despite the reports of Royal Commissions on capital punishment which claimed for it humanity, speed and the certainty of instantaneous death, it remained for him one of the ugliest forms of judicial execution encumbered with horrifying images as precisely lined as a pen drawing: mass victims in the wake of triumphant armies, the pathetic, half-demented victims of seventeenth-century justice, the muted drums of the quarterdecks of ships where the navy exacted its revenge and issued its warning, women convicted in the eighteenth century of infanticide, that ridiculous but sinister ritual of the small black square formally placed atop the judge's wig, the concealed but ordinary-looking door leading from the condemned cell to that last brief walk. It was good that they were all part of history. For a moment the Cadaver Club was a less agreeable place in which to lunch, its eccentricities more repugnant than amusing.

The Snug at the Cadaver Club is well named. It is a small basement room at the rear of the house with two windows and a french door opening on to a narrow paved courtyard bounded by a ten-foot ivied wall. The yard could comfortably accommodate three tables, but the members of the club are not addicted to dining outside, even in the occasional hot spell of an English summer, apparently regarding the habit as a foreign eccentricity incompatible with the proper appreciation of food or the privacy necessary to good talk. To dissuade any member who might be tempted to this indulgence, the courtyard is furnished with terracotta pots of various sizes planted with geraniums and ivy, and space further restricted by a huge stone copy of the Apollo Belvedere propped in the wall against the corner and rumoured to be the gift of an early member of the Club whose wife had banished it from their suburban garden. The geraniums were still in full bloom and the bright pinks and reds glowed through the glass enhancing the immediate impression of welcoming domesticity. The room had obviously once been the kitchen and one wall was still fitted with the original iron grate, its bars and ovens polished now to ebony. The blackened beam above was hung with iron cooking instruments and a row of copper pans, battered but gleaming. An oak dresser ran the whole length of the opposite wall, serving as a receptacle for the display of the gifts and bequests of members which were deemed unsuitable for, or unworthy of, the library cabinet.

Dalgliesh remembered that the Club had an unwritten law that no offering from a member, however inappropriate or bizarre, should be rejected and the dresser, like the whole room, bore witness to the idiosyncratic tastes and hobbies of the donors. Delicate Meissen plates were ranged in incongruous proximity to Victorian ribbon-decorated souvenirs bearing pictures of Brighton and Southend-on-Sea, a toby jug which looked like a fairground trophy stood between a Victorian Staffordshire flatback, obviously original, of Wesley preaching from a double-decker pulpit, and a fine Parian bust of the Duke of Wellington. An assortment of coronation mugs and early Stafford-shire cups was suspended in precarious disorder from the hooks. Beside the door hung a painted glass picture of the burial of Princess Charlotte; above it a stuffed elk's head with an old Panama hat slung on its left horn gazed glassy-eyed with lugubrious disapproval at a large and lurid print of the Charge of the Light Brigade.

The present kitchen was somewhere close; Dalgliesh could hear small agreeable tinklings and from time to time the thud of the food lift descending from the first floor dining-room. Only one of the four tables was set, the linen immaculate, and Dalgliesh and Ackroyd seated themselves beside the window.

The menu and wine list were already to the right of Ackroyd's place. Taking them up, he said: 'The Plants have retired, but we've got the Jacksons now, and I'm not sure that Mrs Jackson's cooking isn't even better. We were lucky to get them. She and her husband used to run a private nursing home but they got tired of the country and wanted to return to London. They dcn't need to work but I think the job suits them. They've kept on with the policy of having only one main dish a day at luncheon and dinner. Very wise. Today, white bean and tuna fish salad followed by rack of lamb with fresh vegetables and a green salad. Then lemon tart and cheese to follow. The vegetables will be fresh. We still get all the vegetables and eggs from young Plant's smallholding. Do you want to see the wine list? Have you a preference?'

'I'll leave that to you.'

Ackroyd cogitated aloud while Dalgliesh, who loved wine but disliked talking about it, let his gaze range appreciatively over the muddle of a room which despite, perhaps because of, its air of eccentric but organized chaos was surprisingly restful. The discordant objects, not carefully placed for effect, had through time achieved a rightness of place. After a lengthy discussion on the merits of the wine list in which Ackroyd apparently expected no contribution from his guest, he fixed on a chardonnay. Mrs Jackson, appearing as if in response to some secret signal, brought with her the smell of hot rolls and an air of bustling confidence.

'Very nice to meet you, Commander. You've got the Snug to yourself this morning, Mr Ackroyd. Mr Jackson will be seeing to the wine.'

After the first course had been served, Dalgliesh said: 'Why is Mrs Jackson dressed as a nurse?'

'Because she is one, I suppose. She used to be a matron. She's a midwife too, I believe, but we've no call for that here.'

Not surprisingly, thought Dalgliesh, since the Club didn't admit women. He said: 'Isn't that goffered cap with streamers going a bit far?'

'Oh, do you think so? I suppose we've got used to it. I doubt if the members would feel at home if Mrs Jackson stopped wearing it now.'

Ackroyd wasted no time in coming to the purpose of the meeting. As soon as they were finally alone he said: 'Lord Stilgoe had a word with me last week in Brooks's. He's my wife's uncle, incidentally. Do you know him?'

'No. I thought he was dead.'

'I can't think how you got that idea.' He prodded at his bean salad irritably and Dalgliesh remembered that he resented any suggestion that someone he knew personally could actually die, and certainly not without the prior knowledge of himself. 'He isn't even as old as he looks, not eighty yet. He's remarkably spry for his age. Actually he's publishing his memoirs. The Peverell Press are bringing them out next spring. That's what he wanted to see me about. Something rather worrying has happened. At least his wife finds it worrying. She thinks he's had a direct threat of murder.'

'And has he?'

'Well, he's received this.'

He took some time in taking the small oblong of paper from his wallet and passing it over to Dalgliesh. The words had been accurately typed on a word processor and the message was unsigned.

'Do you really think it wise to publish with Peverell Press? Remember Marcus Seabright, Joan Petrie and now Sonia Clements. Two authors and your own editor dead in less than twelve months. Do you want to be number four?'

Dalgliesh said: 'More mischievous than threatening, I should have thought, and the malice directed against the Press rather than Stilgoe. There's no doubt that Sonia Clements' death was suicide. She left a note for the coroner and wrote to her sister telling her that she intended to kill herself. I don't recall anything about the first two deaths.'

'Oh, they're straightforward enough, I should have thought. Seabright was over eighty and had a bad heart. He died from an attack of gastroenteritis which brought on a heart attack. Anyway, he was no loss to Peverell Press. He hadn't produced a novel for ten years. Joan Petrie killed herself driving to her country cottage. Accidental death. Petrie had two passions, whisky and fast cars. The only surprise is that she killed herself before she killed someone else. Obviously the poison pen dragged up these two deaths as make weights. But Dorothy Stilgoe is superstitious. She takes the view, why publish with Peverell when there are other publishers?'

'And who is actually in charge now?'

'Oh Gerard Etienne. Very much so. The last chairman and managing director, old Henry Peverell, died in early January and left his shares in the business in equal parts to his daughter Frances and to Gerard. His original partner, Jean-Philippe Etienne, had retired about a year previously, and not before time. His shares also went to Gerard. The two older men ran the firm as if it was their private hobby. Old Peverell always took the view that a gentleman inherited money, he didn't earn it. Jean-Philippe Etienne hadn't taken an active part in the firm for years. His moment of glory, of course, was in the last war where he was a hero of the Resistance in Vichy France, but I don't think he's done anything memorable since. Gerard was waiting in the wings, the crown prince. And now he's well on stage and we're likely to see action if not melodrama.'

'Does Gabriel Dauntsey still run the poetry list?'

'I'm surprised you need to ask, Adam. You mustn't let your passion for catching murderers put you out of touch with real life. Yes, he's still there. He hasn't written a poem himself for over twenty years. Dauntsey's an anthology poet. The best is so good that it keeps reappearing, but I imagine most readers think he's dead. He was a bomber pilot in the last war so he must be well over seventy. It's time he retired. The poetry list at Peverell Press is about all he does nowadays. The other three partners are Gerard's sister Claudia Etienne, James de Witt, who's been with the firm since he left Oxford, and Frances Peverell, the last of the Peverells. But it's Gerard who runs the firm.'

'What is he planning, do you know?'

'Rumour has it that he wants to sell Innocent House and move to Docklands. That won't please Frances Peverell. The Peverells have always had an obsession about Innocent House. It belongs to the partnership now, not to the family, but any Peverell thinks of it as the family home. He's already made other changes, some staff sacked including Sonia Clements. He's right, of course. The firm has got to be dragged into the twentieth century or go under, but he's certainly made enemies. It's significant that they had no trouble at the Press until Gerard took over. That coincidence hasn't escaped Stilgoe, although his wife is still convinced that the malice is directed against her husband personally, not the firm, and against his memoirs in particular.'

'Will Peverell lose much if the book is withdrawn?'

'Not a great deal, I imagine. Of course they'll hype the memoirs as if their disclosures could bring down the Government, discredit the Opposition and end parliamentary democracy as we know it, but I imagine that, like most political memoirs, they'll promise more than they deliver. But I don't see how it can be withdrawn. The book is in production, they won't let it go without a struggle, and Stilgoe won't want to break the contract if it means publicly explaining why. What Dorothy Stilgoe is asking is, was Sonia Clements' death really suicide and did someone interfere with Petrie's Jag? I think she's satisfied enough that old Seabright died from natural causes.'

'So what am I expected to do?'

'There must have been inquests in the last two cases and presumably the police carried out an investigation. Your people could take a look at the papers, have a word with the officers concerned, that sort of thing. Then, if Dorothy could be assured that a senior Metropolitan detective has looked at all the evidence and is satisfied, she might give her husband, and Peverell Press, some peace.'

Dalgliesh said: 'That might serve to satisfy her that Sonia Clements' death was suicide. It will hardly content her if she's superstitious, and I don't see what will. The essence of superstition is that it isn't amenable to reason. She'll probably take the view that an unlucky publisher is as bad as a murderous one. I suppose she isn't seriously suggesting that someone at Peverell Press put an unidentifiable poison in Sonia Clements' wine?'

'No, I don't think she's going as far as that.'

'Just as well or her husband will have his profits eaten up by a libel action. I'm surprised he didn't go straight to the Commissioner or to me direct.'

'Are you? I'm not sure. It would have looked – well, shall we say a little timid, a trifle over-concerned. Besides he doesn't know you, I do. I can understand why he spoke to me first. And of course, one can hardly see him calling in at the local nick, joining the queue of lost-dog owners, assaulted wives and aggrieved motorists and explaining his dilemma to the duty sergeant. Frankly I don't think he believed it would be taken seriously. His view is that, having regard to his wife's concern and that anonymous note, he's justified in asking the police to take a look at what is happening at the Peverell Press.'

The lamb had arrived, pink and succulent and tender enough to be eaten with a spoon. In the few minutes of silence which Ackroyd thought a necessary tribute to a perfectly cooked meal, Dalgliesh recalled the first time he had seen Innocent House.

His father had taken him to London for his eighth birthday treat; they were to spend two whole days sightseeing and stay overnight with a friend, who was a parish priest in Kensington, and his wife. He could remember lying in bed the night before, fitfully sleeping and almost sick with excitement, the cavernous immensity and clamour of the old Liverpool Street Station, his terror of losing his father, of being caught up and swept along with the great army of grey-faced marching people. In the two days in which his father had intended to combine pleasure with education – to his scholarly mind the two were indistinguishable – they had perhaps inevitably tried to do too much. The visit had been overwhelming for an eight-year-old, leaving a confused memory of churches and galleries, restaurants and unfamiliar food, of floodlit towers and the dancing reflection of light on the black creased surface of the water, of sleek, prancing horses and silver helmets, of the glamour and terror of history made manifest in brick and stone. But London had laid on him her spell which no adult experience, no exploration of other great cities had been able to break.

It was on the second day that they had visited Westminster Abbey and later taken a river steamer from Charing Cross pier to Greenwich and he had first seen Innocent House, glittering in the morning sun, seeming to rise like a golden mirage from the shimmering water. He had gazed at it in wonder. His father had explained that the name was derived from Innocent Walk which ran behind the house, at the end of which had once stood an early eighteenth-century magistrates' court. Defendants taken into custody after their first hearing were removed to the Fleet prison; the more fortunate walked down the cobbled lane to freedom. He had started to tell his son something of the house's architectural history, but his voice had been overpowered by the tour-guide's booming commentary, loud enough to be heard by every boat on the river.

'And here, coming up on our left ladies and gentlemen, is one of the most interesting buildings on the Thames: Innocent House, built in 1830 for Sir Francis Peverell, a noted publisher of the day. Sir Francis had visited Venice and had been very impressed by the Ca' d'Oro, the Golden House on the Grand Canal. Those of you who have had holidays in Venice have probably seen it. So he hit on the idea of building his own golden house on the Thames. Pity he couldn't import Venetian weather.' He paused briefly for the expected laughter. 'Today it is the headquarters of a publishing firm, the Peverell Press, so it's still in the family. There's an interesting story about Innocent House. Apparently Sir Francis was so absorbed by it that he neglected his young wife whose money had helped him to build it, and she threw herself from the top balcony and was instantly killed. The legend has it that you can still see the stain of her blood on the marble which can't be cleaned away. It's said that Sir Francis went mad with remorse in his old age and used to go out alone at night trying to get rid of that tell-tale spot. It's his ghost that people claim to see, still scrubbing away at the stain. There are some watermen who don't like sailing too close to Innocent House after dark.'

All eyes on deck had been docilely turned to the house but now, intrigued by this story of blood, the passengers moved to hang over the rail; voices murmured and heads craned as if the legendary stain might still be visible. Eight-year-old Adam's over-vivid imagination had pictured a white-clad woman, blonde hair flying, flinging herself from the balcony like some demented storybook heroine, had heard the final thud and seen the trickle of blood creeping and starting across the marble to drip into the Thames. For years afterwards the house had continued to fascinate him with a potent amalgam of beauty and terror.

The tour-guide had been inaccurate about one fact; it was possible that the suicide story had also been embellished or untrue. He knew now that Sir Francis had been enchanted, not by the Ca' d'Oro which, despite the intricacies of its fine tracings and carvings, he had found, or so he had written to his architect, too asymmetrical for his taste, but by the Palace of Doge Francesco Foscari, and it was the Ca' Foscari which his architect had been instructed to build for him on this cold, tidal river. It should have looked incongruous, a folly, unmistakably Venetian and Venetian of the mid-fifteenth century. And yet it looked as if no other city, no other site would have been right for it. Dalgliesh still found it difficult to understand why it should be so successful, this unashamed borrowing from another age, another country, a softer, warmer air. The proportions had been changed and surely that alone should have rendered Sir Francis's dream an impracticable presumption, but the reduction in scale had been brilliantly carried out and the dignity of the original somehow maintained. There were six great central window arches instead of eight behind the finely carved balconies of the first and second floors, but the marble columns with their decorated pinnules were almost exact copies of the Venetian palace and the central arcades here, as there, were balanced by tall single windows, giving the façade its unity and grace. The great curved door fronted a marble patio leading to a landing-stage and a flight of steps to the river. On either side of the house two brick-built Regency town houses with small balconies, presumably built to house coachmen or other servants, stood like humble sentries of the central magnificence. He had seen it from the river many times since that eighth birthday celebration but had never been inside. He recalled having read that there was a fine Matthew Cotes Wyatt

33

ceiling in the central hall and rather wished he could see it. It would be a pity if Innocent House fell into the hands of philistines.

He asked: 'And what exactly has been going on at Peverell Press? What's worrying Lord Stilgoe apart from his poison pen letter?'

'So you've heard the rumours. Difficult to tell. They're being rather cagey about it and I don't blame them. But one or two little incidents have become common knowledge. Not so little either. The most serious happened just before Easter when they lost the illustrations for Gregory Maybrick's book on the Guy Fawkes conspiracy. Popular history, no doubt, but Maybrick knows his period. They expected to do rather well with it. He'd managed to lay his hands on some interesting contemporary plates, never before published, as well as other written records, and the whole lot were lost. They were on loan from the various owners and he'd more or less guaranteed their safety.'

'Lost? Mislaid? Destroyed?'

'The story is that he delivered them by hand to James de Witt who was editing the book. He's their senior editor and normally responsible for fiction but old Peverell who edited their non-fiction had died about three months earlier and I suppose they either hadn't had time to find a suitable replacement or wanted to save money. Like most houses they're laying off rather than taking on. The rumour is that they can't keep afloat much longer. Not surprising with that Venetian palace to maintain. Anyway, the illustrations were handed over to de Witt in his office and he locked them in his cupboard while Maybrick watched.'

'Not in a safe?'

'My dear boy, we're talking about a publishing house not Cartier's. Knowing Peverells, I'm only surprised that de Witt bothered to lock the cupboard.'

'Was his the only key?'

'Really Adam, you're not detecting now. Actually it was. He kept it in a battered old tobacco tin in his left-hand drawer.'

Where else? thought Dalgliesh. He said: 'Where any member of the staff or any unaccompanied visitor could lay hands on it.'

'Well, someone obviously did. James didn't need to go to the cupboard for a couple of days. The illustrations were due to be delivered personally to the art department the following week. You know that Peverells have put out their artwork to an independent firm?'

'No, I didn't know.'

'More economical, I suppose. It's the same firm that's been doing the jackets for the last five years. Rather well, actually. Peverells have never let their standards slip on book production and design. You can always tell a Peverell book just by handling it. Until now, of course. Gerard Etienne may change that too. Anyway, when de Witt looked for the envelope it had disappeared. Huge fuss, of course. Everyone questioned. Frantic searches. General panic. In the end they had to confess to Maybrick and the owners. You can imagine how they took the news.'

'Did the stuff ever come to light?'

'Not until too late. There were doubts whether Maybrick would want to publish at all but the book was in the catalogue and it was decided to go ahead with alternative illustrations and some necessary changes to the text. A week after they'd finished printing, the envelope and its contents mysteriously reappeared. De Witt found it in his cupboard exactly where he had placed it.'

'Which suggests that the thief had some respect for scholarship and had never intended to destroy the papers.'

'It suggests a number of possibilities, spite against Maybrick, spite against the Press, spite against de Witt, or a somewhat warped sense of humour.'

'Peverells didn't report the theft to the police?'

'No, Adam, they didn't place their confidence in our wonderful boys in blue. I don't want to be unkind but the police haven't an impressive clear-up rate when it comes to domestic burglary. The partners took the view that they stood just as good a chance of success and would cause less upset to staff if they undertook their own enquiry.'

'By whom? Were any of them free of suspicion?'

'That, of course, is the difficulty. They weren't then and they aren't now. I imagine that Etienne adopted the Head Beak's strategy. You know, "If the boy who's responsible will come to my study after prep in confidence and return the documents no more will be heard of the matter." It never worked at school. I don't suppose it was more successful at Peverells. It was obviously an inside job, and it isn't as if they employ a large staff, only about twenty-five people in addition to the five partners. Most of them are old faithfuls of course, and the story is that the few who aren't have alibis.'

'So it's still a mystery.'

35

'And so is the second incident. The second serious incident – there have probably been minor mischiefs which they've managed to keep quiet about. This one concerns Stilgoe so it's just as well that so far they've managed to keep it from him and it hasn't become public property. The old boy really would have something to feed his paranoia. Apparently when the page proofs had been read and a number of alterations agreed with Stilgoe they were packaged and left overnight under the counter in the reception office where they were due to be collected next morning. Someone opened the package and tampered with them, changed a number of the names, altered punctuation, deleted a couple of sentences. Fortunately the printer who received them was intelligent and thought some of the changes odd, so he telephoned to check. The partners have managed, God knows how, to keep this contretemps secret from most of the staff at Innocent House and, of course, from Stilgoe. It would have been extremely damaging to the firm if it had got out. I understand all parcels and papers are locked up overnight now and no doubt they've tightened security in other ways.'

Dalgliesh wondered whether the perpetrator had from the first intended the alterations to be discovered. They seemed to have been made with very little attempt to deceive. It surely wouldn't have been difficult to alter the page proofs in a way which would seriously damage the book without arousing the suspicions of the printer. It was odd, too, that the poison pen hadn't mentioned the alterations to Stilgoe's proofs. Either he or she hadn't known, which would absolve the five partners, or the poison pen had wanted to frighten Stilgoe but not to provide evidence which would justify him in withdrawing the book. It was an interesting little mystery but not one on which he proposed to waste the time of a senior police officer.

Nothing more was said about the Peverell Press until they were taking their coffee in the library. Ackroyd leaned forward and asked a little anxiously, 'Can I tell Lord Stilgoe that you'll try to reassure his wife?'

'I'm sorry, Conrad, but no. I'll get him a note to say that the police have no cause to suspect foul play in any of the cases which concern him. I doubt whether it will do much good if his wife is superstitious, but that is her misfortune and his problem.'

'And the other trouble at Innocent House?'

'If Gerard Etienne believes that the law is being broken and wants the police to investigate he must get in touch with his local station.'

'Just like anybody else?'

'Precisely.'

'You wouldn't be prepared to go to Innocent House and have an informal word with him?'

'No, Conrad. Not even for a sight of the Wyatt ceiling.'

5

On the afternoon of Sonia Clements's cremation Gabriel Dauntsey and Frances Peverell shared a taxi from the crematorium back to number 12 Innocent Walk. Frances was very silent on the journey, sitting a little apart from Dauntsey, gazing out of the window. She was hatless, the light brown hair a shining helmet which curved to touch the collar of her grey coat. Her shoes, tights and handbag were black, and there was a black chiffon scarf knotted at her neck. They were, Dauntsey remembered, the same clothes she had worn at her father's cremation, a contemporary understated mourning, nicely holding the balance between ostentation and a decent respect. The combination of grey and black in its sombre simplicity made her look very young and emphasized what he most liked in her, a gentle old-fashioned formality which reminded him of the young women of his youth. She sat distanced and very still, but her hands were restless. He knew that the ring she wore on the third finger of her right hand had been her mother's engagement ring and he watched while she twisted it obsessively under the black suede of her glove. He wondered for a moment whether to reach out and silently take her hand, but resisted the impulse to a gesture which he told himself might only embarrass them both. He could hardly keep holding her hand all the way back to Innocent Walk.

They were fond of each other; he was, he knew, the one person at Innocent House in whom she felt she could occasionally confide; but neither was demonstrative. They lived a short staircase apart but visited each other only by invitation, each anxious not to intrude or impose on the other, or to initiate an intimacy which the other might find unwelcome or come to regret. As a result, liking each other, enjoying each other's company, they saw less of each other than if they had lived miles apart. When they were together they spoke chiefly of books, poetry, plays they had seen, programmes on the television, seldom of people. Frances was too fastidious to gossip and he was equally reluctant to get drawn into controversy about the new regime. He had his job, his flat on the bottom two floors of number 12

Innocent Walk. Neither might be his much longer, but he was seventy-six, too old to fight. He knew that her flat above his had an attraction for him which it was prudent to resist. Sitting in the high-backed chair, with the curtains drawn against the gentle half-imagined sighing of the river, stretching out his legs before the open fire after one of their rare dinners together when she had left him to make coffee, he would hear her quietly moving about the kitchen and would feel a seductive peace and contentment stealing over him which it would be only too easy to make a regular part of his life.

Her sitting-room stretched the whole length of the house. Everything in it was attractive; the elegant proportions of the original marble fireplace, the oil of an eighteenth-century Peverell with his wife and children above the mantelshelf, the small Queen Anne bureau, the mahogany bookcases on each side of the fire, topped with a pediment and with two fine Parian heads of a veiled bride, the Regency dining table and six chairs, the subtle colours of the rugs glowing against the gold of the polished floor. How simple, now, to establish an intimacy which would open to him this gentle feminine comfort so different from his own bleak and underfurnished rooms below. Sometimes, if she telephoned with an invitation to dinner, he would invent a prior engagement and take himself out to a local pub, filling the long hours in the smoke and clatter, anxious not to return too early since his front door in Innocent Lane lay directly under her kitchen windows.

This evening he felt that she might welcome his company but was unwilling to ask for it. He wasn't sorry. The cremation had been depressing enough without having to discuss its banalities; he had had enough of death for one day. When the taxi drew up in Innocent Walk and she said an almost hurried goodbye and unlocked her front door without once looking back, he felt a sense of relief. But two hours later, after he had finished his soup and the scrambled eggs and smoked salmon which was his favourite evening meal and which he prepared, as always, with care, keeping the gas low, drawing the mixture lovingly from the sides of the pan, adding a final spoonful of cream, he pictured her eating her solitary supper and regretted his selfishness. This wasn't a good night for her to be alone. He telephoned and said: 'I'm wondering, Frances, whether you would care for a game of chess.'

He could tell from the joyous rise in her voice that the suggestion had come as a relief. 'Yes, I would, Gabriel. Do please come up. Yes, I'd love a game.'

Her dining table was still set when he arrived. She always ate with some formality even when alone, but he could see that the meal had been as simple as his own. The cheese board and the fruit bowl were on the table and she had obviously had soup but nothing else. He could see, too, that she had been crying.

She said, smiling, trying to make her voice cheerful: 'I'm so glad you've come up. It gives me an excuse to open a bottle of wine. It's odd how much one dislikes drinking alone. I suppose it's all those early warnings about solitary drinking being the beginning of the slide into alcoholism.'

She fetched a bottle of Château Margaux and he came forward to open it. They didn't speak again until they were settled, glasses in hand, before the fire, when, looking into the flames, she said: 'He should have been there. Gerard should have been there.'

'He doesn't like funerals.'

'Oh Gabriel, who does? And it was awful, wasn't it? Daddy's cremation was bad enough but this was worse. That pathetic clergyman who did his best but who didn't know her and didn't know any of us, trying to sound sincere, praying to the God she didn't believe in, talking about eternal life when she didn't even have a life worth living here on earth.'

He said gently: 'We can't know that. We can't be the judge of another's happiness or unhappiness.'

'She wanted to die. Isn't that evidence enough? At least Gerard came to Daddy's funeral. He more or less had to, though, didn't he? The crown prince saying farewell to the old king. It wouldn't have looked good if he'd stayed away. After all, there were important people there, writers, publishers, the press, people he wanted to impress. There was no one important at today's cremation, so he didn't have to bother. But he ought to have come. After all, he killed her.'

Dauntsey said more firmly: 'Frances, you mustn't say that. There's absolutely no evidence that anything Gerard did or said caused Sonia's death. You know what she wrote in the suicide note. If she had planned to kill herself because Gerard had sacked her I think she would have said so. The note was explicit. You must never say that outside this room. This kind of rumour can be deeply damaging. Promise me – it is important.'

'All right, I promise. I haven't said it to anyone except you, but I'm not the only one at Innocent House who's thinking it, and some are saying it. Kneeling there in that awful chapel I was trying to pray, for Daddy, for her, for all of us. But it was all so meaningless, so futile. All I could think about was Gerard, Gerard who ought to have been sitting there in the front row with us, Gerard who was my lover, Gerard who isn't my lover any more. It's so humiliating. I know now, of course, what it was all about. Gerard thought, "Poor Frances, twenty-nine and still a virgin. I must do something about that. Give her the experience of her life, show her what she's missing." His good deed for the day. His good deed for three months, rather. I suppose I lasted longer than most. And the ending was so sordid, so messy. Isn't it always? Gerard is very good at beginning a love-affair, but he doesn't know how to end it, not with any dignity. But then, nor do I. And I was deluded enough to think that I was different from his other women, that this time he was serious, in love, wanting commitment, marriage. I thought we would run Peverell Press together, live in Innocent House, bring up our children here, even change the name of the firm. I thought that would please him. Peverell and Etienne. Etienne and Peverell. I used to practise the alternatives, trying to decide which sounded better. I thought he wanted what I wanted – marriage, children, a proper home, a shared life. Is that so unreasonable? Oh God, Gabriel, I feel so stupid, so ashamed.'

She had never before spoken so openly to him, never shown the depth of her anguish. It was almost as if she had been silently rehearsing the words, waiting for this moment of relief when, at last, she was with someone she could trust and in whom she could confide. But coming from Frances, who was always so sensitive, reticent and proud, this uncontrolled pouring forth of bitterness and self-disgust appalled him. Perhaps it was the funeral, the memory of that earlier cremation, which had released the pent-up hatred and humiliation. He wasn't sure that he could cope with it but knew that he must try. This fluency of pain demanded more than the soft pabulum of comfort; 'he isn't worth it, forget him, the pain will pass with time'. But that last was true, the pain did pass with time, whether it was the pain of betrayal or the pain of bereavement. Who knew that better than he? He thought: the tragedy of loss is not that we grieve, but that we cease to grieve, and then perhaps the dead are dead at last.

He said gently: 'The things you want – children, marriage, home, sex – are reasonable desires, some would say very proper desires. Children are our only hope of immortality. They aren't things to be ashamed of. It is your misfortune not your shame that Etienne's desires and yours didn't coincide.' He paused, then said, wondering if it were wise, whether she would find the words crudely insensitive: 'James is in love with you.'

'I suppose so. Poor James. He hasn't said so, but he doesn't need to, does he? Do you know, I think I could have loved James if it hadn't been for Gerard. And I don't even like Gerard. I never did, even when I wanted him most. That's what's so terrible about sex, it can exist without love, without liking, even without respect. Oh, I tried to fool myself. When he was insensitive or selfish or crude I made excuses. I reminded myself how brilliant he was, how handsome, how amusing, what a wonderful lover. He was all those things. He is all those things. I told myself that it was unreasonable to apply to Gerard the petty standards one applied to others. And I loved him. When you love, you don't judge. And now I hate him. I didn't know that I could hate, really hate, another person. It's different from hating a thing, a political creed, a philosophy, a social evil. It's so concentrated, so physical, it makes me feel ill. My hate is the last thing I think about at night and I wake up with it every morning. But it's wrong, a sin. It has to be wrong. I feel I'm living in mortal sin and I can't get absolution because I can't stop the hating.'

Dauntsey said: 'I don't think in those terms, sin, absolution. But hate is dangerous. It perverts justice.'

'Oh justice! I've never expected much in the way of justice. And hate has made me so boring. I bore myself. I know I bore you, dear Gabriel, but you're the only one I can talk to and sometimes, like tonight, I feel I have to talk or I might go mad. And you're so wise, that's your reputation anyway.'

He said drily: 'It's easy to get a reputation for wisdom. It's only necessary to live long, speak little and do less.'

'But when you do speak you're worth listening to. Gabriel, tell me what I must do.'

'To get rid of him?'

'To get rid of this pain.'

'There are the usual expedients; drink, drugs, suicide. The first two lead to the third, it's just a slower, more expensive, more humiliating route. I don't advise it. Or you could murder him, but I don't advise that either. Do it in fantasy as ingeniously as you like, but not in reality. Not unless you want to rot for ten years in prison.'

She said: 'Could you stand that?'

'Not for ten years. I might manage three but not more. There are better ways of coping with pain than death, his death or yours. Tell yourself that pain is part of life, to feel pain is to be alive. I envy you. If I could feel such pain I might still be a poet. Value yourself. You're no less a human being because one selfish, arrogant, insensitive man doesn't find you lovable. Do you really need to value yourself by the standard of any man, let alone Gerard Etienne? Remind yourself that the only power he has over you is the power that you give him. Take that power away and you take away the hurt. Remember, Frances, you don't have to stay with the firm. And don't say that there has always been a Peverell at the Peverell Press.'

'There has since 1792, even before we moved into Innocent House. Daddy wouldn't have wanted me to be the last.'

'Someone has to be, someone will be. You owed your father a certain duty in life but it ceased with his death. We can't be in thrall to the dead.'

As soon as the words were out of his mouth he regretted them, half expecting her to ask 'What about you? Aren't you in thrall to the dead, your wife, your lost children?' He went on quickly: 'What would you like to do if you had a free choice?'

'Work with children, I think. Perhaps train as a primary school teacher. I've got my degree. I suppose it would only mean another year's training. And then I think I'd like to work in the country or in a small country town.'

'Then do it. You do have a free choice. But don't go searching for happiness. Find the right job, the right place, the right life. The happiness will come if you're lucky. Most of us get our share of it. Some of us get more than our share even if it's concentrated into a little space of time.'

She said: 'I'm surprised you don't quote Blake, that poem about "joy and pain being woven fine, a clothing for the soul divine". How does it go?

> "Man was made for Joy and Woe;
> And when this we rightly know,
> Thro' the World we safely go."

Only you don't believe in the soul divine, do you?'

'No, that would be the ultimate self-deception.'

'But you do go safely through the world. And you understand about hate. I think I've always known that you hated Gerard.'

He said: 'No, you're wrong, Frances. I don't hate him. I feel nothing for him, nothing at all. And that makes me far more dangerous to him than you can ever be. Hadn't we better start a game?'

He took out the heavy chessboard from the corner cupboard and she moved the table between the armchairs then helped him to set out the pieces. Holding out his clenched fist for her to choose black or white he said: 'I think you ought to give me a pawn, the tribute of youth to age.'

'Nonsense, you beat me last time. We play even.'

She surprised herself. Once she would have given way. It was a small act of self-assertion and she saw him smile as with his stiffened fingers he began to set out the pieces.

6

Miss Blackett went home every night to Weaver's Cottage in West
Marling in Kent where, for the past nineteen years, she had lived with
her older widowed cousin, Joan Willoughby. Their relationship was
affectionate but had never been emotionally intense. Mrs Willoughby
had married a retired clergyman and when he died three years after
the marriage, which Miss Blackett privately suspected was as long as
either partner could have borne, it had seemed natural for his widow
to invite her cousin to give up her unsatisfactory rented flat in
Bayswater and move to the cottage. Early in these nineteen years of
shared life a routine had established itself, evolving rather than
planned, which satisfied them both. It was Joan who managed the
house and was responsible for the garden, Blackie who, on Sundays,
cooked the main meal of the day which was always eaten promptly at
one o'clock, a responsibility which excused her from Matins although
not from Evensong. It was Blackie who, rising first, took early
morning tea to her cousin and made their nightly Ovaltine or cocoa at
half past ten. They holidayed together, for the last two weeks in July,
usually abroad, because neither of them had anyone with a stronger
claim. They looked forward each June to the Wimbledon tennis
championship and enjoyed the occasional weekend visit to a concert,
theatre or art gallery. They told themselves, but did not say aloud,
that they were lucky.

Weaver's Cottage stood on the northern outskirts of the village.
Originally two substantial cottages, it had in the 1950s been converted
into one dwelling by a family with definite ideas about what
constituted rural domestic charm. The tiled roof had been replaced
with reed thatch from which three dormer windows stared out like
protruding eyes; the plain windows were now mullioned and a porch
had been added, covered in summer by climbing roses and clematis.
Mrs Willoughby loved the cottage and if the mullioned windows
made the sitting-room rather darker than she would ideally have
liked, and some of the oak beams were less authentic than others,
these defects were never openly acknowledged. The cottage with its

immaculate thatch and its garden had appeared on too many calendars, had been photographed by visitors too often for her to worry about small details of architectural integrity. The main part of the garden was in the front, and here Mrs Willoughby spent most of her spare hours, tending, planting and watering what was generally admitted to be West Marling's most impressive front garden, designed as much for the pleasure of passers-by as for the occupants of the cottage.

'I aim for something of interest throughout the year,' she would explain to people who paused to admire, and in this she certainly succeeded. But she was a true and imaginative gardener. Plants thrived under her care and she had an instinctive eye for the placing of colour and mass. The cottage might be less than authentic but the garden was unmistakably English. There was a small lawn with a mulberry tree which in spring was surrounded by crocuses, snow-drops and later the bright trumpets of daffodils and narcissi. In the summer the heavily planted beds leading to the porch were an intoxication of colour and scent, while the beech hedge, trimmed low so as not to obscure the view of the glories beyond, was a living symbol of the passing seasons from the first tight, tentative buds to the crisp gold and reds of its autumn glory.

She always returned from the monthly PCC meeting bright-eyed and invigorated. Some people, Blackie reflected, would have found the fortnightly skirmishes with the vicar about his partiality for the new liturgy over the old and his other minor delinquencies dispirit-ing; Joan seemed to thrive on them. She settled herself, plump thighs parted stretching the tweed of her skirt, feet firmly planted, before the pie-edged table and poured the two glasses of amontillado. A dry biscuit cracked between the strong white teeth, the cut glass, one of a set, with its delicate stem looked as if it would snap in her hand.

'It's inclusive language now, if you please. He wants "Through the Night of Doubt and Sorrow" at next Sunday's Evensong, but we're supposed to sing "Person takes the Hand of Person, Marching Fearless through the Night". I soon put a stop to that, supported by Mr Higginson, thankfully. I can forgive that man the price of his bacon and the way he lets that mangy old cat of his sit in the window on the corn flakes when he acts with sense at the PCC which, to do him justice, he usually does. Miss Matlock suggested "Sister Takes the Hand of Sister".'

'What's wrong with that?'

'Nothing, except it's not what the author wrote. Had a good day?'

'No. It hasn't been a good day.'

But Mrs Willoughby's mind was still with the PCC. 'I'm not particularly fond of that hymn. Never have been. I can't think why Miss Matlock's so keen on it. Nostalgia, I suppose. Childhood memories. Not much doubt and sorrow about the congregation at St Margaret's. Too well fed. Too well-off. Still, there will be if the vicar tries to cut out the eight o'clock 1662 Holy Communion on Sundays. There'll be plenty of doubt and sorrow in the parish then.'

'Has he suggested it?'

'Not in so many words, but he's keeping an eye on the size of the congregation. You and I must keep up our attendance and I'll see if I can stir up some of the villagers. All this trendiness is Susan, of course. The man would be perfectly amenable if he weren't egged on by his wife. She's talking of going off to be trained for the diaconate. Next thing they'll be ordaining her priest. They'd both do better in a large inner-city parish. They could have their banjos and guitars and I dare say the people would quite like it. What was your journey like?'

'Not bad. Better tonight than this morning. We were ten minutes late at Charing Cross, a bad beginning to a bad day. It was Sonia Clements's funeral. Mr Gerard didn't go. Too busy, so he said. I suppose she wasn't important enough. Naturally that meant I felt I had to stay.'

Joan said: 'Well that was no hardship. Cremations are always depressing. You can get some satisfaction out of a well-conducted funeral, but not out of a cremation. Which reminds me that the vicar actually proposed using the Alternative Service Book when he buries old Merryweather next Tuesday. I soon put a stop to that. Mr Merryweather was eighty-nine and you know how he hated change. He wouldn't think he'd had a proper Christian burial without the 1662 book.'

When on the previous Tuesday Blackie had returned home with the news of Sonia Clements's suicide, Joan had taken it with remarkable composure. Blackie told herself that she oughtn't to be surprised. Her cousin frequently confounded her by an unexpected response to news and events. Small domestic inconveniences would provoke outrage, a major tragedy was taken with stoic calm. And this tragedy, after all, couldn't be expected to touch her. She had never known, not even met, Sonia Clements.

Breaking the news, Blackie had said: 'I haven't gossiped with the junior staff, of course, but I gather that the general feeling in the office is that she killed herself because Mr Gerard sacked her. I don't suppose he did it tactfully either. Apparently she left a note but it didn't mention losing her job. People take the view, though, that she'd still be here if it wasn't for Mr Gerard.'

Joan's response had been robust. 'But that's ridiculous. Grown women don't kill themselves because they've been sacked. If losing your job was a reason for suicide we'd be having to dig mass graves. It was very inconsiderate of her, very thoughtless. And if she had to kill herself she should have done it somewhere else. After all, it might have been you who'd gone to the little archives room and found her. That wouldn't have been at all pleasant.'

Blackie had said: 'It wasn't very pleasant for Mandy Price, the new temp, but I must say she took it very coolly. Some young girls would have had hysterics.'

'No point in getting hysterics over a dead body. Dead bodies can't harm you. She'll be lucky if she sees nothing worse in life than that.'

Blackie, sipping her sherry, looked across at her cousin from under lowered lids as if seeing her dispassionately for the first time. The solid, almost waistless body, the firm legs with the beginnings of varicose veins above surprisingly shapely ankles, the abundant hair, once a rich brown, still thick and only slightly grey, worn in a heavy bun (a fashion which hadn't changed since Blackie had first known her), the cheerful, weather-coarsened face. A sensible face, people might say. A sensible face for a sensible woman, one of Barbara Pym's excellent women but with none of the gentleness or reticence of a Barbara Pym heroine, applying a ruthless kindness to the problems of the village from bereavements to recalcitrant choirboys, her life as regulated in its pleasures and duties as the liturgical year which gave it shape and focus. And so had Blackie's life once had shape and focus. It seemed to Blackie that she had no control over anything, her life, her job, her emotions, and that in dying Henry Peverell had taken with him an essential part of herself.

Suddenly she said: 'Joan, I don't think I can go on at Peverells. Gerard Etienne is getting intolerable. I'm not even allowed to deal with his personal calls. He takes them on a private line in his office. Mr Peverell used to leave our door ajar, propped open with that draught-excluder snake, Hissing Sid. Mr Gerard keeps it shut and he's had a high cupboard moved against the glass partition to give himself more privacy. It's not very considerate. It cuts off even more of my light. And now I'm expected to house the new temp, Mandy Price, although all the work for her has to be routed through Emma Wainwright, Miss Claudia's PA. She ought to be sitting in with Emma. Now that Mr Gerard has had the partition moved my office is cramped even for one. Mr Peverell would never have agreed to a partition that cut the dining-room across the window and the stuccoed ceiling. He hated the partition and fought against it when the alterations were first made.'

Her cousin said: 'Can't his sister do something? Why not have a word with her?'

'I don't like to complain, particularly not to her. And what could she do? Mr Gerard's the managing director and the chairman. He's ruining the firm and no one can stand up to him. I'm not even sure that they want to, except perhaps for Miss Frances, and he's not going to listen to her.'

'Then leave. You don't have to work there.'

'After twenty-seven years?'

'Long enough for any job, I'd have thought. Retire early. You joined their pension scheme when old Mr Peverell set it up. I thought at the time that was very wise. I advised it, if you remember. You won't get a full pension of course, but there'll be something coming from that. Or you could take a nice little part-time job in Tonbridge. That wouldn't be difficult to find with your skills. But why work? We can manage. And there's plenty to do in the village. I've never let the PCC make use of you while you're at Peverells. As I told the vicar, my cousin is a personal secretary and spends all her day typing. It's unfair to expect her to do it in the evenings and weekends. I've made it my business to protect you. But it would be different once you were retired. Geoffrey Harding is complaining that acting as secretary to the PCC is getting too much for him. You could take that on for a start. And then there's the Literary and Historical Society. They can certainly do with some secretarial help.'

The words, the life they so succinctly described, horrified Blackie. It was as if, in those few ordinary sentences, Joan had pronounced a life sentence. She realized for the first time how unimportant a part West Marling played in her life. She didn't dislike the village; the rows of rather dull cottages, the shaggy green beside a malodorous pond, the modern pub which tried unsuccessfully to look seventeenth-century with a gas-fired open hearth and black-painted beams, even the little church with its pretty broach-spire evoked no emotion as strong as dislike. This was where she lived, ate, slept. But for twenty-seven years the centre of her life had been elsewhere. She had been glad enough to return at night to Weaver's Cottage, to its comfort and order, to her cousin's undemanding companionship, to good meals elegantly served, to the sweet-smelling wood fire in winter, the drink in the garden on warm summer nights. She had liked the contrast between this rural peace and the stimulus and challenges of the office, the raucous life of the river. She had to live somewhere since she couldn't live with Henry Peverell. But now she realized, in an overwhelming moment of revelation, that her life at West Marling would be insupportable without her job.

She saw that life stretching before her in a series of bright disjointed images projected on the mind's screen in a clicking, inexorable sequence; hours, days, weeks, months, years of unfulfilled predictable monotony. The small household chores which would give her the illusion of usefulness, helping in the garden under Joan's supervision, acting as secretary or typing for the PCC or the WI, shopping in Tonbridge on Saturdays, Holy Communion and Evensong on Sundays, planning the excursions which would provide the highlights to the month, not rich enough to escape, with no excuse to justify escape, and nowhere to escape to. And why should she wish to leave? It was a life her cousin found satisfying and psychologically fulfilling, her place in the village hierarchy secure, the cottage her acknowledged property, the garden her continued interest and joy. Most people would think that she, Blackie, was lucky to share it, lucky to live rent-free (they'd know that in the village, that was the kind of fact they knew by instinct), a beautiful home, her cousin's companionship. She would be the less regarded of the two, the less popular, the poor relation. Her job, imperfectly understood in the village but magnified in importance by Joan, had given her dignity. Work did bestow dignity, status, meaning. Wasn't that why people dreaded unemployment, why some men found retirement so traumatic? And she couldn't find herself what Joan described as 'a nice little part-time job' in Tonbridge. She knew what that would mean; working in an office with half-trained girls fresh from school or secretarial college, sexually on-the-make, resented for her efficiency or pitied for her all-too-obvious virginity. How could she lower herself to a part-time job, she who had once been confidential personal assistant to Henry Peverell?

Sitting immobile with a glass of half-drunk sherry before her and staring into its amber glow as if mesmerized, her heart was in tumult, her voice crying wordlessly, 'Oh my darling, why did you leave me? Why did you have to die?'

She had hardly ever seen him outside the office, had never been invited to his flat at number 12, and had never invited him to Weaver's Cottage or spoken to him of her private life. Yet for twenty-seven years he had been central to her existence. She had spent more of her waking hours with him than with any other human being. To her he was always Mr Peverell, and he had called her Miss Blackett to others, Blackie to her face. She couldn't remember that her hands had ever touched his since that first meeting twenty-seven years ago when, as a shy seventeen-year-old fresh from secretarial college, she had come to Innocent House for her interview and he had risen smiling from his desk to greet her. Her typing and shorthand skills had already been tested by the secretary who was leaving him to get married. Now, looking at the handsome scholarly face and into his incredibly blue eyes, she had known that this was the ultimate test. He had said little about the job – but then why should he? Miss Arkwright had already explained in intimidating detail what would be expected of her – but he had asked her about her journey and had said: 'We have a launch which brings some of the staff to work. It can pick you up at Charing Cross pier and bring you to work by the Thames – that is unless you're afraid of water.'

And she had known that this was the test question, that she wouldn't get the job if she disliked the river. 'No,' she said, 'I'm not afraid of water.'

After that she had spoken little, almost incoherent with the thought of coming each day to this glittering palace. At the end of the interview he had said, 'If you think you can be happy here, suppose we both give each other a month's trial.'

At the end of the month he had said nothing, but she knew there was nothing he need say. She had been with him until the day he died.

She remembered the morning of his heart attack. Was it really only eight months ago? The door between their offices had been ajar as it always was, as he liked it to be. The velvet snake with its intricately marked back, its red forked flannel tongue, had been curled at the foot. He had given one call, but in a voice so harsh and strangled that it was hardly recognizable as human and she thought she was hearing some waterman shouting from the river. It had taken her a couple of seconds to realize that this disembodied, alien voice was calling her name. She had leapt from her chair, hearing it skid across the floor, and was at his desk, staring down at him. He was still in his chair, rigid, as if seized by rigor, not daring to move, grasping the arms with white knuckles, his eyes bulging beneath a forehead on which the sweat had started in glistening globules thick as pus. He gasped, 'The pain, the pain! Get a doctor!'

Ignoring the telephone on his desk, she had fled to her own office as if only in that familiar place could she cope. She fumbled with the telephone book, then remembered that his doctor's name and number was in the small black reference book in her desk. She yanked open the drawer and plunged in her hand to find it, trying to remember the name, wanting desperately to return to that horror in the chair yet afraid of what she might find, knowing that she must get help and get it quickly. Then she remembered. Of course, the ambulance. She must call an ambulance. She punched at the telephone keys and heard a voice, calm, authoritative, and gave her message. The urgency, the terror in her voice must have convinced them. The ambulance would be on its way.

She recalled what happened afterwards, not in sequence but in a series of disconnected but vivid pictures. At the door of his office she had just time to glimpse Frances Peverell standing impotently at his side before Gerard Etienne came towards her and, firmly closing the door, said: 'We don't want anyone else in here. He needs air.'

It was to be the first of all the rejections that followed. She remembered the noises as the paramedics worked on him; his head turned from her as they bore him past covered in a red blanket; the sound of someone sobbing, someone who could have been herself; the emptiness of the office, empty, as it was in the morning when she arrived before him, or as it was at night when he left first, but now everlastingly, permanently empty of everything that had given it meaning. She had never seen him again. She had wanted to visit him in hospital and had asked Frances Peverell what time would be convenient, only to be told: 'He's still in intensive care. Only family and the partners are allowed to visit. I'm sorry, Blackie.'

The news had at first been reassuring. He was better, much better. They hoped he would soon be out of the intensive care unit. And then, four days after the first, he had suffered a second, massive, heart attack and had died. At the cremation she had sat in the chapel three pews back, among other members of the staff. No one had consoled her; why should they? She wasn't one of the officially bereaved, not one of the family. When, outside the chapel, inspecting the wreaths of the mourners, unable to help herself she had broken down, Claudia Etienne had looked briefly at her with a mixture of wonder and irritation, as if to say, 'If his daughter and his friends can control themselves, why can't you?' The grief had been made to seem in bad taste, as presumptuous as was her wreath, ostentatious among the family's simple cut flowers. She had remembered overhearing Gerard Etienne's comment made to his sister. 'God, Blackie's overdone it. That wreath wouldn't disgrace a New York Mafia funeral. What's she trying to do, making everyone think she was his mistress?'

And next day, at a small private ceremony, the five partners had thrown his ashes into the Thames from the terrace of Innocent House. She hadn't been asked to take part but Frances Peverell had come into her office and said: 'You might like to join us on the terrace, Blackie. I think my father would have liked you to be there.' She had stood well back, careful not to be in their way. They had stood a little distanced from each other, close to the edge of the terrace. The white ground bones which were all that remained of Henry Peverell were in a tin which looked to her curiously like a biscuit tin. They passed it from hand to hand, took out a fistful of the grains and dropped or flung them into the Thames. She remembered that it had been high tide with a fresh breeze blowing. The river, ochre-brown, had slapped against the jetty walls, sending out small droplets of spray. Frances Peverell's hands had been damp; the fragments of bone had stuck to them and afterwards she had wiped her hands surreptitiously against her skirt. She had been perfectly calm as she had spoken by heart the words from *Cymbeline*, beginning:

> Fear no more the heat o' the sun,
> Nor the furious winter's rages;
> Thou thy worldly task hast done,
> Home art gone and ta'en thy wages.

It seemed to Blackie that they had forgotten to decide on the order of speaking and there was a short silence before James de Witt moved closer to the edge of the terrace and spoke words from the Apocrypha. 'The souls of the righteous are in the hands of God, and there shall no torment touch them.' Afterwards he had let his portion of ashes trickle from his hands as if counting every separate grain.

Gabriel Dauntsey had read a poem by Wilfred Owen which was unfamiliar to her, but afterwards she had looked it up and had wondered a little at his choice.

> I am the ghost of Shadwell Stair.
> Along the wharves by the water-house,
> And through the cavernous slaughter-house,
> I am the shadow that walks there.
>
> Yet I have flesh both firm and cool,
> And eyes tumultuous as the gems
> Of moons and lamps in the full Thames
> When dusk sails wavering down the Pool.

Claudia Etienne had been the briefest, with just two lines:

> The worst that can befall us, measured right,
> Is a long slumber and a long goodnight.

She had spoken them loudly but rather fast with a fierce intensity which gave the impression that she disapproved of the whole charade. After her had come Jean-Philippe Etienne. He hadn't been seen at Innocent House since his retirement a year earlier and had been driven up from his remote house on the Essex coast by his chauffeur, arriving just before the ceremony was due to begin and leaving immediately afterwards without sharing the buffet lunch prepared in the boardroom. But his passage had been the longest and he had read it in a flat voice, holding on to one of the finials of the railings for support. De Witt had told her afterwards that it was from the *Meditations* of Marcus Aurelius but at the time only a brief passage impressed itself on Blackie's mind:

In a word all the things of the body are as a river, and the things of the soul as a dream and a vapour; and life is a warfare and a pilgrim's sojourn, and fame after death is only forgetfulness.

Gerard Etienne had been last. He had flung the ground bones from him as if shaking off all the past, and had spoken words from Ecclesiastes:

For to him that is joined to all the living there is hope; for a living dog is better than a dead lion. For the living know that they shall die; but the dead know not anything, neither have they any more a reward; for the memory of them is forgotten. Also their love, and their hatred, and their envy is now perished; neither have they any more a portion for ever in any thing that is done under the sun.

Afterwards they had turned away silently and gone up to the boardroom to their cold luncheon and wine. And at two o'clock precisely Gerard Etienne had walked without speaking through Blackie's room to the office beyond and had seated himself for the first time in Henry Peverell's chair. The lion was dead and the living dog had taken over.

7

After Sonia Clements's cremation James de Witt declined the invitation of Frances to join her and Gabriel in their taxi, saying instead that he felt in need of a walk and would take the tube from Golders Green Station. The walk from the crematorium was longer than he had expected, but he was glad to be alone. The rest of the Peverell Press staff had been driven home in the undertaker's cars and he couldn't decide which would have been worse, to contemplate Frances's taut unhappy face with no hope of comforting her or to be crushed in an over-full, ostentatious car with a gaggle of junior staff who had preferred a funeral to an afternoon's work and whose tongues, released after the spurious solemnity of the funeral, would have been inhibited by his presence. Even the temp, Mandy Price, had been there. But that was reasonable enough; after all, she had been present at the finding of the body.

The cremation had been a grim affair and for that he blamed himself. He always did blame himself, and sometimes reflected that to have so lively a sense of sin without the religion which could assuage it by absolution was an uncomfortable idiosyncrasy. Miss Clements's sister, the nun, had been at the funeral, appearing as if by magic at the last moment to take her seat at the back, and disappearing again with equal speed at the end, pausing only to shake hands with those of the Peverell Press staff who pressed forward to mutter their condolences. She had previously written to Claudia requesting the firm to make all the funeral arrangements and they should have done better. He should have taken more interest instead of leaving it all to Claudia, which in effect had meant leaving it to Claudia's secretary.

There should, he thought, be a service designed for those without a religion. Probably there was and they could have discovered it if they had taken the trouble. It might be an interesting, and possibly even lucrative, publishing venture, a book of alternative funeral rites for humanists, atheists and agnostics, a formal ceremony of remembrance, a celebration of the human spirit with no reference to its possible continuing existence. Striding to the station, his long coat flapping open, he amused himself selecting passages of prose and verse which might be included. De la Mare's 'Look thy last on all things lovely', for a touch of nostalgic melancholy. Perhaps Oliver Gogarty's 'Non Dolet', Keats' 'Ode to Autumn' if the dead person were old, and Shelley's 'To a Skylark' if he were young. Wordsworth's 'Lines Written Above Tintern Abbey' for the nature worshipper. There could be songs instead of hymns and the slow movement from Beethoven's 'Emperor Concerto' would be an appropriate funeral march. And there was, of course, always the third chapter of Ecclesiastes:

To everything there is a season, and a time to every purpose under the heaven:
A time to be born, and a time to die; a time to plant, and a time to pluck up that which is planted;
A time to kill and a time to heal; a time to break down and a time to build up.

He could have concocted something suitable for Sonia, perhaps including extracts from a book she had commissioned and edited, a commemoration of twenty-four years of service to the firm which the living Sonia would have thought appropriate. It was odd, he thought, how important were these rites of passage, designed surely to comfort and minister to the needs of the living since they could never touch the dead.

He stopped to buy two cartons of semi-skimmed milk and a container of washing-up liquid at the supermarket at Notting Hill Gate before letting himself quietly into the house. It was apparent that Rupert had company, the sound of voices and of music came clearly down the stairs. He had hoped that Rupert would have been alone and wondered, as he so often did, that a man so ill could stand so much noise. But it was, after all, cheerful noise and Rupert stood it only for a limited period. It was he, James, who coped afterwards with the inevitable reaction. Suddenly he felt that he couldn't face any of them. Instead he went into the kitchen and, without taking off his coat, made himself a mug of tea then opened the back door and carried it out with him into the quietness and darkness of the garden and sat down on the wooden bench by the back door. It was a warm evening for late September and, sitting there as the darkness deepened, distanced from the racket and bright lights of Notting Hill Gate by no more than eighty yards, it seemed to him that this small garden held suspended in its quiet air all the remembered sweetness of summer and the loamy richness of autumn.

For ten years, ever since his godmother had left it to him, the house had been a source of unfailing pleasure and contentment. He hadn't expected to enjoy such a keen or self-indulgent satisfaction in ownership, having deceived himself since boyhood with the conviction that, except for his pictures, material possessions were unimportant to him. He knew now that one possession, and that the most solid and permanent, had become central to his life. He liked its unassuming Regency façade, the shuttered windows, the double drawing-room on the first floor looking out over the street at the front and with a conservatory built out at the back, giving a view of his own small garden and those of his neighbours. He liked the eighteenth-century furniture which his godmother had brought with her to the house when comparative poverty had driven her to this then humble street, not yet gentrified, still a little shabby. She had left him everything but her pictures, and here their tastes differed and he didn't repine. The drawing-room was fitted with bookshelves four feet high on every wall, and above them he had hung his own prints and water-colours. The house still retained an air of discriminating femininity but he had no wish to impose upon it a more masculine taste. He came back to it each evening, into the small but elegant hall with its faded wallpaper and its gently curved staircase, with a sense of entering a private, secure and wholly pleasing world. But that was before he took in Rupert.

Rupert Farlow had published his first novel with the Peverell Press fifteen years previously and James could still remember the mixture of excitement and awe with which he had read the manuscript, submitted not through an agent, but to the Press direct, badly typed on unsuitable paper and accompanied by no explanatory letter but merely with Rupert's name and address, as if he challenged the as yet unknown reader to recognize its quality. His second novel, two years later, had been less generously received as second novels often are after a spectacular initial success, but James hadn't been disappointed. Here, confirmed, was a major talent. And then silence. Rupert was no longer seen in London and letters and telephone calls went unanswered. It was rumoured that he was in North Africa, California,

India. And then, briefly, he had reappeared but he had brought no new work with him. There had never been another novel and now there never would be. It was Frances Peverell who mentioned to James that she had heard that Rupert was dying of AIDS and was in a west London hospice. She didn't visit but James did, and continued to visit. Rupert was in remission but the hospice staff were in difficulty about what to do with him. His flat was unsuitable, his landlord unsympathetic, he hated the camaraderie of the hospice. These things emerged without complaint. Rupert never complained except about the trivia of life. He seemed to regard his illness not as a cruel and unjust affliction but as an end ordained and inescapable, to be endured not resented. Rupert was dying with courage and grace, but he was still the old Rupert, malicious or mischievous, tricky or temperamental, as you chose to describe him. Tentatively, afraid that the offer might be resented or misunderstood, James had suggested that Rupert should join him in Hillgate Village. The offer had been accepted and four months earlier Rupert had moved in.

Peace, the old order, the old security, had all vanished. Rupert found difficulty in managing stairs so James had installed a bed for him in the drawing-room and he spent most of the day there or in the conservatory when it was sunny. There was a lavatory and shower on the first floor and a room little bigger than a cupboard which James had made into a kitchen fitted with an electric kettle and a double burner where he could make coffee or toasted sandwiches. The first floor had become, in effect, a small self-contained flat which Rupert had taken over and on which he had imposed his untidy, iconoclastic, mischievous personality. Ironically the house had become less peaceful now that it was home to a dying man. There was a constant stream of callers, Rupert's present and old buddies, his reflexologist, the masseuse who left behind her a smell of exotic oils, Father Michael who came, so Rupert said, to hear his confession but whose ministrations seemed to be regarded by him with the same amused indulgence with which he accepted those concerned with his bodily needs. The friends were seldom there when James was home, except at weekends, although the evidence of their visits met him every evening; flowers, magazines, fruit, bottles of sweet-smelling oils. They gossiped, made coffee, were given drinks. Once he said to Rupert, 'Does Father Michael enjoy his wine?'

'He certainly knows which bottles to bring up.'

'That's all right then.'

James didn't grudge Father Michael his claret as long as the man knew what he was drinking.

He had provided Rupert with a brass hand-bell, strident as a school bell, which he had found in the Portobello Market, so that Rupert could summon him from his bedroom above if he needed help in the night. He now slept badly, half expecting to hear that clamorous summons, imagining, half-awake, the rumble of death-carts in plague-ridden London, the wailing call, 'Bring out your dead'.

He could remember every word of that conversation two months ago, Rupert's watchful ironic eyes, his smiling face daring him to disbelieve.

'I'm just telling you the facts. Gerard Etienne knew that Eric had AIDS, and he made sure that we met each other. I'm not complaining, far from it. I had some choice in the matter. Gerard didn't actually tuck us up in bed together.'

'It's a pity you didn't exercise it, the choice.'

'But I did. I don't pretend that I gave it much thought. You never knew Eric, did you? He was beautiful. Very few people are. Attractive, handsome, sexy, good-looking, all the usual adjectives, but not beautiful. But Eric was. I've always found beauty irresistible.'

'And that's all you required in a lover, physical beauty?'

Rupert had mimicked him, eyes and voice gently mocking.

'And that's all you required in a lover? My dear James, what sort of world do you live in, what sort of person are you? No, that wasn't all I required. Required. Past tense, I notice. It would have been a bit more sensitive to watch your grammar. No it wasn't all. I wanted someone who fancied me too and had certain skills in bed. I didn't ask Eric whether he preferred jazz to chamber music, or opera to ballet, or, more important, what wine he preferred. I'm talking about desire, I'm talking about love. Christ, it's like explaining Mozart to the tone-deaf. Look, let's leave it at this: Gerard Etienne deliberately threw us together. At the time he knew that Eric had AIDS. He might have hoped we'd become lovers, he might have intended us to become lovers, he might not have cared a damn either way. Perhaps he was amusing himself. I don't know what he had in mind. I don't much care. I know what I had in mind.'

'And Eric, knowing he had an infectious disease, didn't tell you? What in God's name was he thinking of?'

'Well, not at first. He told me later. I'm not blaming him, and if I don't you can keep your moral judgements. And I don't know what he was thinking of. I don't pry into my friends' minds. Perhaps he wanted a companion for the last mile or so before he set off to explore that long silence.' He had added: 'Don't you forgive your friends?'

'Forgiveness is hardly a word to use between friends. But then, none of my friends has infected me with a fatal disease.'

'But my dear James, you don't exactly give them the chance, do you?'

He had questioned Rupert with the detached persistence of a trained investigator, needing to force the truth out of him, desperate to know. 'How can you be sure that Etienne knew Eric was ill?'

'James, don't cross-examine me. You sound like a prosecuting counsel. And you do love euphemisms don't you? He knew because Eric told him. Etienne asked him when he could expect another book. The Peverell Press had done rather well with his first travel book. Etienne had got it cheap and probably hoped for the next one on the same terms. Eric told him there wouldn't be one. He hadn't the energy or the inclination. He had other plans for the rest of his life.'

'And those included you.'

'Eventually. It was two weeks after that conversation that Etienne arranged the river trip. Suspicious in itself, wouldn't you say? Not Etienne's kind of jolly at all. Chug chug down dear Old Father Thames to inspect the flood barrier, chug chug back again with smoked salmon sandwiches and champagne. How did you manage to avoid it, by the way?'

'I was in France.'

'So you were. Your second home. Odd that old Etienne has been so content to spend all these years away from his native land. Gerard and Claudia don't go there either, do they? You'd think they might occasionally like to see the place where Papa and his mates had such a jolly time popping away at Germans from behind the rocks. They never go and you can't keep away. What do you do there, check up on him?'

'Why should I do that?'

'It was only a remark, I meant nothing. Anyway, you'll never pin anything on old Etienne. He's been authenticated; there's no doubt there, the genuine hero.'

'Go on about the river trip.'

'Oh, it was the usual thing. Giggling typists, Miss Blackett a little tipsy, red puffy face, that awful virginal archness. She'd brought that draught-excluder snake with her. Hissing Sid they call it. Extraordinary woman. Absolutely no humour, I would have said, except about that snake. Some of the girls hung it over the side threatening to drown it, and one of them pretended to feed it champagne. In the end they wound it round Eric's neck and he wore it all the way home. But that was later. On the way up-river I took refuge in the bow. Eric was standing there alone, perfectly still, like a figurehead. He turned and looked at me.' Rupert paused, and then said almost in a whisper: 'He turned round and looked at me. James, what I've just told you, better forget.'

'No, I shan't do that. Are you telling me the truth?'

'Of course, don't I always?'

'No Rupert, not always.'

Suddenly his reverie was broken. The kitchen door was flung open and Rupert's buddy thrust out his head. 'I thought I heard the front door. We're just off. Rupert was asking if you were back. You usually go straight up.'

'Yes,' he said, 'I usually go straight up.'

'So what are you doing out here?'

He asked it with little curiosity, but James replied: 'Musing on the third chapter of Ecclesiastes.'

'I think Rupert wants you.'

'I'm coming now,' and he mounted, painfully as an old man, to the disorder, the warmth, the exotic overcrowded muddle that was now his sitting-room.

8

It was nine o'clock and on the top floor of a terraced house off Westbourne Grove Claudia Etienne lay in bed with her lover.

She said: 'I wonder why one always feels randy after a funeral. The potent conjunction of death and sex, I suppose. Did you know that Victorian prostitutes used to service their clients in graveyards on the flat tops of the tombs?'

'Hard, cold and sinister. I hope they got piles. It wouldn't turn me on. I'd keep thinking of the rotting body underneath and all those bloated worms creeping in and out of the orifices. Darling, what extraordinary facts you do know. Being with you is an education.'

'Yes,' she said. 'I know it is.' She was wondering whether he, like her, had more than historical facts in mind. 'Being with you', he had said, not 'loving you'.

He turned towards her, propping his head on his hand. 'Was the funeral ghastly?'

'It managed to be tedious and grim at the same time, canned music, a coffin which looked as if it had been recycled, a liturgy revised to offend no one, including God, and a parson who did his best to give the impression that we were engaged in something that had meaning.'

He said: 'When my turn comes I'd like to be burnt on a funeral pyre by the sea like Keats.'

'Shelley.'

'That poet, whoever he was. A hot windy night, no coffin, lots of booze and all one's mates swimming naked then dancing round the fire, all being happily warmed by me. And the ashes could be washed away by the next tide. Do you think if I left instructions in my will someone would arrange it?'

'I shouldn't rely on it. You'll probably end up at Golders Green like the rest of us.'

His bedroom was small and the floor space almost entirely occupied by a five-foot wide Victorian bed in ornamental brass, the high bedposts crowned with knobs. From these Declan had suspended a

Victorian patchwork quilt, in part badly tattered. It hung above them as they made love, lit by the bedside lamp, a rich patterned canopy of gleaming silk and satin. Some shreds of the silk hung down and she had an impulse now to pick at them. The scraps were, she saw, lined with old letters, the black spider-marks of the long-dead hand plainly visible. A family's history, a family's troubles and triumphs pressed down upon them.

His kingdom, and it seemed to her a kingdom, lay beneath them. The shop, the whole property, was owned by Mr Simon – she had never learned his forename – and he rented the top two floors to Declan at a ridiculous sum and paid him with equal frugality for managing the shop. He himself was always there in his black skull-cap to greet favoured customers, sitting at a Dickensian desk just inside the door, but otherwise he took little part in buyirg and selling although he controlled the flow of cash. The front of the house was arranged under his personal supervision, the pick of the furniture, pictures and artefacts displayed to advantage. It was the back of the ground floor which Declan had made his domain. It was a long conservatory of strengthened glass with at each end two palm-trees, the slender trunks of iron, and the fronds, which trembled as the hand brushed against them, sheets of tin painted a bright green. This touch of Mediterranean sun contrasted with the conservatory's faintly ecclesiastical air. Some of the original lower panes of glass had been replaced by oddly shaped pieces of stained glass from demolished churches; a jigsaw of yellow-haired angels and haloed saints, lugubrious apostles, fragments of a nativity scene or of the last supper, domestic vignettes of hands pouring wine into pitchers or lifting loaves of bread. Placed in happy disorder on a variety of tables, piled up on chairs, were the objects acquired by Declan and it was here that his personal customers rummaged, exclaimed, admired and made their discoveries.

And there were discoveries to be made. Declan, as Claudia admitted, had an eye. He loved beauty, variety, oddity. He was extraordinarily knowledgeable in fields of which she knew little. She was as amazed by the things he knew as by the things he didn't know. Occasionally his findings would be promoted to the front of the shop when he would immediately lose interest in them, but his love for all his acquisitions was fickle. 'You do see, Claudia darling, how I had to have it? You do see how I couldn't not buy?' He would stroke, admire, research, gloat over every acquisition, give it pride of place. But three months later it would have mysteriously disappeared to be replaced by the new enthusiasm. There was no attempt at display; objects were jumbled together, the worthless and the good. A Staffordshire commemorative figure of Garibaldi on a Horse, a cracked Bloor Derby sauce tureen, coins and medals, stuffed birds under domed glass, sentimental Victorian water-colours, bronze busts of Disraeli and Gladstone, a heavy Victorian commode, a pair of art-deco gilt wood chairs, a stuffed bear, a heavily encrusted German air force officer's cap.

She had said, examining the latter: 'What are you selling this as, property of the late Field Marshal Hermann Goering?'

She knew nothing about his past. Once he had said in a broad and unconvincing Irish accent, 'Sure, aren't I just a poor Tipperary boy, my ma dead and my pa off God knows where,' but she didn't believe it. There was no hint to background or family in his light, carefully cultivated voice. When they were married – if they were married – she supposed that he would tell her something about himself, and if not she would probably ask. At present an instinct warned her that it was unwise and kept her silent. It was difficult to imagine him with an orthodox past life, parents and siblings, school, a first job. It some-times seemed to her that he was an exotic changeling who had spontaneously materialized in that crowded back room, reaching out acquisitive fingers to the objects of past centuries, but himself having no reality except in the present moment.

They had met six months earlier, sitting in adjacent seats in the tube on a day when there had been a major breakdown on the Central Line. During the seemingly interminable wait before they were instructed to leave the train and make their way along the track, he had glanced at her copy of the *Independent* and, when their eyes had met, had smiled apologetically and said: 'I'm sorry, it's rude I know, but I'm slightly claustrophobic. I always find it easier to cope with these delays when I have something to read. Usually I have.'

She had replied, 'I've finished with it. Do have it. Anyway I've got a book in my briefcase.'

So they had sat together, both reading, neither speaking, but she had been very aware of him. She told herself that this was a result of tension and of a touch of fear. When the instructions to leave the train had at last come there was no panic, but it had been a disagreeable experience and for some very frightening. One or two comedians had reacted to the tension with attempts at crude humour and loud laughter, but most had endured in silence. There had been an elderly woman sitting close to them in obvious distress and they had half-carried her between them, helping her along the track. She told them that she had a heart condition and was asthmatic and was afraid that the dust in the tunnel might cause an attack.

When they reached the station and had left her in the care of one of the nurses on duty, he had turned to Claudia and said: 'I think we deserve a drink. I need one anyway. Shall we find a pub?'

She had told herself that there was nothing like a common peril followed by a shared benevolence to promote intimacy and knew that it would be wiser now to say goodbye and be on her way. Instead she had agreed. By the time they finally parted she knew where it would end. But she had taken her time. She had never begun a love-affair without the private assurance that she was in control, more loved than loving, more likely to cause pain than to be hurt herself. She couldn't be sure of that now.

About a month after they had become lovers he had said: 'Why don't we get married?'

The suggestion – she hardly regarded it as a proposal – was so surprising that for a moment she was silent. He went on: 'Don't you think it would be a good idea?'

She found that she was treating the suggestion seriously without knowing whether to him it was just one more of the ideas he occasionally put forward without expecting her to believe them, and apparently not much caring whether she did or not.

She said slowly: 'If you're serious then the answer is that it would be a very bad idea.'

'All right, let's get engaged. I like the idea of a permanent engagement.'

'That's an illogicality.'

'Why? Old Simon would like it. I could say "I'm expecting my fiancée". He'd be less shocked when you stay the night.'

'He's never shown the slightest sign of being shocked. I doubt whether he would care if we fornicated in the front room provided we didn't frighten the customers or damage the stock.'

But he did occasionally speak of her to old Simon as 'my fiancée', and she felt she could hardly deny the description without making

66

both of them seem foolish or giving the whole thing an importance which it didn't merit. He didn't again mention marriage but she was disconcerted to realize that, with part of her mind, the idea was beginning to take hold.

When she had arrived that evening from the crematorium she had greeted Mr Simon then gone straight into the back room. Declan had been peering at a miniature. She enjoyed watching him with the object with which, however transitory the affection, he was momentarily enthused. It was a picture of an eighteenth-century lady, her décolleté bodice and frilled chemisette painted with great delicacy, the face under the high powdered wig perhaps too sweetly pretty.

He had said: 'Paid for, I imagine, by a wealthy lover. She looks more like a tart than a wife, doesn't she? I think it could be by Richard Corey. If so, it's a find. You do see, darling, how I had to have it?'

'Where did you get it?'

'A woman who had advertised some drawings she thought were originals. They weren't. This is.'

'How much did you pay?'

'Three fifty. She would have taken less. She was pretty desperate. I like to spread a little happiness by paying slightly more than is expected.'

'And it's worth about three times as much, I suppose.'

'About that. Lovely, isn't it? The thing itself I mean. There's a strand of her hair curled in the back. I don't think this should go into the front room, it could be nicked in a second. Old Simon's eyes aren't what they were.'

She said: 'He's looking pretty ill to me. Shouldn't you encourage him to see a doctor?'

'No point, I've tried. He hates doctors. He's terrified they'll send him into hospital and he hates hospitals even more. For him hospitals are places where people die and he doesn't like to think about dying. Not surprising when the rest of your family have been wiped out in Auschwitz.'

Now, turning away from her onto his back and staring up at the patterned silk on which the bedside lamp shed a soft glow, he said: 'Have you spoken to Gerard yet?'

'No, not yet. I'll do that after the next board meeting.'

'Look Claudia, I want this shop. I need it. I've made it. Everything

67

that's different about it is because of me. Old Simon can't sell it to someone else.'

'I know. We'll have to see that he doesn't.'

How strange it was, she thought, this urge to give, to satisfy the lover's every desire as if propitiating him for the burden of being loved. Or was there a deeper irrational belief that he deserved to get what he wanted when he wanted it simply by virtue of being lovable? And when Declan wanted something he wanted it with the insistence of a spoilt child, without reserve, without dignity, without patience. But she told herself that this particular want was adult and rational. The freehold comprising the two flats and all the shop would be a snip at £350,000. Simon wanted to sell, and wanted to sell to him, but he couldn't wait much longer.

She said: 'Has he spoken to you recently? How much longer can we have?'

'He wants a decision by the end of October, but the sooner the better. He yearns to go and lay his old bones in the sun.'

'But he wouldn't find another purchaser in a hurry.'

'No, but he wants to put it on the market if we don't give him a definite answer by then. He'll ask more, of course, than he's asking from me.'

Claudia said slowly: 'I'm going to suggest to Gerard that he buys me out.'

'You mean all your shares in the Peverell Press? Can he afford to?'

'Not without difficulty, but if he agrees he'll find the money.'

'And there's no other way you can get it?'

She thought, I could sell the Barbican flat and move in here, but what sort of solution would that be to anything? She said: 'I haven't got £350,000 sitting on deposit in the bank, if that's what you mean.'

He persisted again: 'Gerard's your brother. Surely he'll help.'

'We aren't close. How could we be? After our mother died we were sent away separately to school. We hardly saw each other until we both started work at Innocent House. He'll buy my shares if he thinks it's to his advantage. Otherwise he won't.'

'When will you ask him?'

'After the board meeting on October the fourteenth.'

'Why wait until then?'

'Because then will be the best time.'

They lay for minutes in silence.

Suddenly she said: 'Look, Declan, let's go on the river on the fourteenth. Why don't you call for me at six-thirty and we'll take the launch down to the Thames Barrier. You've never seen it after dark.'

'I haven't seen it at all. Won't it be cold?'

'Not particularly. Wear something warm. I'll bring a thermos of soup and the wine. It really is worth seeing, Declan, those great hoods rising out of the dark river towering over you. Do come. We could put in at Greenwich for a pub meal.'

'All right,' he said. 'Why not? I'll come. I don't see why you have to fix it now, but I'll come as long as I don't have to meet your brother.'

'I can promise you that.'

'Six-thirty then at Innocent House. We could make it earlier if you like.'

'Six-thirty is the earliest. The launch won't be free until then.'

He said: 'You make it sound important.'

'Yes,' she said. 'Yes, it is important, important for both of us.'

9

Gabriel left Frances as soon as the game was finished, a game he easily won. She saw with compunction that he looked very tired and wondered if he had come up out of compassion for her rather than from his own need for company. The funeral must have been worse for him than for the other partners. He was after all the only member of staff for whom Sonia had appeared to have any affection. Her own tentative attempts at friendship had been subtly rebuffed by Sonia, almost as if being a Peverell disqualified her for intimacy. Perhaps alone among the partners he was feeling a personal grief.

The game had stimulated her mind and she knew that to go to bed now would only result in one of those nights of alternate restlessness and brief periods of sleep which brought her to the morning more tired than if she had never been to bed. On impulse she went to the hall cupboard for her warm winter coat then, putting out the light, opened the window and stepped outside on to the balcony. The night air smelt cold and clean with the familiar tang of the river. Grasping the rail she felt as if she were suspended, disembodied in air. A cluster of low cloud lay over London, stained pink like a lint bandage which had soaked up the city's blood. Then, as she watched, the clouds moved slowly apart and she saw the clear blue-black of the night sky and a single star. A helicopter like a jewelled metallic dragonfly clattered upstream. This was how her father had stood night after night before going to bed. She would be busy in the kitchen after dinner and would come into the sitting-room to find it in darkness except for the one low lamp, and would see the dark shadow of that silent motionless figure standing there looking out over the river.

They had moved to number 12 in 1983 when the firm was expanding in one of its periods of comparative prosperity, and extra office space was needed at Innocent House. Number 12 had been let to a long-standing tenant who had conveniently died, freeing the property to be converted to provide a top flat for herself and her father and a smaller one at the bottom of the house for Gabriel Dauntsey. Her father had accepted the need to move philosophically, had indeed seemed almost to welcome it, and she suspected that it was only after she joined him in 1985 on leaving Oxford that he began to find the flat restrictive, almost claustrophobic.

Her mother, never strong, had died suddenly and unexpectedly of viral pneumonia when Frances was five and she had spent all her childhood with her father and a nurse in Innocent House. Only in adult life had she realized how extraordinary those early years had been, how unsuitable the house as a family home, even for a family diminished by death, to the two of them, father and daughter. She had had no young companions; only a few remaining Georgian squares in the East End which had survived the bombing had become fashionable enclaves for the middle classes. Her playground was the glittering marble hall and the forecourt and here, despite the pro-tective railings, she·was always .closely supervised, permitted no bicycle or ball games. The streets were unsafe for a child and she, with Nanny Bostock, was taken, occasionally by the firm's launch, across the river to a small private school in Greenwich where the emphasis was on gentility rather than the development of questioning intelli-gence, but where she had at least been given a good grounding. But on most days the launch was needed to pick up members of staff from the Thames pier and she and Nanny Bostock would be driven to the Greenwich foot tunnel, and always accompanied on their sub-terranean walk by the chauffeur or by her father for extra safety.

It never occurred to the adults that she found the foot tunnel terrifying and she would have died rather than tell them. She had known from early childhood that her father admired courage above all virtues. She would walk between them, holding their hands in a simulation of childish meekness, trying not to grasp the fingers too hard, keeping her eyes down so that they couldn't see that they were tightly closed, smelling the distinctive tunnel smell, hearing the echo of their feet and picturing above them that great weight of slopping water, terrifying in its power, which one morning would break the tunnel roof and begin to seep through, at first in heavy drops as the tiles cracked and then, suddenly, in a thundering wave, black and evil-smelling, sweeping them off their feet, swirling and rising, until there was nothing between their fighting bodies and screaming mouths but a few inches of space and air. And then not even that.

Five minutes later, they would come up by the lift into the daylight to see the gleaming magnificence of Greenwich Naval College with its twin cupolas and gold-tipped weathervanes. For the child it was like coming out of hell and having her eyes dazzled by the celestial city. Here, too, was the Cutty Sark with her tall masts and slender lines. Her father would tell her about the East India Company's monopoly of trade with the Far East in the eighteenth century and how these great clippers, built for speed, would vie with each other to bring to the British market in record time the perishable and valuable tea of China and India.

From her earliest years her father had told her stories of the river which for him had been almost an obsession, a great artery, endlessly fascinating, constantly changing, bearing on its strong tide the whole history of England. He told her of the rafts and coracles of the first Thames voyagers, the square sails of the Roman ships bringing cargo to Londinium, the Viking long boats with their curved prows. He would describe to her the river of the early eighteenth century when London was the greatest port in the world and the wharfs and quays with their tall masted ships looked like a wind-denuded forest. He told her of the raucous life of the waterfront and the many trades which drew their life from this bloodstream; the stevedores or lumpers, the watermen who worked the lighters which provisioned the vessels as they rode at anchor, suppliers of rope and tackle, boat-builders, ships' bakers, carpenters, rat-catchers, lodging-house keepers, pawnbrokers, publicans, marine store dealers, rich and poor alike, drawing their life from the river. He had described for her the great occasions:, Henry VIII in the gold-crested royal barge being rowed up river to Hampton Court, the long oars sweeping upward in salute; Lord Nelson's body taken up river in 1806 from Greenwich in the barge originally built for Charles II; river festivities; floods and tragedies. She yearned for his love and approbation. She had listened dutifully, had asked the right questions, had instinctively known that this was an interest he assumed that she would share. But she realized now that the deception had only added guilt to her natural reserve and timidity, that the river had become the more terrifying because she could not acknowledge its terrors and her relationship with her father more distant because it was founded on a lie.

But she had made for herself another world and, lying awake at night in that glittering, un-cosy nursery, curled womb-like under the sheets, she would enter its gentle security. In this imaginary life she had a sister and brother and lived with them in a large country rectory. There was a garden with an orchard and a fruit cage and vegetables planted in rows separated by neat box hedges from the wide green lawns. Beyond the garden was a stream, only inches deep, which they could leap across and an old oak with a tree house, snug as a hutch, where they sat and read and scrunched apples. The three of them slept in the nursery, looking out over the lawn and rose garden to the church tower, and there were no raucous voices, no river smell, no image of terror, only tenderness and peace. There was a mother too; tall, fair, with a long blue dress and a half-remembered face, walking towards her across the lawn, arms outstretched for her to leap into because she was the youngest and the best-loved.

There was, she knew, the adult equivalent of this unfrightening world available to her. She could marry James de Witt and move into his charming house in Hillgate Village and have his children, the children she, too, wanted. She could rely on his love, be certain of his kindness, know that whatever problems their marriage might bring there would be no cruelty and no rejection. She might have taught herself, not to desire him, since that was not susceptible to the will, but to find in kindness and gentleness a substitute for desire, so that in time sex with him would become possible, even agreeable, at its lowest a price to be paid for his love, at its highest a pledge of affection and of belief that love could in time beget love. But for three months she had been Gerard Etienne's mistress. After that wonder, that astonishing revelation, she found that she couldn't even bear James to touch her. Gerard, taking her casually, discarding her equally casually, had deprived her even of the consolation of the second best.

It was always the terror of the river, not its romance or its mystery, which had held her imagination and, with Gerard's brutal rejection, these terrors, which she thought she had put away with childhood, reasserted themselves. This Thames was a dark tide of horror; that sodden algae-matted gate, leading into the fastness of the Tower, the thud of the axe, the tide lapping Wapping Old Stairs where pirates were taken and tied to the piles at low water until three tides – the Grace of Wapping – had flowed over them; the stinking hulks lying off Gravesend with their fettered human cargo. Even the river steamers butting upstream, their decks loud with laughter and brightly patterned with holiday-makers, brought back to mind unbidden the greatest of all Thames tragedies when, in 1878, the

73

paddle-steamer *Princess Alice*, returning loaded from a trip to Sheerness, was mown down by a collier and 640 people drowned. It seemed to her now that it was their screams that she heard in the cries of the gulls and, looking down at night at the dark river splattered with light, she could imagine the pale upward faces of the drowned children torn from their mothers' arms floating like frail petals on the dark tide.

When she was fifteen her father had taken her for her first visit to Venice. He had said that fifteen was the earliest age at which a child could appreciate Renaissance art and architecture, but she had suspected even then that he preferred to travel alone and that taking her was a duty which he could no longer reasonably defer, but a duty nevertheless which held some promise of hope for both of them.

It was their first and last holiday together. She had expected bright, hot sun, gaudily clad gondoliers on blue water, gleaming marble palaces, dining alone with him in one of the new dresses chosen for her by the housekeeper, Mrs Rawlings, for the occasion, drinking wine at dinner for the first time. She had longed desperately for the holiday to be a new beginning. It had begun badly. They had had to travel in the school holidays and the city was overcrowded. For the whole ten days the sky had been leaden with intermittent rain, its heavy drops pitting canals as brown as the Thames. Her impression was of constant noise, raucous foreign voices, the terror of losing her father in the crush, of dimly lit old churches in which the attendant would shuffle to switch on the light and illumine a fresco, a painting, an altarpiece. The air would be heavy with incense and the sour mustiness of wet clothes. Her father would edge her to the front of the jostling tourists and whisper to her, explaining the paintings, above the noise of discordant tongues and the distant calls of peremptory guides.

One picture remained strongly in memory. A mother nursing her baby under a stormy sky, a solitary male watcher. She knew that there was something to which she should respond, some mystery of subject and intention, and she longed to share her father's excitement, to say something which, if it couldn't be clever, would at least not cause him to turn away with the silent disapproval to which she had become accustomed. Always at the bad moments there were remembered words. 'Madam was never the same after the child was born. That pregnancy killed her, no doubt about that. And now look what we've

74

got landed with.' The woman, her name and purpose in the house now long forgotten, had probably only meant that what they were faced with was a large unmanageable house without the controlling hand of a mistress, but to the child the meaning of the words had been plain and had remained plain. 'She killed her mother and look what we've got in exchange.'

Another memory of that holiday remained sharp in the years to follow. It was on their first visit to the Accademia and, holding her gently by the shoulder, he had led her to a picture by Vittore Carpaccio, *The Dream of St Ursula*. They were, for once, alone and, standing beside him, aware of the weight of his hand, she had found herself looking at her bedroom in Innocent House. Here were the twin rounded windows with their top half-moons filled with discs of bottle-glass, the corner door ajar, the two vases on the window-shelf so like those at home, the same bed, a delicate four-poster with a high carved headboard and a tasselled fringe. Her father had said: 'See, you sleep in a fifteenth-century Venetian bedroom.'

There was a woman in the bed, resting her head on her hand. Frances had asked, 'Is that lady dead?'

'Dead? Why should she be dead?'

She had heard in his voice the familiar sharpness. She hadn't answered, had said no more. The silence between them lengthened until, with the hand still on her shoulder but pressing more heavily now, or so it seemed, he had turned her away. But she had failed him again. It had always been her fate to be sensitive to his every mood but without the skill or the confidence to meet that mood or respond to his need.

They were divided even by religion. Her mother had been a Roman Catholic, but how devout she neither knew nor had any means of discovering. Mrs Rawlings, a co-religionist employed a year before her mother's death to be half housekeeper to the ailing woman, half child-minder, had been punctilious in taking her every Sunday to Mass but had otherwise ignored her religious education, giving the child the impression that religion was something her father couldn't understand and could barely tolerate, a feminine secret best not spoken of in his presence. They seldom went more than twice to any church. It was as if Mrs Rawlings was a taster of religion, sampling the variety of ritual, architecture, music and sermons on offer, afraid of a premature commitment, of being recognized by the congregation, welcomed as a regular by the priest at the door, enticed into parish activities, perhaps even expected to receive visitors at Innocent House. As Frances grew older she suspected that finding a new church for Sunday morning Mass had become something of a private initiative test for Mrs Rawlings, affording a sense of adventure and providing a measure of variety to her otherwise monotonous week and a lively subject of conversation on their way home.

'Not a very good choir, was it? Hardly up to Oratory standard. We must go to the Oratory again when I've got the energy. Too far for every Sunday but at least the sermon was short. I can't be doing with long sermons. Very few souls saved after the first ten minutes, if you ask me.'

'I don't like that Father O'Brien. That's what he calls himself apparently. Very poor attendance. No wonder he was so friendly at the door. Wanted to entice us back next week, I don't wonder.'

'Nice Stations of the Cross they've got. I like them carved. Those painted ones we saw at St Michael's last week were too gaudy by half. And at least the choirboys had clean surplices, someone did a good job of ironing there.'

After one Sunday morning, when they had heard Mass at a particularly dull church where the rain had clattered like hailstones on the temporary tin roof ('Not our class of person. We won't be going there again.'), Frances had asked: 'Why do I have to go to Mass every Sunday?'

'Because your Ma was RC. That's what your father agreed. The boys would be brought up C of E, tne daughters RC. Well, he got you.'

He had got her. The despised sex. The despised religion.

Mrs Rawlings said: 'There's plenty of religions in the world. Everyone can find something to suit them. All you have to remember is that ours is the only true one. But there's no point in thinking about it too much, not until you have to. I think we'll go back to the cathedral next week. It'll be Corpus Christi. They'll put on a grand show for that, I shouldn't wonder.'

It was a relief to her father and to her when, at twelve, she was sent to the convent. He had come himself to collect her at the end of the first term and she had overheard the Mother Superior's words as she said goodbye to them at the door: 'Mr Peverell, the child has had virtually no instruction in her faith.'

'In my wife's faith. Then, Mother Bridget, I suggest that you instruct her.'

They had with gentle patience done that for her, and much more. They had given her a brief period of security, the sense that she was valued, that it was possible she could be loved. They had prepared her for Oxford, which she supposed she ought to consider a bonus since Mother Bridget had frequently impressed on her that the intention of a true Catholic education was to prepare her for death. They had done that too, but she was less sure that they had prepared her for life. Certainly they hadn't prepared her for Gerard Etienne.

She turned back into the sitting-room, closing the window firmly behind her. The sound of the river became faint, a gentle susurration on the night air. Gabriel had said to her, 'He can have no power over you unless you give it to him.' Somehow she had to find the will and the courage to break that power finally and for ever.

10

Mandy's first four weeks at Innocent House, which began inauspiciously with a suicide and were to end dramatically in murder, seemed in retrospect one of the happiest months of her working life. As always, she adapted quickly to the daily routine of the office and with a few exceptions liked her fellow workers. She was given plenty to do, which suited her, and the work was more varied and more interesting than that which normally came her way.

At the end of her first week Mrs Crealey had asked if she was happy and Mandy had replied that there were worse jobs and that she might as well stick it out for a bit longer, which was as far as she ever went in expressing satisfaction with a job. She had rapidly become accepted at Innocent House; youth and vitality combined with high efficiency are seldom resented for long. Miss Blackett, after a week of staring across at her with repressive severity, had apparently decided that she had known worse temps. Mandy, always quick to recognize her own interest, treated Miss Blackett with a flattering mixture of deference and confidence; fetching her coffee from the kitchen, asking her advice although with no intention of taking it, and accepting some of the duller routine tasks with cheerful goodwill. Privately she thought the poor old thing was pathetic; you had to be sorry for her. It was obvious that Mr Gerard for one couldn't stand the sight of her, and no wonder. Mandy's private opinion was that Miss Blackett was for the chop. They were, in any case, too busy to spend time considering how little they had in common and how much each deplored the other's clothes, hairstyle and attitude to senior staff. Nor was Mandy required to spend every day in Miss Blackett's office. She was frequently called to take shorthand from Miss Claudia or Mr de Witt, and one Tuesday when George was away ill with a violent stomach upset she took over the reception desk and coped with the switchboard with no more than a few misdirected calls.

On the Wednesday and Thursday of her second week she spent two days in the publicity department helping to organize a couple of publicity tours and a signing session and was introduced by Maggie

FitzGerald, Miss Etienne's assistant, to the foibles of authors, those unpredictable and oversensitive creatures on whom, as Maggie reluctantly conceded, the fortunes of Peverell Press ultimately depended. There were the frighteners, who were best left to Miss Claudia to cope with, the timid and insecure who needed constant reassurance before they could utter even one word on a BBC chat-show and for whom the prospect of a literary luncheon induced a mixture of inarticulate terror and indigestion. Equally hard to handle were the aggressively overconfident who, if not restrained, would break free of their minder and leap into any convenient shop with offers to sign their books, thus reducing the carefully-worked-out publicity schedule to chaos. But the worst, Maggie confided, were the conceited, usually those whose books sold the least well, but who demanded first-class fares, five-star hotels, a limousine and a senior member of staff to escort them and who wrote furious letters of complaint if their signings didn't attract a queue round the block. Mandy enjoyed her two days in publicity: the youthful enthusiasm of the staff, cheerful voices calling against the perpetual stridency of the telephone, travellers vociferously welcomed, homing in for a gossip and an exchange of news, the sense of urgency and impending crisis. She returned to her seat in Miss Blackett's room with reluctance.

She was less enthusiastic about requests that she take dictation from Mr Bartrum in charge of accounts who, she confided to Mrs Crealey, was boring, middle-aged, and treated her like something the cat had brought in. The accounts department was in number 10 and, after a stint with Mr Bartrum, Mandy would escape upstairs for a few minutes of chat, flirtation, and the ritual exchange of insults with the three packing-staff. They inhabited their private world of bare floors and trestle tables, of collapsible brown cartons, Sellotape and immense balls of twine, of the distinctive and exciting smell of books fresh from the press. She liked them all; Dave of the bush-ranger hat who, despite his size, had arm muscles like footballs and could shift extraordinary weights; Ken who was tall and lugubrious and silent; and Carl, the warehouse manager who had been with the firm since he was a boy. 'They'll do no good with this one,' he would say, slapping a hand on a carton.

'He can't go wrong,' confided Dave admiringly. 'He can tell a best-seller from a dud just by smelling it. He don't even 'ave to read 'em.'

Her willingness to make tea and coffee for the two PAs and the partners gave her the opportunity for a twice-daily gossip with the cleaner Mrs Demery. Mrs Demery's domain was centred on the large kitchen and adjacent smaller sitting-room on the ground floor at the back of the house. The kitchen was furnished with a rectangular pine table, large enough to seat ten, one gas and one electric stove and a microwave oven, a double sink, a huge refrigerator and a wall fitted with small cupboards. Here, at any time between twelve and two, in a pungent aroma of discordant cooking smells, all but the senior staff ate their sandwiches, heated their foils of oven-ready pasta and curry, made omelettes, boiled eggs, grilled bacon for bacon rolls and brewed their tea and coffee. The five partners never joined them. Frances Peverell and Gabriel Dauntsey went next door to their separate flats at number 12 and the two Etiennes and James de Witt took the launch upstream to lunch in the city, or walked to the Prospect of Whitby or one of the pubs in Wapping High Street. The kitchen, without their inhibiting presence, was the centre of gossip. Here news was received, endlessly discussed, embroidered and disseminated. Mandy would sit in silence in front of her sandwich box, knowing that when she was present the middle-grade staff in particular were unusually discreet. Whatever their feelings about the new chairman or the possible future of the firm, loyalty and a sense of their status forbade open criticism in front of a temp. But when she and Mrs Demery were alone brewing morning coffee or afternoon tea, Mrs Demery had no such inhibitions.

'We thought Mr Gerard and Miss Frances would marry. That's what she thought too, the poor kid. And then there's Miss Claudia and her toy boy.'

'Miss Claudia with a toy boy! Come off it, Mrs D.'

'Well, maybe not a toy boy exactly, although he's young enough. Younger than her anyway. I saw him when he came to Mr Gerard's engagement party. He's good-looking, I'll say that for him. Miss Claudia always had an eye for a good-looking chap. He's in antiques. You know, like the Antiques Road Show. They're supposed to be engaged but I notice she don't wear a ring.'

'But she's quite old, isn't she? And people like Miss Claudia don't bother so much about rings.'

'That Lady Lucinda's got one though, hasn't she? A bloody great emerald set with diamonds. That must have cost Mr Gerard a packet. I don't know why he wants to marry an earl's sister. Young enough to be his daughter, too. I don't think it's decent.'

'Maybe he fancies a wife with a title, Mrs D. You know, Lady Lucinda Etienne. Maybe he likes the sound of that.'

'That don't count for as much as it did, Mandy, not with the way some of these old families behave nowadays. No better than the rest of us. It used to be different when I was a girl, you had some respect for them then. That brother of hers is nothing to write home about, earl or no earl, if you're to believe half of what you read in the papers. Ah well, them that lives longest will see most.' It was Mrs Demery's invariable way of ending a conversation.

On her first Monday, a day so sunny that she could almost believe they were back in the summer, she had watched with some envy while the first set of staff entered the launch at 5.30 to be taken to Charing Cross. On impulse she asked Fred Bowling, the waterman, if she could go for the ride. He made no objection and she jumped in. On the way there he had sat at the wheel in silence as she suspected he always did. But when the party had disembarked and they turned for the journey downstream to Innocent House, she had started asking him questions about the river and had been amazed at his knowledge. There was no building which he couldn't identify, no history which apparently he didn't know, no fellow-waterman whom he couldn't recognize, and few boats which he couldn't name.

It was from him that she learned that Cleopatra's Needle was first erected about 1450 BC in front of the Temple of Isis at Heliopolis, and towed to England to be erected on the river bank in 1878. It was one of a twin and the other stood in Central Park, New York. She could picture the great container with its core of stone thrashing through the turbulent seas of the Bay of Biscay like a great fish. He pointed out Doggett's Coat and Badge public house next to Blackfriars Bridge, and told her about Doggett's Coat and Badge sculling race which has been rowed since 1722 from the Old Swan Inn at London Bridge to the Old Swan Inn at Chelsea, the first single sculling race in the world. His nephew had rowed in it. As they butted under the great pillars of Tower Bridge he could tell her the length of each span and that the High Walk was 142 feet above high water. When they reached Wapping he told her about James Lee, a market gardener from Fulham, who in 1789 had noticed a fine flowering plant in a cottage window which had been brought back by a sailor from Brazil. James Lee bought it for £8 and planted cuttings, and next year made his fortune selling 300 plants at a guinea each.

'Now, what do you think that plant was?'

'I don't know, Mr Bowling, I don't understand about plants.'

'Go on, Mandy, have a guess.'

'It couldn't be a rose?'

'A rose? 'Course it wasn't a rose! There have been roses in England for ever. No, that was a fuchsia.'

Glancing up at him, Mandy saw that the brown creased face, still looking ahead, was quietly smiling. How odd people were, she thought. Nothing he had told her about the splendours and horror of the river was for him as sweetly remarkable as the discovery of that single flower.

As they neared Innocent House Mandy could see the figures of the last two passengers, James de Witt and Emma Wainwright, ready to embark. Darkness had fallen and the river had become as smooth and thick as oil, a black tide which broke into a fishtail of white foam as the launch chugged away. Mandy crossed the patio to her motor bike. She didn't linger. She wasn't superstitious or particularly nervous, but once darkness had fallen Innocent House became more mysterious and a little sinister, even with the two globes of light casting over the marble their soft warm light. She walked with her eyes ahead, willing herself not to look down in case she could see that fabled stain of blood or upwards to the top balcony from which that long-dead distracted wife had hurled herself to her death.

And so the days passed. Going from office to office, willing, conscientious, quickly accepted, there was nothing which escaped Mandy's sharp experienced eyes; Miss Blackett's unhappiness, the casual contempt with which Mr Gerard treated her; Miss Frances's taut white face, stoical in misery; George's anxious eyes following Mr Gerard whenever he passed the reception desk; half-overheard conversations which broke off when she appeared. Mandy knew that the staff were anxious about the future. There hung over the whole of Innocent House an atmosphere of unease, almost foreboding, which she could sense and occasionally even slightly relish, since she felt, as she always did, that she was merely the privileged spectator, the outsider who was under no personal threat, who took her money by the week, owed allegiance to no one and could walk out when she chose. Sometimes at the end of the day when the light began to fade and the river outside was a black tide, and footsteps echoed eerily on the marble of the hall, she would be reminded of the hours before a bad thunderstorm; the deepening darkness, the heaviness and sharp metallic smell of the air, the knowledge that nothing could break this tension but the first crash of thunder and a violent tearing of the skies.

11

It was Thursday 14 October. The partners' meeting at Innocent House was due to begin at ten o'clock in the boardroom and by 9.45, as was his habit, Gerard Etienne had already taken his seat at the oval mahogany table. He sat in the middle of the side which faced the window and the river. By ten o'clock his sister Claudia would be seated on his right and Frances Peverell on his left. James de Witt would be opposite him with Gabriel Dauntsey on his right. The seating hadn't changed since that day nine months earlier when he had formally taken over as chairman and managing director of Peverell Press. On that Thursday his four colleagues had loitered outside the boardroom as if each was reluctant to enter it alone. Joining them he had unhesitatingly thrust open the double mahogany door and, striding confidently into the room, had taken his seat in Henry Peverell's old chair. Behind him the other four partners had entered together and silently seated themselves as if in obedience to some preordained plan which both established and reaffirmed their status in the firm. He had taken Henry Peverell's chair as if by right, and it was by right. Frances, he remembered, had sat pale-faced and almost silent throughout that short meeting and afterwards, drawing him aside, James de Witt had said: 'Need you have taken her father's chair? He's only been dead ten days.'

He felt again that mixture of surprise and mild irritation which the question had provoked at the time. Which chair was he expected to take? What did James want, to waste time while the five of them deferred politely to each other, discussing who should or should not have a river view, playing a kind of unaccompanied musical chairs around the table? The chair with the arms was the managing director's chair and he, Gerard Etienne, was managing director. How could it possibly matter how long old Peverell had been dead? Henry had used this chair, this place at the table, when he was alive, had occasionally raised his eyes to look out over the river in one of his irritating moments of private contemplation while the rest of them had waited patiently for the meeting to resume. But he was dead.

James surely wasn't suggesting that the chair should be left permanently empty as a kind of memorial, that a suitable plaque should be attached to the seat.

He saw the incident as typical of James's overdeveloped and self-indulgent sensitivity, typical too of something else which he found more perplexing and more interesting since it concerned himself. It sometimes seemed to him that the thought processes of other people were so radically different from his that he and they inhabited a different dimension of reason. Facts which to him were self-evident required from his four partners prolonged thought and discussion before, reluctantly, they were accepted; discussions were complicated by confused emotions and personal considerations which seemed to him as irrelevant as they were irrational. He told himself that, for them, reaching a decision was like achieving orgasm with a frigid woman, requiring a tedious amount of foreplay and the expenditure of disproportionate energy. He wondered occasionally whether to present them with the analogy but decided, inwardly smiling, that the pleasantry was best kept to himself. Frances, for one, would not find it amusing. But it would happen again this morning. The choices facing them were stark and inescapable. They could sell Innocent House and use the capital to establish and develop the firm; they could negotiate an arrangement with another publishing house whereby the name Peverell Press would at least be preserved; or they could go out of business. The second option was merely a longer and more tedious route to the last, beginning invariably with public optimism and ending in ignominious extinction. He had no intention of going down that well-trod path. The house must be sold. Frances had to realize, they all had to realize, that they couldn't both keep Innocent House and continue as independent publishers.

He got up from the table and moved over to the window. As he watched a cruise ship suddenly and silently blocked his view, so close that for a moment he could look into a lighted porthole and see, in the half-circle of brightness, the head of a woman, delicate as a cameo, pale arms raised, running her fingers through an aureole of hair, and could imagine that their eyes met in a surprised and fleeting intimacy. He wondered briefly, and with no real curiosity, who it was who shared her cabin – husband, lover, friend? – and what plans they had for the evening. He had none. By established habit he worked late on Thursday nights. He wouldn't see Lucinda until Friday when they had planned a concert on the South Bank followed by dinner at the Bombay Brasserie since Lucinda had expressed a preference for Indian food. He thought of the weekend without excitement but with quiet satisfaction. One of Lucinda's virtues was her decisiveness. Frances, asked where she preferred to eat, would have replied 'Anywhere you like, darling' and if the meal disappointed and he complained, would have said, leaning against him, slipping her arm through his, beguiling him into a good humour, 'It was perfectly edible, not bad really. And what does it matter, darling? We were together.' Lucinda had never suggested that his company could compensate for or excuse a poorly cooked, ill-served dinner. Occasionally he wondered whether, in fact, it did.

12

Etienne said: 'This is a private meeting, Miss Blackett. We have some confidential business to discuss. I'll take my own notes. There's plenty of typing to keep you occupied.'

His voice was dismissive with a note of contempt. Miss Blackett flushed and gave a small, soundless intake of air. Her notebook slid from her fingers and she bent stiffly to pick it up, then rose and walked to the door with a pathetic attempt at dignity.

James de Witt said: 'Was that kind? Blackie has taken the notes of the partners' meeting for over twenty years. She's always sat in.'

'Wasting her time and ours.'

Frances Peverell said: 'You needn't have suggested that we don't trust her.'

'I didn't. All the same, when we get to discussing the mischief here she has to be a suspect. I don't see why she should be treated differently from the rest of the staff. She has no alibi for any of the incidents. She has plenty of opportunity.'

Gabriel Dauntsey said: 'So do I, or any of the five of us here. And haven't we spent enough time discussing the practical joker? It never gets us anywhere.'

'Perhaps. Anyway, that can wait. The important news first. Hector Skolling has upped his offer for Innocent House by another £300,000. Four and a half million. It's the first time in the negotiations that he's used the words "final offer", and when he says that he means it. It's a clear million more than I thought we would have to take. More than it's worth in purely commercial terms, but property is worth what someone is prepared to pay, and Hector Skolling likes the house. After all, his empire is in Docklands. There's a clear distinction between the property he develops for letting and the kind of house he's prepared to live in. I propose to accept verbally today and get the solicitors working on the details so that we can exchange within a month.'

James de Witt said: 'I thought we discussed it at the last meeting but didn't reach a decision. I think if you consult the minutes . . .'

'I don't need to. I'm not running this company on the basis of what Miss Blackett chooses to put in the minutes.'

'Which, incidentally, you haven't yet signed.'

'Exactly. I suggest that in the future we run this monthly meeting with a less formal agenda. You're always saying that this is a partnership of friends and colleagues and that I'm the one who insists on tedious procedures and unnecessary bureaucracy. So why all this formality, agenda, minutes, resolutions, when it comes to the monthly partners' meeting?'

De Witt said: 'It has been found useful. And I don't think I, for one, have ever used the phrase "friends and colleagues".'

Frances Peverell had been sitting bolt upright, her face very white. Now she said: 'You can't sell Innocent House.'

Etienne didn't look at her but kept his eyes on his papers. 'I can. We can. We have to sell if this business is to survive. You can't run an efficient publishing house from a Venetian palace on the Thames.'

'My family has for a hundred and sixty years.'

'I said an efficient publishing business. Your family didn't need to be efficient, they were cushioned with private incomes. Publishing in your grandfather's day wasn't even an occupation for gentlemen, it was a hobby for gentlemen. Today a publisher makes money, and makes it efficiently or goes under. Is that what you want? I don't propose to go under. I intend to make the Peverell Press profitable and after that to make it large.'

Gabriel Dauntsey said quietly: 'So that you can sell it? Make your millions and get out?'

Etienne ignored him.

'I'm getting rid of Sydney Bartrum to begin with. He's a competent enough accountant, but what we want is someone a great deal more than that. I propose to appoint a financial director with the job of finding money for development and setting up a proper financial system.'

De Witt said: 'We have a perfectly good financial system. The auditors have never complained. Sydney has been here for nineteen years. He's an honest, conscientious, hard-working accountant.'

'Exactly. That's what he is and it's all he is. As I said, we need something more. For example, I need to know the margin of profit over gross expenditure of every book we publish. Other houses have that information. How can we cut out the unproductive authors if we don't know who they are? We need someone who will make money for us, not just tell us each year how we spent it. I know how we spent it. If all we need is a competent accountant I can do that myself. I'd expect you to support him, James. He's pathetic, unprepossessing and not particularly efficient. Naturally that makes an immediate appeal. You needs must love the lowest when you see it. You should do something about your bleeding heart syndrome.'

James flushed, but said quietly enough: 'I don't particularly like the man. I cringe every time he calls me Mr de Witt. I suggested that he should say de Witt or James, but he looked at me as if I were proposing an indecency. But he's a perfectly competent accountant and he's been here for nineteen years. He knows the firm, he knows us, he knows the way we work.'

'Used to work, James, used to work.'

Frances said: 'And he only married a year ago. They've got a new baby.'

'What on earth has that to do with whether he's the right man for the job?'

De Witt asked: 'Do you have someone in mind?'

'I've asked Patterson Macintosh, the head-hunters, to put forward some names.'

'That will cost us a few quid. Head-hunters don't come cheap. Odd that nowadays we can't recruit staff without head-hunters, can't improve efficiency without time-and-motion-study experts and have to call in management consultants to tell us how to manage. Half the time these so-called experts are just front-men called in to cut down staff when the management haven't the guts to do it themselves. Have you ever known management consultants who didn't recommend sacking people? It's what they're paid to say, and a cushy little number they've made out of it for themselves.'

Frances said: 'We should have been consulted about all this.'

'You are being consulted.'

'In that case we can stop talking about it now. It isn't going to happen. Innocent House isn't going to be sold.'

'It is if just one of you agrees to sell. That's all it takes. You've forgotten how many shares I own. And the house isn't yours, Fran. Your family sold it to the firm in 1940, remember. All right, they got it too cheap, but they probably didn't give much for its chance of survival given the East End bombing. It was under-insured and, anyway, it couldn't have been replaced. Get this into your head, Fran, it isn't a Peverell house any more. Why are you so worried? You haven't a child. There's no Peverell to inherit.'

Frances flushed and half rose from her chair, but de Witt said quietly: 'Don't, Frances. Don't leave. We all need to discuss this.'

'There's nothing to discuss.'

There was a silence broken by Dauntsey's quiet voice. 'Is my poetry required to earn its 8.5 per cent net or whatever?'

'We'll keep your volumes in print, Gabriel, naturally. There will be a few books we'll have to carry.'

'I must hope that the burden of mine won't be too great.'

'And selling this place will mean turning you out of number twelve. Skolling wants the whole property, the two houses as well as the main building. I'm sorry about that.'

'But I have, after all, lived at number twelve at a ludicrously low rent for over ten years.'

'Well that's the arrangement Henry Peverell agreed with you, and naturally you had a right to take what he gave.' He paused, then added, 'And to go on taking. But you must see, things can't be allowed to go on like this.'

'Oh yes, I do see. Things can't be allowed to go on.'

Etienne went on as if he hadn't heard.

'And it's time to get rid of George. We should have retired him years ago. The switchboard operator is the first contact that people have with the firm. You need a young, vital, attractive girl, not that sixty-eight-year-old man. He is sixty-eight, isn't he? And don't tell me he's been here for twenty-two years. I know how long he's been here, that's just the trouble.'

Frances said: 'He isn't just the switchboard operator. He opens the place up, sees to the burglar alarm, and he's a wonderful handyman.'

'And he needs to be. There's always something going wrong with this house. It's time we moved into a modern, purpose-built, efficiently run building. And we haven't begun to take on board modern technology. You people thought you were being dangerously innovative when you replaced a few of the typewriters with word processors. And there's one other piece of good news. There's a chance that I may be able to entice Sebastian Beacher from his present publishers. He's not at all happy.'

Frances cried out: 'But he's an appallingly bad writer, and he's not much better as a human being.'

'The business of publishing is to give people what they want, not to make moral judgements.'

'You could argue that if you were manufacturing cigarettes.'

'I would argue it if I were manufacturing cigarettes. Or whisky for that matter.'

De Witt said: 'It isn't a true analogy. You could argue that drink is positively beneficial if used in moderation. You can never argue that a bad novel is other than a bad novel.'

'Bad for whom? And what do you mean by bad? Beacher tells a strong story, keeps the action moving, provides that mixture of sex and violence which people apparently want. Who are we to tell readers what is good for them? Anyway, haven't you always argued that the important thing is to get people reading? Let them begin with cheap romantic fiction and they may go on to Jane Austen or George Eliot. I don't see why they should – go on to the classics, I mean. That's your argument, not mine. What's wrong with cheap romantic fiction if that's what they happen to enjoy? It's a pretty condescending attitude to argue that popular fiction is only justified if it leads on to higher things. Well, what you and Gabriel happen to think are higher things.'

Dauntsey said: 'Are you saying that one shouldn't make value judgements? We make them every day of our lives.'

'I'm saying you shouldn't make them for other people. I'm saying that I shouldn't make them as a publisher. Anyway, there's one unanswerable argument; if I'm not allowed to make a profit on popular books, good or bad, I can't afford to publish less popular books for what you see as the discerning minority.'

Frances Peverell turned on him. Her colour was high and she found difficulty in controlling her voice. 'Why do you keep on saying "I"? It's always "I'll do this, I'll publish that". You may be chairman but you aren't the firm. We are. Collectively. The five of us. And we aren't meeting now as the Book Committee. That's next week. We're supposed to be talking about the future of Innocent House.'

'We are. I propose that we accept the offer and put the negotiations in hand.'

'And where do you propose we move to?'

'Offices in Docklands on the river. Downstream possibly. We need to discuss whether we buy or take a long lease, but either's possible. Prices have never been lower. Docklands has never been better value. And now that the Docklands Light Railway is working and the tube is to be extended, access will be easier. We shan't need the launch.'

Frances said: 'And sack Fred after all these years?'

'My dear Frances, Fred is a qualified waterman. Fred will have no problem in getting another job.'

Claudia said: 'It's too hurried, Gerard. I agree that the house will probably have to go, but we don't have to decide this morning. Put something on paper, the figures for example. Let's look at it when we've had time to consider.'

Gerard said: 'And lose the offer?'

'Is that likely? Come off it, Gerard. If Hector Skolling wants the house he isn't going to withdraw because he has to wait a week for an answer. Accept it if that makes you feel happier. We can always take it off the market if we have second thoughts.'

James de Witt said: 'I wanted to talk about Esmé Carling's new novel. At the last meeting you said something about turning it down.'

'*Death on Paradise Island*? I have turned it down. I thought that was agreed.'

De Witt said quietly and slowly as if to a recalcitrant child: 'No, it wasn't agreed. It was briefly discussed and the matter deferred.'

'Like so many of our decisions. You four remind me of that definition of a meeting – a collection of people who prefer to substitute the pleasure of talk for the responsibility of action or the ardour of decision. Something like that. I spoke to Esmé's agent yesterday and gave her the news. I confirmed it in writing with a copy to Carling. I take it that no one here is seriously arguing that Esmé Carling is a good novelist, or even a profitable one. Personally I prefer a writer to be one or the other, preferably both.'

De Witt said: 'We have published worse.'

Etienne turned on him with a small explosion of derision. 'God knows why you support her, James. You're the one who's keen to publish literary novels, Booker Prize candidates, sensitive little works to impress the literary mafia. Five minutes ago you were criticizing me for trying to get Sebastian Beacher. You're not suggesting that *Death on Paradise Island* is going to enhance the reputation of Peverell Press? I mean, I take it that you don't see it as the Whitbread Book of the Year. Incidentally, I'd be a great deal more sympathetic to your so-called Booker books if they occasionally made the Booker shortlist.'

James said: 'I agree it's probably time that we parted from her. It's the means, not the end I object to. I suggested at the last meeting, if you remember, that we should publish her latest and then tactfully say that we're closing the popular mystery list.'

Claudia said: 'Hardly convincing. She's the only author on it.'

James went on, speaking directly to Gerard. 'The book will need careful editing but she'll take that if it's done tactfully. The plot needs strengthening and the middle section is weak. But the description of the island is good. She's excellent at evoking an atmosphere of menace. And the characterization is an improvement on her last. We won't lose on it. We've published her for thirty years. It's a long association. I'd like it to end with goodwill and generosity, that's all.'

Gerard Etienne said: 'It has ended. And we're a publishing house not a charity. I'm sorry, James, she's got to go.'

De Witt said: 'You could have waited until the Book Committee met.'

'I probably would have waited if her agent hadn't rung. Carling was pressing to know if we had fixed publication day and what was proposed by way of a publication party. A party! A wake would have been more appropriate. There was no point in prevaricating. I told her that the book wasn't up to standard and that we didn't propose to publish. I confirmed that in writing yesterday.'

'She'll take it badly.'

'Of course she'll take it badly. Authors always take rejection badly. They equate it with infanticide.'

'What about her back-list?'

'Now there we may be able to make a bit of money.'

Frances Peverell suddenly spoke. 'James is right. We did agree that we'd discuss it again. You had absolutely no authority to speak to Esmé Carling or to Velma Pitt-Cowley. We could perfectly well publish her latest and tell her gently that it had to be the last. Gabriel, you agree, don't you? You think we should have taken *Death on Paradise Island*?'

The four partners looked at Dauntsey and waited as if he were a final court of appeal. The old man had been studying his paper but now he looked up and smiled gently at Frances.

'I don't think that would have softened the blow, do you? You don't reject an author. What you reject is the book. If we publish this latest she'll present us with another and we'll be faced with the same dilemma. Gerard acted prematurely and I imagine not particularly tactfully, but I think the decision was right. A novel is either worth publishing or it isn't.'

'I'm glad we've settled something.' Etienne began shuffling his papers together.

De Witt said: 'As long as you realize that's all that we've settled. No more negotiations about selling Innocent House until we've had another meeting and you've provided us with the figures and a full business plan.'

'You've had a business plan. I gave you one last month.'

'Not one we could understand. We'll meet a week today. It would be helpful if you could circulate the papers a day in advance. And we need alternatives. A business plan on the assumption that Innocent House is sold, a second on the assumption that it isn't.'

Etienne said: 'The second is easily provided. Either we do business with Skolling or we go bankrupt. And Skolling isn't a patient man.'

Claudia said: 'Keep him quiet with a promise. Tell him that if we decide to sell he will get first refusal.'

Etienne smiled. 'Oh no, I don't think I could make that kind of promise. Once his interest becomes public we could attract another £50,000. I don't think it's likely but you never know. The Greyfriars Museum is said to be looking for somewhere to house its collection of maritime paintings.'

Frances Peverell said: 'We're not going to sell Innocent House to Hector Skolling or anyone else. This house is sold over my dead body – or yours.'

13

In the secretaries' office Mandy looked up as Blackie entered, stalked over red-faced to her desk, sat down at her word processor and began typing. After a minute curiosity overcame discretion and Mandy asked: 'What's up? I thought you always took notes at the partners' meeting.'

Blackie's voice was strange, at once harsh but with a small note of triumphant vindication: 'Not any more apparently.'

Chucked out, poor cow, Mandy thought. She said: 'What's so secret then? What are they doing up there?'

'Doing?' Blackie's hands ceased their restless weaving over the keys. 'They're ruining this firm, that's what they're doing. They're sweeping away everything Mr Peverell worked for, cared for, stood for, for over thirty years. They're planning to sell Innocent House. Mr Peverell loved this house. It's been in the family for over a hundred and sixty years. Innocent House is Peverell Press. If one goes they both go. Mr Gerard's been planning to get rid of it ever since Mr Etienne retired and now he's taken over there's no one to stop him. They don't care anyway. Miss Frances won't like it but she's in love with him, and no one takes much notice of Miss Frances. Miss Claudia is his sister and Mr de Witt hasn't the guts to stop him. No one has. Mr Dauntsey might, but he's too old now and past caring. None of them can stand up to Mr Gerard. But he knows what I think. That's why he didn't want me there. He knows I disagree. He knows I'd stop him if I could.'

Mandy saw she was close to tears, but they were tears of anger. Embarrassed, anxious to comfort but uneasily aware that Blackie would later regret this unwonted confidence, she said: 'He can be a right sod. I've seen the way he treats you sometimes. Why don't you leave, try a spot of temping? Ask for your cards and tell him where he can stuff his job.'

Blackie, fighting for control, made an attempt to recover her dignity. 'Don't be ridiculous, Mandy. I've no intention of leaving. I'm a senior personal secretary. I'm not a temp. I never have been and I never will be.'

'There are worse things than temping. What about some coffee, then? I could make it now – no point in waiting – and a couple of chocolate digestives.'

'All right then, but don't waste time gossiping with Mrs Demery. I've got some copy-typing for you when you've finished those letters. And, Mandy, what I said is confidential. I spoke rather more freely than I should have done and I want it kept within these walls.'

Fat chance, thought Mandy. Didn't Miss Blackett realize that it was gossiped about all over the building? She said: 'I can keep my mouth shut. It's no skin off my nose is it? I'll be gone by the time you move from here.'

She was hardly on her feet when the telephone on her desk rang and she heard George's worried voice, but speaking with such conspiratorial quietness that she could hardly hear.

'Mandy, do you know where Miss FitzGerald is? I can't get Blackie out of a partners' meeting and I've got Mrs Carling here. She's demanding to see Mr Gerard and I don't think I can hold her much longer.'

'It's OK, Miss Blackett's here.' Mandy handed over the instrument. 'It's George. Mrs Carling is in reception screaming to see Mr Gerard.'

'Well she can't.'

Blackie took the instrument, but before she could speak the door was flung open and Mrs Carling burst in, thrust Mandy aside and strode straight through to the front office. Immediately she was back confronting them.

'Well, where is he? Where's Gerard Etienne?'

Blackie, attempting dignity, flipped open her desk diary. 'I don't think you have an appointment, Mrs Carling.'

'Of course I haven't a bloody appointment! After thirty years with the firm I don't need an appointment to see my publisher. I'm not a rep trying to sell him advertising space. Where is he?'

'He's in the partners' meeting, Mrs Carling.'

'I thought that was only on the first Thursday.'

'Mr Gerard moved it to today.'

'Then they'll have to interrupt it. They're in the boardroom I suppose.'

She made for the door, but Blackie was quicker and, slipping past her, stood with her back against it.

'You can't go up, Mrs Carling. Partners' meetings are never

interrupted. I have instructions that even urgent telephone calls have to be held.'

'In that case I'll wait until they're through.'

Blackie, still standing, found her typing chair firmly occupied, but remained calm.

'I don't know when that will be. They could send down for sandwiches. And haven't you a signing in Cambridge this lunch-hour? I'll let Mr Gerard know that you called and no doubt he'll get in touch with you when he has a free moment.'

The recent contretemps, the need to re-establish her status before Mandy, made her voice more authoritative than was tactful, but even so the ferocity of the response surprised them. Mrs Carling rose from the chair at a speed which set it spinning and stood so that her face was almost touching Blackie's. She was three inches shorter but it seemed to Mandy that this difference made her more, not less, terrifying. The muscles of the stretched neck stood out like cords, the eyes blazed upwards and beneath the slightly hooked nose the mean little mouth, like a red gash, spat out its venom.

'When he has a free moment! You stupid bitch! You arrogant conceited little fool! Who do you think you're talking to? It's my talent which has paid your wages for the last twenty-odd years and don't you forget it. It's time you realized just how unimportant you are in this firm. Just because you worked for Mr Peverell, and he indulged you and tolerated you and made you feel wanted, you think you can queen it over people who were part of Peverell Press when you were still a snotty-nosed school kid. Old Henry spoiled you, of course, but I can tell you what he really thought of you. And why? Because he told me, that's why. He was sick of you hanging about and gazing at him like a moonstruck cow. He was sick and tired of your devotion. He wanted you out, but he hadn't the guts to sack you. He never did have any guts, poor sod. If he'd had guts Gerard Etienne wouldn't be in charge now. Tell him I want to see him, and it had better be at my convenience, not his.'

Blackie spoke through lips so white and stiff that it seemed to Mandy that they could hardly move. 'It isn't true. You're lying. It isn't true.'

And now Mandy was frightened. She was used to office rows. In over three years of temping she had witnessed some impressive squalls of temperament and like a stalwart little boat had bobbed happily among the strewn wreckage of tumultuous seas. Mandy rather enjoyed a good office row. There was no better antidote to boredom. But this was different. Here, she recognized, was genuine suffering, real adult pain, an adult malice welling out of a hatred which was terrifying. This was grief which could not be assuaged by fresh coffee and a couple of biscuits from the tin Mrs Demery reserved for the partners only. She thought for a terrifying second that Blackie was going to throw back her head and howl with anguish. She wanted to hold out a hand in comfort but instinctively knew that there was no comfort she could give and that the attempt would later be resented.

The door banged. Mrs Carling had swept out.

Blackie said again: 'It's a lie. It's all lies. She doesn't know anything about it.'

'Of course she doesn't,' said Mandy sturdily. 'Of course she's lying, anyone could see that. She's just a jealous bitch. I shouldn't take any notice of her.'

'I'm just going to the bathroom.'

It was apparent that Blackie was about to be sick. Again Mandy wondered whether she could go with her but decided against it. Blackie walked out as stiff as an automaton, almost colliding with Mrs Demery as she came in carrying a couple of parcels.

Mrs Demery said: 'These came in the second post so I thought I'd bring them in. What's wrong with her?'

'She's upset. The partners didn't want her at the meeting and then Mrs Carling arrived demanding to see Mr Gerard and Blackie stopped her.'

Mrs Demery folded her arms and leaned against Blackie's desk. 'I expect she got the letter this morning telling her that they don't want her new novel.'

'How on earth do you know that, Mrs Demery?'

'There's not much happens around here I don't get to know about. There'll be trouble about this, mark my words.'

'If it's not good enough why doesn't she revise it or write another?'

'Because she doesn't think she can, that's why. That's what happens to authors when they get rejected. That's what they're terrified about all the time, losing their talent, writers' block. That's what makes them so tricky to deal with. Tricky, that's what writers are. You have to keep on telling them how wonderful they are or they go to pieces. I've seen it happen before more than once. Now old Mr Peverell knew how to deal with them. He had the right touch with authors had Mr Peverell. With Mr Gerard it's difficult. He's different. He doesn't see why they can't get on with the job and stop whining.'

It was a view with which Mandy had considerable sympathy. She might tell Blackie – and indeed believe it – that Mr Gerard was a sod, but she found him difficult to dislike. She felt that, given the chance, she could cope' with Mr Gerard. But further confidences were interrupted by the return of Blackie much sooner than Mandy had expected. Mrs Demery slipped away and Blackie, without a word, sat again at her keyboard.

For the next hour they worked in an oppressive silence broken only when Blackie issued orders. Mandy was sent to the copy room to make three copies of a recently arrived manuscript which, judging by the first three paragraphs, she thought was unlikely to appear in print, was handed a pile of extremely dull copy-typing and then told to weed out any papers more than two years old from the 'Keep a Little While' drawer. This useful compendium was used by the whole office as a depository for papers for which no one could find an appropriate place but which they were reluctant to throw away. There was little in it under twelve years old and weeding the 'Keep a Little While' drawer was a deeply unpopular chore. Mandy felt that she was being unjustly punished for Blackie's burst of confidence.

The partners' meeting ended earlier than usual and it was only half past eleven when Gerard Etienne, followed by his sister and Gabriel Dauntsey, came briskly through the office and into his own room. Claudia Etienne was pausing to speak to Blackie when the inner door was flung open and he reappeared. Mandy saw that he was containing his temper with difficulty. He said to Blackie: 'Have you taken my private diary?'

'Of course not Mr Gerard. Isn't it in your right-hand desk drawer?'

'If it were I should hardly be asking for it.'

'I made it up to date on Monday afternoon and put it back in the drawer. I haven't seen it since.'

'It was there yesterday morning. If you haven't taken it you had better discover who has. I presume you accept that looking after my diaries is part of your responsibility. If you can't find the diary I should be glad to have the pencil returned. It's gold and I'm rather attached to it.' Blackie's face was scarlet. Claudia Etienne looked on with an amused sardonic lift of her eyebrow. Mandy, scenting battle, studied the outlines in the shorthand notebook as if they had suddenly become incomprehensible.

Blackie's voice was hovering on the edge of hysteria. 'Are you accusing me of theft, Mr Gerard? I've worked in this office for twenty-seven years but –' Her voice broke off.

He said impatiently, 'Don't be a little fool. No one's accusing you of anything.' His eye hit on the snake curled over the handle of the filing cabinet. 'And for God's sake get rid of that bloody snake. Chuck it in the river. It makes this office look like a kindergarten.'

He went into his office and his sister followed. Without a word Blackie took the snake and shut it in her desk drawer.

She said to Mandy, 'What are you staring at? If you haven't any typing to do I can soon find you some. In the mean time you can make me some coffee.'

Mandy, armed with this new gossip for the delectation of Mrs Demery, was happy to oblige.

14

Declan was to arrive for the river trip at half past six, and it was 6.15 when Claudia went in to her brother's office. They were the last two people in the building. Gerard invariably worked late on Thursdays, but it was the night when most of the staff planned to leave early and take advantage of Thursday late-night shopping. He was sitting at his desk in the pool of light from his lamp, but stood up as she entered. His manners to her were always formal, always impeccable. She used to wonder if this was one small ploy to discourage intimacy.

She seated herself opposite him and said without preamble: 'Look, I'll support you about selling Innocent House. I'll go along with all your other plans, come to that. With my support you can easily out-vote the others. But I need cash: £350,000. I want you to buy half of my shares, all of them if you like.'

'I can't afford to.'

'You can when Innocent House is sold. Once the contracts are exchanged you can raise a million or so. With my shares you'll have a permanent overall majority. That will give you absolute power. It's worth paying for. I'll stay on in the firm but with fewer shares, or none.'

He said quietly: 'It's certainly worth thinking about, but not now. And I can't use the money from the sale. That belongs to the partnership. I'll need it anyway for the relocation and my other plans. But you could raise it. You could raise £350,000. If I can, so can you.'

'Not as easily. Not without a great deal of trouble and delay. And I need it urgently. I need it by the end of the month.'

'What for? What are you going to do?'

'Invest in the antique business with Declan Cartwright. He's got the chance of buying the business from old Simon: £350,000 for the four-storey freehold property and all stock. It's a very good price. The old man's devoted to him and would prefer him to have the business, but he can't wait to sell. He's old, he's sick and he's in a hurry.'

'Cartwright's a pretty boy, but at £350,000, isn't he pricing himself rather high?'

'I'm not a fool. The money isn't going to be handed over. It will still be my money invested in a joint business. Declan isn't a fool either. He knows what he's doing.'

'You're thinking of marrying him, are you?'

'I may do. Does it surprise you?'

'It does rather.' He added: 'I think you're fonder of him than he is of you. That's always dangerous.'

'Oh, it's more equal than you think. He feels as much for me as he's capable of feeling, and I feel as much for him as I'm capable of feeling. Our capacities for feeling are unequal, that's all. We both give the other what we have to give.'

'So you propose to buy him?'

'Isn't that how you and I have always got what we wanted, by buying it? And what about you and Lucinda? Are you so sure you're doing the right thing – for you I mean? I'm not worried about her. I'm not deceived by that air of virtuous fragility. She can take care of herself all right. Anyway, her class always do.'

'I mean to marry her.'

'Well you needn't sound so belligerent over it. No one's trying to stop you. Incidentally, are you proposing to tell her the truth about yourself – about us? More to the point, are you going to tell her family?'

'I shall answer reasonable questions. So far they haven't asked any, reasonable or unreasonable. We aren't in the age, thank God, when fathers are asked for their consent and fiancés have to produce some evidence of moral fitness and financial probity. Anyway, there's only her brother. He seems to assume I have a house for her to live in and enough money to keep her in reasonable comfort.'

'But you haven't a house, have you? I can't see her living in the Barbican flat. Nothing like enough room.'

'I think she rather fancies Hampshire. Anyway, we can discuss that nearer the date of the wedding. I shall keep on the Barbican flat. It's handy for the office.'

'Well, I hope it works out. Frankly I give Declan and me the better chance of the two. We don't confuse sex with love. And you may not find this marriage easy to get out of. She'll probably develop religious scruples about divorce. Anyway divorce is vulgar, messy and expensive. OK, she couldn't prevent it after two years of separation but they'd be very uncomfortable years. You wouldn't enjoy public failure.'

'I'm not even married. It's a bit early to start deciding how I'm going to cope with failure. It won't fail.'

'Frankly, Gerard, I don't see what you expect to get out of it, except a beautiful wife eighteen years younger than you.'

'Most people would think that was enough.'

'Only the naïve. It's a recipe for disaster. You aren't royal, you don't have to marry a totally unsuitable virgin just to continue a dynasty. Or is that what this is all about, founding a family? Yes, I believe it is. You've turned conventional in middle age. You want a settled life, children.'

'That seems the most sensible reason for marriage. Some might say the only sensible reason.'

'You've had enough of playing the field so now you're looking for a young, beautiful and preferably well-born virgin. Frankly, I think you'd have been better off with Frances.'

'That was never a possibility.'

'It was for her. I can see how it happened, of course. Here's a virgin of nearly thirty obviously wanting sexual experience and who better to provide it than my clever little brother. But it was a mistake. You've made an enemy of James de Witt and you can't afford that.'

'He's never spoken to me about it.'

'Of course he hasn't. That isn't how James operates. He's a doer not a talker. A word of advice. Don't stand too near the balcony of the upper storeys of Innocent House. One violent death in this house is enough.'

He said calmly: 'Thank you for the warning, but I'm not sure James de Witt would be the chief suspect. After all, if anything happens to me before I marry and make a new will, you'll get my shares, my flat and my life assurance money. You can buy quite a lot of antiques for the best part of two and a half million.'

Claudia was at the door when he spoke again, coolly and without looking up from his paper.

'By the way, the office menace has struck again.'

Claudia turned and said sharply: 'What do you mean? How? When?'

'This afternoon, at twelve-thirty to be precise. Someone sent a fax from here to Better Books in Cambridge cancelling Carling's signing.

She arrived to find the advertisements taken down, the table and chair removed, the hopefuls turned away and most of the books relegated to the back office. Apparently she was incandescent with rage. I rather wish I'd been there to see it.'

'Christ! When did you learn this?'

'Her agent, Velma Pitt-Cowley, rang me at two forty-five when I got back from lunch. She'd been trying to reach me since one-thirty. Carling telephoned her from the shop.'

'And you've kept quiet about it until now?'

'I've had more important things to do this afternoon than swan round the office asking people for alibis. Anyway, that's your job, but I shouldn't make too much of it. I've a good idea this time who was responsible. It's of small importance anyway.'

Claudia said grimly: 'Not to Esmé Carling. You can dislike her, despise her or pity her but don't underestimate her. She could prove a more dangerous enemy than you imagine.'

15

The upstairs room at the Connaught Arms off Waterloo Road was crowded. Matt Bayliss, the licensee, had no doubt about the success of the poetry reading. Already by nine o'clock the bar takings were well up for a Thursday night. The small upstairs room was normally used for lunches – there was little demand for hot dinners at the Connaught Arms – but was also available for the occasional function and it was his brother, who worked for an arts organization, who had persuaded him to cater for the Thursday night event. The plan was for a number of published poets to read their works interposed with readings by any amateurs who cared to take part. A fee of £1 a head had been charged and Matt had set up a cash wine bar at the back of the room. He had no idea that poetry was so popular or that so many of his regulars had ambitions to express themselves in verse. The initial sale of tickets had been satisfactory but there was a steady stream of late arrivals and people from the bar, hearing of the entertainment overhead, were making their way up the narrow staircase, tankards in hand.

Colin's enthusiasms were varied and fashionable: Black Art, Women's Art, Gay Art, Commonwealth Art, Accessible Art, Innovative Art, Art for the People. This event was billed as Poetry for the People. Matt's personal interest was in beer for the people, but he had seen no reason why the two enthusiasms should not be profitably combined. Colin's ambition was to make the Connaught Arms a recognized centre for contemporary verse speaking and a public platform for new poets. Matt, watching his relief barman busily opening bottles of Californian red, discovered in himself an un-expected interest in contemporary culture. He came up from the saloon bar from time to time to sample the entertainment. The verses were to him largely incomprehensible; certainly very few either rhymed or had a discernible metre, which was his definition of poetry; but all were enthusiastically applauded. As most of the amateur poets and the audience smoked, the stagnant air was heavy with the fumes of beer and tobacco.

The advertised star of the evening was Gabriel Dauntsey. He had asked to go on early but most of the poets before him had overstepped their time limits, the amateurs in particular not being susceptible to Colin's muttered hints, and it was nearly 9.30 before Dauntsey made his slow way to the rostrum. He was listened to in a respectful silence and loudly applauded, but Matt guessed that his poems of a war which, for the great majority of those present, was now history, had little relevance to their current preoccupations. Afterwards Colin had pushed his way through the throng to reach him.

'Do you really have to leave? A few of us are thinking of going out for a meal afterwards.'

'I'm sorry, it will be too late for me. Where can I get a taxi?'

'Matt here could ring, but you'll probably get one quicker by walking to Waterloo Road.'

He had slipped away almost unnoticed and unthanked, leaving Matt feeling that somehow they had done badly by the old man.

He was hardly out of the door when an elderly couple came up to him at the bar. The man said: 'Has Gabriel Dauntsey gone? My wife has a first edition of his poems which she'd love him to sign. We can't see him anywhere upstairs.'

Matt said: 'Have you got a car?'

'Parked about three blocks away. It's the nearest we could get.'

'Well he's only just left. He's on foot. If you hurry you could catch him up. You'll probably miss him if you wait to go for the car.'

Hurriedly they left, the woman, book in hand, eager-eyed.

Within three minutes they were back. Across the bar Matt could see them coming in through the door, supporting Gabriel Dauntsey between them. He was holding a blood-stained handkerchief to his brow. Matt made his way across to them.

'What's happened?'

The woman, obviously shaken, said: 'He's been mugged. Three men, two black and one white. They were bending over him, but ran off when they saw us. They got his wallet, though.'

The man looked round for a vacant chair and settled Dauntsey into it. 'We'd better ring the police and an ambulance.'

Dauntsey's voice was stronger than Matt had expected. 'No, no. I'm all right. I don't want either. It's only a graze where I fell.'

Matt looked at him, undecided. He seemed more shaken than hurt.

And what was the point of ringing the police? They didn't have a chance of catching the muggers and this would only be one more minor crime to add to their statistics of crimes reported but unsolved. Matt, while a strong supporter of the police, preferred on the whole not to see them too frequently in his bar.

The woman looked at her husband then said firmly: 'We have to pass St Thomas's Hospital. We'll take him to the casualty department. That would be the wisest plan.'

Dauntsey, apparently, was to have no say in the matter.

They want to get rid of the responsibility as soon as possible, thought Matt, and he didn't blame them. After they had left he made his way upstairs to check on the supply of wine and noticed on a table by the door a pile of slim volumes. He felt a spurt of pity for Gabriel Dauntsey. The poor devil hadn't even waited to sign his books. But perhaps that was just as well. It would have been embarrassing for everyone if he hadn't made a sale.

16

On the following morning, Friday 15 October, Blackie awoke to a weight of apprehension. Her first conscious thought was dread of the day and what might lie ahead. She put on her dressing gown and went down to make the morning tea, wondering whether to wake Joan with the complaint that she had a headache, that she didn't think she'd go into the office today, asking Joan to telephone later with her regrets and promises to be back on Monday. She thrust the temptation aside. Monday would come only too quickly, bringing with it an even heavier weight of anxiety. And not to appear today would look suspicious. Everyone knew that she didn't take days off, that she was never ill. She must go in to work as if this was just an ordinary day.

She could eat no breakfast. Even the thought of eggs and bacon made her nauseous and the first spoonful of cereal clogged her mouth. At the station she bought her usual *Daily Telegraph* but clutched it unopened during the journey, staring out at the flashing kaleidoscope of the Kent suburbs with unseeing eyes.

The launch was five minutes late starting off from Charing Cross pier. Mr de Witt, usually so punctual, came running down the ramp just as Fred Bowling was deciding that he had to cast off.

Mr de Witt said briefly, 'Sorry everyone, I overslept. Good of you to wait. I thought I'd have to take the second boat.'

They were all there now, the usual first boatload: Mr de Witt, herself, Maggie FitzGerald and Amy Holden from publicity, Mr Elton from rights and Ken from the warehouse. Blackie took her usual seat in the prow. She would have liked to have removed herself to the stern and sit alone, but that too might have looked suspicious. It seemed that she was abnormally conscious of her every word and action, as if she were already under interrogation. She heard James de Witt tell the others that Miss Frances had rung him late the previous night to tell him that Mr Dauntsey had been mugged. It had happened after his poetry reading. He had been quickly found by two people who had been at the pub and who had taken him to the casualty department at St Thomas's Hospital. He had suffered more from shock than from the mugging and was all right now. Blackie didn't comment. This was just one more minor mishap, one more piece of bad luck. It seemed unimportant compared to the dragging weight of her own anxiety.

Usually she enjoyed the river trip. She had done it now for over twenty-five years and it had never lost its fascination. But today all the familiar landmarks seemed no more than stage-posts on the journey to disaster: the elegant ironwork of Blackfriars Railway Bridge; Southwark Bridge with the steps on Southwark Causeway from which Christopher Wren was rowed across the river when he supervised the building of St Paul's Cathedral; London Bridge where once the heads of traitors were displayed on spikes at either end; Traitor's Gate, green with algae and weed; and Dead Man's Hole under Tower Bridge where, by tradition, the ashes of the dead were scattered outside the city boundaries; Tower Bridge itself, the white and pale blue of the high walkway with its gleaming gold-tipped badge; HMS Belfast in its Atlantic colours. She saw them all with uncaring eyes. She told herself that this anxiety was ridiculous and unnecessary. She had only one small cause for guilt which perhaps, after all, wasn't really so important or so blameworthy. She had only to keep her nerve and all would be well. But her anxiety, which now amounted to active fear, grew stronger with every minute which brought her closer to Innocent House and it seemed to her that her mood infected the rest of the group. Mr de Witt usually sat in silence, often reading, on the river journey, but the girls were usually cheerful chatterers. This morning all of them fell into silence as the launch slowly rocked to its usual mooring ring to the right of the steps.

De Witt suddenly said: 'Innocent House. Well, here we are . . .'

His voice held a note of spurious jollity as if they had all returned from a boat trip, but his face was stern. She wondered what was the matter with him, what he was thinking. Then slowly, with the others, she carefully made her way up the tide-washed steps onto the marble patio, bracing herself to meet whatever the day had in store.

17

George Copeland, standing behind the protection of his reception desk in embarrassed ineptitude, heard the clatter of feet on the cobbles with relief. So the launch had arrived at last. Lord Stilgoe halted his angry pacing and they both turned to the door. The little group came through in a bunch with James de Witt at the front. Mr de Witt gave one look at George's worried face and asked quickly: 'What's wrong, George?'

It was Lord Stilgoe who answered. Without greeting de Witt he said grimly: 'Etienne's missing. I had an appointment to meet him in his office at nine o'clock. When I arrived there was no one here but the receptionist and the cleaner. It's not the way I expect to be treated. My time is valuable even if Etienne's isn't. I have a hospital appointment this morning.'

De Witt said easily: 'How do you mean, missing? I expect he's got held up in the traffic.'

George broke in: 'He must be here somewhere, Mr de Witt. His jacket is over the chair in his office. I looked there when he didn't reply to my ring. And the front door wasn't locked when I arrived this morning, not with the Banham. I got in with just the Yale. And the alarm hadn't been set. Miss Claudia's just arrived. She's checking now.'

They all moved, as if driven by a common impulse, into the hall. Claudia Etienne, with Mrs Demery at her shoulder, was coming out of Blackie's office.

She said: 'George is right. He must be here somewhere. His jacket is over the chair and his bunch of keys in the top right-hand drawer.' She turned to George. 'You've checked at number ten?'

'Yes, Miss Claudia. Mr Bartrum's arrived but there's no one else in the building. He had a look and rang back. He says that Mr Gerard's Jaguar is there, parked where it was last night.'

'How about the house lights? Were they on when you arrived?'

'No, Miss Claudia. There wasn't a light in his office either. Not anywhere.'

At this moment Frances Peverell and Gabriel Dauntsey appeared. George saw that Mr Dauntsey looked frail. He was walking with a stick and there was a small sticking-plaster on the right of his forehead. No one remarked on it. George wondered if anyone but him had even noticed.

Claudia said: 'You haven't got Gerard at number twelve have you? He seems to have disappeared.'

Frances said: 'He hasn't been with us.'

Mandy, coming in behind and taking off her helmet, said: 'His car is here. I saw it at the end of Innocent Passage when I drove past.'

Claudia said repressively, 'Yes, we know that, Mandy. I'll take a look upstairs. He must be somewhere in the building. The rest of you, wait here.'

She made briskly for the staircase with Mrs Demery at her back. Blackie, as if she hadn't heard the instruction, gave a little gasp and ran clumsily after them. Maggie FitzGerald said, 'Trust Mrs Demery to be in on the act', but her voice was uncertain and when no one commented she blushed as if wishing she hadn't spoken.

The little group moved quietly into a semicircle, almost, George thought, as if gently pushed by an invisible hand. He had switched on the lights in the hall and the painted ceiling glowed above them, seeming to mark with its splendour and permanence their puny preoccupations and unimportant anxieties. All their eyes were turned upwards. George thought that they looked like figures in a religious painting, staring up in anticipation of some supernatural visitation. He waited with them, uncertain whether his place was here or behind his counter. It wasn't for him to initiate action by joining the search. As always he did what he was told, but he was a little surprised that the partners waited with such docility. But why not? It was pointless for a whole crowd of them to go charging round Innocent House. Three searchers were more than enough. If Mr Gerard was in the building Miss Claudia would find him. No one spoke or moved except James de Witt who had stepped quietly to Frances Peverell's side. It seemed to George that they had been waiting, frozen, like actors in a tableau, for hours although it could only have been for a few minutes.

Then Amy, her voice sharp with fear, said: 'Someone's screaming. I heard a scream.' She looked round at them, frantic-eyed.

James de Witt didn't turn to look at her but kept his eyes on the stairs. He said quietly: 'No one screamed. You imagined it, Amy.'

Then it came again, but this time louder and unmistakable, a high desperate cry. They moved forward to the bottom of the stairs but no further. It was as if no one dared to take that first upward step. There was a second's silence, and then the wailing began, at first a distant lament and then rising, getting closer. George, rooted in terror, couldn't identify the voice. It seemed to him as inhuman as the wail of a siren or the scream of a cat in the night.

Maggie FitzGerald whispered: 'Oh my God! My God, what is it?'

And then, with dramatic suddenness, Mrs Demery appeared at the top of the staircase. It seemed to George that she materialized out of the air. She was supporting Blackie, whose wails were now subsiding into low heaving sobs.

James de Witt's voice was low but very clear: 'What is it, Mrs Demery? What's happened? Where's Mr Gerard?'

'In the little archives room. Dead! Murdered! That's what's happened. He's lying up there half-naked and stiff as a bloody board. Some devil has strangled him with that sodding snake. He's got Hissing Sid wound round his neck with its head stuffed in his mouth.'

At last James de Witt moved. He sprang for the stairs. Frances made to follow him, but he turned and said urgently, 'No, Frances, no', and pushed her gently aside. Lord Stilgoe followed him with an old man's ungainly waddle, grasping at the stair rail. Gabriel Dauntsey hesitated for a moment then followed.

Mrs Demery cried: 'Give me a hand, can't you someone? She's a dead weight.'

Frances went immediately to her and placed an arm round Blackie's waist. Looking up at them, George thought that it was Miss Frances who needed support. They came down the stairs together almost carrying Blackie between them. Blackie was moaning and whispering, 'I'm sorry. I'm sorry.' Together they supported her across the hall towards the back of the house while the little group looked after them in appalled silence.

George went back to his desk, to his switchboard. This was his place. This was where he felt secure, in control. This was where he could cope. He could hear voices. The awful sobbing was quieter now but he could hear Mrs Demery's high expostulations and a babble of female voices. He shut them out of his mind. There was a job to be done: he had better do it. He tried to unlock his security cupboard under the counter but his hands were shaking so violently that he couldn't fit the key into the lock. The telephone rang and he jumped violently then fumbled for the headset. It was Mrs Velma Pitt-Cowley, Mrs Carling's agent, wanting to speak to Mr Gerard. George, shocked into initial silence, managed to say that Mr Gerard wasn't available. Even to his ears, his voice sounded high, cracked, unnatural.

'Miss Claudia, then. I suppose she's in.'

'No,' said George, 'No.'

'What's wrong? That's you, isn't it George? What's the matter?'

George, appalled, switched off the call. Immediately the telephone rang again, but he didn't answer and after a few seconds the noise stopped. He gazed at it in trembling impotence. Never before had he acted like this. Time passed, seconds, minutes. And then Lord Stilgoe was towering over the desk and he could smell his breath and feel the force of his triumphant anger.

'Get me New Scotland Yard. I want to speak to the Commissioner. If he's not available, get me Commander Adam Dalgliesh.'

BOOK TWO

Death of a Publisher

18

Detective Inspector Kate Miskin, nudging aside a half-empty packing case, opened the balcony door of her new Docklands flat and, grasping the rail of polished oak, gazed over the shimmering river, up to Limehouse Reach and down to the great curve round the Isle of Dogs. It was only 9.15 in the morning but already an early mist had cleared and the sky, almost cloudless, was brightening to an opaque whiteness with glimpses of soft clear blue. It was a morning more like spring than mid-October, but the river smell was autumnal, strong as the smell of damp leaves and rich earth overlaying the salty tang of the sea. It was full tide and beneath the pin-points of light which flicked and danced on the creased surface of the water like fireflies, she could imagine the strong tug of the flowing current, could almost sense its power. With this flat, this view, one more ambition had been achieved, one more step taken away from that dull box-sized flat at the top of Ellison Fairweather Buildings in which she had spent the first eighteen years of her life.

Her mother had died within days of her birth, her father was unknown and she had been cared for by a reluctant and elderly maternal grandmother, who resented the child who had made her a virtual prisoner in the high-rise flat she dared no longer leave at night to seek the conviviality, the glitter and the warmth of the local pub and who had grown increasingly embittered by her grandchild's intelligence and by a responsibility for which she was unsuited, by age, by health, by temperament. Kate had realized too late, only at the moment of her grandmother's death, how much she had loved her. It seemed to her now that in the moment of that death each had paid to the other a lifetime's arrears of love. She knew that she would never break completely free of Ellison Fairweather Buildings. Coming up to this flat in the large modern lift, surrounded by the carefully packed oil paintings which she herself had painted, she had remembered the lift at Ellison Fairweather, the smeared and filthy walls with their graffiti, the stink of urine, the cigarette ends, the discarded beer cans. It had been frequently vandalized and she and her grandmother had

had to lug their shopping and washing up the seven storeys, pausing at the top of each flight for her grandmother to catch her breath. Sitting there surrounded by their plastic bags, listening to the old lady's wheezings, she had vowed: 'When I'm grown-up I shall get out of this. I shall leave bloody Ellison Fairweather Buildings for ever. I shall never come back again. I shall never be poor again. I shall never have to smell this smell again.'

She had chosen the police service through which to make her escape, resisting the temptation to enter the sixth form or try for university, anxious only to begin earning, to get away. That first Victorian flat in Holland Park had been the beginning. After her grandmother's death she had stayed on for nine months knowing that to leave at once would be a desertion, although she was not sure from what, perhaps from a reality that had to be faced, knowing too that there was expiation to be made, things she had to learn about herself, and that this was the place in which to learn them. The time would come when it would be right to leave and she could close the door with a sense of completion, of putting behind her a past which couldn't be altered, but which could be accepted with its miseries, its horrors – yes, and its joys – reconciled and made part of herself. And now that time had come.

This flat, of course, wasn't what she had originally imagined. She had pictured herself in one of the great converted warehouses near Tower Bridge with high windows and huge rooms, the strong oak rafters and, surely, the lingering smell of spice. But even with a falling property market this had been beyond her means. And the flat, which after careful searching she had chosen, wasn't a poor second. She had taken the highest mortgage possible, believing that it was financially wise to buy the best she could afford. She had one large room, eighteen feet by twelve, and two smaller bedrooms, one with its shower en suite. The kitchen was large enough to eat in and well fitted. The south-west facing balcony, which ran the whole length of the sitting-room, was narrow but still wide enough to take a small table and chairs. She could eat out there in the summer. And she was glad that the furniture originally bought for her first flat hadn't been cheap. The sofa and two chairs in real leather were going to look good and right in this modern setting. It was lucky that she had rejected black in favour of fawn. Black would have looked too smart. And the simple elm table and chairs looked right too.

And the flat had another great advantage. It was at the end of the building and with a double outlook and two balconies. From her bedroom she could see the wide gleaming panorama of Canary Wharf, the tower like an immense cellular pencil with its lead topped with light, the great white curve of the adjoining building, the still water of the old West India Dock and the overhead Docklands Light Railway with its trains like clockwork toys. This city of glass and concrete would become busier as new firms moved in. She would be able to look down on the multicoloured, ever-changing pageant of half a million scurrying men and women leading their working lives. The other balcony looked south-west over the river and the slower immemorial traffic of the Thames; barges, pleasure boats, the launches of the River Police and the Port of London Authority, the cruise liners making their way upstream to berth at Tower Bridge. She loved the stimulus of contrast and here in the flat she could move at will from one world to another, from the new to the old, from still water to the tidal river which T. S. Eliot had called a strong brown god.

The flat was particularly suitable for a police officer, with an entryphone system on the main entrance and two security locks and a chain fitted to her front door. There was a basement garage to which the residents had their own keys. That, too, was important. And the journey to New Scotland Yard wouldn't be too difficult. She was, after all, on the right side of the river. But perhaps she might occasionally travel by river boat to Westminster Pier. She would get to know the river, become part of its life and history. She would wake in the morning to the cry of gulls and step out into this cool white emptiness. Standing now between the glitter of the water and the high, delicate blue of the sky she felt an extraordinary impulse which had visited her before and which she thought must be as close as she could ever get to a religious experience. She was possessed by a need, almost physical in its intensity, to pray, to praise, to say thank you, without knowing to whom, to shout with a joy that was deeper than the joy she felt in her own physical well-being and achievements or even in the beauty of the physical world.

She had left the fitted bookshelves at the old flat, but new ones built to her specification covered the whole of the wall facing the window and on these, kneeling beside a packing case, Alan Scully was arranging her books. She had been surprised how many she had acquired since knowing him. None of these writers had she ever encountered at school but she was grateful now for Ancroft Comprehensive. It had done its best for her. The teachers whom she had once in her arrogance despised she now knew had been dedicated, struggling to impose discipline, to cope with large classes and a dozen different languages, to meet competing needs, to tackle the appalling home problems of some of the children and to get them through the examinations which would at least open the door to something better. But most of her education had happened since school. Behind its bicycle sheds and in its asphalt playground she had learned all that was unimportant about sex and nothing that was important. It was Alan who had done that for her, that and so much else. He had taught her about books, not condescendingly, not seeing himself as some kind of Pygmalion, but wanting to share with someone he loved the things that he loved. And now the time had come for that, too, to end.

She heard his voice: 'If we're taking a break I'll make a coffee. Or are you just admiring the view?'

'Admiring the view. Gloating. What do you think of it, Alan?'

It was the first time he had seen the flat and she had displayed it with something of the pride of a child with a new toy.

'I shall like it when you're finally settled. That is, if I see it when you're finally settled. What about these books? Do you want to separate poetry, fiction, non-fiction? At present we've got Dalgliesh next to Defoe.'

'Defoe? I didn't know I had a Defoe. I don't even like Defoe. Oh, separate I think. And then by author's name.'

'The Dalgliesh is a first edition. Do you feel it necessary to buy him in hardback because he's your boss and you work with him?'

'No. I read his poetry to see if I can understand him better.'

'And do you?'

'Not really. I can't relate the poetry to the man. And when I do, it's terrifying. He notices too much.'

'Not signed, I notice. So you didn't ask.'

'It would embarrass both of us. Don't fiddle with it, Alan. Just put it on the shelf.'

She went over and knelt beside him. He had made no mention of her professional books and she saw that they were neatly piled beside the packing case. One by one she began placing them on the lowest shelf: a copy of the latest Criminal Statistics, the *Police and Criminal Evidence Act 1984*, Blackstone's *Guide to the Criminal Justice Act 1991*, Butterworth's *Police Law*, Keane's *The Modern Law of Evidence*, Clifford Hogan's *Criminal Law*, the *Police Training Manual* and the Sheehy Report. She thought: the collection of a professional woman on the make, and wondered whether in placing them to one side and not mentioning them, Alan was making some kind of comment, perhaps even a subconscious judgement on more than her library. For the first time in years she saw that relationship through the eyes of a detached and critical observer. Here we have a professional woman, successful, ambitious, knowing where she wants to go. Coping every day with the messy detritus of undisciplined lives, she has carefully excluded messiness from her own. One necessary accoutrement of this well-organized self-sufficiency is a lover, intelligent, personable, available when needed, skilful in bed and undemanding out of it. For three years Alan Scully had admirably filled this need. She knew that, in return, she had given affection, loyalty, kindness, understanding; none of these things had been difficult to provide. But was it surprising that, having made his own commitment, he wanted to be more to her than the equivalent of a fashion accessory?

She ground the beans, relishing the fresh coffee smell. No drink ever tasted quite as good as the beans smelled. They drank the coffee sitting on the floor, their backs against a packing case as yet unopened. She said: 'What flight are you taking next Wednesday?'

'The eleven o'clock, BA175. You haven't changed your mind?'

She almost said 'No, I can't Alan, it's impossible,' but stopped herself. It wasn't impossible. She could perfectly well change her mind. The honest answer was that she didn't want to. They had talked over their problem many times before and she knew now that there could be no compromise. She understood what he felt and what he wanted. He wasn't trying to blackmail her. The chance had come for him to work for three years in Princeton and he was anxious to go. It was important to his career, to his future. But he would stay in London, would continue his present job at the library if she would make a commitment to him, would agree to marry him, or at least to live with him, and have his child. It wasn't that he thought her career less important than his; if necessary he would temporarily give up his job and stay at home while she worked. He had always granted her that essential equality. But he was tired of being on the periphery of her life. She was the woman he loved and wanted to spend his life with. He would give up Princeton, but not if it meant continuing as they were, seeing her only when the job permitted, knowing that he was her lover but would never be more.

She said: 'I'm not ready for marriage or for motherhood. Perhaps I never shall be, particularly not for motherhood. I wouldn't be any good at it. I've never had any training, you see.'

'I don't think it requires training.'

'It requires loving commitment. That's one thing I can't give. You can't give what you haven't had.'

He didn't argue or attempt to persuade her. The time for talking was over.

He said: 'At least we've got another five days and we'll have today. Unpacking all this morning, lunch at a riverside pub, maybe the Prospect of Whitby. There ought to be time for that. You've got to eat. What time are you expected back at the Yard?'

She said: 'Two o'clock. I've only got the half day. Daniel Aaron's on leave today so it isn't easy. I'll get off as early as I can and we'll have dinner here tonight. One meal out is enough. We can pick up a Chinese takeaway.'

Alan was carrying the coffee mugs into the kitchen when the telephone rang. He called out: 'Your first call. That's what comes of sending out change-of-address cards. You'll be pestered by friends wishing you luck.'

But the call was short and Kate hardly spoke as she answered it. Putting down the receiver she turned to him.

'It's the Squad. Suspicious death. They want me at once. It's on the river so AD is picking me up here in a Thames Division launch. Sorry, Alan.' She seemed to have spent the last three years saying 'Sorry, Alan'.

They looked at each other in silence for a moment, then he said: 'As it was in the beginning, is now and ever shall be. What do you want me to do, Kate, go on unpacking?'

Suddenly the thought of him here alone was intolerable. 'No,' she said. 'Leave it. I'll do it later. It can wait.'

But he continued unpacking as she changed her clothes from the jeans and sweatshirt, which had been suitable for the dusty job of moving in and then cleaning the flat, to a pair of fawn corduroy trousers, a well-cut tweed jacket and a polo-necked jumper in fine cream wool. She plaited her thick hair high at the back and secured the end of the plait with a slide.

On her return he gave her his usual quick appraising smile and said: 'Your working clothes? I never know whether you dress for Adam Dalgliesh or for the suspects. Obviously it's not for the corpse.'

She said: 'This corpse isn't exactly lying in a ditch.'

It was comparatively new, this jealousy of her boss, and was perhaps both a symptom and the cause of their changing relationship.

They left together in silence. It wasn't until Kate was double-locking the front door after them that he spoke again. He said: 'Shall I see you again before I leave next Wednesday?'

'I don't know, Alan. I don't know.'

But she did know. If this case was as important as it promised to be she would be working a sixteen-hour day, perhaps longer. She would look back on those few hours they had spent together in the flat with pleasure, even with sadness. But what she was feeling now was something more intoxicating, and she felt it whenever she was called to a new case. This was her job, one she had been trained for, one she did well, one she enjoyed. Already knowing that this might be the last time she saw him for years she was moving in thought away from him, mentally bracing herself for the task ahead.

He had parked his car in one of the marked spaces to the right of the forecourt but he didn't get in. Instead he came and waited with her for the approach of the police launch. When its dark blue sleek lines came into view he turned from her without a word and went back to the car. But still he didn't drive away. As the launch drew up Kate knew that he was still watching as the tall dark figure standing in the bow held out a hand to steady her on board.

19

The call came to Inspector Daniel Aaron just as he was approaching
Eastern Avenue. He didn't need to stop the car to take it; the message
was short and clear. A suspicious death at Innocent House, Innocent
Walk. He was to go there immediately. Robbins would be bringing
his murder bag.

The message couldn't have come at a better time. His first reaction
was a surge of excitement that here at last was the major job he had
been longing for. He had only replaced Massingham on the Special
Squad three months ago and was anxious to prove himself. But there
was another reason. He was on his way to his parents' house, in The
Drive, Ilford. It was their fortieth wedding anniversary and a
luncheon party had been arranged with his mother's sister and her
husband. He had applied well in advance for a day's leave knowing
that this was one family occasion he couldn't reasonably ignore, but
he hadn't been looking forward to it. The morning promised a
pretentious but dull lunch at the popular store restaurant his mother
had chosen, followed by an afternoon of boring family chat. He knew
that his aunt regarded him as an uncaring son, an unsatisfactory
nephew, a bad Jew. On this occasion she might not openly voice her
disapproval but this brittle forbearance would hardly lighten the
atmosphere.

He turned into a side road and stopped the car to telephone. It was
going to be a difficult call and he preferred not to be driving while he
made it. As he stabbed out the number he was aware of a confusion of
emotions: relief that he had a valid excuse to miss the luncheon party,
a strong disinclination to break the news, excitement that he was on
his way to a case which promised to be a big one, and the usual
irrational and pleasure-destroying guilt. He had no intention of
wasting time in argument or prolonged explanations. Kate Miskin
might be already at the scene. His parents would have to accept that
he had a job to do.

It was his father who answered the telephone. 'Daniel, haven't
you started out yet? You said you'd come really early, have a

124

quiet time with us before the others arrive. Where are you?'

'I'm on Eastern Avenue. I'm sorry, Father, but I can't come. I've just had a call from the Squad. It's an urgent case. Murder. I have to drive straight to the scene.'

And then his mother's voice as she took over the telephone. 'What is it you're saying, Daniel? Did you say you're not coming? But you must come. You promised. Your aunt and uncle will be here. It's our fortieth wedding anniversary. What is a celebration if I can't have both my sons with me? You promised.'

'I know that I promised. I wouldn't be on Eastern Avenue now if I hadn't intended to come. The call's just come through.'

'But you're on leave. What's the point of having a rest day if they call you back like this? Can't someone else cope? Why does it always have to be you?'

'It doesn't always have to be me. It does today. It's an urgent case. Murder.'

'Murder! And you'd rather be mixed up in murder than be with your parents. Murder. Death. Can't you give a thought to the living?'

'I'm sorry, I have to go now.' He added grimly, 'Have a good lunch', and replaced the receiver.

It had been worse than he had expected. He sat for a few seconds willing himself into calm, fighting down an irritation which was rising to anger. Then he slipped in the clutch, found a convenient driveway to reverse and joined the stream of traffic. He was part now of the morning rush hour, although the words seemed inappropriate to describe this grinding erratic progress. And he was unlucky with the traffic lights. The journey was punctuated by light after light glowing into red with maddening perversity. The scene of violent death to which he was driving with such tedious slowness could not yet even be imagined but, once there, the tasks would take all his thoughts and energies. Physically he was moving away from that Ilford house mile by painful mile, but now he could not banish it or its life from his thoughts.

The family had moved from the Whitechapel terraced house where he was born when he was ten and David thirteen. He still thought of 27 Balaclava Terrace as home. It was one of the few streets not destroyed by enemy bombing, stubbornly surviving while the surrounding flats and houses were demolished in clouds of acrid dust and the great high towers rose up like an alien city. It, too, would have gone but for the eccentricity and determination of an old woman in a neighbouring square whose efforts at preserving something of the old East End had coincided with a shortage of local authority money for their more adventurous plans. So Balaclava Terrace still stood, now no doubt gentrified, a refuge from strident modernity for young executives, housemen from the London Hospital and sharing medical students. None of the family had ever returned. For his parents the move had been the realization of a dream, a dream which was almost terrifying when it promised to become reality, a matter for constant half-understood conversations late into the night. His father, his accountancy examinations completed, had gained a promotion. It was to be a sloughing off of the past, a move north-east which was also a move upwards, a few more miles from that distant Polish village with its unpronounceable name from which his great-grand-father had originally come. It would mean a mortgage, a matter for anxious arithmetic, the weighing of alternatives.

But all had been well. Within six months of moving an unforeseen death in the firm had meant further promotion and with it financial security. There was a modern fitted kitchen in the Ilford house, a three-piece suite for the sitting-room. The women who attended the local synagogue were smartly dressed; now his mother was among the smartest. Daniel suspected that he was the only member of the family who regretted Balaclava Terrace. He was ashamed of the Ilford house and ashamed of himself for despising what had been so hardly won. He thought to himself that if ever he brought Kate Miskin home he would prefer her to see Balaclava Terrace not The Drive, Ilford. But what on earth had Kate Miskin to do with where or how he lived? There was no question of inviting her home. He had worked with her in the special squad for only three months. What on earth had Inspector Kate Miskin to do with his family's life?

He thought he knew the root of his discontent: it lay in envy. Almost from early childhood he had known that his elder brother was his mother's favourite son. She had been thirty-five when David was born and had almost given up hope of a child. The overwhelming love she had felt for her first-born had been a revelation of such intensity that it had absorbed almost all she had to give in maternal affection. Coming three years later, he was welcomed but never obsessively desired. He remembered as a fourteen-year-old seeing a woman gazing into a neighbour's pram at a new baby, and saying,

'So he's number five? Still, they all bring their own love with them, don't they?' He had never felt that he had brought his.

And then when David was eleven he had had his accident. Daniel could still remember the effect on his mother. Her wild eyes as she clung to his father, her face bleached with terror and pain, suddenly the face of a wild stranger, her unbearable sobbing, the long hours spent at David's bedside in the London Hospital while he was left to the care of neighbours. In the end they had had to amputate David's left leg below the knee. She had brought home her maimed elder son with an exultant tenderness as if he had risen from the dead. But Daniel knew that he had no chance of competing. David had been courageous, uncomplaining, an easy child. He had been moody, jealous, difficult. He had also been intelligent. He suspected that he was cleverer than David but had early given up their academic rivalry. It was David who went to London University, read law, had been called to the Bar and had now found a place in a chambers which specialized in criminal cases. And it was as an act of defiance that at eighteen and straight from school he had joined the police.

He told himself, and half believed, that his parents were ashamed of his job. Certainly they never boasted of his successes as they did of David's. He remembered a snatch of conversation at his mother's last birthday dinner. Greeting him at the door she had said: 'I haven't told Mrs Forsdyke that you're a policeman. Of course I shall mention it if she asks what you do.'

His father had said quietly: 'And in Commander Dalgliesh's special squad, Mother, called in to crimes of particular sensitivity.'

He had said with a bitterness which surprised even himself: 'I'm not sure that will help disinfect the shame. And what will the old bat do anyway? Faint into her prawn cocktail? Why should the job worry her, unless her old man's on the fiddle?' Oh God, he had thought, I've started it all again. On her birthday, too. 'Cheer up. You've got one respectable son. You can tell Mrs Forsdyke that David spends his time lying to keep criminals out of gaol and I spend my time lying to get them in.'

Well, they could enjoy criticizing him over their hors d'oeuvre. And Bella would be there, of course. Like David, she was a lawyer but she would have found time for his parents' anniversary. Bella the perfect daughter-in-law-to-be. Bella who was learning Yiddish, who visited Israel twice a year and raised money to help immigrants from

Russia and Ethiopia, who attended Beit Midrash, the Talmudic learning centre at the synagogue, who kept Sabbath; Bella who turned on him her dark reproachful eyes and worried about the state of his soul.

It was no use saying to them, 'I don't believe in it any more.' How much did they believe, either of his parents? Put them on oath in the witness box and ask them whether they really believed that God handed down the Torah to Moses at Sinai and that their lives depended on the right answer. What would they say? He had asked his brother that question and he still remembered the answer. It had surprised him at the time and did so now, opening the disconcerting possibility that there were subtleties in David which he had never understood.

'I should probably lie. There are some beliefs it is worth dying for and that doesn't depend on whether or not they are strictly true.'

His mother, of course, would never bring herself to say, 'I don't care whether you believe or disbelieve, I want you to be here with us on the Sabbath. I want you to be seen in the synagogue with your father and brother'. And it wasn't intellectual dishonesty, although he tried to tell himself that it was. You could argue that few adherents of any religion believed all the dogma of their faith except the fundamentalists and, God knew, they were a bloody sight more dangerous than any non-believer. God knew. How natural it was and how universal to slip into the language of faith. And perhaps his mother was right, although she would never bring herself to speak the truth. The outward forms were important. To practise religion wasn't only a matter of intellectual assent. To be seen in the synagogue was to proclaim; this is where I stand, these are my people, these are the values by which I try to live, this is what generations of my forebears have made me, this is what I am. He remembered his grandfather's words, spoken to him after his bar mitzvah; 'What is a Jew without his belief? What Hitler could not do to us shall we do to ourselves?' The old resentments welled up. A Jew wasn't even allowed his atheism. Burdened with guilt from childhood, he couldn't reject his faith without feeling the need to apologize to the God he no longer believed in. It was always there at the back of his mind, silent witness of his apostasy, that moving army of naked humanity, the young, the middle-aged, the children, flowing like a dark tide into the gas chambers.

And now, halted at yet another red light, thinking of the house that would never be home, seeing with his mind's clear eye the gleaming windows, the looped lace curtains with their bows, the immaculate front lawn, he thought: Why must I define myself by the wrongs others have done to my race? The guilt was bad enough; do I have to carry the burden of innocence also? I'm a Jew, isn't that enough? Do I have to represent to myself and others the evil of mankind?

He had at last reached The Highway and mysteriously as is its habit the traffic had eased and he was making good progress. With luck he would be at Innocent House within five minutes. This death wouldn't be commonplace, this mystery not easily solved. The team wouldn't have been called in to a routine case. For those intimately concerned, perhaps, no death was commonplace and no investigation purely routine. But this was his chance to prove to Adam Dalgliesh that he had been right to choose him as Massingham's replacement and he intended to seize it. There was no priority, personal or professional, which was higher than this.

20

The police launch butted upstream round the northerly bend of the river between Rotherhithe and Narrow Street against a strong current. The breeze was strengthening to a light wind and the morning was colder than it had seemed to Kate on her first wakening. A few clouds, thin trails of white vapour, drifted and dissolved against the pale blue of the sky. She had seen Innocent House before from the river, but when it appeared with dramatic suddenness as they rounded the bend of Limehouse Reach she gave a small gasp of wonder and, glancing up at Dalgliesh's face, caught his brief smile. In the morning sunlight it gleamed with such an unreal intensity that for a moment she thought it was floodlit. As the engine of the police launch died and it was skilfully manoeuvred to the row of hanging tyres to the right of the landing steps she could almost believe that the house was part of a film set, an insubstantial palace of hardboard and paste behind whose ephemeral walls the director, the actors, the lighting men were already busying themselves around the body of the corpse while the make-up girl darted forward to mop a glistening brow and apply a final dollop of artificial blood. The fantasy disconcerted her; she was not prone to play-acting or to flights of imagination, but the sense of a contrived occasion, of being at once an observer and a participant, was difficult to shake off and was strengthened by the posed immobility of the reception party.

There were two men and two women. The women stood a little to the front with a man on each side. They were grouped on the wide marble forecourt as motionless as statues watching the tying-up of the launch with serious and, it seemed, critical faces. There had been time on the short journey for Dalgliesh to give her some briefing and Kate could guess who they were. The tall dark woman must be Claudia Etienne, the dead man's sister, with the last of the Peverells, Frances Peverell, on her left. The older of the two men, who looked well over seventy, would be Gabriel Dauntsey, the poetry editor, and the younger James de Witt. They looked as posed as if a director had carefully arranged them to suit the camera angles, but as Dalgliesh advanced the little group broke up and Claudia Etienne, hand outstretched, came forward to make the introductions. She turned and they followed her down a short cobbled lane and into the side door of the house.

An elderly man was seated at the switchboard behind the reception desk. With his pale smooth face an almost perfect oval, the cheeks splotched with small red circles under gentle eyes, he had the look of an elderly clown. He looked up at them as they entered and Kate saw in the luminous eyes a look of mingled apprehension and appeal. It was a look she had seen before. The police might be needed, even impatiently waited, but they were seldom greeted without anxiety, even by the innocent. For the first couple of seconds she wondered irrelevantly which professions were invited into people's homes without reservation. Doctors and plumbers came high on the list, midwives probably at the top. She wondered what it would feel like to be greeted with the heartfelt words, 'Thank God you're here.' The telephone rang and the old man turned to answer it. His voice was low and very attractive but held an unmistakable note of distress and his hands were shaking.

'Peverell Press. Can I help you? No, I'm afraid Mr Gerard isn't available. Can I get someone else to ring you back later?' He looked up again, this time at Claudia Etienne, and said helplessly: 'It's Matthew Evans's secretary from Fabers, Miss Etienne. He wants to talk to Mr Gerard. It's about next Wednesday's meeting on literary piracy.'

Claudia took the receiver. 'This is Claudia Etienne. Please tell Mr Evans I'll ring him back as soon as I can. We're going to close the office now for the rest of the day. I'm afraid there's been an accident. Tell him Gerard Etienne is dead. I know he'll understand that I can't speak now.'

Without waiting for a response she replaced the receiver, then turned to Dalgliesh. 'There's no point in trying to cover it up, is there? Death is death. It isn't a temporary embarrassment, a little local difficulty. You can't pretend it hasn't happened. Anyway the press will get hold of it soon enough.'

Her voice was harsh, the dark eyes hard. She looked like a woman possessed more by anger than grief. Turning to the receptionist, she said more gently, 'Put a message on the answerphone, George, that the office is closed for the day. Then go and get yourself some strong coffee. Mrs Demery is about somewhere. If any other staff arrive, tell them to go home.'

George said: 'But will they go, Miss Claudia? I mean, they won't want to take it from me surely?'

Claudia Etienne frowned: 'Perhaps not. I suppose I ought to see them. Better still, we'll get Mr Bartrum. He's here somewhere isn't he, George?'

'Mr Bartrum is in his own office in number ten, Miss Claudia. He said he had plenty of work to get on with and wanted to stay. He thought it would be all right as he's not in the main house.'

'Ring him will you, George, and ask him to have a word with me. He can cope with the latecomers. Some of them may have work they can take home. Tell them I shall be speaking to all of them on Monday.'

She turned to Dalgliesh. 'We've been doing that, sending staff home. I hope that's all right. It seemed better not to have too many people on the premises.'

Dalgliesh said. 'We shall need to see them all in time, but that can wait. Who found your brother?'

'I did. Blackie – Miss Blackett, my brother's secretary – was with me and so was Mrs Demery, our cleaner. We went up together.'

'Which of you entered the room first?'

'I did.'

'Then if you could show me the way. Did your brother usually take the lift or the stairs?'

'The stairs. But he didn't normally go up to the top of the house. That's what's so extraordinary, his being in the archives office at all.'

Dalgliesh said: 'Then we'll take the stairs.'

Claudia Etienne said: 'I locked the room after we found my brother's body. Lord Stilgoe has the key. He asked for it so I gave it to him. Why not if it made him happy? I suppose he thought one of us might go back and interfere with the evidence.'

But Lord Stilgoe was already pressing forward. 'I thought it right to take charge of the key, Commander. I have to speak to you in private. I warned you. I knew that we should have a tragedy here sooner or later.'

He held out the key but it was Claudia who took it. Dalgliesh said: 'Lord Stilgoe, do you know how Gerard Etienne died?'

'Of course not, how could I?'

'Then we'll talk later.'

'But I've seen the body, of course. I thought that was only my duty. Abominable. Well, I warned you. It's obvious that this outrage is part of the campaign against me and my book.'

Dalgliesh said: 'Later, Lord Stilgoe.'

He was, as always, taking his time in viewing the body. Kate knew that, however speedily he responded to a murder call, he always arrived with the same unhurried calm. She had seen him put out a restraining hand to an over-enthusiastic detective sergeant with the quiet words, 'Cool it, sergeant. You're not a doctor. The dead can't be resuscitated.'

Now he turned to Claudia Etienne. 'Shall we go up?'

She turned to the three partners who, with Lord Stilgoe, were standing together in a silent group as if waiting for instructions, and said: 'Perhaps you'd better wait in the boardroom. I'll join you as soon as I can.'

Lord Stilgoe said in a voice more reasonable than Kate expected: 'I'm afraid I can't stay any longer, Commander. That's why I made such an early appointment with Mr Etienne. I wanted to discuss progress on my memoirs before I went into hospital for a minor operation. I'm due there at eleven. I don't want to risk losing the bed. I'll telephone either you or the Commissioner at the Yard from the hospital.'

Kate sensed that this suggestion was greeted with relief by de Witt and Dauntsey.

The little group passed through the open doorway into the hall. Kate gave a silent gasp of admiration. For a second her step halted, but she resisted the temptation to let her eyes too obviously range. The police were always invaders of privacy; it was offensive to act as if she were a paying tourist. But it seemed to her that in that one moment of revelation she was aware simultaneously of every detail of the hall's magnificence, the intricate segments of the marble floor, the six mottled marble pillars with their elegantly carved capitals, the richness of the painted ceiling, a gleaming panorama of eighteenth-century London, bridges, spires, towers, houses, masted ships, the whole unified by the blue reaches of the river, the elegant double staircase, the balustrade curving down to end in bronzes of laughing boys riding dolphins and holding aloft the great globed lamps. As they mounted the magnificence was less intrusive, the decorative

133

detail more restrained, but it was through dignity, proportion and elegance that they moved purposefully upwards to the stark desecration of murder.

On the third floor there was a green baize door which stood open. They mounted a narrow stairway, Claudia Etienne leading with Dalgliesh at her shoulder and Kate at the rear. The stairs turned to the right before the final half-dozen treads led them to a narrow hall about ten feet wide, with the grille doors of a lift to the left. The right-hand wall was without doors but there was a closed door on the left and one immediately in front of them which stood open.

Claudia Etienne said: 'This is the archives room where we keep our old records. The small archives office is through here.'

The archives room had obviously once been two rooms, but the central wall had been removed to produce one very long chamber running almost the whole length of the house. The rows of wooden filing racks at right angles to the door and reaching almost to the ceiling were ranged so closely that there could hardly be room to move comfortably between them. Between the rows hung a number of light bulbs without shades. Natural light came from six long windows through which Kate could glimpse the intricate stone carving of a balustrade. They turned to the right, down the clear space about four feet wide between the ends of the shelves and the wall, and came to another door.

Claudia Etienne silently handed Dalgliesh the key. Taking it he said: 'If you can bear to come in I would like you to confirm that the room and your brother's body look exactly as they did when you first entered. If you find that too distressing, don't worry. It will help, but it isn't essential.'

She said: 'It's all right. It's easier for me now than it would be tomorrow. I still can't believe it's real. Nothing about it looks real, nothing about it feels real. I suppose that by tomorrow I'll know that it is real and that the reality is final.'

It was her words which to Kate sounded unreal. There was a strain of falsity, of histrionics in the balanced cadences, as if they had been thought out in advance. But she told herself not to be over-hasty. It was too easy to misinterpret the disorientation of grief. She more than most surely knew how oddly inappropriate the first spoken reaction to shock or bereavement could be. She remembered the wife of a bus driver stabbed to death in an Islington pub, whose first reaction had been to lament that he hadn't changed his shirt that morning or posted the pools coupon. And yet the wife had loved her husband, and genuinely grieved for him.

Dalgliesh took the key from Claudia Etienne. It turned easily in the lock and he opened the door. A sour gaseous smell wafted out like a contagion. The half-naked body seemed to leap up at them with the stark theatricality of death and hang for a moment suspended in unreality, an image bizarre and powerful, staining the quiet air.

He was lying supine, his feet towards the door. He was wearing grey trousers and grey socks. The shoes of fine black leather looked new, the soles almost unscuffed. It was odd, Kate thought, how one noticed such details. The top of his body was naked and a white shirt was bunched in the extended fist of his outstretched right hand. The velvet snake was wound twice round his neck, the tail lying against his chest, the head jammed into the wide-stretched mouth. Above it his eyes, open and glazed, unmistakably the eyes of death, seemed to Kate to hold for a moment a look of outraged surprise. All the colours were strong, unnaturally bright. The rich dark brown of the hair, the face and torso stained an unnatural pinkish red, the stark whiteness of the shirt, the livid green of the snake. The impression of a physical force emanating from the body was so strong that Kate instinctively recoiled and felt the soft bump of her shoulder against Claudia's. She said: 'I'm sorry', and the conventional apology sounded inadequate even if it referred only to that brief physical encounter. Then the image faded and reality reasserted itself. The body became what it was, dead bare flesh, grotesquely adorned, displayed as if on a stage.

And now in a swift glance, standing in the open doorway, she took in the details of the room. It was small, no more than twelve feet by eight, and bleak as an execution shed, the wooden floor uncovered, the walls bare. There was one high narrow window, closed tight shut, and a single white shaded bulb suspended from the middle of the ceiling. From the window frame hung a broken window cord no more than three inches long. To the left of the window was a small Victorian fireplace with coloured tiles of fruit and flowers. The grate had been removed and replaced by an old-fashioned gas fire. Against the opposite wall was a small wooden table holding a modern black angled reading lamp and two wire filing trays each holding a few shabby manila files. Aware that some small detail was incongruous, Kate looked for the remaining length of the window cord and saw it under the table, as if it had been casually kicked or thrown out of the way. Claudia Etienne was still standing at her shoulder. Kate was aware of her stillness, of her breathing, shallow and controlled.

Dalgliesh asked: 'Is this how you found the room? Does anything strike you now which didn't then?'

She said: 'Nothing's changed. Well how could it? I locked the door before we left. I didn't notice much about the room when I – when I found him.'

'Did you touch the body?'

'I knelt by him and felt his face. He was very cold, but I knew he was dead before then. I stayed kneeling by him. When the others had gone, I think . . .' She paused, then went on resolutely, 'I laid my cheek briefly against his.'

'And the room?'

'It looks odd now. I'm not often up here – the last time was when I found Sonia Clements' body – but it looks different, emptier, cleaner. And there's something missing. It's the tape recorder. Gabriel – Mr Dauntsey – dictates on to a tape and the recorder is usually left on the table. And I didn't notice that broken window cord when I first came in. Where's the end? Is Gerard lying on it?'

Kate said: 'It's under the table.'

Claudia Etienne looked at it and said: 'How odd. You'd expect it to be lying by the window.'

She swayed, and Kate put out a supporting hand but the girl shrugged it quickly away.

Dalgliesh said: 'Thank you for coming up with us, Miss Etienne. I know it wasn't easy. That's all I wanted to ask now. Kate, will you . . . ?'

But before Kate could move, Claudia Etienne said: 'Don't touch me. I'm perfectly capable of walking downstairs by myself. I'll be with the others in the boardroom if you need me again.'

But her way down the narrow stairs was impeded. There was the sound of male voices, quick light footsteps. A few seconds later Daniel Aaron came swiftly into the room, followed by two scene-of-crime officers, Charlie Ferris and his assistant.

Aaron said: 'I'm sorry I'm late, sir. The traffic was heavy on the Whitechapel Road.'

His eyes met Kate's and he gave a shrug and a brief, rueful smile. She liked and respected him. She had no difficulty in working with him. He was in every way an improvement on Massingham, but like Massingham he was never happy to find that Kate had got to the scene of crime before him.

21

The four partners had moved together into the boardroom on the first floor less by deliberate intention than by an unspoken feeling that it was wiser to stay together, to hear what words were spoken by the others, to feel at least the spurious comfort of human comradeship, not to retreat to a suspicious isolation. But they were without occupation and each was unwilling to send for files, papers or reading matter in case this demonstrated a callous indifference. The house seemed curiously quiet. Somewhere, they knew, the few staff still on the premises would be conferring, discussing, speculating. There were things they too needed to discuss, a provisional reallocation of work to be agreed, but to do so now seemed as brutally insensitive as robbing the dead.

But, at first their wait was not long. Within ten minutes of his arrival Commander Dalgliesh appeared with Inspector Miskin. As the tall dark figure moved quietly up to the table, four pairs of eyes turned and regarded him soberly as if his presence, at once desired and half-feared, was an intrusion into a common grief. They sat unmoving as he pulled out a chair for the woman police officer and then himself sat down, resting his hands on the table.

He said: 'I'm sorry to have kept you waiting but I'm afraid that waiting and disruption are inevitable after an unexplained death. I shall need to see you separately and I hope to give those interviews before too long. Is there a room here with a telephone I could use without too great inconvenience? I shall need it only for the rest of the day. The incident room will be at Wapping Police Station.'

It was Claudia who replied. 'If you took over the whole house for a month the inconvenience would be slight compared with the inconvenience of murder.'

De Witt broke in quietly, 'If it is murder', and it seemed as if the room, already quiet, grew quieter as they waited for his reply.

'We can't be sure of the cause of death until after the post-mortem. The forensic pathologist will be here shortly and I shall then know when that's likely to be. Then there may be some laboratory investigations which will also take time.'

Claudia said: 'You can use my brother's office. That would seem appropriate. It's on the ground floor, the right-hand front room. You have to go through his PA's office to get to it but Miss Blackett can move out if that's inconvenient. Is there anything else you need?'

'I would like, please, a list of all staff presently employed and the rooms they occupy and the names of any who may have left but were here for the whole of the period during which your practical joker has been at work. I believe that you have already carried out an investigation into these incidents. I need details of the incidents and what, if anything, you have discovered.'

De Witt said: 'So you know about that?'

'The police had been told. It would be helpful too if I could have a plan of the building.'

Claudia said: 'There's one in the files. We had some interior alterations done a couple of years ago and the architect drew up new drawings of the interior and the exterior. The original designs for the house and for its decoration are in the archives, but I don't suppose your interest is primarily architectural.'

'Not at present. What arrangements are there for securing the building? Who holds the keys?'

Miss Etienne said: 'Each of the partners has a set of keys to all the doors. The formal entrance is from the terrace and the river but that door is only used now for big occasions, when most of the guests come by boat. We don't have many of those nowadays. The last one was the joint summer party and celebration of my brother's engagement on the tenth of July. The door from Innocent Walk is the main street door but it's rarely used. Because of the architectural oddity of the house it leads past the servants' quarters and the kitchen. It's always kept locked and bolted. It's still locked and bolted. Lord Stilgoe checked the doors before you arrived.' She seemed about to make some comment on Lord Stilgoe's activities but checked herself and went on: 'The door we use is the side one on Innocent Lane by which you came in. That is normally left open during the day as long as George Copeland is on the switchboard. George has a key to that door, but not the back door or the river frontage. The burglar alarm system is controlled from the panel beside the switchboard. The doors and the windows on three storeys are locked. The system is fairly rudimentary, I'm afraid, but burglary has never really been a problem. The house itself is, of course, almost priceless but few of the pictures, for example, are originals. There is a large safe in Gerard's office and after an incident when the page proofs of Lord Stilgoe's book were tampered with we installed additional locking cupboards in three of the offices and under the reception desk so that any manuscripts or important papers can be locked up at night.'

Dalgliesh asked: 'And who normally arrives first in the morning and unlocks?'

Gabriel Dauntsey said: 'Usually it's George Copeland. He's due to start work at nine o'clock and he's usually on the switchboard by then. He's very reliable. If he does get held up – he lives south of the river – it could be Miss Peverell or me. We each have a flat in number twelve, that's the house to the left of Innocent House. It's a bit haphazard. Whoever arrives first unlocks and switches off the alarm system. The door on Innocent Lane has a Yale and one security lock. This morning George arrived first as usual and found that the security lock hadn't been used. He was able to open the door with the Yale. The alarm system was also switched off so he naturally assumed that one of us had already arrived.'

Dalgliesh asked, 'Which of you four last saw Mr Etienne?'

Claudia said: 'I did. I went into the office to talk to him before I left, just before half past six. He usually worked late on Thursday nights. He was still at his desk. There may have been other people in the building at the time but I think they had all gone. Obviously I didn't check or make a search.'

'Was it generally known that your brother worked late on Thursdays?'

'It was known within the office. Probably other people knew as well.'

Dalgliesh said: 'He seemed as usual? He didn't tell you that he intended to work in the little archives office?'

'He seemed perfectly as usual, and he never mentioned the little archives office. As far as I know it wasn't a room he ever visited. I have no idea why he went up there or why he died there – if, in fact, that is where he died.'

Again the four pairs of eyes looked intensely into Dalgliesh's face. He didn't comment. After formally asking the expected question whether they knew of anyone who might wish Etienne dead and receiving their short and equally expected answers, he got up from his chair and the woman officer, who hadn't spoken, got up too. Then he thanked them quietly and she stood a little aside so that he moved first out of the door.

After they had left there was a silence for half a minute then de Witt said: 'Not exactly the kind of copper from whom one asks the time. Personally I find him terrifying enough to the innocent, so God knows what he does to the guilty. Do you know him, Gabriel? After all you're in the same line of business.'

Dauntsey looked up and said, 'I know his work, of course, but I don't think we've ever met. He's a fine poet.'

'Oh, we all know that. I'm only surprised you've never tried to wean him away from his publisher. Let's hope he's an equally good detective.'

Frances said: 'It's odd though, isn't it, he never asked us about the snake?'

Claudia said sharply: 'What about the snake?'

'He didn't ask us whether we knew where to find it.'

'Oh he will,' said de Witt. 'Believe me, he will.'

22

In the little archives room Dalgliesh asked: 'Did you manage to speak to Dr Kynaston, Kate?'

'No, sir. He's in Australia visiting his son. Doc Wardle's coming. He was in his lab so he shouldn't be long.'

It was an unpropitious start. Dalgliesh was used to working with Miles Kynaston whom he both liked as a man and respected as probably the country's most brilliant forensic pathologist. He had, perhaps unreasonably, taken it for granted that it would be Kynaston who would be squatting by this body, Kynaston's stubby-fingered hands in the latex gloves, fine as a second skin, which would be moving about the corpse with as much gentleness as if these stiff limbs could still tense under his probing hands. Reginald Wardle was a perfectly capable forensic pathologist; he wouldn't otherwise have been employed by the Met. He would do a good job. His report would be as thorough as Kynaston's and would come on time. He would be as effective in the witness box, if it came to that, cautious but definite, unshakeable under cross-examination. But Dalgliesh had always found him irritating and suspected that the mild antipathy, not strong enough to be called dislike or to prejudice their co-operation, was mutual.

Wardle, when called out, came promptly to the murder scene – no one could fault him there – but would invariably stroll in with leisurely unconcern as if to demonstrate the unimportance of violent death, and this corpse in particular, in his private scheme of things. He was apt to sigh and tut-tut over the body, as if the problem it presented was irritating rather than interesting and one which hardly justified the police in dragging him away from the more immediate concerns in his laboratory. He provided the minimum of information at the scene, perhaps from natural caution, but too often giving the impression that the police were unreasonably pressing him for a premature judgement. His most common words spoken over the corpse were: 'Better wait, better wait, Commander. I'll get him on the table soon enough and then we'll know.'

He was, too, a self-publicist. At the scene he might give the impression of a boring and reluctant colleague but, surprisingly, he was a brilliant after-dinner speaker and probably enjoyed more free meals than most of his profession. Dalgliesh, who found it astonishing that a man could actually volunteer for, let alone enjoy, a protracted and usually poor hotel dinner for the satisfaction of getting on his feet afterwards, privately added this fact to the list of Wardle's mild delinquencies. Once in his autopsy room, however, Doc Wardle was a different man. Here, perhaps because this was his acknowledged kingdom, he seemed to take a pride in demonstrating his considerable skills and was ready enough to share opinions and propound theories.

Dalgliesh had worked with Charlie Ferris before and was glad to see him. His nickname of 'the Ferret' was rarely used to his face but it was perhaps too appropriate a soubriquet to be always avoided. He had pale-lashed sharp little eyes, a long nose sensible to every variety of smell and tiny fastidious fingers which could pick up small objects as if by magnetism. He presented an eccentric and occasionally bizarre appearance when on the job, his preferred clothes for a search being tight-fitting cotton shorts or trousers, a sweatshirt, surgeon's latex gloves and a plastic swimming cap. His professional creed was that no murderer left the scene of his crime without depositing some physical evidence and it was his business to find it.

Dalgliesh said: 'Your usual search, Charlie, but we'll need a gas engineer to take out that gas fire and make a report. Tell them it's urgent. If there's rubble blocking the flue I want that sent to the lab with samples of any loose pieces of the chimney lining. It's a very old nursery gas fire with a removable tap. I don't know whether we'll get a useful print from there, almost certainly not. All surfaces of the fire need testing for prints. The window cord is important. I'd like to know if it snapped because of natural wear and tear or was deliberately frayed. I doubt whether you'll get more than an opinion but the lab may be able to help.'

Leaving them to it he knelt by the body, studied it intently for a moment then, putting out his hand, touched the cheek. Was it his imagination and the ruddiness of the skin which made it feel slightly warm to the touch? Or was it that the warmth of his own fingers had for a few seconds given a spurious life to the dead flesh? He moved his hand to the jaw taking care not to dislodge the snake. The flesh was soft, the bone moved under his gentle urging.

He said to Kate and Dan: 'See what you make of the jaw. Be careful. I want the snake in place until after the PM.'

They knelt in turn, Kate first, touched the jaw, looked closely into the face, put their hands to the naked torso.

Daniel said: 'Rigor mortis is well established in the top part of the body but the jaw is free.'

'Which means?'

It was Kate who replied. 'That someone broke the rigor in the jaw some hours after death. Presumably it was necessary in order to stuff the snake into the mouth. But why bother? Why not wind it round his neck? That would make the point just as well.'

Daniel said: 'But less dramatically.'

'Maybe. But forcing open the jaw proves that someone visited the body hours after death. It could have been the murderer – if this is murder. It could have been someone else. We'd never have suspected that there was a second visit to the scene if the snake had been merely wrapped round the neck.'

Daniel said: 'Perhaps it's precisely what the murderer wanted us to know.'

Dalgliesh looked carefully at the snake. It was about five feet long and was obviously intended as a draught excluder. The top of the body was of striped velvet, the bottom of some tougher brown material. Under the softness of the velvet, it felt grainy to his touch.

There were leisurely footsteps approaching through the archives room. Daniel said: 'It sounds as if Doc Wardle has arrived.'

He was over six feet three inches tall, his impressive head jutting above wide bony shoulders from which his ill-fitting and thin jacket drooped as if from a wire coat hanger. With the beaked, mottled nose, barking voice and keen darting eyes under bushy brows so luxuriant and vigorous that they seemed to have a life of their own, he looked and sounded like the stereotype of an irascible colonel. His height could have been a disadvantage in a job where corpses often lay inconveniently concealed in ditches, culverts, cupboards and make-shift graves, but the long body could insinuate itself with unexpected ease, even grace, into the most unaccommodating place. Now he gazed round the room, deploring its stark simplicity and the uninviting business which had dragged him from his microscope, then knelt by the body and let out a lugubrious sigh.

'You'll want the approximate time of death, of course,

Commander. That's always the first question after "Is he dead?" and, yes, he is dead. That's the one fact we can all agree about. Body cold, rigor mortis fully established. One interesting exception, but we'll get on to that later. Suggests he's been dead about thirteen to fifteen hours. The room's warm, unnaturally so for the time of the year. Taken the temperature, have you? Sixty-eight degrees. That and the fact that metabolism was probably fairly pronounced at the time of death could delay the onset of rigor. You've already discussed the interesting anomaly, no doubt. Still, tell me about it Commander. Tell me about it. Or you, Inspector. I can see you're longing to.'

Dalgliesh almost expected him to add, 'It's too much to hope that you could keep your hands off him.' He looked at Kate, who said: 'The jaw is slack. Rigor mortis begins in the face, jaw and neck at five to seven hours after death and is fully established at about twelve hours. It passes off in the same sequence. So either it is already passing off in the jaw, which would put the time of death earlier by some six hours, or the mouth was forcibly opened. I'd say almost certainly the latter. The facial muscles aren't slack.'

Wardle said: 'I sometimes wonder, Commander, why you bother to call out a pathologist.'

Undeterred, Kate went on: 'Which means that the snake's head was put in the mouth not at the time of death but at least five to seven hours later. So the cause of death can't be suffocation, at least not with the snake. But then we never thought that it was.'

Dalgliesh said: 'The staining and the position of the body suggests that he died face downward and was subsequently turned over. It would be interesting to know why.'

Kate suggested: 'Easier to arrange the snake, stuff the head in his mouth?'

'Perhaps.'

Dalgliesh said no more, while Doc Wardle continued his examination. He had already encroached on the pathologist's territory more than was prudent. He had little doubt about the cause of death and wondered whether it was perversity rather than caution which was keeping Wardle silent. It wasn't the first case either of them had seen of carbon monoxide poisoning. The post-mortem lividity, more pronounced than usual because of the blood's slower liquidation, the cherry red coloration of the skin, so bright that the body looked as if it had been painted, were unmistakable and surely definitive.

Wardle said: 'Copy-book, isn't it? Hardly needs a forensic pathologist and a commander of the Met to diagnose carbon monoxide. But don't let's get too excited. Let's get him on the table, shall we? Then the lab leeches can take their blood samples and give us an answer we can rely on. Do you want that snake kept in the mouth?'

'I think so. I'd prefer to leave it undisturbed until the autopsy.'

'Which you'll want done, no doubt, immediately if not sooner.'

'Don't we always?'

'I can do it this evening. We were due at a dinner party which our hostess has cancelled. Sudden attack of flu, or so she claims. Six-thirty at the usual mortuary if you can make it. I'll give them a ring, tell them to expect us. Is the meat wagon on the way?'

Kate said: 'It should arrive any moment.'

Dalgliesh was aware that the PM would go ahead whether or not he could make it, but of course he would be there. Wardle was being unexpectedly co-operative, but then he reminded himself that when the chips were down Wardle invariably was.

23

As soon as he saw Mrs Demery Dalgliesh knew that he would have no trouble with her; he had dealt with her kind before. The Mrs Demerys, in his experience, had no hang-ups about the police, whom they assumed in general to be beneficent and on their side, while seeing no reason to treat them with inordinate respect or to credit male officers with more sense than was commonly found in the rest of the sex. They were, no doubt, as ready to lie as other witnesses when it came to protecting their own, but being honest and unburdened by imagination preferred to tell the truth as being on the whole less trouble and, having told it, saw no reason to torture their consciences with doubts about their own motives or the intentions of other people. They were obstinately firm, unshakeable and occasionally irreverent under cross-examination. Dalgliesh suspected that they found men slightly ridiculous, particularly when dressed in gowns and wigs and given to pontificating in arrogant voices over other people's heads, and had no intention of being lectured to, brow-beaten or put down by those irritating creatures.

Now the latest example of this excellent species settled herself opposite him and gave him a frank appraisal from bright intelligent eyes. Her hair, obviously recently dyed, was a bright orange-gold worn in a style seen in Edwardian photographs; swept up firmly at the back and sides and with a fringe of frizzy curls low on the forehead. With her sharp nose and bright, slightly exophthalmic eyes she reminded Dalgliesh of an exotic and intelligent poodle.

Without waiting for him to begin the conversation she said: 'I knew yer dad, Mr Dalgliesh.'

'Did you, Mrs Demery? When was that? During the war?'

'Yes, that's right. My twin brother and I was evacuated to your village. Remember the Carter twins? Well, of course, you wouldn't. You wasn't even a glint in yer dad's eye then. Oh, he was a lovely gentleman! We wasn't billeted at the rectory, they had the unmarried mothers. We was with Miss Pilgrim in her cottage. Oh God, Mr Dalgliesh, that was a terrible place, that village. I don't know how you put up with it when you was a kid. Put me off the country for life that village did. Mud, rain and that awful stink you get from the farmyard. And talk about boredom!'

'Not much, perhaps, for a city child to do.'

'I wouldn't say that. There was things to do all right, but start doing them and you were in dead trouble.'

'Like damming the village stream?'

'So you heard about that? How was we to know that it would flow into that Mrs Piggott's back kitchen and drown her old cat? Fancy you knowing about that, though.' Mrs Demery's face expressed the liveliest gratification.

'You and your brother are part of the folklore of the village, Mrs Demery.'

'Are we now? That's nice. Remember Mr Stuart's piglets?'

'Mr Stuart does. He's well over eighty now, but there are some events that are branded on the memory.'

'A proper race that was going to be. We got the little buggers lined up, more or less, but after that they was all over the place. Well, mostly all over the Norwich road. But, oh God! That village was a terrible place. The quiet of it! We'd lie awake listening to it, that silence. It was like being dead. And the dark! I never knew darkness like that. Pitch black it was. It was like a great black woolly blanket being pressed down on you until you felt suffocated. Billy and I couldn't stand it. We never had a nightmare till we was evacuated. When our mum came to visit we used to bawl all the time. I can remember those visits, Mum dragging us along that boring old lane and Billy and I howling that we wanted to come home. We told her that Miss Pilgrim wasn't giving us any food and was always after us with the slipper. It was true about the food too, we never had a decent chip the whole time we was there. In the end Mum brought us back home to get a bit of peace. We was all right then. We had a lovely time, especially after the bombing started. We had one of those Anderson shelters in the garden and we were all snug in it with Mum and Gran and Auntie Edie and Mrs Powell from number forty-two when she got bombed out.'

Dalgliesh asked: 'Wasn't it dark in the Anderson shelter?'

'We had our torches, didn't we? And when the raids weren't actually on you could go outside and watch the searchlights. Lovely crisscross patterns they made in the sky. And talk about noise! Those anti-aircraft guns, well it was like a giant tearing up corrugated iron.

Well, as Mum said, if you give your kids a happy childhood there's not much life can do to them after that.'

Dalgliesh felt that it would be unproductive to argue this sanguine view of child rearing. He was about tactfully to suggest that it was time they got down to business when Mrs Demery forestalled him.

'Well, that's enough about the good old days. You'll be wanting to ask me about this murder.'

'So that's how it strikes you, Mrs Demery?'

'Stands to reason. He didn't put that snake around his own neck. Strangled, was he?'

'We shan't know how he died until we get the result of the PM.'

'Well, he looked strangled to me, with his face all pink and that snake's head stuffed in his mouth. Mind you, I've never seen a healthier-looking corpse. Looked better dead than he did alive, and he looked pretty good alive. He was a good looker all right. I always thought he looked a bit like the young Gregory Peck.'

Dalgliesh asked her to describe exactly what had happened since her arrival at Innocent House.

'I come in every weekday except Wednesday from nine until five. On Wednesdays they're supposed to have the whole place thoroughly cleaned by the Superior Office Cleaning Company. At least that's what they call themselves. Inferior Cleaning Company would be more like it. I suppose they do the best they can, but it's not like taking a personal interest in the place. George comes thirty minutes early and lets them in. They're usually through by ten.'

'Who lets you in, Mrs Demery? Do you have keys?'

'No. Old Mr Etienne suggested I did but I didn't want the responsibility. Too many keys in my life already. George usually opens up. Or it could be Mr Dauntsey or Miss Frances. Just depends who's earlier. This morning Miss Peverell and Mr Dauntsey weren't here, but George was and he let me in. Well, I got on quietly enough with my cleaning back in the kitchen. Nothing happened until just before nine, then this Lord Stilgoe turned up, saying he'd got an appointment with Mr Gerard.'

'Were you there at the time?'

'I was as it happened. I was having a bit of a chat with George. Lord Stilgoe was none too pleased to find no one there but the receptionist and me. George had rung round the office trying to find Mr Gerard, and he was suggesting that Lord Stilgoe should wait in the reception area when Miss Etienne arrived. She asked George if Mr Gerard was in his office and George said he'd rung but there was no reply. So she went across the hall to the office and Lord Stilgoe and I followed her. Mr Gerard's jacket was over his chair and the chair was pulled back from the desk, which seemed a bit odd. Then she put her hand in the right-hand drawer and found his keys. Mr Gerard always kept his keys there when he was in his office. The bunch was rather heavy and he hated it dragging on his jacket pocket. Miss Claudia said, "He must be here somewhere. Perhaps he's in number ten with Mr Bartrum." So we went back to the reception room and George said he'd rung number ten. Mr Bartrum had arrived but he hadn't seen Mr Gerard though his Jag was there. Mr Gerard always parked his car in Innocent Passage because it was safer. So Miss Claudia said, "He must be here somewhere. We'd better start looking for him." By then the first boat had arrived and then Miss Frances and Mr Dauntsey.'

'Did Miss Etienne sound worried?'

'More puzzled, if you know what I mean. I said, well I've been through most of the back of the house and on the ground floor, so he isn't in the kitchen. And Miss Claudia said something about well he'd hardly likely to be would he, and started up the stairs with me and Miss Blackett just behind her.'

'You didn't say that Miss Blackett was there.'

'Didn't I? Well she'd arrived all right with the launch. Of course you tend to overlook her now that old Mr Peverell's dead. Anyway she was there, although she was still wearing her coat, and she came up the stairs with us.'

'Three of you to search for one man?'

'Well, that's how it was. I suppose I went out of curiosity. It was a kind of instinct really. I don't know why Miss Blackett went. You'll have to ask her. Miss Claudia said, "We'll start searching at the top of the house", so that's what we did.'

'So she went straight to the archive room?'

'That's right, and then on to the little room beyond. The door wasn't locked.'

'How did she open it, Mrs Demery?'

'How do you mean? She opened it same way you always open a door.'

'Did she fling it wide? Open it gently? Did she seem at all apprehensive?'

'Not that I noticed. She just opened it. And, well, there he was. Lying on his back with his face all pink and that snake wound round his neck with the head stuffed in his mouth. His eyes were open and staring. Horrible they was! Mind you, I could see he was dead at once, though, like I said, I've never seen him looking better. Miss Claudia went over and knelt beside him. She said, "Go and phone the police. And get out of here, both of you." Kind of sharp, she was. Still, it was her brother. I know when I'm not wanted so I got out. I wasn't that anxious to stay.'

'What about Miss Blackett?'

'She was just behind me. I thought she was going to scream but instead of that she made a kind of high wailing noise. I put my arms round her shoulders. She was shaking something terrible. I said, "Come on dearie, come on, there's nothing you can do here." So we went down the stairs. I thought it would be quicker than the lift, which is always getting stuck. But maybe the lift would've been better. I had some trouble getting her down the stairs, she was shaking so much. And once or twice her legs almost gave way. Once I thought I'd just have to dump her and go for help. When we got to the bottom flight there was Lord Stilgoe and Mr de Witt and the rest of them standing there looking up at us. I suppose they saw from my face and the state Miss Blackett was in that something awful had happened. So then I told them. Seemed like they couldn't take it in for a moment, and then Mr de Witt started running up the stairs with Lord Stilgoe and Mr Dauntsey behind him.'

'What happened then, Mrs Demery?'

'I helped Miss Blackett to her chair and went off to find her some water.'

'You didn't ring the police?'

'I thought I'd leave that to the rest of them. The body wasn't going to go away, was it? What was the hurry? Anyway, if I had rung I'd only have done the wrong thing. Lord Stilgoe came back. He went straight to the reception desk and said to George, "Get me New Scotland Yard. I want the Commissioner. Failing him, Commander Adam Dalgliesh." Straight to the top for him, of course. Then Miss Claudia asked me to go and make some strong coffee, so that's what I did. White as a sheet she was. Well, you couldn't wonder, could you?'

Dalgliesh said: 'Mr Gerard Etienne took over as chairman and managing director fairly recently, didn't he? Was he well-liked?'

'Well he wouldn't have been carried out of here in a body bag if he was a little ray of sunshine about the place. Someone didn't like him, that's for sure. Of course, it wasn't easy for him taking over from old Mr Peverell. Everyone respected Mr Peverell. He was a lovely man. But I got on all right with Mr Gerard. I didn't worry him and he didn't worry me. I don't reckon, though, that many about the place will be crying for him. Still, murder is murder and it'll be a shock, no doubt about it. Won't do much good for the firm either, I shouldn't wonder. Now here's an idea. See how this grabs you. Maybe he did it himself, then this joker we've got about the place put the snake round his neck afterwards to show what they thought of him. Might be worth thinking about.'

Dalgliesh didn't say that it had been thought about. He asked: 'Would it surprise you to hear that he had killed himself?'

'Well it would, to tell you the truth. Too pleased with himself for that, I'd have said. Anyway, why should he? OK, so the firm's in a bit of trouble, but what firm isn't? He'd have come through all right. I can't see Mr Gerard doing a Robert Maxwell. Still, who'd have thought it of Robert Maxwell, so there's no knowing really, is there? Mysterious, that's what people are, mysterious. I could tell you a thing or two about the mysteriousness of people.'

Kate broke in: 'Miss Etienne must have been terribly distressed finding him like that. Her own brother.'

Mrs Demery transferred her attention to Kate but seemed none too pleased at this intrusion of a third person into her tête-à-tête. 'Ask a straight question and you'll get a straight answer, Inspector. How distressed was Miss Claudia? That's what you want to know, isn't it? You'll have to ask her. I don't know. She was at the side of the body bending over it and she never turned her face all the time Miss Blackett and I were in the room, which wasn't long. I don't know what she was feeling. I only know what she said.'

' "Get out of here both of you." Rather harsh.'

'Shock, maybe. You work it out for yourselves.'

'Leaving her alone with the body.'

'That's the way she wanted it seemingly. Anyway, I couldn't have stayed. Someone had to help Miss Blackett down the stairs.'

Dalgliesh asked: 'Is it a good place to work, Mrs Demery? Are you happy here?'

'As good as I'm likely to get. Look, Mr Dalgliesh, I'm sixty-three.

OK, that's no great age and I've still got my eyes and legs, and I'm a damned sight better worker than some I could name. But you don't start looking for a new job at sixty-three, and I like work. I'd die of boredom stuck at home. And I'm used to this place, been here nigh on twenty years. It's not everyone's cup of tea, but it suits me. And it's handy – well, more or less. I'm still in Whitechapel. Got a nice little modern flat now.'

'How do you get here?'

'Tube to Wapping, then walk. It's no distance. I'm not afraid of London streets. Been walking London streets before you was thought of. Old Mr Peverell said that he'd send a taxi for me any morning if the journey worried me. He would have too. He was a very special gentleman, was Mr Peverell. That showed what he thought of me. It's nice to be appreciated.'

'It is indeed. Tell me, Mrs Demery, about the cleaning of the archives room, the large one and the small office where Mr Etienne was found. Is that your responsibility, or does the cleaning company do it?'

'I do. The outside cleaners never go as high as the top floor. That started with old Mr Peverell. There's all that paper up there, you see, and he was afraid of them smoking and starting a fire. Besides, those files are confidential. Don't ask me why. I've had a peek at one or two and they're only full of a lot of old letters and manuscripts as far as I can see. It's not as if they keep the staff records there, or anything private like that. Still, Mr Peverell set great store by the archives. Anyway, he agreed I'd be responsible for those two rooms. No one hardly ever goes up there, except Mr Dauntsey, so I don't bother overmuch. No point in it. I usually go up once a month on a Monday and give it a quick dust.'

'Do you vacuum the floor?'

'Might give it a quick go round if it looked as if it needed it. Might not. As I said, there's only Mr Dauntsey uses it and he doesn't make much mess. There's enough to do in the rest of the house without lugging the vacuum cleaner all the way up there and spending time where it isn't needed.'

'I can see that. When did you last clean the little room?'

'I gave it a quick dust three weeks ago last Monday. I'll be up there again next Monday. Leastwise that's what I normally do, but I expect you'll be keeping the door locked.'

'For the time being, Mrs Demery. Shall we go up?'

They took the lift which was slow but smooth enough. The door of the small archives office was open. The gas company engineer hadn't yet arrived but the two scene-of-crime officers and the photographers were still there. At a sign from Dalgliesh they slipped past him and stood waiting.

Dalgliesh said: 'Don't go in, Mrs Demery. Just stand at the door and tell me if you see any change.'

Mrs Demery surveyed the room slowly. Her eyes rested briefly on the white chalked outline of the absent body but she made no comment. With only a few seconds' pause, she said: 'Your chaps been giving it a clean up then, have they?'

'We've done no cleaning, Mrs Demery.'

'Someone has. There's not three weeks' dust here. Look at that mantelpiece and the floor. That floor's been vacuumed. Bloody hell! So he cleaned the room before he did his killing, and with my Hoover!'

She turned to Dalgliesh and he saw in her eyes a dawning mixture of outrage, horror and superstitious awe. Nothing so far about Etienne's death had affected her so deeply as this cleaned and prepared death cell.

'How do you know, Mrs Demery?'

'The Hoover's kept in the utility room on the ground floor, next to the kitchen. When I went to take it out this morning I said to myself, "Someone's been using this."'

'How could you tell?'

'Because it was set for cleaning a smooth floor, not a carpet. There's two settings, you see. When I put it away it was set for cleaning the carpet. The last job I'd done was those carpets in the boardroom.'

'Are you sure, Mrs Demery?'

'Not to swear in a court of law. There are things you can swear to and things you can't. I suppose I could have changed the setting accidentally like. All I know is that when I took it out this morning I said to myself, "Someone's been using this."'

'Did you ask anyone if they had been using it?'

'No one here to ask then was there? Besides, it wouldn't be any of the staff here. Why would any of them be wanting the Hoover? That's my job not theirs. I thought it might be someone from the cleaning company, but that would be odd too. They bring all their own equipment.'

'Was the vacuum cleaner in its usual place?'

'Yes it was. And the flex wound round crossed, just like I left it. But the setting wasn't the same.'

'Is there anything else about this room that strikes you?'

'Well the window cord's gone, hasn't it? I suppose you chaps have taken that away. It was getting a bit old and frayed. I said to Mr Dauntsey when I put my head round the door on Monday that it ought to be replaced and he said he'd have a word with George. George does all the odd jobs around here. Very handy is George. Mr Dauntsey had the window half open at the time. He usually keeps it like that. He didn't seem much worried but, like I said, he was going to have a word with George about it. And that table's been moved. I never move the table when I dust up here. Look for yourself. It's a couple of inches to the right. You can see by that faint line of dirt on the wall where it usually was. And Mr Dauntsey's tape recorder's gone. There used to be a bed here once, but they took that away after Miss Clements killed herself. A nice thing that was too. Two deaths we've had in this room Mr Dalgliesh. I reckon it's time they locked it up for good.'

Before they had finished with Mrs Demery, Dalgliesh asked her to say nothing to anyone about the possible use made of her vacuum cleaner, but with little hope that she would keep the news to herself for long.

After she had left, Daniel said: 'How reliable is that piece of evidence, sir? Could she really tell if the room has been recently cleaned? It could be her imagination.'

'She's the expert, Daniel. And Miss Etienne remarked on the cleanness of the room. On Mrs Demery's admission she doesn't usually bother with the floor. This floor is dustless, even in the corners. Someone has cleaned it recently and it wasn't Mrs Demery.'

24

In the boardroom the four partners still waited. Gabriel Dauntsey and Frances Peverell sat at the oval mahogany table, close but not touching. Frances had her head bowed but was absolutely still. De Witt was at the window, one hand pressed to the pane as if he needed support. Claudia stood intently examining the large copy of a Canaletto of the Grand Canal which hung beside the door. The magnificence of the room both diminished and formalized the burden each bore of fear, grief, anger or guilt. They were like actors in an over-designed play in which a fortune had been lavished on the extravagant set but in which the players were amateurs, the dialogue half-learned, the moves stiff and unpractised. When Dalgliesh and Kate had left the room Frances Peverell had said, 'Leave the door open', and de Witt, without a word, had gone back to leave it ajar. They needed the sense of a world outside, the sound of distant voices however faint, however occasional. The closed door would be too like the vacant chair at the middle of the table, one awaiting Gerard's impatient entry, the other his presiding presence.

Without looking round Claudia said: 'Gerard always disliked this picture. He thought Canaletto overrated, too precise, too flat. He said he could picture the apprentices carefully painting in the waves.'

De Witt said: 'It wasn't Canaletto he disliked, just that picture. He said he was bored with constantly having to explain to visitors that it's only a copy.'

Frances's voice was indistinct. 'He resented it. It reminded him that Grandfather had sold the original at a bad time and for about a quarter of what it was worth.'

'No,' said Claudia firmly. 'He disliked Canaletto.'

De Witt moved slowly from the window. He said: 'The police are taking their time. Mrs Demery is enjoying herself, I imagine, giving her favourite impersonation of a Cockney charwoman, good-natured but sharp-tongued. I hope the Commander appreciates it.'

Claudia turned from her concentrated examination of the painting. 'Since that is what she is you can hardly describe it as an impersonation. Still, she does become garrulous when excited. We must take care that we don't. Become garrulous. Talk too much. Tell the police things they don't need to know.'

De Witt said: 'What things had you in mind?'

'That we weren't precisely united about the future of the firm. The police think in clichés. Since most criminals act in clichés that is probably their strength.'

Frances Peverell raised her head. No one had seen her weep but her face was drained and bloated, the eyes dull under swollen lids, and when she spoke her voice sounded cracked and a little querulous.

'What does it matter if Mrs Demery does talk? What does it matter what we say? No one here has anything to hide. It's obvious what happened. Gerard died of natural causes or an accident and someone, the same person who's been playing tricks in this place, found the body and decided to make a mystery of it. It must have been terrible for you, Claudia, finding him like that, seeing the snake around his neck. But it's all fairly straightforward surely. It has to be.'

Claudia turned on her as vehemently as if they were in the middle of a quarrel. 'What sort of accident? You're suggesting Gerard had an accident? What sort of accident?'

Frances seemed to shrink in her chair but her voice was firm. 'I don't know. I wasn't there when it happened, was I? It was just a suggestion.'

'A bloody stupid one.'

'Claudia,' de Witt's voice was more loving than censorious. 'We mustn't quarrel. We have to keep calm and we have to stay together.'

'How can we stay together? Dalgliesh will want to see us separately.'

'Not physically together. Together as partners. Together as a team.'

As if he hadn't spoken, Frances said: 'Or a heart attack. Or a stroke. He could have had either. It happens to the healthiest of people.'

Claudia said: 'Gerard had a perfectly sound heart. You don't climb the Matterhorn if you've got a weak heart. And I can't imagine any less likely subject for a stroke.'

De Witt's voice was conciliatory. 'We don't know yet how he died. We can't until after the post-mortem. In the mean time what happens here?'

Claudia said: 'We carry on. Of course we carry on.'

'Provided we have the staff. People may not want to stay,

especially if the police suggest that Gerard's death wasn't straight-forward.'

Claudia's laugh was harsh as a sob. 'Straightforward! Of course it wasn't straightforward. He was found dead, half-naked with a toy snake wound round his neck and its head stuffed in his mouth. Even the least suspicious policeman would hardly call that straight-forward.'

'I meant, of course, if they suspect murder. We've all got the word in our minds. Someone may as well speak it.'

Frances said: 'Murdered? Why should anyone murder him? And there wasn't any blood, was there? You didn't find a weapon. And no one could have poisoned him. Poisoned him with what? When could he have taken it?'

Claudia said: 'There are other ways.'

'You mean he was strangled with Hissing Sid? Or suffocated? But Gerard was strong. You'd have to overpower him to do that.' Then, as no one replied, she said, 'Look, I don't know why you're both so anxious to suggest Gerard was murdered.'

De Witt came and sat down beside her. He said gently: 'Frances, no one is suggesting it, we're just facing the possibility. But you're right of course. It's much better to wait until we know how he died. What puzzles me is why he was in the little archives office. I can't remember him ever going up to the top floor, can you Claudia?'

'No, and he couldn't have been working up there. If he decided to do that he wouldn't have left his keys in his desk drawer. You know how punctilious he was about security. The keys were only in that drawer when he was working at his desk. If he left the office for any length of time he'd slip on his jacket and put the bundle of keys back in his pocket. We've all seen him do that often enough.'

De Witt said: 'The fact that he was found in the archives office doesn't necessarily mean that he died there.'

Claudia seated herself opposite him and leaned forward over the table. 'You mean he could have died in his office?'

'Died or been killed there and moved subsequently. He could have died quite naturally at his desk, a stroke or heart attack as Frances suggests, and the body moved later.'

'But that would need considerable strength.'

'Not if you used one of the book trolleys and took the body up by the lift. There's nearly always a trolley waiting at the lift.'

'But surely the police can tell whether a body has been moved after death.'

'Yes, if it's found outdoors. You get traces of soil, twigs, flattened grass, signs of dragging. I'm not sure that it would be so easy with a body discovered in a building. It's one of the possibilities they'll be considering. I suppose they'll condescend to tell us something sooner or later. They're certainly taking their time up there.'

The two of them were talking as if there was no one else in the room. Frances suddenly said: 'Do you have to discuss it as if Gerard's death was some kind of a puzzle, a detective story, something we'd read or seen on television? This is Gerard we're talking about, not a stranger, not a character in a play. Gerard is dead. He's upstairs with that ghastly snake round his neck and we're sitting here as if we didn't care.'

Claudia turned on her a speculative gaze tinged with contempt. 'What do you expect us to do? Sit around in silence? Read a good book? Ask George if the newspapers have been delivered? I think it helps to talk. He was my brother. If I can stay reasonably calm, so can you. You shared his bed, at least temporarily, but you never shared his life.'

De Witt said quietly, 'Did you, Claudia? Did any of us?'

'No, but when this death really hits me, when I really believe what's happened I shall mourn for him, never fear. I shall mourn for him but not yet, not now and not here.'

Gabriel Dauntsey had been sitting gazing ahead out of the window towards the river. Now he spoke for the first time, and the others turned and looked at him as if suddenly remembering that he was there.

He said quietly: 'I think he may have died of carbon monoxide poisoning. The skin was very pink – that's one of the signs apparently – and the room was unnaturally warm. Didn't it strike you, Claudia, that the room was very warm?'

For a moment there was silence, then Claudia said: 'Very little struck me except seeing Gerard and that snake. You mean he could have been gassed?'

'Yes. I'm saying that he could have been gassed.'

The word hissed on the air. Frances said: 'But isn't the new North Sea gas harmless? I thought you couldn't poison yourself any more by putting your head in a gas oven.'

It was de Witt who explained. 'It isn't poisonous to breathe. It's perfectly safe if properly used. But if he lit the gas fire and the room wasn't adequately ventilated the fire could malfunction and produce carbon monoxide. Gerard could have become disorientated and unconscious before he realized what was happening.'

Frances said: 'And afterwards someone found the body, turned off the gas and put the snake round his neck. As I said, it was an accident.'

Dauntsey spoke quietly and calmly. 'It isn't quite as simple as that. Why did he light the fire? It wasn't particularly cold last night. And if he did light it, why did he shut the window? It was shut when I saw his body and I left it open when I last used the room on Monday.'

De Witt said: 'And if he was planning to spend the evening working in the archives long enough to need a fire, why did he leave his jacket and keys in his office? None of it makes sense.'

In the silence that followed Frances suddenly spoke. 'We've forgotten Lucinda. Someone's got to tell her.'

Claudia said, 'God yes! One tends to forget the Lady Lucinda. Somehow I don't imagine that she'll hurl herself into the Thames with grief. There was always something odd about that engagement.'

De Witt said: 'All the same, we can't let her read it in tomorrow's papers or hear it on the South East News. One of us had better ring Lady Norrington. She can break the news to her daughter. It would come best from you, Claudia.'

'I suppose so, as long as I'm not expected to go round and administer comfort. I'd better do it now. I'll ring from my own office, that is if the police aren't in occupation. Having the police here is like having mice in the house. You can sense them scrabbling away even when you don't actually hear or see them and once they're in you feel you'll never get rid of them.'

She got up and walked out, her head held unnaturally high but her step uncertain. Dauntsey tried to get to his feet, but his stiffened limbs seemed unable to respond and it was de Witt who moved quickly to her side. But she shook her head and gently pushed away his supporting arm and was gone.

Less than five minutes later she returned. She said: 'She wasn't in. It's hardly the kind of message you can leave on the answerphone. I'll try again later.'

Frances said: 'What about your father? Isn't he more important?'

'Of course he's more important. I shall drive down to see him tonight.'

The door opened without a preliminary knock, and Detective Sergeant Robbins put his head in.

'Mr Dalgliesh is sorry that he's keeping you waiting longer than he expected. He would be grateful if Mr Dauntsey could come now to the archives office.'

Dauntsey at once got up, but his stiffness after long sitting had made him clumsy. His stick, dislodged from the back of his chair, clattered to the ground. He and Frances Peverell knelt simultaneously to retrieve it and, after what sounded to the others like a short scuffle and a few almost conspiratorial whispers, Frances laid hands on it and, rising red-faced from under the table, handed it to Dauntsey. He leaned on it for a few seconds, then hung it again on the back of the chair and moved towards the door without its aid, slowly but firm-footed.

When he had left Claudia Etienne said: 'I wonder why Gabriel gets the privilege of going first.'

James de Witt answered: 'Probably because he uses the little archives office more than most of us.'

Frances said: 'I don't think I've ever used it. The last time I was there was when they took the bed away. You don't go up there either, do you James?'

'I've never worked up there, at least not for more than half an hour. The last time was about three months ago. I went up to find Esmé Carling's original contract with us. I couldn't find it.'

'You mean you couldn't find her old file?'

'I found her file. I took it into the little archives room to study it. The original contract wasn't there.'

Claudia said, without particular interest: 'That's not surprising. We've had her on the list for thirty years. It was probably misfiled twenty years ago.' And then, with sudden energy: 'Look, I don't see why I should waste time just because Adam Dalgliesh wants to chat with a fellow poet. We don't have to stay in this room.'

Frances sounded doubtful. 'He said he wanted to see us together.'

'Well, he has seen us together. Now he's seeing us separately. When he wants me he'll find me in my office. Tell him that, will you.'

After she had left James said: 'She's right you know. We may not feel like working but it's worse sitting and waiting, looking at that empty chair.'

'But we haven't been looking at it, have we? We've been carefully not looking at it, keeping our eyes elsewhere, almost as if Gerard were an embarrassment. I can't work, but I would like some more coffee.'

'Then let's find it. Mrs Demery must be about somewhere. I'd rather like to hear her version of her interview with Dalgliesh. If that doesn't lighten the atmosphere nothing will.'

They moved together to the door. As they reached it Frances turned to him. 'James, I feel so frightened. I ought to be feeling grief and shock and the horror of it. We were lovers. I did love him once and now he's dead. I ought to be thinking of him, of the awful finality of his death. I ought to be praying for him. I did try but it came out as meaningless words. What I'm feeling is totally selfish, totally ignoble. It's fear.'

'Fear of the police? Dalgliesh isn't a bully.'

'No, it's worse than that. Fear of what's going on here. That snake – whoever did that to Gerard is evil. Don't you find it, the presence of evil in Innocent House? I think I've been feeling it for months. This just seems like the inevitable end, something all the petty mischiefs have been leading up to. My mind ought to be full of grief for Gerard. It isn't, it's full of terror, terror and an awful foreboding that this isn't the end.'

James said gently: 'There aren't any right or wrong emotions. We feel what we feel. I doubt whether any of us feels intense grief, even Claudia. Gerard was a remarkable man but he wasn't lovable. What I try to persuade myself is grief is probably no more than that universal and impotent sadness one always feels at the death of the young, the talented, the healthy. Even that is overlaid by a fascinated curiosity spiced with apprehension.' He turned to her and said: 'I'm here, Frances. When you need me and if you need me, I'm here. I shan't be a nuisance. I shan't thrust myself on you just because shock and fear have made us both vulnerable. I'm just offering you whatever you need when you need it.'

'I know. Thank you, James.'

She put out her hand and for a second laid it against his face. It was the first time she had ever voluntarily touched him. Then she turned to the door and, in turning, missed the spreading radiance of joy and triumph on his face.

25

Twenty years previously Dalgliesh had heard Gabriel Dauntsey reading his poetry in the Purcell Room on the South Bank. He had no intention of telling Dauntsey so, but as he waited for the old man the event came back to him with such clarity that he listened to the approaching footsteps through the archives room with something of the excited expectation of youth. Of the two world wars it was the first which had produced the greater poetry and sometimes he occupied his mind by wondering why this should be so. Was it that the year 1914 had seen the death of innocence, that the cataclysm had swept away more than a brilliant generation? But for a few years – was it only three? – it had seemed that Dauntsey might be the Wilfred Owen of his own time, his very different war. But the promise of those first two volumes had never been fulfilled and he had published nothing more. Dalgliesh told himself that the word promise, with its suggestion of a talent as yet unrealized, was hardly appropriate. One or two of those early poems had represented achievement at a level which few post-war poets had reached.

After that reading Dalgliesh had discovered as much as Dauntsey wanted known of his history; how, living in France, he had been in England on business when war was declared, leaving his wife and two children trapped by the invading Germans; how they had totally disappeared from knowledge and official records so that it was only after years of searching after the war that he had discovered that all three, living under a false name to avoid internment, had been killed in a British bomber raid on occupied France. Dauntsey himself had served in RAF Bomber Command but had been spared the ultimate tragic irony; he had not taken part in that raid. His had been the poetry of modern war, of loss and grief and terror, comradeship and courage, cowardice and defeat. The strong sinuous brutal verses were lit by passages of lyrical beauty, like shells bursting in the mind. The great Lancasters lifting themselves like ponderous beasts with death in their bellies, the dark and silent skies exploding in a cacophony of terror, the boyish crew for whom he, little older, was responsible, climbing clumsily accoutred into that frail metal shell night after night, knowing the arithmetic of survival, that this could be the night when they would fall from the sky like flaming torches. And always the guilt, the sense that this nightly terror, both dreaded and welcomed, was an expiation, that there was a betrayal for which only death could atone, personal betrayal mirroring a greater universal desolation.

And now he was here, an ordinary old man if any old man could be described as ordinary, not bent, but holding himself with disciplined effort as if endurance and courage could successfully overcome the ravages of time. Old age either produces a soft plumpness obliterating character in crinkled nonentity or, as here, strips the face so that the bones stand out like a skeleton temporarily clothed in flesh dry and delicate as paper. But the hair, although grey, was still strong, the eyes as black and darting as Dalgliesh remembered. Now they fixed on him a questioning ironic stare.

Dalgliesh swung round the chair from the table and placed it near the door. Dauntsey sat.

Dalgliesh said: 'You came up with Lord Stilgoe and Mr de Witt. Did anything strike you about this room apart from the presence of the body?'

'Not at first, apart from a disagreeable smell. A corpse, half-naked, grotesquely decorated as that corpse was, assaults the senses. After a minute, perhaps less, I did notice other things, and with unusual clarity. The room struck me as different – odd. It looked stripped, although it wasn't, unnaturally clean, warmer than usual. The body looked so – so disordered; the room so very ordered. The chair was precisely in place, the files as neatly on the table. I noticed, of course, that the tape recorder was missing.'

'Were the files as you had left them?'

'Not as I remember. The two filing trays have been reversed. The tray with the smaller number of files should be on the left. I had two piles, the right higher than the left. I work from left to right with six to ten files at a time, depending on their size. When I finish with a file I transfer it to the right. When all six have been dealt with I return them to the main archives room with a ruler inserted to show how far I've got.'

Dalgliesh said: 'We noticed the ruler in a space on the bottom shelf of the second row. Does that mean that you've only completed one row?'

'It's very slow work. I tend to get interested in old letters even if they aren't worth preserving. I've found quite a lot that are – letters from twentieth-century writers and others who corresponded with Henry Peverell and his father, even if the firm didn't publish them. There are letters from H. G. Wells, Arnold Bennett, members of the Bloomsbury group, some even earlier.'

'What is your system?'

'I dictate a description of the contents of each file and my recommendation either for Destruction, Doubtful, Preserve or Important on the tape recorder. A typist then types a list and periodically the board goes through it. Nothing has actually been thrown out yet. Until we know the future of the firm it seemed unwise to destroy anything.'

'When did you last use this room?'

'On Monday. I worked here all day. Mrs Demery put her head round the door at about ten o'clock but said that she wouldn't disturb me. The place only gets cleaned about one week in four and then superficially. She told me about the frayed window cord and I said I'd mention it to George and get him to do the repair. I haven't spoken to him yet.'

'You hadn't noticed it yourself?'

'I'm afraid not. The window has been open for weeks. I prefer it that way. I suppose I would have noticed when the weather gets colder.'

'How do you heat the room?'

'Always with an electric fire. Actually it belongs to me. I prefer it to the gas fire. I don't mean that I thought the gas fire was unsafe, but I don't smoke so I never seem to have matches when I need them. It was easier to bring the electric reflector fire over from my flat. It's very light and I either carry it back to number twelve with me or leave it here if I propose to work next day. On Monday I took it home.'

'And the door was unlocked when you left the room?'

'Oh yes. I never lock the door. The key is kept in the lock, usually on this side, but I've never used it.'

Dalgliesh said: 'The lock looks comparatively new. Who had it fitted?'

'Henry Peverell. He liked to work up here occasionally. I don't know why, but he was a solitary man. I suppose he thought fitting a lock gave him an added sense of security. But it isn't really new –

much newer than the door, of course, but I think the key has been there for at least five years.'

Dalgliesh said: 'But it hasn't been unused for five years. The lock has been kept oiled, the key turns easily.'

'Does it? I don't use it so I haven't noticed. But it's odd about the oiling. Mrs Demery may have done it but it seems unlikely.'

Dalgliesh said: 'Did you like Gerard Etienne?'

'No, but I respected him. Not for qualities which necessarily deserve respect; I respected him for being so different from me. He had the virtues of his defects. And he was young. He could hardly claim credit or responsibility for that, but it gave him an enthusiasm which most of us here no longer have and which I think the firm needs. We may have complained about what he did or disliked what he proposed to do, but at least he knew where he was going. I suspect we shall feel rudderless without him.'

'Who will take over as managing director?'

'Oh, his sister, Claudia Etienne. The job here goes to the person with the greatest number of shares. As far as I know she will inherit his. That will give her an overall majority.'

Dalgliesh said: 'To do what?'

'I don't know. You'll have to ask her. I doubt whether she knows herself. She's just lost a brother. I doubt whether she's spending much time thinking about the future of Peverell Press.'

Dalgliesh went on to ask Dauntsey how he had spent the previous day and night. Dauntsey looked down with a small wry smile. He was too intelligent not to know that what he was being asked for was his alibi. He was silent for a little time as if marshalling his thoughts. Then he said: 'I was in the partners' meeting from ten o'clock until eleven-thirty. Gerard liked to get it over within two hours, but yesterday we stopped earlier than usual. After the meeting he had a few words with me coming down from the boardroom about the future of the poetry list. I think, too, he was trying to enlist my support for his plan to sell Innocent House and move the firm down-river to Docklands.'

'You saw that as desirable?'

'I saw it as necessary.' He paused, then said, 'Unfortunately.' Again he paused, then continued, speaking slowly and deliberately but with little emphasis, occasionally pausing as if to select one word over another, from time to time frowning as if memory were painful or uncertain. Dalgliesh listened in silence to the monologue.

'After I left Innocent House I went back to my flat to get ready for a luncheon appointment. When I say get ready, I mean merely to run a comb through my hair and wash my hands. I wasn't there long. I took a young poet, Damien Smith, to lunch at the Ivy. Gerard used to say that James de Witt and I spent money on entertaining authors in inverse proportion to their importance to the firm. I thought the boy might enjoy the Ivy. I was due there at one o'clock and was taken by launch to London Bridge and then caught a taxi to the restaurant. We spent two hours over lunch and I was back at my flat about half past three. I made myself a pot of tea and returned to my office here at four. I worked for about an hour and a half.

'The last time I saw Gerard was when I went to the ground-floor lavatory. It's the one at the back of the house next to the shower room. The women usually use the lavatory on the first floor. Gerard was coming out as I went in. We didn't speak but I think he nodded or smiled. There was some kind of passing acknowledgement, that's all. I didn't see him again. I came back to my flat and spent the next two hours in reading over the poems I'd selected for the evening, thinking about them, making coffee. I listened to the BBC six o'clock news. Shortly afterwards Frances Peverell rang me to wish me good luck. She had offered to go with me. I think she thought that someone from the firm ought to be there. We had spoken about it a few days earlier and I managed to dissuade her. One of the poets due to read was Marigold Riley. She's not a bad poet but much of her verse is scatological. I knew that Frances wouldn't enjoy the poetry, the company or the atmosphere. I told her that I would prefer to be on my own, that having her there would make me nervous. It wasn't entirely a lie. I hadn't read my verse for fifteen years. Most of the people there would assume that I was dead. I was already wishing I hadn't agreed to go. Having Frances there, wondering whether she was unhappy, how much she was disliking it all, would only have increased the trauma. I rang for a taxi and left shortly after half past seven.'

Dalgliesh asked: 'How shortly?'

'I rang for the taxi to be in the lane by seven forty-five, and I suppose I kept him waiting a few minutes, not more.' He paused again, then went on: 'What happened at the Connaught Arms will hardly interest you. There were enough people there to confirm my presence. I suppose the reading went rather better than I expected, but it was too crowded and too noisy. I hadn't realized that poetry had become a spectator sport. There was a great deal of drinking and smoking and some of the poets were rather self-indulgent. It all went on too long. I meant to ask the landlord to telephone for a taxi but he was busy talking to a group of people and I slipped out more or less unnoticed. I thought I could pick up a cab at the end of the road, but before I got there I was mugged. There were three of them, I think, two black and one white, but I won't be able to identify them. I was just aware of rushing figures, the strong shove from the back, of hands grabbing at my pockets. It wasn't even a necessary assault. If they had asked I would have handed over my wallet. What else could I do?'

'They got it?'

'Oh yes, they got it. At least it was missing when I looked. The fall stunned me for a moment. When I came to a man and a woman were bending over me. They had been at the reading and were trying to catch me up. I had banged my head when I fell and it was bleeding slightly. I took out my handkerchief and held it to the wound. I asked them to bring me home but they said that they had to drive past St Thomas's Hospital and insisted on leaving me there. They said that I ought to have an X-ray. I could hardly insist that they drove me home or found a cab. They were being very kind, but I don't think they wanted to go too far out of their way. At the hospital I had to wait quite a time. There were more urgent cases in the casualty department. Eventually a nurse dressed the wound on my head and said that I must wait to have an X-ray. That meant another wait. The result of that was satisfactory but they wanted to keep me in for a night's observation. I assured them that I would be well looked after at home and told them that I wasn't prepared to be admitted. I asked them to ring Frances and let her know what had happened and call a taxi. I thought she would probably be watching out for me to hear how the evening went and might be worried when I wasn't back by eleven. It was about half past one when I did get home, and I rang Frances at once. She wanted me to go up to her flat, but I told her I was perfectly all right and what I needed most was a bath. As soon as I'd had one I gave her another ring and she came down at once.'

Dalgliesh said: 'And she didn't insist on coming down to your flat as soon as you returned?'

'No. Frances never intrudes if she thinks someone wants to be alone, and I did want to be alone at least for a little time. I wasn't quite ready to give explanations, hear expressions of sympathy. What I needed was a drink and a bath. I had both and then rang Frances. I knew she was anxious and I didn't want to keep her waiting until the morning to learn what had happened. I thought the whisky would make me feel better, but in fact it made me feel rather sick. I suppose I had some kind of delayed shock. By the time she knocked on the door I wasn't feeling too good. We sat up together for a little time and then she insisted that I went to bed. She said she would stay in the flat in case I needed something in the night. I think she was afraid that I might be a great deal more ill than I made out and that she ought to be at hand to telephone a doctor if anything went wrong. I didn't try to dissuade her, although I knew that all I needed was a night's rest. I thought she would sleep in my spare room but I believe she wrapped herself in a blanket and stayed next door in the sitting-room. When I woke in the morning she was dressed and had made me a cup of tea. She insisted that I should stay at home, but I was feeling a great deal better by the time I was dressed and decided to go into Innocent House. We arrived together in the main hall just after the first launch of the day had arrived. That's when we were told that Gerard was missing.'

Dalgliesh said: 'And that was the first you knew of it?'

'Yes. It was his habit to work later than most of us, particularly on Thursdays. He was usually in later in the morning, except on the days when we had a partners' meeting when he liked to begin promptly at ten. I'd assumed, of course, that he had gone home at about the time I left for my reading.'

'But you didn't see him when you left for the Connaught Arms?'

'No, I didn't see him.'

'Or see anyone entering Innocent House?'

'No one. I saw no one.'

'And when you were given the news that he was dead the three of you went up to the little archives office?'

'Yes, we went up together, Stilgoe, de Witt and myself. It was a natural response to the news, I suppose, the need to see for oneself. James got there first. Stilgoe and I couldn't keep up with him. Claudia was still kneeling by her brother's body when we arrived. She got up and faced us and spread out one arm towards us. It was a curious gesture. It was as if she were displaying this enormity to public gaze.'

'And how long were you in the room?'

'It could only have been less than a minute. It seemed longer. We were bunched together just inside the door, looking, staring, unbelieving, appalled. I don't think anyone spoke. I know I didn't. Everything in the room was extremely vivid. The shock seemed to have jarred my eyes into an extraordinary keenness of perception. I saw every detail of Gerard's body and of the room itself with astonishing clarity. Then Stilgoe spoke. He said: "I'll telephone the police. We can do nothing here. This room must be locked at once and I'll keep the key." He took over. We left together and Claudia locked the door after us. Stilgoe took the key. The rest you know.'

26

During the innumerable discussions of the tragedy which were to occupy the following weeks and months, it was generally agreed by the staff of the Peverell Press that the experience of Marjorie Spenlove had been singular. Miss Spenlove, senior copy editor, had arrived at Innocent House punctually at her usual hour of 9.15. She had murmured a 'good morning' to George who, sitting stricken at his switchboard, hadn't noticed her. Lord Stilgoe, Dauntsey and de Witt were in the little archives room with the body, Mrs Demery was ministering to Blackie in the ground-floor cloakroom surrounded by the rest of the staff and the hall was for a few minutes empty. Miss Spenlove went straight up to her room, took off her jacket and settled down to work. When working she was oblivious to everything except the text before her. It was claimed by Peverell Press that no work copy-edited by Miss Spenlove ever contained an undetected error. She was at her best working on non-fiction, occasionally finding it difficult, with young modern novelists, to distinguish between grammatical mistakes and their cultivated and much-praised natural style. Her expertise went beyond details of the words; no geographical or historical inaccuracy went unchecked, no inconsistencies of weather, topography or dress unnoticed. Authors valued her even though their session with her to approve the final text left them feeling that they had undergone a particularly traumatic session with an intimidating headmistress of the old school.

Sergeant Robbins and a detective constable had searched the premises soon after their arrival. The search had been a little perfunctory; no one could seriously expect that the murderer was still on the premises unless he or she was a member of the staff. But Sergeant Robbins, perhaps excusably, had neglected to look in the small lavatory on the second floor. Descending to fetch Gabriel Dauntsey, his sharp ears detected the sound of a cough from the adjoining office and, opening the door, he found himself confronting an elderly lady working at a desk. Regarding him sternly above her half-moon spectacles she enquired: 'And who may you be?'

'Detective Sergeant Robbins of the Metropolitan Police, madam. How did you get in?'

'Through the door. I work here. This is my office. I am the senior copy editor of Peverell Press. As such I have a right to be here. I very much doubt whether that could be said of you.'

'I'm here on duty, madam. Mr Gerard Etienne has been found dead under suspicious circumstances.'

'You mean someone has murdered him?'

'We can't be sure of that yet.'

'When did he die?'

'We shall know more after the forensic pathologist has reported.'

'How did he die?'

'We don't yet know the cause of death.'

'It seems to me, young man, that there is very little you do know. Perhaps you had better come back when you are better informed.'

Sergeant Robbins opened his mouth then shut it firmly, just managing to prevent himself saying, 'Yes, miss. Very good, miss.' He disappeared, closing the door behind him, and was halfway down the stairs before realizing that he hadn't asked the woman's name. He would, of course, learn it in time. It was a small omission in a brief encounter which, he admitted, hadn't gone well. Being honest and given to mild speculation, he also admitted that part of the reason was the woman's uncanny resemblance in appearance and voice to Miss Addison, who had been his first teacher when he moved up from the infants' school and who had believed that children do best and are happiest when they know from the start who is boss.

Miss Spenlove was more shaken by the news than she had let him see. After completing work on the page she telephoned the switchboard.

'George, could you find Mrs Demery for me?' In seeking information she believed in going to an expert. 'Mrs Demery? There's a young man roaming the building who claims to be a detective sergeant of the Metropolitan Police. He told me that Mr Etienne is dead, possibly murdered. If you know anything about it, perhaps you could come up and enlighten me. And I'm ready for my coffee.'

Mrs Demery, abandoning Miss Blackett to the ministrations of Mandy, was only too eager to oblige.

27

Dalgliesh, with Kate, conducted the remaining interviews with the partners in Gerard Etienne's office. Daniel was occupied in the little archives room where the gas man was already at work dismantling the fire and, when this was completed and samples of any chimney debris despatched to the lab, would go on to Wapping Police Station to set up the incident room. Dalgliesh had already spoken to the station superintendent who had accepted philosophically the need for the intrusion and the temporary use of one of his offices. Dalgliesh hoped that it wouldn't be for long. If this was murder, and he now had no doubt in his own mind that it was, then the number of possible suspects was unlikely to be great.

He had no wish to sit at Etienne's desk, partly because of sensitivity to the feelings of the partners, but principally because a confrontation across four feet of pale oak invested any interview with a formality which was more likely to inhibit or antagonize a suspect than elicit helpful information. There was, however, a small conference table in the same wood, with six chairs, close to the windows, and they seated themselves there. The long walk from the door would be intimidating for all but the most self-possessed, but he doubted whether it would worry Claudia or James de Witt.

The room had obviously once been a dining-room but its elegance had been desecrated by the end partition which cut across the oval stucco decorations on the ceiling and bisected one of the four tall windows which looked out on Innocent Passage. The magnificent marble fireplace with its elegant carving was in Miss Blackett's office. And here in Etienne's office the furniture – desk, chairs, conference table and filing cabinets – was almost aggressively modern. They might have been chosen to be deliberately at odds with the marble pilasters and porphyry entablatures, the two magnificent chandeliers, one almost touching the partition, and the gilt of picture frames against the pale green of the walls. The pictures were conventional rural scenes, almost certainly Victorian. They were well but a little over-painted, too sentimental for his taste. He doubted whether these were the pictures which had originally hung here and he wondered what portraits of the Peverells had once graced these walls. There was still one piece of the original furniture; a marble and bronze wine-table, obviously Regency. So one reminder of past glories, at least, was still in use. He wondered what Frances Peverell thought of the room's desecration and whether now, with Gerard Etienne dead, the partition would be taken down. He wondered, too, if Gerard Etienne had been insensitive to all architecture or only disregarding of this particular house. Was the partitioning, the discordant modern furnishing, his comment on the unsuitability of the room for his purposes, a deliberate rejection of a past which had been dominated by Peverells not Etiennes?

Claudia Etienne walked across the thirty feet towards him with confident grace and seated herself as if she were conferring a favour. She was very pale, but had herself well under control, although he suspected that her hands, plunged in the pockets of her cardigan, would have been more revealing than her taut grave face. He offered his condolences simply and, he hoped, sincerely but she cut him short.

'Are you here because of Lord Stilgoe?'

'No. I'm here because of your brother's death. Lord Stilgoe did get in touch with me indirectly through a mutual friend. He had received an anonymous letter which greatly upset his wife; she saw it as a threat to his life. He asked for an official assurance that the police have no suspicion of foul play in the three deaths concerned with Innocent House, two authors and Sonia Clements.'

'Which you were, of course, able to give.'

'Which the police divisions concerned were able to give. He should have received that assurance about three days ago.'

'I hope it satisfied him. Lord Stilgoe's self-absorption amounts to paranoia. Still, he can hardly suppose that Gerard's death is a deliberate attempt to sabotage his precious memoirs. I still find it strange, Commander, that you are here personally, and in such impressive force. Are you treating my brother's death as murder?'

'As an unexplained and suspicious death. That is why I need to trouble you now. I would be grateful for your co-operation, not only personally, but in explaining to your staff that some invasion of their privacy and interference with their work is inevitable.'

'I think they will understand that.'

'We shall need to take fingerprints for the purpose of elimination.

174

Any not needed in evidence will be destroyed when the case is complete.'

'That will be a new experience for us. If it is necessary, of course, we must accept it. I assume that you will be requiring all of us, particularly the partners, to provide an alibi.'

'I need to know what you were doing, Miss Etienne, and who you were with from six o'clock last night.'

She said: 'You have the unenviable task, Commander, of expressing sympathy at my brother's death while requiring an alibi to prove that I didn't murder him. You do it with some grace. I congratulate you; but then you've had plenty of practice. I was on the river with a friend, Declan Cartwright, last night. When you check with him he'll probably describe me as his fiancée. I prefer to use the word lover. We started off shortly after six-thirty when the launch returned from taking staff to Charing Cross Pier. We were on the river until about ten-thirty, perhaps a little later, when we returned here and I drove him back to his flat off Westbourne Grove. He lives above an antique shop which he manages for the owner. I shall, of course, give you the address. I was with him until two o'clock, then drove back to the Barbican. I have a flat there on the floor beneath that of my brother.'

'It was a long time to spend on the river on an October night.'

'A fine October night. We went downstream to see the Thames Barrier and then returned and put in at Greenwich Pier. We had dinner at Le Papillon in Greenwich Church Street. We booked for eight o'clock and I suppose we were there for about an hour and a half. Then we went upstream beyond Battersea Bridge and returned and, as I've said, were back here shortly after ten-thirty.'

'Did anyone see you, other, of course, than the staff of the restaurant and the other diners?'

'The river wasn't very busy. Even so, plenty of people must have seen us, but that doesn't mean they'll remember us. I was in the wheelhouse and Declan was with me most of the time. We saw at least two police launches on the river. I dare say they will have noticed us. That's their job, isn't it?'

'Did anyone see you when you embarked or on your return?'

'Not as far as I know. We saw and heard no one.'

'And you can think of no person who wished your brother dead?'

'You asked that question before.'

'I'm asking it again now that we're here in private.'

'Are we? Is anything one says to a police officer really private? The answer is the same. I know of no one who hated him enough to kill him. There are probably people who won't be sorry he's dead. No death is universally regretted. Every death advantages someone.'

'Who will be advantaged by this death?'

'I shall. I'm Gerard's heir. That would, of course, have changed once he was married. As it is I inherit his shares in the firm, his Barbican flat, the proceeds of his life insurance. I didn't know him very well, we weren't brought up to be loving siblings. We went to different schools, different universities, had different lives. My Barbican flat is underneath his but we didn't make a habit of dropping in on each other. It would have seemed an invasion of privacy. But I liked him, I respected him. I was on his side. If he was murdered I hope that his killer rots in prison for the rest of his life. He won't, of course. We're so quick to forget the dead and forgive the living. Perhaps we need to show mercy because we're uncomfortably aware that one day we may need it. Incidentally, here are his keys. You asked for a set. I've taken off his car keys and the keys to his flat.'

'Thank you,' said Dalgliesh, taking them. 'I don't need to assure you that they will stay in my possession, or be held by one of my team. Has your father been told that his son is dead?'

'Not yet. I'm going to drive down to Bradwell-on-Sea late this afternoon. He lives as a recluse and doesn't take incoming calls. In any case I would prefer to break it to him personally. Do you want to see him?'

'It's important I do. I'd be grateful if you would ask him if I could see him tomorrow at any time convenient for him.'

'I'll ask but I'm not sure whether he'll agree. He has a strong dislike of visitors. He lives with an elderly French woman who looks after him. Her son is his chauffeur. He's married to a local girl and I imagine they'll take over when Estelle dies. She certainly won't retire. She regards it as a privilege to devote her life to a hero of France. Father, as always, has his life well organized. I tell you this so that you'll know what to expect. I don't think you will be welcome. Is that all?'

'I need, too, to see the next-of-kin of Sonia Clements.'

'Sonia Clements? What possible connection can there be between her suicide and Gerard's death?'

'None as far as I know at present. Does she have next-of-kin, or was there someone she lived with?'

'Only her sister, and they didn't live together for the last three years of her life. She's a nun, a member of a community at Kemptown outside Brighton. They run a hostel for the dying. I think it's called St Anne's Convent. I'm sure the Reverend Mother will allow you to see her. After all the police are like the VAT inspectors, aren't they? However disagreeable or inconvenient their presence, when they call on you, you have to let them in. Is there anything else you want from me?'

'The little archives room will be sealed and I should also like to lock the archives room itself.'

'For how long?'

'For as long as necessary. Will that be very inconvenient?'

'Of course it will be inconvenient. Gabriel Dauntsey is working on the old records. The job is already well behind schedule.'

'I realize that it will be inconvenient. I asked if it will be very inconvenient. The work of the firm can continue without access to those two rooms?'

'Obviously if you think it important, we shall have to manage.'

'Thank you.'

He ended by asking her about the practical joker at Innocent House and the means taken to discover the culprit. The investigation seemed on the whole to have been as superficial as it was unsuccessful.

She said: 'Gerard more or less left it to me, but I didn't get very far. All I could do was to list the incidents as they happened and the number of people who were on the premises at the time or could have been responsible. That meant practically everyone except staff who were off sick or on holiday. It was almost as if the joker deliberately chose times when all the partners and most of the staff were here and could have been responsible. Gabriel Dauntsey has an alibi for the last incident, the fax that was sent yesterday from this office to Better Books in Cambridge. He was on his way at the time to lunch with one of our authors at the Ivy, but the other partners and the senior staff were here. Gerard and I took the launch to Greenwich and had a pub lunch at the Trafalgar Tavern, but we didn't leave here until twenty past one. The fax was sent at twelve-thirty. Carling was due to begin signing at one o'clock. The most recent incident, of course, is the stealing of my brother's diary. That could have been taken from his desk drawer any time on the Wednesday. He missed it first thing yesterday morning.'

Dalgliesh said: 'Tell me about the snake.'

'Hissing Sid? Goodness knows when that first appeared here. About five years ago, I think. Someone left it after a staff Christmas party. It used to be used by Miss Blackett to prop open the door between her room and Henry Peverell's. It's become something of an office mascot. Blackie's attached to it for some reason.'

'And yesterday your brother told her to get rid of it.'

'Mrs Demery told you that, I suppose. Yes, he did. He wasn't in a particularly good mood after the partners' meeting and for some reason the sight of the thing irritated him. She put it in the desk drawer.'

'You saw her do that?'

'Yes. Myself, Gabriel Dauntsey and our temporary shorthand-typist, Mandy Price. I imagine that the news got round the office pretty fast.'

Dalgliesh said: 'Your brother came out of the meeting in a bad temper?'

'I didn't say that. I said he wasn't in a particularly good mood. None of us were. It's no secret that the Peverell Press is in trouble. We have to face up to selling Innocent House if we're to have any hope of staying in business.'

'That must be a distressing prospect for Miss Peverell.'

'I don't think any of us welcomes it. The suggestion that any of us tried to prevent it by harming Gerard is ludicrous.'

Dalgliesh said: 'It was not a suggestion that I have made.'

Then he let her go.

She had just reached the door when Daniel put his head round. He opened it for her and waited to speak until she had left the room.

'The gas engineer is ready to go, sir. It's what we expected. The flue is badly blocked. It looks like rubble from the chimney lining, but there's been a lot of falling grit over the years. He'll provide an official report but he hasn't any doubt about what happened. With the flue in the state it is, that fire was lethal.'

Dalgliesh said: 'Only in a room without adequate ventilation. We've been told that often enough. The lethal combination was the burning fire and the unopenable window.'

Daniel said: 'There was one particularly large piece of rubble wedged against the flue. It could have fallen naturally from the lining of the chimney or been deliberately dislodged. There's really no way of telling. You'd only have to prod parts of that lining and chunks would fall away. Do you want to have a look, sir?'

'Yes, I'll come now.'

'And you want the fire as well as the rubble to go to forensics?'

'Yes, Daniel, all of it.' He had no need to add 'And I want prints, photographs, the lot.' He was, as always, working with experts in violent death.

As they made their way upstairs, he asked: 'Any news of the missing tape recorder or Etienne's diary?'

'Not so far, sir. Miss Etienne made a fuss about checking the desk drawers of the staff who'd been sent home or who are on leave today. I didn't think you'd want to apply for a search warrant.'

'Not necessary at present. I doubt whether it will be. The search can take place on Monday when all the staff are here. If that tape recorder was taken by the murderer for a specific reason it's probably at the bottom of the river. If the office joker took it, it could turn up anywhere. The same goes for the diary.'

Daniel said: 'The recorder was the only one of its kind in the office, apparently. It belonged personally to Mr Dauntsey. All the others are larger and are AC/battery cassette recorders which take the usual two-and-a-half by four inch cassettes. Mr de Witt wonders if you'll see him fairly soon, sir. He has a seriously sick friend living with him and promised that he'd be home early.'

'All right, I'll take him next.'

The gas engineer, already in his coat and ready to go, was vocal in his disapproval, obviously torn between an almost proprietorial interest in the appliance and professional outrage at its misuse.

'Haven't seen a fire of this type for nearly twenty years. It should be in a museum. But there's nothing wrong with the functioning of the fire itself. It's well-made, sturdy. It's the type they used to install in nurseries. The tap's removable, you see, so that the children couldn't accidentally turn it on. You can see plainly enough what happened here, Commander. The flue's totally blocked. This grit must have been coming down for years. God knows when this appliance was last serviced. This was a death waiting to happen. I've seen it before, you too no doubt, and we'll see it again. People can't say they haven't been warned often enough. Gas appliances need air. Without ventilation what you get is malfunctioning and a build-up of carbon monoxide. Gas is a perfectly safe fuel if it's used properly.'

'He'd have been all right with the window open?'

'Should have been. The window is high and rather narrow, but if it'd been properly open he'd have been all right. How did you find him? Asleep in a chair, I suppose. That's usually how it happens. People get a bit dozy, fall asleep and don't wake up.'

Daniel said: 'There are worse ways of going.'

'Not if you're a gas engineer there aren't. It's an insult to the product. You'll be needing a report I suppose, Commander. Well, you'll get it soon enough. He was a young chap, wasn't he? Well, that makes it worse. I don't know why it should but it always does.' He opened the door and looked round the room. 'I wonder why he came up here to work. Odd place to choose. You'd think there'd be plenty of offices in a building this size without wanting to come up here.'

28

James de Witt closed the door behind him and paused for a moment nonchalantly against it as if wondering whether he would after all bother to enter, then walked across the room in easy strides and pulled the empty chair to one side of the table.

'Is it all right if I sit here? Confronting you across the board in this adversarial way is rather intimidating. It brings back unpleasant memories of interviews with one's tutor.' He was casually dressed in dark blue jeans and a loose-fitting ribbed sweater with leather patches on the elbows and shoulders which looked like army surplus. On him it looked almost elegant.

He was very tall, certainly over six feet, and loose-limbed with a suggestion of gawkiness in the long bony wrists. His face, with something of the melancholy humour of a clown, was lean and intelligent, his cheeks flat under the jutting bones. A heavy strand of light brown hair fell across the high forehead. His eyes were narrow, sleepy under heavy lids, but they were eyes which missed little and gave nothing away. When he spoke the soft agreeable drawl was oddly inappropriate to his words.

'I've just seen Claudia. She looks desperately tired. Did you really need to interrogate her? She has, after all, lost an only brother in appalling circumstances.'

Dalgliesh said: 'It was hardly an interrogation. If Miss Etienne had asked us to stop, or if I thought she was too distressed, we would obviously have deferred the interview.'

'And Frances Peverell? It's just as ghastly for her. Can't her interview wait until tomorrow?'

'Not unless she's too distressed to see me now. In this kind of investigation we need to get as much information as possible as soon as possible.'

Kate wondered whether his real concern had been for Frances Peverell rather than Claudia Etienne.

He said: 'I suppose I'm taking Frances's turn. Sorry about that. It's just that my arrangements have temporarily broken down and my friend, Rupert Farlow, will be alone if I don't get back by half past four. Actually, Rupert Farlow is my alibi. I'm assuming that the main purpose of this interview is for me to provide one. I went home yesterday by the launch at five-thirty and was at Hillgate Village by half past six. I took the Circle Line from Westminster to Notting Hill Gate. Rupert can confirm that I was at home with him for the whole evening. Nobody called and, unusually, no one telephoned. It would be helpful if you could make an appointment before you check with him. He's seriously ill now and some days are better for him than others.'

Dalgliesh asked him the usual question, whether he knew anyone who might wish Gerard Etienne dead. He asked: 'Any political enemies for example, using that word in the widest sense?'

'Good God no! Gerard was impeccably liberal, in talk if not in actions. And after all it's the talk that matters. All the correct liberal opinions. He knew what can't be spoken or published in Britain today and he didn't speak it or publish it. He may have thought it, like the rest of us, but that's hardly a crime yet. Actually, I doubt whether he was much interested in political or social affairs, not even as they affected publishing. He'd pretend to a concern if it were expedient but I doubt whether he felt it.'

'What did concern him? What did he feel deeply about?'

'Fame. Success. Himself. The Peverell Press. He wanted to head one of the largest – the largest – and most successful private publishing house in Britain. Music: Beethoven and Wagner in particular. He was a pianist and played rather well. It's a pity his touch with people wasn't as sensitive. His current woman, I suppose.'

'He was engaged?'

'To Earl Norrington's sister. Claudia has telephoned the Dowager. I expect she's broken the news to her daughter by now.'

'And there was no problem about the engagement?'

'Not that I am aware of. Claudia might know but I doubt it. Gerard was reticent about Lady Lucinda. We've all met her, of course. Gerard gave a joint engagement and birthday party for her here on the tenth of July instead of our usual summer bash. I believe he met her in Bayreuth last year but I gained the impression – I could be wrong – that it wasn't Wagner who had taken her there. I think she and her mother were visiting some continental cousins. I really know little else about her. The engagement was surprising, of course. One didn't think of Gerard as socially ambitious, if that's what it was all about. It's not as if Lady Lucinda was bringing money into the firm. Lineage but not lolly. Of course, when these people complain that they are poor they only mean that there is a slight temporary difficulty about paying the heir's fees at Eton. Still, Lady Lucinda certainly counts as one of Gerard's interests. And then there's mountaineering. If you had asked Gerard about his interests he would probably have added mountaineering. To my knowledge he only climbed one mountain in his life.'

Kate asked unexpectedly: 'Which mountain?'

De Witt turned to her and smiled. The smile was unexpected and transformed his face. 'The Matterhorn. That probably tells you as much about Gerard Etienne as you need to know.'

Dalgliesh said: 'Presumably he intended to make changes here. They can't all have been popular.'

'That didn't mean they weren't necessary, still are necessary I suppose. Maintaining this house has been eating up the annual profit for decades. I suppose we could stay on if we halved the list, sacked two-thirds of the staff, took a 30 per cent cut in our own pay and contented ourselves with the back-list and being a very small cult publisher. That wouldn't have suited Gerard Etienne.'

'Or the rest of you?'

'Oh, we grumbled and kicked against the pricks at times but I think we recognized that Gerard was right; it was expand or go under. A publishing house today can't survive on trade publishing. Gerard wanted to take over a firm with a strong legal list – there's one ripe for plucking – and to go into educational publishing. It was all going to take money, not to say energy and a certain amount of commercial aggression. I'm not sure that some of us had the stomach for it. God knows what will happen now. I imagine that we'll have a partners' meeting, confirm Claudia as chairman and MD and defer all disagreeable decisions for at least six months. That would have amused Gerard. He would have seen it as typical.'

Dalgliesh, anxious not to detain him too long, ended by asking him briefly about the practical joker.

'I've no idea who's responsible. We've wasted a lot of time in the monthly partners' meetings talking about it but we've got nowhere. It's odd really. With a total staff of only thirty, you'd imagine that we'd have got some clue by now if only by a process of elimination.

Of course, the great majority of the staff have been with the Press for years and I'd have said that all of them, old and new, were beyond suspicion. And the incidents have happened when practically everyone has been there. Perhaps that was the joker's idea, to make elimination difficult. Most serious, of course, was the disappearance of the artwork for the non-fiction book on Guy Fawkes and the alteration of Lord Stilgoe's proofs.'

Dalgliesh said: 'But neither, in fact, proved catastrophic.'

'As it happens, no. This last business with Hissing Sid seems to be in a different category. The others were directed against the firm, but stuffing the head of that snake into Gerard's mouth was surely an act of malice against him personally. To save you asking, I may as well say that I knew where to find Hissing Sid. I imagine most of the office did by the time Mrs Demery had finished her rounds.'

Dalgliesh thought that it was time to let him go. He said: 'How will you get to Hillgate Village?'

'I've ordered a taxi, it'll be too slow by launch to Charing Cross. I'll be in at half past nine tomorrow if there's anything else you want to know. Not that I think I can help. Oh, I may as well say now that I didn't kill Gerard, nor did I put that snake round his neck. I could hardly hope to persuade him of the virtues of the literary novel by gassing him to death.'

Dalgliesh said: 'So that's how you think he died?'

'Didn't he? Actually it was Dauntsey's idea, I can take no credit for it. But the more I think about it the more credible it appears.'

He left with the same unhurried grace as that with which he had entered.

Dalgliesh reflected that questioning suspects was rather like interviewing candidates as a member of a selection board. There was always the temptation to assess the performance of each and to put forward a tentative opinion before the next applicant was summoned. Today he waited in silence. Kate, as always, sensed that it was wise to keep her counsel, but he suspected that there were one or two pungent comments she would like to have made about Claudia Etienne.

Frances Peverell was the last. She came into the room with something of the docility of a well-trained schoolchild but her composure broke when she saw Etienne's jacket still hanging across the back of his chair.

She said: 'I didn't think this was still here,' and began to move towards it, her hand outstretched. Then she checked herself and turned towards Dalgliesh and he saw that her eyes had brimmed with tears.

He said: 'I'm sorry. Perhaps we should have taken it away.'

She said: 'Claudia might have removed it, perhaps, but she's had other things to think about. Poor Claudia. I suppose she'll have to cope with all his belongings, all his clothes.'

She sat down and looked at Dalgliesh like a patient, waiting for a consultant's opinion. Her face was gentle, the light brown hair with strands of gold was cut in a fringe above straight eyebrows and blue-green eyes. Dalgliesh suspected that the look of strained anxiety in them was more long-standing than a response to the present trauma and he wondered what Henry Peverell had been like as a father. The woman before him had none of the petulant self-absorption of a spoiled only daughter. She looked like a woman who all her life had responded to the needs of others, more used to receiving implied criticism than praise. She had none of Claudia Etienne's self-possession or de Witt's *dégagé* elegance. She was wearing a skirt in a soft blue and fawn tweed with a blue jumper and matching cardigan, but without the usual string of pearls. She could, he thought, have worn exactly the same in the 1930s or 1950s, the unexceptional day clothes of the English gentlewoman; unexciting, conventional, expensive good taste, giving offence to no one.

Dalgliesh said gently: 'I always think that's the worst job after someone dies. Watches, jewellery, books, pictures; these can be given to friends and it seems right and appropriate. But clothes are too intimate to be given as gifts. Paradoxically it seems that we can only bear to think of them being worn not by people we know, but by strangers.'

She said with eagerness as if grateful that he understood: 'Yes, I felt that after Daddy died. In the end I gave all his suits and shoes to the Salvation Army. I hope they found someone who needed them, but it was like clearing him out of the flat, clearing him out of my life.'

'Were you fond of Gerard Etienne?'

She looked down at her folded hands and then straight into his eyes. 'I was in love with him. I wanted to tell you myself because I'm sure you'll find out sooner or later and it's better coming from me. We had an affair but it ended a week before he became engaged.'

'By common consent?'

'No, not by common consent.'

He didn't need to ask her what she had felt at this betrayal. What she had felt, and was still feeling, was written plainly on her face.

He said: 'I'm sorry. Talking about his death can't be easy for you.'

'Not as painful as being unable to talk. Please tell me, Mr Dalgliesh, do you think that Gerard was murdered?'

'We can't be certain yet but it is a probability rather than a possibility. That's why we have to question you now. I'd like you to explain exactly what happened last night.'

'I expect Gabriel – Mr Dauntsey – has explained about the mugging. I didn't go with him to his poetry reading because he was adamant he wanted to be alone. I think he felt I wouldn't enjoy it. But someone from Peverell Press should have gone with him. It was the first time he'd read for about fifteen years and it wasn't right that he should be alone. If I'd been with him perhaps he wouldn't have been mugged. I received the telephone call from St Thomas's at about eleven-thirty saying he was there and would have to wait for an X-ray, and asking if I would be with him if they sent him home. Apparently he was more or less demanding to come back and they wanted to be sure he wouldn't be alone. I was watching out for him from my kitchen window but I missed hearing the taxi. His front door is in Innocent Lane but I think the driver must have turned at the bottom and left him there. He must have rung as soon as he got in. He said he was all right, that there was no fracture and he was going to have a bath. After that he'd be glad if I'd come down. I don't think he really wanted me, but he knew I couldn't be happy if I hadn't made sure he was all right.'

Dalgliesh asked: 'You haven't a key to his flat, then? You couldn't wait for him there?'

'I do have a key and he has a key to my flat. It's a sensible precaution in case there's a fire or flood and we need to gain access when the other is away. But I wouldn't dream of using it unless Gabriel had asked me.'

Dalgliesh asked: 'How long was it before you joined him?'

The answer was, of course, of vital importance. It was possible for Gabriel Dauntsey to have killed Etienne before he set off for the poetry reading at 7.45. The timing would have been tight but it could have been done. But it seemed that the only chance he would have had to return to the scene was after one in the morning.

He asked again: 'How long was it before Mr Dauntsey rang to call you down? Can you be fairly precise?'

'It can't have been long. I suppose about eight or ten minutes, maybe a little shorter. About eight minutes I'd say, just long enough for him to have a bath. His bathroom is under mine. I can't hear it when he runs his bath but I do hear the water running away. Yesterday I was listening for that.'

'And it was about eight minutes before you heard it?'

'I wasn't watching the time. Why should I have been? But I'm sure it wasn't unduly long.' She said, as if the possibility had suddenly struck her: 'But you can't really mean that you suspect Gabriel, that you think he went back to Innocent House and killed Gerard?'

'Mr Etienne was dead long before midnight. What we are considering now is the possibility that the snake was put round his neck some hours after he died.'

'But that would mean that someone went up to the little archives office specially, knowing that he was dead, knowing that he was lying there. But the only person who knew that would be the murderer. You're saying you thought the murderer went back later to the little archives room.'

'If there was a murderer. We can't be sure of that yet.'

'But Gabriel was ill, he'd been mugged! And he's old. He's over seventy. And he's rheumatic. He usually walks with a stick. He couldn't possibly have done it in the time.'

'Are you absolutely sure of that, Miss Peverell?'

'Yes, I'm sure. Besides, he did have a bath. I heard the water running away.'

Dalgliesh said gently: 'But you couldn't tell if it was his bath water.'

'What else could it have been? He didn't just leave his tap running, if that's what you're suggesting. If he had I should have heard it immediately. This water didn't begin running away until about eight minutes after he rang and said he was ready for me. I went down at once. He was wearing his dressing-gown. I could tell he had had a bath. His hair and face were damp.'

'And after that?'

'He'd already had some whisky and didn't want anything else, so I insisted that he went to bed. I was determined to stay the night so he told me where the clean sheets were for the spare bed. I don't think anyone had slept in that room for years and I didn't make up the bed. He fell asleep very quickly and I settled myself in the armchair in the sitting-room in front of the electric fire. I left the door open so that I could hear him, but he didn't wake. I woke before him, shortly after seven, and made a cup of tea. I tried to be quiet but I think he must have heard me moving around. It was about eight o'clock when he woke. Neither of us was in a hurry. We knew that George would open Innocent House. We both had a boiled egg for breakfast and went across shortly after nine o'clock.'

'And you didn't go up to see Mr Etienne's body?'

'Gabriel did. I didn't. I waited with the others at the bottom of the stairs. But when we heard that horrible high wailing I think I knew that Gerard was dead.'

Dalgliesh could see that she was again becoming distressed. He had learned all he needed for the present. He thanked her gently and let her go.

After she had left them they were silent for a moment, then Dalgliesh said: 'Well Kate, we've been presented with more dis-interested and convincing alibis; Claudia Etienne's lover, de Witt's sick house-guest and Frances Peverell, who's obviously incapable of believing that Gabriel Dauntsey could be guilty of a malicious act, let alone murder. She's trying to be honest about the length of time between his coming home and calling her down. She's an honest woman, but I'd guess that her eight minutes was an underestimate.'

Kate said: 'I wonder if she realized that he was giving her an alibi as well as she providing one for him. But of course it isn't important, is it? She could have gone over to Innocent House and done that business with the snake any time before Dauntsey arrived home. And she had every opportunity to kill Etienne. She's got no alibi for earlier yesterday evening. She was quick to pick up that point about the bath water, that he couldn't just have turned on the tap and let it run.'

'No, but there is another possibility. Think about it, Kate.'

Kate thought, then said: 'Of course, it could have been done that way.'

'Which means that we need to know the capacity of that bath. And we need to test the timing. Don't use Dauntsey. Robbins will have to imagine he's a rheumatic seventy-six-year-old. See how long it takes to get from Dauntsey's door in Innocent Lane up to the little archives room, do what had to be done there, and get back.'

'Using the stairs?'

'Time it using both stairs and the lift. With that lift the stairs are probably quicker.'

As they began putting their papers together Kate thought about Frances Peverell. Dalgliesh had been gentle with her, but when was he ever brutal in interrogation? He had been sincere in that comment about the clothes of the dead. All the same it had been remarkably effective in gaining Frances Peverell's confidence. He was probably sorry for the woman, possibly even rather liked her; but no personal feelings would influence him in his investigation. And what about me? Kate asked herself, not for the first time. Wouldn't he show a similar detachment, a comparable ruthlessness, in all aspects of his professional life? She thought: he respects me, he's glad to have me in the team, he trusts me, sometimes I can believe that he likes me. But if I fell down badly on the job, how long would I last?

Dalgliesh said: 'I need to go back to the Yard now for a couple of hours. I'll meet you and Daniel at the mortuary for the PM but I may not be able to stay until it's completed. I've a meeting with the Commissioner and the Minister in the House of Commons at eight o'clock. I don't know when I'll get away from that but I'll come on straight to Wapping and we'll review progress so far.'

It was going to be a long night.

29

It was two minutes to three and Blackie was sitting alone at her desk. She was oppressed by a listlessness which was partly the result of delayed shock, partly fear, but which made any action seem an intolerable exertion. She supposed she could go home, although no one had told her so. There was filing to be done, letters which Gerard Etienne had dictated still to be typed, but it seemed somehow indecent as well as pointless to file papers for which he would now never call and type letters his hand would never sign. Mandy had left half an hour earlier, presumably told that she was no longer wanted. Blackie had watched while she took her red crash-helmet from the bottom drawer of her desk and zipped up her tight leather jacket. Topped with that glittering dome, with her skinny body, the long legs clad in black ribbed leggings, she had been instantly transformed as always into the caricature of an exotic insect.

Her last words to Blackie, spoken with a trace of embarrassed sympathy, had been: 'Look, don't you go losing any sleep over him. I won't, and I quite liked him, what I saw of him. But he was a proper bastard to you. Are you going to be all right, going home I mean?'

She had replied: 'Yes thank you, Mandy. I'm perfectly all right now. It was the shock. After all, I was his PA. You've only known him for a few weeks and as a temporary typist.'

The words, a clumsy attempt to restore her dignity, had sounded even to her own ears repressive and pompous. They had been greeted with a shrug and Mandy had left without another word, her loud goodbyes to Mrs Demery echoing across the hall.

Mandy had been notably cheered by her interview with the police and had immediately gone off to discuss it with Mrs Demery, George and Amy in the kitchen. Blackie would have liked to have joined them but had felt that it would be inappropriate to her status to be found gossiping with the junior staff. She knew, too, that they wouldn't have welcomed her intrusion into their confidences and speculations. On the other hand, she hadn't been invited to join the partners when they were closeted in the boardroom and had been seen by no one except

Mrs Demery when they rang for more coffee and sandwiches. It seemed to her that there was no place in Innocent House where she was wanted or could any longer feel at home.

She thought about Mandy's last words. Was that what Mandy had told the police, that Mr Gerard had treated her, Blackie, like a proper bastard? But of course she had. Why should Mandy keep quiet about anything that had happened at Innocent House, Mandy who was the outsider, who had arrived long after the series of practical jokes had begun, who could take a detached, almost pleasurable, interest in all the excitement, secure in the knowledge of her own innocence, unmoved by personal affections, untouched by personal loyalties. Mandy, whose sharp little eyes missed nothing, would have been a gift to the police. And she had been with them a long time, nearly an hour, longer, surely, than her importance in the firm could justify. Once more, and fruitlessly, since nothing now could be changed, Blackie thought over her own interview. She hadn't been among the first to be called. She had had time to prepare herself, to think about what she would say. And she had thought about it. Fear had sharpened her mind.

It had taken place in Miss Claudia's office and only two of the police had been there, the woman detective inspector and a sergeant. Somehow she had expected to see Commander Dalgliesh and his absence had disconcerted her so that she had answered the first questions uncertain whether the interview had really begun, and half expecting him to come in at the door. She was surprised, too, that the interview wasn't being tape-recorded. The police almost always did that in the detective series which were her cousin's favourite viewing at Weaver's Cottage, but perhaps that came later, when they had a prime suspect and were questioning him or her under caution. And then, of course, she would have a lawyer present. Now she was alone. This time there had been no caution, no suggestion that this was anything but an informal preliminary chat. The woman detective inspector had asked most of the questions while the sergeant had made notes, but he had intervened from time to time without deferring to his senior officer and with the quiet assurance which suggested to her that they were used to working together. Both had been very polite, almost gentle, with her but she hadn't been deceived. They were still interrogators and even their formal expressions of sympathy, their gentleness, were part of their technique. She was surprised, looking back on it, how she had known this and known them for the enemies they were even in the tumult of her fear.

They had begun by asking simple preliminary questions about her length of service in the firm, the method of locking the premises at night, the people who had keys and could control the burglar alarms, the general shape of her day, even her arrangements for lunch. Answering them she had begun to feel more at ease even while she knew that they were designed for just that purpose.

Then Detective Inspector Miskin had said: 'You worked for Mr Henry Peverell for twenty-seven years until he died, then transferred to Mr Etienne when he took over as chairman and managing director in January this year. That must have been a difficult change for you and for the firm.'

She was expecting that. She had her answer ready.

'It was different, of course. I had worked for old Mr Peverell for so long that naturally he confided in me. Mr Gerard was younger and had different methods of working. I had to adapt to a different personality. Every PA does that when she gets a change of boss.'

'You were happy to work for Mr Etienne? You liked him?' This was the sergeant, uncompromising dark eyes compelling her own.

She said: 'I respected him.'

'That's not quite the same thing.'

'You can't always like your boss. I think I was getting used to him.'

'And he to you? What about the rest of the firm? He was making changes, wasn't he? Change always causes some pain, particularly in a long-established organization. We know that at the Yard. Weren't there sackings, threats of sackings, a possible move down-river to new premises, the proposal to sell Innocent House?'

She had said: 'You'll have to ask Miss Claudia. Mr Gerard didn't discuss house policy with me.'

'Unlike Mr Peverell. The change from confidante to ordinary secretary can't have been agreeable.'

She didn't reply. Then Inspector Miskin leaned forward and said confidingly, almost as if they were girls together ready to share a feminine secret: 'Tell us about the snake. Tell us about Hissing Sid.'

So she had told them how the snake had been brought into the office about five years previously at Christmas by a temporary shorthand typist whose name and address no one now could remember. She had left it behind after the Christmas party and it hadn't been discovered until six months later stuffed into the back of the drawer of her desk. Blackie had used it to wind round the handles of the door between her office and that of Mr Peverell. He liked the door to be kept ajar so that he could call for her when he wanted her. Mr Peverell had never liked using the telephone. Hissing Sid had become something of a house mascot, taken on the river outing in the summer and to the Christmas party, but she no longer used the snake to keep the door ajar. Mr Etienne preferred it closed.

The sergeant asked: 'Where was the snake usually kept?'

'Usually curled on top of the left-hand filing cabinet. Sometimes it would be hung or curled round one of the handles.'

'Tell us what happened yesterday. Mr Etienne objected, didn't he, to seeing the snake in the office?'

She said, trying to keep her voice calm, 'He came out of his room and saw Hissing Sid drooping from the handle of the top filing cabinet. He thought it looked inappropriate in an office and told me to get rid of it.'

'And what did you do?'

'I put it in my top right-hand drawer.'

Detective Inspector Miskin said: 'This is very important, Miss Blackett, and I'm sure you are intelligent enough to know why. Who was in the office when you put the snake into the drawer?'

'Only Mandy Price who shares the office with me, Mr Dauntsey and Miss Claudia. Afterwards she went with her brother into his office. Mr Dauntsey gave Mandy a letter to type, then left.'

'And no one else?'

'No one else in the room but I expect some of the people who were mentioned what had happened. I don't think that Mandy would have kept quiet. And anyone looking for the snake would probably have thought of my right-hand drawer. I mean, that was the natural place to put the snake.'

'And you didn't think of throwing it away?'

Thinking back on it she knew now that she had reacted too forcibly to the suggestion, that there had been in her voice a note of angry resentment.

'Get rid of Hissing Sid? No, why should I? Mr Peverell used to like the snake. He found it amusing. It wasn't doing any harm in the office. After all, my office isn't a place where the public normally come. I just put it in the top drawer. I thought perhaps I might take it home.'

They had asked about the earlier visit of Esmé Carling and her insistence on seeing Mr Etienne. She realized that someone must have talked, that none of this was new to them, so she told the truth, or as much of the truth as she could bear to speak.

'Mrs Carling isn't one of our easiest authors and she was extremely angry. I think her agent had told her that Mr Etienne didn't wish to publish her latest book. She was insistent on seeing him but I had to explain that he was in the partners' meeting and that it was impossible to disturb them. She retaliated by being extremely offensive about Mr Peverell and our confidential relationship. I think she thought that I had exerted too much influence in the firm.'

'Did she threaten to come back and see Mr Etienne later in the day?'

'No, nothing like that. Of course, she might have insisted on staying until the meeting was over, but she had a signing at a bookshop in Cambridge.'

'Which was, of course, cancelled by a fax from this office sent at twelve-thirty. Did you send that fax, Miss Blackett?'

She stared straight into the grey eyes. 'No, I didn't.'

'Do you know who did send it?'

'I have no idea. It was during our usual lunch hour. I was in the kitchen heating up a Marks & Spencer packet of spaghetti bolognese for my lunch. People were in and out all the time. I can't remember where anyone was at twelve-thirty precisely. I only know I wasn't in the office.'

'And your office wasn't locked?'

'Of course not. We never lock offices during the day.'

And so it had gone on. Questions about the previous practical jokes, questions about when she had left the office the previous night, her journey home, the time she had arrived, how she had spent the evening. None of that was difficult. Eventually Detective Inspector Miskin had brought the interview to an end but with no sense that it had really finished. When it was over, Blackie had found that her legs were trembling and she had had to grasp the side of her chair firmly for a few seconds before she could be confident of walking to the door without staggering.

She had tried twice to ring Weaver's Cottage but there had been no reply. Joan must be somewhere in the village or shopping in the town; but perhaps that was just as well. This was news best broken in person, not over the telephone. She wondered whether there was any point in ringing again to say that she would be home early, but even picking up the receiver seemed too much effort. While she was trying to rouse herself to action, the door opened and Miss Claudia put her head round.

'Oh, you're still here. The police are happy for people to go now. Didn't anyone tell you? The office is closed anyway. Fred Bowling is ready to take you to Charing Cross in the launch.' Seeing Blackie's face, she added: 'Are you all right, Blackie? I mean, do you want someone to go home with you?'

The thought appalled Blackie. Who was there anyway? Mrs Demery, she knew, was still on the premises making endless jugs of coffee for the partners or the police, but she certainly wouldn't welcome being detailed to make an hour and a half journey into Kent. Blackie could picture that journey, the chatter, the questions, arriving together at Weaver's Cottage, Mrs Demery reluctantly escorting her as if she were a delinquent child or a prisoner under surveillance. Joan would probably feel that she had to give Mrs Demery tea. Blackie imagined the three of them in the cottage sitting-room, Mrs Demery giving her highly coloured version of the day's events, garrulous, vulgar, solicitous in turn, almost impossible to get rid of. She said: 'I'm perfectly all right, thank you, Miss Claudia. I'm sorry I was so stupid. It was just the shock.'

'It was a shock for all of us.'

Miss Claudia's voice was colourless. Perhaps the words weren't meant as a rebuke; they only sounded like one. She paused as if there was something else she needed to say, or perhaps felt she should say, then she added: 'Don't come in on Monday if you still feel distressed. There's no real need. If the police want you again they know where to find you.' And then she was gone.

It was the first time that they had been alone together, however briefly, since the discovery of the body and Blackie wished she had found something to say, some word of sympathy. But what was there to say that was at once truthful and sincere? 'I never liked him and he didn't like me, but I'm sorry he's dead.' And was that really true?

At Charing Cross she was used to being borne along on the rush-hour stream of commuter traffic, purposeful and confident. It was strange to be there in the mid-afternoon with a concourse surprisingly quiet for a Friday and a muted air of indecisive timelessness. An elderly couple, overclad for the journey, the woman obviously in her best, were anxiously scanning the departure board, the man dragging a large suitcase on wheels, the case heavily strapped. At a word from the woman he jerked closer and immediately it thudded over. Blackie watched for a moment, as they tried unsuccessfully to right it, then moved across to help them. But even as she grappled with its unwieldy top-heavy bulk she was aware of their anxious and suspicious eyes, as if fearing that she had designs on their underwear. The task completed, they murmured their thanks and moved off, supporting the case between them and from time to time patting it as if pacifying a recalcitrant dog.

The board showed that Blackie had half an hour to wait, just comfortable time for a coffee. Sipping it, smelling the familiar aroma, comforting her hands around the cup, she thought that this unexpected and early journey would normally have been a small indulgence, the unfamiliar emptiness of the station reminding her not of rush-hour discomforts but of childhood holidays, the leisure for coffee, the reassuring certainty of getting home before dark. But all pleasure was now overburdened by the memory of horror, by that nagging, insistent amalgam of fear and guilt. She wondered whether she would ever again be free of it. But at last she was on her way home. She hadn't made up her mind how far she would confide in her cousin. There were things that she couldn't and mustn't tell her, but at least she would be sure of Joan's common-sense reassurance, of the familiar ordered peace of Weaver's Cottage.

The train, half empty, left on time, but later she could recall nothing of the journey or of unlocking the car in the car park at East Marling, nor of the drive to West Marling and the cottage. All she remembered later was driving up to the front gate and·what then met her eyes. She stared in unbelieving horror. In the autumnal sunshine the garden lay before her, violated, desolate, physically torn up, ripped and thrown aside. At first, disorientated by shock, confused by a memory of the great storms of earlier years, she thought that Weaver's Cottage had been struck by a bizarre and localized tornado. But the thought was momentary. This destruction, more petty, more discriminate, was the work of human hands.

She got out of the car, her limbs seeming no longer part of her, and walked stiffly to the gate, clutching at it for support. And now she could see each separate barbarity. The flowering cherry to the right of the gate, its autumn palettes of bright red and yellow staining the air, had been stripped of all its lower branches, the scars on the bark raw as open wounds. The mulberry tree in the middle of the lawn, Joan's special pride, had been similarly violated and the white slatted bench round the trunk smashed and splintered as if jumped on by heavy boots. The rose bushes, perhaps because of the spikiness of their branches, had been left whole but torn up by their roots and thrown into a heap, and the bed of early Michaelmas daisies and white chrysanthemums, which Joan had planned as a pale drift against the dark hedge, lay in swathes over the path. The rose over the porch had defeated them, but they had ripped down both the clematis and the wistaria, making the front of the cottage look oddly naked and defenceless.

The cottage was empty. Blackie went from room to room calling Joan's name long after it was obvious that she wasn't at home. She was beginning to feel the first prick of real anxiety when she heard the bang of the front gate and saw her cousin wheeling her bicycle down the path. Running from the front door to meet her, she cried out: 'What happened? Are you all right?'

Her cousin showed no surprise at seeing her home hours before the usual time. She said grimly: 'You can see what happened. Vandals. Four of them on motor bikes. I nearly caught them at it. They were roaring off as I got back from the village but they were away before I could get their numbers.'

'You've rung the police?'

'Of course. They're coming from East Marling and taking their time. This wouldn't have happened if we'd still had our village policeman. There's no point in their hurrying. They won't catch them. No one will. And if they do, what will happen to them? Nothing but a small fine or a conditional discharge. My God, if the police can't protect us, they'd better let us arm ourselves. If I'd only had a gun.'

Blackie said: 'You can't shoot people just because they've vandalized your garden.'

'Can't you? I could.'

As they moved into the cottage Blackie saw with amazement and embarrassment that Joan had been crying. The signs were unmistakable; the eyes, unnaturally small and lifeless, still bloodshot, her blotched face an unhealthy grey mottled with raw red patches. This had been a violation against which all her customary calmness and stoicism were powerless. She could more easily have borne an attack on her person. But anger had now taken over from grief and Joan's anger was formidable.

'I've been back to the village to see what else they've done. Nothing much, apparently. They went into the Moonraker's Arms for lunch but got so noisy that Mrs Baker refused to serve them further and Baker pushed them out. Then they began riding round in circles on the village green until Mrs Baker went across and told them it wasn't allowed. By then they were being extremely offensive and jeering, revving up their bikes and making a great deal of noise. However, they did eventually leave when Baker went out and threatened to phone the police. I suppose this was their revenge.'

'Suppose they come back?'

'Oh, they won't come back. Why should they? They'll look for something else beautiful to destroy. My God, what sort of generation have we bred? They're better fed, better educated, better looked after than any previous generation and they behave like vicious louts. What's happened to us? And don't talk to me about unemployment. They may have been unemployed but they could afford expensive motor bikes, and two of them had cigarettes hanging out of their mouths.'

'They're not all like that, Joan. You can't judge a whole generation by the few.'

'You're right, of course. I'm glad you're home.'

It was the first time in their nineteen years together that she had expressed a need for Blackie's support and comfort. She went on: 'It was good of Mr Etienne to let you get away early. What happened? Did someone from the village telephone you to tell you? But they couldn't have. You must've been on your way about the time it happened.'

And then Blackie, concisely but vividly, told her.

The news of this bizarre horror had at least the merit of diverting Joan's mind from the violation of her garden. She sank into the nearest chair as if her legs had given way, but she listened in silence, making no exclamations of disgust or surprise. When Blackie had finished she got up and gazed fixedly for a long quarter of a minute into her cousin's eyes as if to reassure herself that Blackie was still in her right mind. Then she said briskly: 'You'd better stay sitting down. I'll put a match to the fire. We've both had a bad shock and it's important to keep warm. And I'll get the whisky. We need to talk this over.'

As Joan settled her more comfortably into the fireside chair, plumping up the cushions and pulling over the footrest with a solicitude rare to her, Blackie couldn't help noticing that her cousin's voice and face expressed less outrage than a certain grim satisfaction and reflected that there was nothing like the vicarious horror of murder to divert attention from one's own less egregious misfortunes.

Forty minutes later, sitting in front of the crackle of the wood fire, soothed by the warmth and the bite of the whisky which she and her cousin kept for emergencies, she felt for the first time distanced from the traumas of the day. On the rug Arabella delicately stretched and curled her paws in ecstasy, her white fur ruddy from the dancing flames. Joan had lit the oven before they settled down together and Blackie could detect the first savoury smell of lamb casserole seeping through the kitchen door. She realized that she was actually hungry, that it might even be possible to enjoy a meal. Her body felt light, as if a weight of guilt and fear had been physically lifted from her shoulders. Despite her resolution she found herself confiding about Sydney Bartrum.

'You see, I knew he was due for the sack. I typed the letter from Mr Gerard to this headhunting firm. Of course I couldn't directly tell Sydney what was being planned. I've always regarded a PA's job as highly confidential, but it didn't seem right not to warn him. Only married just over a year ago and now they've got a baby daughter. And he's over fifty. He must be. It won't be easy for him to get another job. So I left a copy of the letter on my desk when I knew he was due to see Mr Gerard about the estimates. Mr Gerard always kept him waiting, so I went out of the office and gave him his chance. I felt sure he'd read it. It's human instinct to glance at a letter if it's there in front of you.'

But her action, so alien to her character and normal behaviour, hadn't been prompted by pity. She knew that now, and wondered why she hadn't realized it before. What she had felt was a common cause with Sydney Bartrum; they were both victims of Mr Gerard's barely concealed disdain. She had made her first small gesture of defiance. Was it that which had given her courage for that later, more disastrous rebellion?

Joan said: 'But did he read it?'

'He must have done. He didn't give me away – at least Mr Gerard never mentioned the matter to me or rebuked me for my carelessness. But next day Sydney made an appointment to see him and I think asked if his job was safe. I didn't hear their voices but he wasn't in there long, and when he came out he was crying. Think of that, Joan, a grown man crying.' She added, 'That's why I didn't tell the police.'

'About the crying?'

'About the letter. I didn't tell them any of it.'

'And is that all you didn't tell them?'

'Yes,' lied Blackie, 'that's all.'

'I think you were right.' Mrs Willoughby, strong legs planted apart, hand reaching for the whisky bottle, was judicial. 'Why volunteer information which may be irrelevant and even misleading? If they ask you directly, of course, you'll have to tell the truth.'

'That's what I thought. And we can't even be sure yet that it was murder. I mean he could have died from natural causes, a heart-attack maybe, and someone put the snake around his neck afterwards. That's what most people seem to think. It's exactly the kind of thing the office prankster would do.'

But Mrs Willoughby immediately rejected this convenient theory. 'Oh, I think we can be reasonably sure that it was murder. Whatever happened to the body afterwards you wouldn't have had the police there for so long, and at such senior level, if they had any real doubt. This Commander Dalgliesh, I've heard of him. They wouldn't send an officer of his seniority if they thought it was a natural death. You say, of course, that Lord Stilgoe was the one who telephoned New Scotland Yard. Perhaps that may have influenced the police. A title still has some power. There's always suicide or accident, of course, but neither seems likely from what you've told me. No, if you ask me, this was murder, and an inside job.'

Blackie said: 'But not Sydney. Sydney Bartrum wouldn't hurt a fly.'

'Maybe. But he might swat something a great deal larger and more dangerous. Anyway, the police will check up on all your alibis. It's a pity you went late-night shopping in the West End yesterday and didn't come straight home. I suppose there's no one at Liberty or Jaeger who can speak for you?'

'I don't think so. You see I didn't buy anything. I was only looking, and the stores were very crowded.'

'It's ludicrous, of course, to think that you had anything to do with it, but the police have to treat everyone on the same footing, at least initially. Oh well, there's no point in worrying until we know the exact time of death. Who saw him last? Has that been established?'

'Miss Claudia, I think. She's usually among the last to leave.'

'Except, of course, for his murderer. I wonder how he managed to entice the victim up to the little archives office. I suppose it is where he died. Assuming he was strangled or suffocated with Hissing Sid, then the murderer must have overpowered him first. A strong young man doesn't lie down meekly allowing himself to be murdered. He could have been drugged, of course, or perhaps stunned by a blow sufficiently powerful to knock him out, but not strong enough to break the skin.'

Mrs Willoughby, an avid reader of detective stories, was familiar with fictional murderers adept at this difficult procedure. She went on: 'The drug could have been administered in his afternoon tea. It would need to be tasteless and very slow-acting. Difficult. Or, of course, he could have been throttled with something soft which wouldn't leave a mark, a pair of tights or a stocking. It would be no use for the murderer to use a cord, the mark would show very plainly under the snake. I expect the police have thought of all that.'

'I am sure, Joan, that they have thought of everything.'

Sipping her whisky, Blackie reflected that there was something strangely reassuring about Joan's uninhibited interest in and specula-tion about the crime. Not for nothing were there those five shelves of crime paperbacks in her bedroom, Agatha Christie, Dorothy L. Sayers, Margery Allingham, Ngaio Marsh, Josephine Tey and the few modern writers whom Joan considered fit to join those Golden Age practitioners in fictional murder. After all, why should Joan feel a personal grief? She had only been to Innocent House once, three years previously when she had attended the staff Christmas party. She knew few of the staff except by name. And as she cogitated, the horror of Innocent House began to seem unreal, unfrightening, an elegant literary concoction, without grief, without pain, without loss, the guilt and horror disinfected and reduced to an ingenious puzzle. She stared into the leaping flames from which the image of Miss Marple seemed to rise, handbag protectively clutched to her bosom, the gentle wise old eyes gazing into hers, assuring her that there was nothing to be afraid of, that everything would be all right.

The fire and the whisky combined to induce a somnolent contentment, so that her cousin's voice, fitfully heard, seemed to be coming from a long distance. If they didn't begin dinner soon she would be asleep. Rousing herself she said: 'Isn't it time we thought about eating?'

30

They had met at 6.15 on the steps leading down to the river by Greenwich station between a high wall and the ramp of a boat-house. It was a good and private place to meet. There was a small gritty beach and now, driving home and far from the river, he could still hear the gentle splash of the small spent waves, the grinding and tinny clatter of the pebbles, the backward suck of the tide. Gabriel Dauntsey had arrived first for the assignation but hadn't turned as Bartrum moved up beside him. When he spoke his voice was gentle, almost apologetic.

'I thought we ought to talk, Sydney. I saw you letting yourself into Innocent House yesterday evening. My bathroom window overlooks Innocent Lane. I looked out by chance and glimpsed you. It was about six-forty.'

Sydney had known what he was going to hear and now when the words were spoken he heard them with something very like relief.

He had said, willing Dauntsey to believe him: 'But I came out again almost at once. I swear it. If you'd waited, if you'd been watching for only a minute more you would have seen me. I didn't get any further than the reception room. I lost my nerve. I told myself that it wouldn't have been any use arguing and pleading. Nothing would have moved him, nothing would have done any good. I swear to you, Mr Dauntsey, that I never set eyes on him last night after I left my office.'

'Yes, it wouldn't have done any good. Gerard wasn't susceptible to pleading.' He added, 'Or to threats.'

'How could I threaten him? I was powerless. He could sack me the next week and I couldn't stop him. And if I did anything more to antagonize him he'd have given me one of those cunningly worded references which you can't contest but which make sure that you never get another job. He had me in his power. I'm glad he's dead. If I were a religious man I'd go down on my knees and thank God that he's dead. But I didn't kill him. You have to believe me. If you don't, Mr Dauntsey, my God, who will?'

The figure at his side didn't move or speak but stood staring out over the black waste of the river. At last, humbly, he had asked: 'What are you going to do?'

'Nothing. I had to see you to find out whether you've told the police, whether you propose to tell them. I was asked, of course, whether I'd seen anyone going into Innocent House. We all were. I lied. I lied and I'm proposing to go on lying, but it will be pointless if you've told them or are likely to lose your nerve.'

'No, I didn't tell them. I said I got home at the usual time, just before seven. I rang my wife as soon as I heard the news, before the police arrived, and told her to confirm that I was home on time if anyone rang to ask. It was lucky I was the first one in. I had the office to myself. I hated having to ask her to lie but she didn't think it mattered. She knew that I was innocent, that I hadn't done anything to be ashamed of. I'll explain more fully to her tonight. She'll understand.'

'You rang her before you knew that his death might be murder?'

'I thought it was murder from the start. The snake, that half-naked body. How could that be a natural death?' He added simply: 'Thank you for keeping silent, Mr Dauntsey. I won't forget this.'

'You don't need to thank me. It's the sensible thing to do. I'm not doing you a favour. You don't have to be grateful. It's a matter of common sense, that's all. If the police waste time suspecting the innocent they'll have less chance of catching the guilty. And I haven't quite the confidence I once had that they don't make mistakes.'

He had said, greatly daring: 'And you care about that? You want them to catch the guilty?'

'I want them to find out who put that snake round Gerard's neck and stuffed its head in his mouth. That was an abomination, a desecration of death. I prefer the guilty to be convicted and the innocent vindicated. I suppose most people do. That, after all, is what we mean by justice. But I don't feel personally outraged by Gerard's death, not by any death, not any longer. I doubt whether I have the capacity to feel strongly about anything. I didn't murder him; I have done more than my share of killing. I don't know who did, but this murderer and I have something in common. We didn't have to look our victim in the eyes. There's something particularly ignoble about a murderer who doesn't even have to face the reality of what he has done.'

He had brought himself to the final humiliation: 'My job, Mr

Dauntsey. Do you think it's safe now? It is important to me. You don't know what Miss Etienne has in mind – what any of the partners has in mind? I know that there have to be changes. I could learn new methods if you think it necessary. And I don't mind if you bring someone in over my head if he's better qualified. I can work loyally as a subordinate.' He added with bitterness: 'That's all Mr Gerard thought I was good for.'

Dauntsey had said: 'I don't know what will be decided but I dare say we'll make no major changes for at least six months. And if I have anything to do with it, your job will be safe.'

Then they had turned together and walked without speaking to the side road where both had parked their cars.

31

The house which Sydney and Julie Bartrum had chosen, and which he was buying on the highest mortgage obtainable, was close to Buckhurst Hill Station on a sloping narrow road which was more like a country lane than a suburban street. It was a conventional 1930s house with a front bay window and porch and narrow back garden. Everything in it he and Julie had chosen together. Neither had brought anything from the past except memories. It was this home, this hard-won security, which Gerard Etienne had threatened to take from him with so much else. If he lost his job at fifty-two, what hope would there be of an equal salary? His lump sum would drain away, month after month, until even paying the mortgage became an impossible burden.

She came out of the kitchen as soon as she heard his key in the lock. As always she put out both arms and kissed him on the cheek, but tonight her arms were taut and she clung to him almost desperately.

'Darling, what is it? What's happened? I didn't like to phone you back. You said not to ring.'

'No, that wouldn't have been wise. Darling, there's nothing for you to worry about. Everything is going to be all right.'

'But you said that Mr Etienne is dead. Killed.'

'Come into the sitting-room, Julie, and I'll tell you.'

She sat very close to him and very still while he spoke. Afterwards she said: 'They can't think you had anything to do with it, darling. I mean, that's ridiculous, that's stupid. You wouldn't hurt a soul. You're kind, good, gentle. They can't believe that.'

'Of course they won't. But innocent people do sometimes get harassed, questioned and put under suspicion. Sometimes they even get arrested and tried. It does happen. And I was the last person to leave the office. I had some important work to do and stayed a little late. That's why I rang as soon as I heard the news. It seemed sensible to tell the police that I was home at the usual time.'

'Of course it was, darling. You're right. I'm glad you did.'

He was a little surprised that his request to her to lie had caused her no unease, no guilt. Perhaps women lied more easily than men provided they believed the cause was just. He needn't have worried that he was causing her a crisis of conscience. Like him, she knew where her allegiance lay.

He said: 'Has anyone been in touch – anyone from the police?'

'Someone rang. He said he was a Sergeant Robbins. He just asked what time you got back last night. Nothing else. He didn't give me any information or say that Mr Gerard was dead.'

'And you didn't let on that you knew?'

'Of course not. You'd warned me. I did ask what it was all about and he said you would explain when you got home, that you were all right and that I wasn't to worry.'

So the police had been quick off the mark. Well, that was to be expected. They had wanted to check before he had had time to arrange an alibi.

He said: 'You see what I mean, darling. It really was wise to be prepared.'

'Of course it was. But you don't really think Mr Gerard was murdered?'

'They don't seem to know how he died. Murder's a possibility, but only one. He could have had a heart attack and the snake been put round his neck afterwards.'

'Darling, how terrible! That's a horrible thing for anyone to do. It's wicked.'

He said: 'Don't think about it. It's nothing to do with us. It can't touch us. If we stick to our story, there's nothing anyone can do.'

She had no idea how closely it touched them. This death was his salvation. He hadn't confided in her about the risk to his job or his hatred and fear of Etienne. This had partly been because he didn't want to worry her, but he knew that the main motive had been pride. He needed her to believe that he was successful, respected, invaluable to the firm. Now she need never know the truth. He decided, too, to say nothing of the earlier interview with Dauntsey. Why worry her? Everything was going to be all right.

As usual before supper, they went up together to look at their sleeping daughter. The baby was in the nursery at the back of the house, which he with Julie's help had decorated. She had recently been promoted from the basket crib to the railed cot and lay, as always, pillowless and supine. Julie had explained that this was the recommended position. She didn't speak the words 'to avoid cot death', but both of them knew what she meant. That anything should happen to the child was their greatest unspoken horror. He put out a hand and touched the downy head. It was incredible that any human hair could feel so soft, any scalp so vulnerable. Overcome with love, he wanted to pick up the child and hold her against his cheek, to enfold mother and daughter in an embrace that was strong, eternal and unbreakable, to shield them against all the terrors of the present and all the terrors to come.

This house was his kingdom. He told himself that he had won it by love but he felt for it some of the fierce possessiveness of a conqueror. It was his by right and he would kill a dozen Gerard Etiennes before he lost it. No one before Julie had ever found him lovable. Plain, scrawny, humourless, and shy, he knew that he wasn't lovable, the years in the children's home had taught him that. Your father didn't die, your mother didn't walk out on you, if you were lovable. The staff at the home had done their best according to the received wisdom of the times, but the children hadn't been loved. The caring, like the food, had been carefully allocated to go round. The children knew that they were rejects. He had taken in that knowledge with his porridge. After the children's home there had been a succession of landladies, of bed-sitting-rooms, of small rented flats, of evening classes and examinations, watery cups of coffee, solitary meals in inexpensive restaurants, breakfast cooked in a shared kitchen, of solitary pleasures, solitary, unsatisfying, guilt-inducing sex.

He felt now like a man who all his life had been living under-ground in partial darkness. With Julie he had come up into the sunlight, his eyes dazed by an unimagined world of light and sound and colour and sensation. He was glad that Julie had been previously married, but in their love-making she managed to make him feel that it was she who was inexperienced, who was finding fulfilment for the first time. He told himself that perhaps she was. Sex with her had been a revelation. He could never have believed that it was at once so simple and so marvellous. He was glad, too, with a half-guilty relief, that her first marriage had been unhappy and that Terry had walked out on her. He need never fear that she was comparing him with a first love romanticized and immortalized by death. They spoke rarely of the past; for both of them, the people who lived and walked and spoke in that past were different people. Once, early in their marriage, she had said to him: 'I used to pray that I could find someone to love, someone I could make happy and who could make me happy. Someone who would give me a child. I had almost given up hope. And then I found you. It seems like a miracle, darling, the answer to a prayer.' Her words had exalted him. He felt for a moment as if he was the agent of God himself. He who all his life had known only what it was to feel powerless was filled with an intoxication of power.

He had been happy at Peverell Press until Gerard Etienne took over. He knew himself to be a valued, conscientious accountant. He worked long hours of unpaid overtime. He did what was required of him by Jean-Philippe Etienne and Henry Peverell; and what they required was well within his powers. But then one had retired and the other died, and the young Gerard Etienne had taken his seat in the managing director's chair. He had played little part in the firm for the previous few years but he had been watching, learning, biding his time, taking his Master's degree in business administration, formulating plans which didn't include a fifty-two-year-old accountant with minimal qualifications. Gerard Etienne, young, successful, handsome, rich, who through all his privileged life had grasped what he wanted without compunction, had been going to take from him, Sydney Bartrum, everything which made his life worthwhile. But Gerard Etienne was dead, lying in a police mortuary with a snake stuffed into his mouth.

He tightened his arm around his wife and said: 'Darling, let's go down to supper. I'm hungry.'

32

The street entrance to Wapping Police Station is so unobtrusive that it can easily be missed by the uninitiated. From the Thames its agreeable and unpretentious brick façade and the domestic note of a bay window overlooking the river suggests an old and accommodating utility, the residence of an eighteenth-century merchant, with a preference for living above his warehouse. Standing at the window of the incident room, Daniel looked down at the wide ramp, the three bays of the floating pier with its flotilla of police launches and the discreetly sited stainless steel bath trolley for the reception and hosing-down of drowned bodies, and reflected that few perceptive travellers by water would fail to recognize the function of the house.

He had been busy since he and Sergeant Robbins had arrived, passing through the vehicle parking lot and up the iron staircase into the subdued busyness of the station. He had set up the computers, cleared desks for Dalgliesh, himself and Kate, had spoken to the coroner's officer about arrangements for the post-mortem and the inquest and had liaised with the forensic science laboratory. The photographs taken at the scene had been pinned to the noticeboard, their stark shadowless clarity seeming to reduce horror to an exercise in photographic technique. He had also spoken to Lord Stilgoe in his private room at the London Clinic. Happily the effect of a general anaesthetic, the cosseting of the nurses and the number of his visitors had temporarily diverted Lord Stilgoe's attention from the murder and he had received Daniel's report with surprising equanimity and had not, as expected, demanded Dalgliesh's immediate appearance at his bedside. Daniel had also put the Met's Press Bureau in the picture. When the story broke they would be responsible for setting up press conferences and for liaison with the media. There were a number of details which the police in the interests of their inquiry had no intention of divulging, but the bizarre use of the snake would be known to everyone at Innocent House by tomorrow at the latest and would be round the publishing houses of London and into the papers within hours. The Press Bureau was likely to be busy.

Robbins had moved up beside him, obviously taking his senior's inactivity as the justification for a break. He said: 'It's interesting to be here, isn't it? The oldest police station in the United Kingdom.'

'If you're itching to tell me that the River Police were established in 1798, thirty-one years before the Met, then I know.'

'I don't know whether you've seen their museum, sir. It's in the carpenter's shop of the old boatyard. I was taken round it when I was at Preliminary Training School. They've got some interesting exhibits. Leg irons, police cutlasses, old uniforms, a surgeon's chest, early nineteenth-century records and accounts of the *Princess Alice* disaster. It's a fascinating collection.'

'That probably accounts for the less than enthusiastic welcome. They probably suspect the Met curator of wanting to get his hands on it, or suspect we might nick the choicest exhibits. I like their new toys though.'

Below them the river had erupted into foaming tumult. A couple of high-speed semi-rigid inflatables, bright orange, black and grey, with their crew of two in crash helmets and fluorescent green jackets, skimmed, veered and circled the police launches like dangerous adult playthings before roaring downstream.

Robbins said: 'No seats. I should think those back rolls are hard on the muscles. They must be doing close on forty knots. Do you think there will be time to have another look at the museum, sir?'

'I shouldn't rely on it.'

In Daniel's opinion Sergeant Robbins, who had come into the police service straight from his red-brick university, with a second-class degree in history, was almost too good to be true. Here surely was the epitome of every mother's favourite son; fresh-faced, ambitious without being ruthless, a devout Methodist, engaged, so it was rumoured, to a girl from his church. No doubt after a virtuous engagement they would marry and produce admirable children who would go to the right schools, pass the right exams, cause no grief or pain to their parents and eventually end up interfering with people for their own good, as teachers, social workers, and possibly even policemen. In Daniel's book Robbins should have long ago resigned, disillusioned by a macho ethos which could so easily degenerate into violence, by the necessary compromises and fudges, and by the job itself with its daily evidence of the sleaziness of crime and man's inhumanity to man. Instead he was apparently both unshockable and idealistic. Daniel supposed that he had a secret life; most people did. It was hardly possible to live without one. But Robbins was singularly adept at keeping his hidden. Daniel reflected that it would pay the Home Office to parade him round the country to persuade idealistic school-leavers of the advantages of a police career.

They settled back to work. There was very little time before they were due at the mortuary, but there was no justification for wasting it. Daniel sat down to go through Etienne's papers. Even at his first and cursory glance he had been surprised at the amount of work Gerard Etienne had taken on. The firm published about sixty books a year with a total staff of thirty. Publishing was an alien world to him. He had no idea whether this was average but the administrative structure seemed odd and Etienne's load disproportionate. De Witt was the editorial director with Gabriel Dauntsey assisting him as poetry editor but otherwise, apparently, doing little except for his job in the archives. Claudia Etienne was responsible for sales and publicity, including personnel, and Frances Peverell for contracts and rights. Gerard Etienne, as chairman and managing director, had overseen production, accounts and the warehouse and had had by far the heaviest load.

Daniel was interested, too, in how far Etienne had pushed forward his plans to sell Innocent House. The negotiations with Hector Skolling had been under way for some months and were now advanced. Looking through the minutes of the monthly partners' meetings, he could see little reference to much that was happening. While Dalgliesh and Kate had been busy with the formal interviews, he had learned almost as much by listening to Mrs Demery's gossip and talking to George and the few staff who were in the building. The partners might wish to present the picture of a generally united board with a common purpose, but the evidence so far showed a very different reality.

The phone rang. It was Kate. She was going back to her flat to change. AD had been called to the Yard. They would both see Daniel at the mortuary.

33

The local authority mortuary had recently been modernized but the exterior remained unaltered. It was a single-storey building of grey London brick approached from a short cul-de-sac, the forecourt bounded by an eight-foot wall. Neither noticeboard nor street number proclaimed its function; those who had business there knew how to find it. It presented to the curious an impression of some dull and not particularly flourishing enterprise where goods were delivered in plain vans and unpacked with discretion. To the right of the door was a garage, large enough to accommodate two undertaker's vans, from which double doors led to a small reception area with a waiting room to the left. Here Dalgliesh, arriving a minute before 6.30, found Kate and Daniel already waiting. An attempt had been made to make the waiting-room welcoming with a low round table, four comfortable chairs, and a large TV set which Dalgliesh had never found turned off. Perhaps its purpose was less entertainment than therapy; the lab technicians in their unpredictable spells of leisure needed to exchange, however momentarily, the silent corruption of death for the bright ephemeral images of the living world.

He saw that Kate had exchanged her usual tweed jacket and trousers for denim jeans and jacket, and that her thick plait of blonde hair had been tucked inside a peaked jockey cap. He knew why. He too was informally dressed. The half-sweet, half-citrus smell of the disinfectant became almost unnoticeable after the first half hour but lingered for days in the clothes, permeating his wardrobe with the smell of death. He had early learned to wear nothing that couldn't be thrown into the washing machine, while he obsessively showered, lifting his face under the power-jet as if the sting of the water could physically wash away more than the smell and the sights of the last two hours. He was due to meet the Commissioner at the Minister's room in the House of Commons at eight o'clock. Somehow he must find time to get back to his Queenhithe flat to shower before then.

He remembered vividly – how could he not? – the first post-mortem he had attended as a young detective constable. The murder victim had been a twenty-two-year-old prostitute and there had, he recalled, been difficulty over the formal identification of the body since the police had been unable to trace either relatives or close friends. The white undernourished body stretched out on the tray, with the weals of the lash purple as stigmata, had seemed in its pale frigidity the ultimate mute witness to male inhumanity. Looking round at the crowded PM room, the phalanx of officialdom, he had reflected that Theresa Burns was receiving in death a great deal more attention from the agents of the state than she had received in life. The pathologist then had been Doc McGregor, one of the old school of egregious individualists, a rigid Presbyterian who had insisted on conducting all his post-mortems in the spiritual, if not the physical, odour of sanctity. Dalgliesh remembered his rebuke to a technician who had responded with a brief laugh to a colleague's muttered witticism. 'I'll have no laughter in my mortuary. It's no a frog I'm dissecting here.'

Doc McGregor would have no secular music while he worked and had a preference for the metrical psalms whose lugubrious tempo tended to slow down the speed of the work as well as depressing the spirits. But it had been one of McGregor's post-mortems – that of a murdered child – accompanied by Fauré's *Pie Jesu* that had given Dalgliesh one of his best poems, and he supposed that for this he should be grateful. Wardle cared little what music was played while he worked, so long as it wasn't pop, and today they were to listen to the familiar anodyne melodies of Classic FM.

There were two post-mortem rooms, one with four dissecting tables and a single room. It was this which Reginald Wardle preferred for murder cases, but the room was small and there was the inevitable crush as the experts in violent death jostled for space; the pathologist and his assistant, the two mortuary technicians, four police officers, the laboratory liaison officer, the photographer and assistant, the scene-of-crime officer and fingerprint men, and a trainee pathologist whom Dr Wardle introduced as Dr Manning and announced would take the notes. He had a dislike of using the overhead microphone. In their fawn cotton overalls the group looked, thought Dalgliesh, like a cluster of dilatory removal men. Only the plastic overshoes suggested that theirs might be a more sinister assignment. The technicians were wearing their head-straps but with the visors still up. Later when they received the organs into the bucket and weighed them the visors would be down, protection against AIDS and the more common risk of hepatitis B. Dr Wardle as usual wore only his pale green apron over slacks and shirtsleeves. Like most forensic pathologists he was cavalier about his own safety.

The body, parcelled and sealed in its plastic shroud, lay on the trolley in the outer room. At a word from Dalgliesh the technicians slashed the plastic and tore it aside. There was a small explosion of air like an expelling sigh, and the plastic crackled like a charge of electricity. The body lay exposed like the contents of some great Christmas cracker. The eyes were duller now; only the snake taped to the cheek, its head gagging the mouth, seemed to have life or vitality. Dalgliesh was visited by a strong desire to see it removed – only then could the body be restored to some dignity – and he wondered briefly why it was that he had been insistent it remain in place until the autopsy. It was all he could do to prevent himself from reaching down and tearing it away. Instead he made his formal identification establishing the chain of evidence.

'This is the body I first saw at nine forty-eight on Friday the fifteenth of October at Innocent House, Innocent Walk, Wapping.'

Dalgliesh had a considerable respect for Marcus and Len, both as men and as mortuary technicians. There were some people, a number of them police officers, who found it difficult to believe that a man could voluntarily work in a mortuary unless to satisfy some eccentric if not sinister psychological compulsion, but Marcus and Len seemed blessedly free even from the crude graveyard humour which some professionals used as a defence against horror or distaste, and did their work with a matter-of-fact competence, quietness and dignity which he found impressive. He had seen, too, how much trouble they took to make a body presentable before the next of kin came to view. Many of the bodies they watched being clinically dismembered would be those of the old, diseased, or dead by natural causes, small tragedies, perhaps, to a loved one, but hardly a cause for distress to a stranger. But how, he wondered, did they cope psychologically with the murdered young, the violated, the victims of accident or violence? In an age when every sorrow, even those natural to the human condition, could not apparently be endured without counselling who, if anyone, counselled Marcus and Len? But at least they would be free from the temptation to deify the popular, the rich and the famous. Here in the mortuary was the final equality. What mattered to Marcus and Len was not the number of eminent doctors who had clustered around the deathbed, nor the splendour of the planned obsequies, but the state of decay and whether the corpse would need to be accommodated in the obese refrigerator.

The tray holding the now naked body had been placed on the floor so that the photographer could more easily move around it. When he nodded his satisfaction with the first shots the two technicians gently turned the corpse over, taking care not to dislodge the snake. Finally, with the body face-upwards, the tray was lifted and placed on the supports at the foot of the dissecting table, the round hole over the drain. Doc Wardle made his usual general examination of the body, then turned his attention to the head. He stripped away the tape, gently removed the snake as if it were a biological specimen of extraordinary interest, and began his examination of the mouth, looking, thought Dalgliesh, like an over-enthusiastic dentist. He remembered what Kate Miskin had once confided to him when she had first started working for him and confidence came more easily to her; that it was this part of the autopsy, not the later systematic removal and weighing of all the main organs, that made her squeamish, as if the dead nerves were merely quiescent and could still react as they had in life to the gloved, probing fingers. He was aware of Kate standing a little behind him, but did not glance at her. He could be sure that she wouldn't faint, either now or later, but he guessed that, like him, she was feeling something more than a professional interest in the dismemberment of what had been a young and healthy man – and felt again a small ache of regret that police work demanded so much of gentleness and innocence.

Suddenly Doc Wardle gave a low grunt that was almost a growl, his distinctive noise when he found something of interest.

'Take a look at this, Adam. On the roof of the mouth. A distinct scratch. Post-mortem by the look of it.'

At the scene it had been 'Commander' but now, king of his domain, at ease as always with his work, he had reverted to Dalgliesh's Christian name.

Dalgliesh bent low. He said: 'It looks as if something sharp-edged was forced in or out of the mouth after death. I'd say out by the look of the mark.'

'Difficult to be 100 per cent sure, of course, but that's what it looks like to me. The direction of the scratch is from the back of the palate almost to the top teeth.' Doc Wardle stood aside so that Kate and Daniel could take their turn at peering into the mouth. He added: 'Impossible to say exactly when it happened, of course, except that it was after death. Etienne may have put the thing – whatever it was – in his mouth but someone else took it out.'

Dalgliesh said: 'And with some force, and possibly in a hurry. If it had happened before rigor mortis set in the removal would have been quicker and easier. How much strength would it take to force open the jaw after rigor was established?'

'It's not difficult, of course, and easier if the mouth were partly open and he could get his fingers in and use both hands. A child couldn't do it, but then you aren't looking for a child.'

Kate said: 'If the snake-head was pushed in immediately the sharp object was removed and soon after death couldn't we expect some visible blood stain on the fabric? How much seeping of blood would there have been after death?'

Doc Wardle said: 'Immediately after death? Not a lot. But he wasn't alive when that mark was made.'

They peered at the snake's head together. Dalgliesh said: 'This thing has been played about with at Innocent House for nearly five years. It's easier to imagine a stain than to see it. There's no obvious blood. The lab may give us something. If it was placed in the mouth as soon as the object was pulled out there should be some biological evidence.'

Daniel asked: 'Any idea, Doc, of the kind of object?'

'Well, there are no other marks on the soft tissues or the back of the teeth that I can see, which suggests that it was something that he could fairly easily fit into his mouth, though why the hell he would have wanted to beats me. Still, that's your department.'

Daniel said: 'If it was something he wanted to conceal, why not slip it into his trouser pocket? Hiding it in his mouth meant keeping silent. He could hardly speak normally even with a small object between his tongue and the roof of his mouth. But suppose he knew that he was going to die. Suppose he was trapped in that room with the gas pouring out, the key to the gas tap missing, a window he couldn't open . . .'

Kate broke in: 'But the object would be found on the body later even if he only put it in his pocket.'

'Unless his murderer knew it was there and came back for it. Then hiding it in the mouth made sense, even if it was something the murderer didn't know existed. Putting it in his mouth made sure that it would be found at the PM if not before.'

Kate said: 'But he did know – the murderer I mean. He came back to look for it and I think he found it. He forced open the jaw to get it out, then used the snake to make it look like the work of the practical joker.'

She and Daniel were concentrated on each other. The room could have been empty except for those two. Daniel said: 'But could he really expect that we wouldn't find the scrape?'

'Oh come on, Daniel. He didn't know that he'd scratched the mouth. What he did know was that he had to break the rigor and that we wouldn't miss that. So he used the snake. And if it hadn't been for that scratch we would have fallen for it. We're looking for a murderer who knew something about the timing of rigor and expected the body to be found relatively soon. If the body was to lie undisturbed for another day the snake wouldn't have been necessary.'

They were, Dalgliesh knew, in danger of theorizing in advance of all the facts. The autopsy hadn't yet been completed. There was still no confirmation of the cause of death but he felt reasonably sure, and so, he knew, did Doc Wardle, what the cause of death would prove to be.

Kate asked: 'What kind of object? Something small, sharp-edged? A key? A bunch of keys? A small metal box?'

Dalgliesh said quietly, 'Or the cassette of a small tape recorder?'

Dalgliesh left before the post-mortem was completed. Doc Wardle was explaining to his assistant that the blood samples for the lab must be taken from the femoral vein, not the heart, and why. Dalgliesh doubted whether there was anything further to learn from the autopsy, and if there was he would be told soon enough. There were papers he needed to look over before the meeting at eight o'clock in the House and time was tight. It would have been pointless to go first to the Yard before going to his flat and his driver, William, had collected his briefcase from his office and was waiting now in the forecourt, his amiable chubby face displaying carefully controlled anxiety.

The heavy rain of the afternoon had abated to a thin continuous drizzle and with the window half open he tasted the salt tang of the Thames. The traffic lights on the Embankment smudged the air with crimson and, waiting for them to change, a police horse, its flanks gleaming, stamped its delicate hoofs on the shining tarmac. Darkness had come striding over the city, transforming it into a phantasma-goria of light in which the streets and squares shivered into moving necklaces of white, red and green. He opened his briefcase and drew out his papers for a quick reading of the salient arguments. It was time to shift the gears of his mind to a more immediate – and perhaps in the end more important – preoccupation. Usually he did not find this difficult, but now the earlier images of the mortuary persisted.

Something small, something sharp, had been wrenched out of Etienne's mouth after rigor had set in in the top part of the body. It was possible that object had been a cassette; the removal of the tape recorder certainly suggested that possibility. The inference was that Etienne had dictated the name of his murderer and the killer had later returned to remove the evidence. But his mind rejected this simple hypothesis. Etienne's murderer had taken care that nothing should remain in the room which would enable him to leave a message. The floor and the mantelpiece had been cleaned, all the papers had been removed, Etienne's diary with the gold pencil attached had been stolen the day before. The killer had thought even of that. Etienne hadn't even been able to scrawl his or her name on the bare wooden floor. Why then should the murderer have been so stupid as to leave a tape recorder ready for his victim's use?

There was, of course, another explanation. The tape recorder could have been there for a specific purpose, and if it had been then the case promised to be even more puzzling and more intriguing than it had at first appeared.

34

It was after 10.30 before Dalgliesh returned to the Wapping incident room and Robbins had been sent off duty. Kate and Daniel had bought sandwiches on their drive back from the mortuary and made do with them and coffee as the night wore on. They had already worked a twelve-hour day but it wasn't over yet. Dalgliesh would want to assess progress and have a clear idea where they were going before they entered on the next stage of the enquiry.

He sat for ten minutes studying the papers Daniel had brought from Gerard Etienne's study, then, closing the file without comment, looked at his watch then said: 'Right. So what tentative conclusions have you reached from the facts as far as we know them?'

Daniel broke in immediately as Kate had expected him to. That didn't worry her. They were of equal rank but she had seniority in service and felt no need to emphasize it. There was an advantage in going first; it prevented other people from taking credit for your ideas and showed keenness. On the other hand, there was a certain wisdom in biding one's time. Daniel was taking care over his spiel; probably, she thought, he had been mentally practising it since their return from the mortuary.

He said: 'Natural death, suicide, accident or murder? The first two are out. We don't need the laboratory reports to be sure that this was carbon monoxide poisoning, the post-mortem told us that. Told us too that, otherwise, he died healthy. There is absolutely nothing to indicate suicide, so I don't think we need waste time on that.

'So we come to accident. If this is an accidental death, what are we expected to believe? That Etienne decided for some reason to work up in the archives office, left his jacket on the chair downstairs and his keys in his desk drawer. That he felt cold, lit the fire with matches which we've no evidence he had on him, then got so engrossed in his work that he didn't realize that the fire had started to malfunction until too late. Apart from the obvious inconsistencies, if it happened that way, I suggest that he'd have been found slumped over the table, not lying half-naked on his back with his head towards the fire. At this stage I'm not taking account of the snake. I think we have to make a clear distinction between what happened at the time of death and what happened to the body afterwards. Obviously someone found him after rigor had set in to the top part of the body, but there's no evidence that the person who stuffed the snake in his mouth took off his shirt or moved him from the table to where he was found.'

Kate said: 'He must have taken off his own shirt. It was clutched in his right hand. It looked as if he had taken it off with some idea of using it to put out the fire. I mean, look at the photograph. The right hand is still holding part of the shirt, the rest of it trails across the body. It looks to me as if he died on his face and his killer turned over the body, perhaps using his foot, and then prised open the mouth. Look at the position of the knees, slightly bent. He didn't die in that position. It's consistent with the post-mortem findings that he died on his face. He was crawling across the room towards the fire.'

'OK, I agree. But he couldn't have hoped to put it out, not that way. The shirt would have caught fire.'

'I know he couldn't, but that's what it looks like. Snuffing out the fire may have seemed possible to his confused mind.'

Dalgliesh didn't intervene but listened while they argued it out.

Daniel said: 'That suggests he knew what was happening to him. But if he did, the obvious thing was to open the door and let in air, then turn off the gas.'

'But suppose the door had been locked on the outside and the tap removed from the gas fire. When he tried to open the high window the cord snapped because someone had frayed it to make damned sure it would as soon as it was tugged with any force. The murderer must have first moved out the chairs and table so that Etienne couldn't climb on them to reach the window and break the glass. The window was stuck fast. He couldn't have opened it if he had, not unless he had something to bash it with.'

Daniel said: 'The tape recorder perhaps?'

'Too small, too fragile. All the same, I agree he would have tried. He could have battered the glass with his hands, but there was no evidence of bruising of the knuckles. I think that the furniture must have been moved before he entered the room. We know from the marks on the wall that the table was normally a few inches to the left.'

'That isn't proof. The cleaner could have moved it.'

'I didn't say that it was proof, but it is significant. Both Gabriel

Dauntsey and Mrs Demery said that the table wasn't in the usual position.'

'That doesn't let them out as suspects.'

'I didn't say that it did. Dauntsey is an obvious suspect. No one had better opportunity than he. But if Dauntsey moved out the chairs and table, surely he would have taken trouble to place the table back precisely where it was. Unless, of course, he was in a hurry.' She broke off, then turned to Dalgliesh excitedly. 'And of course, sir, he was in a hurry. He had to be back in the time it would take to bath.'

Daniel said: 'We're going too fast. It's all conjecture.'

'I'd call it logical deduction.'

Dalgliesh spoke for the first time. 'Kate's theory is reasonable; it conforms with all the facts as we know them. But what we haven't got is a scintilla of hard evidence. And don't let's forget the snake. How far have you got with finding out who knew that it was in Miss Blackett's desk drawer, apart of course from Miss Blackett, Mandy Price, Dauntsey and the two Etiennes?'

It was Kate who replied. 'The news was round the office by the afternoon, sir. Mandy told Mrs Demery that Etienne had told Miss Blackett to get rid of it when they were making coffee together in the kitchen, shortly after eleven-thirty. Mrs Demery admits that she may have told one or two people when she took round the afternoon tea trolley. "One or two people" probably means every room in the building. Mrs Demery was a bit vague about what she actually said, but Maggie FitzGerald in publicity is quite certain that they were told that Mr Gerard had instructed Miss Blackett to get rid of the snake and that she'd put it in her desk drawer. Mr Sydney Bartrum in accounts claims that he didn't know. He said that he and his staff had no time to gossip with the office domestics and that they wouldn't have the opportunity anyway. Their department is in number ten and they make their own afternoon tea. De Witt and Miss Peverell have admitted that they knew. Miss Blackett's drawer was the natural place for anyone to look anyway. She had a sentimental affection for Hissing Sid and wouldn't have thrown it away.'

Daniel said: 'Why did Demery bother to pass on the news? It was hardly a major office scandal.'

'No, but it obviously caused a stir. Most of the staff knew or suspected that Gerard Etienne wouldn't be sorry to see the back of Miss Blackett. They were probably wondering how long she'd hold out, whether she'd chuck the job before she was sacked. Any fresh spat between those two was news.'

Dalgliesh said: 'You see the importance of the snake. Either it was wound round Etienne's neck and stuffed into his mouth by the murderer, probably to explain the breaking of the rigor of the jaw, or the joker stumbled on the body and saw the chance of a particularly revolting piece of malice. If the murderer did it, is he or she also the joker? Were these pranks part of a carefully laid plan which goes back as far as the first incident? That would tie up with the frayed window cord. If that was deliberate it was done over a period of time. Or did the murderer realize the significance of the loose jaw and use the snake on impulse to conceal the fact that he'd actually removed some object from Etienne's mouth?'

Daniel said: 'There's another possibility, sir. Suppose the joker finds the body, thinks it's a natural or accidental death, then decides to stir things up by making it look like murder. It could have been he or she who moved the table out of place as well as putting the snake round Etienne's neck.'

Kate objected. 'He couldn't have weakened the window cord, that must have been done earlier. And why bother to shift the table? That could only confuse the issue and make the death look like murder if the joker already knew that Etienne had died from carbon monoxide poisoning.'

'He must have known. He turned off the gas fire.'

Kate said: 'He'd have done that anyway. That small room must have been like a furnace.' She turned to Dalgliesh. 'Sir, I think there's only one theory that fits all the facts. This was intended to look like an accidental death from carbon monoxide poisoning. The murderer planned to be the one to find the body and to find it on his own. All he had to do then was to replace the tap and turn off the gas – a natural reaction anyway – then put back the table and chair, take away the tape and raise the alarm. But he couldn't find the tape, and when he did he couldn't get his hands on it without breaking the rigor in the jaw. He knew that this wouldn't be missed by a competent detective or the forensic pathologists, so he used the snake to suggest that this was an accidental death complicated by the malice of the office joker.'

Daniel objected. 'Why take the tape recorder? I'm talking about the murderer now.'

'Why leave it? He had to remove the tape, he might as well take the recorder. Look, the natural thing would be to chuck it in the Thames.' She turned to Dalgliesh. 'Do you think there's any chance an underwater search could find it, sir?'

Dalgliesh said: 'Extremely unlikely. And if it did the tape wouldn't be intact. The murderer would certainly have erased any messages. I doubt whether the expense of a search would be justified, but you'd better have a word with the people here. Find out what the bottom of the river is like at Innocent House.'

Daniel said: 'There's something else, sir. If the killer wanted to leave a message for his victim, why use the tape? Why not write it? He had to recover it anyway. It would have been as easy to recover a piece of paper, perhaps easier.'

Dalgliesh said: 'But not as safe. If Etienne had time enough before unconsciousness supervened, he could tear up the paper and hide the separate pieces. But if he didn't tear it, paper is easier to conceal than a tape. The murderer knew that he might not have much time. He needed to retrieve that message and find it quickly. And there's another point: a speaking voice can't be ignored, a written message can. The interesting thing about this whole case is why he needed to leave a message at all.'

Daniel said: 'To gloat. To have the last word. To show how clever he was.'

Dalgliesh said: 'Or to explain to someone why he had to die. If that was the reason then the motive for this murder may not be obvious. It may lie in the past, even in the distant past.'

'But if so, why wait until now? If the murderer is here at Innocent House, Etienne could have been killed any time during the last twenty years or so. He's been part of the firm since he left Cambridge. What has happened recently to make this death necessary?'

Dalgliesh said: 'Etienne took over as chairman and MD, he proposed to force the sale of Innocent House, and he became engaged.'

'Do you think the engagement could be relevant, sir?'

'Anything could be, Kate. I'm going to see Etienne's father tomorrow morning. Claudia Etienne drove down to Bradwell-on-Sea early this evening to break the news to him and to ask him to agree to a meeting. She won't be staying the night. I've asked her to meet you at Etienne's flat in the Barbican tomorrow. But the first priority is to check all the alibis, starting with the partners and staff at Innocent

House. Daniel, you and Robbins had better see Esmé Carling. Find out where she went when she left Better Books at Cambridge. There was Gerard Etienne's engagement party on the tenth of July. We need to check the guest list and interview people who were there. You're going to need tact. The line to take is whether they did wander through the house and whether they saw anything odd or suspicious. But we concentrate on the partners. Did anyone see Claudia Etienne and her companion on the river, and at what time? Check with St Thomas's Hospital what time Gabriel Dauntsey was brought in and when he left, and of course on his alibi. I'll be leaving early for Bradwell-on-Sea but I should be back by early afternoon. For the present I think we'd better call it a day.'

35

The partners spent Friday night apart. Standing at her kitchen table, trying to summon the energy to decide what to eat, Frances reflected that this wasn't surprising. They led separate lives away from Innocent House and it sometimes seemed to her that they made a deliberate attempt to distance themselves outside the office, almost as if they wanted to demonstrate that all they had in common was work. They seldom discussed their social engagements and she would occasionally be a guest at the party of another publisher and be surprised to see Claudia's sleek head momentarily appearing in a gap of yelling faces, or be at the theatre with a friend from her convent schooldays and see Dauntsey painfully edging his way along the row ahead. Then they would greet each other as politely as acquaintances. Tonight she sensed that something stronger than habit was holding them apart, that they had grown increasingly reluctant to discuss Gerard's death as the day progressed, and that the frankness of that hour closeted together in the boardroom had been displaced by a wary distrust of intimacy.

James, she knew, had no choice. He needed to go home to Rupert, and she envied him the necessity of obligation. She had never met his friend, never been invited to his house since Rupert's arrival there and she wondered now about their life together. But at least he would have someone with whom he could share the distresses of the day, a day which now seemed inordinate in length. They had, by common unspoken consent, left Innocent House early and she had waited while Claudia locked the door and set the alarm. She had asked, 'Will you be all right, Claudia?' and, even as she spoke, had been struck by the futility, the banality of the question. She had wondered if she ought to offer to go home with Claudia, but was afraid that this might only be seen as a confession of weakness, her own need for company. And Claudia, after all, had her fiancé – if he was her fiancé. She was more likely to turn to him than to Frances.

Claudia had replied: 'All I want at the moment is to get home and be alone.' Then she had added, 'What about you, Frances? Will you be all right?'

The same meaningless, unanswerable question. She wondered how Claudia would have replied if she'd said, 'No, I'm not all right. I don't want to be alone. Stay with me tonight, Claudia. Sleep in my spare room.'

She could, of course, telephone Gabriel. She wondered what he was doing, what he was thinking, in that plain underfurnished apartment beneath her. He too had said, 'Will you be all right, Frances? Ring me if you need company.' She wished that he had said, 'Do you mind if I come up, Frances? I don't want to be alone.' Instead he had placed the onus on her. To ring for him was to confess a weakness, a need, which he might not welcome. What was it about Innocent House, she wondered, that made it so difficult for people to express a human need or to give each other a simple reciprocal kindness?

In the end she opened a carton of mushroom soup and boiled herself an egg. She felt extraordinarily tired. Curled last night in Gabriel's chair, her broken hours of fitful sleep hadn't been the best preparation for a day of almost continuous trauma. But she knew that she wasn't ready for sleep. Instead, after washing up her supper things, she went into the room which had been her father's bedroom and which she had now made into a small sitting-room and sat herself in front of the television. The bright images passed in front of her eyes; the news, a documentary, a comedy, an old film, a modern play. As she pressed the buttons, flicking from channel to channel, the changing faces, grinning, laughing, serious, magisterial, the mouths continually opening and closing were a visual drug, meaning nothing, evoking no emotion, but at least providing a spurious companionship, a fleeting and irrational solace.

At one o'clock she went to bed, taking with her a glass of hot milk laced with a little whisky. It was effective and she slipped away into unconsciousness with the last thought that she was, after all, to enjoy the benison of sleep.

The nightmare returned to her in the early hours, the old familiar nightmare but in a new guise, more terrible, more intensely real. She was walking along the Greenwich tunnel between her father and Mrs Rawlings. They were holding her hands but their grasp was an imprisonment not a comfort. She couldn't run away and there was nowhere to run. Behind her she could hear the cracking of the tunnel roof but she dared not turn her head because she knew that even to look back would be disaster. In front of her the tunnel stretched longer than in life with a circle of bright sunlight at the end. As they walked the tunnel lengthened and the circle became gradually smaller, until it was only a small gleaming saucer and she knew that soon it would recede into a pin-point of light, then disappear. Her father was walking very upright, not looking at her, not speaking. He was wearing the tweed coat with the short cape which he always wore in winter and which she had given to the Salvation Army. He was angry that she had given it away without consulting him, but he had found it and got it back. She wasn't surprised to see the snake wound round his neck. It was a real snake, immense as a cobra, expanding and contracting, draped round his shoulders, hissing with its evil life, ready to crush the breath out of him. And overhead the tiles of the roof were wet and the first large drops were already falling. But she saw that they weren't drops of water, but of blood. And now suddenly she broke free and began to run, screaming, towards that unobtainable pin-point of light while the roof ahead cracked and fell and there rolled towards her, shutting out the last light, the black obliterating wave of death.

She woke to find herself slumped against the window, her hands beating the glass. With consciousness came relief, but the horror of the nightmare remained like a stain on the mind. But at least she knew it for what it was. She went over to her bed and turned on the lamp. It was nearly five o'clock. There was no point now in trying to sleep again. Instead she put on her dressing-gown, drew the curtains and opened the windows. With the darkened room behind her she could see the luminous glimmer of the river and a few high stars. The terror of her dream was passing but it gave way to that other terror from which she had no hope of waking.

Suddenly she thought of Adam Dalgliesh. His flat, too, was on the river, at Queenhithe. She wondered how she knew where he lived, and then remembered some of the press coverage of his last and successful book of poetry. He was a very private man but that fact at least had emerged. It was odd that their lives were linked by this dark tide of history. She wondered if he, too, was wakeful, whether a mile or two upstream his tall dark figure was standing looking out over the same dangerous river.

BOOK THREE

Work in Progress

36

On Saturday 16 October Jean-Philippe Etienne took his morning walk as usual at nine o'clock. Neither the time nor the route varied whatever the season or the weather. He would walk along the narrow ridge of rock between the marshes and the ploughed fields on which the Roman fort of Othona was said to have stood, past the Anglo-Celtic chapel of St Peter-on-the-Wall round the headland to the Blackwater estuary. It was rare for him to meet anyone on his morning perambulation, even in summer when a visitor to the chapel or a bird-watcher might be abroad early, but if he did he would say a courteous good morning, but no more. The locals knew that he had come to Othona House for solitude and had no wish to violate it. He accepted no incoming telephone calls, received no visitors. But this morning at half past ten a visitor would come who could not be refused.

Now in the strengthening light he looked across the calm straits of the estuary to the lights on Mersea Island and thought about this unknown Commander Dalgliesh. The message he had sent to the police by Claudia had been unambiguous; he had no information to offer about his son's death, no theories to propose, no possible explanations of the mystery to put forward, no suspect he could name. His own view was that Gerard had died by accident, however odd or suspicious some of the circumstances. Accidental death seemed likelier than any other explanation, certainly far likelier than murder. Murder. The heavy consonants of horror thudded in his mind, evoking nothing but repugnance and disbelief.

And now, standing as still as if petrified on the narrow strip of gritty beach where the minuscule waves spent themselves in a thin smudge of dirty foam, and watching the lamps across the water die one by one as the day brightened, he paid his son the reluctant tribute of memory. Most of the memories were troubling, but since they besieged his mind and could not be repelled it was perhaps better that they should be accepted, made sense of and disciplined. Gerard had grown to adolescence with one central assurance: he was the son of a hero. That was important to a boy, to any boy, but particularly one as proud as he. He might resent his father, feel himself inadequately loved, undervalued, neglected, but he could do without the love if he had the pride, pride in the name and in what that name stood for. It had always been important to him to know that the man whose genes he carried had been tested as had few of his generation and had not been found wanting. The decades were passing and memories fading, but a man could still be judged by what he had done in those turbulent years of war. Jean-Philippe's reputation was secure, inviolable. The reputation of other heroes of the Resistance had been sullied by the revelations of later years, but never his. The medals that he never now wore had been honestly earned.

Jean-Philippe had watched the effect of that knowledge on Gerard: the compelling need for his father's approbation and respect, the need to compete, to justify himself in his father's eyes. Wasn't that what climbing the Matterhorn when he was twenty-one had been all about? He had never before shown any interest in mountaineering. The exploit had been time-consuming and expensive. He had employed the best Zermatt guide who, reasonably, had decreed a period of some months' hard training before the climb was attempted and had laid down his strict conditions. The party would turn back before the final assault on the summit if he judged Gerard a danger to himself or to others. But they hadn't turned back. The mountain had been conquered. That was something Jean-Philippe hadn't achieved.

And then there was the Peverell Press. Here in his last years Jean-Philippe knew that he had been little more than a passenger, tolerated, undisturbed, no trouble to anyone. Gerard, when power passed into his hands, would transform Peverell Press. And Jean-Philippe had given him that power. He had transferred twenty of his shares in the firm to Gerard, and fifteen to Claudia. Gerard had only to keep the support of his sister to be sure of majority control. And why not? The Peverells had had their day; it was time for the Etiennes to take over.

And still Gerard had come, month after month, to give his account as if he were a steward reporting to his master. He asked for no advice, no approbation. It wasn't for advice or approbation that he came. Sometimes it seemed to Jean-Philippe that the journey was a form of reparation, a penance voluntarily imposed, a filial duty undertaken now when the old man was past caring and letting slip from his stiffened hands those frail cords which bound him to family, to the firm, to life. He had listened, had occasionally commented, but had never brought himself to say: 'I don't want to hear. I'm no longer concerned. You can sell Innocent House, move to Docklands, sell the firm, burn the archives. The last of my interest in Peverell Press was cast from me when I dropped those grains of crushed bone into the Thames. I am as dead to your busy concerns as is Henry Peverell. We are both now beyond caring. Don't think because I can speak to you, still perform some of the functions of a man, that I am alive.' He would sit immobile, and from time to time stretch out a shaking hand for his tumbler of wine, the glass, with its heavy base, so much easier now to manage than a wineglass. His son's voice had come from a distance.

'It's difficult to know whether to buy or rent. In principle I'm for buying. The rents are ridiculously low but they won't be when the leases run out. On the other hand it makes sense to take a short lease for the next five years and free the capital for acquisitions and development. Publishing is about books not property. For the past hundred years Peverell Press have squandered resources on maintaining Innocent House as if the house was the firm. Lose the house and you lose the Press. Bricks and mortar elevated to a symbol, even on the writing paper.'

Jean-Philippe had said: 'Stone and marble.' To Gerard's quick enquiring frown he added, 'Stone and marble, not bricks and mortar.'

'The rear façade is brick. The house is an architectural bastard. People say how brilliantly Charles Fowler wedded late Georgian elegance to fifteenth-century Venetian Gothic, but he'd have done better not to try. Hector Skolling is welcome to Innocent House.'

'Frances will be unhappy.'

He had said it for something to say. He was untouched by Frances's unhappiness. The wine was strong in his mouth. It was good that he could still taste the robust reds.

Gerard had said: 'She'll get over it. All the Peverells feel compelled to love Innocent House, but I doubt if she greatly cares.' Following the association of ideas, he added: 'You saw the announcement of my engagement in last Monday's *Times*?'

'No. I no longer bother with newspapers. The *Spectator* has a summary of the week's main news. That half-page is sufficient to reassure me that the world goes on much as it always has. I hope you'll be happy in your marriage. I was.'

'Yes, I always thought that you and Mother seemed to hit it off rather well.'

Jean-Philippe could smell his embarrassment. The comment in its gross inadequacy had hung between them like a wisp of acrid smoke. Jean-Philippe said quietly: 'I wasn't thinking of your mother.'

And now, gazing across the stretch of quiet water it seemed to him that only in those turbulent and confused days of war had he been truly alive. He had been young, passionately in love, exhilarated by constant danger, stimulated by the ardours of leadership, exalted by a simple and unquestioning patriotism which for him had become a religion. Among the confused loyalties of Vichy France his own had been clear and absolute. Nothing since had touched the wonder, the excitement, the glamour of those years. Never again had he lived every day with such intensity. Even after Chantal had been killed, his resolution hadn't faltered although he was confused by the realization that he blamed the Maquis as much as the occupying Germans for her death. He had never believed that the most effective resistance lay in armed action or in the murder of German soldiers. And then in 1944 had come liberation and triumph, and with it a reaction so unexpected and so strong that it left him demoralized, almost apathetic. Only then, in the moment of triumph, had he space and time to grieve for Chantal. He felt like a man emptied of all capacity for emotion except for this overwhelming grief which in its sad futility seemed part of a greater, a universal grieving.

He had had little stomach for revenge and had watched with sick disgust the shaving of the heads of women accused of 'sentimental relations with the enemy', the vendettas, the purges by the Maquis, the summary justice which executed thirty people in the Puy-de-Dôme without formal trial. He was glad, as was most of the population, when the due process of law was established, but he took no satisfaction in the proceedings or in the verdicts. He had no sympathy for those collaborators who had betrayed the Resistance, or who had tortured or murdered. But in those ambiguous years many collaborators with the Vichy regime had done what they believed right for France, and if the Axis powers had won, perhaps it would have been right for France. Some were decent men who had chosen the wrong side for motives not wholly ignoble, others were weak, some motivated by a hatred of communism, others seduced by fascism's insidious glamour. He could hate none of them. Even his own fame, his own heroism, his own innocence, became repugnant to him.

He had needed to get away from France and had come to London. His grandmother had been English. He spoke the language faultlessly and was familiar with the peculiarities of English customs, all of which helped to soothe his self-imposed banishment. But he hadn't come to England out of any special affection for the country or its people. The countryside was beautiful, but then he had had France. It had been necessary to leave and England was the obvious choice. It was in London at a party – he couldn't now remember which or where – that he had been introduced to Henry Peverell's cousin Margaret. She was pretty, sensitive and appealingly childlike, and had fallen romantically in love with him, in love with his heroism, with his nationality, even with his accent. He had found her uncritical adulation flattering, and it was difficult not to respond with at least affection and a protective warmth for what he saw as her vulnerability. But he had never loved her. He had only loved one human being. With Chantal had died his capacity for any feeling warmer than affection.

But he had married her, taken her for four years to Toronto, and when that self-imposed banishment grew irksome they had returned to London, now with two babies. At Henry's invitation he had joined the Peverell Press, invested his considerable capital in the firm, taken his shares and spent the rest of his working life in that extravagant folly on a northern alien river. He supposed that he had been reasonably content. He knew people thought him rather dull; that didn't surprise him, he bored himself. The marriage had endured. He had made his wife Margaret Peverell as happy as she was capable of being. He suspected that the Peverell women weren't capable of much happiness. She had desperately wanted children and he had dutifully provided her with the son and daughter for which she had hoped. That was how, then and now, he thought of parenthood; the giving of something necessary for his wife's happiness if not for his own and for which, having provided it as he might a ring, a necklace or a new car, he need take no further responsibility since responsibility was handed over with the gift.

And now Gerard was dead and this unknown policeman was coming to tell him that his son had been murdered.

37

Kate and Daniel's appointment to see Rupert Farlow had been fixed for ten o'clock. They knew it would be almost impossible to park in Hillgate Village so left the car at Notting Hill Gate Police Station and walked up the gentle hill under the high limes of Holland Park Avenue. Kate thought how strange it was to be back so soon in this familiar part of London. She had left her flat only three days earlier but it seemed that she had moved away from the area in imagination as well as in fact and that now, coming up to Notting Hill Gate, she saw the raucous urban conglomeration through the eyes of a stranger. But nothing, of course, had changed; the discordant undistinguished 1930s architecture, the plethora of street signs, the railings which made her feel like a herded animal, the long concrete flower beds with their straggling and dust-grimed evergreens, the shop fronts spilling their names in rivers of garish light red, green and yellow, the ceaseless grind of the traffic. There was even the same beggar outside the supermarket with his large Alsatian slumped on a rug at his feet, murmuring to passers-by his appeal for change to buy a sandwich. Behind this busyness lay Hillgate Village in its stuccoed multi-coloured calm.

As they passed the beggar and stood waiting to cross at the traffic lights, Daniel said: 'We've got a few like that where I live. I'd be tempted to pop into the supermarket and buy him a sandwich if I wasn't afraid of provoking a breach of the peace and if he and the dog didn't already look over-fed. Do you ever give?'

'Not to his kind, and not often. Sometimes. I disapprove of myself but I do it. Never more than a quid.'

'To be spent on drink and drugs.'

'A gift should be unconditional. Even a quid. Even to a beggar. And OK, I do know that it's conniving at an offence.'

They had crossed the road at the traffic lights when abruptly he spoke again.

'I ought to go to my cousin's bar mitzvah next Saturday.'

'Then go, that is if it's important.'

'AD won't welcome an application for leave. You know how he is once we're on a case.'

'It doesn't take all day, does it? Ask him. He was very decent when Robbins wanted that day off after his uncle died.'

'That was for a Christian funeral not a Jewish bar mitzvah.'

'What other kind of bar mitzvah is there? And don't be unfair. He isn't like that and you know it. Like I said, if it's important ask, if it isn't don't.'

'Important to whom?'

'How do I know? To the boy I suppose.'

'I hardly know him. I doubt whether he'll care much either way. But we're a small family, he's only got the two cousins. I suppose he'd like me to be there. My aunt would probably prefer me not to be. That way she'll be given another grievance against my mother.'

'You can hardly expect AD to decide whether pleasing your nephew is more important than disobliging your aunt. If it's important to you then go. Why make such a big thing about it?'

He didn't reply, and as they made their way up Hillgate Street she thought, perhaps it's because, for him, it is a big thing. Thinking back on it, the brief conversation surprised her. This was the first time he had even tentatively opened the door to his private life. And she had thought that, like her, he guarded with almost obsessive watchfulness that essentially inviolate portal. In the three months since he had joined the squad they had never spoken of his Jewishness, nor indeed of much else except work. Was he genuinely seeking advice or using her to clear his thoughts? If he needed advice it was surprising that he sought it from her. She had from the first been aware of a defensiveness in him which if not tactfully handled could become tricky, and she slightly resented the need for tact in a professional relationship. Police work was stressful enough without the need to propitiate or accommodate a colleague. But she liked him or, it might be truer to say, was beginning to like him without being sure why. He was sturdily built, hardly taller than she, strong featured, fair haired and with slate-grey eyes which shone like polished pebbles. When he was angry they could darken almost to black. She recognized both his intelligence and an ambition which mirrored her own. And at least he had no hang-up about working with a woman senior to himself or, if he had, was more skilful than most of his colleagues at concealing it. She told herself, too, that she was beginning to find him sexually attractive as if this formal and regular recognition of the fact could guard her against the follies of propinquity. She had seen too many colleagues make a mess of their private and professional lives to risk that kind of involvement, always so much easier to begin than to end.

She said, wanting to match his confidence and fearing that she had been too dismissive: 'There were a dozen different religions among the children at Ancroft Comprehensive. We seemed always to be celebrating some kind of feast or ceremony. Usually it required making a noise and dressing up. The official line was that all religions were equally important. I must say that the result was to leave me with the conviction that they were equally unimportant. I suppose if you don't teach religion with conviction it becomes just one more boring subject. Perhaps I'm a natural pagan. I don't go in for all this emphasis on sin, suffering and judgement. If I had a God I'd like Him to be intelligent, cheerful and amusing.'

He said: 'I doubt whether you'd find him much of a comfort when they herded you into the gas chambers. You might prefer a god of vengeance. This is the street isn't it?'

She wondered if he had wearied of the subject or was warning her off his private ground. She said: 'Yes. It looks as if the high numbers are at the other end.'

There was an entryphone at the left of the door. Kate pressed the bell and when a masculine voice responded said: 'This is Inspector Miskin and Inspector Aaron. We've come to see Mr Farlow. He is expecting us.'

She listened for the buzz which would indicate that the door lock had been released, but instead the same voice said: 'I'll be down.'

The wait of a minute and a half seemed longer. Kate had looked at her watch a second time when the door was opened and they found themselves confronted by a stocky young man, barefoot and wearing tightly fitting trousers in a blue and white check and a white sweatshirt. His hair was cut in very short spikes giving the round head the look of a bristled brush. His nose was wide and chubby and the short round arms with their patina of brown hair looked as softly plump as a child's. Kate thought that he had the snug compactness of a toy bear, needing only a price tag dangling from the earring in his left ear to complete the illusion. But the pale blue eyes meeting hers were initially wary, then changed as she met them to frank antagonism, and when he spoke there was no welcome in his voice. Ignoring the proffered warrant card he said: 'You'd better come up.'

The narrow hall was very warm, the air permeated with an exotic smell, part floral, part spicy, which Kate would have found agreeable if it had been less strong. They mounted the narrow stairs behind their guide and found themselves in a sitting-room which ran the whole length of the house. A curved archway showed where once there must have been the dividing wall. At the rear a small conservatory had been built out to overlook the garden. Kate, who thought that she had brought to an art the ability to take in details of her surroundings without betraying too obvious a curiosity, now noticed nothing but the man they had come to see. He was lying propped up on a single bed to the right of the conservatory and he was obviously dying. She had seen the extremity of emaciation often enough pictured on her television screen; viewing almost routinely in her sitting-room the dead eyes and shrivelled limbs of starvation. But now, encountering it for the first time, she wondered how any human being could be so diminished and still breathe, how the great eyes, which seemed to be floating free in their sockets, could hold her with such a look of intense, slightly ironic amusement. He was enveloped in a dressing-gown of scarlet silk but it could give no glow to the sickly yellow skin. There was a card table close to the head of the bed with a facing chair and two packs of cards ready on the green baize top. It looked as if Rupert Farlow and his companion were about to begin a game of canasta.

His voice was not strong but it did not waver; the essential self was still alive, still heard in its high clear tones. 'Forgive me if I don't get up. The spirit is willing but the flesh is weak. I'm conserving my energies for ensuring that Ray doesn't get a sight of my cards. Do sit down if you can find a seat. Would you like a drink? I know you're not supposed to drink on duty but I insist on regarding this as a social call. Ray, where did you hide the bottle?'

The boy, seated at the card table, made no move. Kate said: 'We won't drink, thank you. And this shouldn't take long. It's about Thursday evening.'

'I thought it might be.'

'Mr de Witt says that he came straight home from the office and was here with you all the evening. Could you confirm that?'

'If that's what James told you then it's true. James never lies. That's one of the things about him that his friends find so trying.'

'And is it true?'

'Naturally. Hasn't he said so?'

'What time did he arrive home?'

'The usual time. About six-thirty, isn't it? He'll tell you. He has told you, surely.'

Kate, who had pushed a heap of magazines to one side, had seated herself on a Victorian sofa opposite the bed. She said: 'How long have you lived here with Mr de Witt?'

Rupert Farlow turned on her his immense, pain-filled eyes, moving his head slowly as if the weight of this denuded skull had become too great for his neck to bear. He said: 'Are you asking how long I've shared this house as opposed, shall we say, to sharing his life, sharing his bed?'

'Yes, that's what I'm asking.'

'Four months, two weeks, three days. He took me in from the hospice. I'm not sure why. Perhaps being with the dying turns him on. It does some people. There was no shortage of visitors at the hospice, I assure you. We're the one charity they can always get volunteers for. Sex and death, a great turn-on. We weren't lovers, incidentally. He's in love with that boringly conventional woman, Frances Peverell. James is depressingly heterosexual. You needn't be frightened to shake his hand or even indulge in more intimate physical contact if you like to try your luck.'

Daniel said: 'He arrived here from work at six-thirty. Did he go out later?'

'Not as far as I know. He went up to bed at about eleven and he was here when I woke at three-thirty and four-fifteen and five forty-five. I made a careful note of the hours. Oh, and he did various messy things for me at about seven o'clock in the morning. He certainly wouldn't have had time between these hours to get back to Innocent House and dispose of Gerard Etienne. But I may as well warn you that I'm not particularly reliable. I would say that anyway. It isn't exactly in my interest to have James carted off to prison, is it?'

Daniel said: 'Nor in your interest to be an accessory to murder.'

'That isn't the worry. If you take James you may as well take me. I should be more of an inconvenience to the criminal justice system than you would be to me. That's the advantage of dying. It hasn't a lot to be said for it but it does put you beyond the power of the police. Still, I must try to be helpful, mustn't I? There is one piece of corroborative evidence. You rang and spoke to James, didn't you, Ray, at about seven-thirty?'

Ray had taken up a second pack of cards and was expertly shuffling them. 'Yeah, that's right, seven-thirty. Rang to enquire. He was here then.'

'There you are then. Wasn't it clever of me to remember?'

Kate said impulsively: 'Are you – surely you must be – the Rupert Farlow who wrote *The Fruit Cage*?'

'Have you read it?'

'A friend gave it to me last Christmas. He managed to find a hardback. Apparently they're rather sought after. He told me that the first edition was sold out and that they didn't reprint.'

'A literate cop. I thought you only got them in fiction. Did you like it?'

'Yes, I liked it.' She paused, then added: 'I thought it was wonderful.'

He raised his head and looked at her. His voice changed and he spoke so softly she could hardly hear the words. 'I was quite pleased with it myself.'

Looking into his eyes she saw, appalled, that they were glistening with tears. The frail body in its crimson shroud trembled and she had an impulse, so strong that she had almost physically to fight it, to move forward and take him in her arms. She looked away and said, trying to make her voice sound normal: 'We won't tire you any more but we may have to come back and ask you to sign a statement.'

'You'll find me at home. Or if I'm not, you'll be unlikely to get a statement. Ray will see you out.'

The three of them walked down the stairs in silence. At the door Daniel turned and said: 'Mr de Witt has told us that no one telephoned this house on Thursday evening, so one of you is either lying or mistaken. Is it you?'

The boy shrugged. 'OK, maybe I was mistaken. That's no great deal. It could have been another night.'

'Or no night? It's dangerous to lie in a murder investigation. Dangerous for you and the innocent. If you have any influence over Mr Farlow you should tell him that the best way he can help his friend is by telling the truth.'

Ray had his hand on the door. He said: 'Don't give me that crap. Why should I? That's what the police always say, that you help yourself and the innocent by telling the truth. Telling the truth to the fuzz is in the fuzz's interest. Don't try telling us it's in ours. And if you want to come back, you'd better ring first. He's too weak to be badgered.'

Daniel opened his mouth, restrained himself and said nothing. The door closed firmly behind them. They walked into Hillgate Street without speaking. Then Kate said: 'I shouldn't have said that about his novel.'

'Why not? What's the harm – that is, if you were being honest.'

'It's because I was being honest that I did the harm. It upset him.' She paused then said: 'What do you think that particular alibi is worth?'

'Not much. But if he sticks to it, and my guess is he will, we're in trouble, no matter what else we manage to grub up about de Witt.'

'Not necessarily. It'll depend on the strength of any further evidence. And if we find the alibi unconvincing so will a jury.'

'If you ever get that chap in front of a jury.'

Kate said: 'There's one thing though. It might just have been chance but I wonder. Obviously that friend of his, Ray, was lying, but how did Farlow know that the alibi was needed for around seven-thirty? Or was it just a lucky guess?'

38

Dalgliesh's appointment with Jean-Philippe Etienne, conveyed by Claudia Etienne, had been made for 10.30, a time which necessitated a comfortably early start from London. The time of the appointment had been surprisingly specific for a man whose day was presumably his own. Dalgliesh wondered if it had been chosen to ensure that, even if the interview were more protracted than expected, Etienne would feel under no obligation to invite him to lunch. This, too, suited him. To lunch alone in a strange place where he was unknown and un-recognized, even if the food proved disappointing, a place where he could eat in the assurance that no one in the world knew who he was and that no telephone could reach him, was a rare pleasure, and he intended after the interview to make the most of it. He had a meeting at the Yard at four o'clock and then would go straight to Wapping to hear Kate's report. There would be no time for a solitary walk or for exploring an interesting-looking church. But after all, a man had to eat.

It was dark when he set out and the day lightened into a dry but sunless morning. But as he shook off the last eastern suburbs and drove between the muted colours of the Essex countryside, the grey canopy lightened into a white transparent haze with the promise that the sun might eventually break through. Beyond the cropped hedges spiked with the occasional wind-distracted tree, the ploughed fields of autumn, stippled with the first green shoots of winter wheat, stretched to the far horizon. He felt a sense of liberation under the wide East Anglian sky, as if the weight of an old and familiar burden had been temporarily lifted.

He thought about the man he was to meet. He was coming to Othona House with few expectations but he was not coming totally unprepared. There had been no time for detailed research into the man's history. He had spent some forty minutes in the London Library and had talked on the telephone to an ex-member of the Resistance living in Paris, whose name had been supplied by a contact at the French Embassy. He now knew something of Jean-Philippe Etienne, hero of the Resistance in Vichy France.

Etienne's father had owned a flourishing newspaper and printing press in Clermont-Ferrand and had been one of the earliest and most active members of the Organisation de Résistance de l'Armée. He had died of cancer in 1941 and his only son, recently married, had both inherited the business and taken over his father's role in the struggle against the Vichy authorities and the German occupiers. Like his father, he was a fervent Gaullist and strongly anti-Communist, distrustful of the Front National because it was founded by Communists, even though many of his own friends, Christians, socialists, intellectuals, were members of the Front. But he was by nature a loner and worked best with his own small, secretly-recruited band. Without quarrelling openly with the major organizations, he had concentrated on propaganda rather than on armed struggle, circulating his own underground paper, distributing Allied leaflets dropped by air, providing London with irregular but invaluable information and attempting even to suborn and demoralize German soldiers by infiltrating propaganda into their camps. His family newspaper continued, but now less a paper of record than a literary journal, its careful, non-political stance enabling Etienne to retain more than his share of printer's ink and paper, all rationed and closely supervised. By careful husbandry and subterfuge he was able to divert resources to his underground press.

For four years he had lived a double life so successfully that he was never suspected by the Germans nor denounced as a collaborator by his fellow résistants. His deep distrust of the Maquis had been reinforced when in 1943 his wife had been killed in a train blown up by one of the more active groups. He had ended the war as a hero, not as well known as Alphonse Rosier, Serge Fischer or Henri Martin, but his name could be found in the index of books on the Vichy Resistance. He had earned his medals and his peace.

Less than two hours after leaving London Dalgliesh had turned off the A12 south-east to Maldon, then east through flat unexciting countryside, and had entered the attractive village of Bradwell-on-Sea with its square-towered church and pink, white and ochre clapboard cottages, the doorways hung with baskets of late chrysanthemums. He marked down the King's Head as a possible place for lunch. A narrow road was signposted to the chapel of St-Peter-on-the-Wall and soon it came into view, a distant high rectangular building standing against the sky. It looked now as it had when he had first been brought there by his father as a ten-year-old, as simply and crudely proportioned as a child's doll's house. There was a rough footpath leading to the chapel separated from the road by a fixed wooden barrier, but the track to Othona House a few hundred yards to the right was open. A signpost, the wood beginning to split and the words almost indecipherable, bore the painted name of the house, and that and the distant sight of the roof and chimneys confirmed that the lane was the only access. Dalgliesh reflected that Etienne could hardly have devised a more effective deterrent to visitors and for a moment he wondered whether to walk the half-mile rather than risk his suspension. Glancing at his watch he saw that it was 10.25. He would arrive precisely on time.

The track to Othona House was deeply rutted, the pot-holes still holding water from the previous night's rain. It was bounded on one side by ploughed fields stretching as far as the eye could see, hedgeless and with no sign of habitation. On the left was a wide ditch bordered by a tangle of blackberry bushes heavy with berries, and beyond them a broken row of gnarled trunks thickly leached with ivy. On both sides of the path the tall dry grasses, already weighted with seed pods, stirred fitfully in the breeze. Under his careful handling the Jaguar lurched and shuddered and he was beginning to regret not parking in the entrance to the land when the track became less pot-holed, the crevasses less deep, and he was able to accelerate for the last hundred yards.

The house, bounded by a high curved wall in brick which looked comparatively modern, was still invisible except for the roof and chimneys, and it was apparent that the entrance faced the sea. He drove round to the right and saw the place clearly for the first time.

It was a small, agreeably proportioned house in mellowed red brick, the façade almost certainly Queen Anne. The central bay was capped with a Dutch parapet, its curve echoing that of the elegant portico of the front door. On either side stretched identical wings with their eight-paned windows under a stone cornice, decorated with carved scallop shells. These were the only indication that the house had been built on the coast but it still seemed oddly out of place, its dignified symmetry and mellow calm more appropriate to a cathedral close than to this bleak and isolated headland. There was no immediate access to the sea. Between the breaking waves and Othona House stretched a hundred yards or so of salt marsh, crossed by innumerable small streams, a sodden and treacherous carpet of soft blues, greens and greys with patches of acid green in which the pools of sea water gleamed as if the marshland had been set with jewels. He could hear the sea, but on this calm day, with only a light wind rustling the reeds, it came to him as gently as a soft expiring sigh.

He rang the bell and heard its muffled peal within the house, but it was over a minute before his ears caught the shuffle of approaching footsteps. There was a rasp of a drawn bolt and he heard the key turn before, slowly, the door was opened.

The woman who stood regarding him with blank incuriosity was old – probably, he thought, nearer eighty than seventy – but there was nothing frail about her full-fleshed solidity. She was wearing a black dress, high-buttoned to the throat and fastened with an onyx brooch surrounded with dull seed pearls. Her legs bulged above black laced boots and her breasts were carried high, shapeless as a bolster over a voluminous white starched apron. Her face was broad, the colour of suet, the cheekbones sharp ridges under the creased, suspicious eyes. Before he could speak, she said: 'Vous êtes le Commandant Dalgliesh?'

'Oui Madame, je viens voir Monsieur Etienne, s'il vous plaît.'

'Suivez-moi.'

Her pronunciation of his name was so bizarre that at first he couldn't recognize it, but her voice was strong and deep, and with a note of confident authority. She might be a servant at Othona House but she was not servile. She stood aside to let him enter and he waited while she closed and secured the door. The bolt above her head was heavy, the key large and old-fashioned, and she had some difficulty in turning it. The veins on her age-blanched and speckled hands stood out like purple cords and the strong work-worn fingers were gnarled.

She led him down a panelled hall to a room at the rear of the house. Pressing her back against the open door as if he were infectious, she announced 'Le Commandant Dalgliesh', then closed the door firmly as if anxious to dissociate herself from this unwanted guest.

The room was surprisingly light after the darkness of the hall. Two tall windows, multi-paned and fitted with shutters, looked out over a treeless garden dissected with stone paths and apparently given over to vegetables and herbs. The only colour was from late geraniums planted in the large terracotta pots which lined the main path. The room was obviously both a library and a sitting-room. Three walls were fitted with bookshelves to a height comfortable to reach, with prints and maps ranged above them. There was a drum table in the middle of the room, its top laden with books. To the left was a stone fireplace with a simple but elegant overmantel. A small fire of wood crackled in the basket-grate.

Jean-Philippe Etienne was sitting in a high buttoned green leather chair to the right of the fire, but made no move until Dalgliesh had almost reached it, when he got to his feet and held out his hand. Dalgliesh felt for no more than two seconds the clasp of the cold flesh. Time, he thought, can reduce all individuality to stereotype. It can soften and plump the ageing features into bland childishness, or strip them to the bone and muscle so that mortality already stares out from the shrivelled eyes. It seemed to him that he could see the outline of every bone, the twitch of every muscle in Etienne's face. His spare figure was still upright, although he walked stiffly, and his dapper elegance held no hint of decrepitude. The grey hair was sparse, brushed back from a high forehead, the jutting nose was long above a wide, almost lipless mouth, the large ears lay flat against the skull and the veins under the high cheekbones looked as if they were about to bleed. He was wearing a velvet jacket with frogged fastening, reminiscent of a Victorian smoking-jacket, above black tightly fitting trousers. Just so might a nineteenth-century landowner have risen stiffly to greet a guest, but this guest, Dalgliesh at once knew, was as little welcome in this elegant library as he had been on arrival.

Etienne motioned him to the chair opposite his own and seated himself, then he said: 'Claudia handed me your letter, but please spare me any renewal of your condolences. They can hardly be sincere. You did not know my son.'

Dalgliesh said: 'It isn't necessary to know a man to feel regret that he should die too young and needlessly.'

'You are, of course, right. The death of the young is always embittered by the injustice of mortality, the young go, the old live on. You will take something? Wine? Coffee?'

'Coffee, please, sir.'

Etienne walked into the passage, closing the door behind him. Dalgliesh could hear him call out, he thought in French. There was an embroidered bell rope to the right of the fireplace, but apparently Etienne did not choose to use it in his relationship with his household. Returning to his chair, he said: 'It was necessary for you to come, I realize that. But there is nothing I can say to help you. I have no idea why my son died, unless it was, as seems most likely, by accident.'

Dalgliesh said: 'There are a number of oddities about his death which suggest that it could have been deliberate. I know that this must be painful for you and I'm sorry.'

'What are those oddities?'

'The fact that he died of carbon monoxide poisoning in a room he rarely visited. A broken window cord which could have snapped when it was tugged so that the window couldn't be opened. A missing tape recorder. A removable tap on the gas fire which could have been removed after the fire was lit. The position of the body.'

Etienne said: 'Nothing you have told me is new. My daughter was here yesterday. The evidence is surely entirely circumstantial. Were there any prints on the gas tap?'

'Only a smudge. The surface is too small for anything useful.'

Etienne said: 'Even taken together these suppositions are less – odd was the word you used? – than the suggestion that Gerard was murdered. Oddities are not evidence. I am ignoring the matter of the snake. I know that there is a malicious prankster at Innocent House. His or her activities scarcely warrant the attention of a Commander of New Scotland Yard.'

'They do, sir, if they complicate, or obscure, or are connected with a murder.'

There were footsteps in the passage. Etienne went at once to the door and opened it for the housekeeper. She came in with a tray bearing a cafetière, a brown jug, sugar and one large cup. She placed the tray on the table and, after a glance at Etienne, immediately left the room. Etienne poured the coffee and brought it over to Dalgliesh. It was apparent that he himself was not to drink, and Dalgliesh wondered if this was a not-very-subtle ploy to put him at a disadvantage. There was no small table by his chair so he placed the coffee cup on the hearth.

Returning to his chair, Etienne said: 'If my son was murdered I want his murderer brought to justice, inadequate as that justice may be. It is not perhaps necessary that I say this, but it is important that I do say it and that you believe me. If you find me unhelpful it is because I have no help to give.'

'Your son had no enemies?'

'I know of none. No doubt he had professional rivals, discontented authors, colleagues who disliked, resented, or were envious of him. That is common for any successful man. I know of no one who would wish to destroy him.'

'Is there anything in his past, or yours? Some old or imagined wrong or injustice that could have caused long-standing resentment?'

Etienne paused before replying, and Dalgliesh was aware for the first time of the silence of the room. Suddenly the wood fire crackled with a small explosion of flame and a shower of sparks fell on to the hearth. Etienne looked into the fire. He said: 'Resentment? The enemies of France were once my enemies and I fought them in the only way I could. Those who suffered may have sons, grandsons. It seems to me ludicrous to imagine they are exacting a vicarious revenge. And then there are my own people, the families of Frenchmen who were shot as hostages because of the activity of the Resistance. Some would say they had a legitimate grievance, but surely, not against my son. I suggest you concentrate your attention on the present not the past and on those people who normally had access to Innocent House. That would seem the obvious line of enquiry.'

Dalgliesh picked up his coffee cup. The coffee, black as he wanted, was still too hot to drink. He replaced it in the hearth and said: 'Miss Etienne has told us that your son visited you regularly. Did you discuss the firm?'

'We discussed nothing. He apparently felt the need to keep me informed of what was happening, but he asked for no advice and I offered none. I have no longer any interest in the firm and I had little for the last five years I worked there. Gerard wanted to sell Innocent House and move to Docklands. There is, I think, no secret about that. He saw it as necessary, and no doubt it was. No doubt it still is. I have a confused memory of our conversations; there was talk of money, acquisitions, staff changes, leases, a possible purchaser for Innocent House. I'm sorry my memory is not more precise.'

'But your years with the firm were not unhappy?'

The question, Dalgliesh saw, was regarded as an impertinence. He had ventured on forbidden ground. Etienne said: 'Neither happy nor unhappy. I made a contribution although, as I say, in the last five years it was an increasingly unimportant one. I doubt whether any other job would have suited me better. Henry Peverell and I went on too long. The last time I visited Innocent House was to help scatter Peverell's ashes in the Thames. I shall not return again.'

Dalgliesh said: 'Your son planned a number of changes, some, no doubt, unwelcome.'

'All change is unwelcome. I am glad to have placed myself beyond its reach. Some of us who dislike aspects of the modern world are fortunate. We need no longer live in it.'

Looking across at him while he at last sipped his coffee, Dalgliesh saw that the man was as tense in his chair as if about to spring from it. He realized that Etienne was a true recluse. Human company, except that of the few people with whom he lived, was intolerable to him for more than a brief span and he was nearing the end of his endurance. It was time to go; nothing else would be learned.

Moments later, as Etienne was accompanying him to the front door, a courtesy which Dalgliesh hadn't expected, he commented on the age and architecture of the house. It was the only thing he had said which stimulated his host to an interested response.

'The façade is Queen Anne, as I expect you know, but the interior is largely Tudor. The original house on this site was much earlier. Like the chapel, it is built on the walls of the old Roman settlement of Othona, hence the name of the house.'

'I thought I might visit the chapel, if I could leave my car here.'

'Of course.'

But the permission was not gracious. It was as if even the presence of the Jaguar on his forecourt was a disturbing intrusion. He was no sooner out of the door when it was firmly closed behind him and he heard the rasp of the lock.

39

Dalgliesh wondered if he would find the chapel door locked but it opened to his hand, and he entered into its silence and simplicity. The air was very cold and smelled of earth and mortar grit, an unecclesiastical smell, domestic and contemporary. The chapel was sparsely furnished. There was a stone altar with a Greek crucifix above it, a few benches, two large jars of dried flowers, one on each side of the altar, and a rack of pamphlets and guides. He folded a note and put it in the box, then took one of the guide-books and sat on a bench to study it, wondering why he should feel this sense of emptiness and mild depression. The chapel was, after all, among the earliest church buildings in England, perhaps the oldest, the sole surviving monument of the Anglo-Celtic Church in this part of England, the foundation of St Cedd who had landed here at the old Roman fort at Othona as early as 653. It had stood here confronting the cold and inhospitable North Sea for thirteen centuries. Here, if anywhere, he should surely have heard the dying echoes of plainsong and the vibration of 1,300 years of muttered prayer.

Whether one found the building holy or empty of holiness was a matter of personal perception, and his failure in this moment to experience more than the out-flowing of tension he could always feel when totally alone was a failure of imagination, not of the place itself. He wished that, sitting there quietly, he could hear the sea, with a need that was almost a longing – that ceaseless rise and fall which, more than any other natural sound, touched mind and heart with a sense of time's inexorable passing, of the centuries of unknown and unknowable human lives with their brief miseries and even briefer joys. But he had come here not to meditate but to think about murder and of murder's more immediate degradations. He put down the guidebook and mentally reviewed the recent interview.

It had been an unsatisfactory visit. His journey had been necessary but it had proved even more unproductive than he had feared. Yet he couldn't shake off the conviction that there was something of importance to be learned at Othona House which Jean-Philippe

Etienne hadn't chosen to tell him. It was possible, of course, that Etienne hadn't told him because it was something he had forgotten, something he thought insignificant, even something which he didn't realize that he knew. Dalgliesh thought again about the central fact of the mystery, the missing tape recorder, the scratches in Gerard Etienne's mouth. This murderer had needed to talk to his victim before he died, to talk to him even while he was dying. He or she had wanted Etienne dead, but had also wanted Etienne to know why he was dying. Was it no more than a murderer's overwhelming vanity, or had there been another reason buried in Etienne's past life? And if so, part of that life was here present in Othona House and he had failed to find it.

He wondered what had brought Etienne at the last to this soggy bulge of an alien country, to this drear, wind-scoured coast where the marsh lay like a sour, disintegrating sponge sopping up the fringes of the cold North Sea. Did he ever long for the mountains of his native province, for the jabber of French voices in street and café, for the sound, the scents and colours of rural France? Had he come to this desolate place to forget the past or to relive it? What had these old unhappy far-off things to do with the death nearly fifty years later of his son, a son by an English mother, born in Canada, murdered in London? What tentacles, if any, had stretched out from those momentous years to wind themselves round Gerard Etienne's neck?

He glanced at his watch. It was still a minute short of 11.30. He would make time to visit the monuments in St George's church in Bradwell, but after that brief visit there would be no possible excuse for not driving back to London to lunch at New Scotland Yard.

He was still sitting, guidebook held loosely in his hand, when the door opened and two elderly women entered. They were shod and dressed for walking, and each carried a small knapsack. They looked disconcerted and a little apprehensive to see him and, thinking that they might not welcome the presence of a solitary male, he said a quick 'Good morning' and left. Turning briefly at the door, he saw that they were already on their knees and wondered what it was they found in this quiet place and whether, if he had come with more humility, he might have found it also.

40

Gerard Etienne's flat was on the eighth floor of the Barbican. Claudia Etienne had said that she would be there to meet them at four o'clock and when Kate rang the door was opened promptly and, without speaking, she stood aside to let them in.

The day was beginning to darken but the large rectangular room was still full of light, as a room will hold warmth when the sun has set. The long curtains in what looked like fine cream linen were drawn back to reveal, beyond the balcony, an attractive view of the lake and the elegant spire of a city church. Daniel's first response was to wish the flat was his, his second that in all his visits to the homes of murder victims he had never seen one so impersonal, so ordered, so uncluttered with the detritus of the dead life. This place looked like a show flat, carefully furnished to attract a purchaser. But it would be a rich purchaser; nothing in this apartment had been inexpensive. And he was wrong to see it as impersonal, it spoke as clearly of its owner as the most overfurnished suburban sitting-room, or any tart's bedroom. He could have played that television game: 'Describe the owner of this apartment'. Male, young, rich, discriminating, organized, unmarried; there was nothing feminine about this room. Obviously musical; the expensive stereo equipment might be expected in any flat of a well-to-do bachelor, but not the grand piano. All the furniture was modern, pale unpolished wood elegantly fashioned into cupboards, bookcases, a desk. At the end of the room, close to a door obviously leading to the kitchen, was a round dining table with six matching chairs. There was no fireplace. The focus of the room was the window, and a long sofa and two armchairs in soft black leather were grouped to face it round a coffee table.

There was only one photograph. On the top of a low bookcase, in a silver frame, was the studio portrait of a girl, presumably Etienne's fiancée. Fine fair hair fell from a central parting to frame a long, delicately boned face, large-eyed, the mouth a little too small but with a full, beautifully curved upper lip. Was this too, Daniel wondered, an acquired expensive object? Feeling that it might be offensive to study it too closely, he turned to the only painting, a large oil of Etienne and his sister hanging on the wall facing the window. In winter, with the curtains drawn, this vivid picture would be the focus of the room, colours, form, brushwork almost aggressively proclaiming the artist's mastery. Perhaps this week or next the sofa and the chairs would have been swung round to face it and for Etienne winter would have officially begun. This identification with the routine of the dead man's life seemed to Daniel irrational and a little disturbing. There was, after all, no evidence here of Etienne's presence, none of the small but pathetic leavings of a life unexpectedly ended; the half-finished meal, the open book placed face-downwards, the unemptied ashtray, the little messes and muddles of ordinary life.

He saw that Kate was studying the oil painting. That was natural enough, she was known to like modern art. She turned to Claudia Etienne. 'This is a Freud, isn't it? It's wonderful.'

'Yes. My father had it painted as a present for Gerard on his twenty-first birthday.'

It was all there, thought Daniel, moving up beside her; the arrogant good looks, the intelligence, the confidence, the assurance that life was his for the taking. Beside the central figure his sister, younger, more vulnerable, looked at the painter with wary eyes as if defying him to do his worst.

Claudia Etienne said: 'Would you like coffee? It won't take long. One could never rely on finding food here – Gerard mostly ate out – but there was always wine and coffee. You can come into the kitchen if you like, but there's nothing to see there. All Gerard's papers are in that bureau. It opens at the side, a concealed catch. You're welcome to look, but you won't get any joy out of prying. Any papers of importance were kept by the bank and all his business papers are at Innocent House. You've got those. Gerard always lived as if he expected to die overnight. There is one thing, though. I found this unopened on the mat. It's dated the thirteenth of October, so probably arrived on Thursday by the second post. I saw no reason not to read it.'

She handed over a plain white envelope. The paper inside was of the same high quality, the address embossed. The handwriting was large, a girlish scrawl. Daniel read it over Kate's shoulder.

Dear Gerard,

This is to tell you that I want to end our engagement. I suppose I ought to say that I'm sorry to hurt you, but I don't think you will be hurt except in your pride. I shall mind more than you, but not very much and not for long. Mummy thinks that we ought to put a notice in *The Times* since we did announce the engagement, but that doesn't seem very important at present. Look after yourself. It was fun while it lasted, but not as much fun as it could have been.

Lucinda

Underneath there was a postscript: 'Let me know if you want me to return the ring.'

Daniel thought that it was as well the letter had been found unopened. If Etienne had received it, it could have been used by a defence counsel to show a motive for suicide. As it was, it was of small importance to their inquiry.

Kate said to Claudia: 'Had your brother any idea that Lady Lucinda was about to break their engagement?'

'Not as far as I know. She's probably regretting that she wrote that letter. She can hardly pose now as the broken-hearted fiancée.'

The desk was modern, plain and outwardly unpretentious, but with an interior cleverly designed with numerous drawers and cubbyholes. It was all in immaculate order: bills paid, a few bills still outstanding, chequebooks for the previous two years bound together with a rubber band, a drawer with a portfolio of his investments. It was obvious that Etienne kept only what was necessary, clearing his life as it went along, shedding inessentials, conducting his social life, such as it was, by telephone not by letter. They had been at the task for only a few minutes when Claudia Etienne returned carrying a tray with a cafetière and three mugs. She placed the tray on the low table and they came over to take up their mugs. They were still standing, Claudia Etienne with her mug in her hand, when there was the sound of a key in the lock.

Claudia gave an extraordinary sound – something between a gasp and a moan – and Daniel saw that her face had become a mask of terror. The coffee mug dropped from her hands and the brown stain spread over the carpet. She bent down to pick it up, her hands scrabbling over the soft surface and shaking so violently that she couldn't replace the mug on the tray. It seemed to Daniel that her terror infected him and Kate so that they, too, gazed with horrified eyes at the closed door.

It was slowly opened and the original of the photograph came into the room. She said: 'I'm Lucinda Norrington. Who are you?' Her voice was high and clear, a child's voice.

Instinctively Kate had moved to steady Claudia, and it was Daniel who answered. 'Police. Detective Inspector Miskin, and I'm Detective Inspector Aaron.'

Claudia had quickly managed to control herself. Clumsily, refusing Kate's help, she got to her feet. Lucinda's letter lay beside the tray on the coffee table. It seemed to Daniel that every eye was on it.

Claudia's voice was harshly guttural. 'Why did you come here?'

Lady Lucinda moved further into the room. 'I came for that letter. I didn't want people to think Gerard had killed himself because of me. After all he didn't, did he? Kill himself I mean.'

Kate said quietly: 'How can you be sure of that?'

Lady Lucinda turned on her her immense blue eyes. 'Because he liked himself too much. People who like themselves don't commit suicide. Anyway he wouldn't kill himself because I chucked him. He didn't love me, he only loved an idea of me.'

Claudia Etienne had found her normal voice. She said: 'I told him that the engagement was foolish, that you were a selfish, over-bred and rather silly girl, but I think I may have been unfair. You're not as silly as I thought. Actually, Gerard never received your letter. I found it here unopened.'

'Then why did you open it? It isn't addressed to you.'

'Someone had to open it. I could have returned it to you but I didn't know who had sent it. I'd never seen your handwriting before.'

Lady Lucinda said: 'May I have my letter?'

Kate replied: 'We should like to keep it for the time being, if we may.'

Lady Lucinda seemed to regard this as a statement rather than a request. She said: 'But it belongs to me. I wrote it.'

'We may only need to keep it for a little time and we don't intend to publish it.'

Daniel, uncertain what the law said about ownership of a letter, wondered whether they had, in fact, any right to take it, and what

256

Kate would do if Lady Lucinda pressed the matter. He wondered, too, why Kate was so anxious to have it. It wasn't as if Etienne had received it. But what proof had they of that? They had only his sister's word that she had found it on the mat unopened. Lady Lucinda made no further objection. She shrugged and turned to Claudia.

'I'm sorry about Gerard. It was an accident, wasn't it? That's the impression you gave Mummy on the telephone. But this morning some of the papers are hinting it could be more complicated. He wasn't murdered, was he?'

Kate said: 'He could have been.'

Again the blue eyes were turned consideringly on her. 'How bizarre. I don't think I've ever known anyone who was murdered, known them personally, I mean.'

She walked over to her photograph and took it in her hands, studying it closely as if she hadn't seen it before and was none too pleased with what the photographer had made of her features. Then she said: 'I'll take this. After all, you won't want it, Claudia.'

Claudia said: 'Strictly speaking none of his possessions should be moved except by his executors or the police.'

'Well the police won't want it either. I don't want it to be here in the empty flat, not if Gerard was murdered.'

So she was not without superstition. The discovery intrigued Daniel. It sat oddly with her cool self-possession. He watched as she studied the photograph and ran a long pink nailed finger caressingly over the glass as if testing it for dust. Then she turned and said to Claudia: 'I suppose there's something I can use to wrap this?'

'There may be a plastic bag in the kitchen drawer, you'd better look. And if there's anything else which belongs to you, now might be a good time to take it.'

Lady Lucinda didn't even trouble to cast her eyes round the room. She said: 'There's nothing else.'

'If you want a coffee bring in another mug. It's freshly made.'

'I don't want coffee, thank you.'

They waited in silence until, in less than a minute, she returned carrying the photograph in a Harrods plastic bag. She was walking to the door when Kate said: 'Lady Lucinda, I wonder if we could ask you a few questions? We would in any case have asked to see you, but now that you're here it will save time for both of us.'

'How much time? I mean, how long is it going to take?'

'Not very long.' Kate turned to Claudia. 'You don't mind if we use this flat for the interview?'

'I don't see how I can prevent you. I suppose you don't expect me to retire to the kitchen?'

'That won't be necessary.'

'Or to the bedroom? That might be more comfortable.'

She was looking fixedly at Lady Lucinda who said calmly: 'I can't tell you. I've never been in Gerard's bedroom.'

She sat in the nearer of the two armchairs and Kate seated herself opposite. Daniel and Claudia sat between them on the sofa.

Kate said: 'When did you last see your fiancé?'

'He isn't my fiancé. He was at the time, though. I saw him last Saturday.'

'Saturday ninth October?'

'I suppose so, if last Saturday was the ninth. We were going to Bradwell-on-Sea to visit his father but the day was wet and Gerard said his father's house was gloomy enough without arriving in the rain and we'd go another time. Instead we went to the Sainsbury Wing at the National Gallery in the afternoon because Gerard wanted to look again at the Wilton Diptych, and then on to the Ritz for tea. I didn't see him that evening because Mummy wanted me to drive down to Wiltshire with her to spend the night and Sunday with my brother. She wanted to talk about marriage settlements before we saw the lawyers.'

'And how was Mr Etienne when you met him on the Saturday, apart from being depressed about the weather?'

'He wasn't depressed about the weather. There wasn't any hurry to see his father. Gerard didn't get depressed about things he couldn't change.'

Daniel said: 'And the things he could change, he changed?'

She turned and looked at him, and suddenly smiled. 'That's right.' She added, 'That was the last time I saw him but it wasn't the last time I spoke to him. We talked on the telephone on Thursday night.'

Kate's voice was carefully controlled: 'You spoke to him two days ago, on the night he died?'

'I don't know when he died. He was found dead yesterday morning, wasn't he? I spoke to him on his private line on the previous evening.'

'At what time, Lady Lucinda?'

258

'At about twenty past seven, I suppose. It might have been a little later but it was certainly before half past seven because Mummy and I were supposed to leave the house at seven-thirty to go to dinner with my godmother and I was already dressed. I thought I would just have time to ring Gerard. I wanted an excuse to make it a short conversation. That's how I can be so sure of the time.'

'What about? You'd already written to break off the engagement.'

'I know. I thought he would have got the letter that morning. I wanted to ask him whether he agreed with Mummy that we ought to put a notice in *The Times* or whether he preferred for us to write to our personal friends and just let the news get around. Of course Mummy now wants me to destroy my letter to Gerard and say nothing. I shan't do that. I can't anyway now you've seen it. But at least she doesn't have to worry about the notice in *The Times*. That will save her a few pounds.'

The pin-prick of venom was so sudden and so quickly withdrawn that Daniel could almost believe he'd missed it. As if she hadn't heard, Kate asked: 'What did he say about the notice, about your broken engagement? Didn't you ask him if he'd received your letter?'

'I didn't ask him anything. We didn't talk at all. He said he couldn't speak then because he had a visitor with him.'

'You're sure of that?'

The high bell-like voice was almost expressionless. 'I'm not sure that he had a visitor. I mean, how could I be? I didn't hear anyone or speak to anyone except Gerard. Perhaps that was just an excuse for not talking to me, but I'm sure that's what he told me.'

'And in those precise words? I want to be absolutely clear about this, Lady Lucinda. He didn't say he wasn't alone or that he had someone with him? He used the word visitor?'

'I've told you. He said he had a visitor with him.'

'And that was between, say, seven-twenty and seven-thirty?'

'Nearer seven-thirty. The car came round for Mummy and me at half past seven.'

A visitor. By an effort of will Daniel prevented himself from glancing at Kate but he knew that their thoughts were in harness. If Etienne had indeed used that word – and the girl seemed positive about it – it surely implied that Etienne was with someone from outside the firm. He would hardly have used the word for a partner or a member of staff. Wouldn't it then be more natural to say 'I'm tied up', or 'In a meeting', or 'I'm busy with a colleague'? And if someone had called on him that night, invited or uninvited, he or she hadn't yet come forward. Why not, if the visit had been innocent, if he'd left Etienne alive and well? There had been no note of any arranged meeting in Etienne's office diary, but that wasn't conclusive. The visitor could have rung him on his private line any time during the day or early evening, or come uninvited and unexpected. But the evidence, such as it was, was circumstantial, like so much evidence in this increasingly baffling case.

But Kate was pressing on, asking Lady Lucinda when she had last been at Innocent House.

'Not since the party on the tenth of July. It was partly for my birthday – I was twenty – and partly as an engagement party.'

Kate said: 'We have the list of guests. I suppose they were free to wander all over the house if they wanted?'

'Some of them did, I think. You know how couples are at parties, they like to get away on their own. I don't think any of the rooms were locked although Gerard said that the staff had been told to put away all their papers safely.'

'You didn't happen to see anyone going to the top of the house, towards the archives room?'

'Well I did actually. It was rather funny. I needed to go to the loo but the one on the first floor which was being used for the women guests was occupied, and then I remembered there was a small one on the top floor and I decided to use that. I went up by the stairs and I saw two people coming down. Not at all the people you'd expect. They looked so guilty, too. It really was weird.'

'Who were they, Lady Lucinda?'

'George, the old man who works on the switchboard in reception and that dull little woman who's married to the accountant, I forget his name, Sydney Bernard or something like that. Gerard introduced me to all the staff and their wives. It was a terrible bore.'

'Sydney Bartrum?'

'That's right, his wife. She was wearing an extraordinary dress in pale blue taffeta with a pink sash.' She turned to Claudia Etienne. 'You remember, don't you, Claudia? A very full skirt covered with pink net and puffed sleeves. Gruesome!'

Claudia said shortly: 'I remember.'

'Did either of them say what they were doing on the top floor?'

'The same as I was, I suppose. She went scarlet and muttered something about using the toilet. They looked extraordinarily alike, the same round faces, the same embarrassment. George looked as if I'd discovered them pilfering the petty cash. It was odd, though, wasn't it? Those two together I mean. George wasn't a guest, of course. He was only there to help with the men's coats and repel gatecrashers. And if Mrs Bartrum wanted the loo, why didn't she ask Claudia or one of the women staff?'

Kate asked: 'Did you mention this to anyone afterwards, to Mr Etienne, for example?'

'No, it wasn't that important, just odd. I'd almost forgotten about it until now. Look, is there anything else you want to know? I think I've been here long enough. If you want to speak to me again you'd better write and I'll try to arrange a meeting.'

Kate said: 'We'd like a statement, Lady Lucinda. Perhaps you could call in at Wapping Police Station as soon as convenient.'

'With my solicitor?'

'If you prefer it, or think it necessary.'

'I don't suppose it is. Mummy said that I might need a solicitor to watch my interests at the inquest, if it came out about the broken engagement, but I don't think I have any interests now, not if Gerard died before he got my letter.'

She got to her feet and shook hands formally with both Kate and Daniel but made no move towards Claudia Etienne. But at the door she turned and it was to Claudia that she spoke.

'He never bothered to make love to me when we were engaged so I don't think the marriage would have been much fun for either of us, do you?' Daniel suspected that, had neither police officer been present, she would have used a coarser expression. She added, 'Oh, you'd better have this,' and laid a key on the coffee table. 'I don't suppose I shall see this flat again.'

She went out closing the door firmly, and a second later they heard the front door close with equal finality.

Claudia said: 'Gerard was a romantic. He divided women into those you have affairs with and those you marry. Most men get over that sexual illusion before they're twenty-one. He was probably reacting against too many sexual conquests made too easily. I wonder how long that marriage would have lasted. Well, there's one dis-illusionment he's been spared. Will you be much longer?'

Kate said: 'Not much longer now.'

Minutes later they were ready to go. Daniel's last picture of Claudia Etienne was of a tall figure standing and looking out over the balcony at the darkening spires of the city. She answered their goodbyes without turning her head and they left her to the silence and emptiness of the flat, quietly closing the doors behind them.

41

Leaving Hillgate Street, Daniel and Kate had picked up the car at Notting Hill Gate Police Station and driven the short distance to Declan Cartwright's shop. It was open, and in the front room an elderly bearded man, wearing a skull-cap and a long black coat, verdigrised with age, was showing a customer a Victorian writing desk, his skeleton-yellow fingers caressing the marquetry on the lid. He was apparently too occupied to hear their entrance even with the clang of the bell, but the customer turned, and the old man looked round.

Kate said: 'Mr Simon? We have an appointment to see Mr Declan Cartwright.'

Even before she could take out her warrant card, he said, 'He's in the back. Straight through. He's in the back', and turned quickly again to the writing desk, his hands shaking so violently that the fingers clattered on the lid. Kate wondered what it was in his past that had produced such fear of authority, such terror of the police.

They made their way through the shop, down three steps and into a kind of conservatory at the back. Among a clutter of miscellaneous objects Declan Cartwright was conferring with a customer. He was large, very swarthy and wearing a coat with an astrakhan collar topped with a rakish trilby, and was studying a cameo through an eyeglass. Kate could only assume that a man who chose to look so like a caricature of a crook would hardly dare actually to be one. As soon as they appeared, Cartwright said: 'Charlie, why don't you buy yourself a drink and think it over? Come back in about half an hour. This is the fuzz arriving. I've got myself mixed up in a murder. Don't look so worried, I didn't do it. It's just that I have to give an alibi for someone who might have done.'

The customer, with a glance at Kate and Daniel, made a nonchalant exit.

Kate again took out her warrant card, but Declan waved it aside. 'That's all right, don't bother. I can recognize the police when I see them.'

He must, she thought, have been an exceptionally pretty child and there was still something childlike in the gamin face with its cluster of undisciplined curls above the high forehead, the huge eyes and the beautifully formed but petulant mouth. But there was a very adult sexuality in the appraisal he gave both her and Daniel. She felt Daniel stiffen at her side and thought: 'Not his type, and certainly not mine.'

Like Farlow, he answered their questions with a half-mocking insouciance, but there was an essential difference. With Farlow they had been aware of an intelligence and a force still dominating the pathetically emaciated body. Declan Cartwright was both weak and frightened, as frightened as old Simon had been but for a different reason. His voice was brittle, his hands restless and his attempts at banter as unconvincing as his accent. He said: 'My fiancée told me that you would be coming. I don't suppose you're here to look at antiques but I've got some nice little pieces of Staffordshire just come in. All legally acquired. I could do you a very good price if you don't think that would be suborning the police in the execution of their duty.'

Kate asked: 'You and Miss Etienne are engaged to be married?'

'I'm engaged to her, but I'm not sure if she's engaged to me. You'll have to ask her. With Claudia being engaged is a fluctuating state. It rather depends on how she's feeling at the time. But we were engaged – at least I think we were – when we went on the river on Thursday night.'

'When did you arrange this trip?'

'Quite a time ago, actually. On the night of Sonia Clements' funeral. You've heard about Sonia Clements, of course.'

Kate said: 'A bit odd, wasn't it, to arrange a river trip so far in advance?'

'Claudia likes to arrange things a week or so ahead. She's a very well-organized woman. Actually there was a reason. Thursday the fourteenth of October was the morning of the partners' meeting. She was going to tell me all about it.'

'And did she tell you all about it?'

'Well she told me that the partners were going to sell Innocent House and move downstream to Docklands and that they were going to sack someone, the accountant I think. I can't remember the details. It was all rather boring.'

Daniel said: 'Hardly worth the trouble of a river trip.'

'Oh, but there are other things you can do on the river than discuss business, even if the cabin is a little cramped. Those great steel hoods of the Thames barrier are very erotic. You two should borrow a police launch. You might surprise yourselves.'

Kate said: 'When did you begin the trip and when did it end?'

'It began at six-thirty when the launch came back from Charing Cross and we took over. It ended at about ten-thirty when we got back to Innocent House and Claudia drove me home. I suppose we got back here at about eleven o'clock. As I expect she told you, she didn't leave here until two o'clock.'

Daniel said: 'I suppose Mr Simon will be able to confirm that? Or doesn't he live here?'

'Actually, I'm afraid he won't. Sorry about that. The poor old darling is getting dreadfully deaf. We always creep up the stairs so as not to disturb him but it's a totally unnecessary precaution. Actually, he might be able to confirm when we arrived. He could have had his door ajar. He sleeps more soundly when he knows the boy is home and safely tucked up. But I doubt whether he heard anything after that.'

Kate said: 'You didn't take your own car, then, to Innocent House?'

'I don't drive, Inspector. I deplore the pollution caused by motor cars and I don't add to it. Isn't that public-spirited of me? There's also the fact that when I tried to learn I found the whole experience so terrifying that I had to keep my eyes permanently closed, and none of the instructors would take me on. I went to Innocent House by tube. Very tedious. I took the Circle Line from Notting Hill Gate to Tower Hill and then picked up a cab. It's easier to go by the Central Line to Liverpool Street and take a cab from there but, in fact, I didn't, if it's of the slightest importance.'

Kate asked him for details of the evening and was unsurprised when he confirmed Claudia Etienne's account.

Daniel said: 'So you were together the whole evening from six-thirty until the early hours of the morning?'

'That's right, Sergeant – you are a sergeant, aren't you? If not, I'm so sorry. It's just that you look so very like a sergeant. We were together from six-thirty until about two in the morning. I don't suppose you're interested in what we were doing between, say, eleven o'clock and two. If you are, you'd better ask Miss Etienne. She'll be able to give an account suitable for your chaste ears. I suppose you'll be wanting all this in the form of a statement?'

It gave Kate considerable satisfaction to say that they would indeed and that he could come to Wapping Police Station to make it.

Under questioning by Kate so gentle and patient that it seemed only to increase his terror, Mr Simon confirmed that he had heard them come in at eleven. He had been listening for Declan because he always slept more soundly knowing that there was someone in the house. That was partly why he had suggested to Mr Cartwright that he should live on the premises. But once he had heard the door, he had settled to sleep. He wouldn't have heard if either of them had subsequently gone out.

Unlocking the car, Kate said: 'Shit scared, wasn't he? Cartwright I mean. D'you think he's a rogue or a fool or both, or just a pretty boy with a taste for baubles? What on earth does an intelligent woman like Claudia Etienne see in him?'

'Oh come on, Kate. Since when has intelligence had anything to do with sex? I'm not sure they aren't incompatible, sex and intelligence I mean.'

'They aren't for me. Intelligence turns me on.'

'Yes I know.'

'What do you mean?' she asked sharply.

'Nothing. I find I do best with pretty, good natured, obliging women who aren't very bright.'

'Like most of your sex. You should try to train yourself out of it. How much do you think that alibi's worth?'

'About as much as Rupert Farlow's. Cartwright and Claudia Etienne could have killed Etienne, taken the launch straight over to Greenwich pier and easily been in the restaurant by eight. There's not a lot of traffic on the river after dark, the chances of anyone seeing them aren't great. Another boring job of checking.'

Kate said: 'He has a motive – both of them have. If Claudia Etienne is fool enough to marry him he'll be getting a wealthy wife.'

Daniel said: 'Do you think he's got the bottle to kill anyone?'

'It didn't need much bottle, did it? All he had to do was entice Etienne into that killing room. He didn't have to stab or bludgeon or strangle. He didn't even have to face his victim.'

'One of them would have had to go back later and do that business with the snake. That would have taken some guts. I can't see Claudia Etienne doing that, not to her brother.'

'Oh I don't know. If she was prepared to kill him, why balk at desecrating the body? Do you want to drive or shall I?'

While Kate took the wheel, Daniel telephoned Wapping. It was apparent that there was news. Replacing the receiver after a few minutes, he said: 'The lab report is in. I've just heard the blood analysis from Robbins in boring detail. There was a blood saturation of 73 per cent. He probably died pretty quickly. Seven-thirty seems about right for the time of death. You get dizziness and headache at 30 per cent, incoordination and mental confusion at 40 per cent, exhaustion at 50 per cent and unconsciousness at 60 per cent. Weakness may come on suddenly because of muscular suboxia.'

Kate asked: 'Anything on the rubble blocking the flue?'

'It came from the chimney. It's the same stuff. But we expected that.'

Kate said: 'We already know that the gas fire isn't defective and we've got no significant prints. What about the window cord?'

'That's rather more difficult. The likelihood is that it was deliberately frayed with some bluntish implement and over a period of time, but they can't be 100 per cent sure. The fibres were crushed and broken, not cut. The rest of the cord was old and in parts weak, but they could see no reason why it should have snapped at that point unless it had been deliberately interfered with. Oh, and there's one other finding. There was a minute stain of mucus on the head of the snake. That means that it was rammed into the mouth immediately or very soon after the sharp object was removed.'

42

On Sunday 17 October Dalgliesh decided to take Kate with him to interview Sonia Clements' sister, Sister Agnes, at her Brighton convent. He would have preferred to go alone, but a convent, even an Anglican one, and even for the son of a rector with High Church tendencies, was unfamiliar ground, to be approached with circumspection. Without a woman as chaperon he might not be permitted to see Sister Agnes except in the presence of the Mother Superior or another nun. He wasn't sure what he expected to get from the visit but his instinct, which he sometimes distrusted but had learned not to ignore, told him that there was something to be learned. The two deaths, so very different, were linked by more than that bare upper room in which one person had chosen to die, the other had fought to live. Sonia Clements had worked at Peverell Press for twenty-four years; it was Gerard Etienne who had sacked her. Was that ruthless decision a sufficient reason for the suicide? And if not, why had she chosen to die? Who, if anyone, might have been tempted to avenge that death?

The weather held. An early mist lifted to promise another day of mellow if fitful sunshine. Even the London air held something of the sweetness of the summer and a light breeze dragged tatters of thin cloud across an azure sky. Making his tedious and circuitous way through the suburbs of South London with Kate at his side, Dalgliesh, with the return of a boyish longing for the sight and sound of the sea, found himself hoping that the convent would be situated on the coast. They spoke little on the journey. Dalgliesh preferred to drive in silence and Kate could tolerate even taciturnity without the need to chat. It was, he reflected, not the least of her virtues. He had called for her at her new flat but had waited in the Jaguar for her to appear rather than taking the lift and ringing her doorbell when she might have felt an obligation to invite him in. He valued his own privacy too much to risk invading hers. She had appeared precisely on time as he had expected. She looked different and he realized how seldom he saw her wearing a skirt. He smiled inwardly, wondering whether she had hesitated over the choice before deciding that her usual trousers might be seen as inappropriate for a visit to a convent. He suspected that, despite his sex, he might be more at home there than Kate.

His hope, never realistic, of stealing five minutes for a brisk walk along the edge of the beach was due to be frustrated. The convent stood on rising ground above a dull but busy main road, separated from it by an eight-foot brick wall. The main gate stood open and, turning in, they saw an ornate building in harsh red brick, obviously Victorian and as obviously designed as an institution, probably to house the first sisters of the order. The four storeys of identical windows placed closely together and ranged with precision reminded Dalgliesh uncomfortably of a prison, a thought which may have occurred to the architect since the incongruous addition of a thin spire at one end of the building and a tower at the other looked like afterthoughts, designed as much to humanize as to embellish. A wide sweep of gravel curved upwards to a front door of almost black oak banded with iron, which would have been more appropriate as the entrance to a Norman keep. To their right they could glimpse a brick-built church, large enough to serve a parish, with a graceless spire and narrow lancet windows. To the left was contrast; a low modern building with a covered terrace and small formal garden, which he guessed was the hospice for the dying.

There was only one car, a Ford, standing in front of the convent and Dalgliesh parked neatly beside it. Pausing outside the car for a moment, he glanced back over the terraced lawns and could at last glimpse the English Channel. Short streets of small coloured houses, pale blue, pink and green, their roofs patterned with a frail geometry of television aerials, ran down in parallel lines to the layered blue of the sea, their precisely ordered domesticity contrasting with the heavy Victorian pile at his back.

There was no sign of life from the main building but, as he turned to lock the car door, he saw a nun turn the corner of the hospice with a patient in a wheelchair. The patient wore a striped white and blue cap with a red bobble and was covered with a rug drawn up to the chin. The nun bent to whisper and the patient laughed, a thin falling trickle of joyous notes on the quiet air.

He pulled the iron chain to the left of the door and heard its echoing clangour even through the thick iron-bounded oak. The square grille slid open and a gentle-faced nun looked out. Dalgliesh gave his name and held out his warrant card. At once the door was opened and the nun, wordless, but still smiling, gestured them to enter. They found themselves in a wide hall which smelled not unpleasantly of mild disinfectant. The floor was chequered with black and white tiles which looked freshly scrubbed and the walls were bare except for a sepia portrait, obviously Victorian, of a formidable grave-faced nun whom Dalgliesh assumed to be the foundress of the order, and a reproduction of Millais' *Christ in the Carpenter's Shop* in an ornate carved wood frame. The nun, still smiling, still wordless, ushered them into a small room to the right of the hall and with a somewhat theatrical gesture silently invited them to sit. Dalgliesh wondered if she was deaf and dumb.

The room was sparsely furnished but was not unwelcoming. The central table, highly polished, held a bowl of late roses and there were two easy chairs covered with faded cretonne set in front of the double windows. The walls were plain except for a large and ornate wood and silver crucifix of horrific realism to the right of the fireplace. It looked, Dalgliesh thought, Spanish and as if it must once have hung in a church. Over the fireplace was a copy in oil of a Madonna offering a bunch of grapes to the Christ Child which it took him some time to identify as Mignard's *La Vierge à la Grappe*. A brass plaque bore the name of the donor. There were four upright dining chairs set in an uninviting line against the right-hand wall, but Dalgliesh and Kate remained standing.

They were not kept waiting long. The door opened and a nun entered with brisk self-assurance and held out her hand.

'You are Commander Dalgliesh and Inspector Miskin? Welcome to St Anne's. I am Mother Mary Clare. We spoke when you telephoned, Commander. Would you and the Inspector care for some coffee?'

The hand which briefly grasped his was plump but cool. He said: 'No thank you, Mother. That is kind of you but we hope not to inconvenience you for too long.'

There was nothing intimidating about her. Her short and sturdy body was dignified by the long blue-grey habit bound with a leather belt, but she looked as comfortable in it as if the formal garb were workaday clothes. A single heavy cross in dark wood hung from a cord round her neck and her face, soft and pale as dough, bulged like a baby's from the constricting wimple. But the eyes behind the steel spectacles were shrewd, and the little mouth, for all its delicate softness, held the promise of an uncompromising firmness. Dalgliesh knew that he and Kate were subject to a scrutiny as keen as it was unobtrusive.

Then, with a little nod, she said: 'I'll send Sister Agnes to you. It's a lovely day, perhaps you would care to walk together in the rose garden.'

It was, Dalgliesh recognized, a command not a suggestion, but he knew that in that first brief encounter they had passed some private test. Had she been less than satisfied he had no doubt that the interview would have taken place in this room and under her supervision. She tugged at the bell-cord and the little smiling nun who had let them in again appeared.

'Will you ask Sister Agnes to be good enough to join us?'

Again they waited in silence, still standing. In less than two minutes the door opened and a tall nun entered alone. The Mother Superior said: 'This is Sister Agnes. Sister, this is Commander Dalgliesh of New Scotland Yard and Inspector Miskin. I have suggested that you might like to walk outside in the rose garden.'

With a valedictory nod but no formal goodbye she was gone.

The nun who confronted them with wary eyes could not have been more different from the Mother Superior. The habit was the same, except that her cross was smaller, but on her it conferred a hieratic dignity, remote and a little mysterious. The Mother Superior had looked dressed for a stint at the kitchen stove; it was difficult to imagine Sister Agnes except at the altar. She was very thin, long-limbed and strong-featured, the wimple emphasizing the high cheekbones, the strong line of the eyebrows and the uncompromising set of the wide mouth.

She said: 'Then shall we look at the roses, Commander?' Dalgliesh opened the door and he and Kate followed her out of the reception room and through the hall on almost silent feet.

She led the way down the grand path to the terraced rose garden. The beds were in three long rows divided by parallel gravel paths, each path four stone steps down from the one above. There would be just room for the three of them to walk abreast, first along the top path, then down the steps, then back along the second path to the second flight of steps and the forty yards of the lowest path before turning, a bleak perambulation carried out in full view of all the convent windows. He wondered if there was a more private garden at the rear of the convent. Even if there was they were not, apparently, expected to walk there.

Sister Agnes paced between them, almost as tall as his six feet two inches, her head held high. She was wearing a long grey cardigan over her habit and with each hand thrust deeply into the opposite cuff as if for warmth. With her bound arms held tightly against her body she reminded Dalgliesh uncomfortably of old pictures he had seen of mental patients in strait-jackets. It seemed that she walked between them like a prisoner under escort, and he wondered if that was how the three of them would appear to any secret watcher from the high windows. The thought, and it was not agreeable, apparently also entered Kate's mind for, muttering an excuse, she dropped a little behind and, kneeling, appeared to be tying the shoelace of her brogues. When she caught up with them she took her place next to Dalgliesh.

It was Dalgliesh who broke the silence. He said: 'It is good of you to see us. I'm sorry to have to trouble you, particularly as it must seem an intrusion on private grief. I need to ask you about the death of your sister.'

' "Intrusion on private grief". That was the telephone message I received from Mother Superior. I suppose they are words you often have to use, Commander.'

'Intrusion is sometimes inseparable from my job.'

'And have you specific questions you hope I can answer, or is this a more general intrusion?'

'A little of both.'

'But you know how my sister died. Sonia killed herself, there is no possible doubt about that. She left a note at the scene. She also posted a letter to me on the morning she died. She didn't think the news was worth a first-class stamp. I received it three days later.'

Dalgliesh said: 'Would you mind telling me what was in the note? I know, of course, what was in the note to the coroner.'

She didn't speak for a few seconds which seemed much longer, then spoke without emphasis as if reciting a piece of prose learned by heart. ' "What I am about to do will seem a sin in your eyes. Please try to understand that what you see as sinful is to me both natural and right. We have made different choices but they lead to the same end. After the vacillating years at least I can be absolute for death. Try not to grieve for me too long; grief is only an indulgence. I could not have had a better sister." '

She said: 'Is that what you want to hear, Commander? It is hardly relevant, surely, to your present inquiry.'

'We have to look at anything which happened at Innocent House in the months before Gerard Etienne died which could have had a bearing even remotely on that death. One is your sister's suicide. The gossip in London literary circles and at Innocent House seems to be that Gerard Etienne drove her to that act. If he did, her friend – a particular friend – might have wished him harm.'

She said: 'I was Sonia's particular friend. She had no particular friends except me, and I had no reason to wish Gerard Etienne dead. I was here on the day or night when he died. That is a fact you can easily check.'

Dalgliesh said: 'I was not suggesting, Sister, that you were in any way personally concerned with Gerard Etienne's death. I am asking if you knew of any other person close to your sister who could have resented the way she died.'

'None except myself. But I resented it, Commander. Suicide is the final despair, the final rejection of God's grace, the ultimate sin.'

Dalgliesh said quietly: 'Then perhaps, Sister, it will receive the ultimate mercy.'

They had reached the end of the first path and together they descended the steps and turned left. Suddenly she said, 'I dislike roses in autumn. They are essentially summer flowers. The December roses are the most depressing, brown and shrivelled buds on a tangle of prickles. I can hardly bear to walk here in December. Like us, roses don't know when to die.'

He said: 'But today we can almost believe it is summer.' He paused, then added: 'I expect you know that Gerard Etienne died from carbon monoxide poisoning and in the same room as your sister. It is unlikely in his case to have been suicide. It could be accidental death, a blocked flue which caused the gas fire to malfunction, but we have to consider a third possibility, that the fire was deliberately tampered with.'

She said: 'You're saying that you believe he was murdered?'

'It can't be ruled out. What I have to ask you is whether you have any reason to believe that your sister could have interfered with the fire. I'm not suggesting it was a plot to kill Etienne. But is it possible that she might have planned a suicide which would look like accidental death and then changed her mind?'

'How can I possibly tell you that, Commander?'

'It was a very long shot, but I had to ask. If anyone is brought to trial for murder it is a possibility that the defence counsel will certainly put forward.'

She said: 'It would have saved a great deal of distress for other people if she had troubled to make her death look like an accident, but suicides so seldom do. It is, after all, the supreme act of aggression and what satisfaction is there in aggression if it hurts only oneself? To make suicide look accidental wouldn't have been so very difficult. I could think of ways, but they don't include dismantling a gas fire and blocking the flue. I'm not sure that Sonia would have known how to do that. She wasn't mechanically minded in life; why should she be so in death?'

'And the note she sent you, that was all? No reason, no explanation?'

'No,' she said. 'No reason, no explanation.'

Dalgliesh went on: 'It seems to have been assumed that your sister killed herself because Gerard Etienne had told her that she had to go. Does that seem likely to you?'

She didn't reply, and after a minute he gently persisted. 'As her sister, as someone who knew her well, does that explanation satisfy you?'

She turned to him and, for the first time, looked him full in the face. 'Is that question relevant to your inquiry?'

'It could be. If Miss Clements knew something about Innocent House, or about one of the people who worked there, something so distressing to her that it contributed to her death, that something could also be relevant to the death of Gerard Etienne.'

Again she turned. She said: 'Is there any question of reopening the manner of my sister's death?'

'Formally? None at all. We know how Miss Clements died. I would like to know why, but the verdict of the inquest was correct. Legally that is the end of it.'

They paced in silence. She seemed to be considering a course of action. He was aware of, or perhaps imagined, the muscles taut with tension of the arm which briefly brushed his own. When she spoke her voice was harsh.

'I can satisfy your curiosity, Commander. My sister died because the two people she cared for most, perhaps the only two people she ever cared for, left her and left her finally. I took my vows the week

274

before she killed herself; Henry Peverell died eight months earlier.'

Until now Kate had been silent. She said: 'You're saying that she was in love with Mr Peverell?'

Sister Agnes turned and looked at her as if noticing her presence for the first time. Then she again turned her head and with an almost imperceptible shiver clasped her arms more tightly across her breast. 'She was his mistress for the last eight years of his life. She called it love. I called it an obsession. I don't know what he called it. They were never seen together in public. The affair was kept deeply secret at his insistence. The room in which they made love was the one in which she died. I always knew when they had been together. Those were the nights when she stayed late at the office. When she came in I could smell him on her.'

Kate protested: 'But why the secrecy? What was he afraid of? Neither was married, they were both adults. This was no one's business but their own.'

'When I asked that question she had her answers ready, or rather his. She said that he had no wish to marry again, that he wanted to stay faithful to the memory of his wife, that he disliked the idea of his private affairs being the subject of office gossip, that the relationship would distress his daughter. She accepted all the excuses. It was enough for her that he apparently needed what she could provide. It may, of course, have been quite simple, that she was adequate to satisfy a physical need but not sufficiently beautiful or young or rich enough to tempt him to marry her. And for him, I think the secrecy added an additional *frisson* to the affair. Perhaps this was what he enjoyed, humiliating her, testing the limits of her devotion, stealing up to that drab little room like a Victorian employer pleasuring his parlour-maid. It was not the sinfulness of the relationship which distressed me most, it was the vulgarity.'

He had not expected such openness, such confidence. But, perhaps, it was not so surprising. She must have endured months of self-imposed silence and now, to two strangers whom she need never see again, the pent-up bitterness was released. She said: 'I am the elder by only eighteen months. We were always very close. He destroyed that. She couldn't have him and her religion so she chose him. He destroyed the confidence between us. How could there be confidence when each of us despised the other's god?'

Dalgliesh said: 'She had no sympathy with your vocation?'

275

'She had no understanding of it. Nor had he. He saw it as a retreat from the world and from responsibility, from sexuality and from involvement, and what he believed she believed. She had known for some time, of course, what I had in mind. I suppose that she hoped no one would have me. There are not many communities which welcome middle-aged postulants. A convent isn't intended as a refuge for the unsuccessful and disillusioned. And she knew, of course, that I had no practical skills to offer. I was – I am – a book-restorer. Reverend Mother still releases me from time to time to work in libraries in London, Oxford and Cambridge, provided that there is a suitable house – I mean a convent – in which I can be lodged. But that work is becoming infrequent. It takes a great deal of time to restore and rebind a valuable book or manuscript, more time than I can be spared for.'

Dalgliesh recalled a visit three years previously to the library at Corpus Christi College in Cambridge when he had been shown the Jerusalem Bible, taken under escort to Westminster Abbey for successive coronations, together with one of the earliest illuminated copies of the New Testament. The recently rebound treasure, lifted lovingly from its special box, had been placed on the padded V-shaped lectern, the pages turned with a wooden spatula to avoid handling. He had looked in wonder across five centuries at the meticulous drawings, still as bright as when the colours had flowed with such gentle precision from the artist's pen, drawings which, in their beauty and essential humanity, had brought him close to tears.

He said: 'Your work here is regarded as more important?'

'It is judged by different criteria. And here my lack of the more commonplace practical skills is no disadvantage. Anyone with a little training can operate a washing machine, wheel patients to the bathroom, give out bedpans. I can't be sure how long even these services will be required. The priest who is our chaplain here is converting to Roman Catholicism following the decision of the Church of England to ordain women. Half of the sisters want to follow him. The future of St Anne's as an Anglican order is in doubt.'

They had now walked the length of the three paths and, turning, began the journey again. Sister Agnes said: 'Henry Peverell wasn't the only person who came between us in the last years of my sister's life. There was Eliza Brady. Oh you needn't trouble to look for her, Commander, she died in 1871. I read about her in a report of an inquest in a Victorian newspaper which I found in a second-hand bookshop in Charing Cross Road and which unhappily I passed over to Sonia. Eliza Brady was thirteen years old. Her father worked for a coal merchant and her mother had died in childbirth. Eliza became the mother to four younger brothers and sisters and the baby. Her father gave evidence at the inquest that Eliza was mother to them all. For fourteen hours a day she worked. She washed, she made the fire, she cooked, she shopped, she cared for the whole of that little family. One morning, when she was drying the baby's napkins on a guard in front of the fire, she leaned on the guard and it collapsed into the flames. She was horribly burnt and died in agony three days later. The story affected my sister powerfully. She said, "So this is the justice of your so-called loving God. This is how he rewards the innocent and the good. He wasn't satisfied with killing her. She had to die horribly, slowly and in agony." My sister became almost obsessed with Eliza Brady. She made her into a kind of cult figure. If she had had a picture of the child she would probably have prayed in front of it, although I don't know to whom.'

Kate protested: 'But if she'd wanted a reason to disbelieve in God why go back to the nineteenth century? There are plenty of contemporary tragedies. She'd only got to look at the television or read the newspaper. She'd only got to think of Yugoslavia. Eliza Brady has been dead for over a hundred years.'

Sister Agnes said: 'That is what I told her, but Sonia replied that justice had nothing to do with time. We shouldn't allow ourselves to be dominated by time. If God is eternal, then His justice is eternal. And so is His injustice.'

Kate asked: 'Before your estrangement from your sister, did you often visit Innocent House?'

'Not often, but I went there occasionally. Actually there was a possibility, months before I decided that I had a vocation, that I might have worked part-time at Innocent House. Jean-Philippe Etienne was very anxious that the archives should be examined and catalogued and apparently he thought I might be a suitable person to do it. The Etiennes have always had an eye for a bargain and he probably guessed that I would work as much for interest as for money. However, Henry Peverell put a stop to that, and, of course, I understood why.'

Dalgliesh asked: 'You knew Jean-Philippe Etienne?'

'I got to know all the partners reasonably well. The two old men, Jean-Philippe and Henry, seemed to be almost wilfully hanging on to a power neither seemed able or willing to exercise. Gerard Etienne was obviously the young Turk, the heir apparent. I never got on particularly well with Claudia Etienne but I liked James de Witt. De Witt is an example of a man who lives a good life without the help of religious belief. There are those who are apparently born with a deficiency of original sin. Goodness in them is hardly a merit.'

Dalgliesh said: 'Surely religious belief isn't necessary to a good life.'

'Perhaps not. Belief in religion may not influence behaviour. The practice of religion surely should.'

Kate said: 'You weren't, of course, at the last party they held. Did you go to any of the earlier parties? Were the visitors able to wander where they wanted throughout the house?'

'I only went to two of the parties. They held one in the summer and one in the winter. There was certainly nothing to prevent visitors from wandering round the house. I don't think many people did. It is hardly courteous to take the opportunity of a party to explore rooms which are generally held to be private. Of course, Innocent House is now mainly offices and perhaps that makes a difference. But the Innocent House parties were fairly formal affairs. The guest list was controlled and Henry Peverell greatly disliked having more than eighty people in the house at one time. Peverell Press has never gone in for the ordinary kind of literary party – too many people invited in case any of their writers are offended at being left out; overcrowded, overheated rooms with guests trying to balance plates of cold food and drink lukewarm inferior white wine while bawling at each other. The majority of guests came by water, so it was fairly easy, I imagine, to repel gatecrashers.'

There was little else to be learned. By common consent they turned at the end of the next path and retraced their steps. In silence they returned with Sister Agnes to the front door, then said their goodbyes without re-entering the convent. She looked at Dalgliesh and Kate with great intensity, holding their eyes, compelling them to a moment of concentrated attention as if by a force of will she could compel them to respect her confidence.

They had hardly turned out of the drive and were waiting at the first red traffic light when Kate's pent-up resentment burst out.

'So that's why the bed was there in the little archives room, why the door had a bolt and lock. My God, what a bastard! Sister Agnes was right, he did sneak up to that room like some Victorian petty despot. He did humiliate her, make use of her. I can imagine what went on up there. The man was a sadist.'

Dalgliesh said quietly: 'You've no evidence for that, Kate.'

'Why the hell did she put up with it? She was an experienced, well-regarded editor. She could have left.'

'She was in love with him.'

'And her sister in love with God. She's looking for peace. I didn't get the impression that she's found it. Even the future of the convent is at risk.'

'The founder of her religion didn't promise it. "I came not to send peace but a sword."' Glancing at her he saw that the text meant nothing to her. He said: 'It was a useful visit. We know now why Sonia Clements died and it was nothing – or little – to do with Gerard Etienne's treatment of her. There is apparently no one living with a motive to avenge her death. We already knew that visitors to Innocent House could wander at will through the house, but it's useful to have Sister Agnes's confirmation. And then there's the interesting piece of information about the archives. According to Sister Agnes it was Henry Peverell who was anxious that she shouldn't be given the job of working on them. It was only after his death that Jean-Philippe Etienne agreed that Gabriel Dauntsey should undertake the job.'

Kate said: 'It would have been more interesting if it had been the Etiennes who wanted the archives left undisturbed. It's obvious why Henry Peverell didn't want Sonia Clements' sister working up there. It would have upset his little arrangements with his mistress.'

Dalgliesh said: 'That's the obvious explanation, and like most obvious explanations it's probably the right one. But there might be something else in the archives that Henry Peverell wanted to leave undisturbed, something he either knew or suspected was there. It's difficult to see, even so, why that should be relevant to Gerard Etienne's death. As you say, it would have been more interesting if it had been the Etiennes who were insisting that the archives were left undisturbed. Even so, I think we're going to have to take a look at those papers.'

'All of them, sir?'

'If necessary, Kate. All of them.'

43

It was now half past nine on Sunday and Daniel and Robbins were working together at the top of Innocent House searching through the files. They were using the desk and chair in the little archives room. The method Daniel had decided upon was for both of them to work their way along the shelves, pulling out any file which looked hopeful and then taking it in to the little archives room for further investigation. It was a discouraging task since neither knew what he was looking for. Daniel had estimated that the task would take weeks with two of them working but they were making better progress than he had expected. If AD's hunch was right and there were papers which could throw a light on Etienne's murder someone must surely have consulted them fairly recently. This meant that the very old nineteenth-century files, many of which had obviously been untouched for a hundred years, could safely be ignored, at least for the present. There was no problem about the light; the unshaded overhead bulbs were only a few feet part. But the job was dusty, tiring and boring and he did it without hope.

Soon after half past nine he decided that enough was enough for one night. He was aware of a disinclination to go back to his Bayswater flat, a reluctance so strong that almost any alternative seemed preferable. He had spent as little time in it as possible since Fenella had departed for the States. They had bought their flat together just eighteen months ago and he had known within weeks of their living together that this commitment to a joint mortgage and a shared life had been a mistake.

She had said: 'We'll have separate rooms, of course, darling. We both need our privacy.'

Later he was to wonder whether he had actually heard the words. Not only did Fenella not need her privacy, she had no intention of allowing him his, less he thought from wilful denial than from a total lack of understanding of what the word meant. He recalled too late what should have been a salutary childhood lesson: a friend of his mother's telling her complacently, 'We've always respected books and learning in our home', while her six-year-old son, unrebuked, systematically tore to pieces the pages of Daniel's copy of *Treasure Island*. That should surely have taught him that what people believed about themselves seldom bore resemblance to how they behaved in reality. Even so, Fenella had set a record in the irreconcilability of belief and action. The flat was always crowded; friends dropped in, were fed in his kitchen, quarrelled and were reconciled on his sofa, took baths in his bathroom, made international calls on his telephone, raided his refrigerator and drank his beer. The flat was never quiet, the two of them never alone. His bedroom became their shared bedroom, largely because Fenella's was usually temporarily occupied by a homeless chum. She drew people to her like a lighted doorway. Hers was the attraction of unbreakable good humour. She would probably have captivated his mother if he had ever allowed them to meet, no doubt by immediately promising to convert to Judaism. Fenella was nothing if not obliging.

Her compulsive gregariousness went with an untidiness which had never ceased to amaze him during their eighteen months together and which he could never reconcile with her fussiness about small items of décor. He remembered her holding up against the sitting-room wall three small prints, vertically mounted on a length of ribbon and surmounted by a bow. 'Just here, darling, or another two inches to the left? What do you think?'

It scarcely seemed to matter when they had a kitchen sink full of unwashed dishes, a bathroom whose door had to be pushed open against the weight of a heap of dirty and malodorous towels, unmade beds and clothes strewn over the bedroom. With this sluttishness over domestic detail went a compulsive need to bathe and to wash her clothes. The flat was perpetually noisy with the thump and whirl of the washing machine and the hiss of the shower.

He recalled how she had announced the end of their relationship: 'Darling, Terry wants me to join him in New York. Next Thursday, actually. He's sent a first-class ticket. I didn't think you'd mind. We haven't been having a lot of fun together recently, have we? Don't you think that something fundamental has gone out of the relationship? Something precious we once had has been lost. Don't you feel that something has just drained away?'

'Apart from my savings.'

'Oh darling, don't be mean. It's so unlike you.'

He had asked: 'What about your job? How will you work in the States? It isn't easy getting a green card.'

'Oh, I shan't bother about a job, not at once. Terry's loaded. He says I can amuse myself decorating his apartment.'

Their parting had been unacrimonious. It was almost impossible, he found, to quarrel with Fenella. He was resigned, even wryly amused, to discover that this amiability went with a keener commercial sense than he had expected.

'Darling, I think you'd better buy me out at half what we paid for the flat, not half what it's worth now. It's gone down terribly, everything has. I'm sure you can get a higher mortgage. And if you pay me my half of what the furniture cost, I'll leave it all for you. You must have something to sit on, sweetie.'

It seemed hardly worthwhile pointing out that he had paid for, although not chosen, most of the furniture and liked none of it. He noticed, too, that the more valuable of her small acquisitions disappeared with her and were presumably now in New York. The tat remained, and he had neither the time nor the will to dispose of it. She had left him with a crippling mortgage, a flat full of furniture he disliked, an outrageous telephone bill consisting mainly of calls to New York and a lawyer's bill he could only hope to pay by instalments. It was the more irritating to find how much he occasionally missed her.

There was a small washroom and lavatory off the landing outside the archives room. While Robbins was washing the dirt of decades from his hands Daniel, on impulse, telephoned Wapping Police Station. Kate wasn't there. He waited, thought for less than a second, then rang her home number.

She answered, and he said: 'What are you doing?'

'Arranging papers. What about you?'

'Disarranging papers. I'm still at Innocent House. Would you care for a drink?'

She hesitated for a couple of seconds, then said: 'Why not. Where do you suggest?'

'The Town of Ramsgate. It's convenient for us both. I'll meet you there in twenty minutes.'

44

Kate parked her car at the bottom of Wapping High Street and walked the fifty yards or so to the Town of Ramsgate. As she approached, Daniel appeared from the alleyway leading to Wapping Old Stairs.

He said: 'I've been looking at Execution Dock. D'you suppose the pirates were alive when they tied them to the piles at low tide and left them until they'd been washed by three tides?'

'I shouldn't think so. They probably hanged them first. The eighteenth-century penal system was barbaric but not that barbaric.'

They pushed open the pub door and were received into the multicoloured glitter and Sunday-night conviviality of a London pub. The narrow seventeenth-century tavern was crowded and Daniel had to edge and push his way through the throng of regulars to get his pint and Kate's half-pint of Charrington's Ale. A man and woman were getting up from two seats at the end of the room close to the door into the garden and Kate quickly secured them. If Daniel had come primarily to talk rather than to drink, this was as good a place as any. The pub was orderly but the noise level high. Against this background babble of voices and sudden guffaws of laughter they could talk with more privacy and less notice than if the bar had been empty.

He was, she sensed, in an odd mood and she wondered whether, in ringing her, he had been looking for a sparring partner rather than a drinking companion. But the call had been welcome. Alan hadn't telephoned and, with the flat now almost in order, the temptation to ring him, to see him once more before he left, had been too strong for comfort. She was glad to be out of the flat and away from temptation.

Daniel's temper had probably been soured by his frustrating evening in the archives. She would take her turn the next evening and probably with as little expectation of success. But if the object wrenched from Etienne's mouth had indeed been a cassette, if this murderer had needed to tell the victim why he had been lured to his death, then the motive might well lie in the past, even in the distant past; an old evil, an imagined wrong, a hidden danger. The decision to examine the old records might be one of AD's famous hunches but like all his hunches, it was rooted in reason.

Looking down into his beer, Daniel said: 'You worked with John Massingham, didn't you, on the Berowne case. Did you like him?'

'He was a good detective, although not as good as he thought. No, I didn't like him. Why?'

He left the question unanswered. 'Nor do I. He and I were detective-sergeants together in H Division. He called me a Jew-boy. I wasn't meant to hear, of course, he would have thought that was rather bad form, insulting a chap to his face. Admittedly his actual words were "our clever little Jew-boy", but somehow I don't think it was meant as a compliment.'

When she didn't comment, he went on: 'When Massingham uses the expression "when I succeed", you know he isn't talking about making Chief Superintendent. What he's talking about is inheriting his dad's title. Chief Constable, the Lord Dungannon. It won't do him any harm. He'll get there before either of us.'

Certainly before me, thought Kate. For her, ambition had to be governed by reality. Someone had to be the first woman Chief Constable. It could be she, but it was folly to count on it. She had probably entered the force ten years too soon.

She said: 'You'll make it, if you really want it.'

'Perhaps. It's not easy being a Jew.'

She could have retorted that it wasn't easy being a woman in the macho world of the police, but that was a common complaint and she had no intention of whining to Daniel. She said: 'It's not easy being illegitimate.'

'Are you? I thought that was fashionable.'

'Not my kind of illegitimate. And so is being a Jew – prestigious anyway.'

'Not my kind of Jew.'

'How is it difficult?'

'You can't be a cheerful atheist like other people. You feel the need to keep explaining to God why you can't believe in him. Then you have a Jewish mother. That is absolutely essential, it comes with the package. If you haven't got a Jewish mother then you aren't a Jew. Jewish mothers want their sons to marry nice Jewish girls, produce Jewish grandchildren and be seen with them in the synagogue.'

'You could do that last occasionally without too much violence to your conscience, if atheists have one.'

'Jewish atheists do. That's the trouble. Let's go and look at the river.'

There was a small garden at the rear of the tavern overlooking the river which, on warm summer nights, could become uncomfortably crowded. But on an October night few of the regulars had any inclination to carry their drinks outside and Kate and Daniel walked out into a cool river-scented silence. The one lamp shining from the wall shed a soft glow over the upturned garden chairs and the tubs of woody-stemmed tangled geraniums. They moved together and rested their glasses on the river wall.

There was a silence. Then Daniel said abruptly: 'We're not going to get this chap.'

She said: 'Why so sure? And why chap? It could be a woman. And why so defeatist? AD is probably the most intelligent detective in Britain.'

'More likely a man. Dismantling and replacing that gas fire is more likely to be the work of a man. Let's assume he's a man anyway. We shan't get him because he's as intelligent as AD and he's got one big advantage: the criminal justice system is on his side, not ours.' This was a familiar gripe. Daniel's almost paranoid distrust of lawyers was one of his obsessions, like his dislike of having his name shortened to Dan. She was used to his complaint that the criminal justice system was less concerned with convicting the guilty than in devising an ingenious and lucrative obstacle course for lawyers to demonstrate their cleverness.

She said: 'That's nothing new. The criminal justice system has favoured criminals for the last forty years. That's a fact we live with. Fools try to get over it by improving the evidence when they know damn well their man is guilty. All that does is discredit the police, set guilty men free and produce more legislation which tips the balance against convictions still further. You know that, we all know it. The answer is to get good honest evidence and make it stick in court.'

'Good evidence in a really serious case is often the evidence of informers and undercover agents. For God's sake Kate, you know that. Now we have to feed that to the defence in advance so we can't use it without putting lives at risk. Do you know how many major cases we've had to abandon in the last six months in the Met alone?'

'That won't happen in this case, will it? When we get the evidence we'll produce it.'

'But we aren't going to get it, are we? Not unless one of them cracks, and they won't. It's all circumstantial. We haven't a single fact which we can link with one of the suspects. Any of them could have done it. One of them did. We could put a case together against any of them. It wouldn't even get to court. The DPP would throw it out. And if it did get to court, can't you imagine what the defence would make of it? Etienne could have gone up to that room for his own purposes. We can't prove that he didn't. He could have been looking for something in the archives, checking an old contract. He doesn't expect to stay long so he leaves his coat and keys in his office. Then he comes upon something which is more interesting than he expects and settles down to study it. He feels cold so he shuts the window, breaking the window cord, and lights the fire. By the time he realizes what's happening he's too disorientated to get to the fire to turn it off. So he dies. Then hours later the firm's mischief-maker finds the body and decides to add a note of morbid mystery to what is, in fact, an unfortunate accident.'

Kate said: 'We've gone over all that. It doesn't really stand up, does it? Why did he collapse next to the fire? Why not go out of the door? Etienne was intelligent, he must have known the risks from a gas fire in a badly ventilated room, so why shut the window?'

'All right, he was trying to open it, not shut it, when the cord broke.'

'Dauntsey says it was open when he last used the room.'

'Dauntsey is the chief suspect; we can ignore that evidence.'

'His counsel won't. You can't build a case by ignoring inconvenient evidence.'

'All right, he was trying either to shut or open the window. We'll leave that.'

'But why light the fire in the first place? It wasn't that cold. Where are these records that so intrigued him? The ones on the table were old contracts from fifty years ago, the writers dead, unremembered. Why should he want to look at those?'

'The mischief-maker changed them. We've no way of knowing what records he was actually looking at.'

'Why should he change them? And if Etienne went to the room to work, where was his pen, his pencil, his Biro?'

'He went to read not to write.'

'He couldn't write, could he? He couldn't even scribble the name of his killer. He had nothing to write with. Someone had stolen his diary with the pencil attached. He couldn't even write the name in dust. There was no dust. And what about that scratch on his palate? That's incontrovertible, that's fact.'

'Connected to no one. We won't be able to prove how that was made unless we can produce the object that made it. And we don't know what made it. We probably never shall know. All we've got is suspicion and circumstantial evidence. We haven't even enough to put one of the suspects under surveillance. Can't you imagine it, the outcry, if we did? Five respectable people, not one of them with a criminal record. And two of them with alibis.'

Kate said: 'Neither of them worth a damn. Rupert Farlow admitted frankly that he'd swear de Witt was with him true or not. And that story of needing him during the night, he was careful to give us the precise times, wasn't he?'

'I imagine you tend to notice the precise time when you're dying.'

'And Claudia Etienne claims she was with her fiancé. He's going to marry a very rich woman, a bloody sight richer than she was a week ago. Do you think he'd hesitate to lie for her if she asked him?'

Daniel said: 'OK. It's easy to disbelieve the alibis, but can we disprove them? And they could be telling the truth, both of them. We can't assume they're lying. And if they are, then Claudia Etienne and de Witt are in the clear. Which leads us back to Gabriel Dauntsey. He had the means and the opportunity and he has no alibi for the half hour before he left for that pub reading.'

Kate said: 'But that goes equally for Frances Peverell and she's the one with a motive. Etienne chucked her for another woman, proposed to sell Innocent House over her head. She had more reason to wish him dead than anyone. And try convincing a jury that a rheumatic man of seventy-six could get up those stairs or take that slow creaking lift, do what he had to do in the little archives room and get back to his flat in about eight minutes. OK, Robbins did that trial run and it was just about possible but not if he had to go down to the ground floor to fetch the snake.'

'We've only Frances Peverell's word for it that it was eight minutes. And they could be in it together. That's always been one of our possibilities. And the bath water running away means nothing.

I've seen that bath, Kate. It's the big old-fashioned solid kind. You could drown a couple of adults in it. All he had to do was to leave the tap on very slowly so that the bath filled up while he was away. Then he steps into it to get himself convincingly wet and rings for Frances Peverell. But my guess is they were fellow conspirators.'

'Daniel, you're not thinking clearly. It's that story about the bath water which puts Frances Peverell in the clear. If they were fellow conspirators why concoct a complicated story about baths, running water and eight minutes? Why not merely say that she was looking out for his taxi, was worried because he was late, and when she saw that he'd arrived she took him up to her own flat and kept him there for the night. She's got a spare room, hasn't she? This is murder, after all. She's not going to be worried about the possibility of gossip.'

'We could prove he hadn't slept in that bed. If she'd told that story we would have got forensic on to it. You can't sleep all night in a bed without some evidence, from hair or sweat.'

'Well, I think she's telling the truth. That alibi is too complicated not to be genuine.'

'That's probably what we're meant to believe. My God, this murderer is clever. Clever and lucky. Think about Sonia Clements for a moment. She killed herself in that room. Why couldn't she have frayed the window cord, bunged up the gas fire flue?'

Kate said: 'Look Daniel, AD and I have checked that this morning, as far as we could anyway. Her sister says she was mechanically inept. And why should she tamper with the fire? In the hope that someone, weeks later, would mysteriously light it, entice Etienne upstairs and lock him in to be poisoned with carbon monoxide?'

'Of course not. But she could have planned to kill herself that way, wanting it to look like an accident, hoping to protect Peverells. Perhaps she had that in mind from the moment old Peverell died. Then when Gerard Etienne sacked her so brutally . . .'

'If he was brutal.'

'Assume he was. After that she no longer cares whether or not she harms the firm, probably wanted to harm it, or at least to harm Etienne. So she no longer bothers to make her death look accidental, kills herself in a more agreeable way with drugs and drink and leaves a suicide note. Kate, I like that. It has a kind of crazy logic about it.'

'More crazy than logical. How would the murderer know that Clements had interfered with the gas? She's hardly likely to have told him. All you've done is to make the accidental death theory more plausible. Your theory is just another gift for the defence. You can hear defence counsel making the most of it. "Ladies and gentlemen of the jury, Sonia Clements had just as much chance as my client of interfering with that gas fire, and Sonia Clements is dead."'

Daniel said: 'OK, let's be optimistic. We catch him, and then what will happen to him? Ten years in prison if he's unlucky, fewer if he behaves himself.'

'You wouldn't want to sling him up by the neck?'

'No. Would you?'

'No I wouldn't want hanging back. I'm not sure, though, that my position is particularly rational. I'm not even sure that it's honest. I happen to believe that the death penalty does deter, so what I'm saying is that I'm willing for innocent people to take a greater chance of being murdered so that I can salve my conscience by saying that we no longer execute murderers.'

Daniel said: 'Did you watch that TV programme last week?'

'The one about the USA correctional institute?'

'Correctional. That's a good word. The inmates were corrected all right. Killed with lethal injection after God knows how many years on death row.'

'Yes, I saw it. You could argue that they got a damn sight easier end than their victims. An easier end than most human beings get, come to that.'

'So you approve of revenge killing?'

'Daniel, I didn't say that. It's just that I couldn't feel much pity. They killed in a state with the death penalty and then seemed aggrieved that the state proposed to carry out what it had legislated for. Not one of them mentioned his victim. No one spoke the word "remorse".'

'One did.'

'Then I must have missed it.'

'That's not all you missed.'

'Are you trying to quarrel?'

'Just trying to find out what you believe.'

'What I believe is my business.'

'Even on matters which concern the job?'

'Particularly on matters which concern the job. Anyway, this doesn't concern the job except indirectly. The programme was intended to make me feel outrage. OK, it was skilfully made. The producer didn't labour the point. You couldn't say it was unfair. But at the end they gave a number to the viewers so that they could ring to express disgust. All I'm saying is that I didn't feel quite the disgust they obviously intended. Anyway, I dislike television programmes which try to tell me what I ought to feel.'

'In that case you'd better stop watching documentaries.'

A police launch, sleek and fast, came into view travelling upstream, its prow searchlight raking the darkness, its wake a white fishtail of foam. Then it was gone and the dishevelled surface subsided into a gentle heaving calm on which the reflected lights of the river pubs threw shining pools of silver. Small beads of foam floated out of the darkness to break against the river wall. A silence fell. They were standing about two feet apart, each looking out over the river. Then simultaneously they turned and their eyes met. Kate couldn't see his expression from the one wall-lamp but she could feel his force and hear his quickened breathing. Suddenly she felt a charge of physical longing so strong that she had to put out a hand and steady herself against the wall to prevent herself from stepping forward into his arms.

He said 'Kate', and made a quick move towards her, but she had known what was coming and she turned quickly aside. The movement was slight but unmistakable. He said gently: 'What's wrong, Kate?' and then, his voice sardonic, 'Wouldn't AD like it?'

'I don't arrange my private life to suit AD.'

He didn't touch her. It would, she thought, have been easier if he had. She said: 'Look, I've chucked a man I love because of the job. Why should I mess it up for someone I don't love?'

'Would it mess it up, your job or mine?'

'Oh Daniel, doesn't it always?'

He said, a little teasingly, 'You did tell me I should train myself to fancy intelligent women.'

'But I didn't offer to be part of the training.'

His low laugh broke the tension. She liked him immensely, not least because, unlike most men, he could take rejection without rancour. But why not? Neither of them could pretend to be in love. She thought, both of us are vulnerable, both a little lonely, but this isn't the answer.

As they turned to go back into the pub, he asked: 'If it were AD here with you now, if he asked you to go home with him, would you?'

She thought for a few seconds, then decided he deserved honesty. 'Probably. Yes I would.'

'And would that be love or sex?'

'Neither,' she said. 'Call it curiosity.'

45

On Monday morning Daniel telephoned the switchboard at Innocent House and asked George Copeland to call in at Wapping during his lunch break. He arrived just after half-past one, bringing into the room with him a weight of apprehension and tension which seemed to encumber the very air. When Kate suggested that the room was warm and that he might like to take off his coat, he did so at once, as if the suggestion had been a command, but looked after it with anxious eyes as Daniel received it and hung it up, as if fearing that this was the first stage of some premeditated divestation. Looking at the childlike face, Daniel thought that it must have changed little since he was a boy. The round cheeks with their moons of red, definite as patches, had the smoothness of rubber, an incongruous contrast to the dry thatch of grey hair. The eyes had a look of strained hopefulness and the voice, attractive but diffident, was, he suspected, more ready to propitiate than to assert. Probably bullied at school, thought Daniel, and been kicked around since. But apparently he had found his niche at Innocent House in a job which seemed to suit him and which he obviously did satisfactorily. How long, he wondered, would that have lasted under the new dispensation?

Kate had settled him opposite her with more courtesy than she would have shown Claudia Etienne, or any of the other male suspects, but he sat facing her across the desk as rigid as a board, his hands like paws, close-fisted, in his lap.

Kate said: 'Mr Copeland, on the night of Mr Etienne's engagement party on the tenth of July you were seen with Mrs Bartrum coming down from the archives floor at Innocent House. What were you doing there?'

The question was gently put, but the effect was as devastating as if Kate had physically pinned him up against the wall and screamed in his face. He seemed literally to sink in his chair and the red moons flamed and grew, then faded, leaving him so pale that Daniel instinctively moved closer, half expecting him to faint.

Kate said: 'Do you admit that you did go to the top floor?'

He found his voice: 'Not to the archives room, not there. Mrs Bartrum wanted to use the toilet. I took her to the one on the top floor and waited outside.'

'Why didn't she use the lavatories in the women's cloakroom on the first floor?'

'She tried, but both cubicles were occupied and there was a queue. She was – she was in a hurry.'

'So you took her upstairs. But why did she ask you, rather than one of the women staff?'

It was a question which, Daniel thought, could more reasonably have been put to Mrs Bartrum. No doubt in time it would be.

Now Copeland was silent. Kate persisted: 'Wouldn't it have been more natural for her to have asked one of the women?'

'It might have been, but she was shy. She didn't know any of them, and I was there on the desk.'

'And she knew you, is that it?' He didn't answer, but he gave a little nod. Kate said: 'How well does she know you?'

And now, looking full in her face, he replied: 'She's my daughter.'

'Mr Sydney Bartrum is married to your daughter? So that explains it. It's all perfectly natural and understandable. She came to you because you're her father. But that isn't generally known, is it? Why the secrecy?'

'If I tell you, does it have to go any further? Do you have to say that I've told?'

'We don't have to tell anyone else except Commander Dalgliesh and it won't then go further unless it's relevant to our inquiry. We can't decide that unless you explain.'

'It was Mr Bartrum – Sydney – who wanted it kept silent. He wanted it kept a secret, at least at the beginning. He's a good husband, he loves her, they're happy together. Her first husband was a brute. She tried to make a success of the marriage but I think it was a relief when he walked out. There had always been other women and he went off with one of them. They got a divorce, but it hit her very hard. She lost all her confidence. Luckily there were no children.'

'How did she meet Mr Bartrum?'

'She came to collect me from work one day. I'm usually the last out, so no one saw her except Mr Bartrum. His car wouldn't start so Julie and I offered him a lift. When he got to his house he invited us in for coffee. I suppose he thought he had to. That's when it began. They started writing to each other. He went down at weekends to Basingstoke, where she lived and worked, to see her.'

'But surely people at Innocent House knew that you had a daughter?'

'I'm not sure. They knew I was a widower but they never asked about my family. It wasn't as if Julie lived with me. She worked in the tax office in Basingstoke and she wasn't often at home. I think they must have known, but they didn't ask about her. That's why the secrecy was so easy when they married.'

'Why shouldn't people know?'

'Mr Bartrum – Sydney – said he wanted to keep his private life private, that his marriage was nothing to do with Peverell Press, that he didn't want the junior staff gossiping about his personal affairs. He didn't invite any of them to the wedding but he did tell the directors that he was married. Well, of course he had to because of changing his tax code. And later he told them about the baby and showed everyone her photograph. He's very proud of her. I think to begin with he didn't want people to know that he'd married – well, that he'd married the receptionist's daughter. Perhaps he was afraid that he'd lose face with the staff here. He was brought up in an orphanage, and forty years ago institutions for children were different from how they are today. He was despised at school, made to feel inferior, and I don't think he ever forgot it. He's always been a little over-concerned about his status in the firm.'

'And what does your daughter think about all this, the secrecy, concealing the fact that Mr Bartrum is your son-in-law?'

'I don't think that worries her. She's probably forgotten by now. It's not as if the firm is part of her life. She's only been in Innocent House once since they were married and that was for Mr Gerard's engagement party. She wanted to see inside the house, see number ten and the room where he worked. She loves him. They've got the baby now, they're happy together. He's changed her life. And it's not as if I don't see them out of the office. I visit nearly every weekend. I see Rosie – the baby – whenever I like.'

He looked from Daniel to Kate, imploring them to understand, then said: 'I know it seems strange and I think Sydney regrets it now. He's more or less said so. But I can see how it happened. He asked us on impulse to keep it secret and the longer we did the more impossible it was to tell the truth. And no one asked. No one was interested in whom he married. No one asked me about my daughter. People are only interested in your family if you talk about them, and even then it's mostly just politeness. They don't really care. It would be very hurtful to Mr Bartrum – to Sydney – if it came out now. And I wouldn't like him to think that I told you. Does it need to go any further?'

'No,' said Kate, 'I don't think it does.'

He seemed reassured and Daniel helped him into his coat. When he came back from seeing him off the premises he found Kate pacing the room in a furious temper.

'Of all the bloody pompous stupid snobs! That man is worth ten of Bartrum. Oh, I can see how it happened, all right, the social insecurity I mean. He's the only one of the senior staff – isn't he? – who hasn't been to Oxbridge. These things seem to matter to your sex. God knows why. And it tells you something about Peverell Press, doesn't it? That man has worked for them for – how long? – nearly twenty years, and they've never even enquired about his daughter.'

Daniel said: 'If they had asked he would have replied that she was now married and very happy, thank you. But why should they enquire? AD doesn't enquire about your home life. Would you want him to? I can see how it began, the first snobbish impulse to keep it secret and then the realization that he had to go on keeping it a secret unless he wanted to look a fool. I wonder how much Bartrum would pay to prevent it being known. At least we know now why Copeland and Mrs Bartrum were on the top floor together. Not that he needed an excuse to be there, he can go up any time. That's one small problem out of the way.'

Kate said: 'Not really. They were all pretty discreet at Innocent House, particularly the partners, but we've heard enough from Mrs Demery and the junior staff to get a good idea of what was going on. With Gerard Etienne as boss, how long do you think either Bartrum or Copeland would have lasted in their jobs? Copeland loves his daughter and she loves her husband – God knows why but apparently she does. They're happy together, they've got a child. There was a lot at stake for both of them, wasn't there, Bartrum and Copeland? And don't forget one thing about George Copeland. He's the handyman. He does the repairs. He's one of the people at Innocent House who would have had no trouble in disconnecting that gas fire. And he could have done it safely at any time. The only person who regularly uses the little archives room is Gabriel Dauntsey and he never lights the gas. He takes in his own electric fire if he needs it. This isn't one small problem out of the way. It's one more bloody complication.'

BOOK FOUR

Evidence in Writing

46

On the evening of Thursday 21 October Mandy left the office an hour later than usual. She was to meet her housemate, Maureen, at the White Horse on the Wanstead Road for a pub meal followed by a gig. The outing was a double celebration; it was Maureen's nineteenth birthday and the drummer in the band, the Devils on Horseback, was her current boyfriend. The gig was due to begin at eight but the party would meet at the pub an hour earlier for a preliminary meal. Mandy had brought a change of clothes to the office in her bike pannier and planned to go straight to the White Horse. The prospect of the evening, and in particular of meeting again the band leader, Roy, whom she had decided that she rather fancied, or was prepared to fancy if the evening went well, had cast a glow of happy anticipation over the day which not even Miss Blackett's silent and almost manic concentration on work could dim. Miss Blackett was now working for Miss Claudia, who had moved into her dead brother's office. Three days after his death Mandy had overheard Mr de Witt encouraging her.

'It's what he would have wanted. You're chairman and managing director now, or will be when we've got round to passing the necessary resolution. We can't just leave the room empty. Gerard wouldn't have wanted it kept as a shrine.'

A few of the staff had left immediately, but those who remained, either by choice or necessity, found themselves bound by an unacknowledged comradeship and shared experience. Together they waited and wondered and, when the partners weren't present, speculated and gossiped. Mandy's bright eyes and keen ears missed nothing. It seemed to her now that Innocent House held her in some mysterious thrall. She came to work each morning energized with a mixture of excitement and anticipation spiced with fear. That small bare room in which, on her first day, she had stood looking down at the body of Sonia Clements possessed her imagination so powerfully that the whole top floor, still securely locked by the police, had assumed some of the terrifying potency of a child's fairy-tale,

Bluebeard's lair, the forbidden territory of horror. She hadn't seen Gerard Etienne's body but in imagination it shone with the vivid imagery of a dream. Sometimes before sleep she would picture the two bodies there together, Miss Clements lying in her sad decrepitude; the half-naked male body sprawled on the floor beside her, would watch terrified while the dull and lifeless eyes blinked and brightened and the snake pulsated into slimy life, red tongue darting to find the dead mouth, the muscles tightening to squeeze out breath. But these imaginings, she knew, were still controllable. Secure in the knowledge of her own innocence, never feeling herself seriously at risk, she could enjoy the half-guilty exhilaration of simulated terror. But she knew that Innocent House was contaminated with a fear which went beyond her self-indulgent imaginings. She would begin to smell the fear like a river fog as she dismounted from her bike in the mornings, and it strengthened and engulfed her as she stepped over the portal. She saw fear in George's anxious gaze as he greeted her, in Miss Blackett's taut face and restless eyes, in Mr Dauntsey's steps as, suddenly an old man, all vigour drained, he drew himself painfully up the stairs. She heard fear in the voices of all the partners.

On the Wednesday morning, just before ten o'clock, Miss Claudia had summoned the staff to a meeting in the boardroom. They had all been there, even George, his switchboard left on the answerphone, and Fred Bowling from the launch. Chairs had been brought in to form a half-circle and the other three partners had sat at the table, Miss Claudia with Miss Peverell on her right and Mr de Witt and Mr Dauntsey on her left. When the call to the meeting came, Miss Blackett had put down the telephone and said, 'You, too, Mandy. You're one of us now', and Mandy, despite herself, had felt a small surge of gratification. They had seated themselves a little self-consciously filling the second row first, and Mandy had been aware of the collected weight of excitement, anticipation and anxiety.

When the last arrival scurried red-faced to her chair in the front row and the door was closed, Miss Claudia said: 'Where is Mrs Demery?'

It was Miss Blackett who answered. 'Perhaps she thought she wasn't included.'

'Everyone is included. Find her will you please, Blackie.'

Miss Blackett hurried out and, within a couple of minutes during which the meeting waited in total silence, reappeared with Mrs

Demery, still wearing her apron. She opened her mouth as if to make some derogatory comment, then, obviously thinking better of it, closed it and took the only remaining chair in the middle of the front row.

Miss Claudia spoke: 'First of all I would like to thank you all for your loyalty. My brother's death and the method of it has been a horrible shock for us all. This is a difficult time for Peverell Press, but I hope and believe that we shall come through it together. We have a responsibility to our authors and to the books which they expect us to publish to the same high standard that has characterized the Peverell Press for over two hundred years. I have now been informed of the result of the inquest. My brother died of carbon monoxide poisoning, obviously from the gas fire in the little archives room. Precisely how that death occurred the police aren't yet able to say. I know that Commander Dalgliesh or one of his officers has already spoken to all of you. There will probably be continued interviews and I know that all of you will do what you can to help the police in their inquiries, as shall we the partners.

'A word about the future. You have probably heard rumours about plans to sell Innocent House and move down-river. All those plans are now in abeyance. Things will continue as they are, at least until the end of the financial year next April. Much will depend on the success of our autumn list and on how well we do over Christmas. The list is particularly strong this year and we are all optimistic. But I have to tell you that there is no prospect of anyone getting a rise in pay during the rest of this year and all the partners have agreed to take a 10 per cent cut. There will be no more changes in the present staff, at least until next April, but inevitably there will have to be some reorganization: I shall be taking over as chairman and managing director, at first in an acting capacity. This means that I shall be responsible for production, accounts and the warehouse as was my brother. Miss Peverell will take over my present responsibilities as sales and publicity director, and Mr de Witt with Mr Dauntsey will add contracts and rights to their editorial responsibilities. We have recruited Virginia Scott-Headley from Herne & Illingworth to assist Maggie in publicity. She is highly competent and experienced and she will also help with the spate of press and outside inquiries about my brother's death. George has been fielding most of it magnificently but when Miss Scott-Headley arrives all those calls will be directed to publicity. I don't think there is anything else I need to say except that

Peverell Press is the oldest independent publisher in the country and all we partners are determined that it shall survive and flourish. That is all. Thank you for coming. Are there any questions?'

There was an embarrassed silence in which people seemed to be steeling themselves to speak. Miss Claudia had taken advantage of it to get up from the table and had quickly led the way from the room.

Afterwards in the kitchen, making Miss Blackett's coffee, Mrs Demery had been more forthcoming.

'They haven't a clue what to do, any of them. That was plain enough. Mr Gerard could be a proper bastard but at least he knew what he wanted and how to get it. They won't be selling Innocent House, Miss Peverell saw to that, I suppose, and Mr de Witt supported her. But if they don't sell the house, how are they going to keep it up? You tell me that. If people here have any sense they'll start putting out feelers for new jobs.'

And now, alone in the office, tidying her desk, Mandy thought what a difference these extra sixty minutes made. Innocent House seemed suddenly to have emptied. As she mounted the staircase to the first-floor women's cloakroom, where she would change, her feet echoed eerily on the marble as if someone unseen was walking a little behind her. Pausing on the landing to look down over the balustrade she saw the two globes of light at the foot of the stairs glowing like floating moons over a hall grown cavernous and mysterious. She hurried over her change, stuffing her office clothes into the tote bag, pulling over her head the short, multi-layered skirt in patchwork cotton with its matching top, pulling on her high glittering boots. Perhaps it was a pity to bike in them but they were tough enough and it was easier than carrying them in the pannier.

How quiet it was! Even the flush of the lavatory roared like an avalanche. It was comforting to see George, wearing his coat and old tweed hat, still behind the reception desk and locking away the three parcels awaiting collection in his security cupboard. The malicious prankster hadn't struck since the murder but the precautions were still in force.

Mandy said: 'Isn't it funny how quiet the place is when people have left? Am I the last?'

'Just me and Miss Claudia. I'm on my way now. Miss Claudia will set the alarms.'

They left together, George pulling the door firmly shut behind them. It had been a day of heavy and incessant rain, dancing on the marble forecourt, streaming against the windows, almost obscuring the grey swell of the river. But now the rain had stopped and in the gleam of George's rear-lights the cobbles of Innocent Passage shone like rows of newly peeled conkers. The air held the first raw bite of winter. Mandy's nose began to run and she rummaged in her bag for a scarf and her handkerchief. She waited to mount her bike until, with maddening slowness, George began reversing his old Metro down the passage. After a second's thought she ran to signal that Innocent Walk was clear. It always was clear, but George invariably reversed out as if the manoeuvre was his daily dice with death. After he had given a valedictory grateful wave and accelerated away she told herself that at least his job was safe now, and was glad. Mrs Demery had told her that there were rumours that Mr Gerard had planned to get rid of him.

Mandy wove in and out of the late commuter traffic with her usual expertise and a cheerful disregard for the occasional toots of affronted motorists, and it was little more than thirty minutes later when she saw before her the mock-Tudor façade of the White Horse festooned with coloured lights. It stood back from the road on a hundred-yard stretch where the lines of suburban houses gave way to a fringe of shrubs and bushes on the edge of Epping Forest. The forecourt was already closely packed with cars, including, she saw, the band's van and Maureen's Fiesta. She rode slowly to the smaller parking space at the rear of the pub and, pulling her tote bag from the pannier, pushed her way down the passage to the women's cloakroom and joined the noisy chaos of girls hanging up coats and changing their shoes under a notice reminding them that these were left at their own risk, queuing for one of the four lavatories and spreading their make-up clobber on to the narrow shelf under the long mirror. It was when she had fought for her place and was rummaging for the plastic toilet bag which held her make-up that Mandy made the heart-lurching discovery. Her purse was missing; the black leather purse which was also a wallet, and held her money, her one credit card and bank card, prized symbols of financial status, and the Yale key to her front door. Her noisy exclamations of dismay alerted Maureen from her careful application of eye-liner.

'Tip everything out. I always do,' she advised, and returned unworried to the task of outlining her eyelids with black.

303

'Fat lot she cares,' murmured Mandy, sweeping Maureen's make-up to one side and emptying the tote-bag's contents. But the purse wasn't there. And then she remembered. She must have caught it up with her scarf and handkerchief on leaving Innocent House. It was probably lying there still on the cobbles. She would have to go back. The consolation was that there was little chance that a passer-by could have found it. Innocent Walk, and Innocent Lane in particular, were always deserted after dark. It would mean missing the meal, but with luck, not more than half an hour of the gig.

And then a thought struck her. She could telephone Mr Dauntsey or Miss Peverell. At least that way she would know whether the purse was there. They might think she had a cheek to ask, but she was confident that neither of them would really mind. She had done very little work for Mr Dauntsey or Miss Peverell, but when she had, both had seemed grateful and been decent to her. It would only take them a minute to look, a few yards to walk. And it wasn't as if it was still raining. It was a nuisance about the key. If the purse was there it would be too late to call for it after the gig. She would have to go home with Maureen or, if Maureen had other plans for the night, wake up Shirl or Pete. But they could hardly complain; she'd been woken up to let them in often enough.

There was a delay while she coaxed the necessary coins for a call box from Maureen, more delay while she waited for one of the two telephone booths to be free, and another minute wasted when she discovered that the directory she needed was in the other booth. She rang Miss Peverell first, but got only the answerphone with its usual message, spoken in Miss Peverell's quiet, almost apologetic voice. There was very little space to manage the directory and it thudded to the floor. Outside a couple of impatient men gesticulated impatiently. Well, they would have to wait. If Mr Dauntsey was in she wouldn't hang up until he'd been to look. She found the number and stabbed the digits. There was no reply. She let the ringing continue long after she had any real hope before replacing the receiver. And now she had no choice. She couldn't bear to spend the evening and night in suspense. She must go back to Innocent House.

She was riding now against the stream of traffic but was hardly aware of the details of the journey, her mind a muddle of anxiety, impatience and irritation. It wouldn't have hurt Maureen to have driven her to Wapping in the Fiesta, but trust Maureen not to miss the chance of a meal. She was becoming aware, too, of her own hunger but told herself that, with luck, she would have time to grab a sandwich from the bar before the gig.

Innocent Walk was, as usual, deserted. The back of Innocent House rose like a dark bastion against the night sky, then, as she looked up, her head flung back, became as insubstantial and unsteady as a cardboard cut-out, reeling against the low scudding clouds stained pink by the lights of the city. The pools in the gutter of the lane had dried now and a freshening breeze caught her at the end of Innocent Lane bringing with it the strong smell of the river. The only signs of life were the lit windows of the top flat at number 12. It looked as if Miss Peverell at least was now at home. She dismounted at the end of Innocent Lane, anxious not to disturb them with the sound of her bike, not wanting to be delayed by questions and explanations. She walked up the lane as delicately as a thief towards the shimmer of the river, to the place where she had parked the Yamaha. There was sufficient light from the lamps on the forecourt to aid her search, but no search was necessary. The purse lay exactly where she had hoped to find it. She gave a small, almost inaudible, whoop of delight and stuffed it deep into the zipped pocket of her jacket.

It was less easy to see the face of her watch, and she moved closer to the river. At each end of the forecourt the two great globes of light supported by bronze dolphins threw shining pools on the heaving surface of the water which as she watched shimmered like a great cloak of black satin, shaken, smoothed and gently billowed by an invisible hand. Mandy glanced at her watch: 8.20. It was later than she thought and suddenly she found her enthusiasm for the gig had waned. The surge of relief at finding her purse had induced a disinclination for further effort and in this mood of contented lethargy the prospect of the cosy claustrophobia of her bed-sitting-room, the kitchen to herself for once, the rest of the evening in front of the television, grew in attraction by the second. There was that video of the Scorsese *Cape Fear* which was due back tomorrow, £2 wasted if she didn't watch it tonight. Now in no hurry, she turned almost without thought to look up at the façade of Innocent House.

The bottom two storeys were faintly lit by the lights from the forecourt, the slender marble pillars gleaming softly against the dead windows, black cavernous openings into an interior which she now knew so well, but which had become mysterious and forbidding.

305

How odd, she thought, that everything inside would be just as it was when she had left; the two word processors under their covers, Miss Blackett's neat desktop with her rack of filing trays, her diary placed precisely at her right hand, the locked cabinet of files, the notice board to the right of the door. All these ordinary things remained even when there was no one there to see them. And there was no one, no one at all. She thought of that small bare room at the top of the house, the room where two people had died. The chair and the table would still be in place, but there would be no bed, no woman's body, no naked man clawing at the bare boards. Suddenly she saw again Sonia Clements' body, but more real, more frightening than when she had seen it in the flesh. And then she remembered what Ken the packer had told her when she had taken a message to number 10 and had stayed gossiping, how Lady Sarah Peverell, wife of the Peverell who had built Innocent House, had thrown herself from the top balcony and smashed to death on the marble.

'You can still see the mark of the blood,' Ken had said, shifting a box of books from the shelf to the trolley. 'Don't let Miss Frances see you looking for it, though. That's not a story the family like to have told. But they can't clean that stain away for all that, and there'll be no luck in this house till they do. And she still walks, does Lady Sarah. You ask any waterman on the river.'

Ken, of course, had been trying to frighten her, but that had been in late September, a day of mellow sunshine, and she had relished the story, only half believing it, feeling an agreeable shiver of self-induced fear. But she had asked Fred Bowling and she remembered his answer. 'There are ghosts enough on this river, but none walk at Innocent House.'

That was before the death of Mr Gerard. Perhaps they walked now.

And now the fear was becoming real. She looked up at the top balcony and imaged the horror of that fall, the flailing limbs, the single cry – surely she must have cried out – the sickening crunch as the body hit the marble. Suddenly there was a wild scream and she started, but it was only a seagull. The bird swooped above her, perched for a moment on the railings, then winged its way down-river.

She was aware that she was getting chilled. The cold was unnatural, seeping out from the marble as if she stood on ice, and the river breeze was colder now, blowing against her face with the first chill of winter. She was taking a last look at the river, glancing down to where the launch lay silent and empty, when her eyes caught a flash of something white at the top of the railings, to the right of the stone steps which led down to the Thames. It looked at first as if someone had tied a handkerchief to the rail. Curious, she walked across and saw that it was a sheet of paper rammed down on to one of the narrow spikes. And there was something else, a gleam of golden metal at the bottom of the rail. Squatting down, a little disorientated by self-induced fear, Mandy took some seconds to recognize it. It was the buckle of a narrow leather strap, the strap of a brown shoulder-bag. The strap strained down to the puckered surface of the water, and beneath that surface something was just visible, something grotesque and unreal, like the domed head of a gigantic insect, its millions of hairy legs stirring gently in the tide. And then Mandy knew that what she was seeing was the top of a human head. At the end of the strap was a human body. And as she gazed down in horror the body shifted in the tide and a white hand rose slowly from the water, its wrist drooping like the stem of a dying flower.

For a few seconds disbelief fought with realization and then, half fainting with shock and terror, she sank to her knees, clutching at the iron railings. She was aware of the cold metal rasping her hands and then the strength of it pressed against her forehead. She knelt there, powerless to move, terror squeezing at her stomach and turning her limbs to stone. In this cold nothingness only her heart was alive, a heart which had become a great ball of burning iron thudding against her ribs as if it could power her through the railings and into the river. She dared not open her eyes; to open them was to see what she could still only half believe; the double leather of the strap straining down to the abomination below.

She didn't know how long she knelt there before she was capable of sense and movement, but gradually she became aware of the strong river smell in her nostrils, the coldness of the marble against her knees, her quietening heart. Her hands were so rigid on the railings that it took painful seconds to prise the fingers away. She drew herself up and then suddenly found strength and purpose.

Running wordlessly across the courtyard, she banged on the first door, Dauntsey's, and pressed his bell. Above, the windows were dark and she wasted no time in waiting for the answer which she knew wouldn't come, but ran round the house into Innocent Walk and pressed Frances Peverell's bell, keeping her right thumb on the button while she hammered on the knocker with her left hand. The response was almost immediate. She couldn't hear the rush of feet on the stairs but the door was thrown open and she saw James de Witt with Frances Peverell at his shoulder. Incoherently she stammered, pointing towards the river, began running and was aware that they were on her heels. And now they were standing together looking down into the river. Mandy found herself thinking, I'm not mad. It wasn't a dream. It's still here.

She heard Miss Peverell say: 'Oh no! Oh please God no!' Then she turned half fainting and was caught in James de Witt's arms, but not before Mandy had seen her make the sign of the cross.

He said: 'It's all right, my darling, it's all right.'

Her voice was half-muffled in his jacket. 'It isn't all right. How can it be all right?' Then she broke free and said with surprising strength and calmness: 'Who is it?'

De Witt didn't look again at the thing in the river. Instead, carefully, he prised the sheet of paper from the railing and peered at it. He said: 'Esmé Carling. This looks like a suicide note.'

Frances said: 'Not again! Not another! What does it say?'

'It's not easy to see.' He turned and held it so that the light from the globe at the end of the railings fell on the paper. There was almost no margin, as if the page had been trimmed to fit the words, and the sharp finial of the railing had pierced and torn the paper. He said: 'It looks as if it's written in her own hand. It's addressed to all of us.'

He smoothed it out and read aloud: ' "To the partners of Peverell Press. God rot you all! For thirty years you've exploited my talent, made money out of me, neglected me as a writer and as a woman, treated me as if my books aren't fit to bear your precious imprint. What do you know about creative writing? Only one of you has written a word and his talent, such as it was, died years ago. It's me, and writers like me, who have kept your house alive. And now you've thrown me over. After thirty years I'm finished, without explanation, without the right of appeal, without a chance to re-write or revise. Finished. Dismissed, as the Peverells have casually dismissed their unwanted servants for generations. Don't you realize that this finishes me as a human being as well as a writer? Don't you know that when a writer can no longer be published she may as well be dead? But at least I can make your name stink throughout London, and believe me I shall. This is only the beginning." '

Frances Peverell said: 'Poor woman. Oh, poor woman. James, why didn't she come and see us?'

'Would that have done any good?'

'It's the same as Sonia. If it had to be done it could have been done differently, with compassion, with some kindness.'

James de Witt said gently: 'Frances, there's nothing we can do for her now. We'd better call the police.'

'But we can't leave her like that! It's too horrible. It's obscene! We must pull her out – try artificial respiration.'

He said patiently: 'Frances, she's dead.'

'But we can't leave her. Please, James, we must try.'

It seemed to Mandy that they had forgotten she was there. Now that she was no longer alone the terrible paralysing fear had faded. The world had become, if not ordinary, at least familiar, manageable. She thought: he doesn't know what to do. He wants to please her but he doesn't want to touch the body. He can't pull it out by himself and can't bear for her to help. She said: 'If you were going to try mouth-to-mouth breathing you ought to have pulled her out at once. It'll be too late now.'

He said, it seemed to Mandy with a great sadness: 'It was always too late. Anyway, the police won't want the body interfered with.'

Interfered with? The words struck Mandy as funny. She fought an impulse to giggle, knowing that if she gave way to giggling she would end by crying. Oh God, she thought, why doesn't he bloody well do something?

She said: 'If you two stay here I could ring the police. Give me the key and tell me where the phone is.'

Frances said dully: 'In the hall. And the door's open – at least I think it's open.' She turned to de Witt, suddenly frantic: 'Oh my God, James, have I locked us out?'

'No,' he said patiently. 'I've got the key. It was in the front door.'

He was about to hand it to Mandy when their ears caught the sound of feet approaching down Innocent Lane and Gabriel Dauntsey and Sydney Bartrum appeared. They were both wearing raincoats and brought with them a sense of the reassuringly normal. Something about the three still figures, faces turned towards them, alerted them and their footsteps quickened to a run.

Dauntsey said: 'We heard voices. Is something wrong?'

Mandy took the key but did not move. There was no hurry anyway; the police couldn't save Mrs Carling. No one could help her now. And now two more faces were peering down, two more voices murmuring their horror.

De Witt said: 'She's left a note. Here, on the railings. A fulmination against the whole lot of us.'

Frances said again: 'Please get her out.'

And now it was Dauntsey who took control. Looking at him, at the skin which in the light of the globes was as sickly green as river weeds, at the lines scarring the face like black wounds, Mandy thought: he's an old, old man. This shouldn't happen to him. What can he do?

He said to de Witt, 'You and Sydney could lift her using the steps. I haven't the strength.'

His words galvanized James who made no further objection but began walking carefully down the slimy steps holding on to the railings. Mandy saw his involuntary shiver at the bite of the cold water on his legs. She thought, the best way would be for Mr de Witt to support the body from the steps and Mr Dauntsey and Mr Bartrum to pull on the strap, but they won't want to do it that way. And, indeed, the thought of watching the drowned face rise slowly from the water while the men pulled on the strap, as if deliberately hanging her again, was so horrible that she wondered how the thought could have come into her mind. Again it seemed to her that they had forgotten her presence. Frances Peverell had moved a little apart, her hands grasping the railings, her eyes fixed on the river. Mandy guessed a little of what she was feeling. She wanted the body brought out of the water, the dreadful strap removed; she needed to stay until that was done but she couldn't bear to watch it happening. But, for Mandy, to look away was more horrible than to watch. If she had to stay it was better to know than to imagine. And of course she had to stay. No one had again taken up her suggestion that she should take the key and ring the police. And there was no hurry. What did it matter if they came later than sooner? Nothing they brought with them, nothing they could do could revive Mrs Carling.

Now de Witt, descending gingerly, was in the water up to his knees. With his right hand he grasped the bottom of the railings and, with his left, he fumbled for the sodden clothing and began drawing the body towards him. The surface of the river broke into ripples and the strap slackened, then strained tight. He said: 'If one of you could undo the buckle I think I could get her on to the steps.'

Dauntsey's voice was calm. He too was holding on to the railings as if for support. 'Don't let her drift away, James. And keep hold of the railings. We don't want you in the river.'

It was Bartrum who came down the first two steps and leaned over to undo the buckle. His hands were pale in the light from the globes, his fingers like swollen sausages. He took his time, fumbling, seeming unaware how the buckle worked.

When at last it was released, de Witt said: 'I'll need both hands. Grasp hold of my jacket will you.'

And now Dauntsey joined Bartrum on the second step. Together they steadied and held tightly to de Witt's jacket while with both hands he drew the body towards him and released the strap from the neck. And now it lay sprawled face-downwards on the steps. De Witt took it by the legs which stuck out from the skirt like thin sticks and Bartrum and Dauntsey each took an arm. The sodden bundle was lifted up the steps and laid prone on the marble. Gently de Witt turned it over. Mandy had only one glimpse of the face, terrible in death, of the open mouth and protruding tongue, the eyes half opened under the crêped lids, the dreadful stigmata of death round her throat, before Dauntsey, with surprising speed, whipped off his coat and laid it over the body. From beneath the tweed a trickle of water, thin at first then stronger, crept over the marble, as dark as blood.

Frances Peverell walked over to the body and knelt beside it. She said, 'Poor woman. Oh, poor woman', and Mandy saw her lips move silently and wondered if she were praying. They waited in silence, the harsh gasps of their breath sounding unnaturally loud on the quiet air. The effort of raising the body from the water seemed to have drained de Witt and Bartrum of strength and decision, and it was Gabriel Dauntsey who took control.

He said: 'Someone had better stay by the body. Sydney and I will wait here. James, you take the women inside and phone the police. And we'll all need hot coffee, or something stronger, and plenty of it.'

47

The front door of number 12 opened onto a narrow, rectangular hall and Mandy followed Frances Peverell and James de Witt up a flight of steep stairs carpeted in pale green. The staircase ended in another hall, squarer and larger with a door immediately ahead. Mandy found herself in a sitting-room which ran the whole length of the front of the house. The two tall windows leading to the balcony were curtained against the night and the river. There was a pile of smokeless coal in the basket by the grate. Mr de Witt took away the brass fireguard and settled Mandy in one of the high-backed chairs. Suddenly they were as solicitous of her as if she were a guest, perhaps, she thought, because fussing over her at least gave them something to do.

Looking down at her, Miss Peverell said: 'Mandy, I'm so very sorry. Two suicides and you found them both. First Miss Clements and now this. What can we give you? Coffee? Brandy? Or there's red wine. But I don't suppose you've eaten, have you? Are you hungry?'

'I am rather.'

She was, in fact, suddenly ravenous for food. The warm savoury smell pervading the flat was almost intolerable. Miss Peverell looked at Mr de Witt. She said: 'We were going to have duck à l'orange. What about you, James?'

'I'm not hungry but I'm sure Mandy is.'

Mandy thought, she's only got enough for two. Probably bought it from M & S. All right for those who can afford it! Miss Peverell had planned a cosy intimate dinner. And trouble, she saw, had been taken. A round table at the far end of the room had been set with white linen, three sparkling glasses at each setting, and a couple of low silver candlesticks with the candles still unlit. Moving closer she saw the salad had already been set out in small wooden bowls, delicate leaves in a variety of green and red, small toasted nuts, slivers of cheese. There was an open bottle of red wine and one of white in a wine cooler. Mandy had no appetite for the salad. What she craved was hot and savoury food.

She could see, too, that Miss Peverell had taken trouble with more than the meal. The blue-green patterned dress with its pleated skirt and over-blouse tied with a bow at the side was real silk and it suited her colouring. Too old for her, of course, too conventional, a bit dull, and the skirt too long. It didn't do much for her figure, which could have looked spectacular if Miss Peverell knew how to dress. The pearls gleaming against the silk were probably real. Mandy hoped Mr de Witt appreciated the efforts made for him. Mrs Demery had told her that he had been in love with Miss Peverell for years. Now with Mr Gerard out of the way it looked as if he was getting somewhere at last.

The duck came served with peas and small new potatoes. Mandy, her social insecurity swept away in a surge of hunger, fell upon it ravenously. They sat at the table with her. Neither ate but they both drank a glass of red wine. They waited on her with anxious care as if they felt somehow responsible for what had happened and were trying to make amends. Miss Peverell pressed her to a second helping of vegetables and Mr de Witt filled her glass. From time to time they went out together into the room she guessed was the kitchen and which overlooked Innocent Passage and she could hear the subdued mutter of their voices and knew that they were saying things they didn't want to say in her presence while watching and listening for the arrival of the police.

Their temporary absence gave her an opportunity to look more closely at the room as she ate. Its elegant simplicity was too formal, too conventional for Mandy's more eccentric and iconoclastic taste, but she admitted to herself that it looked all right if this was the kind of thing you liked and had the money to afford. The colour scheme was conventional enough, soft blue-green with touches of rose-red. The curtains of draped satin hung from simple poles. At each side of the fireplace was an alcove fitted with bookshelves, the spines of the books gleaming in the firelight. On each top shelf was what looked like the marble head of a girl crowned with roses and closely veiled. They were probably meant to be brides but the veils, marvellously delicate and realistic, looked more like shrouds. Morbid, thought Mandy, cramming her mouth with duck. The picture over the mantelpiece was of an eighteenth-century mother holding her two daughters and was obviously original, as was a curious picture of a woman lying in bed in a room which reminded Mandy of her schoolgirl visit to Venice. The two winged armchairs, one on each side of the fire, were covered in plain linen in a faded pink, but only one chair, with its creased seat and back, looked as if it were much used. So that was where Miss Peverell sat, thought Mandy, facing an empty chair and beyond it the river. She supposed that the picture on the right-hand wall was an icon, but couldn't imagine why anyone should want a Virgin Mary who looked so old and black, or an adult-looking baby who obviously hadn't had a decent meal for weeks.

She envied neither the room nor anything in it and thought with satisfaction of the large low attic which was her share of the rented house in Stratford East, the wall opposite the bed with her hats hung on a peg board, in a riotous flowering of ribbon, flowers and coloured felt: the single bed, just wide enough for two when a boyfriend occasionally spent the night, covered with its striped blanket, the drawing board which she used for her designs, the bean-bag cushions which littered the floor, the hi-fi and television, and the deep cupboard which held her clothes. There was only one room which she longed for more.

Suddenly she paused, fork halfway to her mouth, and listened intently. Surely she could hear the grind of car-wheels on the cobbles. Seconds later James and Frances returned from the kitchen.

James de Witt said: 'The police have arrived. Two cars. We couldn't see how many people they've brought.' He turned to Frances Peverell, sounding for the first time uncertain, needing reassurance. 'I wonder if I ought to go down.'

'Oh surely not. They won't want anyone extra there. Gabriel and Sydney can give them the facts. Anyway, I expect they'll come up here when they've finished. They'll want to talk to Mandy. She is the most important witness. She was there first.' She sat down again at the table and said gently: 'I expect you're longing to get home, Mandy, and Mr de Witt or I will take you later, but I think you ought to stay until the police come.'

It had never occurred to Mandy to do otherwise. She said: 'That's OK by me. They'll think I'm bad luck, won't they? Everywhere I go I find a suicide.'

The words were only half in earnest, but to her surprise Miss Peverell cried out: 'Don't say that, Mandy! You mustn't even think like that. That's just superstition. Of course no one will think you're bad luck! Look, Mandy, I don't like to think of you being on your own tonight. Would you like to telephone your parents – your mother? Wouldn't it be better to go home tonight? She could come here to collect you.'

Like a bloody parcel, thought Mandy. She said: 'I don't know where she is,' and was tempted to add, 'You could always try the Red Cow at Hayling Island.'

But the words and the kindness that prompted them touched in her a previously unacknowledged need for female comfort, for the cosiness of that upstairs room off the Whitechapel Road. She wanted to smell the familiar frowst compounded of drink and Mrs Crealey's scent, to curl up in front of the gas fire in the low chair which enclosed her like a womb, to hear outside the comforting rumble of the traffic on Whitechapel Road. She wasn't at ease in this elegant flat, and these people, for all their kindness, weren't her people. She wanted Mrs Crealey.

She said: 'I could telephone the agency. Mrs Crealey might still be there.'

Frances Peverell looked surprised, but led Mandy upstairs into her bedroom. She said, 'It will be more private for you here Mandy, and there's a bathroom next door if you need it.'

The telephone was on the bedside table and above it hung a crucifix. Mandy had seen crucifixes before, usually outside churches, but this one was different. The Christ, almost beardless, looked very young and his head, instead of drooping in death, was flung back, the mouth wide as if he were crying for vengeance or pity to his God. Mandy thought it was not the kind of object she would like to find hanging beside her bed, but she knew that it had power. Religious people prayed before a crucifix and if they were lucky their prayers were answered. It was worth a try. Punching out Mrs Crealey's office number she made herself gaze hard at the silver figure crowned with its bush of thorns and soundlessly formed the words: 'Please make her answer, please let her be there. Please make her answer, please let her be there.' But the telephone continued its intermittent ring and there was no reply.

Less than five minutes later the doorbell rang. James de Witt went down and came back with Dauntsey and Bartrum.

Frances Peverell said: 'What's happening, Gabriel? Is Commander Dalgliesh there?'

'No, just Inspector Miskin and Inspector Aaron. Oh, and there's that young detective sergeant and a photographer. They're waiting now for the police surgeon to arrive and certify that she's dead.'

Frances cried: 'But of course she's dead! They don't need a police surgeon to tell them that.'

'I know, Frances, but it's normal procedure apparently. No, I won't have any wine, thank you. Sydney and I have been drinking at the Sailor's Return since half past seven.'

'Coffee then. What about coffee? You too, Sydney?'

Sydney Bartrum seemed embarrassed. He said: 'No thank you, Miss Peverell. I really have to go. I told my wife that I was meeting Mr Dauntsey for a quick drink and would be a little late, but I'm always home before ten.'

'Of course you must go. She'll be getting worried. Ring her from here.'

'Yes, I think I'd better. Thank you.' He followed her out of the room.

De Witt asked: 'How are they taking it – the police I mean?'

'Professionally. How else would they take it? They aren't saying much. I got the impression they were none too pleased that we'd moved the body, or even read the note for that matter.'

De Witt poured himself another glass of wine.

'What the hell did they expect us to do? And the note was addressed to us. If we hadn't read it, I wonder if they would have told us what it said? They've been keeping us pretty much in the dark about Gerard's death.'

Gabriel said: 'They'll be up here as soon as the van comes to take her away.' He paused, and then added: 'I think I may have seen her arriving. Sydney and I agreed to be at the Sailor's Return at half past seven and when I reached Wapping Way I saw a taxi turning into Innocent Walk.'

'Did you see the passenger?'

'I wasn't really close enough. I probably wouldn't have noticed her anyway. But I did see the driver. He was large and black. The police think that will be helpful in tracing him. Black drivers are still in a minority.'

Bartrum had made his call and now returned. He said with his usual nervous clearing of his throat: 'Well, I'd better be off. Thank you, Miss Peverell, I won't stay for coffee. I want to get home. The police have said I needn't stay. I've told them all I know, that I was with Mr Dauntsey in the pub from seven-thirty. If they want me again I'll be in the office tomorrow morning. Business as usual.'

The false jauntiness of his voice disconcerted them. For a moment, looking up from her meal, Mandy thought that he was going to shake hands all round. Then he turned and left, and Frances Peverell went to show him out. It seemed to Mandy that they were all glad to be rid of him.

An uneasy silence fell; ordinary conversation, the small talk of a dinner party, chat about work, all seemed inappropriate, almost indecent. Innocent House and the horror of death were all they had in common. Mandy sensed that they would have been more at ease without her, that the bonds of shared shock and terror were loosening and that they were reminding themselves that she was only the temporary shorthand-typist, Mrs Demery's companion in gossip, that the whole story would be round Innocent House next day and the less said by them now the better.

From time to time one of them went to telephone Claudia Etienne. From their brief subsequent conversations Mandy gathered that she wasn't at home. There was another number they could try but James de Witt said: 'Better leave it. We'll get her later. There's nothing she can do here anyway.'

And now Frances and Gabriel went out to make coffee and this time James stayed with Mandy. He asked where she lived and she told him. He said he didn't think she ought to go back to an empty house. Would there be anyone at home when she got there? Mandy, lying to save explanations and trouble, said that there would. After that he seemed unable to think of a further question and they sat in silence, listening to the small sounds from the kitchen. Mandy thought that it was like waiting in hospital for some dreaded news, as she had with her mum when her gran underwent her last operation. They had waited in a sparsely furnished, anonymous room in uncompanionable silence, perched on the edge of their chairs, feeling as ill at ease as if they had no right to be there, knowing that somewhere out of sight and sound the experts in life and death were going about their mysterious business while they themselves were powerless to do anything but wait. And this time the wait was not long. They had hardly finished their coffee when they heard the expected ring on the front door. Less than a minute later Inspector Miskin and Inspector Aaron were with them. They were both carrying what looked like large attaché cases. Mandy wondered if these were their murder bags.

Inspector Miskin said: 'We'll talk at greater length after we've got the results of the PM. There are just a few questions now. Who found her?'

'I did,' said Mandy, and wished she wasn't still sitting at the table with the smeared and empty plate in front of her. There seemed something indecent in this evidence of appetite. And why ask anyway, she thought with a spurt of resentment, you know bloody well by now who found her.

'What were you doing here? It was late to be working.' It was Inspector Aaron who spoke.

'I wasn't working.' Mandy was aware that her voice was sulky and took herself in hand. Briefly she described the events of her ill-fated evening.

Inspector Miskin asked: 'When you found your purse where you expected, what made you go to the river?'

'How do I know? Because it was there I suppose.' She added: 'I wanted to look at my watch. It was lighter by the river.'

'And you saw and heard no one else either then or when you arrived?'

'Look, if I had I'd have said so by now. I didn't see anyone or hear anything except the paper on the railings. So I went over to take a look, and that's when I saw the shoulder-bag lying on the ground at the foot of the railings and the straps going down into the river. When I looked down I saw what was at the end of the strap, didn't I?'

Frances Peverell broke in quietly. 'It's human instinct to go to see the river, particularly at night. I always do when I'm near. Does Miss Price have to answer any more questions now? She's told you all she knows. She ought to be at home. She's had a terrible experience.'

Inspector Aaron didn't look at her, but Inspector Miskin spoke, and more gently. 'Do you know what time you arrived back at Innocent House?'

'Eight-twenty. I looked at my watch when I got to the river.'

Inspector Aaron said: 'It was a longish way to come back from the White Horse. Didn't you think of ringing Miss Peverell or Mr Dauntsey and asking them to look for the purse?'

'I did. There was no reply from Mr Dauntsey and Miss Peverell had the answerphone on.'

Frances Peverell said: 'I do that sometimes if I have a visitor. James arrived by taxi just after seven, and I suppose Mr Dauntsey was at the Sailor's Return with Sydney Bartrum.'

'So he has already told us. Did either of you see or hear anything unusual, any sound from Innocent Lane, for example?'

They looked at each other. Frances Peverell said: 'I don't think we'd hear footsteps on the cobbles, not from this room. I was in the kitchen briefly at about eight to prepare the salads. I always do that at the last moment. The kitchen window overlooks Innocent Lane, and I would have heard a taxi then if it had set her down at the usual door to Innocent House. I heard nothing.'

James de Witt said: 'I didn't hear a taxi, and neither Miss Peverell nor I saw or heard anyone or anything in Innocent Lane after my arrival. There were the usual sounds from the river, but muted by the curtains. I think there was a certain amount of noise earlier in the evening but I can't remember when. It certainly wasn't unusual enough to cause us to go out on the balcony and see what was happening. One gets used to noises on the river.'

Inspector Aaron spoke: 'How did you get here tonight, sir, by car?'

'By taxi. I don't drive in London. I ought to have said earlier that I came from home. I wasn't in the office this afternoon. I had a dental checkup.'

Suddenly Frances Peverell said: 'What was in her bag? It looked heavy.'

Inspector Miskin said: 'It is heavy. This is why.'

She took the plastic bag from Inspector Aaron and tipped out the shoulder-bag on to the table.

They watched while she undid the straps. The manuscript was bound in a pale blue manila cover with the name of the novel and of the author in capitals: DEATH ON PARADISE ISLAND BY ESMÉ CARLING. And written across the cover in thick red ink were scrawled the words 'REJECTED – AND AFTER THIRTY YEARS', followed by three huge exclamation marks.

Frances Peverell said: 'So she brought that with her as well as the suicide note. We're all a little to blame. We should have acted with more kindness. But to kill herself ... And to do it like that. The loneliness, and the horror. Poor woman.'

She turned away, and James de Witt moved closer to her but didn't touch her. He said, turning to Inspector Miskin: 'Look, do we have to talk any more tonight? We're all in shock, and it's not as if there's any doubt.'

Inspector Miskin replaced the manuscript in the bag. She said quietly: 'There is always doubt until we know the facts. When did Miss Carling learn that the firm had rejected her novel?'

James de Witt replied: '*Mrs* Carling. She's a widow. She divorced some time ago and her husband died since. She knew the morning Gerard Etienne died. She came into the office to see him but we were at the board meeting and she had to leave for a book signing at Cambridge. But you know all that.'

'The signing that was cancelled before she arrived?'

'Yes, that signing.'

'And has she been in touch with either of you since Mr Etienne's death or with anyone at the firm as far as you know?'

Again de Witt and Frances Peverell looked at each other. De Witt said: 'Not with me. Has she been in touch with you, Frances?'

'No, not a word. It's rather odd when you come to think of it. If only we'd been able to talk, to explain, this might not have happened.'

It was Inspector Aaron who suddenly broke the silence. He said: 'Who was it who decided to pull her out of the river?'

'I did.' Frances Peverell turned on him her mild but reproachful look.

'You surely didn't think you'd be able to resuscitate her?'

'No, I don't think I thought that, but it was so terrible to see her hanging there. So . . .' She paused and then said, 'So inhuman.'

De Witt said: 'We're not all police officers, Inspector, some of us still have human instincts.'

Inspector Aaron flushed, glanced at Inspector Miskin and with difficulty controlled his temper.

Inspector Miskin said quietly: 'Let us hope you manage to retain them. I expect Miss Price would like to go home now. Inspector Aaron and I will drive her.'

Mandy said with the obstinacy of a child: 'I don't want to be driven. I want to go home by myself on the bike.'

Frances Peverell said gently: 'Your bike will be perfectly safe here, Mandy. If you like we could lock it in the garage at number ten.'

'I don't want to leave it in the garage. I want to ride home on it.'

In the end she had her way, but Inspector Miskin insisted on the police car driving behind her. Mandy took some pleasure in weaving in and out of the traffic and making it as difficult as possible for them to keep up with her.

When they got to her house on Stratford High Street, Inspector Miskin, looking up at the darkened windows, said: 'I thought you said there would be someone at home.'

'There is someone at home. They're all in the kitchen. Look, I can look after myself. I'm not a kid, OK? Just get off my back, will you?'

She dismounted and Inspector Aaron got out of the car and helped her lift the Yamaha through the front door and into the hall. Without a word she shut the door firmly after him.

48

Daniel said: 'It wouldn't have hurt her to say thank you. She's a tough cookie that one.'

'She's in shock.'

'Not so shocked she couldn't eat her dinner.'

Wapping Police Station was quiet and they saw only one officer as they mounted the stairs to the incident room. They stood for a moment at the window before drawing the curtains. The clouds had lifted now, and the river flowed wide and calm, bearing its patterns and swirls of light under the prickling of high stars. But there was always an unnatural sense of peace and isolation in a station at night. Even when it was busy, and the calm momentarily broken by loud male voices and heavy footfalls, the air held a peculiar stillness, as if the world outside with its violence, its terrors, could lie in wait but had no power to disturb that essential tranquillity. There was, too, a deepening comradeship; colleagues talked less often but more freely. But they could expect no comradeship at Wapping. She knew that they were to an extent intruders. The police station was offering them hospitality, affording them all the facilities they needed, but they were still outsiders.

Dalgliesh was visiting the Durham Constabulary on some mysterious business of the Commissioner, and she didn't know whether he had yet left for London. She put through her call and was told that he was thought to be still there. They would make an attempt to find him and ask him to ring back.

While waiting, she said: 'You were sure of her alibi? Esmé Carling's, I mean. She was at home the night Etienne died?'

Daniel seated himself at his desk and began playing with the computer. He said, trying to keep the irritation from his voice: 'Yes, I'm sure. You've read my report. She was with the kid, Daisy Reed from the same block of flats. They were together the whole evening and until midnight or after. The kid confirmed it. I wasn't incompetent, if that's what you're suggesting.'

'I'm not. Cool it, Daniel. But she was never really a suspect, was she? The blocked flue, the frayed cord – it all needed too much advance planning. We never saw her as a possible murderess.'

'So you're suggesting that I was too easily satisfied?'

'No, I'm just checking that you were satisfied.'

'Look, I went with Robbins and a WPC from the Juvenile Bureau. I interviewed Esmé Carling and the kid separately. They were together that night, most nights if it comes to that. The mother would be out at her job – stripping, or night-clubbing, or a spot of prostitution, or whatever – and the kid would wait until she'd gone, then sneak off and spend the evening with Carling. Apparently it suited them both. I checked on every detail of that Thursday night and their accounts tallied. The kid didn't want to admit she'd been with Carling at first. She was a bit scared that her mother would stop the arrangement or that the Juvenile Bureau would get in touch with Social Services and she'd end in care. They did of course – get in touch with Social Services, I mean. They could hardly do anything else, given the circumstances. The kid was telling the truth. Why the doubt anyway?'

'But it's odd, isn't it? Here you have a woman whose book has been turned down after thirty years. She comes roaring in fury to Innocent House to have it out with Gerard Etienne. She's prevented from seeing him because he's in a board meeting. Then she goes off to do a signing and discovers on arrival that someone from Innocent House has cancelled it. By then I imagine she was incoherent with rage. So what would you expect her to do? Go home quietly and write a letter or storm back that evening to confront Etienne? She probably knew that he worked late on Thursdays. Nearly everyone concerned with Innocent House seems to have known that. And her behaviour since is odd too. She knew that Gerard Etienne was the one principally responsible for rejecting the manuscript. Now Gerard Etienne is dead. So why didn't she come back and make another attempt to get the book accepted?'

'She probably knew that it wouldn't be any use. The partners wouldn't like to reverse a decision of Etienne's so soon after his death. Anyway, they probably agreed with it.'

Kate went on: 'And there are several odd things about tonight, aren't there? Frances Peverell and de Witt would almost certainly have heard the taxi if it had come up Innocent Lane to the usual entrance. So where exactly did she ask to be dropped?'

'Probably somewhere in Innocent Walk, then she went on foot to the river. She knew that a taxi might be heard on the cobbles of Innocent Lane either by Dauntsey or Miss Peverell. Or she may have been dropped at the end of Innocent Passage. That's the access closest to where she was found.'

'But the gate at the end of the passage is locked. If she got to the river that way, then who opened the gate for her and locked it again? And what about the message? Did it really read to you like a suicide note?'

'It's not typical, perhaps; but, then, what is a typical suicide note? A jury wouldn't have much difficulty in convincing themselves that it's genuine.'

'And written when?'

'I suppose just before she killed herself. It's hardly the kind of thing you concoct in advance and keep handy in case you should suddenly need it.'

'Then why no mention of Gerard Etienne's death? She must have known that he was chiefly responsible for rejecting her novel. Well, of course she knew. Mandy Price and Miss Blackett have both described how she burst into the office to see him. Surely his death must have made a difference to how she felt about Peverell Press. And even if it didn't – if she still felt the same bitterness – isn't it odd that the note doesn't even mention his death?'

Then the telephone rang and Dalgliesh was on the line. Kate gave her report clearly and concisely, explaining that they hadn't been able to contact Doc Wardle who was out on a case but hadn't tried to find a substitute since the body had been moved. It was now at the mortuary. It seemed to Daniel that she listened for a long time without speaking, except for an occasional 'Yes sir'.

Eventually she put down the receiver. She said: 'He's flying back tonight. We're not to interview anyone at Innocent House until we get the results of the PM. They can wait. Tomorrow you're to try and trace the taxi and check whether anyone on the river that night saw anything, including any boat party who passed between seven o'clock and the time before Mandy found the body. We've got the keys to Carling's flat from her bag and apparently there's no next of kin, so we're going there tomorrow morning. It's in Hammersmith. Mount Eagle Mansions. He wants Mrs Carling's agent to meet us there at eleven-thirty. First thing tomorrow he and I are going to re-interview Daisy Reed. And there's something else. Damn it, Daniel, we should have thought of it ourselves. AD wants the scene-of-crime officers here first thing tomorrow to examine the launch. The Peverell Press will have to make other arrangements to collect their staff from Charing Cross. God I feel such a bloody fool. AD must be wondering if we ever see ahead further than our own noses.'

'So he thinks she used the launch to string herself up. It would certainly have been easier.'

'Carling used it – or someone else.'

'But the launch was tied up in its usual place on the other side of the steps.'

'Exactly. So, if it was used, then someone moved it before and after she died. Prove that and we're getting closer to proving that this was murder.'

49

By ten o'clock Gabriel Dauntsey had gone down to let himself into his own flat and James de Witt and Frances were alone. Both realized that they were hungry. Mandy had finished both portions of the duck but neither would have felt equal to its richness. They were in the uncomfortable state of needing food but without being able to think of anything they actually wanted to eat. In the end Frances cooked a large herb omelette and they shared it with more pleasure than either would have thought possible. As if by an unspoken agreement they said little about Esmé Carling's death.

Before Dauntsey left Frances had said: 'We're all responsible, aren't we? None of us really stood up to Gerard. We ought to have insisted on a discussion about Esmé's future. Someone should have seen her, talked to her.'

James had said gently: 'Frances, we couldn't have published that book. I don't mean because it was a commercial book, we need popular fiction. But it was bad popular fiction. It was a bad book.'

And Frances had replied: 'A bad book? The ultimate crime, the sin against the Holy Ghost. Well, she's certainly paid highly for it.'

The bitterness, the irony had surprised him. The comment had been so unlike her. But she had lost some of her old gentleness and passivity since the break-up with Gerard. He saw the change with a tinge of regret, but recognized that this was one more manifestation of his recurrent psychological need to search out and love the vulnerable, the innocent, the hurt and the weak, to give rather than to receive. He knew that it didn't make for an equal relationship, that a constant uncritical kindness could in its subtle condescension be as oppressive to the loved one as cruelty or neglect. Was this how he bolstered his ego, by the knowledge that he was needed, depended upon, admired for a compassion which when he looked at it with honest eyes was a particularly subtle form of emotional patronage and spiritual pride? Was he any better than Gerard for whom sex was part of his personal power game and who got a kick out of seducing a devout virgin because he knew that, for her, surrender had been a mortal sin? He had always loved Frances, he still loved her. He wanted her in his life, in his house, in his bed, as well as in his heart. Perhaps it was possible now that they could love on equal terms.

Tonight he was reluctant to leave her but there was no choice. Rupert's buddy, Ray, had to leave by 11.30 and Rupert was too ill to be alone even for a few hours. And there was another difficulty. He felt that he could hardly suggest that he should spend the night in her spare room without presumption. She might, after all, prefer to confront her private demons alone rather than have the inconvenience of his presence. And there was something more. He wanted to make love to her but it was too important to happen because shock and grief had made her vulnerable so that she came to his bed not from an equal desire but from the need to be comforted. He thought: What a mess we're all in. How hard it is to know ourselves and, when we do, how difficult to change.

But the problem solved itself when he said: 'Are you sure you'll be all right alone, Frances?'

She said firmly: 'Of course I shall. Anyway Rupert needs you at home. There's Gabriel downstairs if I need company, but I shan't need company. I'm used to being alone, James.'

She rang for a taxi and he took the quickest way home, paying off the cab at the Bank and taking the Central Line to Notting Hill Gate.

He saw the ambulance as soon as he turned out of Hillgate Street. His heart jolted. Breaking into a run he saw that the paramedics were already carrying Rupert down the front steps in a chair-stretcher. Nothing could be seen of him but his face above the blanket, a face which, even now in the extremity of weakness and stripped for death, had never for James lost its beauty. Watching the two men as they manoeuvred the stretcher with experienced hands, it seemed to him that it was his own arms that could feel the unbearable lightness of their burden.

He said: 'I'll come with you.'

But Rupert shook his head. 'Better not. They don't want too many people in the ambulance. Ray will come.'

Ray said: 'That's right. I'm going with him.'

They were anxious to get off. Already there were two cars waiting to pass. He climbed into the ambulance and gazed wordlessly into Rupert's face.

Rupert said: 'Sorry about the mess in your sitting-room. I won't be coming back. You'll be able to tidy up and invite Frances now without either of you feeling the need to sterilize all the crockery.'

James said: 'Where are they taking you? The hospice?'

'No, the Middlesex.'

'I'll come and see you tomorrow.'

'Better not.'

Ray was already sitting in the ambulance solidly and comfortably as if it were his rightful place. And it was his rightful place. And now Rupert was speaking again. James bent to hear him. He said: 'That story, about Gerard Etienne. About me and Eric. You didn't believe it?'

'Yes Rupert, I did believe it.'

'It wasn't true. How could it be? It was a nonsense. Surely you know about incubation periods? You believed it because you needed to. Poor James! How you must have hated him. Don't look like that. Don't look so appalled.'

It seemed to James that he had no voice. And when he did speak the words horrified him by their banal futility. 'You'll be all right, Rupert?'

'Yes, I shall be all right. I shall be finally all right. Don't worry and don't visit. Remember what G. K. Chesterton said. "We must learn to love life without ever trusting it." I never have.'

He had no memory of climbing down from the ambulance but he heard the soft slam of the double doors as they were closed firmly in his face. In seconds it had turned the corner but he stood for a long time looking after it, as if it was travelling on a long straight road and he could watch it out of sight.

50

Mount Eagle Mansions, close to Hammersmith Bridge, revealed itself as a large red-brick Victorian block with the shabby uncared-for look of a building languishing between owners. The huge over-embellished Italianate porch, its stucco beginning to crumble, was at odds with the plain façade and gave the block an air of eccentric ambiguity as if the architect had been prevented by the failure of inspiration or money from completing his original design. Judging from the porch, Kate thought this was perhaps fortunate. But the inhabitants had obviously not given up hope of preserving the value of their property. The windows, at least at ground-floor level, were clean, the varied curtains hung in regular folds and a few of the window-sills had been fitted with boxes from which ivy and trailing geraniums hung against the grimy bricks. The letter-box and door-knocker in the form of an immense lion's head were polished to whiteness and there was a large rush mat, obviously new, with 'Mount Eagle Mansions' woven into the bristles. To the right of the door was a row of doorbells, each with a name-card in the adjoining slot. The card for Flat 27, cut from a visiting card, read 'Mrs Esmé Carling' in an ornate script. The card for Flat 29 had the one word 'Reed' in printed capitals. Kate's ring was answered after a few seconds by a female voice in which the tone of grudging resignation was clearly discerned above the crackle of the intercom.

'All right, come on up.'

There was no lift, although the size of the tessellated hall suggested that one had originally been intended. Along one wall was a double row of post boxes, clearly numbered, and against the other a heavy mahogany table, its legs elaborately carved, holding a collection of circulars, readdressed letters and a bundle of old papers tied with string. They were neatly arranged and above them swirls of dried soapy water showed that some attempt had been made to clean the paintwork, although the result had only been to emphasize the grime. The air smelled of furniture polish and disinfectant. Neither Kate nor Dalgliesh spoke, but as they mounted the stairs, past the heavy doors with their eye-holes and double security locks, Kate was aware of a rising excitement mixed with slight apprehension, and wondered whether this was shared by the quiet figure at her shoulder. This was an important interview. By the time they came down this stairway the case could be solved.

Kate was surprised that Esmé Carling couldn't afford something better than a flat in this unimpressive block. It was hardly a prestigious address at which to receive interviewers or journalists, assuming, of course, that she did receive them. But the little they knew of her didn't suggest a literary recluse and she was, after all, fairly well known. She, Kate, had heard of Esmé Carling even if she had never read her. That didn't, of course, mean that her income from writing was large; hadn't she read in some magazine article that, while a few very successful novelists were millionaires, the majority, even the well-regarded, had difficulty in living off their royalties. But her agent would be with them in an hour and there was little point in wasting time cogitating about Esmé Carling the crime writer when all the questions would so soon be answered by the person most qualified to know.

Dalgliesh had chosen to see Daisy even before he examined Mrs Carling's flat and she thought she knew why. It was the child's information that was vital. Whatever secrets lay behind the door of number 27 could wait. The detritus of a murdered life told its own story. The evidence of the victim's pathetic leavings, letters, bills, could be misinterpreted but artefacts didn't lie, they didn't change their story, they didn't fabricate alibis. It was the living who must be interviewed while the shock of murder was still vivid in their minds. A good detective respected grief, sometimes shared it, but was never slow to exploit it, even the grief of a child.

They had reached the door, and before she could lift her hand to the bell Dalgliesh said: 'You do the talking, Kate.'

She replied, 'Yes, sir,' but her heart leapt. Two years ago she would almost have found herself praying, 'Oh God, let me get this right'; now, more experienced, she was confident that she would.

She hadn't wasted time imagining what the child's mother, Shelley Reed, looked like. In police work it was wise not to anticipate reality by premature and manufactured prejudice. But when the chain rasped back and the door was opened she had difficulty in concealing her initial look of surprise. It was hard to believe that this chubby-faced girl, staring at them with the sulky resentment of an adolescent, was the mother of a twelve-year-old. She could hardly have been more than sixteen when Daisy was born. Her face, naked of make-up, still held something of the unformed softness of childhood. The sulky mouth was very full and drooped at the corners. Her wide nose was pierced at one side with a glittering stud matching the studs in her small ears. Her hair, a bright yellow at odds with her heavy dark brows, hung in a fringe almost to her eyes and framed her face in crimped curls. Her eyes were widely spaced and set at an angle under lids so heavy that they looked swollen. Only her figure hinted at maturity. Heavy breasts swung loose under a long jersey of pristine white cotton and her long, well-shaped legs were ensconced in black tights. On her feet she wore house slippers embroidered with Lurex thread. Her hard uncompromising eyes changed as she saw Dalgliesh to a wary respect, as if she recognized a more intractable authority than that of a social worker. And when she spoke Kate detected a note of weary resignation in the ritual defiance.

'You'd better come in, although I don't know what good it'll do. Your chaps have seen Daisy once. The kid has told you all she knows. We co-operated with the police, and what do we get for it but the bloody welfare on our backs. It's not their business how I earn my living. OK, I'm a stripper. So what's wrong with that? I earn a living and I keep my kid. I'm in a job and it's legal, OK? The papers are always complaining about single mothers on social security, well I'm not on any bloody social security but I will be if I have to hang about here all day answering damn silly questions. And we don't want any WPCs from the Juvenile Bureau. That one who came last time with that Jewish chap was a proper cow.'

She hadn't moved during this welcome but now at last, reluctantly, she stepped aside and they moved into a hall so small that it could hardly hold the three of them.

Dalgliesh said: 'I'm Commander Dalgliesh and this is Inspector Miskin who isn't from the Juvenile Bureau. She's a detective, we both are. We're sorry to worry you again, Mrs Reed, but we must talk to Daisy. Does she know that Mrs Carling is dead?'

'Yes, she knows. We all know, don't we? It was on the local news. The next thing you'll be saying is that it wasn't suicide and we did it.'

'Is Daisy distressed?'

'How do I know? She isn't laughing. I never know what that kid's feeling anyway. She'll be distressed all right by the time you lot have finished with her. She's in here – I've rung the school to say she won't be in till the afternoon. And, look, do me a favour. Make it quick, OK? I've got to get out to the shops. And the kid'll be looked after tonight. Don't you start fretting about Daisy. The cleaner here is coming in for the evening. After that you can bloody well ask the welfare to look after her if they're so worried.'

The sitting-room was narrow and gave an impression of cluttered discomfort and an oddness which puzzled Kate until she saw that an artificial fireplace, the mantelshelf crowded with good luck cards and small china ornaments, had been fitted to the external, chimney-less wall. To the right an open door showed a double bed, partly made and strewn with clothes. Mrs Reed went over and quickly closed it. To the right of the door was fitted a curtained rail on which Kate could glimpse a row of tightly packed dresses. There was an immense television set to the left of the door with a sofa facing it and in front of the double window a square table with four chairs. The table was piled high with what looked like school textbooks. A child in a uniform of navy-blue pleated skirt and white blouse turned and faced them.

Kate thought that she had seldom seen a plainer child. She was obviously her mother's daughter but by some trick of the genes the maternal features had been superimposed incongruously on her frail thin face. The eyes behind the spectacles were small and too far apart, the nose broad like that of the mother, the mouth as full and its downward turn more pronounced. But her skin was delicate and an extraordinary colour, a pale greeny-gold like apples seen under water. Her hair, its colour between gold and a pale auburn, hung like strands of silk framing a face which looked more mature than childlike. Kate glanced at Dalgliesh, then turned her eyes quickly away. She knew that what he was feeling was pity and tenderness. She had seen that look before, however quickly disciplined, however fleeting. She was surprised at the surge of resentment it provoked. For all his sensitivity he was no different from any other man. His first reaction on seeing a female was an aesthetic response, pleasure in beauty and a compassionate regret at ugliness. Plain women got used to that look; they had to. But surely a child could be spared that brutal revelation of a universal human unfairness. You could legislate for every kind of discrimination but not this. In everything from jobs to sex the attractive were advantaged, the very plain denigrated and rejected. And this child hadn't even the promise of that distinctive, sexually charged ugliness which, if accompanied by intelligence and imagination, could be so much more erotic than mere prettiness. Nothing could ever be done to turn up the downward droop of that too-heavy mouth, to bring the piggy eyes closer together. In the few seconds before she spoke Kate was aware of a tumble of emotions, not least self-disgust. If Dalgliesh had felt instinctive pity, almost as if the child was maimed, then so had she and she was a woman. She at least could have judged by different criteria. In reply to a wave of the mother's hand, Dalgliesh sat down on the sofa and Kate took a chair opposite Daisy. Mrs Reed plonked herself belligerently at the other end of the sofa and lit a cigarette.

'I'm staying. You're not interviewing the kid without me.'

Dalgliesh said: 'We can't talk to Daisy unless you do stay, Mrs Reed. There are special procedures for interviewing juveniles. It would be helpful if you didn't interrupt, unless you feel we're being unfair.'

Kate took a chair at the table, immediately facing the child, and said gently: 'We are so sorry about your friend, Daisy. Mrs Carling was your friend, wasn't she?'

Daisy opened one of her school books and made a pretence of reading. Without looking up she said: 'She liked me.'

'When people like us we usually like them in return, at least I do. You know that Mrs Carling is dead. She may have killed herself but we can't yet be sure. We need to find out how and why she died. We want you to help us. Will you?'

Then Daisy looked up at her. The small eyes, disconcertingly intelligent, were as hard as an adult's and as judgemental as only a child's can be. She said: 'I don't want to talk to you. I want to talk to the boss-man.' She gazed across at Dalgliesh and said: 'I want to talk to him.'

Dalgliesh said: 'Well, I'm here. But it's the same, Daisy, whoever you speak to.'

'I won't talk except to you.'

Kate, disconcerted, trying to conceal her disappointment and chagrin, rose from her seat but Dalgliesh motioned her to stay and drew up a chair beside her.

Daisy said: 'You think Auntie Esmé was murdered, don't you? What will you do to him when you've caught him?'

'If the court finds him guilty then he'll go to prison. But we can't be certain that Mrs Carling was murdered. We don't yet know how or why she died.'

'Mrs Summers at school says that putting people in prison doesn't do them any good.'

Dalgliesh said: 'Mrs Summers is right. But people aren't usually sent to prison to do them good. Sometimes it's necessary to protect other people, or to deter, or because society cares deeply about what the guilty person has done and the punishment reflects that concern.'

Oh God, thought Kate, are we expected to spend time discussing the case for custodial sentences and the philosophy of judicial punishment? But Dalgliesh was obviously prepared to be patient.

'Mrs Summers says that executing people is barbaric.'

'We don't execute people any longer in this country, Daisy.'

'They do in America.'

'Yes, in some parts of the United States, and in other countries too, but it doesn't happen any longer in Britain. I think you know that, Daisy.'

The child, thought Kate, was being deliberately obstructive. She wondered what Daisy thought she was doing, apart, of course, from playing for time. Silently she cursed Mrs Summers. She had known one or two of her kind in her old schooldays, principally Miss Crighton who had done her best to dissuade her from joining the police on the grounds that they were the oppressive fascist agents of capitalist authority. She would have liked to have asked the child what Mrs Summers would have done with Mrs Carling's murderer, if murderer there was, apart of course from giving him sympathy, counselling him and sending him on a world cruise. Better still, it would have been agreeable to take Mrs Summers to view some of the victims of murder and to face the murder scenes she, Kate, had had to face. Irritated by the resurgence of old prejudices, old resentments which she thought she had conquered, and of memories she preferred to forget, she kept her eyes on Daisy's face. Mrs Reed said nothing but pulled on her cigarette vigorously. The air became disagreeably smoky.

Sitting close to the child, Dalgliesh said: 'Daisy, we need to find out how and why Mrs Carling died. It could have been by her own hand, and it is possible, just possible, that she was murdered. If she was, we have to find out who was responsible. That is our job. That is why we are here. We've come because we think you can help.'

'I've told that inspector and the woman police officer what I knew.'

Dalgliesh didn't reply. The silence and what it implied obviously disconcerted Daisy. After a short pause she said defensively: 'How do I know you won't try to pin Mr Etienne's murder on Auntie Esmé? She said you might try, she thought you might fit her up.'

Dalgliesh said: 'We don't think Mrs Carling had anything to do with Mr Etienne's death. And we won't pin the murder on anyone. What we're trying to do is to find out the truth. I think I know two things about you, Daisy; that you are intelligent and that, if you promise to tell the truth, then it will be the truth. Will you promise?'

'How do I know I can trust you?'

'I'm asking you to trust us. You have to make up your own mind whether you can. That's an important decision for you to have to make, but you can't escape it. Only, don't lie. I would rather you told us nothing than that you lied.'

This is a high-risk strategy, thought Kate. She hoped that they were not now about to hear how Mrs Summers had warned the children never to trust a policeman. Daisy's piggy eyes looked straight into Dalgliesh's. The silence seemed interminable.

Then Daisy said: 'All right. I'll tell the truth.'

Dalgliesh's voice didn't change. He said: 'When Inspector Aaron and the WPC came to see you, you told them that you have been spending your evenings in Mrs Carling's flat to do your homework and have supper with her. Is that true?'

'Yes. Sometimes I went to sleep in her spare room and sometimes on the couch, and then Auntie Esmé would wake me up and bring me back here before Mummy got home.'

Mrs Reed broke in: 'Look, the kid was safe here. I always double-locked the door when I left and she had her own keys. And I left a phone number. What was I bloody well supposed to do? Take her with me to the Club?'

Dalgliesh ignored her. His eyes were still on Daisy.

'What did you do together?'

'I did my homework and sometimes she did some writing, and then we used to watch telly. She let me read her books. She has a lot of books about murders, and she knew all about real-life murders. I used to take my supper in with me and sometimes I would have some of hers.'

'It sounds as if you had happy evenings together. I expect she was glad of your company.'

'She didn't like being alone at night. She said she could hear noises on the stairs and she didn't feel safe even with the door double-locked. She said that someone who had a second pair of keys could be careless with them and then a murderer could get hold of them and come creeping up the stairs and let himself into the flat. Or, she said, he could be on the roof after dark and let himself down with a rope and get in at the window. Sometimes at night she could hear him tapping against the pane. It was always worse when there was something frightening on the telly. She never liked to watch the telly by herself.'

Poor kid, thought Kate. So these were the vividly imagined horrors from which Daisy, left alone night after night, had taken refuge in Mrs Carling's flat. What, she wondered, was Esmé Carling escaping from? Boredom, loneliness, her own imagined fears? It was an unlikely friendship, but each had met the other's need for companionship, a sense of security, the small domestic comforts of a home.

Dalgliesh said: 'And you told Inspector Aaron and the woman police officer from the Juvenile Bureau that you were in Mrs Carling's flat from six o'clock on Thursday the fourteenth of October, the night Mr Etienne died, until she took you home at about midnight. Was that true?'

Here at last was the crucial question and it seemed to Kate that they waited for it with bated breath. The child still gazed calmly at Dalgliesh. They could hear her mother pulling on her cigarette, but she didn't speak.

The seconds passed, then Daisy said: 'No, it wasn't true. Auntie Esmé asked me to lie for her.'

'When did she ask you to do that?'

'On Friday, the day after Mr Etienne was killed, when she met me out of school. She was waiting at the gate. Then she came home with me by bus. We sat upstairs in the bus where there weren't many people and she told me that the police would be asking where she was and I was to tell them that we had spent the evening and the night together. She said they might think she had killed Mr Etienne because she was a crime writer and knew all about murder and because she was very clever at devising plots. She said the police might try to pin it on her because she had a motive. Everyone at

336

Peverell Press knew that she hated Mr Etienne for turning down her book.'

'But you didn't think she'd done it, did you Daisy? Why was that?'

The sharp little eyes still looked into his. 'You know why.'

'Yes, and so does Inspector Miskin. But tell us.'

'If she had done it she would have come here late that night before Mummy was home and asked for the alibi then. She never asked until the body was discovered. And she didn't know when it was Mr Etienne had died. She said I was to be sure to give an alibi for the whole evening and the night. Auntie said we had to tell the same story because the police would try to catch us out. So I told that Inspector everything that had happened except for what we saw on the television, but it had all happened the night before.'

Dalgliesh said: 'That's the most reliable way of fabricating an alibi. Essentially you're telling the truth so you don't have to fear that the other person will say something different. Was that your idea?'

'Yes.'

'We must hope, Daisy, that you don't go in for crime in a serious way. Now this is very important and I want you to think hard before you answer any of my questions. Will you do that?'

'Yes.'

'Did your Aunt Esmé tell you what happened at Innocent House on that Thursday night, the night that Mr Etienne died?'

'She didn't tell me very much. She said that she'd been there and seen Mr Etienne but that he was alive when she left. Someone had rung him to go upstairs and he'd told her he wouldn't be long. But he was long so she got tired of waiting. She said in the end she left.'

'She left without seeing him again?'

'That's what she said. She said she waited and then she got frightened. It's terrible at Innocent House when all the staff have left and it's cold and silent. There was a lady who killed herself there and Mrs Carling says that sometimes her ghost walks. So she didn't wait for Mr Etienne to come back. I asked her if she'd seen the murderer and she said, "No, I didn't see him. I don't know who did it, but I know who didn't do it."'

'Did she say who?'

'No.'

'Did she tell you whether it was a man or a woman, the person who didn't do it?'

337

'No.'

'Daisy, did you gain any impression that she was speaking of a man or a woman?'

'No.'

'Did she tell you anything else about that night? Try to remember her exact words.'

'She did say something, but it didn't make sense, not then. She said, "I heard the voice, but the snake was outside the door. Why was the snake outside the door? And it was a funny time to borrow a vacuum cleaner." She said it very low, as if she was speaking to herself.'

'Did you ask her what she meant?'

'I asked her what kind of snake? Was it a poisonous snake? Did the snake bite Mr Etienne? And she said, "No, it wasn't a real snake, but maybe it was lethal enough in its way." '

Dalgliesh said: ' "I heard the voice, but the snake was outside the door. And it was a funny time to borrow a vacuum cleaner." Are you sure of those words?'

'Yes.'

'She didn't say his voice or her voice?'

'No. She said what I told you. I think she wanted to keep some of it secret. She liked secrets and mysteries.'

'When did she next speak to you about the murder?'

'The day before yesterday when I was here doing my homework. She said she was going on Thursday night to Innocent House to see somebody. She said "They'll have to go on publishing me now. I can make sure of that, anyway." She said she might want me to give her another alibi but she wasn't sure yet. I asked her who she was going to see and she said she wouldn't tell me for the time being, it had to be a secret. I don't think she was ever going to tell me. I think it was too important to tell anyone. I said, "If you're going to see the murderer, he might kill you too", and she said she wasn't that silly, she wasn't going to see any murderer. She said, "I don't know who the murderer is, but I may do after tomorrow night." She didn't say anything else.'

Dalgliesh held out his hand across the table and the child clasped it. He said: 'Thank you Daisy. You've been very helpful. We shall have to ask you to write this down and sign it but not now.'

'And I won't be put in care?'

'I don't think there's any chance of that, is there?' He looked at Mrs

Reed who said grimly: 'That kid goes into care over my dead body.'

She was seeing them out when, apparently on impulse, she slipped out after them and closed the door. Ignoring Kate she spoke directly to Dalgliesh: 'Mr Mason, he's Daisy's headmaster, says she's clever, I mean really clever.'

'I think she is, Mrs Reed. You should be proud of her.'

'He thinks she could get one of them government grants to go to a different school, â boarding school.'

'What does Daisy think?'

'She says she wouldn't mind. She isn't happy at the school where she is. I think she'd like to go but she doesn't like to say so.'

Kate felt a spurt of mild irritation. They needed to get on. There was Mrs Carling's flat to examine and the literary agent was expected at 11.30.

But Dalgliesh showed no sign of impatience. He said: 'Why don't you and Daisy talk it over at length with Mr Mason? Daisy has to be the one to decide.'

Mrs Reed still lingered, looking at him as if there was something else she needed to hear, some reassurance that only he could give.

He said: 'You mustn't think that it's necessarily wrong for Daisy because it happens to be convenient for you. It could be the right thing for both of you.'

'Thank you, thank you,' she whispered and slipped back into the flat.

51

Mrs Carling's flat was one floor down and at the front of the building. The heavy mahogany door was fitted with a keyhole and with two security locks, a Banham and an Ingersoll. The keys turned easily and Dalgliesh pushed open the door against the shifting weight of a pile of post. The hall smelled musty and was very dark. He felt for the light switch and pressed it down to reveal at a glance the simple layout of the flat, a narrow hall with two doors facing him and one at each end. He bent down to pick up the assorted envelopes and saw that they were merely circulars, with two obvious bills and an envelope which exhorted Mrs Carling to open it immediately and win the chance of half a million. There was also a sheet of folded paper with a message in a laborious hand. 'Sorry I can't come tomorrow. Have to go to clinic with Tracey on account of high blood pressure. Hope to see you next Friday. Mrs Darlene Morgan.'

Dalgliesh opened the door immediately ahead and switched on the light. They found themselves in the sitting-room. The two windows overlooking the street were close-shut, the curtains of red velvet half-drawn. At this height there was no risk of prying eyes even from the top deck of buses but the bottom halves of both windows were curtained in a patterned net. The main artificial light came from an inverted glass bowl painted with a faint design of butterflies which hung from a central rose on the ceiling, the glass spotted with the black shrivelled bodies of trapped flies. There were three table lamps with pink-fringed shades, one on a small table beside a fireside chair, one on a square table set between the two windows and the third on a huge roll-top desk against the left-hand wall. As if desperate for light and air, Kate drew back the curtains and pushed open one of the windows then went round the room and switched on all the lights. They breathed the cool air which gave the illusion of country freshness, and looked round at a room they could at last see clearly.

The immediate impression, emphasized by the pink glow of the lamps, was of a cushioned, old-fashioned cosiness which was the more appealing because the owner had made no concessions to popular contemporary taste. The room could have been furnished in the 1930s and left virtually undisturbed. Most of the pieces looked as if they had been inherited; the roll-top desk which held her portable typewriter, the four mahogany dining chairs of discordant shape and age, an Edwardian glass-fronted cabinet in which assorted china objects and part of a tea service had been piled and stacked rather than arranged, two faded rugs so inappropriately placed that Dalgliesh suspected they were concealing holes in the carpet. Only the sofa and two matching armchairs which surrounded the fireplace were comparatively new, furnished with plump cushions and covered in linen patterned with pale pink and yellow roses. The fireplace itself looked original, an ornate contrivance in grey marble with a heavy overmantel, the grate surrounded by a double row of ornamental tiles, of flowers, fruits and birds. At each end of the mantelshelf two collared Staffordshire dogs with golden chains stared with bright-eyed intensity at the opposite wall. Ranged between them was a clutter of ornaments; a George VI and Queen Elizabeth coronation mug, a black japanned box, two diminutive brass candlesticks, a modern porcelain figure of a crinolined woman holding a lap-dog, a cut-glass vase containing a bunch of imitation primroses. Behind the ornaments were two coloured photographs. One looked as if it had been taken at a prize-giving; Esmé Carling stood pointing an imitation gun, surrounded by grinning faces. In the second she was at a book signing. The picture had obviously been carefully posed. A purchaser stood expectantly at her side, head unnaturally bent to get it in the picture, while Mrs Carling, pen raised from the page, smiled beguilingly into the camera. Kate briefly studied it, trying to superimpose on the square marsupial features, the small mouth and slightly hooked nose, that appallingly drowned and violated face which was the first glimpse she had had of Esmé Carling.

Dalgliesh could understand the attraction this homely soft-cushioned room had held for Daisy. On this broad sofa she had read, watched television, briefly slept before being half-carried back to her own room. Here was a refuge from the terror of her imaginings in simulated terror, neatly contained within the covers of books, sanitized, fictionalized, to be tasted, shared, put aside, no more real than and as easily turned off as the dancing flames of the artificial log fire. There had been security here, companionship and, yes, love of a kind if love was the meeting of mutual need. He glanced at the books. The shelves held paperback copies of crime and detective stories, but he noticed that few of the writers were living. Mrs Carling's taste was for women writers of the Golden Age. They all looked well-read. Below them was a shelf of real-life crime: books on the Wallace case, on Jack the Ripper, on the more famous Victorian murders, Adelaide Bartlett and Constance Kent. The lower shelves held leather-bound and gold-titled copies of her own works, an extravagance, Dalgliesh thought, unlikely to have been subsidized by Peverell Press. The sight of this harmless vanity depressed him, evoking a spasm of pity. Who would inherit this accumulated record of a life lived by murder and ended by murder? On what shelf in drawing-room, bedroom or lavatory would they find an honoured or tolerated place? Or would they be bought as a job-lot by some second-hand bookseller and priced as a set, their value enhanced by the horror and appalling appropriateness of her death? Surveying the titles so reminiscent of the 1930s, of village policemen cycling to the scene of the murder, tugging their forelocks to the gentry, of autopsies undertaken by eccentric general practitioners after evening surgery and unlikely denouements in the library, he took them out and glanced at them at random. *Death by Dancing* apparently set in the world of formation ballroom competitions, *Cruising to Murder, Death by Drowning, The Mistletoe Murders*. He replaced them carefully feeling no condescension. Why should he? He told himself that she had probably given pleasure to more people with her mysteries than he had with his poetry. And if the pleasure was different in kind, who was to say that one was inferior to the other? She had at least respected the English language and used it as well as lay in her power. In an age rapidly becoming illiterate that was something. For thirty years she had purveyed the fantasy of murder, the acceptable face of violence, the controllable terror. He hoped that when she had come at last face to face with reality the encounter had been brief and merciful.

Kate had moved into the kitchen. He joined her and together they surveyed the mess. The sink was piled with dirty crockery, the unwashed frying pan was on the stove, and the waste bin was spilling its tins and squashed cartons onto the grimy floor. Kate said: 'She wouldn't have wanted us to find it looking like this. Tough on her that her Mrs Morgan couldn't come this morning.'

Glancing at her he saw the flush rise from her throat and knew that the remark had suddenly struck her as irrational and foolish and that she wished it unspoken.

But their minds had moved in tandem. 'Lord, let me know mine end, and the number of my days: that I may be certified how long I have to live.' Surely few people could pray that prayer with any sincerity. The best one could hope for or want was enough time to tidy away the personal debris, consign one's secrets to the flames or the dustbin and leave the kitchen tidy.

For a couple of seconds, even as he opened the drawers and cupboards, he was back in that Norfolk graveyard hearing his father's voice, an instantaneous image powerful in its intensity and bringing with it the smell of cut hay, newly turned Norfolk earth, of the intoxication of lilies. The parishioners liked the rector's son to be present at village funerals and during the school holidays he always attended, finding a village burial more of an interest than an imposition, sharing the funeral tea afterwards, trying to contain his boyish hunger, while the mourners pressed on him the traditional cooked ham and rich fruit-cake, and murmured their thanks.

'Good of you to come, Mr Adam. Dad would have appreciated it. He was very fond of you, was Dad.'

His mouth sticky with cake, murmuring the expected lie: 'I was very fond of him, Mrs Hodgkin.'

He would stand there watching while old Goodfellow the sexton and the undertaker's men tilted the coffin into that neatly accommodating pit, hearing the soft thud of Norfolk earth on the lid, listening to his father's grave, scholarly voice as the breeze lifted his greying hair and billowed his surplice. And he would picture the man or woman he had known, the shrouded body encased in padded imitation silk, more ostentatiously bedded than it had ever been in life, and would picture every stage of its dissolution: the rotting shroud, the slowly decaying flesh, the final falling-in of the coffin-lid on the denuded bones, and had never from childhood been able to believe that magnificent proclamation of immortality. 'And though worms destroy this body, yet in my flesh shall I see God.'

They moved into Mrs Carling's bedroom but did not linger. It was large, overfurnished, untidy and not very clean. The 1930s dressing table with its triple mirror held a plastic tray patterned with violets containing a jumble of half-empty bottles of hand and body lotions, greasy jars, lipsticks and eye make-up. Without thinking, Kate unscrewed the largest jar of foundation cream and saw its single indentation where Mrs Carling had drawn her finger across the surface. The mark, so ephemeral yet, for a moment, seeming permanent and ineradicable, brought the dead woman's image so vividly to mind that she froze, the jar in her hand, as if she had been caught out in an act of private violation. The eyes in the mirror stared back at her, guilty and a little ashamed. She made herself go over to the wardrobe and open its door. There came out with the rustle of the hanging clothes a smell that brought back other searches, other victims, other rooms, the sweet–sour musty smell of age and failure and death. She closed its door quickly but not before she had seen the three whisky bottles hidden among the row of shoes. She thought: there are moments when I hate my job. But these moments were few and they never lasted long.

The guest bedroom was a narrow, ill-proportioned cell, the one high window giving a view of a brick wall grimed with decades of London dirt and angled with heavy drainpipes. But some attempt, even if misguided, had been made to make the room inviting. The walls and ceiling were covered with a paper of twining honeysuckle, roses and ivy. The curtains, elaborately pleated, were of a matching material and the single divan, placed under the window, had a pale pink coverlet, obviously chosen to match the pink of the roses. The attempt to prettify, to impose on bleak nothingness a feminine intensity, served only to emphasize the room's defects. The décor had obviously been designed for a female guest, but Dalgliesh couldn't imagine a woman sleeping peacefully in this claustrophobic over-patterned cell. Certainly no man could, with the ceiling's synthetic sweetness pressing down on him, the bed too narrow for comfort, the bedside table a fragile reproduction, too small to hold more than the bedside lamp.

The time looking round the flat had not been wasted. Kate remembered one of the first lessons she had been taught as a young detective constable: know the victim. Every victim dies because of who he is, what he is, where he is at one moment of time. The more you know about the victim the closer you are to his murderer. But now as they sat down at Esmé Carling's desk they were in search of more specific evidence.

They were rewarded as soon as they opened it. The desk was tidier and less cluttered than they had expected and lying on the top of a pile of recent unpaid bills were two sheets of paper. The first was obviously a draft of the note found on the railings at Innocent House. There were few alterations; Mrs Carling's final version was little different from her first outpouring of pain and anger. But the writing was a scrawl compared with the firm and careful calligraphy of the final note. Here was confirmation, if it had been needed, that they were her words and written in her hand. Underneath was a draft of a letter in the same hand. It was dated Thursday 14 October.

Dear Gerard,

I have just heard the news from my agent. Yes, from my agent! You haven't even the decency or the courage to tell me direct. You could have asked me to come to talk to you at the office, or it wouldn't have hurt you to take me out to lunch or dinner to break the news. Or are you as mean as you are disloyal and cowardly? Perhaps you were afraid that I would disgrace you by howling in the soup. I'm a great deal tougher than that, as you will discover. Your rejection of *Death on Paradise Island* would still have been unfair, unjustified and ungrateful, but at least I could have said these things to your face. And now I can't even reach you by telephone. I'm not surprised. That bloody woman, Miss Blackett, is good at blocking calls if nothing else. At least it shows that even you are capable of some shame.

Have you any idea what I have done for Peverell Press, long before you had any power? And what a disastrous day for the firm that has proved. I have produced a book a year for thirty years, all reliable sellers, and if sales of the last were disappointing, whose fault is that? What have you ever done to promote me with the vigour and enthusiasm my reputation demands? I'm off to do a signing at Cambridge this afternoon. Who persuaded the bookshop to put that on? I did. I shall go alone as usual. Most publishers see that their top authors are properly accompanied and looked after. But the fans will be there, and they'll buy. I have devoted readers who look to me to provide what no other detective writer apparently does, a fair mystery with good writing and an absence of that sex, violence and filthy language which you apparently think people today want. Well they don't. If you have so little idea of what readers really

345

want you'll drive Peverell Press to bankruptcy even quicker than the publishing world predicts.

I shall, of course, have to consider how best to safeguard my interests. If I move to another publisher I shall expect to take my back-list with me. Don't think you can throw me overboard and still exploit that valuable asset. And there's something else. These mysterious mishaps which are taking place at Peverell Press only began when you took over as Managing Director. If I were you, I'd take care. There have already been two deaths at Innocent House.

Kate said: 'I wonder if this, too, was just a preliminary draft or whether she actually sent in the final version. She usually typed her letters but there's no carbon here. If she did post it, perhaps she thought it would be more forceful hand-written. This could be the copy.'

'The letter wasn't among the correspondence in his office. My guess is that it wasn't sent. Instead she called at Innocent House demanding to see him. When that failed she went to do her Cambridge signing, discovered that it had been cancelled by someone at Peverell Press, returned to London in a state of high indignation and decided to call on Etienne that evening. Most people seem to have known that he worked late on Thursdays. It's possible that she telephoned and told him that she was coming. He could hardly, after all, prevent her. And if she did telephone using his private number the call wouldn't have gone through Miss Blackett.'

Kate said: 'It's odd, if she took the first paper with her, that she didn't take this letter and leave it with him. I suppose it's possible she did and that either Etienne tore it up or the murderer found it and destroyed it.'

Dalgliesh said: 'Unlikely, I think. What seems more likely is that she took with her the fulmination addressed to the partnership perhaps with the object of pinning it to the noticeboard in the reception room. That way the partners would see it and so would all members of the staff and visitors.'

'They'd hardly have left it up, sir.'

'Of course not. But she probably hoped that quite a number of people would see it before it was drawn to the partners' attention. At least it would cause a stir. The fulmination was probably intended as the first blow in her campaign of revenge. She must have had some very bad hours when she first heard of Gerard's death. If she did in fact leave the notice, and possibly also the manuscript of her novel, in the reception room, their presence would prove that she had called at Innocent House that night and after most of the staff had left. She must have been waiting for us to appear, knowing that the presence of the note made her one of the chief suspects. So she arranges her alibi with Daisy. And then when the police do arrive, nothing is said about the note. So either we've missed its significance which is unlikely or someone has removed it. And then the person who did take it down from the noticeboard telephones to reassure her. He or she is able to reassure her because Carling is confident that she is talking to an ally not to a murderer.'

'It hangs together, sir. It's logical and it's credible.'

'It's conjecture, every part of it, Kate. It can't be proved. None of it would stand up in court. It's an ingenious theory which fits all the facts as we know them so far but it's circumstantial. There's just one small piece of corroborative evidence. If she pinned the false suicide note to the noticeboard before she left Innocent House there would have been the marks of one or more drawing pins in the paper. Was that the reason why it was so neatly trimmed down before it was spiked on the railings?'

There was little else of interest in the desk. Mrs Carling received few letters or, if she did, she destroyed them. Those she kept included a bundle of airmail forms tied with a ribbon and kept together in one of the cubby-holes. They were from a woman friend in Australia, a Mrs Marjorie Rampton, but the correspondence had gradually grown more perfunctory and seemed to have petered out. Apart from this there were bundles of letters from fans, all with a carbon of the reply attached to the original letter. Mrs Carling had obviously taken considerable trouble to satisfy her admirers. In the top drawer of the desk there was a file labelled investments with letters from her stockbroker. She had capital of just over £32,000 carefully invested between gilts and equities. In another file was a copy of her will. It was a short document in which she left a legacy of £5,000 to the Authors' Foundation and to a crime writers' club and the bulk of her estate to the friend in Australia. Another file contained papers relating to her divorce fifteen years earlier. Glancing quickly through them, Dalgliesh saw that it had been acrimonious but, from her point of view, not particularly advantageous. The payments had been small and had stopped with Raymond Carling's death five years later. And that was all. The contents of the desk confirmed what Dalgliesh had suspected. Here was a woman who lived for her work. Take that away and what had she left?

52

Velma Pitt-Cowley, Mrs Carling's literary agent, had agreed to be at the flat at 11.30 and arrived six minutes late. She was hardly inside the door before it became apparent that she was in none too good a temper. She burst into the room when Kate opened the door with a speed that suggested that it was she who had been kept waiting, flung herself into the nearer of the two armchairs, then leaned forward to slip the gold chain of her bag from her shoulder and to deposit a bulging briefcase on the carpet beside her. Only then did she deign to bestow any attention on Kate or Dalgliesh. When she did, and her eyes met Dalgliesh's, her mood subtly changed and her first words showed that she was prepared to be gracious.

'Sorry to be late and in such a rush, but you know how it is. I had to go into the office first and I've got a luncheon guest at the Ivy at twelve forty-five. It's pretty important as a matter of fact. The author I'm meeting flew in especially from New York this morning. And things cropped up as they always do if you show your face in the office. You can't trust people with the simplest jobs nowadays. I left as soon as I could but the taxi got snarled up in Theobalds Road. My God, this is terrible about poor Esmé. It's really terrible! What happened? She drowned herself, didn't she? Drowned or hanged herself or both. I mean, that's really sick.'

Having expressed appropriate outrage, Mrs Pitt-Cowley settled herself more elegantly in the chair and drew up the skirt of her formal black suit almost to her crotch to reveal a pair of very long and shapely legs enclosed in nylons so fine that they were no more than a dull sheen on the sharp bones. She had obviously dressed with care for her 12.45 luncheon appointment, and Dalgliesh wondered what privileged client, present or prospective, warranted a smartness which carefully combined professional competence with sexual allure. Beneath the well-fitting jacket with its row of brass buttons she wore a high-necked silk shirt. A hat of black velvet, speared at the front with a golden arrow, was crushed over light brown hair cut in a fringe, just touching the thick, level eyebrows and falling in well-brushed swathes almost to her shoulders. As she spoke she gesticulated; the long fingers, heavily ringed, restlessly patterned the air as if she were communicating to the deaf, and from time to time her shoulders hunched in sudden spasms. The gestures seemed oddly unrelated to her words and it seemed to Dalgliesh that the affectation was less a symptom of nervousness or insecurity than a trick originally designed to draw attention to her remarkable hands but which had now become an unbreakable habit. Her initial testiness had surprised him; in his experience people involved in a spectacular murder, provided they neither grieved for the victim nor felt themselves at risk from the police inquiry, usually relished the vicarious excitement of their brush with violent death and the notoriety of being in the know. He was used to encountering eyes slightly ashamed but avid with curiosity. Bad temper and a preoccupation with one's own concerns at least made a change.

She gazed round the room at the open desk, at the pile of papers on the table, and said: 'God, it's too awful sitting here in her flat, you having to rummage through her things. I know you have to do it, it's your job, but it's sort of uncanny. She seems more present now than when she was actually here. I keep thinking I'll hear her key in the lock and she'll come in, find us like this, uninvited, and raise hell.'

Dalgliesh said: 'Violent death destroys privacy, I'm afraid. Did she commonly raise hell?'

As if she hadn't heard him, Mrs Pitt-Cowley said: 'Do you know what I'd really like now? What I really need is a good strong black coffee. There's no chance of any, I suppose?'

It was Kate she looked at, and Kate who replied. 'There's a jar of coffee grains in the kitchen and a carton of milk in the fridge unopened. Strictly speaking I suppose we should get the bank's permission, but I doubt whether anyone would object.'

When Kate made no immediate move towards the kitchen, Velma gave her a long speculative stare as if assessing the possible nuisance-value of a new typist. Then, with a shrug and a flurry of fingers, she decided on prudence.

'Better not I suppose, although she won't be needing it herself now, will she? But I can't say I fancy drinking it out of one of her cups.'

Dalgliesh said: 'Obviously it's important for us to learn as much about Mrs Carling as we can. That's why we're grateful to you for meeting us here this morning. Her death must have been a shock and I realize that it can't be easy for you coming here. But it is important.'

Mrs Pitt-Cowley's voice and look expressed a passionate intensity. 'Oh, I do see that. I mean, I understand absolutely that you have to ask questions. Obviously I'll help all I can. What did you want to know?'

He asked: 'When did you hear the news?'

'This morning, shortly after seven, before your people rang to ask me to meet you here. Claudia Etienne telephoned. Woke me up, actually. Not exactly pleasant news to start the day. She could have waited, but I suppose she didn't want me to read it in the evening paper or hear it when I got to the office. You know how fast gossip travels in this town. After all I am – I mean I was – Esmé's agent and I suppose she thought that I ought to be one of the first to know and that she ought to be the one to tell me. But suicide! It's bizarre. It's the last thing I'd have expected Esmé to do. Well of course it was the last thing she did. Oh God, I'm sorry. Nothing one says seems adequate at a time like this.'

'So you were surprised at the news?'

'Isn't one always? I mean, even when people who threaten suicide actually do it, it always seems surprising, a bit unreal. But Esmé! And to kill herself like that. I mean it wasn't the most comfortable way to go. Claudia didn't seem very sure how exactly she died. She just said that Esmé had hanged herself from the railings at Innocent House and that the body was found under water. Did she drown or strangle herself or what exactly?'

Dalgliesh said: 'It is possible Mrs Carling died by drowning but we shan't know the cause of death until after the autopsy.'

'But it was suicide? I mean, you're sure about that?'

'We're not sure yet of anything. Can you think of any reason why Mrs Carling should have wanted to end her life?'

'She was upset about Peverell Press rejecting *Death on Paradise Island*. You've heard about that, I suppose. But she was more angry than distressed. Furiously angry in fact. I can imagine her seeking some kind of vengeance on the firm, but not by killing herself. Besides that takes guts. I don't mean that Esmé was a coward, but I can't somehow see her throttling herself or throwing herself in the river. What a way to die! If she really wanted to do away with herself there are easier ways. Take Sonia Clements. You know about that, of course. Sonia killed herself with drugs and booze. That would be my way. I'd have thought it would be Esmé's.'

Kate said: 'But less effective as a public protest.'

'Not so dramatic, I agree. But what's the good of a dramatic public protest if you aren't there to enjoy it? No, if Esmé decided to kill herself it would be in bed, clean sheets, flowers in the room, her best night-dress, a dignified farewell note on the bedside cabinet. She was a great one for appearances.'

Kate, remembering the rooms of suicides she had been called to, the vomit, the soiled bedclothes, the grotesque body stiffened in death, reflected that suicide was seldom as dignified in practice as in imagination. She said: 'When did you last see her?'

'On the evening of the day after Gerard Etienne's death. That would be October fifteenth, the Friday.'

Dalgliesh asked: 'Here or in your office?'

'Here in this room. It was fortuitous really. I mean, I hadn't planned to call. I was dining with Dicky Mulchester of Herne & Illingworth to discuss a client and it occurred to me that his firm might be interested in *Death on Paradise Island*. It was a long shot but they are taking on a few crime writers. I was driving past here to the restaurant when I noticed that there were some parking spaces free down the side road and I thought I'd call in and borrow Esmé's copy of the manuscript. The traffic was lighter than I expected and I had ten minutes in hand. We hadn't spoken since Gerard's death. It's odd, isn't it, how small things decide one's actions? I probably wouldn't have bothered if I hadn't seen the empty space. I was interested, too, in hearing Esmé's reaction to Gerard's death. I couldn't get much out of Claudia. I thought Esmé might have picked up some of the details. She was a great one for gossip. Not that I had much time to spare then. The main reason for calling was to collect the manuscript.'

Dalgliesh asked: 'How did you find her?'

Mrs Pitt-Cowley didn't immediately reply. Her face was thoughtful, the restless hands momentarily stilled. Dalgliesh thought that she was evaluating the interview in the light of subsequent events, seeing it perhaps as more significant than it seemed at the time. At last she said: 'Looking back on it I think she behaved rather oddly. I would have expected her to want to talk about Gerard, how he died, why he died, whether it was murder. She just wouldn't discuss it. She said it was too dreadful and too painful, that she'd been published by

Peverell Press for thirty years and however badly they'd treated her his death had shocked her profoundly. Well, it had shocked us all, but I didn't expect Esmé to feel much personal sorrow. She did tell me that she had an alibi for the previous evening and the night. Apparently she had a neighbour's child in here with her. I remember thinking it a little odd at the time that she bothered to tell me that. After all, no one was going to suspect Esmé of throttling Gerard with a snake, or however it was he died. Oh, and I remember she did ask whether I thought that the partners would change their minds about *Paradise Island* now that Gerard was dead. She always held him mainly responsible for its rejection. I didn't hold out much hope. I pointed out that it had probably been a decision from the whole Book Committee and that anyway the partners wouldn't like to go against Gerard's wishes now that he was dead. Then I suggested that Herne & Illingworth might be interested and asked to borrow her manuscript. She was odd then too. She said she wasn't sure where she'd put it. She'd looked for it that morning and couldn't find it. Then she said that she was too upset to think about *Paradise Island* so soon after Gerard's death. That hardly rang true. After all, she'd asked me only a couple of minutes earlier whether I thought that the partners would change their minds and take it. I don't think she had the manuscript. Either that or she didn't want me to have it. I left soon afterwards. I was only here for about ten minutes in all.'

'And you have spoken to her since?'

'No, not once. That's odd too when I come too think of it. After all, Gerard Etienne was her publisher. I'd have expected her to come into the office if only for a gossip. Usually you couldn't keep her away.'

'How long have you been her agent? Did you know her well?'

'Less than two years, actually. But yes, even in the short time I did get to know her quite well. She saw to that. Actually I inherited her. Her old agent was Marjorie Rampton and Marge took her on with her first book. That's thirty years ago. They were really close. There often is personal friendship between agent and author – you can't do your best for a client if you don't get on with them as well as respecting the work. But with Marge and Esmé it went deeper. Don't misunderstand me, I'm talking about friendship. I'm not hinting at anything, well – sexual. I suppose they had quite a lot in common, both being widows, both childless. They used to take holidays together and I think Esmé asked Marge to be her literary executor. That's going to be a nuisance for someone if she didn't change her will. Marge went to Australia to stay with her nieces as soon as she'd sold the agency to me, and she's still there as far as I know.'

Dalgliesh said, 'Tell us about Esmé Carling. What sort of woman was she?'

'Oh God, this is awful. I mean, what can I say? It seems so disloyal, indecent almost, criticizing her when she's dead, but I can't pretend she was easy. She was one of those clients who are always on the phone or calling in at the office. Nothing's ever right. They always feel you can do more, squeeze a higher advance from the publisher, sell the film rights, get them a TV series. I think she resented losing Marge and thought I wasn't giving her the attention her genius warranted, but actually I was giving her more time than was really justified. I mean, I do have other clients and most of them a damn sight more profitable.'

Kate said: 'More trouble than she was worth?'

Mrs Pitt-Cowley turned on her a speculative, then dismissive glance. 'I wouldn't have put it like that myself, but, if you want the truth, I wouldn't have broken my heart if she'd decided to look for another agent. Look, I hate saying this, but anyone in the office will tell you the same. A lot of it was loneliness, missing Marge, resenting Marge for abandoning her. But Marge was an old toughie. When it came to choosing between her precious nieces and Esmé it was no contest. And I think Esmé knew that her talent was running out. We were in for big trouble. Peverell Press turning down *Death on Paradise Island* was just the beginning.'

'Was that Gerard Etienne?'

'Basically, yes. What Etienne wanted went at Peverell Press. But I doubt whether anyone there really wanted her, except perhaps James de Witt, and he doesn't cut much ice at Peverells. I rang and made a fuss, of course, as soon as I got Gerard's letter. I wasn't getting anywhere. And honestly, the new book really wasn't up to standard, even her standard. Do you know her work at all?'

Dalgliesh said carefully: 'I have heard of her, of course, but never read her.'

'She wasn't that bad. I mean, she could write literate prose, and that's rare enough nowadays. Peverell Press wouldn't have published her otherwise. She wasn't consistent. Just when you thought: God, I can't go on with this boring drivel, she'd produce a really good passage and the book would suddenly come alive. And she had an original idea for her detective – detectives, rather. She had a retired married couple, the Mainwarings, Malcolm and Mavis. He was a retired bank manager, and she'd been a teacher. It was quite neat. Went down well with an ageing population. Reader identification and all that. Bored retired couple haring off after the clues, plenty of time to make murder their hobby, using a lifetime of experience to put one over on the police, the wisdom of old age triumphing over the crass immaturity of youth, that sort of thing. A nice change to have a detective with a touch of arthritis. But they were getting a bit tiresome – the Mainwarings I mean. Esmé had the bright idea of involving Malcolm with young female suspects and Mavis having to rescue him from his entanglements. I suppose she was aiming for light relief, but it had become a bore. I mean, geriatric sex is all right if that happens to turn you on, but people don't want it in popular fiction, and Esmé was getting more explicit with each book. Bodice-rippers with blood. That's not really her market. It wasn't in Malcolm Mainwaring's character. And, of course, she couldn't plot. God, I hate saying this, but she couldn't. You did say you wanted the truth. She used to steal ideas from other writers – only dead writers, of course – and add her own twists. It was becoming a bit obvious. That's what gave Gerard Etienne his chance to turn down *Death on Paradise Island*. He said it was a boring read and the only parts that weren't boring were too like Agatha Christie's *Murder Under the Sun*. I believe he actually uttered the dread word "plagiarism". Then, of course, there was Esmé's other trouble which didn't make her any easier to deal with.'

Velma sketched in the air the outline of St Paul's Cathedral complete with dome, and ended with a pantomime of raising a glass to her lips.

'Are you saying that she was an alcoholic?'

'Getting on that way. You didn't get a hell of a lot of sense out of Esmé after midday. It had got worse in the last six months.'

'So she wasn't making much money?'

'Never did. Esmé was never in the big league. Still she was doing all right, until the last three years. She could live on her writing, which is more than most authors can. She had quite a faithful following of old *aficionados* who'd grown up with the Mainwarings, but as they died off she wasn't attracting younger readers. Last year there was a

355

big slump in paperback sales. I was afraid we were going to lose that contract.'

Kate said: 'Which perhaps accounts for this flat. It isn't exactly a fashionable address.'

'Well it suited her. She was a protected tenant and the rent was low, I mean really low. She'd have been crazy to leave. Actually she told me that she planned to buy a country cottage in the Cotswolds or Herefordshire and was saving her capital for that. Saw herself among the roses and wistaria, I suppose. Personally I think she'd have died of boredom. I've seen it happen before.'

Dalgliesh asked: 'She wrote crime novels, detective stories. Would she be likely to fancy herself as an amateur detective? Try her hand at solving a crime if one came her way?'

'You mean tangling with a real-life murderer, with whoever it was killed Etienne? She'd be crazy. Esmé wasn't a great brain, but she wasn't stupid either. I'm not saying that she lacked courage, she had plenty of guts – especially after a few whiskies – but that would have been plain stupid.'

'She might not think she was tangling with a murderer. Suppose she got an idea about the murder, would she be likely to bring it to us or be tempted to do a little private investigating?'

'She might, if she thought it was safe and she could get something out of it. It would be quite a triumph, wouldn't it? Publicity-wise, I mean. "Woman crime writer outwits Scotland Yard". Yes, I can see her mind working like that. But you're not suggesting that she tried something like that?'

'I was interested whether you thought it was in character.'

'Let's say that it wouldn't surprise me. She was fascinated by real-life crime, detection, murder trials, that sort of thing. Well, you've only got to look at her bookcase. And she had a high opinion of her own cleverness. And she might not see the danger. I don't think she had much imagination, not about real life. OK, I know that sounds odd when I'm talking about a novelist, but she'd lived with fictional murder for so long that I don't think she realized that real-life murder is different, that it isn't something you can control and write up into a plot and neatly solve in the last chapter. And she didn't see Gerard Etienne's body, did she? I don't think she ever saw a dead person in real life. She could only imagine it, and death probably seemed no more real or frightening than her other imaginings. Am I being too sophisticated? I mean, do say if I'm talking the most utter nonsense.'

Performing a complicated manoeuvre with her hands, Mrs Pitt-Cowley cast on Dalgliesh a look of histrionic sincerity which didn't quite conceal the sharper look of enquiry. Dalgliesh reminded himself not to underestimate her intelligence. He said: 'You're not talking nonsense. What will happen now about her latest book?'

'Oh I doubt whether Peverell Press will take it. It would be different, of course, if Esmé had been murdered. A double-murder, publisher and writer brutally done to death within a fortnight. Still, even suicide has publicity value, particularly if it's dramatic. I ought to be able to negotiate quite a satisfactory contract with someone.'

Dalgliesh was tempted to say: 'It's a pity we don't still have the death penalty. You could time publication to coincide with the execution date.'

Mrs Pitt-Cowley, as if aware of his thought, looked for a moment slightly embarrassed, then shrugged and went on: 'Poor Esmé, if she did have the bright idea of getting some free publicity she certainly succeeded. Pity she won't benefit. Nice for her heirs, though.'

Nice for you too, thought Kate. She asked: 'Who does get her money, do you know?'

'No, she never told me that. As I said, Marge was her executor, or one of them. But I'm grateful to say that she never suggested transferring that privilege when I took over the agency. Not that I would have taken it on. I did a lot for Esmé, but there are limits. Honestly, you've no idea what some authors expect. Find them commissions, get them on TV chat shows, feed the cat when they're on holiday, hold their hand through their divorces. For 10 per cent of home sales I'm expected to be agent, nurse, confidante, friend, the lot. I do know that she had no family – at least her ex-husband has a daughter and grandchildren somewhere, in Canada I believe. I can't see Esmé leaving anything to them. But there will be some money, no doubt about that, and my guess is that Marge will get it. I may be able to negotiate a reprint of the early paperbacks.'

Dalgliesh said: 'A profitable client after all, in death if not in life.'

'Well, it's a funny old world, isn't it?'

And with this echo of a lady with whom she had otherwise little in common, Mrs Pitt-Cowley glanced at her watch and bent down to pick up her briefcase and bag.

But Dalgliesh wasn't yet ready to let her go. He said: 'I assume Mrs

Carling told you about the cancellation of her Cambridge signing session.'

'Did she not! Actually she rang me from the shop. I tried to phone Gerard Etienne but I imagine he was at lunch. I got through to him later in the afternoon. Esmé was absolutely incoherent with rage. I mean really incoherent. Perfectly justified, of course. Peverell Press have a lot of explaining to do. I was sorry for the people in the shop, she was obviously taking it out on them but it was hardly their fault. At least, I suppose you could argue that they should have rung Peverell Press as soon as the fax was received to check that it wasn't a hoax, and they probably would have done if the Press had been less secretive about the trouble they were having. The manager was out when the fax came through and the girl who first saw it naturally assumed it was genuine. Well, it was genuine in the sense that it came from Peverell Press. To calm Esmé I told her I would take it up with Gerard myself. I would've done too but for the murder. That did rather put Esmé's grievance into perspective. I still intend to take the matter up with the firm but there is a time and place. Is it all right if I go now? I do have that luncheon appointment.'

Dalgliesh said: 'I've only a few more questions. What was your relationship with Gerard Etienne?'

'You mean my professional relationship?'

'Your relationship.'

Velma Pitt-Cowley sat for a moment entirely in silence. They saw that she was gently smiling, a look that was lubricious, reminiscent. Then she said: 'It was professional. I suppose we spoke on the phone about twice a month on average. I haven't seen him for the last four months. We did sleep together once. That was nearly a year ago. We'd both been to the same launch party. We both stayed to the bitter end. It was nearly midnight and I was rather drunk. Drink wasn't his thing, Gerard hated being out of control. He offered to drive me home and the night ended in the usual way. I suppose you'd call it a one-night stand, except that the word "stand" isn't really appropriate. It never happened again.'

Kate asked: 'Did either of you want it to?'

'Not really. He sent me a spectacular bunch of flowers next day. Gerard wasn't exactly subtle, but I suppose that's some improvement on leaving fifty quid by the bedside. No, I didn't want it to go on. I've got a healthy sense of self-preservation. I don't go round inviting heartbreak. But I thought I'd better mention it. There were plenty of people at that party who might just have guessed how the evening ended. God knows how these things get out but they always do. In case you're wondering, the events of that night and particularly the next morning, which I remember more clearly, left me well-disposed towards him rather than the opposite. But not so well disposed that I invited a second encounter. I suppose you want to ask me where I was on the night he died.'

Dalgliesh said gravely: 'That would be a help, Mrs Pitt-Cowley.'

'Oddly enough I was at that poetry reading at the Connaught Arms when Gabriel Dauntsey read. I left shortly after he'd done his stint. I was with a poet, or someone who describes himself as a poet, and he wanted to stay on, but I'd had enough of noise, uncomfortable chairs and cigarette smoke. Everyone was well tanked-up by then and the party showed no signs of breaking up. I suppose I left at about ten and drove home. So I've no alibi for the rest of the evening.'

'And last night?'

'When Esmé died? But that was suicide, you said so yourself.'

'However she died it is helpful to know where people were at the time.'

'But I don't know when she died. I was at the office until six-thirty and then at home. I was at home all evening and I was alone. Is that what you wanted to know? Look, Commander, I really must go.'

Dalgliesh said: 'Just two final questions. How many copies of the manuscript of *Death on Paradise Island* were in existence, and was Mrs Carling's copy distinctive?'

'I think there were about eight in all. I had to send five to Peverell Press, one for each of the partners. I don't see why they couldn't have copied the manuscript themselves, but that's how they liked it. I only had a couple of copies. Esmé always had her own copy bound with a pale blue cover. A bound copy isn't much use for editing purposes. In fact it's a bloody nuisance. Publishers and readers prefer manuscripts to be submitted with the pages tagged together in chapters, or not tagged at all. But Esmé always wanted her own copy bound.'

'And when you called in here to see Mrs Carling on October fifteenth, the evening after Gerard Etienne died, did you get the impression that she was reluctant to hand over her manuscript, pretending, perhaps that she couldn't find it, or that she didn't in fact any longer have it in her possession?'

As if recognizing the importance of the question, Mrs Pitt-Cowley took her time in answering. Then she said: 'How can I tell? But I do remember that the request disconcerted her. I think she was flustered. And it's difficult to see how she can actually have mislaid the manuscript. She wasn't careless about possessions which were important to her. And it's not as if there's a lot of space here in the flat. She didn't trouble to look for it, either. If you asked me to make a guess, I'd say that the manuscript wasn't any longer in her possession.'

53

When they got back to the car Dalgliesh said: 'I'll drive, Kate.'

She took the left-hand seat and buckled her belt in silence. She liked to drive and knew that she did it well, but when, as now, he chose to take over, she was content to sit quietly beside him and occasionally watch the strong sensitive hands lying lightly on the wheel. Now, glancing quickly at him as they crossed Hammersmith Bridge, she saw in his face a look with which she was familiar; a stern withdrawn self-absorption as if he were stoically enduring a private pain. When she was first recruited to his team she thought that the look was one of controlled anger and feared the sudden bite of cold sarcasm which she suspected was one of his defences against lack of control and which his subordinates had come to dread. They had gathered vital evidence during the last two and a half hours and she longed to hear his reaction, but she knew better than to break the silence. He was driving with his usual quiet competence and it was difficult to believe that part of his mind was elsewhere. Was he worrying about the vulnerability of that child as well as mentally reviewing the evidence she had given? Was he grimly containing his outrage at the planned barbarity of Esmé Carling's death, a death which they now knew had been murder?

In other senior officers this look of stern withdrawal could have been anger at Daniel's incompetence. If Daniel had extracted from the child the truth about what had happened on that Thursday night Esmé Carling might be alive now. But could it really be called incompetence? Both Carling and the child had told the same story and it was a convincing one. Children were good witnesses and they very seldom lied. If she had been sent to interview Daisy, would she have done any better? Would she have done any better this morning if Dalgliesh hadn't been there to intervene? She doubted whether Dalgliesh would say a word of blame, but that wouldn't prevent Daniel from blaming himself. She was heartily glad that she wasn't in his shoes.

They had driven over Hammersmith Bridge before he spoke.

'I think Daisy told us everything she knew, but the omissions are frustrating, aren't they? That one missing word would have made all the difference. The snake was outside the door. Which door? She heard a voice. Male or female? Someone was carrying a vacuum cleaner. Man or woman? But at least we don't have to rely on the implausibility of that suicide note to be sure now that this was murder.'

In the Wapping incident room Daniel was working alone. Kate, embarrassed for him, wanted to leave him with Dalgliesh but it was difficult without the ruse appearing too obvious. Dalgliesh briefly reported the result of their morning visits. Daniel stood up. The action, reminding Kate of a prisoner under sentence, seemed instinctive. His strong face was very pale.

'I'm sorry, sir. I should have broken that alibi. It was a bad mistake.'

'An unfortunate one, certainly.'

'I ought to say, sir, that Sergeant Robbins wasn't convinced. He thought from the first that Daisy was lying and wanted to press her.'

Dalgliesh said: 'That's never easy with a child, is it? If it came to a battle of wills between Daisy and Sergeant Robbins I'm not sure I wouldn't back Daisy.'

It was interesting, thought Kate, that Robbins hadn't trusted the child. He seemed to be able to combine a belief in the essential nobility of man with a reluctance to believe anything any witness said. Perhaps, being religious, he was more ready than Daniel to believe in original sin. But it was generous of Daniel to say what he had. Generous, but perhaps, if she was being cynical, and, knowing AD, it had also been judicious.

He said, as if doggedly determined to make the worst of it: 'But if I hadn't been satisfied, Esmé Carling would be alive today.'

'Possibly. Don't over-indulge in guilt, Daniel. The person responsible for Esmé Carling's death is the person who killed her. What about the post-mortem? Anything unexpected?'

'Death by vagal inhibition, sir. She died as soon as the strap tightened round her neck. She was dead when she was put in the water.'

'Well at least it was swift. What about the launch? Any news from Ferris?'

'Yes sir, good news.' Daniel's face lightened. 'He's found some minute fibres of cloth caught on a small splinter of wood on the cabin floor. They're pink, sir. She was wearing a pink and fawn tweed jacket. With luck the lab will be able to get a match.'

They glanced at each other. Kate knew that each was feeling the same contained exultation. A physical clue at last, something that could be tagged, measured, scientifically examined, produced in court as evidence. They had already checked with Fred Bowling that Esmé Carling hadn't been in the launch since the previous summer. If the fibres matched, then they had proof that she had been killed in the launch. And if she had, who had subsequently moved it to the other side of the steps? Who else but her killer?

Dalgliesh said: 'If the fibres match we can prove that she was in the cabin of the launch yesterday night. The obvious inference is that she died there. It would be a sensible plan on the part of the murderer to choose. He could wait with the body concealed until the river was quiet and choose his moment to string her up unobserved. But even if the fibres connect her to the launch, that doesn't mean they will connect her to the killer. We need to collect the coats and jackets of all the suspects who were on the scene and get them to the lab. Will you see to that Daniel?'

'Including Mandy Price and Bartrum?'

'All of them.'

Kate said: 'All we need now is the minutest thread of pink fibre on one of the coats.'

Dalgliesh said: 'Not all we need. There's one depressing fact, Kate. Most of them will be able to claim that they knelt close to Esmé Carling's body, even touched her. There is more than one way in which a fibre could have got on their clothes.'

Daniel added: 'And what's the betting that this murderer knew damn well what he was about? He'll have taken off his coat before he got close to her, and made damn sure afterwards that he was clean.'

54

Mandy had meant to get to work early next morning but to her astonishment on waking found that she had overslept and that it was already 8.45. She would probably have slept on if Maureen and Mike hadn't indulged in one of their arguments about the availability and the state of the bathroom, carried on as usual by Maureen shouting from the top of the stairs and Mike yelling back from the kitchen. A minute later there was a bang on her bedroom door followed immediately by Maureen bursting in. It was obvious that she was in one of her moods.

'Mandy, that bloody bike of yours takes up all the hall. Why can't you leave it in the front garden like anyone else?'

This was a perennial complaint. Mandy awoke to instant indignation.

'Because some arsehole would steal it, that's why. That bike's staying in the hall.' She added sulkily: 'I suppose it's too much to hope that the bathroom's free.'

'It's free if you can put up with the state it's in. Mike's left the bath filthy as usual. If you want a bath you'll have to clean it yourself. And he's forgotten that this is his week to buy the toilet paper. I don't see why I should do all the thinking and all the work in this house.'

It was obviously going to be one of those days. Neither Maureen nor Mike had been in when she had arrived home the previous evening. She had gone to bed but had tried to stay awake, listening for the door, longing to pour out her story. But it hadn't happened that way. She had fallen asleep despite herself. And now she heard them leave, two loud bangs of the door in quick succession. Maureen hadn't even bothered to enquire why she hadn't returned to the gig.

Things didn't improve when she got to Innocent House. She had looked forward to being first with the news, but there was no chance of that now. The partners had all come in early. George, busy taking a call, threw her a look of desperate appeal as she came in, as if any help would be welcome. It was apparent that the news had spread further than Innocent House.

'Yes, I'm afraid it is true . . . Yes, it does look like suicide . . . No, I'm afraid I haven't any details . . . We don't yet know how she died . . . I'm sorry . . . Yes, the police have been here . . . I'm sorry . . . No, Miss Etienne isn't available at the moment . . . No, Mr de Witt isn't free either. Perhaps one of them could ring you back . . . No, I'm sorry. I don't know when they'll be available.'

He replaced the receiver and said: 'One of Mr de Witt's authors. I don't know how he learned the news. Perhaps he rang publicity and Maggie or Amy told him. Miss Etienne has instructed me to say as little as possible but it isn't easy. People aren't satisfied with speaking to me. They want to talk to one of the partners.'

Mandy said: 'I shouldn't bother with them. Just say "Wrong number" and hang up. If you keep on doing it they'll soon get fed up.'

The hall was empty. The house felt strangely different, unnaturally quiet, a house in mourning. Mandy had expected that the police would be there but there was no sign of their presence. In the office Miss Blackett was sitting at her word processor, staring at the screen as if mesmerized. Mandy had never seen her look so ill. She was very pale and her face seemed suddenly to have become the face of an old woman.

Mandy said: 'Are you all right? You look awful.'

Miss Blackett made an effort at dignified control. 'Of course I'm not all right, Mandy. How can any of us be all right? This is the third death we've had in two months. It's dreadful. I don't know what's happening to the firm. Nothing's gone right with the Peverell Press since Mr Peverell died. And I'm surprised you manage to look so cheerful. After all, you found her.'

She looked close to tears. And there was something else. Miss Blackett was afraid. Mandy could almost smell her terror. She said uneasily: 'Yes, well, I'm sorry she's dead. But it's not as if I knew her, is it? And she was old. And she did do it herself. It was her choice. She must have wanted to die. I mean, it's not like Mr Gerard's death.'

Miss Blackett, face flushed, cried out: 'She wasn't old! How can you say that? And what if she was? The old have as much right to life as you.'

'I never said they hadn't.'

'That's what you implied. You should think before you speak, Mandy. You said that she was old and her death didn't matter.'

'I didn't say that it didn't matter.'

365

Mandy felt that she was becoming embroiled in a vortex of irrational emotion which she had no hope of understanding or controlling. And now she saw that Miss Blackett was almost crying. She was relieved when the door opened and Miss Etienne came in.

'Oh here you are, Mandy. We wondered if you were going to appear. Are you all right?'

'Yes thank you, Miss Etienne.'

'It seems that next week we shall be rather thin on the ground. I suppose you'll want to leave too, once the initial excitement is over.'

'No, Miss Etienne, I'd like to stay.' She added with a flash of financial acumen: 'If some of the staff are leaving and there's more work I think I ought to have a rise.'

Miss Etienne gave her a look which Mandy interpreted as more cynically amused than disapproving. After a few seconds' pause she said: 'All right. I'll speak to Mrs Crealey. An extra ten pounds a week. But the rise won't be a reward for staying. We don't bribe staff to work at Peverell Press, nor do we submit to blackmail. You'll get it because your work warrants it.' She turned to Miss Blackett. 'The police will probably be here this afternoon. They may want to use Mr Gerard's – I mean, my – office again. If so, I'll move upstairs with Miss Frances.'

After she had left Mandy said: 'Why don't you ask for a rise too? We're going to have to take on an extra load unless they recruit some replacements and that may not be too easy. It's like you said. Three deaths in two months. People may think twice about working here.'

Miss Blackett had begun typing, eyes fixed on her shorthand notebook. 'No thank you, Mandy. I don't take advantage of my employers in their hour of need. I have some principles.'

'Oh well, you can afford them I dare say. Seems to me that they've been taking advantage of you for the last twenty-odd years. Still, please yourself. I'll just have a word with Mrs Crealey then I'll make the coffee.'

Mandy had tried to phone Mrs Crealey's office before leaving home but there had been no reply. Now there was, and she gave the news succinctly, keeping to the bare facts and omitting any reference to her own emotions. With Miss Blackett listening with repressive disapproval, it was wise to be as brief and matter-of-fact as possible. The details could wait for their evening session together in the cosy.

She said: 'I've asked for a rise. They're giving me another ten pounds a week. Yeah, that's what I thought. No, I said I'd stay on. I'll come into the office straight from work and we can have a talk.'

She replaced the receiver. It was, she thought, a measure of Miss Blackett's odd mood that she omitted to remind her that she was not supposed to use the office telephone for her private calls.

There were more people in the kitchen than was normal before ten o'clock. Those of the staff who preferred to brew their own morning coffee rather than pay their weekly sub for Mrs Demery's version of the drink seldom appeared before eleven. Pausing at the door Mandy could hear the low buzz of gossiping voices. It stopped when she opened the door and they looked up guiltily, then greeted her with relief and flattering attention. Mrs Demery was there, of course, and so was Emma Wainwright, Miss Etienne's anorexic former PA who was now working for Miss Peverell, together with Maggie FitzGerald and Amy Holden from publicity, Mr Elton from contracts and rights, and Dave from the warehouse who had apparently come over from number 10 with the unconvincing excuse that the warehouse was out of milk. There was a strong smell of coffee and someone had been making toast. The kitchen was cosily conspiratorial but, even here, Mandy could sense fear.

Amy said: 'We thought you might not come in. Poor Mandy! It must have been absolutely ghastly. I should have died. If there's a body on the premises trust you to find it. Go on, tell. Was she drowned, or hanged or what? None of the partners will tell us anything.'

Mandy could have pointed out that it hadn't been she who had found Gerard Etienne's body. Instead she gave her account of the previous night but, even as she spoke, was aware that she was disappointing them. She had looked forward to this moment but now that she was the centre of their curiosity, she felt a curious reluctance to pander to it, almost as if there was something indecent in making Mrs Carling's death the subject of gossip. The picture of that dead sodden face, the make-up washed away so that it looked stripped and defenceless in its ugliness, floated between her and their avid eyes. She couldn't understand what was happening to her, why her emotions should be so confused, so disturbing in their perplexity. What she had said to Miss Blackett had been the truth; she hadn't even known Mrs Carling. She couldn't be feeling grief. She had no reason to feel guilty. What then was she feeling?

Mrs Demery was unaccountably silent. She was quietly setting out cups and saucers on her trolley, but her sharp little eyes darted from face to face as if each held a secret which a moment's inattention might miss.

Maggie said: 'Did you read the suicide note, Mandy?'

'No, but Mr de Witt did. It was all about how badly the partners had behaved to her, how she was going to get her own back. "Make their names stink," I think that's what she wrote. I can't really remember.'

Mr Elton said: 'You knew her better than most, Maggie. You did that big publicity tour with her eighteen months ago. What was she like?'

'She was no trouble. I got on all right with Esmé. She could be a bit demanding but I've been on tours with far worse. And she did care about her fans. Nothing was too much trouble. Always a word when they queued for a signing, and she would personalize every book for them, any message they wanted. Not like Gordon Holgarth. All they ever get from him is a scrawled signature, a scowl and a puff of cigar-smoke in the face.'

'Did you think she was the suicidal type?'

'Is there a suicidal type? I'm not sure what the words mean. But if you're asking me if I'm surprised that she's killed herself, the answer is yes. I am surprised. Very surprised.'

Mrs Demery spoke at last. 'If she did.'

'She must have done, Mrs Demery. She left a note.'

'A funny kind of note if what Mandy remembers is right. I'd need to have a look at that note before I was satisfied. And it's obvious the police aren't. If they were, why have they taken the launch?'

Maggie said: 'Is that why we were collected from Charing Cross by taxi instead of the launch this morning? I thought the launch had broken down. Fred Bowling never said anything about the police when he met us.'

'Told not to, I dare say. But they've taken it all right. Came first thing in the morning and towed it away. I thought they might have done when it wasn't here, so I asked him. It's over at Wapping Police Station.'

Maggie was pouring hot water on to coffee grains. She paused, kettle poised.

'You're not saying, Mrs D, that the police think Mrs Carling was murdered?'

'I don't know what the police think. I know what I think. She wasn't one to commit suicide, not Esmé Carling.'

Emma Wainwright was sitting at the end of the table, her skeletal fingers wrapped round a mug of coffee. She had made no attempt to drink, but was staring down at the thin swirl of foaming milk as if mesmerized with disgust.

Now she looked up and said in her harsh rather guttural voice: 'This is the second body you've found, Mandy, since you arrived at Innocent House. We never had any of this trouble before. They'll be calling you the Typist of Death. If you go on like this you'll find it difficult to get another job.'

Mandy, enraged, spat out her retort. 'Not so difficult as you will. At least I don't look as if I've come out of a concentration camp. You should see yourself. You look disgusting.'

For a few seconds there was a horrified silence. Six pairs of eyes glanced quickly at Emma then looked away. She sat very still, then suddenly stumbled to her feet and hurled the coffee cup across the room into the sink where it smashed spectacularly. Then she gave a high wail, burst into tears and rushed out of the room. Amy gave a little cry and wiped a splash of hot coffee from her cheek.

Maggie was shocked. 'You shouldn't have said that, Mandy. That was cruel. Emma's ill. She can't help it.'

'Of course she can help it. She only does it to upset other people. And she started the row. She called me the Typist of Death. I'm not bad luck. It's not my fault I found them.'

Amy looked at Maggie: 'D'you think I ought to go to her?'

'Better leave her alone. You know how she is. She's upset because Miss Claudia has taken over Blackie as her PA instead of her. She's already told Miss Claudia that she wants to leave at the end of the week. If you ask me I think she's plain scared. I'm not sure that I blame her.'

Torn between angry self-justification and a remorse which was the more disagreeable because she suffered from it so rarely, Mandy felt that she too would enjoy the relief of hurling crockery across the room and bursting into tears. What was happening to them all, to Innocent House, to herself? Was this what violent death did to people? She had expected the day to be pleasantly exciting, filled with comfortable gossip and speculation, herself at the heart of all the interest. Instead it had been hell from the start.

The door opened and Miss Etienne appeared. She said coldly: 'Maggie, Amy and Mandy, there's work to be done. If you've no intention of doing it, it would be better if you said so frankly and went home.'

55

Dalgliesh had said that he wanted to see all the partners in the boardroom at three o'clock and that Miss Blackett should be with them. None of them made any objection either to the summons or to her proposed presence. They had handed over the clothes they had been wearing when Esmé Carling's body was found without argument or question. But then, thought Kate, they were all intelligent people; they hadn't needed to ask why. None of them had requested the presence of a solicitor, and she wondered whether they feared that this might look suspiciously premature, had confidence in their ability to look after their own interests, or were fortified by the knowledge of their innocence.

She and Dalgliesh sat one side of the table with the partners and Miss Blackett facing them. At their last meeting in the boardroom after Gerard Etienne's death she had been aware of a mixture of emotions emanating from them: curiosity, shock, grief and apprehension. Now all she could smell was fear. It was like a contagion. It seemed that they infected each other, and even the air of the room. Only Miss Blackett showed it outwardly. Dauntsey looked very old and sat with the resignation of a geriatric patient awaiting admission. De Witt had seated himself close to Frances Peverell. His eyes were watchful under the heavy lids. Miss Blackett sat forward in her chair with the quivering intentness of a trapped animal. Her face was very white but from time to time hectic blotches spread over her cheeks and forehead like the visitation of a disease. Frances Peverell's face was taut and she ran her tongue over her lips. On her other side Claudia Etienne was outwardly the most composed. She looked as elegant as always and Kate saw that her make-up had been applied with care and wondered whether this was a gesture of defiance or a small but gallant attempt to impose normality on the psychological chaos of Innocent House.

Dalgliesh had laid on the table Esmé Carling's final message. It was now enclosed in a plastic cover. He read it through, his voice almost expressionless. No one spoke. Then, without commenting on it, he said quietly: 'We now believe that Mrs Carling came to Innocent House on the evening of Mr Etienne's death.'

Claudia's voice was sharp: 'Esmé came here? Why?'

'Presumably to see your brother. Is that so improbable? She had learned only the previous day that her new novel had been rejected by Peverell Press. She had tried to see Mr Etienne first thing that morning but had been refused access to him by Miss Blackett.'

Blackie cried: 'But he was in the partners' meeting! No one interrupts the partners' meeting! I was specifically told not even to put through urgent telephone calls.'

Claudia's voice was impatient: 'No one's blaming you, Blackie. Of course you were right not to admit the woman.'

As if there had been no interruption, Dalgliesh continued: 'She went straight from this office to Liverpool Street and her signing at Cambridge only to find that someone from here had sent a fax cancelling it. Was it likely that she would go quietly home and do nothing? You all knew her. Wasn't it much more likely that she would come here and make another attempt to confront Mr Etienne with her grievances, arriving at a time when she expected to find him alone, unprotected by his secretary? It seems to have been generally known that he worked late on Thursdays.'

De Witt said: 'But you must surely have checked, asked her where she was that evening? If you seriously suspect that Gerard was murdered, then Esmé Carling had to be among the suspects.'

'We did check. She provided a very convincing alibi, a child who claimed to have spent the hours from six-thirty to midnight with her in her flat. Her name is Daisy and she has now told us everything she knows. Mrs Carling persuaded her to provide her alibi for that night and admitted that she had been in Innocent House.'

Claudia said: 'And now you're condescending to tell us. Well that makes a change, Commander. It's time we were told something positive. Gerard was my brother. You've been suggesting from the first that his death wasn't an accident and you seem no nearer to explaining how or why he died.'

De Witt said quietly: 'Don't be naïve, Claudia. The Commander isn't confiding in us out of consideration for your sisterly feelings. He's telling us that the child, Daisy, has been questioned and has told everything she knows so there's no point in anyone trying to trace her, suborn her, bribe her or silence her in any way.'

The implication of his words was plain and was so appalling that Kate half expected a chorus of outraged protestations. None came. Claudia flushed deeply and looked as if she were about to remonstrate, then thought better of it. The rest of the partners froze into silence, apparently unwilling to meet each other's eyes. It was as if the remark had opened vistas of conjecture so unwelcome and horrifying that they were best left unexplored.

Dauntsey said, his voice a little too carefully controlled: 'So you have one suspect who is known to have been here, and probably at the relevant time. If she had nothing to hide, why didn't she come forward?'

De Witt added: 'And it's odd when you come to think of it that she's been so silent since. I don't suppose you were expecting a letter of condolence, Claudia, but I'd have expected some word, perhaps a fresh attempt to get us to accept the novel.'

Frances said: 'She probably thought it was tactful to wait a little. It would look pretty callous if she began badgering us so soon after Gerard's death.'

De Witt added: 'It would certainly have been the least propitious time to try to get us to change our mind.'

Claudia said sharply: 'We wouldn't have changed our mind. Gerard was right, it's a bad book. It wouldn't have done our reputation any good, or hers either for that matter.'

Frances said: 'But we could have rejected it with more kindness, seen her, tried to explain to her.'

Claudia turned on her. 'For God's sake, Frances, don't start reopening all that old argument. What good would it have done? Rejection is rejection. She would have resented the decision even if it had been broken to her over champagne and lobster thermidor at Claridge's.'

Dauntsey seemed to have been pursuing his private line of thought. He said: 'I don't see how Esmé Carling could have had anything to do with Gerard's death, but I suppose it's possible she was responsible for putting the snake round his neck. That would seem rather more her style.'

Claudia said: 'You mean she found the body and decided to add a personal comment, as it were?'

Dauntsey went on: 'But then it's hardly likely, is it? Gerard must have been alive when she arrived here. Presumably he let her in.'

Claudia said: 'Not necessarily. He could have left the front door open or ajar that night. It's unlike Gerard to be careless about security, but it's not impossible. She could somehow have gained access after he was dead.'

De Witt said: 'Even if she did, why should she go up to the little archives room?'

They seemed, for the moment, to have forgotten the presence of Dalgliesh and Kate.

Frances said: 'To look for him.'

Dauntsey said: 'But wouldn't she be more likely to wait for him in his office? She would have known that he was somewhere in the building. His jacket was still slung over the back of his chair. Sooner or later he'd be back. And then there's the snake. Would she have known where to find it?'

Having demolished his case, Dauntsey sank again into silence. Claudia glanced from partner to partner as if inviting silent assent to what she proposed to say. Then she looked full at Dalgliesh.

'I can see that this new information that Esmé Carling was in Innocent House on the night Gerard died does put her suicide in a different light. But however she died, the partners couldn't have been concerned. All of us can account for our movements.'

Kate thought: she doesn't want to use the word alibi.

Claudia went on: 'I was with my fiancé, Frances and James were together, Gabriel was with Sydney Bartrum.' She turned to him, her voice suddenly hard: 'Brave of you, Gabriel, to walk to the Sailor's Return alone so soon after your mugging.'

'I have walked alone in my capital city for over sixty years. One mugging isn't going to stop me.'

'And it was convenient that you happened to be leaving just as Esmé's taxi was arriving.'

De Witt said quietly: 'Fortuitous, Claudia, not convenient.'

But Claudia was looking at Dauntsey as if he were a stranger: 'And the pub may be able to confirm when you and Sydney arrived. But it is, of course, about the busiest on the river and with the longest bar, as well as access from the river walk, and you arrived separately. I doubt whether they'll be able to be precise even if anyone remembers two particular customers. You didn't draw attention to yourselves, I suppose?'

Dauntsey said quietly: 'That was not our intention in going there.'

'Why did you? I didn't know you used the Sailor's Return. I shouldn't have thought it was your choice of watering hole. Altogether too raucous. And I hadn't realized that you and Sydney were drinking pals.'

It was, thought Kate, as if they were suddenly conducting a private war. She heard Frances's soft anguished cry: 'Oh don't, please don't!'

De Witt said: 'Is your alibi any more reliable, Claudia?'

She turned on him. 'Or yours, come to that. Are you saying that Frances wouldn't lie for you?'

'She might. I don't know. As it happens she isn't required to. We were together from seven o'clock.'

Claudia said: 'Noticing nothing, seeing nothing, hearing nothing. Totally occupied with each other.' Before de Witt could reply she went on: 'It's odd, isn't it, how momentous events begin with something quite small. If someone hadn't sent that fax cancelling Esmé's signing she might not have come back here that night, wouldn't have seen what she did see, may not have died.'

Blackie could bear it no longer, their barely concealed antipathy, and now this horror. She leapt up and cried: 'Stop it, please stop it! And it isn't true. She killed herself. Mandy found her. Mandy saw. You know she killed herself. The fax has nothing to do with it.'

Claudia said sharply: 'Of course she killed herself. Any other idea is wishful thinking on the part of the police. Why accept suicide when you can go for the more exciting option? And that fax may have been the last straw for Esmé. Whoever sent it bears a heavy responsibility.'

She was gazing fixedly at Blackie, and the heads of the others turned as if Claudia had pulled on an invisible string.

Claudia suddenly said: 'It was you! I thought so. It was you, Blackie! You sent it!'

They watched appalled as Blackie's mouth slowly and silently opened. For what seemed minutes rather than seconds she held her breath, and then she burst into uncontrollable sobbing. Claudia got up from her seat and took her by the shoulders. For a second it looked as if she were going to shake her.

'And what about the rest of the mischief? What about the altered proofs, the stolen artwork? Was that you too?'

'No! No, I swear it. Just the fax. Nothing else. Only that one. She was so unkind about Mr Peverell. She said terrible things. It isn't true he thought I was a nuisance. He cared about me. He relied on me. Oh God, I wish I were dead like him.'

She stumbled to her feet and, still howling, blundered to the door, holding out a hand before her like a blind woman feeling for her way. Frances half rose and de Witt was already on his feet when Claudia grasped his arm.

'For God's sake leave her alone, James. We don't all welcome your shoulder to cry on. Some of us prefer to bear our own misery.'

James flushed and immediately sat down.

Dalgliesh said: 'I think we had better stop now. When Miss Blackett is calmer Inspector Miskin will talk to her.'

De Witt said: 'Congratulations Commander. It was clever of you to get us to do your job for you. It would have been kinder to have questioned Blackie in private but that would have taken longer, wouldn't it, and might have been less successful.'

Dalgliesh said: 'A woman has died and it is my job to discover how and why. I'm afraid that kindness isn't my first priority.'

Frances said, almost in tears, looking across at de Witt: 'Poor Blackie! Oh my God, oh poor Blackie! What are they going to do with her?'

It was Claudia who replied. 'Inspector Miskin will comfort her and then Dalgliesh will grill her. Or, if she's lucky, the other way round. You needn't worry about Blackie. Sending that fax isn't a hanging matter, it isn't even an indictable offence.' She turned violently and spoke to Dauntsey. 'Gabriel, I'm sorry. I'm so terribly sorry. I'm sorry, sorry. I don't know what came over me. My God, we've got to stand together.' When he didn't reply, she said almost beseechingly: 'You don't think it was murder, do you? Esmé's death, I'm saying. You don't think someone killed her?'

Dauntsey said quietly: 'You've heard the Commander read that message she wrote for us. Did that really sound to you like a suicide note?'

56

Mr Winston Johnson was large, black, amiable, apparently unworried by the ambience of a police station and philosophical about losing possible fares by the necessity to call in at Wapping. His voice was a deep attractive bass but its accent was pure Cockney. When Daniel apologized for the need to encroach on his working time he said: 'Don't reckon I've lost much. Picked up a fare wanting Canary Wharf on the way here. A couple of American tourists. Good tippers too. That's why I'm a bit late.'

Daniel passed over a photograph of Esmé Carling. 'This is the fare we're interested in. Thursday night to Innocent Walk. Recognize her?'

Mr Johnson took the photograph in his left hand. 'That's right. Hailed me at Hammersmith Bridge at about half past six. Said she wanted to be at number ten Innocent Walk by seven-thirty. No problem there. It wasn't going to take the best part of an hour, not unless the traffic was extra bad or we'd had a bomb alert and your chaps had closed down one of the roads. We made good time.'

'You mean you got there before seven-thirty.'

'Would've done, but she tapped the glass when we got to the Tower and said she didn't want to be early. Asked me to kill time. I asked her where she'd like to go and she said, "Anywhere, so long as we get to Innocent Walk at seven-thirty." So I took her as far as the Isle of Dogs and drove round a bit, then came back down The Highway. It put a few bob on the fare but I reckon that wasn't her worry. Eighteen pounds in all that cost her, and she gave a tip.'

'How did you approach Innocent Walk?'

'Left off The Highway down Garnet Street, then right off Wapping Wall.'

'Did you see anyone in particular?'

'Anyone in particular? There were one or two chaps around but I can't say I noticed anyone particular. Watching the road, wasn't I?'

'Did Mrs Carling speak to you on the journey?'

'Only what I told you, that she didn't want to get to Innocent Walk until half past seven, so would I drive around, like.'

'And you're sure she wanted number ten Innocent Walk, not Innocent House.'

'Number ten is what she asked for and number ten is where I dropped her. By the iron gates at the end of Innocent Passage. Seemed to me she was anxious not to go further down Innocent Walk. She tapped on the window as soon as I turned into it and said that's as far as she wanted.'

'Did you see whether the gate into Innocent Passage was open?'

'It wasn't standing open. That's not to say it was locked.'

Daniel asked, knowing what the answer would be but needing to get it on record. 'She didn't mention why she was going to Innocent Walk, whether she was meeting anyone, for example?'

'Wasn't my business, was it, guv?'

'Maybe not, but fares do chat occasionally.'

'A darned sight too much, some of them. But this one didn't. Just sat there clutching her bloody great shoulder-bag.'

Another photograph was passed over. 'This shoulder-bag?'

'Could be. Looks like it. Mind you, I couldn't swear to it.'

'Did the bag look full, as if she was carrying something heavy or bulky?'

'Can't help you there, mate. But I did notice that it was slung round her shoulder and it was large.'

'And you can swear that you drove this woman from Hammersmith to Innocent Walk on Thursday and left her alive at the end of Innocent Passage at seven-thirty?'

'Well I certainly didn't leave her dead. Yes I can swear to that all right. Do you want me to make a statement?'

'You've been very helpful, Mr Johnson. Yes, we'd like a statement. We'll take it next door.'

Mr Johnson went out accompanied by the detective constable. Almost immediately the door opened and Sergeant Robbins put his head in. He made no attempt to disguise his excitement.

'Just checking on the river traffic, sir. We've just had a telephone call from the Port of London Authority. It's in reply to that ring I gave them about an hour ago. Their launch, *Royal Nore*, was passing Innocent House last night. Their chairman had a private dinner party on board. The meal was at eight and three of his guests were anxious to see Innocent House so they were out on deck. They reckon the time was about twenty to eight. They can swear, sir, that the body wasn't suspended then and that they saw no one on the forecourt. And there's another thing, sir. They're adamant that the launch was to the left not to the right of the steps. I mean to the left looking from the river.'

Daniel said slowly: 'Bloody hell! So AD's instinct was right. She was killed in the launch. The killer heard the Port of London Authority boat approaching and kept the body out of sight before he strung her up.'

'But why that side of the railings? Why move the boat?'

'In the hope that we wouldn't realize that that's where she was killed. The last thing he wants is to have scene-of-crime officers crawling over that launch. And there's another thing. He met her inside the wrought-iron gates at the bottom of Innocent Passage. He had a key and was waiting for her, standing in the side doorway. It would be safer to keep to that end of the forecourt as far as possible from Innocent House and number twelve.'

Robbins had thought of an objection. 'Wasn't it risky moving the launch? Miss Peverell and Mr de Witt might have heard it from her flat. If they had, surely they'd have come down to investigate.'

'They claim they couldn't even hear a taxi unless it was actually driven over the cobbles of Innocent Lane. It's something we can check, of course. If they did hear an engine they probably thought it was any passing launch on the river. They had the curtains drawn, remember. Of course there's always another possibility.'

'What's that, sir?'

'That it was they who moved the launch.'

57

It was only just 5.30 on Saturday, normally a busy day, but the shop was locked with the closed notice showing through the glass. Claudia rang the bell at the side and within seconds Declan's figure appeared and the door was unbolted. As soon as she was through he gave a quick look down both sides of the street, then locked the door again behind her.

She said: 'Where's Mr Simon?'

'In hospital. That's where I've been. He's very ill. He thinks it's cancer.'

'What do they say, the people at the hospital?'

'They're going to do some tests. I could see that they think it's serious. I made him call in Dr Cohen – that's his GP – this morning and he said, "For God's sake, why didn't you see me earlier?" Simon knows he isn't going to come out of hospital, he told me. Look, come into the back room, won't you, it'll be more comfortable there.'

He neither kissed her nor touched her.

She thought, he's speaking to me as if I were a customer. Something had happened to him, something more than old Simon's illness. She had never seen him like this before. He seemed to be possessed by a mixture of excitement and terror. His eyes looked almost wild and his skin glistened with sweat. She could smell him, an alien feral smell. She followed him into the conservatory. All three bars of the wall-mounted electric fire were on and the room was very warm. The familiar objects looked strange, diminished, the petty leavings of dead and unregarded lives.

She didn't sit but stood watching him. He seemed unable to keep still, pacing the few yards of free space like a caged animal. He was more formally dressed than usual and the unfamiliar tie and jacket were at odds with his almost manic restlessness, the dishevelled hair. She wondered how long he had been drinking. There was a bottle of wine, two-thirds empty, and a single stained glass among the clutter on one of the tables. Suddenly he stopped the restless pacing and turned to her, and she saw in his eyes a look of mingled pleading, shame and fear.

He said: 'The police have been here. Look Claudia, I had to tell them about Thursday, the night that Gerard died. I had to tell them that you left me at Tower Pier, that we weren't together all the time.'

She said: 'Had to? What do you mean, had to?'

'They forced it out of me.'

'What with, thumb-screws and hot pincers? Did Dalgliesh twist your arms and slap your face? Did they take you to Notting Hill nick and punch you up, cleverly leaving no bruises? We know how good they are at that, we watch the TV.'

'Dalgliesh wasn't here. It was that Jew-boy and a sergeant. Claudia, you don't know what it was like. They think that that novelist, Esmé Carling, was murdered.'

'They can't know that.'

'I'm telling you, that's what they think. And they know I had a motive for Gerard's murder.'

'If it was murder.'

'They knew that I needed cash, that you'd promised to get it for me. We could've moored the launch at Innocent House and done it together.'

'Only we didn't.'

'They don't believe that.'

'Did they say that directly, any of it?'

'No, but they didn't need to. I could see what they were thinking.'

She said patiently: 'Look, if they seriously suspected you they would have had to question you under caution at a police station and tape record the interview. Is that what they did?'

'Of course not.'

'They didn't invite you to go with them to the station, tell you that you could call a lawyer?'

'Nothing like that. They did say at the end that I must call in at Wapping and make a statement.'

'So what did they really do?'

'Kept on about was I really sure that we'd been together all the time, that you'd driven me back here from Innocent House. How much better it was to tell the truth. The inspector used the words "accessory to murder", I'm sure he did.'

'Are you? I'm not.'

'Anyway, I told them.'

She said quietly and through lips that no longer seemed her own: 'You realize what you've done? If Esmé Carling was murdered then probably Gerard was too, and if he was, the same person was responsible for both deaths. It would be too much of a coincidence to have two murderers in one firm. All you've done is to get yourself suspected of two deaths, not one.'

He was almost crying. 'But we were together here when Esmé died. You came here straight from work. I let you in. We were together the whole evening. We were making love. I told them that.'

'But Mr Simon wasn't here when I arrived, was he? No one saw me but you. So what proof have we?'

'But we were together! We've got an alibi – we both have an alibi!'

'But are the police going to believe it now? You've admitted that you lied about the night of Gerard's death; why shouldn't you be lying again about the night when Esmé died? You were so anxious to save your own skin that you hadn't the sense to see that you were dropping yourself deeper in the shit.'

He turned from her and poured more wine into the glass. He held out the bottle and said: 'Do you want some? I'll get a glass.'

'No thank you.'

Again he turned away from her. 'Look,' he said, 'I don't think we ought to see each other again. Not for quite a time anyway. I mean, we oughtn't to be seen together until all this is cleared up.'

She said: 'Something else has happened, hasn't it? It's not only the alibi.'

It was almost laughable how his face changed. The look of shame and fear gave way to a flush of excitement, a sly satisfaction. How like a child he is, she thought, and wondered what new toy had come within his grasp. But she knew that the contempt she felt was more for herself than for him.

He said, willing her to understand: 'There is something else. It's rather good really. It's Simon. He's sent for his solicitor. He's going to make a will leaving me the whole of the business and the property. Well, there's no one else to leave it to, is there? He's got no relations. He knows he'll never get to the sun now, so I might as well have it. He'd rather me than the government.'

'I see,' she said. And she did see. She was no longer necessary. The money she had inherited from Gerard was no longer required. She said, keeping her voice calm, 'If the police seriously suspect you, and I very much doubt whether they do, not seeing each other isn't going to make any difference. If anything it will look more suspicious. That's exactly how two guilty people would behave. But you're right. We won't see each other again, not ever if I can help it. You don't need me and I certainly don't need you. You have a certain farouche charm and a mild entertainment value, but you're hardly the world's greatest lover, are you?'

She was surprised that she could walk to the door without faltering, but she had a little difficulty with the bolts. She found that he was close behind her. He said, his voice almost pleading: 'But you can see how it looked. You asked me to go on the river with you. You said it was important.'

'It was important. I was going to speak to Gerard after the partners' meeting, remember? I thought I might have something good to tell you.'

'And then you asked me for an alibi. You asked me to say that we were together until two o'clock. You rang from the archives room as soon as you were alone with the body. You just had time. And it was the first thing you thought about. You told me what to say. You forced me to lie.'

'And you've told the police that, of course.'

'You could see how it looked to them, how it will look to anyone. You took the launch back on your own. You were alone at Innocent House with Gerard. You've inherited his flat, his shares, his life assurance money.'

She felt the strength of the door against her back. She turned to face him and she saw the dawning of fear in his eyes as she spoke.

'So aren't you afraid to be with me? Aren't you terrified to be here alone with me? I've already killed two people, why should I worry about a third? Perhaps I'm a homicidal maniac, you can't be sure, can you? God, Declan! Do you really believe I killed Gerard, a man worth ten of you, just to buy you this place and that pathetic collection of junk which you acquire to try and convince yourself that your life has a meaning, that you're a man?'

She couldn't remember opening the door, but she heard it close firmly behind her. The night seemed to her very cold and she found that she was shivering violently. So it has ended, she thought, ended in bitterness, acrimony, cheap sexual insult, humiliation. But then, doesn't it always? She pushed her hands deep into her coat pockets and hunching her shoulders into her collar walked briskly to where she had parked the car.

BOOK FIVE

Final Proof

58

It was early Monday evening and Daniel was working alone in the archives room. He wasn't sure what had brought him back to these close-packed, musty-smelling shelves unless it was to perform a self-imposed penance. It seemed that he couldn't even for a moment put out of his mind his blunder over Esmé Carling's alibi. It wasn't only Daisy Reed who had deceived him; Esmé Carling had too, and she, he could have pressed more strongly. Dalgliesh hadn't referred again to the mistake, but it wasn't one he was likely to forget. Daniel didn't know which was worse, AD's forbearance or Kate's tact.

He worked on, taking each pile of about ten files into the little archives room. It was warm enough; he had been provided with a small electric fire. But the room wasn't comfortable. Without the fire, the cold struck with an immediate chill which was almost unnatural; with it the room soon became unpleasantly warm. He wasn't superstitious. He had no sense that the ghosts of the unquiet dead were the watchers of his solitary, methodical search. The room was bleak, soulless, commonplace, evoking only a vague unease born paradoxically not of horror's contagion but of its absence.

He had taken out the next tranche of files on a top shelf when he saw behind them a small parcel of brown paper done up with old string. Taking it to the table, he struggled with the knots and finally got it undone. It was an old leather-covered Prayer Book measuring about six inches by four with the initials F.P. engraved in gold on the cover. The Prayer Book had obviously been well used; the initials were almost indecipherable. He opened it at the first brown stiff page and saw in crude writing the superscription: 'Printed by John Baskett, Printers to the Kings most Excellent Majesty and the Assigns of Thomas Newcomb, and Henry Hills, Deceas'd. 1716. *Cum Privilegio.*' He turned the pages with some interest. There were thin red lines down each margin and the middle of the page. He knew little of the Anglican Prayer Book but he turned the stiff brown pages with some interest, noting that there was a special 'Form of Prayer with Thanksgiving to be used yearly upon the Fifth of November, for the happy Deliverance of King James I and Parliament from the most Traitorous and Bloody intended Massacre by Gunpowder'. He doubted whether this was still part of the Anglican liturgy.

It was then that the sheet of paper fell out of the back of the book. It was folded once, whiter than the pages of the Prayer Book but as thick. There was no superscription. The message was written in black ink, the hand uncertain, but the words were as plain as the day they were penned:

I, Francis Peverell, write this with my own hand on the Fourth of September 1850 at Innocent House, in my last agony. The disease that has laid its hold on me for the past eighteen months will soon have finished its work, and by the grace of God I shall be free. My hand has written those words, "by the grace of God", and I shall not delete them. I have neither strength nor time for re-writing. But the most that I can expect from God is the grace of extinction. I have no hope of Heaven and no fear of the pains of Hell, having suffered my Hell here on earth for the last fifteen years. I have refused all palliatives for my present agony. I have not touched the laudanum of oblivion. Her death was more merciful than mine. This, my confession, can bring no relief to mind or body since I have not sought absolution nor confessed my sin to a living soul. Nor have I made restitution. What restitution can a man make for the murder of his wife?

I write these words because justice to her memory demands that the truth be told. Yet I still cannot bring myself to make public confession, nor to lift from her memory the stain of suicide. I killed her because I needed her money to finish the work on Innocent House. I had spent what she brought as a marriage-portion but there were funds tied up and denied to me that would come to me on her death. She loved me but she would not pass them over. She saw my love of the house as an obsession and a sin. She thought that I cared more for Innocent House than for her or for our children, and she was right.

The deed could not have been more easy. She was a reserved woman whose shyness and disinclination for company meant that she had no intimate acquaintances. All her family were dead. She was known by the servants to be unhappy and, in preparation for her death, I confided to certain of my colleagues and friends that I was worried about her health and spirits. On the twenty-fourth of September on a calm autumnal night I called her up to the third floor telling her I had something to show her. We were alone in the house, except for the servants. She came out to me where I stood on the balcony. She was a slight woman and it was only a second's work to lift her bodily and cast her to her death. Then, without hurrying, I went swiftly downstairs to the library and was there, sitting quietly reading, when they brought me the terrible news. I was never suspected. Why should I be? They would not suspect a respected man of murdering his wife.

I have lived for Innocent House and killed for it but, since her death, the house has given me no joy. I leave this confession to be handed in each generation to the eldest son. I implore all who read it to keep my secret. It will come first to my son, Francis Henry, and then in time to his son, and to all my descendants. I have nothing to hope for in this world or the next, and no message to give. I write because it is necessary before I die that I tell the truth.

At the bottom he had signed his name and the date.

After reading the confession, Daniel sat still for a full two minutes, considering. He wondered why these words, speaking to him over a century and a half, should have affected him so powerfully. He felt that he had no right to read them, that the proper course was to replace the paper in the Prayer Book, re-wrap the book and place it back on the shelf. But he supposed that he ought at least to let Dalgliesh know what he had found. Was this confession the reason why Henry Peverell had been so unwilling to have the archives examined? He must have known of its existence. Was he shown it when he came of age, or had it been mislaid before then and become part of family folklore, whispered about but never actually acknowledged? Had Frances Peverell been shown it when she came of age, or had the words 'eldest son' always been taken literally? But it surely had no relevance to Gerard Etienne's murder. This was a Peverell tragedy, a Peverell shame, as old as the paper on which it was confessed. He could understand that the family would want it kept secret. It would be disagreeable whenever the house was admired to have to confess that it had been built with money obtained by murder. After a little thought he replaced the paper, carefully reparcelled the Prayer Book and left it on one side.

There were footsteps, light but definite, approaching through the archives room. And now, for a second, remembering that murdered wife, he was touched with a slight shiver of superstitious awe. Then sense reasserted itself. These were the footsteps of a living woman and he knew whose.

Claudia Etienne stood in the doorway. She said without preamble: 'Will you be long?'

'Not very long. Perhaps an extra hour, maybe less.'

'I shall be leaving at half past six. I'm turning off the lights except on the stairs. Will you turn those off when you leave and set the alarm?'

'Of course.'

He opened the nearer file and appeared to be studying it. He didn't want to talk to her. It would be unwise now to be drawn into any conversation without the presence of a third party.

She said: 'I'm sorry I lied about my alibi for Gerard's death. It was partly fear, mostly the wish to avoid complications. But I didn't kill him, none of us did.' He didn't reply, nor did he look at her. She said, with a note of desperation: 'How long is this going to go on? Can't you tell me? Haven't you any idea? The coroner hasn't even released my brother's body for cremation. Can't you understand what that's doing to me?'

Then he looked up at her. If he had been capable of pity for her, seeing her face, he would have felt it then. 'I'm sorry,' he said, 'I can't discuss it now.'

Without another word she turned abruptly and left. He waited till the footsteps had faded then went out and locked the door of the archives room. He should have remembered that Dalgliesh wanted it kept secure at all times.

59

At 6.25 Claudia locked away the files she had been working on and went upstairs to wash and fetch her coat. The house was ablaze with light. Since Gerard's death she had hated working alone in the darkness. Now chandeliers, wall sconces, the great globes at the foot of the stairs, illumined the splendour of painted ceilings, the intricacies of carved wood and the pillars of coloured marble. Inspector Aaron could turn the lights off on the way down. She wished she hadn't given way to the impulse to go to the little archives room. She had hoped that, seeing him alone, she might have extracted some information about the progress of the inquiry, some idea when it was likely to end. The thought had been folly, the result humiliation. She wasn't a person to him. He didn't see her as a human being, a woman who was alone, afraid, burdened with unexpected and onerous responsibilities. To him, to Dalgliesh, to Kate Miskin she was only one, and perhaps the chief, of their suspects. She wondered whether every murder investigation dehumanized all those caught up in it.

Most of the staff parked their cars behind the locked gate in Innocent Passage. Claudia was the only one who used the garage. She was very fond of her Porsche 911. It was now seven years old, but she wanted no replacement and disliked leaving it ungaraged. She unlocked the door of number 10, moved across the passage and opened the door into the garage. Putting up a hand to the light she pressed it down. There was no response; obviously the bulb had gone. And then, as she stood there irresolute, she was aware of the sound of gentle breathing, the knowledge, immediate and terrifying, that someone was standing there in the darkness. And at that moment the noose of leather came down over her head and tightened round her neck. She was jerked violently backwards, and felt the crack of the concrete momentarily stunning her and then its scrape against the back of her skull.

It was a long strap. She tried to reach out to struggle with whoever was holding it, but there was no strength in her arms, and every time she tried to move the noose tightened and her mind swam through an agony of pain and terror into brief unconsciousness. She thrashed feebly on its end like a hooked and dying fish, her feet scrabbling ineffectively for a hold on the rough concrete.

And then she heard his voice. 'Lie still, Claudia. Lie still and listen. Nothing will happen while you lie still.'

She ceased her struggles and at once the dreadful throttling eased. His voice was speaking quietly, persuasively. She heard what he said and her numbed brain at last understood. He was telling her that she had to die, and why.

She wanted to shout out that it was a terrible mistake, that it wasn't true, but her voice was throttled and she knew that only by lying totally motionless could she stay alive. He was explaining now that it would look like suicide. The strap would be tied to the fixed wheel of the car, the engine would be left running. She would be dead by then but it was necessary to him that the garage should be full of a fatal gas. He explained this to her patiently, almost kindly, as if it were important to him that she should understand. He told her that she had no alibi for either of the murders now. The police would think she had killed herself from fear of arrest or remorse.

And now he had finished. She thought: I won't die. I won't let him kill me. I won't die, not here, not like this, hauled about like an animal on this garage floor. She summoned up her will. She thought: I must pretend to be dead, fainted, half dead. If I can get him off his guard I can twist round and seize the strap. I can overpower him if only I can get to my feet.

She summoned up her strength for this last move. But he had been waiting for just this, he was ready. As soon as she moved, the noose was jerked taut again and this time it did not slacken.

He waited until at last the body's dreadful contortions were stilled, the last gurglings silenced. Then he let go of the strap and, bending, listened for the absent breath. He got up and, taking the bulb from his pocket, stretched up and replaced it in the socket in the low ceiling. Now, with the garage lit, he could see to take the keys from her pocket unlock the car and tie the end of the strap round the wheel. His gloved hands worked swiftly and without fumbling. Lastly he turned on the engine. Her body lay sprawled as if she had flung herself from the open door of the car, knowing that either the noose or the fatal exhaust fumes would finish her off. And it was at that moment that he heard the footsteps coming down the passage towards the garage door.

60

It was 6.27. In Frances Peverell's flat the phone rang. As soon as James spoke her name she knew that something was wrong.

She said at once: 'James, what is it?'

'Rupert Farlow is dead. He died in hospital an hour ago.'

'Oh James, I'm so terribly sorry. Were you with him?'

'No. Ray was. He only wanted Ray. It's so strange, Frances. When he was living here the house was almost intolerable. Sometimes I dreaded coming home to the mess, the smells, and the disruption. But now he's dead I want it to look as it did then. I hate it. It's prissy, affected, boringly conventional, just a show house for someone who's dead at heart. I want to smash it.'

She said: 'Would it help if I came over?'

'Would you, Frances?' She heard the note of relief in his voice with joy. 'You're sure it won't be any trouble?'

'Of course it won't be a trouble. I'll come at once. It's not half-past six yet, Claudia may still be here. If she is I'll get her to drop me at the Bank and take the Central Line. That'll be the quickest. If she has left, I'll call a cab.'

She put down the receiver. She was sorry about Rupert but she had only met him once, years before, when he had come to Innocent House. And surely for him this long-expected death, awaited in such uncomplaining agony, must have come as a release. But James had called for her, needed her, wanted her to be with him. She was possessed with joy. Grabbing her jacket and scarf from the hall peg, she almost flung herself down the stairs and ran into Innocent Lane. But the door to Innocent House was locked and there was no light shining through the window of the reception room. Claudia had left. She ran into Innocent Walk thinking that she might still catch her getting out the car, but could see that the garage door was closed. She was too late.

She decided to call for a cab from the wall telephone in the passage at number 10. That would be quicker than going back to her own flat. It was as she came up to the garage doors that she heard unmistakably the sound of a running engine. This surprised and disconcerted her. Claudia's Porsche, her beloved 911, was too old to have a catalytic converter. Surely she realized that it was unsafe to run her engine in a closed garage? It was unlike Claudia to be careless.

The door to number 10 was locked. That wasn't surprising; Claudia always came into the garage this way and locked the door behind her. But it was strange to find the light still on in the passage and the side door to the garage ajar. Calling Claudia's name, she dashed to it and threw it open.

The light was on, a harsh, cruel, shadowless light. She stood transfixed, every nerve and muscle paralysed by a second of instantaneous revelation and horror. He was kneeling by the body, but now he got to his feet and came quietly across to her blocking the door. She looked into his eyes. They were the same eyes, wise, a little tired, eyes that had seen too much and for far too long.

She whispered: 'Oh no! Gabriel, not you. Oh no.'

She didn't scream. She was as incapable of screaming as she was of movement. When he spoke it was in the same gentle remembered voice.

'I'm sorry, Frances. You do see, don't you, that I can't possibly let you go?'

And then she swayed and felt herself falling into the merciful dark.

61

In the little archives room Daniel looked at his watch. Six o'clock. He had been here for two hours. But the time hadn't been wasted. At least he had found something. The two hours of searching had been rewarded. It might not be relevant to the investigation, but it had some interest. When he showed the confession to the team, AD might feel that his hunch had been vindicated, even if less fruitfully than he had hoped, and call off the search. There was no reason why he shouldn't stop now.

But success had revived his interest and he was nearly at the end of a row. He might as well take down and examine the last thirty or so files along the top shelf. He preferred a job to have a defined and tidy ending, and it was still early. If he left he would feel obliged to go back to Wapping. He didn't feel at the moment that he wanted to confront either Kate's understanding or her pity. He moved the step-ladder further along the row.

The file, bulky but not abnormally so, was lodged tightly between two others and as he pulled at them it slipped from the shelf. A few papers, detached, fell over his head like heavy leaves. He carefully dismounted and gathered them up. The rest of the papers were tagged together, presumably in date order. Two things struck him. The file cover was of heavy manila and obviously very old, while some of the papers looked fresh and clean enough to have been filed within the last five years. The file was unnamed, but among the early papers he was scrabbling together the word 'Jew' caught his eye time and time again. He took it with him to the table in the little archives room.

The papers were not numbered and he could only assume that they were in the correct order, but one, undated, caught his eye. It was a proposal for a novel, inexpertly typed and unsigned. It was headed *Submission to the Partners of the Peverell Press*. He read:

The background and the universal and unifying theme of this novel, provisionally to be called *Original Sin*, is the co-operation of the Vichy regime in France with the deportation of Jews from France between 1940 and 1944. During these four years nearly 76,000 Jews were deported, the great majority to die in concentration camps in Poland and Germany. The book will tell the story of one family divided by war in which a young Jewish mother and her four-year-old twins are trapped in France by the invasion, are hidden by friends and are provided with false papers, but are subsequently betrayed to be deported and murdered in Auschwitz. The novel will explore the effect of this betrayal – one small family among thousands of the victims – on the woman's husband, on the betrayed and on the betrayers.

Working through the papers he could see no response to this proposal and no communication from the Peverell Press. The file contained what were obviously working and research papers. The novel had been well researched, extraordinarily well researched for a proposed work of fiction. The writer had either visited or written to a remarkable variety of international and national organizations over the years. The Archives Nationales in Paris and Toulouse, the Centre de Documentation Juive Contemporaine in Paris, Harvard University, the Public Record Office and the Royal Institute of International Affairs in London and the West German Federal Archives in Koblenz. There were extracts, too, taken from the journals of the Resistance movement, l'Humanité, Témoignage Chrétien and Le Franc-Tireur, and minutes from prefects in the unoccupied zone. He let them pass in front of his eyes, letters, reports, scraps of official documents, copies of minutes, eyewitness accounts. The record was both broad-based and in places peculiarly precise; the number of deportees, the times of the trains, the part played by the policy of Pierre Laval, even changes in the German power hierarchy in France during the spring and summer of 1942. It was quickly apparent that the researcher had taken care to ensure that nowhere should his name appear. Letters from him had his signature and address cut off or blacked out, letters to him had the name and address of the sender but all other identifying marks had been obliterated. There was no evidence that any of this particular research had been used, that the book had even been started, let alone finished.

It increasingly became apparent that the researcher was particularly interested in one region and one year. The novel, if that was what it was, was becoming more focused. It was as if a cluster of searchlights had played over a wide terrain highlighting an incident, an interesting configuration, a single figure, a moving train, but had now co-ordinated their beams to illumine a single year: 1942. It was a year in which the Germans had demanded a great increase in deportations from the unoccupied zone. The Jews, after being rounded up, had been taken either to the Vel d'Hiv or to Drancy, a huge apartment complex in a suburb north-east of Paris. It was this camp which served as the staging post to Auschwitz. There were three eyewitness reports in the file: one was from a French nurse who had worked with a paediatrician in Drancy for fourteen months until she could no longer stand the accumulated misery, and two from survivors, apparently in reply to a specific inquiry from the researcher. One woman wrote:

I was rounded up on 16 August 1942 by the Gardes Mobiles. I was reassured because they were French and were very correct at the time I was arrested. I did not know then what would happen to me but I remember that I did not feel that it would be too bad. I was told what possessions I could take with me and medically examined before I was in transit. I was sent to Drancy and it was there I met the young mother with the twins. Her name was Sophie. I cannot recall the names of the children. She had been first in Vel d'Hiv but was later transferred to Drancy. I remember her and the children well although we did not speak very often. She told me little about herself, except that she had been living under a false name near Aubière. All her concern was for her children. At the time we were in the same hut with fifty other inmates. We lived in great squalor. There was a shortage of beds and straw for mattresses, the only food was cabbage soup and we were suffering from dysentery. Many people died in Drancy, I think over 400 in the first ten months. I can remember the wails of the children and the groans of the dying. For me Drancy was as bad as Auschwitz. I went merely from one room in hell to another.

The second survivor from the same camp wrote of the same horrors, although more graphically, but had no memory of a young mother or her twins.

Daniel was turning the papers as if in a trance. He knew now where the journey was leading him and here at last was the proof: a letter written by a Marie-Louise Robert from Quebec. It was hand-written in French with a typed translation attached.

My name is Marie-Louise Robert and I am a Canadian citizen, the widow of Emile Edouard Robert, a French-Canadian. I met him and married him in Canada in 1958. He died two years ago. I was born in 1928 so was fourteen in 1942. I lived with my widowed mother and grandfather on his small farm on the Puy-de-Dôme area of France, outside Aubière which is just south-east of Clermont-Ferrand. Sophie and the twins came to us in April 1941. It is difficult now that I am old to remember how much I knew at the time and how much I learned afterwards. I was an inquisitive girl and resented being kept out of the adults' concerns and treated as if I were a child, too immature to be trusted. I was not told at the time that Sophie and the children were Jews but I learned that later. There were many people and organizations in France at that time which helped Jews at great risk to themselves, and Sophie and the twins were sent to my parents by a Christian organization of this kind. I never knew its name. At the time I was told she was just a friend of the family who had come to us to be safe from bombing. My uncle Pascal worked for Monsieur Jean-Philippe Etienne at his publishing and printing firm in Clermont-Ferrand. I think I did know at the time that Pascal was part of the Resistance, but I'm not sure that I knew that Monsieur Etienne was head of the organization. It was in July 1942 that the police came to take Sophie and the twins away. As soon as they arrived my mother told me to get out of the house and stay in the barn till she called me. I went to the barn but I crept back and listened. I could hear screaming and the children crying. Then I heard a car and a van being driven away. When I went back into the house my mother was crying too, but wouldn't tell me what had happened.

That night Pascal came to the house and I crept down the stairs to listen. My mother was angry with him, but he said he hadn't betrayed Sophie or the twins, that he wouldn't have put my mother and grandfather in danger, that it must have been Monsieur Etienne. I forgot to say that it was Pascal who forged the false papers for Sophie and the twins. That was his job in the Resistance, although I am not sure whether I knew this at the time. He told my mother to do nothing, to say nothing. There were reasons for these things. However, my mother did go to see Monsieur Etienne the next day, and when she came back she spoke to my grandfather. I don't think that they cared then whether I heard or not. I was sitting quietly reading in the room when they spoke. She said to my grandfather that Monsieur Etienne had admitted that he had betrayed Sophie to the authorities, but that it had been necessary. It was because he was trusted and his friendship valued that she would not be punished for harbouring Jews. It was thanks to his relationship with the Germans that Pascal had not been deported as slave labour. He had asked my mother what was more important to her: the honour of France, the safety of her family or three Jews. Afterwards no one ever spoke about Sophie and the twins. It was as if they hadn't existed. If I asked about them, my mother would just say, "It is finished. It is over." The money from the organization kept coming, although it was not very much, and my grandfather said that we should keep it. We were very poor at the time. I think someone did write to enquire about Sophie eighteen months after she and the children were taken away, but my mother wrote back that the authorities were becoming suspicious and that Sophie had left and gone to friends at Lyons and she didn't know the address. Then the money stopped.

I am the only member of my family left. My grandfather died in 1946 and my mother of cancer a year later. Pascal was killed on his motorcycle in 1954. After my marriage I never went back to Aubière. There is nothing else I can remember about Sophie and the children except that I missed the children very much when they were gone.

That paper was dated 18 June 1989. Dauntsey had taken over forty years of his part-time searching to find Marie-Louise Robert and his final proof. But he had gone even further. The last paper on the file dated 20 July 1990 was in German, again with a translation attached. He had tracked down one of the German officers at Clermont-Ferrand. In bald sentences and official language an old man, retired and living in Bavaria, had for a few minutes relived one small incident of a half-remembered past. The truth of the betrayal was confirmed.

There was one final piece of evidence on the file and it was in an envelope. Daniel opened it and found a photograph, black and white, over fifty years old and fading, but still clear. It had obviously been taken by an amateur and it showed a smiling, dark-haired girl, gentle-eyed, with an arm round each of her children. The children, un-smiling, leaned against their mother and gazed huge-eyed at the camera as if knowing the importance of this moment, that the click of the shutter would fix for ever their frail mortality. He turned it over and read: 'Sophie Dauntsey. 1920–1942. Martin and Ruth Dauntsey. 1938–1942.'

He closed the file and sat for a moment so still that he might have been a statue. Then he got up and, moving into the archives room, began pacing between the racks, stopping occasionally to thump his palm against the metal struts. He was possessed by an emotion which he recognized as anger but which was like no anger he had ever felt before. He heard a strange inhuman noise and knew that he was groaning aloud with the pain and the horror of it. He had no thought of destroying the evidence; that he couldn't do and didn't for one moment consider. But he could warn Dauntsey, let him know that they were already close and that at last they had the missing motive. He was for a moment surprised that Dauntsey hadn't retrieved and shredded the papers. They weren't needed any more. No court of law would see them. They hadn't been collected with such patience, such thoroughness over half a century to be presented to a court of law. Dauntsey had been judge and jury, prosecutor and plaintiff. Perhaps he would have destroyed them if the room hadn't been locked, if Dalgliesh hadn't reasoned that the motive for this crime lay in the past, and that the missing evidence could be evidence in writing.

Suddenly the telephone rang, harsh and insistent as an alarm. He stopped his pacing and stood frozen, as if to answer it could shatter his intense preoccupation with the clamorous irrelevancies of the outside world. But it continued to ring. He went to the wall telephone and heard Kate's voice.

'You were a long time answering.'

'I'm sorry. I was pulling out files.'

'Are you all right, Daniel?'

'Yes. Yes, I'm all right.'

She said: 'We've heard from the lab. The fibres match. Carling was killed in the launch. But there are no fibres on any of the suspects' clothing. I suppose that was too much to hope. So we're a little further on, but not much. AD is thinking of questioning Dauntsey tomorrow – tape recorded and under caution. We shan't get anywhere but I suppose we have to try. He's not going to crack. None of them will.'

He heard for the first time in her voice the faint questioning note of despair. She said, 'Have you found anything interesting?'

'No,' he said. 'Nothing interesting. I'm leaving now. I'm going home.'

62

He put the photograph back in the envelope and the envelope in his pocket, then he replaced all the files on the top shelf, the manila folder among them. He put out the lights and unlocked and relocked the door. Claudia Etienne had left all the lights on the stairs shining for him and as he descended he turned them off one by one. He turned on the lights on the ground floor to see his way. Each action was deliberate, portentous, as if each had a unique value. He took a final look at the great domed ceiling, plunged the hall into darkness, set the alarms and finally turned out the light in the reception room and left Innocent House, locking the door behind him. He wondered if he would ever enter it again, and smiled ironically at the thought that he, resolved on the unforgivable perfidy, the great iconoclasm, could still be meticulous about the things which didn't matter.

There was no sign of life from the small side windows of number 12. He rang Dauntsey's bell, looking up at the darkened windows. There was no reply. Perhaps he was with Frances Peverell. He hurried down the lane into Innocent Walk and it was then that, glancing to the left, he saw Dauntsey's cream Rover just moving off from in front of the garage. Instinctively he ran a few steps toward it but realized that there was no point in calling after it. Dauntsey wouldn't hear above the sound of the engine and the rumble of wheels on the cobbles.

He dashed to where his Golf GTI was parked in Innocent Lane and set off in pursuit. He had to see Dauntsey tonight. Tomorrow might be too late. Dauntsey had only half a minute's start, but that could be crucial if he had a clear turn at the top of Garnet Road and into The Highway. But he was lucky. He was in time to see the car turn right, heading east towards the Essex suburbs, not towards central London.

For the next five miles he was able to keep the Rover within sight. The homeward build-up of traffic was still heavy, a glittering, slow-moving mass of metal, and even by skilful weaving, and driving which was more selfish than orthodox, he was making slow progress. From time to time he lost Dauntsey, only to find when the traffic slightly cleared that he was still on the same road. And Daniel guessed now where he was heading. He grew more certain with every mile, and when at last they approached the A12 he no longer had any doubt. But at every light, every pause, every stretch of clear road his mind focused on the two murders which had led him to this chase, to this resolve.

He saw the whole plan now in its brilliance, its initial simplicity. Etienne's murder had been planned to look like an accident, had been devised in all its details over weeks, probably months, the ideal moment patiently awaited. The police had always known that Dauntsey was the obvious suspect. No one could more easily work undisturbed in the little archives room. He had probably locked the door while he dismantled the fire, dislodged the rubble from the chimney lining, replaced the fire with its flue effectively blocked. The window cord had been deliberately weakened over weeks. And he had chosen the obvious night for the murder, a Thursday when Etienne was known to work late and alone. He had timed it for half past seven, just before he left for the Connaught Arms. Had that engagement been fortuitous, arising by luck on the night he had chosen? Or had he chosen that particular night because of the poetry reading? It would have been easy enough to concoct some other appointment, but it had always seemed strange that he bothered with the poetry reading. No other well-known poet had been present and the event was hardly of major literary importance. He would have waited his moment to slip into Innocent House unobserved once everyone but Etienne had left, would have crept up quietly to the little archives room. But even if Etienne had come out of his office unexpectedly and seen him he would have made no comment. Why should he? Dauntsey had a key to the building, he was a partner, he could come and go as he chose. Etienne would have assumed he was going upstairs to fetch a necessary paper or papers from his third-floor office before leaving for the Connaught Arms.

And then what? The final preparations would have been made about an hour earlier. Daniel could picture every action and the sequence of every action. Dauntsey had carried the table and the chair and placed them in the space outside the door; it was important that Etienne should have no way of reaching the window. The room was cleaned. There must be no dust or dirt in which Etienne could smear his killer's name. His diary with the pencil attached had already been stolen in case Etienne brought it up in his jacket or trouser pocket.

Next Dauntsey lit the gas fire and turned it full on before removing the tap so that the fumes would begin to build up before his victim arrived. Lastly the tape recorder was placed on the floor and plugged in. Dauntsey had wanted Etienne to know that he was about to die, that there was no chance of escape, that in this isolated and empty building no one would hear the shouting and banging on the door, exertion which would only make his end more speedy, that his death was as inevitable as if he had been thrust into the gas chamber at Auschwitz. Above all, he had needed Etienne to know why it was that he had to die.

So the scene was set for murder. Then just before 7.30 Dauntsey had rung Etienne's office from the telephone by the door of the little archives room. What would he have said? 'Come up at once, I've found something here. It's important.' Etienne would, of course, have come. Why not? Mounting the stairs he might have wondered whether Dauntsey had discovered a clue to the identity of the practical joker. It hardly mattered what he thought. The call was from a man he trusted and had no reason to fear. The voice would have been urgent, the message intriguing. Of course he would have gone up.

The killing ground had been prepared, cleaned and empty. And what then? Dauntsey would have been waiting by the door. There would have been no more than a quick exchange of words.

'What is it, Dauntsey?' Had his voice been impatient, a little arrogant?

'It's in here, in the little archives room. See for yourself. There's a message on that tape recorder. Listen to it and you'll understand.'

And Etienne, puzzled but unsuspecting, had walked into the room and to his death.

The door was quickly closed, the key turned and removed. Hissing Sid had already been hidden among the files in the archives room. Dauntsey laid the snake along the bottom of the door, ensuring that even this small amount of ventilation was blocked. There was nothing more to do at present. He could leave for his poetry reading.

He had planned to be back from the Connaught Arms by about ten to do what he had to do. And he could take his time. The door would have to be opened for some minutes to disperse the fumes. Then he would replace the tap on the gas fire and restore the room to its previous appearance. The tables and chairs would be carried back, the filing trays arranged as they were on the table. Wasn't there something else he must have thought of? It would be sensible to add another file to the existing pile, papers which Etienne might reasonably have discovered, searched for, been interested in, a file which could have brought him up to the little archives room; an old contract, something relating perhaps to Esmé Carling. Dauntsey could have extracted it earlier and kept it hidden misfiled among other papers ready for use. He would then have left, making sure that the door key was on the inside of the lock, taking the snake with him.

He could have worked without hurry, probably moving through Innocent House by torchlight but knowing that he could safely put on the light once he was in the little archives room. He would have gone down to Etienne's office and brought up his jacket and keys, hanging the jacket on the back of the chair, placing the keys on the top of the table. Of course he couldn't have replaced the dust on the mantelshelf above the fire and on the floor. But would anyone really have noticed the exceptional cleanliness of the room if the death had from the start looked accidental?

And the scene would have spoken for itself. Here was Etienne studying a file which obviously interested him. He must have been prepared to work there for some time, since he had come up with his jacket and his keys and had lit the fire. He had closed the window, snapping the cord as he did so. The body would probably have been found either slumped over the table or on its face, as if crawling towards the fire. The only puzzle would have been why he hadn't realized what was happening to him and at once opened the door. But one of the earliest symptoms of carbon monoxide poisoning was disorientation. There would have been no broken rigor of the jaw, no need to stuff the snake-head into the mouth. It would have been an almost perfect example of accidental death.

But for Dauntsey it had gone dreadfully wrong. The mugging, the hours wasted in hospital, the late return, had upset all his plans. Now, home at last and with Frances waiting, he had very little time and must act with extraordinary speed, and when he was physically at his weakest. But his mind was still functioning. He turned on the bath tap very slowly so that the bath would be about filled by the time he returned. He had probably thrown off his clothes and worn only his dressing gown; there would be an advantage in entering the little archives room naked. But he had to go back and go back that night. After the accident it would be highly suspicious if he were first in Innocent House the next morning. Most vital of all, he needed to retrieve that tape, that damning tape with its confession of murder.

Etienne had listened to the tape; Dauntsey at least had had that satisfaction. His victim had known that he was doomed but he had, brilliantly, hit on his own small revenge. Determined that the evidence should be found, he had placed the tape in his mouth. And then, disorientated, he had obviously had some idea of trying to put out the fire by smothering it with his shirt and had been crawling across the floor when unconsciousness supervened. How long had it taken Dauntsey to find the tape? Obviously not very long. But he had had to break the rigor of the jaw to get it and he knew now that there was no longer any hope that this death could be passed off as accidental. Was that why he had later co-operated so fully with the police, had drawn attention to the missing tape recorder, even to the cleanliness of the room? They were facts which the police would find out from other people; it was prudent to get in first. And there had been no time to do more than hurriedly replace the table and chair. He hadn't even noticed that the table had been replaced with the other side next to the wall so that the position of the files was altered, or that there was a small mark on the wall which showed that it had been moved. And there was no time now to find Etienne's jacket and keys.

But what to do about the forcing open of the mouth? Hissing Sid, the snake, must have been an inspiration. There it was ready to hand. He need waste no time fetching it. All he had to do was wind it round Etienne's neck and stuff its head into his mouth. He had embarked on the series of malicious pranks to confuse the investigation if Etienne's death wasn't accepted as suicide. He couldn't have guessed how vital that ploy was to prove.

But leaving he had noticed Esmé Carling's blue-bound manuscript on the low table in the reception room and seen her message pinned to the wall. It must have been a moment of panic, but it would quickly have subsided. Esmé Carling had almost certainly left Innocent House before he called Etienne upstairs. Perhaps he had paused for a moment wondering whether to check, and then decided that this was pointless. Obviously she had gone leaving the manuscript and the message as a public proclamation of her outrage. Would she tell the police that she had been present or keep quiet? On the whole he thought that she would keep quiet. But he had decided to take both the manuscript and the note. Dauntsey was a murderer who thought ahead, even thought ahead as far as the necessity for her death.

63

Frances slipped in and out of full consciousness, waking to a half-fuddled comprehension, then sinking back as her mind briefly touched reality, rejected its horror, and took refuge again in oblivion. When she became fully conscious she lay for a few minutes, totally still, hardly breathing, assessing her situation in small mental steps as if this gradual acceptance could make reality more bearable. She was alive. She was lying on her left side on the floor of a car covered by a rug. Her ankles were bound and her hands tied behind her back. She was gagged with something soft, she thought it must be her silk scarf. The car's progress was uneven and once it stopped and she felt the gentle jar as the brakes were applied. They must be halted at a traffic light. That meant they were travelling in traffic. She wondered if she could manage to dislodge the blanket by wriggling, but with her hands and feet tied found that it was too firmly tucked around her. But at least she could vigorously move her body. If they were in traffic it was possible that a passing motorist might look through the window and see the heaving blanket and wonder. Hardly had the thought come to her than the car started again and moved smoothly on.

She was alive. She must hang on to that. Gabriel might intend to kill her, but he could easily have done so while she lay unconscious in the garage. Why hadn't he? It couldn't be that he wanted to show her mercy. What mercy had he shown to Gerard, to Esmé Carling, to Claudia? She was in the hands of a murderer. The word, thudding into her mind, woke the terror which had been lying dormant ever since she had regained consciousness. It swept over her, primitive, uncontrollable, a humiliating wave, annihilating thought and will. She knew now why he hadn't killed her in the garage. Claudia's murder, like the other two, was to look like accidental death or suicide. He couldn't leave two bodies on the garage floor. He had to get rid of her, but it must be in a different way. What had he in mind? Her complete disappearance? A killing which Dalgliesh would have no hope of solving since there would be no body? She remembered reading somewhere that it wasn't necessary to produce a body to prove murder, but Gabriel might not realize that. He was mad, he had to be mad. Even now he might be planning, thinking, wondering how best to dispose of her. Whether to drive to the edge of a cliff and tumble her into the sea, to bury her in some ditch, still bound, to tip her into an old mine shaft where she would die of thirst and hunger, alone, never to be found. Image succeeded image, each more horrifying than the last. The terrifying fall through the dark air into the crashing waves, the suffocating wet leaves and earth stamped down into her eyes and mouth, the vertical tunnel of the mine shaft where she would slowly starve to death in claustrophobic agony.

The car was riding more smoothly now. They must have thrown off the last tentacles of London and be in open country. By an effort of will she calmed herself. She was alive. She must hold on to that. There was still hope, and if in the end she had to die she would try to die bravely. Gerard and Claudia, both agnostics, would have died with courage even if they hadn't been allowed to die with dignity. What was her religion worth if it couldn't help her to do the same?

She said an act of contrition, then prayed for the souls of Gerard and Claudia and, last of all, prayed for herself and for her own safety. The well-worn comforting words brought their assurance that she was not alone. Then she tried to plan. Not knowing what he had in mind for her, it was difficult to decide on alternative courses of action, but one fact was certain. She couldn't believe he was strong enough to carry her body unaided. That meant he would at least have to free her ankles. She was younger, stronger than he and could easily out-distance him. If she had the chance she would run for her life. But whatever happened at the end she wouldn't plead for mercy.

In the mean time she must try to prevent her limbs from becoming too stiff. Her hands, wrenched behind her back, were tied with something soft, perhaps his tie or socks. He would not, after all, have come prepared for more than one victim. But he had done the job efficiently. She could not wriggle free. Her ankles were as strongly if more comfortably tied. But even bound she could tense and relax the muscles of her legs, and to make even this small preparation for escape gave her strength and courage. She told herself, too, that she mustn't lose hope of rescue. How long would James wait before he discovered she was missing? He would probably take no action for an hour, imagining she was held up in the traffic or the underground.

But then he would ring number 12 and, getting no answer, would try Claudia's Barbican flat. Even then he might not be seriously worried. But surely he wouldn't wait more than an hour and a half. Perhaps he would take a taxi to number 12. Perhaps, if she were lucky, even hear the sound of the running engine in the garage. Once Claudia's body was found and Dauntsey's absence known, all police forces would be alerted to intercept the car. She must hang on to that hope.

And still he drove. Unable to see her watch she could only guess at the time and had no idea of the direction in which they travelled. She didn't waste energy wondering why Gabriel had killed. That was fruitless; only he could tell her that, and perhaps at the end he would. Instead she thought about her own life. What had it been but a series of compromises? What had she given her father but a timid acquiescence which had only reinforced his insensitivity and contempt? Why had she come so meekly into the firm at his bidding to be trained to take over contracts and rights? She could do the work well enough; she was conscientious and methodical, punctilious about detail; but it wasn't what she had wanted to do with her life. And Gerard? In her heart she had known his sexual exploitation for what it was. He had treated her with contempt because she had made herself contemptible. Who was she? What was she? Frances Peverell, meek, obliging, gentle, uncomplaining, the appendage of her father, her lover, the firm. Now when her life might be nearing its end she could at least say, 'I am Frances Peverell. I am myself.' If she lived to marry James, she could at least be offering an equal partnership. She had found the courage to face death, but that, after all, was not so difficult. Thousands, including children, did it every day. It was time she found an equal courage to face life.

And now she felt curiously at peace. From time to time she said a prayer, mentally spoke the lines of a favourite poem, looked back on moments of joy. She even tried to doze and might have succeeded if the car hadn't suddenly jolted her mind awake. Gabriel must be driving over rough country. The Rover lurched, rolled, struck potholes, bounded from side to side, and she rolled with it. And then there was another stretch, but less uneven, probably, she thought, a country track. And then the car stopped and she heard him open his door.

64

In Hillgate Village James glanced at the carriage clock on the mantelpiece. It ˙was 7.42, just over an hour since he had rung Frances. She should have arrived by now. He did again the quick calculation he had been making during the last sixty minutes. There were ten stations between the Bank and Notting Hill Gate. Allow two minutes per station, say twenty minutes for the journey, and fifteen to get to the Bank. But perhaps she had missed Claudia and had had to ring for a taxi. Even so the journey shouldn't have taken sixty minutes, not even in the rush hour and in central London, not unless there had been an unusual hold-up, roads closed or a terrorist alert. He rang Frances's flat again. As expected there was no reply. Then once more he tried Claudia's number, again unsuccessfully. That didn't surprise him. She might have driven straight on to see Declan Cartwright, or had a theatre or a dinner engagement. There was no reason why Claudia should be at home. He switched on the radio to the local London station. Another ten minutes passed before there was the news flash. Travellers were warned of a hold-up on the Central Line. No reason was given, which usually meant an IRA alert, but four stations between Holborn and Marble Arch were closed. So that was the explanation. It could be another hour before Frances arrived. There was nothing to do but wait in patience.

He paced the sitting-room. Frances was slightly claustrophobic. He knew how much she hated using the Greenwich foot tunnel. She disliked travelling by underground. She wouldn't be trapped there now if she hadn't wanted to hurry to his side. He hoped that the lights were on in the train, that she wasn't sitting there unfriended in total darkness. And suddenly he had an extraordinarily vivid and disturbing image of Frances, abandoned, dying, in a dark enclosing tunnel somewhere far from him, unreachable and alone. He thrust it out of his mind as a morbid imagining and looked at the clock again. He would wait half an hour and try to get through to London Transport and find out if the line was open, how long the delay was likely to be. He went over to the window and, moving behind the curtains, stared down on the lighted street willing her to appear.

65

And now at last Daniel was on the A12 and the road was clearer. He kept within the speed limit; it would be disastrous if he were caught by a police patrol. But Dauntsey would be equally careful not to attract attention, not to be held up. To that extent they were driving on equal terms, but he had the faster car. He planned how best to get ahead once his quarry was in sight. In normal circumstances Dauntsey would almost certainly know the car, would probably recognize him even at a glance, but it was unlikely that he knew he was being followed. He wouldn't be watching for a pursuer. The best plan would be to wait until the road was busy then take his chance to overtake in a stream of traffic.

And now for the first time he remembered Claudia Etienne. It horrified him that the possibility of her danger hadn't occurred to him in his concern to get to Dauntsey and warn him. But she would be all right. He had last seen her when she proposed to go home and she must be safe now. Dauntsey was ahead of him in his Rover. The only risk was that she had decided to visit her father and might even now be on her way to Othona House. But that was one more reason for getting there first. There was no point in trying to stop Dauntsey, to overtake him, wave him down. Dauntsey wouldn't stop unless forced to. Daniel needed to speak to him, to warn him, but in calmness, not by ramming his car. The last scene of this tragedy was to be played out in peace.

And then at last he caught sight of the Rover. They were now nearing the Chelmsford by-pass and the traffic was building up. He waited his moment and then joined the stream of cars in the overtaking lane and shot past.

Esmé Carling must have had a few very bad days after the news of the discovery of the body. She would have expected the police to arrive with questions about the notice pinned to the board, the discarded manuscript. But he and Robbins had come with their harmless questions about an alibi and the alibi had been provided. She had kept her nerve admirably, he had to give her that. Never once had he suspected that there was more to learn. And after that? What thoughts had gone through her mind? Had Dauntsey telephoned her first or had she got in touch with him? Almost certainly the latter. Dauntsey would have had no need to kill her if she hadn't told him that she'd actually seen him walking downstairs carrying the vacuum cleaner. He, too, must have had some very bad moments. He, too, had kept his nerve. Esmé Carling has said nothing and he must have thought he was safe.

And then would have come the telephone call, the suggestion that they should meet, the implied threat that unless her book was published she would go to the police. The threat was, of course, baseless. She couldn't go to the police without revealing that she, too, had been in Innocent House that night. She had as strong a motive for getting rid of Etienne as anyone. But she was a woman whose mind, ingenious, scheming, devious, a little obsessional, had its limitations. She was not clear-thinking nor was she highly intelligent.

How exactly, he wondered, had Dauntsey enticed her to that meeting? Did he say that he knew or suspected who had killed Etienne and that together they could arrive at the truth and enjoy a joint triumph? Had they reached at least a provisional understanding that she would remain silent and he would return the manuscript and the paper and ensure that her book was published? She had told Daisy Reed that Peverell Press would have to publish. Who else but one of the partners could have given her that assurance? Had he presented himself in that brief conversation as her defender and saviour, or as a fellow conspirator? They would now never know unless Dauntsey chose to tell them.

One thing was certain; Esmé Carling had gone to that interview without fear. She hadn't known who the murderer had been but she was confident she knew who it couldn't have been. She had been the visitor in Etienne's office when the call came through and, at first, had waited for him to return. Then, growing impatient, she had gone up to the little archives room, glimpsing Dauntsey carrying down the vacuum cleaner as she was about to leave Miss Blackett's office. Outside the door she had seen the snake and heard the voice. Someone inside the room was speaking. The door was not substantial and she probably realized that it wasn't Etienne's voice. When the body was discovered, she could be certain that Dauntsey at least was innocent. She had seen him herself walking down the stairs while

Etienne was still alive and in the little archives room talking with his killer.

How had he managed that alibi for Esmé Carling's murder? But of course; he and Bartrum had been the only two left alone with her body before the police arrived. Wasn't it Dauntsey who had suggested that the women should be taken indoors, that he and Bartrum would wait by the body? He must have arranged his alibi then. But it was surprising that Bartrum had agreed. Had Dauntsey promised to support him in keeping his job? To get him promotion? Or was there an existing obligation to be repaid? Whatever the reason, the alibi had been given. And the pub at which they had met half an hour later than they claimed had been well-chosen. No one at the Sailor's Return had been able to say precisely when two particular customers had entered that large, raucous and overcrowded tavern.

The murder itself would have presented few problems, the only moment of danger the moving of the launch. But that, of course, would have been necessary. He needed the launch; only in the safety of its cabin could he kill, unseen both from the land and the river. Esmé Carling had been a thin woman and not heavy, but Dauntsey was seventy-six and it would have been easier to string her up from the launch than to manoeuvre her body, dead or alive, down the slippery tide-washed steps. And moving the launch would be safe enough if he kept the engine low. The only person living close was Frances and Dauntsey knew from experience how little could be heard from her sitting-room with the curtains drawn. And even if she had heard the noise of an engine, would she really have taken the trouble to investigate? This, after all, was a common sound of the river. But after the murder the launch had to be moved back. He couldn't be certain that there wouldn't be a trace of her, however small, in the cabin, particularly if there was a struggle. It was important that no one should associate the launch with her death.

She had come to this last fatal appointment by taxi. That must have been by Dauntsey's suggestion, and his suggestion, too, that she should be put down at the end of Innocent Passage. He would be waiting there in the shadows, standing in the doorway. What had he told her? That they could speak in greater privacy if they went on the river? He would have placed the manuscript and her message to the partners ready in the cabin. What else would have been there? A rope for the strangling, a scarf, a belt? But he must have hoped that she would be carrying her usual shoulder-bag with the strong strap. He must have seen her with it often enough.

And now, with his eyes fixed on the road ahead, his hands lightly on the wheel, Daniel pictured the scene in that narrow cabin. How long would they have talked? Perhaps not at all. She must already have told Dauntsey on the telephone that she had seen him at Innocent House coming down the stairs carrying the vacuum cleaner. That in itself was damning. There was nothing else he needed to know from her. It would have been easiest and safest to waste no time. Daniel could see Dauntsey standing a little aside, politely waiting for her to enter the cabin first, the strap of her bag over her shoulder. Then the quick flick upwards of the strap, the falling and thrashing on the cabin floor, the old hands ineffectively clutching at the leather noose as with both hands he tugged it tight. There must have been at least a second of horrified realization before merciful unconsciousness blacked out her mind for ever.

And this was the man he was driving to warn, not because there could now be any escape for him, but because even the horror of Esmé Carling's death seemed only one small and inevitable part of a greater and more universal tragedy. All her life she had fabricated mysteries, exploited coincidence, arranged facts to conform to theory, manipulated her characters, relished the self-importance of vicarious power. It was her tragedy that in the end she had confused fiction with real life.

It was after he had left Maldon and turned south by the B1018 that Daniel got lost. He had earlier stopped the car in a lay-by for a minute to consult the map, resenting every second of lost time. The shorter route to Bradwell-on-Sea was by a left-hand turn off the B1018 and through the villages of Steeple and St Lawrence. He folded the map away and drove on through the dark, desolate landscape. But the road, wider than he had expected, stretched on with two left-hand turns which he hadn't remembered from the map, and with no sign of the first village. Some instinct which he had never been able to explain told him that he was driving south, not east. He stopped at a crossroads to consult a signpost and by the lights of the car saw the name Southminster. Somehow he had got himself on to the more southerly and longer road. The darkness was intense and thick as a fog. And then the clouds moved from the moon and he saw a roadside pub, closed and derelict, two brick-built cottages with dim

416

lights behind their curtains, and a single wind-distorted tree with a fragment of a white notice nailed to the bark, fluttering like a pinioned bird. On either side of the road the desolate country lay wind-scoured and eerie in the moon's cold light.

He drove on. The road with its twists and turns seemed endless. The wind was strengthening now, gently buffeting the car. And here at last was the right-hand turn to Bradwell-on-Sea and he saw that he was passing through the outskirts of the village to the squat tower of the church and the lights of the pub. He turned once again, towards the marshlands and the sea. There was no sign of Dauntsey's car and he couldn't tell which of them would reach Othona House first. He only knew that for both of them this would be the journey's end.

66

He opened the rear door. After the enclosing darkness, the smell of petrol, of the rug, of her own fear, the fresh moonlit air touched her face like a blessing. She could hear nothing but the sighing of the wind, see nothing but his dark form leaning over her. His hands stretched towards her and he fumbled the gag. She felt the brush of his fingers momentarily against her cheek. Then he bent and untied her ankles. The knots were not difficult. If her hands had been free she could have untied them herself. He didn't need to cut them free. Did that mean that he hadn't a knife? But she was no longer worried about her own safety. Suddenly she knew that he hadn't brought her here to kill her. He had other, and for him more important, preoccupations.

He said, with a voice as ordinary, as gentle, as the voice she had known, relied upon, liked to hear: 'Frances, if you turn over I can get more easily at your hands.'

It could have been her rescuer speaking, not her gaoler. She turned, and it took only a few seconds to free her. She tried to ease her legs out of the car but they were stiff and he put out his hand to help.

She said: 'Don't touch me.'

The words were indistinct. The gag had been tighter than she had thought and her jaw was fixed in a painful rictus. But he understood. He stepped back at once and watched while she dragged herself out and stood upright, leaning against the car for support. This was the moment for which she had planned, the chance to outrun him, it hardly mattered where. But he had turned from her and she knew that there was no need to run, no point in trying to escape. He had brought her here from necessity, but she was no longer dangerous, no longer important. His thoughts were elsewhere. She could try to stumble away on her cramped legs but he wouldn't prevent her and he wouldn't follow. He was moving away from her, staring at the dark outline of a house and she could feel the intensity of his gaze. For him this was the end of a long journey.

She said: 'Where are we? What place is this?'

He said, his voice carefully controlled: 'Othona House. I've come to see Jean-Philippe Etienne.'

They went together to the front door. He rang the bell. She could hear its peal even through the strong oak. The wait was not long. They could hear the rasp of the bolt, the turn of the key in the lock and the door opened. The stocky figure of an old woman dressed in black stood outlined against the light of the hall.

She said: 'Monsieur Etienne vous attend.'

Gabriel turned to Frances. 'I don't think you've met Estelle, Jean-Philippe's housekeeper. You're all right now. In a few minutes you can telephone for help. Estelle will look after you in the mean time if you go with her.'

She said: 'I don't need looking after. I'm not a child. You brought me here against my will. Now I'm here, I'm staying with you.'

Estelle led them down a long stone-floored passage to the back of the house, then stood aside and motioned them to enter. The room, obviously a study, was dark-panelled, the air stagnant with the pungent sweetness of wood smoke. In the stone fireplace the flames leapt like tongues and the wood crackled and hissed. Jean-Philippe Etienne was seated in a high winged chair to the right of the fire. He didn't get up. Standing against the window, facing the door, was Inspector Aaron. He was wearing a sheepskin jacket, its bulkiness emphasizing the stockiness of his figure. His face was very pale, but as a log of wood crashed and flared it glowed for a moment into ruddy life. His hair was windswept, dishevelled. He must, thought Frances, have arrived just before them and parked his car out of sight.

Ignoring her, he said directly to Dauntsey, 'I've been following you. I need to talk to you.'

He took an envelope from his pocket and, drawing out a photograph, laid it on the table. He watched Dauntsey's face in silence. No one moved.

Dauntsey said: 'I know what you've come to say, but the time for speaking is over. You are here not to talk but to listen.'

And now for the first time Aaron seemed aware of Frances's presence. He said sharply, almost accusingly: 'Why are you here?'

Frances's mouth still ached but her voice was strong and clear. 'Because I was brought here by force. I was bound and gagged. Gabriel has killed Claudia. He strangled her in the garage. I saw her body. Aren't you going to arrest him? He's killed Claudia and he killed the other two.'

Etienne had got to his feet but now he gave a curious sound, something between a groan and a sigh, and sank back into his chair. Frances ran to him. She said: 'I'm sorry, I'm so sorry, I should have told you more gently.' Then, looking up, she saw Inspector Aaron's horrified face.

He turned to Dauntsey and said almost in a whisper: 'So you did finish the job.'

'Don't blame yourself, Inspector. You couldn't have saved her. She was dead before you left Innocent House.'

He spoke directly to Jean-Philippe Etienne. 'Stand up, Etienne. I want you to stand.'

Etienne rose slowly from his chair and reached for his cane. With its help he got to his feet. He made an obvious effort to steady himself but swayed and might have fallen if Frances hadn't moved forward and put her arms around his waist. He didn't speak, but gazed at Dauntsey.

Dauntsey said: 'Stand behind your chair. You can use it for support.'

'I don't need support.' Firmly he removed Frances's arm. 'It was only a temporary stiffness after sitting. I'm not standing behind the chair as if I were in the dock. And if you have come here as a judge, I thought it was usual to take the plea before the trial and to punish only if there is a verdict of guilty.'

'There has been a trial. I've conducted the trial for over forty years. Now I'm asking you to admit that you handed over my wife and children to the Germans, that in fact you sent them to be murdered in Auschwitz.'

'What were their names?'

'Sophie Dauntsey, Martin and Ruth. They were going under the name Loiret. They had forged documents. You were one of the few people who knew that, who knew that they were Jews, who knew where they were living.'

Etienne said calmly: 'The names mean nothing. How can I be expected to remember? They weren't the only Jews I informed on to Vichy and the Germans. How am I expected to remember the individual names or the families? I did what was necessary at the time. A great number of French lives depended on me. It was

420

important that the Germans continued to trust me if I were to get my allocation of paper, ink and resources for the underground press. How can I be expected to remember one woman and two children after fifty years?'

Dauntsey said: 'I remember them.'

'And now you have come for your revenge. Is it still sweet even after fifty years?'

'This isn't revenge, Etienne. This is justice.'

'Oh don't deceive yourself, Gabriel. This is revenge. Justice doesn't require that you come finally to tell me what you have done. Call it justice if it comforts your conscience. It's a strong word, I hope you know what it means. I'm not sure that I do. Perhaps the representative of the law can help us.'

Daniel said: 'It means an eye for an eye and a tooth for a tooth.'

Dauntsey was still gazing at Jean-Philippe. 'I have taken no more than you took, Etienne. A son and a daughter for a son and a daughter. You murdered my wife but yours was already dead when I learned the truth.'

'Yes, she was beyond your malice. And mine.'

He said the last two words so quietly that Frances wondered if she had really heard them.

Gabriel went on: 'You killed my children; I have killed yours. I have no posterity; you will have none. After Sophie's death I could never love another woman. I don't believe that our existence here has a meaning or that we have any future after death. Since there is no God there can be no divine justice. We have to make justice for ourselves and make it here on earth. It has taken me nearly fifty years but I have made my justice.'

'It would have been more effective if you had acted sooner. My son had his youth, his young manhood. He had success, the love of women. You couldn't take those away from him. Your children had none of them. Justice should be speedy as well as effective. Justice doesn't wait for fifty years.'

'What has time to do with justice? Time takes away our strength, our talent, our memories, our joys, even our capacity to grieve. Why should we let it take away the imperative of justice? I had to be certain, and that, too, was justice. It took me over twenty years to trace two vital witnesses. Even then I was in no hurry. I couldn't have stood ten years or more of prison and now I shan't have to. Nothing is impossible to bear at seventy-six. Then your son got engaged. There might have been a child. Justice required that only two should die.'

Etienne said: 'And is that why you left your publishers and came to Peverell Press in 1962? Did you suspect me then?'

'I was beginning to. The strands of my inquiry were beginning to come together. It seemed sensible to get close to you. And you were, I remember, glad enough to have me and my money.'

'Of course. Henry Peverell and I thought that we were getting a major talent. You should have kept your energies for your poetry, Gabriel, not wasted them on a useless obsession born of your own guilt. It was hardly your fault that your wife and children were trapped in France. You were imprudent in leaving them at that time, of course, but no more. You left them and they died. Why try to purge that guilt by murdering the innocent? But murdering the innocent is your forte, isn't it? You took part in the bombing of Dresden. Nothing I have done can compete with the horror and magnitude of that achievement.'

Daniel said, almost in a whisper: 'That was different. That was the awful necessity of war.'

Etienne turned on him: 'And so it was for me, the necessity of war.' He paused, and when he spoke again Frances could hear in his voice the barely controlled note of triumph. 'If you want to act like God, Gabriel, you should first ensure that you have the wisdom and knowledge of God. I have never had a child. I caught a viral infection when I was thirteen; I am totally infertile. My wife needed a son and a daughter and to satisfy her maternal obsession I agreed to provide them. Gerard and Claudia were adopted in Canada and brought back with us to England. They are not related by blood either to each other or to me. I promised my wife that the truth would never be publicly known but Gerard and Claudia were both told when they were fourteen. The effect on Gerard was unfortunate. Both children should have been told from the start.'

Frances knew that Gabriel didn't need to ask if this was the truth. She had to force herself to look at him. For a moment she saw him physically crumble, the muscles of face and body seeming to disintegrate even as she watched. He had been an old man but one with force, intelligence and will. Now everything that was alive in him drained away in front of her eyes. Quickly she moved towards him but he put out a restraining hand. Now, slowly and painfully, he forced himself to stand upright. He tried to speak but no words came. Then he turned and made for the door. No one spoke, but they followed him out through the hall and into the night and watched while he walked towards the narrow ridge of rock at the edge of the marsh.

Frances ran after him and, catching him up, seized him by his jacket. He tried to shake her off but she clung on and his strength was failing. It was Daniel, running up behind them, who clasped her in his arms and carried her bodily away. She tried to struggle free but his arms were like iron bands. She watched helplessly as Gabriel walked forward into the marsh.

Daniel said: 'Let him be. Let him be.'

She called back to Jean-Philippe Etienne: 'Go after him! Stop him! Make him come back!'

Daniel said quietly, 'Come back for what?'

'But he'll never reach the sea.'

It was Etienne coming up beside them who spoke. 'He doesn't need to reach it. Those pools are deep. A man can drown in a foot of water if he wants to die.'

They stood watching. Frances was still held in Daniel's arms. Suddenly she was aware of the beating of his heart thudding against her own. The stumbling figure was dark against the night sky. It rose, then fell, then reared itself up and fought on. Again the clouds moved and by the light of the moon they could see him more clearly. From time to time he would fall, but then would rise to his feet again, looking immense as a giant, arms raised as if in a curse or a last beseeching gesture. Frances knew that he was fighting to reach the sea, longing to walk out into its cold immensity, further and deeper, until he could splash forward into that final blessed oblivion.

And now he was down again, and this time he didn't rise. Frances thought she could see the glitter of the moonlight on the surface of the pool. It seemed to her that almost all his body was submerged. But she could no longer see him clearly. He was just one more dark low hump amongst all the tussocks of this sodden wasteland. They waited in silence, but there was no movement. He had become part of the marshland and of the night. Now Daniel released her and she moved and stood a little apart. The silence was absolute. And at last she thought she could hear the sea, a faint susurration, less a sound than a pulse beat on the quiet air.

They were turning towards the house when the night vibrated

with a harsh metallic groan which grew rapidly into a rattle. Overhead were the twin lights of a helicopter. They watched as it circled three times then landed on the field beside Othona House. Frances thought, so they have found Claudia's body. James must have got tired of waiting for her and in the end gone back to Innocent House to search.

She stood on the edge of the field, still a little apart from the others and saw the three figures running crouched under the great blades, then standing upright and moving towards her, over the gritty field and the wind-torn grass, Commander Dalgliesh, Inspector Miskin and James. Etienne moved forward to meet them. They stood in a group talking together. She thought, let Etienne tell them. I shall wait.

Then Dalgliesh detached himself and came up to her. He didn't touch her but he bent from his tall height and looked intently into her face.

'Are you all right?'

'I am now.'

He smiled and said: 'We'll talk very soon. De Witt insisted on coming with us. It was less trouble to let him have his way.'

He walked on to join Etienne and Kate and together they went towards Othona House.

Frances thought, 'I am myself at last. I have something worth giving him.' She didn't run towards the waiting figure. She didn't call out to him. It was slowly, but with all the intensity of her being, that she walked over the windswept grass and into his waiting arms.

Daniel heard the approach of the helicopter but he didn't move. He stood on the narrow ridge of rock still looking out over the saltings to the sea. He waited in solitary patience until he heard the approaching footsteps and Dalgliesh was at his side.

He said: 'Was he under arrest?'

'No, sir. I didn't come to arrest him, I came to warn him. I didn't caution him. I did speak but they weren't the words you would have spoken. I let him go.'

'You let him go deliberately? He didn't break free?'

'No, sir. He didn't break free.' He added, so softly that he doubted whether Dalgliesh heard the words: 'But he's free now.'

Dalgliesh turned away and went back to the house. He had learned what he needed to know. No one else came near. Daniel felt isolated in a moral quarantine, standing on the edge of the marshes, on the edge of the world. He thought he saw a trembling light, bright as phosphorous, burning and darting among the humps of marram grass and the black pools of stagnant water. He couldn't see the small breaking waves but he could hear the sea, a soft eternal moaning like a universal grief. And then the clouds moved and the moon with its shaved side, so nearly full, shed its cold light on the marsh and on that distant fallen figure. He sensed a shadow at his side. Turning he saw that it was Kate. It was with astonishment and pity that he realized her face was wet with tears.

He said: 'I wasn't trying to help him escape. I knew that there could be no escape. But I couldn't bear to see him handcuffed, in the dock, in prison. I wanted to give him the chance to take his own path home.'

She said: 'Daniel, you fool. You bloody fool.'

He turned to her and said: 'What will he do?'

'AD? What do you think he'll do? Oh God, Daniel, you could have been so good, you were so good.'

He said: 'Etienne couldn't even remember their names. He could hardly remember what he'd done. He felt no guilt, no remorse. A mother and two small children. They didn't exist. They weren't human. He would have given more thought to putting down a dog. He didn't think of them as people. They were expendable. They didn't count. They were Jews.'

She cried: 'And Esmé Carling? Old, plain, childless, alone. Not a very good writer. Was she expendable? All right, she didn't have a lot. A flat, someone else's kid to spend the evenings with, a few photographs, her books. What right had he to decide that her life didn't count?'

He said bitterly: 'You're so confident, aren't you, Kate. So certain you know what's right. It must be comforting, never having to face a moral dilemma. The criminal law and police regulations: they provide all you need, don't they?'

She said: 'I'm certain about some things. I'm certain about murder. How could I be a police officer if I weren't?'

Dalgliesh came over to them. He said in a voice as ordinary as if they were companionably together in that Wapping incident room: 'The Essex Police won't attempt to recover the body until daylight. I want you to drive Kate back to London. Do you feel able to do that?'

'Yes, sir. I'm perfectly fit to drive.'

'If you aren't, Kate will take over. Mr de Witt and Miss Peverell will come with me in the helicopter. They'll want to get back as soon as possible. I'll see you both later tonight at Wapping.'

He stood with Kate at his side until the three figures had joined the pilot and entered the helicopter. The machine roared into life and the great blades slowly revolved, spun into a haze, became invisible. The helicopter lifted and lurched into the sky. Etienne and Estelle were on the edge of the field looking up at it. He thought bitterly: they look like sightseers. It's a wonder they're not waving goodbye.

He said to Kate: 'There's something I've left in the house.'

The front door stood open. She came with him through the hall and into the study, walking behind him so that he shouldn't feel like a prisoner under escort. The light had been turned off in the room but the flames of the fire threw dancing gules over the walls and ceilings and stained the polished surface of the table with a ruddy glow, as if it had been smeared with blood.

The photograph was still there. He was for a moment surprised that Dalgliesh hadn't taken it. But then he remembered. It didn't matter. There would be no trial now, no exhibits, no need to produce it as evidence in court. It wasn't needed any more. It was of no importance.

He left it on the table and, turning to join Kate, walked with her in silence to the car.